GREAT SHORT STORIES OF THE WORLD

A Collection of Complete Short
Stories chosen from the Literatures
of all Periods and Countries by
BARRETT H. CLARK
& MAXIM LIEBER
with an introduction by
GERDA CHARLES

SPRING BOOKS • LONDON

Published by

Spring Books

Westbook House · Fulham Broadway · London

Originally published by William Heinemann Ltd

This edition published 1964

Printed in Czechoslovakia

by Polygrafia 3, Praha

T 1283

Preface to Original Edition

THIS collection marks the first attempt to bring together in a single volume a characteristic group of the outstanding examples of the Short Story as it has been practised by writers of almost every race, from the earliest days of civilization down to the present century. Its purpose is not to show, by a series of texts chosen on academic grounds, how the form developed, but to bring together the best examples of every form by which men have endeavoured to entertain and instruct their fellows.

No art is more spontaneous than that of the short story, and though it may be proved that lyric poetry came earlier to the dignity of literature, it is certain that stories of some sort were told as soon as man became articulate. The period covered in the present collection embraces nearly five thousand years, but there can be no reasonable doubt that the Egyptian tales that open the volume, the first of their kind known to us, are the finished products of an art that was practised thousands of years before these were written. And since the beginning of civilization as we know it, there has been no break in the tradition of tale-telling: the demand for stories is as strong and insatiable in man to-day as it was before he discovered how to make stone weapons.

Of recent years there has been a good deal of theorizing about the Short Story as an art form. A whole literature of theory has come into being in order to explain the work of Maupassant and Poe and O. Henry, as well as to guide the would-be writer. Several theorists have maintained that the Short Story (as opposed to the story that is short) is an invention of the Nineteenth Century, that it must be unified, that it must concern itself with but a single anecdote or episode or situation, that it must be of a certain length; in a word, that it must conform to certain *a priori* principles. These theories are often interesting and ingenious, but so far as they have influenced the writers of stories, they are of little importance.

The editors of this collection have approached their task of selection with open minds: they have not allowed themselves to be influenced by any theory of what a short story should be, except that which requires that it be interesting of its kind. While it is quite true that Maupassant was a more highly inspired artist than say the Seventeenth Century Dutchman Jacob Cats, it does not follow that Cats' fable which is printed in the pages that follow, is not a story because *The Necklace* is a masterpiece.

So, without confining themselves to any theory of classification, the editors have chosen a wide variety of stories designed to appeal to the general reader, and perhaps to the student as well, in the belief that what has delighted the Chinese from time immemorial, the ancient Egyptians, the Jewish shepherds and warriors of Biblical times, the Greeks of Homer's days and the Romans of Cæsar's, will appeal with equal force to the inhabitants of the civilized world of the Twentieth Century.

Despite the indefatigable efforts of editors and publishers in unearthing the little-known or quite forgotten tales of certain countries or peoples, and the bewilderingly numerous collections of stories published in sets of many volumes, it has never before been possible for the reader to make the acquaintance of so many stories as are here brought together within the covers of a single volume. It has even been necessary to translate the work of several writers unknown to readers of English, and in many cases to make known through translation some particular story hitherto not accessible. The volume, therefore, besides being the first to include examples of stories of practically the entire world, introduces several new writers to English and American readers. Among the stories that appear here for the first time in English are those by the Hungarians Mikszath and Molnar; the Spanish-American Darío, Blanco-Fombóna and García-Calderón; the Dutchman Heijermans; the Pole Prus; the Bulgarian Elin-Pelin; the Jugoslavs Matoš, Lazarevich, and Cankar; and the Belgian Lemonnier.

That *Great Short Stories of the World* is not as nearly perfect a collection as the editors and publisher would have liked to make it is a foregone conclusion. Has ever any anthology entirely pleased its maker? Has it ever pleased every critic and every reader? It is hardly necessary to state that the first limitation imposed upon the editors was that of space. It was not, of course, possible to include more than a comparatively small number of the great stories available; it was not possible to include many stories which, like Vigny's *Laurette*, were too long; it was inadvisable to reprint too many of the stories that were in every other collection, but on the other hand it would not have done to omit all the recognized masterpieces, like Maupassant's *Necklace*. To include stories even from those countries which had made the most important contributions to the world's store of tales was in itself a hazardous undertaking, but when it came to selecting precisely what stories should be chosen to give an adequate notion of the richness and variety of a country like France, it seemed at first a rather hopeless task. How, for instance, was it possible to give the reader a fair notion of the beautiful stories of the Thirteenth and Fourteenth Centuries? It was imperative that out of a possible hundred only two or three should be chosen.

In the case of modern writers, the difficulties were much greater. Every one has his favourite authors and favourite stories. It was not the intention of the editors to bring this collection up to the minute: the works of our immediate contemporaries are easily accessible. If certain contemporaries like Cabell and Anderson, Bojer and Gorky are included, it is either because they have their roots in the Nineteenth Century or that they represent in a general way some modern trend that seems more or less permanent, and because their work is intrinsically worth printing in a collection of this sort.

Finally, came considerations of copyright. In almost every instance both publishers and writers have been helpful in allowing copyright stories to be reprinted, but occasionally it has been necessary to omit the work of certain authors because either the publisher or the agent was unable to see his way clear to co-operating with the editors.

Although the final selection of all stories is a matter for which the editors are alone responsible, the lists were submitted to and passed upon by a number of specialists, particularly in the case of those sections whose literature was little known. These persons have enabled the editors to make their work more inclusive and more genuinely representative of all peoples and nations than would otherwise have been possible. But while every effort has been made to show, both by the stories themselves and by the brief notes, what each nation and race has contributed to the art of the Short Story, the attitude of the editors throughout has been that of every true teller of tales: it is their wish that these stories shall be read and enjoyed by the general public. They were written not for critics and historians, editors of anthologies and specialists, but for all mankind. They have tried to bear in mind that the Short Story is a "tale which holdeth children from play and old men from the chimney corner."

To many publishers, both English and American, thanks are due for their courtesy and assistance in the use of copyright material. Specific acknowledgment is made in connection with the separate stories. For constant and invaluable assistance of every sort the editors take this occasion to thank Cecile S. Clark, Irma Lieber, and Mr. Guy Holt. A number of authors have themselves granted permission to reprint and in some instances given valuable advice regarding what stories to use. Acknowledgment is hereby gratefully made to Maxim Gorky, George Moore, James Branch Cabell, Per Hallström, Johan Bojer, Arthur Morrison, and Abraham Raisin. Among the many advisers and translators who have helped in the preparation of one or more sections, the editors are especially grateful to Miss Hanna Astrup Larsen, Dr. Isaac Goldberg, Dr. A. C. van P. Huizinga, Mrs. Velma S. Howard, Prof. Sarka B. Hrbkova, Mr. Gray Casement, Mr. Rajner Hlacha, Mr. Ivan Mladineo, Mr. Adamantios Polisoides, and Mr. George Gorn.

THE EDITORS

PUBLISHER'S NOTE

Every care has been taken to discover the owners of all copyrighted stories, but if any necessary acknowledgments have been omitted, or any stories included without due permission, we trust the copyright-holders will accept our apologies.

Introduction

THE short story is one of the oldest forms of creative writing in the world. Compared with it formal poetry is a stripling and the novel a babe in arms. Yet, though the habit of short story making has not or ever will be allowed to die, the mode itself suffers eclipse from time to time. Always in being, it is not always in fashion. The Elizabethans preferred drama, the eighteenth century the Romantic poem, the Victorians the novel. In this country its heyday was probably from about 1880 to the late 1920s; a "magazine" era when periodicals were bought because the public actually wanted to read the stories printed in them. This was the magic time when editors regarded short stories (and their authors) as objects of respect, prestige givers no less, and to be solicited, courted and encouraged accordingly... to say nothing of paid! In the 'Twenties, for instance, magazines of repute were quite prepared to pay several hundred pounds for a good story from a well-known writer. Kipling in the 'Nineties received fabulous sums for some of his tales.

There were, it is true, exceptions. Katharine Mansfield, whose posthumous reputation later ballooned her almost into sainthood, received practically nothing for her best stories even when they managed to get themselves published—which wasn't all that often during her lifetime. But the exceptions *were* exceptions. The short story in general was admired, looked forward to, bought.

The decline from this condition of sunshine to the present climate of cool near-indifference is in many ways a puzzling one, hard to explain. The short story, as has frequently been pointed out, bears less relation to the novel than one might think, its true affinity being the cinema—not to say the television screen. It is concerned with quick image rather than long drawn out exposition, it lends itself to the swift glance rather than the slow stare. Its appeal is more coffee bar than restaurant. All this, one would think, would make it ideal fare for our lunch counter civilization used to short snatches and the constant change and flicker of screen and scene with nothing allowed to stay too long for fear of an Admass yawn. And yet this simply is not so and has not happened. The short story has not only been ousted from its high position: the very journals which supported it have gradually disappeared. And this is true not only of this country

but all over the world. In America for instance, even as I write, some
of the last strongholds of the good story-magazine are struggling, game
but dying, towards their end. The market for the short story as a
work of art is almost gone. Only the pulps, produced for semi-
literates, really flourish.

The explanations are many and various as to why this should have
happened. They range from the general decline in reading habits to
the rise of Do-It-Yourself—with television as everybody's whipping
boy. My own part-explanation of this situation is that the contemporary neglect of the short story is not because people don't like it—
at its most supple, most subtle, most satisfying best. The trouble with
the short story is that it is *short*. That is, in an age swamped with
"giant" offers, deafened by contending claims of Super Pack, Family
Size, Mile High, Jumbo, even the more discriminating mind has been
unconsciously pressurized into the belief that anything smaller than
the biggest simply isn't worth buying. We are all so conditioned to
the idea of the "bargain offer", to buying in bulk because that way
we feel we're somehow saving not only in money but in energy and
effort also, that to pay an average price for an average measure is to
feel oneself cheated.

One of the great advantages of this anthology therefore is that it
not only offers fare of the finest quality but happens also, by happy
accident, to do so in the kind of quantity most satisfying to present-day
conceptions of worth. The fact that it provides sheer, splendid value
for money should be neither despised nor overlooked. To be a bargain
is not necessarily the least of virtues so long as—and this is of course
the crux of the matter—the quality turns out to be first-rate, long-
wearing and handsome.

It would of course be absurd to pretend that there are not—and
bound to be for each reader—omissions or inclusions which madden,
particularly as we come nearer our own time: no Lawrence, no Isaac
Babel, no Conan Doyle ... and how gladly we would exchange, say,
Arthur Morrison for Joyce. But these are the kind of complaints no
anthologist in the world can escape. To choose from amongst the
Great Short Stories *of the World* is the kind of job which requires an
almost inexhaustible memory, a degree of sheer mental stamina, a
continually renewed freshness of judgment and vitality of opinion.
The editors of this volume not only gave evidence of these virtues in
abundance, they also exercised the necessary eclecticism which has
provided, it is reasonable to say, something for every taste. They have
been flexible, easy, unprejudiced, delightfully unstuffy. Starting with
two tales (extraordinarily modern in basic theme) from Ancient Egypt
they have ranged down the centuries, taking from Greek, Roman and
Biblical sources what are no less marvellous because familiar stories,

proceeding through the hardly less ancient treasures of Indian, Persian and Arabic literatures and the legacies of China and Japan, and on to Europe, South America and the United States.

Many of the stories which had to be specially translated into English for the first time for this volume serve as splendid introduction to writers of enormous reputation in their own countries such as the Hungarian writer, Molnar and the Spanish-American, García Calderón. Both these writers have come to be well known to English-speaking readers, but a new name even now to most of us would be that of Matilde Serao, an Italian writer with close affinities to Jane Austen, whose story, *Lulu's Triumph*, a witty, deeply penetrating and altogether enchanting tale sparkles up out of the heap of other jewels with an effect of most happy discovery.

But perhaps best of all the functions performed by the editors is that of reminder. One forgets just how superb a story—read hastily perhaps when young because one has been told it is a masterpiece—is for example Maupassant's *The Necklace*. How little the trick ending matters after all. One has forgotten the sad, humorous, disillusioned warmth of Shalom Aleichem's *The Passover Guest*. One has—again in youth—passed over too quickly the quiet, human magic of Sarah Orne Jewett's New England sketches of which *Miss Tempy's Watchers* is so perfect an example. One has forgotten the cynicism (so entirely of our time that it seems impossible that he should be not living now, but nineteen hundred years ago) of Petronius. Again and again as one goes through this volume one is struck with what one might call the "surprise of modernity" — that application to all times which is after all the ultimate test of a work of art. And this though a large proportion of these tales deals with magic in the primitive sense... fairies, demons, transmogrifications. But whatever the characters, whether mythological or mortal, animal or spirit, their use is invariably to act as moral pointers to the good or bad of human conduct. However charmed or remote in time they are it is this quality which in the end gives all these stories their permanent value and place in literature.

I cannot finish without reference to the original editors' introductions to each country's contribution as well as to each separate story: little masterpieces of compressed comment, relevant facts and information, invaluable to the student as well as absorbingly interesting to the general reader. They add a final distinction to this welcome reissue of a volume already graced by some of the choicest blooms from five thousand years of creative flowering in the imaginations of men.

GERDA CHARLES

Contents

PERSIA

ARABIA

GREAT BRITAIN

GERMANY

FRANCE

ITALY

RUSSIA

POLAND

YIDDISH

THE SCANDINAVIAN COUNTRIES

NORWAY

SWEDEN

BELGIUM

JUGOSLAVIA

CZECHOSLOVAKIA

MODERN GREECE

ROUMANIA

GREAT
SHORT STORIES
OF THE WORLD

Ancient Egypt

INTRODUCTION

IN determining the development of the short story in Egypt, it is necessary to study the inscriptions on papyri and stone monuments, a process which the archæologists are better fitted to accomplish than the literary historians, for there appears to have been little development in the form, and the earliest do not differ radically from the later stories, such as the two here included.

The few Egyptian tales that have survived may date back as early as the Thirtieth Century B.C. So far as can be determined, they are indigenously Egyptian, having Egyptian names, backgrounds, and customs. They are not only an invaluable commentary on the lives of the men of those times, but also genuinely moving and interesting stories.

The tales from Egypt have an extraordinary interest in that they are the very earliest examples that we possess. That they were the earliest in order of composition is naturally an open question: before the year 3000 B.C. we can only conjecture. How many thousands of years before that time the plots were invented we cannot know, but the art with which *The Two Brothers* and *Setna and the Magic Book* are contrived indicates that they are comparatively late products.

By the time Egypt was conquered by Alexander the Great, the ancient literature of the country had been superseded.

THE TWO BROTHERS

(ANPU AND BATA)

(Anonymous: about 1400 B.C.)

THE manuscript of this story, one of the oldest in the world, came from the workshop of the scribe Anena, who flourished in the reigns of Rameses II, Menephtah, and Seti II. The work of an unknown author, it is one of the finest examples of the short story in existence.

3

The theme, which has been used numberless times, is easily recognizable as that of the story of Potiphar's wife. It has also been used in *The History of Prince Amziad and Prince Aisad* in *The Arabian Nights*, and later by Dante in *The Divine Comedy*.

As in all great art, we are here impressed by the modernity of the author's attitude, which is only another way of saying that he understood his characters and was an accomplished artist.

The translation here used is that by William Flinders Petrie in *Egyptian Tales*, Vol. 2, published in 1895 by Methuen & Co., by whose permission it is here reprinted. The original manuscript is a part of the so-called Madame d'Orbiney Papyrus. There is no title in the original story.

THE TWO BROTHERS

(ANPU AND BATA)

ONCE there were two brethren, of one mother and one father; Anpu was the name of the elder, and Bata was the name of the younger. Now, as for Anpu he had a house, and he had a wife. But his little brother was to him as it were a son; he it was who made for him his clothes; he it was who followed behind his oxen to the fields; he it was who did the plowing; he it was who harvested the corn; he it was who did for him all the matters that were in the field. Behold, his younger brother grew to be an excellent worker, there was not his equal in the whole land; behold, the spirit of a god was in him.

Now after this the younger brother followed his oxen in his daily manner; and every evening he turned again to the house, laden with all the herbs of the field, with milk and with wood, and with all things of the field. And he put them down before his elder brother, who was sitting with his wife; and he drank and ate, and he lay down in his stable with the cattle. And at the dawn of day he took bread which he had baked, and laid it before his elder brother; and he took with him his bread to the field, and he drave his cattle to pasture in the fields. And as he walked behind his cattle, they said to him, "Good is the herbage which is in that place"; and he listened to all that they said, and he took them to the good place which they desired. And the cattle which were before him became exceeding excellent, and they multiplied greatly.

Now at the time of plowing his elder brother said unto him: "Let us make ready for ourselves a goodly yoke of oxen for plowing, for the land has come out from the water: it is fit for plowing. Moreover, do thou come to the field with corn, for we will begin the plowing in the morrow morning." Thus said he to him; and his younger brother did all things as his elder brother had spoken unto him to do them.

And when the morn was come, they went to the fields with their things; and their hearts were pleased exceedingly with their task in the beginning of their work. And it came to pass after this that as they were in the field they stopped for corn, and he sent his younger brother, saying, "Haste thou, bring to us corn from the farm." And the younger brother found the wife of his elder brother, as she was sitting tying her hair. He said to her: "Get up, and give to me corn, that I may run to the field, for my elder brother hastened me; do not delay." She said to him: "Go, open the bin, and thou shalt take to thyself according to thy will, that I may not drop my locks of hair while I dress them."

The youth went into the stable; he took a large measure, for he desired to take much corn; he loaded it with wheat and barley; and he went out carrying it. She said to him, "How much of the corn that is wanted, is that which is on thy shoulder?" He said to her: "Three bushels of barley, and two of wheat, in all five; these are what are upon my shoulder." Thus said he to her. And she conversed with him, saying, "There is great strength in thee, for I see thy might every day." And her heart knew him with the knowledge of youth. And she arose and came to him, and conversed with him, saying, "Come, stay with me, and it shall be well for thee, and I will make for thee beautiful garments." Then the youth became like a panther of the south with fury at the evil speech which she had made to him; and she feared greatly. And he spake unto her, saying: "Behold, thou art to me as a mother, thy husband is to me as a father, for he who is elder than I has brought me up. What is this wickedness that thou hast said to me? Say it not to me again. For I will not tell it to any man, for I will not let it be uttered by the mouth of any man." He lifted up his burden, and he went to the field and came to his elder brother; and they took up their work, to labor at their task.

Now afterward, at eventime, his elder brother was returning to his house; and the younger brother was following after his oxen, and he loaded himself with all the things of the field; and he brought his oxen before him, to make them lie down in their stable which was in the farm. And behold the wife of the elder brother was afraid for the words which she had said. She took a parcel of fat, she became like one who is evilly beaten, desiring to say to her husband, "It is thy younger brother who has done this wrong." Her husband returned in the even, as was his wont of every day; he came unto his house; he found his wife ill of violence; she did not give him water upon his hands as he used to have, she did not make a light before him, his house was in darkness, and she was lying very sick. Her husband said to her, "Who has spoken with thee?" Behold she said: "No one has spoken with me except thy younger brother. When he came to take for thee corn he found me sitting alone; he said to me, 'Come, let us stay together, tie up thy hair.' Thus spake he to me. I did not listen to him, but thus spake I to him: 'Behold, am I not thy mother, is not thy elder brother to thee as a father?' And he feared, and he beat me to stop me from making report to thee, and if thou lettest him live I shall die. Now behold he is coming in the evening; and I complain of these wicked words, for he would have done this even in daylight."

And the elder brother became as a panther of the south; he sharpened his knife; he took it in his hand; he stood behind the door of his stable to slay his younger brother as he came in the evening to bring his cattle into the stable.

Now the sun went down, and he loaded himself with herbs in his daily manner. He came, and his foremost cow entered the stable, and she said to her keeper, "Behold thou thy elder brother standing before thee with his knife to slay thee; flee from before him." He heard what his first cow had said; and the next entering, she also said likewise. He looked beneath the door of the stable; he saw the feet of his elder brother; he was standing behind the door, and his knife was in his hand. He cast down his load to the ground, and betook himself to flee swiftly; and his elder brother pursued after him with his knife. Then the younger brother cried out unto Ra Harakhti, saying, "My good Lord! Thou art he who divides the evil from the good." And Ra stood and heard all his cry; and Ra made a wide water between him and his elder brother, and it was full of crocodiles; and the one brother was on one bank, and the other on the other bank; and the elder brother smote twice on his hands at not slaying him. Thus did he. And the younger brother called to the elder on the bank, saying: "Stand still until the dawn of day; and when Ra ariseth, I shall judge with thee before him, and he discerneth between the good and the evil. For I shall not be with thee any more forever; I shall not be in the place in which thou art; I shall go to the valley of the acacia."

Now when the land was lightened, and the next day appeared, Ra Harakhti arose, and one looked unto the other. And the youth spake with his elder brother, saying: "Wherefore camest thou after me to slay me in craftiness, when thou didst not hear the words of my mouth? For I am thy brother in truth, and thou art to me as a father, and thy wife even as a mother: is it not so? Verily, when I was sent to bring for us corn, thy wife said to me, 'Come, stay with me'; for behold this has been turned over unto thee into another wise." And he caused him to understand of all that happened with him and his wife. And he swore an oath by Ra Harakhti, saying, "Thy coming to slay me by deceit with thy knife was an abomination." Then the youth took a knife, and cut off of his flesh, and cast it into the water, and the fish swallowed it. He failed; he became faint; and his elder brother cursed his own heart greatly; he stood weeping for him afar off; he knew not how to pass over to where his younger brother was, because of the crocodiles. And the younger brother called unto him, saying: "Whereas thou hast devised an evil thing, wilt thou not also devise a good thing, even like that which I would do unto thee? When thou goest to thy house thou must look to thy cattle, for I shall not stay in the place where thou art; I am going to the valley of the acacia. And now as to what thou shalt do for me; it is even that thou shalt come to seed after me, if thou perceivest a matter, namely, that there are things happening unto me. And this is what shall come to pass, that I shall draw out my soul, and I shall put it upon the top of the flowers of the acacia, and when the acacia is cut down, and it falls to the ground, and thou comest to seek for it, if thou searchest for it seven years do not let thy heart be wearied. For thou wilt find it, and thou must put it in a cup of cold water, and expect that I shall live again, that I may make answer to what has been done wrong. And thou shalt know of this, that is to say, that things are happening to me, when one shall give to thee a cup of beer in thy hand, and it shall be troubled; stay not then, for verily it shall come to pass with thee."

And the youth went to the valley of the acacia; and his elder brother went unto his house; his hand was laid on his head, and he cast dust on his head; he came to his house, and he slew his wife, he cast her to the dogs, and he sat in mourning for his younger brother.

Now many days after these things, the younger brother was in the valley of the acacia; there was none with him; he spent his time in hunting the beasts of the desert, and he came back in the even to lie down under the acacia, which bore his soul upon the topmost flower. And after this he built himself a tower with his own hands, in the valley of the acacia; it was full of all good things, that he might provide for himself a home.

And he went out from his tower, and he met the Nine Gods, who were walking forth to look upon the whole land. The Nine Gods talked one with another, and they said unto him: "Ho! Bata, bull of the Nine Gods, art thou remaining alone? Thou hast left thy village for the wife of Anpu, thy elder brother. Behold his wife is slain. Thou hast given him an answer to all that was transgressed against thee." And their hearts were vexed for him exceedingly. And Ra Harakhti said to Khnumu, "Behold, frame thou a woman for Bata, that he may not remain alive alone." And Khnumu made for him a mate to dwell with him. She was more beautiful in her limbs than any woman who is in the whole land. The essence of every god was in her. The seven Hathors came to see her: they said with one mouth, "She will die a sharp death."

And Bata loved her very exceedingly, and she dwelt in his house; he passed his time in hunting the beasts of the desert, and brought and laid them before her. He said: "Go not outside, lest the sea seize thee; for I cannot rescue thee from it, for I am a woman like thee; my soul is placed on the head of the flower of the acacia; and if another find it, I must fight with him." And he opened unto her his heart in all its nature.

Now after these things Bata went to hunt in his daily manner. And the young girl went to walk under the acacia which was by the side of her house. Then the sea saw her, and cast its waves up after her. She betook herself to flee from before it. She entered her house. And the sea called unto the acacia, saying, "Oh, would that I could seize her!" And the acacia brought a lock from her hair, and the sea carried it to Egypt, and dropped it in the place of the fullers of Pharaoh's linen. The smell of the lock of hair entered into the clothes of Pharaoh; and they were wroth with the fullers of Pharaoh, saying, "The smell of ointment is in the clothes of Pharaoh." And the people were rebuked every day, they knew not what they should do. And the chief fuller of Pharaoh walked by the bank, and his heart was very evil within him after the daily quarrel with him. He stood still, he stood upon the sand opposite to the lock of hair, which was in the water, and he made one enter into the water and bring it to him; and there was found in it a smell, exceeding sweet. He took it to Pharaoh; and they brought the scribes and the wise men, and they said unto Pharaoh: "This lock of hair belongs to a daughter of Ra Harakhti: the essence of every god is in her, and it is a tribute to thee from another land. Let messengers go to every strange land to seek her: and as for the messenger who shall go to the valley of the acacia, let many men go with him to bring her." Then said his Majesty, "Excellent exceedingly is what has been said to us"; and they sent them. And many days after these things the people who were sent to strange lands came to give report unto the King: but there came not those who went to the valley of the acacia, for Bata had slain them, but let one of them return to give a report to the King. His Majesty sent many men and soldiers, as well as horsemen, to bring her back. And there was a woman among them, and to her had been given in her hand beautiful ornaments of a woman. And the girl came back with her, and they rejoiced over her in the whole land.

And his Majesty loved her exceedingly, and raised her to high estate; and he spake unto her that she should tell him concerning her husband. And she said, "Let the acacia be cut down, and let one chop it up." And they sent men and soldiers with their weapons to cut down the acacia; and they came to the acacia, and they cut the flower upon which was the soul of Bata, and he fell dead suddenly.

And when the next day came, and the earth was lightened, the acacia was cut down. And Anpu, the elder brother of Bata, entered his house, and washed his hands; and one gave him a cup of beer, and it became troubled; and one gave him another of wine, and the smell of it was evil. Then he took his staff, and his sandals, and likewise his clothes, with his weapons of war; and he betook himself forth to the valley of the acacia. He entered the tower of his younger brother, and he found him lying upon his mat; he was dead. And he wept when he saw his younger brother verily lying dead. And he went out to seek the soul of his younger brother under the acacia tree, under which his younger brother lay in the evening. He spent three years in seeking for it, but found it not. And when he began the fourth year, he desired in his heart to return into Egypt; he said, "I will go to-morrow morn." Thus spake he in his heart.

Now when the land lightened, and the next day appeared, he was walking under the acacia; he was spending his time in seeking it. And he returned in the evening, and labored at seeking it again. He found a seed. He returned with it. Behold this was the soul of his younger brother. He brought a cup of cold water, and he cast the seed into it: and he sat down, as he was wont. Now when the night came his soul sucked up the water; Bata shuddered in all his limbs, and he looked on his elder brother; his soul was in the cup. Then Anpu took the cup of cold water, in which the soul of his younger brother was; Bata drank it, his soul stood again in its place, and he became as he had been. They embraced each other, and they conversed together.

And Bata said to his elder brother: "Behold I am to become as a great bull, which bears every good mark; no one knoweth its history, and thou must sit upon my back. When the sun arises I shall be in the place where my wife is, that I may return answer to her; and thou must take me to the place where the King is. For all good things shall be done for thee; for one shall lade thee with silver and gold, because thou bringest me to Pharaoh, for I become a great marvel, and they shall rejoice for me in all the land. And thou shalt go to thy village."

And when the land was lightened, and the next day appeared, Bata became in the form which he had told to his elder brother. And Anpu sat upon his back until the dawn. He came to the place where the King was, and they made his Majesty to know of him; he saw him, and he was exceeding joyful with him. He made for him great offerings, saying, "This is a great wonder which has come to pass." There were rejoicings over him in the whole land. They presented unto him silver and gold for his elder brother, who went and stayed in his village. They gave to the bull many men and many things, and Pharaoh loved him exceedingly above all that is in this land.

And many days after these things, the bull entered the purified place; he stood in the place where the princess was; he began to speak with her, saying, "Behold, I am alive indeed." And she said to him, "And, pray, who art thou?" He said to her, "I am Bata. I perceived when thou causedst that they should destroy the acacia of Pharaoh, which was my abode, that I might not be suffered to live. Behold, I am alive indeed, I am as an ox." Then the princess feared exceedingly for the words that her husband had spoken to her. And he went out from the purified place.

And his Majesty was sitting, making a good day with her: she was at the table of his Majesty, and the King was exceeding pleased with her. And she said to his Majesty, "Swear to me by God, saying, 'What thou shalt say, I will obey it for thy sake.' " He hearkened unto all that she said, even this. "Let me eat of the liver of the ox, because he is fit for naught." Thus spake she to him. And the King was exceeding sad at her words, the heart of Pharaoh grieved him greatly. And after the land was lightened, and the next day appeared, they proclaimed a great feast with offerings to the ox. And the King sent one of the chief butchers of his Majesty, to cause the ox to be sacrificed. And when he was sacrificed, as he was upon the shoulders of the people, he shook his neck, and he threw two drops of blood over against the two doors of his Majesty. The one fell upon the one side, on the great door of Pharaoh, and the other upon the other door. They grew as two great Persea trees, and each of them was excellent.

And one went to tell unto his Majesty, "Two great Persea trees have grown, as a great marvel of his Majesty, in the night by the side of the great gate of his Majesty." And there was rejoicing for them in all the land, and there were offerings made to them.

And when the days were multiplied after these things, his Majesty was adorned with the blue crown, with garlands of flowers on his neck, and he was upon the chariot of pale gold, and he went out from the palace to behold the Persea trees: the princess also was going out with horses behind his Majesty. And his Majesty sat beneath one of the Persea trees, and it spake thus with his wife: "Oh, thou deceitful one, I am Bata, I am alive, though I have been evilly entreated. I knew who caused the acacia to be cut down by Pharaoh at my dwelling. I then became an ox, and thou causedst that I should be killed."

And many days after these things the princess stood at the table of Pharaoh, and the King was pleased with her. And she said to his Majesty, "Swear to me by God, saying, 'That which the princess shall say to me I will obey it for her.' " And he hearkened unto all she said. And he commanded, "Let these two Persea trees be cut down, and let them be made into goodly planks." And he hearkened unto all she said. And after this his Majesty sent skilful craftsmen, and they cut down the Persea trees of Pharaoh; and the princess, the royal wife, was standing looking on, and they did all that was in her heart unto the trees. But a chip flew up, and it entered into the mouth of the princess;

she swallowed it, and after many days she bore a son. And one went to tell his Majesty, "There is born to thee a son." And they brought him, and gave to him a nurse and servants; and there were rejoicings in the whole land. And the King sat making a merry day, as they were about the naming of him, and his Majesty loved him exceedingly at that moment, and the King raised him to be the royal son of Kush.

Now after the days had multiplied after these things, his Majesty made him heir of all the land. And many days after that, when he had fulfilled many years as heir, his Majesty flew up to heaven. And the heir said, "Let my great nobles of his Majesty be brought before me, that I may make them to know all that has happened to me." And they brought also before him his wife, and he judged with her before him, and they agreed with him. They brought to him his elder brother; he made him hereditary prince in all his land. He was thirty years King of Egypt, and he died, and his elder brother stood in his place on the day of burial.

Excellently finished in peace, for the ka of the scribe of the treasury Kagabu, of the treasury of Pharaoh, and for the scribe Hora, and the scribe Meremapt. Written by the scribe Anena, the owner of this roll. He who speaks against this roll, may Tahuti smite him.

SETNA AND THE MAGIC BOOK

(Anonymous: about 1400 B.C.)

THE manuscript of this story was found during the Nineteenth Century in the tomb of a Coptic monk. Nothing is known of the author, but it is assumed that he lived not long after the time of the probable origin of the Egyptian short story. *Setna and the Magic Book* is one of those wonder tales that have from time immemorial evoked the admiration of the world, and particularly of the Orientals. Whether or not the Egyptians actually believed all they were told in a fairy tale is an idle conjecture: but it seems probable that the strange happenings described in this story were accepted by many. Even the present age of science has not entirely banished a belief in magic: some of the finest of modern tales are based upon an ineradicable belief in the supernatural.

The translation here used is that by William Flinders Petrie in *Egyptian Tales*, Vol. 2, published in 1895 by Methuen and Co., by whose permission it is here reprinted. The original manuscript is a part of the so-called Doulaq Papyrus. There is no title to the original story, the title here used being that given it by the transcriber.

SETNA AND THE MAGIC BOOK

THE mighty King User-maat.ra (Rameses the Great) had a son
named Setna Kha.em.uast who was a great scribe, and very
learned in all the ancient writings. And he heard that the magic book
of Thoth, by which a man may enchant heaven and earth, and know
the language of all birds and beasts, was buried in the cemetery of
Memphis. And he went to search for it with his brother An.he.hor.eru;
and when they found the tomb of the King's son, Na.nefer.ka.ptah,
son of the King of Upper and Lower Egypt, Mer.neb.ptah, Setna
opened it and went in.

Now in the tomb was Na.nefer.ka.ptah, and with him was the *ka* of
his wife Ahura; for though she was buried at Koptos, her *ka* dwelt at
Memphis with her husband, whom she loved. And Setna saw them
seated before their offerings, and the book lay between them. And
Na.nefer.ka.ptah said to Setna, "Who are you that break into my
tomb in this way?" He said, "I am Setna, son of the great King User.-
maat.ra, living forever, and I come for that book which I see between
you." And Na.nefer.ka.ptah said, "It cannot be given to you." Then
said Setna, "But I will carry it away by force."

Then Ahura said to Setna, "Do not take this book; for it will bring
trouble on you, as it has upon us. Listen to what we have suffered
for it."

AHURA'S TALE

"We were the two children of the King Mer.neb.ptah, and he loved
us very much, for he had no others; and Na.nefer.ka.ptah was in his
palace as heir over all the land. And when we were grown, the King
said to the Queen, 'I will marry Na.nefer.ka.ptah to the daughter of
a general, and Ahura to the son of another general.' And the Queen
said, 'No; he is the heir, let him marry his sister, like the heir of a king;
none other is fit for him.' And the King said, 'That is not fair; they
had better be married to the children of the general.'

"And the Queen said, 'It is you who are not dealing rightly with
me.' And the King answered, 'If I have no more than these two children, is it right that they should marry one another? I will marry
Na.nefer.ka.ptah to the daughter of an officer, and Ahura to the son of
another officer. It has often been done so in our family.'

"And at a time when there was a great feast before the King, they
came to fetch me to the feast. And I was very troubled, and did not
behave as I used to do. And the King said to me, 'Ahura, have you
sent someone to me about this sorry matter, saying, "Let me be married to my elder brother"?' I said to him, 'Well, let me marry the son

of an officer, and he marry the daughter of another officer, as it often happens so in our family.' I laughed, and the King laughed. And the King told the steward of the palace, 'Let them take Ahura to the house of Na.nefer.ka.ptah to-night, and all kinds of good things with her.' So they brought me as a wife to the house of Na.nefer.ka.ptah; and the King ordered them to give me presents of silver and gold, and things from the palace.

"And Na.nefer.ka.ptah passed a happy time with me, and received all the presents from the palace; and we loved one another. And when I expected a child, they told the King, and he was most heartily glad; and he sent me many things, and a present of the best silver and gold and linen. And when the time came, I bore this little child that is before you. And they gave him the name of Mer-ab, and registered him in the book of the 'House of life.'

"And when my brother Na.nefer.ka.ptah went to the cemetery of Memphis, he did nothing on earth but read the writings that are in the catacombs of the kings, and the tablets of the 'House of life,' and the inscriptions that are seen on the monuments, and he worked hard on the writings. And there was a priest there called Nesi-ptah; and as Na.-nefer.ka.ptah went into a temple to pray, it happened that he went behind this priest, and was reading the inscriptions that were on the chapels of the gods. And the priest mocked him and laughed. So Na.-nefer.ka.ptah said to him. 'Why are you laughing at me?' And he replied, 'I was not laughing at you, or if I happened to do so, it was at your reading writings that are worthless. If you wish so much to read writings, come to me, and I will bring you to the place where the book is which Thoth himself wrote with his own hand, and which will bring you to the gods. When you read but two pages in this you will enchant the heaven, the earth, the abyss, the mountains, and the sea; you shall know what the birds of the sky and the crawling things are saying; you shall see the fishes of the deep, for a divine power is there to bring them up out of the depth. And when you read the second page, if you are in the world of ghosts, you will become again in the shape you were in on earth. You will see the sun shining in the sky, with all the gods, and the full moon.'

"And Na.nefer.ka.ptah said: 'By the life of the King! Tell me of anything you want done, and I'll do it for you, if you will only send me where this book is.' And the priest answered Na.nefer.ka.ptah, 'If you want to go to the place where the book is, you must give me 100 pieces of silver for my funeral, and provide that they shall bury me as a rich priest.' So Na.nefer.ka.ptah called his lad and told him to give the priest 100 pieces of silver; and he made them do as he wished, even everything that he asked for. Then the priest said to Na.nefer.ka.ptah: 'This book is in the middle of the river at Koptos, in an iron box; in the iron box is a bronze box; in the bronze box is a sycamore box; in the sycamore box is an ivory and ebony box; in the ivory and ebony box is a silver box; in the silver box is a golden box, and in that is the book. It is twisted all round with snakes and scorpions and all the other crawling things around the box in which the book is; and there is a deathless snake by the box.' And when the priest told Na.nefer.ka.-ptah, he did not know where on earth he was, he was so much delighted.

"And when he came from the temple he told me all that had happened to him. And he said: 'I shall go to Koptos, for I must fetch this book; I will not stay any longer in the north.' And I said, 'Let me dissuade you, for you prepare sorrow and you will bring me into trouble in the Thebaid.' And I laid my hand on Na.nefer.ka.ptah, to keep him from going to Koptos, but he would not listen to me; and he went to the King, and told the King all that the priest had said. The King asked him, 'What is it that you want?' and he replied, 'Let them give me the royal boat with its belongings, for I will go to the south with Ahura and her little boy Mer-ab, and fetch this book without delay.' So they gave him the royal boat with its belongings, and we went with him to the haven, and sailed from there up to Koptos.

"Then the priests of Isis of Koptos, and the high-priest of Isis, came down to us without waiting, to meet Na.nefer.ka.ptah, and their wives also came to me. We went into the temple of Isis and Harpokrates; and Na.nefer.ka.ptah brought an ox, a goose, and some wine, and made a burnt-offering and a drink-offering before Isis of Koptos and Harpokrates. They brought us to a very fine house, with all good things; and Na.nefer.ka.ptah spent four days there and feasted with the priests of Isis of Koptos, and the wives of the priests of Isis also made holiday with me.

"And the morning of the fifth day came; and Na.nefer.ka.ptah called a priest to him, and made a magic cabin that was full of men and tackle. He put the spell upon it, and put life in it, and gave them breath, and sank it in the water. He filled the royal boat with sand, and took leave of me, and sailed from the haven: and I sat by the river at Koptos that I might see what would become of him. And he said, 'Workmen, work for me, even at the place where the book is.' And they toiled by night and by day; and when they had reached it in three days, he threw the sand out, and made a shoal in the river. And then he found on it entwined serpents and scorpions and all kinds of crawling things around the box in which the book was; and by it he found a deathless snake around the box. And he laid the spell upon the entwined serpents and scorpions and all kinds of crawling things which were around the box, that they should not come out. And he went to the deathless snake, and fought with him, and killed him; but he came to life again, and took a new form. He then fought again with him a second time; but he came to life again, and took a third form. He then cut him in two parts, and put sand between the parts, that he should not appear again.

"Na.nefer.ka.ptah then went to the place where he found the box. He uncovered a box of iron, and opened it; he found then a box of bronze, and opened that; then he found a box of sycamore wood, and opened that; again, he found a box of ivory and ebony, and opened that; yet, he found a box of silver, and opened that; and then he found a box of gold; he opened that, and found the book in it. He took the book from the golden box, and read a page of spells from it. He enchanted the heaven and the earth, the abyss, the mountains, and the sea; he knew what the birds of the sky, the fish of the deep, and the beasts of the hills all said. He read another page of the spells, and saw the sun shining in the sky, with all the gods, the full moon, and the stars in their shapes; he saw the fishes of the deep, for a divine power was present that brought them up from the water. He then read the spell upon the workmen that he had made, and taken from the haven, and said to them, 'Work for me, back to the place from which I came.' And they toiled night and day, and so he came back to the place where I sat by the river of Koptos; I had not drunk nor eaten anything, and had done nothing on earth, but sat like one who is gone to the grave.

"I then told Na.nefer.ka.ptah that I wished to see this book, for which we had taken so much trouble. He gave the book into my hands; and when I read a page of the spells in it I also enchanted heaven and earth, the abyss, the mountains, and the sea. I also knew what the birds of the sky, the fishes of the deep, and the beasts of the hills all said. I read another page of the spells, and I saw the sun shining in the sky with all the gods, the full moon, and the stars in their shapes; I saw the fishes of the deep, for a divine power was present that brought them up from the water. As I could not write, I asked Na.nefer.ka.ptah, who was a good writer, and a very learned one; he called for a new piece of papyrus, and wrote on it all that was in the book before him. He dipped it in beer, and washed it off in the liquid; for he knew that if it were washed off, and he drank it, he would know all that there was in the writing.

"We returned back to Koptos the same day, and made a feast before Isis of Koptos and Harpokrates. We then went to the haven and sailed, and went northward of Koptos. And as we went on Thoth discovered all that Na.nefer.ka.ptah had done with the book; and Thoth hastened to tell Ra, and said, 'Now know that my book and my revelation are with Na.nefer.ka.ptah, son of the King Mer.neb.ptah. He has forced himself into my place, and robbed it, and seized my box with the writings, and killed my guards who protected it.' And Ra replied to him, 'He is before you, take him and all his kin.' He sent a power from heaven with the command, 'Do not let Na.nefer.ka.ptah return safe

to Memphis with all his kin.' And after this hour, the little boy Mer-ab,
going out from the awning of the royal boat, fell into the river: he
called on Ra, and everybody who was on the bank raised a cry. Na.-
nefer.ka.ptah went out of the cabin, and read the spell over him; he
brought his body up because a divine power brought him to the surface. He read another spell over him, and made him tell of all that
happened to him, and of what Thoth had said before Ra.

"We turned back with him to Koptos. We brought him to the Good
House, we fetched the people to him, and made one embalm him; and
we buried him in his coffin in the cemetery of Koptos like a great and
noble person.

"And Na.nefer.ka.ptah, my brother, said: 'Let us go down, let us
not delay, for the King has not yet heard of what has happened to him,
and his heart will be sad about it.' So we went to the haven, we sailed,
and did not stay to the north of Koptos. When we were come to the
place where the little boy Mer-ab had fallen into the water, I went out
from the awning of the royal boat, and I fell into the river. They called
Na.nefer.ka.ptah, and he came out from the cabin of the royal boat; he
read a spell over me, and brought my body up, because a divine power
brought me to the surface. He drew me out, and read the spell over
me, and made me tell him of all that had happened to me, and of what
Thoth had said before Ra. Then he turned back with me to Koptos, he
brought me to the Good House, he fetched the people to me, and made
one embalm me, as great and noble people are buried, and laid me in
the tomb where Mer-ab my young child was.

"He turned to the haven, and sailed down, and delayed not in the
north of Koptos. When he was come to the place where we fell into
the river, he said to his heart: 'Shall I not better turn back again to
Koptos, that I may lie by them? For, if not, when I go down to
Memphis, and the King asks after his children, what shall I say to him?
Can I tell him, "I have taken your children to the Thebaid, and killed
them, while I remained alive, and I have come to Memphis still alive"?'
Then he made them bring him a linen cloth of striped byssus; he made
a band, and bound the book firmly, and tied it upon him. Na.nefer.ka.-
ptah then went out of the awning of the royal boat and fell into the
river. He cried on Ra; and all those who were on the bank made an
outcry, saying: 'Great woe! Sad woe! Is he lost, that good scribe and
able man that has no equal?'

"The royal boat went on, without anyone on earth knowing where
Na.nefer.ka.ptah was. It went on to Memphis, and they told all this to
the King. Then the King went down to the royal boat in mourning,
and all the soldiers and high-priests of Ptah were in mourning, and all
the officials and courtiers. And when he saw Na.nefer.ka.ptah, who was
in the inner cabin of the royal boat—from his rank of high scribe—he

lifted him up. And they saw the book by him; and the King said, 'Let one hide this book that is with him.' And the officers of the King, the priests of Ptah, and the high-priest of Ptah, said to the King, 'Our Lord, may the King live as long as the sun! Na.nefer.ka.ptah was a good scribe, and a very skilful man.' And the King had him laid in his Good House to the sixteenth day, and then had him wrapped to the thirty-fifth day, and laid him out to the seventieth day, and then had him put in his grave in his resting-place.

"I have now told you the sorrow which has come upon us because of this book for which you ask, saying, 'Let it be given to me.' You have no claim to it; and, indeed, for the sake of it, we have given up our life on earth."

And Setna said to Ahura, "Give me the book which I see between you and Na.nefer.ka.ptah; for if you do not I will take it by force." Then Na.nefer.ka.ptah rose from his seat and said: "Are you Setna, to whom my wife has told of all these blows of fate, which you have not suffered? Can you take this book by your skill as a good scribe? If, indeed, you can play games with me, let us play a game, then, of 52 points." And Setna said, "I am ready," and the board and its pieces were put before him. And Na.nefer.ka.ptah won a game from Setna; and he put the spell upon him, and defended himself with the game board that was before him, and sunk him into the ground above his feet. He did the same at the second game, and won it from Setna, and sunk him into the ground to his waist. He did the same at the third game, and made him sink into the ground up to his ears. Then Setna struck Na.nefer.ka.ptah a great blow with his hand. And Setna called his brother An.he.hor.eru and said to him, "Make haste and go up upon earth, and tell the King all that has happened to me, and bring me the talisman of my father Ptah, and my magic books."

And he hurried up upon earth, and told the King all that had happened to Setna. The King said, "Bring him the talisman of his father Ptah, and his magic books." And An.he.hor.eru hurried down into the tomb; he laid the talisman on Setna, and he sprang up again immediately. And then Setna reached out his hand for the book, and took it. Then—as Setna went out from the tomb—there went a Light before him, and Darkness behind him. And Ahura wept at him, and she said: "Glory to the King of Darkness! Hail to the King of Light! All power is gone from the tomb." But Na.nefer.ka.ptah said to Ahura: "Do not let your heart be sad; I will make him bring back this book, with a forked stick in his hand, and a fire-pan on his head." And Setna went out from the tomb, and it closed behind him as it was before.

Then Setna went to the King, and told him everything that had happened to him with the book. And the King said to Setna, "Take back the book to the grave of Na.nefer.ka.ptah, like a prudent man, or else he will make you bring it with a forked stick in your hand, and a fire-pan on your head." But Setna would not listen to him; and when Setna had unrolled the book he did nothing on earth but read it to everybody.

After that it happened one day, when Setna was walking near the temple of Ptah, he saw a woman of such beauty that another could not be found to equal her. On her there was much gold, and with her were fifty-two servants. From the time that Setna beheld her, he no longer knew the part of the world he lived in. He called his page, saying, "Do not delay going to the place where that woman is and finding out who she is." The young page made no delay. He addressed the maidservant who walked behind her, and questioned her, "What person is that?" She said to him, "She is Tbubui, daughter of the prophet of Bastit, who now goes to make her prayer before Ptah." When the young man had returned to Setna, he recounted all the words she had said to him with-out exception. Setna said to the young man, "Go and say thus to the maidservant, 'Setna-Khamois, son of the Pharaoh Usimares it is who sends me, saying, "I will give thee ten pieces of gold that thou mayest pass an hour with me. If there is necessity to have recourse to violence he will do it, and he will take thee to a hidden place, where no one in the world will find thee."'" When the young man had returned to the place where Tbubui was, he addressed the maidservant, and spake with her, but she exclaimed against his words, as though it were an insult to speak them. Tbubui said to the young man, "Cease to speak to that wretched girl; come and speak to me." The young man ap-proached the place where Tbubui was; he said to her, "I will give thee ten pieces of gold if thou wilt pass an hour with Setna-Khamois, the son of Pharaoh Usimares. If there is necessity to have recourse to vio-lence, he will do so, and will take thee to a hidden place where no one in the world will find thee." Tbubui said, "Go, say to Setna, 'I am a hierodule, I am no mean person; if thou dost desire to have thy pleas-ure of me, thou shalt come to Bubastis into my house. All will be ready there, and thou shalt have thy pleasure of me, and no one in the world shall know it, and I shall not have acted like a woman of the streets.'" When the page had returned to Setna, he repeated to him all the words that she had said without exception, and he said, "Lo, I am satisfied." But all who were with Setna began to curse.

Setna caused a boat to be fetched, he embarked, and delayed not to arrive at Bubastis. He went to the west of the town, until he came to a house that was very high; it had a wall all round it, it had a garden on the north side, there was a flight of steps in front of it. Setna inquired saying. "Whose is this house?" They said to him, "It is the house of Tbubui." Setna entered the grounds, and he marveled at the pavilion situated in the garden while they told Tbubui; she came down, she took the hand of Setna, and she said to him, "By my life! the journey to the house of the priest of Bastit, lady of Ankhutaui, at which thou art arrived, is very pleasant to me. Come up with me." Setna went up by the stairway of the house with Tbubui. He found the upper story of the house sanded and powdered with sand and powder of real lapis lazuli and real turquoise. There were several beds there, spread with stuffs of royal linen, and also many cups of gold on a stand. They filled a golden cup with wine and placed it in the hand of Setna and Tbubui said to him, "Will it please thee to rest thyself?" He said to her, "That is not what I wish to do." They put scented wood on the fire, they brought perfumes of the kind that are supplied to Pharaoh, and Setna made a happy day with Tbubui. "Let us accomplish that for which we have come here." She said to him, "Thou shalt arrive at thy house, that where thou art. But for me, I am a hierodule, I am no mean person. If thou desirest to have thy pleasure of me, thou shalt make me a contract of sustenance, and a contract of money on all the things and all the goods that are thine." He said to her, "Let the scribe of the school be brought." He was brought immediately, and Setna caused to be made in favor of Tbubui a contract for maintenance, and he made her in writing a dowry of all the things, all the goods that were his. An hour passed, one came to say this to Setna, "Thy children are below." He said, "Let them be brought up." Tbubui arose; she put on a robe of fine linen and Setna beheld all her limbs through it, and his desire increased yet more than before. Setna said to Tbubui, "Let us accomplish now that for which I came." She said to him, "Thou shalt arrive at thy house, that where thou art. But for me, I am a hierodule; I am no mean person. If thou desirest to have thy pleasure of me, thou wilt cause thy children to subscribe to my writing that they may not seek a quarrel with my children on the subject of thy possessions." Setna had his children fetched and made them subscribe to the writing. Setna said to Tbubui, "Let me now accomplish that for which I came." She said to him, "Thou shalt arrive at thy house, that where thou art. But for me, I am a hierodule; I am no mean person. If thou dost desire to have thy pleasure of me, thou shall cause thy children to be slain, so that they may not seek a quarrel with my children on account of thy possessions." Setna said, "Let the crime be committed on them of which the desire has entered thy heart." She caused the children of Setna to be slain before him, she had them thrown out below the window, to the dogs and cats, and they ate their flesh, and he heard them while he was drinking with Tbubui. Setna said to Tbubui, "Let us accomplish that for which we have come here, for all that thou hast said before me has been done for thee." She said to him, "Come into this chamber." Setna entered the chamber; he lay down on a bed of ivory and ebony, in order that his love might be rewarded, and Tbubui lay down by the side of Setna. He stretched out his hand to touch her; she opened her mouth widely and uttered a loud cry.

When Setna came to himself he was in a place of a furnace without any clothing on his back. After an hour Setna perceived a very big man standing on a platform, with quite a number of attendants beneath his feet, for he had the semblance of a Pharaoh. Setna was about to raise himself but he could not arise for shame, for he had no clothing on his back. This Pharaoh said, "Setna, what is the state in which you are?" He said, "It is Na.nefer.ka.ptah who has had all this done to me." This Pharaoh said, "Go to Memphis; thy children, lo! they wish for thee. Lo! they are standing before Pharaoh." Setna spake before this Pharaoh, "My great lord the king—mayest thou have the duration of Ra—how can I arrive at Memphis, for I have no raiment in the world on my back?" This Pharaoh called a page who was standing near him and commanded him to give a garment to Setna. This Pharaoh said, "Setna, go to Memphis. Thy children, behold they live, behold they are standing before the king."

So Setna went to Memphis, and embraced his children for that they were alive. And the King said to him, "Were you not drunk to do so?" Then Setna told all things that had happened with Tbubui and Na.nefer.ka.ptah. And the King said, "Setna, I have already lifted up my hand against you before, and said, 'He will kill you if you do not take back the book to the place you took it from." But you have never listened to me till this hour. Now, then, take the book to Na.nefer.ka.-ptah, with a forked stick in your hand, and a fire-pan on your head."

So Setna went out from before the King, with a forked stick in his hand, and a fire-pan on his head. He went down to the tomb in which was Na.nefer.ka.ptah. And Ahura said to him, "It is Ptah, the great god, that has brought you back safe." Na.nefer.ka.ptah laughed, and he said, "This is the business that I told you before." And when Setna had praised Na.nefer.ka.ptah, he found it as the proverb says, "The sun was in the whole tomb." And Ahura and Na.nefer.ka.ptah besought Setna greatly. And Setna said, "Na.nefer.ka.ptah, is it aught disgraceful (that you lay on me to do)?" And Na.nefer.ka.ptah said, "Setna, you know this, that Ahura and Mer-ab, her child, behold! they are in Koptos; bring them here into this tomb, by the skill of a good scribe. Let it be impressed upon you to take pains, and to go to Koptos to bring them here." Setna then went out from the tomb to the King, and told the King all that Na.nefer.ka.ptah had told him.

The King said, "Setna, go to Koptos and bring back Ahura and Mer-ab." He answered the King, "Let one give me the royal boat and its belongings." And they gave him the royal boat and its belongings, and he left the haven, and sailed without stopping till he came to Koptos.

And they made this known to the priests of Isis at Koptos and to the high priest of Isis; and behold they came down to him, and gave him their hand to the shore. He went up with them and entered into the temple of Isis of Koptos and of Harpokrates. He ordered one to offer for him an ox, a goose, and some wine, and he made a burnt-offering and a drink-offering before Isis of Koptos and Harpokrates. He went to the cemetery of Koptos with the priests of Isis and the high-priest of Isis. They dug about for three days and three nights, for they searched even in all the catacombs which were in the cemetery of Koptos; they turned over the steles of the scribes of the "double house of life," and read the inscriptions that they found on them. But they could not find the resting-place of Ahura and Mer-ab.

Now Na.nefer.ka.ptah perceived that they could not find the resting place of Ahura and her child Mer-ab. So he raised himself up as a venerable, very old ancient, and came before Setna. And Setna saw him, and Setna said to the ancient: "You look like a very old man; do you know where is the resting-place of Ahura and her child Mer-ab?" The ancient said to Setna: "It was told by the father of the father of my father to the father of my father, and the father of my father has told it to my father; the resting-place of Ahura and of her child Mer-ab is in a mound south of the town of Pehemato." And Setna said to the ancient, "Perhaps we may do damage to Pehemato, and you are ready to lead one to the town for the sake of that." The ancient replied to Setna: "If one listens to me, shall he therefore destroy the town of Pehemato! If they do not find Ahura and her child Mer-ab under the south corner of their town may I be disgraced." They attended to the ancient, and found the resting-place of Ahura and her child Mer-ab under the south corner of the town of Pehemato. Setna laid them in the royal boat to bring them as honored persons, and restored the town of Pehemato as it originally was. And Na.nefer.ka.ptah made Setna to know that it was he who had come to Koptos, to enable them to find out where the resting-place was of Ahura and her child Mer-ab.

So Setna left the haven in the royal boat, and sailed without stopping, and reached Memphis with all the soldiers who were with him. And when they told the King he came down to the royal boat. He took them as honored persons escorted to the catacombs, in which Na.nefer.ka.ptah was, and smoothed down the ground over them.

This is the completed writing of the tale of Setna Kha.em.uast, and Na.nefer.ka.ptah, and his wife Ahura, and their child Mer-ab. It was written in the thirty-fifth year, the month Tybi.

Ancient Greece

INTRODUCTION

THERE is no land without its story-tellers, and in the dawn of Hellenic civilization we find the half-legendary author of the *Iliad* and the *Odyssey* telling tales—some of them so long and elaborate as to be called epics, and some of them brief enough to be classed as short stories. Though the actual composition of the earliest Greek stories dates from a thousand or fifteen hundred years after the Egyptian tales, there is no doubt that they were sung or recited centuries before the great epics assumed the form in which they are now known.

The poet Hesiod, somewhat later than Homer, but before the opening of the Golden Age of Greek literature (Fifth Century, B.C.), inserted into his longer mythical and didactic works episodes which are, as a matter of fact, short stories, though they are inferior in workmanship to the ingenious tales with which Herodotus enlivens the pages of his fascinating *History*. Herodotus was much more of an artist than a mere recorder of facts. He was determined at all costs to make his work readable. Other and later historians strove to imitate him, and their books are full of anecdotes and episodes many of which might be extracted to demonstrate the gradual development of the form. Plutarch, in particular, was fond of relating incidents to illustrate the *Lives* of his heroes.

Though the fable probably originated in India, it was given a particular form in the so-called Beast Fable of the Greeks. This is a short story told in order to point a moral, in which respect it is not essentially different from most other stories, ancient and modern. It was in Greece that a collection of beast fables accumulated, and was attributed to a certain Æsop, of whom we have no authentic knowledge. That they are short and deal ostensibly with animals instead of human beings in no way prevents their inclusion in a collection of this sort. The best of them are masterpieces in the art of condensed narrative. Though the works attributed to Æsop are now lost, they have been preserved in translated or adapted form by the Latin fabulist, Phædrus.

It was after the close of the great epoch of Greek literature that the art of prose fiction arose in Greece. Antonius Diogenes, Xenophon of Ephesus, Achilles Tatius, Lucian, Parthenius, Longus and Heliodorus belong more especially among the writers of pure fiction. There were occasional exceptions, like Apollonius of Rhodes, who sought inspiration in the myths of the past, and developed the more or less crude incidents of the ancients into comely, if occasionally affected, stories. But the romance itself was originated by Xenophon of Ephesus, Longus, and Heliodorus, and later developed by Achilles Tatius and Chariton. Still, the short story as an independent form was apparently not recognized. In *The Robbers of Egypt*, which is the first chapter of Heliodorus' *Æthiopian Romance*, we find a complete and unified short story. The *Daphnis and Chloe* of Longus is an early example of the "long-short" story.

Long before the final extinction of Greek romance the Greek forms had been carried over into the Roman world, where they were to flourish for a time, disappear, and then a thousand years later bloom again under the touch of the Italians.

HOMER

(About 1000 B.C.)

THE first mention of Homer dates from the Seventh Century B.C., but when he lived, or indeed whether he ever lived at all, are questions that have never been solved. *The Iliad* and *The Odyssey* were probably composed about a thousand years before the Christian era. The short story, as we know it, was not of course a recognized literary form, but *Eumæus' Tale*, in *The Odyssey*, happens to be an excellent example. It is told to Odysseus by the old swine-herd.

The present version, purposely reduced by the editors to more or less colloquial prose, is based upon three translations. There is no title in the original.

EUMÆUS' TALE

(From *The Odyssey*, Book XV)

"THERE is an island over beyond Ortygia—perchance thou hast heard tell of it—where the sun turns. It is a goodly island, though not very vast, with rich herds and flocks, and much grain and wine. There is no dearth, and no illness visits poor mortals. When men grow old there, Apollo of the Silver Bow, in company with Artemis, comes to them and kills them gently with his shafts. On the island are two cities, which divide all the land between them. My father was king over all, Ctesius son of Ormenus, a godlike man.

"To this land came the Phœnicians, famous sailors greedy for merchandise, bringing many things in their dark ship. There was in my father's palace a Phœnician woman, tall and lovely, and skilful in making beautiful things with her hands; her the Phœnicians deceived by their guile. As she was washing clothes near the hollow ship, one of them conquered her; love beguiles many women, even the noblest. The Phœnician asked her who she was and from what land, and she straightway showed him the high palace of my father, and said, 'I come from Sidon, rich in bronze, and am the daughter of the wealthy Arybas. The Taphians, who are pirates, seized me as I was coming from the fields, brought me to this land, and sold me for a great price to my present master.' Then he who had conquered her said in answer, 'Wouldst thou return once more to thy home with us, to see again the high palace of thy father, and see thy mother? They are yet alive, and are reputed to be wealthy.'

"Then the woman made answer to him and said, 'This may be, if you sailors will swear to bring me home safely.' Thus she answered, and the sailors swore as she bade them, and after they had sworn, the woman spake to them: 'Say naught now; let none of you speak to me when you see me in the street, or even by the well, lest it be known and told to the old man here, and he suspect me and tie me fast and bring death to you all. But keep in mind the plan, and hasten to bring your freight for the homeward voyage. When your ship is full laden, send a messenger quickly to the palace for me, and I will bring gold, all I can lay hand upon. And there is more, besides, that I would bring with me: I am nursing a child for my master, a darling boy who runs about with me; I would bring him with me on the ship. He should bring a high price, if you sell him among men of other lands and other speech.'

"Then she departed to the fair halls. But the sailors remained among us a whole year, and gathered great wealth for their hollow ship, and when it was laden and ready to sail, a messenger was sent to tell the woman. A crafty man with a golden and amber chain came to the halls of my father. My mother and the maidens in the palace were looking upon the chain and holding it, offering the man a price for it, while he made signs in silence to the woman. Then he betook himself to the hollow ship. The woman then took me by the hand and led me out of the house. At the doorway she found the cups and tables of the guests who had feasted and waited upon my father: they had gone out to the meeting-place where councils were held. And the woman concealed three cups in her bosom, and carried them away, while I followed her innocently. The sun sank and darkness came. Going quickly, we reached the harbor and the swift ship of the Phœnicians; the sailors went aboard, taking us with them, and sailed over the ocean, Zeus giving us favoring winds. We sailed continuously day and night for six days, but when Zeus, son of Cronos, brought the seventh, Artemis the huntress struck down the woman and she fell like a swallow to the bottom of the ship. The sailors threw her overboard, to the seals and the fishes, and I sorrowed. With the help of wind and wave they came to Ithaca, where Laertes bought me. It was thus that I first beheld this place."

ÆSOP

(6th Century, B.C.?)

ÆSOP was "not a poet," says Gilbert Murray, "but the legendary author of a particular type of story." This type is known as the Beast Fable, a brief incident related in order to point a simple moral. According to tradition Æsop was a foreign slave of the Sixth Century B.C. Whether the fables of ancient India, such as those in the *Hitopadesa*, influenced the ancient Greeks and Romans is a question still debated by scholars. At any rate there is a striking similarity, both in treatment and subject-matter, between the Fables of Æsop, Phædrus and Avianus, and those which delighted the Indians.

The present translation was made by James and published first in 1848.

THE COUNTRY MOUSE AND THE TOWN MOUSE

ONCE upon a time a Country Mouse who had a friend in town invited him, for old acquaintance' sake, to pay him a visit in the country. The invitation being accepted in due form, the Country Mouse, though plain and rough and somewhat frugal in his nature opened his heart and store, in honor of hospitality and an old friend. There was not a carefully stored-up morsel that he did not bring forth out of his larder, peas and barley, cheese-parings and nuts, hoping by quantity to make up what he feared was wanting in quality, to suit the palate of his dainty guest. The Town Mouse, condescending to pick a bit here and a bit there, while the host sat nibbling a blade of barley-straw, at length exclaimed, "How is it, my good friend, that you can endure the dullness of this unpolished life? You are living like a toad in a hole. You can't really prefer these solitary rocks and woods to streets teeming with carriages and men. On my honor, you are wasting your time miserably here. We must make the most of life while it lasts.

A mouse, you know, does not live forever. So come with me and I'll show you life and the town." Overpowered with such fine words and so polished a manner, the Country Mouse assented; and they set out together on their journey to town. It was late in the evening when they crept stealthily into the city, and midnight ere they reached the great house, where the Town Mouse took up his quarters. Here were couches of crimson velvet, carvings in ivory, everything in short that denoted wealth and luxury. On the table were the remains of a splendid banquet, to procure which all the choicest shops in the town had been ransacked the day before. It was now the turn of the courtier to play the host; he places his country friend on purple, runs to and fro to supply all his wants, presses dish upon dish and dainty upon dainty, and as though he were waiting on a king, tastes every course ere he ventures to place it before his rustic cousin. The Country Mouse, for his part, affects to make himself quite at home, and blesses the good fortune that had wrought such a change in his way of life; when, in the midst of his enjoyment, as he is thinking with contempt of the poor fare he has forsaken, on a sudden the door flies open, and a party of revellers returning from a late entertainment, bursts into the room. The affrighted friends jump from the table in the greatest consternation and hide themselves in the first corner they can reach. No sooner do they venture to creep out again than the barking of dogs drives them back in still greater terror than before. At length, when things seemed quiet, the Country Mouse stole out from his hiding place, and bidding his friend good-bye, whispered in his ear, "Oh, my good sir, this fine mode of living may do for those who like it; but give me my barley-bread in peace and security before the daintiest feast where Fear and Care are in waiting."

HERODOTUS

(484—424 B.C.)

HERODOTUS, the Father of History, is celebrated as a teller of tales. These he introduced into his *History* partly for purposes of elucidation and example, but partly also because he enjoyed writing them. The story that follows is, according to Professor Murray "all but pure fairy" tale, and is probably based on an Indian original. For the first time in Greek literature we have a short story as unified and free from unessential details as the most rigid modern critic could desire.

The present version, which comprises Chapter CXXI of the Second Book of the *History*, is from the standard translation by George Rawlinson, first published in 1858. There is no title in the original.

KING RHAMPSINITUS AND THE THIEF

(From the *History*, Book II)

KING RHAMPSINITUS was possessed, they said, of great riches in silver—indeed to such an amount, that none of the princes, his successors, surpassed or even equaled his wealth. For the better custody of this money, he proposed to build a vast chamber of hewn stone, one side of which was to form a part of the outer wall of his palace. The builder, therefore, having designs upon the treasures, contrived, as he was making the building, to insert in this wall a stone which could easily be removed from its place by two men, or even one. So the chamber was finished, and the king's money stored away in it.

Time passed, and the builder fell sick; when finding his end approaching, he called for his two sons, and related to them the contrivance he had made in the king's treasure-chamber, telling them it was for their sakes he had done it, so that they might always live in affluence. Then he gave them clear directions concerning the mode of removing the stone, and communicated the measurements, bidding them carefully keep the secret, whereby they would be Comptrollers of the Royal Exchequer so long as they lived. Then the father died, and the sons were not slow in setting to work; they went by night to the palace, found the stone in the wall of the building, and having removed it with ease, plundered the treasury of a round sum.

When the king next paid a visit to the apartment he was astonished to see that the money was sunk in some of the vessels wherein it was stored away. Whom to accuse, however, he knew not, as the seals were all perfect, and the fastenings of the room secure. Still each time that he repeated his visits, he found that more money was gone. The thieves in truth never stopped, but plundered the treasury ever more and more.

At last the king determined to have some traps made, and set near the vessels which contained his wealth. This was done, and when the thieves came, as usual, to the treasure chamber, and one of them entering through the aperture, made straight for the jars, suddenly he found himself caught in one of the traps. Perceiving that he was lost, he instantly called his brother, and telling him what had happened, entreated him to enter as quickly as possible and cut off his head, that when his body should be discovered it might not be recognized, which would have the effect of bringing ruin upon both. The other thief thought the advice good, and was persuaded to follow it; then, fitting the stone into its place, he went home, taking with him his brother's head.

When day dawned, the king came into the room, and marveled

greatly to see the body of the thief in the trap without a head, while the building was still whole, and neither entrance nor exit was to be seen anywhere. In this perplexity he commanded the body of the dead man to be hung up outside the palace wall, and set a guard to watch it, with orders that if any persons were seen weeping or lamenting near the place, they should be seized and brought before him. When the mother heard of this exposure of the corpse of her son, she took it sorely to heart, and spoke to her surviving child, bidding him devise some plan or other to get back the body, and threatening that if he did not exert himself she would go herself to the king and denounce him as a robber.

The son said all he could to persuade her to let the matter rest, but in vain: she still continued to trouble him, until at last he yielded to her importunity, and contrived as follows: Filling some skins with wine, he loaded them on donkeys, which he drove before him till he came to the place where the guards were watching the dead body, when, pulling two or three of the skins towards him, he untied some of the necks which dangled by the asses' sides. The wine poured freely out, whereupon he began to beat his head and shout with all his might, seeming not to know which of the donkeys he should turn to first.

When the guards saw the wine running, delighted to profit by the occasion, they rushed one and all into the road, each with some vessel or other, and caught the liquor as it was spilling. The driver pretended anger, and loaded them with abuse; whereon they did their best to pacify him, until at last he appeared to soften, and recover his good humor, drove his asses aside out of the road, and set to work to re-arrange their burdens; meanwhile, as he talked and chatted with the guards, one of them began to rally him, and make him laugh, where-upon he gave them one of the skins as a gift. They now made up their minds to sit down and have a drinking-bout where they were, so they begged him to remain and drink with them. Then the man let himself be persuaded, and stayed.

As the drinking went on, they grew very friendly together, so presently he gave them another skin, upon which they drank so copiously that they were all overcome with liquor, and growing drowsy, lay down, and fell asleep on the spot. The thief waited till it was the dead of the night, and then took down the body of his brother; after which, in mockery, he shaved off the right side of all the soldiers' beards, and so left them. Laying his brother's body upon the asses, he carried it home to his mother, having thus accomplished the thing that she had required of him.

When it came to the king's ears that the thief's body was stolen away, he was sorely vexed. Wishing, therefore, whatever it might cost, to catch the man who had contrived the trick, he had recourse (the priest said) to an expedient which I can scarcely credit. He announced that he would bestow his own daughter upon the man who would narrate to her the best story of the cleverest and wickedest thing done by himself. If any one in reply told her the story of the thief, she was to lay hold of him, and not allow him to get away.

The daughter did as her father willed, whereon the thief, who was well aware of the king's motive, felt a desire to outdo him in craft and cunning. Accordingly he contrived the following plan: He procured the corpse of a man lately dead, and cutting off one of the arms at the shoulder, put it under his dress, and so went to the king's daughter. When she put the question to him as she had done to all the rest, he replied that the wickedest thing he had ever done was cutting off the head of his brother when he was caught in a trap in the king's treasury, and the cleverest was making the guards drunk and carrying off the body. As he spoke, the princess caught at him, but the thief took advantage of the darkness to hold out to her the hand of the corpse. Imagining it to be his own hand, she seized and held it fast; while the thief, leaving it in her grasp, made his escape by the door.

The king, when word was brought him of this fresh success, amazed at the sagacity and boldness of the man, sent messengers to all the towns in his dominions to proclaim a free pardon for the thief, and to promise him a rich reward, if he came and made himself known. The thief took the king at his word, and came boldly into his presence; whereupon Rhampsinitus, greatly admiring him, and looking on him as the most knowing of men, gave him his daughter in marriage. "The Egyptians," he said, "excelled all the rest of the world in wisdom, and this man excelled all other Egyptians."

APOLLONIUS OF RHODES

(3rd Century B.C.)

ALTHOUGH he was a late writer in the epic form, Apollonius treated ancient mythical material, but from the standpoint of a scholar and a literary stylist. He left his native land, Rhodes, and settled in Alexandria, then the centre of the cultured world. The tale of Phineus is not new, but the details which embellish it, and the verbal pyrotechnics which he lavished upon it, are highly characteristic of the decadent period in which it was written.

The present translation is that of R. C. Seaton, in the Loeb edition, William Heinemann, London, 1912. There is no title to the story in the original.

PHINEUS AND THE HARPIES

(From *The Argonautica*, Book III)

THERE Phineus, son of Agenor, had his home by the sea, Phineus, who above all men endured most bitter woes because of the gift of prophecy which Leto's son had granted him aforetime. And he reverenced not a whit even Zeus himself, for he foretold unerringly to men his sacred will. Wherefore Zeus sent upon him a lingering old age, and took from his eyes the pleasant light, and suffered him not to have joy of the dainties untold that the dwellers-around ever brought to his house when they came to inquire the will of heaven. But on a sudden, swooping through the clouds, the Harpies, with their crooked beaks, incessantly snatched the food away from his mouth and hands, and at times not a morsel of food was left, at others but a little, in order that he might live and be tormented. And they poured forth over all a loathsome stench; and no one dared not merely to carry food to his mouth, but even to stand at a distance, so foully reeked the remnants of the meal. But straightway when he heard the voice and the tramp of the band he knew that they were the men passing by, at whose coming Zeus's oracle had declared to him that he should have joy of his food. And he rose from his couch, like a lifeless dream, bowed over his staff, and crept to the door on his withered feet, feeling the walls; and as he moved, his limbs trembled for weakness and age; and his parched skin was caked with dirt, and naught but the skin held his bones together. And he came forth from the hall and sat on the threshold of the courtyard; and a dark stupor covered him, and it seemed that the earth reeled round beneath his feet, and he lay in a strengthless trance, speechless. But when they saw him they gathered round and marveled, and he at last drew labored breath from the depths of his chest and spoke among them with prophetic utterance:

"Listen, bravest of all the Hellenes, if it be truly ye, whom by a king's ruthless command Jason is leading on the ship Argo in quest of the fleece. It is ye truly. Even yet my soul by its divinations knows everything. Thanks I render to thee, O King, son of Leto, plunged in bitter affliction though I be. I beseech you by Zeus, the god of suppliants, the sternest foe to sinful men, and for the sake of Phœbus and Hera herself under whose especial care ye have come hither, help me, save an ill-fated man from misery, and depart not uncaring, and leaving me thus as ye see. For not only has the Fury set her foot on my eyes and I drag on to the end a weary old age, but besides my other woes a woe hangs over me, the bitterest of all. The Harpies, swooping down from some unseen den of destruction, ever snatch the food from my mouth, and I have no device to aid me. But it were easier, when I long for a meal, to escape my own thoughts than them, so swiftly do they fly through the air. But if haply they do leave me a morsel of food, it reeks of decay and the stench is unendurable, nor could any mortal bear to draw near, even for a moment, no, not if his heart were wrought of adamant. But necessity, bitter and insatiate, compels me to abide, and abiding to put food into my accursed belly. These pests, the oracle declares, the sons of Boreas shall restrain, and no strangers are they that shall ward them off if indeed I am Phineus who was once renowned among men for wealth and the gift of prophecy, and if I am the son of my father Agenor; and when I ruled among the Thracians, by my bridal gifts I brought home their sister Cleopatra to be my wife."

So spake Agenor's son, and deep sorrow seized each of the heroes, and especially the two sons of Boreas. And brushing away a tear, they drew nigh, and Zetes spake as follows, taking in his own the hand of the grief-worn sire:

"Unhappy one, none other of men is more wretched than thou, methinks. Why upon thee is laid the burden of so many sorrows? Hast thou with baneful folly sinned against the gods through thy skill in prophecy? For this are they greatly wroth with thee? Yet our spirit is dismayed within us for all our desire to aid thee, if indeed the god has granted this privilege to us two. For plain to discern to men of earth are the reproofs of the immortals. And we will never check the Harpies when they come, for all our desire, until thou hast sworn that for this we shall not lose the favor of heaven."

Thus he spake; and towards him the aged sire opened his sightless eyes and lifted them up and replied with these words:

"Be silent, store not up such thoughts in thy heart, my child. Let the son of Leto be my witness, he who of his gracious will taught me the lore of prophecy, and be witness the ill-starred doom which possesses me, and this dark cloud upon my eyes, and the gods of the underworld —and may their curse be upon me if I die perjured thus—no wrath of heaven will fall upon you two for your help to me."

Then were those two eager to help him because of the oath. And quickly the younger heroes prepared a feast for the aged man, a last prey for the Harpies; and both stood near him, to smite with the sword those pests when they swooped down. Scarcely had the aged man touched the food when they forthwith, like bitter blasts or flashes of lightning, suddenly darted from the clouds, and swooped down with a yell, fiercely craving for food; and the heroes beheld them and shouted in the midst of their onrush. But they, at the cry, devoured everything and sped away over the sea afar, and an intolerable stench remained. And behind them the two sons of Boreas, raising their swords, rushed in pursuit. For Zeus imparted to them tireless strength; but without Zeus they could not have followed, for the Harpies used ever to outstrip the blasts of the west wind when they came to Phineus, and when they left him. And, as when, upon the mountain-side, hounds, cunning in the chase, run in the track of horned goats or deer, and as they strain a little behind, gnash their teeth upon the edge of their teeth in vain; so Zetes and Calias rushing very near, just grazed the Harpies in vain with their fingertips. And assuredly they would have torn them to pieces despite heaven's will when they had overtaken them far off at the Floating Islands, had not swift Iris seen them and leaped down from the sky from heaven above and checked them with these words:

"It is not lawful, O sons of Boreas, to strike with your swords the Harpies, the hounds of mighty Zeus; but I myself will give you a pledge, that hereafter they shall not draw near to Phineus."

With these words she took an oath by the water of Styx, which to all the gods is most dread and most awful, that the Harpies would never thereafter again approach the home of Phineus, son of Agenor, for so it was fated. And the heroes, yielding to the oath, turned back their flight to the ship. And, on account of this, men called them the Islands of Turning, though aforetime they had called them the Floating Islands. And the Harpies and Iris parted. They entered their den in Minoan Crete; but she sped up to Olympus, soaring aloft on her swift wings.

Meantime the chiefs carefully cleansed the old man's squalid skin, and, with due selection, sacrificed sheep which they had borne away from the spoil of Amycus. And when they had laid a huge supper in the hall, they sat down and feasted, and with them feasted Phineus ravenously, delighting his soul as in a dream. And there, when they had taken their fill of food and drink, they kept awake all night, waiting for the sons of Boreas. And the aged sire himself sat in the midst, near the hearth, telling of the end of their voyage and the completion of their journey.

HELIODORUS

(3rd Century, A.D.)

HELIODORUS was one of the earliest writers of the novel, or romance. Though he lived long after the close of the Golden Age of Greek literature, he is (together with Longus) the initiator of the novel form. But like many novelists (even modern novelists, who are supposed to know better), he interspersed his romance with episodes which are in themselves short stories. The very first chapter of the *Æthiopian Romance*, which is here reprinted, is such a story.

The present version is slightly modified and modernized from the early English translation by Thomas Underdowne. There is no title to the story in the original.

THE ROBBERS OF EGYPT

(From *The Æthiopica*, or *Æthiopian Romance*, Book I)

AT the first smile of day, when the sun was just beginning to shine on the summits of the hills, men whose custom was to live by rapine and violence ran to the top of a cliff and stretched toward that mouth of the Nile which is called Heracleot. Standing awhile, they viewed the sea underneath them, and when they had looked a good season afar off into the same and could see nothing which could put them in the hope of prey, they cast their eyes toward the neighboring shore, where a ship lay moored, without sailors but full-freighted; which thing they who were afar off might easily conjecture, for the cargo brought the water up to the ship's third loading-line. But on the shore every place was full of men newly slain, some quite dead, some half dead, some whose bodies yet panted and plainly declared that there had been a battle fought of late. There could be seen no signs or tokens of any just quarrel, but only some poor confused remnants of an unlucky banquet which had ended so. For the tables were furnished with delicate dishes, some whereof lay in the hands of those that were slain, having served as weapons in the battle so suddenly begun. Other tables covered such as had crept under them to hide themselves, as they thought. Besides, the cups were overthrown and fallen from the hands, either of them that drank or those who had, instead of stones, used them. For that sudden mischief wrought new devices, and taught them instead of weapons to use their pots. Of those who lay there, one was wounded with an ax, another was hurt with the shells of fishes, whereof on the shore there was great plenty; another was battered with a club, many burnt by fire, and the rest by divers other means, but most of all were slain with arrows. To be brief, God showed a wonderful sight in so small a space, imbruing wine with blood, joining battle with banqueting, mingling indifferently slaughter with drinking, and killing with quaffings, providing such a sight for the thieves of Egypt to gaze at. For they, when they had looked upon these things a good while from the hill, could not understand what that sight meant, forasmuch as they saw some slain there, but the conquerors could they see nowhere. A manifest victory, but no spoils taken away, a ship without mariners, but, as concerning other things, untouched, as if she had been kept with a guard of many men, and lay at road in a peaceful harbor.

But though they knew not what the thing meant, they still had regard for gain, and deeming themselves to be victors, hurried with all speed to seize their booty. They were but a little way from the ship when they saw a sight more perplexing than the rest a great deal.

A maid endowed with excellent beauty, who almost might be supposed a goddess, sat upon a rock seeming not a little to be grieved with that present mischance, but for all that of excellent courage. She had a garland of laurel on her head, a quiver on her back; to her left shoulder a bow was fastened, and her left arm hung carelessly down. Her right elbow she rested upon her thigh, holding her cheek in her hand, looking downward without moving her head, beholding a certain young man who lay before her, the which was sore wounded and seemed to lift up himself as if he had been awakened out of a dead sleep, almost of death itself. Yet was he in this case of singular beauty, and although his cheeks were besprinkled with blood, his whiteness did appear so much the more. He was constrained for grief to close his eyes, but the sight of the maiden drew them towards her, and they must needs see, because they saw her. As soon as he came to himself he heaved a deep sigh and uttered these words very faintly, "And art thou safe indeed, my sweetheart?" quoth he. "Or hast thou by thy death augmented the slaughter? Canst thou not endure, even after death, to be separated from me, that now a vision of thy spirit haunts this place of trouble?" "Nay," answered the maid, "on you doth all my estate depend, for good or ill, for this cause, you see"—showing a knife in her hand—"this has hitherto been waiting, and only by the chance of your recovery was restrained."

As soon as she had said thus, she leaped from the stone, and they who were on the hill, as well for wonder as also for the fear they had, as if they had been stricken with lightning, ran every man to hide them in the bushes there beside. For she seemed to them a thing of greater price, and more heavenly when she stood upright, and her arrows with the sudden moving of her body gave a clash on her shoulders, her apparel wrought with gold glistened against the sun, and her hair under the garland, blown about with the wind, covered a great part of her back. The thieves were greatly afraid; and even more than what they saw did their ignorance of what had happened before terrify them. Some of them said indeed it was a goddess—Artemis, or Isis, the lady of the land—others declared it was a priestess of the gods who, replenished with divine fury, had made the great slaughter which there appeared. And they every man gave his verdict, because they knew not yet the truth. But she, hastily running to the young man, embraced him, wept for sorrow, kissed him, wiped away his blood and made pitiful moan, scarcely believing that she held him in her arms. Which things when the Egyptians had seen, they turned their opinions: "And are these," said they, "the works of a goddess? Would a goddess kiss a dead man with such compassion?" They determined therefore with themselves that it was best to take heart of grace, and draw near to find out the truth. When they had therefore encouraged each other a little, they ran down and found the maid busy in dressing the young man's wounds, and coming behind her, suddenly stood still, and durst neither speak nor do anything more for their lives.

When she heard the noise around her, and saw their shadows before her eyes, she lifted herself up a little and looked back, but then at once stooped down again, no whit dismayed by the strange color of their skin, nor yet abashed to see the thieves in harness, but applying herself only to bind up his wounds that lay before her. Such is the force of earnest desire and true love: it despiseth all outward chances, be they pleasant or otherwise, only beholding that which it loveth, and thereabout bestoweth all diligence and travail. But when the thieves passed by and stood before her, and seemed as though they would enterprise somewhat, she lifted herself up again and beholding them black and ill-favored, said: "If you be the spirits of those who are slain here, you trouble us wrongfully, for most of you were slain by your own hands. As for us, if we slew any, we did it but in our own defense to repel the violence which was proffered to my virginity. But if you be men alive, it seemeth you are thieves, and you have come here in good season. Rid us, I pray, from these present miseries, and by death finish this our unhappy tragedy." Thus did she sorrowfully lament. But they, not understanding what she said, left them there, accounting their weakness a sufficient guard, and hastened to the ship, and brought out that which was in the same, paying no regard to other things whereof therein was great store, but every man bearing out as much as he could, of gold, silver, precious stones and silk. And when they thought they had enough, and there was such plenty as might satisfy even a thief's greed, laying their booty on the shore, they fell to dividing it into portions such as they could carry, not according to the worth and value of what they had, but contenting themselves with equality of weight. As for the young man and the maid, they would take order for them afterwards.

In the meantime, another company of thieves, whereof two horsemen were captains, came toward them: which thing as soon as those saw that had been there before, having no courage to oppose them, they ran away as fast as they could, without taking with them any part of the prey, that they might give their enemy no occasion to pursue them. For they were in number but ten, and those who came upon them were three times as many. And so the maid and her companion, though not yet prisoners, were again in durance. But the robbers, although they were eager for the spoil, yet, partly because they knew not what those things signified which they saw, and partly also for fear, stayed themselves a while, thinking that the former slaughter had been made by the thieves that had been there before. But when they beheld the maid in her fine foreign dress, who despised the dangers that hung over her head as if they had been none, and altogether employed her care to ease the young man's wounds, taking his grief as heavily as her own sorrow, they not only marveled at her beauty and high spirit but were wonderfully moved by the comeliness of the wounded man's person. Such was the seemliness of his countenance, and tallness of his stature, as he lay before them. For by this time he was a little mended, and his person had recovered its old handsomeness again. At length, after they had beheld them a good while, he drew near who was their master, and laid hand on the maid, and bade her arise and follow him. She, although she understood not what he said, conjecturing what he wished her to do, drew the young man with her, himself holding her fast, and pointing with a knife to her breast, threatened that she would kill herself if they carried them not away both together. Which thing when the master, partly by her talk but more plainly by her gesture, understood, hoping also to use the young man's help in great affairs when he recovered, he alighted himself from his horse and commanded his harness-bearer likewise so to do, and set his prisoners upon them. Then, ordering the rest when they had gathered up the prey to follow them, he himself like a lackey ran by their side and stayed them upright, if by reason of their infirmity they were likely to fall. Surely this deed was not without glory; for he who was their master now waited upon them, and he who took them prisoners was content to serve them. Such is the impression that nobility makes, and such the force of comeliness, which can subdue the disposition of thieves and bring under the wild and savage.

Ancient Rome

INTRODUCTION

IT is a commonplace of literary history that Roman art was largely imitated or derived from the Greek, and in particular that Roman literature contributed little to the world's store of masterpieces. Yet among the Romans the short story was esteemed more highly and was often more skilfully developed than it was among the Greeks.

The first of the stories chosen is from the historian Livy. Before his day there is very little material from which to select, although if the earlier writers of epic and history were better known to us, we might have found stories in the works of Livius Andronicus, Ennius, and the historians, most of whose writings have been lost. In the *Letters* of Cicero are numerous incidents falling within our category, but none of them of sufficient intrinsic interest to warrant their inclusion in this volume. Livy's *History* abounds in episodes, many of them related with a certain matter-of-factness that characterizes a great deal of Latin prose writing. Still, *Horatius at the Bridge* is a stirring tale rendered doubly effective by its simplicity.

Ovid was a born teller of stories, and though he borrowed largely from the Greeks and was a fastidious poet intent upon achieving a refined and elegant style, the numerous myths which he treats at length in his *Metamorphoses* include half a dozen of the loveliest stories ever written.

Other poets and historians and miscellaneous writers—Valerius Maximus, Varro, Statius, Tacitus and Suetonius—tried their hand at story-telling, and even Vergil in his *Æneid* recounted episodes that are genuine stories, but none of them could rival the technical skill with which the minor poet Phædrus turned the Æsopian fables and every-day incidents of life and history into graceful and appealing tales. Like the earlier fabulists, Phædrus preached little sermons. The most interesting parts of his work are the little anecdotes, like the one included in this volume; these are miniature stories. The other famous Roman fabulist was Avianus who, rediscovered in the Middle Ages, exerted a profound and lasting influence in France and Germany. But his work is neither so finished nor so attractive as that of Phædrus.

Many genuine stories are found in the personal correspondence of the time, chiefly among the published collections of Cicero and Pliny the Younger. Pliny wrote several short stories which he elaborated with conscious skill, for he wrote with a view to publication. Throughout all modern literature we find stories, indeed lengthy stories (see Richardson), related through the medium of letters. This is a deliberate device employed to lend to the narrative an air of actuality. It would be enlightening to know whether Pliny wrote his *Haunted House* as a literary experiment, or whether he really believed the story. But supposing he related it as a fact—supposing even that all the facts were to be proved scientifically correct, would it be any the less a good story?

Petronius belonged to a different world in which Latin prose had lost a good deal of its rigid dignity, and like the literature of the late Hellenistic period in Greece, was characterized by a facile cynicism on the part of the writers, and an over-luxuriance of style. The writers were very numerous, poets, historians, satirists, and even scientists interspersing their writings with tales of haunted houses, ghosts, and all the supernatural apparitions that are the stock-in-trade of the story-writer. Petronius and Apuleius, however, stood head and shoulders above the rest of their contemporaries and followers. *The Matron of Ephesus*, hackneyed though its theme may be, is a masterpiece of satirical fiction, while *The Dream* is one of a dozen tales of mystery and imagination which constitute the chief glory of *The Golden Ass*. That rambling romance, it will be remembered, also contains the enchanting *Cupid and Psyche*, which is far too long for inclusion in a collection of this sort.

Just at what point Roman literature ended is a matter to be determined by the historians, but after the Fifth Century A.D. it becomes increasingly difficult to designate any tale as unmistakably Roman.

Then foreigners began to change the face of the Empire, Christianity damped the ardour of the artist and stifled the imagination of the storyteller. It is not until the dawn of modern times, some six or seven centuries afterward, when the fragments of Roman stories were again taken up and imbedded in the curious mediæval mosaics of the *Gesta Romanorum* and the *Hundred Ancient Tales*, that we realize that the art of tale-telling had never been forgotten.

Throughout the break-up of Rome and the barbarian invasions, through the darkest years of the Tenth Century, the Latin traditions were preserved in the manuscripts of the monasteries, and on the lips of singers, minstrels, acrobats, and actors.

With Apuleius and Petronius the short story, as a literary-form, achieved a decided technical advance over the efforts of the Greeks. With these later writers the story was told largely for its own sake, and not to illustrate a moral truth or glorify the deeds of the Roman people.

LIVY

(59 B.C.—17 A.D.)

TITUS LIVIUS, known to us under the English title of Livy, though born
in the provinces at Padua, spent most of his life at the capital, where
he was a teacher and writer of history. His *History of Rome* was a
monumental work, of which only a part has come down to us. Like
practically all the historians of antiquity (and most of the moderns, for
that matter) he introduces stories and anecdotes on hearsay evidence,
using them in order to glorify his country or to drive home a lesson.
Horatius at the Bridge is a case in question, and though it may be founded
on fact, it is probably apocryphal in detail.

The present translation (including Chapters IX and X of Book II)
is a revision of that made by D. Spillan, published in the Bohn edition
in 1872. There is no title in the original.

HORATIUS AT THE BRIDGE

(From the *History*, Book II)

BY this time the Tarquins had fled to Lars Porsena, king of Clusium. There, with advice and entreaties, they besought him not
to suffer them, who were descended from the Etrurians and of the same
blood and name, to live in exile and poverty; and advised him not to
let this practice of expelling kings to pass unpunished. Liberty, they
declared, had charms enough in itself; and unless kings defended their
crowns with as much vigor as the people pursued their liberty, the
highest must be reduced to a level with the lowest; there would be
nothing exalted, nothing distinguished above the rest; hence there
must be an end of regal government, the most beautiful institution
both among gods and men. Porsena, thinking it would be an honor to
the Tuscans that there should be a king at Rome, especially one of the
Etrurian nation, marched towards Rome with an army. Never before
had such terror seized the Senate, so powerful was the state of Clusium
at the time, and so great the renown of Porsena. Nor did they only
dread their enemies, but even their own citizens, lest the common
people, through excess of fear should, by receiving the Tarquins into
the city, accept peace even though purchased with slavery. Many
concessions were therefore granted to the people by the Senate during
that period. Their attention, in the first place, was directed to the
markets, and persons were sent, some to the Volscians, others to

Cumæ, to buy up corn. The privilege of selling salt, because it was farmed at a high rate, was also taken into the hands of the government, and withdrawn from private individuals; and the people were freed from port-duties and taxes, in order that the rich, who could bear the burden, should contribute; the poor paid tax enough if they educated their children. This indulgent care of the fathers accordingly kept the whole state in such concord amid the subsequent severities of the siege and famine, that the highest as well as the lowest abhorred the name of king; nor was any individual afterwards so popular by intriguing practices as the whole Senate was by their excellent government.

Some parts of the city seemed secured by the walls, others by the River Tiber. The Sublician Bridge wellnigh afforded a passage to the enemy, had there not been one man, Horatius Cocles (fortunately Rome had on that day such a defender) who, happening to be posted on guard at the bridge, when he saw the Janiculum taken by a sudden assault and the enemy pouring down thence at full speed, and that his own party, in terror and confusion, were abandoning their arms and ranks, laying hold of them one by one, standing in their way and appealing to the faith of gods and men, he declared that their flight would avail them nothing if they deserted their post; if they passed the bridge, there would soon be more of the enemy in the Palatium and Capitol than in the Janiculum. For that reason he charged them to demolish the bridge, by sword, by fire, or by any means whatever; declaring that he would stand the shock of the enemy as far as could be done by one man. He then advanced to the first entrance of the bridge, and being easily distinguished among those who showed their backs in retreating, faced about to engage the foe hand to hand, and by his surprising bravery he terrified the enemy. Two indeed remained with him from a sense of shame: Sp. Lartius and T. Herminius, men eminent for their birth, and renowned for their gallant exploits. With them he for a short time stood the first storm of the danger, and the severest brunt of the battle. But as they who demolished the bridge called upon them to retire, he obliged them also to withdraw to a place of safety on a small portion of the bridge that was still left. Then casting his stern eyes toward the officers of the Etrurians in a threatening manner, he now challenged them singly, and then reproached them, slaves of haughty tyrants who, regardless of their own freedom, came to oppress the liberty of others. They hesitated for a time, looking round one at the other, to begin the fight; shame then put the army in motion, and a shout being raised, they hurled weapons from all sides at their single adversary; and when they all stuck in his upraised shield, and he with no less obstinacy kept possession of the bridge, they endeavored to thrust him down from it by one push, when the crash of the falling bridge was heard, and at the same time a shout of the Romans raised for joy at having completed their purpose, checked their ardor with sudden panic. Then said Cocles: "Holy Father Tiber, I pray thee, receive these arms, and this thy soldier, in thy propitious stream." Armed as he was, he leaped into the Tiber, and amid showers of darts, swam across safe to his party, having dared an act which is likely to obtain with posterity more fame than credit. The state was grateful for such valor; a statue was erected to him in the comitium, and as much land given to him as he could plow in one day. The zeal of private individuals was also conspicuous among his public honors. For amid the great scarcity, each contributed something, according to his supply depriving himself of his own support.

OVID

(43 B.C.—18 A.D.?)

PUBLIUS OVIDIUS NASO, better known to readers of English as Ovid, was born not far from Rome, and spent the latter part of his life in exile. *The Metamorphoses*, his most ambitious work, is an attempt to reshape in metrical form the chief stories of Greek mythology, and several from Roman mythology. *Orpheus and Eurydice*, one of the most human of the legends of antiquity, is a graceful piece of writing. Its "point" is as clear and as cleverly turned as you will find in any ancient tale.

The present translation is based by the editors upon two early versions, the one very literal, the other a paraphrase. The story, which has no title in the original, appears in the Tenth Book of the *Metamorphoses*.

ORPHEUS AND EURYDICE

(From *The Metamorphoses*, Book X)

THENCE Hymenæus, clad in a saffron-colored robe, passed through the unmeasured spaces of the air and directed his course to the region of the Ciconians, and in vain was invoked by the voice of Orpheus. He presented himself, but brought with him neither auspicious words, nor a joyful appearance, nor happy omen. The torch he held hissed with a smoke that brought tears to the eyes, though it was without a flame. The issue was more disastrous than the omen; for the new bride, while strolling over the grass attended by a train of Naiads, was killed by the sting of a serpent on her ankle.

After the Rhodopeian bard had bewailed her in the upper realms, he dared, that he might try the shades below as well, to descend to the Styx by the Tænarian Gate, and amid the phantom inhabitants, he went to Persephone and him who held sway over the dark world. Touching the strings of his harp and speaking, he thus addressed them: "Oh, ye deities of the world that lies beneath the earth, to which we all come at last, if I be permitted to speak, laying aside the artful expressions of a deceitful tongue, I have not descended hither from curiosity to see dark Tartarus nor to bind the threefold throat of the Medusæan monster bristling with serpents. My wife is the cause of my coming, into whom a serpent which she trod on suffused its poison, and cut short the thread of her years. I wished to be able to endure this, and I will not deny that I have striven to do so. But love has proved stronger. That god is well-known in the regions above; whether he be so here as well, I am uncertain. Yet I think that even here he is, and if the story of the rape of former days is true, 'twas love that brought you two together. By these places filled with terrors, by this vast chaos and by the silence of these boundless realms, I entreat you, weave over again the quickspun thread of the life of Eurydice.

"To you we all belong, and having stayed but a little while above, sooner or later we all hasten to your abode. Hither are we all hastening. This is our last home, and you possess indisputable dominion over the human race. She, too, when in due time she shall have completed her allotted number of years, will be under your sway. The enjoyment of her I entreat as a favor, but if the fates deny me this privilege on behalf of my wife, I have determined that I will never return to earth. Triumph, then, in the death of us both!"

As he spoke and touched the strings of his lyre, the bloodless spirits wept. Tantalus no longer caught at the retreating water; the wheel of Ixion stood still in amazement; the birds ceased to tear at the liver of Tityus, and the granddaughters of Belus paused at their urns. Thou, too, Sisyphus, didst seat thyself on the stone. The story is that then for the first time the cheeks of the Eumenides, overcome by the music of Orpheus, were wet with tears; nor could the royal consort, nor he who ruled the infernal regions endure to deny his request. And they called for Eurydice. She advanced at a slow pace from among the shades newly arrived, for she was lame from her wound.

The Rhodopeian hero received her and at the same time was told the condition that he turn not back his eyes until he had passed the Avernian Valley, lest the grant be revoked. They ascended the path in silence, steep, dark, and enveloped in deepening gloom. Now they were arrived at last at a point not far below the verge of the upper earth. Orpheus, fearing lest Eurydice should fall, and impatient to behold her once again, turned his eyes, and at once she sank back again. Hapless woman, stretching out her hands and struggling for the arms of her lover, she caught nothing but empty air. Dying a second time, she complained not of her husband, for why should she complain of being beloved? Then she pronounced the last farewell, which he scarcely heard, and again was she hurried back whence she had come.

And Orpheus was astounded and perplexed by this two-fold death of his wife.

PHÆDRUS

(15 B.C.?—55 A.D.?)

It was the chief distinction of this writer to have collected the *Fables* of Æsop (or whoever it was who wrote Æsop's works) and rewritten them for the Romans. His collection is the earliest of its kind which has survived. Not all his Fables, however, are based upon Æsop. *The Ship-wreck of Simonides* is either an original composition or was taken from another source. Phædrus was a Thracian slave, and later a freedman, in the service of the Emperor Augustus. He once declared that the fable was invented as a "device whereby slavery could find a voice," a definition which throws considerable light on Phædrus' life, even if it fails to explain the origin of the Fable form.

The present text was first published in the Bohn edition of Phædrus in 1848.

THE SHIPWRECK OF SIMONIDES

A LEARNED man has always a fund of riches in himself. Simonides, who wrote such excellent lyric poems, the more easily to support his poverty, began to make a tour of the celebrated cities of Asia, singing the praises of victors for such reward as he might receive. After he had become enriched by this kind of gain, he resolved to return to his native land by sea (for he was born, it is said, in the island of Ceos). Accordingly he embarked in a ship, which a dreadful tempest, together with its own rottenness, caused to founder at sea. Some gathered together their girdles, others their precious effects, which formed the support of their existence. One who was over in-quisitive, remarked: "Are you going to save none of your property, Simonides?" He made reply: "All my possessions are about me." A few only made their escape by swimming, for the majority, being weighed down by their burdens, perished. Some thieves too made their appearance, and seized what each person had saved, leaving him naked. Clazomenæ, an ancient city, chanced to be near; to which the shipwrecked persons repaired. Here a person devoted to the pursuits of literature, who had often read the lines of Simonides, and was a very great admirer of him though he had never seen him, knowing from his very language who he was, received him with the greatest pleasure into his house, and furnished him with clothes, money, and attendants. The others meanwhile were carrying about their pictures, begging for victuals. Simonides chanced to meet them; and, as soon as he saw them, remarked: "I told you that all my property was about me; what you have endeavored to save is lost."

PETRONIUS

(Died 66 A.D.)

GAIUS PETRONIUS ARBITER was born some time early in the First Century of the Christian era, and committed suicide in the year 66. Writer, government official, dilettante and friend of Nero, he "had idled into fame," as Tacitus tells us. His best-known work, *The Satyricon*, is a strange straggling sort of satirical novel, into which he introduced this short masterpiece, *The Matron of Ephesus*. The tale is supposed to be in the manner of one of the so-called lost Milesian Tales, a collection renowned for its cynical outlook on humanity in general and woman in particular. This brief story (in one form or another) is to be found running through all literature, especially the literature written by men. The present version is a revision (by the editors) of two older versions.

THE MATRON OF EPHESUS

(From *The Satyricon*)

A CERTAIN matron of Ephesus was so notably pure that women came from afar to look upon her. When her husband was buried, she was not satisfied with the usual custom of following the body with loosened hair and beating her breast in the presence of the people: she accompanied her dead spouse right into the sepulcher—which was in the Greek style, underground—and there remained to watch and weep by day and by night. Her parents and relations were unable to prevent her from thus torturing herself, and remaining in the sepulcher to die of hunger. The civil officials at last left in despair.

The matron lived through the fifth day without eating, and was grieved for by all as a shining example to all womenkind. A faithful maidservant sat by the wretched woman, shed the appropriate number of tears, and kept the lamp burning.

Word spread through the city, and every one agreed that it was a unique example of conjugal love and fidelity.

Meantime, the provincial governor crucified certain thieves near the sepulcher where the matron was weeping over the body of her late husband, and a soldier was commanded to keep guard over the crosses, to prevent the bodies from being taken down and buried. The following night he perceived a light shining brightly among the trees and heard the moans of the woman. Like all human beings, he was curious, and desired to know who was groaning, and what was the cause of it. He therefore entered the sepulcher, and on seeing a beautiful woman, stopped short and was as deeply moved as though he had seen an omen or a ghost from the nether world. The moment he set eyes on the body and remarked the matron's tears, and her face scarred by the marks of fingernails, he understood: she was desperate in her love for the man who was dead. He then brought his frugal supper into the sepulcher, and begged the matron not to give way so to a grief that was useless, nor break her heart in weeping. All men, he said, had the same fate and the same last resting-place. But she was ill-pleased by such commonplace consolation, and smote her breast more violently than ever, tearing out her hair and throwing it upon the body before her. Still, the young soldier did not leave. He tried to give the woman food. Though she resisted, her maidservant was won over by the smell of the wine, and stretched out her hand for the supper that was offered her. After she was fortified by food and drink, she strove to win over her mistress. "How," she asked, "will you be benefited, if you starve to death and bury yourself alive, dying before Destiny has demanded your soul? Do you imagine that your mourning can be acceptable to the body or the soul of a man who is dead and buried? Why not rather begin your life anew? Why not forget this misguided fidelity—adhered to only by women—and enjoy the daylight as long as the gods allow? This cold body ought to be a warning to you to enjoy life to the utmost."

Now, generally, one gives heed when one is asked to eat food or to live, and the matron was both hungry and thirsty after five days' fasting; she allowed her resolution to be broken. She ate as greedily as the maidservant had eaten. Those who are well-fed are easily tempted, and the soldier set about to conquer the matron's virtue, by the same pleasant and persuasive means he had used before. The chaste matron perceived that he was an attractive young man, and by no means a fool. The maidservant was sympathetic, and quoted the words, "Do you seek to struggle against a passion that is pleasing to you? Do you not remember in whose country you are?"

To make a long story short, having overcome certain of the matron's scruples, the soldier succeeded in overcoming her remaining scruples.

They were together not only on that first night, but on the second and the third. The gates of the sepulcher were closed, so that if any friend or stranger had come, he would have imagined that the very virtuous woman had died in the presence of her husband's body. The soldier was greatly pleased by the matron's charms, and with their uninterrupted love; he bought such delicate viands as his pay would permit, and brought them to the sepulcher when darkness came.

The parents of one of the thieves who had been crucified, perceiving that the soldier was not strictly guarding the crosses, took down the body of their son and buried it. Next morning, seeing the body gone, the soldier knew what his punishment would be, and went and told the woman. He would, he declared, kill himself with his sword rather than be sentenced by a military court, and told her to make room for her lover to lie beside her late husband. But the lady was as compassionate as she was pure. "May the gods forbid," said she, "that I should lay eyes at one time on the corpses of the two men who are dearest to me! It were better to hang up a dead body than to kill a breathing man." And therewith she told the soldier to take the husband's body from its place and put it upon the cross that was vacant. The soldier at once acted upon the matron's clever suggestion, and the next day people wondered how the dead man had been able to crucify himself.

PLINY THE YOUNGER

(62—113 A.D.)

THE *Letters* of Pliny the Younger (known in Latin as C. Plinius Cæcilius Secundus) give a pleasant and varied picture of Roman life at a time when the satirists were depicting it in lurid hues. Pliny was a gentleman of refinement who found time, in spite of his career as a lawyer and a high government official, to write many letters to his friends, with a view, as we happen to know, to publication. Several of these letters are neither more nor less than short stories. *The Haunted House* is simply the recital of an incident in a letter to his friend Sura, and is one of the best of the ancient ghost stories. Needless to say, it is a type that has been used time and again.

The text is from an early English translation, and comprises *Letter* 27 of the Seventh Book. There is no title in the original.

THE HAUNTED HOUSE

(*Letter* to Sura, Book VII)

THERE was at Athens a mansion, spacious and commodious, but of evil repute and dangerous to health. In the dead of night there was a noise as of iron, and, if you listened more closely, a clanking of chains was heard, first of all from a distance, and afterwards hard by. Presently a specter used to appear, an ancient man sinking with emaciation and squalor, with a long beard and bristly hair, wearing shackles on his legs and fetters on his hands, and shaking them. Hence the inmates, by reason of their fears, passed miserable and horrible nights in sleeplessness. This want of sleep was followed by disease, and, their terrors increasing, by death. For in the daytime as well, though the apparition had departed, yet a reminiscence of it flitted before their eyes, and their dread outlived its cause. The mansion was accordingly deserted and, condemned to solitude, was entirely abandoned to the dreadful ghost. However, it was advertised, on the chance of some one, ignorant of the fearful curse attached to it, being willing to buy or to rent it. Athenodorus the philosopher came to Athens and read the advertisement. When he had been informed of the terms, which were so low as to appear suspicious, he made inquiries, and learned the whole of the particulars. Yet none the less on that account, nay, all the more readily, did he rent the house. As evening began to draw on, he ordered a sofa to be set for himself in the front part of the house, and called for his notebooks, writing implements, and a light. All his servants he dismissed to the interior apartments, and for himself applied his soul, eyes, and hand to composition, that his mind might not, from want of occupation, picture to itself the phantoms of which he had heard, or any empty terrors. At the commencement there was the universal silence of night. Soon the shaking of irons and the clanking of chains was heard, yet he never raised his eyes nor slackened his pen, but hardened his soul and deadened his ears by its help. The noise grew and approached: now it seemed to be heard at the door, and next inside the door. He looked round, beheld and recognized the figure he had been told of. It was standing and signaling to him with its finger, as though inviting him. He, in reply, made a sign with his hand that it should wait a moment, and applied himself afresh to his tablets and pen. Upon this the figure kept rattling its chains over his head as he wrote. On looking round again, he saw it making the same signal as before, and without delay took up a light and followed it. It moved with a slow step as though oppressed by its chains, and after turning into the courtyard of the house vanished suddenly and left his company.

On being thus left to himself, he marked the spot with some grass and leaves which he plucked. Next day he applied to the magistrates, and urged them to have the spot in question dug up. There were found there some bones attached to and intermingled with fetters; the body to which they had belonged, rotted away by time and the soil, had abandoned them thus naked and corroded to the chains. They were collected and interred at the public expense, and the house was ever afterwards free from the spirit, which had obtained due sepulture.

The above story I believe on the strength of those who affirm it. What follows I am myself in a position to affirm to others. I have a freedman, who is not without some knowledge of letters. A younger brother of his was sleeping with him in the same bed. The latter dreamed he saw some one sitting on the couch, who approached a pair of scissors to his head, and even cut the hair from the crown of it. When day dawned he was found to be cropped round the crown, and his locks were discovered lying about. A very short time afterwards a fresh occurrence of the same kind confirmed the truth of the former one. A lad of mine was sleeping, in company with several others, in the pages' apartment. There came through the windows (so he tells the story) two figures in white tunics, who cut his hair as he lay, and departed the way they came. In his case, too, daylight exhibited him shorn, and his locks scattered around. Nothing remarkable followed, except, perhaps, this, that I was not brought under accusation, as I should have been, if Domitian (in whose reign these events happened) had lived longer. For in his desk was found an information against me which had been presented by Carus; from which circumstance it may be conjectured—inasmuch as it is the custom of accused persons to let their hair grow—that the cutting off of my slaves' hair was a sign of the danger which threatened me being averted.

I beg, then, that you will apply your great learning to this subject. The matter is one which deserves long and deep consideration on your part; nor am I, for my part, undeserving of having the fruits of your wisdom imparted to me. You many even argue on both sides (as your way is), provided you argue more forcibly on one side than the other, so as not to dismiss me in suspense and anxiety, when the very cause of my consulting you has been to have my doubts ended.

APULEIUS

(Born *ca.* 125 A.D.)

LUCIUS APULEIUS, author of *The Golden Ass*, was born and educated in northern Africa. He practised law, was an indefatigable traveller, a ceaseless investigator into religious ceremonies and mysteries, and a writer of considerable skill and imagination. Many stories, including *Cupid and Psyche* and *The Dream*, are introduced into the rambling narrative of his celebrated romance. Like many other literary men, he was publicly accused of writing indecent literature. Like Pliny's *Haunted House*, *The Dream* is one of those lurid ghost-stories which apparently pleased the readers of the early Christian era. They continue to do so.

The present text is a modernized version of the classic translation by Adlington, which first appeared in 1566. There is no title in the original.

THE DREAM

(From *The Golden Ass*)

BUT I could in no wise sleep for the great fear which was in my heart, until it was about midnight, and then I began to slumber. But, alas! behold suddenly the chamber doors broke open, and locks, bolts, and posts fell down, that you would verily have thought that some thieves had presently come to have spoiled and robbed us. And my bed whereon I lay, being a truckle-bed, fashioned in the form of a cradle, and one of the feet broken and rotten, by violence was turned upside down, and I likewise was overwhelmed and covered lying in the same. And while I lay on the ground covered in this sort, I peeped under the bed to see what would happen. And behold there entered in two old women, the one bearing a burning torch, and the other a sponge and a naked sword; and so in this habit they stood about, Socrates being fast asleep. Then she which bare the sword said unto the other, "Behold, sister Panthia, this is my dear and sweet heart, this is he who little regarding my love, doth not only defame me with reproachful words, but also intendeth to run away." Which said, she pointed toward me that lay under the bed, and showed me to Panthia. "This is he," quoth she, "which is his counselor, and persuadeth him to forsake me, and now being at the point of death, he lieth prostrate on the ground covered with his bed, and hath seen all our doings, and hopeth to escape scot-free from my hands; but I will cause that he shall repent himself too late, nay rather forthwith, of his former intemperate language, and his present curiosity." Which words when I heard, I fell into a cold sweat, and my heart trembled with fear, insomuch that the bed over me did likewise rattle and shake. Then spake Panthia unto Meroe and said, "Sister, let us by and by tear him in pieces." Then Meroe answered, "Nay, rather let him live, and bury the corpse of this poor wretch in some hole of the earth"; and therewithal she turned up the head of Socrates on the other side, and thrust her sword up to the hilt into the left part of his neck, and received the blood that gushed out, into a pot, that no drop thereof fell beside: which things I saw with mine own eyes; and as I think to the intent that she might alter nothing that pertained to sacrifice, which she accustomed to make, she thrust her hand down into the internals of his body, and searching about at length brought forth the heart of my miserable companion, Socrates, who having his throat cut in such sort, yielded out a dreadful cry and gave up the ghost. Then Panthia stopped the wide wound of his throat with the sponge, and said, "O sponge, sprung and made of the sea, beware that thou pass not by running river." When this was ended, they went their ways, and the doors closed fast, the posts stood in their old places, and the locks and bolts were shut again. But I that lay upon the ground like one without soul, naked and cold, like to one that were more than half dead, yet reviving myself, and appointed as I thought for the gallows, began to say, "Alas! what shall become of me to-morrow, when my companion shall be found murdered here in the chamber? To whom shall I seem to tell any similitude of truth, whenas I shall tell the truth indeed? They will say, 'If thou wert unable to resist the violence of the women, yet shouldst thou have cried for help: wouldst thou suffer the man to be slain before thy face and say nothing? Or why did they not slay thee likewise? Why did they spare thee that stood by and saw them commit that horrible fact? Wherefore although thou hast escaped their hands, yet thou shalt not escape ours.' " While I pondered these things with myself the night passed on, and so I resolved to take my horse before day, and go forward on my journey.

Howbeit the ways were unknown to me: and thereupon I took up my packet, unlocked and unbarred the doors, but those good and faithful doors, which in the night did open of their own accord, could then scantly be opened with their keys. And when I was out I cried, "O sirrah hostler, where art thou? Open the stable-door, for I will ride away by and by." The hostler lying behind the stable-door upon a pallet and half asleep, "What (quoth he), do you not know that the ways be very dangerous? what mean you to rise at this time of night? If you, perhaps guilty of some heinous crime, be weary of your life, yet think you not that we are such sots that we will die for you." Then said I, "It is wellnigh day, and moreover, what can thieves take from him that hath nothing? Dost thou not know, fool as thou art, if thou be naked, if ten giants should assail thee, they could not spoil or rob thee?" Whereunto the drowsy hostler, half asleep and turning on the other side, answered, "What know I whether you have murdered your companion whom you brought in yesternight or no, and now seek the means to escape away?" O Lord, at that time, I remember, the earth seemed to open, and methought I saw at hellgate the dog

Cerberus ready to devour me; and then I verily believed that Meroe did not spare my throat moved with pity, but rather cruelly pardoned me to bring me to the gallows. Wherefore I returned to my chamber, and there devised with myself in what sort I should finish my life. And therewithal I pulled out a piece of rope wherewith the bed was corded, and tied one end thereof about a rafter by the window, and with the other end I made a sliding knot, and stood upon my bed, and so put my neck into it, and when I leaped from the bed thinking verily to strangle myself and so die, behold the rope, being old and rotten, burst in the middle, and I fell down tumbling upon Socrates that lay under: and even at that same very time the hostler came in crying with a loud voice and said, "Where are you that made such haste at midnight, and now lies wallowing abed?" Whereupon (I know not whether it was by my fall, or by the great cry of the hostler) Socrates as waking out of a sleep, did rise up first and said, "It is not without cause that strangers do speak evil of all such hostlers, for this caitiff in his coming in, and with his crying out, I think under a color to steal away something, has waked me out of a sound sleep." Then I rose up, joyful with a merry countenance, saying, "Behold, good hostler, my friend, my companion and my brother whom thou didst falsely affirm to be slain by me this night." And therewithal I embraced my friend Socrates and kissed him, and took him by the hand and said, "Why tarry we? Why lose we the pleasure of this fair morning? let us go": and so I took up my packet, and paid the charges of the house and departed.

And we had not gone a mile out of the town but it was broad day, and then I diligently looked upon Socrates' throat to see if I could espy the place where Meroe thrust in her sword; but when I could not perceive any such thing, I thought with myself, What a madman am I, that being overcome with wine yesternight have dreamed such terrible things! behold, I see Socrates is sound, safe and in health. Where is his wound? where is the sponge? where is his great and new cut? And then I spake to him and said, "Verily it is not without occasion that physicians of experience do affirm, that such as fill their gorges abundantly with meat and drink shall dream of dire and horrible sights: for I myself, not tempering my appetite yesternight from pots of wine, did seem to see this night strange and cruel visions, that even yet I think myself sprinkled and wet with human blood." Whereunto Socrates laughing made answer, "Nay, verily, I myself dreamed this night that my throat was cut, and that I felt the pain of the wound, and that my heart was pulled out of my belly, and the remembrance thereof makes me now to fear, for my knees do so tremble that I can scarce go any further; and therefore I would fain eat somewhat to strengthen and revive my spirits." Then said I, "Behold here thy breakfast"; and therewithal I opened my scrip that hanged upon my shoulder, and gave him bread and cheese, and we sat down under a great plane tree, and I ate part with him. And while I beheld him eating greedily, I perceived that he waxed meager and pale, and that his lively color faded away, insomuch that being in great fear, and remembering those terrible furies of whom I lately dreamed, the first morsel of bread that I put in my mouth (which was but very small) did so stick in my jaws, that I could neither swallow it down, nor yet yield it up, and moreover the small time of our being together increased my fear: and what is he that seeing his companion die in the highway before his face, would not greatly lament and be sorry? But when that Socrates had eaten sufficiently, he waxed very thirsty, for indeed he had well-nigh devoured all a whole cheese: and behold evil fortune! there was behind the plane tree a pleasant running water as clear as crystal, and I said unto him, "Come hither, Socrates, to this water and drink thy fill." And then he rose and came to the river, and kneeled down upon the side of the bank to drink; but he had scarce touched the water with his lips, whenas behold the wound of his throat opened wide, and the sponge suddenly fell into the water, and after issued out a little remnant of blood, and his body being then without life, had fallen into the river, had I not caught him by the leg and so pulled him up. And after that I had lamented a good space the death of my wretched companion, I buried him in the sands there by the river.

Biblical Literature

INTRODUCTION

IT is not surprising that the stories scattered so profusely through the *Bible*, the *Apocrypha*, and the *Talmud*, should be mostly moral tales. They were told in order to illustrate a theological or ethical contention or law, to glorify the race or nation to which the teller belonged, to attract and hold the interest of the listener. All of them were related by Jews, and all, even the parables of Jesus, bear the imprint of the Oriental imagination. The stories of *Ruth* and *Susanna*, from the *Old Testament* and the *Apocrypha*, are the earliest examples in this little group of Biblical tales. *Ruth* is the type of story that could easily be expanded into a novel, while *Susanna* conforms more exactly to the modern conception of what a short story ought to be. These two have been chosen from a great storehouse of prose narrative, which was designed in the first place to appeal to simple-minded shepherds and tradespeople.

In the *New Testament* we find among many other beautiful stories the parables. These are in reality fables, told by Jesus for exactly the same reason that the fables of Æsop or of Phædrus were told, to drive home a moral lesson. If Jesus spoke his parables exactly as they are written, he must be accounted one of the world's greatest artists. *The Prodigal Son* is a perfect model of the short story. The other tale included here, *The Raising of Lazarus*, though somewhat longer and more diffuse, is no less perfect.

The Talmud, which is the orthodox Jewish commentary on the *Old Testament*, bristles with short moral tales. To develop the art of the Jewish short story would necessitate tracing it from the earliest chapters of the *Old Testament*, through *The Talmud*, with all its accumulation of commentary upon commentary, through a long period of oral tradition up to modern times. There are still sporadic writers in the Hebrew language, though for the most part the modern Jewish writers (when they have not, like Israel Zangwill, written in the language of the country of their adoption) have employed the modern Yiddish dialect.

The literature of the *New Testament* (which was written in late Greek) is difficult to classify. It is Jewish, of course, but permeated by a

53

distinctly non-Hebraic spirit. The influence exerted by the narratives of the *New Testament* has been enormous, but it is rather religious and theological than artistic. The spirit of this literature has penetrated the thought, life, habits and art of the entire Occidental world.

THE BOOK OF RUTH

(From the *Old Testament*)

INTO the extremely complicated questions of authorship, origin and development of the Old Testament it is not necessary to enter. *Ruth* is one of the most beautifully conceived and finely written narratives of all Biblical literature. Although it has its place in the ethical scheme of the Old Testament, it seems to have been written with an artistic zest and freedom from constraint that are rare in the religious literature of any race.

The text used here is that printed in Volume IV of *Ancient Hebrew Literature*, in Everyman's Library, published in 1907 by J. M. Dent and Sons, by whose permission it is here included. (The last sentence has been omitted, as it has nothing to do with the story.)

THE BOOK OF RUTH

NOW it came to pass in the days when the judges ruled, that there was a famine in the land. And a certain man of Beth-lehem-judah went to sojourn in the country of Moab, he, and his wife, and his two sons. And the name of the man was Elimelech, and the name of his wife Naomi, and the name of his two sons Mahlon and Chilion, Ephra-thites of Beth-lehem-judah. And they came into the country of Moab, and continued there.

And Elimelech Naomi's husband died; and she was left, and her two sons. And they took them wives of the women of Moab; the name of the one was Orpah, and the name of the other Ruth: and they dwelled there about ten years. And Mahlon and Chilion died also both of them; and the woman was left of her two sons and her husband.

Then she arose with her daughters-in-law, that she might return from the country of Moab: for she had heard in the country of Moab how that the Lord had visited His people in giving them bread. Wherefore she went forth out of the place where she was, and her two daughters-in-law with her; and they went on the way to return unto the land of Judah. And Naomi said unto her two daughters-in-law:— "Go, return each to her mother's house: the Lord deal kindly with you,

as ye have dealt with the dead, and with me. The Lord grant you that
ye may find rest, each of you in the house of her husband." Then she
kissed them; and they lifted up their voice, and wept. And they said
unto her:—"Surely we will return with thee unto thy people."

And Naomi said:—"Turn again, my daughters: why will ye go with
me? are there yet any more sons in my womb, that they may be your
husbands? Turn again, my daughters, go your way; for I am too old
to have an husband. If I should say, I have hope, if I should have an
husband also to-night, and should also bear sons; would ye tarry for
them till they were grown? would ye stay for them from having husbands? nay, my daughters; for it grieveth me much for your sakes that
the hand of the Lord is gone out against me."

And they lifted up their voice, and wept again: and Orpah kissed
her mother-in-law; but Ruth clave unto her. And she said:—"Behold,
thy sister-in-law is gone back unto her people, and unto her gods:
return thou after thy sister-in-law." And Ruth said:—"Intreat me
not to leave thee, or to return from following after thee: for whither
thou goest, I will go; and where thou lodgest, I will lodge: thy people
shall be my people, and thy God my God: where thou diest, will I die,
and there will I be buried: the Lord do so to me, and more also, if
ought but death part thee and me."

When she saw that she was steadfastly minded to go with her, then
she left speaking unto her. So they two went until they came to Beth-
lehem. And it came to pass, when they were come to Beth-lehem, that
all the city was moved about them, and they said:—"Is this Naomi?"
And she said unto them:—"Call me not Naomi, call me Mara: for the
Almighty hath dealt very bitterly with me. I went out full, and the
Lord hath brought me home again empty: why then call ye me Naomi,
seeing the Lord hath testified against me, and the Almighty hath
afflicted me?"

So Naomi returned, and Ruth the Moabitess, her daughter-in-law,
with her, which returned out of the country of Moab: and they came to
Beth-lehem in the beginning of barley harvest. And Naomi had a kinsman of her husband's, a mighty man of wealth, of the family of Elimelech; and his name was Boaz. And Ruth the Moabitess said unto
Naomi:—"Let me now go to the field, and glean ears of corn after
him in whose sight I shall find grace." And she said unto her:—"Go,
my daughter." And she went, and came, and gleaned in the field after
the reapers: and her hap was to light on a part of the field belonging
unto Boaz, who was of the kindred of Elimelech.

And, behold, Boaz came from Beth-lehem, and said unto the reapers:
—"The Lord be with you." And they answered him:—"The Lord bless
thee." Then said Boaz unto his servant that was set over the reapers:
—"Whose damsel is this?" And the servant that was set over the reapers

answered and said:—"It is the Moabitish damsel that came back with Naomi out of the country of Moab: and she said, I pray you, let me glean and gather after the reapers among the sheaves: so she came, and hath continued even from the morning until now, that she tarried a little in the house." Then said Boaz unto Ruth:—"Hearest thou not, my daughter? Go not to glean in another field, neither go from hence, but abide here fast by my maidens: let thine eyes be on the field that they do reap, and go thou after them: have I not charged the young men that they shall not touch thee? and when thou art athirst, go unto the vessels, and drink of that which the young men have drawn." Then she fell on her face, and bowed herself to the ground, and said unto him:—"Why have I found grace in thine eyes, that thou shouldest take knowledge of me, seeing I am a stranger?" And Boaz answered and said unto her:—"It hath fully been shewed me, all that thou hast done unto thy mother-in-law since the death of thine husband: and how thou hast left thy father and thy mother, and the land of thy nativity, and art come unto a people which thou knewest not heretofore. The Lord recompense thy work, and a full reward be given thee of the Lord God of Israel, under whose wings thou art come to trust."

Then she said:—"Let me find favor in thy sight, my lord; for that thou hast comforted me, and for that thou has spoken friendly unto thine handmaid, though I be not like unto one of thine handmaidens." And Boaz said unto her:—"At mealtime come thou hither, and eat of the bread, and dip thy morsel in the vinegar." And she sat beside the reapers: and he reached her parched corn, and she did eat, and was sufficed, and left. And when she was risen up to glean, Boaz commanded his young men, saying:—"Let her glean even among the sheaves, and reproach her not: and let fall also some of the handfuls of purpose for her, and leave them, that she may glean them, and rebuke her not."

So she gleaned in the field until even, and beat out that she had gleaned: and it was about an ephah of barley. And she took it up, and went into the city: and her mother-in-law saw what she had gleaned: and she brought forth, and gave to her that she had reserved after she was sufficed. And her mother-in-law said unto her:—"Where hast thou gleaned to-day? and where wroughtest thou? blessed be he that did take knowledge of thee." And she shewed her mother-in-law with whom she had wrought, and said:—"The man's name with whom I wrought to-day is Boaz." And Naomi said unto her daughter-in-law: —"Blessed be he of the Lord, who hath not left off His kindness to the living and to the dead." And Naomi said unto her:—"The man is near of kin unto us, one of our next kinsmen." And Ruth the Moabitess said:—"He said unto me also, Thou shalt keep fast by my young men, until they have ended all my harvest." And Naomi said unto Ruth her daughter-in-law:—"It is good, my daughter, that thou go out with his maidens, that they meet thee not in any other field." So she kept fast by the maidens of Boaz to glean unto the end of barley harvest and of wheat harvest; and dwelt with her mother-in-law.

Then Naomi her mother-in-law said unto her:—"My daughter, shall I not seek rest for thee, that it may be well with thee? And now is not Boaz of our kindred, with whose maidens thou wast? Behold, he winnoweth barley to-night in the threshing-floor. Wash thyself therefore, and anoint thee, and put thy raiment upon thee, and get thee down to the floor: but make not thyself known unto the man, until he shall have done eating and drinking. And it shall be, when he lieth down, that thou shalt mark the place where he shall lie, and thou shalt go in, and uncover his feet, and lay thee down; and he will tell thee what thou shalt do." And she said unto her:—"All that thou sayest unto me I will do."

And she went down unto the floor, and did according to all that her mother-in-law bade her. And when Boaz had eaten and drunk, and his heart was merry, he went to lie down at the end of the heap of corn: and she came softly, and uncovered his feet, and laid her down. And it came to pass at midnight, that the man was afraid, and turned himself: and, behold, a woman lay at his feet. And he said:—"Who art thou?" And she answered:—"I am Ruth thine handmaid: spread therefore thy skirt over thine handmaid; for thou art a near kinsman." And he said:—"Blessed be thou of the Lord, my daughter: for thou hast shewed more kindness in the latter end than at the beginning, inasmuch as thou followedst not young men, whether poor or rich. And now, my daughter, fear not; I will do to thee all that thou requirest: for all the city of my people doth know that thou art a virtuous woman. And now it is true that I am thy near kinsman: howbeit there is a kinsman nearer than I. Tarry this night, and it shall be in the morning, that if he will perform unto thee the part of a kinsman, well; let him do the kinsman's part: but if he will not do the part of a kinsman to thee, then will I do the part of a kinsman to thee, as the Lord liveth: lie down until the morning."

And she lay at his feet until the morning: and she rose up before one could know another. And he said:—"Let it not be known that a woman came into the floor." Also he said:—"Bring the vail that thou hast upon thee, and hold it." And when she held it, he measured six measures of barley, and laid it on her: and she went into the city. And when she came to her mother-in-law, she said:—"Who art thou, my daughter?" And she told her all that the man had done to her. And she said:—"These six measures of barley gave he me; for he said to me, Go not empty unto thy mother-in-law." Then said she:—"Sit still, my daughter, until thou know how the matter will fall: for the man will not be in rest, until he have finished the thing this day."

Then went Boaz up to the gate, and sat him down there: and, behold, the kinsman of whom Boaz spake came by; unto whom he said:
—"Ho, such a one! turn aside, sit down here." And he turned aside, and sat down. And he took ten men of the elders of the city, and said:
—"Sit ye down here." And they sat down. And he said unto the kinsman:— "Naomi, that is come again out of the country of Moab, selleth a parcel of land, which was our brother Elimelech's: and I thought to advertise thee, saying, Buy it before the inhabitants, and before the elders of my people. If thou wilt redeem it, redeem it: but if thou wilt not redeem it, then tell me, that I may know: for there is none to redeem it beside thee; and I am after thee." And he said: "I will redeem it." Then said Boaz:—"What day thou buyest the field of the hand of Naomi, thou must buy it also of Ruth the Moabitess, the wife of the dead, to raise up the name of the dead upon his inheritance." And the kinsman said:—" I cannot redeem it for myself, lest I mar mine own inheritance: redeem thou my right to thyself; for I cannot redeem it." Now this was the manner in former time in Israel concerning redeeming and concerning changing, for to confirm all things; a man plucked off his shoe, and gave it to his neighbor: and this was a testimony in Israel. Therefore the kinsman said unto Boaz:
—"Buy it for thee." So he drew off his shoe.

And Boaz said unto the elders, and unto all the people:—"Ye are witnesses this day, that I have bought all that was Elimelech's, and all that was Chilion's and Mahlon's of the hand of Naomi. Moreover, Ruth the Moabitess, the wife of Mahlon, have I purchased to be my wife, to raise up the name of the dead upon his inheritance, that the name of the dead be not cut off from among his brethren, and from the gate of his place: ye are witnesses this day." And all the people that were in the gate, and the elders, said:—"We are witnesses. The Lord make the woman that is come into thine house like Rachel and like Leah, which two did build the house of Israel: and do thou worthily in Ephratah, and be famous in Beth-lehem: and let thy house be like the house of Pharez, whom Tamar bare unto Judah, of the seed which the Lord shall give thee of this young woman."

So Boaz took Ruth, and she was his wife: and when he went in unto her, the Lord gave her conception, and she bare a son. And the women said unto Naomi:—"Blessed be the Lord, which hath not left thee this day without a kinsman, that his name may be famous in Israel. And he shall be unto thee a restorer of thy life, and a nourisher of thine old age: for thy daughter-in-law, which loveth thee, which is better to thee than seven sons, hath born him." And Naomi took the child, and laid it in her bosom, and became nurse unto it. And the women her neighbors gave it a name, saying:—"There is a son born to Naomi"; and they called his name Obed: he is the father of Jesse, the father of David.

THE HISTORY OF SUSANNA

(From *The Apocrypha*)

SUSANNA was originally a part of the Book of Daniel, but was set apart as apocryphal, because it "was not in Hebrew." It is none the less a story of remarkable vividness, told with skill and dramatic power.

The text used here is that printed in Volume IV of *Ancient Hebrew Literature*, in Everyman's Library, published in 1907 by J. M. Dent and Sons, by whose permission it is here included.

THE HISTORY OF SUSANNA

THERE dwelt a man in Babylon, called Joakim: and he took a wife, whose name was Susanna, the daughter of Chelcias, a very fair woman, and one that feared the Lord. Her parents also were righteous, and taught their daughter according to the law of Moses. Now Joakim was a great rich man, and had a fair garden joining unto his house: and to him resorted the Jews; because he was more honorable than all others. The same year were appointed two of the ancients of the people to be judges, such as the Lord spake of, that wickedness came from Babylon from ancient judges, who seemed to govern the people. These kept much at Joakim's house: and all that had any suits in law came unto them.

Now when the people departed away at noon, Susanna went into her husband's garden to walk. And the two elders saw her going in every day, and walking; so that their lust was inflamed toward her. And they perverted their own mind, and turned away their eyes, that they might not look unto heaven, nor remember just judgments. And albeit they both were wounded with her love, yet durst not one shew another his grief. For they were ashamed to declare their lust, that they desired to have to do with her. Yet they watched diligently from day to day to see her. And the one said to the other:—"Let us now go home: for it is dinner time." So when they were gone out, they parted the one from the other, and turning back again they came to the same place; and after that they had asked one another the cause, they acknowledged their lust: then appointed they a time both together, when they might find her alone.

And it fell out, as they watched a fit time, she went in as before with two maids only, and she was desirous to wash herself in the garden: for it was hot. And there was nobody there save the two elders, that had hid themselves, and watched her. Then she said to her maids:

"Bring me oil and washing balls, and shut the garden doors, that I may wash me." And they did as she bade them, and shut the garden doors, and went out themselves at privy doors to fetch the things that she had commanded them: but they saw not the elders, because they were hid.

Now when the maids were gone forth, the two elders rose up, and ran unto her, saying:—"Behold, the garden doors are shut, that no man can see us, and we are in love with thee; therefore consent unto us, and lie with us. If thou wilt not, we will bear witness against thee, that a young man was with thee: and therefore thou didst send away thy maids from thee." Then Susanna sighed, and said:—"I am straitened on every side: for if I do this thing, it is death unto me: and if I do it not, I cannot escape your hands. It is better for me to fall into your hands, and not do it, than to sin in the sight of the Lord." With that Susanna cried with a loud voice: and the two elders cried out against her. Then ran the one, and opened the garden door. So when the servants of the house heard the cry in the garden they rushed in at a privy door, to see what was done unto her. But when the elders had declared their matter, the servants were greatly ashamed: for there was never such a report made of Susanna.

And it came to pass the next day, when the people were assembled to her husband Joakim, the two elders came also full of mischievous imagination against Susanna to put her to death: and said before the people, "Send for Susanna, the daughter of Chelcias, Joakim's wife." And so they sent. So she came with her father and mother, her children, and all her kindred. Now Susanna was a very delicate woman, and beauteous to behold. And these wicked men commanded to uncover her face (for she was covered) that they might be filled with her beauty. Therefore her friends and all that saw her wept. Then the two elders stood up in the midst of the people, and laid their hands upon her head. And she weeping looked up toward heaven: for her heart trusted in the Lord. And the elders said:—"As we walked in the garden alone, this woman came in with two maids, and shut the garden doors, and sent the maids away. Then a young man, who there was hid, came unto her, and lay with her. Then we that stood in a corner of the garden, seeing this wickedness, ran unto them. And when we saw them together, the man we could not hold: for he was stronger than we, and opened the door, and leaped out. But having taken this woman, we asked who the young man was, but she would not tell us: these things do we testify."

Then the assembly believed them, as those that were the elders, and judges of the people: so they condemned her to death. Then Susanna cried out with a loud voice, and said:—"O everlasting God, that knowest the secrets, and knowest all things before they be: Thou knowest that they have borne false witness against me, and, behold, I must die; whereas I never did such things as these men have maliciously invented against me." And the Lord heard her voice. Therefore when she was led to be put to death, the Lord raised up the holy spirit of a youth, whose name was Daniel: who cried with a loud voice:—"I am clear from the blood of this woman." Then all the people turned them toward him, and said:—"What mean these words that thou hast spoken?"

So he standing in the midst of them said:—"Are ye such fools, ye sons of Israel, that without examination or knowledge of the truth ye have condemned a daughter of Israel? Return again to the place of judgment: for they have borne false witness against her." Wherefore all the people turned again in haste, and the elders said unto him:—"Come, sit down among us, and shew it us, seeing God hath given thee the honor of an elder." Then said Daniel unto them:—"Put these two aside one far from another, and I will examine them." So when they were put asunder one from another, he called one of them, and said unto him:—"O thou that art waxen old in wickedness, now thy sins which thou hast committed aforetime are come to light: for thou hast pronounced false judgment, and hast condemned the innocent, and hast let the guilty go free; albeit the Lord saith, The innocent and righteous shalt thou not slay. Now then, if thou hast seen her, tell me, Under what tree sawest thou them companying together?" Who answered:—"Under a mastic tree." And Daniel said:—"Very well; thou hast lied against thine own head; for even now the angel of God hath received the sentence of God to cut thee in two."

So he put him aside, and commanded to bring the other, and said unto him:—"O thou seed of Canaan, and not of Juda, beauty hath deceived thee, and lust hath perverted thine heart. Thus have ye dealt with the daughters of Israel, and they for fear companied with you: but the daughter of Juda would not abide your wickedness. Now therefore tell me, Under what tree didst thou take them companying together?" Who answered:—"Under an holm tree." Then said Daniel unto him:—"Well; thou hast also lied against thine own head: for the angel of God waiteth with the sword to cut thee in two, that He may destroy you." With that all the assembly cried out with a loud voice, and praised God, who saveth them that trust in Him.

And they arose against the two elders, for Daniel had convicted them of false witness by their own mouth: and according to the law of Moses they did unto them in such sort as they maliciously intended to do to their neighbor: and they put them to death. Thus the innocent blood was saved the same day. Therefore Chelcias and his wife praised God for their daughter Susanna, with Joakim her husband, and all the kindred, because there was no dishonesty found in her.

From that day forth was Daniel had in great reputation in the sight of the people.

THE PRODIGAL SON

(From the *New Testament*, Luke XV)

THE PRODIGAL SON is a parable, spoken by Jesus in praise of forgiveness.
It is one of the great stories of the world, and is justly regarded as
a perfect model of the art of story-telling.

The present text is taken from the King James version. There is
no title to the story in the original.

THE PRODIGAL SON

AND he said, A certain man had two sons: and the younger of
them said to his father, Father, give me the portion of goods that
falleth to me. And he divided unto them his living. And not many days
after the younger son gathered all together, and took his journey into
a far country, and there wasted his substance with riotous living. And
when he had spent all, there arose a mighty famine in that land; and
he began to be in want. And he went and joined himself to a citizen
of that country; and he sent him into his fields to feed swine. And he
would fain have filled his belly with the husks that the swine did eat:
and no man gave unto him. And when he came to himself, he said,
How many hired servants of my father's have bread enough and to
spare, and I perish with hunger! I will arise and go to my father, and
will say unto him, Father, I have sinned against heaven, and before
thee, and am no more worthy to be called thy son: make me as one
of thy hired servants. And he arose, and came to his father. But when
he was yet a great way off, his father saw him, and had compassion,
and ran, and fell on his neck, and kissed him. And the son said unto
him, Father, I have sinned against heaven, and in thy sight, and am no
more worthy to be called thy son. But the father said to his servants,
Bring forth the best robe, and put it on him; and put a ring on his
hand, and shoes on his feet: and bring hither the fatted calf, and kill it;
and let us eat, and be merry: For this my son was dead, and is alive
again; he was lost, and is found. And they began to be merry.

Now his elder son was in the field: and as he came and drew nigh to
the house, he heard music and dancing. And he called one of the
servants, and asked what these things meant. And he said unto him,
Thy brother is come; and thy father hath killed the fatted calf, because
he hath received him safe and sound. And he was angry, and would
not go in: therefore came his father out, and entreated him. And he
answering said to his father, Lo these many years do I serve thee,

neither transgressed I at any time thy commandment: and yet thou never gavest me a kid, that I might make merry with my friends: but as soon as this thy son was come, which hath devoured thy living with harlots, thou hast killed for him the fatted calf. And he said unto him, Son, thou art ever with me, and all that I have is thine. It was meet that we should make merry, and be glad: for this thy brother was dead, and is alive again; and was lost, and is found.

THE RAISING OF LAZARUS

(From the *New Testament*, John XI)

THOUGH this story is part of the larger narrative of the Gospel of St. John, it is a perfect example of the short story. The details that lead up to the dramatic climax are at first sight not entirely relevant. It is only after the story has been read in its entirety that we perceive the consummate art of the preparatory sentences. Balzac was, many centuries later, to apply this method to the writing of his novels.

The text is taken from the King James version. There is no title to the story in the original.

THE RAISING OF LAZARUS

NOW a certain man was sick, named Lazarus, of Bethany, the town of Mary and her sister Martha. (It was that Mary which anointed the Lord with ointment, and wiped his feet with her hair, whose brother Lazarus was sick.) Therefore, his sister sent unto him saying, Lord, behold, he whom thou lovest is sick. When Jesus heard that, he said, This sickness is not unto death, but for the glory of God, that the Son of God might be glorified thereby.

Now Jesus loved Martha, and her sister, and Lazarus. When he had heard therefore that he was sick, he abode two days still in the same place where he was. Then after that saith he to his disciples, Let us go into Judæa again. His disciples say unto him, Master, the Jews of late sought to stone thee; and goest thou thither again? Jesus answered, Are there not twelve hours in the day? If any man walk in the day, he stumbleth not, because he seeth the light of this world. But if a man walk in the night, he stumbleth, because there is no light in him. These things said he: and after that he saith unto them, Our friend Lazarus sleepeth; but I go, that I may awake him out of sleep. Then said his disciples, Lord, if he sleep, he shall do well. Howbeit Jesus spake of his death: but they thought that he had spoken of taking of rest in sleep. Then Jesus said unto them plainly, Lazarus is dead. And I am glad for your sakes that I was not there, to the intent ye may believe; nevertheless let us go unto him. Then said Thomas, which is called Didymus, unto his fellow disciples, Let us also go, that we may die with him.

Then when Jesus came, he found that he had lain in the grave four days already. Now Bethany was nigh unto Jerusalem about fifteen furlongs off: and many of the Jews came unto Martha, and Mary, to comfort them concerning their brother. Then Martha, as soon as she heard that Jesus was coming, went and met him, but Mary sat still in the house. Then said Martha unto Jesus, Lord, if thou hadst been here, my brother had not died. But I know, that even now, whatsoever thou wilt ask of God, God will give it thee. Jesus saith unto her, Thy brother shall rise again. Martha saith unto him, I know that he shall rise again in the resurrection at the last day. Jesus said unto her, I am the resurrection and the life: he that believeth in me, though he were dead, yet shall he live: and whosoever liveth and believeth in me shall never die. Believest thou this? She saith unto him, Yea, Lord; I believe that thou art the Christ, the son of God, which should come into the world. And when she had so said, she went her way, and called Mary her sister secretly, saying, The Master is come, and calleth for thee. As soon as she heard that, she arose quickly and came unto him.

Now Jesus was not yet come into the town, but was in that place where Martha met him. The Jews then which were with her in the house, and comforted her, when they saw Mary, that she rose up hastily and went out, followed her saying, She goeth unto the grave to weep there. Then when Mary was come where Jesus was, and saw him, she fell down at his feet, saying unto him, Lord, if thou hadst been here, my brother had not died. When Jesus therefore saw her weeping, and the Jews also weeping which came with her, he groaned in the spirit, and was troubled, and said, Where have ye laid him? They said unto him, Lord, come and see. Jesus wept. Then said the Jews, Behold how he loved him! And some of them said, Could not this man, which opened the eyes of the blind, have caused that even this man should not have died? Jesus therefore again groaning in himself cometh to the grave. It was a cave, and a stone lay upon it. Jesus said, Take ye away the stone. Martha, the sister of him that was dead, saith unto him, Lord, by this time he stinketh: for he hath been dead four days. Jesus saith unto her, Said I not unto thee, that, if thou wouldest believe, thou shouldest see the glory of God? Then they took away the stone from the place where the dead was laid. And Jesus lifted up his eyes, and said, Father, I thank thee that thou hast heard me. And I knew that thou hearest me always: but because of the people which stand by I said it, that they may believe that thou hast sent me. And when he thus had spoken, he cried with a loud voice, Lazarus, come forth. And he that was dead, came forth, bound hand and foot with grave-clothes. And his face was bound about with a napkin. Jesus saith unto them, Loose him, and let him go. Then many of the Jews which came to Mary, and had seen the things which Jesus did, believed on him.

RABBI AKIVA

(From *The Talmud*)

THE TALMUD is a great collection of law, ritual, precept, and example, which was composed during the period extending from the First Century B.C. to the Fourth Century A.D. The work was the result of a vast amount of compilation begun, so far as the actual writing is concerned, in the year 219 A.D. by Rabbi Jehudah Hanassi. About the year 500 A.D. it was complete, having been combined with a good deal of material brought together since the first parts were written down. The colossal work is interspersed throughout with parables, like *Rabbi Akiva* and *The Jewish Mother*, all of which were used for purposes of illustration.

The texts of these stories are based, by the editors, upon two early translations. There are no titles to the stories in the original.

RABBI AKIVA

THE Rabbis tell us that once the Roman Government made a decree forbidding Israel to study the law. Thereupon Pappus, son of Yehudah, one day found Rabbi Akiva teaching it openly to many whom he had gathered round him to hear it. "Akiva," he said, "dost not thou fear the Government?" "Listen," was the reply, "and I will tell thee how it is through a parable. It is the same with me as with the fishes which a fox, walking by a river's bank, saw darting distractedly to and fro in the stream; and, speaking to them, inquired, 'From what, pray, are ye fleeing?' 'From the nets,' they answered, 'which the sons of men have set to snare us.' 'Why, then,' rejoined the fox, 'not try the dry land with me, where we can live together, as our fathers managed to live before us?' 'Surely,' they exclaimed, 'thou art not he of whom we have heard as the most cunning of animals; for in this thing thou art not wise, but foolish. For if we have cause to fear where it is natural for us to live, how much more reason have we to do so where we must die!' Exactly so," continued Akiva, "is it with us who study the law, in which it is written, 'He is thy life and the length of thy days'; for if we suffer while studying the law, how much more shall we suffer if we neglect it?" Not many days afterward it is related that Rabbi Akiva was arrested and thrown into prison. It so happened that they led him out for execution just at the time when "Hear, O Israel!" was being repeated, and as they gashed his flesh with currycombs, and as he was with longdrawn breath uttering the word One, his soul departed from him. Then there came forth a voice from heaven saying, "Blessed art thou, Rabbi Akiva, for thy soul and the word One left thy body together."

THE JEWISH MOTHER

(From *The Talmud*)

ONCE upon a time a Jewish mother together with her seven sons suffered martyrdom at the hands of the Emperor. The sons, ordered by the latter to do homage to the Imperial idols, declined, and justified their disobedience by each quoting a simple text from the Scriptures. When the seventh was brought forth, it is said that Cæsar, for appearance' sake, offered to spare him if he would only stoop and pick up a ring from the ground which had been dropped on purpose. "Alas for thee, oh, Cæsar!" replied the boy; "if thou art so zealous for thine honor, how much more so ought we to be for that of the Holy One—blessed be He!" When he was led away to the place of execution, his mother begged and obtained leave to give him a last kiss. "Go, my child," she said, "and say to Abraham, Thou didst build an altar for the sacrifice of one son, but I have raised altars for seven sons." Then she turned away and threw herself headlong from the roof and died. The echo of a voice was heard exclaiming, "The joyful mother of children."

Ancient India

INTRODUCTION

SANSKRIT is the classical language of the Hindus of ancient India. Practically the whole of that extraordinary literature which began with the *Vedas* and culminated some time before the close of the Middle Ages, was written in Sanskrit.

Our knowledge of the earliest period is vague. The *Vedas* were composed perhaps before the days of Homer. Beginning perhaps about 500 B.C. and extending to about the time of Christ, is the period of the epics, during which the *Mahabharata* and *Ramayana* were probably written. Both these monumental poems are full of episodes containing at least the material for short stories.

But for the purpose of this volume, the outstanding contribution of the ancient Hindus were the fables and tales, most of which are found in large collections. The earliest of these is doubtless the *Jataka*, or Buddhist "birth-stories," which were in existence at least as early as the Fourth Century B.C. The *Panchatantra* may be as old as the *Jataka* stories; both are rooted in a common source. Many centuries later an unknown author revised certain parts of the *Panchatantra* and produced the book known as the *Hitopadesa*, which may be as recent as the Fourteenth Century A.D.

Most of these stories are directly didactic, but for the historian in search of the origin of certain types, the question of the fable and its Indian or Greek origin, is one of the most fascinating in all literature. There are those who claim that the tales in the *Panchatantra* and the *Jataka* stories are the source of all the fables in the Occident, and others who believe that it was the Hindus who took the fable form from the ancient Greeks.

Of the other collections of stories the most varied is the famous *Katha-sarit-Sagara*, or *Ocean of Streams of Stories*, written about 1070 A.D. by Somadeva. This was based upon a much earlier collection, which is now lost.

The influence of the Sanskrit tales on the art of the story is almost impossible to estimate: translations and revisions of Sanskrit tales and fables were made as early as the Sixth Century B.C., and modern research is demonstrating beyond any doubt the fact that the Ancient Hindus have furnished ideas and literary forms to other nations ever since the dawn of history.

THE ASS IN THE LION'S SKIN

(Anonymous: 500 B.C.?—380 B.C.?)

THE *Jataka* or "Birth-story" is found in one form or another in several collections, one of which was well known as early as the Fourth Century B.C. It is a brief incident, usually in fable form, showing one incarnation of the Buddha, and drawing from the fable a little moral. The *Jataka* may actually have influenced the ancient Greeks and given rise to the Æsop legends, but whether or not that is true, they constitute the "oldest, most complete, and most important collection of folk-lore extant."

Nothing whatsoever is known of the author or authors of the particular collection from which this story is taken. It is reprinted from *Buddhist Birth Stories [Nidana-Katha]*, by T. W. Rhys Davids, London, 1880, by permission of the publishers, Kegan Paul, Trench, Trübner and Co.

THE ASS IN THE LION'S SKIN

(From the *Jataka* Collections)

ONCE upon a time, while Brahma-datta was reigning in Benares, the future Buddha was born one of a peasant family; and when he grew up, he gained his living by tilling the ground.

At that time a hawker used to go from place to place, trafficking in goods carried by an ass. Now at each place he came to, when he took the pack down from the ass's back he used to clothe him in a lion's skin, and turn him loose in the rice and barley-fields, and when the watchmen in the fields saw the ass, they dared not go near him, taking him for a lion. So one day the hawker stopped in a village; and while he was getting his own breakfast cooked, he dressed the ass in a lion's skin and turned him loose in a barley-field. The watchmen in the field dared not go up to him; but going home, they published the news. Then all the villagers came out with weapons in their hands; and blowing chanks, and beating drums, they went near the field and shouted. Terrified with the fear of death, the ass uttered a cry— the cry of an ass!

And when he knew him then to be an ass, the future Buddha pronounced the first stanza —

> "This is not a lion's roaring,
> Nor a tiger's, nor a panther's;
> Dressed in a lion's skin,
> 'Tis a wretched ass that roars!"

But when the villagers knew the creature to be an ass, they beat him till his bones broke; and, carrying off the lion's skin, went away. Then the hawker came, and seeing the ass fallen into so bad a plight, pronounced the second stanza:

> "Long might the ass,
> Clad in a lion's skin,
> Have fed on barley green,
> But he brayed,
> And that moment he came to ruin."

And even while he was yet speaking the ass died on the spot!

THE DOVE AND THE CROW

(Anonymous: 2nd Century B.C. or later)

It is thought that the collection of fables now known as the *Panchatantra* had assumed definite shape at least as early as the Sixth Century A.D., and it is possible that it dates back to the Second Century B.C. Nothing is known of the author. The little stories that make up the collection are mostly Beast Fables, which were originally designed to instruct young princes. "Panchatantra" means "five books."

The present story, from the second book or *Tantra*, is reprinted from *Ancient Indian Fables and Stories*, by permission of the publisher, John Murray. It has no title in the original.

THE DOVE AND THE CROW

(From the *Panchatantra*)

WHEN Vishnu Sarma had finished telling and expounding these fables, his pupils were lost in admiration of their teacher, whose wisdom had been so clearly marked by his dexterous mingling of amusement with instruction. They rose and all three fell at his feet, thanking him for the wise lessons he had given them; they assured him that henceforth they would regard him as their guru and that they hoped with his help and advice to rise from the state of ignorance in which they had hitherto been. They prayed him to continue the work so happily begun and to give them more of his interesting lessons.

Vishnu Sarma was charmed to see that his pupils were well disposed and noticed with satisfaction that his plan had so far succeeded. He continued his task with enthusiasm and proceeded to tell them fresh fables.

"Now," said Vishnu Sarma, "listen, my young princes, to the fable I am going to tell you. In the complex nature of this life we must all help one another. It is by this mutual help that the weak escape the dangers, to which they are exposed from the strong, as you shall now hear."

A certain dove, by name Chitrani, had built her nest on the top of the mountain Kanakachala and was living there comfortably with her family. At the foot of the mountain dwelt a crow. One day Vega-Varma (such was the crow's name) was flying round in search of food when he noticed a fowler spreading his nets in the way. He was frightened at sight of the danger and at once returned home.

The dove Chitrani passed by the same place with her family, but being off their guard, they all flew into the net and were captured. What was to be done? How could they escape from certain death? There was in fact no escape, no hope of obtaining their liberty. Already the fowler was running up to seize his prey, when all at once under the impulse of danger they took to flight together, carrying with them the net that enclosed them. So they succeeded in escaping, and the fowler, who had reckoned upon his capture, was not a little surprised when he saw them fly away with his nets. But they reached their home in safety still entangled in the nets into which they had flown.

When the crow saw them coming in this strange chariot, he hastened to meet them; and as soon as Chitrani saw him, she told him of their adventures and asked him to help them by disentangling the nets. The crow replied that he could not free them, but suggested a rat of the name of Hiranya Varma who lived close by and who could help them. Accordingly Chitrani called the rat, who came up at once, and when he saw the captives he began to scold Chitrani for her imprudence and folly which had brought them to this pass. Chitrani defended herself and quoted the maxim: "No one, be he never so wise or prudent, can escape his destiny." Then the rat, pitying the poor doves, called his fellows, and they all set to work to gnaw the knots of the nets, so that very soon they had freed Chitrani and her family.

The crow, who had seen the signal service performed by the rat for the doves, was anxious to make friends with him; he hoped also to obtain a useful ally should occasion arise. He accordingly made overtures to him; but the rat replied that they were of totally different species, the one living in the air and the other in the earth; he did not see the use of the close friendship of two creatures between whom Nature had fixed such a wide gulf.

But the crow insisted. Matters of personal interest and friendship, he said, are decided by our inclination. We do not consider distance or the difference of condition. So the rat yielded and they swore a close friendship. One day when they were out together they happened to meet a deer; they stopped him and asked his name and where he was going. The deer said he was called Chitranga, told them his story, and asked if he might join them. They readily consented, and so the three struck up a lasting friendship.

One day while they were out together and were very thirsty, in their search for water they found a well into which a tortoise had fallen. As soon as she saw the three friends she begged them to take her out of her prison and to put her somewhere where she could live in comfort. Pitying her plight, they rescued her and took her to a spring of clear water; and she, mindful of this service, also became their friend.

For a long time the four lived happily together, but one day when the deer had gone away to graze he fell into the snare of a hunter. But when the rat saw that his friend the deer was so long in returning, he guessed that he had met with an accident. So he called the crow and told him what he feared and advised him to fly up and try to discover their friend. This the crow did, and after looking about for some time, at last saw poor Chitranga in the snare struggling hard to get out, but in vain.

The crow at once told Hiranya Varma what had happened to their friend, and he, calling his fellow-rats, sallied out to help him. They soon set him free. Chitranga went home with his friends and the accident was soon forgotten. But later on, when the four friends were resting quietly in the shade of a tree, they were suddenly disturbed by the unexpected sight of a crowd of hunters. This alarmed them. The crow and the deer could easily avoid pursuit, but not so the rat, and least of all the tortoise. The other two would not leave them to the mercy of the hunters, who were coming on quickly, and so the deer undertook to attract attention to himself in order to save the life of his friends. He pretended to be lame. The hunters, seeing him limp and apparently hardly able to hold himself up, all ran to capture the easy prey. But the deer led them a long dance, sometimes quickening his pace, sometimes slowing down, until at last, having made them follow for a long time, he fairly used his four legs and was soon out of sight. Meanwhile the tortoise and the rat had found a place of safety out of reach of the hunters.

Once more the four friends were united and lived quietly together; these dangers had taught them the value of true unity and of sincere friendship, and by experience they learned how the weak need to support one another.

SOMADEVA

(Flourished about 1070 A.D.)

SOMADEVA (Soma with the Brahminical suffix *deva*) was a poet of
Kashmir. His celebrated collection, the *Ocean of Streams of Stories*,
based upon Buddhist stories, traditions, and an earlier collection of tales,
is one of the most voluminous and interesting of its kind in Sanskrit
literature.

    The present story, translated by C. H. Tawney, appeared in *The
Ocean of Story*, Vol. I, Book IV, Chap. 21, of the complete edition in
ten volumes edited by N. M. Penzer, and published in 1924–25 by
Chas. J. Sawyer, Ltd., by whose permission it is here included.

THE STORY OF DEVADATTA

(From the *Katha-Sarit-Sagara*)

IN old time there was a certain petty monarch of the name of Jayadatta, and there was born to him a son, named Devadatta. And
that wise king, wishing to marry his son, who was grown up, thus
reflected: "The prosperity of kings is very unstable, being like a cour-
tesan to be enjoyed by force; but the prosperity of merchants is like
a woman of good family; it is steady and does not fly to another man.
Therefore I will take a wife to my son from a merchant's family, in
order that misfortune may not overtake his throne, though it is surrounded with many relations." Having formed this resolve, that king
sought for his son the daughter of a merchant in Pātaliputra named
Vasudatta. Vasudatta for his part, eager for such a distinguished alliance, gave that daughter of his to the prince, though he dwelt in
a remote foreign land.

    And he loaded his son-in-law with wealth to such an extent that he
no longer felt much respect for his father's magnificence. Then King
Jayadatta dwelt happily with that son of his who had obtained the
daughter of that rich merchant. Now one day the merchant Vasudatta
came, full of desire to see his daughter, to the palace of his connection
by marriage, and took away his daughter to his own home. Shortly
after the King Jayadatta suddenly went to heaven, and that kingdom
was seized by his relations, who rose in rebellion; through fear of them
his son Devadatta was secretly taken away by his mother during the
night to another country.

    Then that mother, distressed in soul, said to the prince: "Our feudal lord is the emperor who rules the eastern region; repair to him, my son; he will procure you the kingdom."

When his mother said this to him, the prince answered her: "Who will respect me if I go there without attendants?" When she heard that, his mother went on to say: "Go to the house of your father-in-law, and get money there, and so procure followers; and then repair to the emperor." Being urged in these words by his mother, the prince, though full of shame, slowly plodded on and reached his father-in-law's house in the evening. But he could not bear to enter at such an unseasonable hour, for he was afraid of shedding tears, being bereaved of his father and having lost his worldly splendor; besides, shame withheld him.

So he remained in the veranda of an almshouse near, and at night he suddenly beheld a woman descending with a rope from his father-in-law's house, and immediately he recognized her as his wife, for she was so resplendent with jewels that she looked like a meteor fallen from the clouds; and he was much grieved thereat. But she, though she saw him, did not recognize him, as he was emaciated and begrimed, and asked him who he was. When he heard that, he answered: "I am a traveler." Then the merchant's daughter entered the almshouse, and the prince followed her secretly to watch her. There she advanced towards a certain man, and he towards her, and asking why she had come so late, he bestowed several kicks on her. Then the passion of the wicked woman was doubled, and she appeased him, and remained with him on the most affectionate terms.

When he saw that, the discreet prince reflected: "This is not the time for me to show anger, for I have other affairs in hand; and how could I employ against these two contemptible creatures, this wife of mine and the man who has done me this wrong, this sword which is to be used against my foes? Or what quarrel have I with this adulteress, for this is the work of malignant desire that showers calamities upon me, showing skill in the game of testing my firmness? It is my marriage with a woman below me in rank that is in fault, not the woman herself; how can a female crow leave the male crow to take pleasure in a cuckoo?"

Thus reflecting, he allowed that wife of his to remain in the society of her paramour; for in the minds of heroes possessed with an ardent desire of victory, of what importance is woman, valueless as a straw? But at the moment when his wife ardently embraced her paramour there fell from her ear an ornament thickly studded with valuable jewels. And she did not observe this, but at the end of her interview, taking leave of her paramour, returned hurriedly to her house as she came. And that unlawful lover also departed somewhere or other.

Then the prince saw that jeweled ornament, and took it up; it flashed with many jewel-gleams, dispelling the gathering darkness of despondency, and seemed like a hand-lamp obtained by him to assist him in searching for his lost prosperity. The prince immediately perceived that it was very valuable, and went off, having obtained all he required, to Kanyākubja; there he pledged that ornament for a hundred thousand gold pieces, and after buying horses and elephants went into the presence of the emperor. And with the troops which he gave him he marched, and slew his enemies in fight, and recovered his father's kingdom; and his mother applauded his success.

Then he redeemed from pawn that ornament, and sent it to his father-in-law to reveal that unsuspected secret; his father-in-law, when he saw that earring of his daughter's, which had come to him in such a way, was confounded, and showed it to her. She looked upon it, lost long ago like her own virtue; and when she heard that it had been sent by her husband she was distracted, and called to mind the whole circumstance: "This is the very ornament which I let fall in the almshouse the night I saw that unknown traveler standing there; so that must undoubtedly have been my husband come to test my virtue, but I did not recognize him, and he picked up this ornament."

While the merchant's daughter was going through this train of reflection, her heart, afflicted by the misfortune of her unchastity having been discovered, in its agony, broke. Then her father artfully questioned a maid of hers who knew all her secrets, and found out the truth, and so ceased to mourn for his daughter; as for the prince, after he recovered the kingdom, he obtained as wife the daughter of the emperor, won by his virtues, and enjoyed the highest prosperity.

THE JACKAL

(Anonymous: 14th Century A.D., or earlier)

NOTHING is known of the author of the *Hitopadesa*, a manual of didactic fables composed—on the basis of the *Panchatantra*—before the year 1373 A.D.

The present story—which has no title in the original—is reprinted from Charles Wilkins' translation, London, 1787.

THE JACKAL

(From the *Hitopadesa*)

A CERTAIN jackal, as he was roaming about the borders of a town, just as his inclinations led him, fell into a dyer's vat; but being unable to get out, in the morning he feigned himself dead. At length, the master of the vat, which was filled with indigo, came, and seeing a jackal lying with his legs uppermost, his eyes closed, and his teeth bare, concluded that he was dead, and so, taking him out, he carried him a good way from the town, and there left him. The sly animal instantly got up, and ran into the woods; when, observing that his coat was turned blue, he meditated in this manner: "I am now of the finest color! what great exaltation may I not bring about for myself?" Saying this, he called a number of jackals together, and addressed them in the following words: "Know that I have lately been sprinkled king of the forests, by the hands of the goddess herself who presides over these woods, with a water drawn from a variety of choice herbs. Observe my color, and henceforward let every business be transacted according to my orders." The rest of the jackals, seeing him of such a fine complexion, prostrated themselves before him, and said: "According as Your Highness commands!" By this step he made himself honored by his own relations, and so gained the supreme power over those of his own species, as well as all the other inhabitants of the forests. But after a while, finding himself surrounded by a levee of the first quality, such as the tiger and the like, he began to look down upon his relations; and, at length, he kept them at a distance. A certain old jackal, perceiving that his brethren were very much cast down at this behavior, cried: "Do not despair! If it continue thus, this imprudent friend of ours will force us to be revenged. Let me alone to contrive his downfall. The lion, and the rest who pay him court, are taken by his outward appearance; and they obey him as their king, because they are not aware that he is nothing but a jackal: do something then by which he may be found out. Let this plan be pursued: Assemble all of you in a body about the close of the evening, and set up one general howl in his hearing; and I'll warrant you, the natural disposition of his species will incline him to join in the cry; for,

> Whatever may be the natural propensity of anyone is very hard to be overcome. If a dog were made king, would he not gnaw his shoe straps?

And thus the tiger, discovering that he is nothing but a jackal, will presently put him to death." The plan was executed, and the event was just as it had been foretold.

Persia

INTRODUCTION

THE short story in Persia had its origin among the wandering story-tellers, who sometimes invented their plots (so far as any one ever invents a plot), but more commonly borrowed them from the extensive store of legends or folk-tales, Semitic or Mohammedan in origin. No story-teller's repertory was complete unless it included tales of treasure or of love. The motive of these characteristic stories was extremely simple: one set out to amass a fortune, either by cunning or outright theft; or else one pursued some woman who was acclaimed as the perfection of maidenly beauty. In any event, the hero almost invariably succeeded in his quest and lived happy ever after. The obstacles in the way of achievement, whether the quest was treasure or a beautiful woman, formed the basis of the story, and when these were of a supernatural character the teller excelled in the invention of particularly ingenious obstacles. The introduction of supernatural elements was to be expected among a people whose imaginations had been stimulated by long ages of wandering in the uninhabited spots of the earth, and the Persian story-teller delighted in mixing his facts with fancy.

The Golden Age of the Persian story was about the Eleventh Century A.D. Since that time there has been little activity on the part of the novelist or the short story writer.

The Persians added to the art they so zealously practised a decorative element that was wanting in the Sanscrit stories, from which they largely borrowed, but apart from this they would deserve enduring fame for having transmitted to the Arabians the celebrated *Arabian Nights*.

ABUL KASIM MANSUR FIRDAWSÍ

(935—1025 A.D.)

ABUL KASIM MANSUR FIRDAWSÍ was born in the city of Tus, in Persia, in 935. He left the city of his birth to join the famous court of Mahmud of Ghazna, but not before he had completed a rough draft of his justly famous *Shah-Nama*, or *Book of Kings*. About forty

76

years he devoted to this wonderful epic, an account of the glories of Irán from its very beginnings and one of the great contributions to classic literature. It is related that Mahmud promised Firdawsí a fortune for his epic. When it was finally finished in 1010, the monarch broke his promise. Later, repenting of his misdeed, he sent the poet the promised gold, which arrived just as this ill-treated immortal was being buried.

The present version of *Jamshid and Zuhak*, a single episode from *The Book of the Kings*, is from the translation by Reuben Levy, M.A., copyrighted in 1923 by the Oxford University Press, by whose permission it is here reprinted.

JAMSHID AND ZUHAK

IN the days when the world was young, there was a king who, from his capital in Irán, ruled the earth for seven hundred years. His name was Jamshid, and he was indeed a mighty monarch, for men and divs and birds and peris all obeyed him. The world grew prosperous under him, for he said: "I will prevent evildoers from working ill, and will guide all men aright."

For fifty years he concerned himself with weapons of war, to open the path to glory for the valiant, and made helmets and lances and coats of mail. Then he turned to the making of garments for his people. He prepared stuffs of linen, of wool, of beaver skins and of rich brocade, and taught the people how to weave; and when the material was ready he showed them how to clean it and make it into garments. This being achieved, he devoted a space of time to seeking out the precious stones, and discovered such treasured things as ruby, yellow amber, silver, and gold. Then he invented perfumes, such as balm, camphor and pure musk, aloes, umber and rose-water. Thereafter he discovered medicine, remedies against every sickness, and the means of preserving health and of curing wounds. Thereby he made the world contented and was himself happy.

Three hundred years passed, and in that time death was unknown. There was neither pain nor sorrow, and the divs were kept in slavery, so that they never troubled men. But as time went on, the king became so powerful that he could see nothing in all the earth save himself, and by his arrogance incurred the anger of the gods.

Now there lived at this time in Arabia a king among the desert chieftains and the captain of many armed bands of horsemen. He possessed flocks and herds of goats, camels, and sheep, each a thousand strong, as well as cows and Arab horses. This generous king had a son Zuhak, who was brave, light-hearted, and care-free, and who was constantly engaged in wars against his enemies.

It happened one day that Iblis, the god of the divs, came to the palace disguised as a nobleman, and so pleased the young prince that he turned aside from his brave and noble way in order to follow the wicked div. Iblis rejoiced greatly, and said: "I know many things which none can learn except from me." "Teach me them," said the young man, "and do not delay." "First," said Iblis, "you must swear an oath not to reveal my secrets to any man." "I swear," said Zuhak, "and I will do everything you tell me." "Then," said Iblis to him, "why should there be any other man but you, illustrious prince, in the palace? Of what use is a father when he has a son like you? Take his throne, for it belongs to you, and if you follow my counsel, you will be a great king on the earth."

When Zuhak heard this he pondered long, for he loved his father. He said: "I cannot do it. Tell me something else, for that is not possible." Iblis replied in fury, "If you do not carry out my commands and if you break the oath you swore to me, my bonds will remain attached to your neck for ever." Zuhak submitted, and said: "How am I to bring this about?"

"I, Iblis, will prepare the means, and raise you to the sun. You have but to keep silence."

Now the king had around his palace a garden in which he took great delight, and here, often rising before dawn, he would walk, without even one slave to carry his torch. On the path the div dug a deep pit, covered it with brushwood, and spread earth on the top. Early the following morning, before the sun was up, the Arab king awoke and went out into the cold air of dawn. As he approached the fatal pit his star paled, but he disregarded its warning, and, falling into the chasm, was slain. Thus perished this pious man who had scarce ever spoken a harsh word to his son.

Iblis, his plan accomplished, then approached Zuhak again, and said: "When you have turned your heart towards me, you may obtain all that you desire. Renew but your oath, and the entire world will be your kingdom; the wild beasts, the birds, and the fishes will be your subjects." And with these words he vanished.

Soon afterwards Iblis assumed the guise of a young man of ready speech and agile form, and presented himself to Zuhak, saying that he was an excellent cook. The prince engaged him, and by his royal command delivered to him the keys of his kitchen. Now the design of Iblis was to make the prince abandon his eating of herbs and to persuade him to the eating of meat. He began by preparing yolk of egg for him, which in a short time gave him great vigor of body. Zuhak was pleased and commended his cook, who said, "To-morrow I will prepare for your Majesty a dish than which nought is more perfect." And the next day, when the blue dome of heaven was lighted by the red ruby of the sun, he prepared a dish of partridge and of silver pheasant, which the Arab ruler ate; and thus he abandoned his imprudent mind to the power of Iblis, who, on the third day, placed upon the table a mixture of birds and lambs' flesh. On the fourth day, when the meal was brought, the king feasted on the flesh of a young calf seasoned with rose-water, old wine, and pure musk. The meal filled him with delight at the skill of his cook, and, summoning him, he said, "Think what it is that you desire, and ask it of me." Iblis replied, "I have but one request to make of the king (may he live prosperous forever), but that is an honor too great for me; it is that I may be permitted to kiss his shoulders and to touch them with my eyes and face."

Zuhak suspected nothing of his intention, and said: "I grant your wish; it may be that some honor will thereby accrue to your name," and he bared his shoulders to him as to a friend. Iblis kissed them and vanished from the earth. But from each of Zuhak's shoulders appeared a black serpent, and Zuhak became sick at heart and sought on all sides for a remedy. Finally he bade that the serpents be cut off close to his shoulder, but they grew again. Every physician and wise man in the kingdom tried his remedies, but all in vain. The last to come was Iblis himself, who appeared as a physician before Zuhak. "It was inevitable," said he, "that this should happen. Leave the serpents and do not cut them off while there is life in them. To appease them you must feed them on the brains of men, which alone will at last slay them."

While these events were taking place at the court of Arabia, great tumults filled the land of Irán. The arrogance of Jamshid had set his subjects in revolt against him, and a great army marched towards Arabia from the highlands of Irán. They had heard that in Arabia there was a man with a serpent's face that inspired terror in men, and to him they went in order to elect him as their king. Zuhak eagerly returned with them and was crowned, and, turning his eyes towards the throne of Jamshid, began to treat the world familiarly as if it were the ring upon his finger. Jamshid fled before him, and for a hundred years was seen by no man, till Zuhak fell upon him without warning in the confines of China and put him to death. Thus perished his pride from the earth.

For a thousand years Zuhak occupied the throne and the world submitted to him, so that goodness died away and was replaced by evil. Every night during that long period two youths were slain to provide the serpents' food. Now in the king's country there remained two men of purity, of Persian race, the one Irmail the Pious, and the other Girmail the Clear-sighted. It happened that they met one day and talked of many matters great and small; of the unjust king, of his army, and of his horrible custom. The one said: "We ought, by the art of the kitchen, to introduce ourselves into the king's household and apply our wits to saving the unfortunates who lose their lives each day." Setting to work, they learned the art of cookery, and succeeded in entering the king's kitchen. There, after no long time, they were entrusted with the preparation of the king's meal, and they contrived to mix the brains of a sheep with those of one of the youths who was brought for slaughter. The other one they saved alive and dismissed secretly, saying to him: "Escape in secret, beware of visiting any inhabited town; your portion in the world must be the desert and the mountain."

In this manner they saved two hundred men, of whom is born the race of Kurds, who know not any fixed abode, whose houses are tents; and who have in their hearts no fear of God.

While Zuhak still had forty years to live, one night he dreamed a dream, and he saw three royal warriors emerge, two of them aged, and another, younger, who walked between them, and who had the form of a cypress and the visage of a king. His girth and his gait were those of a prince, and he carried a club with a bull's head. He advanced straight upon Zuhak, smote him upon the forehead with his club, tied him hand and foot with thongs, and overwhelmed him with shame and torments.

Zuhak awoke with a great cry of fear, that brought his wife, Arnawaz, and his attendants running to him in alarm. Arnawaz, as she approached, cried out to him: "O king, confide in me and tell me what has happened. You sleep in your palace securely; everything that is in the world obeys you; savage beasts, divs, and men are your guardians; the earth with its seven climes is your domain; all, from the firmament to the depths of the seas, is yours. Why then do you leap thus from your bed? Tell us." Zuhak replied: "My dream must be kept secret, for were I to reveal it, you would despair of my life." "Perhaps, if you reveal it," said Arnawaz, "we may find a remedy, for no ill exists that has not its remedy." The king was persuaded by this, and told what he had seen in his dream. "This is not a matter that you may neglect," exclaimed the queen on hearing it. "Summon from every country the sages that can read the stars, examine all sources, and seek thus to learn the secret. Discover what he is whose hand threatens you; man, div, or peri; and when you know, then immediately apply your remedy." And the king approved the counsel of this silver swan.

The world, plunged in night, was black as a raven's wing; suddenly light dawned upon the mountains as though the sun had scattered rubies upon the azure of the firmament. Wherever there were wise counselors the king sought them out and assembled them in his palace, where he told the whole company of his trouble, and sought their advice. The lips of the noblemen were dried with fear, their cheeks paled, and their hearts filled with anguish. "For," said each to himself, "if we disclose what must happen, he will die, and if we remain silent, then we must bid adieu to life." Thus they remained hesitating for three days. And on the fourth day, Zuhak assembled them again and in rage asked for their counsel, and menaced them with death if they withheld from him their knowledge of the future.

At length there stood out from among the noble counselors one who was their chief, whose conduct was upright and whose heart was filled with wisdom. He loosened his tongue before Zuhak, and spoke thus: "Empty thine heart of vain hope, for no one is born save to die. There have been many kings before you worthy of the throne of power, they saw much of grief and much of joy; and, when their long days had flowed past, they died. Were you a rampart of iron securely founded, the turn of the skies would break you too, and you would disappear. There will be some one who will inherit your throne and will overturn your fortunes. His name is Faridun, but he is not yet born, and the time to fear him is not yet. He will grow like a tree destined to bear fruit, and when he has reached manhood his head will touch the moon. Then he will demand your girdle and your crown, your throne and your diadem. He will carry upon his shoulder a club of steel, and with his bull-headed mace he will strike you and drag you from your palace."

"What reason has he for hating me?" cried out the impure Zuhak.

"Because his father will die at your hands."

The king heard and thought on this, fell from his throne, and swooned away. When his senses returned to him, he mounted again upon his throne and sent out searchers, both secret and public, to seek for traces of Faridun. He sought no rest or sleep or food, and bright day became gloomy to him.

Thus passed a long space of time, while the serpent-man remained prey to his terror. Faridun was born, and the lot of the whole world was thereby destined to change. The youth grew up like a cypress, and he was resplendent with all the glory of majesty. He was like the shining sun, as needful to the world as rain, an adornment to the mind like knowledge. Zuhak filled the earth with sound and fury, searching everywhere for Faridun son of Abtin. The earth became straitened for Abtin, who fled and struggled; but he was finally caught in the lion's net.

Meantime Faridun was well secured by his mother, and was safe. The king ceased not night or day to be in anguish concerning him. One day he seated himself on his ivory throne, and, putting his crown upon his head, summoned all his nobles. To them he spoke thus: "O you men of virtue, noble and prudent, I have a hidden enemy, as all men know. I despise no enemy however feeble, for I fear lest fortune betray me. I must increase my army, and will have it of men, divs, and peris. I desire you to aid me, for I cannot bear my torment alone. You must write for me a declaration that as king I have sown nought but the seed of good, that I have spoken nought save the words of truth, that I have never frustrated justice." All the noblemen, in fear of the king, consented to his demand, and all, old and young, declared what the serpent-man desired.

But suddenly at the gate of the palace was heard the voice of one crying out for justice. The complainant was brought before the king, who asked who had done him wrong. The man cried out, struck his head with his hands on seeing the monarch, and said: "I am Kawa, O king; I demand justice. Grant me justice. I have come in haste, and it is you whom I accuse in the bitterness of my heart. I had seventeen sons, and now there remains but one. Give me back this one, my only son; think how my heart will burn with grief, the whole length of my life. What crime have I committed? Even tyranny must have a pretext, and I am an innocent man, a blacksmith. You must render count to me for what you have done, and the world will be astonished thereby. It will see, by the account you will render to me, what my lot on earth has been, and how I have been compelled to give my sons to feed your serpents."

The king looked harshly upon him on hearing these words, gave back the man's son, and strove to soothe him with words. Lastly he asked Kawa to sign the declaration of the nobles, but he, trembling with rage, tore and trampled on it and emerged shouting with a mighty anger. The crowd in the market-place gathered round him, and to them and the whole world he appealed to aid him in obtaining justice. He took off the apron which blacksmiths wear, tied it to a lance and marched through the bazaars crying: "Illustrious men, you that adore God, who desire to be delivered from the clutches of Zuhak, let us go to Faridun and let us rest in the shadow of his sovereignty."

Having ascertained where Faridun lay hiding, he set out with a great troop of men, and after no long time reached his abode. The young prince saw the standard made of the blacksmith's apron, and accepted it as a good omen. Then, tarrying only while a suit of armor was made for him, he began his march at the head of his army, which moved as speedily as the wind. Soon they reached the Tigris River and the city of Baghdad. Arrived there, Faridun sent his greeting to the guardian of the crossing, and said: "Send me boats and ships, that I and my army may cross." But the guardian sent back answer: "The king has given me secret command that no man may cross without his sealed order."

Faridun heard the messenger with anger. The swift stream inspired him with no fear, and he with his warriors tightened girdle and plunged into it with their horses. Having crossed, they made their way to the royal city of Zuhak. On coming within a mile of it Faridun saw a palace whose walls were raised higher than Saturn, as if it had been built to tear the stars from the sky. It shone like Jupiter in the celestial sphere. From its vastness and magnificence Faridun knew it to be the palace of the monster-king, and, turning to his companions, he said: "I fear one that has been able from dust and stones to rear so mighty a structure. I fear some secret bond between fortune and him, but it is better to fling ourselves into battle than to delay here." Thus he spoke, and, giving rein to his spirited horse, he raised his club and rushed like a flame past the wardens of the gate and into the palace. He dashed to the ground a talisman which Zuhak had set up against him, and struck down all that offered resistance; he placed his foot upon the throne of Zuhak, seized the royal crown, and took his place.

A servant of Zuhak saw what had happened, and mounting a swift horse brought the tale to his master: "O king of a proud people, there are tokens that portend the fall of your fortunes. Three heroes have come from a strange land with an army. The youngest remains always between the two elder, his stature is that of a prince, his face that of a king. He carries a mighty club like a great rock, and he has seated himself upon the throne."

Zuhak, in great haste, prepared to return with an army of divs and men. By devious ways he flung his army against the terraces and gates of the palace, thinking of nought but vengeance. But the army of Faridun and the inhabitants of the town fought together in the battle, and their mass was like a mountain.

Meantime rage incited Zuhak to further enterprise. Covering himself from head to foot with armor, that none might know him, in the confusion he climbed unseen into the palace by means of a rope of sixty cubits. But he was recognized and pursued and, in his rage, leaped from the battlements to the ground. Faridun advanced, swift as the wind, and smote Zuhak with his club through his helmet to his head. But a faithful counselor held his hand, saying, "His time is not yet come. He is broken but not dead. Let him be placed to spend the rest of his days in the depths of the rocks, where neither his friends nor his vassals can find him."

So Faridun prepared thongs of lion skin, and bound Zuhak's hands and feet and body, in such manner that a wild elephant could not have broken the bonds. He bore the monster, thus tightly bound, to the height of the lofty mountain of Damawand, and there, in a narrow bottomless chasm, he chained him. And there Zuhak remains suspended until the ill he wrought shall have vanished from the earth.

THE SAILOR AND THE PEARL MERCHANT

THE author of th following story is unknown. It was gathered with others in Persia, ought to England and presented to the Bodleian Library.

The Story of the ailor and the Pearl Merchant is a splendid example of the Persian story-eller's fantastic and magical art.

The present versin is from a translation by Reuben Levy, M.A., of MS. Ouseley 231 Bodleian Library. Copyright, 1923, by Oxford University Press, by hose permission it is here reprinted.

THE SAILOR ND THE PEARL MERCHANT

IT is related that in te city of Basrah there was a man, Abu'l Fawaris, who was the chief of the sailors of the town, for in the great ocean there was no ort at which he had not landed. One day, as he sat on the seashore, wih his sailors round him, an old man arrived in a ship, landed where Abu'l Fawaris was sitting, and said: "Friend, I desire you to give me you ship for six months, and I will pay you whatever you desire." "I demand a thousand gold dinars," said the sailor, and at once received he gold from the old man, who, before departing, said that he would come again on the next day, and warned Abu'l Fawaris that there was o be no holding back.

The sailor took home his goll, made his ship ready, and then, taking leave of his wife and sons, he went down to the shore, where he found the old man waiting for him vith a slave and twenty ass-loads of empty sacks. Abu'l Fawaris greeed him, and together they loaded the ship and set sail. Taking a particular star for their mark, they sailed for three months, when an island appeared to one side of them. For this the old man steered, and they soon landed upon it. Having loaded his slave with some sacks, the old man with his companions set out towards a mountain which they could see in the distance. This they reached after some hours of travel, and climbed to the summit, upon which they found a broad plain where more than two hundred pits had been dug. The old man then explained to the sailor that he was a merchant, and that he had, on that spot, found a mine of jewels. "Now that I have given you my confidence," he continued, "I expect faithfulness from you too. I desire you to go down into this pit and send up sufficient pearls to fill these sacks. Half I will give to you, and we shall be able to spend the rest of our lives in luxury." The sailor thereupon asked how the pearls had found their way into these pits, to which the old man replied that there was a passage connecting the pits with the sea. Along this passage oysters swam, and settled in the pits, where by chance he had come upon them. He explained further that he had only brought the sailor because he needed help; but he desired not to disclose the matter to any one else.

With great eagerness then the sailor descended into the pit, and there found oysters in great numbers. The old man let down a basket to him, which he filled again and again, until at last the merchant cried out that the oysters were useless, for they contained no pearls. Abu'l Fawaris therefore left that pit, and descended into another, where he found pearls in great number. By the time night fell he was utterly wearied, and called out to the old man to help him out of the pit. In reply the merchant shouted down that he intended to leave him in the pit, for he feared that Abu'l Fawaris might kill him for the sake of the jewels. With great vehemence the sailor protested that he was innocent of any such intention, but the old man was deaf to his entreaties, and, making his way back to the ship, sailed away.

For three days Abu'l Fawaris remained, hungry and thirsty. As he struggled to find a way out he came upon many human bones, and understood that the accursed old man had betrayed many others in the same fashion. In desperation he dug about, and at last he saw a small opening, which he enlarged with his hands. Soon it was big enough for him to crawl through, and he found himself in the darkness, standing upon mud. Along this he walked carefully, and then felt himself suddenly plunged to his neck in water, which was salt to the taste; and he knew that he was in the passage that led to the sea. He swam along in this for some way, till, in front of him, there appeared a faint light. Greatly heartened by the sight of it, he swam vigorously until he reached the mouth of the passage. On emerging, he found himself facing the sea, and threw himself on his face to give thanks for his delivery. Then he arose, and a little distance from him he found the cloak which he had left behind when he set out for the mountain; but of the old merchant there was no sign, and the ship had disappeared.

Full of trouble and despondency, he sat down at the water's brink, wondering what he was to do. As he gazed at the sea there came into view a ship, and he saw that it was filled with men. At sight of it the sailor leaped from his place; snatching his turban from his head, he waved it with all his might in the air, and shouted at the top of his voice. But as they approached he decided not to tell his rescuers the truth of his presence there; therefore when they landed and asked how he came to be on the island he told them that his ship had been wrecked at sea, that he had clung to a plank and been washed to the shore.

They praised his good fortune at his escape, and in reply to his questions with regard to the place of their origin, told him that they had sailed from Abyssinia, and were then on their way to Hindustan. At this, Abu'l Fawaris hesitated, saying that he had no business in Hindustan. They assured him, however, that they would meet ships going to Basrah, and would hand him over to one of them. He agreed then to go with them, and for forty days they sailed without seeing any inhabited spot. At last he asked them whether they had not mistaken their way, and they admitted that for five days they had been sailing without knowing whither they were going or what direction to follow. All together therefore set themselves to praying, and remained in prayer for some time.

Soon afterwards, as they sailed, something in appearance like a minaret emerged from the sea, and they seemed to behold the flash of a Chinese mirror. Also they perceived that their ship, without their rowing, and without any greater force of wind, began to move at great speed over the water. In great amazement the sailors ran to Abu'l Fawaris and asked him what had come to the ship that it moved so fast. He raised his eyes, and groaned deeply as in the distance he saw a mountain that rose out of the sea. In terror he clapped his hand to his eyes and shouted out: "We shall all perish! My father continually warned me that if ever I lost my way upon the sea I must steer to the East; for if I went to the West I would certainly fall into the Lion's Mouth. When I asked him what the Lion's Mouth was, he told me that the Almighty had created a great hole in the midst of the ocean, at the foot of a mountain. That is the Lion's Mouth. Over a hundred leagues of water it will attract a ship, and no vessel which encounters the mountain ever rises again. I believe that this is the place and that we are caught."

In great terror the sailors saw their ship being carried like the wind against the mountain. Soon it was caught in the whirlpool, where the wrecks of ten thousand ancient ships were being carried around in the swirling current. The sailors and merchants in the ship crowded to Abu'l Fawaris, begging him to tell them what they could do. He cried out to them to prepare all the ropes which they had in the ship; he would then swim out of the whirlpool and on to the shore at the foot of the mountain, where he would make fast to some stout tree. Then they were to cast their ropes to him and so he would rescue them from their peril. By great good fortune the current cast him out upon the shore, and he made the rope of his ship fast to a stout tree.

Then, as soon as was possible, the sailor climbed to the top of the mountain in search of food, for neither he nor his shipmates had eaten for some days. When he reached the summit he found a pleasant plain stretching away in front of him, and in the midst of it he saw a lofty arch, made of green stone. As he approached it and entered, he observed a tall pillar made of steel, from which there hung by a chain a great drum of Damascus bronze covered with a lion's skin. From the arch also hung a great tablet of bronze, upon which was engraved the following inscription: "O thou that dost reach this place, know that when Alexander voyaged round the world and reached the Lion's Mouth, he had been made aware of this place of calamity. He was therefore accompanied by four thousand wise men, whom he summoned and whom he commanded to provide a means of escape from this calamitous spot. For long the philosophers pondered on the matter, until at last Plato caused this drum to be made, whose quality is that if any one, being caught in the whirlpool, can come forth and strike the drum three times, he will bring out his ship to the surface."

When the sailor had read the inscription, he quickly made his way to the shore and told his fellows of it. After much debate he agreed to risk his life by staying on the island and striking the drum, on condition that they would return to Basrah on their escape, and give to his wife and sons one-half of what treasure they had in the ship. He bound them with an oath to do this, and then returned to the arch. Taking up a club he struck the drum three times, and as the mighty roar of it echoed from the hills, the ship, like an arrow shot from a bow, was flung out of the whirlpool. Then with a cry of farewell to Abu'l Fawaris from the crew, they sailed to Basrah, where they gave one-half the treasure which they had to the sailor's family.

With great mourning the wife and family of Abu'l Fawaris celebrated his loss; but he, after sleeping soundly in the archway and giving thanks to his Maker for preserving him alive, made his way again to the summit of the mountain. As he advanced across the plain he saw black smoke arising from it, and also in the plain were rivers, of which he passed nine. He was like to die of hunger and weariness, when suddenly he perceived on one side a meadow, in which flocks of sheep were grazing. In great joy he thought that he was at last reaching human habitation, and as he came towards the sheep, he saw with them a youth, tall in stature as a mountain, and covered with a tattered cloak of red felt, though his head and body were clad in mail. The sailor greeted him, and received greeting in reply, and also the question "Whence come you?" Abu'l Fawaris answered that he was a man upon whom catastrophe had fallen, and so related his adventures to the shepherd. He heard it with a laugh, and said: "Count yourself fortunate to have escaped from that abyss. Do not fear now, I will bring you to a village." Saying this he set bread and milk before him and bade him eat. When he had eaten he said: "You cannot remain here all day, I will take you to my house, where you may rest for a time."

Together they descended to the foot of the mountain, where stood a gateway. Against it leaned a mighty stone, which a hundred men could not have lifted, but the shepherd, putting his hand into a hole in the stone, lifted it away from the gateway and admitted Abu'l Fawaris. Then he restored the stone to its place, and continued on his way.

When the sailor had passed through the gateway he saw before him a beautiful garden in which were trees laden with fruit. In the midst of them was a kiosk, and this, the sailor thought, must be the shepherd's house. He entered and looked about from the roof, but though he saw many houses there was no person in sight. He descended therefore, and walked to the nearest house, which he entered. Upon crossing the threshold he beheld ten men, all naked and all so fat that their eyes were almost closed. With their heads down upon their knees, all were weeping bitterly. But at the sound of his footsteps they raised their heads and called out "Who are you?" He told them that the shepherd had brought him and offered him hospitality. A great cry arose from them as they heard this. "Here," they said, "is another unfortunate who has fallen, like ourselves, into the clutch of this monster. He is a vile creature, who in the guise of a shepherd goes about and seizes men and devours them. We are all merchants whom adverse winds have brought here. That div has seized us and keeps us in this fashion."

With a groan the sailor thought that now at last he was undone. At that moment he saw the shepherd coming, saw him let the sheep into the garden, and then close the gateway with the stone before entering the kiosk. He was carrying a bag full of almonds, dates, and pistachio nuts, with which he approached, and, giving it to the sailor, he told him to share it with the others. Abu'l Fawaris could say nothing, but sat down and ate the food with his companions. When they had finished their meal, the shepherd returned to them, took one of them by the hand, and then in sight of them all, slew, roasted, and devoured him. When he was sated, he brought out a skin of wine and drank until he fell into a drunken sleep.

Then the sailor turned to his companions and said: "Since I am to die, let me first destroy him; if you will give me your help, I will do so." They replied that they had no strength left; but he, seeing the two long spits on which the ogre had roasted his meat, put them into the fire until they were red hot, and then plunged them into the monster's eyes.

With a great cry the shepherd leaped up and tried to seize his tormentor, who sprang away and eluded him. Running to the stone, the shepherd moved it aside and began to let out the sheep one by one, in the hope that when the garden was emptier he could the more easily capture the sailor. Abu'l Fawaris understood his intention: without delay, he slew a sheep, put on the skin and tried to pass through. But the shepherd knew as soon as he felt him that this was not a sheep, and leaped after him in pursuit. Abu'l Fawaris flung off the pelt, and ran like the wind. Soon he came to the sea, and into this he plunged, while the shepherd after a few steps returned to the shore, for he could not swim.

Full of terror the sailor swam till he reached the other side of the mountain. There he met an old man who greeted him, and, after hearing his adventure, fed him and took him to his house. But soon, to his horror, Abu'l Fawaris found that this old man also was an ogre. With great cunning he told the ogre's wife that he could make many useful implements for her house, and she persuaded her husband to save him. After many days in the house, he was sent away to the care of a shepherd, and put to guard sheep. Day by day he planned to escape, but there was only one way across the mountain and that was guarded.

One day, as he wandered in a wood, he found in the hollow trunk of a tree a store of honey, of which he told the shepherd's wife when he went home. The next day, therefore, the woman sent her husband with Abu'l Fawaris, telling him to bring home some of the honey; but, on the way, the sailor leaped upon him and bound him to a tree. Then, taking the shepherd's ring, he returned and told the woman that her husband had given him leave to go, and that he sent his ring in token of this. But the woman was cunning and asked: "Why did not my husband come himself to tell me this?" Seizing him by the cloak, she told him that she would go with him and find out the truth. The sailor, however, tore himself free, and again fled to the sea, where he thought that he might escape death. In haste and terror he swam for many hours, until at last he espied a ship full of men, who steered towards him and took him on board. Full of wonder they asked how he came there, and he related to them all his adventures.

It happened by great good fortune that the ship's captain had business at one place only on the coast, and that from there he was sailing to Basrah. In the space of a month, therefore, Abu'l Fawaris was restored to his family, to the joy of them all.

The many dangers and sufferings of the sailor had turned his hair white. For many days he rested, and then, one day, as he walked by the seashore, that same old man who had before hired his ship again appeared. Without recognizing him, he asked if he would lend his ship on hire for six months. Abu'l Fawaris agreed to do so for a thousand dinars of gold, which the old man at once paid to him, saying that he would come in a boat on the morrow, ready to depart.

When the ancient departed, the sailor took home the money to his wife, who bade him beware not to cast himself again into danger. He replied that he must be avenged not only for himself, but also for the thousand Muslims whom the villainous old man had slain.

The next day, therefore, the sailor took on board the old man and a black slave, and for three months they sailed, until they once more reached the island of pearls. There they made fast the ship on the shore, and taking sacks, they ascended to the top of the mountain. Once arrived there, the old man made the same request to Abu'l Fawaris as before, namely, that he should go down into the pits and send up pearls. The sailor replied that he was unacquainted with the place, and preferred that the old man should go down first, in order to prove that there was no danger. He answered that there was surely no danger; he had never in his life harmed even an ant, and he would of a certainty never send Abu'l Fawaris down into the pits if he knew any peril lay there. But the sailor was obstinate, saying that until he knew how to carry it out, he could not undertake the task.

Very reluctantly, therefore, the old man allowed himself to be lowered into the first pit by a basket and a rope. He filled the basket with oysters and sent it up, crying out: "You see, there is nothing to do harm in this pit. Draw me up now, for I am an old man and have no more strength left." The sailor replied, "Now that you are there, it were better if you remained there to complete your task. To-morrow I myself will go into another pit and will send up so many pearls as to fill the ship." For a long time the old man worked, sending up pearls, and at last he cried out again, "O my brother, I am utterly wearied, draw me out now." Then the sailor turned upon him with fury, and cried out: "How is it that thou dost see ever thine own trouble and never that of others? Thou misbegotten dog, art thou blind that thou dost not know me? I am Abu'l Fawaris, the sailor, whom long ago you left in one of these pits. By the favor of Allah I was delivered, and now it is your turn. Open your eyes to the truth and remember what you have done to so many men." The old man cried aloud for mercy, but it availed him nothing, for Abu'l Fawaris brought a great stone and covered up the mouth of the pit. The slave too he overwhelmed with threats, and then together they carried down the pearls to the ship, in which they set sail. In three months they arrived at Basrah. There Abu'l Fawaris related his adventures, to the amazement of all. Thenceforward he abandoned the sea and adopted a life of ease. Finally he died, and this story remains in memory of him. And Allah knoweth best.

Arabia

INTRODUCTION

THE literature of the Arab originated in the improvisations of stories and poems among the pre-Mohammedan inhabitants of Arabia. These were the oral recitations of the people, transmitted from generation to generation. It is improbable that anything was actually collected and reduced to writing before the Ninth or Tenth Century A.D., although some time during the Ninth Century Al-Asma'i brought together the elements that make up the *Romance of Antar*, one of the stories from which is here reprinted. This coloured and romantic accumulation of poetic stories and legends is the great epic of Arabian literature.

The Arabs are noted for nomadic existence, but there were also town dwellers in Arabia who appreciated a less simple story than the recitations of the wandering inhabitants of the desert and therefore imported several cycles or collections of tales, of which the supreme masterpiece is the celebrated *Thousand Nights and One Night*, better known as the *Thousand and One Nights*, or simply the *Arabian Nights*. These famous tales had been translated from the Sanskrit (with certain elaborations) into the Persian, from which the Arabs borrowed them, though they added so much in the way of details and literary style that the collection may be considered an original contribution. These made their appearance in the Arabic somewhere between the Tenth and Fourteenth Centuries of our epoch.

It is hazardous to attribute to any one person the actual invention of a literary form, but it is customary to designate Hamadhani (968-1054) as the first writer of stories in Arabic. His art was practised and improved upon by Al-Hariri (1054-1122), whose *Lectures* constitute an imposing array of fanciful tales. The *Golden Meadows* of Mas'udi, composed during the Tenth Century, are interesting rather as commentaries upon contemporary life and manners than as tales.

After the appearance of the *Arabian Nights*, there was little more in Arabian literature in the way of short stories to be added. Modern literature is of relatively little importance.

The Arabian tale, although it was not altogether indigenous, has established itself, at least in the minds of Occidentals, as a sort of symbol of the romance of the Orient. There was a gorgeousness of local color, a riot of sensuous imagery in the best of the Arabian stories, that later writers have sought in vain to imitate.

AL-ASMA'I

(9th Century, A.D.)

PRACTICALLY nothing is known of the collector of the material that makes up the epical *Romance of Antar. Khaled and Djaida*, which is taken from that epic, is not so finished and skilful a narrative as the best of the tales in the *Arabian Nights*: it belongs rather to the type of episode which Homer introduced into the *Odyssey*, or the author of *Beowulf* into that work. Yet there is in it that element of wonder which the world's great story-tellers knew so well how to use, and a certain delicate art that spins out an incident to the delight of idle listeners.

The present text is based upon the translation by T. Hamilton: *A Bedoueen Romance*, London, 1820. There is no title to the original story.

KHALED AND DJAIDA

(From *The Romance of Antar*)

MOHARIB and Zahir were two brothers, by the same father and mother; the Arabians call them "germane". Both were eminent for their courage and daring. But Moharib was chief of the clan, and Zahir was his minister, subject to his authority, giving him counsel and advice. It happened that a violent dispute and quarrel arose between them. Zahir retired to his tent, sorrowing and not knowing what to do. "What is the matter with you?" demanded his wife. "Why are you troubled? What has happened? Has anyone displeased or insulted you—the greatest of Arabian chiefs?" "What am I to do?" said Zahir; "he who has injured me is one I cannot lay hands on, or wrong; my companion in private, my brother in the world. Oh, if it had been any other, I would have shown him what kind of man he was at odds with, and made an example of him before the chiefs of our people!" "Leave him in the enjoyment of his possessions," cried his wife, and, to persuade her husband to do this, she recited verses from a contemporary poet, dissuading a man from accepting an insult even from his parents.

Zahir accepted the advice of his wife. He made preparations for departure, took down his tents, loaded his camels, and started off towards the camp of the Saad clan, with whom he was allied. Nevertheless, he felt a pang at separating himself from his brother—and thus he spoke: "On starting a journey which takes me from you, I shall seem a thousand years on the way, each year carrying me a thousand leagues. . . . Even though the favors you heap upon me be worth a thousand Egypts, and each Egypt had a thousand Niles, they would all be despised. I shall be happy with little so long as I am far from you. In my absence, I shall recite this verse, which is worth more than a necklace of fine pearls: 'When a man is insulted on the soil of his clan, there is nothing to do but to leave it; you, who have so wickedly injured me, ere long shall feel the power of the beneficent divinity, for he is your judge and mine, unchangeable and everlasting.'"

Zahir proceeded on his journey, until he reached the Saad tribe, and dismounted from his horse. He was cordially welcomed and pressed to dwell among them. His wife was soon to become a mother, and he said to her: "If a son be given us, he will be welcome; but if it be a daughter, conceal her sex, and allow people to think we have a boy, so that my brother may have no reason to crow over us." When her time came Zahir's wife brought forth a daughter. They agreed that her name should be Djaida, but that in public she should be known as Djonder, that people might think her a boy. In order to promote this belief, they feasted and entertained early and late for many days.

About the same time Moharib, the other brother, had a son born to him, whom he called Khaled. He chose this name out of gratitude to God, because, since his brother's departure, his affairs had prospered.

The two children in time reached maturity, and their fame spread far and wide among the Arabians. Zahir had taught his daughter to ride horseback, and trained her in all the accomplishments fitting to a brave and daring warrior. He accustomed her to the severest labor, and the most perilous enterprises. When he went to war, he put her among the other Arabs of the clan, and among these horsemen she soon took her rank as one of the most valiant of them. And thus it came to pass that she outstripped all her comrades, and would even attack the lions in their dens. At last her name inspired the greatest terror; when she had conquered a champion she never failed to cry out: "I am Djonder, son of Zahir, horseman of the clans."

For his part, her cousin Khaled distinguished himself likewise by his brilliant courage. His father Moharib, a wise and prudent chieftain, had built places of entertainment for strangers; and horsemen found a welcome there. Khaled had grown up in the company of warriors. In this school his spirit had been moulded, here he had learned to ride, and had become at last an intrepid warrior, and a fear inspiring hero. It was soon perceived by the army that his spirit and valor were unconquerable.

Now at last he heard news of his cousin Djonder, and his eagerness to see and know him and witness his skill in arms became extreme. But he was unable to satisfy this desire because of the dislike his father showed for his cousin, his uncle's son. Khaled's curiosity remained unsatisfied until the death of his father Moharib, which put him in possession of rank, riches and land. He followed the example of his father in entertaining strangers, protecting the weak and unfortunate, and giving clothing to the naked. He continued also to sweep the plains on horseback in company with his warriors, and thus became greater in bodily strength and courage. After some time, gathering together a number of precious gifts, he set out, in company with his mother, to visit his uncle. He did not draw rein until he reached the dwelling of Zahir, who was very glad to see him, and made magnificent preparations for his entertainment; for the uncle had heard news on several occasions of this nephew's worth and valor. Khaled also visited his cousin. He saluted her, pressed her to his bosom, and kissed her forehead, thinking that she was a young man. He felt the keenest pleasure when he was in her company, and remained for ten days with his uncle, taking part in the tournaments and contests of horsemen and warriors. As for his cousin, the moment she had seen how handsome and valiant Khaled was, she fell violently in love with him. She was unable to sleep; she could not eat; and her love drew to such a pitch that feeling her heart completely lost to him, she spoke to her mother, saying: "Oh, mother, if my cousin should leave without taking me with him, I shall die of grief at his absence." Then her mother was touched with pity for her, and spoke no reproaches, feeling that they would be in vain. "Djaida," she said, "conceal your feelings, and restrain yourself from grief. You have done nothing wrong, for your cousin is the man of your choice, and is of your own race and blood. Like him, you are beautiful and attractive; like him, brave and skilful in horsemanship. Tomorrow morning, when his mother comes to us, I will lay before her the whole matter; we will soon afterwards give you to him in marriage, and at last we shall all return to our own country."

Zahir's wife waited patiently until the following morning, when Khaled's mother arrived. She then presented her daughter, whose head she uncovered so as to allow the hair to fall over her shoulders. At the sight of such charms Khaled's mother was immeasurably astonished, and exclaimed: "What! is not this your son Djonder?" "No! it is Djaida —behold, the moon of beauty! She at last has risen." She then went on to tell her all that had passed between herself and her husband, and how and why they had concealed the sex of their child. "Dear kinswoman," answered Khaled's mother, still quite surprised, "among all the daughters of Arabia who have been famed for their beauty I have never seen one more lovely than this one. What is her name?" "I have already told you that her name is Djaida, and my special purpose in telling you the secret is to offer you these charms, for I ardently wish to marry my daughter to your son, so that we may all be able to return to our own land." Khaled's mother at once assented to this proposal, and said: "The possession of Djaida will surely render my son very happy." She rose immediately and went to look for Khaled, and told him all that she had seen and learned, not failing to praise especially the charms of Djaida. "By the faith of an Arab," said she, "never, oh, son, have I seen in the desert, or in any city, a girl like your cousin; not even the most beautiful. Nothing is so perfect as she, nothing lovelier and more attractive. Hasten, my son, to see your uncle and ask him for his daughter in marriage. You will be happy indeed if he grants your prayer. Go, my son, and waste no time in winning her."

On hearing these words Khaled cast his eyes on the ground; and remained for some time thoughtful and gloomy. Then he answered: "Mother, I cannot remain here longer. I must return home in company with my horsemen and troops. I have no intention of saying more to my cousin; I am convinced that she is a girl whose temper and philosophy are uncertain; her character and mode of speech are destitute of stability and propriety. I have always been accustomed to live with warriors, on whom I spend my wealth, and with whom I win a soldier's fame. As for my cousin's love for me, it is the weakness of a woman, a young girl." He then put on his armor, mounted his horse, bade his uncle farewell, and announced his intention of leaving on the moment. "What means this haste?" cried Zahir. "I can remain here no longer," answered Khaled, and, putting his horse to a gallop, he plunged into the wilderness. His mother, after relating to Djaida the conversation she had had with her son, mounted a camel and proceeded on her way towards her own country.

The sensitive soul of Djaida felt keenly this indignity. She brooded over it—sleepless and without appetite. Some days afterwards, as her father was preparing to make a foray with his horsemen against his enemies, his glance fell on Djaida, and seeing how changed she was in face, and dejected in spirit, he refrained from saying anything, thinking and hoping that she would surely become herself again after a short time.

Scarcely was Zahir out of sight of his tents, when Djaida, who felt herself nigh unto death, and whose melancholy was quite insupportable, said to her mother: "Mother, I feel that I am dying, while this miserable Khaled is still in the vigor of life. I should like, if God grants me the power, to make him experience the fury of death, the bitterness of its pang and torture." So saying, she rose like a lioness, donned her armor, and mounted her horse, informing her mother she was going on a hunting expedition. Swiftly, and without stopping, she made her way over rocks and mountains, her excitement increasing as she approached the dwelling-place of her cousin. As she was disguised, she entered, without being recognized, into the tent where strangers were received. But her visor was lowered, like that of a horseman of Hijaz. Slaves and servants welcomed her, offered her hospitality, behaving towards her as to one of the guests, and the most noble personages of the country. That night Djaida took rest; but the following day she took part in the military exercises, challenged many warriors, and exhibited so much skill and bravery, that she called forth great astonishment among all the spectators. Long before midday the horsemen of her cousin were forced to acknowledge her superiority over themselves. Khaled wished to witness her prowess, and, astonished at the sight of such skill, he offered to match himself with her. Djaida entered the contest with him, and then both of them joining in combat tried, one after another, all the methods of attack and defense, until the shades of night came upon them. When they separated neither one was hurt, and none could say which was the victor. Thus Djaida, while rousing the admiration of the spectators, perceived the annoyance they felt on finding their chief equaled in fight by so skilful an opponent. Khaled ordered his antagonist to be treated with every care and honor, and then retired to his tent, his mind filled with thoughts of this conflict. Djaida remained for three days at her cousin's dwelling-place. Every morning she presented herself on the field of combat and remained under arms until the fall of night. She enjoyed it greatly, still keeping her identity concealed, whilst Khaled, on the other hand, made no inquiries, and asked no questions of her, as to who she was and to what clan she might belong.

On the morning of the fourth day, while Khaled, according to his custom, rode out over the plain, and passed close to the tents reserved for strangers, he caught sight of Djaida mounting her horse. He saluted her, and she returned his salute. "Noble Arab," said Khaled, "I would ask you one question. Until this moment I have failed in courtesy towards you, but I now beg of you in the name of that God who has given you such great dexterity in arms, tell me who you are, and to what noble princes are you allied? For I have never met your equal among brave warriors. Answer me, I beseech you, for I am most impatient to learn." Djaida smiled, and raising her visor, made answer: "Khaled, I am a woman, not a warrior. I am your own cousin Djaida, who offered herself to you, and desired to give herself to you; but you refused her—from the pride you felt in your passion for arms." As she spoke she turned her horse suddenly, pressed the spurs into him, and galloped off at full speed in the direction of her own country.

Khaled, covered with confusion, withdrew to his tent, not knowing what to do, and not knowing what would be the end of the passionate love which he suddenly felt surging within him. He was seized with a violent disgust for all his warlike habits and tastes, which had reduced him to the melancholy plight in which he now found himself. His distaste for women was suddenly changed into love. He sent for his mother and recounted to her all that had occurred. "My son," said she, "all these circumstances ought to render Djaida still dearer to you. Wait patiently a little, until I have been able to go and ask her hand of her mother." She thereupon mounted her camel at once, and started off through the desert on the tracks of Djaida, who immediately on her arrival home had told her mother everything that had happened. As soon as Khaled's mother had arrived, she threw herself into the arms of her relative and demanded Djaida in marriage for her son, for Zahir had not yet returned from his expedition. When Djaida heard from her mother the request of Khaled, she said, "This shall never be, even though I be forced to drink the cup of death. What occurred at his tents was brought about by me to quench the fire of my grief and unhappiness, and soothe the anguish of my soul."

On hearing these words Khaled's mother, disappointed, went back to her son, who was tortured by the cruelest anxiety. He rose suddenly to his feet, for his love had reached the point of despair, and asked uneasily what were the feelings of his cousin. When he learned the answer of Djaida his distress became overwhelming, for her refusal served only to increase his passion. "What can be done, my mother," he exclaimed. "I see no way of escaping from this predicament," she replied, "excepting that you assemble all your horsemen from among the Arabian sheiks, and among those with whom you are on friendly terms. Wait until your uncle returns from the campaign, and then, surrounded by all your followers, go to him, and in the presence of the assembled warriors, demand of him the hand of his daughter in marriage. If he denies that he has a daughter, tell him everything that has happened, and urge him until he gives in to your demand." This advice, and the plan that was proposed moderated the grief of Khaled. The moment he learned that his uncle had returned home, he assembled chiefs of his family and told his story to them. They were all much astonished, and Madi Kereb, one of Khaled's bravest companions, could not help saying: "This is a strange thing; we have always heard it said that your uncle had a son named Djonder, but now the truth is known. You are indeed the man who has the best right to the daughter of your uncle. It is therefore our best course to present ourselves in a body and prostrate ourselves before him, requesting him to return to his family and not give his daughter to any stranger." Khaled, without waiting to hear more, took with him a hundred of his bravest horsemen, those who had been brought up with Moharib and Zahir from their earliest childhood, and having provided themselves with presents even more costly than those they had taken before, they started off on their journey, and marched until they came to the clan of Saad. Khaled began by complimenting his uncle on his fortunate return from war, but no one could be more astounded than Zahir at this second visit, particularly when he saw his nephew with all the chieftains of his family. It never occurred to him that his daughter Djaida had anything to do with Khaled's return; he thought that his nephew simply wished to persuade him to return to his native land. He offered them every hospitality, provided them with tents and entertained them in great magnificence. He ordered camels and sheep killed, and offered a banquet, furnishing his guests with all things needful and proper for a period of three days. On the fourth day Khaled arose, and after thanking his uncle for all his courtesy, asked him for his daughter's hand, and begged him to return to his own land. Zahir denied that he had any child except his son Djonder, but Khaled told him all that he had learned, and all that had passed between himself and Djaida. On hearing these words Zahir was overcome with shame and cast his eyes to the ground. He remained for some time plunged in thought, and after reflecting that the affair must needs proceed from bad to worse, he addressed those present in the following words: "Kinsmen, I can no longer delay acknowledging this secret; therefore, she shall be married to her cousin as soon as possible, for of all the men I know, he is most worthy of her." He offered his hand to Khaled, who at once clasped it in presence of the chiefs who were witnesses to the contract. The dowry was agreed upon at five hundred brown black-eyed camels, and a thousand camels loaded with the choicest products of Yemen. The clan of Saad, among which Zahir had lived, were excluded from all part in this matter.

When Zahir had asked his daughter's consent to this arrangement, Djaida was overwhelmed with confusion at the course her father had taken. Since he let the girl clearly understand that he did not wish her to remain unmarried, she at last replied: "Father, if my cousin desires to have me in marriage, I shall not enter into his tent until he undertakes to slaughter at my wedding a thousand camels, among those which belong to Gheshem, son of Malik, 'The Brandisher of Spears.' Khaled agreed to this; but the sheiks and warriors did not leave Zahir before he had collected his possessions for transportation to his own land. No sooner were these preparations finished than Khaled marched forth at the head of a thousand horsemen, with whose assistance he conquered the clan of Aamir. Having thrice wounded "The Brandisher of Spears," and slain a great number of his champions, he carried off their goods and brought back from their country a richer spoil even than Djaida had demanded. Loaded with booty he returned, and was intoxicated with his success. But when he asked that a day should be fixed for the wedding, Djaida begged him to approach and spoke these words to him: "If you desire me to become your wife, fulfil first of all my wishes, and keep the engagement I make with you. This is my demand: that on the day of my marriage, some nobleman's daughter, a free-born woman, hold the bridle of my camel; she must be the daughter of a prince of the highest rank, in order that I may be most honored of all the daughters of Arabia." Khaled consented, and set about to carry out . her wishes. That same day he started with his horsemen, and crossed plains and valleys, searching the land of Ymer, until he reached the country of Hijar and the hills of Sand. In that place he attacked the tribe-family of Moawich, son of Mizal. He fell upon them like a tempest, and cutting a way with his sword through the opposing horsemen, took prisoner Amima, daughter of Moawich, at the very moment when she was betaking herself to flight.

Having accomplished feats which rendered useless the resistance of the skilful heroes, after having scattered all the clans in flight, and carried off all the wealth of all the Arabs in that country, he returned home. But he did not wish to approach his tents until he had gathered in all the wealth he had left at various points and places in the desert.

The young girls marched before him sounding their cymbals and other musical instruments. All the clan rejoiced; and when Khaled appeared, he distributed clothing to widows and orphans, and invited his companions and friends to the banquet he was preparing for his wedding. All the Arabs of the country came in a vast assemblage to the marriage. He caused them to be regaled with abundance of flesh and wine. But while all the guests gave themselves up to feasting and pleasure, Khaled, accompanied by ten slaves, prepared to scour the wild and marshy places of the country, in order to attack in their lairs the lions and lionesses and their cubs, and carry them to the tents, in order to provide meat for all those who attended the festival.

But Djaida had been informed beforehand of this plan. She disguised herself in a coat of mail, mounted her horse, and left the tents; since three days of festivities still remained, she quickly followed Khaled into the desert, and met him face to face in a cavern. She flung herself upon him with the impetuosity of a wild animal, and attacked him furiously, crying aloud, "Arab! dismount from your horse, take off your coat of mail and your armor; if you hesitate, I will run this lance through your heart." Khaled was determined at once to resist her in this demand. They engaged in a furious combat. The struggle lasted for well over an hour, when the warrior saw in the eyes of his adversary an expression which frightened him. He mounted his horse again, and having wheeled round his steed from the place of combat, exclaimed: "By the faith of an Arab, I beg of you to tell me what horseman of the desert you are; for I feel that your attack and the violence of your blows are irresistible.

You have prevented me from accomplishing what I had intended, and everything that I had eagerly wished to do." On hearing these words Djaida raised her visor, allowing him to see her face. "Khaled," she cried, "is it necessary for the girl you love to attack wild beasts, in order that the daughters of Arabia may learn that this is not the sole privilege of a warrior?" At this stinging rebuke Khaled was overcome with shame. "By the faith of an Arab," he replied, "no one but you can conquer me; but is there any man in this country who has challenged you, or have you come here merely to prove to me the extent of your valor?" "By the faith of an Arab," replied Djaida, "I came into this desert solely for the purpose of helping you hunt wild beasts, that your warriors might not reproach you for choosing me as your wife." At these words Khaled was thrilled with astonishment and admiration, that such spirit and resolution should have been exhibited by Djaida.

Thereupon both of them dismounted from their horses and entered into a cavern. Khaled seized two ferocious wild beasts, and Djaida attacked and carried off a lion and two lionesses. After these exploits they exchanged congratulations, and Djaida was happy to be with Khaled. "Meanwhile," she said, "I shall not allow you to leave our tents until after our marriage." She immediately left him in great haste and betook herself to her own dwelling.

Khaled then proceeded to rejoin the slaves he had left a little way off, and commanded them to carry to the tents the beasts he had slain. Trembling with fright at the view of what Khaled had done, they extolled him with admiration above all other champions.

Meanwhile the feasts went on, and all who came were welcomed with magnificence. The maidens clashed their cymbals; slaves waved their swords in the air, and young girls sang from morning till evening. In the midst of such rejoicings Djaida and Khaled were married. Amima, daughter of Moawich, held the reins of the young bride's camel, and both men and women exalted the name of Djaida.

ABOU HASSAN THE WAG

(Anonymous: 10th to 14th Century, A.D.)

THE chief glory of Arabian prose literature is the celebrated collection known to us as *The Thousand and One Nights*. Out of this voluminous treasure store *Abou Hassan the Wag* has been chosen as an example of one of the numerous types of story to be found in it. This tale is rich in Oriental colour, furnishing as it does the humorous details of that craftiness which the Arab delights in—at least in the stories he tells and listens to. The story is among the best of the *Nights*.

The present version is translated by Edward William Lane, whose edition was first published in London in 1839. It is from the 271st to the 290th Night (Breslau ed.). The complete title is *The Story of Abou Hassan the Wag, or The Sleeper Awakened.*

THE STORY OF ABOU HASSAN THE WAG

OR THE SLEEPER AWAKENED

(From *The Thousand and One Nights*)

THERE was a merchant of Bagdad in the reign of the Caliph Haroun Alrashid, and he had a son named Abou Hassan the Wag. And this merchant died, leaving to his son his vast wealth; whereupon Abou Hassan divided his property into two equal portions, one of which he laid aside, and of the other he expended. He took as his familiar friends a number of the sons of the merchants, and others, and gave himself up to the delights of good drinking and good eating, until all the wealth that he had appropriated to this purpose was consumed. And upon this he repaired to his associates, and relations, and boon-companions, and exposed to them his case, showing them how little property remained in his possession; but none of them paid any regard to him, or uttered a word in reply. So he returned to his mother with a broken heart, and told her of the treatment that he had experienced from his associates, that they would neither do him justice nor even reply to him. But she said, O Abou Hassan, thus are the sons of this age: as long as thou hast anything, they draw thee near to them; and when thou hast nothing, they cast thee off. She was grieved for him, and he sighed and wept.

He then sprang up, and went to the place in which was deposited the other half of his wealth, and upon this he lived agreeably. He took an oath that he would not thenceforth associate with any one of those whom he knew, but only with the stranger, and that he would not associate with any person but for one night, and on the following morning would not recognize him. Accordingly, every night he went forth and seated himself on the bridge, and when a stranger passed by him, he invited him to an entertainment, and took him to his house, where he caroused with him that night, until the morning: he then dismissed him; and after that he would not salute him if he saw him.

Thus he continued to do for a whole year; after which, as he was sitting one day upon the bridge as usual, to see who might come toward him, Alrashid and certain of his domestics passed by in disguise; for the caliph had experienced a contraction of the bosom and had come forth to amuse himself among the people. So Abou Hassan laid hold upon him, and said to him, O my master, hast thou any desire for a repast and beverage? And Alrashid complied with his request, saying to him, Conduct us. And Abou Hassan knew not who was his guest. The caliph proceeded with him until they arrived at Abou Hassan's house: and when Alrashid entered, he found in it a saloon, such that if thou beheldest it, and lookedst towards its walls, thou wouldst behold wonders; and if thou observedst its conduits of water, thou wouldst see a fountain incased with gold. And after he had seated himself there, Abou Hassan called for a slave girl, like the twig of the Oriental willow, who took a lute and sang. And when Alrashid heard her, he said, Thou has performed well. God bless thee! Her eloquence pleased him, and he wondered at Abou Hassan and his entertainment.

He then said to Abou Hassan, O young man, who art thou? Acquaint me with thy history, that I may requite thee for thy kindness. But Abou Hassan smiled, and replied, O my master, far be it from me that what hath happened should recur, and that I should be in thy company again after this time, And why so? said the caliph; and why wilt thou not acquaint me with thy case? So Abou Hassan told his story, and when the caliph heard it, he laughed violently, and said, By Allah, my brother, thou art excusable in this matter. Then a dish of roast goose was placed before him, and a cake of fine bread; and Abou Hassan sat, and cut off the meat, and put morsels into the mouth of the caliph, and they continued eating until they were satisfied; when the basin and ewer were brought, with the kali; and they washed their hands. After this Abou Hassan lighted for his guests three candles and three lamps, spread the wine cloth, and brought clear, strained, old, perfumed wine, the odor of which was like fragrant musk, and, having filled the first cup, said, O my boon-companion, bashfulness is dismissed from us, with thy permission. Thy slave is by thee. May I never be afflicted by the loss of thee! And he drank the cup, and filled the second, which he handed to the caliph, waiting upon him as a servant. And the caliph was pleased with his actions, and the politeness of his words, and said within himself, By Allah, I will certainly requite him for this! Abou Hassan then, after he had kissed the cup, handed it to the caliph, who accepted it from his hand, kissed it and drank it, and handed it back to him. Abou Hassan still continued serving him, saying, Drink, and may it be attended with health and vigor. And they drank and caroused until midnight.

After this the caliph said to his host, O Abou Hassan, is there any service that thou wouldst have performed, or any desire that thou wouldst have accomplished? And Abou Hassan answered, In our neighborhood is a mosque to which belong an imam and four sheiks, and whenever they hear music or any sport, they incite the judge against me, and impose fines upon me, and trouble my life, so that I suffer torment from them. If I had them in my power, therefore, I would give each of them a thousand lashes, that I might be relieved from their excessive annoyance.

Alrashid replied, May Allah grant thee the accomplishment of the wish! And without his being aware of it, he put into a cup a lozenge of bhang, and handed it to him; and as soon as it had settled in his stomach, he fell asleep immediately. Alrashid then arose and went to the door, where he found his young men waiting for him, and he ordered them to convey Abou Hassan upon a mule, and returned to the palace, Abou Hassan being intoxicated and insensible. And when the caliph had rested himself in the palace, he called for his vizier Giafar, and Abdallah the son of Tahir, the Judge of Bagdad, and certain of his chief attendants, and said to them all, In the morning when ye see this young man (pointing to Abou Hassan) seated on the royal couch, pay obedience to him, and salute him as caliph, and whatsoever he commandeth you, do it. Then going to his female slaves, he directed them to wait upon Abou Hassan, and to address him as Prince of the Faithful: after which he entered a private closet, and, having let down a curtain over the entrance, slept.

So when Abou Hassan awoke, he found himself upon the royal couch with the attendants standing around, and kissing the ground before him; and a maid said to him, O our lord, it is the time for morning prayer. Upon which he laughed, and, looking round about him, he beheld a pavilion whose walls were adorned with gold and ultramarine, and the roof bespotted with red gold, surrounded by chambers with curtains of embroidered silk hanging before their doors; and he saw vessels of gold, and chinaware, and crystal, and furniture, and carpets spread, and lighted lamps, and female slaves, and eunuchs, and other attendants; whereat he was perplexed in his mind, and said, By Allah, either I am dreaming, or this is Paradise, and the Abode of Peace. And he closed his eyes. So a eunuch said to him, O my lord, this is not thy usual custom, O Prince of the Faithful. And he was perplexed at his case, and put his head into his bosom, and then began to open his eyes by little and little, laughing, and saying, What is this state in which I find myself? And he bit his finger; and when he found that the bite pained him, he cried, Ah! and was angry. Then raising his head, he called one of the female slaves, who answered him, At thy service, O Prince of the Faithful! And he said to her, What is thy name? She answered, Cluster of Pearls. And he said, Knowest thou in what place I am, and who I am? Thou art the Prince of the Faithful, she answered, sitting in thy palace, upon the royal couch. He replied, I am perplexed at my case; my reason hath departed, and it seemeth that I am asleep: but what shall I say of my yesterday's guest? I imagine nothing but that he is a devil, or an enchanter, who hath sported with my reason.

All this time the caliph was observing him from a place where Abou Hassan could not see him. And Abou Hassan looked toward the chief eunuch, and called to him. So he came, and kissed the ground before him, saying to him, Yes, O Prince of the Faithful. And Abou Hassan said to him, Who is the Prince of the Faithful? Thou, he answered. Abou Hassan replied, Thou liest. And addressing another eunuch, he said to him, O my chief, as thou hopest for Allah's protection, tell me, am I the Prince of the Faithful? Yea, by Allah, answered the eunuch; thou art at this present time the Prince of the Faithful, and the caliph of the Lord of all creatures. And Abou Hassan, perplexed at all that he beheld, said, In one night do I become Prince of the Faithful! Was I not yesterday Abou Hassan; and to-day am I Prince of the Faithful? He remained perplexed and confounded until the morning, when a eunuch advanced to him, and said to him, May Allah grant a happy morning to the Prince of the Faithful! And he handed to him a pair of shoes of gold stuff, reticulated with precious stones and rubies; and Abou Hassan took them, and after examining them a long time, put them into his sleeve. So the eunuch said to him, These are shoes to walk in. And Abou Hassan replied, Thou hast spoken truth. I put them not into my sleeve but in my fear lest they should be soiled. He therefore took them forth, and put them on his feet. And shortly after, the female slaves brought him a basin of gold and a ewer of silver, and poured the water upon his hands; and when he had performed the ablution, they spread for him a prayer carpet; and he prayed; but knew not how to do so. He continued his inclinations and prostrations until he had performed twenty rekahs; meditating and saying within himself, By Allah, I am none other than the Prince of the Faithful, in truth; or else this is a dream, and all these things occur not in a dream. He therefore convinced himself, and determined in his mind that he was the Prince of the Faithful; and he pronounced the salutations, and finished his prayers. They then brought him a magnificent dress, and, looking at himself as he sat upon the couch, he retracted, and said, All this is an illusion, and a machination of the Genii.

And while he was in this state, lo, one of the mamlouks came in and said to him, O Prince of the Faithful, the chamberlain is at the door, requesting permission to enter. Let him enter, replied Abou Hassan. So he came in, and, having kissed the ground before him, said, Peace be on thee, O Prince of the Faithful! And Abou Hassan rose, and descended from the couch to the floor; whereupon the chamberlain exclaimed, Allah! Allah! O Prince of the Faithful! Knowest thou not that all

men are thy servants, and under thy authority, and that is it not proper
for the Prince of the Faithful to rise to anyone! Abou Hassan was then
told that Giafar the Barmecide, and Abdallah the son of Tahir, and
the chiefs of the mamlouks, begged permission to enter. And he gave
them permission. So they entered, and kissed the ground before him,
each of them addressing him as Prince of the Faithful. And he was
delighted at this, and returned their salutation; after which he called
the judge, who approached him, and said, At thy service, O Prince of
the Faithful! And Abou Hassan said to him, Repair immediately to
such a street, and give a hundred pieces of gold to the mother of Abou
Hassan the Wag, with my salutation; then take the imam of the mosque, and the four sheiks, inflict upon each of them a thousand lashes;
and when thou hast done that, write a bond against them, confirmed
by oath, that they shall not reside in the street, after thou shalt have paraded them through the city, mounted on beasts, with their faces to the
tails, and hast proclaimed before them, This is the recompense of those
who annoy their neighbors. And beware of neglecting that which I
have commanded thee to do. So the judge did as he was ordered. And
when Abou Hassan had exercised his authority until the close of the
day, he looked toward the chamberlain and the rest of the attendants,
and said to them, Depart.

He then called for a eunuch who was near at hand, and said to him,
I am hungry, and desire something to eat. And he replied, I hear and
obey; and led him by the hand into the eating chamber, where the attendants placed before him a table of rich viands; and ten slave girls,
high-bosomed virgins, stood behind his head. Abou Hassan, looking at
one of these, said to her, What is thy name? She answered, Branch of
Willow. And he said to her, O Branch of Willow, who am I? Thou
art the Prince of the Faithful, she answered. But he replied, Thou liest,
by Allah, thou slut! Ye girls are laughing at me. So she said, Fear Allah,
O Prince of the Faithful; this is thy palace, and the female slaves are
thine. And upon this he said within himself, It is no great matter to be
effected by God, to whom be ascribed might and glory! Then the slave
girls led him by the hand to the drinking chamber, where he saw what
astonished the mind; and he continued to say within himself, No doubt
these are of the Genii, and this person who was my guest is one of the
kings of the Genii, who saw no way of requiting and compensating me
for my kindness to him but by ordering his slaves to address me as
Prince of the Faithful. All these are of the Genii. May Allah then deliver me from them happily! And while he was thus talking to himself,
lo, one of the slave girls filled for him a cup of wine; and he took it
from her hand and drank it; after which, the slave girls plied him with
wine in abundance; and one of them threw into his cup a lozenge of
bhang; and when it had settled in his stomach, he fell down senseless.

Alrashid then gave orders to convey him to his house; and the servants did so, and laid him on his bed, still in a state of insensibility. So when he recovered from his intoxication, in the latter part of the night, he found himself in the dark; and he called out, Branch of Willow! Cluster of Pearls! But no one answered him. His mother, however, heard him shouting these names, and arose and came, and said to him, What hath happened to thee, O my son, and what hath befallen thee? Art thou mad? And when he heard the words of his mother, he said to her, Who art thou, O ill-omened old woman, that thou addressest the Prince of the Faithful with these expressions? She answered, I am thy mother, O my son. But he replied, Thou liest: I am the Prince of the Faithful, the lord of the countries and the people. Be silent, she said, or else thy life will be lost. And she began to pronounce spells, and to recite charms over him, and said to him, It seemeth, O my son, that thou hast seen this in a dream, and all this is one of the ideas suggested by the devil. She said to him, I give thee good news, at which thou wilt be rejoiced. And what is it? said he. She answered, The caliph gave orders yesterday to beat the imam and the four sheiks, and caused a bond to be written against them, confirmed by oath, that they shall not transgress henceforth against anyone by their impertinent meddling; and he sent me a hundred pieces of gold, with his salutation. And when Abou Hassan heard these words from his mother, he uttered a loud cry, with which his soul almost quitted the world; and he exclaimed, I am he who gave orders to beat the sheiks, and who sent thee the hundred pieces of gold, with my salutation, and I am the Prince of the Faithful.

Having said this, he rose up against his mother, and beat her with an almond stick, until she cried out, O ye faithful. And he beat her with increased violence, until the neighbors heard her cries and came to her relief. He was still beating her, and saying to her, O ill-omened old woman, am I not the Prince of the Faithful? Thou has enchanted me! And when the people heard his words, they said, This man hath become mad. And not doubting his insanity, they came in and laid hold upon him, bound his hands behind him, and conveyed him to the madhouse. There every day they punished him, dosing him with abominable medicines, and flogging him with whips, making him a madman in spite of himself. Thus he continued, stripped of his clothing, and chained by the neck to a high window, for the space of ten days; after which his mother came to salute him. And he complained to her of his case. So she said to him, O my son, fear God in thy conduct: if thou wert Prince of the Faithful, thou wouldst not be in this predicament. And when he heard what his mother said, he replied, By Allah, thou hast spoken truth. It seemeth that I was asleep, and dreamed that they made me caliph, and assigned me servants and female slaves. So his mother said to him, O my son, verily Satan doeth more than this. And he replied, Thou hast spoken truth, and I beg forgiveness of God for the actions committed by me.

They therefore took him forth from the madhouse, and conducted him into the bath; and when he recovered his health, he prepared food and drink, and began to eat. But eating by himself was not pleasant to him; and he said to his mother, O my mother, neither life nor eating by myself is pleasant to me. She replied, If thou desire to do according to thy will, thy return to the madhouse is most probable. Paying no attention, however, to her advice, he walked to the bridge to seek for himself a cup-companion. And while he was sitting there, lo, Alrashid came to him in the garb of a merchant; for, from the time of his parting with him he came every day to the bridge, but found him not till now. As soon as Abou Hassan saw him, he said to him, A friendly welcome to thee, O King of the Genii! So Alrashid said, What have I done to thee? What more couldst thou do, said Abou Hassan, than thou hast done to me, O filthiest of the Genii? I have suffered beating, and entered the madhouse, and they pronounced me a madman. All this was occasioned by thee. I brought thee to my abode, and fed thee with the best of my food; and after that thou gavest thy devils and thy slaves entire power over me, to make sport with my reason from morning to evening. Depart from me, therefore, and go thy way.

The caliph smiled at this, and, seating himself by his side, addressed him in courteous language, and said to him, O my brother, when I went forth from thee, I inadvertently left the door open, and probably the devil went in to thee. Abou Hassan replied, Inquire not respecting that which happened to me. And what possessed thee, he added, that thou leftest the door open, so that the devil came in to me, and that such and such things befell me? And he related to the caliph all that had happened to him from first to last, while Alrashid laughed, but concealed his laughter: after which the caliph said to him, Praise be to God that He hath dispelled from thee that which thou hatest, and that I have seen thee again in prosperity!

But Abou Hassan replied, I will not take thee again as my boon-companion, nor as an associate to sit with me; for the proverb saith, He who stumbleth against a stone and returneth to it, is to be blamed and reproached: and with thee, O my brother, I will not carouse, nor will I keep company with thee: since I have not found thy visit to be followed by good fortune to me. The caliph, however, said, I have been the means of the accomplishment of thy desire with regard to the imam and the sheiks. Yes, replied Abou Hassan. And Alrashid added, Perhaps something will happen to thee that will rejoice thy heart more than that. Then what dost thou desire of me? said Abou Hassan. My desire, answered Alrashid, is to be thy guest this night. And at length-

Abou Hassan said, On the condition that thou swear to me by the inscription on the seal of Solomon the son of David (on both of whom be peace!) that thou wilt not suffer thy Afrites to make sport with me. And Alrashid replied, I hear and obey.

So Abou Hassan took him to his abode, and put the food before him and his attendants, and they ate as much as satisfied them; and when they had finished eating, the servants placed before them the wine and exhilarating beverages, and they continued drinking and carousing until the wine rose into their heads. Abou Hassan then said to the caliph, O my boon-companion, in truth I am perplexed respecting my case. It seemeth that I was Prince of the Faithful, and that I exercised authority, and gave and bestowed: and truly, O my brother, it was not a vision of sleep. But the caliph replied, This was the result of confused dreams. And having said this, he put a piece of bhang into the cup, and said, By my life, drink this cup. Verily I will drink it from thy hand, replied Abou Hassan. So he took the cup, and when he had drank it his head fell before his feet. The caliph then arose immediately, and ordered his young men to convey Abou Hassan to the palace, and to lay him upon his couch, and commanded the female slaves to stand around him; after which he concealed himself in a place where Abou Hassan could not see him, and ordered a slave girl to take her lute and strike its chords over Abou Hassan's head, and desired the other slave girls to play upon their instruments.

It was then the close of the night, and Abou Hassan, awaking, and hearing the sounds of the lutes, and tambourines, and flutes, and the singing of the slave girls, cried out, O my mother! Whereupon the slave girls answered, At thy service, O Prince of the Faithful! And when he heard this, he exclaimed, There is no strength nor power but in God, the High, the Great! Come to my help this night; for this night is more unlucky than the former! He reflected upon all that had happened to him with his mother, and how he had beaten her, and how he had been taken into the madhouse, and he saw the marks of the beating that he had suffered there. Then looking at the scene that surrounded him, he said, These are all of them of the Genii, in the shapes of human beings! I commit my affairs unto Allah! And looking toward a mamlouk by his side, he said to him, Bite my ear, that I may know if I be asleep or awake. The mamlouk said, How shall I bite thine ear, when thou art the Prince of the Faithful? But Abou Hassan answered, Do as I have commanded thee, or I will strike off thy head. So he bit it until his teeth met together, and Abou Hassan uttered a loud shriek. Alrashid (who was behind a curtain in a closet), and all who were present, fell down with laughter, and they said to the mamlouk, Art thou mad, that thou bitest the ear of the caliph? And Abou Hassan said to them, Is it not enough, O ye wretches of Genii, that hath befallen me? But ye are not in fault: the fault is your chief's, who transformed you from the shapes of Genii into the shapes of human beings. I implore help against you this night by the Verse of the Throne, and the Chapter of Sincerity, and the two Preventives! Upon this Alrashid exclaimed from behind the curtain, Thou hast killed us, O Abou Hassan! And Abou Hassan recognized him, and kissed the ground before him, greeting him with a prayer for the increase of his glory and the prolongation of his life. Alrashid then clad him in a rich dress, gave him a thousand pieces of gold, and made him one of his chief boon-companions.

Abou Hassan, after this, became a greater favorite with the caliph than all the other boon-companions, so that he sat with the caliph and his wife the Lady Zobeide, the daughter of Kasim, and he married her female treasurer, whose name was Nouzatalfuad. With this wife he resided, eating, and drinking, and enjoying a delightful life, until all the money that they possessed had gone; whereupon he said to her, O Nouzatalfuad! And she answered, At thy service. I desire, said he, to practise a trick upon the caliph, and thou shalt practise a trick upon the Lady Zobeide, and we will obtain from them immediately two hundred pieces of gold, and two pieces of silk. Do what thou desirest, replied she: and what, she asked, is it? He answered, We will feign ourselves dead. I will die before thee, and lay myself out: then do thou spread over me a napkin of silk, and unfold my turban over me, and tie my toes, and put upon my stomach a knife and a little salt; after which, dishevel thy hair, and go to thy Lady Zobeide, and tear thy vest, and slap thy face, and shriek. So she will say to thee, What is the matter with thee? And do thou answer her, May thy head long survive Abou Hassan the Wag; for he is dead! Whereupon she will mourn for me, and weep, and will order her female treasurer to give thee a hundred pieces of gold, and a piece of silk, and will say to thee, Go, prepare his corpse for burial, and convey it forth to the grave. So thou shalt receive from her the hundred pieces of gold, and the piece of silk, and come hither. And when thou comest to me, I will rise, and thou shalt lay thyself down in my place, and I will go to the caliph, and say to him, May thy head long survive Nouzatalfuad! And I will tear my vest and pluck my beard; upon which he will mourn for thee, and will say to his treasurer, Give to Abou Hassan a hundred pieces of gold, and a piece of silk: and he will say to me, Go, prepare her corpse for burial, and convey it forth to the grave. So I will come to thee. And Nouzatalfuad was delighted with this, and replied, Truly this is an excellent stratagem!

She forthwith closed his eyes, and tied his feet, covered him with the napkin, and did all that her master told her; after which she tore her vest, uncovered her head, and disheveled her hair, and went in to the Lady Zobeide, shrieking and weeping. When the Lady Zobeide, therefore, beheld her in this condition, she said to her, What is this state in which I see thee, and what hath happened unto thee, and what hath caused thee to weep? And Nouzatalfuad wept and shrieked, and said, O my mistress, may thy head long survive Abou Hassan the Wag; for he is dead! And the Lady Zobeide mourned for him, and said, Poor Abou Hassan the Wag! Then, after weeping for him a while, she ordered the female treasurer to give to Nouzatalfuad a hundred pieces of gold and a piece of silk, and said, O Nouzatalfuad, go, prepare his body for burial, and convey it forth. So she took the hundred pieces of gold and the piece of silk, and, returning to her abode full of joy, went in to Abou Hassan, and acquainted him with what had happened to her; upon which he arose and rejoiced, and girded his waist and danced, and took the hundred pieces of gold, with the piece of silk, and laid them up.

He then extended Nouzatalfuad, and did with her as she had done with him; after which he tore his vest, and plucked his beard, and disordered his turban, and ran without stopping until he went in to the caliph, who was in his hall of judgment; and in the condition above described, he beat his bosom. So the caliph said to him, What hath befallen thee, O Abou Hassan? and he wept, and said, Would that thy boon-companion had never been, nor his hour come to pass! The caliph therefore said to him, Tell me. He replied, May thy head long survive, O my lord, Nouzatalfuad! And the caliph exclaimed, There is no deity but God! and struck his hands together. He then consoled Abou Hassan, and said to him, Mourn not: I will give thee a slave in her stead. And he ordered his treasurer to give him a hundred pieces of gold, and a piece of silk. The treasurer therefore did as he was commanded, and the caliph said to Abou Hassan, Go, prepare her corpse for burial, and convey it forth, and make a handsome funeral for her. And he took what the caliph gave him, and went to his abode joyful, and going in to Nouzatalfuad, said to her, Arise; for our desire is accomplished. She therefore arose, and he put before her the hundred pieces of gold and the piece of silk. So she rejoiced; and they put these pieces of gold on the other pieces, and the piece of silk on the former one, and sat conversing and laughing at each other.

But as to the caliph, when Abou Hassan parted from him, and went with the pretense of preparing the corpse of Nouzatalfuad for burial, he mourned for her, and, having dismissed the council, arose and went in, leaning upon Mesrour his executioner, to console the Lady Zobeide for the loss of her slave girl. He found her, however, sitting weeping, and waiting for his arrival, that she might console him for the loss of Abou Hassan the Wag. The caliph said, May thy head long survive thy slave girl, Nouzatalfuad! But she replied, O my lord, Allah preserve my slave girl! Mayest thou long survive thy boon-companion Abou

Hassan the Wag; for he is dead! And the caliph smiled, and said to his eunuch, O Mesrour, verily women are of little sense. By Allah, was not Abou Hassan just now with me? Upon this the Lady Zobeide said, after uttering a laugh from an angry bosom, Wilt thou not give over thy jesting? Is not the death of Abou Hassan enough, but thou must make my slave girl to be dead, as though we had lost them both, and thou must pronounce me of little sense? The caliph replied, Verily Nouzatalfuad is the person who is dead. And the Lady Zobeide rejoined, In truth he was not with thee, nor, didst thou see him; and none was with me just now but Nouzatalfuad, who was mourning and weeping, with her clothes rent in pieces; and I exhorted her to have patience, and gave her a hundred pieces of gold, and a piece of silk; and I was waiting for thee, that I might console thee for the loss of thy boon-companion Abou Hassan the Wag; and I was going to send for thee. On hearing this the caliph laughed, and said, None is dead but Nouzatalfuad. And the Lady Zobeide said, No, no, O my lord; none is dead but Abou Hassan. But the caliph now became enraged; the vein between his eyes, which was remarkable in members of the family of Hashim, throbbed, and he called out to Mesrour the Executioner, saying to him, Go forth and repair to the house of Abou Hassan the Wag, and see which of the two is dead.

Mesrour, therefore, went forth running. And the caliph said to the Lady Zobeide, Wilt thou lay me a wager? She answered, Yes, I will, and I say that Abou Hassan is dead. And I, replied the caliph, lay a wager, and say that none is dead but Nouzatalfuad; and our wager shall be, that I stake the Garden of Delight against thy pavilion, the Pavilion of the Pictures. And they sat waiting for Mesrour to return with the information. Now as to Mesrour, he ran without ceasing until he entered the by-street in which was the house of Abou Hassan the Wag. Abou Hassan was sitting reclining against the window, and, turning his eyes, he saw Mesrour running along the street. So he said to Nouzatalfuad, It seemeth that the caliph, after I went forth from him, dismissed the court, and hath gone in to the Lady Zobeide to console her, and that she, on his arrival, hath arisen and consoled him, and said to him, May God largely compensate thee for the loss of Abou Hassan the Wag! whereupon the caliph hath said to her, None is dead but Nouzatalfuad. May thy head long survive her! And she hath replied, None is dead but Abou Hassan the Wag, thy boon-companion. And he hath said again to her, None is dead but Nouzatalfuad. So they have become obstinate, and the caliph hath been enraged, and they have laid a wager, in consequence of which Mesrour the Executioner hath been sent to see who is dead. It is therefore the more proper that *thou* lay thyself down, that he may see thee, and go and inform the caliph, who will thereupon believe my assertion.

Accordingly, Nouzatalfuad extended herself, and Abou Hassan covered her with her veil, and seated himself at her head, weeping. And lo, Mesrour the eunuch came up into the house of Abou Hassan, and saluted him, and saw Nouzatalfuad stretched out; upon which he uncovered her face, and exclaimed, There is no deity but God! Our sister Nouzatalfuad is dead! How speedy was the stroke of fate! May Allah have mercy upon her, and acquit thee of responsibility! He then returned, and related what had happened before the caliph and the Lady Zobeide, laughing as he spoke. So the caliph said to him, O thou accursed, this is not a time for laughing. Tell us which of them is dead. He therefore replied, By Allah, O my lord, verily Abou Hassan is well, and none is dead but Nouzatalfuad. And upon this the caliph said to Zobeide, Thou has lost thy pavilion in thy play. And he laughed at her, and said, O Mesrour, relate to her what thou sawest. So Mesrour said to her, In truth, O my mistress, I ran incessantly until I went in to Abou Hassan in his house; whereupon I found Nouzatalfuad lying dead, and Abou Hassan sitting at her head, weeping; and I saluted him, and consoled him, and seated myself by his side; and, uncovering the face of Nouzatalfuad, I beheld her dead, with her face swollen: I therefore said to him, Convey her forth presently to the grave, that we may pray over her. And he replied, Yes. And I came, leaving him to prepare her corpse for burial, in order to inform you. Upon this the caliph laughed, and said, Tell it again and again to thy mistress, the person of little sense. But when the Lady Zobeide heard the words of Mesrour, she was enraged, and said, None is deficient in sense but he who believeth a slave. And she abused Mesrour, while the caliph continued laughing; and Mesrour was displeased, and said to the caliph, He spoke truth who said that women are deficient in sense and religion.

The Lady Zobeide then said, O Prince of the Faithful, thou sportest and jestest with me, and this slave deceiveth me for the purpose of pleasing thee; but I will send and see which of them is dead. The caliph replied, Do so. And she called to an old woman, a confidential slave, and said to her, Repair quickly to the house of Nouzatalfuad, and see who is dead, and delay not thy return. And she threw money to her. So the old woman went forth running, the caliph and Mesrour laughing. The old woman ran without ceasing until she entered the street, when Abou Hassan saw her and knew her; and he said to his wife, O Nouzatalfuad, it seemeth that the Lady Zobeide hath sent to us to see who is dead, and hath not believed what Mesrour hath said respecting thy death: wherefore she hath sent the old woman to ascertain the truth of the matter. It is therefore more proper now for *me* to be dead, that the Lady Zobeide may believe thee.

Then Abou Hassan laid himself along, and Nouzatalfuad covered him, and bound his eyes and his feet, and seated herself at his head, weeping. And the old woman came in to Nouzatalfuad, and saw her sitting at the head of Abou Hassan, weeping, and enumerating his merits; and when Nouzatalfuad saw the old woman, she shrieked, and said to her, See what hath befallen me! Abou Hassan hath died and left me single and solitary! Then she shrieked again, and tore her clothes in pieces, and said to the old woman, O my mother, how good he was! The old woman replied, Truly thou art excusable; for thou hadst become habituated to him, and he had become habituated to thee. And knowing how Mesrour had acted to the caliph and the Lady Zobeide, she said to Nouzatalfuad, Mesrour is about to cause a quarrel between the caliph and the Lady Zobeide. And what is this cause of quarrel, O my mother? said Nouzatalfuad. The old woman answered, O my daughter, Mesrour hath come to them and told them that thou wast dead, and that Abou Hassan was well. O my aunt, replied Nouzatalfuad, I was just now with my lady, and she gave me a hundred pieces of gold and a piece of silk; and see thou my condition, and what hath befallen me. I am perplexed; and what shall I do, single and solitary? Would that I had died, and that he had lived! Then she wept, and the old woman wept with her, and advancing, and uncovering the face of Abou Hassan, saw his eyes bound, and swollen from the bandage. And she covered him, and said, Truly, O Nouzatalfuad, thou hast been afflicted for Abou Hassan. And she consoled her, and went forth from her running until she went on to the Lady Zobeide, when she related to her the story; on hearing which, the Lady Zobeide laughed, and said, Tell it to the caliph who hath pronounced me of little sense, and caused this ill-omened, lying slave to behave arrogantly toward me. But Mesrour said, Verily this old woman lieth; for I saw Abou Hassan in good health, and it was Nouzatalfuad who was lying dead. The old woman replied, It is thou who liest, and thou desirest to excite a quarrel between the caliph and the Lady Zobeide. Mesrour rejoined, None lieth but thou, O ill-omened old woman, and thy lady believeth thee, for she is disordered in mind. And upon this the Lady Zobeide cried out at him, enraged at him and at his words; and she wept.

At length the caliph said to her, I lie, and my eunuch lieth, and thou liest, and thy female slave lieth. The right course, in my opinion, is this, that we four go together to see who among us speaketh truth. So Mesrour said, Arise with us, that I may bring misfortunes upon this ill-omened old woman, and bastinade her for her lying. O thou imbecile in mind! exclaimed the old woman: is thy sense like mine? Nay, thy sense is like that of the hen. And Mesrour was enraged at her words, and would have laid violent hands upon her; but the Lady Zobeide, having pushed him away from her, said to him, Immediately will her veracity be distinguished from thine, and her lying from thine. They all four arose, laying wagers with each other, and went forth and walked from the gate of the palace until they entered the gate of the street in which dwelt Abou Hassan the Wag: when Abou Hassan saw them, and said to his wife Nouzatalfuad, In truth, everything that is slippery is not a pancake, and not every time the jar is struck doth it escape unbroken. It seemeth that the old woman hath gone and related the story to her lady and acquainted her with our case, and that she hath contended with Mesrour the eunuch, and they have laid wagers respecting our death: so the caliph, and the eunuch, and the Lady Zobeide, and the old woman have all four come to us. And upon this Nouzatalfuad arose from her extended position, and said, What is to be done? Abou Hassan answered her, We will both feign ourselves dead, and lay ourselves out and hold in our breath. And she assented to his proposal.

They both stretched themselves along, bound their feet, closed their eyes, and held in their breath, lying with their heads in the direction of the kebla, and covered themselves with the veil. Then the caliph, and Zobeide, and Mesrour, and the old woman entered the house of Abou Hassan the Wag, and found him and his wife extended as if they were dead. And when the Lady Zobeide saw them, she wept, and said, They continued to assert the death of my female slave until she actually died; but I imagine that the death of Abou Hassan so grieved her that she died after him in consequence of it. The caliph, however, said, Do not prevent me with thy talk and assertions; for she died before Abou Hassan, because Abou Hassan came to me with his clothes torn in pieces, and with his beard plucked, and striking his bosom with two clods and I gave him a hundred pieces of gold, with a piece of silk, and said to him, Go, prepare her body for burial, and I will give thee a concubine better than her, and she shall serve in her stead: and it appears that her loss was insupportable to him; so he died after her. I have therefore overcome thee, and gained thy stake. But the Lady Zobeide replied in many words, and a long dispute ensued between them.

The caliph then seated himself at the heads of the two pretended corpses, and said, By the tomb of the Apostle of Allah (God favor and preserve him!), and by the tombs of my ancestors, if anyone would acquaint me which of them died before the other, I would give him a thousand pieces of gold. And when Abou Hassan heard these words of the caliph, he quickly rose and sprang up, and said, It was I who died first, O Prince of the Faithful. Give me the thousand pieces of gold, and so acquit thyself of the oath that thou hast sworn. Then Nouzatalfuad arose and sat up before the caliph and the Lady Zobeide, who rejoiced at their safety. But Zobeide chid her female slave. The caliph and the Lady Zobeide congratulated them both on their safety, and knew this pretended death was a stratagem for the purpose of obtaining the gold: so the Lady Zobeide said to Nouzatalfuad, Thou shouldst have asked of me what thou desiredst without this proceeding, and not have tortured my heart on thine account. I was ashamed, O my mistress, replied Nouzatalfuad. But as to the caliph, he was almost senseless from laughing, and said, O Abou Hassan, thou hast not ceased to be a wag, and to do wonders and strange acts. Abou Hassan replied, O Prince of the Faithful, this stratagem I practised in consequence of the dissipation of the wealth that I received from thy hand; for I was ashamed to ask of thee a second time. When I was alone, I was not tenacious of wealth; but since thou hast married me to this female slave who is with me, if I possessed all thy wealth I should make an end of it. And when all that was in my possession was exhausted, I practised this stratagem, by means of which I obtained from thee these hundred pieces of gold and the piece of silk, all of which are an alms of our lord. And now make haste in giving me the thousand pieces of gold, and acquit thyself of thine oath.

At this the caliph and the Lady Zobeide both laughed; and after they had returned to the palace, the caliph gave to Abou Hassan the thousand pieces of gold, saying to him, Receive them as a gratuity on account of thy safety from death. In like manner, also, the Lady Zobeide gave to Nouzatalfuad a thousand pieces of gold, saying to her the same words. Then the caliph allotted to Abou Hassan an ample salary and ample supplies, and he ceased not to live with his wife in joy and happiness, until they were visited by the terminator of delights and the separator of companions, the devastator of palaces and houses, and the replenisher of the graves.

Great Britain

INTRODUCTION

THE history of the short story in Great Britain can be traced back to the very earliest epoch, before even the formation of the language itself. By varying one's definition of the term "short story," it is possible to fix a date as early as the Seventh or the Eighth Century A.D., or as late as the days of Addison, a thousand years after. The first example chosen for this collection is a brief episode from the Anglo-Saxon epic tale of *Beowulf*. When "our own branch of the Teutonic race migrated from the Continent, among the furniture it deemed too precious to be left behind was, apparently, the group of legends from which sprang *Beowulf*." (Walker.) Apart from such largely mythological works, we find in the ecclesiastical literature (particularly in the writings of Bede and Alfred) little stories which were used in sermons. These were popular for centuries, and in the form of apologues and fables were in later times collected into such books as the Thirteenth Century *South English Legendary*.

To trace the many and diverse influences—French, German, Scandinavian and Celtic—that operated to produce the tales and poetical romances of the Middle Ages, is here out of the question. It is sufficient to state that tales and traditional lore from all these sources were told and retold by poets and singers, priests and kings, each adapting the old material to his own ends. Of the writers who flourished in England before the time of Malory, only a few are represented in this volume: the authors of the stories in *The Mabinogion* and the *Gesta Romanorum*, and Geoffrey of Monmouth.

Chaucer's contribution to English literature is, of course, of the first importance, but his original prose tales are neither very short nor very interesting. His contemporaries, Langland and Gower, were somewhat better equipped, bringing as they did a sense of proportion into their otherwise inferior work. In the period between Chaucer and the end of the Fifteenth Century, when the *Morte d'Arthur* appeared, there is, except for the *Gesta Romanorum*, very little to detain us in our rapid survey of the development of the short story.

When the ideas of the Italian Renaissance were at last introduced into England, there were several writers ready to translate, adapt, and imitate the stories of Boccaccio and his followers. Among the first of the English collections of tales was Painter's famous *Palace of Pleasure* (1566-67), to which Shakespeare was indebted for more than one of his plots. Though the Elizabethans never altogether assimilated the Italian tale, men like Green occasionally produced clever imitations. Thomas Deloney was an exceptional figure: his homely and realistic stories of middle- and lower-class life are still worth reading. The other fiction writers—Lyly and Lodge and the rest—were preoccupied rather with evolving a literary style than with the telling of effective stories.

Between the age of Elizabeth and that of Anne there is little to record. With the advent of Addison and Defoe a new epoch opened. Addison has so long been praised as a stylist that it is time we remembered him as a story writer. His narratives in *The Spectator* are among the very best specimens of their kind in English literature. And to Defoe is due the credit not only for his epoch-making *Robinson Crusoe*, but for his remarkable realistic tales, *The Cock-Lane Ghost* and *The Apparition of Mrs. Veal*.

The little moral tale, as told by Addison and Steele, was taken up by Hawkesworth, Johnson, and Goldsmith, while even the novelists (in particular Laurence Sterne) delighted to break the thread of their long narratives in order to introduce episodes that are true short stories. By the end of the Eighteenth Century there were comparatively few writers who did anything with the story, and although Scott and Dickens wrote brief narratives, and an occasional Lover or Carleton devoted his life to the exploitation of character in the briefer narrative form, it was not until after the middle of the Nineteenth Century that the short story came into its own. The second half of the last century, not only in England, but throughout Europe and America, was an age of great fiction—both in the novel and the short story.

There is no use in repeating the names of the great story writers of modern times; it is enough to say that nearly all the novelists of Victorian and later days wrote short tales as well as long ones.

In more recent times we have seen the development of the short story in the hands of specialists, like Kipling and Morrison, Jacobs and Merrick, writers who regard the story as an independent literary form deserving a life-time of application and care.

GRENDEL'S RAID

(Anonymous: About 7th Century, A.D.)

THE poet who wrote the first important extant specimen of Anglo-Saxon literature was probably an inhabitant of Anglia, and except that he wrote *Beowulf* late in the Seventh Century or early in the

Eighth (not later than 752), we know nothing of him. Apart from its intrinsic merits, *Beowulf* is the "oldest surviving epic of any Teutonic people." It is partly mythological, but it does contain a certain amount of historical fact. The grim tale here included is a crude but stirring narrative.

The present version, translated from the Anglo-Saxon by J. R. C. Hall, is from *Beowulf and the Finnsburg Fragment*, published in London in 1911 by George Allen and Unwin, by whose permission it is here reprinted. There is no title in the original.

GRENDEL'S RAID

(From *Beowulf*)

THEN came Grendel, advancing from the moor, under the misty slopes; God's anger rested on him. The deadly foe thought to entrap one of the human race in the high Hall: he strode beneath the clouds in such wise that he might best discern the wine-building, the gold chamber of men, resplendent with adornment. Nor was that the first time that he had visited Hrothgar's home. Never in the days of his life, before or since, did he discover a braver warrior and hall-guards.

So this creature, deprived of joys, came journeying to the hall. The door, fastened by four bands, opened straightway, when he touched it with his hand. Thus, bent on destruction, for he was swollen with rage, he tore away the entrance of the building.

Quickly, after that, the fiend stepped onto the fair-paved floor, advanced in angry mood; out of his eyes there started a weird light, most like a flame. He saw many men in the hall, a troop of kinsmen, a band of warriors, sleeping all together. Then his spirit exulted; he, the cruel monster, resolved that he would sever the soul of every one of them from his body before day came; for the hope of feasting full had come to him. That was no longer his fortune, that he should devour more of human kind after that night. Hygelac's mighty kinsman kept watching how the murderous foe would set to work with his sudden snatchings. The monster was not minded to put it off, but quickly seized a sleeping warrior as a first start, rent him undisturbed, bit his sinews, drank the blood from his veins, swallowed bite after bite, and soon he had eaten up all of the dead man, even his feet and hands.

Forward and nearer he advanced, and then seized with his hands the doughty warrior on his bed—the fiend reached out towards him with his claw. He (Beowulf) at once took in his evil plans, and pressed heavily on his (Grendel's) arm. Instantly the master of crimes realized that never in this middle-world, these regions of earth, had he met with a mightier hand-grip in any other man. He became affrighted in soul and spirit, but he could get away no faster for all that. His mind was bent on getting off,—he wished to flee into the darkness and go back to the herd of devils. His case was unlike anything he had met with in his lifetime there before. Then Hygelac's brave kinsman was mindful of his evening speech: he stood erect and grasped him tight,—his fingers burst. The monster was moving out; the chief stepped forward too. The infamous creature thought to slip further off, wheresoever he could, and to flee away thence to his fen-refuge; he knew the power of his fingers was in the foeman's grip. That was a sorry journey which the baleful fiend had made to Heorot!

The warrior's hall resounded, there was panic among all the Danes, the castle-dwellers, the nobles and the heroes every one. Both the raging wardens of the house were furious; the building rang again. Then was it a great wonder that the wine-hall was proof against the savage fighters,—that the fair earthly dwelling did not fall to the ground; yet it was (made) firm enough for it, inside and out, by means of iron clamps, forged with curious art. There, where the foemen fought, many a mead-bench adorned with gilding, started from the sill, as I have heard. Before that, veterans of the Scyldings weened that no man could shatter it, splendid and horn-bedecked, in any wise, or ruin it by craft, although the embrace of fire might swallow it in smoke.

A sound arose, startling enough; a horrible fear clung to the North Danes, to everyone who heard the shrieking from the wall—(heard) the adversary of God chant his grisly lay, his song of non-success,—the prisoner of hell wailing over his wound. He held him fast who was strongest of men in might in this life's day!

The defender of nobles would not by any means let the murderous visitor escape alive,—he did not count his (Grendel's) life (-days) of use to any of the people. There many a noble of Beowulf's company brandished an old ancestral weapon—they wished to protect the life of their lord, of their famous chief, if so be they might. They did not know, brave-minded men of war, when they took part in the contest, and thought to hew at him on every side, and to hunt out his life, that no war-bill on earth, no best of sabers, could touch the cursed foe, for that he used enchantment against conquering weapons, every sort of blades.

In this life's day his breaking-up was to be pitiable—the alien spirit was to journey far into the power of fiends. Then he who of yore had accomplished much of the joy of his heart, of crime against mankind, he, the rebel against God, discovered this—that his bodily frame was no help to him, but that the bold kinsman of Hygelac had him by the hands. While he lived, each was abhorrent to the other. The horrible wretch suffered deadly hurt, on his shoulder gaped a wound past remedy, the sinews sprang asunder, the tendons burst. Glory in fight was granted to Beowulf; Grendel, sick to death, must needs flee thence under the fen-fastnesses—seek out his joyless dwelling;—he knew too well that the end of his life had come, the (daily-) number of his days. After that bloody contest, the desire of all the Danes had come to pass!

GEOFFREY OF MONMOUTH

(1100?—1154?)

OUR information about Geoffrey of Monmouth is very limited. He was probably of Welsh origin, and lived in the Welsh Marches, not far from the scenes of the most famous exploits of Arthur and his knights. His *Chronicle* has been aptly called a "romance-history." The twelve books or chapters of which it is composed are stories of the early (actual or imaginary) rulers of Britain. Among the finest of these are stories of King Lear, King Arthur, and the one here reprinted. *Esyllt and Sabrina* is one of the loveliest of all the early English tales.

The present version, translated from the original Latin by Louisa J. Menzies, is reprinted from *Legendary Tales of the Ancient Britons*, London, 1864.

ESYLLT AND SABRINA

(From the *Chronicle of Geoffrey of Monmouth*)

IT was about three thousand years ago that there lived a fierce warrior, named Hymyr, the Hun, whose chief delight it was to voyage about over the mighty sea, and to make descents upon fruitful lands and take to himself by rapine and violence the produce of the long toil of the husbandman and the artisan; nor was he always content with stores of corn, treasure of gold, of silver, and apparel; many fair children did he carry off from burning homesteads, young maidens, and even wives, who sorrowed in vain for slaughtered husbands and brothers, and bore in pale resignation the stern rule of the tyrant and his haughty queen.

Once Hymyr fitted out a great armament, and voyaging up the river Albis, carried off from its banks the fair daughter of a German King, whom he found playing with her maidens in a flowery meadow; then he coasted along the shore of Frisia, a terror to the husbandmen, and, forasmuch as he had heard that there was much and singular wealth in the island of Albion, newly named Britain, from its King Brutus, he turned the heads of his ships northward, and came to the part of the island that lies towards the Great Bear, and which was then called Albany. Landing here with his fierce sea-robbers, he easily defeated Albanactus, the king, who came hastily to meet him with raw levies, for he was but newly come to his throne, and was thinking of nothing less than invasion.

Then Hymyr had a joyous time of it, he reveled and feasted in the halls of Albanactus, and so pleasant did the country, seem in his eyes, with its great rows of purple mountains, its gleaming lakes abounding in fish, and its forests teeming with game, that he was in no hurry to take to the sea again: so he hunted and feasted till the summer was past its prime, eating the good fruits of the earth, and making the land desolate of men. Then news came to him that Albanactus, the king, was marching up from the south with an army of tried warriors, the warriors of Locrinus, his brother, King of Loegria, for so the southern part of Briatin was named, and that Locrinus himself was with them.

Then Hymyr might have got on board his ships and sailed away as he had been wont to do, but the gods had maddened him with long good fortune, and nothing seemed good to him but to go and meet the brothers; for he thought in his heart that he would slay them both, and possess their lands; but the gods had willed it otherwise. The armies met at a great river, half way down the island, and, because, the brothers were afraid to cross in the face of the enemy, they remained in their camp on the right bank of the river till they could construct rafts to cross in safety; but Hymyr had brought his ships round the coast, and impatient of delay, he went on board of them, and crossed the arm of the sea at the river's mouth, and his men came down on the compact lines of the brothers with shouting and boasting more like a rabble of revelers than tried soldiers going into battle.

Then there was fierce fighting on both sides, and the Huns knew at last what was the manliness of the Britons, and repented them in blood and agony of their rash boasting; and Hymyr, their chief, flying to his ships, was carried away by the current of the river, and drowned; and the river perpetuates the memory of his defeat and death, even to this day; for the men of the country call it the Humber, as it was called at that time from Hymyr, the Hun.

When Hymyr was dead, his men, such, at least, as remained of them, laid down their arms, and gave themselves up to the Kings Locrinus and Albanactus, who received them kindly, and gave them waste lands to till, and ordered that they should be supplied with corn till their own crops were grown. Then all the treasure stored up in the ships was brought to the kings, and they were amazed at the costly garments, at the precious vessels plundered from the glowing west, at the armor, and at the rich furniture, spoil of palaces; and while they were admiring these things, lo! there came to them from the ships the fair princess

Esyllt, led in triumph by the soldiers who had found her cowering among the sails, for she knew not whether the defeat of Hymyr were a cause of sorrow or rejoicing to her.

The warlike bearing of the sturdy Britons tended little to reassure her, and she came slowly and fearfully to the tent where the princes were inspecting the spoil; but when the eyes of Locrinus lighted on her, albeit her looks were bent on the ground, and her long hair almost hid her features, love suddenly flooded his soul, and he stood like one smitten by the powerful wand of a magician; but when at length he gathered power to speak, and bade her be of good cheer, the sound of his noble voice and his kind words, made the damsel lift her eyes with a touch of hope; and when she beheld the broad brow of the king, and all his presence radiant with youth and love, the color came into her cheeks and she stood revealed in all her beauty.

Then King Locrinus knew what is the bliss of the gods who live forever, but because he would not have the princess stand as a captive and unattended in a place so public, he caused her to be conducted in all honor to his own tent, and spoke to his brother in this wise:—

"Brother, take the goodly ships, the armor, and the spoil; haply thou wilt find thy palace but an empty barn, and all thy costly things wasted by the riot of the slain sea-robber; but leave to me the fair Princess Esyllt, for my soul cleaveth to her, that I may make her my wife; she is of noble parentage and deserveth well to be a queen."

"Alas! my brother," replied Albanactus, "what frenzy hath seized thy mind? The captive is passing fair, and doubtless of noble lineage, but art not thou affianced to the Lady Guendolen, the only child of Corineus, our father's trusty comrade? How, think you, will the haughty chieftain brook it, if he hears that his daughter is set at naught for a captive?"

The face of Locrinus darkened, and he answered from a heavy heart:—

"I never loved the proud Guendolen; who could love her? but because Corineus wished it, and because I thought it well to have him for a friend rather than a foe, I consented to take her. But, brother, then I had seen no damsel whom I desired to call my wife; now the gods hold out to me a joy which is like their own; I will grasp it if I die for it."

Seeing him so set upon the matter, Albanactus said no more, but gathered his spoil together, and having made costly presents to his brother for his timely help, marched homewards where affairs were eagerly calling for him to restore law and order to his lands.

Then Locrinus straightway took the Princess Esyllt for his wife, and delighted in her more and more: for she was as prudent as she was beautiful, and she loved the king, her deliverer, with the love of a true wife, and of a noble princess.

But when Corineus, the giant-slayer, heard that Locrinus had taken a foreign princess to be his wife, and that she sat beside him on his throne to the open scorn of Guendolen, his daughter, he arose in great wrath, and swore a mighty oath, that he would either make him put away his wife and marry the Lady Guendolen, to whom he was affianced, or that one of the two should never eat bread more; and gathering together a band of Cornish men, sons of the giants, and taking with him Guendolen, his daughter, he marched eastward, passing like an angry meteor through town and hamlet, for wrath drove him like a scourge.

King Locrinus, hearing of his coming, and boding ill of the issue, hid his wife privily in a shepherd's cottage, and caused a rumor to be spread that at the terror of the coming of the Giant-slayer, his queen had fallen into the pangs of premature labor, and that she and her infant had both perished; and to add greater faith to the tale, he had funeral rites performed, and went heavily as one who mourneth, and put on mourning garments.

These tidings, meeting Corineus on the way, somewhat slaked the fury of his wrath, and halting, he sent forward a messenger to Locrinus, to demand of him that he would fulfil his contract with the Lady Guendolen.

The King with a sad heart assented, but would that the marriage should be deferred for the present that he might furnish himself, with fitting ceremony to do honor to his bride; but Corineus would hear nothing of delay, and resuming his onward course burst furiously into the city of Trinovant, where Locrinus abode, and breaking unannounced into the presence of the King bade him keep to his covenant, and take the Lady Guendolen at once to his throne.

The fierce countenance of Corineus was not less terrible because it was furrowed by age, and set round with strong white hair, and a beard like a trail of autumn cloud; the muscles stood out like serpents from his bare arms, and his loose garment of Tyrian purple left to view a broad patch of the shaggy breast against which, as in a vise, he had crushed the ribs of the monster Gogmagog. Such as Corineus was, such were his followers; shaggy-browed, iron-sinewed, ample in stature, resolute in purpose, and ruthless in action, they waited but a sign from their chief to dash like wolves upon the homesteads of the peaceful subjects of the King, or to tear him to pieces in his own halls. Then Locrinus sadly gave way, priests whom Corineus had brought with him performed the rites that united a frowning bride to a bridegroom in a mourning habit, and the haughty Guendolen sat in the place of Esyllt.

Little love was there between Locrinus and his new queen, as you may well guess; for the daughter of Corineus was not one to win love;

but the more she saw that the heart of her husband was turned away from her, the more did she exult in the submission that her father had forced upon him, and triumph in the power that her high place gave her.

Esyllt, meanwhile, tarried sadly in the shepherd's cottage, wearying for the coming of her lord; the daily pain of his absence left her little thought for her changed fortunes, or for the lost throne; if she could only see him she thought she could be content to die, and day by day she sat upon the lonely shore looking out on the immeasurable waters, or climbed to the trackless downs, if perchance he might be coming by sea or by land; and when she came back weary and faint to the cottage, she could find little comfort in the talk of the shepherd and his wife, who told such tales of the wrath and of the strength of the great Prince Corineus, that the poor lady trembled to think of her dear lord, and lay awake half the night weeping and praying to the gods to protect him.

At length, however, King Locrinus, on pretense of hunting, contrived to steal away from Guendolen, and to visit the lonely Esyllt, and the hearts of both were refreshed, and the spark of life which was dying out in Esyllt's bosom shot up again into a bright flame, like a waning lamp newly fed with oil; and they dared even to think of a time when their troubles might be at an end, and the gods, to whom all things are possible, might give them back something of their old happiness. But because the King loved Esyllt better than his life, and because he feared everything from the jealousy of Guendolen if she should in any way discover that Esyllt lived, he fitted up a secret chamber, curiously contrived years ago by his father Brutus, for the deposit of treasure or for other need; and thither he conveyed the princess in the night, and hid her there for seven weary years. She had not been there many days, when a daughter was born to her, and care for the new life that had opened in the grave as it were, caused the princess herself to take fresh hold on life, and gave her strength to bear the privation of the blessed gifts of the sun for all those years.

The little Sabrina, it was so Esyllt named her daughter, pined not for what she knew not of; the pale light of the lamp which burnt day and night in the chamber could not ripen the color in her cheeks or the laughter on her lips as the goodly sun does; but she grew ever more sweet and fair, her one pleasure to watch the motion of her mother's hands as she busily plied the loom, counting the threads and marking with great joy the pattern as it sprung into shape under her creative fingers; and so for seven long years they lived, companions only to each other, and looking fondly for the short visit which Locrinus from time to time was able to pay them. But when the seven years were ended, news came from Cornwall that a sudden sickness had seized Corineus, and that he was dead. And Locrinus straightway resolved to divorce his Queen Guendolen, whose haughty and cruel temper made the lives of all about her bitter to them, and to bring the imprisoned Esyllt to light again, and place her once more on the throne. When Guendolen heard the purpose of the King, and that Esyllt was still alive, her anger was very fierce; but forasmuch, as there were none who loved her in Loegria, as Cornwall was far away, and in great confusion at the death of Corineus, she dissembled her wrath, and taking with her her son Madoc, she went back to her own Duchy of Cornwall, thinking of nothing but how she might revenge herself.

But Locrinus fetched home his Queen Esyllt and his little daughter Sabrina in great state, and brought them to his palace in Trinovant; and the whole land rejoiced, as the earth rejoices and covers herself with beauty, when the east wind is driven back to his caverns, and the genial western breeze dimples the lakes and calls forth the lingering flowers. But those who were near enough to see her marveled much at the pale countenance of the Queen, and at the face of the little princess, who sat like one dazzled and sorely perplexed by the side of her mother.

In truth the glory of the upper world was well nigh too much for the child, she hid herself from the light and from the sounds, and languished for the still chamber which had been her home; the crowding faces, the gay dresses, and the obsequious manners of the many attendants about the court bewildered her, and she glided about like a silent shadow after her mother, weary and faint in spirit; but as months passed on, the strangeness of things wore off, and she grew to endure, and finally to love the open air; but it was ever the paths of shady forests that pleased her most, where the sunlight came tempered through countless leaves, and pale primroses and lurking violets formed a chaplet that pleased her better than roses and lilies. Her sweet nature made her very courteous to those about her, and she learned with aptitude the arts that were taught her, so that men praised her beauty and her princely carriage; but her cheeks remained ever colorless, and the smile that played on her features like moonlight on the waters was never broken up into laughter.

And so it was, that when she was grown to be a fair damsel, and the King her father was thinking to which of the foreign princes whom the fame of her beauty had drawn to his court, he should give her in marriage, so as to strengthen his own hands and secure the throne to her, tidings came that the Lady Guendolen and Madoc her son were making ready to march eastward, and boasted that they would slay Locrinus and take Esyllt and her daughter alive.

Then the King bestirred himself, and gathering his troops marched to meet them, taking with him the Queen and the Princess, for he thought them safe nowhere but with him, neither would they let him go alone, for they saw that his soul foreboded evil, and that his heart was heavy within him. And so it was that the armies met together at a river just on the frontiers of Cambria, and a great battle was fought in which King Locrinus was slain by an arrow, and Esyllt and her daughter fell into the hands of Guendolen.

When they were brought before the daughter of Corineüs, the stern Princess gazed unmoved on the sorrow-stricken pair, no touch of pity stirring her bosom, but with fierce and angry words she reviled them, heaping insults on the head of the slain King, and triumphing savagely in her victory. To all this Esyllt said not a word, she only embraced her daughter, who clung to her in silent terror. Then Guendolen gave orders that both should be taken and flung without more ado into the river that was flowing by, and six fierce Cornish men, sons of the giants, sprung forward to seize them; but Esyllt lifted her head, and looking straight into the eyes of Guendolen, spoke to her in this wise:—

"Princess, if I have wronged thee, the gods have richly avenged thee, seeing that I did it unwillingly, yea even unwittingly. The fate thou adjudgest to me and to this child is a merciful one; I seek not to change it—it is better to fall into the power of the gods; add to it yet this favor—let not the hands of thy warriors come upon the maiden, seeing she is a Princess, and the daughter of Locrinus. Behold we go whither thou biddest us. May the gods receive us!"

So saying, she walked down the green meadow to the amber river leading her daughter by the hand, and when they came to the brink, and the murmuring water kissed their feet, the Queen Esyllt turned her face to the setting sun, silently saluting it, then folding her daughter in her arms, she plunged with her into the bosom of the stream, and no one saw them more; but the name of the Princess clung to the river, and men as they wander by the Glassy Severn dream even yet of the gentle Sabrina, dwelling in the halls of the River Gods, and ready to hearken to the cry of the innocent, and to lend her help to the oppressed.

THE HUMBLING OF JOVINIAN

(Anonymous: 13th Century)

THE famous collection of mediæval tales gathered together under the title *Deeds of the Romans (Gesta Romanorum)* was compiled in Latin by an unidentified preacher some time between the Twelfth and the Fourteenth Centuries in England. The collection comprises two hundred and fifteen stories, that "might be use d to enforce and enliven lessons from the pulpit." Each tale is written round some actual or imaginary Roman emperor. The writer was indebted for his material to the floating legends and traditions of the Middle Ages, to actual history, and to the fables and tales of the Arabs and other Oriental peoples. First printed in 1473, the tales of the *Gesta Romanorum* have been utilized time and again by Shakespeare and other writers of succeeding ages.

The present version is reprinted from the translation by C. Swan, published in London in 1824.

THE HUMBLING OF JOVINIAN

(From the *Gesta Romanorum*)

WHEN Jovinian was emperor, he had very great power, and as he lay in bed reflecting upon the extent of his dominions, his heart was elated.

"Is there," he impiously asked, "is there any other god than me?" Amid such thoughts he fell asleep.

In the morning, he reviewed his troops, and said, "My friends, after breakfast we will hunt."

Preparations being made accordingly, he set out with a large retinue. During the chase, the emperor felt such extreme oppression from the heat, that he believed his very existence depended upon a cold bath. As he anxiously looked around, he discovered a sheet of water at no great distance. "Remain here," said he to his guard, "until I have refreshed myself in yonder stream." Then spurring his steed, he rode hastily to the edge of the water. Alighting, he stripped off his clothes, and experienced the greatest pleasure from its invigorating freshness and coolness. But whilst he was thus employed, a person similar to him in every respect—in countenance and gesture—arrayed himself unperceived in the emperor's dress, and then mounting his horse, rode off to the attendants. The resemblance to the sovereign was such that no doubt was entertained of the reality; and straightway command was issued for their return to the palace.

Jovinian, however, having quitted the water, sought in every possible direction for his horse and clothes, and to his utter astonishment, could find neither. Vexed beyond measure at the circumstance (for he was completely naked, and saw no one near to assist him), he began to reflect upon what course he should pursue. "Miserable man that I am," said he, "to what a strait am I reduced! There is, I remember, a knight who lives close by; I will go to him, and command his attendance and service. I will then ride on to the palace and strictly investigate the cause of this extraordinary conduct. Some shall smart for it."

Jovinian proceeded, naked and ashamed, to the castle of the aforesaid knight, and beat loudly at the gate. The porter, without unclosing the wicket, inquired the cause of the knocking. "Open the gate," said the enraged emperor, "and you will see who I am." The gate was opened; and the porter, struck with the strange appearance he exhibited, replied, "In the name of all that is marvelous, what are you?" "I am," said he, "Jovinian, your emperor; go to your lord, and command him from me to supply the wants of his sovereign. I have lost both horse and clothes."

"Infamous ribald!" shouted the porter, "just before thy approach, the Emperor Jovinian, accompanied by the officers of his household, entered the palace. My lord both went and returned with him; and but even now sat with him at meat. But because thou hast called thyself the emperor, however madly, my lord shall know of thy presumption." The porter entered, and related what had passed. Jovinian was introduced, but the knight retained not the slightest recollection of his master, although the emperor remembered him. "Who are you?" said the knight, "and what is your name?" "I am the Emperor Jovinian," rejoined he; "canst thou have forgotten me? At such a time I promoted thee to a military command." "Why, thou most audacious scoundrel," said the knight, "darest thou call thyself the emperor? I rode with him myself to the palace, from whence I am this moment returned. But thy impudence shall not go without its reward. Flog him," said he, turning to his servants. "Flog him soundly, and drive him away."

This sentence was immediately executed, and the poor emperor, bursting into a convulsion of tears, exclaimed, "Oh, my God, is it possible that one whom I have so much honored and exalted should do this? Not content with pretending ignorance of my person, he orders these merciless villains to abuse me! However, it will not be long unavenged. There is a certain duke, one of my privy councilors, to whom I will make known my calamity. At least, he will enable me to return decently to the palace." To him, therefore, Jovinian proceeded, and the gate was opened at his knock. But the porter, beholding a naked man, exclaimed in the greatest amaze, "Friend, who are you, and why come you here in such a guise?" He replied, "I am your emperor; I have accidentally lost my clothes and my horse, and I have come for succor to your lord. Inform the duke, therefore, that I have business with him." The porter, more and more astonished, entered the hall, and told of the man outside. "Bring him in," said the duke. He was brought in, but neither did he recognize the person of the emperor. "What art thou?" was again asked, and answered as before. "Poor mad wretch," said the duke, "a short time since, I returned from the palace, where I left the very emperor thou assumest to be. But ignorant whether thou art more fool or knave, we will administer such remedy as may suit both. Carry him to prison, and feed him with bread and water." The command was no sooner delivered, than obeyed; and the following day his naked body was submitted to the lash, and again cast into the dungeon.

Thus afflicted, he gave himself up to the wretchedness of his untoward condition. In the agony of his heart, he said: "What shall I do? Oh! what will be my destiny! I am loaded with the coarsest contumely, and exposed to the malicious observation of my people. It were better to hasten immediately to my palace, and there discover myself—my wife will know me; surely, my wife will know me!" Escaping, therefore, from his confinement, he approached the palace and beat upon the gate. The same questions were repeated, and the same answers returned. "Who art thou?" said the porter. "It is strange," replied the aggrieved emperor, "it is strange that thou shouldst not know me; thou, who hast served me so long!" "Served *thee*!" returned the porter indignantly; "thou liest abominably. I have served none but the emperor." "Why," said the other, "thou knowest that I am he. Yet, though you disregard my words, go, I implore you, to the empress; communicate what I will tell thee, and by these signs, bid her send the imperial robes, of which some rogue has deprived me. The signs I tell thee of are known to none but to ourselves." "In verity," said the porter, "thou art specially mad; at this very moment my lord sits at table with the empress herself. Nevertheless, out of regard for thy singular merits, I will intimate thy declaration within; and rest assured thou wilt presently find thyself most royally beaten." The porter went accordingly, and related what he had heard. But the empress became very sorrowful, and said: "Oh, my lord, what am I to think? The most hidden passages of our lives are revealed by an obscene fellow at the gate, and repeated to me by the porter, on the strength of which he declares himself the emperor, and my espoused lord!" When the fictitious monarch was apprised of this, he commanded him to be brought in. He had no sooner entered, than a large dog, which crouched upon the hearth, and had been much cherished by him, flew at his throat, and, but for timely prevention, would have killed him. A falcon also, seated upon her perch, no sooner beheld him than she broke her jesses and flew out of the hall. Then the pretended emperor, addressing those who stood about him, said: "My friends, hear what I will ask of yon ribald. Who are you? and what do you want?" "These questions," said the suffering man, "are very strange. You know I am the emperor and master of this place." The other, turning to the nobles who sat or stood at the table, continued: "Tell me, on your allegiance, which of us two is your lord and master?" "Your majesty asks us an easy thing," replied they, "and need not to remind us of our allegiance. That obscene wretch cannot be our sovereign. You alone are he, whom we have known from childhood; and we intreat that this fellow may be severely punished as a warning to others how they give scope to their mad presumption." Then turning to the empress, the usurper said: "Tell me, my lady, on the faith you have sworn, do you know this man who calls himself thy lord and emperor?" She answered: "My lord, how can you ask such a question? Have I not known thee more than thirty years, and borne thee many children? Yet, at one thing I do admire. How can this fellow have acquired so intimate a knowledge of what has passed between us?"

The pretended emperor made no reply, but addressing the real one, said: "Friend, how darest thou to call thyself emperor? We sentence thee, for this unexampled impudence, to be drawn, without loss of time, at the tail of a horse. And if thou utterest the same words again, thou shalt be doomed to an ignominious death." He then commanded his guards to see the sentence put in force, but to preserve his life. The unfortunate emperor was now almost distracted; and urged by his despair, wished vehemently for death. "Why was I born?" he exclaimed. "My friends shun me, and my wife and children will not acknowledge me. But there is my confessor, still. To him will I go; perhaps he will recollect me, because he has often received my confessions." He went accordingly, and knocked at the window of his cell. "Who is there?" said the confessor. "The Emperor Jovinian," was the reply; "open the window and I will speak to thee." The window was opened; but no sooner had he looked out than he closed it again in great haste. "Depart from me," said he, "accursed thing: thou art not the emperor, but the devil incarnate." This completed the miseries of the persecuted man; and he tore his hair, and plucked up his beard by the roots. "Woe is me," he cried, "for what strange doom am I reserved?" At this crisis, the impious words which, in the arrogance of his heart, he had uttered crossed his recollection. Immediately he beat again at the window of the confessor's cell, and exclaimed: "For the love of Him who was suspended from the cross, hear my confession." The recluse opened the window, and said, "I will do this with pleasure"; and then Jovinian acquainted him with every particular of his past life; and principally how he had lifted himself up against his Maker.

The confession made, and absolution given, the recluse looked out of his window, and directly knew him. "Blessed be the most high God," said he, "now I do know thee. I have here a few garments: clothe thyself, and go to the palace. I trust that they also will recognize thee." The emperor did as the confessor directed. The porter opened the gate, and made a low obeisance to him. "Dost thou know me?" said he. "Very well, my lord!" replied the menial; "but I marvel that I did not observe you go out." Entering the hall of his mansion, Jovinian was received by all with a profound reverence. The strange emperor was at that time in another apartment with the queen; and a certain knight going to him, said, "My lord, there is one in the hall to whom everybody bends; he so much resembles you, that we know not which is the emperor." Hearing this, the usurper said to the empress, "Go and see if you know him." She went, and returned greatly surprised at what she saw. "Oh, my lord," said she, "I declare to you that I know not whom to trust." "Then," returned he, "I will go and determine you." And taking her hand he led her into the hall and placed her on the throne beside him. Addressing the assembly, he said, "By the oaths you have taken, declare which of us is your emperor." The empress answered: "It is incumbent on me to speak first; but heaven is my witness, that I am unable to determine which is he." And so said all. Then the feigned emperor spoke thus: "My friends, hearken! That man is your king and your lord. He exalted himself to the disparagement of his Maker; and God, therefore, scourged and hid him from your knowledge. But his repentance removes the rod; he has now made ample satisfaction, and again let your obedience wait upon him. Commend yourselves to the protection of heaven." So saying, he disappeared. The emperor gave thanks to God, and surrendering to Him all his oul, lived happily and finished his days in peace.

LLUDD AND LLEVELYS

(Anonymous: Some Time Before 14th Century)

Nor only is nothing known of the author of this story, but it is hardly possible to make a good guess within several centuries of the date of its composition. *The Mabinogion*, from which it is taken, is the title given to a collection of translations made from the Welsh by Lady Charlotte Guest some eighty years ago, in which she included twelve old Welsh romances. The literature of early Wales was extremely rich; from it sprang a host of stories, of which the most important were those treating of King Arthur and his court. In the words of Lady Guest, Welsh literature has "strong claims to be considered the cradle of European romance."

The present tale, translated by Lady Guest, is reprinted from *The Mabinogion*, Everyman's Library, by permission of the publisher, J. M. Dent and Sons.

LLUDD AND LLEVELYS

(From *The Mabinogion*)

BELI the great, the son of Manogan, had three sons, Lludd and Caswallawn, and Nynyaw; and according to the story he had a fourth son called Llevelys. And after the death of Beli, the kingdom of the Island of Britain fell into the hands of Lludd, his eldest son; and Lludd ruled prosperously, and rebuilt the walls of London, and encompassed it about with numberless towers. And after that he bade the citizens build houses therein, such as no houses in the kingdoms could, equal. And moreover he was a mighty warrior, and generous and liberal in giving meat and drink to all that sought them. And though he had many castles and cities this one loved he more than any. And he dwelt therein most part of the year, and therefore was it called Caer Lludd, and at last Caer London. And after the stranger-race came there, it was called London, or Lwndrys.

Lludd loved Llevelys best of all his brothers, because he was a wise and discreet man. Having heard that the king of France had died leaving no heir except a daughter, and that he had left all his possessions in her hands, he came to Lludd his brother, to beseech his counsel and aid. And that not so much for his own welfare, as to seek to add to the glory and honor and dignity of his kindred, if he might go to France to woo the maiden for his wife. And forthwith his brother conferred with him, and this counsel was pleasing unto him.

So he prepared ships and filled them with armed knights, and set forth towards France. And as soon as they had landed, they sent messengers to show the nobles of France the cause of the embassy. And by the joint counsel of the nobles of France and of the princes, the maiden was given to Llevelys, and the crown of the kingdom with her. And thenceforth he ruled the land discreetly, and wisely, and happily, as long as his life lasted.

After a space of time had passed, three plagues fell on the Island of Britain, such as none in the islands had ever seen the like of. The first was a certain race that came, and was called the Coranians; and so great was their knowledge, that there was no discourse upon the face of the Island, however low it might be spoken, but what, if the wind met it, it was known to them. And through this they could not be injured.

The second plague was a shriek which came on every May-eve, over every hearth in the Island of Britain. And this went through people's hearts, and so scared them that men lost their hue and their strength, and the women their children, and the young men and the maidens lost their senses, and all the animals and trees and the earth and the waters were left barren.

The third plague was, that however much of provisions and food might be prepared in the king's courts, were there even so much as a year's provision of meat and drink, none of it could ever be found, except what was consumed in the first night. And two of these plagues, no one ever knew their cause, therefore was there better hope of being freed from the first than the second and third.

And thereupon King Lludd felt great sorrow and care, because that he knew not how he might be freed from these plagues. And he called to him all the nobles of his kingdom, and asked counsel of them what they should do against these afflictions. And by the common counsel of the nobles, Lludd the son of Beli went to Llevelys his brother, king of France, for he was a man great of counsel and wisdom, to seek his advice.

And they made ready a fleet, and that in secret and in silence, lest that race should know the cause of their errand, or any besides the king and his counselors. And when they were made ready, they went into their ships, Lludd and those whom he chose with him. And they began to cleave the seas towards France.

And when these tidings came to Llevelys, seeing that he know not the cause of his brother's ships, he came on the other side to meet him, and with him was a fleet vast of size. And when Lludd saw this, he left all the ships out upon the sea except one only; and in that one he came to meet his brother, and he likewise with a single ship came to meet him. And when they were come together, each put his arms about the other's neck, and they welcomed each other with brotherly love.

After that Lludd had shown his brother the cause of his errand, Llevelys said that he himself knew the cause of the coming to those lands. And they took counsel together to discourse on the matter otherwise than thus, in order that the wind might not catch their words, nor the Coranians know what they might say. Then Llevelys caused a long horn to be made of brass, and through this horn they discoursed. But whatsoever words they spoke through this horn, one to the other, neither of them could hear any other but harsh and hostile words. And when Llevelys saw this, and that there was a demon thwarting them and disturbing through this horn, he caused wine to be put therein to wash it. And through the virtue of the wine the demon was driven out of the horn. And when their discourse was unobstructed, Llevelys told his brother that he would give him some insects whereof he should keep some to breed, lest by chance the like affliction might come a second time. And other of these insects he should take and bruise in water. And he assured him that it would have power to destroy the race of the Coranians. That is to say, that when he came home to his kingdom he should call together all the people both of his own race and of the race of the Coranians for a conference, as though with the intent of making peace between them; and that when they were all together, he should take this charmed water, and cast it over all alike. And he assured him that the water would poison the race of the Coranians, but that it would not slay or harm those of his own race.

"And the second plague," said he, "that is in thy dominion, behold it is a dragon. And another dragon of a foreign race is fighting with it, and striving to overcome it. And therefore does your dragon make a fearful outcry. And on this wise mayest thou come to know this. After thou hast returned home, cause the Island to be measured in its length and breadth, and in the place where thou dost find the exact central point, there cause a pit to be dug, and cause a cauldron full of the best mead that can be made to be put in the pit, with a covering of satin over the face of the cauldron. And then, in thine own person do thou remain there watching, and thou wilt see the dragon fighting in the form of terrific animals. And at length they will take the form of dragons in the air. And last of all, after wearying themselves with fierce and furious fighting, they will fall in the form of two pigs upon the covering, and they will sink in, and the covering with them, and they will draw it down to the very bottom of the cauldron. And they will drink up the whole of the mead; and after that they will sleep. Thereupon do thou immediately fold the covering around them, and bury them in a kistvaen, in the strongest place thou hast in thy dominions, and hide them in the earth. And as long as they shall bide in that strong place no plague shall come to the Island of Britain from elsewhere.

"The cause of the third plague," said he, "is a mighty man of magic, who takes thy meat and thy drink and thy store. And he through illusions and charms causes every one to sleep. Therefore it is needful for thee in thy own person to watch thy food and thy provisions. And lest he should overcome thee with sleep, be there a cauldron of cold water by thy side, and when thou art oppressed with sleep, plunge into the cauldron."

Then Lludd returned back unto his land. And immediately he summoned to him the whole of his own race and of the Coranians. And as Llevelys had taught him, he bruised the insects in water, the which he cast over them all together, and forthwith it destroyed the whole tribe of the Coranians, without hurt to any of the Britons.

And some time after this, Lludd caused the Island to be measured in its length and in its breadth. And in Oxford he found the central point, and in that place he caused the earth to be dug, and in that pit a cauldron to be set, full of the best mead that could be made, and a covering of satin over the face of it. And he himself watched that night. And while he was there, he beheld the dragons fighting. And when they were weary they fell, and came down upon the top of the satin, and drew it with them to the bottom of the cauldron. And when they had drunk the mead they slept. And in their sleep, Lludd folded the covering around them, and in the securest place he had in Snowdon, he hid them in a kistvaen. Now after that this spot was called Dinas Emreis, but before that, Dinas Ffaraon. And thus the fierce outcry ceased in his dominions.

And when this was ended, King Lludd caused an exceeding great banquet to be prepared. And when it was ready, he placed a vessel of cold water by his side, and he in his own proper person watched it. And as he abode thus clad with arms, about the third watch of the night, lo, he heard many surpassing fascinations and various songs. And drowsiness urged him to sleep. Upon this, lest he should be hindered from his purpose and be overcome by sleep, he went often into the water. And at last, behold, a man of vast size, clad in strong, heavy armor, came in, bearing a hamper. And, as he was wont, he put all the food and provisions of meat and drink into the hamper, and proceeded to go with it forth. And nothing was ever more wonderful to Lludd, than that the hamper should hold so much.

And thereupon King Lludd went after him and spoke unto him thus. "Stop, stop," said he, "though thou hast done many insults and much spoil erewhile, thou shalt not do so any more, unless thy skill in arms and thy prowess be greater than mine."

Then he instantly put down the hamper on the floor, and awaited him. And a fierce encounter was between them, so that the glittering fire flew out from their arms. And at last Lludd grappled with him, and fate bestowed the victory on Lludd. And he threw the plague to the earth. And after he had overcome him by strength and might, he besought his mercy. "How can I grant thee mercy," said the king, "after all the many injuries and wrongs that thou has done me?" "All the losses that ever I have caused thee," said he, "I will make the atonement for equal to what I have taken. And I will never do the like from this time forth. But thy faithful vassal will I be." And the king accepted this from him.

And thus Lludd freed the Island of Britain from the three plagues. And from thenceforth until the end of his life, in prosperous peace did Lludd the son of Beli rule the Island of Britain. And this Tale is called the Story of Lludd and Llevelys. And thus it ends.

SIR THOMAS MALORY

(Flourished Late 15th Century)

PRACTICALLY nothing is known of this first great writer of English prose romance. Malory's significance in the development of the English language is, for our purposes, not so vital a matter as his contribution to the art of story-telling. His vast compilation, which is a rewritten version of the outstanding episodes in the Arthurian cycle, was printed by Caxton in 1485, and, due to the rapid spread of books through the recently invented printing-press, Malory's influence was far greater than it would otherwise have been. "Malory," says Edmund Gosse, "tinges the whole English character; he is the primal fount of our passion for adventure, and of our love for active chivalry."

The present version is reprinted from *Malory's History of King Arthur and the Quest of the Holy Grail*, London, 1886. There is no title in the original text.

LAUNCELOT'S TOURNEY

(From the *Morte d'Arthur*)

AND then the Queen let make a privy dinner in the city of London, unto the knights of the Round Table; and all was to show outward that she had a great joy in all other knights of the Round Table, as she had in Sir Launcelot. All only at that dinner she had Sir Gawaine and his brethren; that is to say, Sir Agravaine, Sir Gaheris, Sir Gareth, and Sir Mordred. Also there was Sir Bors de Ganis, Sir Blamor de Ganis, Sir Bleoberis de Ganis, Sir Galihud, Sir Galihodin, Sir Ector de Maris, Sir Lionel, Sir Palomides, and his brother, Sir Safre; la Cote mal Tail, Sir Persuant, Sir Ironside, Sir Brandiles, Sir Kaye the seneschal, Sir Mador de la Port, Sir Patrice a knight of Ireland, Sir Aliducke, Sir Astomore, and Sir Pinell le Savage, the which was cousin unto Sir Lamoracke de Galis, the good knight, the which Sir Gawaine and brethren slew by treason. And so these knights should dine with the Queen in a privy place by themselves; and there was made a great feast of all manner of dainty meats and drinks. But Sir Gawaine had a custom that he used daily at dinner and at supper, that he loved well all manner of fruits, and in especial apples and pears; and, therefore, whosoever dined of feasted, Sir Gawaine would commonly purvey for good fruit for him: and so did the Queen; for, to please Sir Gawaine, she let purvey for him of all manner of fruits. For Sir Gawaine was a passing hot knight of nature; and this Sir Pinell hated Sir Gawaine, because of his kinsman, Sir Lamoracke de Galis: and, therefore, for pure envy and hate, Sir Pinell poisoned certain apples for to poison Sir Gawaine withal. And so this was well unto the end of the meat; and so it befell, by misfortune, that a good knight, named Sir Patrice, cousin unto Sir Mador de la Port, took one of the poisoned apples: and, when he had eaten it, he swelled till he burst; and there Sir Patrice fell down dead suddenly among them. Then every knight leaped from the board, ashamed, and enraged for wrath nigh out of their wits; for they wist not what to say, considering that Queen Guenever made the feast and dinner, they all had suspicion upon her. "My lady, the Queen," said Sir Gawaine, "wit ye well, madam, that this dinner was made for me: for all folks, that know my conditions, understand well that I love fruit; and now I see well I had been near slain: therefore, madam, I dread me least ye will be shamed." Then the Queen stood still, and was right sore abashed, that she wist not what to say. "This shall not be ended so," said Sir Mador de la Port; "for here have I lost a full noble knight of my blood: and, therefore, upon this shame and despite I will be revenged to the uttermost." And thereupon Sir Mador appealed Queen Guenever of the death of his cousin, Sir Patrice. Then stood they all still, that none of them would speak a word against him; for they had a great suspicion unto Queen Guenever, because she let make the dinner. And the Queen was so sore abashed, that she could none otherwise do, but wept so heartily, that she fell in a swoon. With this noise and sudden cry came unto them King Arthur, and marveled greatly what it might be; and, when he wist of their trouble, and the sudden death of that good knight, Sir Patrice, he was a passing heavy man.

And ever Sir Mador stood still before King Arthur, and ever he appealed Queen Guenever of treason. For the custom was such at that time, that all manner of shameful death was called treason. "Fair lords," said King Arthur, "me repenteth sore of this trouble, but the cause is so, we may not have to do in this matter; for I must be a rightful judge, and that repenteth me that I may not do battle for my wife; for, as I deem, this deed came never of her, and therefore I suppose we shall not be all destitute, but that some good knight shall put his body in jeopardy, rather than she should be burnt in a wrong quarrel. And, therefore, Sir Mador, be not so hasty; for it may happen she shall not be all friendless: and, therefore, desire thou the day of battle, and she shall purvey her of some good knight, which shall answer you, or else it were to me great shame, and unto all my court." "My gracious lord," said Sir Mador, "ye must hold me excused: for, though ye be our King in that degree, ye are but a knight as we are, and ye are sworn unto knighthood as we are: and, therefore, I pray you, that ye will not be displeased; for there is none of the twenty knights that were bidden for to come unto this dinner, but all they have great suspicion unto the Queen. What say ye all, my lords?" said Sir Mador. Then they answered by and by, and said, that they "could not excuse the Queen; for why she made the dinner: and either it must come by her, or by her servants." "Alas!" said the Queen, "I made this dinner for a good intent, and never for any evil (so God help me in my right!) as I was never purposed to do such evil deeds, and that I report me unto God." "My lord, the King," said Sir Mador, "I require you heartily, as ye be a righteous king, give me a day that I may have justice." "Well," said King Arthur

"I give you a day this day fifteen days, that ye be ready armed on horseback in the meadow beside Westminster; and, if it so fall that there be any knight to encounter with you, there may ye do your best, and God speed the right: and, if it so fall that there be no knight at that day, then must my Queen be burnt, and there shall ye be ready to have her judgment." "Well I am answered," said Sir Mador; and every knight went where it liked him. So, when the King and the Queen were together, the King asked the Queen how this case befell. Then answered the Queen, "So God me help, I wot not how, or in what manner." "Where is Sir Launcelot?" said King Arthur. "An he were here, he would not grudge to do battle for you." "Sir," said the Queen, "I cannot tell you where he is; but his brother, and all his kinsmen, deem that he is not within this realm." "That sore repenteth me," said King Arthur; "for an he were here, he would full soon stint this strife. Then I will counsel you," said the King, "that ye go unto Sir Bors, and pray him to do that battle for you for Sir Launcelot's sake: and, upon my life, he will not refuse you. For right well I perceive," said King Arthur, "that none of all those twenty knights, without more, that were with you in fellowship together at your dinner, where Sir Patrice was so traitorously slain, that will do battle for you, nor none of them will say well of you; and that shall be great slander for you in this court." "Alas!" said the Queen, "I cannot do withal: but now I miss Sir Launcelot; for, an he were here, he would put me full soon unto my heart's ease." "What aileth you," said King Arthur, "that ye cannot keep Sir Launcelot on your side? For wit ye well," said King Arthur, "whosoever hath the noble knight, Sir Launcelot, on his part, hath the most man of worship in the world on his side. Now, go your way," said the King unto the Queen, "and require Sir Bors to do battle for you for Sir Launcelot's sake."

So the Queen departed from the King, and sent for Sir Bors into her chamber; and when he was come, she besought him of succor. "Madam," said he, "what would ye that I do? for I may not which my worship have to do in this matter, because I was at the same dinner, for dread that any of those knights would have me in suspicion. Also, madam," said Sir Bors, "now miss ye Sir Launcelot; for he would not have failed you, neither in right, nor yet in wrong, as ye have well proved when ye have been in danger; and now have ye driven him out of this country, by whom ye and we all were daily worshiped. Therefore, madam, I greatly marvel me how ye dare for shame require me to do any thing for you, insomuch as ye have chased him out of your country, by whom I was borne up and honored." "Alas! fair knight," said the Queen, "I put me wholly in your grace; and all that is done amiss I will amend, as ye will counsel me." And therewith she kneeled down upon both her knees, and besought Sir Bors to have mercy upon her, "for I shall have a shameful death, and thereto I never offended." Right so came King Arthur, and found the Queen kneeling before Sir Bors. Then Sir Bors took her up, and said, "Madam, ye do to me great dishonor." "Ah! gentle knight," said King Arthur, "have mercy upon my Queen, for I am now in a certain that she is now untruly defamed; and, therefore, courteous knight," said the King, "promise her to do battle for her: I require you for the love of Sir Launcelot." "My lord," said Sir Bors, "ye require me of the greatest thing that any man may require me; and wit ye well if I grant to do battle for the Queen, I shall wrath many of my fellowship of the Round Table; but, as for that," said Sir Bors, "I will grant my lord, for my lord Sir Launcelot's sake, and for your sake, I will at that day be the Queen's champion, unless that there come by adventure a better knight than I am to do battle for her." "Will ye promise this," said the King, "by your faith?" "Yes, sir," said Sir Bors, "of that will I not fail you, nor her both: but if that there come a better knight than I am, then shall he have the battle." Then were the King and the Queen passing glad, thanked him heartily, and so departed.

So then Sir Bors departed secretly upon a day, and rode unto Sir Launcelot there as he was with the hermit by Sir Brastias, and told him of all his adventures. "Ah! Jesu," said Sir Launcelot, "this is happily come as I would have it, and therefore I pray you make you ready to do battle; but look that ye tarry till ye see me come as long as ye may, for I am sure Sir Mador is a hot knight, if he be chafed, for the more ye suffer him, the hastier will he be to do battle." "Sir," said Sir Bors, "let me deal with him; doubt ye not ye shall have all your will." Then departed Sir Bors from him, and came unto the court again. Then was it noised in all the court that Sir Bors should do battle for the Queen; wherefore many knights were greatly displeased with him, that he should take upon him to do battle in the Queen's quarrel; for there were but few knights in the court but that they deemed the Queen was in the wrong, and that she had done that treason. So Sir Bors answered thus unto his fellows of the Round Table, "Wit ye well, my fair lords, it were shame unto us all, and we suffered to see the most noble queen of the world for to be shamed openly, considering that her lord and our lord is the man of most worship of the world, and the most christened; and he hath always worshiped us all in all places." Many knights anwered him again, and said, "As for our most noble King Arthur, we love him and honor him as well as ye do; but as for Queen Guenever, we love her not, for because she is a destroyer of good knights." "Fair lords," said Sir Bors, "me seemeth, ye say, not as ye should say, for never yet in all my days knew I, nor heard say, that ever she was a destroyer of any good knight; but at all times as far as I ever could know, she was always a maintainer of good knights; and always she hath been large and free of her goods to all good knights, and the most bounteous lady of her gifts and her good grace that ever I saw, or heard speak of; and therefore it were great shame (said Sir Bors) unto us all to our most noble King's wife, if we suffer her to be shamefully slain: and wit ye well (said Sir Bors) I will not suffer it; for I dare say so much the Queen is not guilty of Sir Patrice's death, for she ought him never none evil will, nor none of the twenty knights that were at that dinner; for I dare well say that it was for good love she had us to dinner, and not for no malice, and that I doubt not shall be proved hereafter; for howsoever the game goeth, there was treason among some of us." Then some said to Sir Bors, "We may well believe your words." And so some of them were well pleased, and some were not pleased.

The day came on fast until the even that the battle should be. Then the Queen sent for Sir Bors, and asked him "how he was disposed." "Truly, madam," said he, "I am disposed in likewise as I promised you; that is to say, I shall not fail you, unless by adventure there come a better knight than I to do battle for you; then, madam, am I discharged of my promise." "Will ye," said the Queen, "that I tell my lord, King Arthur, thus?" "Do as it shall please you, madam," said Sir Bors. Then the Queen went unto the King, and told him the answer of Sir Bors. "Have ye no doubt," said the King, "of Sir Bors, for I call him now one of the best knights of the world, and the most profitablest man; and this is past forth until the morrow." And the King and the Queen, and all the knights that were there at that time, drew them to the meadow beside Winchester, whereas the battle should be. And so when the King was come with the Queen, and many knights of the Round Table, then the Queen was put there in the constable's ward, and there was made a great fire about the iron stake, that an Sir Mador de la Port had the better she should be burnt; such a custom was used in those days, that neither for favor, nor for love, nor for affinity, there should be none other but right wise judgment as well upon a King as upon a knight, as well upon a Queen as upon another poor lady.

So in the meanwhile came in Sir Mador de la Port, and took the oath before the King, that Queen Guenever did this treason unto his cousin, Sir Patrice, and unto his oath he would prove it with his body, hand for hand, who that would say the contrary thereto. Right so came Sir Bors de Ganis, and said "that as for Queen Guenever she is in the right, and that will I make good with my hands, that she is not culpable of this treason that is put upon her." "Then make thee ready," said Sir Mador, "and we shall soon prove whether thou be in the right or I." "Sir," said Sir Bors, "wit ye well I know thee for a good knight, not for then I shall not fear thee so greatly, but I trust unto Almighty God, my Maker, I shall be able enough to withstand thy malice; but thus much have I promised my lord, King Arthur, and my lady, the Queen, that I shall do battle for her in this case to the uttermost, only that there came a better knight than I am, and discharged me." "Is that all?" said Sir Mador. "Either come thou off and do battle with me, or else say nay." "Take your horse," said Sir Bors, "and as I suppose ye shall not tarry long, but that ye shall be answered." Then either departed to their tents, and made them ready to mount upon horseback as they thought best. And anon Sir Mador de la Port came into the field with his shield on his shoulder, and a spear in his hand, and so rode about the place, crying unto King Arthur, "Bid your champion come forth an he dare." Then was Sir Bors ashamed, and took his horse, and came to the list end; and then was he ware whereas came out of a wood there fast by, a knight, all armed at all points, upon a white horse, with a strong shield and of strange arms; and he came riding all that he might run. And so he came to Sir Bors, and said, "Fair knight, I pray you, be not displeased, for here must a better knight than ye are have this battle; therefore I pray you to withdraw you; for I would ye knew I have had this day a right great journey, and this battle ought to be mine, and so I promised you when I spake with you last, and with all my heart I thank you for your good will." Then Sir Bors rode unto King Arthur, and told him how there was a knight come that would have the battle for to fight for the Queen. "What knight is he?" said King Arthur. "I cannot show you," said Sir Bors, "but such a covenant made he with me for to be here this day. Now, my lord," said Sir Bors, "here am I discharged."

Then the King called unto the knight, and asked him "if he would fight for the Queen?" Then he answered unto the King, "Therefore came I hither; and, therefore, Sir King," he said, "tarry me no longer, for I may not tarry; for anon as I have finished this battle, I must depart hence, for I have to do many matters elsewhere: for wit ye well," said that knight, "this is dishonor unto you, all knights of the Round Table, to see and know so noble a lady and so courteous a Queen, as Queen Guenever is, thus to be rebuked and shamed among you." Then marveled they all what knight that might be, that so took the battle upon him; but there was not one that knew him but if it were Sir Bors. "Then," said Sir Mador de la Port unto the King, "now let me wit with whom I shall have to do withal." And then they rode to the list's end, and there they couched their spears, and ran the one against the other with all their mights: and Sir Mador's spear brake all to pieces; but Sir Launcelot's spear held, and bare Sir Mador's horse and all backward to the ground, and had a great fall; but mightily and suddenly he avoided his horse, and dressed his shield before him, and then drew his sword, and bade that other knight alight and do battle with him on foot. Then that knight descended lightly from his horse like a valiant man, and put his shield afore him, and drew out his sword. And so they came eagerly to battle, and either gave other many sad

strokes, tracing and traversing, racing and foyning, and hurtling together with their swords, as they had been two wild boars.

Thus were they fighting nigh an hour; for this Sir Mador was a full
strong knight, and mightily proved in many strong battles. But, at the
last, the knight smote Sir Mador groveling upon the ground, and the
knight stepped near him for to have pulled Sir Mador flat-long upon
the ground. And therewith, all suddenly, Sir Mador arose; and, in his
arising, he smote that knight through the thigh, that the blood ran out
right fiercely. And when he felt himself so wounded, and saw his blood,
he let him arise upon his feet, and then he gave him such a buffet upon
the helm that he fell flat-long to the ground. And therewith he strode
to him, for to have pulled off his helm from his head; and then Sir
Mador prayed that knight to save his life; and so he yielded him as an
overcome knight, and released the Queen of his quarrel. "I will not
grant thee life," said the knight, "but only that you freely release the
Queen forever, and that no manner of mention be made upon Sir
Patrice's tomb that ever Queen Guenever consented to that treason."
"All this shall be done," said Sir Mador; "and clearly I discharge my
quarrel forever." Then the knights' porters of the list took up Sir Mador, and led him to his tent; and the other went straight to the stairfoot, whereas King Arthur sat. And by that time was the Queen come
unto the King, and either kissed other lovingly. And, when the King
saw that knight, he stooped unto him, and thanked him; and in likewise did the Queen: and then the King prayed him to pull off his helm,
and to rest him, and to take a sup of wine. And then he put off his helm
to drink, and then every knight knew that he was the noble knight, Sir
Launcelot.

ROBERT GREENE

(1560?—1592)

GREENE was born at Norwich about 1560. He went both to Cambridge and Oxford, and then seems to have lived a wild and irregular
life in London. He wrote plays, pamphlets, novels and stories and
despite his popularity he died in poverty at an early age. Greene was
one of the few Elizabethan writers who turned his hand to the composition of short tales. Two of his romances contain several examples,
and here and there in his other writings he has introduced a story in
the style of *Roberto's Tale*. In an age that had not learned to copy the
technical finish of the Italians, Greene managed, as this story shows,
to surpass most of his predecessors in the art of elimination.

ROBERTO'S TALE

(From *Greene's Groatsworth of Wit Bought with a Million of Repentance*)

IN the North parts there dwelt an old squire that had a young daughter his heir, who had (as I know, Madam Lamilia, you have had) many youthful gentlemen that long time sued to obtain her love. But she, knowing her own perfection (as women are by nature proud), would not to any of them vouchsafe favor, insomuch that they, perceiving her relentless, showed themselves not altogether witless, but left her to her fortune when they found her frowardness. At last it fortuned, among other strangers, a farmer's son visited her father's house, on whom, at the first sight, she was enamored; he likewise on her. Tokens of love passed between them; either acquainted other's parents of their choice, and they kindly gave their consent. Short tale to make, married they were, and great solemnity was at the wedding feast.

A young gentleman that had been long a suitor to her, vexing that the son of a farmer should be so preferred, cast in his mind by what means, to mar their merriment, he might steal away the bride. Hereupon he confers with an old beldam called Mother Gunby dwelling thereby, whose counsel being taken, he fell to his practise and drift, and proceeded thus. In the afternoon, when dancers were very busy, he takes the bride by the hand and after a turn or two tells her in her ear he has a secret to impart unto her, appointing her in any wise, in the evening, to find a time to confer with him. She promised she would, and so they parted. Then goes he to the bridegroom and with protestations of entire affection, protests the great sorrow he takes at that which he must utter, whereon depended his especial credit, if it were known the matter by him should be discovered. After the bridegroom's promise of secrecy, the gentleman tells him that a friend of his received that morning from the bride a letter, wherein she willed him with some sixteen horse to await her coming at a park side; for that she detested him in her heart as a base country hind, whom her father compelled her to marry. The bridegroom, almost out of his wits, began to bite his lip. "Nay," said the gentleman, "if you will by me be advised, you shall save her credit, win her by kindness, and yet prevent her wanton complot." "As how?" said the bridegroom. "Marry, thus," said the gentleman: "In the evening (for till the guests be gone she intends not to gad) get you on horseback, and seem to be of the company that attends her coming. I am appointed to bring her from the house to the park, and from thence fetch a winding compass of a mile about, but to turn unto old Mother Gunby's house, where her lover (my friend) abides. When she alights, I will conduct her to a chamber far from his lodging, but when the lights are out and she expecting her adulterous copes-mate, yourself (as reason is) shall prove her bedfellow, where privately you may reprove her, and in the morning early return home without trouble. As for the gentleman my friend, I will excuse her absence to him by saying, She mocked thee with her maid instead of herself, whom, when I knew at her lighting, I disdained to bring her unto his presence." The bridegroom gave his hand it should be so.

Now by the way we must understand this Mother Gunby had a daughter who all that day sat heavily at home with a willow garland, for that the bridegroom (if he had dealt faithfully) should have wedded her before any other. But men, Lamilia, are inconstant: money nowadays makes the match, or else the match is marred. But to the matter: the bridegroom and the gentleman thus agreed. He took his time, conferred with the bride, persuaded her that her husband notwithstanding his fair show at the marriage had sworn to his old sweetheart, neighbor Gunby's daughter, to be that night her bedfellow, and if she would bring her father, his father and her friends to the house at midnight, they should find it so. At this the young gentlewoman, inwardly vexed to be by a peasant so abused, promised, if she saw likelihood of his slipping away, that then she would do as he directed.

All this thus sorting, the old woman's daughter was trickly attired, ready to furnish this pageant, for her old mother provided all things necessary. Well, supper past, dancing ended, all the guests would home, and the bridegroom pretending to bring some friend of his home, got his horse and to the park side he rode, and stayed with the horsemen that attended the gentleman. Anon came Marian like mistress bride, and, mounted behind the gentleman, away they passed, fetched their compass, and at last alighted at an old wife's house, where suddenly she is conveyed to her chamber, and the bridegroom sent to keep her company; where he had scarce devised how to begin his exhortation, but the father of his bride knocked at the chamber door. At which being somewhat amazed yet thinking to turn it to a jest, sith his wife (as he thought) was in bed with him, he opened the door saying, "Father, you are heartily welcome. I wonder how you found us out here. This device to remove ourselves was with my wife's consent, that we might rest quietly, without the maids and bachelors disturbing us."

"But where is your wife?" said the gentleman.

"Why, here in bed," quoth the other.

"My daughter had been your wife, for sure I am to-day she was given you in marriage."

"You are merrily disposed," said the bridegroom. "What! Think you I have another wife?"

"I think but as you speak," quoth the gentleman, "for my daughter is below, and you say your wife is in the bed."

"Below!" said he. "You are a merry man," And with that, casting on a night-gown, he went down where, when he saw his wife, the gentleman his father, and a number of his friends assembled, he was so confounded that how to behave himself he knew not, only he cried out that he was deceived. At this the old woman arrived, and making herself ignorant of all the whole matter, inquires the cause of that sudden tumult. When she was told the new bridegroom was found in bed with her daughter, she exclaimed against so great an injury. Marian was called *in quorum;* she justified it was by his allurement. He, being condemned by all their consents, was judged unworthy to have the gentlewoman unto his wife, and compelled (for escaping of punishment) to marry Marian; and the young gentleman (for his care in discovering the farmer's lewdness) was recompensed with the gentlewoman's everduring love.

DANIEL DEFOE

(1659?—1731)

DANIEL FOE—later changed to Defoe—was born in London, probably in 1659, of a lower middle-class family of Dissenters. He lived an active life as a hack-writer, earning a livelihood for the most part by writing political pamphlets, satires—in a word paid propaganda—for one or other of the powerful parties. He was also engaged in business, and edited a periodical for nine years. He was once imprisoned for two years because of his bitter satire, *The Shortest Way with Dissenters.* It has not yet been possible to identify all his very numerous writings. It was not until he reached the age of sixty that he began to write the works by which he is best known. The first of these was *Robinson Crusoe,* celebrated as one of the world's favorite books. But some years earlier he had written a few sketches, the best of which appears in the following pages. It is a most convincing bit of realistic writing. It was first published in 1706 in pamphlet form, and later revised.

The present is a reprint from the latest revised edition, in which spelling and punctuation have been modernized.

TRUE RELATION OF THE APPARITION OF ONE MRS. VEAL

THIS thing is so rare in all its circumstances, and on so good authority, that my reading and conversation have not given me anything like it. It is fit to gratify the most ingenious and serious inquirer. Mrs. Bargrave is the person to whom Mrs. Veal appeared after her death; she is my intimate friend, and I can avouch for her reputation for these fifteen or sixteen years, on my own knowledge; and I can affirm the good character she had from her youth to the time of my acquaintance. Though, since this relation, she is calumniated by some people that are friends to the brother of Mrs. Veal who appeared to think the relation of this appearance to be a reflection, and endeavor what they can to blast Mrs. Bargrave's reputation and to laugh the story out of countenance. But by the circumstances thereof, and the cheerful disposition of Mrs. Bargrave, notwithstanding the ill usage of a very wicked husband, there is not yet the least sign of dejection in her face; nor did I ever hear her let fall a desponding or murmuring expression; nay, not when actually under her husband's barbarity, which I have been a witness to, and several other persons of undoubted reputation.

Now you must know Mrs. Veal was a maiden gentlewoman of about thirty years of age, and for some years past had been troubled with fits, which were perceived coming on her by her going off from her discourse very abruptly to some impertinence. She was maintained by an only brother, and kept his house in Dover. She was a very pious woman, and her brother a very sober man, to all appearance; but now he does all he can to null and quash the story. Mrs. Veal was intimately acquainted with Mrs. Bargrave from her childhood. Mrs. Veal's circumstances were then mean; her father did not take care of his children as he ought, so that they were exposed to hardships. And Mrs. Bargrave in those days had as unkind a father, though she wanted neither for food nor clothing; while Mrs. Veal wanted for both, insomuch that she would often say, "Mrs. Bargrave, you are not only the best, but the only friend I have in the world; and no circumstance of life shall ever dissolve my friendship." They would often condole each other's adverse fortunes, and read together *Drelincourt upon Death*, and other books; and so, like two Christian friends, they comforted each other under their sorrow.

Some time after, Mr. Veal's friends got him a place in the custom-house at Dover, which occasioned Mrs. Veal, by little and little, to fall off from her intimacy with Mrs. Bargrave, though there was never any such thing as a quarrel; but an indifference came on by degrees, till at last Mrs. Bargrave had not seen her in two years and a half, though above a twelvemonth of the time Mrs. Bargrave hath been absent from Dover, and this last half-year has been in Canterbury about two months of the time, dwelling in a house of her own.

In this house, in the eighth of September, one thousand seven hundred and five, she was sitting alone in the forenoon, thinking over her unfortunate life, and arguing herself into a due resignation to Providence, though her condition seemed hard: "And," said she, "I have been provided for hitherto, and doubt not but I shall be still, and am well satisfied that my afflictions shall end when it is most fit for me."

And then took up her sewing work, which she had no sooner done but she hears a knocking at the door; she went to see who was there, and this proved to be Mrs. Veal, her old friend, who was in a riding habit. At that moment of time the clock struck twelve at noon.

"Madam," says Mrs. Bargrave, "I am surprised to see you, you who have been so long a stranger"; but told her she was glad to see her, and offered to salute her, which Mrs. Veal complied with, till their lips almost touched, and then Mrs. Veal drew her hand across her own eyes, and said, "I am not very well," and so waived it. She told Mrs. Bargrave she was going a journey, and had a great mind to see her first. "But," says Mrs. Bargrave, "how can you take a journey alone? I am amazed at it, because I know you have a fond brother." "Oh," says Mrs. Veal, "I gave my brother the slip, and came away, because I had so great a desire to see you before I took my journey." So Mrs. Bargrave went in with her into another room within the first, and Mrs. Veal sat her down in an elbow-chair, in which Mrs. Bargrave was sitting when she heard Mrs. Veal knock. "Then," says Mrs. Veal, "my dear friend, I am come to renew our old friendship again, and beg your pardon for my breach of it; and if you can forgive me, you are the best of women." "Oh," says Mrs. Bargrave, "do not mention such a thing; I have not had an uneasy thought about it." "What did you think of me?" says Mrs. Veal. Says Mrs. Bargrave, "I thought you were like the rest of the world, and that prosperity had made you forget yourself and me." Then Mrs. Veal reminded Mrs. Bargrave of the many friendly offices she did her in former days, and much of the conversation they had with each other in the times of their adversity; what books they read, and what comfort in particular they received from Drelincourt's *Book of Death*, which was the best; she said, on the subject ever wrote. She also mentioned Dr. Sherlock, and two Dutch books, which were translated, wrote upon death, and several others. But Drelincourt, she said, had the clearest notions of death and of the future state of any who had handled that subject. Then she asked Mrs. Bargrave whether she had Drelincourt. She said, "Yes." Says Mrs. Veal, "Fetch it." And so Mrs. Bargrave goes upstairs and brings it down. Says Mrs. Veal, "Dear Mrs. Bargrave, if the eyes of our faith were as open as the eyes of our body, we should see numbers of angels about us for our guard. The notions we have of Heaven now are nothing like what it is, as Drelincourt says; therefore be comforted under your afflictions, and believe that the Almighty has a particular regard to you, and that your afflictions are marks of God's favor; and when they have done the business they are sent for, they shall be removed from you. And believe me, my dear friend, believe what I say to you, one minute of future happiness will infinitely reward you for all your sufferings. For I can never believe" (and claps her hand upon her knee with great earnestness, which, indeed, ran through most of her discourse) "that ever God will suffer you to spend all your days in this afflicted state. But be assured that your afflictions shall leave you, or you them, in a short time." She spake in that pathetical and heavenly manner that Mrs. Bargrave wept several times, she was so deeply affected with it.

Then Mrs. Veal mentioned Doctor Kendrick's *Ascetic*, at the end of which he gives an account of the lives of the primitive Christians. Their pattern she recommended to our imitation, and said, "Their conversation was not like this of our age. For now," says she, "there is nothing but vain, frothy discourse, which is far different from theirs. Theirs was to edification, and to build one another up in faith, so that they were not as we are, nor are we as they were. But," said she, "we ought to do as they did; there was a hearty friendship among them; but where is it now to be found?" Says Mrs. Bargrave, "It hard is indeed to find a true friend in these days." Says Mrs. Veal, "Mrs. Norris has a fine copy of verses, called *Friendship in Perfection*, which I wonderfully admire. Have you seen the book?" says Mrs. Veal. "No," says Mrs. Bargrave, "but I have the verses of my own writing out." "Have you?" says Mrs. Veal; "then fetch them"; which she did from above stairs, and offered them to Mrs. Veal to read, who refused, and waived the thing, saying, "holding down her head would make it ache"; and then desiring Mrs. Bargrave to read them to her, which she did. As they were admiring *Friendship*, Mrs. Veal said, "Dear Mrs. Bargrave, I shall love you forever." In these verses there is twice used the word Elysian. "Ah!" says Mrs. Veal, "these poets have such names for Heaven." She would often draw her hand across her own eyes, and say, "Mrs. Bargrave, do not you think I am mightily impaired by my fits?" "No," says Mrs. Bargrave; "I think you look as well as ever I knew you."

After this discourse, which the apparition put in much finer words than Mrs. Bargrave said she could pretend to, and as much more as she can remember—for it cannot be thought that an hour and three quarter's conversation could all be retained, though the main of it she thinks she does—she said to Mrs. Bargrave she would have her write a letter to her brother, and tell him she would have him give rings to such and such; and that there was a purse of gold in her cabinet, and that she would have two broad pieces given to her cousin Watson.

Talking at this rate, Mrs. Bargrave thought that a fit was coming upon her, and so placed herself on a chair just before her knees, to keep her from falling to the ground, if her fits should occasion it; for the elbow-chair, she thought, would keep her from falling on either side. And to divert Mrs. Veal, as she thought, took hold of her gown-sleeve several times, and commended it. Mrs. Veal told her it was a scoured silk, and newly made up. But, for all this, Mrs. Veal persisted in her request, and told Mrs. Bargrave she must not deny her. And she would have her tell her brother all their conversation when she had the opportunity. "Dear Mrs. Veal," says Mrs. Bargrave, "it is much better, methinks, to do it yourself." "No," says Mrs. Veal, "though it seems impertinent to you now, you will see more reasons for it hereafter." Mrs. Bargrave, then, to satisfy her importunity, was going to fetch a pen and ink, but Mrs. Veal said, "Let it alone now, but do it when I am gone; but you must be sure to do it"; which was one of the last things she enjoined her at parting, and so she promised her.

Then Mrs. Veal asked for Mrs. Bargrave's daughter. She said she was not at home. "But if you have a mind to see her," says Mrs. Bargrave, "I'll send for her." "Do," says Mrs. Veal; on which she left her, and went to a neighbor's to see her; and by the time Mrs. Bargrave was returning, Mrs. Veal was without the door in the street, in the face of the beast-market, on a Saturday (which is market-day), and stood ready to part as soon as Mrs. Bargrave came to her. She asked her why she was in such haste. She said she must be going, though perhaps she might not go her journey till Monday; and told Mrs. Bargrave she hoped she should see her again at her cousin Watson's before she went whither she was going. Then she said she would take her leave of her, and walked from Mrs. Bargrave, in her view, till a turning interrupted the sight of her, which was three-quarters after one in the afternoon.

Mrs. Veal died the seventh of September, at twelve o'clock at noon, of her fits, and had not above four hours' senses before her death, in which time she received the sacrament. The next day after Mrs. Veal's appearance, being Sunday, Mrs. Bargrave was mightily indisposed with a cold and sore throat, that she could not go out that day; but on Monday morning she sends a person to Captain Watson's to know if Mrs. Veal was there. They wondered at Mrs. Bargrave's inquiry, and sent her word she was not there, nor was expected. At this answer, Mrs. Bargrave told the maid she had certainly mistook the name or made some blunder. And though she was ill, she put on her hood and went herself to Captain Watson's, though she knew none of the family, to see if Mrs. Veal was there or not. They said they wondered at her asking, for that she had not been in town; they were sure, if she had, she would have been there. Says Mr. Bargrave, "I am sure she was with me on Saturday almost two hours." They said it was impossible, for they must have seen her if she had. In comes Captain Watson, while they were in dispute, and said that Mrs. Veal was certainly dead, and the escutcheons were making. This strangely surprised Mrs. Bargrave, when she sent to the person immediately who had the care of them, and found it true. Then she related the whole story to Captain Watson's family; what gown she had on, and how striped; and that Mrs. Veal told her that it was scoured. Then Mrs. Watson cried out, "You have seen her indeed, for none knew but Mrs. Veal and myself that the gown was scoured." And Mrs. Watson owned that she described the gown exactly; "for," said she, "I helped her to make it up." This Mrs. Watson blazed all about the town, and avouched the demonstration of truth of Mrs. Bargrave's seeing Mrs. Veal's apparition. And Captain Watson carried two gentlemen immediately to Mrs. Bargrave's house to hear the relation from her own mouth. And when it spread so fast that gentlemen and persons of quality, the judicious and skeptical part of the world, flocked in upon her, it at last become such a task that she was forced to go out of the way; for they were in general extremely satisfied of the truth of the thing, and plainly saw that Mrs. Bargrave was no hypochondriac, for she always appears with such a cheerful air and pleasing mien that she has gained the favor and esteem of all the gentry, and it is thought a great favor if they can but get the relation from her own mouth. I should have told you before that Mrs. Veal told Mrs. Bargrave that her sister and brother-in-law were just come down from London to see her. Says Mrs. Bargrave, "How came you to order matters so strangely?" "It could not be helped," said Mrs. Veal. And her brother and sister did come to see her, and entered the town of Dover just as Mrs. Veal was expiring. Mrs. Bargrave asked her whether she would drink some tea. Says Mrs. Veal, "I do not care if I do; but I'll warrant you this mad fellow"—meaning Mrs. Bargrave's husband— "has broke all your trinkets." "But," says Mrs. Bargrave, "I'll get something to drink in for all that"; but Mrs. Veal waived it, and said, "It is no matter; let it alone," and so it passed.

All the time I sat with Mrs. Bargrave, which was some hours, she recollected fresh sayings of Mrs. Veal. And one material thing more she told Mrs. Bargrave, that old Mr. Bretton allowed Mrs. Veal ten pounds a year, which was a secret, and unknown to Mrs. Bargrave till Mrs. Veal told her.

Mrs. Bargrave never varies in her story, which puzzles those who doubt of the truth, or are unwilling to believe it. A servant in the neighbor's yard adjoining to Mrs. Bargrave's house heard her talking to somebody an hour of the time Mrs. Veal was with her. Mrs. Bargrave went out to her next neighbor's the very moment she parted with Mrs. Veal, and told her what ravishing conversation she had had with an old friend, and told the whole of it. Drelincourt's *Book of Death* is, since this happened, bought up strangely. And it is to be observed that, notwithstanding all the trouble and fatigue Mrs. Bargrave has undergone upon this account, she never took the value of a farthing, nor suffered her daughter to take anything of anybody, and therefore can have no interest in telling the story.

But Mr. Veal does what he can to stifle the matter, and said he would see Mrs. Bargrave; but yet it is certain matter of fact that he has been at Captain Watson's since the death of his sister, and yet never went near Mrs. Bargrave; and some of his friends report her to be a liar, and that she knew of Mr. Bretton's ten pounds a year. But the person who pretends to say so has the reputation to be a notorious liar among persons whom I know to be of undoubted credit. Now, Mr. Veal is more of a gentleman than to say she lies, but says a bad husband has crazed her; but she needs only present herself, and it will effectually confute that pretense. Mr. Veal says he asked his sister on her death-bed whether she had a mind to dispose of anything. And she said no. Now the things which Mrs. Veal's apparition would have disposed of were so trifling, and nothing of justice aimed at in her disposal, that the design of it appears to me to be only in order to make Mrs. Bargrave satisfy the world of the reality thereof as to what she had seen and heard, and to secure her reputation among the reasonable and understanding part of mankind. And then again, Mr. Veal owns that there was a purse of gold; but it was not found in her cabinet, but in a comb-box. This looks improbable; for that Mrs. Watson owned that Mrs. Veal was so very careful of the key of her cabinet that she would trust nobody with it; and if so, no doubt she would not trust her gold out of it. And Mrs. Veal's often drawing her hands over her eyes, and asking Mrs. Bargrave whether her fits had not impaired her, looks to me as if she did it on purpose to remind Mrs. Bargrave of her fits, to prepare her not to think it strange that she should put her upon writing to her brother, to dispose of rings and gold, which looks so much like a dying person's bequest; and it took accordingly with Mrs. Bargrave as the effect of her fits coming upon her, and was one of the many instances of her wonderful love to her and care of her, that she should not be affrighted, which, indeed, appears in her whole management, particularly in her coming to her in the daytime, waiving the salutation, and when she was alone; and then the manner of her parting, to prevent a second attempt to salute her.

Now, why Mr. Veal should think this relation a reflection—as it is plain he does, by his endeavoring to stifle it—I cannot imagine; because the generality believe her to be a good spirit, her discourse was so heavenly. Her two great errands were, to comfort Mrs. Bargrave in her affliction, and to ask her forgiveness for her breach of friendship, and with a pious discourse to encourage her. So that, after all, to suppose that Mrs. Bargrave could hatch such an invention as this, from Friday noon to Saturday noon—supposing that she knew of Mrs. Veal's death the very first moment—without jumbling circumstances, and without any interest, too, she must be more witty, fortunate, and wicked, too, than any indifferent person, I dare say, will allow. I asked Mrs. Bargrave several times if she was sure she felt the gown. She answered, modestly, "If my senses be to be relied on, I am sure of it." I asked her if she heard a sound when she clapped her hand upon her knee. She said she did not remember she did, but said she appeared to be as much a substance as I did who talked with her. "And I may," said she, "be as soon persuaded that your apparition is talking to me now as that I did not really see her; for I was under no manner of fear, and received her as a friend, and parted with her as such. I would not," says she, "give one farthing to make any one believe it; I have no interest in it; nothing but trouble is entailed upon me for a long time, for aught I know; and, had it not come to light by accident, it would never have been made public." But now she says she will make her own private use of it, and keep herself out of the way as much as she can; and so she has done since. She says she had a gentleman who came thirty miles to her to hear the relation; and that she had told it to a roomful of people at the time. Several particular gentlemen have had the story from Mrs. Bargrave's own mouth.

This thing has very much affected me, and I am as well satisfied as I am of the best-grounded matter of fact. And why we should dispute matter of fact, because we cannot solve things of which we can have no certain or demonstrative notions, seems strange to me; Mrs. Bargrave's authority and sincerity alone would have been undoubted in any other case.

JOSEPH ADDISON
(1672–1719)

BORN in Wiltshire in 1672, of a respected and cultured family, Joseph Addison went to Oxford, and began his literary life by writing Latin verses. In 1699 he travelled on the Continent by way of preparation for a political career. But on the death of the King in 1703 his hopes of advancement were shattered. The next year, however, he celebrated Marlborough's victory at Blenheim in his poem *The Campaign*, which attracted considerable notice. In 1709 he collaborated with his friend Richard Steele in the recently founded periodical, *The Tatler*, and later in the better-known *Spectator*, contributing essays and sketches and several charmingly written tales which are among the most finished and neatly turned stories in the language.

THE STORY OF AN HEIR
(From *The Spectator*)

AS I was yesterday taking the air with my friend Sir Roger, we were met by a fresh-colored ruddy young man who rid by us full speed, with a couple of servants behind him. Upon my inquiry who he was, Sir Roger told me that he was a young gentleman of a considerable estate, who had been educated by a tender mother that lived not many miles from the place where we were. She is a very good lady, says my friend, but took so much care of her son's health that she has made him good for nothing. She quickly found that reading was bad for his eyes, and that writing made his head ache. He was let loose among the woods as soon as he was able to ride on horseback, or to carry a gun upon his shoulder. To be brief, I found, by my friend's account of him, that he had got a great stock of health, but nothing else; and that if it were a man's business only to live, there would not be a more accomplished young fellow in the whole country.

The truth of it is, since my residing in these parts I have seen and heard innumerable instances of young heirs and elder brothers who either from their own reflecting upon the estates they are born to, and therefore thinking all other accomplishments unnecessary, or from hearing these notions frequently inculcated to them by the flattery of their servants and domestics, or from the same foolish thought prevailing in those who have the care of their education, are of no manner of use but to keep up their families, and transmit their lands and houses in a line to posterity.

This makes me often think on a story I have heard of two friends, which I shall give my reader at large, under feigned names. The moral of it may, I hope, be useful, though there are some circumstances which make it rather appear like a novel, than a true story.

Eudoxus and Leontine began the world with small estates. They were both of them men of good sense and great virtue. They prosecuted their studies together in their earlier years, and entered into such a friendship as lasted to the end of their lives. Eudoxus, at his first setting out in the world, threw himself into a court, where by his natural endowments and his acquired abilities he made his way from one post to another, till at length he had raised a very considerable fortune. Leontine on the contrary sought all opportunities of improving his mind by study, conversation and travel. He was not only acquainted with all the sciences, but with the most eminent professors of them throughout Europe. He knew perfectly well the interests of its princes, with the customs and fashions of their courts, and could scarce meet with the name of an extraordinary person in the *Gazette* whom he had not either talked to or seen. In short, he had so well mixed and digested his knowledge of men and books, that he made one of the most accomplished persons of his age. During the whole course of his studies and travels he kept up a punctual correspondence with Eudoxus, who often made himself acceptable to the principal men about court by the intelligence which he received from Leontine. When they were both turned of forty (an age in which, according to Mr Cowley, *there is no dallying with life*) they determined, pursuant to the resolution they had taken in the beginning of their lives, to retire, and pass the remainder of their days in the country. In order to this, they both of them married much about the same time. Leontine, with his own and his wife's fortune, bought a farm of three hundred a year, which lay within the neighborhood of his friend Eudoxus, who had purchased an estate of as many thousands. They were both of them fathers about the same time, Eudoxus having a son born to him, and Leontine a daughter; but to the unspeakable grief of the latter, his young wife (in whom all his happiness was wrapped up) died in a few days after the birth of her daughter. His affliction would have been insupportable, had not he been comforted by the daily visits and conversations of his friend. As they were one day talking together with their usual intimacy, Leontine, considering how incapable he was of giving his daughter a proper education in his own house, and Eudoxus, reflecting on the ordinary behavior of a son who knows himself to be the heir of a great estate, they both agreed upon an exchange of children, namely that the boy should be bred up with Leontine as his son, and that the girl should live with Eudoxus as his daughter, till they were each of them arrived at years of discretion. The wife of Eudoxus, knowing that her son could not be so advantageously brought up as under the care of Leontine, and considering at the same time that he would be perpetually under her own eye, was by degrees prevailed upon to fall in with the project. She therefore took Leonilla, for that was the name of the girl, and educated her as her own daughter. The two friends on each side had wrought themselves to such an habitual tenderness for the children who were under their direction, that each of them had the real passion of a father, where the title was but imaginary. Florio, the name of the young heir that lived with Leontine, though he had all the duty and affection imaginable for his supposed parent, was taught to rejoice at the sight of Eudoxus, who visited his friend very frequently, and was dictated by his natural affection, as well as by the rules of prudence, to make himself esteemed and beloved by Florio. The boy was now old enough to know his supposed father's circumstances, and that therefore he was to make his way in the world by his own industry. This consideration grew stronger in him every day, and produced so good an effect, that he applied himself with more than ordinary attention to the pursuit of everything which Leontine recommended to him. His natural abilities, which were very good, assisted by the directions of so excellent a counselor, enabled him to make a quicker progress than ordinary through all the parts of his education. Before he was twenty years of age, having finished his studies and exercises with great applause, he was removed from the university to the Inns of Court, where there are very few that make themselves considerable proficients in the studies of the place, who know they shall arrive at great estates without them. This was not

Florio's case; he found that three hundred a year was but a poor estate for Leontine and himself to live upon, so that he studied without inter-mission till he gained a very good insight into the constitution and laws of his country.

I should have told my reader, that whilst Florio lived at the house of his foster-father he was always an acceptable guest in the family of Eudoxus, where he became acquainted with Leonilla from her infancy. His acquaintance with her by degrees grew into love, which in a mind trained up in all the sentiments of honor and virtue became a very un-easy passion. He despaired of gaining an heiress of so great a fortune, and would rather have died than attempted it by any indirect methods. Leonilla, who was a woman of the greatest beauty joined with the greatest modesty, entertained at the same time a secret passion for Flo-rio, but conducted herself with so much prudence that she never gave him the least intimation of it. Florio was now engaged in all those arts and improvements that are proper to raise a man's private fortune, and give him a figure in his country, but secretly tormented with that pas-sion which burns with the greatest fury in a virtuous and noble heart, when he received a sudden summons from Leontine to repair to him in the country the next day. For it seems Eudoxus was so filled with the report of his son's reputation that he could no longer withhold making himself known to him. The morning after his arrival at the house of his supposed father, Leontine told him that Eudoxus had something of great importance to communicate to him; upon which the good man em-braced him and wept. Florio was no sooner arrived at the great house that stood in his neighborhood, but Eudoxus took him by the hand, after the first salutes were over, and conducted him into his closet. He there opened to him the whole secret of his parentage and education, concluding after this manner: *I have no other way left of acknowledging my gratitude to Leontine, than by marrying you to his daughter. He shall not lose the pleasure of being your father by the discovery I have made to you. Leonilla too shall be still my daughter; her filial piety, though misplaced, has been so exem-plary that it deserves the greatest reward I can confer upon it. You shall have the pleasure of seeing a great estate fall to you, which you would have lost the relish of had you known yourself born to it. Continue only to deserve it in the same man-ner you did before you were possessed of it. I have left your mother in the next room. Her heart yearns towards you. She is making the same discoveries to Leo-nilla which I have made to yourself.* Florio was so overwhelmed with this profusion of happiness, that he was not able to make a reply, but threw himself down at his father's feet, and amidst a flood of tears, kissed and embraced his knees, asking his blessing, and expressing in dumb show those sentiments of love, duty, and gratitude that were too big for utterance. To conclude, the happy pair were married, and half Eu-doxus' estate settled upon them. Leontine and Eudoxus passed the remainder of their lives together; and received in the dutiful and affectionate behavior of Florio and Leonilla the just recompense, as well as the natural effects, of that care which they had bestowed upon them in their education.

OLIVER GOLDSMITH

(1728—1774)

GOLDSMITH's family were Irish people of English descent. Oliver Goldsmith was born in County Longford, Ireland. He went to Trinity College, Dublin, and after his graduation in 1749, began the study of medicine at Edinburgh. After a short period in Scotland he left for the Continent, where he wandered from country to country. After his return to London in 1756 his early essays and verses attracted the attention of Dr. Johnson, and he became a member of the illustrious group that gathered round that literary monarch. The years between 1759 and 1773 were the most productive of his entire career. *The Vicar of Wakefield*, which is a landmark in the development of prose fiction, appeared in 1766. Like Addison and Steele and other of the periodical essayists, Goldsmith wrote several short stories of high merit. *The Disabled Soldier* was first printed in the *Citizen of the World*, in 1760.

THE DISABLED SOLDIER

(From the *Citizen of the World*)

NO observation is more common, and at the same time more true, than that one half of the world are ignorant how the other half lives. The misfortunes of the great are held up to engage our attention; are enlarged upon in tones of declamation; and the world is called upon to gaze at the noble sufferers: the great, under the pressure of calamity, are conscious of several others sympathizing with their distress; and have, at once, the comfort of admiration and pity.

There is nothing magnanimous in bearing misfortunes with fortitude, when the whole world is looking on: men in such circumstances will act bravely even from motives of vanity: but he who, in the vale of obscurity, can brave adversity; who without friends to encourage, acquaintances to pity, or even without hope to alleviate his misfortunes, can behave with tranquillity and indifference, is truly great: whether peasant or courtier, he deserves admiration, and should be held up for our imitation and respect.

While the slightest inconveniences of the great are magnified into calamities; while tragedy mouths out their sufferings in all the strains of eloquence, the miseries of the poor are entirely disregarded; and yet some of the lower ranks of people undergo more real hardships in one day, than those of a more exalted station suffer in their whole lives. It is inconceivable what difficulties the meanest of our common sailors and soldiers endure without murmuring or regret; without passionately declaiming against providence, or calling their fellows to be gazers on their intrepidity. Every day is to them a day of misery, and yet they entertain their hard fate without repining.

With what indignation do I hear an Ovid, a Cicero or a Rabutin complain of their misfortunes and hardships, whose greatest calamity was that of being unable to visit a certain spot of earth, to which they had foolishly attached an idea of happiness. Their distresses were pleasures, compared to what many of the adventuring poor every day endure without murmuring. They ate, drank, and slept; they had slaves to attend them, and were sure of subsistence for life; while many of their fellow creatures are obliged to wander without a friend to comfort or assist them, and even without shelter from the severity of the season.

I have been led into these reflections from accidentally meeting, some days ago, a poor fellow, whom I knew when a boy, dressed in a sailor's jacket, and begging at one of the outlets of the town, with a wooden leg. I knew him to have been honest and industrious when in the country, and was curious to learn what had reduced him to his present situation. Wherefore, after giving him what I thought proper, I desired to know the history of his life and misfortunes, and the manner in which he was reduced to his present distress. The disabled soldier, for such he was, though dressed in a sailor's habit, scratching his head, and leaning on his crutch, put himself into an attitude to comply with my request, and gave me his history as follows:

"As for my misfortunes, master, I can't pretend to have gone through any more than other folks; for, except the loss of my limb, and my being obliged to beg, I don't know any reason, thank Heaven, that I have to complain. There is Bill Tibbs, of our regiment, he has lost both his legs, and an eye to boot; but, thank Heaven, it is not so bad with me yet.

"I was born in Shropshire; my father was a laborer, and died when I was five years old, so I was put upon the parish. As he had been a wandering sort of a man, the parishioners were not able to tell to what parish I belonged, or where I was born, so they sent me to another parish, and that parish sent me to a third. I thought in my heart, they kept sending me about so long, that they would not let me be born in any parish at all; but at last, however, they fixed me. I had some disposition to be a scholar, and was resolved at least to know my letters:

but the master of the workhouse put me to business as soon as I was able to handle a mallet; and here I lived an easy kind of life for five years. I only wrought ten hours in the day, and had my meat and drink provided for my labor. It is true, I was not suffered to stir out of the house, for fear, as they said, I should run away; but what of that? I had the liberty of the whole house, and the yard before the door, and that was enough for me. I was then bound out to a farmer, where I was up both early and late; but I ate and drank well; and liked my business well enough, till he died, when I was obliged to provide for myself; so I resolved to go seek my fortune.

"In this manner I went from town to town, worked when I could get employment, and starved when I could get none; when, happening one day to go through a field belonging to a justice of peace, I spied a hare crossing the path just before me; and I believe the devil put it into my head to fling my stick at it. Well, what will you have on't? I killed the hare, and was bringing it away, when the justice himself met me; he called me a poacher and a villain, and collaring me, desired I would give an account of myself. I fell upon my knees, begged his worship's pardon, and began to give a full account of all that I knew of my breed, seed, and generation; but though I gave a very true account, the justice said I could give no account; so I was indicted at the sessions, found guilty of being poor, and sent up to London to Newgate, in order to be transported as a vagabond.

"People may say this and that of being in jail, but, for my part, I found Newgate as agreeable a place as ever I was in in all my life. I had my belly full to eat and drink, and did no work at all. This kind of life was too good to last forever; so I was taken out of prison, after five months, put on board of ship, and sent off, with two hundred more, to the plantations. We had but an indifferent passage, for being all confined in the hold, more than a hundred of our people died for want of sweet air; and those that remained were sickly enough, God knows. When we came ashore we were sold to the planters, and I was bound for seven years more. As I was no scholar, for I did not know my letters, I was obliged to work among the negroes; and I served out my time, as in duty bound to do.

"When my time was expired, I worked my passage home, and glad I was to see old England again, because I loved my country. I was afraid, however, that I should be indicted for a vagabond once more, so did not much care to go down into the country, but kept about the town, and did little jobs when I could get them.

"I was very happy in this manner for some time till one evening, coming home from work, two men knocked me down, and then desired me to stand. They belonged to a press-gang. I was carried before the justice, and as I could give no account of myself, I had my choice left, whether to go on board a man-of-war, or list for a soldier. I chose the latter, and in this post of a gentleman, I served two campaigns in Flanders, was at the battles of Val and Fontenoy, and received but one wound through the breast here; but the doctor of our regiment soon made me well again.

"When the peace came on I was discharged; and as I could not work, because my wound was sometimes troublesome, I listed for a landman in the East India Company's service. I have fought the French in six pitched battles; and I verily believe that if I could read or write, our captain would have made me a corporal. But it was not my good fortune to have any promotion, for I soon fell sick, and so got leave to return home again with forty pounds in my pocket. This was at the beginning of the present war, and I hoped to be set on shore, and to have the pleasure of spending my money; but the Government wanted men, and so I was pressed for a sailor, before ever I could set a foot on shore.

"The boatswain found me, as he said, an obstinate fellow: he swore he knew that I understood my business well, but that I shammed Abraham, to be idle; but God knows, I knew nothing of sea-business, and he beat me without considering what he was about. I had still, however, my forty pounds, and that was some comfort to me under every beating; and the money I might have had to this day, but that our ship was taken by the French, and so I lost all.

"Our crew was carried into Brest, and many of them died, because they were not used to live in a jail; but for my part, it was nothing to me, for I was seasoned. One night, as I was asleep on the bed of boards, with a warm blanket about me, for I always loved to lie well, I was awakened by the boatswain, who had a dark lantern in his hand. 'Jack,' says he to me, 'will you knock out the French sentry's brains?' 'I don't care,' says I, striving to keep myself awake, 'if I lend a hand.' 'Then, follow me,' says he, 'and I hope we shall do business.' So up I got, and tied my blanket, which was all the clothes I had, about my middle, and went with him to fight the Frenchman. I hate the French, because they are all slaves, and wear wooden shoes.

"Though we had no arms, one Englishman is able to beat five French at any time; so we went down to the door where both the sentries were posted, and rushing upon them, seized their arms in a moment, and knocked them down. From thence nine of us ran together to the quay, and seizing the first boat we met, got out of the harbor and put to sea. We had not been here three days before we were taken up by the Dorset privateer, who were glad of so many good hands; and we consented to run our chance. However, we had not as much luck as we expected. In three days we fell in with the *Pompadour* privateer of forty guns, while we had but twenty-three, so to it we went, yard-arm and yard-arm. The fight lasted three hours, and I verily believe we should have taken the Frenchman, had we but had some more men left behind; but unfortunately we lost all our men just as we were going to get the victory.

"I was once more in the power of the French, and I believe it would have gone hard with me had I been brought back to Brest; but by good fortune we were retaken by the *Viper*. I had almost forgotten to tell you that in that engagement I was wounded in two places; I lost four fingers off the left hand, and my leg was shot off. If I had had the good fortune to have lost my leg and use of my hand on board a king's ship, and not aboard a privateer, I should have been entitled to clothing and maintenance during the rest of my life; but that was not my chance: one man is born with a silver spoon in his mouth, and another with a wooden ladle. However, blessed be God, I enjoy good health, and will forever love liberty and old England. Liberty, property, and old England, forever, huzza!"

Thus saying, he limped off, leaving me in admiration at his intrepidity and content; nor could I avoid acknowledging that an habitual acquaintance with misery serves better than philosophy to teach us to despise it.

SIR WALTER SCOTT

(1771—1832)

WALTER SCOTT, founder of the romantic historical novel, was born in Edinburgh in 1771. He entered his father's law office, but before long gave up law for literature. His first works were ballads and long narrative poems. In 1814 he published the novel *Waverley*, which established his position as a writer. At the very height of his brilliant career he found himself morally obliged to pay off an enormous debt, and spent the rest of his life trying to do so. Scott wrote several short stories. *The Bridal of Janet Dalrymple*, not so well known as the far longer *Wandering Willie's Tale* from *Redgauntlet*, is a well-written and (for Scott) surprisingly short and closely-woven narrative.

The present edition is reprinted from the volume, *Scottish Love Tales*, London, no date.

THE BRIDAL OF JANET DALRYMPLE

MISS JANET DALRYMPLE, daughter of the first Lord Stair, and Dame Margaret Ross, had engaged herself without the knowledge of her parents to the Lord Rutherford, who was not acceptable to them either on account of his political principles, or his want of fortune. The young couple broke a piece of gold together, and pledged their troth in the most solemn manner; and it is said the young lady imprecated dreadful evils on herself should she break her plighted faith. Shortly after, a suitor who was favored by Lord Stair, and still more so by his lady, paid his addresses to Miss Dalrymple. The young lady refused the proposal, and being pressed on the subject, confessed her secret engagement. Lady Stair, a woman accustomed to universal submission (for even her husband did not dare to contradict her), treated this objection as a trifle, and insisted upon her daughter yielding her consent to marry the new suitor, David Dunbar, son and heir to David Dunbar of Baldoon, in Wigtonshire. The first lover, a man of very high spirit, then interfered by letter, and insisted on the right he had acquired by his troth plighted with the young lady. Lady Stair sent him for answer, that her daughter, sensible of her undutiful behavior in entering into a contract unsanctioned by her parents, had retracted her unlawful vow, and now refused to fulfil her engagement with him.

The lover in return declined positively to receive such an answer from anyone but his mistress in person; and as she had to deal with a man who was both of a most determined character, and of too high condition to be trifled with, Lady Stair was obliged to consent to an interview between Lord Rutherford and her daughter. But she took care to be present in person, and argued the point with the disappointed and incensed lover with pertinacity equal to his own. She particularly insisted on the Levitical law, which declares, that a woman shall be free of a vow which her parents dissent from. This is the passage of Scripture she founded on:

"If a man vow a vow unto the Lord, or swear an oath to bind his soul with a bond; he shall not break his word, he shall do according to all that proceedeth out of his mouth.

"If a woman also vow a vow unto the Lord, and bind herself by a bond, being in her father's house in her youth;

"And her father hear her vow, and her bond wherewith she hath bound her soul, and her father shall hold his peace at her: then all her vows shall stand, and every bond wherewith she hath bound her soul shall stand.

"But if her father disallow her in the day that he heareth; not any of her vows, or of her bonds wherewith she hath bound her soul, shall stand: and the Lord shall forgive her, because her father disallowed her."—Numbers xxx. 2, 3, 4, 5.

While the mother insisted on these topics, the lover in vain conjured the daughter to declare her own opinion and feelings. She remained totally overwhelmed, as it seemed—mute, pale, and motionless as a statue. Only at her mother's command, sternly uttered, she summoned strength enough to restore to her plighted suitor the piece of broken gold, which was the emblem of her troth. On this he burst forth into a tremendous passion, took leave of the mother with maledictions, and as he left the apartment, turned back to say to his weak, if not fickle, mistress, "For you, madam, you will be a world's wonder"; a phrase by which some remarkable degree of calamity is usually implied. He went abroad, and returned not again. If the last Lord Rutherford was the unfortunate party, he must have been the third who bore that title, and who died in 1685.

The marriage betwixt Janet Dalrymple and David Dunbar of Baldoon now went forward, the bride showing no repugnance, but being absolutely passive in everything her mother commanded or advised. On the day of the marriage, which, as was then usual, was celebrated by a great assemblage of friends and relations, she was the same—sad, silent, and resigned, as it seemed, to her destiny. A lady, very nearly connected with the family, told the author that she had conversed on the subject with one of the brothers of the bride, a mere lad at the time, who had ridden before his sister to church. He said her hand, which lay on his as she held her arm round his waist, was as cold and damp as marble. But, full of his new dress, and the part he acted in the procession, the circumstance, which he long afterwards remembered with bitter sorrow and compunction, made no impression on him at the time.

The bridal feast was followed by dancing; the bride and bridegroom retired as usual, when of a sudden the most wild and piercing cries were heard from the nuptial chamber. It was then the custom, to prevent any coarse pleasantry which old times perhaps admitted, that the key of the nuptial chamber should be intrusted to the brideman. He was called upon, but refused at first to give it up, till the shrieks became so hideous that he was compelled to hasten with others to learn the cause. On opening the door, they found the bridegroom lying across the threshold, dreadfully wounded, and streaming with blood. The bride was then sought for. She was found in the corner of the large chimney, having no covering save her shift, and that dabbled in gore. There she sat grinning at them, mopping and mowing, as I heard the expression used; in a word, absolutely insane. The only words she spoke were, "Tak up your bonny bridegroom." She survived this horrible scene little more than a fortnight, having been married on the 24th of August, and dying on the 12th of September, 1669.

The unfortunate Baldoon recovered from his wounds, but sternly prohibited all inquiries respecting the manner in which he had received them. If a lady, he said, asked him any question upon the subject, he would neither answer her nor speak to her again while he lived; if a gentleman, he would consider it as a mortal affront, and demand satisfaction as having received such. He did not very long survive the dreadful catastrophe, having met with a fatal injury by a fall from his horse, as he rode between Leith and Holyrood House, of which he died the next day, 28th March, 1682. Thus a few years removed all the principal actors in this frightful tragedy.

Various reports went abroad on this mysterious affair, many of them very inaccurate, though they could hardly be said to be exaggerated. It was difficult at that time to become acquainted with the history of a Scottish family above the lower rank; and strange things sometimes took place there, into which even the law did not scrupulously inquire.

The credulous Mr. Law says, generally, that the Lord President Stair had a daughter, who "being married, the night she was *bride in* [that is, bedded bride], was taken from her bridegroom and *harled* [dragged] through the house (by spirits, we are given to understand), and soon afterwards died. Another daughter," he says, was "possessed by an evil spirit."

My friend, Mr. Sharpe, gives another edition of the tale. According to his information, it was the bridegroom who wounded the bride. The marriage, according to this account, had been against her mother's inclination, who had given her consent in these ominous words: "You may marry him, but soon shall you repent it."

I find still another account darkly insinuated in some highly scurrilous and abusive verses. They are docketed as being written "Upon the late Viscount Stair and his family, by Sir William Hamilton of Whitelaw. The marginals by William Dunlop, writer in Edinburgh, a son of the Laird of Househill, and nephew to the said Sir William Hamilton." There was a bitter and personal quarrel and rivalry betwixt the author of this libel, a name which it richly deserves, and Lord President Stair; and the lampoon, which is written with much more malice than art, bears the following motto:

> "Stair's neck, mind, wife, sons, grandson, and the rest,
> Are wry, false, witch, pests, parricide, possessed."

This malignant satirist, who calls up all the misfortunes of the family, does not forget the fatal bridal of Baldoon. He seems, though his verses are as obscure as unpoetical, to intimate, that the violence done to the bridegroom was by the intervention of the foul fiend to whom the young lady had resigned herself, in case she should break her contract with her first lover. His hypothesis is inconsistent with the account given in the note upon Law's Memorials, but easily reconcilable to the family tradition.

> "In al Stair's offspring we no difference know,
> They doe the females as the males bestow;
> So he of's daughter's marriage gave the ward,
> Like a true vassal, to Glenluce's Laird;

He knew what she did to her suitor plight,
If she her faith to Rutherfurd should slight,
Which, like his own, for greed he broke outright.
Nick did Baldoon's posterior right deride,
And, as first substitute, did seize the bride;
Whate'er he to his mistress did or said,
He threw the bridegroom from the nuptial bed,
Into the chimney did so his rival maul,
His bruised bones ne'er were cured but by the fall."

One of the marginal notes ascribed to William Dunlop applies to the above lines. "She had betrothed herself to Lord Rutherford under horrid imprecations, and afterwards married Baldoon, his nevoy, and her mother was the cause of her breach of faith."

The same tragedy is alluded to in the following couplet and note:

"What train of curses that base brood pursues,
When the young nephew wed's old uncle's spouse."

The note on the word *uncle* explains it as meaning "Rutherfoord, who should have married the Lady Baldoon, was Baldoon's uncle." The poetry of this satire on Lord Stair and his family was, as already noticed, written by Sir William Hamilton of Whitelaw, a rival of Lord Stair for the situation of President of the Court of Session; a person much inferior to that great lawyer in talents, and equally ill-treated by the calumny or just satire of his contemporaries, as an unjust and partial judge. Some of the notes are by that curious and laborious antiquary, Robert Milne, who, as a virulent Jacobite, willingly lent a hand to blacken the family of Stair.

Another poet of the period, with a very different purpose, has left an elegy, in which he darkly hints at and bemoans the fate of the ill-starred young person, whose very uncommon calamity Whitelaw, Dunlop, and Milne thought a fitting subject for buffoonery and ribaldry. This bard of milder mood was Andrew Symson, before the Revolution minister of Kirkinner, in Galloway, and after his expulsion as an Episcopalian, following the humble occupation of a printer in Edinburgh. He furnished the family of Baldoon, with which he appears to have been intimate, with an elegy on the tragic event in their family. In this piece he treats the mournful occasion of the bride's death with mysterious solemnity.

The verses bear this title—"On the unexpected death of the virtuous Lady Mrs. Janet Dalrymple, Lady Baldoon, younger," and afford us the precise dates of the catastrophe, which could not otherwise have been easily ascertained. "Nupta August 12. Domum Ducta August 24. Obiit September 12. Sepult. September 30, 1669." The form of the elegy is a dialogue betwixt a passenger and a domestic servant. The first, recollecting that he had passed that way lately, and seen all around enlivened by the appearances of mirth and festivity, is desirous to know what had changed so gay a scene into mourning. We preserve the reply of the servant as a specimen of Mr. Symson's verses, which are not of the first quality:

> "———————— Sir, 'tis truth you've told,
> We did enjoy great mirth; but now, ah me!
> Our joyful song's turned to an elegie.
> A virtuous lady, not long since a bride,
> Was to a hopeful plant by marriage tied,
> And brought home hither. We did all rejoice,
> Even for her sake. But presently our voice
> Was turn'd to mourning for that little time
> That she'd enjoy: She waned in her prime,
> For Atropos, with her impartial knife,
> Soon cut her thread, and therewithal her life;
> And for the time we may it well remember,
> It being in unfortunate September;
> Where we must leave her till the resurrection,
> 'Tis then the Saints enjoy their full perfection."

SAMUEL LOVER

(1797?—1868)

SAMUEL LOVER was born in Dublin of an English Protestant family. He studied painting at an early age, and though he continued to practise that art, he soon discovered his talent for writing. Many of his most delightful sketches of Irish life appeared in various Dublin periodicals in the early thirties. In 1832 he published his *Legends and Stories of Ireland*, in which *The White Trout* is found. The best known of his novels is *Handy Andy*.

The White Trout is reprinted from Yeats' *Irish Fairy and Folk Tales;* New York, no date.

THE WHITE TROUT

THERE was wanst upon a time, long ago, a beautiful lady that lived in a castle upon the lake beyant, and they say she was promised to a king's son, and they wor to be married, when all of a sudden he was murthered, the crathur (Lord help us), and threwn into the lake above, and so, of course, he couldn't keep his promise to the fairy lady—and more's the pity.

Well, the story goes that she went out iv her mind, bekase av loosin' the king's son—for she was tendher-hearted, God help her, like the rest iv us!—and pined away after him, until at last, no one about seen her, good or bad; and the story wint that the fairies took her away.

Well, sir, in coorse o' time, the White Throut, God bless it, was seen in the sthrame beyant, and sure the people didn't know what to think av the crathur, seein' as how a *white* throut was never heard av afor, nor since; and years upon years the throut was there, just where you seen it this blessed minit, longer nor I can tell—aye throth, and beyant the memory o' th' ouldest in the village.

At last the people began to think it must be a fairy; for what else could it be?—and no hurt nor harm was iver put an the white throut, until some wicked sinners of sojers kem to these parts, and laughed at all the people, and gibed and jeered them for thinkin' o' the likes; and one o' them in partic'lar (bad luck to him; God forgi' me for saying it!) swore he'd catch the throut and ate it for his dinner—the black-guard!

Well, what would you think o' the villainy of the sojer? Sure enough he cotch the throut, and away wid him home, and puts an the fryin'-pan, and into it he pitches the purty little thing. The throut squeeled all as one as a christian crathur, and, my dear, you'd think the sojer id split his sides laughin'—for he was a harden'd villain; and when he thought one side was done, he turns it over to fry the other; and, what would you think, but the divil a taste of a burn was an it at all at all; and sure the sojer thought it was a *quare* throut that could not be briled. "But," says he, "I'll give it another turn by and by," little thinkin' what was in store for him, the haythen.

Well, when he thought that side was done he turns it agin, and lo and behold you, the divil a taste more done that side was nor the other. "Bad luck to me," says the sojer, "but that bates the world," says he; "but I'll thry you agin, my darlint," says he, "as cunnin' as you think yourself"; and so with that he turns it over and over, but not a sign of the fire was on the purty throut. "Well," says the desperate villain— (for sure, sir, only he was a desperate villain *entirely*, he might know he was doing a wrong thing, seein' that all his endeavors was no good) —"Well," says he, "my jolly little throut, maybe you're fried enough, though you don't seem over well dress'd; but you may be better than you look, like a singed cat and a tit-bit afther all," says he; and with that he ups with his knife and fork to taste a piece o' the throut; but, my jew'l, the minit he puts his knife into the fish, there was a murtherin' screech, that you'd think the life id lave if you hurd it, and away jumps the throut out av the fryin'-pan into the middle o' the flure; and an the spot where it fell, up riz a lovely lady—the beautifullest crathur that eyes ever seen, dressed in white, and a band o' goold in her hair, and a sthrame o' blood runnin' down her arm.

"Look where you cut me, you villain," says she, and she held out her arm to him —and, my dear, he thought the sight id lave his eyes.

"Couldn't you lave me cool and comfortable in the river where you snared me, and not disturb me in my duty?" says she.

Well, he thrimbled like a dog in a wet sack, and at last he stammered out somethin', and begged for his life, and ax'd her ladyship's pardin, and said he didn't know she was on duty, or he was too good a sojer not to know betther nor to meddle wid her.

"I *was* on duty, then," says the lady; "I was watchin' for my true love that is comin' by wather to me," says she, "an' if he comes while I'm away, an' that I miss iv him, I'll turn you into a pinkeen, and I'll hunt you up and down for evermore, while grass grows or wather runs."

Well, the sojer thought the life id lave him, at the thoughts iv his bein' turned into a pinkeen, and begged for mercy; and with that says the lady:

"Renounce your evil coorses," says she, "you villain, or you'll repint it too late; be a good man for the futhur, and go to your duty reg'lar, and now," says she, "take me back and put me into the river again, where you found me."

"Oh, my lady," says the sojer, "how could I have the heart to drownd a beautiful lady like you?"

But before he could say another word, the lady was vanished, and there he saw the little throut an the ground. Well, he put it in a clean plate, and away he runs for the bare life, for fear her lover would come while she was away; and he run, and he run, even till he came to the cave agin, and threw the throut into the river. The minit he did, the wather was as red as blood for a little while, by rayson av the cut, I suppose, until the sthrame washed the stain away; and to this day there's a little red mark an the throut's side, where it was cut.

Well, sir, from that day out the sojer was an altered man, and re-formed his ways, and went to his duty reg'lar, and fasted three times a week—though it was never fish he tuk an fastin' days, for afther the fright he got, fish id never rest an his stomach—savin' your presence.

But anyhow, he was an altered man, as I said before, and in coorse o' time he left the army, and turned hermit at last; and they say he *used to pray evermore for the soul of the White Throut.*

CHARLES DICKENS

(1812–1870)

THE son of a government clerk, Charles Dickens was born at Portsea in 1812. His family moved to London shortly after his birth. The early London life of the Dickens family was utilized in several of the son's novels, especially in *David Copperfield*. His first great success was with the *Pickwick Papers*, which appeared serially in 1836. Then followed the novels which have become celebrated and are read the world over. Dickens was an indefatigable writer, editor and, later in life, a public reader. He wrote a number of short stories, of which *The Old Man's Tale of the Queer Client* is probably the most skilfully constructed and best written. It is related by one of the characters in the *Pickwick Papers*.

THE OLD MAN'S TALE OF THE QUEER CLIENT

(From the *Pickwick Papers*)

"IT matters little," said the old man, "where, or how, I picked up this brief history. If I were to relate it in the order in which it reached me, I should commence in the middle, and when I had arrived at the conclusion, go back for a beginning. It is enough for me to say that some of its circumstances passed before my own eyes. For the remainder I know them to have happened, and there are some persons yet living who will remember them but too well.

"In the Borough High Street, near St. George's Church, and on the same side of the way, stands, as most people know, the smallest of our debtor's prisons, the Marshalsea. Although in later times it has been a very different place from the sink of filth and dirt it once was, even its improved condition holds out but little temptation to the extravagant, or consolation to the provident. The condemned felon has as good a yard for air and exercise in Newgate, as the insolvent debtor in the Marshalsea Prison.

"It may be my fancy, or it may be that I cannot separate the place from the old recollections associated with it, but this part of London I cannot bear. The street is broad, the shops are spacious, the noise of passing vehicles, the footsteps of a perpetual stream of people—all the busy sounds of traffic, resound in it from morn to midnight, but the streets around are mean and close; poverty and debauchery lie festering in the crowded alleys; want and misfortune are pent up in the narrow prison; an air of gloom and dreariness seems, in my eyes at least, to hang about the scene, and to impart to it a squalid and sickly hue.

"Many eyes, that have long since been closed in the grave, have looked round upon that scene lightly enough, when entering the gate of the old Marshalsea Prison for the first time: for despair seldom comes with the first severe shock of misfortune. A man has confidence in untried friends, he remembers the many offers of service so freely made by his boon companions when he wanted them not; he has hope—the hope of happy inexperience—and however he may bend beneath the first shock, it springs up in his bosom, and flourishes there for a brief space, until it droops beneath the blight of disappointment and neglect. How soon have those same eyes, deeply sunken in the head, glared from faces wasted with famine, and sallow from confinement, in days when it was no figure of speech to say debtors rotted in prison, with no hope of release, and no prospect of liberty! The atrocity in its full extent no longer exists, but there is enough of it left to give rise to occurrences that make the heart bleed.

"Twenty years ago, that pavement was worn with the footsteps of a mother and child, who, day by day, so surely as the morning came, presented themselves at the prison gate; often, after a night of restless misery and anxious thoughts, were they there, a full hour too soon, and then the young mother turning meekly away, would lead the child to the old bridge, and raising him in her arms to show him the glistening water, tinted with the light of the morning's sun, and stirring with all the bustling preparations for business and pleasure that the river presented at that early hour, endeavor to interest his thoughts in the objects before him. But she would quickly set him down, and, hiding her face in her shawl, give vent to the tears that blinded her; for no expression of interest or amusement lighted up his thin and sickly face. His recollections were few enough, but they were all of one kind: all connected with the poverty and misery of his parents. Hour after hour had he sat on his mother's knee, and with childish sympathy watched the tears that stole down her face, and then crept quietly away into some dark corner, and sobbed himself to sleep. The hard realities of the world, with many of its worst privations—hunger and thirst, and cold and want—had all come home to him, from the first dawnings of reason; and though the form of childhood was there, its light heart, its merry laugh, and sparkling eyes, were wanting.

"The father and mother looked on upon this, and upon each other, with thoughts of agony they dared not breathe in words. The healthy, strong-made man, who could have borne almost any fatigue of active exertion, was wasting beneath the close confinement and unhealthy atmosphere of a crowded prison. The slight and delicate woman was sinking beneath the combined effects of bodily and mental illness. The child's young heart was breaking.

"Winter came, and with it weeks of cold and heavy rain. The poor girl had removed to a wretched apartment close to the spot of her husband's imprisonment; and though the change had been rendered necessary by their increasing poverty, she was happier now, for she was nearer him. For two months, she and her little companion watched the opening of the gate as usual. One day she failed to come, for the first time. Another morning arrived, and she came alone. The child was dead.

"They little know, who coldly talk of the poor man's bereavements, as a happy release from pain to the departed, and a merciful relief from expense to the survivor—they little know, I say, what the agony of those bereavements is. A silent look of affection and regard when all other eyes are turned coldly away—the consciousness that we possess the sympathy and affection of one being when all others have deserted us—is a hold, a stay, a comfort, in the deepest affliction, which no wealth could purchase, or power bestow. The child had sat at his parents' feet for hours together, with his little hands patiently folded in each other, and his thin wan face raised towards them. They had seen him pine away, from day to day; and though his brief existence had been a joyless one, and he was now removed to that peace and rest which, child as he was, he had never known in this world, they were his parents, and his loss sunk deep into their souls.

"It was plain to those who looked upon the mother's altered face, that death must soon close the scene of her adversity and trial. Her husband's fellow-prisoners shrank from obtruding on his grief and misery, and left to himself alone the small room he had previously occupied in common with two companions. She shared it with him: and lingering on without pain, but without hope, her life ebbed slowly away.

"She had fainted one evening in her husband's arms, and he had borne her to the open window, to revive her with the air, when the light of the moon falling full upon her face showed him a change upon her features, which made him stagger beneath her weight, like a helpless infant.

"'Set me down, George,' she said faintly. He did so, and seating himself beside her, covered his face with his hands, and burst into tears.

"'It is very hard to leave you, George,' she said, 'but it is God's will, and you must bear it for my sake. Oh! how I thank Him for having taken our boy! He is happy, and in Heaven now. What would he have done here without his mother!'

"'You shall not die, Mary, you shall not die!' said the husband, starting up. He paced hurriedly to and fro, striking his head with his clenched fists; then reseating himself beside her, and supporting her in his arms, added more calmly, 'Rouse yourself, my dear girl. Pray, pray do. You will revive yet.'

"'Never again, George; never again,' said the dying woman. 'Let them lay me by my poor boy now, but promise me that if ever you leave this dreadful place, and should grow rich, you will have us removed to some quiet country churchyard, a long, long way off—very far from here, where we can rest in peace. Dear George, promise me you will.'

"'I do, I do,' said the man throwing himself passionately on his knees before her. 'Speak to me, Mary, another word; one look—but one!'

"He ceased to speak: for the arm that clasped his neck grew stiff and heavy. A deep sigh escaped from the wasted form before him; the lips moved, and a smile played upon the face; but the lips were pallid, and the smile faded into a rigid and ghastly stare. He was alone in the world.

"That night, in the silence and desolation of his miserable room, the wretched man knelt down by the dead body of his wife, and called on God to witness a terrible oath, that from that hour he devoted himself to revenge her death and that of his child; that thenceforth to the last moment of his life, his whole energies should be directed to this one object; that his revenge should be protracted and terrible; that his hatred should be undying and inextinguishable; and should hunt its object through the world.

"The deepest despair, and passion scarcely human, had made such fierce ravages on his face and form, in that one night, that his companions in misfortune shrunk affrighted from him as he passed by. His eyes were bloodshot and heavy, his face a deadly white, and his body bent as if with age. He had bitten his underlip nearly through in the violence of his mental suffering, and the blood which had flowed from the wound had trickled down his chin, and stained his shirt and neckerchief. No tear or sound of complaint escaped him: but the unsettled look, and disordered haste with which he paced up and down the yard denoted the fever which was burning within.

"It was necessary that his wife's body should be removed from the prison, without delay. He received the communication with perfect calmness, and acquiesced in its propriety. Nearly all the inmates of the prison had assembled to witness its removal; they fell back on either side when the widower appeared; he walked hurriedly forward, and stationed himself, alone, in a little railed area close to the lodge gate, from whence the crowd, with an instinctive feeling of delicacy, had retired. The rude coffin was borne slowly forward on men's shoulders. A dead silence pervaded the throng, broken only by the audible lamentations of the women, and the shuffling steps of the bearers on the stone pavement. They reached the spot where the bereaved husband stood: and stopped. He laid his hand upon the coffin, and mechanically adjusting the pall with which it was covered, motioned them onward. The turnkeys in the prison lobby took off their hats as it passed through, and in another moment the heavy gate closed behind it. He looked vacantly upon the crowd, and fell heavily to the ground.

"Although for many weeks after this he was watched, night and day, in the wildest ravings of fever, neither the consciousness of his loss, nor the recollection of the vow he had made, ever left him for a moment. Scenes changed before his eyes, place succeeded place, and event followed event, in all the hurry of delirium; but they were all connected in some way with the great object of his mind. He was sailing over a boundless expanse of sea, with a blood-red sky above, and the angry waters, lashed into fury beneath, boiling and eddying up on every side. There was another vessel before them, toiling and laboring in the howling storm: her canvas fluttering in ribbons from the mast, and her deck thronged with figures who were lashed to the sides, over which huge waves every instant burst, sweeping away some devoted creatures into the foaming sea. Onward they bore, amidst the roaring mass of water, with a speed and force which nothing could resist; and striking the stern of the foremost vessel, crushed her beneath their keel. From the huge whirlpool which the sinking wreck occasioned, arose a shriek so loud and shrill—the death-cry of a hundred drowning creatures, blended into one fierce yell—that it rung far above the war-cry of the elements, and echoed and reechoed till it seemed to pierce air, sky, and ocean. But what was that—that old gray head that rose above the water's surface, and with looks of agony, and screams for aid, buffeted with the waves! One look, and he had sprung from the vessel's side, and with vigorous strokes was swimming towards it. He reached it; he was close upon it. They were *his* features. The old man saw him coming and vainly strove to elude his grasp. But he clasped him tight, and dragged him beneath the water. Down, down with him, fifty fathoms down; his struggles grew fainter and fainter, until they wholly ceased. He was dead; he had killed him, and had kept his oath.

"He was traversing the scorching sands of a mighty desert, barefooted and alone. The sand choked and blinded him; its fine thin grains entered the very pores of his skin, and irritated him almost to madness. Gigantic masses of the same material, carried forward by the wind, and shone through by the burning sun, stalked in the distance like pillars of living fire. The bones of men, who had perished in the dreary waste, lay scattered at his feet; a fearful light fell on everything around; so far as the eye could reach, nothing but objects of dread and horror presented themselves. Vainly striving to utter a cry of terror, with his tongue cleaving to his mouth, he rushed madly forward. Armed with supernatural strength, he waded through the sand, until exhausted with fatigue and thirst, he fell senseless on the earth. What fragrant coolness revived him; what gushing sound was that? Water! It was indeed a well; and the clear fresh stream was running at his feet. He drank deeply of it, and throwing his aching limbs upon the bank, sank into a delicious trance. The sound of approaching footsteps aroused him. An old gray-headed man tottered forward to slake his burning thirst. It was *he* again! He wound his arms round the old man's body, and held him back. He struggled, and shrieked for water, for but one drop of water to save his life! But he held the old man firmly, and watched his agonies with greedy eyes; and when his lifeless head fell forward on his bosom, he rolled the corpse from him with his feet.

"When the fever left him, and consciousness returned, he awoke to find himself rich and free: to hear that the parent who would have let him die in jail—*would!* who *had* let those who were far dearer to him than his own existence die of want and sickness of heart that medicine cannot cure—had been found dead on his bed of down. He had had all the heart to leave his son a beggar, but proud even of his health and strength, had put off the act till it was too late, and now might gnash his teeth in the other world, at the thought of the wealth his remissness had left him. He awoke to this, and he awoke to more. To recollect the purpose for which he lived, and to remember that his enemy was his wife's own father—the man who had cast him into prison, and who, when his daughter and her child sued at his feet for mercy, had spurned them from his door. Oh, how he cursed the weakness that prevented him from being up, and active, in his scheme of vengeance!

"He caused himself to be carried from the scene of his loss and misery, and conveyed to a quiet residence on the sea coast, not in the hope of recovering his peace of mind or happiness, for both were fled forever; but to restore his prostrate energies, and meditate on his darling object. And here, some evil spirit cast in his way the opportunity for his first, most horrible revenge.

"It was summer-time; and wrapped in his gloomy thoughts, he would issue from his solitary lodgings early in the evening, and wandering along a narrow path beneath the cliffs, to a wild and lonely spot that had struck his fancy in his ramblings, seat himself on some fallen fragment of the rock, and burying his face in his hands, remain there for hours—sometimes until night had completely closed in, and the long shadows of the frowning cliffs above his head cast a thick black darkness on every object near him.

"He was seated here, one calm evening, in his old position, now and then raising his head to watch the flight of a sea-gull, or carry his eye along the glorious crimson path, which, commencing in the middle of the ocean, seemed to lead to its very verge where the sun was setting, when the profound stillness of the spot was broken by a loud cry for help; he listened, doubtful of his having heard aright, when the cry was repeated with even greater vehemence than before, and starting to his feet, he hastened in the direction whence it proceeded.

"The tale told itself at once; some scattered garments lay on the beach; a human head was just visible above the waves at a little distance from the shore; and an old man, wringing his hands in agony, was running to and fro, shrieking for assistance. The invalid, whose strength was now sufficiently restored, threw off his coat, and rushed towards the sea, with the intention of plunging in, and dragging the drowning man ashore.

"Hasten here, sir, in God's name; help, help, sir, for the love of Heaven. He is my son, sir, my only son!' said the old man, frantically, as he advanced to meet him. 'My only son, sir, and he is dying before his father's eyes!'

"At the first word the old man uttered, the stranger checked himself in his career, and, folding his arms, stood perfectly motionless.

"'Great God!' exclaimed the old man, recoiling. 'Heyling!'

"The stranger smiled, and was silent.

"'Heyling!' said the old man, wildly: 'My boy, Heyling, my dear boy, look, look!' Gasping for breath, the miserable father pointed to the spot where the young man was struggling for life.

"'Hark!' said the old man. 'He cries once more. He is alive yet. Heyling, save him, save him!'

"The stranger smiled again, and remained immovable as a statue.

"'I have wronged you,' shrieked the old man, falling on his knees, and clasping his hands together. 'Be revenged; take my all, my life; cast me into the water at your feet, and, if human nature can repress a struggle, I will die, without stirring hand or foot. Do it, Heyling, do it, but save my boy; he is so young, Heyling, so young to die!'

"'Listen,' said the stranger, grasping the old man fiercely by the wrist: 'I will have life for life, and here in one. *My* child died, before his father's eyes, a far more agonizing and painful death than that young slanderer of his sister's worth is meeting while I speak. You laughed—laughed in your daughter's face, where death had already set his hand—at our sufferings, then. What do you think of them now? See there, see there!'

"As the stranger spoke, he pointed to the sea. A faint cry died away upon its surface; the last powerful struggle of the dying man agitated the rippling waves for a few seconds: and the spot where he had gone down into his early grave was indistinguishable from the surrounding water.

"Three years had elapsed, when a gentleman alighted from a private carriage at the door of a London attorney, then well known as a man of no great nicety in his professional dealings; and requested a private interview on business of importance. Although evidently not past the prime of life, his face was pale, haggard, and dejected; and it did not require the acute perception of the man of business, to discern at a glance that disease or suffering had done more to work a change in his appearance than the mere hand of time could have accomplished in twice the period of his whole life.

"'I wish you to undertake some legal business for me,' said the stranger.

"The attorney bowed obsequiously, and glanced at a larger packet which the gentleman carried in his hand. His visitor observed the look, and proceeded:

"'It is no common business,' said he, 'nor have these papers reached my hands without long trouble and great expense.'

"The attorney cast a still more anxious look at the packet: and his visitor, untying the string that bound it, disclosed a quantity of promissory note, with copies, of deeds and other documents.

"'Upon these papers,' said the client, 'the man whose name they bear, has raised, as you will see, large sums of money, for some years past. There was a tacit understanding between him and the men into whose hands they originally went—and from whom I have by degrees purchased the whole, for treble and quadruple their nominal value—that these loans should be from time to time renewed, until a given period had elapsed. Such an understanding is nowhere expressed. He has sustained many losses of late; and these obligations accumulating upon him at once would crush him to the earth.'

"'The whole amount is many thousands of pounds,' said the attorney, looking over the papers.

"'It is,' said the client.

"'What are we to do?' inquired the man of business.

"'Do!' replied the client, with sudden vehemence. 'Put every engine of the law in force, every trick that ingenuity can devise and rascality execute; fair means and foul; the open oppression of the law, aided by all the craft of its most ingenious practitioners. I would have him die a harassing and lingering death. Ruin him, seize and sell his lands and goods, drive him from house and home, and drag him forth a beggar in his old age, to die in a common jail.'

"'But the costs, my dear sir, the costs of all this,' reasoned the attorney when he had recovered from his momentary surprise. 'If the defendant be a man of straw, who is to pay the costs, sir?'

"'Name any sum,' said the stranger, his hand trembling so violently with excitement that he could scarcely hold the pen he seized as he spoke; 'any sum, and it is yours. Don't be afraid to name it, man. I shall not think it dear, if you gain my object.'

"The attorney named a large sum, at hazard, as the advance he should require to secure himself against the possibility of loss; but more with the view of ascertaining how far his client was really disposed to go, than with any idea that he would comply with the demand. The stranger wrote a check upon his banker, for the whole amount, and left him.

"The draft was duly honored, and the attorney, finding that his strange client might be safely relied upon, commenced his work in earnest. For more than two years afterwards, Mr. Heyling would sit whole days together, in the office, poring over the papers as they accumulated, and reading again and again, his eyes gleaming with joy, the letters of remonstrance, the prayers for a little delay, the representations of the certain ruin in which the opposite party must be involved, which poured in, as suit after suit, and process after process, was commenced. To all applications for a brief indulgence, there was but one reply—the money must be paid. Land, house, furniture, each in its turn, was taken under some one of the numerous executions which were issued; and the old man himself would have been immured in prison had he not escaped the vigilance of the officers, and fled.

"The implacable animosity of Heyling, so far from being satiated by the success of his persecution, increased a hundred-fold with the ruin he inflicted. On being informed of the old man's flight, his fury was unbounded. He gnashed his teeth with rage; tore the hair from his head, and assailed with horrid imprecations the men who had been entrusted with the writ. He was only restored to comparative calmness by repeated assurances of the certainty of discovering the fugitive. Agents were sent in quest of him, in all directions; every stratagem that could be invented was resorted to, for the purpose of discovering his place of retreat; but it was all in vain. Half a year had passed over, and he was still undiscovered.

"At length, late one night, Heyling, of whom nothing had been seen for many weeks before, appeared at his attorney's private residence, and sent up word that a gentleman wished to see him instantly. Before the attorney, who had recognized his voice from above stairs, could order the servant to admit him, he had rushed up the staircase, and entered the drawing-room, pale and breathless. Having closed the door, to prevent being overheard, he sank into a chair, and said, in a low voice:

"'Hush! I have found him at last.'

"'No!' said the attorney. 'Well done, my dear sir; well done.'

"'He lies concealed in a wretched lodging in Camden Town,' said Heyling. 'Perhaps it is as well we *did* lose sight of him, for he has been living alone there, in the most abject misery, all the time, and he is poor —very poor.'

"'Very good,' said the attorney. 'You will have the capture made tomorrow, of course?'

"'Yes,' replied Heyling. 'Stay! no! The next day. You are surprised at my wishing to postpone it,' he added, with a ghastly smile; 'but I had forgotten. The next days is an anniversary in his life: let it be done then.'

"'Very good,' said the attorney. 'Will you write down instructions for the officer?'

"'No; let him meet me here, at eight in the evening, and I will accompany him myself.'

"They met on the appointed night, and, hiring a hackney coach, directed the driver to stop at that corner of the old Pancras Road, at which stands the parish workhouse. By the time they alighted there, it was quite dark; and, proceeding by the dead wall in front of the Veterinary Hospital, they entered a small by-street, which is, or was at that time called Little College Street, and which, whatever it may be now, was in those days a desolate place enough, surrounded by little else than fields and ditches.

"Having drawn the traveling cap he had on half over his face, and muffled himself in his cloak, Heyling stopped before the meanest-looking house in the street, and knocked gently at the door. It was at once opened by a woman, who dropped a curtsey of recognition, and Heyling, whispering the officer to remain below, crept gently upstairs, and, opening the door of the front room, entered at once.

"The object of his search and his unrelenting animosity, now a decrepit old man, was seated at a bare deal table, on which stood a miserable candle. He started on the entrance of the stranger, and rose feebly to his feet.

"'What now, what now?' said the old man. 'What fresh misery is this? What do you want here?'

"'A word with _you_,' replied Heyling. As he spoke, he seated himself at the other end of the table, and, throwing off his cloak and cap, disclosed his features.

"The old man seemed instantly deprived of the power of speech. He fell backward in his chair, and clasping his hands together, gazed on the apparition with a mingled look of abhorrence and fear.

"'This day six years,' said Heyling, 'I claimed the life you owed me for my child's. Beside the lifeless form of your daughter, old man, I swore to live a life of revenge. I have never swerved from my purpose for a moment's space; but if I had, one thought of her uncomplaining, suffering look, as she drooped away, or of the starving face of our innocent child, would have nerved me to my task. My first act of requital you well remember: this is my last.'

"The old man shivered, and his hands dropped powerless by his side.

"'I leave England to-morrow,' said Heyling, after a moment's pause. 'To-night I consign you to the living death to which you devoted her—a hopeless prison—'

"He raised his eyes to the old man's countenance, and paused. He lifted the light to his face, set it gently down, and left the apartment.

"'You had better see to the old man,' he said to the woman, as he opened the door and motioned the officer to follow him into the street. 'I think he is ill.' The woman closed the door, ran hastily upstairs, and found him lifeless.

"Beneath a plain gravestone, in one of the most peaceful and secluded churchyards in Kent, where wild flowers mingle with the grass, and the soft landscape around forms the fairest spot in the garden of England, lie the bones of the young mother and her gentle child. But the ashes of the father do not mingle with theirs; nor, from that night forward, did the attorney ever gain the remotest clue to the subsequent history of his queer client."

WILKIE COLLINS

(1824—1889)

WILLIAM WILKIE COLLINS was born at London in 1824. Like his friend Dickens, he was a voluminous writer of novels and tales, an editor and a dramatist. He was rather more interested in the short story form than Dickens, and a more accomplished master of it. *A Terribly Strange Bed* is one of the best known examples of the tale that is related for the sake of the thrill.

The story is reprinted from the volume *After Dark*, first published in London, 1856.

A TERRIBLY STRANGE BED

SHORTLY after my education at college was finished, I happened to be staying at Paris with an English friend. We were both young men then, and lived, I am afraid, rather a wild life, in the delightful city of our sojourn. One night we were idling about the neighborhood of the Palais Royal, doubtful to what amusement we should next betake ourselves. My friend proposed a visit to Frascati's; but his suggestion was not to my taste. I knew Frascati's, as the French saying is, by heart; had lost and won plenty of five-franc pieces there, merely for amusement's sake, until it was amusement no longer, and was thoroughly tired, in fact, of all the ghastly respectabilities of such a social anomaly as a respectable gambling-house.

"For Heaven's sake," said I to my friend, "let us go somewhere where we can see a little genuine, blackguard, poverty-stricken gaming, with no false gingerbread glitter thrown over it at all. Let us get away from fashionable Frascati's, to a house where they don't mind letting in a man with a ragged coat, or a man with no coat, ragged or otherwise."

"Very well," said my friend, "we needn't go out of the Palais Royal to find the sort of company you want. Here's the place just before us; as blackguard a place, by all report, as you could possibly wish to see."

In another minute we arrived at the door, and entered the house.

When we got upstairs, and had left our hats and sticks with the door-keeper, we were admitted into the chief gambling-room. We did not find many people assembled there. But, few as the men were who looked up at us on our entrance, they were all types—lamentably true types—of their respective classes.

We had come to see blackguards; but these men were something worse. There is a comic side, more or less appreciable, in all blackguardism: here there was nothing but tragedy—mute, weird tragedy. The quiet in the room was horrible. The thin, haggard, long-haired young man, whose sunken eyes fiercely watched the turning up of the cards, never spoke; the flabby, fat-faced, pimply player, who pricked his piece of pasteboard perseveringly, to register how often black won, and how often red, never spoke; the dirty, wrinkled old man, with the vulture eyes and the darned great-coat, who had lost his last sou, and still looked on desperately after he could play no longer, never spoke. Even the voice of the croupier sounded as if it were strangely dulled and thickened in the atmosphere of the room. I had entered the place to laugh, but the spectacle before me was something to weep over. I soon found it necessary to take refuge in excitement from the depression of spirits which was stealing on me. Unfortunately I sought the nearest excitement, by going to the table and beginning to play. Still more unfortunately, as the event will show, I won—won prodigiously; won incredibly; won at such a rate that the regular players at the table crowded round me; and staring at my stakes with hungry, superstitious eyes, whispered to one another that the English stranger was going to break the bank.

The game was Rouge et Noir. I had played at it in every city in Europe, without, however, the care or the wish to study the Theory of Chances—that philosopher's stone of all gamblers! And a gambler, in the strict sense of the word, I had never been. I was heart-whole from the corroding passion for play. My gaming was a mere idle amusement. I never resorted to it by necessity, because I never knew what it was to want money. I never practised it so incessantly as to lose more than I could afford, or to gain more than I could coolly pocket without being thrown off my balance by my good luck. In short, I had hitherto frequented gambling-tables—just as I frequented ball-rooms and opera-houses—because they amused me, and because I had nothing better to do with my leisure hours.

But on this occasion it was very different—now, for the first time in my life, I felt what the passion for play really was. My successes first bewildered, and then, in the most literal meaning of the word, intoxicated me. Incredible as it may appear, it is nevertheless true, that I only lost when I attempted to estimate chances, and played according to previous calculation. If I left everything to luck, and staked without any care or consideration, I was sure to win—to win in the face of every recognized probability in favor of the bank. At first some of the men present ventured their money safely enough on my color; but I speedily increased my stakes to sums which they dared not risk. One after another they left off playing, and breathlessly looked on at my game.

Still, time after time, I staked higher and higher, and still won. The excitement in the room rose to fever pitch. The silence was interrupted by a deep-muttered chorus of oaths and exclamations in different languages, every time the gold was shoveled across to my side of the table—even the imperturbable croupier dashed his rake on the floor in a (French) fury of astonishment at my success. But one man present preserved his self-possession, and that man was my friend. He came to my side, and whispering in English, begged me to leave the place, satisfied with what I had already gained. I must do him the justice to say that he repeated his warnings and entreaties several times, and only left me and went away, after I had rejected his advice (I was to all intents and purposes gambling drunk) in terms which rendered it impossible for him to address me again that night.

Shortly after he had gone, a hoarse voice behind me cried, "Permit me, my dear sir—permit me to restore to their proper place, two napoleons which you have dropped. Wonderful luck, sir! I pledge you my word of honor, as an old soldier, in the course of my long experience in this sort of thing, I never saw such luck as yours—never! Go on, sir—*Sacre mille bombes!* Go on boldly, and break the bank!"

I turned round and saw, nodding and smiling at me with inveterate civility, a tall man, dressed in a frogged and braided surtout.

If I had been in my senses, I should have considered him, personally, as being rather a suspicious specimen of an old soldier. He had goggling, bloodshot eyes, mangy mustaches, and a broken nose. His voice betrayed a barrack-room intonation of the worst order, and he had the dirtiest pair of hands I ever saw—even in France. These little personal peculiarities exercised, however, no repelling influence on me. In the mad excitement, the reckless triumph of that moment, I was ready to "fraternize" with anybody who encouraged me in my game. I accepted the old soldier's offered pinch of snuff; clapped him on the back, and swore he was the honestest fellow in the world—the most glorious relic of the Grand Army that I had ever met with. "Go on!" cried my military friend, snapping his fingers in ecstasy—"Go on, and win! Break the bank—*Mille tonnerres!* my gallant English comrade, break the bank!"

And I *did* go on—went on at such a rate, that in another quarter of an hour the croupier called out, "Gentlemen, the bank has discontinued for to-night." All the notes, and all the gold in that "bank," now lay in a heap under my hands; the whole floating capital of the gambling house was waiting to pour into my pockets!

"Tie up the money in your pocket-handkerchief, my worthy sir," said the old soldier, as I wildly plunged my hands into my heap of gold. "Tie it up, as we used to tie up a bit of dinner in the Grand Army; your winnings are too heavy for any breeches-pockets that ever were sewed. There! that's it—shovel them in, notes and all! *Credie!* what luck! Stop! another napoleon on the floor. *Ah! sacre petit polisson de Napoleon!* have I found thee at last? Now then, sir—two tight double knots each way with your honorable permission, and the money's safe. Feel it! feel it, fortunate sir! hard and round as a cannon-ball—*A bas* if they had only fired such cannon-balls at us at Austerlitz—*nom d'une pipe!* if they only had! And now, as an ancient grenadier, as an ex-brave of the French army, what remains for me to do? I ask what? Simply this, to entreat my valued English friend to drink a bottle of champagne with me, and toast the goddess Fortune in foaming goblets before we part!"

"Excellent ex-brave! Convivial ancient grenadier! Champagne by all means! An English cheer for an old soldier! Hurrah! hurrah! Another English cheer for the goddess Fortune! Hurrah, hurrah! hurrah!"

"Bravo! the Englishman; the amiable, gracious Englishman, in whose veins circulates the vivacious blood of France! Another glass? *A bas!*— the bottle is empty! Never mind! *Vive le vin!* I, the old soldier, order another bottle, and half a pound of *bonbons* with it!"

"No, no, ex-brave; never—ancient grenadier! *Your* bottle last time; *my* bottle this! Behold it! Toast away! The French Army! the great Napoleon! the present company! the croupier! the honest croupier's wife and daughters—if he has any! the ladies generally! everybody in the world!"

By the time the second bottle of champagne was emptied, I felt as if I had been drinking liquid fire—my brain seemed all aflame. No excess in wine had ever had this effect on me before in my life. Was it the result of a stimulant acting upon my system when I was in a highly excited state? Was my stomach in a particularly disordered condition? Or was the champagne amazingly strong?

"Ex-brave of the French Army!" cried I, in a mad state of exhilaration, "*I* am on fire! how are *you?* You have set me on fire! Do you hear, my hero of Austerlitz? Let us have a third bottle of champagne to put the flame out!"

The old soldier wagged his head, rolled his goggle-eyes, until I expected to see them slip out of their sockets; placed his dirty forefinger by the side of his broken nose; solemnly ejaculated "Coffee!" and immediately ran off into an inner room.

The word pronounced by the eccentric veteran seemed to have a magical effect on the rest of the company present. With one accord they all rose to depart. Probably they had expected to profit by my intoxication; but finding that my new friend was benevolently bent on preventing me from getting dead drunk, had now abandoned all hope of thriving pleasantly on my winnings. Whatever their motive might be, at any rate they went away in a body. When the old soldier returned and sat down again opposite to me at the table, we had the room to ourselves. I could see the croupier, in a sort of vestibule which opened out of it, eating his supper in solitude. The silence was now deeper than ever.

A sudden change, too, had come over the "ex-brave." He assumed a portentously solemn look; and when he spoke to me again, his speech was ornamented by no oaths, enforced by no finger-snapping, enlivened by no apostrophes or exclamations.

"Listen, my dear sir," said he, in mysteriously confidential tones— "listen to an old soldier's advice. I have been to the mistress of the house (a very charming woman, with a genius for cookery!) to impress on the the necessity of making us some particularly strong and good coffee. You must drink this coffee in order to get rid of your little amiable exaltation of spirits before you think of going home—you *must*, my good and gracious friend! With all that money to take home tonight, it is a sacred duty to yourself to have your wits about you. You are known to be a winner to an enormous extent by several gentlemen present to-night, who, in a certain point of view, are very worthy and excellent fellows; but they are mortal men, my dear sir, and they have their amiable weaknesses! Need I say more? Ah, no, no! you understand me! Now, this is what you must do—send for a cabriolet when you feel quite well again—draw up all the windows when you get into it—and tell the driver to take you home only through the large and well-lighted thoroughfares. Do this; and you and your money will be safe. Do this; and to-morrow you will thank an old soldier for giving you a word of honest advice."

Just as the ex-brave ended his oration in very lachrymose tones, the coffee came in, ready poured out in two cups. My attentive friend handed me one of the cups with a bow. I was parched with thirst, and drank it off at a draft. Almost instantly afterward I was seized with a fit of giddiness, and felt more completely intoxicated than ever. The room whirled round and round furiously; the old soldier seemed to be regularly bobbing up and down before me like the piston of a steam-engine. I was half deafened by a violent singing in my ears; a feeling of utter bewilderment, helplessness, idiocy, overcame me. I rose from my chair, holding on by the table to keep my balance; and stammered out that I felt dreadfully unwell—so unwell that I did not know how I was to get home.

"My dear friend," answered the old soldier—and even his voice seemed to be bobbing up and down as he spoke—"my dear friend, it would be madness to go home in *your* state; you would be sure to lose your money; you might be robbed and murdered with the greatest ease. *I* am going to sleep here: *do* you sleep here, too—they make up capital beds in this house—take one; sleep off the effects of the wine, and go home safely with your winnings to-morrow—to-morrow, in broad daylight."

I had but two ideas left: one, that I must never let go hold of my handkerchief full of money; the other, that I must lie down somewhere immediately, and fall off into a comfortable sleep. So I agreed to the proposal about the bed, and took the offered arm of the old soldier, carrying my money with my disengaged hand. Preceded by the croupier, we passed along some passages and up a flight of stairs into the bedroom which I was to occupy. The ex-brave shook me warmly by the hand, proposed that we should breakfast together, and then, followed by the croupier, left me for the night.

I ran to the wash-hand stand; drank some of the water in my jug; poured the rest out, and plunged my face into it; then sat down in a chair and tried to compose myself. I soon felt better. The change for my lungs, from the fetid atmosphere of the gambling-house to the cool air of the apartment I now occupied, the almost equally refreshing change for my eyes, from the glaring gaslights of the "salon" to the dim, quiet flicker of one bedroom-candle, aided wonderfully the restorative effects of cold water. The giddiness left me, and I began to feel a little like a reasonable being again. My first thought was of the risk of sleeping all night in a gambling-house; my second, of the still greater risk of trying to get out after the house was closed, and of going home alone at night through the streets of Paris with a large sum of money about me. I had slept in worse places than this on my travels; so I determined to lock, bolt, and barricade my door, and take my chance till the next morning.

Accordingly, I secured myself against all intrusion; looked under the bed, and into the cupboard; tried the fastening of the window; and then, satisfied that I had taken every proper precaution, pulled off my upper clothing, put my light, which was a dim one, on the hearth among a feathery litter of wood-ashes, and got into bed, with the handkerchief full of money under my pillow.

I soon felt not only that I could not go to sleep, but that I could not even close my eyes. I was wide awake, and in a high fever. Every nerve in my body trembled—every one of my senses seemed to be preternaturally sharpened. I tossed and rolled, and tried every kind of position and perseveringly sought out the cold corners of the bed, and all to no purpose. Now I thrust my arms over the clothes; now I poked them under the clothes; now I violently shot my legs straight out down to the bottom of the bed; now I convulsively coiled them up as near my chin as they would go; now I shook out my crumpled pillow, changed it to the cool side, patted it flat, and lay down quietly on my back; now I fiercely doubled it in two, set it up on end, thrust it against the board of the bed, and tried a sitting posture. Every effort was in vain; I groaned with vexation as I felt that I was in for a sleepless night.

What could I do? I had no book to read. And yet, unless I found out some method of diverting my mind, I felt certain that I was in the condition to imagine all sorts of horrors; to rack my brain with forebodings of every possible and impossible danger; in short, to pass the night in suffering all conceivable varieties of nervous terror.

I raised myself on my elbow, and looked about the room—which was brightened by a lovely moonlight pouring straight through the window—to see if it contained any pictures or ornaments that I could at all clearly distinguish. While my eyes wandered from wall to wall, a remembrance of Le Maistre's delightful little book, "Voyage autour de ma Chambre," occurred to me. I resolved to imitate the French author, and find occupation and amusement enough to relieve the tedium of my wakefulness, by making a mental inventory of every article of furniture I could see, and by following up to their sources the multitude of associations which even a chair, a table, or a wash-hand stand may be made to call forth.

In the nervous, unsettled state of my mind at that moment, I found it much easier to make my inventory than to make my reflections, and thereupon soon gave up all hope of thinking in Le Maistre's fanciful track—or, indeed, of thinking at all. I looked about the room at the different articles of furniture, and did nothing more.

There was, first, the bed I was lying in; a four-post bed, of all things in the world to meet with in Paris—yes, a thorough clumsy British four-poster, with a regular top lined with chintz—the regular fringed valance all round—the regular stifling, unwholesome curtains, which I remembered having mechanically drawn back against the posts without particularly noticing the bed when I first got into the room. Then there was the marble-topped wash-hand stand, from which the water I had spilled, in my hurry to pour it out, was still dripping, slowly and more slowly, on to the brick floor. Then two small chairs, with my coat, waistcoat, and trousers flung on them. Then a large elbow-chair covered with dirty white dimity, with my cravat and shirt collar thrown over the back. Then a chest of drawers with two of the brass handles off, and a tawdry, broken china inkstand placed on it by way of ornament for the top. Then the dressing-table, adorned by a very small looking-glass, and a very large pincushion. Then the window—an unusually large window. Then a dark old picture, which the feeble candle dimly showed me. It was the picture of a fellow in a high Spanish hat, crowned with a plume of towering feathers. A swarthy, sinister ruffian, looking upward, shading his eyes with his hand, and looking intently upward—it might be at some tall gallows on which he was going to be hanged. At any rate, he had the appearance of thoroughly deserving it.

This picture put a kind of constraint upon me to look upward too—at the top of the bed. It was a gloomy and not an interesting object, and I looked back at the picture. I counted the feathers in the man's hat—they stood out in relief—three white, two green. I observed the crown of his hat, which was of a conical shape, according to the fashion supposed to have been favored by Guido Fawkes. I wondered what he was looking up at. It couldn't be at the stars; such a desperado was neither astrologer nor astronomer. It must be at the high gallows, and he was going to be hanged presently. Would the executioner come into possession of his conical crowned hat and plume of feathers? I counted the feathers again—three white, two green.

While I still lingered over this very improving and intellectual employment, my thoughts insensibly began to wander. The moonlight shining into the room reminded me of a certain moonlight night in England—the night after a picnic party in a Welsh valley. Every incident of the drive homeward, through lovely scenery, which the moonlight made lovelier than ever, came back to my remembrance, though I had never given the picnic a thought for years; though, if I had *tried* to recollect it, I could certainly have recalled little or nothing of that scene long past. Of all the wonderful faculties that help to tell us we are immortal, which speaks the sublime truth more eloquently than memory? Here was I, in a strange house of the most suspicious character, in a situation of uncertainty, and even of peril, which might seem to make the cool exercise of my recollection almost out of the question; nevertheless, remembering, quite involuntarily, places, people, conversations, minute circumstances of every kind, which I had thought forgotten forever; which I could not possibly have recalled at will, even under the most favorable auspices. And what cause had produced in a moment the whole of this strange, complicated, mysterious effect? Nothing but some rays of moonlight shining in at my bedroom window.

I was still thinking of the picnic—of our merriment on the drive home—of the sentimental young lady who *would* quote *Childe Harold* because it was moonlight. I was absorbed by these past scenes and past amusements, when, in an instant, the thread on which my memories hung snapped asunder; my attention immediately came back to present things more vividly than ever, and I found myself, I neither knew why nor wherefore, looking hard at the picture again.

Looking for what?

Good God! the man had pulled his hat down on his brows! No! the hat itself was gone! Where was the conical crown? Where the feathers —three white, two green? Not there! In place of the hat and feathers, what dusky object was it that now hid his forehead, his eyes, his shading hand?

Was the bed moving?

I turned on my back and looked up. Was I mad? drunk? dreaming? giddy again? or was the top of the bed really moving down—sinking slowly, regularly, silently, horribly, right down throughout the whole of its length and breadth—right down upon me, as I lay underneath?

My blood seemed to stand still. A deadly, paralyzing coldness stole all over me as I turned my head round on the pillow and determined to test whether the bed-top was really moving or not, by keeping my eye on the man in the picture.

The next look in that direction was enough. The dull, black, frowsy outline of the valance above me was within an inch of being parallel with his waist. I still looked breathlessly. And steadily and slowly—very slowly—I saw the figure, and the line of frame below the figure, vanish, as the valance moved down before it.

I am, constitutionally, anything but timid. I have been on more than one occasion in peril of my life, and have not lost my self-possession for an instant; but when the conviction first settled on my mind that the bed-top was really moving, was steadily and continuously sinking down upon me, I looked up shuddering, helpless, panic-stricken, beneath the hideous machinery for murder, which was advancing closer and closer to suffocate me where I lay.

I looked up, motionless, speechless, breathless. The candle, fully spent, went out; but the moonlight still brightened the room. Down and down, without pausing and without sounding, came the bed-top, and still my panic terror seemed to bind me faster and faster to the mattress on which I lay—down and down it sank, till the dusty odor from the lining of the canopy came stealing into my nostrils.

At that final moment the instinct of self-preservation startled me out of my trance, and I moved at last. There was just room for me to roll myself sidewise off the bed. As I dropped noiselessly to the floor, the edge of the murderous canopy touched me on the shoulder.

Without stopping to draw my breath, without wiping the cold sweat from my face, I rose instantly on my knees to watch the bed-top. I was literally spellbound by it. If I had heard footsteps behind me, I could not have turned round; if a means of escape had been miraculously provided for me, I could not have moved to take advantage of it. The whole life in me was, at that moment, concentrated in my eyes.

It descended—the whole canopy, with the fringe round it, came down—down—close down; so close that there was not room now to squeeze my finger between the bed-top and the bed. I felt at the sides, and discovered that what had appeared to me from beneath to be the ordinary light canopy of a four-post bed was in reality a thick, broad mattress, the substance of which was concealed by the valance and its fringe. I looked up and saw the four posts rising hideously bare. In the middle of the bed-top was a huge wooden screw that had evidently worked it down through a hole in the ceiling, just as ordinary presses are worked down on the substance selected for compression. The frightful apparatus moved without making the faintest noise. There had been no creaking as it came down; there was now not the faintest sound from the room above. Amidst a dead and awful silence I beheld before me—in the Nineteenth Century, and in the civilized capital of France—such a machine for secret murder by suffocation as might have existed in the worst days of the Inquisition, in the lonely inns among the Hartz Mountains, in the mysterious tribunals of Westphalia! Still, as I looked on it, I could not move, I could hardly breathe, but I began to recover the power of thinking, and in a moment I discovered the murderous conspiracy framed against me in all its horror.

My cup of coffee had been drugged, and drugged too strongly. I had been saved from being smothered by having taken an overdose of some narcotic. How I had chafed and fretted at the fever fit which had preserved my life by keeping me awake! How recklessly I had confided myself to the two wretches who had led me into this room, determined, for the sake of my winnings, to kill me in my sleep by the surest and most horrible contrivance for secretly accomplishing my destruction! How many men, winners like me, had slept, as I had proposed to sleep, in that bed, and had never been seen or heard of more! I shuddered at the bare idea of it.

But ere long all thought was again suspended by the sight of the murderous canopy moving once more. After it had remained on the bed— as nearly as I could guess—about ten minutes, it began to move up again. The villains who worked it from above evidently believed that their purpose was now accomplished. Slowly and silently, as it had descended, that horrible bed-top rose toward it former place. When it reached the upper extremities of the four posts, it reached the ceiling too. Neither hole nor screw could be seen; the bed became in appearance an ordinary bed again—the canopy an ordinary canopy—even to the most suspicious eyes.

Now, for the first time, I was able to move—to rise from my knees—to dress myself in my upper clothing—and to consider of how I should escape. If I betrayed by the smallest noise that the attempt to suffocate me had failed, I was certain to be murdered. Had I made any noise already? I listened intently, looking toward the door.

No! No footsteps in the passage outside—no sound of a tread, light or heavy, in the room above—absolute silence everywhere. Besides locking and bolting my door, I had moved an old wooden chest against it, which I had found under the bed. To remove this chest (my blood ran cold as I thought of what its contents *might* be!) without making some disturbance was impossible; and, moreover, to think of escaping through the house, now barred up for the night, was sheer insanity. Only one chance was left me—the window. I stole to it on tiptoe.

My bedroom was on the first floor, above an entresol, and looked into the back street. I raised my hand to open the window, knowing that on that action hung, by the merest hair-breadth, my chance of safety. They keep vigilant watch in a House of Murder. If any part of the frame cracked, if the hinge creaked, I was a lost man! It must have occupied me at least five minutes, reckoning by time—five *hours* reckoning by suspense—to open that window. I succeeded in doing it silently—in doing it with all the dexterity of a house-breaker—and then looked down into the street. To leap the distance beneath me would be almost certain destruction! Next, I looked round at the sides of the house. Down the left side ran a thick water-pipe—it passed close by the outer edge of the window. The moment I saw the pipe, I knew I was saved. My breath came and went freely for the first time since I had seen the canopy of the bed moving down upon me!

To some men the means of escape which I had discovered might have seemed difficult and dangerous enough—to *me* the prospect of slipping down the pipe into the street did not suggest even a thought of peril. I had always been accustomed, by the practise of gymnastics, to keep up my school-boy powers as a daring and expert climber; and knew that my head, hands, and feet would serve me faithfully in any hazards of ascent or descent. I had already got one leg over the window-sill, when I remembered the handkerchief filled with money under my pillow. I could well have afforded to leave it behind me, but I was revengefully determined that the miscreants of the gambling-house should miss their plunder as well as their victim. So I went back to the bed and tied the heavy handkerchief at my back by my cravat.

Just as I had made it tight and fixed it in a comfortable place, I thought I heard a sound of breathing outside the door. The chill feeling of horror ran through me again as I listened. No! Dead silence still in the passage—I had only heard the night air blowing softly into the room. The next moment I was on the window-sill—and the next I had a firm grip on the water-pipe with my hands and knees.

I slid down into the street easily and quietly, as I thought I should, and immediately set off at the top of my speed to a branch "Prefecture" of Police, which I knew was situated in the immediate neighborhood. A "Sub-prefect," and several picked men among his subordinates, happened to be up, maturing, I believe, some scheme for discovering the perpetrator of a mysterious murder which all Paris was talking of just then. When I began my story, in a breathless hurry and in very bad French, I could see that the Sub-prefect suspected me of being a drunken Englishman who had robbed somebody; but he soon altered his opinion as I went on, and before I had anything like concluded, he shoved all the papers before him into a drawer, put on his hat, supplied me with another (for I was bareheaded), ordered a file of soldiers, desired his expert followers to get ready all sorts of tools for breaking open doors and ripping up brick flooring, and took my arm, in the most friendly and familiar manner possible, to lead me with him out of the house. I will venture to say that when the Sub-prefect was a little boy, and was taken for the first time to the play, he was not half as much pleased as he was now at the job in prospect for him at the gambling-house!

Away we went through the streets, the Sub-prefect cross-examining and congratulating me in the same breath as we marched at the head of our formidable *posse comitatus*. Sentinels were placed at the back and front of the house the moment we got to it, a tremendous battery of knocks was directed against the door; a light appeared at a window; I was told to conceal myself behind the police—then came more knocks, and a cry of "Open in the name of the law!" At that terrible summons bolts and locks gave way before an invisible hand, and the moment after the Sub-prefect was in the passage, confronting a waiter half dressed and ghastly pale. This was the short dialogue which immediately took place:

"We want to see the Englishman who is sleeping in this house?"

"He went away hours ago."

"He did no such thing. His friend went away; *he* remained. Show us to his bedroom!"

"I swear to you, Monsieur le Sous-prefect, he is not here! He—"

"I swear to you, Monsieur le Garçon, he is. He slept here—he didn't find your bed comfortable—he came to us to complain of it—here he is among my men—and here am I ready to look for a flea or two in his bedstead. Renaudin!" (calling to one of the subordinates, and pointing to the waiter), "collar that man, and tie his hands behind him. Now, then, gentlemen, let us walk upstairs!"

Every man and woman in the house was secured—the "Old Soldier" the first. Then I identified the bed in which I had slept, and then we went into the room above.

No object that was at all extraordinary appeared in any part of it. The Sub-prefect looked round the place, commanded everybody to be silent, stamped twice on the floor, called for a candle, looked attentively at the spot he had stamped on, and ordered the flooring there to be carefully taken up. This was done in no time. Lights were produced, and we saw a deep raftered cavity between the floor of this room and the ceiling of the room beneath. Through this cavity there ran perpendicularly a sort of case of iron thickly greased; and inside the case appeared the screw, which communicated with the bed-top below. Extra lengths of screw, freshly oiled; levers covered with felt; all the complete upper works of a heavy press—constructed with infernal ingenuity so as to join the fixtures below, and when taken to pieces again to go into the smallest possible compass—were next discovered and pulled out on the floor. After some little difficulty the Sub-prefect succeeded in putting the machinery together, and, leaving his men to work it, descended with me to the bedroom. The smothering canopy was then lowered, but not so noiselessly as I had seen it lowered. When I mentioned this to the Sub-prefect, his answer, simple as it was, had a terrible significance, "My men," said he, "are working down the bed-top for the first time — the men whose money you won were in better practise."

We left the house in the sole possession of two police agents—every one of the inmates being removed to prison on the spot. The Sub-prefect, after taking down my "procès verbal" in his office, returned with me to my hotel to get my passport. "Do you think," I asked, as I gave it to him, "that any men have really been smothered in that bed, as they tried to smother *me?*"

"I have seen dozens of drowned men laid out at the Morgue," answered the Sub-prefect, "in whose pocketbooks were found letters stating that they had committed suicide in the Seine, because they had lost everything at the gaming-table. Do I know how many of those men entered the same gambling-house that *you* entered? won as *you* won? took that bed as *you* took it? slept in it? were smothered in it? and were privately thrown into the river, with a letter of explanation written by the murderers and placed in their pocketbooks? No man can say how many or how few have suffered the fate from which you have escaped. The people of the gambling-house kept their bedstead machinery a secret from us—even from the police! The dead kept the rest of the secret for them. Good-night, or rather good-morning, Monsieur Faulkner! Be at my office again at nine o'clock—in the meantime, au revoir!"

The rest of my story is soon told. I was examined and reexamined; the gambling-house was strictly searched all through from top to bottom; the prisoners were separately interrogated; and two of the less guilty among them made a confession. I discovered that the Old Soldier was the master of the gambling-house—*justice* discovered that he had been drummed out of the army as a vagabond years ago; that he had been guilty of all sorts of villainies since; that he was in possession of stolen property, which the owners identified; and that he, the croupier, another accomplice, and the woman who had made my cup of coffee, were all in the secret of the bedstead. There appeared some reason to doubt whether the inferior persons attached to the house knew anything of the suffocating machinery; and they received the benefit of that doubt, by being treated simply as thieves and vagabonds. As for the Old Soldier and his two head myrmidons, they went to the galleys; the woman who had drugged my coffee was imprisoned for I forget how many years; the regular attendants at the gambling-house were considered "suspicious," and placed under "surveillance"; and I became, for one whole week (which is a long time), the head "lion" in Parisian society. My adventure was dramatized by three illustrious play-makers, but never saw theatrical daylight; for the censorship forbade the introduction on the stage of a correct copy of the gambling-house bedstead.

One good result was produced by my adventure, which any censorship must have approved: it cured me of ever again trying "Rouge et Noir" as an amusement. The sight of a green cloth, with packs of cards and heaps of money on it, will henceforth be forever associated in my mind with the sight of a bed canopy descending to suffocate me in the silence and darkness of the night.

THOMAS HARDY

(1840—1928)

THOMAS HARDY was born in Dorsetshire in 1840. At an early age he went to Dorchester to study architecture, and later to London. His first novel (published 1871) was read and appreciated by George Meredith, who saw it in MS. After its publication Hardy returned to Dorchester, where he lived for over fifty years. Among his many volumes of fiction there are four collections of short stories. Hardy's chief qualities—his grasp of character and his ability to create atmosphere—are observable in his short tales quite as clearly as in his greater and more extensive novels.

The present story is reprinted, by permission of the publisher, from *A Group of Noble Dames*, Macmillan and Co.

SQUIRE PETRICK'S LADY

(From *A Group of Noble Dames*)

FOLK who are at all acquainted with the traditions of Stapleford Park will not need to be told that in the middle of the last century it was owned by that trump of mortgagees, Timothy Petrick, whose skill in gaining possession of fair estates by granting sums of money on their title-deeds has seldom if ever been equaled in our part of England. Timothy was a lawyer by profession, and agent to several noblemen, by which means his special line of business became opened to him by a sort of revelation. It is said that a relative of his, a very deep thinker, who afterwards had the misfortune to be transported for life for mistaken notions on the signing of a will, taught him considerable legal lore, which he creditably resolved never to throw away for the benefit of other people, but to reserve it entirely for his own.

However, I have nothing in particular to say about his early and active days, but rather of the time when, an old man, he had become the owner of vast estates by the means I have signified—among them the great manor of Stapleford, on which he lived, in the splendid old mansion now pulled down; likewise estates at Marlott, estates near Sherton Abbas, nearly all the borough of Millpool, and many properties near Ivell. Indeed, I can't call to mind half his landed possessions, and I don't know that it matters much at this time of day, seeing that he's been dead and gone many years. It is said that when he bought an estate he would not decide to pay the price till he had walked over every single acre with his own two feet, and prodded the soil at every point with his own spud, to test its quality, which, if we regard the extent of his properties, must have been a stiff business for him.

At the time I am speaking of he was a man over eighty, and his son was dead; but he had two grandsons, the eldest of whom, his namesake, was married, and was shortly expecting issue. Just then the grandfather was taken ill, for death, as it seemed, considering his age. By his will the old man had created an entail (as I believe the lawyers call it), devising the whole of the estates to his elder grandson and his issue male, failing which, to his younger grandson and his issue male, failing which, to remoter relatives, who need not be mentioned now.

While old Timothy Petrick was lying ill, his elder grandson's wife, Annetta, gave birth to her expected child, who, as fortune would have it, was a son. Timothy, her husband, though sprung of a scheming family, was no great schemer himself; he was the single one of the Petricks then living whose heart had ever been greatly moved by sentiments which did not run in the groove of ambition; and on this account he had not married well, as the saying is, his wife having been the daughter of a family of no better beginnings than his own; that is to say, her father was a country townsman of the professional class. But she was a very pretty woman, by all accounts, and her husband had seen, courted, and married her in a high tide of infatuation, after a very short acquaintance, and with very little knowledge of her heart's history. He had never found reason to regret his choice as yet, and his anxiety for her recovery was great.

She was supposed to be out of danger, and herself and the child progressing well, when there was a change for the worse, and she sank so rapidly that she was soon given over. When she felt that she was about to leave him, Annetta sent for her husband, and, on his speedy entry and assurance that they were alone, she made him solemnly vow to give the child every care in any circumstances that might arise, if it should please Heaven to take her. This, of course, he readily promised. Then, after some hesitation, she told him that she could not die with a falsehood upon her soul, and dire deceit in her life; she must make a terrible confession to him before her lips were sealed forever. She thereupon related an incident concerning the baby's parentage which was not as he supposed.

Timothy Petrick, though a quick-feeling man, was not of a sort to show nerves outwardly; and he bore himself as heroically as he possibly could do in this trying moment of his life. That same night his wife died; and while she lay dead, and before her funeral, he hastened to the bedside of his sick grandfather, and revealed to him all that had happened—the baby's birth, his wife's confession, and her death, beseeching the aged man, as he loved him, to bestir himself now, at the eleventh hour, and alter his will so as to dish the intruder. Old Timothy, seeing matters in the same light as his grandson, required no urging against allowing anything to stand in the way of legitimate inheritance; he executed another will, limiting the entail to Timothy, his grandson, for life, and his male heirs thereafter to be born; after them to his other grandson, Edward, and Edward's heirs. Thus the newly born infant, who had been the center of so many hopes, was cut off and scorned as none of the elect.

The old mortgagee lived but a short time after this, the excitement of the discovery having told upon him considerably, and he was gathered to his fathers like the most charitable man in his neighborhood. Both wife and grandparent being buried, Timothy settled down to his usual life as well as he was able, mentally satisfied that he had, by prompt action, defeated the consequences of such dire domestic treachery as had been shown towards him, and resolving to marry a second time as soon as he could satisfy himself in the choice of a wife.

But men do not always know themselves. The imbittered state of Timothy Petrick's mind bred in him by degrees such a hatred and mistrust of womankind that though several specimens of high attractiveness came under his eyes, he could not bring himself to the point of proposing marriage. He dreaded to take up the position of husband a second time, discerning a trap in every petticoat, and a Slough of Despond in possible heirs. "What has happened once, when all seemed so fair, may happen again," he said to himself. "I'll risk my name no more." So he abstained from marriage, and overcame his wish for a lineal descendant to follow him in the ownership of Stapleford.

Timothy had scarcely noticed the unfortunate child that his wife had borne, after arranging for a meager fulfilment of his promise to her to take care of the boy, by having him brought up in his house. Occasionally, remembering his promise, he went and glanced at the child, saw that he was doing well, gave a few special directions, and again went his solitary way. Thus he and the child lived on in the Stapleford mansion-house till two or three years has passed by. One day he was walking in the garden, and by some accident left his snuff-box on a bench. When he came back to find it he saw the little boy standing there; he had escaped his nurse, and was making a plaything of the box, in spite of the convulsive sneezings which the game brought in its train. Then the man with the incrusted heart became interested in the little fellow's persistence in his play under such discomforts; he looked in the child's face, saw there his wife's countenance, though he did not see his own, and fell into thought on the piteousness of childhood—particularly of despised and rejected childhood, like this before him.

From that hour, try as he would to counteract the feeling, the human necessity to love something or other got the better of what he had called his wisdom, and shaped itself in a tender anxiety for the youngster Rupert. This name had been given him by his dying mother when, at her request, the child was baptized in her chamber, lest he should not survive for public baptism; and her husband had never thought of it as a name of any significance till, about this time, he learned by accident that it was the name of the young Marquis of Christminster, son of the Duke of Southwesterland, for whom Annetta had cherished warm feelings before her marriage. Recollecting some wandering phrases in his wife's last words, which he had not understood at the time, he perceived at last that this was the person to whom she had alluded when affording him a clew to little Rupert's history.

He would sit in silence for hours with the child, being no great speaker at the best of times; but the boy, on his part, was too ready with his tongue for any break in discourse to arise because Timothy Petrick had nothing to say. After idling away his mornings in this manner, Petrick would go to his own room and swear in long, loud whispers, and walk up and down, calling himself the most ridiculous dolt that ever lived, and declaring that he would never go near the little fellow again; to which resolve he would adhere for the space, perhaps, of a day. Such cases are happily not new to human nature, but there never was a case in which a man more completely befooled his former self than in this.

As the child grew up, Timothy's attachment to him grew deeper, till Rupert became almost the sole object for which he lived. There had been enough of the family ambition latent in him for Timothy Petrick to feel a little envy when, some time before this date, his brother Edward had been accepted by the Honorable Harriet Mountclere, daughter of the second viscount of that name and title; but having discovered, as I have before stated, the paternity of his boy Rupert to lurk in even a higher stratum of society, those envious feelings speedily dispersed. Indeed, the more he reflected thereon, after his brother's aristocratic marriage, the more content did he become. His late wife took softer outline in his memory, as he thought of the lofty taste she had displayed, though only a plain burgher's daughter, and the justification for his weakness in loving the child—the justification that he had longed for—was afforded now in the knowledge that the boy was by nature, if not by name, a representative of one of the noblest houses in England.

"She was a woman of grand instincts, after all," he said to himself, proudly. "To fix her choice upon the immediate successor in that ducal line—it was finely conceived! Had he been of low blood like myself or my relations she would scarce have deserved the harsh measure that I have dealt out to her and her offspring. How much less, then, when such groveling tastes were farthest from her soul! The man Annetta loved was noble, and my boy is noble in spite of me."

The after-clap was inevitable, and it soon came. "So far," he reasoned, "from cutting off his child from inheritance of my estates, as I have done, I should have rejoiced in the possession of him! He is of pure stock on one side at least, while in the ordinary run of affairs he would have been a commoner to the bone."

Being a man, whatever his faults, of good old beliefs in the divinity of kings and those about 'em, the more he overhauled the case in this light the more strongly did his poor wife's conduct in improving the blood and breed of the Petrick family win his heart. He considered what ugly, idle, hard-drinking scamps many of his own relations had been; the miserable scriveners, usurers, and pawnbrokers that he had numbered among his forefathers, and the probability that some of their bad qualities would have come out in a merely corporeal child, to give him sorrow in his old age, turn his black hairs gray, his gray hairs white, cut down every stick of timber, and Heaven knows what all, had he not, like a skilful gardener, minded his grafting and changed the sort; till at length this right-minded man fell down on his knees every night and morning and thanked God that he was not as other meanly descended fathers in such matters.

It was in the peculiar disposition of the Petrick family that the satisfaction which ultimately settled in Timothy's breast found nourishment. The Petricks had adored the nobility, and plucked them at the same time. That excellent man Izaak Walton's feelings about fish were much akin to those of old Timothy Petrick, and of his descendants in a lesser degree, concerning the landed aristocracy. To torture and to love simultaneously is a proceeding strange to reason, but possible to practise, as these instances show.

Hence, when Timothy's brother Edward said slightingly one day that Timothy's son was well enough, but that he had nothing but shops and offices in his backward perspective, while his own children, should he have any, would be far different, in possessing such a mother as the Honorable Harriet, Timothy felt a bound of triumph within him at the power he possessed of contradicting that statement if he chose.

So much was he interested in his boy in this new aspect that he now began to read up chronicles of the illustrious house ennobled as the Dukes of Southwesterland, from their very beginning in the glories of the Restoration of the blessed Charles till the year of his own time. He mentally noted their gifts from royalty, grants of lands, purchases, intermarriages, plantings, and buildings; more particularly their political and military achievements, which had been great, and their performances in arts and letters, which had been by no means contemptible. He studied prints of the portraits of that family, and then, like a chemist watching a crystallization, began to examine young Rupert's face for the unfolding of those historic curves and shades that the painters Vandyke and Lely had perpetuated on canvas.

When the boy reached the most fascinating age of childhood, and his shouts of laughter rang through Stapleford House from end to end, the remorse that oppressed Timothy Petrick knew no bounds. Of all people in the world this Rupert was the one on whom he could have wished the estates to devolve; yet Rupert, by Timothy's own desperate strategy at the time of his birth, had been ousted from all inheritance of them; and, since he did not mean to remarry, the manors would pass to his brother and his brother's children, who would be nothing to him, whose boasted pedigree on one side would be nothing to his Rupert's.

Had he only left the first will of his grandfather alone!

His mind ran on the wills continually, both of which were in existence, and the first, the canceled one, in his own possession. Night after night, when the servants were all abed, and the click of safety-locks sounded as loud as a crash, he looked at that first will, and wished it had been the second and not the first.

The crisis came at last. One night, after having enjoyed the boy's company for hours, he could no longer bear that his beloved Rupert should be dispossessed, and he committed the felonious deed of altering the date of the earlier will to a fortnight later, which made its execution appear subsequent to the date of the second will already proved. He then boldly propounded the first will as the second.

His brother Edward submitted to what appeared to be not only injontestible fact, but a far more likely disposition of old Timothy's procerty; for, like many others, he had been much surprised at the limitptions defined in the other will, having no clew to their cause. He aoined his brother Timothy in setting aside the hitherto accepted document, and matters went on in their usual course, there being no dispositions in the substituted will differing from those in the other, except such as related to a future which had not yet arrived.

The years moved on. Rupert had not yet revealed the anxiously expected historic lineaments which should foreshadow the political abilities of the ducal family aforesaid, when it happened on a certain day that Timothy Petrick made the acquaintance of a well-known physician of Budmouth, who had been the medical adviser and friend of the late Mrs. Petrick's family for many years, though after Annetta's marriage, and consequent removal to Stapleford, he had seen no more of her, the neighboring practitioner who attended the Petricks having then become her doctor as a matter of course. Timothy was impressed by the insight and knowledge disclosed in the conversation of the Budmouth physician, and the acquaintance ripening to intimacy, the physician alluded to a form of hallucination to which Annetta's mother and grandmother had been subject—that of believing in certain dreams as realities. He delicately inquired if Timothy had ever noticed anything of the sort in his wife during her lifetime; he, the physician, had fancied that he discerned germs of the same peculiarity in Annetta when he attended her in her girlhood. One explanation begat another, till the dumbfounded Timothy Petrick was persuaded in his own mind that Annetta's confession to him had been based on a delusion.

"You look down in the mouth!" said the doctor, pausing.

"A bit unmanned. 'Tis unexpected-like," sighed Timothy.

But he could hardly believe it possible; and, thinking it best to be frank with the doctor, told him the whole story which, till now, he had never related to living man, save his dying grandfather. To his surprise, the physician informed him that such a form of delusion was precisely what he would have expected from Annetta's antecedents at such a physical crisis in her life.

Petrick prosecuted his inquiries elsewhere; and the upshot of his labors was, briefly, that a comparison of dates and places showed irrefutably that his poor wife's assertion could not possibly have foundation in fact. The young Marquis of her tender passion—a highly moral and brightminded nobleman—had gone abroad the year before Annetta's, marriage, and had not returned until after her death. The young girl's love for him had been a delicate ideal dream—no more.

Timothy went home, and the boy ran out to meet him; whereupon a strangely dismal feeling of discontent took possession of his soul. After all, then, there was nothing but plebeian blood in the veins of the heir to his name and estates; he was not to be succeeded by a noble-natured line. To be sure, Rupert was his son; but that glory and halo he believed him to have inherited from the ages, outshining that of his brother's children, had departed from Rupert's brow forever; he could no longer read history in the boy's face and centuries of domination in his eyes.

His manner towards his son grew colder and colder from that day forward; and it was with bitterness of heart that he discerned the characteristic features of the Petricks unfolding themselves by degrees. Instead of the elegant knife-edged nose, so typical of the Dukes of Southwesterland, there began to appear on his face the broad nostril and hollow bridge of his grandfather Timothy. No illustrious line of politicians was promised a continuator in that graying blue eye, for it was acquiring the expression of the orb of a particularly objectionable cousin of his own; and, instead of the mouth-curves which had thrilled Parliamentary audiences in speeches now bound in calf in every well-ordered library, there was the bull-lip of that very uncle of his who had had the misfortune with the signature of a gentleman's will, and had been transported for life in consequence.

To think how he himself, too, had sinned in this same matter of a will for this mere fleshly reproduction of a wretched old uncle whose very name he wished to forget! The boy's Christian name, even, was an imposture and an irony, for it implied hereditary force and brilliancy to which he plainly would never attain! The consolation of real sonship was always left him certainly; but he could not help groaning to himself, "Why cannot a son be one's own and somebody else's likewise?"

The Marquis was shortly afterwards in the neighborhood of Stapleford, and Timothy Petrick met him, and eyed his noble countenance admiringly. The next day, when Petrick was in his study, somebody knocked at the door.

"Who's there?"

"Rupert."

"I'll Rupert thee, you young impostor! Say, only a poor commonplace Petrick!" his father grunted. "Why didn't you have a voice like the Marquis I saw yesterday?" he continued, as the lad came in. "Why haven't you his looks, and a way of commanding as if you'd done it for centuries—hey?"

"Why? How can you expect it, father, when I'm not related to him?"

"Ugh! Then you ought to be!" growled his father.

ROBERT LOUIS STEVENSON

(1850—1894)

STEVENSON was born in Edinburgh in 1850. He studied first for the law, and then turned to writing. His earliest books were essays and travel sketches. In the early eighties he tried his hand at short stories, and throughout his career he turned often to the short story medium for the expression of a mood or the recounting of a picturesque episode. He travelled a great deal, both in Europe and in the United States, and, ever in search of a climate that would suit his frail health, he went in 1889 to Samoa, where he lived with his family until his death in 1894. Stevenson is a romantic of the line of Scott and Dumas, but differing from his masters in that he was primarily a literary writer, whose first care was the perfection of a beautiful style.

Thrawn Janet first appeared in a magazine in 1882, and was included in the volume *The Merry Men,* published in 1886 by Chatto and Windus, by whose permission, and that of Mr. Lloyd Osbourne, it is here reprinted.

THRAWN JANET

THE Reverend Murdoch Soulis was long minister of the moorland parish of Balweary, in the vale of Dule. A severe, bleak-faced old man, dreadful to his hearers, he dwelt in the last years of his life, without relative or servant or any human company, in the small and lonely manse under the Hanging Shaw. In spite of the iron composure of his features, his eye was wild, scared, and uncertain; and when he dwelt, in private admonitions, on the future of the impenitent, it seemed as if his eye pierced through the storms of time to the terrors of eternity. Many young persons, coming to prepare themselves against the season of the Holy Communion, were dreadfully affected by this talk. He had a sermon on 1st Peter, v. and 8th, "The devil as a roaring lion," on the Sunday after every seventeenth of August, and he was accustomed to surpass himself upon that text both by the appalling nature of the matter and the terror of his bearing in the pulpit. The children were frightened into fits, and the old looked more than usually oracular, and were, all that day, full of those hints that Hamlet deprecated. The manse itself, where it stood by the water of Dule among some thick trees, with the Shaw overhanging it on the one side, and on the other many cold, moorish hilltops rising toward the sky, had begun, at a very early period of Mr. Soulis's ministry, to be avoided in the dusk hours by all who valued themselves upon their prudence; and guid-men sitting at the clachan alehouse shook their heads together at the thought of passing late by that uncanny neighborhood. There was one spot, to be more particular, which was regarded with especial awe. The manse stood between the high road and the water of Dule, with a gable to each; its back was toward the kirktown of Balweary, nearly half a mile away; in front of it, a bare garden, hedged with thorn, occupied the land between the river and the road. The house was two stories high, with two large rooms on each. It opened not directly on the garden, but on a causewayed path, or passage, giving on the road on the one hand, and closed on the other by the tall willows and elders that bordered on the stream. And it was this strip of causeway that enjoyed among the young parishioners of Balweary so infamous a reputation. The minister walked there often after dark, sometimes groaning aloud in the instancy of his unspoken prayers; and when he was from home, and the manse door was locked, the more daring schoolboys ventured, with beating hearts, to "follow my leader" across that legendary spot.

This atmosphere of terror, surrounding, as it did, a man of God of spotless character and orthodoxy, was a common cause of wonder and subject of inquiry among the few strangers who were led by chance or business into that unknown, outlying country. But many even of the people of the parish were ignorant of the strange events which had marked the first year of Mr. Soulis's ministrations; and among those who were better informed, some were naturally reticent, and others shy of that particular topic. Now and again, only, one of the older folk would warm into courage over his third tumbler, and recount the cause of the minister's strange looks and solitary life.

Fifty years syne, when Mr. Soulis cam' first into Ba'weary, he was still a young man—a callant, the folk said—fu' o' book learnin' and grand at the exposition, but, as was natural in sae young a man, wi' nae leevin' experience in religion. The younger sort were greatly taken wi' his gifts and his gab; but auld, concerned, serious men and women were moved even to prayer for the young man, whom they took to be a self-deceiver, and the parish that was like to be sae ill-supplied. It was before the days o' the moderates—weary fa' them; but ill things are like guid—they baith come bit by bit, a pickle at a time; and there were folk even then that said the Lord had left the college professors to their ain devices, an' the lads that went to study wi' them wad hae done

mair and better sittin' in a peat-bog, like their forebears of the persecution, wi' a Bible under their oxter and a speerit o' prayer in their heart.
There was nae doubt, onyway, but that Mr. Soulis had been ower lang
at the college. He was careful and troubled for mony things besides the
ae thing needful. He had a feck o' books wi' him—mair than had ever
been seen before in a' that presbytery; and a sair wark the carrier had
wi' them, for they were a' like to have smoored in the Deil's Hag between this and Kilmackerlie. They were books o' divinity, to be sure,
or so they ca'd them; but the serious were o' opinion there was little
service for sae mony, when the hail o' God's Word would gang in the
neuk of a plaid. Then he wad sit half the day and half the nicht forbey,
which was scant decent—writin', nae less; and first, they were feared
he wad read his sermons; and syne it proved he was writin' a book
himsel', which was surely no fittin' for ane of his years an' sma' experience.

Onyway it behooved him to get an auld, decent wife to keep the
manse for him an' see to his bit denners; and he was recommended to
an auld limmer—Janet M'Clour, they ca'd her—and sae far left to
himsel' as to be ower persuaded. There was mony advised him to the
contrar, for Janet was mair than suspeckit by the best folk in Ba'weary.
Lang or that, she had had a wean to a dragoon; she hadnae come forrit
for maybe thretty year; and bairns had seen her mumblin' to hersel' up
on Key's Loan in the gloamin', whilk was an unco time an' place for a
God-fearin' woman. Howsoever, it was the laird himsel' that had first
tauld the minister o' Janet; and in thae days he wad have gane a far
gate to pleesure the laird. When folk tauld him that Janet was sib to
the deil, it was a' superstition by his way of it; an' when they cast up
the Bible to him an' the witch of Endor, he wad threep it doun their
thrapples that thir days were a' gane by, and the deil was mercifully
restrained.

Weel, when it got about the clachan that Janet M'Clour was to be
servant at the manse, the folk were fair mad wi' her an' him thegether;
and some o' the guidwives had nae better to dae than get round her
door cheeks and chairge her wi' a' that was ken't again her, frae the
sodger's bairn to John Tamson's twa kye. She was nae great speaker;
folk usually let her gang her ain gate, an' she let them gang theirs, wi'
neither Fairguid-een nor Fair-guid-day; but when she buckled to she
had a tongue to deave the miller. Up she got, an' there wasnae an auld
story in Ba'weary but she gart somebody lowp for it that day; they
couldnae say ae thing but she could say twa to it; till, at the hinder end,
the guidwives up and claught haud of her, and clawed the coats aff her
back, and pu'd her doun the clachan to the water o' Dule, to see if she
were a witch or no, soum or droun. The carline skirled till ye could
hear her at the Hangin' Shaw, and she focht like ten; there was mony

a guidwife bure the mark of her neist day, an' mony a lang day after; and just in the hettest o' the collieshangie, wha suld come up (for his sins) but the new minister.

"Women," said he (and he had a grand voice), "I charge you in the Lord's name to let her go."

Janet ran to him—she was fair wud wi' terror—an' clang to him an' prayed him, for Christ's sake, save her frae the cummers; an' they, for their pairt, tauld him a' that was ken't, and maybe mair.

"Woman," says he to Janet, "is this true?"

"As the Lord sees me," says she, "as the Lord made me, no a word o't. Forbye the bairn," says she, "I've been a decent woman a' my days."

"Will you," says Mr. Soulis, "in the name of God, and before me, His unworthy minister, renounce the devil and his works?"

Weel, it wad appear that when he askit that, she gave a girn that fairly frichtit them that saw her, an' they could hear her teeth play dirl thegether in her chafts; but there was naething for it but the ae way or the ither; an' Janet lifted up her hand and renounced the deil before them a'.

"And now," said Mr. Soulis to the guidwives, "home with ye, one and all, and pray to God for His forgiveness."

And he gied Janet his arm, though she had little on her but a sark, and took her up the clachan to her ain door like a leddy of the land; an' her skreighin' and laughin' as was a scandal to be heard.

There were mony grave folk lang ower their prayers that nicht; but when the morn cam' there was sic a fear fell upon a' Ba'weary that the bairns hid theirsels, and even the men-folk stood and keekit frae their doors. For there was Janet comin' doun the clachan—her or her like-ness, nane could tell—wi' her neck thrawn, and her heid·on ae side, like a body that has been hangit, and a girn on her face like an unstreakit corp. By an' by they got used wi' it, and even speered at her to ken what was wrang; but frae that day forth she couldnae speak like a Christian woman, but slavered and played click wi' her teeth like a pair o' shears; and frae that day forth the name o' God cam' never on her lips. Whiles she wad try to say it, but it michtnae be. Them that kenned best said least; but they never gied that Thing the name o' Janet M'Clour; for the auld Janet, by their way o't, was in muckle hell that day. But the minister was neither to haud nor to bind; he preached about naething but the folks' cruelty that had gi'en her a stroke of the palsy; he skelpt the bairns that meddled her; and he had her up to the manse that same nicht and dwalled there a' his lane wi' her under the Hangin' Shaw.

Well, time gaed by: and the idler sort commenced to think mair lichtly o' that black business. The minister was weel thocht o'; he was aye late at the writing, folk wad see his can'le doun by the Dule water after twal' at e'en; and he seemed pleased wi' himsel' and upsitten as at first, though a' body could see that he was dwining. As for Janet she cam' an' she gaed; if she didnae speak muckle afore, it was reason she should speak less then; she meddled naebody; but she was an eldritch thing to see, an' nane wad hae mistrysted wi' her for Ba'weary glebe. About the end o' July there cam' a spell o' weather, the like o't never was in that countryside; it was lown an' het an' heartless; the herds could-nae win up the Black Hill, the bairns were ower weariet to play; an' yet it was gousty too, wi' claps o' het wund that rumm'led in the glens, and bits o' shouers that slockened naething. We aye thocht it but to thun'er on the morn; but the morn cam', and the morn's morning, and it was aye that same uncanny weather, sair on folks and bestial. Of a' that were the waur, nane suffered like Mr. Soulis; he could neither sleep nor eat, he tauld his elders; an' when he wasnae writin' at his weary book, he wad be stravaguin' ower a' the contryside like a man pos-sessed, when a' body else was blythe to keep caller ben the house.

Abune Hangin' Shaw, in the bield o' the Black Hill, there's a bit in-closed grund wi' an iron yett; and it seems in the auld days, that was the kirkyaird o' Ba'weary, and consecrated by the Papists before the blessed licht shone upon the kingdom. It was a great howff o' Mr. Soulis's, onyway; there he would sit an' consider his sermons; and in-deed it's bieldy bit. Weel, as he cam' ower the wast end o' the Black Hill, ae day, he saw first twa, an' syne fower, an' syne seeven corbie craws fleein' round an' round abune the auld kirkyaird. They flew laigh and heavy, an' squawked to ither as they gaed; and it was clear to Mr. Soulis that something had put them frae their ordinar. He wasnae easy fleyed, an' gaed straucht up to the wa's; an' what suld he find there but a man, or the appearance of a man, sittin' in the inside upon a grave. He was of a great stature, an' black as hell, and his een were singular to see. Mr. Soulis had heard tell o' black men, mony's the time; but there was something unco about this black man that daunted him. Het as he was, he took a kind o' cauld grue in the marrow o' his banes; but up he spak for a' that; an' says he: "My friend, are you a stranger in this place?" The black man answered never a word; he got upon his feet, an' begude to hirstle to the wa' on the far side; but he aye lookit at the minister; an' the minister stood an' lookit back, till a' in a meenute the black man was over the wa' an' rinnin' for the bield o' the trees. Mr. Soulis, he hardly kenned why, ran after him; but he was sair for-jaskit wi' his walk an' the het, unhalesome weather; and rin as he likit, he got nae mair than a glisk o' the black man amang the birks, till he won doun to the foot o' the hillside, an' there he saw him ance mair, gaun, hap, step, an' lowp, ower Dule water to the manse.

Mr. Soulis wasnae weel pleased that this fearsome gangrel suld mak' sae free wi' Ba'weary manse; an' he ran the harder, an', wet shoon, ower the burn, an' up the walk; but the deil a black man was there to see. He stepped out upon the road, but there was naebody there; he gaed a' ower the gairden, but, na, nae black man. At the hinder end, and a bit feared as was but natural, he lifted the hasp and into the manse; and there was Janet M'Clour before his een, wi' her thrawn craig, and nane sae pleased to see him. And he aye minded sinsyne, when first he set his een upon her, he had the same cauld and deidly grue.

"Janet," says he, "have you seen a black man?"

"A black man?" quo' she. "Save us a'! Ye're no wise, minister. There's nae black man in a' Ba'weary."

But she didnae speak plain, ye maun understand; but yam-yam-mered, like a powney wi' the bit in its moo.

"Weel," says he, "Janet, if there was nae black man, I have spoken with the Accuser of the Brethren."

And he sat down like ane wi' a fever, an' his teeth chittered in his heid.

"Hoots," says she, "think shame to yoursel', minister"; an' gied him a drap brandy that she keept aye by her.

Syne Mr. Soulis gaed into his study amang a' his books. It's a lang, laigh, mirk chalmer, perishin' cauld in winter, an' no very dry even in the tap o' the simmer, for the manse stands near the burn. Sae doun he sat, and thocht of a' that had come an' gane since he was in Ba'weary, an' his hame, an' the days when he was a bairn an' ran daffin' on the braes; and that black man aye ran in his heid like the owercome of a sang. Aye the mair he thocht, the mair he thocht o' the black man. He tried the prayer, an' the words wouldnae come to him; an' he tried, they say, to write at his book, but he couldnae mak' nae mair o' that. There was whiles he thocht the black man was at his oxter, an' the swat stood upon him cauld as well-water; and there was other whiles, when he cam' to himself, like a christened bairn and minded naething.

The upshot was that he gaed to the window an' stood glowrin' at Dule water. The trees are unco thick, an' the water lies deep an' black under the manse; an' there was Janet washin' the cla'es wi' her coats kilted. She had her back to the minister, an' he, for his pairt, hardly kenned what he was lookin' at. Syne she turned round an' shawed her face; Mr. Soulis had the same cauld grue as twice that day afore, an' it was borne in upon him what folk said, that Janet was deid lang syne, an' this was a bogle in her clay cauld flesh. He drew back a pickle and he scanned her narrowly. She was tramp-trampin' in the cla'es, croon-in' to hersel'; and eh! Gude guide us, but it was a fearsome face. Whiles she sang louder, but there was nae born o' woman that could tell the words o' her sang; an' whiles she lookit side-lang doun, but there was naething there for her to look at. There gaed a scunner through the flesh upon his banes; and that was Heeven's advertisement. But Mr. Soulis just blamed himsel', he said, to think sae ill of a puir, auld afflicted wife that hadnae a freend froby himsel'; and he put up a bit prayer for him and her, an' drank a little caller water—for his heart rose again the meat—an' gaed up to his naked bed in the gloaming.

That was a nicht that has never been forgotten in Ba'weary, the nicht o' the seeventeenth of August, seeventeen hun'er an' twal'. It had been het afore, as I hae said, but that nicht it was hetter than ever. The sun gaed doun amang unco-lookin' clouds; it fell as mirk as the pit; no a star, no a breath o' wund; ye couldnae see your han' before your face, and even the auld folk cuist the covers frae their beds and lay pechin' for their breath. Wi' an' that he had upon his mind, it was gey and unlikely Mr. Soulis wad get muckle sleep. He lay an' he tummled; the gude, caller bed that he got into brunt his very banes; whiles he slept, and whiles he waukened; whiles he heard the time o' nicht, and whiles a tyke yowlin' up the muir, as if somebody was deid; whiles he thocht he heard bogles claverin' in his lug, an' whiles he saw spunkies in the room. He behooved, he judged, to be sick; an' sick he was— little he jaloosed the sickness.

At the hinder end, he got a clearness in his mind, sat up in his sark on the bedside, and fell thinkin' ance mair o' the black man an' Janet. He couldnae weel tell how—maybe it was the cauld to his feet—but it cam' in upon him wi' a spate that there was some connection between thir twa, an' that either or baith o' them were bogles. And just at that moment, in Janet's room, which was neist to his, there cam' a stramp o' feet as if men were wars'lin', an' then a loud bang; an' then a wund gaed reishling round the fower quarters of the house; an' then a' was aince mair as seelent as the grave.

Mr. Soulis was feared for neither man nor deevil. He got his tinder box, an' lighted a can'le, an' made three steps o't ower to Janet's door. It was on the hasp, an' he pushed it open, an' keeked bauldly in. It was a big room, as big as the minister's ain, an' plenished wi' grand, auld, solid gear, for he had naething else. There was a fower-posted bed wi' auld tapestry; and a braw cabinet of aik, that was fu' o' the minister's divinity books, an' put there to be out o' the gate; an' a wheen duds o' Janet's lying here and there about the floor. But nae Janet could Mr. Soulis see; nor ony sign of a contention. In he gaed (an' there's few that wad ha'e followed him) an' lookit a' round, an' listened. But there was naethin' to be heard, neither inside the manse nor in a' Ba'weary parish, an' naethin' to be seen but the muckle shadows turnin' round the can'le. An' then a' at aince, the minister's heart played dunt an' stood stock-still; an' a cauld wund blew amang the hairs o' his heid. Whaten a weary sicht was that for the puir man's een! For there was

Janet hangin' frae a nail beside the auld aik cabinet: her heid aye lay on her shouther, her een were steeked, the tongue projekit frae her mouth, and her heels were twa clar abune the floor.

"God forgive us all!" thocht Mr. Soulis; "poor Janet's dead."

He cam' a step nearer to the corp; an' then his heart fair whammled in his inside. For by what cantrip it wad ill-beseem a man to judge, she was hingin' fae a single nail an' by a single wursted thread for darnin' hose.

It's an awfu' thing to be your lane at nicht wi' siccan prodigies o' darkness; but Mr. Soulis was strong in the Lord. He turned an' gaed his ways oot o' that room, and lockit the door ahint him; and step by step, doon the stairs, as heavy as leed; and set doon the can'le on the table at the stairfoot. He couldnae pray, he couldnae think, he was dreepin' wi' caul' swat, an' naething could he hear but the dunt-dunt-duntin' o' his ain heart. He micht maybe have stood there an hour, or maybe twa, he minded sae little; when a' o' a sudden he heard a laigh, uncanny steer upstairs; a foot gaed to an' fro in the cha'mer whaur the corp was hingin'; syne the door was opened, though he minded weel that he had lockit it; an' syne there was a step upon the landin', an' it seemed to him as if the corp was lookin' ower the rail and doun upon him whaur he stood.

He took up the can'le again (for he couldnae want the licht) and, as saftly as ever he could, gaed straucht out o' the manse an' to the far end o' the causeway. It was aye pitmirk; the flame o' the can'le, when he set it on the grund, brunt steedy and clear as in a room; naething moved, but the Dule water seepin' and sabbin' doon the glen, an' yon unhaly footstep that cam' ploddin' doun the stairs inside the manse. He kenned the foot ower weel, for it was Janet's; and at ilka step that cam' a wee thing nearer, the cauld got deeper in his vitals. He commended his soul to Him that made an' keepit him; "and O Lord," said he, "give me strength this night to war against the powers of evil."

By this time the foot was comin' through the passage for the door; he could hear a hand skirt alang the wa', as if the fearsome thing was feelin' for its way. The saughs tossed an' maned thegether, a lang sigh cam' ower the hills, the flame o' the can'le was blawn aboot; an' there stood the corp of Thrawn Janet, wi' her grogram goun an' her black mutch, wi' the heid aye upon the shouther, an' the girn still upon the face o't—leevin', ye wad hae said—deid, as Mr. Soulis weel kenned—upon the threshold o' the manse.

It's a strange thing that the saul of man should be that thirled into his perishable body; but the minister saw that, an' his heart didnae break.

She didnae stand there lang; she began to move again an' cam' slowly toward Mr. Soulis whaur he stood under the saughs. A' the life o' his body, a' the strength o' his speerit, were glowerin' frae his een. It seemed she was gaun to speak, but wanted words, an' made a sign wi' the left hand. There cam' a clap o' wund, like a cat's fuff; oot gaed the can'le, the saughs skrieghed like folk; an' Mr. Soulis kenned that, live or die, this was the end o't.

"Witch, beldam, devil!" he cried, "I charge you, by the power of God, begone—if you be dead, to the grave—if you be damned, to hell."

An' at that moment the Lord's ain hand out o' the Heevens struck the Horror whaur it stood; the auld, deid, desecrated corp o' the witch-wife, sae lang keepit frae the grave and hirsled round by deils, lowed up like a brunstane spunk and fell in ashes to the grund; the thunder followed, peal on dirling peal, the rairing rain upon the back o' that; and Mr. Soulis lowped through the garden hedge, and ran, wi' skelloch upon skelloch, for the clachan.

That same mornin', John Christie saw the Black Man pass the Muckle Cairn as it was chappin' six before eicht, he gaed by the change-house at Knockdow; an' no lang after, Sandy M'Lellan saw him gaun linkin' doun the braes frae Kilmackerlie. There's little doubt it was him that dwalled sae lang in Janet's body; but he was awa' at last; and sinsyne the deil has never fashed us in Ba'weary.

But it was a sair dispensation for the minister; lang, lang he lay ravin' in his bed; and frae that hour to this, he was the man ye ken the day.

OSCAR WILDE

(1854–1900)

WILDE was born in Dublin in 1854, the son of distinguished parents. His mother, Lady Wilde, was famous for her volumes of Irish stories. Wilde went first to Trinity College, Dublin, and later to Oxford. His first published work was a volume of poems in 1881. From that time until 1895 he wrote plays, poems, essays, a novel, and several short stories and fairy tales. Wilde's jewelled style was never employed to better purpose than in the group of tales from which *The Selfish Giant* has been selected. In 1895 he was sentenced to two years' hard labour as a result of a notorious trial. After his release he travelled in Italy and France, and died in 1900 at Paris.

The Selfish Giant is reprinted, by permission of Mr. Philip Nutt, from *The Happy Prince and Other Tales*, published by Gerald Duckworth and Co.

THE SELFISH GIANT

E VERY afternoon, as they were coming from school, the children used to go and play in the Giant's garden.

It was a large lovely garden, with soft green grass. Here and there over the grass stood beautiful flowers like stars, and there were twelve peach-trees that in the Spring-time broke out into delicate blossoms of pink and pearl, and in the autumn bore rich fruit. The birds sat on the trees and sang so sweetly that the children used to stop their games in order to listen to them. "How happy we are here!" they cried to each other.

One day the Giant came back. He had been to visit his friend the Cornish ogre, and had stayed with him for seven years. After the seven years were over he had said all that he had to say, for his conversation was limited, and he determined to return to his own castle. When he arrived he saw children playing in the garden.

"What are you doing there?" he cried in a very gruff voice, and the children ran away.

"My own garden is my own garden," said the Giant; "anyone can understand that, and I will allow nobody to play in it but myself." So he built a high wall all round it, and put up a notice-board.

> TRESPASSERS
> WILL BE
> PROSECUTED

He was a very selfish Giant.

The poor children had now nowhere to play. They tried to play on the road, but the road was very dusty and full of hard stones, and they did not like it. They used to wander round the high wall when their lessons were over, and talk about the beautiful garden inside. "How happy we were there," they said to each other.

Then the Spring came, and all over the country there were little blossoms and little birds. Only in the garden of the Selfish Giant it was still winter. The birds did not care to sing in it, as there were no children, and the trees forgot to blossom. Once a beautiful flower put its head out from the grass, but when it saw the notice-board it was so sorry for the children that it slipped back into the ground again, and went off to sleep. The only people who were pleased were the Snow and the Frost. "Spring has forgotten this garden," they cried, "so we will live here all the year round." The Snow covered up the grass with her great white cloak, and the Frost painted all the trees silver. Then they invited the North Wind to stay with them, and he came. He was wrapped in furs, and he roared all day about the garden, and blew the chimney-pots down. "This is a delightful spot," he said; "we must ask the Hail on a visit." So the Hail came. Every day for three hours he rattled on the roof of the castle till he broke most of the slates, and then he ran round and round the garden as fast as he could go. He was dressed in gray, and his breath was like ice.

"I can not understand why the Spring is so late in coming," said the Selfish Giant, as he sat at the window and looked out at his cold white garden; "I hope there will be a change in the weather."

But the Spring never came, nor the Summer. The Autumn gave golden fruit to every garden, but to the Giant's garden she gave none. "He is too selfish," she said. So it was always Winter there, and the North Wind, and the Hail, and the Frost, and the Snow danced about through the trees.

One morning the Giant was lying awake in bed when he heard some lovely music. It sounded so sweet to his ears that he thought it must be the King's musicians passing by. It was really only a little linnet singing outside his window, but it was so long since he had heard a bird sing in his garden that it seemed to him to be the most beautiful music in the world. Then the Hail stopped dancing over his head, and the North Wind ceased roaring, and a delicious perfume came to him through the open casement. "I believe the Spring has come at last," said the Giant; and he jumped out of bed and looked out.

What did he see?

He saw a most wonderful sight. Through a little hole in the wall the children had crept in, and they were sitting in the branches of the trees. In every tree that he could see there was a little child. And the trees were so glad to have the children back again that they had covered themselves with blossoms, and were waving their arms gently above the children's heads. The birds were flying about and twittering with delight, and the flowers were looking up through the green grass and laughing. It was a lovely scene, only in one corner it was still winter. It was the farthest corner of the garden, and in it was standing a little boy. He was so small that he could not reach up to the branches of the tree, and he was wandering all round it, crying bitterly. The poor tree was still quite covered with frost and snow, and the North Wind was blowing and roaring above it. "Climb up, little boy," said the Tree, and it bent its branches down as low as it could; but the boy was too tiny.

And the Giant's heart melted as he looked out. "How selfish I have been!" he said; "now I know why the Spring would not come here. I will put that poor little boy on the top of the tree, and then I will knock down the wall, and my garden shall be the children's playground for ever and ever." He was really very sorry for what he had done.

So he crept downstairs and opened the front door quite softly, and went out into the garden. But when the children saw him they were so frightened that they all ran away, and the garden became winter again. Only the little boy did not run, for his eyes were so full of tears that he did not see the Giant coming. And the Giant stole up behind him and took him gently in his hand, and put him up into the tree. And the tree broke at once into blossoms, and the birds came and sang on it, and the little boy stretched out his two arms and flung them round the Giant's neck, and kissed him. And the other children, when they saw that the Giant was not wicked any longer, came running back, and with them came the Spring. "It is your garden now, little children," said the Giant, and he took a great axe and knocked down the wall. And when the people were going to market at twelve o'clock they found the Giant playing with the children in the most beautiful garden they had ever seen.

All day long they played, and in the evening they came to the Giant to bid him good-bye.

"But where is your little companion?" he said: "the boy I put into the tree." The Giant loved him the best because he had kissed him.

"We don't know," answered the children; "he has gone away."

"You must tell him to be sure and come here to-morrow," said the Giant. But the children said that they did not know where he lived, and had never seen him before; and the Giant felt very sad.

Every afternoon, when school was over, the children came and played with the Giant. But the little boy whom the Giant loved was never seen again. The Giant was very kind to all the children, yet he longed for his first little friend, and often spoke of him. "How I would like to see him!" he used to say.

Years went over, and the Giant grew very old and feeble. He could not play about any more, so he sat in a huge armchair, and watched the children at their games, and admired his garden. "I have many beautiful flowers," he said; "but the children are the most beautiful flowers of all."

One winter morning he looked out of his window as he was dressing. He did not hate the Winter now, for he knew that it was merely the Spring asleep, and that the flowers were resting.

Suddenly he rubbed his eyes in wonder, and looked and looked. It certainly was a marvelous sight. In the farthest corner of the garden was a tree quite covered with lovely white blossoms. Its branches were all golden, and silver fruit hung down from them, and underneath it stood the little boy he had loved.

Downstairs ran the Giant in great joy, and out into the garden. He hastened across the grass, and came near to the child. And when he came quite close his face grew red with anger, and he said, "Who hath dared to wound thee?" For on the palms of the child's hands were the prints of two nails, and the prints of two nails were on the little feet.

"Who hath dared to wound thee?" cried the Giant; "tell me, that I may take my big sword and slay him."

"Nay!" answered the child; "but these are the wounds of Love."

"Who art thou?" said the Giant, and a strange awe fell on him, and he knelt before the little child.

And the child smiled on the Giant, and said to him, "You let me play once in your garden, to-day you shall come with me to my garden, which is Paradise."

And when the children ran in that afternoon, they found the Giant lying dead under the tree, all covered with white blossoms.

GEORGE MOORE

(1852–1933)

GEORGE MOORE was born in County Mayo, in 1852, of a well-to-do family. At an early age he wished to become a painter, and went to Paris for that purpose. Finding that he had no real gift for painting, he turned to literature. His earliest efforts were plays and imitative verses. He spent the period between 1872 and 1882 in Paris, and when he returned to London to earn his livelihood, he was a confirmed Naturalist of the school of Zola. Under Zola's influence he wrote his first successful novel, *A Mummer's Wife*. During the eighties and nineties he wrote several novels of contemporary English and Irish life, including his masterpiece, *Esther Waters*. Most of Moore's short stories are in the volume *The Untilled Field* (1903). These are beautifully written studies of Irish life.

Julia Cahill's Curse is reprinted from *The Untilled Field*, by permission of the publisher, William Heinemann. Copyright, 1903.

JULIA CAHILL'S CURSE

"AND what has become of Margaret?"
"Ah, didn't her mother send her to America as soon as the baby was born? Once a woman is wake here she has to go. Hadn't Julia to go in the end, and she the only one that ever said she didn't mind the priest?"

"Julia who?" said I.

"Julia Cahill."

The name struck my fancy, and I asked the driver to tell me her story.

"Wasn't it Father Madden who had her put out of the parish, but she put her curse on it, and it's on it to this day."

"Do you believe in curses?"

"Bedad I do, sir. It's a terrible thing to put a curse on a man, and the curse that Julia put on Father Madden's parish was a bad one, the divil a worse. The sun was up at the time, and she on the hilltop raising both her hands. And the curse she put on the parish was that every year a roof must fall in and a family go to America. That was the curse, your honor, and every word of it has come true. You'll see for yourself as soon as we cross the mearing."

"And what has become of Julia's baby?"

"I never heard she had one, sir."

He flicked his horse pensively with his whip, and it seemed to me that the disbelief I had expressed in the power of the curse disinclined him for further conversation.

"But," I said, "who is Julia Cahill, and how did she get the power to put a curse upon the village?"

"Didn't she go into the mountains every night to meet the fairies, and who else could've given her the power to put a curse upon the village?"

"But she couldn't walk so far in one evening."

"Them that's in league with the fairies can walk that far and much farther in an evening, your honor. A shepherd saw her; and you'll see the ruins of the cabins for yourself as soon as we cross the mearing, and I'll show you the cabin of the blind woman that Julia lived with before she went away."

"And how long is it since she went?"

"About twenty year, and there hasn't been a girl the like of her in these parts since. I was only a gossoon at the time, but I've heard tell she was as tall as I'm myself, and as straight as a poplar. She walked with a little swing in her walk, so that all the boys used to be looking after her, and she had fine black eyes, sir, and she was nearly always laughing. Father Madden had just come to the parish; and there was courting in these parts then, for aren't we the same as other people—we'd like to go out with a girl well enough if it was the custom of the country. Father Madden put down the ball alley because he said the boys stayed there instead of going into Mass, and he put down the cross-road dances because he said dancing was the cause of many a bastard, and he wanted none in his parish. Now there was no dancer like Julia; the boys used to gather about to see her dance, and whoever walked with her under the hedges in the summer could never think about another woman. The village was cracked about her. There was fighting, so I suppose the priest was right: he had to get rid of her. But I think he mightn't have been as hard on her as he was.

"One evening he went down to the house. Julia's people were well-to-do people, they kept a grocery-store in the village; and when he came into the shop who should be there but the richest farmer in the country, Michael Moran by name, trying to get Julia for his wife. He didn't go straight to Julia and that's what swept him. There are two counters in that shop, and Julia was at the one on the left as you go in. And many's the pound she had made for her parents at that counter. Michael Moran says to the father, 'Now, what fortune are you going to give with Julia?' And the father says there was many a man who would take her without any; and that's how they spoke, and Julia listening quietly all the while at the opposite counter. For Michael didn't know what a spirited girl she was, but went on arguing till he got the father to say fifty pounds, and thinking he had got him so far he said, 'I'll never drop a flap to her unless you give the two heifers.' Julia never said a word, she just sat listening. It was then that the priest came in. And over he goes to Julia. 'And now,' says he, 'aren't you proud to hear that you'll have such a fine fortune, and it's I that'll be glad to see you married, for I can't have any more of your goings-on in my parish. You're the encouragement of the dancing and courting here, but I'm going to put an end to it.' Julia didn't answer a word, and he went over to them that were arguing about the sixty pounds. 'Now, why not make it fifty-five?' says he. So the father agreed to that, since the priest had said it, and all three of them thought the marriage was settled. 'Now what will you be taking, Father Tom?' says Cahill, 'and you, Michael?' Sorra one of them thought of asking her if she was pleased with Michael; but little did they know what was passing in her mind, and when they came over to the counter to tell her what they had settled, she said, 'Well, I've just been listening to you, and 'tis well for you to be wasting your time talking about me,' and she tossed her head, saying she would just pick the boy out of the parish that pleased her best. And what angered the priest most of all was her way of saying it—that the boy that would marry her would be marrying herself and not the money that would be paid when the book was signed or when the first baby was born. Now it was agin girls marrying according to their fancy that Father Madden had set himself. He had said in his sermon the Sunday before that young people shouldn't be allowed out by themselves at all, but that the parents should make up the marriages for them. And he went fairly wild when Julia told him the example she was going to set. He tried to keep his temper, sir, but it was getting the better of him all the while. And Julia said, 'My boy isn't in the parish now, but maybe he is on his way here, and he may be here to-morrow or the next day.' And when Julia's father heard her speak like that he knew that no one would turn her from what she was saying, and he said, 'Michael Moran, my good man, you may go your way: you will never get her.' Then he went back to hear what Julia was saying to the priest, but it was the priest that was talking. 'Do you think,' says he, 'I am going to let you go on turning the head of every boy in the parish? Do you think', says he, 'I'm going to see you gallivanting with one and then with the other? Do you think I am going to see fighting and quarreling for your like? Do you think I am going to hear stories like I heard last week about poor Patsy Carey, who has gone out of his mind, they say, on account of your treatment? No', says he, 'I'll have no more of that. I'll have you out of my parish, or I'll have you married.' Julia didn't answer the priest; she tossed her head, and went on making up parcels of tea and sugar, and getting the steps and taking down candles, though she didn't want them, just to show the priest that she didn't mind what he was saying. And all the while her father trembling, not knowing what would happen, for the priest had a big stick, and there was no saying that he wouldn't strike her. Cahill tried to quiet the priest, he promising him that Julia shouldn't go out any more in the evenings, and bedad, sir, she was out the same evening with a young man and the priest saw them, and the next evening she was out with another and the priest saw them, nor was she minded at the end of the month to marry any of them. Then the priest went down to the shop to speak to her a second time, and he went down again a third time, though what he said the third time no one knows, no one being there at the time. And next Sunday he spoke out, saying that a disobedient daughter would have the worst devil in hell to attend on her. I've heard tell that he called her the evil spirit that set men mad. But most of the people that were there are dead or gone to America, and no one rightly knows what he did say, only that the words came out of his mouth, and the people when they saw Julia crossed themselves, and even the boys that were most mad after Julia were afraid to speak to her. Cahill had to put her out.''

"Do you mean to say that the father put his daughter out?"

"Sure, didn't the priest threaten to turn him into a rabbit if he didn't, and no one in the parish would speak to Julia, they were so afraid of Father Madden, and if it hadn't been for the blind woman that I was speaking about a while ago, sir, it is to the Poor House she'd have to go. The blind woman has a little cabin at the edge of the bog—I'll point it out to you, sir; we do be passing it by—and she was with the blind woman for nearly two years disowned by her own father. Her clothes wore out, but she was as beautiful without them as with them. The boys were told not to look back, but sure they couldn't help it.

"Ah, it was a long while before Father Madden could get shut of her. The blind woman said she wouldn't see Julia thrown out on the roadside, and she was as good as her word for well-nigh two years, till Julia went to America, so some do be saying, sir, whilst others do be saying she joined the fairies. But 'tis for sure, sir, that the day she left the parish Pat Quinn heard a knocking at his window and somebody asking if he would lend his cart to go to the railway station. Pat was a heavy sleeper and he didn't get up, and it is thought that it was Julia who wanted Pat's cart to take her to the station; it's a good ten mile; but she got there all the same!"

"You said something about a curse?"

"Yes, sir. You'll see the hill presently. And a man who was taking some sheep to the fair saw her there. The sun was just getting up and he saw her cursing the village, raising both her hands, sir, up to the sun, and since that curse was spoken every year a roof has fallen in, sometimes two or three."

I could see he believed the story, and for the moment I, too, believed in an outcast Venus becoming the evil spirit of a village that would not accept her as divine.

"Look, sir, the woman coming down the road is Bridget Coyne. And that's her house," he said, and we passed a house built of loose stone without mortar, but a little better than the mud cabins I had seen in Father MacTurnan's parish.

"And now, sir, you will see the loneliest parish in Ireland."

And I noticed that though the land was good, there seemed to be few people on it, and, what was more significant, that the untilled fields were the ruins, for they were not the cold ruins of twenty, or thirty, or forty years ago when the people were evicted and their village turned into pasture—the ruins I saw were the ruins of cabins that had been lately abandoned, and I said:

"It wasn't the landlord who evicted these people."

"Ah, it's the landlord who would be glad to have them back, but there's no getting them back. Every one here will have to go, and 'tis said that the priest will say Mass in an empty chapel, sorra a one will be there but Bridget, and she'll be the last he'll give communion to. It's said, your honor, that Julia has been seen in America, and I'm going there this autumn. You may be sure I'll keep a lookout for her."

"But all this is twenty years ago. You won't know her. A woman changes a good deal in twenty years."

"There will be no change in her, your honor. Sure, hasn't she been with the fairies?"

ARTHUR MORRISON

(1863–1945)

ARTHUR MORRISON is one of the few writers of his period—for he belongs to the "School" of the Nineties—whose work is still widely popular. He is known almost exclusively for his small volume of stories called *Tales of Mean Streets*, from which *That Brute Simmons* has been selected. The entire collection, says Mencken, reveals "the amazing life of the London East End, the sewer of England and of Christendom."

Reprinted from *Tales of Mean Streets*, Methuen, 1894, by permission of the publishers.

THAT BRUTE SIMMONS

SIMMONS'S infamous behavior toward his wife is still matter for profound wonderment among the neighbors. The other women had all along regarded him as a model husband, and certainly Mrs. Simmons was a most conscientious wife. She toiled and slaved for that man, as any woman in the whole street would have maintained, far more than any husband had a right to expect. And now this was what she got for it. Perhaps he had sudenly gone mad.

Before she married Simmons, Mrs. Simmons had been the widowed Mrs. Ford. Ford had got a berth as donkey-man on a tramp steamer, and that steamer had gone down with all hands off the cape—a judgment, the widow woman feared, for long years of contumacy which had culminated in the wickedness of taking to the sea, and taking to it as a donkey-man, an immeasurable fall for a capable engine-fitter. Twelve years as Mrs. Ford had left her still childless, and childless she remained as Mrs. Simmons.

As for Simmons, he, it was held, was fortunate in that capable wife. He was a moderately good carpenter and joiner, but no man of the world, and he wanted to be one. Nobody could tell what might not have happened to Tommy Simmons if there had been no Mrs. Simmons to take care of him. He was a meek and quiet man, with a boyish face and sparse, limp whiskers. He had no vices (even his pipe departed him after his marriage), and Mrs. Simmons had ingrafted on him divers exotic virtues. He went solemnly to chapel every Sunday, under a tall hat, and put a penny—one returned to him for the purpose out of his week's wages—in the plate. Then, Mrs. Simmons overseeing, he took off his best clothes and brushed them with solicitude and pains.

On Saturday afternoons he cleaned the knives, the forks, the boots, the kettles and the windows, patiently and conscientiously. On Tuesday evenings he took the clothes to the mangling. And on Saturday nights he attended Mrs. Simmons in her marketing, to carry the parcels.

Mrs. Simmons's own virtues were native and numerous. She was a wonderful manager. Every penny of Tommy's thirty-six or thirty-eight shillings a week was bestowed to the greatest advantage, and Tommy never ventured to guess how much of it she saved. Her cleanliness in housewifery was distracting to behold. She met Simmons at the front door whenever he came home, and then and there he changed his boots for slippers, balancing himself painfully on alternate feet on the cold flags. This was because she scrubbed the passage and doorstep turn about with the wife of the downstairs family, and because the stair-carpet was her own. She vigilantly supervised her husband all through the process of "cleaning himself" after work, so as to come between her walls and the possibility of random splashes; and if, in spite of her diligence, a spot remained to tell the tale, she was at pains to impress the fact on Simmons's memory, and to set forth at length all the circumstances of his ungrateful selfishness. In the beginning she had always escorted him to the ready-made clothes shop, and had selected and paid for his clothes—for the reason that men are such perfect fools, and shopkeepers do as they like with them. But she presently improved on that. She found a man selling cheap remnants at a street corner, and straightway she conceived the idea of making Simmons's clothes herself. Decision was one of her virtues, and a suit of uproarious check tweeds was begun that afternoon from the pattern furnished by an old one. More: it was finished by Sunday, when Simmons, overcome by astonishment at the feat, was indued in it, and pushed off to chapel ere he could recover his senses. The things were not altogether comfortable, he found; the trousers clung tight against his shins, but hung loose behind his heels; and when he sat, it was on a wilderness of hard folds and seams. Also his waistcoat collar tickled his nape, but his coat collar went straining across from shoulder to shoulder, while the main garment bagged generously below his waist. Use made a habit of his discomfort, but it never reconciled him to the chaff of his shopmates; for as Mrs. Simmons elaborated successive suits, each one modeled on the last, the primal accidents of her design developed into principles, and grew even bolder and more hideously pronounced. It was vain for Simmons to hint—as hint he did—that he shouldn't like her to overwork herself, tailoring being bad for the eyes, and there was a new tailor's in the Mile End Road, very cheap, where... "Ho yus," she retorted, "you're very consid'rit I dessay sittin' there actin' a livin' lie before your own wife, Thomas Simmons, as though I couldn't see through you like a book; a lot you care about overworkin' me as long as *your* turn's served throwin' away money like dirt in the street on a lot o' swindling tailors an' me workin' an' slavin' 'ere to save a 'apenny an' this is my return for it; any one 'ud think you could pick up money in the 'orseroad an' I b'lieve I'd be thought better of if I laid in bed all day like some would, that I do." So that Thomas Simmons avoided the subject, nor even murmured when she resolved to cut his hair.

So his placid fortune endured for years. Then there came a golden summer evening when Mrs. Simmons betook herself with a basket to do some small shopping, and Simmons was left at home. He washed and put away the tea-things, and then he fell to meditating on a new pair of trousers, finished that day and hanging behind the parlor door. There they hung, in all their decent innocence of shape in the seat, and they were shorter of leg, longer of waist, and wilder of pattern than he had ever worn before. And as he looked on them the small devil of original sin awoke and clamored in his breast. He was ashamed of it, of course, for well he knew the gratitude he owed his wife for those same trousers, among other blessings. Still, there the small devil was, and the small devil was fertile in base suggestions, and could not be kept from hinting at the new crop of workshop gibes that would spring at Tommy's first public appearance in such things.

"Pitch 'em in the dust-bin!" said the small devil, at last; "it's all they're fit for."

Simmons turned away in sheer horror of his wicked self, and for a moment thought of washing the tea-things over again by way of discipline. Then he made for the back room, but saw from the landing that the front door was standing open, probably by the fault of the child downstairs. Now, a front door standing open was a thing that Mrs. Simmons would *not* abide; it looked low. So Simmons went down, that she might not be wroth with him for the thing when she came back; and, as he shut the door, he looked forth into the street.

A man was loitering on the pavement, and prying curiously about the door. His face was tanned, his hands were deep in the pockets of his unbraced blue trousers, and well back on his head he wore the high-crowned peaked cap topped with a knob of wool, which is affected by Jack ashore about the docks. He lurched a step nearer to the door, and: "Mrs. Ford ain't in, is she?" he said.

Simmons stared at him for a matter of five seconds, and then said: "Eh?"

"Mrs. Ford as was, then—Simmons now, ain't it?"

He said this with a furtive leer that Simmons neither liked nor understood.

"No," said Simmons, "she ain't in now."

"You ain't her 'usband, are ye?"

"Yus."

The man took his pipe from his mouth, and grinned silently and long. "Blimy," he said, at length, "you look the sort o' bloke she'd like." And with that he grinned again. Then, seeing that Simmons made ready to shut the door, he put a foot on the sill and a hand against the panel. "Don't be in a 'urry, matey," he said; "I come 'ere t'ave a little talk with you, man to man, d'ye see?" And he frowned fiercely.

Tommy Simmons felt uncomfortable, but the door would not shut, so he parleyed. "Wotjer want?" he asked. "I dunno you."

"Then if you'll excuse the liberty, I'll interdooce meself, in a manner of speaking." He touched his cap with a bob of mock humility. "I'm Bob Ford," he said, "come back out o' kingdom-come, so to say. Me as went down with the 'Mooltan'—safe dead five years gone. I come to see my wife."

During this speech Thomas Simmons's jaw was dropping lower and lower. At the end of it he poked his fingers up through his hair, looked down at the mat, then up at the fanlight, then out into the street, then hard at his visitor. But he found nothing to say.

"Come to see my wife," the man repeated. "So now we can talk it over—as man to man."

Simmons slowly shut his mouth, and led the way upstairs mechanically, his fingers still in his hair. A sense of the state of affairs sunk gradually into his brain, and the small devil woke again. Suppose this man *was* Ford? Suppose he did claim his wife? Would it be a knockdown blow? Would it hit him out?—or not? He thought of the trousers, the tea-things, the mangling, the knives, the kettles and the windows; and he thought of them in the way of a backslider.

On the landing Ford clutched at his arm, and asked, in a hoarse whisper: "Ow long 'fore she's back?"

" 'Bout a hour, I expect," Simmons replied, having first of all repeated the question in his own mind. And then he opened the parlor door.

"Ah," said Ford, looking about him, "you've bin pretty comf'table. Them chairs an' things"—jerking his pipe toward them—"was hers —mine, that is to say, speaking straight, and man to man." He sat down, puffing meditatively at his pipe, and presently: "Well," he continued, " 'ere I am agin, ol' Bob Ford dead an' done for—gawn down in the 'Mooltan.' On'y I *ain't* done for, see?"—and he pointed the stem of his pipe at Simmons's waistcoat—"I ain't done for, 'cause why? Cons'kence o' bein picked up by a ol' German sailin'-utch an' took to 'Frisco 'fore the mast. I've 'ad a few years o' knockin' about since then, an' now"—looking hard at Simmons—"I've come back to see my wife."

"She—she don't like smoke in 'ere," said Simmons,·as it were, at random.

"No, I bet she don't," Ford answered, taking his pipe from his mouth, and holding it low in his hand. "I know 'Anner. 'Ow d'you find 'er? Do she make ye clean the winders?"

"Well," Simmons admitted, uneasily, "I—I do 'elp 'er sometimes, o' course."

"Ah! An' the knives too, I bet, an' the bloomin' kittles. I know. Wy"—he rose and bent to look behind Simmons's head—"s'elp me, I b'lieve she cuts yer 'air! Well, I'm damned! Jes' wot she would do, too."

He inspected the blushing Simmons from divers points of vantage. Then he lifted a leg of the trousers hanging behind the door. "I'd bet a trifle," he said, "she made these 'ere trucks. Nobody else 'ud do 'em like that. Damme—they're wuss'n wot you're got on."

The small devil began to have the argument all its own way. It this man took his wife back, perhaps he'd have to wear those trousers.

"Ah!" Ford pursued, "she ain't got no milder. An' my davy, wot a jore!"

Simmons began to feel that this was no longer his business. Plainly, 'Anner was this other man's wife, and he was bound in honor to acknowledge the fact. The small devil put it to him as a matter of duty.

"Well," said Ford, suddenly, "time's short, an' this ain't business. I won't be 'ard on you, matey. I ought prop'ly to stand on my rights, but seein' as you're a well-meanin' young man, so to speak, an' all settled an' a-livin' e're quiet an' matrimonual, I'll"—this with a burst of generosity—"damme, yus, I'll compound the felony, an' take me 'ook. Come, I'll name a figure, as man to man, fust an' last, no less an' no more. Five pound does it."

Simmons hadn't five pounds—he hadn't even five pence—and he said so. "An' I wouldn't think for to come between a man an' 'is wife," he added, "not on no account. It may be rough on me, but it's a dooty. I'll 'ook it."

"No," said Ford, hastily, clutching Simmons by the arm, "dont' do that. I'll make it a bit cheaper. Say three quid—come, that's reasonable, ain't it? Three quid ain't much compensation for me goin' away forever—where the stormy winds do blow, so to say—an' never as much as seein' me own wife agin for better nor wuss. Between man an' man now—three quid; an' I'll shunt. That's fair, ain't it?"

"Of course it's fair," Simmons replied, effusively. "It's more'n fair; it's noble—downright noble, I call it. But I ain't goin' to take a mean advantage o' your good-'artedness, Mr. Ford. She's your wife, an' I oughtn't to 'a' come between you. I apologize. You stop an' 'ave yer proper rights. It's me as ought to shunt, an' I will." And he made a step toward the door.

" 'Old on," quoth Ford, and got between Simmons and the door;

"don't do things rash. Look wot a loss it'll be to you with no 'ome to go to, an' nobody to look after ye, an' all that. It'll be dreadful. Say a couple—there, we won't quarrel, jest a single quid, between man an' man, an' I'll stand a pot o' the money. You can easy raise a quid—the clock 'ud pretty nigh do it. A quid does it; an' I'll—"

There was a loud double-knock at the front door. In the East End a double-knock is always for the upstairs lodgers.

"Oo's that?" asked Bob Ford, apprehensively.

"I'll see," said Thomas Simmons in reply, and he made a rush for the staircase.

Bob Ford heard him open the front door. Then he went to the window, and just below him, he saw the crown of a bonnet. It vanished, and borne to him from within the door there fell upon his ear the sound of a well-remembered female voice.

"Where ye goin' now with no 'at?" asked the voice, sharply.

"Awright, 'Anner—there's—there's somebody upstairs to see you," Simmons answered. And, as Bob Ford could see, a man went scuttling down the street in the gathering dusk. And behold, it was Thomas Simmons.

Ford reached the landing in three strides. His wife was still at the front door, staring after Simmons. He flung into the back room, threw open the window, dropped from the wash-house roof into the back-yard, scrambled desperately over the fence, and disappeared into the gloom. He was seen by no living soul. And that is why Simmons's base desertion—under his wife's very eyes, too—is still an astonishment to the neighbors.

Germany

INTRODUCTION

THE contribution of German writers to the technical development
and the sum total of the world's stories has been especially rich.
Owing doubtless to the political vicissitudes of the German-speaking
peoples, and to the widely varying elements that combined through
the ages to produce it, the short-story literature of the Germans offers
a greater diversity in subject-matter and treatment than that of France
or Italy or Spain. There is a substratum of pre-Christian folklore and
tradition that has persisted through the centuries, lending to the stories
of even the most recent writers a certain air of romance and mystery
that is often lacking among the best productions of other lands.

The earliest specimen of German vernacular literature, the *Lay of
Hildebrand*, a precious document dating from the early Ninth Century,
happens to be a well-told short story. The author was an Austrian, but
it must be remembered that German literature as a whole embraces
certain adjacent countries which, like parts of Switzerland and Austria,
are essentially German, racially and intellectually.

As early as the second decade of the Eleventh Century there existed
a fairly well-defined fiction form. *Ruodlieb*, though it is too long for
inclusion in this volume, is a genuine long-short story. It was written
about the year 1030. Not long afterward came the romances and Lays
of chivalry, like the *Gudrun*, and somewhat later *The Lay of the Nibelungs*. During the Twelfth and Thirteenth Centuries the courtly romances flourished; it was the age of the great Minnesingers, Wolfram von
Eschenbach, Hartmann von Aue, and Gottfried von Strassburg, all of
whom drew largely on France for their plots and characters. It is
possible to select from the romances of these an infinity of episodes,
like *The Coming of Gandin* (which appears in the following pages),
which are true short stories.

With the decline of Chivalry and the growth of the merchant classes,
the courtly tales languished. They gave way to such realistic work as
Wernher the Gardner's *Farmer Helmbrecht* (1250), and *Reynard the
Fox* which, though in fable-form, was a realistic work. This was fol-
lowed by several imitations. Passing rapidly now to the period of the
Reformation, we find a growing literature of and by the people—often

formless and rambling, like Brant's *Ship of Fools*, which dates from the early Sixteenth Century. Far better artistically is Wickram's *Galmy* (1519), usually regarded as the first German novel.

The same century was especially rich in the collections of episodes like the celebrated *Till Eulenspiegel*, Pauli's *Jest and Earnest*, and the Faust chapbooks. These popular works were accumulations of folklore, history, gossip, and the odds and ends of other literatures. The Italian Renaissance had also affected Germany, and influences from France continued as before. Boccaccio and Rabelais, together with their followers and imitators, were well-known by the end of the Sixteenth Century.

Of a more original character is the work of Moscherosch, Grimmelhausen and his follower, Christian Weise. Grimmelhausen was the creator of the famous character of Simplicissimus. The *Adventures* of that remarkable person are still read with interest.

Under the influence of the pseudo-classical Gottsched, about the middle of the Eighteenth Century, a new era dawned. Its most important contribution was the short verse fable and tale, which was perfected by Gellert, though others, like Lessing, tried their hand at it. By the end of the century, the *Storm and Stress* and later the Romantic movements, helped on by Goethe and Schiller, the Schlegels and several others, prepared the way for the first of the moderns, Hauff and Hoffmann and Zschokke.

The Nineteenth Century produced a large number of romantic writers who, in common with the French, evolved a highly finished type of short story. Supreme among these writers were Keller and Heyse, though the novelists Freytag, Auerbach, Spielhagen, Baumbach, and Reuter (to mention only a few) all wrote short tales. Toward the end of the century the short story became with certain writers, like Ludwig Thoma and others, the vehicle for the interpretation of peasant life, while with writers like Schnitzler and Bahr, Hartleben and Wedekind, it was largely an expression of the Time Spirit of all Europe.

The more recent writers, like Heinrich and Thomas Mann, Zweig, Wassermann, Sternheim and Kellermann have developed new varieties of form, and reveal the influence of the Russians to a marked extent.

THE LAY OF HILDEBRAND

(Anonymous: Early 9th Century, A.D.)

THE fragmentary *Lay of Hildebrand* is the very earliest surviving specimen of literature in the German language. Beyond the fact that he was an Austrian, nothing is known of the writer. The fragment consists of sixty-nine lines of verse, and relates the greater part of an incident which belongs to the much longer Dietrich saga. Fortunately, what we possess of *The Lay of Hildebrand* is really, so far as it goes, a short story in itself. It bears a striking resemblance to the old story of Sohrab and Rustem.

The present version is reprinted from W. Taylor's *Historic Survey of German Poetry*, etc., London, 1830. There is no title in the original.

THE LAY OF HILDEBRAND

I HAVE heard say that Hildebrand and Amelung agreed to go on a warlike expedition. These kinsmen made ready their horses, prepared their war-shirts and girded on their chain-hilted swords.

As they rode to the meeting of heroes Hildebrand, Hildebrand's son (he was one of the wise and questioned in few words), said to his companion: "If thou wilt tell me who was thy father and of what people thou art sprung. I will give thee three garments."

"I am a child of the Huns," answered Amelung, "and our old people have told me that my father's name was Hildebrand. In former times he came from the east, flying the enmity of Otto-asa, and put himself with Theodoric and his blades.

"He left behind in the land a bride in childbed and a child without inheritance; and went to the south with Theodoric, where he stood many brunts.

"He was a man without connections, not a match for Otto-asa; but he was a good soldier, while he strove under Theodoric, acquired domains, was his people's father, and dear to brave men. I do not believe that he is living."

"My worthy god Irmin in heaven above," quoth Hildebrand, "do not let me fight with so near a kinsman." Then he untwisted golden bracelets from his arm, and imperial rings which his king had given him, saying: "This I give thee not without good will. I am thy father Hildebrand."

Amelung answered: "With willing soul be gifts taken, tit for tat. Thou art not of his age. Craftily thou seekest to deceive me: but I will convict thee out of thy own mouth. Thou art so advanced in years, and thou must be older than he. And shipwrecked men told me that he died by the Wendel-Sea in the west."

Then Hildebrand answered: "I well see thou hast in thy breast no Lord God, and carest nought for his kingdom. Go now, so God be willing," said Hildebrand; "I would we were parted. Sixty summers have I wandered out of my country, and sometimes I have joined archers but in no borough did ever fasten my legs: and now my nearest kinsman would aim his battle-ax at my neck, or I must bind his legs.

Yet you may now easily, if your valor is up, win the spoils of the dead from one you should venerate, if you have any sense of right. He would be a base Ostrogoth," continued Hildebrand, "who should refuse thee battle, seeing thou so greatly desirest it. Good commoners, be judges which it is who flinches in the field, and which it is who ought to have our two coats of mail."

Then they let them fly their ashen spears with such force that they stuck in the shields. Then they struck together their stone axes, and uplifted hostilely their white shields, till their loins and bellies quivered.

But the lady Utta rushed in between them: "I know," said she, "the cross of gold which I gave him for his shield; this is my Hildebrand. You, Amelung, sheath your sword; this is your father."

Then she led both champions into her hall, and gave them meat and wine and many embraces.

SIEGFRIED AND KRIEMHILD

(Anonymous: End of 12th Century)

THE unknown writer of the *Nibelungenlied*, or *Lay of the Nibelungs*, was an Austrian. Nothing is known of him except that he wrote his celebrated ballad-epic toward the end of the Twelfth Century. Rediscovered toward the end of the Eighteenth Century, the *Lay* is, in the words of Prof. Calvin Thomas, "a powerful poem and a human document of many-sided interest." The component episodes are related with great vivacity, and the characters developed by means of a powerful imagination. The *Lay* was founded upon earlier versions of various legends, traditions, and songs that were current in pre-Christian times. Many of the same stories are found in the two Icelandic *Eddas* and in the *Volsunga Saga*.

The present version comprises two chapters, or "Adventures" (the fourth and fifth) of *The Fall of the Nibelungs*, translated by Margaret Armour, Everyman's Library. Reprinted by permission of the publishers, J. M. Dent and Sons. There is no title in the original.

SIEGFRIED AND KRIEMHILD

(From *The Lay of the Nibelungs*)

NOW there were brought into Gunther's land strange tidings by envoys sent from afar by foreign princes that hated him; and when they heard the message they were troubled. The kings were as I will tell you: Ludger of the Saxons, a high and mighty prince; and Ludgast of Denmark, and many bold warriors with them.

These envoys, sent by his foemen, came into Gunther's land, and the strangers, were asked their business, and brought before the king.

The king greeted them fair, and said, "I know not who hath sent you hither, and would hear it." So spake the good king, and they greatly feared his wrath.

"If thou wilt have our message, O king, we will tell it plain, and name thee the princes that have sent us. They are Ludgast and Ludger, and will come against thee into thy land. Thou art fallen in their displeasure, and we know that they bear thee bitter hate. They come hither with an armed force to Worms by the Rhine—they and their warriors. Wherefore be warned. Inside of twelve days they will ride. If thou hast trusty friends, let it appear now; let them help thee to keep thy castles and thy country, for, or long, there will be smiting of helmets and shields here. Or wouldst thou treat with them, then declare it straightway, that thy foemen come not nigh thee to thy hurt, and that goodly knights perish not thereby."

"Tarry a while—ye shall have answer betimes—that I may bethink me," said the good king. "If I have true liegemen, I will not hide it from them, but will take counsel with them on this hard matter."

Heavy enow of his cheer was Gunther. He pondered the message secretly in his heart, and summoned Hagen, and others of his men, and sent to the court in haste for Gernot. His best knights drew round him, and he said, "Without cause, and with a mighty array, foemen come hither against us into our land."

Thereto answered Gernot, a hardy and bold warrior, "We shall hinder that with our swords. They only perish that fate dooms. Let them die. They shall not turn me from honor. Our foemen are welcome."

Spake Hagen of Trony then, "Methinketh that were unwise. Ludgast and Ludger are proud men withal, and we can hardly in so few days muster our men." Therefore the bold knight said, "Tell Siegfried."

They bade lodge the envoys in the town. Albeit they were his foemen, Gunther, the great king, commanded the folk to entreat them well—rightly he did so—till that he knew the friends that would stand by him.

The king was heavy of his cheer, and Siegfried, the good knight, saw that he was downcast, but wist not the reason, and asked King Gunther what ailed him. "I marvel much," said Siegfried, "that thou takest no part in our sports as heretofore." And Gunther, the doughty knight, anwered him, "Not to every man may I declare the secret heaviness of my heart; only unto true friends shall the heart tell its dole."

Siegfried changed color, and grew red and white, and he said to the king, "I have denied thee naught, and now I would help thee. If thou seekest friends, I will be one of them, and stand to it truly to my life's end."

"Now God requite thee, Sir Siegfried, for I like thy word; and albeit thy might availed me nothing, I would rejoice none the less that thou art well-minded toward me; as much and more will I do to thee if I live. I will tell thee the cause of my trouble. Envoys from my foemen have brought a message that with an army they will come against me; such inroad of warriors hath not been aforetime in this country."

"Be not sorrowful for that," answered Siegfried; "be of good cheer, and do now as I say. I will win for thee honor and profit or ever thy foemen reach this land. Had thy stark adversaries thirty thousand warriors at their back, and I but one thousand, I would withstand them— trust me for that."

King Gunther answered, "Thou shalt be well paid for this."

"Give me a thousand of thy knights, since of mine own I have but twelve here with me, and I will keep thy land for thee. The hand of Siegfried will serve thee truly. Hagen shall help us in this, and also Ortwin, Dankwart, and Sindolt, thy loving knights, and eke Folker, the bold man, who shall bear the standard: better knight thou wilt not find. Bid the envoys return to their country; tell them they shall see us there soon enow. So shall our castles go scatheless."

The king let summon his kinsmen and his liegemen, and Ludger's messengers went to the court. They were glad to be gone. Gunther, the good king, gave them gifts and an escort, whereat they were well content.

Spake Gunther, "Thou shalt say this wise to my haughty foemen: 'They did wisely to turn from their journey, for if my friends fail me not, and they seek me here in my land, they will find work enow.'"

They brought out rich gifts for the envoys, whereof Gunther had to spare, and these said not "nay." Then they took their leave, and departed rejoicing.

When the messengers were come again to Denmark, and told Ludgast how that the Rhine-men would ride thither, he was wroth at their boldness. They made report to him of the many brave men Gunther had, and how that they had seen a knight there amidst of them that hight Siegfried, a hero from the Netherland, the which was heavy news for Ludgast.

When they of Denmark heard it, they hasted the more to summon their friends, till that Ludgast had ready for the onset twenty thousand warriors withal.

On like manner Ludger of Saxony summoned his men to the number of forty thousand, ready to march into Burgundy.

The same also did King Gunther to his liegemen, and to his brothers with their vassals, and to Hagen and his knights. These were sorry enow at the news; by reason thereof many a knight looked on death.

They hasted and made ready for the journey. Brave Folker bare the standard. They purposed to cross the Rhine from Worms. Hagen of Trony led the force. Sindolt and bold Hunolt were there, that they might deserve King Gunther's gold; also Hagen's brother Dankwart, and Ortwin, fit men and worthy for the undertaking.

"Sit thou at home, O King," spake Siegfried. "Since thy knights are willing to follow me, stay here by the women and be of good cheer; for, by my troth, I will guard for thee both goods and honor. I will see to it, that they that seek thee here at Worms by the Rhine bide where they are; we will pierce deep into their country, till their vaunting is turned to sorrow."

They passed from the Rhine through Hesse against Saxony, where the battle was fought afterward. With plunder and with fire they laid waste the land, the which both the princes found to their cost.

When they were come to the marches, the warriors hasted forward, and Siegfried began to ask them, "Which of us shall guard the rest from surprise?" More to their hurt the Saxons never took the field.

They answered, "Let bold Dankwart guard the younger knights. He is a good warrior. So shall we come in less scathe by Ludger's men. He and Ortwin shall guard the rear."

"I myself will ride forward," said Siegfried, "and spy out the foe, that I may know rightly who the warriors be."

Fair Sieglind's son did on his armor in haste. He gave his knights in charge to Hagen and bold Gernot when he set out. He rode into Saxony all alone, and won honor by his quest. He perceived a great host encamped on a field, that loomed mightily against him, beyond the strength of one man: forty thousand or more. And the high heart of Siegfried rejoiced.

One of the enemy's knights kept watch warily, and perceived Siegfried, and Siegfried him, and they glared fiercely on each other. I will tell you who he was that kept watch. On his arm he bare a glittering shield of gold. It was King Ludgast that kept ward over his host.

The noble stranger pricked toward him fiercely. Ludgast dressed him also. They put spurs to their horses and smote with all their strength on the shields with their spears, that it was like to go hard with the king. On their horses, pricked forward by the spur, the princes bare down on each other like the wind. Then they wheeled round deftly—these two fierce men—and fell to hacking with their swords. Sir Siegfried smote, that the field rang therewith; the hero with his mighty blade struck sparks from Ludgast's helmet. Fiercely fought the prince of the Netherland, and Ludgast, likewise, dealt many a grim blow. Each drove with all his might at the other's shield. The combat was spied by thirty of Ludgast's men, but Siegfried, by means of three deep wounds and grisly that he dealt Ludgast through his white harness, overcame the king or these knights came up. His sword drew blood with each stroke, that King Ludgast came in evil plight, and begged for his life, offering his land as the price thereof, and said that his name was Ludgast.

His knights hasted to his rescue, for they had seen the encounter at the ward-post. Siegfried would have led him thence, but thirty of Ludgast's men rode at him. With mighty blows the stark warrior kept his rich captive; and soon his hands did even deadlier deeds. He smote the thirty men dead in his defense, save one that fled and told what had happed, the truth whereof was proven by his bloody helmet.

They of Denmark were aghast when they heard their king was taken captive; they told it to his brother, who fell in a great fury by reason of the disaster.

So the mighty Ludgast was taken by Siegfried's prowess, and given in charge to Hagen. When that good knight heard that it was Ludgast he was not sorry.

They bade raise the standard of Burgundy. "Forward!" cried Siegfried. "More shall be done or the day end, if I lose not my life. The Saxon women shall rue it. Hearken now, ye men of the Rhine. I can lead you to Ludger's army. There ye will see helmets hewn by the good hands of heroes. They shall be in evil case or we turn again."

Then Gernot and his men sprang to horse. The banner was unfurled by Folker, the minstrel knight. He rode before the host, and they all made them ready for battle. They numbered not more than a thousand men, and thereto the twelve strangers. The dust rose from their path, and they rode through the land, their shields flashing.

The Saxons, also, were come up, bearing well-sharpened swords. So hath the story been told me. The swords in the heroes' hands dealt grim blows in defense of their castles and their land.

The marshal led the army, and Siegfried was come forward with the twelve men that he had with him from the Netherland. Many a hand was bloody that day in the battle. Sindolt and Hunolt and eke Gernot smote many heroes dead in the fight, that were bold enow till they felt their prowess. For their sake sorrowed women not a few. Folker and Hagen and Ortwin, the fierce warriors, quenched the flash of many helmets with blood. Dankwart, also, did wonders. The Danes proved their mettle, and loud were heard the hurtling of shields and the clash of sharp swords swung mightily. The Saxons, bold in strife, made havoc enow. Wide were the wounds hewn by the men of Burgundy when they rushed to the encounter. Blood ran down the saddles. So was honor wooed of these knights bold and swift. Loud rang the keen swords in the hands of the heroes of the Netherland, when they rode with their lord into the fray. They rode with Siegfried like good knights. None from the Rhine kept pace with him. By reason of Siegfried's hand streams of blood ran from bright helmets, till that he lit on Ludgast amidst of his men. Thrice he pierced through the army of the Saxons, and thrice returned. Hagen, by this time, was come up with him, that helped him in his quest. They slew many a brave knight.

When bold Ludger found Siegfried with Balmung, the good sword, swung aloft, wherewith he made a mighty slaughter, he was wroth, and of his mood full grim. With a fierce rush and clash of swords the warriors came together. So exceeding furious was their onset that the host gave way. Terrible was their hate. The Saxon king knew well that his brother was taken captive, and he was wroth thereat; but he knew it not for Siegfried's work till now. They had blamed Gernot. Now he found out the truth. Ludger smote so hard that Siegfried's horse reeled under him. But when he was come to, Siegfried was more terrible than afore. Hagen and Gernot, Dankwart and Folker, stood by him. The dead lay in heaps. Sindolt and Hunolt and Ortwin the knight slew many in the strife. The princes held together in the fray. Bright spears in the hands of heroes flashed above the helmets, that clave the shining bucklers in twain. Many a massy shield was red with blood. In the fierce encounter many men fell from their horses. Bold Siegfried and King Ludger strove together, and lances whizzed, and sharp spears. Ludger's shield-plate flew off through the strength of Siegfried's hand. Then the hero of the Netherland thought to have gotten the victory over the Saxons that were hard pressed. Ha! what polished bucklers doughty Dankwart brake!

Of a sudden Ludger espied a crown that was painted on Siegfried's shield, and he knew the mighty man, and cried aloud to his friends, "Forbear, my men all. I have seen the son of Siegmund, even bold Siegfried. The Devil hath sent him hither into Saxony." He bade lower the standard, and sued for peace. They granted this, yet he was compelled by Siegfried to go captive into Gunther's land.

With one accord they ceased from the strife. They threw down their shivered helmets and shields. Blood-red were they all by the hands of the Burgundians. They took captive whom they listed, for they had the power.

Gernot and Hagen gave order to convey the wounded on litters. They led five hundred noble knights as prisoners to the Rhine.

The vanquished warriors rode back to Denmark. Nor had the Saxons fought so as to win them honor, and they were downcast. The dead were mourned by their friends.

They sent the weapons to the Rhine on sumpters. So wondrously had Siegfried done, that all Gunther's men praised him.

Sir Gernot sent word to Worms, and throughout the whole land, to their friends, how it had sped with them; for as bold knights and honorable they had fought. The pages hasted and told it, and the glad news rejoiced the loving ones that had sorrowed. The noble women ceased not from questioning how it had fared with the great king's men.

Kriemhild bade a messenger to her in secret; publicly she durst not, for to one of them she bare dear heart's love.

When the messenger was come to her chamber, Kriemhild, the beautiful maiden, spake him fair. "Now tell me glad tidings; thou shalt have gold therefor; and, sayest thou sooth, I will ever be beholden to thee. How sped my brother Gernot in the battle, and the rest of my friends? Are there many dead? Who did most valiantly? Now tell me."

Whereto the messenger answered truthfully, "We had no coward among us. Yet since thou wilt hear it, noble princess, none rode in the thick of the fight like the knight of the Netherland. Marvelous was the work of Siegfried's hand. All that the knights did in battle—Dankwart and Hagen and the rest—though with honor fought they all, was but as a wind matched with the prowess of Siegfried, the son of Siegmund. Many heroes have they slain, yet of the deeds of Siegfried, done in battle, none shall tell to the end. By reason of him many maidens mourn for their kin. Low lieth the dear one of many a bride. Loud smote he on the helmets, that they ran blood. In all things he is a knight bold and good.

"Ortwin of Metz, also, won worship. Whoso came within range of his sword lieth wounded or dead. Thy brother, too, made fierce havoc in the battle. To his prowess must all testify. The proud Burgundians have so fought that none may question their honor. For many a saddle was emptied by them when the field rang loud with gleaming swords. On such wise fought the knights of the Rhine that their foemen had done better to flee. The brave men of Trony rode fiercely in the strife. Hagen with his hand slew many, whereof Burgundy shall hear. So valiantly fought Sinolt and Hunolt, Gernot's men, and eke Rumolt, that Ludger may well rue that he ever met thy kinsmen by the Rhine. But the mightiest deeds, first and last, were done by Siegfried. He bringeth rich captives into Gunther's land, that his strength hath conquered by reason whereof King Ludgast and his brother, Ludger of Saxony, suffer dole. For list to the marvel, noble queen: both these princes hath Siegfried's hand taken. Never have so many captives been led into this land as come hither now through his prowess."

The maiden was glad at the tale.

"Of unwounded men they bring five hundred or more, and eighty red biers (I say sooth) of the wounded, fallen, the most part, by Siegfried's might. They that arrogantly withstood the knights of the Rhine are now Gunther's captives. Our men lead them hither rejoicing."

When she had heard the news aright, her fair cheek reddened, and her lovely face was the color of the rose, because it had gone well with young and noble Siegfried, and he was come with glory out of peril. She joyed for her kinsmen also, as in duty bound. And she said, "Thou hast spoken well; for guerdon thereof thou shalt have costly raiment, and ten golden marks that I will bid them bear to thee." It is good to tell glad tidings to rich women.

He got his envoy's fee of gold and vesture, and the fair maids hasted to the window and looked down the road, where the high-hearted warriors rode home. They drew nigh, whole and wounded, and heard the greeting of friends, unashamed. Light of heart Gunther rode to meet them, for now his grim care was turned to joy. He received his own men well and also the strangers. Not to have thanked them that were come to his court, for that they had done valiantly in battle, would have been unseemly in so great a king. And he asked tidings of his friends, and who were slain. None were lost to him save sixty only, and these were mourned as many a hero hath been mourned since.

They that were unhurt brought many battered shields and shivered helmets back to Gunther's land. The warriors sprang down from their horses before the palace, and there was a joyful noise of welcome.

Order was given to lodge the knights in the town, and the king commanded that his guests should be courteously entreated, and that the wounded should be seen to and given good chambers. So he approved himself generous to his foes. He said to Ludger, "Thou art welcome! Much scathe have I suffered through thee; yet, if I prosper henceforth, I will consider myself well paid. God reward my warriors, for well have they served me!"

"Thou hast cause to thank them," answered Ludger, "for nobler captives were never won for a king; and gold without stint shall be thine, if thou do well by me and my friends."

Said Gunther, "Ye shall both go free. Yet I must have a pledge that my foemen quit not my land till peace be sealed betwixt us." And they promised, it and gave their hand thereon. They led them to their quarters to rest, and saw the wounded men laid softly in their beds. They set before them that were whole meat and good wine, and never were men merrier. They bare battered shields away into safe keeping; and the bloody saddles, of which there were enow, they hid, that the women might not grieve thereat. Many a weary knight was there.

The king entreated his guests right royally, and the land was full of friends and of strangers. He bade see to the sore wounded ones whose pride was brought low. To them that were skilled in leech craft they offered a rich fee of unweighed silver and yellow gold, that they might heal the heroes of their wounds gotten in battle; the king sent also precious gifts to his guests. They that thought to ride home were bidden stay as friends. And the king took counsel how he might reward his liege men that had done valiantly for his sake.

Sir Gernot said, "Let them go hence for the present, and summon them after six weeks to a hightide. Many will then be whole that now lie sick of their wounds."

Siegfried of the Netherland would have taken leave also, but, when King Gunther knew his intent, he besought him lovingly to tarry, the which Siegfried had not done but for Gunther's sister's sake. He was too rich to take money, albeit he well deserved it; the king loved him, and also the king's kinsmen that had seen the deeds wrought by his hand in battle. So, for love of the maiden, he agreed to tarry, that haply he might win to see her, the which, or long came, to pass; for he knew her to his heart's desire, and rode home joyfully afterward to his father's land.

The young knights obeyed the king's command willingly, and practised daily at the tourney. Seats were raised on the stand before Worms for the guests that were coming into Burgundy.

When it was time for them to arrive, fair Kriemhild heard the news, that they were about to hold a hightide with their friends. Then the beautiful women busied them with their kirtles and their headgear that they were to wear.

Uta, the great queen, heard of the proud knights that were coming, and gorgeous robes were taken from their wrapping-cloths. For love of her children she bade them bring forth the garments. Many women and maidens were adorned therewith, and, of the young knights of Burgundy, not a few. To many of the strangers, also, she gave goodly apparel.

A vast multitude of them that would attend the hightide drew daily to the Rhine; and unto those that came for love of the king horses were given and goodly raiment, and to each his place, even unto two and thirty princes of the highest and the best. So they tell us.

And the women vied with one another in their attire. Giselher, the youth, and Gernot, and their two squires, rested not from welcoming both friends and strangers. They gave courtly greeting unto the warriors.

The guests brought with them to the Rhine, to the tourney, saddles worked in ruddy gold, and finely wrought shields, and knightly apparel. And the sick rejoiced, and they that lay on their beds sore wounded forgot that death is an hard thing. When the rumor of the festival was noised abroad, no man took heed more of them that groaned, for each thought only how he might sojourn there as a guest. Joy without measure had all they that were found there, and gladness and rejoicing were in Gunther's land.

On Whitsun morning, there drew toward the hightide a goodly company of brave men, fairly clad: five thousand or more, and they made merry far and wide, and strove with one another in friendly combat.

Now Gunther knew well how, truly and from his heart, the hero of the Netherland loved his sister whom he had not yet seen, and whose beauty the people praised before that of all other maidens.

And he said, "Now counsel me, my kinsmen and my lieges, how we may order this hightide, that none may blame us in aught; for only unto such deeds as are good pertaineth lasting fame."

Then answered Ortwin, the knight, to the king, "If thou wilt win for thyself glory from the hightide, let now the maidens that dwell with honor in our midst appear before us. For what shall pleasure or glad a man more than to behold beautiful damsels and fair women? Bid thy sister come forth and show herself to thy guests."

And this word pleased the knights.

"That will I gladly do," said the king; and they that heard him rejoiced. He sent a messenger to Queen Uta, and besought her that she would come to the court with her daughter and her women-folk.

And these took from the presses rich apparel, and what lay therein in wrapping-cloths; they took also brooches, and their silken girdles worked with gold, and attired themselves in haste. Many a noble maiden adorned herself with care, and the youths longed exceedingly to find favor in their eyes, and had not taken a rich king's land in lieu thereof. And they that knew not one another before looked each upon each right gladly.

The rich king commanded an hundred men of his household, his kinsmen and hers, to escort his sister, their swords in their hands. Uta, with an hundred and more of her women, gorgeously attired, came forth from the female apartments, and many noble damsels followed after her daughter. The knights pressed in upon them, thinking thereby to behold the beautiful maiden.

And lo! the fair one appeared, like the dawn from out the dark clouds. And he that had borne her so long in his heart was no more aweary, for the beloved one, his sweet lady, stood before him in her beauty. Bright jewels sparkled on her garments, and bright was the rose red of her hue, and all they that saw her proclaimed her peerless among maidens.

As the moon excelleth in light the stars shining clear from the clouds, so stood she, fair before the other women, and the hearts of the warriors were uplifted. The chamberlains made way for her through them that pressed in to behold her. And Siegfried joyed, and sorrowed likewise, for he said in his heart, "How should I woo such as thee? Surely it was a vain dream; yet I were liefer dead than a stranger to thee."

Thinking thus he waxed oft white and red; yea, graceful and proud stood the son of Sieglind, goodliest of heroes to behold, as he were drawn on parchment by the skill of a cunning master. And the knights fell back as the escort commanded, and made way for the high-hearted women, and gazed on them with glad eyes. Many a dame of high degree was there.

Said bold Sir Gernot, the Burgundian, then, "Gunther, dear brother, unto the gentle knight, that hath done thee service, show honor now before thy lieges. Of this counsel I shall never shame me. Bid Siegfried go before my sister, that the maiden greet him. Let her, that never greeted knight, go toward him. For this shall advantage us, and we shall win the good warrior for ours."

Then Gunther's kinsmen went to the knight of the Netherland, and said to him, "The king bids thee to the court that his sister may greet thee, for he would do thee honor."

It rejoiced Siegfried that he was to look upon Uta's fair child, and he forgot his sorrow.

She greeted him mild and maidenly, and her color was kindled when she saw before her the high-minded man, and she said, "Welcome, Sir Siegfried, noble knight and good." His courage rose at her words, and graceful, as beseemed a knight, he bowed himself before her and thanked her. And love that is mighty constrained them, and they yearned with their eyes in secret. I know not whether, from his great love, the youth pressed her white hand, but two love-desirous hearts, I trow, had else done amiss.

Nevermore, in summer or in May, bore Siegfried in his heart such high joy as when he went by the side of her whom he coveted for his dear one. And many a knight thought, "Had it been my hap to walk with her, as I have seen him do, or to lie by her side, certes, I had suffered it gladly! Yet never, truly, hath warrior served better to win a queen." From what land soever the guests came, they were ware only of these two. And she was bidden kiss the hero. He had never had like joy before in this world.

Said the King of Denmark then, "By reason of this high greeting many good men lie low, slain by the hand of Siegfried, the which hath been proven to my cost. God grant he return not to Denmark!"

Then they ordered to make way for fair Kriemhild. Valiant knights in stately array escorted her to the minster, where she was parted from Siegfried. She went thither followed by her maidens; and so rich was her apparel that the other women, for all their striving, were as naught beside her, for to glad the eyes of heroes she was born.

Scarce could Siegfried tarry till they had sung mass, he yearned so to thank her for his gladness, and that she whom he bore in his heart had inclined her desire toward him, even as his was to her, which was meet. Now when Kriemhild was come forth to the front of the minster, they bade the warrior go to her again, and the damsel began to thank him, that before all others he had done valiantly. And she said, "Now, God requite thee, Sir Siegfried, for they tell me thou hast won praise and honor from all knights."

He looked on the maid right sweetly, and he said, "I will not cease to serve them. Never, while I live, will I lay head on pillow, till I have brought their desire to pass. For love of thee, dear lady, I will do this."

And every day of twelve, in the sight of all the people, the youth walked by the side of the maiden as she went to the court. So they showed their love to the knight.

And there was merriment and gladness and delight in the hall of Gunther, without and within, among the valiant men. Ortwin and Hagen did many wonderful deeds, and if any devised a sport, warriors, joyous in strife, welcomed it straightway. So were the knights proven before the guests, and they of Gunther's land won glory. The wounded also came forth to take part with their comrades, to skirmish with the buckler, and to shoot the shaft, and waxed strong thereby, and increased their might.

Gunther gave order that, for the term of the hightide, they should set before them meats of the daintiest, that he might fail in naught as a king, nor the people blame him.

And he came to his guests, and said, "Receive my gifts ere ye go hence, and refuse not the treasure that I would share with you."

The Danes made answer, "Ere we turn again to our land, make thou a lasting peace with us. We have need of such, that have many dear friends, slain by thy warriors."

Ludgast and eke the Saxon were healed of their wounds gotten in battle, but many tarried behind, dead.

Then Gunther sought Siegfried and said, "Now counsel me in this. On the morrow our guests ride forth, and they desire of me and mine a lasting covenant. What they offer I will tell thee: as much gold as five hundred horses may carry, they will give me to go free."

And Siegfried answered, "That were ill done. Send them forth without ransom, that they ride no more hither as foemen. And they shall give thee the hand thereon for surety."

"What thou counselest I will do. They shall depart as thou sayest."

And they told it to his enemies; also that none desired their gold. They said it to the war-tired men, by reason of whom the dear ones of their own land sorrowed.

And the king took shields full of treasure, and divided it among them without weighing it, five hundred marks and more. Gernot, the brave knight, counseled him thereto. And they took their leave, for they were aweary for home. And they passed before Kriemhild and Queen Uta; never were knights dismissed more courteously.

The chambers were void when they left, nevertheless the king abode there still with his lieges and his vassals and knights. And these ceased not to go before Kriemhild.

Then Siegfried, the hero, had also taken leave, for he thought not to attain his desire. But the king heard of it, and Giselher the youth turned him back. "Whither ridest thou, Sir Siegfried? Prithee yield to me in this. Go not from among our knights, and Gunther, and his men. Here are fair maidens enow that thou mayest behold at will."

Said bold Sir Siegfried, "Let stand the horses, bear hence the shields. I would have ridden forth and turned again to my land, but Giselher hath changed my intent."

So he abode among them through love, nor in any land had it been sweeter for him. And Kriemhild, the fair maiden, he saw daily, by reason of whose beauty he tarried.

They passed the time in sports and feats of chivalry. But his heart was weary with love; yea, for love he sorrowed then, and, after, died miserably.

GOTTFRIED VON STRASSBURG

(Died about 1210)

GOTTFRIED was one of the most famous of that group of Minnesingers which included Hartmann von Aue and Wolfram von Eschenbach. These were the most popular writers of the so-called romances of knighthood. Gottfried's *Tristan* was a working-over of a French version of the tale (now existing only in fragmentary form) by Thomas the Trouvère. The German work is a many-coloured story of love and adventure, direct, simple, and devoid of the finer subtleties of psychology. *The Coming of Gandin* is one of the complete episodes which abound throughout the romance.

The present version, translated by Jessie L. Weston, is reprinted by her permission from *Tristan and Iseult*, published by David Nutt in 1899. There is no title in the original.

THE COMING OF GANDIN

(From *Tristan and Iseult*)

FOR in these days a ship came to Mark's haven in Cornwall, and there landed from it a knight, a noble baron of Ireland, named Gandin; he was rich, handsome, and courteous, so manly and strong of limb that all Ireland spake of his valor.

Fairly clad, without shield or spear, he came riding to the king's court. On his back he bare a lute adorned with gold and precious stones, a-strung as a lute should be.

He dismounted, entered the palace, and greeted Mark and Iseult in fitting wise. Many a time and in many ways had he served the queen in her own land, through his knighthood, and the great love he bare her, and for her sake had he journeyed hither from Ireland.

Then Iseult knew him, and greeted him courteously. "God save thee, Sir Gandin."

"Gramercy, fair Iseult, fair and fairer than gold in the eyes of Gandin!"

Iseult spake softly to the king, saying who the knight was and whence he came; and Mark hearkened, wondering much why he bare a lute, and in sooth so did all the folk, for such was not the wont of wandering knights. Nevertheless would Mark do him all the honor he might, both for his own sake and for that of Iseult, since he was the queen's countryman; so he bade the stranger sit beside him, and spake to him of his folk and land, and of knightly deeds.

When the feast was ready, and water was brought round to the guests to wash their hands, then did the courtiers pray the stranger to play the lute before them. The king and queen said nought, they would leave it to his own will; and when he took no heed of their prayers, the courtiers mocked him, calling him "The Knight of the Lute," "The Prince with the Penance"; and Gandin said nought, but sat beside King Mark, and ate and drank, and heeded them not.

When the feast was over, and the tables borne away, then King Mark prayed him, an he could, to pleasure them awhile with his skill on the lute; but Gandin answered: "Sire, I may not, save that I know what my reward may be."

"Sir Knight, what meanest thou? Dost thou desire aught of my possessions? If so, 'tis granted; let us but hearken thy skill, and I will give thee whatever thou desirest."

"So be it," spake the knight of Ireland.

Then he sang a lay which pleased them all well, so that the king desired him to sing another. The traitor laughed in his heart. "Tell me," he said, "what thou wilt, that I may play even as shall please thee."

Now when he had sung another lay, Gandin arose and stood before the king, holding the lute in his hand. "Sir King," he said, "bethink thee of what thou didst promise me."

And Mark answered: "Of good will will I do it. Tell me what wilt thou?"

"Give me Iseult," quoth the knight.

"Friend," said Mark, "whatever else thou desirest thou shalt have, but this may not be."

"Verily, Sir King," said Gandin, "I will neither much nor little, but Iseult alone."

The King spake: "Of a truth, that shall not be!"

"Sire, wilt thou then break thy promise? If thou be thus forsworn, henceforth shall men hold thee unworthy to be king of any land. Bid them read the right of kings, and if this be not so, then will I renounce my claim. Or, dost thou, or any other say that thou didst not swear to give me what I asked, then will I assert my right against thee, or against whomsoever the court may choose. My body shall be overcome with fight ere I renounce my claim. Choose thou a knight to ride in the ring against me, and I will prove by combat that fair Iseult is mine."

The king looked all about and on either side if he might find one who would dare to uphold his cause; but there was no man who would set his life on such a wager, nor would Mark himself fight for his queen, for Gandin was so strong and valiant that none durst take up his challenge.

Now Tristan had ridden forth to the woods to hunt, and as he came homeward to the court he heard on the way the news of what had chanced. 'Twas all true: Gandin had led the queen, weeping and lamenting bitterly from the palace to the seashore. On the shore was pitched a tent, rich and costly, wherein he led the queen that they might wait till tide and river rose and floated the bark, which now lay high on the sand.

When Tristan heard the tale from beginning to end, he mounted his horse and took his harp in his hand, and rode swiftly, even to the haven. There he turned aside secretly, to a grove, made his horse fast to the bough of a tree, and with his harp in his hand took his way to the tent. The knight of Ireland sat there, armed, beside the weeping queen, whom he strove hard to comfort, but little might it avail, till he saw Tristan and his harp.

He greeted Gandin, saying: "God save thee, fair minstrel!"

"Gramercy, gentle knight."

"Sir," he said, "I have hastened hither. Men have told me thou art come from Ireland: I too am from thence. I pray thee, of thine honor, take me back to mine own land."

The Irish knight made answer: "That will I do; but sit thee down, play to me, and if thou canst comfort my lady, whom thou seest weeping sorely, I will give thee the fairest garment that is in this tent."

" 'Tis a fair offer, Sir Knight," said Tristan. "I have good hope that I may do so; and her grief be not so great that it will stay not for any man's playing, she must needs be consoled."

Therewith he harped so sweetly that the notes crept into Iseult's heart and bare her thoughts so far hence that she ceased weeping, and thought but of her love.

Now, when the lay was ended, the water had come up to the bark, and it floated, so that they on board cried to the haven: "Sir, sir, come aboard; if my lord Tristan comes whilst thou art yet ashore, we shall have but an ill time! Folk and land alike are in his power—also he himself, so they say, is of such wondrous daring, so valiant and strong, he will likely do thee a mischief."

This was unpleasing to Gandin, and he said angrily: "Now may heaven hate me if I stir hence a moment earlier for that! Comrade, play me the Lay of Dido; thou dost harp so sweetly that I must needs love thee for it. Now play, and banish my lady's sorrow. Out of love for thee will I bear thee hence with her and me, and will give thee all I have promised thee, yea, and more!"

"So be it," quoth Tristan.

The minstrel touched his harp again; and he played so sweetly that Gandin listened eagerly, and Iseult was all intent on the music. And when it had ended the knight took the queen by the hand, and would lead her aboard, but by now was the tide so high and running so strong that no man might reach the bark save on horseback. "What shall we do now," asked Gandin. "How may my lady come aboard?"

"See, Sir Knight," quoth the minstrel, "since I am sure thou wilt take me hence with thee, I think but little of what I have here in Cornwall. I have a horse near by; I ween he shall be tall enough to carry my lady, thy friend, over to the bark without the sea wetting her."

Gandin said: "Good minstrel, haste, bring thy horse hither, and take also the robe I promised thee."

Tristan fetched his horse swiftly, and when he came back he swung his harp behind him and cried: "Now, knight of Ireland, give me my lady, I will carry her before me through the water."

"Nay, minstrel, thou shalt not touch her; I will carry her myself."

"Nay, sir," said fair Iseult, " 'tis needless to say he shall not touch me. Know the truth, I go not aboard save the minstrel bear me."

Then Gandin led her to Tristan. "Comrade," he said, "have a care of her—carry her so gently that I shall be ever grateful to thee."

Now as soon as Tristan held Iseult he spurred his steed forward, and when Gandin saw it he spake in wrath: "Ha, fool, what dost thou?"

"Nay, nay, fool Gandin," quoth Tristan, " 'tis thou who art the fool; what thou didst steal from King Mark by the lute, that I do bear away with my harp. Thou didst betray, now art thou betrayed. Tristan has followed thee till he has befooled thee! Friend, thou hast indeed given me a rich garment, even the richest that thy tent did hold."

With that Tristan rode his way, leaving Gandin, beyond measure sorrowful; his loss and his shame cut him to the heart; mourning, he returned over-seas.

Tristan and Iseult rode homeward, rejoicing in their love; and when they came to the palace, Tristan led the queen to King Mark, and spake bitterly: "Sire, God knoweth, if thou dost hold thy queen so dear as thou sayest, 'tis a great folly to give her up lightly for mere lute or harp play! The world may well mock! Whoever saw a queen the chattel of a lay? Henceforth bethink thee, and guard my lady better."

BRUIN THE BEAR AND REYNARD THE FOX

(Anonymous: about 1230).

NOTHING is known of the writer of the first version of the celebrated *Reynard the Fox*. The problem of the origin of the book is complicated, but it is generally agreed that a series of incidents attributed to an Alsatian writer of the late Twelfth Century was the basis of the book as it stands in the version here used. This was printed in 1498, though it was probably written about 1230. *Reynard* was soon afterwards translated into nearly every language of Europe. The book, in one form or another, has been a popular favourite among all classes of readers, and has for centuries been rewritten to suit the tastes of each generation.

The present version, translated by Thomas Roscoe, is reprinted from Roscoe's *German Novelists*, London, no date. It is Chapter IV of *The Pleasant History of Reynard the Fox*. The full title of the chapter is *How Bruin the Bear Sped with Reynard the Fox*, followed by a brief description.

BRUIN THE BEAR AND REYNARD THE FOX

(From *Reynard the Fox*)

THE next morning away went Sir Bruin the bear in quest of the fox, armed against all kinds of plots and deceit whatsoever; and as he went along through a dark forest in which Reynard had a by-path which he used when he was out hunting or being hunted, he saw a high mountain, over which he must pass to reach Malepardus. For though Reynard had many houses, Malepardus is his chief and most ancient castle, and there he resorted both for defense and pleasure. When Bruin at length came to the place, he found the gates close shut; at which, after he had knocked, sitting upon his tail, he called aloud,

"Sir Reynard, are you at home? I am Bruin, your kinsman, sent by the king to summon you to court, to answer the many foul accusations laid at your door. His majesty hath taken a great vow if you fail to appear to the summons, your life shall answer for your contempt, and your whole goods and honors become confiscated to the crown. Therefore, fair kinsman, be advised by your friend, and come with me to court, in order to shun the fate that will otherwise overtake you": so said the bear. Reynard, who was lying near the gate, as was his custom, basking in the sun, hearing these words, departed into one of his holes, Malepardus being full of many intricate and curious apartments, through which he could pass in case of danger or for objects of prey, where he determined to commune with himself awhile how best he might counterplot, and bring the bear into disgrace, while he added to his own credit, for he detested the bear; and at last coming forth, said, "Is it you, dear uncle Bruin? you are exceeding welcome, and excuse my delay in saying so; but the truth is, that when you began to speak I was saying my vespers, and devotion must not be neglected for any worldly concerns. Yet I believe he hath done you no good service, nor do I thank him who hath sent you hither, a long and weary journey, in which your sweat and toil far exceed the worth of the labor performed. It is certain, that had you not come, I had tomorrow attended the court of mine own accord. As it is, however, my regret is much diminished, because your counsel just at this time may turn to my double benefit. Alas! uncle, could his majesty find no meaner a messenger than your noble self to employ in these trivial affairs? Truly it appears strange to me, especially since, next his royal self, you are of greatest renown, both in point of blood and riches. For my part, I would that we were both at court, as I fear our journey will be exceedingly troublesome. To say truth, since my entire abstinence from flesh, I have lived upon strange new meats, which have very much disagreed with me, and swelled my body as if it was about to burst." "Alas! dear cousin," said the bear, "what kind of meat can it be that makes you so ill?" "Uncle," he replied, "what will it avail you to know? The food was simple and mean: we poor gentry are no lords, you know, but are glad to eat from necessity what others taste for mere wantonness. Yet not to delay you, that which I ate was honeycombs, large, full, and very pleasant. But, impelled by hunger, I ate so very immoderately that I was afterwards infinitely distempered." "Ay!" quoth Bruin; "honeycombs, do you say? Hold you them in such slight respect, nephew? Why, sir, it is food for the greatest emperors in the world. Help me, fair nephew, to some of these honeycombs, and command me while I live; for only a small share I will be your servant everlastingly." "You are jesting with me, surely, uncle," replied the fox. "Jest with you!" cried Bruin; "beshrew my heart, then; for I am in such serious good earnest, that for a single lick of the same you shall count me among the most faithful of your kindred." "Nay, if you be," returned Reynard, "I will bring you where ten of you would not be able to eat the whole at a meal. This I do out of friendship, for I wish to have yours in return, which above all things I desire." "Not ten of us," cried the bear, "not ten of us! it is impossible; for had I all the honey between Hybla and Portugal, I could eat the whole of it very shortly myself." "Then know, uncle, that near at hand there dwells a husbandman named Lanfert, who is master of so much that you could not consume it in seven years, and this, for your love and friendship's sake, I will put into your possession." Bruin, now mad for the honey, swore that for one good meal he would stop the mouths of all Reynard's enemies. Smiling at his easy credulity, the latter said, "If you would wish for seven ton, uncle, you shall have it"; and these words pleased the bear so much, and made it so pleasant, that he could not actually stand for laughing. "Well," thought the fox, "this is good fortune; though I will assuredly lead him where he shall laugh more in reason." He then said, "Uncle, we must lose no time, and I will spare no pains, such as I would not undertake for any of my kin." The bear gave him thanks, and away they went together, the fox promising as much honey as he could carry, but meaning as many stripes as he could undergo. At length they came to Lanfert's house, the sight of which made the bear caper for joy. This Lanfert was a stout brawny carpenter, who the other day had brought into his yard a large oak, which he had begun to cleave, and struck into it two wedges, so that the cleft lay a great way open, at which the fox rejoiced, as it was just what he wished. Then, with a smiling countenance, turning to the bear, "Behold now," he said, "dear uncle, and be careful of yourself; for within this tree is contained so much honey, that if you can get to it you will find it immeasurable; yet be cautious, good uncle, and eat moderately. The combs are sweet and good, but a surfeit is always dangerous, and may prove troublesome on your journey, which I would not for the world, as no harm can happen to you but must redound to my dishonor." "Concern not yourself for me, faith, nephew Reynard; I am not such a fool but I can temper my appetite if I can only get at the honey." "True, I was perhaps too bold to say what I did, my best uncle; so I pray you enter in at the end, and you shall there find what you want." With all haste the bear entered the tree with his fore feet forward, and thrust his head into the hole quite over the ears. When the fox saw this, he instantly ran and pulled the wedges out of the tree, so that the bear remained locked fast. Neither flattery nor anger now availed the bear, for his nephew had got him in so fast a prison, that it was impossible to free himself by any maneuver. What profited him his great strength and valor now? They only served to irritate and annoy him; and deprived of all relief, he began to howl and bray, to scratch and tumble, and make such a noise, that Lanfert came running hastily out of the house to see what was the matter. He held a sharp hook in his hand, and while the bear lay tearing and roaring in the tree, the fox cried out in scorn, "He is coming, uncle! I fear you will not like the honey; is it good? Do not eat too much; pleasant things are apt to surfeit, and you will delay your journey back to court. If your belly be too full, Lanfert will give you drink to digest it." Having said which, he set off towards his castle again. Lanfert, finding that the bear was taken fast, ran to his neighbors and desired them to come. The tidings spreading through the town, there was neither man, woman, nor child but ran to see; some with one weapon and some with another, goads, rakes, and broom-staves, and whatever they could lay hands on. The priest bore the handle of a large cross, the clerk had holy water, and the priest's wife, Dame Jullock, brought her distaff, as she happened to be spinning: nay, the old beldams came that had never a tooth in their heads. Hearing the approach of this army, Bruin fell into great fear, there being none but himself to withstand them; and as they came thundering down upon him, he struggled so fiercely that he contrived to get his head out of jeopardy by leaving behind the best part of the skin, along with his ears, insomuch that never age beheld a more foul ugly beast; for the blood covered his face and hands, leaving his claws and skin behind him, so that he could hardly move or see. It was an ill market he came to, for in spite of this torment Lanfert and his crew came upon him, and so belabored him with staves, and hooks, and rakes, that it might well be a warning to every one taken in misery, showing how the weakest must evermore go to the wall. This Bruin cruelly experienced, every one venting their fury upon his hide, even Houghlin with his crooked leg, and Ludolf with the long broad nose; the one armed with a leaden mall, and the other with an iron scourge. None lashed so hard as Sir Bertolf with the long fingers, and none annoyed him more than Lanfert and Ortam, one being armed with a sharp Welsh hook, and the second with a crooked staff heavily leaded at the end, with which he used to play at stab-ball. There was Burkin and Armes Ablequack, Bane the priest with his cross-handle, and Jullock his wife. All these so belabored the poor bear that his life was in extreme jeopardy; he sat and sighed sadly during the massacre, but the thundering weight of Lanfert's fierce blows was the most cruel to bear; for Dame Podge, at Casport, was his mother, and his father was Marob, the staple-maker, a passing stout man when he was alone. From him Bruin received such a shower of stones, at the same time that Lanfert's brother wielded him a savage blow upon the pate, that he could no longer see nor hear, but made a desperate plunge into the adjoining river, through a cluster of old wives standing by, many of whom he threw into the water, which was broad and deep, among whom was the parson's wife. Seeing her floating there like a sea-mew, the holy man left off striking the bear, crying out, "Help, oh, help! Dame Jullock is in the water! I absolve the man, woman, or child that saves her, from all their sins and transgressions, past and to come, and I remit all penance." Hearing this, all left the pursuit of the bear to succor Dame Jullock, upon which Bruin cut the stream with fresh strength, and swam away. The priest only pursued him, crying in great rage, "Turn, villain, turn, that I may be revenged upon thee!" But the bear, having the advantage of the stream, heeded not his calling, for he was proud of the triumph of having escaped from them. He bitterly cursed the honey the honey tree, and more bitterly the fox, who had not only betrayed him, but made him lose his hood from his face and his leather gloves from his fingers. In this condition he swam about three miles down the stream, when he grew so very weary that he was obliged to seek a landing. The blood trickled down his face; he sighed, and drew his breath so short that it seemed as if his last hour was come.

Meanwhile the fox, on his way home, had stolen a fat pullet, and running through a by-path to elude pursuit, he now came towards the river with infinite joy. For he never doubted but the bear was slain, and he therefore said, "My fortune is made, for my greatest enemy at the court is dead, and no one can suspect me." But as he spoke, looking towards the river-side, he espied the bear lying down to ease his grievous wounds. At this sight Reynard's heart misgave him, and he railed bitterly against Lanfert the carpenter, cursing him for a silly fool, that did not know how to kill a bear in a trap. "What madman," he cried, "would have lost such good venison? so fat and wholesome, and which lay taken to his hand. A wise man would have been proud of the fortune which thou, like a fool, hast neglected." Thus fretting and chiding, he came to the river, where he found the bear covered with wounds, which Reynard alone had caused. Yet he said in scorn as he passed, "Monsieur, Dieu vous garde!" "O thou foul red villain!" said the bear to himself. "What impudence can equal thine?" But the fox continued his speech: "What, uncle, have you forgotten everything at Lanfert's, or have you paid for the honeycombs you stole? I would rather pay for them myself than that you should incur any disgrace, the honey was good, you may have plenty more at the same price. If Good uncle, tell me before I go, into what order you mean to enter, that you wear this new-fashioned hood? Will you be a monk, an abbot, or a friar? He that shaved your crown seems also to have cropped your ears; your forelock is lost, and your leather gloves are gone. Fie, sloven! go not bareheaded! They say you can sing *peccavi* rarely." These taunts made Bruin mad with rage; but because he could not take revenge, he was obliged to let him talk on. At last, to avoid him, he plunged again into the river and landed on the other side, where he began to meditate how best he might reach the court; for he had lost both his ears and his talons, and could scarcely walk. Yet of necessity he must move forward, which he could only do by setting his buttocks upon the ground, and tumbling his body over and over. In this manner he first rolled about half a mile, then rested, and rolled another half-mile, until by dint of perseverance he tumbled his way to court. Witnessing his strange method of approach, a number of courtiers gazed upon him as a sort of prodigy, little deeming that it was the famous Sir Bruin the bear.

The king himself was the first who recognized him, and he said, "It is Sir Bruin my servant: what villains have wounded him thus? Where can he have been, that he could contrive it—to bring his death as it were back with him? let us hear what tidings he has got." "O my dread sovereign lord the king," cried out the bear, "I have to complain grievously. Behold how I am massacred; a massacre I humbly beseech you to revenge on that false malignant Reynard, who hath wrought me this foul disgrace and slaughter, merely because I have done your royal pleasure in conveying him a summons to court." His majesty then said, "How durst he do this thing? Now, by my crown I swear, I will take such revenge as shall make the traitor tremble, and remember the foul deed." So forthwith the king summoned his whole council, and consulted how and in what way to proceed most efficaciously against the wily fox. At length, after much discussion, it was unanimously concluded that he should be again summoned to appear and answer his transgressions in person. The party now appointed to execute the summons was Tibert the cat, being equally recommended for his gravity and his wisdom; an appointment likewise well pleasing to the king.

EULENSPIEGEL AND THE MERCHANT

(Anonymous: about 1500)

THE earliest known version of *Eulenspiegel* dates from 1515, though an edition is said to have been printed in 1483. Nothing at all is known about the author. The merry pranks of Eulenspiegel, like the adventures of Reynard and his companions, formed the basis of several collections of adventures in the late Sixteenth and early Seventeenth Centuries. They were utilized in the Nineteenth Century by the Belgian Charles de Coster. The original book, in the words of Roscoe, is "a national storehouse of amusement from which each successive generation has largely drawn." Like most of the books of its kind, it was derived from fables and popular traditions.

The present version, translated by Thomas Roscoe, is reprinted from Roscoe's *German Novelists*, London, no date. It is one of the separate adventures and has only a descriptive note by way of title.

EULENSPIEGEL AND THE MERCHANT

(From *Eulenspiegel, the Merry Jester*)

IN the town of Herdellem there resided a rich merchant, who, happening one day to be walking in one of his own fields, a short way out of the city, saw Howleglass lying on the green. He inquired who he was. To this Howleglass replied, "I am a cook without a master, and I have been a cook's servant, otherwise a scullion; but that is now not a place for me." The merchant said, "If you like to become my servant, I will give you good board and wages, besides your clothes; you shall have a trial, for my wife is continually bickering one after another with all her cooks." Howleglass promised to do his best to please him; and his new master asked his name, to which our hero replied that it was Bartholomew. "The name," said the merchant, "is too long; you shall be called *Dol*." "Sir," said Howleglass, "just as you like best, it pleases me well." "Then come," added his master, "you are the sort of man I want; let us go directly into my garden to gather herbs for the young boiled chickens, as to-morrow I have a party coming, and we must make merry with the best cheer." So they went to the house, and when the merchant's wife saw them come in, she said, "Heyday, master mine, what kind of a servant have you brought us here? Are you afraid lest the bread should be left to grow moldy? What is he for?" "Oh, you shall see that, my dear, to-morrow. Here, Dol, take this pannier, and follow me to the shambles."

Away they went, and the merchant bought some pieces of roasting meat, saying on his return, "Now, Dol, remember when you put this sirloin down to-morrow, that you leave it to do coolly at a distance, so as not to catch or singe; the boiling piece you may put on a good deal earlier."

"Very good, master," said Howleglass, "it shall be done." So the next morning he rose betimes and brought the meat he was to boil near the fire. But that which he intended to roast he stuck upon the spit, and placed it at a cool distance as he had been told (namely, in the cellar between two barrels of beer) from the fire. Now, before the merchant's guests had assembled, he went to see that all was going on well in the kitchen (for his wife was a fine lady), and he inquired whether the dinner was almost ready, to which Howleglass made answer, "Yes, everything but the roast beef." "Everything but!" exclaimed the merchant; "and where is that?" "It is on the spit," answered Howleglass; "it is doing cool at a distance, as you desired, in the coolest place in the house, which is the beer cellar. You did not say when you would like to have it roasted." While his master was discussing this point with Howleglass, the guests began to arrive, to whom he candidly related the incident, at which some looked grave and others laughed, while his lady was least of all satisfied with the joke. Indeed, she proposed an ejectment of the new cook from the premises forthwith.

"My love," said the merchant, "give yourself no kind of uneasiness about that! To-morrow I am going to Gollai, and he must see me there; but on my return he shall be discharged." Then they all proceeded to dinner, and made as good cheer as they could upon what they had got. In the evening when all was over, his master called Howleglass, and said, "Dol, see that my coach is in readiness early to-morrow morning, for I and the priest are going as far as Gollai, so look that it be well cleaned and greased." Accordingly when the whole family were abed, Howleglass proceeded to grease the chariot well both inside and out. And in the morning our merchant and the priest mounted to drive off; but slip went the priest wherever he laid his hand or foot! And he had many a time nearly broken his neck as they drove along. "What the deuce," he cried, "can it be that it is so thick and greasy?"

So they stopped and called Howleglass in a great passion, inquiring what vile work he had been doing, and swore and threatened dreadfully. Just then a wagon-load of straw luckily went by, and the unhappy party purchased a small quantity, with which to purify the well-bedizened chariot. Quite enraged, the merchant cried out, "Off to the gallows, you rascal!" and soon after Howleglass saw one not far from the roadside, and driving the chariot right underneath it, he was proceeding very leisurely to unharness the horses. "What is it that you are about, villain?" said his master. "Why," replied Howleglass, "did not you order me to drive off to the gallows? where I thought I was to set you down." On looking up, the priest and the merchant sure enough saw the gibbet; upon which his master, being seized with a panic, commanded him to back, and drive right away as hard as he could flog. Hearing this, Howleglass dashed neck and nothing through the mud, so that by the horrible pulling and tearing, the vehicle came straight in two, the hinder part remaining with the merchant and the priest stuck in the mud, and the other proceeding with Howleglass and the horses just as if nothing had happened. At length with much shouting and running the merchant overtook his driver, and was beginning to inflict summary vengeance upon him, when the priest came up and prevented him; and in this fashion they contrived to accomplish their journey, and so home again. Well! his wife inquired how the merchant had enjoyed his journey? "Oh, delightful," cried the merchant, "now that we are safely returned." Then he called Howleglass, saying, "To-night eat and drink to your heart's content, for tomorrow you quit this house. I cannot keep you, you are too great a malicious rascal for me." "All right, master," said Howleglass. And in the morning when the merchant went out, he again said, "Eat and drink, take as much as you like, but do not let me find you here when I come home from church." So while the family was at church, Howleglass proceeded as he had been ordered to take what he liked; and very shortly he had almost completely gutted the house. In short, the merchant met him with a whole load of his goods in the street as he was coming from church. "Ha! my honest cook," he cried, "what are you dressing now?" "What you commanded me to do," replied Howleglass: "you informed me that I might take what I liked, and rid the house of me." "Leave these things where they are," exclaimed the merchant, "and go to the devil if you please." Howleglass said, "I do everything that my masters order me, and yet I cannot live in peace." So he quitted the merchant in a huff, whom he was sorry again to have met with, while the former had his goods conveyed back to the house.

DOCTOR FAUST AND THE USURER

(Anonymous: Late 16th Century)

THE author of the so-called Chapbook of Dr. Faust was in all probability a Lutheran pastor. The first known edition appeared in 1587. It is a loosely constructed collection of incidents more or less remotely centred in the actual career of Dr. Faust, who died some fifty years before. It is a "curious patchwork of genuine folk tales that were really current about Doctor Faust... and learned demonological rubbish taken from preexistent treatises." A version of this chapbook fell into the hands of Christopher Marlowe; to this we owe *Dr. Faustus*, as well as the *Faust* of Goethe.

The present version, translated by Thomas Roscoe, is reprinted from Roscoe's *German Novelists*, London, no date. It is one of the separate incidents in the *Life*. It bears only a long description by way of title.

DOCTOR FAUST AND THE USURER

(From *The History of Dr. J. Faust...*, etc.)

IT used to be an old saying that the conjuror, "charm he never so wisely," for the year together, was never half a stiver richer in the world for his pains. Now Doctor Faustus began to experience the truth of this, inasmuch as the grand promises made by his demon in their first contract were mere bubbles, well worthy of their proprietor —a liar and the father of lies. For he had led the Doctor to believe that he was compelled into the service and overreached by him, so that vast riches would flow in upon him. Four years of his demon's apprenticeship had yet to run, though he was still not a whit the richer either in gold or goods, for all that Mephistopheles had done. It was agreed likewise he was to partake only of the best fare that could be obtained at princes' courts wheresoever he should travel, as we have already seen. On this account he had held a variety of disputations with his familiar demon, which generally ended, however, by his inviting some boon companions to come and banquet with him. At length, finding himself in want of ready cash, he was compelled to apply to a certain Jew, with whom in the first instance he agreed for sixty dollars, which he promised to return in the space of one month. This being expired, the Jew went to demand his dollars with the interest which was become due, when the Doctor replied to his application as follows: "Jew, I have no money; and I have no means, just now, of procuring any. However, if you are willing to accept good security, I think we can come to terms. I will give you either an arm or a leg, whichever shall best please you, and which shall be made over to you as a pledge of mortgage; though under this one condition: that as soon as I shall have the money forthcoming, you will be prepared to restore to me my leg." Now, the Jew, being naturally every good Christian's enemy, thought to himself, I am glad of this, but he must be a most singular genius to think of pawning me his life and blood for the sake of money. What can I do with such security as this? But meanwhile Doctor Faustus, taking out a saw, was very leisurely sawing off his leg, which he handed to the Jew (though it was all mere illusion), repeating the same condition that he was to return it the moment he should obtain the money, as he (the Doctor) knew how to set it in its place again. So the Jew, not a little pleased with his contract, marched off with the Doctor's leg. When he had kept it, however, a short time, he began to think, What shall I do with this rogue of a Christian's limb? If I carry it about with me I shall be poisoned with the stench, besides its being of no further use to him when he shall want it, however good a security, for what more could he give? Being at length quite puzzled in which way to act for the best, one day as he was crossing over a bridge, weary with calculating *pro et contra*, he threw the Doctor's leg into the water, and thought himself well rid of it. Doctor Faustus, fully aware of what had passed, sent notice to the Jew three days afterwards that he was ready to repay him the money. The latter repented now that he had been so hasty, but he went. The first question put by the Doctor was what he had done with his pledge. "What have I done!" replied the Jew. "What could I do with it? It was of no use, and I threw it away." The Doctor on hearing this took the Jew roundly to task, declaring that he must have his leg again, come what would, or that he (the Jew), must look for the consequences. Alarmed at the violence of the Doctor's threats, the unlucky Israelite at length consented to adjust the matter by further advancing sixty dollars, in order to avoid the terrors of the law.

CHRISTIAN GELLERT

(1715–1769)

THE son of a Saxon clergyman, Christian Fürchtegott (meaning Christian Fear-God) Gellert is said to have exemplified by his life the meaning of his names. For years a victim of ill-health and a hypochondriac, he spent the last part of his life lecturing on poetry at the University of Leipzig. He wrote plays, novels, fables and tales, but is to-day remembered only for his *Fables and Tales* in verse (1746–1748). These are written in a sprightly manner, and are conceived and executed with a delicacy that was rare among the German writers of Gellert's day.

The *Sick Wife*, one of the *Fables and Tales*, is translated especially for this volume, by Barrett H. Clark.

THE SICK WIFE

WHO can estimate the innumerable evils that constantly threaten the health and well-being of mankind? It is needful that we inquire into their causes, for the more we know of the dangers the better able are we to avoid trouble.

The fair young Sulpicia, dearly beloved of her husband, went off one day to visit a friend. Though she left home in the best of health, she returned half dead, it seemed, and at once threw herself down upon her bed. Could it be that her circulation had suddenly stopped?

Her clothes were loosened, and three pairs of hands made busy to assist her. None too many, forsooth!.

The poor young husband dissolved in a flood of tears: who could fail to be affected by so serious a situation? It was still too early, after but a single year of marriage, to wish to be rid of his wife! So he sent immediately for a physician. The youthful Æsculapius appeared on the scene in full regalia. Seating himself on the edge of the patient's bed, he assumed an expression as much as to say he had precisely the right remedy. He felt the wife's pulse, and wondered to himself what his medical books recommended in a case of this sort. But he ordered pen and ink to be brought him at once, and sat down to write. A servant was sent post-haste, and meantime the husband inquired what could be the trouble with his wife? The physician looked at him and smiled:

"You ask me what is the matter? There is really no need to tell you that. You know, it is a very good sign when young wives fret and complain!"

At this news the husband was overjoyed.

The night passed. The patient drank her potion, but it had no effect upon her at all. Another physician had to be summoned.

Patience! At last they were about to discover what really ailed the woman. The second physician was in no doubt: she was coming down with the smallpox!

Well, first she was going to become a mother, and then it was a case of smallpox!

Say no more, Doctors, and prescribe nothing further, for one of you at least is entirely in the wrong! Rather leave her in the hands of Nature and to the mercies of her own comfortable bed. No matter how dangerous the disease, it is not half so dangerous as the Doctor's cures.

Patience! Perhaps she will recover to-day.

Her good husband never left her side, and not a half-hour passed but he asked her a hundred times if she didn't feel a little better? My good fellow, what use is that? Will your talk not make her worse?

She spoke in gasps. It was easy to see by her speech that the pain was increasing. Alas, poor woman! Death seemed at hand. It would be a blessed release from her agony.

But hark! Who knocks? It must be the Doctor? No.

It was a tailor, bringing a dress. Ha, he comes in good time!

"Is it," asks the wife with great difficulty, "my funeral dress? Alas, I will look quite as pale. Had Heaven permitted me to live, I would have ordered a dress like that, of the same kind of material. The tailor would know just how to make it. He made one for my friend. It's the loveliest dress in the whole world. Last time I called on her she wore it. Ah, how short is life. All is vanity!"

Take courage, grief-stricken husband! You hear, do you not, that your wife can at last speak with considerable ease? Don't lose hope. The breath has not yet left her body.

The tailor left the room, and the husband went out with him, and the two spoke secretly together behind the closed door. The tailor swore mighty oaths, and went off to do what he promised. He returned before evening, and went in to Sulpicia who, still in bed, thanked him heartily for coming.

What did the tailor bring with him?

He proceeded at once to unroll something that was wrapped in cloth. What a wonderful sight to behold! The selfsame cloth, the rich and marvelous dress! But what was it doing there? Surely the young wife could not hope to wear it?

"My dearest angel," said her husband, "I would give everything I possess to see you well again and wearing this dress!"

"Oh, I am so ill," began the wife, "I am not even strong enough to deny you anything. I will get up from this bed, so that you may see this very day how the dress becomes me."

The screen was brought, and the poor woman, as weak as though she had lain in bed a whole year, got up. After she was completely dressed out in her finery, she sat down and drank coffee. Well at last! There was no trace of any illness.

A dress was what had ailed her, and a dress was the only effective remedy. A tailor had cured what no physician could so much as diagnose.

JAKOB GRIMM

(1775–1863)

WILHELM GRIMM

(1776–1859)

THE BROTHERS GRIMM, as they are still affectionately called, were both scholars of high repute, and both professors at the University of Berlin. Though they contributed a great deal to the science of philology and the history of literature, their fame rests chiefly on their collections of folk-tales, issued under the title *Children's and Household Stories*, in 1812 and 1814. These were the result of personal investigation and travel. *Little Briar-Rose* is only one of their many charming tales. It is to be observed that in the work of the Brothers Grimm the writers have moulded each story with a conscious art: they are not to be classified as scientists, but artists.

The present version, anonymously translated, is reprinted from an undated London edition of the *Tales of the Brothers Grimm*.

LITTLE BRIAR-ROSE

(From *Children's and Household Stories*)

LONG ago there was a king and a queen. They said every day, "Oh, if we only had a child!" and still they never got one. Then it happened, when once the queen was bathing, that a frog crept ashore out of the water, and said to her, "Your wish shall be fulfilled. Before a year passes you shall bring a daughter into the world."

What the frog said, happened, and the queen had a little girl that was so beautiful that the king could not contain himself for joy, and made a great feast. He invited not only his relatives, friends, and acquaintances, but also the wise women, that they might be gracious and kind to the child. Now, there were thirteen of them in his kingdom; but because he had only twelve gold plates for them to eat from, one of them had to stay at home. The feast was splendidly celebrated, and when it was over the wise women gave the child their wonderful gifts. One gave her virtue, another beauty, another wealth, and so with everything that people want in the world. But when eleven had spoken, suddenly the thirteenth came in. She wished to avenge herself, because she had not been asked; and without greeting or looking at anyone, she cried out, "In her fifteenth year the king's daughter shall wound herself on a spindle, and fall down dead." And without saying another word, she turned around and left the hall. All were frightened. When the twelfth came up, who had her wish still to give, since she could not remove the sentence, but only soften it, she said, "Yet it shall not be a real death, but only a hundred years' deep sleep, into which the king's daughter shall fall."

The king, who wanted to save his dear child from harm, sent out an order that all the spindles in the kingdom should be burned. But in the girl the gifts of the wise women were all fulfilled; for she was so beautiful, good, kind, and sensible, that nobody who saw her could help loving her. It happened that just on the day when she was fifteen years old the king and queen were not at home, and the little girl was left quite alone in the castle. Then she went wherever she pleased, looked in the rooms and chambers, and at last she got to an old tower.

She went up the narrow winding stairs, and came to a little door. In the keyhole was a rusty key, and when she turned it the door sprang open, and there in a little room sat an old woman with a spindle, and spun busily her flax. "Good-day, Aunty," said the king's daughter; "what are you doing there?" "I am spinning," said the old woman, and nodded. "What sort of a thing is that that jumps about so gaily?" said the girl. She took the spindle and wanted to spin, too. But she had hardly touched the spindle before the spell was fulfilled, and she pricked her finger with it.

At the instant she felt the prick she fell down on the bed that stood there, and lay in a deep sleep. And this sleep spread over all the castle. The king and queen, who had just come home and entered the hall, began to go to sleep, and all the courtiers with them. The horses went to sleep in the stalls, the dogs in the yard, the doves on the roof, the flies on the wall, yes, the fire that was flickering on the hearth grew still and went to sleep. And the roast meat stopped sputtering, and the cook, who was going to take the cook-boy by the hair because he had forgotten something, let him go and slept. And the wind was still, and no leaf stirred in the trees by the castle.

But all around the castle a hedge of briars grew, that got higher every year and at last surrounded the whole castle and grew up over it, so that nothing more could be seen of it, not even the flag on the roof. But the story went about in the country of the beautiful sleeping Briar-Rose (for so the king's daughter was called); so that from time to time kings' sons came and tried to get through the hedge into the castle. But they could not; for the briars, as though they had hands, clung fast together, and the young men stuck fast in them, could not get out again, and died a wretched death. After long, long years, there came again a kings' son to that country, and heard how an old man told about the briar hedge; that there was a castle behind it, in which a wonderfully beautiful king's daughter called Briar-Rose had been sleeping for a hundred years, and that the king and the queen and all the court were sleeping with her. He knew, too, from his grandfather that many kings' sons had already come and tried to get through the briar hedge, but had all been caught in it and died a sad death. Then the young man said, "I am not afraid. I will go and see the beautiful Briar-Rose." The good old man might warn him as much as he pleased; he did not listen to his words.

But now the hundred years were just passed, and the day was come when Briar-Rose was to wake again. So when the king's son went up to the briars, they were just great beautiful flowers that opened of their own accord and let him through unhurt; and behind him they closed together as a hedge again. In the yard he saw the horses and the mottled hounds lying and sleeping; on the roof perched the doves, their heads stuck under their wings; and when he came into the house the flies were sleeping on the wall, in the kitchen the cook still held up his hand as though to grab the boy, and the maid was sitting before the black hen that was to be plucked. Then he went further, and in the hall saw all the courtiers lying and sleeping, and upon their throne lay the king and the queen. Then he went further, and all was so still that you could hear yourself breathe; and at last he came to the tower and opened the door of the little room where Briar-Rose was sleeping. There she lay, and she was so beautiful that he could not take his eyes off her; and he bent down and gave her a kiss. But just as he touched her with the kiss, Briar-Rose opened her eyes, awoke, and looked at him very kindly. Then they went downstairs together; and the king awoke, and the queen, and all the courtiers, and made great eyes at one another. And the horses in the yard got up and shook themselves, the hounds sprang about and wagged their tails, the doves on the roof pulled out their heads from under their wings, looked around and flew into the field, the flies on the wall went on crawling, the fire in the kitchen started up and blazed and cooked the dinner, the roast began to sputter again, and the cook gave the boy such a box on the ear that he screamed, and the maid finished plucking the hen. Then the wedding of the king's son with Briar-Rose was splendidly celebrated, and they lived happy till their lives' end.

E. T. A. HOFFMANN

(1776–1822)

ERNST THEODOR AMADEUS HOFFMANN was a master of one particular type of short story, which was to a great extent a product of the romantic tendencies of his times. His earliest collection of tales, *Fantasy Pieces in the Manner of Callot,* are characterized by those qualities of fantasy and mystery with which his name is always associated. The collection under the title of *The Serapion Brethren,* is set within a "frame-narrative of the story-telling club in Berlin, where Hoffmann spent the last six years of his life as judge of a criminal court." Poe was especially indebted to Hoffmann in the composition of his stories, as were several of the most important Nineteenth Century fiction writers all over Europe.

The present translation, by Alexander Ewing, is reprinted from *The Serapion Brethren,* Bohn Library, London, by permission of the publishers, G. Bell and Sons.

THE STORY OF SERAPION

(From *The Serapion Brethren*)

YOU know that some years ago I spent a considerable time in B——, a place in one of the pleasantest districts of the South of Germany. As my habit is, I used to take long walks in the surrounding country by myself, without any guide, though I should often have been the better for one. On one of these occasions I got into a piece of thickly wooded country and lost my way; the farther I went, the less could I discover the smallest vestige of a human footstep. At last the wood grew less thick, and I saw, not far from me, a man in a hermit's brown robe, with a broad straw hat on his head, and a long, wild black beard, sitting on a rock by the side of a deep ravine, gazing, with folded hands, thoughtfully into the distance. This sight had something so strange, unexpected, and out of the common about it that I felt a shiver of eeriness and awe. One can scarcely help such a feeling when what one has only heretofore seen in pictures, or read of in books, suddenly appears before one's eyes in actual, everyday life. Here was an anchorite of the early ages of Christianity, in the body, seated in one of Salvator Rosa's wild mountain scenes. But it soon occurred to me that probably a monk on his peregrinations was nothing uncommon in that part of the country. So I walked up to him, and asked if he could tell me the shortest way out of the wood to the high road leading to B——. He looked at me from head to foot with a gloomy glance, and said, in a hollow and solemn voice:

" 'I know well that it is merely an idle curiosity to see me, and to hear me speak which has led you to this desert. But you must perceive that I have no time to talk with you now. My friend Ambrosius of Camaldoli is returning to Alexandria. Travel with him.'

"With which he arose and walked down into the ravine.

"I felt as if I must be in a dream. Presently I heard the sound of wheels close by. I made my way through the thickets, and found myself in a forest track, where I saw a countryman going along in a cart. I overtook him, and he shortly brought me to the high road leading to B——. As we went along I told him my adventure, and asked if he knew who the extraordinary man in the forest was.

" 'Oh, sir,' he said, 'that was the worthy man who calls himself Priest Serapion, and who has been living in these woods for some years, in a little hut which he built himself. People say he's not quite right in his head, but he is a nice, good gentleman, never does any harm, and edifies us of the village with pious discourses, giving us all the good advice that he can.'

"I had come across the anchorite some six or eight miles from B——, so I concluded that something must be known of him there, and this proved to be the case. Dr. S—— told me all the story. This hermit had once been one of the most brilliant intellects, one of the most universally accomplished men in M——; and belonging, as he did, to a very distinguished family, he was naturally appointed to an important diplomatic post as soon as he had completed his studies: the duties of this office he discharged with great ability and energy. Moreover, he had remarkable poetical gifts, and everything he wrote was inspired by a most brilliant fancy, a mind and imagination which sounded the profoundest depths of all subjects. His incomparable humor, and the unusual charm of his character made him the most delightful of companions imaginable. He had risen from step to step of his career, and was on the point of being despatched on an important diplomatic mission, when he disappeared, in the most incomprehensible fashion, from M——. All search for him was fruitless, and conjecture and inquiry were baffled by a combination of circumstances.

"After a time there appeared amongst the villages, in the depths of the Tyrolese mountains, a man in a brown robe, who preached in these hamlets, and then went away into the wildest parts of the forests, where he lived the life of a hermit. It chanced one day that Count P—— saw this man (who called himself Priest Serapion), and at once recognized him as his unfortunate nephew, who had disappeared from M——. He was taken into custody, became violent, and all the skill of the best doctors in M—— could do nothing to alleviate his terrible condition. He was taken to the lunatic asylum at B——, and there the methodical system, based upon profound psychological knowledge, pursued by the medical man then in charge of that institution, succeeded in bringing about a condition of much less excitement, and greater quietness in the form of his malady. Whether this doctor, true to his theory, gave the patient an opportunity of escaping, or whether he himself found the means of doing so, escape he did, and was lost sight of for a considerable time.

"Serapion appeared, ultimately, in the country some eight miles from B——, where I had seen him; and the doctor declared that if any true compassion was to be shown him, he should not be again driven into a condition of wild excitement; but that, if he was to be at peace, and, after his fashion, happy, he should be left in these woods in perfect freedom, to do just as he liked; in which case he, the said doctor, would be responsible for the consequences. Accordingly, the police authorities were content to leave him to a distant and imperceptible supervision by the officials of the nearest village, and the result bore out what the doctor had said. Serapion built himself a little hut, pretty, and, under the circumstances, comfortable. He made chairs and tables, wove mats of rushes to lie upon, and laid out a garden where he grew flowers and vegetables. In all that did not touch the idea that he was the hermit Serapion who fled into the Theban desert in the days of the Emperor Decius, and suffered martyrdom in Alexandria, his mind was completely unaffected. He could carry on the most intellectual conversation, and often showed traces of the brilliant humor and charming individuality of character for which he had been remarkable in his former life. The aforesaid doctor declared him to be completely incurable, and strongly deprecated all attempts to restore him to the world and to his former pursuits and duties.

"You will readily understand that I could not drive this anchorite of mine out of my thoughts, and that I experienced an irresistible longing to see him again. But just picture to yourselves the excess of my folly! I had no less an undertaking in my mind that that of attacking Serapion's fixed idea at its very roots. I read Pinel, Reil, every conceivable book on insanity which I could lay my hands on. I fondly believed that it might be reserved for *me*, an amateur psychologist and doctor, to cast some rays of light into Serapion's darkened intelligence. And I did not omit, either, to make myself acquainted with the stories of all the Serapions (there were no fewer than eight of them) treated of in the histories of saints and martyrs.

"Thus equipped, I set out one fine morning in search of my anchorite.

"I found him working in his garden with hoe and spade, singing a devotional song. Wild pigeons, for which he had strewed an abundant supply of food, were fluttering and cooing round him, and a young deer was peeping through the leaves on the trellis. He was evidently living in the closest intimacy with the woodland creatures. Not the faintest trace of insanity was visible in his face; it bore a quiet expression of remarkable serenity and happiness; and all this confirmed what Dr. S—— in B—— had told me. When he heard of my projected visit to the anchorite, he advised me to go some fine, bright, pleasant morning, because he said, his mind would be less troubled then and he would be more inclined to talk to a stranger, whereas at evening he would shun all intercourse with mankind.

"As soon as he saw me he laid down his spade, and came towards me in a kind and friendly manner. I said that, being weary with a longish journey, I should be glad if he would allow me to rest with him for a little while.

" 'You are heartily welcome,' he said, 'The little which I can offer you in the shape of refreshment is at your service.'

"And he took me to a seat of moss in front of his hut, brought out a little table, set on bread, magnificent grapes, and a can of wine, and hospitably begged me to eat and drink. He sat down opposite to me, and ate bread with much appetite, washing it down with draughts of water.

"In good sooth I did not see how I was to lead the conversation to my subject—how I was to bring my psychological science to bear upon this peaceful, happy man. At last I pulled myself together and began:

" 'You style yourself Serapion, reverend sir?'

" 'Yes, certainly,' he answered. 'The Church has given me that name.'

" 'Ancient ecclesiastical history,' I continued, 'mentions several celebrated holy men of that name. An abbot Serapion, known for his good works—the learned Bishop Serapion alluded to by Hieronimus in his book *De Viris Illustribus*. There was also a monk Serapion, who (as Heraclides relates in his *Paradise*) on one occasion, coming from the Theban desert to Rome, ordered a virgin, who had joined him—saying she had renounced the world and its pleasures—to prove this by walking with him naked in the streets of Rome, and repulsed her when she hesitated, saying, "You still live the life of Nature, and are careful for the opinions of mankind. Think not that you are anything great or have overcome the world." If I am not mistaken, reverend sir, this was the "filthy monk" (Heraclides himself so styles him) who suffered a terrible martyrdom under the Emperor Decius—his limbs being torn asunder at the joints, and his body thrown down from a lofty rock.'

" 'That was so,' said Serapion, turning pale, and his eyes glowing with a somber fire. 'But Serapion the martyr, had no connection with that monk, who, in the fury of his asceticism, did battle against human nature. *I* am Serapion the martyr, to whom you allude.'

" 'What?' I cried, with feigned surprise. '*You* believe that you are that Serapion who suffered such a hideous martyrdom so many hundred years ago?'

" 'That,' said Serapion with much calmness, 'may appear incredible to you, and I admit that it must sound very wonderful to many who cannot see further than the points of their own noses. However, it is as I tell you. God's omnipotence permitted me to survive my martyrdom, and to recover from its effects, because it was ordained, in His mysterious providence, that I had still to pass a certain period of my existence, to His praise and glory, here in the Theban desert. There is nothing now to remind me of the tortures which I suffered except sometimes a severe headache, and occasional violent cramps and twitchings in my limbs.'

" 'Now,' thought I, 'is the time to commence my cure.'

"I made a wide circumbendibus, and talked in an erudite style concerning the malady of 'Fixed Idea', which attacks people, marring, like one single discord, the otherwise harmonious organisms. I spoke of the scientific man who could not be induced to rise from his chair for fear he would break the windows across the street with his nose. I mentioned the Abbot Molanus, who conversed most rationally upon every subject, but would not leave his room because he thought he was a barleycorn, and the hens would swallow him. I came to the fact that to confound oneself with some historical character was a frequent form of Fixed Idea. 'Nothing more absurd and preposterous,' I said, 'could possibly be imagined than that a little bit of woodland country eight miles from B——, daily frequented by country folk, sportsmen, and people walking for exercise was the Theban desert, and he himself that ascetic who suffered martyrdom many centuries ago.'

"Serapion listened in silence. He seemed to feel what I said, and to be struggling with himself in deep reflection. So that I thought it was time to strike my decisive blow. I stood up, took him by both hands, and cried, loudly and emphatically:

" 'Count P——, awake from the pernicious dream which is enthralling you; throw off that abominable dress, and come back to your family, which mourns your loss, and to the world where you have such important duties to discharge.'

"Serapion gazed at me with a somber, penetrating gaze. Then a sarcastic smile played about his lips and cheeks, and he said, slowly and solemnly:

" 'You have spoken, sir, long, and, as *you* consider, wisely and well. Allow *me*, in turn, to say a few words in reply. Saint Anthony, and all the men of the Church who have withdrawn from the world into solitude, were often visited by vexing spirits, who, envying the inward peace and contentment of their souls, carried on with them lengthy contests, until they had to lie down conquered in the dust. And such is *my* fortune also. Every now and then there appear to me emissaries, sent by Satan, who try to persuade me that I am Count P—— of M——, and that I ought to betake myself to the life of Courts, and all sorts of unholiness. Were it not for the efficacy of prayer, I should take these people by the shoulders, turn them out of my little garden, and carefully barricade it against them. But I need not do so in your case; for *you* are, most unmistakably, the very feeblest of all the adversaries who have ever come to me, and I can vanquish *you* with your own weapons—those of ratiocination. It is insanity that is in question between us. But if one of us two is suffering from that sad malady, it is evident that *you* are so in a much greater degree than I. You maintain that it is a case of Fixed Idea that I believe myself to be Serapion the martyr—and I am quite aware that many persons hold the same opinion, or pretend that they do. Now, if I am really insane, none but a lunatic can think that he could *argue* me out of the Fixed Idea which insanity has engendered in me. Were such a proceeding possible, there would soon be no madmen on the face of the earth, for men would be able to rule, and command, their mental power, which is not their own, but merely lent to them for a time by that Higher Power which disposes of them. But if I am *not* mad, and if I am really Serapion the martyr, it is insane to set about arguing me out of that, and leading me to adopt the Fixed Idea that I am Count P—— of M——. You say that Serapion the martyr lived several centuries ago, and that, consequently, I cannot be that martyr, presumably for the reason that human beings cannot remain so long on this earth. Well, as regards this, the notion of time is just as *relative* a notion as that of number; and I may say to you that, according to the notion of time which I have in *me*, it is scarcely three *hours* (or whatever appellation you may choose to give to the divisions of time) since I was put to martyrdom by the Emperor Decius. But, leaving this on one side, can you assert, in opposition to me, that a life of such length as I say I have lived, is unexampled and contrary to human nature? Have you cognizance of the precise length of the life of every human being who has existed in all this wide world, that you can employ the expression "unexampled" in this pert and decisive manner? Do you compare God's omnipotence to the wretched art of the clockmaker, who can't save his lifeless machinery from destruction? You say this place where we are is not the Theban desert, but a little woodland district eight miles from B——, daily frequented by country folk, sportsmen and others. *Prove* that to me.'

"Here I thought I had my man.

" 'Come with me,' said I, 'and in a couple of hours we shall be in B——, and what I assert will be proved.'

" 'Poor blinded fool,' said Serapion. 'What a wide distance lies between us and B——! But put the case that I went with you to some town which you call B——; would you be able to convince me that we had been traveling for two hours only, and the place we had arrived at was really B——? If I were to assert that you were insane, and suppose the Theban desert is a little bit of wooded country, and far-away Alexandria the town of B—— in the south of Germany, what would you say in reply? Our old discussion would go on forever. Then there is another point which you ought seriously to consider. You must, I should suppose, perceive that I, who am talking with you, am leading the peaceful and happy life of a man reconciled with God. It is only after having passed through martyrdom that such a life dawns upon the soul. And if it has pleased the Almighty to cast a veil over what happened before my martyrdom, is it not a terrible and diabolical action to try to tear that veil away?'

"With all my wisdom, I stood confounded and silenced in the presence of this insane man! With the very rationality of his irrationality he had beaten me completely out of the field, and I saw the folly of my undertaking in all its fulness. Still more than that, I felt the reproach contained in what he had last said as deeply as I was astounded at the dim remembrance of his previous life which shone through it like some lofty, invulnerable higher spirit.

"Serapion seemed to be reading my thoughts, and, looking me full in the face with an expression of the greatest kindliness, he said:

" 'I never took you for an evil-disposed adversary, and I see I was not mistaken. You may have been instigated by somebody—perhaps by the Evil One himself—to come here to vex and try me, but I am sure it was not a spontaneous act of yours. And perhaps the fact that you found me other than you expected, may have strengthened you in your expression of the doubts which you have suggested. Although I in no sense deviate from the devoutness beseeming him who has given up his life to God and the Church, that cynicism of asceticism into which many of my brethren have fallen—thereby giving proof of the weakness, nay, utter destruction of their mental vigor, instead of its boasted strength—is utterly foreign to me! You expected to find the Monk Serapion pale and haggard, wasted with fast and vigil, all the horror of visions, terrible as those which drove even St. Anthony to despair, in his somber face, with quivering knees scarce able to support him, in a filthy robe, stained with his blood. You find a placid, cheerful man. But I, too, have passed through those tortures, and have overcome them and survived. And when I awoke with shattered limbs and fractured skull, the spirit dawned, and shone bright within me, restoring my mind and my body to health. May it please Heaven speedily to grant to *you* also, my brother, even here on earth, a peace and happiness such as those which daily refresh and strengthen *me*. Have no dread of the terror of the deepest solitude. It is only there that a life like this can dawn upon the pious soul.'

"Serapion, who had spoken with genuine priestly unction, raised, in silence, his eyes to Heaven with an expression of blissful gratitude. How could I feel otherwise than awe-struck! A madman, congratulating himself on his condition, looking upon it as a priceless gift from Heaven, and, from the depths of his heart, wishing me a similar fate!

"I was on the point of leaving him, but he began in an altered tone, saying:

" 'You would, probably, scarcely suppose that this wild inhospitable desert is often almost too full of the noise and bustle of life to be suitable for my silent meditations. Every day I receive visits from the most remarkable people of the most diverse kinds. Ariosto was here yesterday, and Dante and Petrarch afterwards. And this evening I expect Evagrus, the celebrated father, with whom I shall discuss the most recent ecclesiastical affairs, as I did poetry yesterday. I often go up to the top of that hill there, whence the towers of Alexandria are to be seen distinctly in clear weather, and the most wonderful and interesting events happen before my eyes. Many people have thought *that* incredible, too, and considered that I only *fancy* I see before me, in actual life, what is merely born in my mind and imagination. Now

I say *that* is the most incomprehensible piece of folly that can exist. What is it, except the mind, which takes cognizance of what happens around us in time and space? What is it that hears, and feels, and sees? Is it the lifeless mechanism which we call eyes, ears, hands, etc., and not the mind? Does the mind give form and shape to that peculiar world of its own which has space and time for its conditions of existence, and *then* hand over the functions of seeing, hearing, etc., to some *other* principle inherent in us? How illogical! Therefore, if it is the mind only which takes cognizance of events around us, it follows that that which it has taken cognizance of *has* actually occurred. Last evening only, Ariosto was speaking of the images of his fancy, and saying he had created in his brain forms and events which had never existed in time and space. I at once denied the possibility of this, and he was obliged to allow that it was only from lack of a higher knowledge that a poet would box up within the narrow limits of his brain that which, by virtue of his peculiar seer gift, he was enabled to see in full life before him. But the complete acquirement of this higher knowledge only comes after martyrdom, and is strengthened by the life in profound solitude. You don't appear to agree with me; probably you don't understand me here. Indeed how could a child of this world, however well disposed, understand an anchorite consecrated in all his works and ways to God. Let me tell you what happened before my eyes, as I was standing this morning at sunrise at the top of that hill.'

"He then related a regular romance, with a plot and incidents such as only the most imaginative poet could have constructed. The characters and events stood out with such a vivid, plastic relief, that it was impossible—carried away as one was by the magic spell of them—to help believing, as if in a species of dream, that Serapion had actually witnessed them from the hilltop. This romance was succeeded by another, and that by another, by which time the sun stood high above us in the noontide sky. Serapion then rose from his seat, and looking into the distance, said: 'Yonder comes my brother Hilarion, who, in his overstrictness, always blames me for being too much given to the society of strangers.'

"I understood the hint, and took my leave, asking if I should be allowed to pay him another visit. Serapion answered with a gentle smile, 'My friend, I thought you would be eager to get away from this wilderness, so little adapted to your mode of life. But if it is your pleasure to take up your abode for a time in my neighborhood, you will always be welcome to my cottage and my little garden. Perhaps it may be granted to me to convert him who came to me as an adversary. Farewell, my friend.'

"I am wholly unable to characterize the impression which my visit to him had made upon me. Whilst his condition, his methodical madness in which he found the joy of his life, produced the weirdest effect upon me, his extraordinary poetical genius filled me with amazement, and his kindly, peaceful happiness, instinct with the quietest resignation of the purest mind, touched me unspeakably. I thought of Ophelia's sorrowful words:

"'O what a noble mind is here o'erthrown! etc.'

Yet I could not make plaint against the Omnipotence, which probably had, in this mysterious fashion, steered his bark away from reefs, which might have wrecked it, into this secure haven.

"The oftener I went to see him, the more attached to him I became. I always found him happy, and disposed to converse, and I took great care never again to essay my rôle of the psychological doctor. It was wonderful with what acuteness and penetration he spoke of life in all its aspects, and most remarkable of all, how he deduced historical events from causes wholly remote from all ordinary theories on the subject. When sometimes—notwithstanding the striking acuteness of those divinations of his—I took it upon me to object that no work on history made any mention of the circumstances which he alluded to, he would answer, with his quiet smile, that probably no historian in the world knew as much about them as he did, seeing that he had them from the very lips of the people concerned, when they came to see him.

"I was obliged to leave B—— and it was three years before I could go back there. It was late in Autumn, about the middle of November —the 14th, if I do not mistake—when I set out to pay my anchorite a visit. Whilst I was still at a distance, I heard the sound of the little bell which hung above his hut, and was filled with gloomy forebodings, without apparent cause. At last I reached the cottage and went in.

"Serapion was lying on his mat, with his hands folded on his breast. I thought he was sleeping, and went softly up to him. Then I saw that he was dead."

GOTTFRIED KELLER

(1819–1890)

KELLER, one of the most distinguished writers of Switzerland, is claimed by the Germans because he wrote in their language. The son of a Swiss mechanic, he spent a dreamy and aimless youth. He lived a great part of his life in Zürich. It was not until after his death that he was recognized as one of the masters of German literature. Professor Thomas declares that his "books are on the whole the very best reading to be found in the whole range of Nineteenth Century

German fiction." He wrote almost entirely of his beloved Switzerland. His *Seven Legends* (1872), in which *A Legend of the Dance* first appeared, is one of his most beautiful books.

The present version, translated by Martin Wyness, is reprinted, by permission of the publishers, from *Seven Legends*, Gowans & Gray, Glasgow, 1911.

A LEGEND OF THE DANCE

ACCORDING to Saint Gregory, Musa was the dancer among the saints. The child of good people, she was a bright young lady, a diligent servant of the Mother of God, and subject only to one weakness, such an uncontrollable passion for the dance that when the child was not praying she was dancing, and that on all imaginable occasions. Musa danced with her playmates, with children, with the young men, and even by herself. She danced in her own room and every other room in the house, in the garden, in the meadows. Even when she went to the altar it was to a gracious measure rather than a walk, and even on the smooth marble flags before the church door, she did not scruple to practice a few hasty steps.

In fact, one day when she found herself alone in the church, she could not refrain from executing some figures before the altar, and, so to speak, dancing a pretty prayer to the Virgin Mary. She became so oblivious of all else that she fancied she was merely dreaming when she saw an oldish but handsome gentleman dancing opposite her and supplementing her figures so skilfully that the pair got into the most elaborate dance imaginable. The gentleman had a royal purple robe, a golden crown on his head, and a glossy black curled beard, which age had touched as with streaks of starlight. At the same time music sounded from the choir where half a dozen small angels stood, or sat with their chubby little legs hanging over the screen, and fingered or blew their various instruments. The urchins were very pleasant and skilful. Each rested his music on one of the stone angels with which the choir screen was adorned, except the smallest, a puffy-cheeked piper who sat crosslegged and contrived to hold his music with his pink toes. He was the most diligent of them all. The others dangled their feet, kept spreading their pinions, one or other of them, with a rustle, so that their colors shimmered like doves' breasts, and they teased each other as they played.

Musa found no time to wonder at all this until the dance, which lasted a pretty long time, was over; for the merry gentleman seemed to enjoy himself as much as the maid, who felt as if she were dancing about in heaven. But when the music ceased and Musa stood there panting, she began to be frightened in good earnest, and looked in astonishment at the ancient, who was neither out of breath nor warm, and who now began to speak. He introduced himself as David, the Virgin Mary's royal ancestor, and her ambassador. He asked if she would like to pass eternal bliss in an unending pleasure dance, compared with which the dance they had just finished could only be called a miserable crawl.

To this she promptly answered that she would like nothing better. Whereupon the blessed King David said again that in that case she had nothing more to do than to renounce all pleasure and all dancing for the rest of her days on earth and devote herself wholly to penance and spiritual exercises, and that without hesitation or relapse. The maiden was taken aback at these conditions, and asked whether she must really give up dancing altogether. She questioned indeed whether there was any dancing in Heaven; for there was a time for everything. This earth looked very fit and proper for dancing; it stood to reason that Heaven must have very different attractions, else death were a superfluity.

But David explained to her that her notions on the subject were erroneous, and proved from many Bible texts, and from his own example that dancing was assuredly a sanctified occupation for the blessed. But what was wanted just now was an immediate decision, Yes or No, whether she wished to enter into eternal joy by way of temporal self-denial, or not. If she did not, then he would go farther on; for they wanted some dancers in Heaven.

Musa stood, still doubtful and undecided, and fumbled anxiously with her finger-tips in her mouth. It seemed too hard never to dance again from that moment, all for the sake of an unknown reward. At that, David gave a signal, and suddenly the musicians struck up some bars of a dance of such unheard-of bliss and unearthliness that the girl's soul leaped in her body, and her limbs twitched; but she could not get one of them to dance, and she noticed that her body was far too heavy and stiff for the tune. Full of longing, she thrust her hand into the King's and made the promise which he demanded.

Forthwith he was no more to be seen, and the angel-musicians whirred and fluttered and crowded out and away through an open window. But, in mischievous childish fashion, before going they dealt the patient stone angels a sounding slap on the cheeks with their rolled-up music.

Musa went home with devout step, carrying that celestial melody in her ears; and having laid all her dainty raiment aside, she got a coarse gown made and put it on. At the same time she built herself a cell at the end of her parents' garden, where the deep shade of the trees lingered, made a scant bed of moss and from that day onward separated herself from all her kindred, and took up her abode there as a penitent and saint. She spent all her time in prayer, and often disciplined herself with a scourge. But her severest penance consisted in holding her limbs stiff and immovable, for whenever she heard a sound, the twitter of a bird or the rustling of the leaves in the wind, her feet twitched as much as to tell her they must dance.

As this involuntary twitching would not forsake her, and often seduced her to a little skip before she was aware, she caused her tender feet to be fastened together by a light chain. Her relatives and friends marveled day and night at the transformation, rejoiced to possess such a saint, and guarded the hermitage under the trees as the apple of their eye. Many came for her counsel and intercession. In particular, they used to bring young girls to her who were rather clumsy on their feet, for it was observed that everyone whom she touched at once became light and graceful in gait.

So she spent three years in her cell, but by the end of the third year Musa had become almost as thin and transparent as a summer cloud. She lay continually on her bed of moss, gazed wistfully into Heaven, and was convinced that she could already see the golden sandals of the blessed, dancing and gliding about through the azure.

At last one harsh autumn day the tidings spread that the saint lay on her death-bed. She had taken off her dark penitential robe, and caused herself to be arrayed in bridal garments of dazzling white. So she lay with folded hands and smilingly awaited the hour of death. The garden was all filled with devout persons, the breezes murmured, and the leaves were falling from the trees on all sides. But suddenly the sighing of the wind changed into music, which appeared to be playing in the tree-tops, and as the people looked up, lo, all the branches were clad in fresh green, the myrtles and pomegranates put out blossom and fragrance, the earth decked itself with flowers, and a rosy glow settled upon the white, frail form of the dying saint.

That same instant she yielded up her spirit. The train about her feet sprang asunder with a sharp twang, Heaven opened wide all around, full of unbounded radiance so that all could see in. Then they saw many thousands of beautiful young men and maidens in the utmost splendor, dancing circle upon circle farther than the eye could reach. A magnificent King enthroned on a cloud, with a special band of small angels seated on its edge, bore down a little way towards earth, and received the form of the sainted Musa from before the eyes of all the beholders who filled the garden. They saw, too, how she sprang into the open Heaven and immediately danced out of sight among the jubilant radiant circle.

That was a high feast-day in Heaven. Now the custom (to be sure, it is denied by Saint Gregory of Nyssa, but stoutly maintained by his namesake of Nazianza) on feast-days was to invite the nine Muses, who sat for the rest of their time in Hell and to admit them to Heaven that they might be of assistance. They were well entertained, but once the feast was over had to go back to the other place.

When, now, the dances and songs and all the ceremonies had come to an end and the heavenly company sat down, Musa was taken to a table where the nine Muses were being served. They sat huddled together half scared, glancing about with their fiery black or dark-blue eyes. The busy Martha of the Gospels was caring for them in person. She had on her finest kitchen-apron and a tiny little smudge on her white chin and was pressing all manner of good things on the Muses in the friendliest possible way, but when Musa and Saint Cecilia and some other artistic women arrived and greeted the shy Pierians cheerfully, and joined their company, they began to thaw, grew confidential, and the feminine circle became quite pleasant and happy. Musa sat beside Terpsichore, and Cecilia between Polyhymnia and Euterpe, and all took one another's hands. Next came the little minstrel urchins and made up to the beautiful women with an eye to the bright fruit which shone on the ambrosial table. King David himself came and brought a golden cup, out of which all drank, so that gracious joy warmed them. He went round the table, not omitting as he passed to chuck pretty Erato under the chin. While things were going on so favorably at the Muses' table, Our Gracious Lady herself appeared in all her beauty and goodness, sat down a few minutes beside the Muses, and kissed the august Urania with the starry coronet tenderly upon the lips, when she took her departure, whispering to her that she would not rest until the Muses could remain in Paradise forever.

But that never came about. To declare their gratitude for the kindness and friendliness which had been shown them, and to prove their goodwill, the Muses took counsel together and practised a hymn of praise in a retired corner of the Underworld. They tried to give it the form of the solemn chorals which were the fashion in Heaven. They arranged it in two parts of four voices each, with a sort of principal part, which Urania took, and they thus produced a remarkable piece of vocal music.

The next time a feast-day was celebrated in Heaven, and the Muses again rendered their assistance, they seized what appeared to be a favorable moment for their purpose, took their places, and began their song. It began softly, but soon swelled out mightily, but in those regions it sounded so dismal, almost defiant and harsh, yet so wistful and mournful that first of all a horrified silence prevailed, and next the whole assembly was seized with a sad longing for earth and home, and broke into universal weeping.

A sigh without end throbbed throughout Heaven. All the Elders and Prophets started up in dismay while the Muses, with the best of intentions, sang louder and more mournfully, and all Paradise, with the Patriarchs and Elders and Prophets and all who ever walked or lay in green pastures, lost all command of themselves. Until at last, the High and Mighty Trinity Himself came to put things right, and reduced the too zealous Muses to silence with a long reverberating peal of thunder.

Then quiet and composure were restored to Heaven, but the poor nine Sisters had to depart and never dared enter it again from that day onward.

PAUL HEYSE

(1830—1914)

HEYSE was one of the most distinguished and highly respected German writers of the past century. Poet, novelist, dramatist, critic, he "created a new standard of style and artistic finish for the novelette." *The Fury* appeared in Heyse's first collection of stories, which was published in 1855. It is generally regarded as one of the very best stories in the German language.

Reprinted from the volume *Tales from the German of Paul Heyse,* New York, 1878, D. Appleton & Co., publishers, by whose permission it is here used. The original title is *L'Arrabbiata.*

THE FURY

THE day had scarcely dawned. Over Vesuvius hung one broad gray stripe of mist, stretching across as far as Naples, and darkening all the small towns along the coast. The sea lay calm. Along the shore of the narrow creek that lies beneath the Sorrento cliffs, fishermen and their wives were at work already, some with giant cables drawing their boats to land, with the nets that had been cast the night before, while others were rigging their craft, trimming the sails, or fetching out oars and masts from the great grated vaults that have been built deep into the rocks for shelter to the tackle overnight. Nowhere an idle hand; even the very aged, who had long given up going to sea, fell into the long chain of those who were hauling in the nets. Here and there, on some flat housetop, an old woman stood and spun, or busied herself about her grandchildren, whom their mother had left to help her husband.

"Do you see, Rachela? yonder is our padre curato," said one to a little thing of ten, who brandished a small spindle by her side;

"Antonio is to row him over to Capri. Madre Santissima! but the reverend signore's eyes are dull with sleep!" and she waved her hand to a benevolent-looking little priest, who was settling himself in the boat, and spreading out upon the bench his carefully tucked-up skirts.

The men upon the quay had dropped their work to see their pastor off, who bowed and nodded kindly, right and left.

"What for must he go to Capri, granny?" asked the child. "Have the people there no priest of their own, that they must borrow ours?"

"Silly thing!" returned the granny. "Priests they have in plenty—and the most beautiful of churches, and a hermit too, which is more than we have. But there lives a great signora, who once lived here; she was so very ill! Many's the time our padre had to go and take the Most Holy to her, when they thought she could not live the night. But with the Blessed Virgin's help she got strong and well, and was able to bathe every day in the sea. When she went away, she left a fine heap of ducats behind her for our church, and for the poor; and she would not go, they say, until our padre promised to go and see her over there, that she might confess to him as before. It is quite wonderful, the store she lays by him! Indeed, and we have cause to bless ourselves for having a curato who has gifts enough for an archbishop, and is in such request with all the great folks. The Madonna be with him!" she cried, and waved her hand again, as the boat was about to put from shore.

"Are we to have fair weather, my son?" inquired the little priest, with an anxious look toward Naples.

"The sun is not yet up," the young man answered; "when he comes, he will easily do for that small trifle of mist."

"Off with you, then! that we may arrive before the heat."

Antonio was just reaching for his long oar to shove away the boat, when suddenly he paused, and fixed his eyes upon the summit of the steep path that leads down from Sorrento to the water. A tall and slender girlish figure had become visible upon the heights, and was now hastily stepping down the stones, waving her handkerchief. She had a small bundle under her arm, and her dress was mean and poor. Yet she had a distinguished if somewhat savage way of throwing back her head, and the dark tress wreathed around it was like a diadem.

"What have we to wait for?" inquired the curato.

"There is someone coming who wants to go to Capri—with your permission, padre. We shall not go a whit the slower. It is a slight young thing, but just eighteen."

At that moment the young girl appeared from behind the wall that bounds the winding path.

"Laurella!" cried the priest. "And what has she to do in Capri?"

Antonio shrugged his shoulders. She came up with hasty steps, her eyes fixed straight before her.

"Ha! l'Arrabiata! good-morning!" shouted one or two of the young boatmen. But for the curato's presence, they might have added more; the look of mute defiance with which the young girl received their welcome appeared to tempt the more mischievous among them.

"Good-day, Laurella!" now said the priest. "How are you? Are you coming with us to Capri?"

"If I may, padre."

"Ask Antonio there; the boat is his. Every man is master of his own, I say, as God is master of us all."

"There is half a carlino, if I may go for that?" said Laurella, without looking at the young boatman.

"You need it more than I," he muttered, and pushed aside some orange-baskets to make room: he was to sell the oranges in Capri, which little isle of rocks has never been able to grow enough for all its visitors.

"I do not choose to go for nothing," said the girl, with a slight frown of her dark eyebrows.

"Come, child," said the priest; "he is a good lad, and had rather not enrich himself with that little morsel of your poverty. Come now, and step in," and he stretched out his hand to help her, "and sit you down by me. See, now, he has spread his jacket for you, that you may sit the softer. Young folks are all alike; for one little maiden of eighteen they will do more than for ten of us reverend fathers. Nay, no excuse, Tonino. It is the Lord's own doing, that like and like should hold together."

Meantime Laurella had stepped in, and seated herself beside the padre, first putting away Antonio's jacket without a word. The young fellow let it lie, and, muttering between his teeth, he gave one vigorous push against the pier, and the little boat flew out into the open bay.

"What are you carrying there in that little bundle?" inquired the padre, as they were floating on over a calm sea, now just beginning to be lighted up with the earliest rays of the rising sun.

"Silk, thread, and a loaf, padre. The silk is to be sold at Anacapri, to a woman who makes ribbons, and the thread to another."

"Spun by yourself?"

"Yes, sir."

"You once learned to weave ribbons yourself, if I remember right?"

"I did, sir; but mother has been much worse, and I cannot stay so long from home; and a loom to ourselves we are not rich enough to buy."

"Worse, is she? Ah! dear, dear! when I was with you last, at Easter, she was up."

"The spring is always her worst time. Ever since those last great storms, and the earthquakes she has been forced to keep her bed from pain."

"Pray, my child. Never slacken your prayers and petitions that the Blessed Virgin may intercede for you; and be industrious and good, that your prayers may find a hearing."

After a pause: "When you were coming toward the shore, I heard them calling after you. 'Good-morning, l'Arrabiata!' they said. What made them call you so? It is not a nice name for a young Christian maiden, who should be meek and mild."

The young girl's brown face glowed all over, while her eyes flashed fire.

"They always mock me so, because I do not dance and sing, and stand about to chatter, as other girls do. I might be left in peace, I think; I do *them* no harm."

"Nay, but you might be civil. Let others dance and sing, on whom this life sits lighter; but a kind word now and then is seemly even from the most afflicted."

Her dark eyes fell, and she drew her eyebrows closer over them, as if she would have hidden them.

They went on a while in silence. The sun now stood resplendent above the mountain chain; only the tip of Mount Vesuvius towered beyond the group of clouds that had gathered about its base; and on the Sorrento plains the houses were gleaming white from the dark green of their orange-gardens.

"Have you heard no more of that painter, Laurella?" asked the curato—"that Neapolitan, who wished so much to marry you?" She shook her head. "He came to make a picture of you. Why would you not let him?"

"What did he want it for? There are handsomer girls than I. Who knows what he would have done with it? He might have bewitched me with it, or hurt my soul, or even killed me, mother says."

"Never believe such sinful things!" said the little curato very earnestly. "Are not you ever in God's keeping, without whose will not one hair of your head can fall? and is one poor mortal with an image in his hand to prevail against the Lord? Besides, you might have seen that he was fond of you; else why should he want to marry you?"

She said nothing.

"And wherefore did you refuse him? He was an honest man, they say, and comely; and he would have kept you and your mother far better than you ever can yourself, for all your spinning and silk-winding."

"We are so poor!" she said passionately; "and mother has been ill so long, we should have become a burden to him. And then I never should have done for a signora. When his friends came to see him, he would only have been ashamed of me."

"How can you say so? I tell you the man was good and kind; he would even have been willing to settle in Sorrento. It will not be so easy to find another, sent straight from heaven to be the saving of you, as this man, indeed, appeared to be."

"I want no husband—I never shall," she said, very stubbornly, half to herself.

"Is this a vow? or do you mean to be a nun?"

She shook her head.

"The people are not so wrong who call you wilful, although the name they give you is not kind. Have you ever considered that you stand alone in the world, and that your perverseness must make your sick mother's illness worse to bear, her life more bitter? And what sound reason can you have to give for rejecting an honest hand, stretched out to help you and your mother? Answer me, Laurella."

"I have a reason," she said reluctantly, and speaking low; "but it is one I cannot give."

"Not give! not give to me? not to your confessor, whom you surely know to be your friend—or is he not?"

Laurella nodded.

"Then, child, unburden your heart. If your reason be a good one, I shall be the very first to uphold you in it. Only you are young, and know so little of the world. A time may come when you will find cause to regret a chance of happiness thrown away for some foolish fancy now."

Shyly she threw a furtive glance over to the other end of the boat, where the young boatman sat, rowing fast. His woollen cap was pulled deep down over his eyes; he was gazing far across the water, with averted head, sunk, as it appeared, in his own meditations.

The priest observed her look, and bent his ear down closer.

"You did not know my father?" she whispered, while a dark look gathered in her eyes.

"Your father, child! Why, your father died when you were ten years old. What can your father (Heaven rest his soul in paradise!) have to do with this present perversity of yours?"

"You did not know him, padre; you did not know that mother's illness was caused by him alone."

"And how?"

"By his ill-treatment of her; he beat her and trampled upon her. I well remember the nights when he came home in his fits of frenzy. She never said a word, and did everything he bade her. Yet he would beat her so, my heart felt ready to break. I used to cover up my head and pretend to be asleep, but I cried all night. And then, when he saw her lying on the floor, quite suddenly he would change, and lift her up and kiss her till she screamed and said he smothered her. Mother forbade me ever to say a word of this; but it wore her out. And in all these long years since father died, she has never been able to get well again. And if she should soon die—which God forbid!—I know who it was that killed her."

The little curato's head wagged slowly to and fro; he seemed uncertain how far to acquiesce in the young girl's reasons. At length he said: "Forgive him, as your mother has forgiven! And turn your thoughts from such distressing pictures, Laurella; there may be better days in store for you, which will make you forget the past."

"Never shall I forget that!" she said, and shuddered. "And you must know, padre, it is the reason why I have resolved to remain unmarried. I never will be subject to a man, who may beat and then caress me. Were a man now to want to beat or kiss me, I could defend myself; but mother could not—neither from his blows nor kisses—because she loved him. Now, I will never so love a man as to be made ill and wretched by him."

"You are but a child, and you talk like one who knows nothing at all of life. Are all men like that poor father of yours? Do all ill-treat their wives, and give vent to every whim and gust of passion? Have you never seen a good man yet? or known good wives, who live in peace and harmony with their husbands?"

"But nobody ever knew how father was to mother; she would have died sooner than complain or tell of him, and all because she loved him. If this be love—if love can close our lips when they should cry out for help—if it is to make us suffer without resistance, worse than even our worst enemy could make us suffer—then, I say, I never will be fond of mortal man."

"I tell you you are childish; you know not what you are saying. When your time comes, you are not likely to be consulted whether you choose to fall in love or not." After a pause, he added, "And that painter: did you think he could have been cruel?"

"He made those eyes I have seen my father make, when he begged my mother's pardon and took her in his arms to make it up. I know those eyes. A man may make such eyes, and yet find it in his heart to beat a wife who never did a thing to vex him! It made my flesh creep to see those eyes again."

After this she would not say another word. The curato also remained silent. He bethought himself of more than one wise saying, wherewith the maiden might have been admonished; but he refrained, in consideration of the young boatman, who had been growing rather restless toward the close of this confession.

When, after two hours' rowing, they reached the little bay of Capri, Antonio took the padre in his arms, and carried him through the last few ripples of shallow water, to set him reverently down upon his legs on dry land. But Laurella did not wait for him to wade back and fetch her. Gathering up her little petticoat, holding in one hand her wooden shoes and in the other her little bundle, with one splashing step or two she had reached the shore. "I have some time to stay at Capri," said the priest. "You need not wait—I may not perhaps return before tomorrow. When you get home, Laurella, remember me to your mother; I will come and see her within the week. You mean to go back before it gets dark?"

"If I find an opportunity," answered the girl, turning all her attention to her skirts.

"I must return, you know," said Antonio, in a tone which he believed to be one of great indifference. "I shall wait here till the Ave Maria. If you should not come, it is the same to me."

"You must come," interposed the little priest; "you never can leave your mother all alone at night. Is it far you have to go?"

"To a vineyard by Anacapri."

"And I to Capri. So now God bless you, child—and you, my son."

Laurella kissed his hand, and let one farewell drop, for the padre and Antonio to divide between them. Antonio, however, appropriated no part of it to himself; he pulled off his cap exclusively to the padre, without even looking at Laurella. But after they had turned their backs, he let his eyes travel but a short way with the padre, as he went toiling over the deep bed of small, loose stones; he soon sent them after the maiden, who, turning to the right, had begun to climb the heights, holding one hand above her eyes to protect them from the scorching sun. Just before the path disappeared behind high walls, she stopped, as if to gather breath, and looked behind her. At her feet lay the marina; the rugged rocks rose high around her; the sea was shining in the rarest of its deep blue splendor. The scene was surely worth a moment's pause. But, as chance would have it, her eyes, in glancing past Antonio's boat, met Antonio's own, which had been following her as she climbed.

Each made a slight movement, as persons do who would excuse themselves for some mistake; and then, with her darkest look, the maiden went her way.

Hardly one hour had passed since noon, and yet for the last two Antonio had been sitting waiting on the bench before the fishers' tavern. He must have been very much preoccupied with something, for he jumped up every moment to step out into the sunshine, and look carefully up and down the roads, which, parting right and left, lead to the only two little towns upon the island. He did not altogether trust the weather, he then said to the hostess of the osteria; to be sure, it was clear enough, but he did not quite like that tint of sea and sky. Just so it had looked, he said, before the last awful storm, when the English family had been so nearly lost; surely she must remember it?

No, indeed, she said, she didn't.

Well, if the weather should happen to change before night, she was to think of him, he said.

"Have you many fine folk over there?" she asked him, after a while.

"They are only just beginning; as yet, the season has been bad enough; those who came to bathe, came late."

"The spring came late. Have you not been earning more than we at Capri?"

"Not enough to give me macaroni twice a week, if I had had nothing but the boat—only a letter now and then to take to Naples, or a gentleman to row out into the open sea, that he might fish. But you know I have an uncle who is rich; he owns more than one fine orange-garden; and, 'Tonino,' says he to me, 'while I live you shall not suffer want; and when I am gone you will find that I have taken care of you.' And so, with God's help, I got through the winter."

"Has he children, this uncle who is rich?"

"No, he never married; he was long in foreign parts, and many a good piastre he has laid together. He is going to set up a great fishing business, and set me over it, to see the rights of it."

"Why, then you are a made man, Tonino!"

The young boatman shrugged his shoulders. "Every man has his own burden," said he, starting up again to have another look at the weather, turning his eyes right and left, although he must have known that there can be no weather side but one.

"Let me fetch you another bottle," said the hostess; "your uncle can well afford to pay for it."

"Not more than one glass; it is a fiery wine you have in Capri, and my head is hot already."

"It does not heat the blood; you may drink as much of it as you like. And here is my husband coming; so you must sit a while, and talk to him."

And in fact, with his nets over his shoulder, and his red cap upon his curly head, down came the comely padrone of the osteria. He had been taking a dish of fish to that great lady, to set before the little curato. As soon as he caught sight of the young boatman, he began waving him a most cordial welcome; and he came to sit beside him on the bench, chattering and asking questions. Just as his wife was bringing her second bottle of pure unadulterated Capri, they heard the crisp sand crunch, and Laurella was seen approaching from the left-hand road to Anacapri. She nodded slightly in salutation; then stopped, and hesitated.

Antonio sprang from his seat. "I must go," he said. "It is a young Sorrento girl, who came over with the signor curato in the morning. She has to get back to her sick mother before night."

"Well, well, time enough yet before night," observed the fisherman; "time enough to take a glass of wine. Wife, I say, another glass!"

"I thank you! I had rather not"; and Laurella kept her distance.

"Fill the glasses, wife; fill them both, I say; she only wants a little pressing."

"Don't," interposed the lad. "It is a wilful head of her own she has; a saint could not persuade her to do what she does not choose." And, taking a hasty leave, he ran down to the boat, loosened the rope, and stood waiting for Laurella. Again she bent her head to the hostess, and slowly approached the water, with lingering steps. She looked around on every side, as if in hopes of seeing some other passenger. But the marina was deserted. The fishermen were asleep, or rowing about the coast with rods or nets; a few women and children sat before their doors, spinning or sleeping; such strangers as had come over in the morning were waiting for the cool of the evening to return. She had not time to look about her long; before she could prevent him, Antonio had seized her in his arms and carried her to the boat, as if she had been an infant. He leaped in after her, and with a stroke or two of his oar they were in deep water.

She had seated herself at the end of the boat, half turning her back to him, so that he could only see her profile. She wore a sterner look than ever; the low, straight brow was shaded by her hair; the rounded lips were firmly closed; only the delicate nostril occasionally gave a wilful quiver. After they had gone on a while in silence, she began to feel the scorching of the sun; and, unloosening her bundle, she threw the handkerchief over her head, and began to make her dinner of the bread; for in Capri she had eaten nothing.

Antonio did not stand this long; he fetched out a couple of the oranges with which the baskets had been filled in the morning. "Here is something to eat to your bread, Laurella," he said. "Don't think I kept them for you; they had rolled out of the basket, and I only found them when I brought the baskets back to the boat."

"Eat them yourself; bread is enough for me."

"They are refreshing in this heat, and you have had to walk so far."

"They gave me a drink of water, and that refreshed me."

"As you please," he said, and let them drop into the basket.

Silence again. The sea was smooth as glass. Not a ripple was heard against the prow. Even the white sea-birds that roost among the caves of Capri pursued their prey with soundless flight.

"You might take the oranges to your mother," again commenced Tonino.

"We have oranges at home; and when they are gone, I can go and buy some more."

"Nay, take these to her, and give them to her with my compliments."

"She does not know you."

"You could tell her who I am."

"I do not know you either."

It was not the first time that she had denied him thus. One Sunday of last year, when that painter had first come to Sorrento, Antonio had chanced to be playing *boccia* with some other young fellows in the little piazza by the chief street.

There, for the first time, had the painter caught sight of Laurella, who, with her pitcher on her head, had passed by without taking any notice of him. The Neapolitan, struck by her appearance, stood still and gazed after her, not heeding that he was standing in the very midst of the game, which, with two steps, he might have cleared. A very ungentle ball came knocking against his shins, as a reminder that this was not the spot to choose for meditation. He looked round, as if in expectation of some excuse. But the young boatman who had thrown the ball stood silent among his friends, in such an attitude of defiance that the stranger had found it more advisable to go his ways and avoid discussion. Still, this little encounter had been spoken of, particularly at the time when the painter had been pressing his suit to Laurella. "I do not even know him," she said indignantly, when the painter asked her whether it was for the sake of that uncourteous lad she now refused him. But she had heard that piece of gossip, and known Antonio well enough when she had met him since.

And now they sat together in this boat, like two most deadly enemies, while their hearts were beating fit to kill them. Antonio's usually so good-humored face was heated to scarlet; he struck the oars so sharply that the foam flew over to where Laurella sat, while his lips moved as if muttering angry words. She pretended not to notice, wearing her most unconscious look, bending over the edge of the boat, and letting the cool water pass between her fingers. Then she threw off her handkerchief again, and began to smooth her hair, as though she had been alone. Only her eyebrows twitched, and she held up her wet hands in vain attempts to cool her burning cheeks.

Now they were well out in the open sea. The island was far behind, and the coast before them lay yet distant in the hot haze. Not a sail was within sight, far or near—not even a passing gull to break the stillness. Antonio looked all round, evidently ripening some hasty resolution. The color faded suddenly from his cheek, and he dropped his oars. Laurella looked round involuntarily—fearless, yet attentive.

"I must make an end of this," the young fellow burst forth. "It has lasted too long already! I only wonder that it has not killed me! You say you do not know me? All and this time you must have seen me pass you like a madman, my whole heart full of what I had to tell you; and then you only made your crossest mouth, and turned your back upon me."

"What had I to say to you?" she curtly replied. "I may have seen that you were inclined to meddle with me, but I do not choose to be on people's wicked tongues for nothing. I do not mean to have you for a husband—neither you nor any other."

"Nor any other? So you will not always say! You say so now, because you would not have that painter. Bah, you were but a child! You will feel lonely enough yet, some day; and then, wild as you are, you will take the next best who comes to hand."

"Who knows? which of us can see the future? It may be that I will change my mind. What is that to you?"

"What is it to me?" he flew out, starting to his feet, while the small boat leaped and danced. "What is it to me, you say? You know well enough! I tell you, that man shall perish miserably to whom you shall prove kinder than you have been to me!"

"And to you, what did I ever promise? Am I to blame if you be mad? What right have you to me?"

"Ah! I know," he cried, "my right is written nowhere. It has not been put in Latin by any lawyer, nor stamped with any seal. But this I feel: I have just the right to you that I have to heaven, if I die an honest Christian. Do you think I could look on and see you go to church with another man, and see the girls go by and shrug their shoulders at me?"

"You can do as you please. I am not going to let myself be frightened by all those threats. I also mean to do as I please."

"You shall not say so long!" and his whole frame shook with passion. "I am not the man to let my whole life be spoiled by a stubborn wench like you! You are in my power here, remember, and may be made to do my bidding."

She could not repress a start, but her eyes flashed bravely on him. "You may kill me if you dare," she said slowly.

"I do nothing by halves," he said, and his voice sounded choked and hoarse. "There is room for us both in the sea. I cannot help thee, child"—he spoke the last words dreamily, almost pitifully—"but we must both go down together—both at once—and now!" he shouted, and snatched her in his arms. But at the same moment he drew back his right hand; the blood gushed out; she had bitten him fiercely.

"Ha! can I be made to do your bidding?" she cried, and thrust him from her, with one sudden movement. "Am I here in your power?" and she leaped into the sea, and sank.

She rose again directly; her scanty skirts clung close; her long hair, loosened by the waves, hung heavy about her neck. She struck out valiantly, and, without uttering a sound, she began to swim steadily from the boat toward the shore.

With senses benumbed by sudden terror, he stood, with outstretched neck, looking after her, his eyes fixed as though they had just been witness to a miracle. Then, giving himself a shake, he seized his oars, and began rowing after her with all the strength he had, while all the time the bottom of the boat was reddening fast with the blood that kept streaming from his hand.

Rapidly as she swam, he was at her side in a moment. "For the love of our most Holy Virgin," he cried, "get into the boat! I have been a madman! God alone can tell what so suddenly darkened my brain. It came upon me like a flash of lightning and set me all on fire. I knew not what I did or said. I do not even ask you to forgive me, Laurella, only to come into the boat again and not to risk your life!"

She swam on as though she had not heard him.

"You can never swim to land. I tell you it is two miles off. Think of your mother! If you should come to grief, I should die of horror."

She measured the distance with her eye, and then, without answering him one word, she swam up to the boat, and laid her hands upon the edge; he rose to help her in. As the boat tilted over to one side with the girl's weight, his jacket that was lying on the bench slipped into the water. Agile as she was, she swung herself on board without assistance, and gained her former seat. As soon as he saw that she was safe, he took to his oars again, while she began quietly wringing out her dripping clothes, and shaking the water from her hair. As her eyes fell upon the bottom of the boat, and saw the blood, she gave a quick look at the hand, which held the oar as if it had been unhurt.

"Take this," she said, and held out her handkerchief. He shook his head, and went on rowing. After a time she rose, and, stepping up to him, bound the handkerchief firmly round the wound, which was very deep. Then, heedless of his endeavors to prevent her, she took an oar, and, seating herself opposite him, began to row with steady strokes, keeping her eyes from looking toward him—fixed upon the oar that was scarlet with his blood. Both were pale and silent. As they drew near land, such fishermen as they met began shouting after Antonio and gibing at Laurella; but neither of them moved an eyelid, or spoke one word.

The sun stood yet high over Procida when they landed at the marina. Laurella shook out her petticoat, now nearly dry, and jumped on shore. The old spinning woman, who in the morning had seen them start, was still upon her terrace. She called down, "What is that upon your hand, Tonino? Jesus Christ! the boat is full of blood!"

"It is nothing, comare," the young fellow replied. "I tore my hand against a nail that was sticking out too far; it will be well to-morrow. It is only this confounded ready blood of mine, that always makes a thing look worse than it is."

"Let me come and bind it up, comparello. Stop one moment; I will go and fetch the herbs, and come to you directly."

"Never trouble yourself, comare. It has been dressed already; to-morrow morning it will be all over and forgotten. I have a healthy skin, that heals directly."

"Addio!" said Laurella, turning to the path that goes winding up the cliffs. "Good-night!" he answered, without looking at her; and then taking his oars and baskets from the boat, and climbing up the small stone stairs, he went into his own hut.

He was alone in his two little rooms, and began to pace them up and down. Cooler than upon the dead calm sea, the breeze blew fresh through the small unglazed windows, which could only be closed with wooden shutters. The solitude was soothing to him. He stooped before the little image of the Virgin, devoutly gazing upon the glory round the head (made of stars cut out in silver paper). But he did not want to pray. What reason had he to pray, now that he had lost all he had ever hoped for?

And this day appeared to last forever. He did so long for night! for he was weary, and more exhausted by the loss of blood than he would have cared to own. His hand was very sore. Seating himself upon a little stool, he untied the handkerchief that bound it; the blood, so long repressed, gushed out again; all round the wound the hand was swollen high.

He washed it carefully, cooling it in the water, then he clearly saw the marks of Laurella's teeth.

"She was right," he said; "I was a brute, and deserved no better. I will send her back the handkerchief by Giuseppe to-morrow. Never shall she set eyes on me again." And he washed the handkerchief with the greatest care, and spread it out in the sun to dry.

And having bound up his hand again, as well as he could manage with his teeth and his left hand, he threw himself upon his bed, and closed his eyes.

He was soon waked up from a sort of slumber by the rays of the bright moonlight, and also by the pain of his hand; he had just risen for more cold water to soothe its throbbings, when he heard the sound of someone at the door. Laurella stood before him.

She came in without a question, took off the handkerchief she had tied over her head, and placed her little basket upon the table; then she drew a deep breath.

"You are come to fetch your handkerchief," he said. "You need not have taken that trouble. In the morning I would have asked Giuseppe to take it to you."

"It is not the handkerchief," she said quickly. "I have been up among the hills to gather herbs to stop the blood; see here." And she lifted the lid of her little basket.

"Too much trouble," he said, not in bitterness—"far too much trouble. I am better, much better; but if I were worse, it would be no more than I deserve. Why did you come at such a time? If any one should see you? You know how they talk, even when they don't know what they are saying."

"I care for no one's talk," she said, passionately. "I came to see your hand, and put the herbs upon it; you cannot do it with your left."

"It is not worth while, I tell you."

"Let me see it then, if I am to believe you."

She took his hand, that was not able to prevent her, and unbound the linen. When she saw the swelling, she shuddered, and gave a cry: "Jesus Maria!"

"It is a little swollen," he said; "it will be over in four-and-twenty hours."

"She shook her head. "It will certainly be a week before you can go to sea."

"More likely a day or two; and if not, what matters?"

She had fetched a basin, and began carefully washing out the wound, which he suffered passively, like a child. She then laid on the healing leaves, which at once relieved the burning pain, and finally bound it up with the linen she had brought with her.

When it was done: "I thank you," he said. "And now, if you would do me one more kindness, forgive the madness that came over me; forget all I said and did. I cannot tell how it came to pass; certainly it was not your fault—not yours. And never shall you hear from me again one word to vex you."

She interrupted him. "It is who I have to beg your pardon. I should have spoken differently. I might have explained it better, and not enraged you with my sullen ways. And now that bite—"

"It was in self-defense; it was high time to bring me to my senses. As I said before, it is nothing at all to signify. Do not talk of being forgiven; you only did me good, and I thank you for it. And now, here is your handkerchief; take it with you."

He held it to her, but yet she lingered, hesitated, and appeared to have some inward struggle. At length she said: "You have lost your jacket, and by my fault; and I know that all the money for the oranges was in it. I did not think of this till afterward. I cannot replace it now; we have not so much at home—or if we had, it would be mother's. But this I have—this silver cross. That painter left it on the table the day he came for the last time. I have never looked at it all this while, and do not care to keep it in my box; if you were to sell it? It must be worth a few piastres, mother says. It might make up the money you have lost; and if not quite, I could earn the rest by spinning at night when mother is asleep."

"Nothing will make me take it," he said shortly, pushing away the bright new cross which she had taken from her pocket.

"You must," she said; "how can you tell how long your hand may keep you from your work? There it lies; and nothing can make me so much as look at it again."

"Drop it in the sea, then."

"It is no present I want to make you; it is no more than is your due; it is only fair."

"Nothing from you can be due to me; and hereafter when we chance to meet, if you would do me a kindness, I beg you not to look my way. It would make me feel you were thinking of what I have done. And now good-night; and let this be the last word said."

She laid the handkerchief in the basket, and also the cross, and closed the lid. But when he looked into her face, he started. Great heavy drops were rolling down her cheeks; she let them flow unheeded.

"Maria Santissima!" he cried. "Are you ill? You are trembling from head to foot!"

"It is nothing," she said; "I must go home"; and with unsteady steps she was moving to the door, when suddenly she leaned her brow against the wall, and gave way to a fit of bitter sobbing. Before he could go to her she turned upon him suddenly, and fell upon his neck.

"I cannot bear it!" she cried, clinging to him as a dying thing to life—"I cannot bear it! I cannot let you speak so kindly, and bid me go, with all this on my conscience. Beat me! trample on me! curse me! Or if it can be that you love me still, after all I have done to you, take me and keep me, and do with me as you please; only do not send me away so!" She could say no more for sobbing.

Speechless, he held her a while in his arms. "If I can love you still!" he cried at last. "Holy Mother of God! Do you think that all my best heart's blood has gone from me through that little wound? Don't you hear it hammering now, as though it would burst my breast and go to you? But if you say this to try me, or because you pity me, I can forget it. You are not to think you owe me this, because you know what I have suffered for you."

"No!" she said very resolutely, looking up from his shoulder into his face, with her tearful eyes; "it is because I love you; and let me tell you, it was because I always feared to love you that I was so cross. I will be so different now. I never could bear again to pass you in the street without one look! And lest you should ever feel a doubt, I will kiss you, that you may say, 'She kissed me'; and Laurella kisses no man but her husband."

She kissed him thrice, and, escaping from his arms: "And now good-night, amor mio, cara vita mia!" she said. "Lie down to sleep, and let your hand get well. Do not come with me; I am afraid of no man, save of you alone."

And so she slipped out, and soon disappeared in the shadow of the wall.

He remained standing by the window, gazing far out over the calm sea, while all the stars in heaven appeared to flit before his eyes.

The next time the little curato sat in his confessional, he sat smiling to himself. Laurella had just risen from her knees after a very long confession.

"Who would have thought it?" he said musingly—"that the Lord would so soon have taken pity upon that wayward little heart? And I had been reproaching myself for not having adjured more sternly that ill demon of perversity. Our eyes are but shortsighted to see the ways of Heaven! Well, may God bless her, I say, and let me live to go to sea with Laurella's eldest born rowing me in his father's place! Ah! well, indeed! l'Arrabiata!"

ARTHUR SCHNITZLER

(1862—1931)

ARTHUR SCHNITZLER, born in Vienna in 1862, was one of the most distinguished figures in Austrian literature, and a dramatist and fiction writer of international renown. His delicately written and finely conceived short stories are among the very best of their kind. *The Triple Warning* is a philosophical and metaphysical parable related in the author's best and most brilliant style.

The present version is translated especially for this collection by Barrett H. Clark, from the volume *Masks and Miracles*.

THE TRIPLE WARNING

IN the morning mist, shot through with the blue of the heavens, a youth was making his way toward the beckoning mountains. His heart thrilled to the rhythmical beat of all the world. Without a care or worry he went on for hours over the level country when, on reaching the edge of a forest, a voice rang out, sounding at once near at hand and far-off, and very mysterious:

"Go not through this forest, youth, unless thou wouldst commit murder."

The youth stood still in astonishment, looked in every direction, and seeing nowhere any sign of a living being, concluded that it was a spirit that had addressed him. But his innate courage would not permit him to heed the strange call, and reducing his gait only a little, he proceeded on his way without misgiving, his senses keenly alert, in order that he might be prepared for a meeting with the unknown enemy that had warned him. But he met no one, nor heard any suspicious sound as, unchallenged, he emerged out of the deep shadows of the trees into the open. Under the last wide boughs he sank down for a short rest, allowing his eyes to wander out across a wide meadow toward the mountains, from among which one peak rose aloft, naked and sharply outlined. This was his ultimate goal.

But scarcely had he arisen again when for the second time the mysterious voice was heard, sounding at once near at hand and far-off, mysteriously, but more earnestly than before:

"Go not through this meadow, youth, unless thou wouldst bring ruin to thy Fatherland."

The youth's pride this time forbade his taking heed; he even smiled at the rigmarole, which was delivered with the air as of one concealing something very important, and hurried on, not knowing whether impatience or unrest hastened his steps. The damp mist of evening descended upon the plain as he at last stood facing the rocky wall below his goal. Hardly had he set foot upon the bare surface of the stone, when the voice rang out again, near at hand and far-off, mysteriously, but more threateningly than before:

"No farther, youth, else wilt thou suffer death."

The youth laughed loudly and, without haste or hesitation, went on his way. And the less clear the ascending path became, the more did his chest expand, and finally on the bravely conquered peak his head was illumined by the last light of day.

"Here I am!" he called out in a tone of triumph. "If this was a test, O good or evil spirit, then have I won! No murder weighs on my conscience, unharmed slumbers my Fatherland below, and I still live. Whosoever thou art, I am stronger than thou, for I did not believe thee, and I did right."

Whereupon came a great sound as of thunder from the mountain sides, and at the same time exceeding close at hand:

"Youth, thou errest!" And the overpowering weight of the words felled the wanderer. He stretched himself out on the edge of rock as though he intended to rest there, and with an ironical curl of the lips he said half to himself:

"So it appears that I have committed murder without knowing it!"

"Thy careless foot has crushed a worm," the answer thundered back. And the youth answered with indifference:

"I see: neither a good nor an evil spirit spoke to me, but a spirit with a sense of humor. I was not aware that such hovered about among us mortals."

And again the voice resounded in the fading twilight of the heights:

"Art thou then no longer the same youth whose heart only this morning thrilled to the rhythmical beat of all the world? Is thy soul so dead that thou art untouched by the happiness and sorrow of even a worm?"

"Is that thy meaning?" replied the youth, wrinkling his forehead. "In that event am I a hundred—a thousand times guilty, like other mortals, whose careless steps have innocently destroyed tiny creatures without number."

"Against this particular thing wast thou warned. Dost thou know to what purpose this worm was destined in the eternal scheme of things?"

With sunken head the youth made answer:

"Since I neither knew nor could know that, thou must humbly confess that in my wandering through the forest I have committed precisely the one of many possible murders that it was thy will to prevent. But how I have contrived in my way over the fields to bring ruin to my Fatherland, I am really most curious to learn."

"Sawest thou, youth, the bright-colored butterfly," came the whispered answer, "that fluttered once to the right of thee?"

"Many butterflies did I see, as well as the one thou mentionest."

"Many butterflies! Ah, many did the breath from thy lips drive far from their way; but the one I speak of was driven off to the east, winging its way far and wide until it flew over the golden fence that encloses the royal park. From that butterfly will be born the caterpillar which next year, one hot summer afternoon, will crawl over the white neck of the young queen, awakening her so suddenly from her sleep that her heart will stand still in her breast, and the fruit of her womb languish and die. Thus the king's brother will inherit the kingdom instead of the rightful heir, whom thou wilt have cheated of his life; vicious, malicious, and cruel, he will so rule as to bring his people to despair, madness, and finally, in a frantic effort to save himself, he will plunge his country into a terrible war, and thus bring thy dear Fatherland to ruin. And on no one but thou rests the blame for all this, thou whose breath drove the colored butterfly eastwards across the meadow until it flew over the golden fence of the king's park."

The youth shrugged his shoulders:

"How, O invisible spirit, can I deny that all this that thou prophesiest will come to pass, since on earth one thing always follows from another, and often the most terrible events are caused by the most trivial things, and the most trivial events by the most terrible things? And why should I believe this particular prophecy, since the other, threatening me with death should I mount these steps, has not come to pass?"

"He who mounts those steps," rang out the terrible voice, "must turn back and descend them, if he wishes to mix with mankind again. Hast thou pondered that?"

The youth stopped suddenly and for a moment it seemed as though he would take the safe path downwards, but fearing the impenetrable night that encircled him, he clearly perceived that for so hazardous an enterprise he would require the light of day, and in order to make sure that he would have all his wits at his command on the morrow, he lay down again on the narrow ledge, longing ardently for the sleep that strengthens. As he lay there motionless, his thoughts keeping him awake, he opened his tired eyelids, while anxious shudders ran through his heart and veins. The dizzy precipice was ever before his eyes: that way lay the only road back to life. He who until then had been always sure of his path, now felt in his soul a doubt he had never before experienced, that deepened and caused him ever greater agony, until he could no longer bear it. He therefore decided rather to attempt forthwith what could not be avoided than to await the light in a torment of incertitude. Again he arose, ready for the venture without the blessed light of day, to conquer with faltering steps the dangerous path. But hardly had he set foot into the darkness when he realized as though condemned by an irrevocable judgment, that his fate was to be fulfilled without delay. He called out into the emptiness in anger and sorrow:

"O Invisible Spirit, who hast three times warned me and whom I have thrice refused to believe, O Spirit to whom I now bow down as to one stronger than I, tell me, ere thou destroyest me, who thou art?"

Again the voice rang out, stiflingly close at hand and immeasurably far away:

"No mortal hath yet known me. Many names have I: the superstitious call me Destiny, fools call me Luck, and the pious call me God. To those who deem themselves wise I am that Power which was in the Beginning and continues without end through all Eternity."

"Then I curse thee in this my last moment," shouted the youth with the bitterness of death in his heart. "If thou art indeed the Power that was in the Beginning and continues without end through all Eternity, then was it fated that all should happen as it did—that I should go through the forest and commit murder, that I should cross the meadow and bring ruin upon my Fatherland, that I should climb this rock and here find death—all this despite thy warning. But why was I condemned to hear thee speak to me thrice, if thy warning was not to help me? And why, oh, irony of ironies! must I in this my last moment whimper my feeble question to thee?"

An answer was made to the youth, stern and terrible, in a peal of mysterious laughter that echoed to the utmost confines of the invisible heavens. As he tried to catch the words the earth moved and sank from under his feet. He fell, deeper than a million bottomless pits, amid all the lurking nights of time, that have been and will be, from the Beginning to the End of all things.

HERMANN SUDERMANN

(1857–1928)

SUDERMANN was born in East Prussia in 1857, and educated at the Universities of Königsberg and Berlin. He was one of the foremost leaders of the dramatic movement of the nineties, though to-day he is regarded as definitely belonging to the past. But his stories of East Prussian and Lithuanian life, and his novels, are written with a fine imaginative power, and are still read both in Germany and abroad.

The present version, translated by Grace I. Colbron, is reprinted by permission of the publisher, from *Short Story Classics*, published and copyright by P. F. Collier's Sons, New York, 1907.

A NEW-YEAR'S EVE CONFESSION

THANKS be to God, dear lady, that I may once more sit beside you for a peaceful chat. The holiday tumult is past, and you have a little leisure for me again.

Oh, this Christmas season! I believe that it was invented by some evil demon expressly to annoy us poor bachelors, to show us the more clearly all the desolation of our homeless existence. For others a source of joy, it is for us a torture. Of course, I know, we are not all entirely lonely—for us also the joy of making others happy may blossom, that joy upon which rests the whole secret of the blessed holiday mood. But the pleasure of joining in the happiness of others is tainted for us by a touch of self-irony partly, and also by that bitter longing to which—in contrast to homesickness—I would give the name of "marriage sickness."

Why didn't I come to pour out my heart to you? you ask, you pitying soul, you—you that can give of your sympathy in the same rich measure that others of your sex save for their dainty malices. There's a reason. You remember what Speidel says in his delightful *Lonely Sparrows*, which you sent me the day after Christmas, with a true perception of my state of mind? "The bachelor by instinct," he says, "does not desire comfort. Once he is unhappy, he wishes to have the full enjoyment of his unhappiness."

Besides the "lonely sparrow" whom Speidel portrays, there is another sort of bachelor, the so-called "friend of the family." By this I do not mean those professional wreckers of homes, in whose eyes the serpent glitters as they settle down comfortably at the hospitable hearthstone. I mean the good uncle, papa's former school friend, who rocks the baby on his knee while he reads the magazine essays to mamma, carefully omitting all the doubtful portions.

I know men who give up their entire lives to the service of some family whose friendship they have won—men who live on without desire by the side of a beautiful woman whom in their hearts they secretly adore. You doubt me? Oh, it is the words "without desire" that disturb you? You are right, perhaps. In the depth of even the tamest heart some wild desire lies, but—understand me here—it lies bound in chains.

As an instance I would like to tell you about a conversation which took place day before yesterday, on New Year's Eve, between two old, two very old, gentlemen. It is my secret how I came to know of this conversation, and I ask you not to let it go any further. May I begin, then?

Picture to yourself, as a setting for my story, a high-ceilinged room, old-fashioned in furnishings, lighted by a green-shaded, impertinently bright hanging-lamp of the sort our parents had in use before the era of petroleum. The cone of light that goes out from the flame falls upon a round, white-clothed table, upon which stands the various ingredients for a New-Year's punch, while several drops of oil show out broadly in the center of the table.

My two old gentlemen sat half in the shadow of the green lampshade, moldering ruins both, from long-past days, bowed and trembling, gazing before them with the dull glance of the dimming eyes of age. One, the host, is evidently an old officer, as you would recognize at once from his carefully wound cravat, his pointed, sharply cut mustache, and his martial eyebrows. He sits holding the handle of his roller-chair like a crutch tightly clasped in both hands. He is motionless except for his jaws, which move up and down ceaselessly with the motion of chewing. The other, who sits near him on the sofa, a tall, spare figure, his narrow shoulders crowned by the high-domed head of a thinker, draws occasional thin puffs of smoke from a long pipe which is just about to go out. Among the myriad wrinkles of his smooth-shaven, dried-up face, framed in a wreath of snow-white curls, there lurked a quiet, gentle smile, a smile which the peace of resignation alone can bring to the face of age.

The two were silent. In the perfect stillness of the room the soft bubbling of the burning oil mingled with the soft bubbling of the tobacco juice. Then, from the darkness of the background, the hanging clock began to announce hoarsely the eleventh hour. "This is the hour when she would begin to make the punch," said the man with the domed forehead. His voice was soft, with a slight vibration.

"Yes, this is the time," repeated the other. The sound of his speech was hard, as if the rattle of command still lingered in it.

"I did not think it would be so desolate without her," said the first speaker again.

The host nodded, his jaws moving.

"She made the New-Year's punch for us four-and-forty times," continued his friend.

"Yes, it's as long as that since we moved to Berlin, and you became our friend," said the old soldier.

"Last year at this time we were all so jolly together," said the other. "She sat in the armchair there, knitting socks for Paul's eldest. She worked busily, saying she must finish it by twelve o'clock. And she did finish it. Then we drank our punch and spoke quite calmly of death. And two months later they carried her away. As you know, I have written a fat book on the 'Immortality of the Idea.' You never cared much about it—I don't care for it myself now that your wife is dead. The entire Idea of the Universe means nothing to me now."

"Yes, she was a good wife," said the husband of the dead woman; "she cared for me well. When I had to go out for service at five o'clock in the morning, she was always up before me to look after my coffee. Of course she had her faults. When she got into philosophizing with you—h'm."

"You never understood her," murmured the other, the corners of his mouth trembling in controlled resentment. But the glance that rested long on his friend's face was gentle and sad, as if a secret guilt pressed upon his soul.

After a renewed pause, he began:

"Franz, there is something I want to tell you, something that has long troubled me, something that I do not want to carry with me to my grave."

"Well, fire away," said the host, taking up the long pipe that stood beside his chair.

"There was once—something—between your wife and me."

The host let his pipe fall back again, and stared at his friend with wide-opened eyes.

"No jokes, please, doctor," he said finally.

"It is bitter earnest, Franz," replied the other. "I have carried it about with me these forty years, but now it is high time to have it out with you."

"Do you mean to say that the dead woman was untrue to me?" cried the husband angrily.

"For shame, Franz," said his friend with a soft, sad smile.

The old soldier murmured something and lit his pipe.

"No, she was as pure as God's angels," continued the other. "It is you and I who are the guilty ones. Listen to me. It is now forty-three years ago; you had just been ordered here as captain to Berlin, and I was teaching at the University. You were a gay bird then, as you know."

"H'm," remarked the host, raising his trembling old hand to his mustache.

"There was a beautiful actress with great black eyes and little white teeth—do you remember?"

"*Do* I? Bianca was her name," answered the other as a faded smile flashed over his weather-beaten, self-indulgent face. "Those little white teeth could bite, I can tell you."

"You deceived your wife, and she suspected it. But she said nothing and suffered in silence. She was the first woman who had come into my life since my mother's death. She came into it like a shining star, and I gazed up to her in adoration as one might adore a star. I found the courage to ask her about her trouble. She smiled and said that she was not feeling quite strong yet—you remember it was shortly after the birth of your Paul. Then came New-Year's Eve—forty-three years ago to-night. I came in at eight o'clock as usual. She sat over her embroidery and I read aloud to her while we waited for you. One hour after another passed and still you did not come. I saw that she grew more and more uneasy, and began to tremble. I trembled with her. I knew where you were, and I feared you might forget the hour of midnight in the arms of that woman. She had dropped her work, I read no longer. A terrible silence weighed upon us. Then I saw a tear gather under her eyelid and drop slowly down upon the embroidery in her lap. I sprang up to go out and look for you. I felt myself capable of tearing you away from that woman by force. But at the same moment she sprang up also from her seat—this very same place where I am sitting now.

" 'Where are you going?' she cried, terror in every feature. 'I am going to fetch Franz,' I said. And then she screamed aloud: 'For God's sake, *you* stay with me at least—don't *you* forsake me also.'

"And she hurried to me, laid both hands on my shoulders and buried her tear-bedewed face on my breast. I trembled in every fiber, no woman had ever stood so near me before. But I controlled myself, and soothed and comforted her—she was so sadly in need of comfort. You came in soon after. You did not notice my emotion, your cheeks were burning, your eyes heavy with the fatigue of love. Since that evening a change had come over me, a change that frightened me. When I had felt her soft arms around my neck, when I had felt the fragrance of her hair, the shining star fell from its heaven, and—a woman stood before me, beautiful, breathing love. I called myself a villain, a betrayer, and to sooth my conscience somewhat I set about separating you from your mistress. Fortunately I had some money at my disposal. She was satisfied with the sum I offered her, and—"

"The devil!" exclaimed the old soldier in surprise; "then you were the cause of that touching farewell letter that Bianca sent me—in which she declared that she must give me up—although her heart would break?"

"Yes, I was the cause of it," said his friend. "But listen, there is more to tell. I had thought to purchase peace with that money, but the peace did not come. The wild thoughts ran riot all the more madly in my brain. I buried myself in my work—it was just about that time that I was working out the plan of my book on the 'Immortality of the Idea'—but still could not find peace. And thus the year passed and New-Year's Eve came round again. Again we sat together here, she and I. You were at home this time, but you lay sleeping on the sofa in the next room. A merry Casino dinner had tired you. And as I sat beside her, and my eyes rested on her pale face, then memory came over me with irresistible power. Once more I would feel her head on my breast, once more I would kiss her—and then—the end, if need be. Our eyes met for an instant; I seemed to see a secret understanding, an answer in her glance. I could control myself no longer; I fell at her feet and buried my burning face in her lap.

"I lay there motionless for two seconds perhaps, then I felt her soft hand rest cool upon my head, and her voice, soft and gentle, spoke the words: 'Be brave, dear friend; yes, be brave—do not deceive the man sleeping so trustfully in the next room.' I sprang up and gazed about, bewildered. She took a book from the table and handed it to me. I understood, opened it at random, and began to read aloud. I do not know what it was I read, the letters danced before my eyes. But the storm within my soul began to abate, and when twelve o'clock struck, and you came in sleepily for the New-Year's wishes, it was as if that moment of sin lay far, far behind me, in days that had long passed.

"Since that day I have been calmer. I knew that she did not return my love, and that I had only pity to hope from her. Years passed, your children grew up and married, we three grew old together. You gave up your wild life, forgot the other women, and lived for one alone, as I did. It was not possible that I should ever cease to love her, but my love took on another shape; earthly desires faded, and a bond of the spirit grew up between us. You have often laughed when you heard us philosophizing together. But if you had known how close were our souls at such moments you would have been very jealous. And now she is dead, and before the next New-Year's Eve comes round we two may follow her. It is, therefore, high time that I rid myself of this secret and say to you, 'Franz, I sinned against you once, forgive me.' "

He held out an imploring hand toward his friend; but the other answered, grumbling: "Nonsense. There is nothing to forgive. What you told me there, I knew it long ago. She confessed it herself forty years ago. And now I will tell you why I ran after other women until I was an old man—because she told me then that you were the one and only love of her life."

The friend stared at him without speaking, and the hoarse clock began to strike—midnight.

France

INTRODUCTION

THERE are probably more short stories, as there is assuredly a longer and more continuous development of the form, in the French than in any other literature of the world. In the earliest efforts of native writers, long before the close of the Middle Ages, are to be found the seeds of those lively and often beautiful forms that flourished from the Twelfth to the Sixteenth Centuries—*Fabliaux, Lays,* devotional and miraculous tales. From the epic *Chansons de geste,* beginning with the *Song of Roland,* throughout the whole period in which these remarkable poems thrived, the *trouvères* and troubadours incorporated independent and unified anecdotes and episodes into their long romances of chivalry and gallantry. These were in effect romantic and religious stories, treating of war and love and wonder and pious devotion.

But the earliest examples of independent tales are found in the *Fabliaux.* Although these were written in verse, they were the delight of the middle and lower classes: the verse was scarcely poetry, it was only a medium for the telling of the story. Of the hundred and fifty examples that survive out of the many thousands written, the first *Fabliau* dates from 1159, and the last from 1340. Most of them were anonymous, but among the few names of writers that have come down to us is that of Bernier, which is still remembered, because he wrote the exquisite *Divided Horsecloth.* The famous poet Rutebœuf also wrote *Fabliaux,* but he is better known for his other productions. For several reasons—still a matter of dispute among literary historians—the *Fabliau* suddenly disappeared about the middle of the Fourteenth Century. The other more or less similar forms—like the *Lay,* the *Miracle* and the *Devotional Tale*—still continued sporadically up to the end of the Middle Ages.

The *trouvères* and troubadours and minstrels who went over into Sicily and Italy and were instrumental in establishing there a vernacular literature, took with them their stories, which reappeared in prose form and in a more skilful guise some centuries later in the work of Boccaccio and his followers. Many of them were again treated by later French writers, Rabelais and Marguerite de Navare and

294

Antoine de Saintré, editor of the French *Hundred New Tales*. Rabelais was followed by imitators, like Noël du Fail, Bonaventure des Périers and Béroalde de Verville, all of whom added their share to the development of the story form.

With the opening of the Seventeenth Century the short story was overshadowed by the drama and the long-winded sentimental romance, although such writers as D'Alcripé, Tallement des Réaux, Camus, and Sorel assiduously applied themselves to the form. Toward the end of the century a new form was developed through the art of La Fontaine and Charles Perrault, whose fables and fairy tales are unsurpassed.

The Eighteenth Century, with its new philosophy, its scepticism, and its preoccupation with literary form, saw the rise of the philosophical and the moral tale. Fénelon began the Oriental, a variety of the moral tale, in the late sixteen hundreds. In England the same type was employed with success by Addison in the *Spectator* papers, and later by Dr. Johnson and Goldsmith. In France Voltaire was the supreme master of the form. Marmontel developed his own type of moral tale, with its extreme sentimentality. It is toward the close of the century that, as in England and Germany and Italy, we detect the first symptoms of a radical change in subject-matter and method of treatment. The same spirit that affected Mrs. Radcliffe and Monk Lewis in England, operated upon certain French forerunners of the romantic-fantastic "school." Influences from England and Germany were strong in the work of such writers as Gérard de Nerval and Alfred de Musset.

With the dawn of the Nineteenth Century we come to the modern short story. The number of writers in France who assiduously applied themselves to the writing of short stories without ulterior motives or philosophical and moral purpose was enormous. In the hands of Balzac, Musset, Gautier, Vigny, Mérimée, Nodier, and a host of others, the short story became a pure work of art. To Balzac is due much of the credit for bringing about a complete break with the past in this respect. As the century progressed, the form was adopted by nearly all the great writers of fiction: Flaubert, George Sand, Adam, Anatole France, Daudet, Zola, Coppée, Maupassant, Richepin, and the rest.

The modern short story is one of the most highly perfected branches of French literature. There is something in the language that seems to make it a fit medium for the conveyance of this kind of fiction; at any rate the French short story at its best has never been surpassed.

BERNIER

(12th or 13th Century, A.D.)

NOTHING is known of the author of this story except his name, which is signed on the MS. *The Divided Horsecloth* is one of the best examples of a type that flourished in France during the Twelfth and Thirteenth Centuries: the *Fabliau* is a short story in verse differing principally from the *Lay* and the *Pious* or *Devotional Tale* by its simple style and its appeal, which is directed rather to the middle classes than the nobility. This particular story has been very popular with later writers, among whom both Montaigne and Browning have made use of it.

The present version is translated by Eugene Mason, in the volume *Aucassin and Nicolette and Other Medieval Romances and Legends*. Published in Everyman's Library, J. M. Dent and Sons, by whose permission it is here reprinted.

THE DIVIDED HORSECLOTH

EACH owes it to his fellows to tell as best he may, or, better still, to write with fair enticing words, such deeds and adventures as are good and profitable for us to know. For as men come and go about their business in the world, many things are told them which it is seemly to keep in remembrance. Therefore, it becomes those who say and relate, diligently and with fair intent to keep such matters in thought and study, even as did our fathers before us. Theirs is the school to which we all should pass, and he who would prove an apt scholar, and live beyond his day, must not be idle at his task. But the world dims our fine gold: the minstrel is slothful, and singers forget to sing, because of the pain and travail which go to the finding of their songs. So without waiting for any to-morrow, I will bring before you a certain adventure which chanced, even as it was told to me.

Some seven years ago it befell that a rich burgess of Abbeville departed from the town, together with his wife, his only son, and all his wealth, his goods and plenishing. This he did like a prudent man, since he found himself at enmity with men who were stronger and of more substance than he. So, fearing lest a worse thing should bechance him, from Abbeville he went up to Paris. There he sought a shop and dwelling, and paying his service, made himself vassal and burgess of the King. The merchant was diligent and courteous, his wife smiling and gracious, and their son was not given over to folly, but went soberly, even as his parents taught him. Much were they praised of their neighbors, and those who lived in the same street often set foot in their dwelling. For very greatly are those loved and esteemed by their fellows who are courteous in speech and address. He who has fair words in his mouth receives again sweet words in his ear, and foul words and foul deeds bring naught but bitterness and railing. Thus was it with this prudent merchant. For more than seven years he went about his business, buying and selling, concerning himself with matters of which he had full knowledge, putting by of his earnings a little every day, like a wise and worthy citizen. So this wealthy merchant lived a happy blameless life, till, by the will of God, his wife was taken from him, who had been his companion for some thirty years. Now these parents had but one only child, a son, even as I have told you before. Very grievously did he mourn the death of her who had cherished him so softly, and lamented his mother with many tears, till he came nigh to swoon. Then, to put a little comfort in his heart, his father said to him:

"Fair son, thy mother is dead, and we will pray to God that He grant her mercy in that day. But dry now thine eyes and thy face, for tears can profit thee nothing. By that road we all must go, neither can any man pass Death upon the way, nor return to bring us any word. Fair son, for thee there is goodly comfort. Thou art a young bachelor, and it is time to take thee a wife. I am full of years, and so I may find thee a fair marriage in an honorable house I will endow thee with my substance. I will now seek a bride for thee of birth and breeding—one of family and descent, one come of ancient race, with relations and friends a gracious company, a wife from honest folk and from an honest home. There, where it is good and profitable to be, I will set thee gladly, nor of wealth and moneys shalt thou find a lack."

Now in that place were three brethren, knights of high lineage, cousins to mighty lords of peerage, bearing rich and honorable blazons on their shields. But these knights had no heritage, since they had pawned all that they owned of woods and houses and lands, the better to take their pleasure at the tourney. Passing heavy and tormented were these brethren because in no wise might they redeem their pledge. The eldest of these brothers had a daughter, but the mother of the maid was dead. Now this damsel owned in Paris a certain fair house, over against the mansion of the wealthy merchant. The house was not of her father's heritage, but came to her from her mother, who had put the maid in ward to guardians, so that the house was free from pledge. She received in rent therefrom the sum of twenty Paris pounds every year, and her dues were paid her right willingly. So the merchant, esteeming her a lady of family and estate, demanded her hand in marriage of her father and of all her friends. The knight inquired in his turn of the means and substance of the merchant, who answered very frankly:

"In merchandise and in moneys I have near upon fifteen hundred pounds. Should I tell you that I had more, I should lie, and speak not the truth. I have besides one hundred Paris pounds, which I have gained in honest dealings. Of all this I will give my son the half."

"Fair sir," made answer the knight, "in no wise can this be agreed to. Had you become a Templar, or a White or a Black monk you would have granted the whole of your wealth either to the Temple or your Abbey. By my faith, we cannot consent to so grudging an offer, certes, sir merchant, no."

"Tell me then what you would have me do."

"Very willingly, fair, dear sir. We would that you grant to your son the sum and total of your substance, so that he be seized of all your wealth, and this in such fashion that neither you, nor any in your name, may claim return of any part thereof. If you consent to this the marriage can be made, but otherwise he shall never wed our child and niece."

The merchant turned this over for a while, now looking upon his son, now deep in thought. But very badly he was served of all his thought and pondering. For at the last be made reply to him and said:

"Lord, it shall even be done according to your will. This is our covenant and bargain, that so your daughter is given to my son I will grant him all that I have of worth. I take this company as witness that here I strip myself of everything I own, so that naught is mine, but all is his, of what I once was seized and possessed."

Thus before the witnesses he divested himself utterly of all his wealth, and became naked as a peeled wand in the eyes of the world, for this merchant now had neither purse nor penny, nor wherewithal to break his fast, save it were given him by his son. So when the words were spoken and the merchant altogether spoiled, then the knight took his daughter by the hand and handfasted her with the bachelor, and she became his wife.

For two years after this marriage the husband and the dame lived a quiet and peaceful life. Then a fair son was born to the bachelor, and the lady cherished and guarded him fondly. With them dwelt the merchant in the same lodging, but very soon he perceived that he had given himself a mortal blow in despoiling himself of his substance to live on the charity of others. But perforce he remained of their household for more than twelve years, until the lad had grown up tall, and began to take notice, and to remember that which often he heard of the making of his father's marriage. And well he promised himself that it should never go from mind.

The merchant was full of years. He leaned upon his staff, and went bent with age, as one who searches for his lost youth. His son was weary of his presence, and would gladly have paid for the spinning of his shroud. The dame, who was proud and disdainful, held him in utter despite, for greatly he was against her heart. Never was she silent, but always was she saying to her lord:

"Husband, for love of me, send your father upon his business. I lose all appetite just for the sight of him about the house."

"Wife," answered he, "this shall be done according to your wish."

So because of his wife's anger and importunity, he sought out his father straightway, and said:

"Father, father, get you gone from here. I tell you that you must do the best you can, for we may no longer concern ourselves with you and your lodging. For twelve years and more we have given you food and raiment in our house. Now all is done, so rise and depart forthwith, and fend for yourself, as fend you must."

When the father heard these words he wept bitterly, and often he cursed the day and the hour in which he found he had lived too long.

"Ah, fair, sweet son, what is this thou sayest to me! For the love of God turn me not from thy door. I lie so close that thou canst not want my room. I require of thee neither seat in the chimney corner, nor soft bed of feathers, no, nor carpet on the floor; but only the attic, where I may bide on a little straw. Throw me not from thy house because I eat of thy bread, but feed me without grudging for the short while I have to live. In the eyes of God this charity will cover all thy sins better than if thou went in haircloth next the flesh."

"Fair father," replied the bachelor, "preach me no preachings, but get you forth at once, for reason that my wife would have you gone."

"Fair son, where then shall I go, who am esteemed of nothing worth?"

"Get you gone to the town, for amongst ten thousand others very easily you may light on good fortune. Very unlucky you will be if there you cannot find a way to live. Seek your fortune bravely. Perchance some of your friends and acquaintances will receive you into their houses."

"Son, how then shall men take me to their lodging, when you turn me from the house which I have given you? Why should the stranger welcome that guest whom the son chases from his door? Why should I be received gladly by him to whom I have given naught, when I am evilly entreated of the rich man for whose sake I go naked?"

"Father," said he, "right or wrong, I take the blame upon my own head; but go you must because it is according to my will."

Then the father grieved so bitterly that for a little his very heart would have broken. Weak as he was, he raised himself to his feet and went forth from the house, weeping.

"Son," said he, "I commend thee to God; but since thou wilt that I go, for the love of Him give me at least a portion of packing cloth to shelter me against the wind. I am asking no great matter; nothing but a little cloth to wrap about me, because I am but lightly clad, and fear to die for reason of the cold."

Then he who shrank from any grace of charity made reply:

"Father, I have no cloth, so neither can I bestow, nor have it taken from me."

"Fair, sweet son, my heart trembles within me, so greatly do I dread the cold. Give me, then, the cloth you spread upon your horse, so that I come to no evil."

So he, seeing that he might not rid himself of his father save by the granting of a gift, and being desirous above all that he should part, bade his son to fetch this horsecloth. When the lad heard his father's call he sprang to him, saying:

"Father, what is your pleasure?"

"Fair son," said he, "get you to the stable, and if you find it open give my father the covering that is upon my horse. Give him the best cloth in the stable, so that he may make himself a mantle or a habit, or any other sort of cloak that pleases him."

Then the lad, who was thoughtful beyond his years, made answer: "Grandsire, come now with me."

So the merchant went with him to the stable, exceedingly heavy and wrathful. The lad chose the best horsecloth he might find in the stable, the newest, the largest, and the most fair; this he folded in two, and drawing forth his knife, divided the cloth in two portions. Then he bestowed on his grandfather one half of the sundered horsecloth.

"Fair child," said the old man, "what have you done? Why have you cut the cloth that your father has given me? Very cruelly have you treated me, for you were bidden to give me the horsecloth whole. I shall return and complain to my son thereof."

"Go where you will," replied the boy, "for certainly you shall have nothing more from me."

The merchant went forth from the stable.

"Son," said he, "chastise now thy child, since he counts thy word as nothing but an idle tale, and fears not to disobey thy commandment. Dost thou not see that he keeps one half of the horsecloth?"

"Plague take thee!" cried the father; "give him all the cloth."

"Certes," replied the boy, "that will I never do, for how then shall you be paid? Rather will I keep the half until I am grown a man, and then give it to you. For just as you have chased him from your house, so I will put you from my door. Even as he has bestowed on you all his wealth, so, in my turn, will I require of you all your substance. Naught from me shall you carry away, save that only which you have granted to him. If you leave him to die in his misery, I wait my day, and surely will leave you to perish in yours."

The father listened to these words, and at the end sighed heavily. He repented him of the evil that he purposed, and from the parable that his child had spoken took heed and warning. Turning himself about towards the merchant, he said:

"Father, return to my house. Sin and the Enemy thought to have caught me in the snare, but, please God, I have escaped from the fowler. You are master and lord, and I render all that I have received into your hands. If my wife cannot live with you in quiet, then you shall be served and cherished elsewhere. Chimney corner, and carpet, pillow and bed of feathers, at your ease you shall have pleasure in them all. I take St. Martin to witness that never will I drink stoup of wine, never carve morsel from dish, but that yours shall be the richer portion. Henceforth you shall live softly in the ceiled chamber, near by a blazing fire, clad warmly in your furred robe, even as I. And all this is not of charity, but of your right, for, fair, sweet father, if I am rich it is because of your substance."

Thus the brave witness and the open remonstrance of a child freed his father from the bad thoughts that he harbored. And deeply should this adventure be considered of those who are about to marry their children. Let them not strip themselves so bare as to have nothing left. For he who gives all, and depends upon the charity of others, prepares a rod for his own back.

THE PRIEST AND THE MULBERRIES

(Anonymous: 12th or 13th Century)

PRACTICALLY nothing is known of the author of this pleasant little *Fabliau*. Compared with the great majority of surviving stories of its kind, it is remarkably free from the coarseness which characterizes the *Fabliau*, particularly when it deals with the clergy.

The present version is translated by Eugene Mason, in the volume *Aucassin and Nicolette and Other Medieval Romances and Legends*. Published in Everyman's Library, J. M. Dent and Sons, by whose permission it is here reprinted. The title of the story in the original is *The Priest Who Ate Mulberries*.

THE PRIEST AND THE MULBERRIES

A CERTAIN priest having need to go to market, caused his mare to be saddled and brought to his door. The mare had carried her master for two years, and was high and well nourished, for during these years never had she known thirst nor hunger, but of hay and of oats ever had she enough and to spare. The priest climbed to the saddle and set out upon his journey, and well I remember that it was the month of September, for in that season mulberries grow upon the bushes in great plenty and abundance. The priest rode upon his way repeating his hours, his matins and his vigils. As he drew near the gate of the town the path ran through a certain deep hollow, and raising his eyes from his book the priest marked a bush thick with mulberries, bigger, blacker and more ripe than any he had ever seen. Desire entered his heart, for very covetous was he of this fair fruit, and gradually checking the pace of his mare, he presently caused her to stand beside the bush. Yet one thing still was wanting to his delight. The mulberries near the ground were set about with spines and thorns, whilst the sweetest of all hung so high upon the tree that in no wise could he reach them from his seat. This thing the priest saw, so in a while he climbed up, and stood with his two feet upon the saddle, whence by leaning over a little he could pluck the fruit. Then he chose the fairest, the ripest, and the sweetest of all these mulberries, eating them as swiftly and greedily as he might, whilst the mare beneath him moved never a whit. Now, when this priest had eaten as many mulberries as he was able, he glanced downwards, and saw that the mare was standing still and coy, with her head turned towards the bank of that deep road. Thereat the priest rejoiced very greatly, for his two feet were yet upon the saddle, and the mare was very tall.

"God!" said he, "if any one now should cry 'Gee up!' " He thought and spoke the words at the same moment, whereat the mare was suddenly frighted, and springing forward on the instant tumbled the luckless priest into the bush where the thorns and briars grew sharpest and thickest. There he lay in that uneasy bed, nor might move from one side to the other, backwards or forwards, for all the money in the mint.

The mare galloped straight to her own stable, but when the priest's household saw her return in this fashion they were greatly discomforted. The servants cursed her for an evil and a luckless jade, whilst the cook maid swooned like any dame, for well she believed that her master was dead. When they were returned a little to themselves they ran to and fro, here and there, about the country searching for the priest, and presently on their way to the market town they drew near to that bush where their master yet lay in much misease. On hearing their words bewailing his piteous case, the priest raised a lamentable voice, and cried:

"Diva, Diva, do not pass me by. This bush is an uneasy bed, and here I lie very hurt and troubled and utterly cast down. Do you not see how my blood is staining these thorns, and briars a vermeil red?"

The servants hurried to the bush, and stared upon the priest.

"Sir," said they, "who has flung you herein?"

"Alas," answered he, "'tis sin that has undone me. This morning when I rode this way reading in my Book of Hours, I desired over greatly to eat of the mulberries growing hereon, and so I fell into the sin of gluttony. Therefore this bush gat hold upon me. But help me forth from this place, for I wish now for no other thing but to have a surgeon for my hurts, and to rest in my own house."

Now by this little story we may learn that the prudent man does not cry aloud all he may think in his heart, since by so doing many an one has suffered loss and shame, as we may see by this fable of the Priest and the Mulberries.

MARIE DE FRANCE

(About 1150—1200)

ALL that is positively known of the author of this *Lay* is that she wrote in Norman French, that her name was Marie, and that she was "of France." It is even thought that she may have been an English subject. Her collection of *Lays*, or romantic love tales, was immensely popular both in France and England. Both in her *Fables* and *Lays* she utilized old materials. *The Lay of the Two Lovers* is one of the most charming of the French *Lays*.

The present version is translated by Eugene Mason, in the volume *French Medieval Romances from the Lays of Marie de France*. Published in Everyman's Library, J. M. Dent and Sons, by whose permission it is here reprinted.

THE LAY OF THE TWO LOVERS

ONCE upon a time there lived in Normandy two lovers, who were passing fond, and were brought by Love to Death. The story of their love was bruited so abroad, that the Bretons made a song in their own tongue, and named this song the Lay of the Two Lovers.

In Neustria—that men call Normandy—there is verily a high and marvelously great mountain, where lie the relics of the Two Children. Near this high place the King of those parts caused to be built a certain fair and cunning city, and since he was lord of the Pistrians, it was known as Pistres. The town yet endures, with its towers and houses, to bear witness to the truth; moreover the country thereabouts is known to us all as the Valley of Pistres.

This King had one fair daughter, a damsel sweet of face and gracious of manner, very near to her father's heart, since he had lost his Queen. The maiden increased in years and favor, but he took no heed to her trothing, so that men—yea, even his own people—blamed him greatly for this thing. When the King heard thereof he was passing heavy and

dolent, and considered within himself how he might be delivered from
this grief. So then, that none should carry off his child, he caused it to
be proclaimed, both far and near, by script and trumpet, that he alone
should wed the maid, who would bear her in his arms to the pinnacle
of the great and perilous mountain, and that without rest or stay.
When this news was noised about the country, many came upon the
quest. But strive as they would they might not enforce themselves more
than they were able. However mighty they were of body, at the last
they failed upon the mountain, and fell with their burthen to the
ground. Thus, for a while, was none so bold as to seek the high Princess.

Now in this country lived a squire, son to a certain count of that
realm, seemly of semblance and courteous, and right desirous to win
that prize, which was so coveted of all. He was a welcome guest at the
Court, and the King talked with him very willingly. This squire had
set his heart upon the daughter of the King, and many a time spoke
in her ear, praying her to give him again the love he had bestowed upon
her. So seeing him brave and courteous, she esteemed him for the gifts
which gained him the favor of the King, and they loved together in
their youth. But they hid this matter from all about the Court. This
thing was very grievous to them, but the damoiseau thought within
himself that it were good to bear the pains he knew, rather than to
seek out others that might prove sharper still. Yet in the end, altogether
distraught by love, this prudent varlet sought his friend, and showed
her his case, saying that he urgently required of her that she would
flee with him, for no longer could he endure the weariness of his days.
Should he ask her of the King, well he knew that by reason of his love
he would refuse the gift, save he bore her in his arms up the steep
mount. Then the maiden made answer to her lover, and said:

"Fair friend, well I know you may not carry me to that high place.
Moreover should we take to flight, my father would suffer wrath and
sorrow beyond measure, and go heavily all his days. Certainly my love
is too fond to plague him thus, and we must seek another counsel, for
this is not to my heart. Hearken well. I have kindred in Salerno, of
rich estate. For more than thirty years my aunt has studied there the
art of medicine, and knows the secret gift of every root and herb. If you
hasten to her, bearing letters from me, and show her your adventure,
certainly she will find counsel and cure. Doubt not that she will discover some cunning simple, that will strengthen your body, as well as
comfort your heart. Then return to this realm with your potion, and
ask me at my father's hand. He will deem you but a stripling, and set
forth the terms of his bargain, that to him alone shall I be given who
knows how to climb the perilous mountain, without pause or rest,
bearing his lady between his arms."

When the varlet heard this cunning counsel of the maiden, he rejoiced greatly, and thanking her sweetly for her rede, craved permission to depart. He returned to his own home, and gathering together a goodly store of silken cloths most precious, he bestowed his gear upon the pack horses, and made him ready for the road. So with a little company of men, mounted on swift palfreys, and most privy to his mind, he arrived at Salerno. Now the squire made no long stay at his lodging, but as soon as he might, went to the damsel's kindred to open out his mind. He delivered to the aunt the letters he carried from his friend, and bewailed their evil case. When the dame had read these letters with him, line by line, she charged him to lodge with her awhile, till she might do according to his wish. So by her sorceries, and for the love of her maid, she brewed such a potion that no man, however wearied and outworn, but by drinking this philter, would not be refreshed in heart and blood and bones. Such virtue had this medicine, directly it were drunken. This simple she poured within a little flacket, and gave it to the varlet, who received the gift with great joy and delight, and returned swiftly to his own land.

The varlet made no long sojourn in his home. He repaired straightway to the Court, and, seeking out the King, required of him his fair daughter in marriage, promising, for his part, that were she given him, he would bear her in his arms to the summit of the mount. The King was no wise wroth at his presumption. He smiled rather at his folly, for how should one so young and slender succeed in a business wherein so many mighty men had failed? Therefore he appointed a certain day for this judgment. Moreover he caused letters to be written to his vassals and his friends—passing none by—bidding them to see the end of this adventure. Yea, with public cry and sound of trumpet he bade all who would, come to behold the stripling carry his fair daughter to the pinnacle of the mountain. And from every region round about men came to learn the issue of this thing. But for her part the fair maiden did all that she was able to bring her love to a good end. Ever was it fast day and fleshless day with her, so that by any means she might lighten the burden that her friend must carry in his arms.

Now on the appointed day this young dansellon came very early to the appointed place, bringing the flacket with him. When the great company were fully met together, the King led forth his daughter before them; and all might see that she was arrayed in nothing but her smock. The varlet took the maiden in his arms, but first he gave her the flacket with the precious brewage to carry, since for pride he might not endure to drink therefrom, save at utmost peril. The squire set forth at a great pace, and climbed briskly till he was halfway up the mount. Because of the joy he had in clasping his burden, he gave no thought to the potion. But she—she knew the strength was failing in his heart.

"Fair friend," said she, "well I know that you tire: drink now, I pray you, of the flacket, and so shall your manhood come again at need."

But the varlet answered:

"Fair love, my heart is full of courage; nor for any reason will I pause, so long as I can hold upon my way. It is the noise of all this folk—the tumult and the shouting—that makes my steps uncertain. Their cries distress me, I do not dare to stand."

But when two-thirds of the course was won, the grasshopper would have tripped him off his feet. Urgently and often the maiden prayed him, saying:

"Fair friend, drink now of thy cordial."

But he would neither hear, nor give credence to her words. A mighty anguish filled his bosom. He climbed upon the summit of the mountain, and pained himself grievously to bring his journey to an end. This he might not do. He reeled and fell, nor could he rise again, for the heart had burst within his breast.

When the maiden saw her lover's piteous plight, she deemed that he had swooned by reason of his pain. She kneeled hastily at his side, and put the enchanted brewage to his lips, but he could neither drink nor speak, for he was dead, as I have told you. She bewailed his evil lot, with many shrill cries, and flung the useless flacket far away. The precious potion bestrewed the ground, making a garden of that desolate place. For many saving herbs have been found there since that day by the simple folk of that country, which from the magic philter derived all their virtue.

But then the maiden knew that her lover was dead, she made such wondrous sorrow, as no man had ever seen. She kissed his eyes and mouth, and falling upon his body, took him in her arms, and pressed him closely to her breast. There was no heart so hard as not to be touched by her sorrow; for in this fashion died a dame, who was fair and sweet and gracious beyond the wont of the daughters of men.

Now the King and his company, since these two lovers came not again, presently climbed the mountain to learn their end. But when the King came upon them lifeless, and fast in that embrace, incontinent he fell to the ground, bereft of sense. After his speech had returned to him, he was passing heavy, and lamented their doleful case, and thus did all his people with him.

Three days they kept the bodies of these two fair children from earth, with uncovered face. On the third day they sealed them fast in a goodly coffin of marble, and by the counsel of all men, laid them softly to rest on that mountain where they died. Then they departed from them, and left them together, alone.

Since this adventure of the Two Children this hill is known as the Mountain of the Two Lovers, and their story being bruited abroad, the Breton folk have made a Lay thereof, even as I have rehearsed before you.

MARGUERITE DE NAVARRE

(1492—1549)

MARGUERITE D'ANGOULÊME, daughter of the Duc d'Angoulême and sister of François I, was the second wife of the King of Navarre, and grandmother of Henry IV of France. A woman of culture and learning, and of immense political ability, she was a writer of considerable importance. But among all her varied literary works none is more popular than her famous collection of tales under the title of the *Heptameron*, a volume more or less based on the *Decameron* of Boccaccio. These tales are for the most part intended to teach manners, wisdom and courtesy, and though they are no longer a practical or useful Book of Etiquette, they are still readable. Marguerite was a shrewd observer of men, and showed in the best of her stories a feeling for character and a love of nature. The *Heptameron* was not published until after her death, though the stories circulated in MS. during her lifetime.

The present tale is reprinted from an anonymous translation published in London in 1894. It is the fifty-sixth story, and has for title only a lengthy descriptive paragraph.

THE PIOUS LADY AND THE GRAY FRIAR

(From the *Heptameron*, Tale 56)

A FRENCH lady, whilst sojourning at Padua, was informed that there was a Gray Friar in the Bishop's prison there, and finding that everyone spoke jestingly about him, she inquired the reason. She was told that this Gray Friar, who was an old man, had been confessor to a very honorable and pious widow lady, mother of only one daughter, whom she loved so dearly as to be at all pains to amass riches for her and to find her a good husband. Now, seeing that her daughter was grown up, she was unceasingly anxious to find her a husband who might live with them in peace and quiet, a man, that is, of a good conscience, such as she deemed herself to possess. And since she had heard some foolish preacher say that it were better to do evil by the counsel of theologians than to do well through the belief in the inspiration of the Holy Spirit, she had recourse to her Father Confessor, a man already old, a doctor of theology and one who was held to lead a holy life by the whole town, for she felt sure that, with his counsel and good prayers, she could not fail to find peace both for herself and for her daughter. After she had earnestly begged him to choose for her daughter such a husband as he knew a woman that loved God and her honor ought to desire, he replied that first of all it was needful to implore the grace of the Holy Spirit with prayer and fasting, and then, God guiding his judgment, he hoped to find what she required.

So the Friar retired to think over the matter; and whereas he had heard from the lady that she had got five hundred ducats together to give to her daughter's husband, and that she would take upon herself the charge of maintaining both husband and wife with lodgment, furniture and clothes, he bethought himself that he had a young comrade of handsome figure and pleasant countenance, to whom he might give the fair maiden, the house, the furniture, maintenance and food, whilst he himself kept the five hundred ducats to gratify his burning greed. And when he spoke to his comrade of the matter, he found that they were both of one mind upon it.

He therefore returned to the lady and said:

"I verily believe that God has sent his angel Raphael to me as he did to Tobit, to enable me to find a perfect husband for your daughter. I have in my house the most honorable gentleman in Italy, who has sometimes seen your daughter and is deeply in love with her. And so to-day, whilst I was at prayer, God sent him to me, and he told me of his desire for the marriage, whereupon, knowing his lineage and kindred and notable descent, I promised him to speak to you on the matter. There is, indeed, one defect in him, of which I alone have knowledge, and it is this: Wishing to save one of his friends whom another man was striving to slay, he drew his sword in order to separate them; but it chanced that his friend slew the other, and thus, although he himself had not dealt a blow, yet inasmuch as he had been present at a murder, and had drawn his sword, he became a fugitive from his native town. By the advice of his kinsfolk he came hither in the garb of a scholar, and he dwells here unknown, until his kinsfolk shall have ended the matter; and this he hopes will shortly be done. For this reason, then, it would be needful that the marriage should be performed in secret, and that you should suffer him to go in the daytime to the public lectures and return home every evening to sup and sleep."

"Sir," replied the worthy woman, "I look upon what you tell me as of great advantage to myself, for I shall at least have by me what I most desire in the world."

Thereupon the Gray Friar brought his comrade, bravely attired with a crimson satin doublet, and the lady was well pleased with him. And as soon as he was come the betrothal took place, and, immediately after midnight, a mass was said and they were married. Then they went to bed together until daybreak, when the bridegroom told his wife that to escape discovery he must needs return to the college.

After putting on his crimson satin doublet and his long robe, without forgetting his coif of black silk, he bade his wife, who was still in bed, good-by, promising that he would come every evening to sup with her, but that at dinner they must not wait for him. So he went away and left his wife, who esteemed herself the happiest woman alive to have found so excellent a match. And the young wedded Friar returned to the old father and brought him the five hundred ducats, as had been agreed between them when arranging the marriage.

In the evening he failed not to return and sup with her, who believed him to be her husband, and so well did he make himself liked by her and by his mother-in-law, that they would not have exchanged him for the greatest prince alive.

This manner of life continued for some time, but God in His kindness takes pity upon those that are deceived without fault of their own, and so in His mercy and goodness it came to pass that one morning the lady and her daughter felt a great desire to go and hear mass at St. Francis, and visit their good father confessor through whose means they deemed themselves so well provided, the one with a son-in-law and the other with a husband. It chanced that they did not find the confessor aforesaid nor any other that they knew, and, while waiting to see whether the father would come, they were pleased to hear high mass, which was just beginning. And whilst the young wife was giving close heed to the divine service and its mystery, she was stricken with astonishment on seeing the Priest turn himself about to pronounce the *Dominus vobiscum*, for it seemed to her that it was her husband or else his very fellow. She uttered, however, not a word, but waited till he should turn round again, when, looking still more carefully at him, she had no doubt that it was indeed he. Then she twitched her mother, who was deep in contemplation, and said:

"Alas! madam, what is it that I see?"

"What is it?" said her mother.

"That is my husband," she replied, "who is singing mass, or else 'tis one as like him as can be."

"I pray you, my daughter," replied the mother, who had not carefully observed him, "do not take such a thought into your head. It is impossible that men who are so holy should have practised such deceit. You would sin grievously against God if you believed such a thing."

Nevertheless the mother did not cease looking at him, and when it came to the *Ita missa est* she indeed perceived that no two sons of the same mother were ever so much alike. Yet she was so simple that she would fain have said, "O God, save me from believing what I see." Since her daughter was concerned in the matter, however, she would not suffer it to remain in uncertainty, and resolved to learn the truth.

When evening was come, and the husband (who had perceived nothing of them) was about to return, the mother said to her daughter:

"We shall now, if you are willing, find out the truth concerning your husband. When he is in bed I will go to him, and then, while he is not thinking, you will pluck off his coif from behind, and we shall see whether he be tonsured like the Friar who said mass."

As it was proposed, so was it done. As soon as the wicked husband was in bed, the old lady came and took both his hands as though in sport—her daughter took off his coif, and there he was with his fine tonsure. At this both mother and daughter were as greatly astonished as might be, and forthwith they called their servants to seize him and bind him fast till the morning, nor did any of his excuses or fine speeches avail him aught.

When day was come, the lady sent for her confessor, making as though she had some great secret to tell him, whereupon he came with all speed, and then, reproaching him for the deceit that he had practised on her, she had him seized like the other. Afterwards she sent for the officers of justice, in whose hands she placed them both. It is to be supposed that if the judges were honest men they did not suffer the offense to go unpunished.

FRANÇOIS RABELAIS

(149–?–1553?)

RABELAIS was born at Chinon in Touraine during the last years of the Fifteenth Century. He studied medicine at Montpellier and then went to Lyon, where he practised and began writing. It was during the 30's that he began publishing *Gargantua and Pantagruel*. Somewhat later, he was physician to Cardinal Du Bellay, and toward the end of his life he entered the priesthood, though after a short while he left it. He died about 1553.

A great scholar and Humanist, one of the giant figures of literature, Rabelais sang the praises of life in his magnificent books. In these are found occasional episodes, like the two included in this collection, that entitle Rabelais to an important place among the writers of short tales.

The present version of these tales is from the old translation of *The Lives, Heroic Deeds... of Gargantua and His Son Pantagruel*, by Sir Thomas Urquhart and Peter Le Motteux. The first story is from Chapter XXXIV, the second from Chapter XXXVII, of the Third Book. Neither story has any title in the original.

HE WHO MARRIED A DUMB WIFE

(From *Gargantua and Pantagruel*, Book 3)

WELCOME, in good faith, my dear Master, welcome; it did me good to hear you talk, the Lord be praised for all. I do not remember to have seen you before now, since the last time that you acted at Montpellier, with our ancient friends, Anthony Saporra, Guy Bourguyer, Balthasar Noyer, Tolly, Jhon Quentin, Francis Robinet, Jhon Perdrier, and Francis Rabelais, the Moral Comedy of him who had espoused and married a Dumb Wife. I was there, quoth Epistemon; the good honest man, her husband, was very earnestly urgent to have the fillet of her tongue untied, and would needs have her speak by all means: At his desire some pains were taken on her, and partly by the industry of the physician, other part by the expertness of the surgeon, the encyliglotte, which she had under her tongue, being cut, she spoke and spoke again; yea, within few hours she spoke so loud, so much, so fiercely, and so long, that her poor husband returned to the same physician for a recipe to make her hold her peace: There are (quoth the physician) many proper remedies in our art, to make dumb women speak, but there are none, that ever I could learn therein, to make them silent. The only cure which I have found out, is their husband's deafness. The wretch became within few weeks thereafter, by virtue of some drugs, charms or enchantments, which the physician had prescribed unto him, so deaf, that he could not have heard the thundering of nineteen hundred cannons at a salvo. His wife, perceiving that indeed he was as deaf as a door-nail, and that her scolding was but in vain, sith that he heard her not, she grew stark mad. Some time after, the doctor asked for his fee of the husband; who answered, That truly he was deaf, and so was not able to understand what the tenure of his demand might be. Whereupon the leech bedusted him with a little, I know not what, sort of powder; which rendered him a fool immediately: so great was the stiltificating virtue of that strange kind of pulverized dose. Then did this fool of a husband and his mad wife join together, falling on the doctor and the surgeon, did so scratch, bethwack, and bang them, that they were left half dead upon the place, so furious were the blows which they received: I never in my lifetime laughed so much, as at the acting of that buffoonery.

THE ROAST-MEAT SELLER

A T Paris, in the Roast-meat Cookery of the Petit Chastelet, before
the cook-shop of one of the roast-meat sellers of that lane, a certain hungry porter was eating his bread, after he had by parcels kept it
awhile above the reek and steam of a fat goose on the spit, turning at
a great fire, and found it so besmoaked with the vapor, to be savory;
which the Cook observing, took no notice, till after having ravined his
Penny Loaf, whereof no Morsel has been unsmoakified, he was about
discamping and going away; but by your leave, as the Fellow thought
to have departed thence shot-free, the Master-Cook laid hold upon
him by the Gorget, demanded payment for the smoak of his roast-
meat. The Porter answered, that he had sustained no loss at all; that
by what he had done there was no diminution made of the flesh, that
he had taken nothing of his, and that therefore he was not indebted to
him in anything: As for the smoak in question, that, although he had
not been there, it would howsoever have been evaporated: Besides
that, before that time it had never been seen nor heard, that roast-
meat smoak was sold upon the streets of Paris. The Cook hereto replied,
That he was not obliged nor any way bound to feed and nourish for
nought a Porter whom he had never seen before with the smoak of his
roast-meat; and thereupon swore, that if he would not forthwith content and satisfie him with present payment for the repast which he had
thereby got, that he would take his crooked staves from off his back;
which instead of having loads thereafter laid upon them, should serve
for fuel to his kitchen fires. Whilst he was going about so to do, and to
have pulled them to him by one of the bottom rungs, which he had
caught in his hand, the sturdy Porter got out of his gripes, drew forth
the knotty cudgel, and stood to his own defence. The altercation
waxed hot in words, which moved the gaping hoydens of the sottish
Parisians to run from all parts thereabouts to see what the issue would
be of that babling strife and contention. In the interim of this dispute,
to very good purpose, Seiny Jhon the Fool and Citizen of Paris, hapen-
ed to be there, whom the Cook perceiving, said to the Porter, Wilt thou
refer and submit unto the noble Seiny Jhon, the decision of the difference and controversie which is betwixt us? Yes, by the blood of a goose,
answered the Porter, I am content. Seiny Jhon the Fool, finding that
the Cook and Porter had compromised the determination of their
variance and debate to the discretion of his award and arbitrament;
after that the reasons on either side whereupon was grounded the
mutual fierceness of their brawling jar had been to the full displayed
and laid open before him, commanded the Porter to draw out of the
fab of his belt a piece of money, if he had it. Whereupon the Porter

immediately without delay, in reverence to the authority of such a judicious umpire, put the tenth part of a silver Phillip into his hand. This little Phillip Seiny Jhon took, then set it on his left shoulder, to try by feeling if it was of a sufficient weight; after that, laying it on the palm of his hand he made it ring and tingle, to understand by the ear if it was of a good alloy in the metal whereof it was composed: Thereafter he put it to the ball or apple of his left eye, to explore by the sight if it was well stamped and marked; all which being done, in a profound silence of the whole doltish people, who were there spectators of this pageantry, to the great hope of the Cooks, and despair of the Porters Prevalency in the suit that was in agitation, he finally caused the Porter to make it sound several times upon the stal of the Cooks Shop. Then with a presidential majesty holding his Bable (scepter-like) in his Hand, muffling his head with a hood of marten skins, each side whereof had the resemblance of an ape's face, sprucified up with ears of pasted paper, and having about his neck a buckled ruff, raised, furrowed, and ridged, with ponting sticks of the shape and fashion of small organpipes; he first, with all the force of his lungs, coughed two or three times, and then with an audible voice pronounced this following sentence, The Court declareth, That the Porter, who ate his Bread at the Smoak of the Roast, hath civilly paid the Cook with the Sound of his Money: And the said Court Ordaineth, That every one return to his own Home, and attend his proper Business, without Cost and Charges, and for a Cause. This verdict, award and arbitrament of the Parisian Fool, did appear so equitable, yea, so admirable to the aforesaid doctors, that they very much doubted, if the matter had been brought before the Sessions for Justice of the said Place, or that the Judges of the Rota at Rome had been umpires therein; or yet that the Areopagites themselves had been the deciders thereof, if by any one part, or all of them together, it had been so judicially sententiated and awarded.

CHARLES PERRAULT

(1628—1703)

PERRAULT, one of several talented brothers who graced the age of Louis XIV, was a scholar, government official, and writer. He lived a life devoid of extraordinary events, except for the celebrated Quarrel of the Ancients and Moderns in which he fought a long contest with Boileau and other believers in the superiority of the ancient over the modern writers. Toward the end of his life he wrote eleven fairy tales (published 1697), based on traditional stories. He was the first to give a literary form to *Little Red Riding-Hood, Cinderella, Puss in Boots, The*

Sleeping Beauty, and half a dozen other household stories, which are destined to last as long as children enjoy fairy tales.

The present version, revised from an early English translation, is reprinted from an anonymously translated edition of the *Fairy Tales of Perrault,* London, no date.

LITTLE RED RIDING-HOOD

(From *Tales of My Mother Goose*)

ONCE upon a time there lived in a certain village a little country girl, the prettiest creature was ever seen. Her mother was excessively fond of her, and her grandmother doted on her still more. This good woman got made for her a little red riding-hood; which became the girl so extremely well that everybody called her Little Red Riding-Hood.

One day her mother, having made some custards, said to her:

"Go, my child, and see how thy grandmamma does, for I hear she has been very ill; carry her a custard, and this little pot of butter."

Little Red Riding-Hood set out immediately to go to her grandmother, who lived in another village. As she was going through the wood, she met with Gaffer Wolf, who had a very great mind to eat her up, but he durst not, because of some fagot-makers hard by in the forest. He asked her whither she was going. The poor child, who did not know that it was dangerous to stay and hear a wolf talk, said to him:

"I am going to see my grandmamma, and carry her a custard and a little pot of butter from my mamma."

"Does she live far off?" said the wolf.

"Oh, ay," answered Little Red Riding-Hood. "It is beyond that mill you see there, at the first house in the village."

"Well," said the wolf, "and I'll go and see her too. I'll go this way and you go that, and we shall see who will be there soonest."

The wolf began to run as fast as he could, taking the nearest way, and the little girl went by that farthest about, diverting herself in gathering nuts, running after butterflies, and making nosegays of such little flowers as she met with. The wolf was not long before he got to the old woman's house. He knocked at the door—tap, tap!

"Who's there?"

"Your grandchild, Little Red Riding-Hood," replied the wolf, counterfeiting her voice, "who has brought you a custard and a little pot of butter, sent you by mamma."

The good grandmother, who was in bed, because she was somewhat ill, cried out:

"Pull the bobbin and the latch will go up." The wolf pulled the bobbin, and the door opened; and then presently he fell upon the good woman and ate her up in a moment, for it was above three days that he had not touched a bit. He then shut the door, and went into the grand-mother's bed, expecting Little Red Riding-Hood, who came sometime afterward and knocked at the door—tap, tap!

"Who's there?"

Little Red Riding-Hood, hearing the big voice of the wolf, was at first afraid; but, believing her grandmother had got a cold and was hoarse, answered:

" 'Tis your grandchild, Little Red Riding-Hood, who has brought you a custard and little pot of butter mamma sends you."

The wolf cried out to her, softening his voice as much as he could: "Pull the bobbin and the latch will go up."

Little Red Riding-Hood pulled the bobbin, and the door opened. The wolf, seeing her come in, said to her, hiding himself under the bedclothes:

"Put the custard and the little pot of butter upon the stool, and come and lie down with me."

Little Red Riding-Hood undressed herself and went into bed, when, being greatly amazed to see how her grandmother looked in her night-clothes, she said to her:

"Grandmamma, what great arms you have got!"

"That is the better to hug thee, my dear!"

"Grandmamma, what great legs you have got!"

"That is to run the better, my child!"

"Grandmamma, what great ears you have got!"

"That is to hear the better, my child!"

"Grandmamma, what great eyes you have got!"

"It is to see the better, my child!"

"Grandmamma, what great teeth you have got!"

"That is to eat thee up!"

And, saying these words, this wicked wolf fell upon Little Red Riding-Hood, and ate her all up.

JEAN DE LA FONTAINE

(1621—1695)

One of the great figures of the age of Louis XIV, Jean de La Fontaine was born at Château-Thierry in 1621. He studied at Rheims and Paris, though he returned to his home afterward. In 1647 he married and entered the government service. He left his wife shortly after his marriage, and placed himself under the protection of several persons of rank and power. In 1668 the first collection of his *Fables* was published, and the following year his *Tales* in verse. He wrote a romance and several plays besides, was elected to membership in the French Academy, and died in 1695.

La Fontaine's *Fables* are by all counts his greatest achievement. These are, in the words of Lanson, "a picture of human life and French society." Based on Æsop and Phædrus and the other fabulists, the little masterpieces of La Fontaine are highly artistic literary performances. *The Four Friends* represents the ultimate perfection of this type of fable.

The present version is translated by Barrett H. Clark, and appears for the first time in this collection.

THE FOUR FRIENDS

(From *The Fables*)

A RAT, a raven, a tortoise, and a gazelle were once upon a time the greatest friends imaginable. This happy friendship first began in a home which was unknown to any human being. However, there is no place safe from humankind, be it in the densest wood, under the deepest river, or on the highest peaks where eagles perch. One day the graceful gazelle was disporting herself when by ill-luck a barking hound (that ferocious servant of ferocious man) found her trail and followed the scent. The gazelle ran on and on.

At meal-time the rat addressed his friends: "Brothers, how comes it that we are only three to-day? Is Miss Gazelle so fickle that she has forgotten us?" Up spoke the tortoise: "Now, if I were a bird, like the raven, I would at once take flight and learn what accident had befallen our fleet-footed sister, and where. My dear rat, it is shameful to doubt her affection for us." Whereupon the raven flew off, and from a distance caught sight of the unfortunate gazelle—he could recognize her face—all tangled up in a snare, and suffering agonies. So back he flew and gave the alarm. He was no fool, and he thought it would be foolish to ask the why and wherefore, the when and how of the poor sufferer, as would some pedantic schoolmaster, and thereby lose the chance of saving the victim.

The three friends, on hearing the sad news, took counsel and deliberated. Two voted to hurry to the spot where the poor gazelle was lying. "Our friend with the shell," said the raven, "might very well remain here to keep watch over the house; when would such a slow creeper reach the spot? Why, the gazelle would be dead." So without further discussion the other two flew to the assistance of the gazelle. But the tortoise was also set on going. Bewailing his inability to walk fast and cursing fate for having made him carry his house on his back, he trudged on behind the others.

Rongemail (that was the rat's name) cut the snare. Was not that fortunate? But just then the huntsman came along. "Who has set loose my gazelle?" he cried. Rongemail quickly scurried into a hole in the ground; the raven flew up into a tree, and the gazelle ran off into the woods. The huntsman, now very angry and seeing no trace of his prey, caught sight of the tortoise and forgot his anger. "Why," he asked himself, "lose courage because my snare has not worked this time? Here is something for my supper." And so saying, he put the tortoise into his bag.

The poor tortoise would have met his fate had not the raven told the gazelle, who came forth from her hiding-place, pretending to be lame. The man, eager for the chase, threw his bag to one side, and Rongemail immediately opened it as he had opened the snare, thus depriving the huntsman of a supper on his friend the tortoise.

VOLTAIRE

(François-Marie Arouet)

(1694–1779)

VOLTAIRE was born in Paris in 1694. His early education was received at a Jesuit school. He began writing verses at an early age, and though his father wished him to study law, he continued to write. He was several times imprisoned for libellous verses and often forced to go into exile. A good part of his life he spent away from France. For over half a century he dominated the intellectual and artistic life of Europe, writing plays, histories, pamphlets, stories and satires. He was one of the greatest French writers and one of the most influential thinkers of modern times. His stories, of which he wrote a fairly large number, are philosophical and satirical tracts cast into narrative form. *Memnon* is what is known as a philosophical tale: it is one of the keenest satires Voltaire ever wrote.

The present version, anonymously translated, appeared originally in *Romances, Tales, and Smaller Pieces of M. de Voltaire*, vol. I, London, 1794.

MEMNON THE PHILOSOPHER, OR HUMAN WISDOM

MEMNON one day took it into his head to become a great philosopher. There are few men who have not, at some time or other, conceived the same wild project. Says Memnon to himself, To be a perfect philosopher, and of course to be perfectly happy, I have nothing to do but to divest myself entirely of passions; and nothing is more easy, as everybody knows. In the first place, I will never be in love; for, when I see a beautiful woman, I will say to myself, These cheeks will one day grow wrinkled, these eyes be encircled with vermilion, that bosom become flabby and pendant, that head bald and palsied. Now I have only to consider her at present in imagination, as she will afterwards appear; and certainly a fair face will never turn my head.

In the second place, I will be always temperate. It will be in vain to tempt me with good cheer, with delicious wines, or the charms of society. I will have only to figure to myself the consequences of excess, an aching head, a loathing stomach, the loss of reason, of health, and of time. I will then only eat to supply the waste of nature; my health will be always equal, my ideas pure and luminous. All this is so easy that there is no merit in accomplishing it.

But, says Memnon, I must think a little of how I am to regulate my fortune; why, my desires are moderate, my wealth is securely placed with the Receiver General of the finances of Nineveh: I have wherewithal to live independent; and that is the greatest of blessings. I shall never be under the cruel necessity of dancing attendance at court: I will never envy anyone, and nobody will envy me; still, all this is easy. I have friends, continued he, and I will preserve them, for we shall never have any difference; I will never take amiss anything they may say or do; and they will behave in the same way to me. There is no difficulty in all this.

Having thus laid his little plan of philosophy in his closet, Memnon put his head out of the window. He saw two women walking under the plane trees near his house. The one was old, and appeared quite at her ease. The other was young, handsome, and seemingly much agitated: she sighed, she wept, and seemed on that account still more beautiful. Our philosopher was touched, not, to be sure, with the beauty of the lady (he was too much determined not to feel any uneasiness of that kind) but with the distress which he saw her in. He came downstairs and accosted the young Ninevite in the design of consoling her with philosophy. That lovely person related to him, with an air of great simplicity, and in the most affecting manner, the injuries she sustained from an imaginary uncle; with what art he had deprived her of some imaginary property, and of the violence which she pretended to dread from him. "You appear to me," said she, "a man of such wisdom that if you will condescend to come to my house and examine into my affairs, I am persuaded you will be able to draw me from the cruel embarrassment I am at present involved in." Memnon did not hesitate to follow her, to examine her affairs philosophically and to give her sound counsel.

The afflicted lady led him into a perfumed chamber, and politely made him sit down with her on a large sofa, where they both placed themselves opposite to each other in the attitude of conversation, their legs crossed; the one eager in telling her story, the other listening with devout attention. The lady spoke with downcast eyes, whence there sometimes fell a tear, and which, as she now and then ventured to raise them, always met those of the sage Memnon. Their discourse was full of tenderness, which redoubled as often as their eyes met. Memnon took her affairs exceedingly to heart, and felt himself every instant more and more inclined to oblige a person so virtuous and so unhappy. By degrees, in the warmth of conversation, they ceased to sit opposite; they drew nearer; their legs were no longer crossed. Memnon counseled her so closely and gave her such tender advices that neither of them could talk any longer of business nor well knew what they were about.

At this interesting moment, as may easily be imagined, who should come in but the uncle; he was armed from head to foot, and the first thing he said was, that he would immediately sacrifice, as was just, the sage Memnon and his niece; the latter, who made her escape, knew that he was well enough disposed to pardon, provided a good round sum were offered to him. Memnon was obliged to purchase his safety with all he had about him. In those days people were happy in getting so easily quit. America was not then discovered, and distressed ladies were not nearly as dangerous as they are now.

Memnon, covered with shame and confusion, got home to his own house; there he found a card inviting him to dinner with some of his intimate friends. If I remain at home alone, said he, I shall have my mind so occupied with this vexatious adventure that I shall not be able to eat a bit, and I shall bring upon myself some disease. It will therefore be prudent in me to go to my intimate friends, and partake with them of a frugal repast. I shall forget in the sweets of their society that folly I have this morning been guilty of. Accordingly, he attends the meeting; he is discovered to be uneasy at something, and he is urged to drink and banish care. A little wine, drunk in moderation, comforts the heart of god and man: so reasons Memnon the philosopher, and he becomes intoxicated. After the repast, play is proposed. A little play with one's intimate friends is a harmless pastime. He plays and loses all that is in his purse, and four times as much on his word. A dispute arises on some circumstances in the game, and the disputants grow warm: one of his intimate friends throws a dice box at his head, and strikes out one of his eyes. The philosopher Memnon is carried home to his house, drunk and penniless, with the loss of an eye.

He sleeps out his debauch, and when his head has got a little clear, he sends his servant to the Receiver General of the finances of Nineveh to draw a little money to pay his debts of honor to his intimate friends. The servant returns and informs him that the Receiver General had that morning been declared a fraudulent bankrupt and that by this means an hundred families are reduced to poverty and despair. Memnon, almost beside himself, puts a plaster on his eye and a petition in his pocket, and goes to court to solicit justice from the king against the bankrupt. In the saloon he meets a number of ladies all in the highest spirits, and sailing along with hoops four-and-twenty feet in circumference. One of them, who knew him a little, eyed him askance, and cried aloud, "Ah! What a horrid monster!" Another, who was better acquainted with him, thus accosts him, "Good-morrow, Mr. Memnon. I hope you are very well, Mr. Memnon. La, Mr. Memnon, how did you lose your eye?" And, turning upon her heel, she tripped away without waiting an answer. Memnon hid himself in a corner and waited for the moment when he could throw himself at the feet of the monarch. That moment at last arrived. Three times he kissed the earth, and presented his petition. His gracious majesty received him very favorably, and referred the paper to one of his satraps, that he might give him an account of it. The satrap takes Memnon aside and says to him with a haughty air and satirical grin, "Hark ye, you fellow with the one eye, you must be a comical dog indeed, to address yourself to the king rather than to me; and still more so, to dare to demand justice against an honest bankrupt, whom I honor with my protection, and who is nephew to the waiting-maid of my mistress. Proceed no further in this business, my good friend, if you wish to preserve the eye you have left."

Memnon, having thus in his closet resolved to renounce women, the excesses of the table, play and quarreling, but especially having determined never to go to court, had been in the short space of four-and-twenty hours, duped and robbed by a gentle dame, had got drunk, had gamed, had been engaged in a quarrel, had got his eye knocked out, and had been at court where he was sneered at and insulted.

Petrified with astonishment, and his heart broken with grief, Memnon returns homeward in despair. As he was about to enter his house, he is repulsed by a number of officers who are carrying off his furniture for the benefit of his creditors: he falls down almost lifeless under a plane tree. There he finds the fair dame, of the morning, who was walking with her dear uncle; and both set up a loud laugh on seeing Memnon with his plaster. The night approached, and Memnon made his bed on some straw near the walls of his house. Here the ague seized him, and he fell asleep in one of the fits, when a celestial spirit appeared to him in a dream.

It was all resplendent with light: it had six beautiful wings, but neither feet nor head nor tail, and could be likened to nothing. "What art thou?" said Memnon. "Thy good genius," replied the spirit. "Restore to me then my eye, my health, my fortune, my reason," said Memnon; and he related how he had lost them all in one day. "These are adventures which never happen to us in the world we inhabit," said the spirit. "And what world do you inhabit?" said the man of affliction. "My native country," replied the other, "is five hundred millions of leagues distant from the sun, in a little star near Sirius, which you see from hence." "Charming country!" said Memnon. "And are there indeed no jades to dupe a poor devil, no intimate friends that win his money, and knock out an eye for him, no fraudulent bankrupts, no satraps that make a jest of you while they refuse you justice?" "No," said the inhabitant of the star, "we have nothing of what you talk of; we are never duped by women, because we have none among us; we never commit excesses at table, because we neither eat nor drink; we have no bankrupts, because with us there is neither silver nor gold; our eyes cannot be knocked out because we have not bodies in the form of yours; and satraps never do us injustice because in our world we are all equal." "Pray, my lord," then said Memnon, "without women and without eating how do you spend your time?" "In watching," said the genius, "over the other worlds that are entrusted to us; and I am now come to give you consolation." "Alas!" replied Memnon, "why did you not come yesterday to hinder me from committing so many indiscretions?" "I was with your elder brother Hassan," said the celestial being. "He is still more to be pitied than you are. His Most Gracious Majesty the Sultan of the Indies, in whose court he has the honor to serve, has caused both his eyes to be put out for some small indiscretion; and he is now in a dungeon, his hands and feet loaded with chains." " 'Tis a happy thing truly," said Memnon, "to have a good genius in one's family, when out of two brothers one is blind of an eye, the other blind of both: one stretched upon straw, the other in a dungeon." "Your fate will soon change," said the animal of the star. "It is true, you will never recover your eye, but, except that, you may be sufficiently happy if you never again take it into your head to be a perfect philosopher." "It is then impossible?" said Memnon. "As impossible as to be perfectly wise, perfectly strong, perfectly powerful, perfectly happy. We ourselves are very far from it. There is a world indeed where all this is possible; but, in the hundred thousand millions of worlds dispersed over the regions of space, everything goes on by degrees. There is less philosophy, and less enjoyment on the second than in the first, less in the third than in the second, and so forth till the last in the scale, where all are completely fools." "I am afraid," said Memnon, "that our little terraqueous globe here is the madhouse of those hundred thousand millions of worlds of which Your Lordship does me the honor to speak." "Not quite," said the spirit, "but very nearly; everything must be in its proper place." "But are those poets and philosophers wrong, then, who tell us that everything is for the best?" "No, they are right, when we consider things in relation to the gradation to the whole universe." "Oh! I shall never believe it till I recover my eye again," said poor Memnon.

J. F. MARMONTEL

(1723–1799)

MARMONTEL, born in the Limousin of artisan parents, came early into popular esteem, and, when only a boy, was awarded several prizes for poetry. He wrote to Voltaire, who thought his verses showed an aptitude for finance, and got him a position in Paris. There until the eve of the Revolution he lived a happy and prosperous life. He wrote plays, verses, romances, tales, literary criticism. Popular at court, protected by powerful nobles, he enjoyed the society of the philosophers and writers of his time. His *Moral Tales*, from which *Lausus and Lydia* is taken, were widely read throughout Europe. Amusing as it may seem, *Lausus and Lydia* was considered a very pathetic story in its day. It does, however, possess merits of clarity and skilful construction. It may be considered a good example of a much-practised type of story in vogue in the Eighteenth Century, in which the author employs a foreign background—often of some imaginary Oriental land—for the purpose of exemplifying a moral or philosophical point.

The present version is reprinted from *Moral Tales by M. Marmontel*, translated by C. Dennis and R. Lloyd, London, 1771.

LAUSUS AND LYDIA

(From the *Moral Tales*)

THE character of Mezentius, King of Tyrrhene, is well known. A bad prince and a good father, cruel and tender by turns. He had nothing of the tyrant, nothing that showed violence as long as his desires knew no obstacle; but the calm of this haughty soul was the repose of a lion.

Mezentius had a son named Lausus, whose valor and beauty rendered him famous among the young heroes of Italy. Lausus had attended Mezentius in the war against the King of Præneste. His father, at the very summit of joy, saw him, covered with blood, fighting and vanquishing by his side. The King of Præneste, driven out of his territories and seeking safety in flight, had left in the hands of the conqueror a treasure more precious than his crown, a princess at that age wherein the heart has only the virtues of nature, and nature has all the charms of innocence and beauty. Everything that the Graces in tears possess, either noble or affecting, was painted on Lydia's countenance. In her grief, courage, and dignity, one might discover the daughter of kings amongst the crowd of slaves. She received the first compliments of her enemies without haughtiness, without acknowledgment, as an homage due to her rank, the noble sentiments of which were not weakened by ill fortune.

She heard her father named, and at that name lifted up to heaven her fine eyes filled with tears. All hearts were moved. Mezentius himself, astonished, forgot his pride and age. Prosperity, which hardens weak souls, softens proud hearts, and nothing can be gentler than an hero after a victory. If the savage heart of old Mezentius was not able to resist the charms of his captive, what was the impression on the virtuous soul of young Lausus? He mourned over his exploits; he reproached himself with his victory: it cost Lydia tears. "Let her avenge herself," said he; "let her hate me as much as I love her; I have deserved it but too much." But an idea still more distressful presents itself to his imagination. He sees Mezentius, astonished, softened, pass on a sudden from rage to clemency. He judged rightly that humanity alone had not effected the revolution, and the fear of having his father for a rival completed his confusion.

At the age of Mezentius jealousy follows closely upon love. The tyrant observed the eyes of Lausus with an uneasy attention; he saw extinguished in them all at once the joy and ardor which had lighted up the face of the young hero on his first victory. He saw him disturbed: he caught some looks which it was but too easy to understand. From that instant he considered himself as betrayed; but nature interposed and suspended his rage. A tyrant, even in his fury, constrains himself to think that he is just; and before he condemned his son Mezentius labored to convict him. He began by dissembling his own passion with so much art that the prince looked on his former fears as vain, and considered the attentions of love as nothing more than the effects of clemency. At first he affected to allow Lydia all the appearances of liberty, but the tyrant's court was full of spies and informers, the usual retinue of men of power who, not being able to make themselves beloved, place their greatness in being feared.

His son was no longer afraid of paying Lydia a respectful homage. He mingled with his sentiments an interest so delicate and tender, that Lydia very soon began to reproach herself for the hatred which she thought she entertained for the blood of her enemy; while Lausus lamented that he had contributed to Lydia's misfortunes. He called the gods to witness that he would do all in his power to repair them. "The King my father," says he, "is as generous after victory as intractable before battle: satisfied with victory, he is incapable of oppression. It is easier than ever for the King of Præneste to engage him to a peace that shall be glorious to both. That peace will dry up your tears, beautiful Lydia; but will it efface the remembrance of their crime who caused you to shed them? Why did I not see all my blood flow rather than those tears?"

Lydia's replies, which were full of modesty and greatness, betrayed to Lausus no warmer emotion than that of gratitude: though at the bottom of her heart she was but too sensible of the care he took to console her. She sometimes blushed for having listened to him with complaisance; but her father's interests made it a law to her to avail herself of such a support. In the meantime their conference growing more frequent became also more animated, more interesting, more intimate; and love made its way insensibly through respect and gratitude, as a flower which, in order to blow, opens the slight texture in which it is enfolded.

Deceived more and more by the feigned tranquillity of Mezentius, the credulous Lausus flattered himself that he should very soon see his duty accord with his inclination, and nothing in the world, in his opinion, was easier than to reconcile them. The treaty of peace which he had meditated, was reduced to two articles: to restore to the King of Præneste his crown and his territories, and to make his marriage with the princess the bond of union between the two powers. He communicated this project to Lydia. The confidence he placed in it, the advantages he saw accruing from it, the transports of joy which the idea alone inspired him with, surprised the lovely captive into a smile, mingled with tears. "Generous Prince," said she to him, "may Heaven fulfill the wishes you pour out for my father! I shall not be sorry that I am made a pledge of peace and the token of gratitude." This touching reply was accompanied with a look still more touching. The tyrant was informed of all. His first transport would have hurried him to sacrifice his rival, but his son was the only support of his crown, the only barrier between the people and him: the same stroke would have rendered him completely odious to his subjects and have taken from him the only defender whom he could oppose to the public hatred. Fear is the ruling passion of tyrants. Mezentius resolved to dissemble. He ordered his son into his presence, talked to him with good humor and bade him prepare to set out the next day for the frontiers of his territory, where he had left his army. The prince endeavored to conceal the grief which wrung his soul, and set out without having time to take leave of Lydia.

The very day of Lausus' departure, Mezentius had caused honorable conditions of peace to be proposed to the King of Præneste, the first article of which was his marriage with the daughter of the vanquished monarch. That unfortunate monarch hesitated not to consent, and the same ambassador that offered him peace brought back his agreement for an answer.

Lausus had in the court a friend, who had been attached to him from his infancy. A remarkable resemblance to the young prince had been the means of making the fortune of the young man, who was called Phanor, but they resembled each other still more in their disposition than their figure; the same inclinations, the same virtues. Lausus and Phanor seemed to have but one soul. Lausus at parting had confided to Phanor his passion and his despair. The latter was therefore inconsolable on hearing of the marriage of Lydia with Mezentius: he thought it his duty to acquaint the prince with it. The situation of the lover at this news cannot be described; his heart was troubled, his reason forsook him, and in the distraction of blind sorrow, he wrote to Lydia the warmest and most imprudent letter that love ever dictated. Phanor was charged with the delivery of it. He went to her at the hazard of his life, if he should be discovered. He was so. Mezentius, enraged, ordered him to be laden with irons and dragged to a frightful prison.

However, everything was prepared for a celebration of this unhappy marriage. We may justly conclude that the feast was suitable to the character of Mezentius. Wrestling, the cestus, gladiators, combats between men and animals bred up to carnage, everything that barbarity has invented for its amusements was to have graced the pomp: nothing was wanting to this bloody spectacle but persons to fight against the wild beasts; for it was customary to expose to these fights none but criminals condemned to die, and Mezentius, who on any suspicion was always eager to put the innocent to death, retarded still less the punishment of the guilty. There remained in the prisons none but the faithful friend of Lausus. "Let him be exposed," said Mezentius; "let him fall a prey to devouring lions: the traitor deserves a more cruel death, but this best suits his crime, and my vengeance, and his punishment is a feast worthy of injured love!"

Lausus having in vain expected the answer of his friend, impatiently gave way to affright. "Should we be discovered," said he, "should I have lost my friend by my fatal imprudence! Lydia herself! Ah, I tremble! No, I cannot live any longer in this dreadful uncertainty."

He set out; he disguised himself carefully. He arrived, and heard the reports spread among the people; learned that his friend was in chains, and that the next day was to unite Lydia with Mezentius. He learned that they were preparing the feast which was to precede the festival; they were to see the unhappy Phanor a prey to wild beasts. He shrunk at this recital; a deadly chillness spread through all his veins; he came again to himself, but lost in distraction he fell upon his knees and cried out, "Great gods, restrain my hand, my despair terrifies me! Let me die honorably!" Resolved to deliver his dear Phanor, though he should perish in his stead, he flew to the gates of the prison; but how was he to enter? He addressed himself to the slave whose office it was to carry food to the prisoners. "Open your eyes," said he, "and know me; I am Lausus, I am the son of the King. I except an important service from you. Phanor is confined here: I will see him, I will. I have but one way to come at him: give me your clothes, and fly! There are the pledges of my acknowledgment. Withdraw yourself from the vengeance of my father. If you betray me, you rush on your ruin; if you assist me in my undertaking, my favor shall find you in the very heart of the deserts."

The weak and timorous slave yielded to his promises and threats. He assisted the prince in disguising himself, and disappeared, after having told him the hour at which he was to present himself, and the conduct he was to observe in order to deceive the vigilance of the guards. Night approached and the moment arrived. Lausus presented himself, assuming the name of the slave. The bolts of the dungeon opened with a dismal sound. By the feeble glimmering of a torch, he penetrated into this mansion of horror; he advanced and listened: the accents of a moaning voice struck his ear; he knew it to be the voice of his friend. He saw him lying down in the corner of the cell covered with rags, consumed with weakness, the paleness of death on his countenance, and the fire of despair in his eyes. "Leave me," said Phanor to him, taking him for the slave; "away with these odious nourishments: suffer me to die. Alas," added he, sending forth cries interrupted by sighs, "alas! my dear Lausus is still more unhappy than I. Oh, gods above! If he knows the state to which he has reduced his friend!" "Yes," cried Lausus, throwing himself on his bosom, "yes, my dear Phanor, he does know it, and he partakes of it!" "What do I see?" cried Phanor transported. "Ah, Lausus, my Prince!" At these words both of them lost the use of their senses, locked in each other's arms. Their hearts met, and their sighs intermingled. They remained for a long time mute and immovable, stretched out on the floor of the dungeon. Grief stifled their voices, and they answered each other only by embracing more closely, and bathing one another with their tears. Lausus, at last coming to himself, "Let us lose no time," said he; "take these clothes, get hence and leave me here." "What, I! Great gods, can I be so vile! Ah, Lausus, could you believe it? Ought you to propose it to me?" "I know you well," said the Prince, "but you should also know me. The sentence is pronounced, your punishment is prepared, you must die or fly." "Fly!" "Hear me: my father is violent, but he is not without sensibility. Nature asserts her right over his heart. If I deliver you from death I have only to melt him to compassion for myself; and his arm, when lifted up against a son, will be easily disarmed." "He would strike," said Phanor, "and your death would be my crime: I cannot abandon you." "Well, then," said Lausus, "remain here, but at your death you shall see mine also. Depend not on my father's clemency; it would be in vain for him to pardon me: think not that I would pardon myself. This hand, which wrote the fatal letter that condemns you, this hand which, even after its crime is still the hand of your friend, shall reunite us in your own despite." In vain would Phanor have insisted. "Let us argue no longer," interrupted Lausus; "you can say nothing to me that can equal the shame of surviving my friend, after I have destroyed him. Your pressing earnestness makes me blush, and your prayers are an affront. I will answer for my own safety if you will fly. I swear to die if you will stay and perish. Choose: the moments now are precious."

Phanor knew his friend too well to pretend to shake his resolution. "I consent," said he, "to let you try the only means of safety that is left us; but live if you would have me live: your scaffold shall be mine." "I readily believe it," said Lausus, "and your friend esteems you too much to desire you to survive him." At these words they embraced, and Phanor went out of the dungeon in the habit of the slave, which Lausus had just thrown off.

What a night! What a dreadful night for Lydia! Alas, how shall we paint the emotions that arose in her soul, that divided, tore it between love and virtue? She adored Lausus, she detested Mezentius, she was sacrificing herself to her father's interests, delivering herself up to the object of her hatred, tearing herself forever from an adored lover. They led her to the altar as it were to punishment. Barbarous Mezentius! Thou art content to reign over the heart by violence and fear! It suffices thee that thy consort trembles before thee as a slave before his master. Such is love in the heart of a tyrant. Yet, alas! it is for him alone that she is hereafter to live: it is to him that she is going to be united. If she resists, she must betray her lover and her father: a refusal would discover the secret of her soul, and if Lausus were suspected to be dear to her, he were undone. It was in this cruel agitation that Lydia awaited the day. The terrible day arrived. Lydia, dismayed and trembling, saw herself decked out not as a bride to be presented at the altar of Love and Hymen, but as one of those innocent victims that a barbarous piety crowned with flowers before it sacrificed them.

They led her to the place where the spectacle was to be exhibited; the people assembled there in multitudes, and the sports began. I shall not stop to describe the engagements at the cestus, at wrestling, at the sword: a more dreadful object engages our attention.

An enormous lion advances. At first, with a calm pride, he traverses the arena, throwing his dreadful looks round the amphitheater that environs him; a confused murmur announces the terror that he inspires. In a short time the sound of clarions animates him; he replies by his roarings; his shaggy mane is erected around his monstrous head; he lashes his loins with his tail, and the fire begins to issue from his sparkling eyeballs. The affrighted populace wish and dread to see the wretch appear who is to be delivered up to the rage of this monster. Terror and pity seize on every breast. The combatant, whom Mezentius' guards themselves had taken for Phanor, presents himself. Lydia could not distinguish him. The horror with which she was seized obliged her to turn away her eyes from this spectacle, which shocks the sensibility of her tender soul. Alas! what would she feel if she knew that Phanor, the dear friend of Lausus, was the criminal whom they have selected; if she knew that Lausus himself had taken his friend's place, and that it was he who was going to fight!

Half-naked, his hair disheveled, he walked with an intrepid air; a poniard for the attack, a buckler for defense, are the only arms by which he was protected. Mezentius, prepossessed, sees in him only the guilty Phanor. His own blood is drunk, Nature is blind; it is his own son whom he delivers up to death, and his bowels are not moved. Resentment and revenge stifle every other sentiment. He saw with a barbarous joy the fury of the lion rising by degrees. Lausus, impatient, provoked the monster and urged him to the combat. He advanced toward him; the lion sprang forward. Lausus avoided him. Thrice the enraged animal made toward him with his foaming jaws, and thrice Lausus escaped his murderous fangs.

In the meantime Phanor learned what was happening. He ran up, bearing down the multitude before him, while his piercing cries made the amphitheater resound. "Stop, Mezentius! Save your son, for it is he! It is Lausus who is engaged!" Mezentius looked and knew Phanor, who hastened toward him. "Oh, ye gods, what do I see! My people, assist me! Throw yourselves on the arena, save my son from the jaws of death!" At the name of Lausus, Lydia fell down dead on the steps of the amphitheater: her heart cold, her eyes covered with darkness. Mezentius saw only his son, now in imminent danger. A thousand hands strive in vain for his defense: the monster pursued him and would have devoured him before they could have come to his assistance. But, oh, incredible wonder! Unlooked-for happiness! Lausus, eluding the bounds of the furious animal, struck him a mortal wound and his sword was drawn reeking from the lion's heart. He fell amid torrents of blood spat forth from the foaming jaws. The universal alarm now changed into triumph, and the people replied to Mezentius' doleful cries only by shouts of admiration and joy. These shouts recalled Lydia to life: she opened her eyes and saw Lausus at Mezentius' feet, holding in one hand the bloody dagger, and in the other his dear and faithful Phanor. "It is I," said he to his father, "I alone who am culpable. Phanor's crime was mine: it was my duty to explain it. I forced him to resign his place, and was about to kill myself if he refused. I live, I owe my life to him, and if your son be still dear to you, you owe your son to him, but if your vengeance is not appeased, our days are in your hands. Strike, we will perish together, our hearts have sworn it." Lydia, trembling at this discourse, viewed Mezentius with suppliant eyes, overflowing with tears. The tyrant's cruelty could not withstand this trial. The cries of Nature and the voice of remorse put to silence jealousy and revenge. He remained for a long time immovable and dumb, casting by turns looks of trouble and confusion on the culprits before him, looks in which love, hatred, indignation, and pity succeeded to one another. All trembled around the tyrant. Lausus, Phanor, Lydia, and a multitude innumerable waited with terror the first words that he was to pronounce. He submitted at last, in spite of himself, to that virtue whose ascendancy overpowered him, and passing of a sudden with impetuous violence from rage to tenderness, he threw himself into his son's arms. "Yes," said he, "I pardon thee, and I pardon also thy friend. Live, love one another; but there remains one sacrifice more for me to make thee, and thou hast just now rendered thyself worthy of it. Receive it, then," said he with a new effort; "receive this hand, the gift of which is dearer to thee than life. It is thy valor which has forced it from me; it is that alone could have obtained it."

HONORÉ DE BALZAC

(1799—1850)

BORN at Tours in 1799, Balzac left his native city at an early age and after various attempts at making a living went into the publishing business in Paris. Failing at that, he set to work more earnestly than ever at writing, and until the end of his life he toiled incessantly at the series of novels and tales which have rendered him famous as one of the great novelists of the world. In his *Human Comedy*, Balzac included several short stories, which are among the very first of their kind; in them the short story is at last entirely free of the past. His work has that contemporary quality that is one of the distinguishing marks of all great art.

The Mysterious Mansion is grouped among the *Scenes from Private Life*. It is one of the great stories of modern times.

The present version, anonymously translated, is reprinted from *Great Short Stories*, Collier's Sons, New York. The original title of the story is *La Grande Bretêche*.

THE MYSTERIOUS MANSION

ABOUT a hundred yards from the town of Vendôme, on the borders of the Loire, there is an old gray house, surmounted by very high gables, and so completely isolated that neither tanyard nor shabby hostelry, such as you may find at the entrance to all small towns, exists in its immediate neighborhood.

In front of this building, overlooking the river, is a garden, where the once well-trimmed box borders that used to define the walks now grow wild as they list. Several willows that spring from the Loire have grown as rapidly as the hedge that encloses it, and half conceal the house. The rich vegetation of those weeds that we call foul adorns the sloping shore. Fruit trees, neglected for the last ten years, no longer yield their harvest, and their shoots form coppices. The wall-fruit grows like hedges against the walls. Paths once graveled are overgrown with moss, but, to tell the truth, there is no trace of a path. From the height of the hill, to which cling the ruins of the old castle of the Dukes of Vendôme, the only spot whence the eye can plunge into this enclosure, it strikes you that, at a time not easy to determine, this plot of land was the delight of a country gentleman, who cultivated roses and tulips and horticulture in general, and who was besides a lover of fine fruit. An arbor is still visible, or rather the débris of an arbor, where there is a table that time has not quite destroyed. The aspect of this garden of bygone days suggests the negative joys of peaceful, provincial life, as one might reconstruct the life of a worthy tradesman by reading the epitaph on his tombstone. As if to complete the sweetness and sadness of the ideas that possess one's soul, one of the walls displays a sun-dial decorated with the following commonplace Christian inscription: "Ultimam cogita!" The roof of this house is horribly dilapidated, the shutters are always closed, the balconies are covered with swallows' nests, the doors are perpetually shut, weeds have drawn green lines in the cracks of the flights of steps, the locks and bolts are rusty. Sun, moon, winter, summer, and snow have worn the paneling, warped the boards, gnawed the paint. The lugubrious silence which reigns there is only broken by birds, cats, martins, rats and mice, free to course to and fro, to fight and to eat each other. Everywhere an invisible hand has graven the word *mystery*.

Should your curiosity lead you to glance at this house from the side that points to the road, you would perceive a great door which the children of the place have riddled with holes. I afterward heard that this door had been closed for the last ten years. Through the holes broken by the boys you would have observed the perfect harmony that existed between the façades of both garden and courtyard. In both the same disorder prevails. Tufts of weed encircle the paving-stones. Enormous cracks furrow the walls, round whose blackened crests twine the thousand garlands of the pellitory. The steps are out of joint, the wire of the bell is rusted, the spouts are cracked. What fire from heaven has fallen here? What tribunal has decreed that salt should be strewn on this dwelling? Has God been blasphemed, has France been here betrayed? These are the questions we ask ourselves, but get no answer from the crawling things that haunt the place. The empty and deserted house is a gigantic enigma, of which the key is lost. In bygone times it was a small fief, and bears the name of the Grande Bretêche.

I inferred that I was not the only person to whom my good landlady had communicated the secret of which I was to be the sole recipient, and I prepared to listen.

"Sir," she said, "when the Emperor sent the Spanish prisoners of war and others here, the Government quartered on me a young Spaniard who had been sent to Vendôme on parole. Parole notwithstanding he went out every day to show himself to the sous-préfet. He was a Spanish grandee! Nothing less! His name ended in os and dia, something like Burgos de Férédia. I have his name on my books; you can read it if you like. Oh! but he was a handsome young man for a Spaniard; they are all said to be ugly. He was only five feet and a few inches high, but he was well-grown; he had small hands that he took such care of; ah! you should have seen! He had as many brushes for his hands as a woman for her whole dressing apparatus! He had thick black hair, a fiery eye, his skin was rather bronzed, but I liked the look of it. He wore the finest linen I have ever seen on any one, although I have had princesses staying here, and, among others, General Bertrand, the Duke and Duchess d'Abrantès, Monsieur Decazes, and the King of Spain. He didn't eat much; but his manners were so polite, so amiable, that one could not owe him a grudge. Oh! I was very fond of him, although he didn't open his lips four times in the day, and it was impossible to keep up a conversation with him. For if you spoke to him, he did not answer. It was a fad, a mania with them all, I heard say. He read his breviary like a priest, he went to Mass and to all the services regularly. Where did he sit? Two steps from the chapel of Madame de Merret. As he took his place there the first time he went to church, nobody suspected him of any intention in so doing. Besides, he never raised his eyes from his prayer-book, poor young man!

After that, sir, in the evening he would walk on the mountains, among the castle ruins. It was the poor man's only amusement, it reminded him of his country. They say that Spain is all mountains! From the commencement of his imprisonment he stayed out late. I was anxious when I found that he did not come home before midnight; but we got accustomed to this fancy of his. He took the key of the door, and we left off sitting up for him. He lodged in a house of ours in the Rue des Casernes. After that, one of our stable-men told us that in the evening when he led the horses to the water, he thought he had seen the Spanish grandee swimming far down the river like a live fish. When he returned, I told him to take care of the rushes; he appeared vexed to have been seen in the water. At last, one day, or rather one morning, we did not find him in his room; he had not returned. After searching everywhere, I found some writing in the drawer of a table, where there were fifty gold pieces of Spain that are called doubloons and were worth about five thousand francs; and ten thousand francs' worth of diamonds in a small sealed box. The writing said, that in case he did not return, he left us the money and the diamonds, on condition of paying for Masses to thank God for his escape, and for his salvation. In those days my husband had not been taken from me; he hastened to seek him everywhere.

"And now for the strange part of the story. He brought home the Spaniard's clothes, that he had discovered under a big stone, in a sort of pilework by the river-side near the castle, nearly opposite to the Grande Bretêche. My husband had gone there so early that no one had seen him. After reading the letter, he burned the clothes, and according to Count Fédéria's desire we declared that he had escaped. The sous-préfet sent all the gendarmerie in pursuit of him; but brust! they never caught him. Lepas believed that the Spaniard had drowned himself. I, sir, don't think so; I am more inclined to believe that he had something to do with the affair of Madame de Merret, seeing that Rosalie told me that the crucifix, that her mistress thought so much of, that she had it buried with her, was of ebony and silver. Now in the beginning of his stay here, Monsieur de Fédéria had one in ebony and silver, that I never saw him with later. Now, sir, don't you consider that I need have no scruples about the Spaniard's fifteen thousand francs, and that I have a right to them?"

"Certainly; but you haven't tried to question Rosalie?" I said.

"Oh, yes, indeed, sir; but to no purpose! the girl's like a wall. She knows something, but it is impossible to get her to talk."

After exchanging a few more words with me, my landlady left me a prey to vague and gloomy thoughts, to a romantic curiosity, and a religious terror not unlike the profound impression produced on us when by night, on entering a dark church, we perceive a faint light under high arches; a vague figure glides by—the rustle of a robe or cassock is heard, and we shudder.

Suddenly the Grande Bretêche and its tall weeds, its barred windows, its rusty ironwork, its closed doors, its deserted apartments, appeared like a fantastic apparition before me. I essayed to penetrate the mysterious dwelling, and to find the knot of its dark story—the drama that had killed three persons. In my eyes Rosalie became the most interesting person in Vendôme. As I studied her, I discovered the traces of secret care, despite the radiant health that shone in her plump countenance. There was in her the germ of remorse or hope; her attitude revealed a secret, like the attitude of a bigot who prays to excess, or of the infanticide who ever hears the last cry of her child. Yet her manners were rough and ingenuous—her silly smile was not that of a criminal, and could you but have seen the great kerchief that encompassed her portly bust, framed and laced in by a lilac and blue cotton gown, you would have dubbed her innocent. No, I thought, I will not leave Vendôme without learning the history of the Grande Bretêche. To gain my ends I will strike up a friendship with Rosalie, if needs be.

"Rosalie," said I, one evening.

"Sir?"

"You are not married?"

She started slightly.

"Oh, I can find plenty of men, when the fancy takes me to be made miserable," she said, laughing.

She soon recovered from the effects of her emotion, for all women, from the great lady to the maid of the inn, possess a composure that is peculiar to them.

"You are too good-looking and well favored to be short of lovers. But tell me, Rosalie, why did you take service in an inn after leaving Madame de Merret? Did she leave you nothing to live on?"

"Oh, yes! But, sir, my place is the best in all Vendôme."

The reply was one of those that judges and lawyers would call evasive. Rosalie appeared to me to be situated in this romantic history like the square in the midst of a chessboard. She was at the heart of the truth and chief interest; she seemed to me to be bound in the very knot of it. The conquest of Rosalie was no longer to be an ordinary siege—in this girl was centered the last chapter of a novel, therefore from this moment Rosalie became the object of my preference.

One morning I said to Rosalie: "Tell me all you know about Madame de Merret."

"Oh!" she replied in terror, "do not ask that of me, Monsieur Horace."

Her pretty face fell—her clear, bright color faded—and her eyes lost their innocent brightness.

"Well, then," she said, at last, "if you must have it so, I will tell you about it; but promise to keep my secret!"

"Done! my dear girl, I must keep your secret with the honor of a thief, which is the most loyal in the world."

Were I to transcribe Rosalie's diffuse eloquence faithfully, an entire volume would scarcely contain it; so I shall abridge.

The room occupied by Madame de Merret at the Bretêche was on the ground floor. A little closet about four feet deep, built in the thickness of the wall, served as her wardrobe. Three months before the eventful evening of which I am about to speak, Madame de Merret had been so seriously indisposed that her husband had left her to herself in her own apartment, while he occupied another on the first floor. By one of those chances that it is impossible to foresee, he returned home from the club (where he was accustomed to read the papers and discuss politics with the inhabitants of the place) two hours later than usual. His wife supposed him to be at home, in bed and asleep. But the invasion of France had been the subject of a most animated discussion; the billiard-match had been exciting, he had lost forty francs, an enormous sum for Vendôme, where every one hoards, and where manners are restricted within the limits of a praiseworthy modesty, which perhaps is the source of the true happiness that no Parisian covets. For some time past Monsieur de Merret had been satisfied to ask Rosalie if his wife had gone to bed; and on her reply, which was always in the affirmative, had immediately gained his own room with the good temper engendered by habit and confidence. On entering his house, he took it into his head to go and tell his wife of his misadventure, perhaps by way of consolation. At dinner he found Madame de Merret most coquettishly attired. On his way to the club it had occurred to him that his wife was restored to health, and that her convalescence had added to her beauty. He was, as husbands are wont to be, somewhat slow in making this discovery. Instead of calling Rosalie, who was occupied just then in watching the cook and coachman play a difficult hand at brisque, Monsieur de Merret went to his wife's room by the light of a lantern that he deposited on the first step of the staircase. His unmistakable step resounded under the vaulted corridor. At the moment that the Count turned the handle of his wife's door, he fancied he could hear the door of the closet I spoke of close; but when he entered Madame de Merret was alone before the fireplace. The husband thought ingenuously that Rosalie was in the closet, yet a suspicion that jangled in his ear put him on his guard. He looked at his wife and saw in her eyes I know not what wild and hunted expression.

"You are very late," she said. Her habitually pure, sweet voice seemed changed to him.

Monsieur de Merret did not reply, for at that moment Rosalie entered. It was a thunderbolt for him. He strode about the room, passing from one window to the other, with mechanical motion and folded arms.

"Have you heard bad news, or are you unwell?" inquired his wife timidly, while Rosalie undressed her.

He kept silent.

"You can leave me," said Madame de Merret to her maid; "I will put my hair in curl papers myself."

From the expression of her husband's face she foresaw trouble, and wished to be alone with him. When Rosalie had gone, or was supposed to have gone (for she stayed in the corridor for a few minutes), Monsieur de Merret came and stood in front of his wife, and said coldly to her:

"Madame, there is someone in your closet!" She looked calmly at her husband and replied simply:

"No, sir."

This answer was heartrending to Monsieur de Merret; he did not believe in it. Yet his wife had never appeared to him purer or more saintly than at that moment. He rose to open the closet door; Madame de Merret took his hand, looked at him with an expression of melancholy, and said in a voice that betrayed singular emotion:

"If you find no one there, remember this, all will be over between us!" The extraordinary dignity of his wife's manner restored the Count's profound esteem for her, and inspired him with one of those resolutions that only lack a vaster stage to become immortal.

"No," said he, "Josephine, I will not go there. In either case it would separate us forever. Hear me, I know how pure you are at heart, and that your life is a holy one. You would not commit a mortal sin to save your life."

At these words Madame de Merret turned a haggard gaze upon her husband.

"Here, take your crucifix," he added. "Swear to me before God that there is no one in there; I will believe you, I will never open that door."

Madame de Merret took the crucifix and said:

"I swear."

"Louder," said the husband, "and repeat 'I swear before God that there is no one in that closet'. "

She repeated the sentence calmly.

"That will do," said Monsieur de Merret, coldly.

After a moment of silence:

"I never saw this pretty toy before," he said, examining the ebony crucifix inlaid with silver, and most artistically chiseled.

"I found it at Duvivier's, who bought it of a Spanish monk when the prisoners passed through Vendôme last year."

"Ah!" said Monsieur de Merret, as he replaced the crucifix on the nail, and he rang. Rosalie did not keep him waiting. Monsieur de Merret went quickly to meet her, led her to the bay window that opened on to the garden and whispered to her:

"Listen! I know that Gorenflot wishes to marry you, poverty is the only drawback, and you told him that you would be his wife if he found the means to establish himself as a master mason. Well! go and fetch him, tell him to come here with his trowel and tools. Manage not to awaken any one in his house but himself; his fortune will be more than your desires. Above all, leave this room without babbling, otherwise—" He frowned. Rosalie went away, he recalled her.

"Here, take my latchkey," he said. "Jean!" then cried Monsieur de Merret, in tones of thunder in the corridor. Jean, who was at the same time his coachman and his confidential servant, left his game of cards and came.

"Go to bed, all of you," said his master, signing to him to approach; and the Count added, under his breath: "When they are all asleep— *asleep*, d'ye hear?—you will come down and tell me." Monsieur de Merret, who had not lost sight of his wife all the time he was giving his orders, returned quietly to her at the fireside and began to tell her of the game of billiards and the talk of the club. When Rosalie returned she found Monsieur and Madame de Merret conversing very amicably.

The Count had lately had all the ceilings of his reception rooms on the ground floor repaired. Plaster of Paris is difficult to obtain in Vendôme; the carriage raises its price. The Count had therefore bought a good deal, being well aware that he could find plenty of purchasers for whatever might remain over. This circumstance inspired him with the design he was about to execute.

"Sir, Gorenflot has arrived," said Rosalie in low tones.

"Show him in," replied the Count in loud tones.

Madame de Merret turned rather pale when she saw the mason.

"Gorenflot," said her husband, "go and fetch bricks from the coach-house, and bring sufficient to wall up the door of this closet; you will use the plaster I have over to coat the wall with." Then calling Rosalie and the workman aside:

"Listen, Gorenflot," he said in an undertone, "you will sleep here to-night. But to-morrow you will have a passport to a foreign country, to a town to which I will direct you. I shall give you six thousand francs for your journey. You will stay ten years in that town; if you do not like it, you may establish yourself in another, provided it be in the same country. You will pass through Paris, where you will await me. There I will insure you an additional six thousand francs by contract, which will be paid to you on your return, provided you have fulfilled the conditions of our bargain. This is the price for your absolute silence as to what you are about to do to-night. As to you, Rosalie, I will give you ten thousand francs on the day of your wedding, on condition of your marrying Gorenflot; but if you wish to marry, you must hold your tongues; or—no dowry."

"Rosalie," said Madame de Merret, "do my hair."

The husband walked calmly up and down, watching the door, the mason, and his wife, but without betraying any insulting doubts. Madame de Merret chose a moment when the workman was unloading bricks and her husband was at the other end of the room to say to Rosalie: "A thousand francs a year for you, my child, if you can tell Gorenflot to leave a chink at the bottom." Then out loud, she added coolly:

"Go and help him!"

Monsieur and Madame de Merret were silent all the time that Gorenflot took to brick up the door. This silence, on the part of the husband, who did not choose to furnish his wife with a pretext for saying things of a double meaning, had its purpose; on the part of Madame de Merret it was either pride or prudence. When the wall was about half-way up, the sly workman took advantage of a moment when the Count's back was turned, to strike a blow with his trowel in one of the glass panes of the closet-door. This act informed Madame de Merret that Rosalie had spoken to Gorenflot.

All three then saw a man's face; it was dark and gloomy with black hair and eyes of flame. Before her husband turned, the poor woman had time to make a sign to the stranger that signified: Hope!

At four o'clock, toward dawn, for it was the month of September, the construction was finished. The mason was handed over to the care of Jean, and Monsieur de Merret went to bed in his wife's room.

On rising the following morning, he said carelessly:

"The deuce! I must go to the Mairie for the passport." He put his hat on his head, advanced three steps toward the door, altered his mind and took the crucifix.

His wife trembled for joy. "He is going to Duvivier," she thought. As soon as the Count had left, Madame de Merret rang for Rosalie; then in a terrible voice:

"The trowel, the trowel!" she cried, "and quick to work! I saw how Gorenflot did it; we shall have time to make a hole and to mend it again."

In the twinkling of an eye, Rosalie brought a sort of mattock to her mistress, who with unparalleled ardor set about demolishing the wall. She had already knocked out several bricks and was preparing to strike a more decisive blow when she perceived Monsieur de Merret behind her. She fainted.

"Lay Madame on her bed," said the Count coldly. He had foreseen what would happen in his absence and had set a trap for his wife; he had simply written to the mayor, and had sent for Duvivier. The jeweller arrived just as the room had been put in order.

"Duvivier," inquired the Count, "did you buy crucifixes of the Spaniards who passed through here?"

"No, sir."

"That will do, thank you," he said, looking at his wife like a tiger. "Jean," he added, "you will see that my meals are served in the Countess's room; she is ill, and I shall not leave her until she has recovered."

The cruel gentleman stayed with his wife for twenty days. In the beginning, when there were sounds in the walled closet, and Josephine attempted to implore his pity for the dying stranger, he replied, without permitting her to say a word:

"You have sworn on the cross that there is no one there."

PROSPER MÉRIMÉE

(1803–1870)

BORN in Paris in 1803, Mérimée spent the greater part of his life in the government service and in travelling. In later years he became a senator. His chief works are his stories and the novel *Carmen*. Mérimée was one of the earliest authors who were content to write for the purpose of giving æsthetic pleasure, and is considered, with Gautier, one of the chief exponents of the Art for Art's Sake theory. His stories are written with great deliberation and care. *Mateo Falcone* is a masterpiece of its kind.

The present version, anonymously translated, is reprinted by permission from *International Short Stories*, P. F. Collier's Sons, New York. Copyright, 1910.

MATEO FALCONE

ON leaving Porto-Vecchio from the northwest and directing his steps towards the interior of the island, the traveler will notice that the land rises rapidly, and after three hours' walking over tortuous paths obstructed by great masses of rock and sometimes cut by ravines, he will find himself on the border of a great mâquis. The mâquis is the domain of the Corsican shepherds and of those who are at variance with justice. It must be known that, in order to save himself the trouble of manuring his field, the Corsican husbandman sets fire to a piece of woodland. If the flames spread farther than is necessary, so much the worse! In any case he is certain of a good crop from the land fertilized by the ashes of the trees which grow upon it. He gathers only the heads of his grain, leaving the straw, which it would be unnecessary labor to cut. In the following spring the roots that have remained in the earth without being destroyed send up their tufts of sprouts, which in a few years reach a height of seven or eight feet. It is this kind of tangled thicket that is called a mâquis. They are made up of different kinds of trees and shrubs, so crowded and mingled together at the caprice of nature that only with an axe in hand can a man open a passage through them, and mâquis are frequently seen so thick and bushy that the wild sheep themselves cannot penetrate them.

If you have killed a man, go into the mâquis of Porto-Vecchio. With a good gun and plenty of powder and balls, you can live there in safety. Do not forget a brown cloak furnished with a hood, which will serve you for both cover and mattress. The shepherds will give you chestnuts, milk and cheese, and you will have nothing to fear from justice nor the relatives of the dead except when it is necessary for you to descend to the city to replenish your ammunition.

When I was in Corsica in 18—, Mateo Falcone had his house half a league from this mâquis. He was rich enough for that country, living in noble style—that is to say, doing nothing—on the income from his flocks, which the shepherds, who are a kind of nomads, lead to pasture here and there on the mountains. When I saw him, two years after the event that I am about to relate, he appeared to me to be about fifty years old or more. Picture to yourself a man, small but robust, with curly hair, black as jet, an aquiline nose, thin lips, large, restless eyes, and a complexion the color of tanned leather. His skill as a marksman was considered extraordinary even in his country, where good shots are so common. For example, Mateo would never fire at a sheep with buckshot; but at a hundred and twenty paces, he would drop it with a ball in the head or shoulder, as he chose. He used his arms as easily at night as during the day. I was told this feat of his skill, which will, perhaps, seem impossible to those who have not traveled in Corsica. A lighted candle was placed at eighty paces, behind a paper transparency about the size of a plate. He would take aim, then the candle would be extinguished, and, at the end of a moment, in the most complete darkness, he would fire and hit the paper three times out of four.

With such a transcendent accomplishment, Mateo Falcone had acquired a great reputation. He was said to be as good a friend as he was a dangerous enemy; accommodating and charitable, he lived at peace with all the world in the district of Porto-Vecchio. But it is said of him that in Corte, where he had married his wife, he had disembarrassed himself very vigorously of a rival who was considered as redoubt-

able in war as in love; at least, a certain gun-shot which surprised this
rival as he was shaving before a little mirror hung in his window was
attributed to Mateo. The affair was smoothed over and Mateo was
married. His wife Giuseppa had given him at first three daughters
(which infuriated him), and finally a son, whom he named Fortunato,
and who became the hope of his family, the inheritor of the name. The
daughters were well married: their father could count at need on the
poniards and carbines of his sons-in-law. The son was only ten years
old, but he already gave promise of fine attributes.

On a certain day in autumn, Mateo set out at an early hour with his
wife to visit one of his flocks in a clearing of the mâquis. The little
Fortunato wanted to go with them, but the clearing was too far away;
moreover, it was necessary someone should stay to watch the house;
therefore the father refused: it will be seen whether or not he had
reason to repent.

He had been gone some hours, and the little Fortunato was tranquilly stretched out in the sun, looking at the blue mountains, and
thinking that the next Sunday he was going to dine in the city with his
uncle, the Caporal, when he was suddenly interrupted in his meditations by the firing of a musket. He got up and turned to that side of
the plain whence the noise came. Other shots followed, fired at irregular intervals, and each time nearer; at last, in the path which led
from the plain to Mateo's house, appeared a man wearing the pointed
hat of the mountaineers, bearded, covered with rags, and dragging
himself along with difficulty by the support of his gun. He had just
received a wound in his thigh.

This man was an outlaw, who, having gone to the town by night to
buy powder, had fallen on the way into an ambuscade of Corsican
light-infantry. After a vigorous defense he was fortunate in making his
retreat, closely followed and firing from rock to rock. But he was only
a little in advance of the soldiers, and his wound prevented him from
gaining the mâquis before being overtaken.

He approached Fortunato and said: "You are the son of Mateo Falcone?"—"Yes."

"I am Gianetto Saupiero. I am followed by the yellow-collars. Hide
me, for I can go no farther."

"And what will my father say if I hide you without his permission?"

"He will say that you have done well."

"How do you know?"

"Hide me quickly; they are coming."

"Wait till my father gets back."

"How can I wait? Malediction! They will be here in five minutes
Come, hide me, or I will kill you."

Fortunato answered him with the utmost coolness:

"Your gun is empty, and there are no more cartridges in your belt."

"I have my stiletto."

"But can you run as fast as I can?"

He gave a leap and put himself out of reach.

"You are not the son of Mateo Falcone! Will you then let me be captured before your house?"

The child appeared moved.

"What will you give me if I hide you?" said he, coming nearer.

The outlaw felt in a leather pocket that hung from his belt, and took out a five-franc piece, which he had doubtless saved to buy ammunition with. Fortunato smiled at the sight of the silver piece; he snatched it, and said to Gianetto:

"Fear nothing."

Immediately he made a great hole in a pile of hay that was near the house. Gianetto crouched down in it and the child covered him in such a way that he could breathe without it being possible to suspect that the hay concealed a man. He bethought himself further, and, with the subtlety of a tolerably ingenious savage, placed a cat and her kittens on the pile, that it might not appear to have been recently disturbed. Then, noticing the traces of blood on the path near the house, he covered them carefully with dust, and, that done, he again stretched himself out in the sun with the greatest tranquillity.

A few moments afterwards, six men in brown uniforms with yellow collars, and commanded by an Adjutant, were before Mateo's door. This Adjutant was a distant relative of Falcone's. (In Corsica the degrees of relationship are followed much further than elsewhere.) His name was Tiodoro Gamba; he was an active man, much dreaded by the outlaws, several of whom he had already entrapped.

"Good day, little cousin," said he, approaching Fortunato; "how tall you have grown. Have you seen a man go past here just now?"

"Oh! I am not yet so tall as you, my cousin," replied the child with a simple air.

"You soon will be. But haven't you seen a man go by here, tell me?"

"If I have seen a man go by?"

"Yes, a man with a pointed hat of black velvet, and a vest embroidered with red and yellow."

"A man with a pointed hat, and a vest embroidered with red and yellow?"

"Yes, answer quickly, and don't repeat my questions!"

"This morning the curé passed before our door on his horse, Piero. He asked me how papa was, and I answered him—"

"Ah, you little scoundrel, you are playing sly! Tell me quickly which way Gianetto went? We are looking for him, and I am sure he took this path."

"Who knows?"

"Who knows? It is I know that you have seen him."

"Can any one see who passes when they are asleep?"

"You were not asleep, rascal; the shooting woke you up."

"Then you believe, cousin, that your guns make so much noise? My father's carbine has the advantage of them."

"The devil take you, you cursed little scapegrace! I am certain that you have seen Gianetto. Perhaps, even, you have hidden him. Come, comrades, go into the house and see if our man is there. He could only go on one foot, and the knave has too much good sense to try to reach the mâquis limping like that. Moreover, the bloody tracks stop here."

"And what will papa say?" asked Fortunato with a sneer. "What will he say if he knows that his house has been entered while he was away?"

"You rascal," said the Adjutant, taking him by the ear, "do you know that it only remains for me to make you change your tone? Perhaps you will speak differently after I have given you twenty blows with the flat of my sword."

Fortunato continued to sneer.

"My father is Mateo Falcone," said he with emphasis.

"You little scamp, you know very well that I can carry you off to Corte or to Bastia. I will make you lie in a dungeon, on straw, with your feet in shackles, and I will have you guillotined if you don't tell me where Gianetto is."

The child burst out laughing at this ridiculous menace. He repeated: "My father is Mateo Falcone."

"Adjutant," said one of the soldiers in a low voice, "let us have no quarrels with Mateo."

Gamba appeared evidently embarrassed. He spoke in an undertone with the soldiers who had already visited the house. This was not a very long operation, for the cabin of a Corsican consists only of a single square room, furnished with a table, some benches, chests, housekeeping utensils and those of the chase. In the meantime, little Fortunato petted his cat and seemed to take a wicked enjoyment in the confusion of the soldiers and of his cousin.

One of the men approached the pile of hay. He saw the cat, and gave the pile a careless thrust with his bayonet, shrugging his shoulders as if he felt that his precaution was ridiculous. Nothing moved; the boy's face betrayed not the slightest emotion.

The Adjutant and his troop were cursing their luck. Already they were looking in the direction of the plain, as if disposed to return by the way they had come, when their chief, convinced that menaces would produce no impression of Falcone's son, determined to make a last effort, and try the effect of caresses and presents.

"My little cousin," said he, "you are a very wide-awake little fellow. You will get along. But you are playing a naughty game with me; and if I wasn't afraid of making trouble for my cousin, Mateo, the devil take me, but I would carry you off with me."

"Bah!"

"But when my cousin comes back I shall tell him about this, and he will whip you till the blood comes for having told such lies."

"You don't say so!"

"You will see. But hold on!—be a good boy and I will give you something."

"Cousin, let me give you some advice: if you wait much longer Gianetto will be in the mâquis and it will take a smarter man than you to follow him."

The Adjutant took from his pocket a silver watch worth about ten crowns, and noticing that Fortunato's eyes sparkled at the sight of it, said, holding the watch by the end of its steel chain:

"Rascal! you would like to have such a watch as that hung around your neck, wouldn't you, and to walk in the streets of Porto-Vecchio proud as a peacock? People would ask you what time it was, and you would say: 'Look at my watch.'"

"When I am grown up, my uncle, the Caporal, will give me a watch."

"Yes; but your uncle's little boy has one already; not so fine as this either. But then, he is younger than you."

The child sighed.

"Well! Would you like this watch, little cousin?"

Fortunato, casting sidelong glances at the watch, resembled a cat that has been given a whole chicken. It feels that it is being made sport of, and does not dare to use its claws; from time to time it turns its eyes away so as not to be tempted, licking its jaws all the while, and has the appearance of saying to its master, "How cruel your joke is!"

However, the Adjutant seemed in earnest in offering his watch. Fortunato did not reach out his hand for it, but said with a bitter smile:

"Why do you make fun of me?"

"Good God! I am not making fun of you. Only tell me where Gianetto is and the watch is yours."

Fortunato smiled incredulously, and fixing his black eyes on those of the Adjutant tried to read there the faith he ought to have had in his words.

"May I lose my epaulettes," cried the Adjutant, "if I do not give you the watch on this condition. These comrades are witnesses; I cannot deny it."

While speaking he gradually held the watch nearer till it almost touched the child's pale face, which plainly showed the struggle that was going on in his soul between covetousness and respect for hospitality. His breast swelled with emotion; he seemed about to suffocate. Meanwhile the watch was slowly swaying and turning, sometimes brushing against his cheek. Finally, his right hand was gradually stretched toward it; the ends of his fingers touched it; then its whole weight was in his hand, the Adjutant still keeping hold of the chain. The face was light blue; the cases newly burnished. In the sunlight it seemed to be all on fire. The temptation was too great. Fortunato raised his left hand and pointed over his shoulder with his thumb at the hay against which he was reclining. The Adjutant understood him at once. He dropped the end of the chain and Fortunato felt himself the sole possessor of the watch. He sprang up with the agility of a deer and stood ten feet from the pile, which the soldiers began at once to overturn.

There was a movement in the hay, and a bloody man with a poniard in his hand appeared. He tried to rise to his feet, but his stiffened leg would not permit it and he fell. The Adjutant at once grappled with him and took away his stiletto. He was immediately secured, notwithstanding his resistance.

Gianetto, lying on the earth and bound like a fagot, turned his head towards Fortunato, who had approached.

"Son of—!" said he, with more contempt than anger.

The child threw him the silver piece which he had received, feeling that he no longer deserved it; but the outlaw paid no attention to the movement, and with great coolness said to the Adjutant:

"My dear Gamba, I cannot walk; you will be obliged to carry me to the city."

"Just now you could run faster than a buck," answered the cruel captor; "but be at rest. I am so pleased to have you that I would carry you a league on my back without fatigue. Besides, comrade, we are going to make a litter for you with your cloak and some branches, and at the Crespoli farm we shall find horses."

"Good," said the prisoner. "You will also put a little straw on your litter that I may be more comfortable."

While some of the soldiers were occupied in making a kind of stretcher out of some chestnut boughs and the rest were dressing Gianetto's wound, Mateo Falcone and his wife suddenly appeared at a turn in the path that led to the mâquis. The woman was staggering under the weight of an enormous sack of chestnuts, while her husband was sauntering along, carrying one gun in his hands, while another was slung across his shoulders, for it is unworthy of a man to carry other burdens than his arms.

At the sight of the soldiers Mateo's first thought was that they had come to arrest him. But why this thought? Had he then some quarrels with justice? No. Ne enjoyed a good reputation. He was said to have a particularly good name, but he was a Corsican and a highlander, and there are few Corsican highlanders who, in scrutinizing their memory, cannot find some peccadillo, such as a gun-shot, dagger-thrust, or similar trifles. Mateo more than others had a clear conscience; for more than ten years he had not pointed his carbine at a man, but he was always prudent, and put himself into a position to make a good defense if necessary. "Wife," said he to Giuseppa, "put down the sack and hold yourself ready."

She obeyed at once. He gave her the gun that was slung across his shoulders, which would have bothered him, and, cocking the one he held in his hands, advanced slowly towards the house, walking among the trees that bordered the road, ready at the least hostile demonstration, to hide behind the largest, whence he could fire from under cover. His wife followed closely behind, holding his reserve weapon and his cartridge-box. The duty of a good housekeeper, in case of a fight, is to load her husband's carbines.

On the other side the Adjutant was greatly troubled to see Mateo advance in this manner, with cautious steps, his carbine raised, and his finger on the trigger.

"If by chance," thought he, "Mateo should be related to Gianetto, or if he should be his friend and wish to defend him, the contents of his two guns would arrive amongst us a certainly as as letter in the post; and if he should see me, notwithstanding the relationship!"

In this perplexity he took a bold step. It was to advance alone towards Mateo and tell him of the affair while accosting him as an old acquaintance, but the short space that separated him from Mateo seemed terribly long.

"Hello! old comrade," cried he. "How do you do, my good fellow? It is I, Gamba, your cousin."

Without answering a word, Mateo stopped, and in proportion as the other spoke, slowly raised the muzzle of his gun so that it was pointing upward when the Adjutant joined him.

"Good-day, brother," said the Adjutant, holding out his hand. "It is a long time since I have seen you."

"Good-day, brother."

"I stopped while passing, to say good-day to you and to cousin Pepa here. We have had a long journey to-day, but have no reason to complain, for we have captured a famous prize. We have just seized Gianetto Saupiero."

"God be praised!" cried Giuseppa. "He stole a milch goat from us last week."

These words reassured Gamba.

"Poor devil!" said Mateo. "He was hungry."

"The villain fought like a lion," continued the Adjutant, a little mortified. "He killed one of my soldiers, and not content with that, broke Caporal Chardon's arm; but that matters little, he is only a Frenchman. Then, too, he was so well hidden that the devil couldn't have found him. Without my little cousin, Fortunato, I should never have discovered him."

"Fortunato!" cried Mateo.

"Fortunato!" repeated Giuseppa.

"Yes, Gianetto was hidden under the hay-pile yonder, but my little cousin showed me the trick. I shall tell his uncle, the Caporal, that he may send him a fine present for his trouble. Both his name and yours will be in the report that I shall send to the Attorney-general."

"Malediction!" said Mateo in a low voice.

They had rejoined the detachment. Gianetto was already lying on the litter ready to set out. When he saw Mateo and Gamba in company he smiled a strange smile, then, turning his head towards the door of the house, he spat on the sill, saying:

"House of a traitor."

Only a man determined to die would dare pronounce the word traitor to Falcone. A good blow with the stiletto, which there would be no need of repeating, would have immediately paid the insult. However, Mateo made no other movement than to place his hand on his forehead like a man who is dazed.

Fortunato had gone into the house when his father arrived, but now he reappeared with a bowl of milk which he handed with downcast eyes to Gianetto.

"Get away from me!" cried the outlaw, in a loud voice. Then, turning to one of the soldiers, he said:

"Comrade, give me a drink."

The soldier placed his gourd in his hands, and the prisoner drank the water handed to him by a man with whom he had just exchanged bullets. He then asked them to tie his hands across his breast instead of behind his back.

"I like," said he, "to lie at my ease."

They hastened to satisfy him; then the Adjutant gave the signal to start, said adieu to Mateo, who did not respond, and descended with rapid steps towards the plain.

Nearly ten minutes elapsed before Mateo spoke. The child looked with restless eyes, now at his mother, now at his father, who was leaning on his gun and gazing at him with an expression of concentrated rage.

"You begin well," said Mateo at last with a calm voice, but frightful to one who knew the man.

"Oh, father!" cried the boy, bursting into tears, and making a forward movement as if to throw himself on his knees. But Mateo cried, "Away from me!"

The little fellow stopped and sobbed, immovable, a few feet from his father.

Giuseppa drew near. She had just discovered the watch-chain, the end of which was hanging out of Fortunato's jacket.

"Who gave you that watch?" demanded she in a severe tone.

"My cousin, the Adjutant."

Falcone seized the watch and smashed it in a thousand pieces against a rock.

"Wife," said he, "is this my child?"

Giuseppa's cheeks turned a brick-red.

"What are you saying, Mateo? Do you know to whom you speak?"

"Very well, this child is the first of his race to commit treason."

Fortunato's sobs and gasps redoubled as Falcone kept his lynx-eyes upon him. Then he struck the earth with his gun-stock, shouldered the weapon, and turned in the direction of the mâquis, calling to Fortunato to follow. The boy obeyed. Giusepppa hastened after Mateo and seized his arm.

"He is your son," said she with a trembling voice, fastening her black eyes on those of her husband to read what was going on in his heart.

"Leave me alone," said Mateo. "I am his father."

Giuseppa embraced her son, and bursting into tears entered the house. She threw herself on her knees before an image of the Virgin and prayed ardently. In the meanwhile Falcone walked some two hundred paces along the path and only stopped when he reached a little ravine which he descended. He tried the earth with the butt-end of his carbine, and found if soft and easy to dig. The place seemed to be convenient for his design.

"Fortunato, go close to that big rock there."

The child did as he was commanded, then he kneeled.

"Say your prayers."

"Oh, father, father, do not kill me!"

"Say your prayers!" repeated Mateo in a terrible voice.

The boy, stammering and sobbing, recited the Pater and the Credo. At the end of each prayer the father loudly answered, "Amen!"

"Are those all the prayers you know?"

"Oh! father, I know the Ave Maria and the litany that my aunt taught me."

"It is very long, but no matter."

The child finished the litany in a scarcely audible tone.

"Are you finished?"

"Oh! my father, have mercy! Pardon me! I will never do so again. I will beg my cousin, the Caporal, to pardon Gianetto."

He was still speaking. Mateo raised his gun, and, taking aim, said:

"May God pardon you!"

The boy made a desperate effort to rise and grasp his father's knees, but there was not time. Mateo fired and Fortunato fell dead.

Without casting a glance on the body, Mateo returned to the house for a spade with which to bury his son. He had gone but a few steps when he met Giuseppa, who, alarmed by the shot, was hastening hither.

"What have you done?" cried she.

"Justice."

"Where is he?"

"In the ravine. I am going to bury him. He died a Christian. I shall have a mass said for him. Have my son-in-law, Tiodoro Bianchi, sent for to come and live with us."

THÉOPHILE GAUTIER

(1811–1872)

THÉOPHILE GAUTIER was born at Tarbes in the south of France in 1811. He came to Paris as an infant. In 1830 he published his first volume of poems. He was, with Victor Hugo and others, one of the prominent initiators of the so-called Romantic Movement in French literature. His finest novel, *Mlle. de Maupin,* appeared in 1835. For many years he wrote art, dramatic, and literary criticisms, poems, stories, ballets and pantomimes, and a number of charming impressionistic travel books. Gautier is one of the most accomplished poets of the external and visible world: his style is vivid, jewelled, and sensuous. His short stories are exotic, highly polished literary exercises, though some of them, like *The Mummy's Foot,* are intrinsically fascinating for their plot and atmosphere.

The present version, translated by Lafcadio Hearn, is reprinted, by permission of the publisher, from the volume, *One of Cleopatra's Nights,* published by Brentano's.

THE MUMMY'S FOOT

I HAD entered, in an idle mood, the shop of one of those curiosity-venders, who are called *marchands de bric-à-brac* in that Parisian *argot* which is so perfectly unintelligible elsewhere in France.

You have doubtless glanced occasionally through the windows of some of these shops, which have become so numerous now that it is fashionable to buy antiquated furniture, and that every petty stock-broker thinks he must have his *chambre au moyen âge.*

There is one thing there which clings alike to the shop of the dealer in old iron, the wareroom of the tapestry-maker, the laboratory of the chemist, and the studio of the painter:—in all those gloomy dens where a furtive daylight filters in through the window-shutters, the most manifestly ancient thing is dust;—the cobwebs are more authentic than the guimp laces; and the old pear-tree furniture on exhibition is actually younger than the mahogany which arrived but yesterday from America.

The warehouse of my *bric-à-brac* dealer was a veritable Capharnaum; all ages and all nations seemed to have made their rendezvous there; an Etruscan lamp of red clay stood upon a Boule cabinet, with ebony panels, brightly striped by lines of inlaid brass; a duchess of the court of Louis XV nonchalantly extended her fawn-like feet under a massive table of the time of Louis XIII with heavy spiral supports of oak, and carven designs of chimeras and foliage intermingled.

Upon the denticulated shelves of several sideboards glittered immense Japanese dishes with red and blue designs relieved by gilded hatching; side by side with enameled works by Bernard Palissy, representing serpents, frogs, and lizards in relief.

From disemboweled cabinets escaped cascades of silver-lustrous Chinese silks and waves of tinsel, which an oblique sunbeam shot through with luminous beads; while portraits of every era, in frames more or less tarnished, smiled through their yellow varnish.

The striped breastplate of a damascened suit of Milanese armor glittered in one corner; Loves and Nymphs of porcelain; Chinese Grotesques, vases of *céladon* and crackle-ware; Saxon and old Sèvres cups encumbered the shelves and nooks of the apartment.

The dealer followed me closely through the tortuous way contrived between the piles of furniture; warding off with his hands the hazardous sweep of my coat-skirts; watching my elbows with the uneasy attention of an antiquarian and a usurer.

It was a singular face that of the merchant:— an immense skull, polished like a knee, and surrounded by a thin aureole of white hair, which brought out the clear salmon tint of his complexion all the more strikingly, lent him a false aspect of patriarchal *bonhomie*, counteracted, however, by the scintillation of two little yellow eyes which trembled in their orbits like two louis-d'or upon quicksilver. The curve of his nose presented an aquiline silhouette, which suggested the Oriental or Jewish type. His hands—thin, slender, full of nerves which projected like strings upon the finger-board of a violin, and armed with claws like those on the terminations of bats' wings—shook with senile trembling; but those convulsively agitated hands became firmer than steel pincers or lobsters' claws when they lifted any precious article— an onyx cup, a Venetian glass, or a dish of Bohemian crystal. This strange old man had an aspect so thoroughly rabbinical and cabalistic that he would have been burnt on the mere testimony of his face three centuries ago.

"Will you not buy something from me to-day, sir? Here is a Malay kreese with a blade undulating like flame: look at those grooves contrived for the blood to run along, those teeth set backwards so as to tear out the entrails in withdrawing the weapon—it is a fine character of ferocious arm, and will look well in your collection: this two-handed sword is very beautiful—it is the work of Josepe de la Hera; and this *colichemarde*, with its fenestrated guard—what a superb specimen of handicraft!"

"No; I have quite enough weapons and instruments of carnage;—I want a small figure, something which will suit me as a paper-weight; for I cannot endure those trumpery bronzes which the stationers sell, and which may be found on everybody's desk."

The old gnome foraged among his ancient wares, and finally arranged before me some antique bronzes—so-called, at least; fragments of malachite; little Hindoo or Chinese idols—a kind of poussah toys in jadestone, representing the incarnations of Brahma or Vishnoo, and wonderfully appropriate to the very undivine office of holding papers and letters in place.

I was hesitating between a porcelain dragon, all constellated with warts—its mouth formidable with bristling tusks and ranges of teeth—and an abominable little Mexican fetish, representing the god Zitzili-putzili *au naturel*, when I caught sight of a charming foot, which I at first took for a fragment of some antique Venus.

It had those beautiful ruddy and tawny tints that lend to Florentine bronze that warm living look so much preferable to the gray-green aspect of common bronzes, which might easily be mistaken for statues in a state of putrefaction: satiny gleams played over its rounded forms, doubtless polished by the amorous kisses of twenty centuries; for it seemed a Corinthian bronze, a work of the best era of art—perhaps molded by Lysippus himself.

"That foot will be my choice," I said to the merchant, who regarded me with an ironical and saturnine air, and held out the object desired that I might examine it more fully.

I was surprised at its lightness; it was not a foot of metal, but in sooth a foot of flesh—an embalmed foot—a mummy's foot: on examining it still more closely the very grain of the skin, and the almost imperceptible lines impressed upon it by the texture of the bandages, became perceptible. The toes were slender and delicate, and terminated by perfectly formed nails, pure and transparent as agates; the great toe, slightly separated from the rest, afforded a happy contrast, in the antique style, to the position of the other toes, and lent it an aerial lightness—the grace of a bird's foot;—the sole, scarcely streaked by a few almost imperceptible cross lines, afforded evidence that it had never touched the bare ground, and had only come in contact with the finest matting of Nile rushes, and the softest carpets of panther skin.

"Ha, ha!—you want the foot of the Princess Hermonthis,"—exclaimed the merchant, with a strange giggle, fixing his owlish eyes upon me—"ha, ha, ha!—for a paper-weight!—an original idea!—artistic idea! Old Pharaoh would certainly have been surprised had some one told him that the foot of his adored daughter would be used for a paper-weight after he had had a mountain of granite hollowed out as a receptacle for the triple coffin, painted and gilded—covered with hieroglyphics and beautiful paintings of the Judgment of Souls,"—continued the queer little merchant, half audibly, as though talking to himself!

"How much will you charge me for this mummy fragment?"

"Ah, the highest price I can get; for it is a superb piece: if I had the match of it you could not have it for less than five hundred francs; —the daughter of a Pharaoh! nothing is more rare."

"Assuredly that is not a common article; but, still, how much do you want? In the first place let me warn you that all my wealth consists of just five louis: I can buy anything that costs five louis, but nothing dearer;—you might search my vest pockets and most secret drawers without even finding one poor—five-franc piece more."

"Five louis for the foot of the Princess Hermonthis! that is very little, very little indeed; 'tis an authentic foot," muttered the merchant, shaking his head, and imparting a peculiar rotary motion to his eyes. "Well, take it, and I will give you the bandages into the bargain," he added, wrapping the foot in an ancient damask rag—"very fine! real damask—Indian damask which has never been redyed; it is strong, and yet it is soft," he mumbled, stroking the frayed tissue with his fingers, through the trade-acquired habit which moved him to praise even an object of so little value that he himself deemed it only worth the giving away.

He poured the gold coins into a sort of mediæval alms-purse hanging at his belt, repeating:

"The foot of the Princess Hermonthis, to be used for a paper-weight!"

Then turning his phosphorescent eyes upon me, he exclaimed in a voice strident as the crying of a cat which has swallowed a fish-bone:

"Old Pharaoh will not be well pleased; he loved his daughter—the dear man!"

"You speak as if you were a contemporary of his: you are old enough, goodness knows! but you do not date back to the Pyramids of Egypt," I answered, laughingly, from the threshold.

I went home, delighted with my acquisition.

With the idea of putting it to profitable use as soon as possible, I placed the foot of the divine Princess Hermonthis upon a heap of papers scribbled over with verses, in themselves an undecipherable mosaic work of erasures; articles freshly begun; letters forgotten, and posted in the table drawer instead of the letter-box—an error to which absent-minded people are peculiarly liable. The effect was charming, *bizarre*, and romantic.

Well satisfied with this embellishment, I went out with the gravity and price becoming one who feels that he has the ineffable advantage over all the passers-by whom he elbows, of possessing a piece of the Princess Hermonthis, daughter of Pharaoh.

I looked upon all who did not possess, like myself, a paper-weight so authentically Egyptian, as very ridiculous people; and it seemed to me that the proper occupation of every sensible man should consist in the mere fact of having a mummy's foot upon his desk.

Happily I met some friends, whose presence distracted me in my infatuation with this new acquisition: I went to dinner with them; for I could not very well have dined with myself.

When I came back that evening, with my brain slightly confused by a few glasses of wine, a vague whiff of Oriental perfume delicately titillated my olfactory nerves: the heat of the room had warmed the natron, bitumen, and myrrh in which the *paraschistes*, who cut open the bodies of the dead, had bathed the corpse of the princess;—it was a perfume at once sweet and penetrating—a perfume that four thousand years had not been able to dissipate.

The Dream of Egypt was Eternity: her odors have the solidity of granite, and endure as long.

I soon drank deeply from the black cup of sleep: for a few hours all remained opaque to me; Oblivion and Nothingness inundated me with their somber waves.

Yet light gradually dawned upon the darkness of my mind; dreams commenced to touch me softly in their silent flight.

The eyes of my soul were opened; and I beheld my chamber as it actually was; I might have believed myself awake, but for a vague consciousness which assured me that I slept, and that something fantastic was about to take place.

The odor of the myrrh had augmented in intensity; and I felt a slight headache, which I very naturally attributed to several glasses of champagne that we had drunk to the unknown gods and our future fortunes.

I peered through my room with a feeling of expectation which I saw nothing to justify: every article of furniture was in its proper place; the lamp, softly shaded by its globe of ground crystal, burned upon its bracket; the water-color sketches shone under their Bohemian glass; the curtains hung down languidly; everything wore an aspect of tranquil slumber.

After a few moments, however, all this calm interior appeared to become disturbed; the woodwork cracked stealthily; the ash-covered log suddenly emitted a jet of blue flame; and the disks of the pateras seemed like great metallic eyes, watching, like myself, for the things which were about to happen.

My eyes accidentally fell upon the desk where I had placed the foot of the Princess Hermonthis.

Instead of remaining quiet—as behooved a foot which had been embalmed for four thousand years—it commenced to act in a nervous manner; contracted itself, and leaped over the papers like a startled frog;—one would have imagined that it had suddenly been brought into contact with a galvanic battery: I could distinctly hear the dry sound made by its little heel, hard as the hoof of a gazelle.

I became rather discontented with my acquisition, inasmuch as I wished my paper-weights to be of a sedentary disposition, and thought it very unnatural that feet should walk about without legs; and I commenced to experience a feeling closely akin to fear.

Suddenly I saw the folds of my bed-curtain stir; and heard a bumping sound, like that caused by some person hopping on one foot across the floor. I must confess I became alternately hot and cold; that I felt a strange wind chill my back; and that my suddenly rising hair caused my nightcap to execute a leap of several yards.

The bed-curtains opened and I beheld the strangest figure imaginable before me.

It was a young girl of a very deep coffee-brown complexion, like the bayadere Amani, and possessing the purest Egyptian type of perfect beauty: her eyes were almond-shaped and oblique, with eyebrows so black that they seemed blue; her nose was exquisitely chiseled, almost Greek in its delicacy of outline; and she might indeed have been taken for a Corinthian statue of bronze, but for the prominence of her cheekbones and the slightly African fulness of her lips, which compelled one to recognize her as belonging beyond all doubt to the hieroglyphic race which dwelt upon the banks of the Nile.

Her arms, slender and spindle-shaped, like those of very young girls, were encircled by a peculiar kind of metal bands and bracelets of glass beads; her hair was all twisted into little cords; and she wore upon her bosom a little idol-figure of green paste, bearing a whip with seven lashes, which proved it to be an image of Isis: her brow was adorned with a shining plate of gold; and a few traces of paint relieved the coppery tint of her cheeks.

As for her costume, it was very odd indeed.

Fancy a *pagne* or skirt all formed of little strips of material bedizened with red and black hieroglyphics, stiffened with bitumen, and apparrently belonging to a freshly unbandaged mummy.

In one of those sudden flights of thought so common in dreams I heard the hoarse falsetto of the *bric-à-brac* dealer, repeating like a monotonous refrain the phrase he had uttered in his shop with so enigmatical an intonation:

"Old Pharaoh will not be well pleased: he loved his daughter, the dear man!"

One strange circumstance, which was not at all calculated to restore my equanimity, was that the apparition had but one foot; the other was broken off at the ankle!

She approached the table where the foot was starting and fidgeting about more than ever, and there supported herself upon the edge of the desk. I saw her eyes fill with pearly-gleaming tears.

Although she had not as yet spoken, I fully comprehended the thoughts which agitated her: she looked at her foot—it was indeed her own—with an exquisitely graceful expression of coquettish sadness; but the foot leaped and ran hither and thither, as though impelled on steel springs.

Twice or thrice she extended her hand to seize it, but could not succeed.

Then commenced between the Princess Hermonthis and her foot—which appeared to be endowed with a special life of its own—a very fantastic dialogue in a most ancient Coptic tongue, such as might have been spoken thirty centuries ago in the syrinxes of the land of Ser: luckily, I understood Coptic perfectly well that night.

The Princess Hermonthis cried, in a voice sweet and vibrant as the tones of a crystal bell:

"Well, my dear little foot, you always flee from me; yet I always took good care of you. I bathed you with perfumed water in a bowl of alabaster; I smoothed your heel with pumice-stone mixed with palm oil; your nails were cut with golden scissors and polished with a hippopotamus tooth; I was careful to select *tatbebs* for you, painted and embroidered and turned up at the toes, which were the envy of all the young girls in Egypt: you wore on your great toe rings bearing the device of the sacred Scarabæus; and you supported one of the lightest bodies that a lazy foot could sustain."

The foot replied, in a pouting and chagrined tone:

"You know well that I do not belong to myself any longer;—I have been bought and paid for; the old merchant knew what he was about; he bore you a grudge for having refused to espouse him;—this is an ill turn which he has done you. The Arab who violated your royal coffin in the subterranean pit of the necropolis of Thebes was sent thither by him: he desired to prevent you from being present at the reunion of the shadowy nations in the cities below. Have you five pieces of gold for my ransom?"

"Alas, no!—my jewels, my rings, my purses of gold and silver, they were all stolen from me," answered the Princess Hermonthis, with a sob.

"Princess," I then exclaimed, "I never retained anybody's foot unjustly;—even though you have not got the five louis which it cost me, I present it to you gladly: I should feel unutterably wretched to think that I were the cause of so amiable a person as the Princess Hermonthis being lame."

I delivered this discourse in a royally gallant, troubadour tone, which must have astonished the beautiful Egyptian girl.

She turned a look of deepest gratitude upon me; and her eyes shone with bluish gleams of light.

She took her foot—which surrendered itself willingly this time—like a woman about to put on her little shoe, and adjusted it to her leg with much skill.

This operation over, she took a few steps about the room, as though to assure herself that she was really no longer lame.

"Ah, how pleased my father will be!—he who was so unhappy because of my mutilation, and who from the moment of my birth set a whole nation at work to hollow me out a tomb so deep that he might preserve me intact until that last day, when souls must be weighed in the balance of Amenthi! Come with me to my father;—he will receive you kindly; for you have given me back my foot."

I thought this proposition natural enough. I arrayed myself in a dressing-gown of large-flowered pattern, which lent me a very Pharaonic aspect; hurriedly put on a pair of Turkish slippers, and informed the Princess Hermonthis that I was ready to follow her.

Before starting, Hermonthis took from her neck the little idol of green paste, and laid it on the scattered sheets of paper which covered the table.

"It is only fair," she observed smilingly, "that I should replace your paper-weight."

She gave me her hand, which felt soft and cold, like the skin of a serpent; and we departed.

We passed for some time with the velocity of an arrow through a fluid and grayish expanse, in which half-formed silhouettes flitted swiftly by us, to right and left.

For an instant we saw only sky and sea.

A few moments later obelisks commenced to tower in the distance: pylons and vast flights of steps guarded by sphinxes became clearly outlined against the horizon.

We had reached our destination.

The princess conducted me to the mountain of rose-colored granite, in the face of which appeared an opening so narrow and low that it would have been difficult to distinguish it from the fissures in the rock, had not its location been marked by two stelæ wrought with sculptures.

Hermonthis kindled a torch, and led the way before me.

We traversed corridors hewn through the living rock: their walls, covered with hieroglyphics and paintings of allegorical processions, might well have occupied thousands of arms for thousands of years in their formation;—these corridors, of interminable length, opened into square chambers, in the midst of which pits had been contrived, through which we descended by cramp-irons or spiral stairways;— these pits again conducted us into other chambers, opening into other corridors, likewise decorated with painted sparrow-hawks, serpents coiled in circles, the symbols of the *tau* and *pedum*—prodigious works of art which no living eye can ever examine—interminable legends of granite which only the dead have time to read through all eternity.

At last we found ourselves in a hall so vast, so enormous, so immeasurable, that the eye could not reach its limits; files of monstrous columns stretched far out of sight on every side, between which twinkled livid stars of yellowish flame;—points of light which revealed further depths incalculable in the darkness beyond.

The Princess Hermonthis still held my hand, and graciously saluted the mummies of her acquaintance.

My eyes became accustomed to the dim twilight, and objects became discernible.

I beheld the kings of the subterranean races seated upon thrones— grand old men, though dry, withered, wrinkled like parchment, and blackened with naphtha and bitumen—all wearing *pshents* of gold, and breastplaces and gorgets glittering with precious stones; their eyes immovably fixed like the eyes of sphinxes, and their long beards whitened by the snow of centuries. Behind them stood their peoples, in the stiff and constrained posture enjoined by Egyptian art, all eternally preserving the attitude prescribed by the hieratic code. Behind these nations, the cats, ibises, and crocodiles contemporary with them—rendered monstrous of aspect by their swathing bands—mewed, flapped their wings, or extended their jaws in a saurian giggle.

All the Pharaohs were there—Cheops, Chephrenes, Psammetichus, Sesostris, Amenotaph—all the dark rulers of the pyramids and syrinxes—on yet higher thrones sat Chronos and Xixouthros—who was contemporary with the deluge; and Tubal Cain, who reigned before it.

The beard of King Xixouthros had grown seven times around the granite table, upon which he leaned, lost in deep reverie—and buried in dreams.

Further back, through a dusty cloud, I beheld dimly the seventy-two pre-Adamite Kings, with their seventy-two peoples—forever passed away.

After permitting me to gaze upon this bewildering spectacle a few moments, the Princess Hermonthis presented me to her father Pharaoh, who favored me with a most gracious nod.

"I have found my foot again!—I have found my foot!" cried the Princess, clapping her little hands together with every sign of frantic joy: "it was this gentleman who restored it to me."

The races of Kemi, the races of Nahasi—all the black, bronzed, and copper-colored nations repeated in chorus:

"The Princess Hermonthis has found her foot again!"

Even Xixouthros himself was visibly affected.

He raised his heavy eyelids, stroked his mustache with his fingers, and turned upon me a glance weighty with centuries.

"By Oms, the dog of Hell, and Tmei, daughter of the Sun and of Truth! this is a brave and worthy lad!" exclaimed Pharaoh, pointing to me with his scepter, which was terminated with a lotus-flower.

"What recompense do you desire?"

Filled with that daring inspired by dreams in which nothing seems impossible, I asked him for the hand of the Princess Hermonthis;—the hand seemed to me a very proper antithetic recompense for the foot.

Pharaoh opened wide his great eyes of glass in astonishment at my witty request.

"What country do you come from? and what is your age?"

"I am a Frenchman; and I am twenty-seven years old, venerable Pharaoh."

"——Twenty-seven years old! and he wishes to espouse the Princess Hermonthis, who is thirty centuries old!" cried out at once all the Thrones and all the Circles of Nations.

Only Hermonthis herself did not seem to think my request unreasonable.

"If you were even only two thousand years old," replied the ancient King, "I would willingly give you the Princess; but the disproportion is too great; and, besides, we must give our daughters husbands who will last well: you do not know how to preserve yourselves any longer; even those who died only fifteen centuries ago are already no more than a handful of dust;—behold! my flesh is solid as basalt; my bones are bars of steel!

"I shall be present on the last day of the world, with the same body and the same features which I had during my lifetime: my daughter Hermonthis will last longer than a statue of bronze.

"Then the last particles of your dust will have been scattered abroad by the winds; and even Isis herself, who was able to find the atoms of Osiris, would scarce be able to recompose your being.

"See how vigorous I yet remain, and how mighty is my grasp," he added, shaking my hand in the English fashion with a strength that buried my rings in the flesh of my fingers.

He squeezed me so hard that I awoke, and found my friend Alfred shaking me by the arm to make me get up.

"O you everlasting sleeper!—must I have you carried out into the middle of the street, and fireworks exploded in your ears? It is after noon; don't you recollect your promise to take me with you to see M. Aguado's Spanish pictures?"

"God! I forgot all, all about it," I answered, dressing myself hurriedly; "we will go there at once; I have the permit lying on my desk."

I started to find it;—but fancy my astonishment when I beheld, instead of the mummy's foot I had purchased the evening before, the little green paste idol left in its place by the Princess Hermonthis!

VILLIERS DE L'ISLE ADAM

(1838–1889)

COUNT VILLIERS DE L'ISLE ADAM, born in Brittany in 1838, led a strange life. "Born without average will-power," says Huneker, "except the will to imagine beautiful and strange things, all his years he fought the contending impulses of his dual nature." He was the very model of a bohemian. His strange tales, the best of which are collected under the title *Cruel Tales*, are fantastic prose poems in the manner of Poe. *The Torture of Hope*, according to Huneker, recalls Poe at his best.

The present version, anonymously translated, is reprinted from an American collection of tales, not dated. It is from the volume of *Cruel Tales*.

THE TORTURE OF HOPE

MANY years ago, as evening was closing in, the venerable Pedro Arbuez d'Espila, sixth prior of the Dominicans of Segovia, and third Grand Inquisitor of Spain, followed by a *fra redemptor*, and preceded by two familiars of the Holy Office, the latter carrying lanterns, made their way to a subterranean dungeon. The bolt of a massive door creaked, and they entered a mephitic *in pace*, where the dim light revealed between rings fastened to the wall a bloodstained rack, a brazier and a jug. On a pile of straw, loaded with fetters and his neck encircled by an iron carcan, sat a haggard man, of uncertain age, clothed in rags.

This prisoner was no other than Rabbi Aser Abarbanel, a Jew of Aragon, who—accused of usury and pitiless scorn for the poor—had been daily subjected to torture for more than a year. Yet "his blindness was as dense as his hide," and he had refused to abjure his faith.

Proud of a filiation dating back thousands of years, proud of his ancestors—for all Jews worthy of the name are vain of their blood—he descended Talmudically from Othoniel and consequently from Ipsiboa, the wife of the last judge of Israel, a circumstance which had sustained his courage amid incessant torture. With tears in his eyes at the thought of this resolute soul rejecting salvation, the venerable Pedro Arbuez d'Espila, approaching the shuddering rabbi, addressed him as follows:

"My son, rejoice: your trials here below are about to end. If in the presence of such obstinacy I was forced to permit, with deep regret, the use of great severity, my task of fraternal correction has its limits. You are the fig tree which, having failed so many times to bear fruit, at last withered, but God alone can judge your soul. Perhaps Infinite Mercy will shine upon you at the last moment! We must hope so. There are examples. So sleep in peace to-night. To-morrow you will be included in the *auto da fé*: that is, you will be exposed to the *quémadero*, the symbolical flames of the Everlasting Fire: it burns, as you know, only at a distance, my son; and Death is at least two hours (often three) in coming, on account of the wet, iced bandages with which we protect the heads and hearts of the condemned. There will be forty-three of you. Placed in the last row, you will have time to invoke God and offer to Him this baptism of fire, which is of the Holy Spirit. Hope in the Light, and rest."

With these words, having signed to his companions to unchain the prisoner, the prior tenderly embraced him. Then came the turn of the *fra redemptor*, who, in a low tone, entreated the Jew's forgiveness for what he had made him suffer for the purpose of redeeming him; then the two familiars silently kissed him. This ceremony over, the captive was left, solitary and bewildered, in the darkness.

Rabbi Aser Abarbanel, with parched lips and visage worn by suffering, at first gazed at the closed door with vacant eyes. Closed? The word unconsciously roused a vague fancy in his mind, the fancy that he had seen for an instant the light of the lanterns through a chink between the door and the wall. A morbid idea of hope, due to the weakness of his brain, stirred his whole being. He dragged himself toward the strange *appearance*. Then, very gently and cautiously, slipping one finger into the crevice, he drew the door toward him. Marvelous! By an extraordinary accident the familiar who closed it had turned the huge key an instant before it struck the stone casing, so that the rusty bolt not having entered the hole, the door again rolled on its hinges.

The rabbi ventured to glance outside. By the aid of a sort of luminous dusk he distinguished at first a semicircle of walls indented by winding stairs; and opposite to him, at the top of five or six stone steps, a sort of black portal, opening into an immense corridor, whose first arches only were visible from below.

Stretching himself flat he crept to the threshold. Yes, it was really a corridor, but endless in length. A wan light illumined it: lamps suspended from the vaulted ceiling lightened at intervals the dull hue of the atmosphere—the distance was veiled in shadow. Not a single door appeared in the whole extent! Only on one side, the left, heavily grated loopholes, sunk in the walls, admitted a light which must be that of evening, for crimson bars at intervals rested on the flags of the pavement. What a terrible silence! Yet, yonder, at the far end of that passage there might be a doorway of escape! The Jew's vacillating hope was tenacious, for it was *the last*.

Without hesitating, he ventured on the flags, keeping close under the loopholes, trying to make himself part of the blackness of the long walls. He advanced slowly, dragging himself along on his breast, forcing back the cry of pain when some raw wound sent a keen pang through his whole body.

Suddenly the sound of a sandaled foot approaching reached his ears. He trembled violently, fear stifled him, his sight grew dim. Well, it was over, no doubt. He pressed himself into a niche and, half lifeless with terror, waited.

It was a familiar hurrying along. He passed swiftly by, holding in his clenched hand an instrument of torture—a frightful figure—and vanished. The suspense which the rabbi had endured seemed to have suspended the functions of life, and he lay nearly an hour unable to move. Fearing an increase of tortures if he were captured, he thought of returning to his dungeon. But the old hope whispered in his soul that divine *perhaps*, which comforts us in our sorest trials. A miracle had happened. He could doubt no longer. He began to crawl toward the chance of excape. Exhausted by suffering and hunger, trembling with pain, he pressed onward. The sepulchral corridor seemed to lengthen mysteriously, while he, still advancing, gazed into the gloom where there *must* be some avenue of escape.

Oh! oh! He again heard footsteps, but this time they were slower, more heavy. The white and black forms of two inquisitors appeared, emerging from the obscurity beyond. They were conversing in low tones, and seemed to be discussing some important subject, for they were gesticulating vehemently.

At this spectacle Rabbi Aser Abarbanel closed his eyes: his heart beat so violently that it almost suffocated him; his rags were damp with the cold sweat of agony; he lay motionless by the wall, his mouth wide open, under the rays of a lamp, praying to the God of David.

Just opposite to him the two inquisitors paused under the light of the lamp—doubtless owing to some accident due to the course of their argument. One, while listening to his companion, gazed at the rabbi! And, beneath the look—whose absence of expression the hapless man did not at first notice—he fancied he again felt the burning pincers scorch his flesh, he was to be once more a living wound. Fainting, breathless, with fluttering eyelids, he shivered at the touch of the monk's floating robe. But—strange yet natural fact—the inquisitor's gaze was evidently that of a man deeply absorbed in his intended reply, engrossed by what he was hearing; his eyes were fixed—and seemed to look at the Jew *without seeing him.*

In fact, after the lapse of a few minutes, the two gloomy figures slowly pursued their way, still conversing in low tones, toward the place whence the prisoner had come; HE HAD NOT BEEN SEEN! Amid the horrible confusion of the rabbi's thoughts, the idea darted through his brain: "Can I be already dead that they did not see me?" A hideous impression roused him from his lethargy: in looking at the wall against which his face was pressed, he imagined he beheld two fierce eyes watching him! He flung his head back in a sudden frenzy of fright, his hair fairly bristling! Yet, no! No. His hand groped over the stones: it was the *reflection* of the inquisitor's eyes, still retained in his own, which had been refracted from two spots on the wall.

Forward! He must hasten toward that goal which he fancied (absurdly, no doubt) to be deliverance, toward the darkness from which he was now barely thirty paces distant. He pressed forward faster on his knees, his hands, at full length, dragging himself painfully along, and soon entered the dark portion of this terrible corridor.

Suddenly the poor wretch felt a gust of cold air on the hands resting upon the flags; it came from under the little door to which the two walls led.

Oh, Heaven, if that door should open outward. Every nerve in the miserable fugitive's body thrilled with hope. He examined it from top to bottom, though scarcely able to distinguish its outlines in the surrounding darkness. He passed his hand over it: no bolt, no lock! A latch! He started up, the latch yielded to the pressure of his thumb: the door silently swung open before him.

"Halleluia!" murmured the rabbi in a transport of gratitude as, standing on the threshold, he beheld the scene before him.

The door had opened into the gardens, above which arched a starlit sky, into spring, liberty, life! It revealed the neighboring fields, stretching toward the sierras, whose sinuous blue lines were relieved against the horizon. Yonder lay freedom! Oh, to escape! He would journey all night through the lemon groves, whose fragrance reached him. Once in the mountains and he was safe! He inhaled the delicious air; the breeze revived him, his lungs expanded! He felt in his swelling heart the the *Veni foràs* of Lazarus! And to thank once more the God who had bestowed this mercy upon him, he extended his arms, raising his eyes toward Heaven. It was an ecstasy of joy!

Then he fancied he saw the shadow of his arms approach him—fancied that he felt these shadowy arms inclose, embrace him—and that he was pressed tenderly to someone's breast. A tall figure actually did stand directly before him. He lowered his eyes—and remained motionless, gasping for breath, dazed, with fixed eyes, fairly driveling with terror.

Horror! He was in the clasp of the Grand Inquisitor himself, the venerable Pedro Arbuez d'Espila, who gazed at him with tearful eyes, like a good shepherd who had found his stray lamb.

The dark-robed priest pressed the hapless Jew to his heart with so fervent an outburst of love, that the edges of the monachal haircloth rubbed the Dominican's breast. And while Aser Abarbanel with protruding eyes gasped in agony in the ascetic's embrace, vaguely comprehending that *all the phases of this fatal evening were only a prearranged torture, that of* Hope, the Grand Inquisitor, with an accent of touching reproach and a look of consternation, murmured in his ear, his breath parched and burning from long fasting:

"What, my son! On the eve, perchance, of salvation—you wished to leave us?"

ALPHONSE DAUDET

(1840–1897)

ALPHONSE DAUDET, one of the masters of the Naturalistic School of modern France, was born at Nîmes in 1840. He made his literary début in 1858 with a volume of verse. He was both novelist and short story writer, but the *Contes du Lundi* and *Lettres de mon Moulin* are now read in preference to *Sappho* and *Jack*. The Tartarin books are perhaps an exception: they are little masterpieces of humour and observation. The *Contes du Lundi* (1873) contain some of Daudet's most delicate and appealing stories. In *The Last Lesson* there is a spontaneity and feeling which is characteristic of all his best work.

The present version, anonymously translated, is reprinted from *Great Short Stories*, P. F. Collier Sons, New York, 1909. Copyright, 1909, by the Frank A. Munsey Co., by whose permission it is here used.

THE LAST LESSON

I STARTED for school very late that morning and was in great dread of a scolding, especially because M. Hamel had said that he would question us on participles, and I did not know the first word about them. For a moment I thought of running away and spending the day out of doors. It was so warm, so bright! The birds were chirping at the edge of the woods; and in the open field back of the sawmill the Prussian soldiers were drilling. It was all much more tempting than the rule for participles, but I had the strength to resist, and hurried off to school.

When I passed the town hall there was a crowd in front of the bulletin-board. For the last two years all our bad news had come from there—the lost battles, the draft, the orders of the commanding officer —and I thought to myself, without stopping:

"What can be the matter now?"

Then, as I hurried by as fast as I could go, the blacksmith, Wachter, who was there, with his apprentice, reading the bulletin, called after me:

"Don't go so fast, bub; you'll get to your school in plenty of time!"

I thought he was making fun of me, and reached M. Hamel's little garden all out of breath.

Usually, when school began, there was a great bustle, which could be heard out in the street, the opening and closing of desks, lessons repeated in unison, very loud, with our hands over our ears to understand better, and the teacher's great ruler rapping on the table. But now it was all so still! I had counted on the commotion to get to my desk without being seen; but, of course, that day everything had to be as quiet as Sunday morning. Through the window I saw my classmates, already in their places, and M. Hamel walking up and down with his terrible iron ruler under his arm. I had to open the door and go in before everybody. You can imagine how I blushed and how frightened I was.

But nothing happened. M. Hamel saw me and said very kindly:

"Go to your place quickly, little Franz. We were beginning without you."

I jumped over the bench and sat down at my desk. Not till then, when I had got a little over my fright, did I see that our teacher had on his beautiful green coat, his frilled shirt, and the little black silk cap, all embroidered, that he never wore except on inspection and prize days. Besides, the whole school seemed so strange and solemn. But the thing that surprised me most was to see, on the back benches that were always empty, the village people sitting quietly like ourselves; old Hauser, with his three-cornered hat, the former mayor, the former postmaster, and several others besides. Everybody looked sad; and Hauser had brought an old primer, thumbed at the edges, and he held it open on his knees with his great spectacles lying across the pages.

While I was wondering about it all, M. Hamel mounted his chair, and, in the same grave and gentle tone which he had used to me, said: "My children, this is the last lesson I shall give you. The order has come from Berlin to teach only German in the schools of Alsace and Lorraine. The new master comes to-morrow. This is your last French lesson. I want you to be very attentive."

What a thunderclap these words were to me!

Oh, the wretches; that was what they had put up at the town-hall!

My last French lesson! Why, I hardly knew how to write! I should never learn any more! I must stop there, then! Oh, how sorry I was for not learning my lessons, for seeking birds' eggs, or going sliding on the Saar! My books, that had seemed such a nuisance a while ago, so heavy to carry, my grammar, and my history of the saints, were old friends now that I couldn't give up. And M. Hamel, too; the idea that he was going away, that I should never see him again, made me forget all about his ruler and how cranky he was.

Poor man! It was in honor of this last lesson that he had put on his fine Sunday clothes, and now I understood why the old men of the village were sitting there in the back of the room. It was because they were sorry, too, that they had not gone to school more. It was their way of thanking our master for his forty years of faithful service and of showing their respect for the country that was theirs no more.

While I was thinking of all this, I heard my name called. It was my turn to recite. What would I not have given to be able to say that dreadful rule for the participle all through, very loud and clear, and without one mistake? But I got mixed up on the first words and stood there, holding on to my desk, my heart beating, and not daring to look up. I heard M. Hamel say to me:

"I won't scold you, little Franz; you must feel bad enough. See how it is! Every day we have said to ourselves: 'Bah! I've plenty of time. I'll learn it to-morrow.' And now you see where we've come out. Ah, that's the great trouble with Alsace; she puts off learning till to-morrow. Now those fellows out there will have the right to say to you: 'How is it; you pretend to be Frenchmen, and yet you can neither speak nor write your own language?' But you are not the worst, poor little Franz. We've all a great deal to reproach ourselves with.

"Your parents were not anxious enough to have you learn. They preferred to put you to work on a farm or at the mills, so as to have a little more money. And I? I've been to blame also. Have I not often sent you to water my flowers instead of learning your lessons? And when I wanted to go fishing, did I not just give you a holiday?"

Then, from one thing to another, M. Hamel went on to talk of the French language, saying that it was the most beautiful language in the world—the clearest, the most logical; that we must guard it among us and never forget it, because when a people are enslaved, as long as they hold fast to their language it is as if they had the key to their prison. Then he opened a grammar and read us our lesson. I was amazed to see how well I understood it. All he said seemed so easy, so easy! I think, too, that I had never listened so carefully, and that he had never explained everything with so much patience. It seemed almost as if the poor man wanted to give us all he knew before going away, and to put it all into our heads at one stroke.

After the grammar, we had a lesson in writing. That day M. Hamel had new copies for us, written in a beautiful round hand: France, Alsace, France, Alsace. They looked like little flags floating everywhere in the school-room, hung from the rod at the top of our desks. You ought to have seen how every one set to work, and how quiet it was! The only sound was the scratching of the pens over the paper. Once some beetles flew in; but nobody paid any attention to them, not even the littlest ones, who worked right on tracing their fish-hooks, as if that was French, too. On the roof the pigeons cooed very low, and I thought to myself:

"Will they make them sing in German, even the pigeons?"

Whenever I looked up from my writing I saw M. Hamel sitting motionless in his chair and gazing first at one thing, then at another, as if he wanted to fix in his mind just how everything looked in that little school-room. Fancy! For forty years he had been there in the same place, with his garden outside the window and his class in front of him, just like that. Only the desks and benches had been worn smooth; the walnut-trees in the garden were taller, and the hop-vine that he had planted himself twined about the windows to the roof. How it must have broken his heart to leave it all, poor man; to hear his sister moving about in the room above, packing their trunks! For they must leave the country next day.

But he had the courage to hear every lesson to the very last. After the writing, we had a lesson in history, and then the babies chanted their ba, be bi, bo, bu. Down there at the back of the room old Hauser had put on his spectacles and, holding his primer in both hands, spelled the letters with them. You could see that he, too, was crying; his voice trembled with emotion, and it was so funny to hear him that we all wanted to laugh and cry. Ah, how well I remember it, that last lesson!

All at once the church-clock struck twelve. Then the Angelus. At the same moment the trumpets of the Prussians, returning from drill, sounded under our windows. M. Hamel stood up, very pale, in his chair. I never saw him look so tall.

"My friends," said he, "I—I—" But something choked him. He could not go on.

Then he turned to the blackboard, took a piece of chalk, and, bearing on with all his might, he wrote as large as he could:

"Vive La France!"

Then he stopped and leaned his head against the wall, and, without a word, he made a gesture to us with his hand:

"School is dismissed—you may go."

EMILE ZOLA

(1840—1903)

EMILE ZOLA was one of the most extraordinary writers of the last century. With limitless energy and scrupulous pains he constructed an imposing edifice of novels and tales, the epic of a certain French family. He preached the doctrine of Naturalism, believing that every novel or story should be based upon what he called a "human document". Opinions still differ as to his importance as an artist. There is no doubt, however, that he influenced most of the fiction writers who have followed him. The prevailing tone of his work is tragic and the details sordid, but he occasionally turned to the purely fantastic. In the *Tales for Nanon* (1864), one of his very earliest productions, he delights in relating a number of delicate fairy tales. *The Fairy Amoureuse* is one of the most charming of these tales.

The present version is translated by Barrett H. Clark, and appears in this collection for the first time in English.

THE FAIRY AMOUREUSE

DO you hear the rain, Nanon, beating against the windows? And the wind sighing through the long corridor? It's a horrid night, a night when poor wretches shiver before the gates of the rich, who dance indoors in rooms bright with many gilded chandeliers. Take off those silk slippers of yours, and come sit on my knee before the blazing hearth. Lay aside your gorgeous finery: I'm going to tell you a pretty fairy tale this evening.

Once upon a time, Nanon, there stood on the top of a mountain an ancient castle, somber and forbidding to look upon. It was a mass of turrets and ramparts and portcullises with heavy clanking chains; men-at-arms clad in steel from top to toe stood guard night and day on its battlements. Of those who came to the castle only warriors found a welcome at the hands of its master, Count Enguerrand.

If you had seen this old warrior stalking through the long galleries, and heard the sudden outbursts of his dry and menacing voice, you would have trembled with fright, just like his niece Odette, a pious and pretty little lady. Have you ever seen an Easter daisy among the nettles and briars open its petals in the early morning to the first kiss of the sun? Odette was like that, living among the rough knights in attendance on her uncle. Whenever she caught sight of him she would suddenly stop playing, and her eyes fill with tears. She had grown tall and fair, and often sighed with a vague desire for she knew not what; and every time the Lord Enguerrand appeared she was seized with an unspeakable and growing dread.

She had her room in a turret in a distant part of the castle, and spent her time embroidering lovely banners; she found repose in praying to God and in looking out of her window at the emerald landscape and the azure sky. How often, at night, had she risen from her bed and gone to the window to gaze at the stars! How often had the heart of this sixteen-year-old child leaped up toward the vasty spaces of the heavens, asking her radiant sisters of the firmament what it was that so troubled her! And after these sleepless nights, these first stirrings of her yet unconscious love, she would have strange promptings urging her to embrace the rough old knight her uncle. But a short answer or a stern glance would check her impulse, and all atremble she would take up her needle again. You are sorry, Nanon, for the poor child: she was like a fresh-scented flower whose loveliness and scent are alike spurned.

One day as poor Odette was sitting at her window following with her eyes the flight of two doves, she heard a soft voice far below her at the foot of the castle wall. She leaned out and saw a handsome young man who, with a song on his lips, demanded hospitality of the inmates of the castle. Though she listened intently, she could not understand what he said, but the sweet voice made her heart heavy, and the tears ran slowly down her cheeks, wetting the sprig of marjoram which she held in her hand.

But the castle gates were not opened, and a man-at-arms cried out from the walls:

"Stand back. Only soldiers are admitted here."

Odette continued to look out of the window. She let slip the flower from her hand, still wet with her tears. It fell near the feet of the singer who, raising his eyes and seeing the fair hair of the girl, kissed the sprig and turned away, though he stopped at every step to look back. After he had disappeared, Odette went to her prie-dieu and prayed a long time. She gave thanks to heaven, she knew not why;

she felt happy, though she did not suspect the reason of her happiness. And that night she dreamed a beautiful dream. She saw again the sprig of marjoram she had thrown to the young man. Slowly, out of the midst of the quivering leaves, there emerged a tiny fairy, with flame-colored wings, a crown of myosotis and a long robe of green, the color of hope.

"Odette," said the fairy in a soothing voice, "I am the Fairy Amoureuse. It was I who sent the young man Lois to you this morning— the young man with the enchanting voice. It was I who, seeing your tears, wanted to dry them. I go about the world seeking lonely hearts and bringing together those who sigh in solitude. I visit the peasant's hut as well as the lord's manor, and at times I see fit to unite the shepherd's crook with the king's scepter. I sow flowers under the feet of those I protect. I enthrall them with bonds so precious and sweet that their hearts throb with joy. My home is among the green things that grow, the forest paths, and in winter-time among the glowing logs on the hearth, in the rooms of husbands and wives. Wherever I set my foot there are kisses and tenderness. Cry no more, Odette, I am Amoureuse, the good Fairy, who have come to dry your tears."

Then she disappeared again into her flower, which closed once more and became an ordinary bud.

You know, of course, Nanon, that the Fairy Amoureuse really exists. Watch her dancing in our own home, and pity the poor people who don't believe in her.

When Odette awoke next morning a ray of sunshine lighted up her room, the song of a bird rose to her high tower and the morning breeze, scented with the first kiss of the flowers, caressed her bright tresses. She rose, happy, and spent the whole day singing, hoping that the Fairy's prophecy would come true. Sometimes she would scan the countryside, smiling at each swiftly flying bird, and feeling within her breast something that made her happy and forced her to clap her hands with joy.

When evening came she descended into the great hall. Near the Count Enguerrand was a knight who listened respectfully to what the old man was saying. Odette seated herself before the fireplace, where a cricket was chirping, and busily plied her ivory distaff.

As she worked, she cast glances from time to time at the stranger knight, and once she caught sight of the sprig of marjoram, which he held tight in one hand. By that sign, and by his sweet voice, she recognized Lois. She almost cried aloud for joy, but in order to conceal her blushes she leaned forward toward the glowing logs, and shook the fire with a long iron rod. The flames darted upwards in a brilliant array, and all at once out of the shower of sparks the Fairy Amoureuse sprang up smiling. Shaking from her green silk robe the bits of burning wood that looked like grains of pure gold, she made off into the great hall where, invisible to the Count, she stood just behind the two young people, while the old warrior went on busily relating the details of a frightful battle with the Infidels. The Fairy spoke in a soothing undertone:

"You must love each other, my children. Leave to the old the memories of youth, and the telling of long tales by the fireside. Let your kisses be the only sound to mingle with the crackling logs. Later will be time enough to mitigate the sorrows of old age by remembering the happy hours long past. When you love at sixteen, words are of no avail: à single look tells more than a lengthy discourse. Love each other, my children, and let old age prate."

Then she covered the two with her wings so completely that the Count, who was explaining how the Giant Buch the Iron-headed was killed by a great blow from the hand of Giralda of the Heavy Sword, could not see when Lois implanted his first kiss on the brow of the trembling Odette.

Now I must tell you, Nanon, about those beautiful wings of the Fairy Amoureuse. They were as transparent as glass and as delicate as the wings of a fly. But when two lovers are in danger of being seen, they grow and grow and become so thick and so opaque that they shut off the view of anything behind them and prevent anyone's hearing the kisses. And so the old man went on and on with his wondrous tale, while Lois continued to caress the fair Odette, right in the presence of the wicked old lord.

Good heavens, what wonderful wings they were! Young girls, I am told, discover them for themselves, and more than one has succeeded in concealing herself from her grandparents. Isn't that so, Nanon?

Well, when the Count had at last brought to a close his lengthy discourse, the Fairy Amoureuse disappeared again into the fire, and Lois withdrew after thanking his host and throwing a farewell kiss to Odette. The girl was so happy that she dreamed that night of mountains studded with flowers made bright by millions of stars, each of them a thousand times more radiant than the sun.

Next morning she went down into the garden, wandering from arbor to arbor. In one of them she came upon a man-at-arms, bowed to him and was about to pass on, when she noticed a sprig of marjoram in his hand, still wet with tears, and recognized again her Lois. He had come to the castle under a new disguise. He made her sit down on a grassy bank near a fountain, and they gazed into each other's eyes, delighted to be able to see each other's features by the light of day. The warblers sang, and the two lovers felt that the Fairy Amoureuse must surely be hovering about in the air near them.

I shan't tell you all that the discreet old oak-trees heard that morning. It was pleasant to watch the boy and the girl sitting there chatting hour after hour, so long indeed that one warbler found ample time to build herself a nest in a nearby bush.

Suddenly the heavy footsteps of Count Enguerrand were heard in the garden walk. The lovers trembled, but the water of the fountain rippled more sweetly than ever, and Amoureuse rose out of the crystal stream, a smile on her face. She covered the lovers with her wings, and quickly slipped between them and the Count, who was greatly surprised to hear voices and yet see no one at all.

Holding her friends in her embrace, she repeated to them in a soft undertone:

"I am she who protects love, who closes the eyes and ears of those who no longer love. Fear nothing, dear lovers: love each other in this beautiful clear sunlight, in these garden walks, by the side of these fountains, wherever you happen to be. I am with you, watching over you. God has sent me among men, and they who scoff at sacred things shall never interrupt you. God gave me these beautiful wings, telling me, 'Go, and let the hearts of the young rejoice!' Love each other, while I keep guard over you."

Then she darted off, gathering dew off the foliage (her only nourishment), and taking with her in her joyous round Odette and Lois, whose arms were ever interlaced.

You will ask me what the lovers did next? Really, my dear, I hardly dare tell you. I'm afraid you would not believe me, or be jealous of *their* happiness, and refuse to return my kisses. Naughty girl, you are curious, aren't you? I see I shall have to satisfy your curiosity.

Know then, that the Fairy flew hither and thither until nightfall, and when she tried to separate her lovers, she found them so reluctant that she had to give them a good talking-to. It seems (for her voice was low) that she said things so beautiful that their faces lighted up and their eyes opened wide from happiness. And after she had done speaking and they consented to her proposal, she touched their foreheads with her magic wand.

Suddenly—oh, Nanon, how big your eyes are! And how you would tap your little foot if I were to refuse to tell you the sequel! Suddenly, Lois and Odette were changed into stalks of marjoram, so large and magnificent that only a fairy could have made them so. There they were, side by side, so close that their leaves were entwined. Marvelous flowers they were; they would bloom forever, and eternally mingle their perfumes and their dew.

As for the Count Enguerrand, they say he consoled himself by relating every single night the story of the Giant Buch the Iron-Headed and how he was killed by a great blow from the hand of Giralda of the Heavy Sword.

And now, Nanon, when we go to the country, we shall look for the two magic marjorams and ask them in which flower we may find the Fairy Amoureuse. Perhaps, my dear, there is a little moral hidden in this tale. However, I have told it to you here, as we sit stretched out before the hearth, just in order to make you forget the December rain beating against our windows, and in the hope that it will inspire you to love a little more the young man who told it to you.

FRANÇOIS COPPÉE

(1842–1908)

COPPÉE, the poet of the poor and humble, lived a long and uneventful life. His volumes of verse are characterized by qualities of sentiment and simplicity. But his novels, plays, and short stories, especially the last, are an integral part of his literary work. These, says Brander Matthews, "have qualities of their own; they have sympathy, poetry, and a power of suggesting pictures not exceeded, I think, by those of either M. de Maupassant or M. Daudet."

The present version, translated by Walter Learned, is reprinted from *Ten Tales by François Coppée,* by permission of the publisher, Harper & Brothers.

THE SUBSTITUTE

HE was scarcely ten years old when he was first arrested as a vagabond.

He spoke thus to the judge:

"I am called Jean François Leturc, and for six months I was with the man who sings and plays upon a cord of catgut between the lanterns at the Place de la Bastille. I sang the refrain with him, and after that I called, 'Here's all the new songs, ten centimes, two sous!' He was always drunk, and used to beat me. That is why the police picked me up the other night. Before that I was with the man who sells brushes. My mother was a laundress, her name was Adèle. At one time she lived with a man on the ground-floor at Montmartre. She was a good work-woman and liked me. She made money because she had for customers waiters in the cafés, and they use a good deal of linen. On Sundays she used to put me to bed early so that she could go to the ball. On weekdays she sent me to Les Frères, where I learned to read. Well, the sergent-de-ville whose beat was in our street used always to stop before our windows to talk with her—a good-looking chap, with a

medal from the Crimea. They were married, and after that everything
went wrong. He didn't take to me, and turned mother against me.
Every one had a blow for me, and so, to get out of the house, I spent
whole days in the Place Clichy, where I knew the mountebanks. My
father-in-law lost his place, and my mother her work. She used to go
out washing to take care of him; this gave her a cough—the steam...
She is dead at Lamboisière. She was a good woman. Since that I have
lived with the seller of brushes and the catgut scraper. Are you going
to send me to prison?"

He said this openly, cynically, like a man. He was a little ragged
street-arab, as tall as a boot, his forehead hidden under a queer mop
of yellow hair.

Nobody claimed him, and they sent him to the Reform School.

Not very intelligent, idle, clumsy with his hands, the only trade he
could learn there was not a good one—that of reseating straw chairs.
However, he was obedient, naturally quiet and silent, and he did not
seem to be profoundly corrupted by that school of vice. But when, in
his seventeenth year, he was thrown out again on the streets of Paris,
he unhappily found there his prison comrades, all great scamps, exercising their dirty professions: teaching dogs to catch rats in the sewers,
and blacking shoes on ball nights in the passage of the Opera—amateur wrestlers, who permitted themselves to be thrown by the Hercules
of the booths—or fishing at noontime from rafts; all of these occupations he followed to some extent, and, some months after he came out
of the house of correction, he was arrested again for a petty theft—
a pair of old shoes prigged from a shop-window. Result: a year in
the prison of Sainte Pélagie, where he served as valet to the political
prisoners.

He lived in much surprise among this group of prisoners, all very
young, negligent in dress, who talked in loud voices, and carried their
heads in a very solemn fashion. They used to meet in the cell of one
of the oldest of them, a fellow of some thirty years, already a long time
in prison and quite a fixture at Sainte Pélagie—a large cell, the walls
covered with colored caricatures, and from the window of which one
could see all Paris—its roofs, its spires, and its domes—and far away
the distant line of hills, blue and indistinct upon the sky. There were
upon the walls some shelves filled with volumes and all the old para-
phernalia of a fencing-room: broken masks, rusty foils, breastplates,
and gloves that were losing their tow. It was there that the "politicians" used to dine together, adding to the everlasting "soup and
beef," fruit, cheese, and pints of wine which Jean François went out
and got by the can—a tumultuous repast interrupted by violent disputes, and where, during the dessert, the "Carmagnole" and "Ça
Ira" were sung in full chorus. They assumed, however, an air of great

dignity on those days when a newcomer was brought in among them, at first entertaining him gravely as a citizen, but on the morrow using him with affectionate familiarity and calling him by his nickname. Great words were used there: Corporation, Responsibility, and phrases quite unintelligible to Jean François—such as this, for example, which he once heard imperiously put forth by a frightful little hunchback who blotted some writing-paper every night:

"It is done. This is the composition of the Cabinet: Raymond, the Bureau of Public Instruction; Martial, the Interior; and for Foreign Affairs, myself."

His time done, he wandered again around Paris, watched afar by the police, after the fashion of cockchafers, made by cruel children to fly at the end of a string. He became one of those fugitive and timid beings whom the law, with a sort of coquetry, arrests and releases by turn—something like those platonic fishers who, in order that they may not exhaust their fish-pond, throw immediately back into the water the fish which has just come out of the net. Without a suspicion on his part that so much honor had been done to so sorry a subject, he had a special bundle of memoranda in the mysterious portfolios of the Rue de Jérusalem. His name was written in round hand on the gray paper of the cover, and the notes and reports, carefully classified, gave him his successive appellations: "Name, Leturc"; "the prisoner Leturc," and, at last, "the criminal Leturc."

He was two years out of prison, dining where he could, sleeping in night lodging-houses and sometimes in lime-kilns, and taking part with his fellows in interminable games of pitch-penny on the boulevards near the barriers. He wore a greasy cap on the back of his head, carpet slippers, and a short white blouse. When he had five sous he had his hair curled. He danced at Constant's at Montparnasse; bought for two sous to sell for four at the door of Bobino, the jack of hearts or the ace of clubs serving as a countermark; sometimes opened the door of a carriage; led horses to the horse-market. From the lottery of all sorts of miserable employments he drew a goodly number. Who can say if the atmosphere of honor which one breathes as a soldier, if military discipline might not have saved him? Taken, in a cast of the net, with some young loafers who robbed drunkards sleeping on the streets, he denied very earnestly having taken part in their expeditions. Perhaps he told the truth, but his antecedents were accepted in lieu of proof, and he was sent for three years to Poissy. There he made coarse playthings for children, was tattooed on the chest, learned thieves' slang and the penal code. A new liberation, and a new plunge into the sink of Paris; but very short this time, for at the end of six months at the most he was again compromised in a night robbery, aggravated by climbing and breaking—a serious affair, in which he played an obscure rôle, half dupe and half fence. On the whole his complicity was evident, and he was sent for five years at hard labor. His grief in this adventure was above all in being separated from an old dog which he had found on a dungheap, and cured of the mange. The beast loved him.

Toulon, the ball and chain, the work in the harbor, the blows from a stick, wooden shoes on bare feet, soup of black beans dating from Trafalgar, no tobacco money, and the terrible sleep in a camp swarming with convicts; that was what he experienced for five broiling summers and five winters raw with the Mediterranean wind. He came out from there stunned, was sent under surveillance to Vernon, where he worked some time on the river. Then, an incorrigible vagabond, he broke his exile and came again to Paris. He had his savings, fifty-six francs, that is to say, time enough for reflection. During his absence his former wretched companions had dispersed. He was well hidden, and slept in a loft at an old woman's, to whom he represented himself as a sailor, tired of the sea, who had lost his papers in a recent shipwreck, and who wanted to try his hand at something else. His tanned face and his calloused hands, together with some sea phrases which he dropped from time to time, made his tale seem probable enough.

One day when he risked a saunter in the streets, and when chance had led him as far as Montmartre, where he was born, an unexpected memory stopped him before the door of Les Frères, where he had learned to read. As it was very warm the door was open, and by a single glance the passing outcast was able to recognize the peaceable school-room. Nothing was changed: neither the bright light shining in at the great windows, nor the crucifix over the desk, nor the rows of benches with the tables furnished with inkstands and pencils, nor the table of weights and measures, nor the map where pins stuck in still indicated the operations of some ancient war. Heedlessly and without thinking, Jean François read on the blackboard the words of the Evangelist which had been set there as a copy:

"Joy shall be in heaven over one sinner that repenteth, more than over ninety and nine just persons, which need no repentance."

It was undoubtedly the hour for recreation, for the Brother Professor had left his chair, and, sitting on the edge of a table, he was telling a story to the boys who surrounded him with eager and attentive eyes. What a bright and innocent face he had, that beardless young man, in his long black gown, and white necktie, and great ugly shoes, and his badly cut brown hair streaming out behind! All the simple figures of the children of the people who were watching him seemed scarcely less childlike than his; above all when, delighted with some of his own simple and priestly pleasantries, he broke out in an open and frank peal of laughter which showed his white and regular teeth, a peal so contagious that all the scholars laughed loudly in their turn. It was such a sweet, simple group in the bright sunlight, which lighted their dear eyes and their blond curls.

Jean François looked at them for some time in silence, and for the first time in that savage nature, all instinct and appetite, there awoke a mysterious, a tender emotion. His heart, that seared and hardened heart, unmoved when the convict's cudgel or the heavy whip of the watchman fell on his shoulders, beat oppressively. In that sight he saw again his infancy; and closing his eyes sadly, the prey to torturing regret, he walked quickly away.

Then the words written on the blackboard came back to his mind

"If it wasn't too late, after all!" he murmured; "if I could again, like others, eat honestly my brown bread, and sleep my fill without nightmare! The spy must be sharp who recognizes me. My beard, which I shaved off down there, has grown out thick and strong. One can burrow somewhere in the great ant-hill, and work can be found. Whoever is not worked to death in the hell of the galleys comes out agile and robust, and I learned there to climb ropes with loads upon my back. Building is going on everywhere here, and the masons need helpers. Three francs a day! I never earned so much. Let me be forgotten, and that is all I ask."

He followed his courageous resolution; he was faithful to it, and after three months he was another man. The master for whom he worked called him his best workman. After a long day upon the scaffolding, in the hot sun and the dust, constantly bending and raising his back to take the hod from the man at his feet and pass it to the man over his head, he went for his soup to the cook-shop, tired out, his legs aching, his hands burning, his eyelids stuck with plaster, but content with himself, and carrying his well-earned money in a knot in his handkerchief. He went out now without fear, since he could not be recognized in his white mask, and since he had noticed that the suspicious glances of the policeman were seldom turned on the tired workman. He was quiet and sober. He slept the sound sleep of fatigue. He was free!

At last—oh, supreme recompense!—he had a friend!

He was a fellow-workman like himself, named Savinien, a little peasant with red lips who had come to Paris with his stick over his shoulder and a bundle on the end of it, fleeing from the wine-shops and going to mass every Sunday. Jean François loved him for his piety, for his candor, for his honesty, for all that he himself had lost, and so long ago. It was a passion, profound and unrestrained, which transformed him by fatherly cares and attentions. Savinien, himself of a weak and egotistical nature, let things take their course, satisfied only in finding a companion who shared his horror of the wine-shop.

The two friends lived together in a fairly comfortable lodging, but their resources were very limited. They were obliged to take into their room a third companion, an old Auvergnat, gloomy and rapacious, who found it possible out of his meager salary to save something with which to buy a place in his own country. Jean François and Savinien were always together. On holidays they together took long walks in the environs of Paris, and dined under an arbor in one of those small country inns where there are a great many mushrooms in the sauces and innocent rebusses on the napkins. There Jean François learned from his friend all that lore of which they who are born in the city are ignorant: learned the names of the trees, the flowers, and the plants; the various seasons for harvesting; he heard eagerly the thousand details of a laborious country life—the autumn sowing, the winter chores, the splendid celebrations of harvest and vintage days, the sound of the mills at the water-side, and the flails striking the ground, the tired horses led to water, and the hunting in the morning mist; and, above all, the long evenings around the fire of vineshoots, that were shortened by some marvelous stories. He discovered in himself a source of imagination before unknown, and found a singular delight in the recital of events so placid, so calm, so monotonous.

One thing troubled him, however: it was the fear lest Savinien might learn something of his past. Sometimes there escaped from him some low word of thieves' slang, a vulgar gesture—vestiges of his former horrible existence—and he felt the pain one feels when old wounds reopen; the more because he fancied that he sometimes saw in Savinien the awakening of an unhealthy curiosity. When the young man, already tempted by the pleasures which Paris offers to the poorest, asked him about the mysteries of the great city, Jean François feigned ignorance and turned the subject; but he felt a vague inquietude for the future of his friend.

His uneasiness was not without foundation. Savinien could not long remain the simple rustic that he was on his arrival in Paris. If the gross and noisy pleasures of the wine-shop always repelled him, he was profoundly troubled by other temptations, full of danger for the inexperience of his twenty years. When spring came he began to go off alone, and at first he wandered about the brilliant entrance of some dancing-hall, watching the young girls who went in with their arms around each other's waists, talking in low tones. Then, one evening, when lilacs perfumed the air and the call to quadrilles was most captivating, he crossed the threshold, and from that time Jean François observed a change, little by little, in his manners and his visage. He became more frivolous, more extravagant. He often borrowed from his friend his scanty savings, and he forgot to repay. Jean François, feeling that he was abandoned, jealous and forgiving at the same time, suffered and was silent. He felt that he had no right to reproach him, but with the foresight of affection he indulged in cruel and inevitable presentiments.

One evening, as he was mounting the stairs to his room, absorbed in his thoughts, he heard, as he was about to enter, the sound of angry voices, and he recognized that of the old Auvergnat who lodged with Savinien and himself. An old habit of suspicion made him stop at the landing-place and listen to learn the cause of the trouble.

"Yes," said the Auvergnat, angrily, "I am sure that some one has opened my trunk and stolen from it the three louis that I had hidden in a little box; and he who has done this thing must be one of the two companions who sleep here, if it were not the servant Maria. It concerns you as much as it does me, since you are the master of the house, and I will drag you to the courts if you do not let me at once break open the valises of the two masons. My poor gold! It was here yesterday in its place, and I will tell you just what it was, so that if we find it again nobody can accuse me of having lied. Ah, I know them, my three beautiful gold-pieces, and I can see them as plainly as I see you. One piece was more worn than the others; it was of greenish gold, with a portrait of the great emperor. The other was a great old fellow with a queue and epaulettes; and the third, which had on it a Philippe with whiskers, I had marked with my teeth. They don't trick me. Do you know that I only wanted two more like that to pay for my vineyard? Come, search these fellows' things with me, or I will call the police! Hurry up!"

"All right," said the voice of the landlord; "we will go and search with Maria. So much the worse for you if we find nothing, and the masons get angry. You have forced me to it."

Jean François' soul was full of fright. He remembered the embarrassed circumstances and the small loans of Savinien and how sober he had seemed for some days. And yet he could not believe that he was a thief. He heard the Auvergnat panting in his eager search, and he pressed his closed fists against his breast as if to still the furious beating of his heart.

"Here they are!" suddenly shouted the victorious miser. "Here they are, my louis, my dear treasure; and in the Sunday vest of that little hypocrite of Limousin! Look, landlord, they are just as I told you. Here is the Napoleon, the man with a queue, and the Philippe that I have bitten. See the dents! Ah, the little beggar with the sanctified air. I should have much sooner suspected the other. Ah, the wretch! Well, he must go to the convict prison."

At this moment Jean François heard the well-known step of Savinien coming slowly up the stairs.

He is going to his destruction, thought he. Three stories. I have time!

And, pushing open the door, the entered the room, pale as death, where he saw the landlord and the servant stupefied in a corner, while the Auvergnat, on his knees, in the disordered heap of clothes, was kissing the pieces of gold.

"Enough of this," he said, in a thick voice; "I took the money, and put it in my comrade's trunk. But that is too bad. I am a thief, but not a Judas. Call the police; I will not try to escape, only I must say a word to Savinien in private. Here he is."

In fact, the little Limousin had just arrived, and seeing his crime discovered, believing himself lost, he stood there, his eyes fixed, his arms hanging.

Jean François seized him forcibly by the neck, as if to embrace him; he put his mouth close to Savinien's ear, and said to him in a low, supplicating voice:

"Keep quiet."

Then turning towards the others:

"Leave me alone with him. I tell you I won't go away. Lock us in if you wish, but leave us alone."

With a commanding gesture he showed them the door.

They went out.

Savinien, broken by grief, was sitting on the bed, and lowered his eyes without understanding anything.

"Listen," said Jean François, who came and took him by the hands. "I understand! You have stolen three gold-pieces to buy some trifle for a girl. That costs six months in prison. But one only comes out from there to go back again, and you will become a pillar of police courts and tribunals. I understand it. I have been seven years at the Reform School, a year at Sainte Pélagie, three years at Poissy, five years at Toulon. Now, don't be afraid. Everything is arranged. I have taken it on my shoulders."

"It is dreadful," said Savinien; but hope was springing up again in his cowardly heart.

"When the elder brother is under the flag, the younger one does not go," replied Jean François. "I am your substitute, that's all. You care for me a little, do you not? I am paid. Don't be childish—don't refuse. They would have taken me again one of these days, for I am a runaway from exile. And then, do you see, that life will be less hard for me than for you. I know it all, and I shall not complain if I have not done you this service for nothing, and if you swear to me that you will never do it again. Savinien, I have loved you well, and your friendship has made me happy. It is through it that, since I have known you, I have been honest and pure, as I might always have been, perhaps, if I had had, like you, a father to put a tool in my hands, a mother to teach me my prayers. It was my sole regret that I was useless to you, and that I

deceived you concerning myself. To-day I have unmasked in saving
you. It is all right. Do not cry, and embrace me, for already I hear
heavy boots on the stairs. They are coming with the *posse*, and we
must not seem to know each other so well before those chaps."

He pressed Savinien quickly to his breast, then pushed him from
him, when the door was thrown wide open.

It was the landlord and the Auvergnat, who brought the police.
Jean François sprang forward to the landing-place, held out his hands
for the handcuffs, and said, laughing, "Forward, bad lot!"

To-day he is at Cayenne, condemned for life as an incorrigible.

ANATOLE FRANCE

(Anatole Thibault)

(1844–1924)

ANATOLE FRANCE was born at Paris in 1844 and lived there most of
his life. He was *par excellence* a man of letters. For over forty years he
has written about Paris, the ancient world and the Middle Ages, endowing each novel or story with the philosophy of enlightened scepticism which is his contribution to modern thought.

Among the several volumes of stories he has written, *L'Etui de nacre*
includes some of his very best. From this is taken *Our Lady's Juggler*,
which is a retelling of one of the most beautiful of the French mediæval
tales.

The present version is translated for this collection by Barrett
H. Clark, by permission of Anatole France's English publishers,
John Lane, Ltd., the Bodley Head.

OUR LADY'S JUGGLER

IN the days of King Louis there lived a poor juggler by the name of
Barnabas, a native of Compiègne, who wandered from city to city
performing tricks of skill and prowess.

On fair days he would lay down in the public square a worn and
aged carpet, and after having attracted a group of children and idlers
by certain amusing remarks which he had learned from an old juggler,
and which he invariably repeated in the same fashion without altering
a word, he would assume the strangest postures, and balance a pewter
plate on the tip of his nose. At first the crowd regarded him with
indifference, but when, with his hands and head on the ground he

threw into the air and caught with his feet six copper balls that glittered in the sunlight, or when, throwing himself back until his neck touched his heels, he assumed the form of a perfect wheel and in that position juggled with twelve knives, he elicited a murmur of admiration from his audience, and small coins rained on his carpet.

Still, Barnabas of Compiègne, like most of those who exist by their accomplishments, had a hard time making a living. Earning his bread by the sweat of his brow, he bore rather more than his share of those miseries we are all heir to through the fault of our Father Adam.

Besides, he was unable to work as much as he would have liked, for in order to exhibit his wonderful talents, he required—like the trees—the warmth of the sun and the heat of the day. In winter time he was no more than a tree stripped of its leaves, in fact, half-dead. The frozen earth was too hard for the juggler. Like the cicada mentioned by Marie de France, he suffered during the bad season from hunger and cold. But, since he had a simple heart, he suffered in silence.

He had never thought much about the origin of wealth nor about the inequality of human conditions. He firmly believed that if this world was evil the next could not but be good, and this faith upheld him. He was not like the clever fellows who sell their souls to the devil; he never took the name of God in vain; he lived the life of an honest man, and though he had no wife of his own, he did not covet his neighbor's, for woman is the enemy of strong men, as we learn by the story of Samson which is written in the Scriptures.

Verily, his mind was not turned in the direction of carnal desire, and it caused him far greater pain to renounce drinking than to forego the pleasure of women. For, though he was not a drunkard, he enjoyed drinking when the weather was warm. He was a good man, fearing God, and devout in his adoration of the Holy Virgin. When he went into a church he never failed to kneel before the image of the Mother of God and to address her with this prayer:

"My Lady, watch over my life until it shall please God that I die, and when I am dead, see that I have the joys of Paradise."

One evening, after a day of rain, as he walked sad and bent with his juggling balls under his arm and his knives wrapped up in his old carpet seeking some barn where he might go supperless to bed, he saw a monk going in his direction, and respectfully saluted him. As they were both walking at the same pace, they fell into conversation.

"Friend," said the monk, "how does it happen that you are dressed all in green? Are you perchance going to play the part of the fool in some mystery?".

"No, indeed, father," said Barnabas. "My name is Barnabas, and my business is that of juggler. It would be the finest calling in the world if I could eat every day."

"Friend Barnabas," answered the monk, "be careful what you say. There is no finer calling than the monastic. The priest celebrates the praise of God, the Virgin, and the saints; the life of a monk is a perpetual hymn to the Lord."

And Barnabas replied: "Father, I confess I spoke like an ignorant man. My estate cannot be compared to yours, and though there may be some merit in dancing and balancing a stick with a denier on top of it on the end of your nose, it is in no wise comparable to your merit. Father, I wish I might, like you, sing the Office every day, especially the Office of the Very Holy Virgin, to whom I am specially and piously devoted. I would willingly give up the art by which I am known from Soissons to Beauvais, in more than six hundred cities and villages, in order to enter the monastic life."

The monk was touched by the simplicity of the juggler, and as he was not lacking in discernment, he recognized in Barnabas one of those well-disposed men of whom Our Lord has said, "Let peace be with them on earth." And he made answer therefore:

"Friend Barnabas, come with me and I will see that you enter the monastery of which I am the Prior. He who led Mary the Egyptian through the desert put me across your path in order that I might lead you to salvation."

Thus did Barnabas become a monk. In the monastery which he entered, the monks celebrated most magnificently the cult of the Holy Virgin, each of them bringing to her service all the knowledge and skill which God had given him.

The Prior, for his part, wrote books, setting forth, according to the rules of scholasticism, all the virtues of the Mother of God. Brother Maurice copied these treatises with a cunning hand on pages of parchment, while Brother Aléxandre decorated them with delicate miniatures representing the Queen of Heaven seated on the throne of Solomon, with four lions on guard at the foot of it. Around her head, which was encircled by a halo, flew seven doves, the seven gifts of the Holy Spirit: fear, piety, knowledge, power, judgment, intelligence, and wisdom. With her were six golden-haired virgins: Humility, Prudence, Retirement, Respect, Virginity, and Obedience. At her feet two little figures, shining white and quite naked, stood in suppliant attitudes. They were souls imploring, not in vain, Her all-powerful intercession for their salvation. On another page Brother Aléxandre depicted Eve in the presence of Mary, that one might see at the same time sin and its redemption, woman humiliated, and the Virgin exalted. Among the other much-prized pictures in his book were the Well of Living Waters, the Fountain, the Lily, the Moon, the Sun, and the Closed Garden, of which much is said in the Canticle; the Gate of Heaven and the City of God. These were all images of the Virgin.

Brother Marbode, too, was one of the cherished children of Mary. He was ever busy cutting images of stone, so that his beard, his eyebrows and his hair were white with the dust, and his eyes perpetually swollen and full of tears. But he was a hardy and a happy man in his old age, and there was no doubt that the Queen of Paradise watched over the declining days of Her child. Marbode represented Her seated in a pulpit, Her forehead encircled by a halo, with an orb of pearls. He was at great pains to make the folds of Her robe cover the feet of Her of whom the prophet has said, "My beloved is like a closed garden."

At times he represented Her as a graceful child, and Her image seemed to say, "Lord, Thou art My Lord!"

There were also in the Monastery poets who composed prose writings in Latin and hymns in honor of the Most Gracious Virgin Mary; there was, indeed, one among them—a Picard—who translated the Miracles of Our Lady into rimed verses in the vulgar tongue.

Perceiving so great a competition in praise and so fine a harvest of good works, Barnabas fell to lamenting his ignorance and simplicity.

"Alas!" he sighed as he walked by himself one day in the little garden shaded by the Monastery wall, "I am so unhappy because I cannot, like my brothers, give worthy praise to the Holy Mother of God to whom I have consecrated all the love in my heart. Alas, I am a stupid fellow, without art, and for your service, Madame, I have no edifying sermons, no fine treatises nicely prepared according to the rules, no beautiful paintings, no cunningly carved statues, and no verses counted off by feet and marching in measure! Alas, I have nothing!"

Thus did he lament and abandon himself to his misery.

One evening when the monks were talking together by way of diversion, he heard one of them tell of a monk who could not recite anything but the *Ave Maria*. He was scorned for his ignorance, but after he died there sprang from his mouth five roses, in honor of the five letters in the name Maria. Thus was his holiness made manifest.

In listening to this story, Barnabas was conscious once more of the Virgin's beneficence, but he was not consoled by the example of the happy miracle, for his heart was full of zeal and he wanted to celebrate the glory of His Lady in Heaven.

He sought for a way in which to do this, but in vain, and each day brought him greater sorrow, until one morning he sprang joyously from his cot and ran to the chapel, where he remained alone for more than an hour. He returned thither again after dinner, and from that day onward he would go into the chapel every day the moment it was deserted, passing the greater part of the time which the other monks dedicated to the pursuit of the liberal arts and the sciences. He was no longer sad and he sighed no more. But such singular conduct aroused the curiosity of the other monks, and they asked themselves why Brother Barnabas retired alone so often, and the Prior, whose business it was to know everything that his monks were doing, determined to observe Barnabas. One day, therefore, when Barnabas was alone in the chapel, the Prior entered in company with two of the oldest brothers, in order to watch, through the bars of the door, what was going on within.

They saw Barnabas before the image of the Holy Virgin, his head on the floor and his feet in the air, juggling with six copper balls and twelve knives. In honor of the Holy Virgin he was performing the tricks which had in former days brought him the greatest fame. Not understanding that he was thus putting his best talents at the service of the Holy Virgin, the aged brothers cried out against such sacrilege. The Prior knew that Barnabas had a simple soul, but he believed that the man had lost his wits. All three set about to remove Barnabas from the chapel, when they saw the Virgin slowly descend from the altar and, with a fold of her blue mantle, wipe the sweat that streamed over the juggler's forehead.

Then the Prior, bowing his head down to the marble floor, repeated these words:

"Blessed are the pure in heart, for they shall see God."

"Amen," echoed the brothers, bowing down to the floor.

GUY DE MAUPASSANT

(1850—1893)

De Maupassant was born at the Château de Miromesnil in 1850. Distinguished though he is as a master of the novel form, and in spite of the fact that his half-dozen novels are powerful and significant works, it is his stories, of which he wrote several hundred, that constitute his chief claim to immortality. He is one of the first modern writers who consistently applied himself to the development of the short story as a separate literary form.

The Necklace is generally conceded to be one of Maupassant's most highly finished achievements. Though it belongs technically to the "surprise" type so ingeniously utilized at a later date by O. Henry, the surprise which marks the point of the tale is introduced not for its own sake alone, but in order to reveal at a stroke the tragedy through which Mathilde has lived.

The present version, translated by Jonathan Sturges, is reprinted by permission of the publisher, from The Odd Number, Harper & Brothers.

THE NECKLACE

SHE was one of those pretty and charming girls who are sometimes, as if by a mistake of destiny, born in a family of clerks. She had no dowry, no expectations, no means of being known, understood, loved, wedded, by any rich and distinguished man; and she let herself be married to a little clerk at the Ministry of Public Instruction.

She dressed plainly because she could not dress well, but she was as unhappy as though she had really fallen from her proper station; since with women there is neither caste nor rank; and beauty, grace, and charm act instead of family and birth. Natural fineness, instinct for what is elegant, suppleness of wit, are the sole hierarchy, and make from women of the people the equals of the very greatest ladies.

She suffered ceaselessly, feeling herself born for all the delicacies and all the luxuries. She suffered from the poverty of her dwelling, from the wretched look of the walls, from the worn-out chairs, from the ugliness of the curtains. All those things, of which another woman of her rank would never even have been conscious, tortured her and made her angry. The sight of the little Breton peasant who did her humble housework aroused in her regrets which were despairing, and distracted dreams. She thought of the silent ante-chambers hung with Oriental tapestry, lit by tall bronze candelabra, and of the two great footmen in knee-breeches who sleep in the big armchairs, made drowsy by the heavy warmth of the hot-air stove. She thought of the long *salons* fitted up with ancient silk, of the delicate furniture carrying priceless curiosities, and of the coquettish perfumed boudoirs made for talks at five o'clock with intimate friends, with men famous and sought after, whom all women envy and whose attention they all desire.

When she sat down to dinner, before the round table covered with a table-cloth three days old, opposite her husband, who uncovered the soup tureen and declared with an enchanted air, "Ah, the good *pot-au-feu!* I don't know anything better than that," she thought of dainty dinners, of shining silverware, of tapestry which peopled the walls with ancient personages and with strange birds flying in the midst of a fairy forest; and she thought of delicious dishes served on marvelous plates, and of the whispered gallantries which you listen to with a sphinx-like smile, while you are eating the pink flesh of a trout or the wings of a quail.

She had no dresses, no jewels, nothing. And she loved nothing but that; she felt made for that. She would so have liked to please, to be envied, to be charming, to be sought after.

She had a friend, a former schoolmate at the convent, who was rich, and whom she did not like to go and see any more, because she suffered so much when she came back.

But, one evening, her husband returned home with a triumphant air, and holding a large envelope in his hand.

"There," said he, "here is something for you."

She tore the paper sharply, and drew out a printed card which bore these words:

> "The Minister of Public Instruction and Mme. Georges Ramponneau request the honor of M. and Mme. Loisel's company at the palace of the Ministry on Monday evening, January 18th."

Instead of being delighted, as her husband hoped, she threw the invitation on the table with disdain, murmuring:

"What do you want me to do with that?"

"But, my dear, I thought you would be glad. You never go out, and this is such a fine opportunity. I had awful trouble to get it. Every one wants to go; it is very select, and they are not giving many invitations to clerks. The whole official world will be there."

She looked at him with an irritated eye, and she said, impatiently:

"And what do you want me to put on my back?"

He had not thought of that; he stammered:

"Why the dress you go to the theater in. It looks very well, to me."

He stopped, distracted, seeing that his wife was crying. Two great tears descended slowly from the corners of her eyes towards the corners of her mouth. He stuttered:

"What's the matter? What's the matter?"

But, by a violent effort, she had conquered her grief, and she replied, with a calm voice, while she wiped her wet cheeks:

"Nothing. Only I have no dress, and therefore I can't go to this ball. Give your card to some colleague whose wife is better equipped than I."

He was in despair. He resumed:

"Come, let us see, Mathilde. How much would it cost, a suitable dress, which you could use on other occasions, something very simple?"

She reflected several seconds, making her calculations and wondering also what sum she could ask without drawing on herself an immediate refusal and a frightened exclamation from the economical clerk.

Finally, she replied, hesitatingly:

"I don't know exactly, but I think I could manage it with four hundred francs."

He had grown a little pale, because he was laying aside just that amount to buy a gun and treat himself to a little shooting next summer on the plain of Nanterre, with several friends who went to shoot larks down there, of a Sunday.

But he said:

"All right. I will give you four hundred francs. And try to have a pretty dress."

The day of the ball drew near, and Mme. Loisel seemed sad, uneasy, anxious. Her dress was ready, however. Her husband said to her one evening:

"What is the matter? Come, you've been so queer these last three days."

And she answered:

"It annoys me not to have a single jewel, not a single stone, nothing to put on. I shall look like distress. I should almost rather not go at all."

He resumed:

"You might wear natural flowers. It's very stylish at this time of the year. For ten francs you can get two or three magnificent roses."

She was not convinced.

"No; there's nothing more humiliating than to look poor among other women who are rich."

But her husband cried:

"How stupid you are! Go look up your friend Mme. Forestier, and ask her to lend you some jewels. You're quite thick enough with her to do that."

She uttered a cry of joy:

"It's true. I never thought of it."

The next day she went to her friend and told of her distress.

Mme. Forestier went to a wardrobe with a glass door, took out a large jewel-box, brought it back, opened it, and said to Mme. Loisel:

"Choose, my dear."

She saw first of all some bracelets, then a pearl necklace, then a Venetian cross, gold, and precious stones of admirable workmanship. She tried on the ornaments before the glass, hesitated, could not make up her mind to part with them, to give them back. She kept asking:

"Haven't you any more?"

"Why, yes. Look. I don't know what you like."

All of a sudden she discovered, in a black satin box, a superb necklace of diamonds; and her heart began to beat with an immoderate desire. Her hands trembled as she took it. She fastened it around her throat, outside her high-necked dress, and remained lost in ecstasy at the sight of herself.

Then she asked, hesitating, filled with anguish:

"Can you lend me that, only that?"

"Why, yes, certainly."

She sprang upon the neck of her friend, kissed her passionately, then fled with her treasure.

The day of the ball arrived. Mme. Loisel made a great success. She was prettier than them all, elegant, gracious, smiling, and crazy with joy. All the men looked at her, asked her name, endeavored to be introduced. All the attachés of the Cabinet wanted to waltz with her. She was remarked by the minister himself.

She danced with intoxication, with passion, made drunk by pleasure, forgetting all, in the triumph of her beauty, in the glory of her success, in a sort of cloud of happiness composed of all this homage, of all this admiration, of all these awakened desires, and of that sense of complete victory which is so sweet to woman's heart.

She went away about four o'clock in the morning. Her husband had been sleeping since midnight, in a little deserted ante-room, with three other gentlemen whose wives were having a very good time.

He threw over her shoulders the wraps which he had brought, modest wraps of common life, whose poverty contrasted with the elegance of the ball dress. She felt this and wanted to escape so as not to be remarked by the other women, who were enveloping themselves in costly furs.

Loisel held her back.

"Wait a bit. You will catch cold outside. I will go and call a cab."

But she did not listen to him, and rapidly descended the stairs. When they were in the street they did not find a carriage; and they began to look for one, shouting after the cabmen whom they saw passing by at a distance.

They went down towards the Seine, in despair, shivering with cold. At last they found on the quay one of those ancient noctambulant coupés which, exactly as if they were ashamed to show their misery during the day, are never seen round Paris until after nightfall.

It took them to their door in the Rue des Martyrs, and once more, sadly, they climbed up homeward. All was ended for her. And as to him, he reflected that he must be at the Ministry at ten o'clock.

She removed the wraps, which covered her shoulders, before the glass, so as once more to see herself in all her glory. But suddenly she uttered a cry. She had no longer the necklace around her neck!

Her husband, already half-undressed, demanded:

"What is the matter with you?"

She turned madly towards him:

"I have—I have—I've lost Mme. Forestier's necklace."

He stood up, distracted.

"What!—how?—Impossible!"

And they looked in the folds of her dress, in the folds of her cloak, in her pockets, everywhere. They did not find it.

He asked:

"You're sure you had it on when you left the ball?"

"Yes, I felt it in the vestibule of the palace."

"But if you had lost it in the street we should have heard it fall. It must be in the cab."

"Yes. Probably. Did you take his number?"

"No. And you, didn't you notice it?"

"No."

They looked, thunderstruck, at one another. At last Loisel put on his clothes.

"I shall go back on foot," said he, "over the whole route which we have taken, to see if I can't find it."

And he went out. She sat waiting on a chair in her ball dress, without strength to go to bed, overwhelmed, without fire, without a thought.

Her husband came back about seven o'clock. He had found nothing.

He went to Police Headquarters, to the newspaper offices, to offer a reward; he went to the cab companies—everywhere, in fact, whither he was urged by the least suspicion of hope.

She waited all day, in the same condition of mad fear before this terrible calamity.

Loisel returned at night with a hollow, pale face; he had discovered nothing.

"You must write to your friend," said he, "that you have broken the clasp of her necklace and that you are having it mended. That will give us time to turn round."

She wrote at his dictation.

At the end of a week they had lost all hope.

And Loisel, who had aged five years, declared:

"We must consider how to replace that ornament."

The next day they took the box which had contained it, and they went to the jeweler whose name was found within. He consulted his books.

"It was not I, madame, who sold that necklace; I must simply have furnished the case."

Then they went from jeweler to jeweler, searching for a necklace like the other, consulting their memories, sick both of them with chagrin and with anguish.

They found, in a shop at the Palais Royal, a string of diamonds which seemed to them exactly like the one they looked for. It was worth forty thousand francs. They could have it for thirty-six.

So they begged the jeweler not to sell it for three days yet. And they made a bargain that he should buy it back for thirty-four thousand francs, in case they found the other one before the end of February.

Loisel possessed eighteen thousand francs which his father had left him. He would borrow the rest.

He did borrow, asking a thousand francs of one, five hundred of another, five louis here, three louis there. He gave notes, took up ruinous obligations, dealt with usurers, and all the race of lenders. He compromised all the rest of his life, risked his signature without even knowing if he could meet it; and, frightened by the pains yet to come, by the black misery which was about to fall upon him, by the prospect of all the physical privations and of all the moral tortures which he was to suffer, he went to get the new necklace, putting down upon the merchant's counter thirty-six thousand francs.

When Mme. Loisel took back the necklace Mme. Forestier said to her, with a chilly manner:

"You should have returned it sooner, I might have needed it."

She did not open the case, as her friend had so much feared. If she had detected the substitution, what would she have thought, what would she have said? Would she not have taken Mme. Loisel for a thief?

Mme. Loisel now knew the horrible existence of the needy. She took her part, moreover, all on a sudden, with heroism. That dreadful debt must be paid. She would pay it. They dismissed their servant; they changed their lodgings; they rented a garret under the roof.

She came to know what heavy housework meant and the odious cares of the kitchen. She washed the dishes, using her rosy nails on the greasy pots and pans. She washed the dirty linen, the shirts, and the dish-cloths, which she dried upon a line; she carried the slops down to the street every morning, and carried up the water, stopping for breath at every landing. And, dressed like a woman of the people, she went to the fruiterer, the grocer, the butcher, her basket on her arm, bargaining, insulted, defending her miserable money sou by sou.

Each month they had to meet some notes, renew others, obtain more time.

Her husband worked in the evening making a fair copy of some tradesman's accounts, and late at night he often copied manuscript for five sous a page.

And this life lasted ten years.

At the end of ten years they had paid everything, everything, with the rates of usury, and the accumulations of the compound interest.

Mme. Loisel looked old now. She had become the woman of impoverished households—strong and hard and rough. With frowsy hair, skirts askew, and red hands, she talked loud while washing the floor with great swishes of water. But sometimes, when her husband was at the office, she sat down near the window, and she thought of that gay evening of long ago, of that ball where she had been so beautiful and so fêted.

What would have happened if she had not lost that necklace? Who knows? who knows? How life is strange and how changeful! How little a thing is needed for us to be lost or to be saved!

But, one Sunday, having gone to take a walk in the Champs Elysées to refresh herself from the labors of the week, she suddenly perceived a woman who was leading a child. It was Mme. Forestier, still young, still beautiful, still charming.

Mme. Loisel felt moved. Was she going to speak to her? Yes, certainly. And now that she had paid, she was going to tell her all about it. Why not?

She went up.

"Good-day, Jeanne."

The other, astonished to be familiarly addressed by this plain good-wife, did not recognize her at all, and stammered:

"But—madame!—I do not know—You must have mistaken."

"No. I am Mathilde Loisel."

Her friend uttered a cry.

"Oh, my poor Mathilde! How you are changed!"

"Yes, I have had days hard enough, since I have seen you, days wretched enough—and that because of you!"

"Of me! How so?"

"Do you remember that diamond necklace which you lent me to wear at the ministerial ball?"

"Yes Well?"

"Well, I lost it."

"What do you mean? You brought it back."

"I brought you back another just like it. And for this we have been ten years paying. You can understand that it was not easy for us, us who had nothing. At last it is ended, and I am very glad."

Mme. Forestier had stopped.

"You say that you bought a necklace of diamonds to replace mine?"

"Yes. You never noticed it, then! They were very like."

And she smiled with a joy which was proud and naïve at once.

Mme. Forestier, strongly moved, took her two hands.

"Oh, my poor Mathilde! Why, my necklace was paste. It was worth at most five hundred francs!"

Italy

INTRODUCTION

ITALY never wholly lost the traditions of Rome. Geographically, linguistically, and racially, the Italians considered themselves the heirs of the Roman Empire. Yet, during the course of the Middle Ages, Italy was overrun in war after war by invaders from the North, who brought with them the songs and lays of the minstrels. Oriental influence was also strong, especially in the South, and the earliest traces of vernacular literature are found in Sicily.

The Italians have excelled in poetry and tales. The first great figure was Dante, and the first collection of prose fiction is the *Hundred Ancient Tales*, an accumulation of fables, legends, and more extended stories, collected from many sources. The *Novela*, or short story, developed from this early collection, and with Boccaccio, the first great writer of Italian prose, it reached its perfection. It seems that the *Novela* was one of those forms that exactly suited the taste of an entire people, and for nearly three hundred years it was assiduously developed. Boccaccio was followed by a dozen others, some of whom, like Masuccio and Bandello and Sacchetti, treated aspects of life which had been neglected by their master.

It was by no means an easy task to eliminate from this collection writers like Luigi da Porto, Granucci, Fortini, Doni and Basile, while including samples of the work of contemporaries in no wise superior, but there was no use in including twenty or thirty examples of *Novele* simply because all were good of their kind.

The tragic tale, the joke, the tale of foreign romantic background, the legend of antiquity, the contemporary tale of low-life, are all recounted with gusto by these energetic Italians. The majority of *Novele* are coarse, crude, cruel and, to the modern taste, shocking; yet among them we occasionally discover a lovely thing like Boccaccio's *Falcon*, or a lengthy story like Da Porto's *Novel of Juliet*, proving that the most robust writer could at times turn his hand to a delicate and moving narrative.

Because of the wide choice offered in the collected *Novele* of fifty writers, it was not necessary to extract from the epics and long prose romances of Ariosto, Tasso, Sannazaro and many others, what would in effect be simply *Novele* in another form.

With the decline of the Renaissance and the political power of the Italian states and republics, came a corresponding decline in the art of the tale. An occasional exception is seen, as in the little stories of Carlo Gozzi toward the end of the Eighteenth Century, but these have little relation to the old Italian tradition, which had meantime been absorbed by the rest of Europe. The epics and romances and *Novele* were early discovered and borrowed by the English dramatists, and by writers of every sort throughout Europe.

With the beginning of the Nineteenth Century came the Romanticists, Manzoni, Foscolo and the rest. These were poets and novelists, to whom the *Novela* meant very little. Their influence extended far into the century, and only with the advent of the naturalist Verga was there a return to the short story. And then it had no relation whatsoever to the art practised by Boccaccio. With Verga, De Amicis, Serao, Fogazzaro, and D'Annunzio, we are in the midst of the modern European literary movement.

The notation "no title in the original," made in several instances after the notes on Boccaccio, Ser Giovanni, Sacchetti, Masuccio, Bandello, Firenzuola, Grazzini, Cinthio, and Gozzi, means that the title given in this collection is furnished by the editors. The Italian editions usually offer a lengthy synopsis of the story.

THE BELL OF ATRI

(Anonymous: 13th or 14th Century)

THE HUNDRED ANCIENT TALES is a collection of short stories containing the earliest examples of prose fiction in the Italian language. They originated, in all probability, in Southern France, where the Troubadours flourished who brought over into Italy the material that was used by the first Italian writers. When and by whom these tales were written is not known.

How short can a short story be? *The Bell of Atri* is, of course, not a highly developed work of art, yet it is complete and effective. Longfellow used it in a rather long poem, but he added little that was essential to the narrative.

The present version is translated by Thomas Roscoe and reprinted from his *Italian Novelists*, London, no date. The full title of the story is *Concerning an Alarm Bell Instituted in the Time of King Giovanni*.

THE BELL OF ATRI

(The Hundred Ancient Tales, Novel 14)

IN the reign of King Giovanni d'Atri, there was ordered to be erected a certain great bell for the especial use of individuals who might happen to meet with any grievous injuries, when they were to ring as loudly as they could, for the purpose of obtaining redress. Now it so fell out that the rope in the course of time was nearly worn away, on which a bunch of snakeweed had been fastened to it, for the convenience of the ringers. One day a fine old courser belonging to a knight of Atri, which being no longer serviceable, had been turned out to run at large, was wandering near the place. Being hard pressed by famine, the poor steed seized hold of the snakeweed with his mouth, and sounded the bell pretty smartly. The council, on hearing the clamor, immediately assembled, as if to hear the petition of the horse, whose appearance seemed to declare that he required justice. Taking the case into consideration, it was soon decreed that the same cavalier whom the horse had so long served while he was young should be compelled to maintain him in his old age; and the king even imposed a fine in similar instances to the same effect.

GIOVANNI BOCCACCIO

(1313–1375)

BOCCACCIO is one of the supreme figures in Italian literature. Great as a reformer of the language, he was at the same time a born teller of tales. He tells us that he wrote stories at the age of seven. He was an enthusiastic traveller and observer of his fellow-men, a scholar, a scientist, and an official of the Florentine state. His most famous book, *The Decameron*, a collection of a hundred stories, was written soon after the great plague of 1348, which serves as a framework for the telling of the tales. Boccaccio took his material from fables, the histories of Greece and Rome and of the Orient, and occasionally from contemporary life. His best stories have been adapted by Shakespeare and a hundred others in plays, poems, and prose fiction.

The present version is translated by Thomas Roscoe and reprinted from his *Italian Novelists*, London, no date. The story has no title in the original.

THE FALCON

(The Decameron, 5th Day, Novel 9)

COPPO DI BORGHESE DOMENICHI, who was of our city, and a man of reverence and authority in his day, and from his virtues and manners, much more than from the nobility of his descent, worthy of everlasting remembrance, being now advanced in years, often took pleasure in the narration of past events, to which his retentive memory and pleasing delivery lent an unusual attraction. Among other interesting events he narrated to us that there once lived in Florence a youth called Federigo, son of Messer Philippo Alberighi, who for feats of arms and accomplishments was held in higher esteem than any cavalier of his age in Tuscany. This young man became deeply enamored of a lady called Monna Giovanna, reputed in her time one of the most beautiful and agreeable women in Florence; and in order to win her affections he gave a succession of tournaments, feasts, and banquets, and spared no expense in his entertainments. But this lady, not less discreet than beautiful, paid no regard to all that was done in her honor, nor condescended to notice the author of it. Federigo, thus spending all his property, and acquiring none in return, was soon stripped of his wealth, and became suddenly impoverished, having nothing now remaining but a small farm, on the produce of which he found a bare subsistence; yet he still retained a favorite falcon, which for her rare qualities was nowhere to be matched. Being thus unable to live any longer in the city in the style he was accustomed to, and being more than ever enamored of the lady, he departed to his little estate in the country, and there, without inviting any one to his house, he amused himself with his falcon, and endured his poverty with tranquil patience. It happened that when Federigo was reduced to this extremity, the husband of Monna Giovanna fell sick, and feeling the approach of death, made his will, leaving his possessions, which were very great, to an only son now growing up, and in the event of the son's death, to Monna Giovanna, whom he dearly loved; and he had no sooner subscribed his will than he died. Monna Giovanna having thus become a widow, went according to the custom of our ladies to pass her year of mourning in retirement, removing to one of her estates very near to the farm of Federigo. Hereupon it happened that her son was accustomed to visit Federigo, and taking great delight in hawks and dogs, and having often seen Federigo's falcon, he became wonderfully fond of it and ardently longed to possess it, but did not venture to ask for it, as he well knew how dear it was to its owner. Within a short time after this the boy fell sick. His mother, who had no other child, and loved him to excess, stood over him the whole day to tend and comfort him, often asking him and entreating him to tell her if there were anything in the world he desired, as, if it were possible to procure it, he should have it. The youth, after a repetition of these questions, at length said, "My dear mother, if you could by any means procure me Federigo's falcon, I think I should recover from my sickness." The lady hearing a request so far out of her power, began to consider what she might do to gratify her son's wish. She knew that Federigo had long loved her, but had never received from her so much as a single glance in return. How then (she reflected) shall I send or go to beg this falcon, which from all I hear is the best bird that ever flew, and moreover is now Federigo's sole maintenance; and how can I be guilty of so great a rudeness as to deprive a gentleman who has no other pleasure remaining, of this his only recreation? Thus troubled in her thoughts, she knew not what to reply to her son. Her maternal love, however, at last prevailed, and she determined to attempt to gratify his wishes, but resolved not to send, but to go herself to Federigo. She then said to her son, "My dear son, be comforted, and get well, for I promise you that the first thing in the morning, I will go myself for the falcon, and bring it to you." This promise brought a beam of joy into the boy's countenance, and the same day he showed evident signs of amendment. The next morning Monna Giovanna, taking with her another lady as a companion, proceeded to Federigo's humble habitation, and inquired for him. As it happened not to be a day fit for hawking, he was in his garden, and desired one of his people to go to the gate. He was beyond measure surprised when he heard that Monna Giovanna was asking for him, and ran in great joy to meet her. As soon as she saw him approach she gracefully moved to meet him, and respectfully saluting him, said, "Federigo, I am come to recompense you in some sort for the evil you have received at my hands, at a time when you loved me more than was wise on your part, and the recompense I intend is to make myself and my companion your guests at dinner to-day." To which Federigo with great humility replied, "Alas, madam! I do not recollect to have received any evil at your hands, but so much good that, if it were ever in my power, I should be happy, for the love I have borne you, and more so for the honor of this visit, to expend my fortune a second time in your honor"; and thus speaking, he respectfully led her into his house, and thence conducted her into his garden, and there, not having any other person to introduce her to, said, "Madam, this good woman, the wife of my husbandman, will wait on you whilst I prepare our table." Living in extreme poverty, Federigo was seldom in a state to receive any one in his house, and this morning being less prepared than usual, and finding nothing to show respect to a lady in whose honor he had entertained such numbers of people, he was grieved beyond measure, and stood in great perplexity, inveighing against his evil fortune as a man bereft of his senses, and running hither and thither, and finding neither money nor provision; and the hour being late, and his desire being great to show the lady some mark of attention, happening to cast his eyes on his favorite falcon, which was resting on its perch in his chamber, and seeing no other resource, he seized the poor bird, and finding it fat and in good condition, thought it would be a dish worthy of the lady, without further hesitation he wrung its neck, and giving it to a girl, ordered her to pluck it and place it on the spit and carefully roast it. He then spread on his table a napkin of snowy whiteness, one of the few things which yet remained to him of his former possessions, and after some time, with a cheerful aspect returned into the garden to the lady, and told her that a dinner, the best he could provide, was prepared for her. On this the lady with her companion went and seated themselves at the table, where Federigo with great courtesy waited on them, whilst they unknowingly ate his favorite bird. When they had risen from table, after some agreeable conversation, it seemed to the lady to be now a proper time to make known the purpose of her visit, and turning politely to Federigo, she thus spoke: "Calling to recollection your past life, Federigo, and remembering my reserve, which you perhaps esteemed hardheartedness and cruelty, I doubt not that you will wonder at my presumption when you learn the object of my visit; but if you now had, or ever had had children, and knew the strength of a parent's affection, I feel assured that you would in some measure pardon me; and though you have none, I, who have a dear and beloved son, cannot yet forego the common affections of a mother. I am, then, by maternal love and duty compelled to ask of you the gift of a possession which I know is indeed very dear to you, and justly so, since your evil fortune has left you no other comfort in your adversity. The gift then I ask is your falcon, which my son is so desirous of possessing, that if I do not obtain it for him, I fear it will so far aggravate the illness under which he labors, that I shall lose him. On this account, therefore, I entreat you, not by the love which you profess for me (by which you ought in no degree to be governed), but by the magnanimity of your character, which is better manifested in a courtesy of this kind than in any other way, that you would do me the favor to bestow it on me, so that by this gift I may be enabled to preserve the life of my dear and only son, and I shall myself be for ever indebted to you." Federigo thus hearing the request of the lady, and seeing it out of his power to gratify her, as he had served his falcon for dinner, began in her presence to weep most bitterly, and became unable to utter a word in reply. The lady supposing that Federigo's grief arose from his affection to his falcon, and his regret to part with it, and expecting a refusal, prepared herself for the worst. "Since the hour, most honored lady," began Federigo, "that

I first fixed my affection on you, I have always found Fortune most perverse and cruel to me, but all her blows I consider light in comparison with the one she has now dealt me, seeing that you have condescended to visit my house, which when I was rich you would not deign to enter, and entreat me for so small a gift; for she has so contrived that it is not in my power to grant it you, and why it is not, you shall briefly hear. When you informed me that you meant to honor me with your company to dinner, considering your rank, and that it was only proper that I should pay you due honor by procuring every delicacy in my power, as is becoming on such occasions, and recollecting the falcon which you now request of me, and its many excellent qualities, I considered it a dish not unworthy to be placed before you, and I therefore this morning served it up to you roasted at dinner, a thing which at the time I considered most opportune, but finding now that you wish to possess the falcon alive for your sick son, my inability to gratify you grieves me so far that I think I shall never know happiness more." In confirmation of his words he then produced the feathers and beak and talons of the poor bird. Monna Giovanna at this recital reprehended him for killing so fine a falcon for a lady's dinner, at the same time, however, highly commending in her own mind his magnanimity, which it had not been in the power of Fortune to abase. The lady having thus lost all chance of possessing the falcon, and despairing of the recovery of her son, thanked Federigo for the honor done her, and for his intended good-will, and departed very much dejected. Her son, either through pining for the falcon, or from his complaint being aggravated by disappointment, died a few days after, to the great grief of his mother. After having for some time indulged her sorrow and tears, her brothers seeing that she was left extremely rich, and was still young, entreated her to marry again. This she was not desirous of doing, but finding herself constantly assailed by their request, and recollecting the noble conduct of Federigo, and this last instance of his magnanimity in having sacrificed the finest falcon in the world out of respect to her, she said to her brothers, "I should willingly, if it were agreeable to you, remain in my present state, but if you insist that I marry, I will assuredly take no one for my husband but Federigo de gli Alberighi." On which her brothers, smiling, replied, "What folly is this? Would you marry a man who is a beggar?" To this she answered, "Brothers, I well know that the matter is as you state it, but I choose rather a man that hath need of wealth, than wealth that hath need of a man." The brothers seeing her fixed determination, and knowing the genuine worth of Federigo, notwithstanding his poverty, bestowed their sister on him with all her fortune. Federigo thus unexpectedly found himself united to a beautiful lady whom he had long dearly loved, and passed the remainder of his days in peace and happiness.

SER GIOVANNI

(Flourished about 1380)

THIS writer was called simply Ser Giovanni Il Fiorentino, the Florentine. Very little is known about him, except that he was a notary who lived in Florence and began his collection of tales called *Il Pecorone*, or *The Dunce*, in 1378. He was influenced by his great contemporary Boccaccio. Like *The Decameron*, the *Pecorone* is set within a fictitious framework: a young man falls in love with a nun, becomes a chaplain and during the hours he is able to see her, the two exchange stories.

Like most of the brilliant writers of *novele*, Giovanni excels in the quality of raciness. Many of his tales are based upon history, with a plentiful admixture of anecdotes, true and untrue. *Galgano* is somewhat exceptional among the stories of the time, in that it reveals a delicacy and reticence that seem to have appealed but rarely to the full-blooded Italians of the early Renaissance.

The present version is translated by Thomas Roscoe and reprinted from his *Italian Novelists*, London, no date. The story has no title in the original.

GALGANO

(*Il Pecorone*, 1st Day, Novel 1)

HAVING agreed upon the manner in which they were to meet each other in the convent parlor, as we have already stated, the two lovers were true to the appointed hour. With mutual pleasure and congratulations, they seated themselves at each other's side, when Friar Auretto, in the following words, began: "It is now my intention, my own Saturnina, to treat you with a little love-tale, founded on some incidents which really occurred, not very long ago, in Siena. There resided there a noble youth of the name of Galgano, who, besides his birth and riches, was extremely clever, valiant, and affable, qualities which won him the regard of all ranks of people in the place. But I am very sorry to add that, attracted by the beauty of a Sienese lady, no other, you must know, than the fair Minoccia, wedded to our noble cavalier, Messer Stricca (though I beg this may go no further), our young friend unfortunately, and too late, fell passionately in love with her.

"So violently enamored did he shortly become, that he purloined her glove, which he wore with her favorite colors wherever he went at tilts and tourneys, at rich feasts and festivals, all of which he was proud to hold in honor of his love: yet all these failed to render him agreeable to the lady, a circumstance that caused our poor friend Galgano no little pain and perplexity. A prey to the excessive cruelty and indifference of one dearer to him than his own life, who neither noticed nor listened to him, he still followed her like her shadow, contriving to be near her at every party, whether a bridal or a christening, a funeral or a play. Long and vainly, with love-messages after love-messages, and presents after presents, did he sue; but never would the noble lady deign to receive or listen to them for a moment, ever bearing herself more reserved and harshly as he more earnestly pressed the ardor of his suit.

"It was thus his fate to remain subject to this very irksome and overwhelming passion until, wearied out, at length he would break into words of grief and bitterness against his 'bosom's lord'. 'Alas! dread master of my destiny,' he would say, 'O Love! can you behold me thus wasting my very soul away, ever loving but never beloved again? See to it, dread lord, that you are not, in so doing, offending against your own laws!' And so, unhappily dwelling upon the lady's cruelty, he seemed fast verging upon despair; then again humbly resigning himself to the yoke he bore, he resolved to await some interval of grace, watching, however vainly, for some occasion of rendering himself more pleasing to the object he adored.

"Now it happened that Messer Stricca and his consort went to pass some days at their country seat near Siena; and it was not long before the lovesick Galgano was observed to cross their route, to hang upon their skirts, and to pass along the same way, always with the hawk upon his hand, as if violently set upon bird-hunting. Often, indeed, he passed so close to the villa where the lady dwelt, that one day being seen by Messer Stricca, who recognized him, he was very familiarly entreated to afford them the pleasure of his company; 'and I hope', added Messer Stricca, 'that you will stay the evening with us.' Thanking his friend very kindly for the invitation, Galgano, strange to say, at the same time begged to be held excused, pleading another appointment, which he believed—he was sorry—he was obliged to keep. 'Then,' added Messer Stricca, 'at least step in and take some little refreshment': to which the only reply returned was, 'A thousand thanks, and farewell, Messer Stricca, for I am in haste.' The moment the latter had turned his back, our poor lover began to upbraid himself bitterly for not availing himself of the invitation, exclaiming, 'What a wretch am I not to accept such an offer as this! I should at least have seen her—her whom from my soul I cannot help loving beyond all else in the world.'

"As he thus went, meditating upon the same subject along his solitary way, it chanced that he sprung a large jay, on which he instantly gave his hawk the wing, which pursuing its quarry into Messer Stricca's gardens and there striking true, the ensuing struggle took place. Hearing the hawk's cry, both he and his lady ran towards the garden balcony, in time to see, and were surprised at the skill and boldness of the bird in seizing and bringing down its game. Not in the least aware of the truth, the lady inquired of her husband to whom the bird belonged. 'Mark the hawk,' replied Messer Stricca; 'it does its work well; it resembles its master, who is one of the handsomest and most accomplished young men in Siena, and a very excellent young fellow, too; —yes, it does well.' 'And who may that be?' said his wife, with a careless air. 'Who,' returned he, 'but the noble Galgano—the same, love, who just now passed by. I wish he had come in to sup with us, but he would not. He is certainly one of the finest and best-tempered men I ever saw.' And so saying, he rose from the window, and they went to supper. Galgano, in the meanwhile, having given his hawk the call, quietly pursued his way; but the praises lavished upon him by her husband made an impression upon the lady's mind such as the whole of his previous solicitations had failed to produce. However strange, she dwelt upon them long and tenderly. It happened that about this very time, Messer Stricca was chosen ambassador from the Sienese to the people of Perugia, and setting out in all haste, he was compelled to take a sudden leave of his lady. I am sorry to have to observe that the moment the cavalcade was gone by, recalling the idea of her noble lover, the lady likewise despatched an embassy to our young friend, entreating him, after the example of her husband, to favor her with his company in the evening. No longer venturing to refuse, he sent a grateful answer back that he would very willingly attend. And having heard tidings of Messer Stricca's departure for Perugia, he set out at a favorable hour in the evening, and speedily arrived at the the house of the lady to whom he had been so long and so vainly attached.

"Checking his steed in full career, he threw himself off, and the next moment found himself in her presence, falling at her feet and saluting her with the most respectful and graceful carriage. She took him joyously by the hand, bidding him a thousand tender welcomes, and setting before him the choicest fruits and refreshments of the season. Then inviting him to be seated, he was served with the greatest variety and splendor; and more delicious than all, the bright lady herself presided there, no longer frowning and turning away when he began to breathe the story of his love and sufferings into her ear. Delighted and surprised beyond his proudest hopes, Galgano was profuse in his expressions of gratitude and regard, though he could not quite conceal his wonder at this happy and unexpected change; entreating, at length, as a particular favor, that she would deign to acquaint him with its blessed cause. 'That will I do soon,' replied the glowing beauty;

'I will tell you every word, and wherefore did I send for you'; and she looked into his face with a serene and pure yet somewhat mournful countenance. 'Indeed,' returned her lover, a little perplexed, 'words can never tell half of what I felt, dear lady, when I heard you had this morning sent for me, after having desired and followed you for so long a time in vain.' 'Listen to me, and I will tell you, Galgano; but first sit a little nearer to me, for, alas! I love you. A few days ago, you know, you passed near our house when hawking, and my husband told me that he saw you, and invited you in to supper, but you would not come. At that moment your hawk sprang and pursued its prey, when seeing the noble bird make such a gallant fight, I inquired to whom it belonged, and my husband replied, "To whom should it belong but to the most excellent young man in Siena"; and that it did well to resemble you, as he had never met a more pleasing and accomplished gentleman. 'Did he—did he say that?' interrupted her lover. 'He did indeed, and much more, praising you to me over and over; until hearing it, and knowing the tenderness you have long borne me, I could not resist the temptation of sending for you hither'; and, half blushes, half tears, she confessed that she was no longer indifferent to him, and that such was the occasion of it. 'Can the whole of this be true?' exclaimed Galgano. 'Alas! too true,' she replied. 'I know not how it is, but I wish he had not praised you so.' After struggling with himself a few moments, the unhappy lover withdrew his hand from hers, saying, 'Now God forbid that I should do the least wrong to one who has so nobly expressed himself, and who has ever shown so much kindness and courtesy to me.' Then suddenly rising, as with an effort, from his seat, he took a gentle farewell of the lady, not without some tears shed on both sides; both loving, yet respecting each other. Never afterwards did this noble youth allude to the affair in the slightest way, but always treated Messer Stricca with the utmost regard and reverence during his acquaintance with the family."

FRANCO SACCHETTI

(Ca. 1335–Ca. 1400)

ANOTHER of the Fourteenth Century writers who fell under the influence of Boccaccio is Franco Sacchetti. Sacchetti, though he was prominent in Florentine political affairs, was essentially a writer and poet. His collection of stories, the *Novelliero*, contains some three hundred tales, the best of which are racy anecdotes of contemporary life, related with wit and humour. They constitute an invaluable picture of the life of the lower classes of the day.

The Two Ambassadors falls into the category of the joke story, so cleverly elaborated more than five hundred years later by O. Henry. But, unlike many of its kind, it is intrinsically interesting because of the multiplicity of human touches with which the writer has been able to make his characters live.

The present version is translated by Thomas Roscoe and reprinted from his *Italian Novelists*, London, no date. The story has no title in the original.

THE TWO AMBASSADORS

(*Novelliero*, Novel 31)

AT the period when the city of Arezzo was under the sway of Bishop Guido, the people of Casentino had occasion to send two ambassadors, requiring of him certain articles they were desirous should be granted them. Having been informed of the particulars of their mission, they were told to hold themselves in readiness for their departure on the ensuing morning. Preparing their luggage in all haste, the two ambassadors accordingly set out on their way; and they had not traveled many miles, before one of them, addressing his companion, said, "Do you recollect all the particulars which they informed us of in so hasty a way?" And the other replied that he feared he hardly did. "But," said his companion, "I relied chiefly upon you"; to which the other rejoined, "And I trusted to you;" while each regarding the other, exclaimed, "We are in a pretty scrape then! What shall we do?" At length the one said, "I will tell you what: let us go on to the next inn, and perhaps after a good dinner we shall remember them better: yes, we shall be sure to remember them." "That is well said," added his companion; and jogging on together, half asleep and half awake, about three o'clock they contrived to reach the first inn. As it was a matter so nearly connected with their embassy, they ordered dinner directly, racking their brains in the meantime to recover some of the articles they had lost. Having taken their seats at table, they luckily found the wine good; and so it was that they were more pleased with this circumstance than sorry for the mission they had forgotten. Indeed it was so excellent, that they repeatedly emptied their glasses, toasting all their friends in town until they became half stupefied, so that, far from recollecting their embassy after dinner, they were in no condition even to talk about it, and hardly knowing where they were, they both dropped asleep.

On rousing themselves once more, one of them inquired of the other whether he had yet succeeded. "I know not," was the reply; "but I know that our host's is the best wine I ever drank: the truth is, I have never thought about it since dinner, and now I hardly know where I am." "And I declare it has been the same with me," answered his friend; "the Lord only knows what we shall do! However, we will stay here to-day and to-night, for the night is always favorable to memory; we cannot fail to recollect the whole." To this the other agreed; and they stayed there the remainder of the day, repeating the experiment of the wine, frequently finding themselves in the clouds, where, however, they found nothing of their mission. The same story was repeated at supper; and they afterwards with difficulty found their way to bed. At breakfast the next morning the inquiry was as vainly repeated, both declaring that they had not so much as dreamed about the matter, and that they had not got the most distant notion of it, having never slept so soundly in all their lives. "The devil is in the wine, I think," cried one; "let us mount horse again, and see what that will do; it will come when we are not thinking about it on the road." So they again set out, occasionally asking each other as they went, "Well, have you got it yet?" "No; have you?" "Not I, indeed." And in this way they journeyed along till they came to Arezzo, where they alighted at one of the first hotels. There they retired into a private room, for the purpose of putting their heads seriously together, as it was high time to recollect what was their business. But I am sorry to add, it was all in vain; and such was their hopeless condition, that one said, "Come, let us go; and God help us at the worst!" "But will He help us?" said the other. "What must we say? what do we know about the matter?" "Well, but we must go through with the business; so let us go and do our best." So, trusting to Fortune, they requested an audience of the bishop, saying they had some matters of importance to communicate to him; and being introduced into his presence, they made a very low obeisance, and remained silent. Upon this the bishop with great dignity approached them, and taking them by the hand, said, "You are welcome, gentlemen; what tidings of import may you bring?" Each of the ambassadors now looked at the other, and bowing, said, "Do you speak!" "No, sir," was the reply; "do you speak, sir; I cannot think of it;" till at length the boldest of the two, addressing the bishop, observed: "We come, my lord, as ambassadors from your poor servants of Casentino, and I can assure your Grace that both those who send us and we who are sent are equally devoted to you; but, please your Grace, we are all of us men of fact, but of few words: our mission was intrusted to us in haste; and whatever may be the occasion of it, either our assembly must have informed us wrong, or we have in some way misunderstood them. Nevertheless, we humbly recommend both them and ourselves to your Grace's good offices; though what possessed them to send us on such a mission, or ourselves to come, we cannot exactly say." The good bishop, like a wise man, only patting them on the shoulder, said,

"Well, well, my friends, it is all right; go home, and say to my dear children of Casentino that I shall always be happy to serve them every way in my power; so much so, that henceforward they need be at no expense in appointing ambassadors to my court; let them only write to me, and I will reply agreeably to their wishes."

The bishop then taking leave of them, our ambassadors resumed their way, saying as they went, "Let us take care not to fall into the same error on our return." "But," said one, "we cannot easily do that; we have got nothing to remember." "Yet we must have our wits about us," returned the other; "for they will ask what we said in our oration, and what was the reply. For if the good people were to suspect that our embassy, like many others, was all a joke, they would never employ us again; and farewell to our occupation—it is gone." To this the more politic of the two replied, "Oh, leave that to me; we will continue in office, trust me. I will tell them such a story about the embassy, and what passed on both sides, as would deceive wiser heads than theirs. The bishop shall say such polite things of them as shall make them in good humor with themselves for an age to come. I will tell them of the letter, and how he thinks himself highly honored by their alliance." "That is well thought," said the other; "and let us spur along a little, that we may get in time for dinner at the same inn—you know where." "That is well thought," echoed the other; and mending their pace at the idea of the Frontignac, they soon dismounted, all in a heat, and without waiting for dinner, called out for some of the same wine. "Good sirs," replied the waiter, "we have some better than ever;" and the ambassadors kept him pretty sharply employed in drawing the bottles, until the wine began to get low, and their politic heads somewhat too elevated. Grieved to hear this, these patterns of diplomacy were compelled to mount again, and the next stage or two brought them into the presence of their employers, where, finding it easier to recollect their own lies than the truths which had been reposed in them, they mystified the good people in such a manner that they were highly pleased with the success of the embassy. They talked in so bold and lofty a tone of the orations they had delivered, that some of the audience compared them to Tully and Quintilian; and the thanks of the assembly being unanimously voted to them, they were afterwards promoted to other offices of great honor and emolument. Nor will this appear very extraordinary if we reflect on the sort of people, of a higher rank than our heroes, whom we every day see entrusted with public missions, and who are about as much suited to their business as a common trooper taken from the ranks; and yet they write long letters, assuring the Government that they are busied day and night in the affairs of the nation, and that all the lucky events which fall out are wholly to be imputed to their skill. Did they tell truth, however, they would own that they had as little merit in bringing them about as a cabbage, or any other vegetating substance, though they are richly recompensed and promoted to the highest honors, in consideration of the ingenious lies and forgeries which they pass upon their countrymen.

MASUCCIO (GUARDATO)

(Flourished latter half of 15th Century)

MASUCCIO was born at Salerno, of noble parentage. He was a resident at the Court of Naples, in the capacity of secretary, for the greater part of his life. His fifty tales, collected in a volume called the *Novellino*, are vivid pictures both of the peasants and lower burgher classes, and of the nobility. *The Cavalier of Toledo* is furnished with a contemporary background and reveals the writer's skill in relating a romantic episode with skill and sympathy. Masuccio has the distinction of having written one of the earliest stories in the series that gave Shakespeare his *Romeo and Juliet*.

The present version is translated by Thomas Roscoe and reprinted from his *Italian Novelists*, London, no date. The story has no title in the original.

THE CAVALIER OF TOLEDO

(Novellino, Novel 50)

THE last in my collection of those noble and virtuous actions which I have always been desirous of commemorating, is one related to me by a distinguished foreigner, which, as being strictly true, it is with equal pride and pleasure I proceed to detail. There resided some time ago in the famous city of Toledo a cavalier named Messer Piero Lopez d'Aiala, of high and ancient lineage, whose only son, a fine and spirited youth of the name of Aries, had the misfortune to engage in a nocturnal brawl. Both parties, in one of which was the king's particular favorite, drawing their swords, Messer Aries, engaging with the latter, passed his weapon through his body on the spot. On discovering the rank of his adversary, aware of the royal favor enjoyed by him, and dreading the indignation of his monarch, the youth resolved to take flight, and being furnished by his father with horses and attendants, he set out to try his fortunes in another land. And hearing of the sanguinary war then waging between the English and the French in the territories of the latter, he resorted without delay to the scene of action, burning with the hope of signalizing himself during the campaign. Arriving in the French army, he had the good fortune to alight at the quarters of the Count d'Armagnac, captain-general of the king's forces, and related to the royal house of France. With his permission, the young Castilian employed the remains of his small resources in equipping himself for battle, in which he so greatly signalized himself, both by his courage and his conduct, as well in open field as in the siege, that he became at once admired and celebrated by his own party and dreaded by his adversaries. In the course of time he rose so high in the esteem of his commander, no less than of the French monarch, that he was entrusted and honored above any other favorites of the court, being in a little while promoted to the rank of campo-major, and acquitting himself in such a manner that he was consulted in almost every action. The campaign being concluded with great honor and advantage on the part of the French, with the aid of the young and enterprising Castilian, both armies were compelled by the severity of the season to retire into winter quarters, and, with the chief part of the general officers and cavaliers, our noble adventurer sought the gaieties of Paris.

In order to celebrate his successes in the most popular way, the king sent an invitation to all his chief lords and barons to be present with their ladies at an appointed festival, along with their followers and companions-in-arms. First in the train of favorite nobles, magnificently arrayed in the honors he had won, appeared the Count d'Armagnac, accompanied by his lovely and only daughter, whose charms attracted every eye. The joyous and splendid feast began, and was celebrated throughout many happy days with all the pleasures which love, and mirth, and music could afford; and still the star whose brightness eclipsed the beauties of the rest was the eye of the Count's fair daughter. And as if to show that her taste was in no way inferior to her beauty and accomplishments, having glanced her eye through the ranks of youth and chivalry marshalled around her, it ever returned and rested on the fine features of the Spanish cavalier, the music of whose fame and virtues had already sounded sweet in her ears. Too incautiously dwelling on these, the idea took her fancy captive, until she at last became so deeply interested in him, that whenever she passed the day without seeing or conversing with him she felt her existence a burden to her. Possessing no one in whom she could confide, in spite of all her struggles, her feelings, when in his presence, half betrayed the secret which preyed upon her heart: her eyes, her voice, and her very motions, when in his presence, or addressing him, all expressed far deeper and softer emotions than language dared to reveal. Nor was the object of them either so cold or so inexperienced as not to be sensible of the impression he had made. But although he thought her the most beautiful woman he had ever seen, the numerous favors he had received from the Count, her father, were so great as to banish every idea of his own gratification in attaching her affections to himself. With this virtuous resolve, he affected to misunderstand the nature of her impassioned feelings, assuming an apparent calmness in his manners, and a coldness, which struck a pang to the unhappy lady's heart. Unable longer to contend with the variety of emotions which shook her bosom and hourly preyed upon her life, she resolved, with the impulse of despair, to upbraid him for his cruelty, to unfold her love, and to die. And, half blinded with streaming tears, she committed her unhappy secret to paper, filled with the very soul of wretched passion, an appeal which no heart of marble, much less that of a fond lover, could have withstood. The conclusion was, that she had resolved to die rather than to survive the weakness of betraying her unhappy love. The young page to whom she confided the letter, conceiving from her manner that it contained something of high importance, and fearful of the result, bore it immediately to the Count, his master. It is impossible to express her father's surprise and grief on learning the extravagance and folly of which this, his only daughter, had been guilty; but every noble spirit shunning infamy and disgrace beyond death itself, may form some idea of his sensations. In this afflicting circumstance he adopted and rejected a thousand various plans of punishing his unworthy child; but as he felt that it ought to be something proportionate to the intolerable pain which she had thus inflicted upon him, he first determined to try the worth and firmness of the young Castilian, and took his measures accordingly. Having carefully wrapped and sealed the letter, he returned it to the boy with orders to deliver it to Messer Aries, and having waited for a reply, to bring it immediately back to him. These orders being promptly complied with, the young cavalier received it with a throb of ecstasy as he caught the name of his beloved; yet having already prepared his mind by strict discipline and self-control, he persevered in braving the fascinating danger. Armed strong in rectitude, he replied with all the delicacy and honor of a true knight to the lady's letter, beseeching her in conclusion rather to inflict any kind of punishment upon him, even unto death, than tempt him either in thought or word to presume on what might offend the honor and dignity of the Count, her father. Dreading, nevertheless, to hurt the feelings of her he loved, and aware of the fatal consequences of scorned or disappointed affections in a woman's soul, he implied the high honor and gratification he should have experienced in indulging such lofty hopes. "Would you venture," he continued, "to throw yourself upon your father's confidence, revealing to him every feeling of your breast (fully sensible as I am of the inequality of our lot), and were it possible that should smile upon our loves, then, only then, might we pronounce ourselves blest; but otherwise forget me—hate me; for when I dwell on the obligations I owe to your father, neither beauty nor ambition, nor any charms or treasures upon earth, shall lead me to sully, in any manner or degree, the brightness of his name."

Having despatched his answer by the same discreet little mesenger, he awaited in much fear and anxiety the result of the strange circumstances in which he was so deeply engaged. The page instantly ran to his master with the above reply, whose previous sorrow and indignation were much diminished on perusing the noble sentiments entertained by the cavalier, and such was his admiration and regard, that he even became gentle and loving as before to his beautiful but weak and unhappy girl. Under these feelings, without saying a word to his daughter, he hastened into the presence of his sovereign, to whom in no slight agitation he recounted the whole of the affair; and after unfolding his own feelings and sentiments on the subject, he entreated that the king would graciously deign to offer his advice. Gifted with great natural sagacity and prudence, the monarch expressed himself by no means surprised at the weak conduct shown by the young lady, being nothing, he declared, very strange or unusual; but he could scarcely prevail upon himself to believe the extraordinary resolution and constancy displayed by the cavalier. However high he had estimated his worth, he had never imagined him capable of such true greatness of soul, in thus sacrificing both ambition and love at the shrine of duty and fidelity.

The king then advised, or rather commanded, him to adopt the most generous resolution in his power; and sending forthwith for the noble Castilian, he closed the door on his attendants, and seizing him affectionately by the hand, he exclaimed, "I have long been sensible, Aries, of your high worth, evinced in all your actions, since you first joined my armies under the patronage of the Count. There has been nothing wanting to complete the excellence of your character, save an occasion to display the hidden force and rectitude of your principles, in the trial of which you have acquitted yourself so nobly, so honorably, and respected the persons whom you loved. I am rejoiced to think that your virtues in peace are equal to the courage and skill you so well displayed in war. We are truly indebted to you, and must endeavor to find such a reward as you may like, such as may evince our gratitude for your good deeds, and commemorate your virtue to later times. I have heard the whole of your generous conduct from the lips of the Count, and if nobility of mind and the best qualities of the heart may entitle you to the lady's love, you not only deserve her, but the very highest and richest princess in the state. But she is beautiful, she loves you, and you are at liberty, when you so please, to take her for your wife." The

Count then likewise came forward, and confirming everything the king had said, tenderly embraced the cavalier, considering himself honored in possessing such a son-in-law.

Equally surprised and rejoiced at the unexpected turn of affairs in his favor, the Castilian, with singular modesty, replied, "Although I am aware that the high authority of your majesty and the noble qualities of the Count are sufficient to exalt me to any degree of rank, I am at the same time too sensible of the inequality of my own birth and fortunes to venture upon such a step as you have generously proposed. Permit me to be near your majesty, and to serve you to the utmost of my ability, as I have hitherto done; but let your majesty and the Count both take it again into consideration how far the subject of your favor may be worthy of so high an honor." But the generous monarch persisted in his intentions, and in order to bring the affair to a speedy and happy termination, he commanded that a sumptuous festival should be held the ensuing day in his palace, which took place in the most gay and magnificent style. Proud trains of lords and cavaliers and gay bevies of ladies, with music, dance, and song, gave life and spirit to the scene. In the midst of these proceedings, the fair daughter of the Count, who had remained ignorant of all the previous explanations, was led forward, arrayed in her bridal ornaments; at the same moment, Messer Aries, the Castilian cavalier, was proclaimed by the heralds without to the applauding people, captain-general of the king's armies, and immediately afterwards the monarch presented the young bride at the altar, where the noble cavalier received her hand.

The most rapturous surprise and joy beamed in the eyes of the lovers and the guests as this novel and happy ceremony was announced through the assembly. The feast and the dance revived with double spirit. Congratulations, commendations, and inquiries poured in on all sides upon the happy parties, until their union became the favorite topic no less of the court than of the people. Murmurs of applause ran through the rooms as the cavalier led forth his beautiful and happy bride to reap, at her father's castle, the fruits of his virtue and his valor.

NICCOLO MACCHIAVELLI

(1464—1527)

MACCHIAVELLI is best known to the world as author of a famous book on statecraft, entitled *The Prince*, and of a *History of Florence*. Like many of the remarkable men of his time, he was an inquiring and many-sided person: statesman, intriguer, political theorist, dramatist, and story-teller. *Belphagor*, exceptional among early Italian stories, is not part of a collection, and was published after the author's death. This tale is a spirited retelling of an old subject, familiar to every student of comparative literature.

The present version is translated by Thomas Roscoe, and reprinted from his *Italian Novelists*, London, no date.

BELPHAGOR

WE read in the ancient archives of Florence the following account, as it was received from the lips of a very holy man, greatly respected by every one for the sanctity of his manners at the period in which he lived. Happening once to be deeply absorbed in his prayers, such was their efficacy, that he saw an infinite number of condemned souls, belonging to those miserable mortals who had died in their sins, undergoing the punishment due to their offences in the regions below. He remarked that the greater part of them lamented nothing so bitterly as their folly in having taken wives, attributing to them the whole of their misfortunes. Much surprised at this, Minos and Rhadamanthus, with the rest of the infernal judges, unwilling to credit all the abuse heaped upon the female sex, and wearied from day to day with its repetition, agreed to bring the matter before Pluto. It was then resolved that the conclave of infernal princes should form a committee of inquiry, and should adopt such measures as might be deemed most advisable by the court in order to discover the truth or falsehood of the calumnies which they heard. All being assembled in council, Pluto addressed them as follows: "Dearly beloved demons! Though by celestial dispensation and the irreversible decree of fate this kingdom fell to my share, and I might strictly dispense with any kind of celestial or earthly responsibility, yet, at it is more prudent and respectful to consult the laws and to hear the opinion of others, I have resolved to be guided by your advice, particularly in a case that may chance to cast some imputation upon our government. For the souls of all men daily arriving in our kingdom still continue to lay the whole blame upon their wives, and as this appears to us impossible, we must be careful how we decide in such a business, lest we also should come in for a share of their abuse, on account of our too great severity; and yet judgment must be pronounced, lest we be taxed with negligence and with indifference to the interests of justice. Now, as the latter is the fault of a careless, and the former of an unjust judge, we, wishing to avoid the trouble and the blame that might attach to both, yet hardly seeing how to get clear of it, naturally enough apply to you for assistance, in order that you may look to it, and contrive in some way that, as we have hitherto reigned without the slightest imputation upon our character, we may continue to do so for the future."

The affair appearing to be of the utmost importance to all the princes present, they first resolved that it was necessary to ascertain the truth, though they differed as to the best means of accomplishing this object. Some were of opinion that they ought to choose one or more from among themselves, who should be commissioned to pay a visit to the world, and in a human shape endeavor personally to ascertain how far such reports were grounded in truth. To many others it appeared that this might be done without so much trouble merely by compelling some of the wretched souls to confess the truth by the application of a variety of tortures. But the majority being in favor of a journey to the world, they abided by the former proposal. No one, however, being ambitious of undertaking such a task, it was resolved to leave the affair to chance. The lot fell upon the arch-devil Belphagor, who, previous to the Fall, had enjoyed the rank of archangel in a higher world. Though he received his commission with a very ill grace, he nevertheless felt himself constrained by Pluto's imperial mandate, and prepared to execute whatever had been determined upon in council. At the same time he took an oath to observe the tenor of his instructions, as they had been drawn up with all due solemnity and ceremony for the purpose of his mission. These were to the following effect:—*Imprimis*, that the better to promote the object in view, he should be furnished with a hundred thousand gold ducats; secondly, that he should make use of the utmost expedition in getting into the world; thirdly, that after assuming the human form he should enter into the marriage state; and lastly, that he should live with his wife for the space of ten years. At the expiration of this period, he was to feign death and return home, in order to acquaint his employers, by the fruits of experience, what really were the respective conveniences and inconveniences of matrimony. The conditions further ran, that during the said ten years he should be subject to all kinds of miseries and disasters, like the rest of mankind, such as poverty, prisons, and diseases into which men are apt to fall, unless, indeed, he could contrive by his own skill and ingenuity to avoid them. Poor Belphagor having signed these conditions and received the money, forthwith came into the world, and having set up his equipage, with a numerous train of servants, he made a very splendid entrance into Florence. He selected this city in preference to all others, as being most favorable for obtaining an usurious interest of his money; and having assumed the name of Roderigo, a native of Castile, he took a house in the suburbs of Ognissanti. And because he was unable to explain the instructions under which he acted, he gave out that he was a merchant, who having had poor prospects in Spain, had gone to Syria, and succeeded in acquiring his fortune at Aleppo, whence he had lastly set out for Italy, with the intention of marrying and settling there, as one of the most polished and agreeable countries he knew.

Roderigo was certainly a very handsome man, apparently about thirty years of age, and he lived in a style of life that showed he was in pretty easy circumstances, if not possessed of immense wealth. Being, moreover, extremely affable and liberal, he soon attracted the notice of many noble citizens blessed with large families of daughters and small incomes. The former of these were soon offered to him, from among whom Roderigo chose a very beautiful girl of the name of Onesta, a daughter of Amerigo Donati, who had also three sons, all grown up, and three more daughters, also nearly marriageable. Though of a noble family and enjoying a good reputation in Florence, his father-in-law was extremely poor, and maintained as poor an establishment. Roderigo, therefore, made very splendid nuptials, and omitted nothing that might tend to confer honor upon such a festival, being liable, under the law which he received on leaving his infernal abode, to feel all kinds of vain and earthly passions. He therefore soon began to enter into all the pomps and vanities of the world, and to aim at reputation and consideration among mankind, which put him to no little expense. But more than this, he had not long enjoyed the society of his beloved Onesta, before he became tenderly attached to her, and was unable to behold her suffer the slightest inquietude or vexation. Now, along with her other gifts of beauty and nobility, the lady had brought into the house of Roderigo such an insufferable portion of pride, that in this respect Lucifer himself could not equal her; for her husband, who had experienced the effects of both, was at no loss to decide which was the more intolerable of the two. Yet it became infinitely worse when she discovered the extent of Roderigo's attachment to her, of which she availed herself to obtain an ascendancy over him and rule him with a rod of iron. Not content with this, when she found he would bear it, she continued to annoy him with all kinds of insults and taunts, in such a way as to give him the most indescribable pain and uneasiness. For what with the influence of her father, her brothers, her friends, and relatives, the duty of the matrimonial yoke, and the love he bore her, he suffered all for some time with the patience of a saint. It would be useless to recount the follies and extravagancies into which he ran in order to gratify her taste for dress, and every article of the newest fashion, in which our city, ever so variable in its nature, according to its usual habits, so much abounds. Yet, to live upon easy terms with her, he was obliged to do more than this; he had to assist his father-in-law in portioning off his other daughters; and she next asked him to furnish one of her brothers with goods to sail for the Levant, another with silks for the West, while a third was to be set up in a goldbeater's establishment at Florence. In such objects the greatest part of his fortune was soon consumed. At length the Carnival season was at hand; the festival of St. John was to be celebrated, and the whole city, as usual, was in a ferment. Numbers of the noblest families were about to vie with each other in the splendor of their parties, and the Lady Onesta, being resolved not to be outshone by her acquaintance, insisted that Roderigo should exceed them all in the richness of their feasts. For the reasons above stated, he submitted to her will; nor, indeed, would he have scrupled at doing much more, however difficult it might have been, could he have flattered himself with a hope of preserving the peace and comfort of his household, and of awaiting quietly the consummation of his ruin. But this was not the case, inasmuch as the arrogant temper of his wife had grown to such a height of asperity by long indulgence, that he was at a loss in what way to act. His domestics, male and female, would no longer remain in the house, being unable to support for any length of time the intolerable life they led. The inconvenience which he suffered in consequence of having no one to whom he could entrust his affairs it is impossible to express. Even his own familiar devils, whom he had brought along with him, had already deserted him, choosing to return below rather than submit longer to the tyranny of his wife. Left, then, to himself, amidst this turbulent and unhappy life, and having dissipated all the ready money he possessed, he was compelled to live upon the hopes of the returns expected from his ventures in the East and the West. Being still in good credit, in order to support his rank he resorted to bills of exchange; nor was it long before, accounts running against him, he found himself in the same situation as many other unhappy speculators in that market. Just as his case became extremely delicate, there arrived sudden tidings both from East and West that one of his wife's brothers had dissipated the whole of Roderigo's profits in play, and that while the other was returning with a rich cargo uninsured, his ship had the misfortune to be wrecked, and he himself was lost. No sooner did this affair transpire than his creditors assembled, and supposing it must be all over with him, though their bills had not yet become due, they resolved to keep a strict watch over him in fear that he might abscond. Roderigo, on his part, thinking that there was no other remedy, and feeling how deeply he was bound by the Stygian law, determined at all hazards to make his escape. So taking horse one morning early, as he luckily lived near the Prato gate, in that direction he went off. His departure was soon known; the creditors were all in a bustle; the magistrates were applied to, and the officers of justice, along with a great part of the populace, were despatched in pursuit. Roderigo had hardly proceeded a mile before he heard this hue and cry, and the pursuers were soon so close at his heels that the only resource he had left was to abandon the highroad and take to the open country, with the hope of concealing himself in the fields. But finding himself unable to make way over the hedges and ditches, he left his horse and took to his heels, traversing fields of vines and canes, until he reached Peretola, where he entered the house of Matteo del Bricca, a laborer of Giovanna del Bene. Finding him at home, for he was busily providing fodder for his cattle, our hero earnestly entreated him to save him from the hands of his adversaries close behind, who would infallibly starve him to death in a dungeon, engaging that if Matteo would give him refuge, he would make him one of the richest men alive, and afford him such proofs of it before he took his leave as would convince him of the truth of what he said; and if he failed to do this, he was quite content that Matteo himself should deliver him into the hands of his enemies.

Now Matteo, although a rustic, was a man of courage, and concluding that he could not lose anything by the speculation, he gave him his hand and agreed to save him. He then thrust our hero under a heap of rubbish, completely enveloping him in weeds; so that when his pursuers arrived they found themselves quite at a loss, nor could they extract from Matteo the least information as to his appearance. In this dilemma there was nothing left for them but to proceed in the pursuit, which they continued for two days, and then returned, jaded and disappointed, to Florence. In the meanwhile, Matteo drew our hero from his hiding-place, and begged him to fulfil his engagement. To this his friend Roderigo replied: "I confess, brother, that I am under great obligations to you, and I mean to return them. To leave no doubt upon your mind, I will inform you who I am;" and he proceeded to acquaint him with all the particulars of the affair; how he had come into the world, and married, and run away. He next described to his preserver the way in which he might become rich, which was briefly as follows. As soon as Matteo should hear of some lady in the neighborhood being said to be possessed, he was to conclude that it was Roderigo himself who had taken possession of her; and he gave him his word, at the same time, that he would never leave her until Matteo should come and conjure him to depart. In this way he might obtain what sum he pleased from the lady's friends for the price of exorcising her; and having mutually agreed upon this plan, Roderigo disappeared.

Not many days elapsed before it was reported in Florence that the daughter of Messer Ambrogio Amedei, a lady married to Buonajuto Tebalducci, was possessed by the devil. Her relations did not fail to apply every means usual on such occasions to expel him, such as making her wear upon her head St. Zanobi's cap, and the cloak of St. John of Gualberto; but these had only the effect of making Roderigo laugh. And to convince them that it was really a spirit that possessed her, and that it was no flight of the imagination, he made the young lady talk

Latin, hold a philosophical dispute, and reveal the frailties of many of her acquaintance. He particularly accused a certain friar of having introduced a lady into his monastery in male attire, to the no small scandal of all who heard it, and the astonishment of the brotherhood. Messer Ambrogio found it impossible to silence him, and began to despair of his daughter's cure. But the news reaching Matteo, he lost no time in waiting upon Ambrogio, assuring him of his daughter's recovery on condition of his paying him five hundred florins, with which to purchase a farm at Peretola. To this Messer Ambrogio consented; and Matteo immediately ordered a number of masses to be said, after which he proceeded with some unmeaning ceremonies calculated to give solemnity to his task. Then approaching the young lady, he whispered in her ear: "Roderigo, it is Matteo that is come. So do as we agreed upon, and get out." Roderigo replied: "It is all well; but you have not asked enough to make you a rich man. So when I depart I will take possession of the daughter of Charles, king of Naples, and I will not leave her till you come. You may then demand whatever you please for your reward; and mind that you never trouble me again." And when he had said this, he went out of the lady, to the no small delight and amazement of the whole city of Florence.

It was not long again before the accident that had happened to the daughter of the king of Naples began to be buzzed about the country, and all the monkish remedies having been found to fail, the king, hearing of Matteo, sent for him from Florence. On arriving at Naples, Matteo, after a few ceremonies, performed the cure. Before leaving the princess, however, Roderigo said: "You see, Matteo, I have kept my promise and made a rich man of you, and I owe you nothing now. So, henceforward you will take care to keep out of my way, lest as I have hitherto done you some good, just the contrary should happen to you in future." Upon this Matteo thought it best to return to Florence, after receiving fifty thousand ducats from his majesty, in order to enjoy his riches in peace, and never once imagined that Roderigo would come in his way again. But in this he was deceived; for he soon heard that a daughter of Louis, king of France, was possessed by an evil spirit, which disturbed our friend Matteo not a little, thinking of his majesty's great authority and of what Roderigo had said. Hearing of Matteo's great skill, and finding no other remedy, the king despatched a messenger for him, whom Matteo contrived to send back with a variety of excuses. But this did not long avail him; the king applied to the Florentine council, and our hero was compelled to attend. Arriving with no very pleasant sensations at Paris, he was introduced into the royal presence, when he assured his majesty that though it was true he had acquired some fame in the course of his demoniac practice, he could by no means always boast of success, and that some devils were of such a desperate character as not to pay the least attention to threats, enchantments, or even the exorcisms of religion itself. He would, nevertheless, do his majesty's pleasure, entreating at the same time to be held excused if it should happen to prove an obstinate case. To this the king made answer, that be the case what it might, he would certainly hang him if he did not succeed. It is impossible to describe poor Matteo's terror and perplexity on hearing these words; but at length mustering courage, he ordered the possessed princess to be brought into his presence. Approaching as usual close to her ear, he conjured Roderigo in the most humble terms, by all he had ever done for him, not to abandon him in such a dilemma, but to show some sense of gratitude for past services and to leave the princess. "Ah! thou traitorous villain!" cried Roderigo, "hast thou, indeed, ventured to meddle in this business? Dost thou boast thyself a rich man at my expense? I will now convince the world and thee of the extent of my power, both to give and to take away. I shall have the pleasure of seeing thee hanged before thou leavest this place." Poor Matteo finding there was no remedy, said nothing more, but, like a wise man, set his head to work in order to discover some other means of expelling the spirit; for which purpose he said to the king, "Sire, it is as I feared: there are certain spirits of so malignant a character that there is no keeping any terms with them, and this is one of them. However, I will make a last attempt, and I trust that it will succeed according to our wishes. If not, I am in your majesty's power, and I hope you will take compassion on my innocence. In the first place, I have to entreat that your majesty will order a large stage to be erected in the center of the great square, such as will admit the nobility and clergy of the whole city. The stage ought to be adorned with all kinds of silks and with cloth of gold, and with an altar raised in the middle. To-morrow morning I would have your majesty, with your full train of lords and ecclesiastics in attendance, seated in order and in magnificent array, as spectators of the scene at the said place. There, after having celebrated solemn mass, the possessed princess must appear; but I have in particular to entreat that on one side of the square may be stationed a band of men with drums, trumpets, horns, tambours, bagpipes, cymbals, and kettledrums, and all other kinds of instruments that make the most infernal noise. Now, when I take my hat off, let the whole band strike up, and approach with the most horrid uproar towards the stage. This, along with a few other secret remedies which I shall apply, will surely compel the spirit to depart."

These preparations were accordingly made by the royal command; and when the day, being Sunday morning, arrived, the stage was seen crowded with people of rank and the square with the people. Mass was celebrated, and the possessed princess conducted between two bishops, with a train of nobles, to the spot. Now, when Roderigo beheld so vast a concourse of people, together with all this awful preparation, he was almost struck dumb with astonishment, and said to himself, "I wonder what that cowardly wretch is thinking of doing now? Does he imagine I have never seen finer things than these in the regions above —ay! and more horrid things below? However, I will soon make him repent it, at all events." Matteo then approaching him, besought him to come out; but Roderigo replied, "Oh, you think you have done a fine thing now! What do you mean to do with all this trumpery? Can you escape my power, think you, in this way, or elude the vengeance of the king? Thou poltroon villain, I will have thee hanged for this!" And as Matteo continued the more to entreat him, his adversary still vilified him in the same strain. So Matteo, believing there was no time to be lost, made the sign with his hat, when all the musicians who had been stationed there for the purpose suddenly struck up a hideous din, and ringing a thousand peals, approached the spot. Roderigo pricked up his ears at the sound, quite at a loss what to think, and rather in a perturbed tone of voice he asked Matteo what it meant. To this the latter returned, apparently much alarmed: "Alas, dear Roderigo, it is your wife; she is coming for you!" It is impossible to give an idea of the anguish of Roderigo's mind and the strange alteration which his feelings underwent at that name. The moment the name of "wife" was pronounced, he had no longer presence of mind to consider whether it were probable, or even possible, that it could be she. Without replying a single word, he leaped out and fled in the utmost terror, leaving the lady to herself, and preferring rather to return to his infernal abode and render an account of his adventures than run the risk of any further sufferings and vexations under the matrimonial yoke. And thus Belphagor again made his appearance in the infernal domains, bearing ample testimony to the evils introduced into a household by a wife; while Matteo, on his part, who knew more of the matter than the devil, returned triumphantly home, not a little proud of the victory he had achieved.

MATTEO BANDELLO

(1480–*ca.* 1560)

BANDELLO, a Lombard noble by birth, is, next to Boccaccio, the most celebrated of the Italian story-tellers, and he, like his predecessor, furnished Shakespeare with plots and ideas. He resided both in Milan and Mantua, as a member of an ecclesiastical order and later was made a Bishop by Henry II of France, in which country he spent the latter part of his life. His adventurous life is, in Symonds' words, an exciting *novela* in itself. The *Novelle*, a collection of stories placed in a fictious framework, is characterized by what appears to the Anglo-Saxon a certain exaggerated violence. Many of his stories are discreditable anecdotes about the church, and were used with considerable effect as weapons by the leaders of the Reformation.

A King in Disguise is characteristic of Bandello's art, if not of his violence. The story has been traced to Oriental sources, and has, since Bandello wrote it, been used by several other writers.

The present version is translated by Thomas Roscoe and reprinted from his *Italian Novelists*, London, no date. The story has no title in the original.

A KING IN DISGUISE

(*Novelle*, Part I, Novel 57)

IT is really superfluous, my noble friends and patrons, to use so many kind entreaties, when a single word from you would be enough, by way of command, to induce me, as you seem to wish, to give you some account of my most remarkable adventures, in addition to what you have already heard of my travels in Africa. With the manners and customs of the people, as well as with their peculiar religious opinions, I believe you are now pretty well acquainted, insomuch that I no longer need to dwell upon these. You are aware that I have been a traveler from the time I was a boy of fifteen, when I set out from my native city of Genoa, in company with Messer Niccolo Cattanio, whose extensive mercantile connections induced him to visit various parts of Barbary. With him I first arrived at the city of Orano, situated on the shores of the Mediterranean, and belonging to the kingdom of the same name. Numbers of the Genoese were accustomed to resort thither, and there is a large place of traffic named from that circumstance the Lodge of the Genoese. My friend Cattanio was highly respected there, and even in great credit with the king; so much so as to have obtained various privileges from him, in consideration of the able and beneficial manner in which he promoted the commerce of his subjects. Residing there during several years, I acquired an excellent knowledge of the language, manners, and peculiar practices of the people, when I was at length prevailed upon to join a party of Oranese merchants, to whom I had been recommended, through Cattanio's influence, by their king. They were men of approved worth and of the kindest manners, and with them I prepared to make a commercial tour through the country, visiting various regions of Africa, in which we discovered many great and populous cities. In several of these countries we met with seminaries of instruction, with their regular professors of different sciences, paid and appointed by the people. There are, moreover, different hospitals instituted for the relief of the impoverished and distressed, who are there supplied with a regular subsistence, it being a principle of their religion to bestow alms, as pleasing in the sight of God. And I solemnly aver that I have met with more instances of true charity and kindness from what are termed these uncivilized people than I ever had the good fortune to do among those who are called Christians. Among other splendid places, I visited a noble city, built in the age of King Mansor, who had likewise been supreme pontifex or high priest of Morocco. Some of their national chronicles were here exhibited to me, composed in the Arabic character, which bore ample witness to the diligence with which they record the most remarkable public events. Being very well versed in the language, I amused myself with perusing various portions of them, but more particularly those relating to the times of King Mansor. I thence learned that among other amusements he was immoderately fond of the chase; and it one day so happened, that being on a hunting excursion, he was surprised by a terrific storm, which, with irresistible fury laying waste both corn and woodlands, soon dispersed his courtiers on all sides in search of shelter. Mistaking his way in the confusion which ensued, King Mansor, separated at length from his companions, wandered through the forest until night-fall, and such was the tempestuous raging of the winds, that, almost despairing of finding shelter, he checked his steed, doubtful which way he should venture to proceed. From the terrific darkness of the sky, relieved only by sheets of flashing light shooting across the far horizon, he was fearful of going farther, lest he should incur still greater danger, either by riding into pitfalls or the deep marshes bordering the forest grounds. As he thus stood, listening to the distant thunder and the raving of the storm, he stretched his view in vain to discover some signs of human existence; until, on proceeding a few more steps, a light suddenly appeared at only a short distance from him. It was from the window of a poor fisherman's hut, who earned his livelihood by catching eels in the adjacent pools and marshes. On hearing the voice of the king, who rushed forward with a shout of joy on beholding a human habitation, the fisherman hastened to the assistance of the bewildered traveler, whom he believed to have lost his way in the storm. Inquiring who called, King Mansor approached near, and entreated him, if he possessed the least charity, to direct him the shortest path to the residence of the monarch. "The king's court," replied the poor man, "is distant from this place above ten long miles." "Yet I will make it worth your trouble, friend, to guide me thither; consent to oblige me, and you shall have no reason to complain," said the king. "Though you were King Mansor himself," returned the fisherman, "who entreated as much, I would not venture upon it at this hour of the night, and such a night as this is; for I should render myself guilty, perhaps, of leading our honored monarch into destruction. The night is dark, and the waters are out around us." "But why should you, friend, be so very solicitous about the safety of the king?" "Oh," replied the good man, "because I honor him more than I do any one else, and love him more than myself." "But what good has he ever done you," asked the king, "that you should hold him in such high esteem? Methinks you would be rather more comfortably lodged and clothed were you any extraordinary favorite of his." "Not so," answered the fisherman; "for tell me, Sir Knight, what greater favor can I receive from my honored king, in my humble sphere, than to be protected in the enjoyment of my house and goods, and the little earnings which I make! All I have I owe to his kindness, to the wisdom and justice with which he rules over his subjects, preserving us in peace or protecting us in war from the inroads of the Arabs, as well as all other enemies. Even I, a poor fisherman, with a wife and little family, am not forgotten, and enjoy my poverty in peace. He permits me to fish for eels wherever I please, and take them afterwards to the best market I can find, in order to provide for my little ones. At any hour, night or day, I go out or I come in just as I like, to or fro, in my humble dwelling; and there is not a single person in all these neighboring woods and valleys who has ever dared to do me wrong. To whom am I indebted for all this, but to him for whom I daily offer up my prayers to God and our holy prophet to watch over his preservation? But why do I talk, when I see you, Sir Knight, before me, dripping from the pelting of this pitiless storm? Deign to come within, and receive what shelter my poor cabin will afford; to-morrow I will conduct you to the king, or wherever else you please."

Mansor now freely availed himself of the invitation, and dismounting from his horse, sought refuge from the still raging storm. The poor steed likewise shared the accommodation prepared in a little outhouse for the good man's ass, partaking of the corn and hay. Seated by the side of a good fire, the king was employed in drying himself and recruiting his exhausted strength, while the wife was busily cooking the eels for his royal supper. When they were served, having a decided distaste for fish, he somewhat anxiously inquired whether there was no kind of meat for which he might exchange them. The fisherman very honestly declared that it was true he had a she-goat with a kid; and perceiving that his guest was no unworthy personage, he directly offered to serve it up to table; which having done, he presented the king with those parts generally esteemed the best and the most delicious. After supper, the monarch retiring to his rustic couch, reposed his wearied limbs and slumbered until the sun was up.

At the appointed hour he once more mounted his steed, attended by his kind host, who now took upon himself the office of a guide. They had scarcely proceeded beyond the confines of the marshes, when they encountered several of the king's party, calling aloud in the utmost anxiety and searching for their royal master in every direction. Unbounded was the joy and congratulation of the courtiers on thus meeting with him safe and uninjured. The king then turning round to the poor fisherman, informed him that he was the monarch whom he had so much praised, and whom he had so humanely and honorably received the foregoing evening, and that he might rely upon him that his singular courtesy and good-will should not go unrewarded.

Now, there were certain hunting-lodges which the king had erected in those parts for the convenience which they afforded in his excursions, and several of his nobles had likewise adorned the surrounding country with various seats and other dwellings, so as to give a pleasing relief to the prospect. With the view of bestowing a handsome remuneration upon the good fisherman, the grateful monarch gave orders that the pools and marshes adjacent to these dwellings should be drained. He then circumscribed the limits of a noble city, comprehending the palaces and houses already erected, and after conferring upon it various rich immunities, by which it shortly became both very populous and powerful, he named the place Cesar Elcabir or the Great Palace, and presented it as a token of his gratitude to the honest fisherman.

At the period when his sons succeeded to it, no city throughout the king's dominions was to be compared with it in point of splendor and beauty of appearance. During the time I remained there it was filled with merchants and artisans of every description. The mosques were extremely grand, nor were the colleges and hospitals less worthy of admiration. As they have but few good wells, the cisterns and other public conduits are very large and numerous. The inhabitants of the places I visited are in general liberal and kind-hearted men, of simple manners, and neat and plain in their dress and appearance. The gardens are at once spacious and beautiful, abounding in all kinds of fruits, which supply a weekly market, the emporium of all the surrounding country. It is situated not above eighteen miles distant from Azella, now called Arzilla, in the possession of the Portuguese.

Now, simple as the whole of this story may appear, it will at least be found to inculcate one beautiful moral: it teaches us to behave with courtesy towards every one, courtesy being, like virtue, its own reward, and sure of meeting sooner or later, as in the instance of the poor fisherman, that reward here below.

ANGOLO FIRENZUOLA

(1493–1546)

ONE of the most brilliant of the Renaissance scholars and poets, Angolo Firenzuola belonged to the group that scandalized even his contemporaries by associating with the notorious Aretino. Born near Pistoja in Tuscany, he became, like many a worldly writer of his time, a monk, and he may even have risen to the dignity of abbot. He lived for a time in Rome and then returned to his native Tuscany, to the city of Prato. His poetry is still admired by the critics, and his scholarly achievements are mentioned with respect. But the best of his stories are read with pleasure. He laid no claims to originality, and most of his plots he borrowed. *The Friar of Novara* is none the less a sprightly story.

The present version in translated by Thomas Roscoe, and reprinted from his *Italian Novelists*, London, no date. The story has no title in the original.

THE FRIAR OF NOVARA

(*Novelle*, Novel 10)

IT was a privilege enjoyed by the relater of the tenth or last story of the day, in Boccaccio's *Decameron*, occasionally to leave the beaten track, and enter upon any fresh subject which might be thought most agreeable; an example which, in the present instance, as I am the last in the series, I intend to follow. Proclaiming a truce, therefore, to our love adventures, which have occupied us nearly the whole of the day, I wish to amuse you with some account of a certain friar of Novara who flourished about twenty years ago. You hardly need to be told that, among all ranks and conditions of men, the good people to be met with are more rare than those of an opposite description; so that I trust you will not be very greatly surprised to hear that in the holy brotherhood there are not a few who fall short of perfection, and even of what the rules of their order require. Nor ought we to think it strange that the vice of avarice, which bears such sway in the courts of princes, both spiritual and temporal, should sometimes take up her residence in the cloisters of the poor brothers.

It happened that in the town of Novara, a very pretty city of Lombardy, there dwelt a rich widow lady, whose name was Donna Agnes. She had worn her weeds with persevering sorrow ever since the death of her dear Gaudenzio de' Piotti, who, besides her dowry, which was very handsome for a lady in those parts, had left her other possessions that put her very much at her ease, even though she should prefer worshipping his memory to any new connection. She had borne him, moreover, four boys, whose education would now devolve upon her alone. But this excellent and considerate husband was scarcely laid at rest in the ground before tidings of this his last will and testament reached the ears of the superior of the convent of San Nazaro, situated a little way beyond the gate of San Agabio. This same good monk was commissioned by the society to keep an eye upon testamentary donations, so that no widow should pass him by without affording at least her mite and assuming the girdle of the seraphic St. Francis. Having been once admitted as lay sisters into their order, many of these devotees were in the habit of frequenting their congregation, and offering up prayers for the souls of their deceased friends, expressing their gratitude to the poor brethren in the shape of fine Bologna sausages and pasties, and were occasionally induced, in their zeal for imitating the good works of the blessed Fra Ginepro and other renowned saints, to endow some little chapel for the convenience of the order, where they might represent the glorious history of St. Francis, as he was seen preaching to the birds in the desert, engaged in kneading the holy bread, or at the moment when the Angel Gabriel brought him his saintly slippers. The chapel once built, it was not very difficult to raise sufficient from the same quarter to defray an annual festival in honor of the saint's holy stripes, and to celebrate every Monday a mass for the souls of all his followers who might still happen to be suffering the pains of purgatory. But as, consistent with their profession of poverty, the good brethren could not openly avail themselves of these gifts, they adopted the ingenious method of endowing their holy buildings, and holding the property as appurtenant to the sacristies, imagining they could thus as easily impose upon Heaven as upon us poor credulous mortals here below; as if their real motives, and all the envy, pride, and covetousness concealed under the large cowls of pursy monks were not fully as evident to an all-seeing eye as those vices that are more clearly apparent in the broad light of the day. These are they who, instead of begging their bread barefoot, or preaching to the people as they ought to do wherever they appear, prefer sitting at ease in their well-stored monasteries, supplied with delicate changes of shoes and linen, some five pair of Cordova slippers, silk stockings, and sweet, dainty fare. And when they can muster sufficient exertion, or it is quite necessary for them to go abroad, they mount their mules, as elegantly attired as themselves, or pretty palfreys, whose paces are of the easiest, so as never to produce a feeling of fatigue. They are equally cautious not to burden the mind with too much study, finding the truth of the Scripture observation, that it is indeed "a weariness to the flesh"; besides the holy dread they entertain, as in the case of Lucifer, of its producing pride, and thus incurring the risk of a fall from their state of monastic innocence and simplicity.

But to return to our devout inspector of the property of rich widows. It is certain that he followed so closely in pursuit of the lady in question, and made so much noise in his poor wooden clogs, that for peace' sake she was soon compelled to add her name to those of the third order, an arrangement from which the poor brethren drew a regular supply of alms, besides warm jackets and richly worked tunics. But, not content with this, and imagining nothing done while anything remained to do, he placed monks round her all day long, to remind her of the superior efficacy of endowing a whole chapel, if she really consulted the benefit of her soul. The lady, however, having four sons, at first thought it rather hard to rob them of their substance in favor of the monks, and being, like some of her sex, by no means liberally inclined, she tried to amuse them for some time with fair words, though resolved in her own mind to stick fast to her property. Just about the period that the good brethren imagined they had brought her over to their purpose and succeeded in obtaining the mention of their new chapel in her will, it happened that she was taken suddenly ill, and, in spite of all medical assistance, died. Before breathing her last, she sent in haste for the superior of San Nazaro to receive her dying confessions, who, imagining he was now about to reap the harvest of his toils in laying such long siege to the widow's purse, very frankly told her how necessary it was, after having made confession, to show a little more charity towards her own soul while it remained yet in her power, and not to rely upon her sons offering up any sort of compensation for her sins in the way of alms and masses after her decease. It was his duty to remind her of the fate of her friend Donna Leonora Caccia, the wife of Messer Cervagio, doctor of laws, who, at the time he spoke, was suffering in purgatory through the wicked neglect of her sons, who had never burnt a single taper since the day of her funeral. Alarmed at the idea of being in a similar predicament, and feeling extremely weak and troubled, such was the impression of the monk's oratory, that she was just on the point of yielding her consent and calling for her will; but still balancing between the opposite interests of her soul and of her family, she declared that she would make up her mind before he should return again on the morrow. The good priest, shaking his head, reminded her of the danger of delay in a case of such paramount importance, and, under pain of great future suffering, hinted at the propriety of the alteration being made before his return the next day. In the meanwhile, the widow's second son, Agabio, having in some way got scent of this negotiation, communicated his fears to his brothers, who agreed with him that it was of the utmost consequence to overhear what should take place on the priest's return. So when Fra Serafino, the superior, arrived the next day, with the intention of concluding the bargain, Agabio took a station which enabled him to hear every word that passed; and such, he found, was the effect of the monk's eloquence, and so dreadful his denunciations of purgatory, that the poor lady was glad to receive absolution upon condition of leaving the sum of two hundred ducats for the purpose of endowing and ornamenting a chapel. Another hundred was to be appropriated to the purchase of the sacred vessels and other articles requisite to the celebration of mass in proper style, besides an annual festival and a service for the souls of the dead. To these was be to added a small farm, situated very conveniently for the use of the poor brotherhood, at Camigliano, worth at least three thousand ducats; in consideration of which, having arranged everything necessary respecting the title, and that the whole should be drawn up by a regular notary as soon as possible, the happy monk absolved the good widow and took his leave.

Agabio, who had heard all that passed, lost no time in acquainting his brothers, all of whom were of opinion that it was not an affair to be trifled with. So, after consulting some of their friends, they proceeded to their mother's chamber, and with some difficulty, by help of a less fastidious confessor, who absolved her on easier terms, they prevailed upon her to leave her will as it was. This done, they next despatched a confidential servant with a message to the wily monk in their mother's name, begging that he would no longer give himself the trouble of calling, as her sons, having got to hear the nature of his business, were bent upon doing him some grievous mischief in case they should meet with him at her house; that she begged him at the same time not to make himself at all anxious upon the subject, as the holy brotherhood would find everything arranged to their entire satisfaction in her last bequest.

Upon receiving these tidings, Fra Serafino took the hint, and giving himself no little credit for his successful negotiation, he abstained from troubling the lady further. But in a few days he had the gratification of hearing that she had breathed her last, and directly hastened, according to his instructions, to the house of Ser Tomeno, the notary, who had already been apprised by Agabio in what way he was to act. By him he was informed that he ought immediately to wait upon Agabio and his brothers, into whose hands he had committed the will the day before, when he might possibly hear of something to his advantage. Without replying a single word, the delighted friar hastened to inspect its contents, and after duly condoling with the young men upon their loss, he came at once to the point, and requested Agabio to let him see the will. The latter, expressing his surprise at his question, requested to know the reason of his troubling himself with affairs that no way concerned him; an observation at which the holy man began to express his dissatisfaction, but was threatened by Agabio with no very pleasing consequences in case he did not forthwith proceed to take sanctuary in his own monastery. Not in the least daunted, however, at this reception, the wily monk made his bow with a malicious smile, and departed without deigning to say a word; and calling upon a certain Messer Niccola, procurator to the order, he put five soldi into his hands, and requested to know his opinion. Having heard the particulars of the case, Messer Niccola, without further hesitation, sent a summons to Ser Tomeno, Agabio's notary, citing him to appear before the bishop's vicar with a copy of the last will and testament of the deceased.

Ser Tomeno, the moment he had perused this document, lost no time in acquainting Agabio with the progress of the affair, and he, desiring nothing better, took his attorney along with him, and called privately at the house of the vicar, who happening to be a particular friend of his, heard the whole proceedings from beginning to end—the good friar's long and difficult negotiation, Agabio's stratagems to counteract him, and the commencement of the present process. Now the vicar, as belonging to the order of the priesthood, was by no means overburdened with affection towards the friars, and expressed his satisfaction at hearing what had passed. Upon the following day, at the hour appointed for the parties to make their appearance, came Fra Serafino, accompanied by the procurator of his convent, both of whom were extremely noisy, and bent upon obtaining a sight of the will immediately. Agabio, in answer to their appeal, said, "Good Messer Vicar, may it please your reverence, I have not the slightest objection to the production of the will, provided that all the parties whose names are therein mentioned consent to fulfil the articles according to the letter, of whatever nature they may be."

"Say no more," interrupted the vicar; "all that is very clear; for our laws are very particular on this point, and whoever comes in for the benefit must also incur the inconvenience of such bequests. Let us have this document, then; it is only what is lawful and reasonable," and Agabio, instantly taking a scroll out of his pocket, handed it to the opposite notary for perusal. After running over the leading particulars relating to the heirs, and several legacies inserted for the purpose of giving the whole a greater air of reality, he came to the part that concerned the friar, the tenor of which ran in the following manner: "*Item,* I will and bequeath, for the better preservation of my son's fortune and for the general benefit of all the widows in Novara, that there be given by the hands of my own children the amount of fifty lashes upon the back of Fra Serafino, at this time being the guardian or superior of the convent of San Nazaro; and that the said lashes be of the best and soundest in the power of my sons' hands to inflict. And be it further stated, that these are intended to serve as an example to the rest of his brotherhood how they venture in future to impose upon poor credulous women or feeble old dotards, basely and maliciously persuading them to disinherit and impoverish their own flesh and blood for the purpose of ornamenting cells and chapels."

Here the risible muscles of the notary would permit him to proceed no further, and his laugh was speedily caught and re-echoed through the whole court; insomuch that the poor friar, overwhelmed with ridicule and confusion, sought to make good his escape, and find the way back to his convent, though fully resolved in his own mind to bring the whole affair, in form of appeal, before the high apostolic chamber. But he was not destined to end the matter in quite so honorable a manner; for Agabio, seizing fast hold of his gown, exclaimed, "Tarry a little, holy father! why are you in such a hurry! I am come here for the purpose of fulfilling the conditions of the will, and these must be complied with"; and then appealing to the vicar, while he held the good father tight by his band, "I require to know from you, as the judge, why Father Serafino should not be entitled to the benefit of his bequest, mounted on the great horse, and receive from my hands the amount of the legacy due to him. If this be not granted, I shall feel bound to appeal to a superior tribunal against the undue partiality and injustice of this court." The good vicar, receiving the whole of this with an air of mock solemnity, turning towards Agabio, replied, "My good Messer Agabio, your beneficent intentions respecting the worthy father no one surely can dispute; but I daresay he will be inclined to rest satisfied with them, without insisting upon the execution of the deed; in particular, as it might possibly bring some degree of scandal upon his cloth, while at the same time that it would be painful to him, such inheritance would produce no sort of benefit to the holy brotherhood. Besides, if he be so truly disinterested as not to wish to accept the kind bequest of your mother, I hardly see how you can venture to force it upon him, and I would rather permit him to take his leave, with the noble consciousness that he bears no marks of your favor along with him."

Upon this hint Fra Serafino acted, and, full of mingled rage, fear, and vexation, retreated to his own abode, which he did not again quit for many days, out of apprehension of the ridicule of the people. His punishment, however, was followed by the desired effect; for from that time forth he was never known to solicit widow ladies for their fortunes to endow chapels, especially such as had families of sons, by whom he might again run the risk of being severely handled. As it was, he had the good fortune to escape martyrdom from their hands, and contrived to digest his spleen and disappointment by patience, as every good Christian ought. According, however, to a different version of the story, trumped up, it is supposed, by some of the friars for the credit of their order (and as I was myself informed by one of them), that same wicked vicar had soon reason to repent of the part he bore in the affair, having to pay no less a fine than five hundred florins.

GIOVANBATTISTA GIRALDI CINTHIO

(1504–1573)

CINTHIO is another of the famous Italian story-tellers to whom Shakespeare is indebted for a good plot: the story of Othello was lifted from the collection called the *Hecatommithi*. Cinthio is best known for his gruesome subjects and the violence of his methods of treatment. Of noble birth, he spent the greater part of his life in a secretarial position at the court of Ferrara. As critic, dramatist and novelist, he is one of the important figures in the literature of his country.

Original plots are rare, and *The Greek Merchant* can claim no other originality than that of treatment. But is that not enough? Like most of the Italian tales we have included, it is gracefully turned, and maintains its interest up to the last moment.

The present version is translated by Thomas Roscoe, and reprinted from his *Italian Novelists*, London, no date. The story has no title in the original.

THE GREEK MERCHANT

(*Hecatommithi*, 1st Decade, Novel 9)

THERE was a Greek merchant from Corfu, who having trafficked in various parts of Italy, at length settled in Mantua. His name was Filargiro, one of the most avaricious characters in the world; for though he had realized a handsome property, all his thoughts were bent upon amassing more and more, his avarice still increasing with the increase of his wealth. It happened that on returning one day from a sale of some of his goods, with a purse of four hundred gold crowns, while engaged in transacting other business, he was unlucky enough to lose the whole sum, nor was he aware of his loss until he reached home. Arriving there, he opened an immense chest containing many thousand crowns, and on preparing to add the four hundred to the number, he was struck dumb with astonishment to find that they were gone. He uttered an exclamation of horror every time he put his hand into each of his pockets, till convinced at last that his loss was but too true, he ran off in great consternation along the path he had come, inquiring of the very dogs he met on the way whether they had seen or seized upon his treasure. He was quite confounded when he reached the place where he had first received the money, without obtaining the least tidings of it. Almost overwhelmed with despair, he suddenly bethought him, as a last resource, to apply to the Marquis, entreating that a public crier might be instantly sent forth, and offering the sum of forty crowns for the recovery of his treasure. With great courtesy the Marquis acceded to this request, expressing himself at the same time concerned to witness the excessive affliction under which the unfortunate Filargiro seemed to labor. The reward was accordingly proclaimed, and the gold soon afterwards made its appearance in the hands of one of those aged old ladies, who, being great devotees, always walk with their eyes upon the ground as they come from church. In this way she discovered the lost treasure, and fearful lest her conscience should be loaded with such a weight of gold, though extremely poor, she would have been very greatly perplexed in what way to act, had she not luckily heard the crier announcing the reward of forty crowns, which she hoped she might receive with a safe conscience. Observing her destitute appearance, the Marquis very humanely inquired whether she had any means of procuring her subsistence, and whether she had no one to assist her. "I have nothing," she replied, "but what I gain by the work of my hands and the help of one daughter; we weave and spin, signor, to earn as much as we want, living in the fear of the Lord in the best way we are able. My daughter, to be sure, I should wish to see married before I die, but I have nothing to give her for a portion." The Marquis, on hearing the poor woman's account of herself, highly praised her integrity in thus restoring what she might so easily have reserved for herself and for a marriage-portion for her daughter; observing that it was an action of which he feared that few others, under the same temptation, would have been capable. He then summoned the merchant, informing him that the lost treasure was found, and requesting him at the same time to put into the poor woman's hands the stated reward. The raptures of the miser were truly amusing when he beheld and seized upon the gold, even in the presence of the Marquis; but on hearing the demand of the stipulated sum, his countenance again fell, and he began to think how he could possibly withhold the promised reward. Having numbered the pieces once or twice exactly over, though he found them perfectly correct, he turned towards the old woman, saying, "There are four-and-thirty ducats short of the sum which I put into this bag." The old lady appeared extremely confused at this accusation, exclaiming in a distressed tone to the Marquis, "Oh, signor, can that be possible? Is it likely I should have stolen thirty-four ducats, when I had it in my power to possess myself of the whole? No; believe me, noble signor, I swear, as I value my hopes of heaven, that I have restored the exact sum which I found on my return from church; not a single farthing have I taken out." But the miserly old wretch continuing to affirm most solemnly that the ducats were in the same bag with the crowns, and that she must consider them as a sufficient remuneration, the affair seemed to perplex the Marquis not a little. Yet when he reflected that the old miser had only mentioned the four hundred crowns in the first instance, he began to suspect his design of imposing upon the poor woman in order to save the paltry sum offered as a reward. The Marquis felt the utmost indignation at the discovery of this deceit, believing no punishment to be too severe for this despicable breach of faith; but checking his rising passion for a moment, he reflected that the most effectual chastisement he could bestow upon the miser's attempt to impose upon the magistracy would be to make him fall into the very snare he had laid for another. With this view he thus addressed the merchant: "And why did you not mention the full amount of your loss before proclaiming the reward?" "I overlooked it; I quite forgot it," was the reply. "But it seems somewhat strange that you, who appear so particular about trifles, should not have recollected the circumstance of the ducats. And as far as I can understand, you wish to recover what is not your own. I mean to say that this bag of gold could never have belonged to you at all, since the sum you first mentioned is not to be found in it. I imagine the real owner to be myself, since a servant of mine lost exactly the sum here contained on the very same day you pretend to have lost yours." The Marquis then turned towards the old woman, observing, "Since it is clear that the money is none of his, but mine, and you have had the good luck to find it, pray keep it: the whole is your own; present it as a wedding-gift to your daughter. If it should happen that you meet with another purse, containing the ducats as well as the crowns, belonging to this gentleman, I beg you will return it to him without demanding any reward." The poor lady expressed her gratitude to the Marquis for this generous mark of his favor, and promised to observe his directions in everything. The wretched merchant, finding that the Marquis had truly penetrated into his motives, and that there was not a chance of succeeding in his nefarious design, declared that he was now quite willing to pay the reward he had promised, if she restored the remaining money, which was indisputably his own. But it was now too late. The Marquis turning towards him with an angry air, threatened to punish him for such a disgraceful attempt to defraud another of so large a sum, since, from his own account, it could not possibly be his. "Get out of my presence, and beware how you exasperate me further. If this good woman should be fortunate enough to meet with the purse, with the exact amount you mention, she has promised to restore it to you untouched. That I think is enough."

Without venturing to answer a single word, the unhappy Filargiro was compelled to leave the place, unaccompanied by his newly recovered treasure, and filled with sorrow and regret at having refused to fulfil the conditions he had made. The poor old woman, on the other hand, went away overjoyed with her unexpected good fortune, and full of gratitude to the Marquis. She hastened to impart the happy tidings to her daughter, who, after having long indulged a vain attachment, had at length the pleasure of being united to the object of her choice, at the expense of the avaricious old merchant.

CARLO GOZZI
(1720–1806)

AFTER the first outburst of the Renaissance, Italy entered upon a period of intellectual and artistic decline extending into the Nineteenth Century; the Eighteenth, a fertile period in other countries, contains but one notable Italian figure, Count Carlo Gozzi. He is generally remembered for his plays but his fairy tales are quite as charming. His work exerted considerable influence over the German Romanticists, especially Schiller and E. T. A. Hoffmann.

The present version is translated by Thomas Roscoe, and reprinted from his *Italian Novelists*, London, no date. The story has no title in the original.

THE VENETIAN SILK-MERCER

HAPPENING to recollect an amusing incident that occurred in my own times at the Church of Santi Ermacora and Fortunato (which the Venetians, making two saints into one, call the Church of Santo Marcuola), I will repeat it to you as follows. Messer Gherardo Benvenga was a Venetian silk-mercer, a very pleasant and good kind of man, and as creditable as you would wish to find any tradesman. Rising early, as usual, one Sunday morning, being the day he had fixed upon, to save time, for the payment of the half year's rent of his shop, he was no sooner washed and dressed than he counted out the money. "First of all," he says, "I will go to mass, after putting these ten sequins in my purse, and when I have heard mass, I will just step and despatch this other little affair." He had no sooner said it than he snatched up his mantle, crossed himself devoutly, and sallied forth. Passing along near the said church, he heard, by the tinkling of a little bell, that the mass was going out. "Oh," he cried, "it is going, full of unction." So he hastens into the church, touches the holy water, and approaches the altar where the priest pronounces the *introido*. He knelt upon a form, where there was no other person except a very pleasing and good-natured looking lady, adorned in the Venetian fashion, with a Florentine petticoat and a black silk vest, apparently just from the mercer's, trimmed with sleeves of the finest lace, along with gold rings, bracelets of the richest chain gold, and a necklace set with beautiful diamonds; while, full of devotion and modesty, she held a very prettily bound book in her hands, from which she was singing hymns like an angel. Messer Gherardo turned his eyes towards her a few moments, anxious to profit by so lovely and edifying an example, without the least alloy of any more terrestrial feeling, and accordingly drew a little psalter from his pocket, and began, quite absorbed within himself, and shaking his head with emotion, to join in the anthem.

The mass being at length over, Messer Gherardo bethought himself, according to courteous custom, of making a chaste obeisance to the lady; but while he was preparing, she had already passed, and he followed, marveling within himself in what manner she would have returned his intended civility. On getting out, he instinctively took the road to pay his ten pieces to the landlord, an agent for one of the noble Morosini family, and knocking at the door, he said, "I am come here to pay money as usual, but you have never yet returned my calls to pay me anything; come and look at my shop some day;" and in this jocular strain he thrust his hand into his purse, feeling on all sides without finding a single sequin. "Am I out of my wits?" he cried. "What is this?" and he rolled his eyes like a demoniac, as if under the operation of the bitterest torments. At length, feeling something hard sticking in a corner of his purse, and hastily seizing it, he drew forth a beautiful bracelet of fine gold with diamond clasps, amounting to the value of some two hundred ducats. The poor tradesman was half petrified at the sight. At first he believed it to be the effect of witchcraft, then a trick; and was altogether so much at a loss, that turning briskly round, while the agent grinned in his face, he ran down the steps without saying a single word. "Messer Gherardo, good Messer Gherardo," he cried, as he held pen and paper in hand to give him a receipt, "what is the matter?" Then looking out of the window, he beheld him running along at a furious pace, every one making way for him. The agent, shaking his head (for he now thought him a little beside himself), returned to his accounts, regretting only that he had not received the money; while Messer Gherardo, who had all his wits about him as far as his interest was concerned, hastened to the house of his friend the goldsmith, anxious to ascertain the value of the toy, in lieu of the sum he had lost. When he heard it amounted to at least two hundred ducats, he suddenly bethought him of the richly dressed lady who stood near him at mass, imagining he had seen it upon her arm, but of this he was not certain. He next conjectured she had played him a trick, but neither the time nor place seemed to warrant such a supposition. Besides he did not know her, nor she him, though he wished to learn where she lived. "I think I have guessed it though now," he exclaimed, as if a sudden bright thought had struck him. "My purse lay beside me; I was buried in profound devotion, and she, wanting money, thrust her hand into my money-bag, and by accident left the bracelet behind her." Yet how to reconcile this, he thought, with so much fashion, beauty, and devotion as she displayed. He felt ashamed of such an accusation, and tried to banish it from his mind. He resolved, however, to keep the bracelet and quietly await the result; then returning in better spirits to settle his account with the agent, not without some jeers, he pretended to have forgotten the money, which, having now paid, he felt much happier and easier, and, with a smile on both sides, they took leave.

The next day Messer Gherardo, walking along the streets, observed, upon turning a corner, affixed to a pillar the following advertisement in large letters: "*Lost or stolen, a rich gold bracelet, with handsome diamond clasps; whoever will restore it to the owner, by leaving it at the sacristy of Santo Marcuola, shall receive a handsome reward.*" Messer Gherardo, thunderstruck at these words, read them again and again, as he would otherwise have had no scruples in retaining the bracelet. As it was, however, such was the singularity of the case, that he could not help laughing as he directed his steps towards the said sacristy, where, upon his arrival, he inquired for the curate. Taking him on one side, he said, "My reverend father, my business with you is no other than a confession, and if you will give me permission, I will inform you. But you must grant me one condition, without which I must take my leave as I came." "Speak out," replied the curate; "what is it? If proper, it is granted." "Then," returned Messer Gherardo, "I am the man who found the bracelet; but I will never restore it, except it be to the lady herself. Now I beg you will not attribute this to any suspicion, or any improper motive; only it will be far preferable, on the lady's account, that I should return it to her without other witnesses. If you will be so good as to point out her abode to me, you may rely upon it that I will go forthwith, like a good subject of the Catholic Church, and return it to the owner; otherwise you must excuse me. I shall keep the bracelet, and without the slightest scruples of conscience." The curate replied, "To any person who should restore such an ornament I have received orders to give three sequins, that he might treat himself to a good dram; but as to you, signor, you are perhaps not in want of one." "Signor," retorted Messer Gherardo, "I would not return it for a hundred sequins; but if I may restore it into the lady's own hands, I will require nothing." "My son," replied the curate, "I would recommend to you to entertain a little more reverence and holy fear of Heaven. Surely you would not keep what is not yours; but as you seem resolved to restore it only to the lady, so be it. I will call my clerk, since you are so very obstinate, and he shall point out to you her dwelling." So, after accompanying him a little way, the little fat clerk said, "That is it, signor," pointing to a very handsome-looking and spacious house; and upon gaining admission he was shown up a magnificent staircase into a large saloon, the walls all covered with silk linings, the sight of which made the mercer's heart glow; and such was his confusion at the idea of his temerity in entering, that he could scarcely ascertain the quality of the silk. At first he thought of making his escape, imagining that he had committed some gross blunder, and might be running his head into a great scrape. While doubtful in what way to act, but gradually edging out, a maidservant advanced from the staircase, crying, "Who is it? Pray who are you and what do you want?" Half struck dumb, with his hat held politely in his hand, Messer Gherardo replied, "I wish to see the lady of the house, and, if perfectly convenient to her ladyship, to be permitted to speak with her"; and this he said in his usual style when waiting on the great to receive commissions. "Madam," cried the girl, calling to her mistress in an adjacent apartment, "it is a gentleman who wishes to speak to you about some business." "Then let him come. Why do not you show him in?" answered a voice that startled our poor tradesman, as he hastened to obey her commands. Sitting in an easy-chair, he discovered, on entering, the same identical beautiful lady whom he had seen at mass, a surprise that had almost cost him his life, for a few degrees more would infallibly have amounted to a fit of apoplexy. The lady looked full at Messer Gherardo, and grew pale as the wife of Lot when she was turned into a pillar of salt; in fact, she had nearly swooned away; for it had never entered into her head, when she first missed her bracelet, that she could have left it behind on withdrawing her hand out of the old gentleman's purse. But such was her hurry to secure the ten pieces, which she effectually did, as she observed him absorbed in his devotions, that it is hardly surprising she was not aware of the loss of it when it came unclasped. On the other hand, she councluded she must have lost it on the road from church, or she would never have had the folly to advertise it. Little did she think, then, such shame and exposure were reserved for her. But Heaven, that frequently punishes guilty mortals in a way they least expect, never fails to overtake offenders. Messer Gherardo, in his turn, fixed his eyes upon the lady, whose looks were still directed towards him, neither of them uttering a word. At length, however, our tradesman, being naturally possessed of much presence of mind and discrimination, further disciplined by his habit of attending to all ranks and descriptions of purchasers, pulled the fatal bracelet from his pocket, and holding it by one end, proceeded to observe: "I am at a loss, madam, to say in what manner the accident occurred; it is plain that you lost this bracelet, but the wretch has stolen ten sequins out of my purse. Yet you see I have caught him, and hold him fast by the hair;" showing the bracelet in his hand; "and if he refuses to make restitution of my money, which is my heart's blood, I will put him into such durance that you will never have the pleasure of beholding the offender again. I know that he is a familiar friend, very dear to you, and that you love him as well as woman ever loved such pretty things. For the sake of your reputation and of your family, then, I would advise you to pay his fine, or I will take such revenge upon him as will prove very disagreeable to you. If, on the other hand, you consent to pay what he owes me, the scandal of this affair shall go no further than ourselves, and I will set the thief free; not, however, without desiring you to give him a word of advice for the future, and a little correction at your hands, such as he will remember to the latest day of his life." In spite of her confusion, the lady could not avoid bursting into a fit of laughter as he concluded; and upon recovering her presence of mind, she adopted the most prudent course, by walking to her desk and taking out ten sequins, perhaps the identical pieces she had pilfered, and which had arrested the guilty bracelet in the very act. Turning towards Messer Gherardo, she said: "I vow, my dear signor, that the moment the rogue had committed the deed, he ran away from me, dreading my displeasure. Here is the money he stole; and since you are pleased to set him at liberty and to keep the affair secret, which I entreat you to do, I shall consider myself eternally bound to you. As you say, I will keep him in order for the future, and prevent the possibility of his becoming guilty of such an offense again." She then counted the pieces into his hand, and received the bracelet in return; and after a few more ceremonies, the good man took his leave. It is certain that this lady was a woman of fashion, of respectable family and connections, the wife of a wealthy citizen, too fond of gaiety and extravagance. Her husband not supplying her fast enough with money for dresses and play, she was in the habit of drawing from other resources, in the manner we have here detailed. It is thus that our errors and vices obscure the intellect and lead us gradually into the abyss of ruin.

GIOVANNI VERGA

(1840—1922)

WITH Verga we find ourselves in modern times. The dawn of the Nineteenth Century found Italy in the full flood of that romanticism that was popularized by Byron and Scott. The figure of Manzoni dominated Italian fiction until the end of the Nineteenth Century.

Verga was born in Catania, Sicily, in 1840. His most significant
work is his stories of Sicilian peasant life. The most celebrated is
Cavalleria Rusticana, which was later adapted as the libretto of Mas-
cagni's opera. Even the music has not entirely deprived the tale of its
moving power. Verga is reckoned as one of the forerunners in the
modern Italian dramatic movement.

The present version is translated by Frederic Taber Cooper. Copyright, 1907, by P. F. Collier and Son, and here reprinted by permission of P. F. Collier & Son Company.

CAVALLERIA RUSTICANA

AFTER Turridu Macca, Mistress Nunzia's son, came home from
soldiering, he used to strut every Sunday, peacock-like, in the
public square, wearing his rifleman's uniform, and his red cap that
looked just like that of the fortune-teller waiting for custom behind the
stand with the cage of canaries. The girls all rivaled each other in making eyes at him as they went their way to mass, with their noses down
in the folds of their shawls; and the young lads buzzed about him like
so many flies. Besides, he had brought back a pipe, with the king on
horseback on the bowl, as natural as life; and he struck his matches on
the back of his trousers, raising up one leg as if he were going to give
a kick. But for all that, Master Angelo's daughter Lola had not once
shown herself, either at mass or on her balcony, since her betrothal to
a man from Licodia, who was a carter by trade, and had four Sortino
mules in his stable. No sooner had Turridu heard the news than, holy
great devil! but he wanted to rip him inside out, that was what he
wanted to do to him, that fellow from Licodia. However, he did
nothing to him at all, but contended himself with going and singing
every scornful song he knew beneath the fair one's window.

"Has Mistress Nunzia's Turridu nothing at all to do," the neighbors
asked, "but pass his nights in singing, like a lonely sparrow?"

At last he came face to face with Lola, on her way back from praying
to Our Lady of Peril; and at sight of him she turned neither white nor
red, as though he were no concern of hers.

"It is a blessing to have sight of you!" said he.

"Oh, friend Turridu, I was told that you came back around the first
of the month."

"And I too was told many other things besides!" he answered. "So
it is true that you are going to marry Alfio the carter?"

"If such is the will of God!" answered Lola, drawing together beneath her chin the two corners of her kerchief.

"You do the will of God by taking or leaving as it pays you best!

And it was the will of God that I should come home from so far away to hear such fine news, Mistress Lola!"

The poor fellow still tried to make a show of indifference, but his voice had grown husky; and he walked on ahead of the girl with a swagger that kept the tassel of his cap dancing back and forth upon his shoulders. It really hurt the girl to see him with such a long face, but she had not the heart to deceive him with fair words.

"Listen, friend Turridu," she said at length, "you must let me go on to join the other girls. What would folks be saying if we were seen together?"

"That is true," replied Turridu; "now that you are to marry Alfio, who has four mules in his stable, it won't do to set people talking. My mother, on the other hand, poor woman, had to sell our one bay mule, and that little bit of vineyard down yonder on the highroad, during the time that I was soldiering. The time is gone when the Lady Bertha span; and you no longer give a thought to the time when we used to talk together from window to courtyard, and when you gave me this handkerchief just before I went away, into which God knows how many tears I wept at going so far that the very name of our land seemed forgotten. But now good-bye, Mistress Lola, let us square accounts and put an end to our friendship."

Mistress Lola and the carter were married; and on the following Sunday she showed herself on her balcony, with her hands spread out upon her waist, to show off the big rings of gold that her husband had given her.

Turridu kept passing and repassing through the narrow little street, with his pipe in his mouth and his hands in his pockets, pretending indifference and ogling the girls; but inwardly he was eating his heart out to think that Lola's husband had all that gold, and that she pretended not even to notice him as he passed by.

"I'd like to take her from under his very eyes, the dirty dog!" he muttered.

Across from Alfio's house lived Master Cola, the vine-grower, who was rich as a porker, so they said, and had an unmarried daughter. Turridu said so much, and did so much, that Master Cola took him into his employ; then he began to haunt the house and make pretty speeches to the girl.

"Why don't you go and say all these fine things to Mistress Lola?" Santa answered him.

"Mistress Lola is a big lady! Mistress Lola is wife of one of the crowned heads now!"

"I suppose I am not good enough for the crowned heads."

"You are worth a hundred such as Lola; and I know one fellow who would never so much as look at Mistress Lola or her patron saint when you are around. For she isn't fit even to carry your shoes for you, indeed she isn't!"

"When the fox found that he couldn't reach the grapes—"

"He said, 'How lovely you are, you sweet little grape!'"

"Oh! come, hands off, friend Turridu."

"Are you afraid I am going to eat you?"

"No, I am not afraid of you nor of him you serve."

"Ah! your mother was from Licodia, we all know that. Your blood boils quickly! Oh! I could eat you up with my eyes!"

"Then eat me up with your eyes, and leave no crumbs; but meanwhile pick up that bundle of twigs for me."

"For your sake I would pick up the whole house, that I would!"

To hide her blushes, she threw at him the fagot she happened to have in her hands, but for a wonder missed him.

"Cut it short! Talking doesn't bind fagots."

"If I was rich, I should be looking for a wife just like you, Santa!"

'I shall not marry a crowned head, as Mistress Lola did; but I shall have my dower, as well as she, when the Lord sends me the right man."

"We know that you are rich, yes, we know that!"

"If you know so much, then stop talking, for my father will soon be here, and I don't care to have him catch me in the courtyard."

The father began to make a wry face, but the girl pretended not to notice, for the tassel of the rifleman's hat had set her heartstrings quivering and was forever dancing before her eyes. After the father had put Turridu out of the door, the daughter opened her window to him, and would stand chatting with him all the evening, until the whole neighborhood could talk of nothing else.

"I am crazy about you," Turridu would say; "I am losing my sleep and my appetite."

"I don't believe it!"

"I wish I was the son of Victor Emmanuel, so that I could marry you!"

"I don't believe it!"

"By our Lady, I could eat you up, like a piece of cake!"

"I don't believe it!"

"On my honor!"

"Oh, mother mine!"

Lola, listening night after night, hidden behind a pot of sweet basil, turning first pale and then red, one day called down to Turridu: "How is it, friend Turridu, that old friends no longer greet each other?"

"Alas!" sighed Turridu, "blessed is he who may greet you!"

"If you care to give me greeting, you know where my home is," answered Lola.

Turridu came back to greet her so often that Santa took notice of it, and closed her window in his face. The neighbors pointed him out with a smile or a nod of the head when he passed by in his rifleman's uniform. Lola's husband was away, making a circuit of the village fairs with his mules.

"On Sunday I mean to go to confession, for last night I dreamt of black grapes," said Lola.

"Wait a while, wait a while!" begged Turridu.

"No, now that Easter is so near, my husband would want to know why I have not been to confession."

"Ahah!" murmured Master Cola's Santa, waiting for her turn on her knees before the confessional where Lola was washing herself clean of her sins. "On my soul, it is not to Rome I would send you to do penance!"

Friend Alfio came home with his mules and a pretty penny of profit, and brought his wife a present of a fine new dress for the holidays.

"You do well to bring her presents," his neighbor Santa said to him, "for while you are away your wife has been trimming up the honor of your house!"

Master Alfio was one of those carters who wear the cap well down over one ear, and to hear his wife talked of in this fashion made him change color as though he had been stabbed. "Holy big devil!" he exclaimed, "if you have not seen aright, I won't leave you eyes to weep with, you and your whole family!"

"I have forgotten how to weep!" answered Santa; "I did not weep even when I saw with these very eyes Mistress Nunzia's son, Turridu, go in at night to your wife's house."

"Then it is well," replied Alfio; "many thanks to you."

Now that the husband was home again, Turridu no longer wasted his days in the little street, but drowned his sorrow at the tavern with his friends; and on Easter eve they had on the table a big dish of sausage. When Master Alfio came in, just from the way he fastened his eyes upon him, Turridu understood what business he had come on, and laid his fork down upon his plate.

"How can I serve you, friend Alfio?" he asked.

"Nothing important; friend Turridu, it is some time since I have seen you, and I wanted to talk with you of the matter that you know about."

Turridu had at once offered him a glass, but Alfio put it aside with his hand. Then Turridu arose and said to him: "Here I am, friend Alfio."

The carter threw an arm around his neck.

"If you will come to-morrow morning down among the prickly pears of Canziria, we can talk of this affair, friend Turridu."

"Wait for me on the highroad at sunrise, and we will go together."

With these words they exchanged the kiss of challenge. Turridu seized the carter's ear between his teeth, and thus solemnly bound himself not to fail him.

The friends had all silently withdrawn from the dish of sausage, and accompanied Turridu all the way to his home. Mistress Nunzia, poor woman, was accustomed to wait for him late every night.

"Mother," said Turridu, "do you remember when I went away to be a soldier, and you thought that I was never coming back! Give me a kiss, such as you gave me then, for to-morrow I am going on a long journey!"

Before daybreak he took his clasp-knife, which he had hidden under the straw at the time he went away as a conscript, and started with it for the prickly pears of Canziria.

"Holy Mother, where are you going in such a rage?" sobbed Lola in terror as her husband started to leave the house.

"I am not going far," anwered Alfio, "but it will be far better for you if I never come back."

Lola, in her night-gown, prayed at the foot of her bed, and pressed to her lips the rosary which Fra Bernardino had brought her from the Holy Land, and recited all the Ave Marias that there were beads for.

"Friend Alfio," began Turridu after he had walked quite a bit of the way beside his companion, who remained silent, with his cap drawn over his eyes, "as true as God himself, I know that I am in the wrong, and I ought to let you kill me. But before I came here, I saw my old mother, who rose early to see me start, on the pretext that she had to tend the chickens; but her heart must have told her the truth. And as true as God himself, I am going to kill you like a dog, sooner than have the poor old woman weeping for me."

"So much the better," replied Master Alfio, stripping off his jacket, "strike your hardest, and so will I."

They were both worthy foes. Turridu received the first thrust, and was quick enough to catch it on his arm. When he paid it back, he gave good measure, and aimed for the groin.

"Ah, friend Turridu, you have really made up your mind to kill me?"

"Yes, I told you so; ever since I saw my old mother going out to feed the chickens, her face floats all the time before my eyes."

"Then open your eyes wide," Alfio called to him, "for I am going to square accounts with you."

And as he stood on guard, crouching ever, so as to hold his left hand upon his wound, which was aching, and with his elbow almost touching the ground, he suddenly caught up a handful of dust and threw it into his opponent's eyes.

"Oh!" howled Turridu, "I am done for!"

He sought to save himself by making desperate leaps backward; but Alfio overtook him with another blow in the stomach and a third in the throat.

"And the third is for the honor of my house that you made free with. Now, perhaps, your mother will forget to feed her chickens."

Turridu stumbled about for a moment here and there among the prickly pears, and then fell like a log. The blood gurgled in a crimson foam out of his throat, and he had no chance even to gasp out, "Oh, mother mine!"

ANTONIO FOGAZZARO

(1842–1911)

BORN at Vicenza in northern Italy, Fogazzaro led a very active life, both as senator and writer. Though he studied at first for the law, he was soon able to devote himself largely to writing. His novels (and in particular *The Saint*) brought him international fame. During his most prolific period he wrote a few volumes of exquisite short stories, among which one of the best is *The Peasant's Will*. It is wholly representative of this writer's art, serene, sympathetic, natural.

The present version is translated by Walter Brooks, and is reprinted from his volume, *Retold in English*. Copyright, 1905, by Brentano's, by whose permission it is here included.

THE PEASANT'S WILL

IN my earlier days I was the assistant of Lawyer X——, of Vincenza, when one day in August, about ten o'clock in the morning, a young peasant of Rettorgole came into the office and begged the lawyer to go with him to his home for the purpose of drawing up the will of his father who was, as he expressed it, "mal da morte."

My principal assented, and, wishing me to accompany him, we all three started off, squeezed into a rickety country cart without springs and drawn by a sorry nag of uneven gait. The seat which we occupied was cushionless and hardly added to the comfort of two not over-stout individuals, each accustomed to his own easy-chair. X——'s face wore an expression of agony, and he cried out at every jolt. I suffered in silence, and the peasant imperturbably described the illness of his father, a certain Matteo Cucco, nicknamed "L'orbo da Rettorgole," because he had only one eye. "But he can see more with that one than most people could with three," remarked the afflicted and respectful son.

We were hardly outside the city when we left the main road and turned into a narrow and muddy lane running through a succession of low-lying meadows, where the cart jolted even more than ever, but fortunately we were not long in arriving at our destination. We found there a miserable tumble-down house planted in the midst of mud and mire. A stable, open below and with a hay-loft above, was built against one end of it, and combined to provide shelter under the same roof for man and beast.

X—— and I were about to enter the kitchen when our conductor informed us that the sick man was not in the house. The heat and filth of his room had become such as to make it necessary to remove him to the hay-loft. Entrance to this was to be had only by climbing a ladder made of a single pole with pegs driven through it at intervals to serve as primitive rungs.

X——immediately flew in a passion at the idea of such indignity, and declared it preposterous to expect him to mount a ladder of that sort; he said he would rather return to town. The young peasant who was holding the ladder below kept assuring him that it was entirely safe, and another peasant who, attracted by the talk, had come to the opening into the loft, also took hold of the ladder, and shouted—

"Come up, Signore, don't be afraid! It's strong."

Being younger, and accustomed to feats of mountain climbing, besides being urged on by curiosity, I determined upon the ascent, and moving cautiously, succeeded in reaching the loft without mishap. X——, emboldened by my success, finally changed his mind and followed.

In the loft was a miserable and filthy straw bed, and lying upon it was an old man in rags, with features like wrinkled parchment, one eye entirely closed, and the other almost devoid of life. Though he breathed with difficulty, he did not appear to be suffering. Two men stood near him, one on either side, both lean and crafty-looking, and with cleanly shaven faces. One had a branch in his hand and was engaged in fanning away the flies from the face of the old man, while the other kept putting in the toothless mouth dry bread and small bits of cheese.

"Magnè, pare; eat, father!" he said in his peasant dialect.

A little distance off on a bundle of hay sat an old woman holding her face in her hands, and farther away still were several peasants, evidently witnesses, talking in a low voice. A table, chair and inkstand stood ready for our use. We were told that the dying man had received absolution early the same morning, and that while he was unable to speak he understood everything, and would make his wishes known by signs.

As X——hesitated, under the circumstances, to proceed with the making of the will, the sons volunteered to put their father to the proof.

Leaning over the dying man, the one who had been administering the bread and cheese shouted in his ear, "Pare, you left me the pig?"

The old man shook his head: "No."

"Did you leave it to Tita?"

There was a nod: "Yes."

"And the field of Polegge, to whom will that go?"

The old man directed his one eye toward the young peasant who had brought us.

"To Gigio; is that what you mean ."

Again he nodded.

"Now you see, Sior," the son concluded, turning to X——, "I am not mistaken."

The latter, however, was not yet satisfied and began to question the wife, the old woman crouching in the hay. With a sudden outburst of words she confirmed what had been said in regard to her husband, and insisted that he was in full possession of all his faculties, since only half an hour before he had objected to the veterinary bleeding one of the oxen which had fallen sick. She added that she knew exactly his intentions as to the distribution of the property.

While she seemed agitated and spoke in an excited manner, she was to all appearances telling the truth, and had no intention of deceiving the lawyer in her answers to his questions concerning the heirs and the amount of property. According to her statements there were only the three children, the sons now present, and the property consisted of about fifty acres of good farm land, part at Polegge and part in Rettorgole, another house, live-stock, farm implements, and numerous small articles.

What the old woman had said was confirmed by her sons, and also by the other witnesses. The lawyer suggested that the estate be divided in some general manner among the heirs, but this was objected to by all: wife, sons and witnesses as well. They insisted that it was the wish of the old man to assign everything specifically.

One of the witnesses, a man of rather better appearance and manners than the rest, came forward, and offering his snuff-box to the lawyer with an evident air of commiseration for the ignorance of his fellows, and of satisfaction at his own superior knowledge said:

"Matteo is near his end, and there is no time to settle the distribution in a strictly legal manner."

X—— thereupon concluded to let the matter go, and when I had made ready to write down from his dictation, he began his questioning, and by means of nods and shakes, of the head there passed to the ownership of Gigio, Tita and Checco, the three sons of the testator, the houses, the land, cattle, horses, pigs, etc., even to the broken-down cart.

"And your wife," exclaimed X——. "Do you not wish to leave something to your wife?"

The old man shook his head, and all, including the wife herself, agreed that this was his recognized wish.

"But," said X——, "the law particularly provides for cases such as this, and we must not disregard it."

"Sior," said the old woman, stoically, "law or no law, I will not touch anything. I will go hungry now and starve in the future sooner than do so."

My principal thereupon allowed the woman to have her way, and began to read the items of the will in a loud voice. I had given him my seat and was standing beside him while he read.

Just then a cock flew through the opening of the loft and began to crow, and turning in the direction of the sound I saw a young peasant woman, flushed and out of breath, with a babe in her arms.

"What are they doing here?" she cried out, fixing upon me two flashing eyes, "are they robbing me and my child?"

At this remark confusion ensued, and the old woman and all three of her sons sprang up and rushed upon the newcomer.

X—— rose to his feet and commanded them all to be still.

"Who is this woman?" he asked, authoritatively. The mother hastily replied:

"I will tell you, Sior, who she is. She is our daughter, but she is good-for-nothing. I want you to understand that her father will not give her a single thing——"

"What, you too, mother?" interrupted the girl bitterly. "I can stand my brothers treating me like a dog, but you, mother—I don't care for them, but you—you are my own mother, and yet you would betray me. What can you say against me, and what against my husband?"

"Enough, enough," cried X——. "Shame on you all. The very first who opens his mouth I will have arrested for perjury."

The sons were white with rage, the witnesses shrunk away in terror, and mother and daughter glared at one another with a look of hatred and menace, but no one dared utter a word as X—— furiously tore the will into fragments.

All of a sudden the daughter started forward, and without hindrance from any one went straight to where the dying man lay, and put the babe down by his side.

"Pare!" she cried. "Pare! do you want me to die of hunger? At least leave me a bowl of 'polenta' for my child!" A scowl passed over the face of the old man, and unable to show any other sign of hostility he closed his one remaining eye.

I shall never forget the picture of the two heads on the pillow: the beginning and the end of life. One with the laughing eyes and dimpled rosy cheeks of the "bambino," and the other a dying man's contracted features, with hollow face darkened by the shadow of death. The idea that the evil spirit was hovering above both, ready to claim one of the two as his victim, caused me to shudder.

At this point the village priest appeared, a simple, kind-hearted man whom I had met once before. He saw the child on the bed and thought a reconciliation had been effected.

"So at last all is well. God be praised!" he said, feelingly. He leaned over and felt the pulse of the dying man.

The child began to cry, and its mother made a move to take it in her arms, but the priest would not permit.

"Leave the 'bambino' there," he said. "Matteo's time has come. Let him pass to the other world with an angel to guide him," and he commenced to recite the prayers for the dying.

X——, with little liking for such scenes, preferred to risk the descent of the ladder, and I hastened to assist him, but before going down myself, I turned to satisfy my curiosity with one last look.

Sons and witnesses had disappeared, I could not tell where. The young mother had taken her babe and was busy trying to quiet it with kisses and caresses, as if the child alone was worthy of attention; and the old woman, faithful to the last to the man whom she had slaved for with a brutish devotion, was kneeling by his side, praying.

I descended the ladder and with X—— wandered back to the town along fields of ripening grain, across meadows gay with flowers, and under rows of poplar trees joined together by festoons of vines from which hung clusters of already darkening grapes; and as we went along I wondered how all this innocence of nature, this beauty of flower and this blessing of fruit, could nourish in the human heart such despicable greed and bitter hatred.

"I cannot understand," I said to X——; "it seems to me there must be something wrong in the methods which man employs for making use of all the glorious gifts of God."

"I fear that is true," he replied, "and that the mistake arises from the worst and most original of all sins—the sin of selfishness. But let us leave its solution to the Creator and to mankind. Together they will surely some time find a remedy."

EDMONDO DE AMICIS

(1846–1908)

DE AMICIS is best known to the world as the author of the children's classic, *Cuore*. De Amicis was a follower of the tradition of Manzoni, and wrote graceful travel books and novels, short stories and poems. Of his delicately conceived tales, *Mendicant Melody* is one of the most charming. It forms a fitting contrast to the wild and savage beauty of D'Annunzio.

The present version is translated by Walter Brooks, and is reprinted from his volume, *Retold in English*. Copyright, 1905, by Brentano's, by whose permission, and that of Signor Ugo de Amicis, it is here included.

MENDICANT MELODY

I WONDER who is the sadder in this world of hunger, he who sings or he who listens?

I often think how much of this sadness I witnessed sitting by my study window in the house in which I spent fifteen years of my life, and looking out into the courtyard where the compassion of the landlord permitted all the singing and listening misery of Turin to enter.

This pitiful vagabond music came there to bemoan and entreat at all hours of the day, and under all conditions; sometimes I heard it at sunrise, and sometimes at the closing in of night.

There were moribund tenor voices still persistent in imploring the penny and refusing to be subdued by the rain; there were the childish notes of a song almost smothered by large flakes of falling snow, and sentimental ditties, accompanied by the rumbling of thunder, and interrupted by the singer stopping to shield his eyes from blinding flashes of lightning. And more than once in the burning heat of an August day, when the sun fairly baked the walls, and the whole house seemed stupefied in this flaming air and this dead silence, arose the voice of an unfortunate one whose very song gave evidence of a day passed without food.

What pitiful and manifold stanzas of melodious misery! All conditions from infancy, which commences to sing before knowing how to form its words, to decrepit old age, which has lost the power to form them, but still sings.

Every infirmity, every deformity, every aspect of misfortune and grief came under my window; from the mountaineer who sang a melancholy song in a dialect known only in the valleys of the Alps, to the Sicilian boy who, warbling all the way, had travelled the length of the Peninsula, and whose first notes caused me to lift my head and see a vision of an azure gulf with a leafy crown of orange trees.

Evidences of poverty and misery and signs, of a life of hardship were manifested by the instruments themselves; the voice of weariness and anguish cried out in the squeaking violins, the discordant harps, the coughing and wheezing flutes and trombones, and the loosely strung tambourines held out by tired hands to receive charity.

From time to time I heard a voice melodious, but impaired by ill-usage, the remains of a former glory, which drew the curious to the window and gave their faces an expression of sorrow that such a precious article should be destroyed. The accent and modulation were those of the stage, and the story could be readily divined: from the theater to the café, from the café to the tavern, from the tavern to the courtyard, and then to the hospital. And was it strange that the singer continued in adversity to ask bread of the art which had so lavishly provided for him in better days, when so many without voice, without ear, without musical sense, resort to song as a means of livelihood? But how pitiful the open mouth from which no melody issues, this childish pretense intended to save the last vestige of shame at asking, without giving something in return.

Then the blind would come, led by companions who could still distinguish a faint glimmer of daylight, and must provide sight for two; then old men and women in peasant costumes, singing with shrill voices the same monotonous song, the only one perchance they had known in the hamlet where they were born, lank and long-haired, with sinister features and casting thievish glances about. Children came also, even the tiny ones, pretty in spite of their rags, the cords of their necks swelling, and all the forces of their emaciated bodies working in unison in their efforts to sing. What will be their lot, poor little forsaken songbirds? While other children sing from sheer happiness, their singing is surely a punishment.

I heard head notes and notes from the nose, intermittent as over broken keys or tremulous like the bleating of a lamb; voices squeaking and hollow, scarcely to be recognized as human; bass voices which sang tenor airs; baritone singing soprano, all lost to shame of discord, and audaciously omitting the high notes or substituting false ones of their own with the barefaced effrontery of a quack who feels he can cheat with impunity. All the injury which the human vocal organs can suffer —the crimes they can commit were there.

What strange subterranean passages of sentiment and tone, from the lively airs of the opera-bouffe to the plaintive entreaties directed toward deserted windows!

"Signori, something for charity's sake! Take compassion on a poor unfortunate!"

And what an extraordinary and incredible mutilation and confusion of musical motives and words which give the impression of the bewildering song of a dreamer or the delirium of a musical maniac!

There came often a whole family, father, mother, and a nestful of children, who stood in a group in the center of the court and sang all together with wide-open mouths, each one on his own account, like a shipwrecked family on a raft calling desperately for succor to a far-off vessel.

I remember also a diminutive hunchback who used to play upon a trombone larger than himself, out of which, with closed eyes, he blew distressing and threatening notes having no connection at all with one another. When he had finished he would remain for a time perfectly motionless, neither looking about nor asking alms, as though he feared to lower his dignity, and if he received nothing he would go away, head erect, wrapped in a superb silence.

And what impressed me deeply was an old man with a battered high hat, his long white hair falling over his shoulders, who, following a tune of his own, with an energy and seriousness worthy of inspiration, would pound together two bent and weather-beaten cymbals, producing a noise resembling the successive breaking of window-panes. Every time his image comes to my mind I hear again the saddening clatter of his dilapidated cymbals as he dragged himself down the road, shaking his head mournfully, the prey of disappointments and troubles.

Oh, unfortunate music, what martyrdom is yours! Your divine art turned adrift never seems so desolate as when at certain hours of the day it makes its appeal to busy households where there is no spare time even for compassion. While you play and sing the cobbler hammers his last, the smith his anvil, and all hurry hither and thither without lowering a voice. Carts enter and depart and your tones are drowned by the cries of itinerant vendors of vegetables and brooms. Your verses of romance, of love, of the moon, and of paradise ascend in a vapor of soapsuds and mingle with the clatter of dishes, the bawling of children, the scolding of housewives, and the prosaic worries of every-day life.

The exhausted and famished tenor sings to the capon hanging outside an upper window, as he inhales the appetizing aroma of the roast cooking in the kitchen on the ground floor, and while he scratches and scrapes his violin a dog sets up a howl, boys stand and jeer, and the curious rise from the table and with mouths full appear at the windows.

Alas! alas! what cruel contrasts and what bitter ironies! The tightened heartstrings respond with the one pitiful note, "The penny for food."

Instead of experiencing a feeling of irritation at all these discordant voices and all these instruments of auricular torment, my heart turned in unconscious admiration toward this superhuman art which is the refuge of derelict creatures too old or not old enough to work; toward this much-outraged melody which obtains for unfortunate humanity the crust of bread, otherwise sought often in vain from the charity of fellowman, and which although offending the ear gives compensation by recalling vague memories and awakening in the heart echoes of other harmonies.

It is often the sufferer's sole means of convening to us the knowledge of those miseries of which we are either ignorant or from which we turn away our heads when the appeal is mute.

There sometimes came to me at night in one confused mass all the thousands of tunes which I had heard in the court these many years. They shook and rattled the window-panes like a musical tempest, and seemed to be the combined voices of all humanity which suffers, and of all the unfortunates who, nailed to the cross of destiny, live in pain and die in desperation.

A blind youth sang in a thin but pleasing tone a mournful ballad which had for its refrain "Ma la voce, la voce la so," ("but the voice, yes, I know the voice") and told how a lover had lost his loved one, but how, after death, her voice had continued to reverberate in his heart like a perpetual echo.

Did the poor mendicant singer who flung his melody through an open window conceive the thoughts which were awakened, like a voice calling from the past in the mind of an invisible listener? Did he imagine for a moment that behind the blank wall was one who sighed, and who, when he bade the poor singer be silent and depart, hastened to recall his words and secretly to throw him a piece of money that he might repeat the song and might even come another time to awaken once more the sad memory of a voice vibrating with a thousand echoes through an overflowing heart?

"Ma la voce, la voce la so."

MATILDE SERAO

(1856–1927)

MATILDE SERAO was born at Patras, Greece, in 1856, and was the most distinguished of the older generation of modern Italian women writers. She began her literary career as a follower of Zola, and later developed the psychological novel. She wrote chiefly of the life about Naples. *Lulu's Triumph* is a short story as well as a study in character, and in spite of its length it conforms rigidly to the qualifications demanded by the strictest critics.

The present version is translated by Elise Lathrop. It is reprinted by permission of the publisher, P. F. Collier & Son.

LULU'S TRIUMPH

SOFIA did not raise her eyes from her work, and her slim fingers fairly flew over the delicate lace. But Lulu wandered about the room, moving the ornaments on the shelves or opening a drawer to gaze absently into it. It was clear that she wished either to do or to say something, but was abashed by her elder sister's grave manner. She hummed a few bars of a song, recited a verse, but Sofia appeared not to hear. Then Lulu, who was not blessed with too much patience, decided to put the question boldly, and, planting herself in front of her sister, she asked:

"Sofia, do you know what Mademoiselle Jeannette told me?"

"Assuredly nothing very interesting."

"Now that is an answer dry and cold enough to give one a chill even in summer! Where do you get your ice, oh, my glacial sister?"

"Lulu, you are a veritable baby!"

"Now, that is just where you mistake, idol of my heart. I am not a baby, for I am going to be married."

"What?"

"And that is just what Jeannette told me."

"What nonsense! I do not understand a word of what you are saying."

"Very good, I will now tell you all, as they say in plays. It will be a narrative—but will Your Seriousness lend me your whole attention?"

"Yes, yes, but be quick."

"The day of the races is the time and the Field of Mars the place. You were not there; you preferred your everlasting books."

"If you wander so from the subject I will not listen to you any longer."

"You must listen to me; this secret is suffocating me, killing me."

"Are you beginning again?"

"I will stop, I will stop. Well, then, at the races we sat in the front row on the grand stand. Paolo Lovato came and presented a handsome young man to us, Roberto Montefranco. After the usual greetings and vague compliments, they found places directly behind us; we exchanged a few words until the signal for the start of the horses was heard. You remember that I favored Gorgon, without foreseeing how ungrateful she was to be to me—one must resign one's self to ingratitude even with beasts. A cloud of dust quite hid the horses. 'Gorgon wins!' I cried. 'No,' said Montefranco, smilingly, 'Lord Lavello.' I was vexed at his contradiction; but he continued smiling and contradicting me; we ended by making a wager. Finally, after half an hour of palpitation and anxiety, I learned that Gorgon had played me false, that I had lost and Montefranco had won; only fancy! I tell him that I will pay at once; he bows and replies that there is plenty of time. I meet him on the Chiaja, throw him an interrogative glance, and he contents himself with bowing and smiling in a mysterious manner. It is the same at the theater, everywhere. I live in the greatest curiosity. Roberto is handsome, twenty-six years old, and this morning Montefranco *père*, my future father-in-law, had a two hours' conference with mamma."

"Oh!"

"Signs of attention on the part of my audience? Well, I knew about his visit from Jeannette. So the marriage is arranged. One momentous detail remains to be settled; when shall I go to the mayor's office, and shall I wear a gray or a tan colored gown? Shall I wear a hat with streamers or without?"

"How you run on!"

"Run? Why, of course; there are no obstacles. Roberto and I will love each other madly, our parents are content—"

"And you would marry a man that way?"

"What does 'that way' mean? It is such an elastic word."

"Without knowing him, without loving him?"

"But I do know him, I have seen him at the races and when out walking. I adore him! Day before yesterday I refused to take luncheon because I had not seen him, and instead drank three cups of coffee, trying to commit suicide."

"And he?"

"He wishes to marry me, therefore he loves me!" replied Lulu, triumphantly. But seeing Sofia's face pale, she repented of this imprudent remark, and bending over her sister, asked affectionately:

"Have I said anything wrong?"

"No, dear, no; you are right. When one loves one marries. It is difficult to awaken love," and she sighed softly.

"Awaken love, awaken love!" repeated Lulu, in an irritated manner. "It is very easy, Sofia; but when one has a serious brow, like you, sad eyes, and unsmiling lips; when one goes and sits in a corner thinking, while every one else is dancing and jesting; when one reads instead of laughing, and instead of living, dreams; and when one cultivates an old and lackadaisical manner, though still young, then it is difficult to be loved."

Sofia lowered her head and made no reply. Her lips quivered slightly, as though she were suppressing a sob.

"Have I hurt you again?" asked Lulu. "It is because I should like to see you beloved, surrounded with affection, to see you a bride—How nice it would be if we were to be married on the same day!"

"That is foolish; I shall be an old maid."

"No, miss, I forbid it, you wicked creature. If Roberto is a nice fellow he absolutely must have a bachelor brother; I wish it!"

At this moment their mother entered the room in walking dress.

"Are you going out, mamma?" asked Lulu.

"Yes, dear, I am going to the notary's."

"Oh! to the notary's. That is a serious business."

"You will soon learn, Miss Tease. Sofia, come with me for a moment."

"And has Sofia, too, some dark dealings with the notary?"

"Lulu, when will you learn to be serious?"

"Very soon, mamma; you will see."

She opened the door for her mother and sister to pass out, made two low courtesies, murmuring: "Madame, Mademoiselle!" When they had left the room she called to them from the threshold, with a burst of laughter:

"Talk, talk away! I will pretend that I know nothing about it."

As a general thing Roberto Montefranco was not a great thinker; he had not time to be. What with luncheons, horseback rides, calls, and dinners, his days flew by, and his evenings he passed pleasantly with his fiancée, Lulu. Then there were tiresome matters to be attended to, some appointments with his lawyer, contracts to be signed, some old debts to be settled, to say nothing of preparations for his house and for the wedding trip. He had barely time even for his half-hour's reading and fifteen minutes' loitering at the door of his café. So he was never seen absorbed in profound reflection, nor was he ever known to be engaged in solving some social problem, for Roberto had nothing of the tragic or heroic in his character. Rather, he was of a serene temperament, and many envied him for it.

But this afternoon he lay stretched out in an armchair, one leg crossed over the other, a book in his hand, with the fixed determination of reading. The book was interesting; yet, new and strange as it may seem, the reader had become very absent-minded. In fact, he was more than that; he was nervous and restless. He never turned a page, because after reading a couple of lines the letters seemed to leave their printed places, to dance about, become confused, disappear. Roberto had involuntarily taken a journey into the unknown regions of thought.

"Papa is satisfied, my aunts all have sent me their blessings, my girl cousins are angry, my friends at the café congratulate me ironically, my true friends clasp my hand; therefore I am doing well to marry. I can not deny that Lulu is very pretty; when she fixes her eyes so full of mischief upon me, when she laughs and shows her little white teeth, I want to take her charming little head between my hands and kiss her over and over again. And she has an excellent disposition, a character of gold, always merry, good-natured, ready for a jest, witty, full of pranks, never melancholy. We shall agree excellently. I can not endure serious looks, especially in people I love. It always seems to me that such looks conceal a secret grief, a grief with which I am unacquainted, and which I cannot alleviate, or of which I am perhaps the involuntary cause. Sofia, my future sister-in-law, has the faculty of irritating me with her cold, impassive face. Whenever she appears my intelligence seems to shrivel up, the smile leaves my lips; and even should the most beautiful spring sun be shining, for me it turns into a gray

November day. I no longer have the courage to joke even with Lulu; that Sofia drives all joy away. She may have noticed the unpleasant impression she makes upon me, for she speaks to me without looking at me, does not shake hands, answers in the fewest possible words. She has noticed my dislike for her. Perhaps she is offended by it.

"Lulu always laughs. She is very young. She never says a serious word to me, and even if she wishes to, it always seems as though she were ridiculing. She loves me, but not madly. To be frank, mine is not a mad passion either; better so. For my part, I have two theories firmly established in my mind: an engaged couple should be of like dispositions, and, secondly, they should never begin with a violent passion. This is our case, and Lulu and I will be very happy. We shall take a trip through Italy, but without haste, taking short journeys, enjoying every comfort, stopping where we please, seeing even the most insignificant things. We will thus occupy three months; no, that will not be enough, let us say four months; I shall be glad to get Lulu away for a certain time from the doleful society of Sofia. But, I ask, is it natural that that girl should be so serious at her age? She must be twenty-three. She is not plain. In fact, she has beautiful eyes, and the carriage of a queen. If she were not so severe she would please. I wager that she will be an old maid; perhaps that is her secret torment, perhaps a love affair, some unfortunate love affair?—I am curious to know the cause of her seriousness—I shall ask Lulu when we are alone—

"Lulu is fond of bonbons, she told me so that second evening I went to her house. How she nibbles them! How they disappear between her little red lips, and after a moment what a false air of compunction she assumes—because there are no more. She is dear, dear, dear! She confided to me in a low tone that when it thunders she is frightened, and goes and hides her head among the pillows; that she has always dreamed of having a gown of black velvet, with a very long train, and with white lace at the neck and sleeves. She assures me that she shall be jealous, jealous as a Spaniard, and that she shall buy a little dagger with a handle inlaid with gold, with which to take vengeance. She is adorable when she repeats these absurdities to me, with her childish air of conviction. Even Sofia is forced to smile sometimes, and how it brightens her face! That Sofia, that Sofia! who will ever learn to know her!"

The book fell from his knees to the floor, the young man started at the sound, looked about in surprise, as though unable to recognize himself. It was actually he, Roberto Montefranco, caught in *flagrante delicto*, meditating.

Twilight was descending like a rain of gray ashes. Sofia, standing at the window that opened out on to the balcony, was gazing down into the crowded, noisy street. It was the hour in which the Via Toledo becomes dangerous because of the great number of large and small carriages that pass up and down in a continuous stream. Sofia seemed looking for some one; suddenly a vivid flush passed over her face, she bent her head slightly, then suddenly paled, and turned back into the room. A minute later Lulu entered like a whirlwind, slamming doors, overturning chairs that she might hurry the more.

"What are you doing here, Donna Sofia Santangelo? Are you reading?"

"Yes, I was reading."

"And you did not even care to stand on the balcony?"

"And if I had?"

"Pshaw! I had to stay upstairs, for Albina, the dressmaker, had brought my gown for this evening, and all the while I was trembling with impatience, for I wanted to be here. Yesterday evening I told Roberto to wear his gray overcoat, to have Selim harnessed to the cart, and to pass at half-past six. Who knows if he obeyed me!"

"Roberto passed here in the cart, and wearing his gray overcoat."

"Good gracious! How do you know all this? I thought you were reading?"

"I was in the window."

"And you recognized Roberto, although you never look at him? Wonderful! Did he bow to you?"

"Yes."

"How did he take off his hat?"

"Why—as he always does."

"And you bowed to him?"

"Do you think me lacking in manners?"

"At least you smiled at him?"

"No—that is, I do not know."

"You are not nice, Sofia. And yesterday evening Roberto spoke to me about you."

"Telling you that I was not nice?"

"No, but, asking me the cause of your reserved character, so different from mine. Then I recited a fine panegyric to him; I told him that you were better, more amiable, more loving than I, that your only fault was in concealing all these good qualities. Only fancy, he listened to me with the greatest interest; finally, he asked me about your aversion to him—"

"Aversion!"

"That is what he said, and, do you know, he is not so entirely wrong; you treat him with so little cordiality. But even on this point I defended you; I told a fib, for I said that you liked him very much indeed, and that you esteemed him greatly—"

"Lulu!"

"I know that it is not true, but Roberto is so fond of you, is it not ungrateful of you to treat him like a stranger?"

Sofia threw her arms around her sister's neck and kissed her; Lulu held her for an instant, and murmured in a caressing voice:

"Why do you not love Roberto a little?"

The other made a sudden abrupt movement and drew away, without saying a word.

"Oh, well!" said Lulu, shrugging her shoulders and changing the subject. "Are you really not coming with us this evening?"

"No, I have a headache; you can go with mamma."

"As usual. I shall go just the same, because I shall have a very good time."

"Is—Roberto going with you?"

"No; he is going to his club, where there is a directors' meeting. I am going to profit by it and go to the Dellinos' ball, and shall dance until to-morrow morning."

"And when he knows of it?"

"So much the better. He will learn from now on to leave me free; I do not wish him to acquire bad habits."

"You love him very little, it seems to me."

"Very much, in my own way. But I must hurry away to dress. It will take me at least two hours."

Sofia stood listening to the noise of the departing carriage which bore away her mother and sister. She was left alone, quite alone, as she had always wished to be left. As a child, when some wrong or injustice had been done her, she had cried all alone, when she was in bed, in the dark, and the habit had remained with her. Now, alone in the great drawing-room, beneath the brightly lighted chandelier, her hands inert, her head resting against the back of her chair, her face wore an expression of great sorrow, the vivid reflection of a serious inward conflict. Certainly in these moments of complete solitude the consciousness of a great grief came over her; the sentiment of the reality, long repulsed, became clear, distinct, cruel.

The sound of footsteps startled her. It was Roberto. Seeing her alone, he paused, hesitating; but supposing the rest of the family to be in another room, he advanced. Sofia had risen at once, agitated.

"Good evening, Sofia."

"Good evening—"

They were both embarrassed.

"Heavens, how unpleasant this Sofia is!" thought Roberto.

Meanwhile the girl recovered herself, composing her features, which once more took on a severe expression. They sat down at some distance from each other.

"Your mother is well?"

"Quite well, thank you."

"And—Lulu?"

"She, too, is very well."

There was silence. Roberto experienced a strange sensation as of joy filled with bitterness.

"Lulu is occupied?" he asked.

Sofia checked a slight movement of impatience.

"She is at the Dellinos' ball with mamma," she continued rapidly, as if to anticipate other questions.

Since Sofia was alone, then, and if he did not wish to be the most discourteous of men, he ought to remain and chat with her. At this thought Roberto was seized with an almost irresistible desire to flee. Yet he did not move.

"I came here because there was not the required number of us at my club," he finally said, as if to excuse his presence.

"Lulu did not expect you—I am sorry—"

"Oh, it does not matter," interrupted Roberto.

The interruption was too quick, and hardly flattering to the absent one.

"And you did not go?" he resumed.

"No, you know I am not very fond of balls."

"Do you prefer reading?"

"Yes, very much."

"Are you not afraid of doing yourself harm?"

"I have good eyes," replied Sofia, raising them to the face of her questioner.

"And beautiful ones," thought Roberto, "but expressionless. I meant—"

"Moral injury, perhaps. I do not think so. From the books that I read I always derive great peace."

"Do you need peace?"

"We all need peace."

Sofia's voice was grave, resonant. Roberto took pleasure in it, as though he were hearing it for the first time. He seemed to find himself face to face with a woman hitherto unknown to him, and who was revealing herself to him in every word and gesture. Sofia had lost her coldness, she even looked at him, smiled at him, and spoke to him as to a friend. What had been between them before this? What was happening now?

"When I like a book," continued Roberto, "I always feel the greatest desire to know the author, to know if he or she is good, if he has suffered, if he too has loved—"

"Perhaps you would be disillusionized. Authors always describe the love of others, never their own."

"Possibly out of respect?"

"From jealousy, I think. There are cases in which love is the only treasure hidden in a soul."

But the voice of Sofia did not change as she said these words. Her face wore such a frank expression, her tone was so simple, so pure, so convinced, that Roberto felt no surprise at hearing her discuss love with such sureness. Nothing now surprised him; everything seemed natural, to be expected. Even this evening, passed alone with this strange girl, seemed to him something predestined and long awaited. When they separated they gazed directly into each other's faces, as though they wished to be sure of recognizing each other again. Sofia held out her hand, Roberto took it and bowed over it; a portière fell heavily behind him. They were parted.

When the charm of Sofia's presence and conversation had ceased, Roberto felt confused, his brain in a turmoil. He was both gay and melancholy, would have liked to die, and was yet full of life. He did not know what to think of Lulu, of himself, or of his future.

Sofia was very happy, very happy. For this reason she wept, sobbing heartily, her head buried in her pillow.

Three months had passed, Lulu's marriage was still postponed. Every once in a while her mother, who did not understand this delay, would call her daughter aside and ask her the cause.

"I wish to wait," Lulu replied; "I need to know Roberto better."

In fact, the girl had become observing. She went about as usual, sang as usual, laughed, joked, but often interrupted these pleasant occupations to study her sister, or to listen closely to Roberto's every word. The former was often seen with lips compressed, her eyebrows drawn together with an air of great attention.

Then Lulu looked about her. And about her strange things were happening, Roberto was no longer serene and hilarious as usual, but thoughtful, pale, and agitated. He spoke briefly and absently; to many things in which he had formerly been interested he now seemed quite indifferent; sometimes with a great effort he succeeded in controlling himself, becoming once more what he had been before, but only for a short time. He had never been accustomed to dissimulation, and succeeded badly; his passion and inner torment were revealed in his eyes.

A different Sofia, too, made her appearance at this time; that is to say, a nervous, restless Sofia, who at times embraced her sister with effusion, sometimes remained for hours without seeing her, rather avoiding her. Fleeting blushes rose to her cheeks, feverish flushes; a flame burned in her eyes; her voice was now deep and full of emotion, now dry and strident; her hands shook. At night she did not sleep. Lulu often rose, and went with bare feet to listen at her door, and heard

Sofia toss about and weep. If questioned, Sofia declared that there was nothing the matter; always the same reply.

When Roberto and Sofia met—and this happened every day—the change that had taken place in both of them became evident. Remarks were rare, replies were either too prompt or too vague, there were odd glances; sometimes for whole evenings they did not speak, but each studied the movements of the other. They never sat beside each other; yet Roberto always found an excuse for picking up the work or the book that Sofia had touched. Sometimes when she did not come into the room, Roberto, always more and more uneasy, stared at the closed door, answering absently to what was said. Sometimes only five minutes after Sofia's appearance he would take his hat and leave. The girl was growing pale, black circles appeared under her eyes. Finally, she decided not to let herself be seen. Every evening for a week she shut herself in her room, trembling with impatience, trying to smother her unhappiness.

One evening Lulu entered her room. "Will you do me a favor?" she asked.

"What do you want?"

"I have a note to write," said Lulu. "Roberto is alone, out on the terrace. Will you go and keep him company?"

"But I—"

"Do you wish to stay shut up here? Does it cost you so much to please me?"

"Will you come back soon?"

"I only want time to write four lines."

Sofia turned toward the terrace, trying to summon courage for the ordeal. She paused on the threshold. Roberto was walking up and down; she went up to him.

"Lulu sends me," she said in a low voice.

"You forced yourself to come?"

"Forced—no."

She trembled throughout her whole frame; Roberto was near her, his face transfigured with passion.

"What have I done to you, Sofia?"

"Nothing, you have done nothing. Do not look at me like that," she implored, terrified.

"You know then, Sofia, that I love you very dearly?"

"Oh! hush, Roberto, for pity's sake hush! If Lulu were to hear us!"

"I do not love Lulu. I love you, Sofia."

"That is treachery."

"I know it, but I love you. I will go away—"

"Well?" cried Lulu in the distance, appearing from another door. "Well, have you two made peace?"

But there was no reply. Sofia fled, hiding her face in her hands; and Roberto remained motionless, silent, as though stunned.

"Roberto!" cried Lulu.

"Lulu."

"What has happened?"

"Nothing; I am going."

And without even taking leave of her, he too went away with a despairing gesture. Lulu followed him with her eyes, and stood there absorbed in thought.

"One here, the other there," she murmured; "and previous to that? Enough! I must take a hand in it."

"And so for all these excellent reasons I cannot marry Roberto Montefranco," Lulu finally said to her mother.

"They are absurd reasons, my daughter," replied the mother, shaking her head.

"In short, must I tell you frankly and plainly that Roberto does not please me, and that I am not going to marry him?"

"It is at least frank; but it is no more than a whim. Roberto loves you."

"He will console himself."

"You have exchanged promises."

"We can retract them. We are no longer living in the days when people were married by force."

"What will the world say?"

"Mother, let us define the world."

"People."

"And who is Mr. People? I do not know him; I am not obliged to be unhappy for the sake of Mr. People."

"You are a terrible girl! But how am I to arrange it with Roberto? What am I to say to him?"

"What you wish. That is what you are my mother for."

"Oh, indeed! To remedy the wrongs you have done. There will be a scandal."

"I do not think so; you can say it politely, with pretty manners. Indeed, I think you might even speak badly of me—call me capricious, frivolous, childish; say that I would be a very bad wife, that I am not at all serious, that I am lacking in dignity, that my sister is—"

"Your sister? Are you losing your mind, Lulu?"

"Pshaw! you could easily say that. At present Roberto and Sofia are indifferent to each other but if they come to know each other better they might appreciate each other, and then—who can say? You would be praised as a good mother for having married off the elder daughter first."

"In fact—"

"I shall not go husbandless; I am barely eighteen years old. And I wish to amuse myself; I wish to dance a great deal; I wish to enjoy my happy youth with my dear, kind little mother—"

"You are a little rogue," replied the mother, moved, and embracing her daughter.

"Then we understand each other? Announce the ugly news to Roberto politely, but add that we must always be friends, that we hope to see him often. If these two are to fall in love with each other they will do so; it is predestined."

"But do you believe, naughty Lulu, that matters will all come right? You know that I hate quarrels."

"Oh, unconvinced mother! Oh, mother, more unbelieving than Saint Thomas! Yes, yes, out of my wide experience I assure you that there will be no scandal. Roberto is a gentleman, and will not expect me to marry him without loving him."

"What seems to me impossible is the affair with Sofia—"

"Nothing is more possible than the impossible," gravely replied Lulu.

"My dear, so many axioms! Enough. Let us leave it all to time; perhaps time will regulate our affairs. All of which does not change the fact that you are a scatterbrain."

"And very capricious—"

"Lacking in judgment—"

"And a whimsical creature. I am everything you like; lecture me, I deserve it. Come; have you nothing to say? I am waiting."

"Give me a kiss, and go to bed. Good night, baby."

"Thank you, mamma. Good night."

"It is better so," thought the good mother. "Lulu is too young yet. Every day one sees the sad consequences of these marriages of convenience. May Heaven free us from them! It is better so."

"Uff!" said Lulu, taking a deep breath. "What diplomacy I was forced to use, what art in order to convince mamma! I would make a perfect ambassador. What a triumph! Not like a triumph of love, to be sure, but it is Lulu's triumph!"

She paused outside her sister's door and listened. She heard every now and then a repressed sigh. Poor Sofia had lost her peace of mind.

"Sleep, Slofia, sleep," Lulu murmured softly, kissing the lock of the door almost as though she were kissing her sister's brow; "calm yourself and rest. I have worked for you this evening."

And the generous girl fell asleep, happy and content in the thought of the happiness of the sister she loved.

Time, good old time, the eternal wise old gentleman, accomplished his task. Lulu asked herself whether this unmarried sister who acted as bridesmaid should wear a gown of blue silk or a simple one of straw-colored foulard with lace. She asked Roberto if there would be a great many bonbons for her, and Sofia if she would give her that pretty embroidered handkerchief that was like a zephyr, a cloud. Roberto and Sofia, knowing what the girl's heart was capable of, smiled at her gay thoughtlessness, and loved her, and looked upon her as their Providence.

"For I have always maintained," said Roberto Montefranco to a friend, speaking of his marriage, "that a couple should be of opposite tastes. Extremes touch. Thus they will understand each other, will mingle, will form a complete whole, while those of similar tastes are like two parallel lines; they walk on together, but never meet. And then when there is love—! I have always said so."

GABRIELE D'ANNUNZIO

(1863—1938)

D'ANNUNZIO was born at Pescara in the Abruzzi in 1863. His first literary work was a volume of verses, published when he was only sixteen. His first novel appeared in 1889, and he afterwards became famous also as a poet and dramatist. His short stories, of which he wrote a number, are memorable pictures of the half-savage peasant-folk in the mountains of his native district. He excelled in the description of vivid landscapes, and in the delineation of elemental types on the one hand, and of decadent overcivilized moderns on the other.

The present version is translated by Louis Lozowick. It appeared originally in the *Pagan* magazine, and is here reprinted by permission of the editor.

THE HERO

THE big banners of St. Gonselvo, brought upon the square, floated heavily in the wind. Men of herculean stature, with faces flushed and necks strained, carried them gingerly.

After the victory over the people of Radusa the population of Mascalico celebrated this September feast with unexampled splendor. Intense religious fervor raised their souls to exaltation. The entire population was sacrificing its rich autumnal harvest to the glory of their patron Saint. From window to window across the street, women stretched their nuptial veils. The men decorated the doors with green wreaths, and spread flowers on the threshold of their houses. A wind was blowing and everything swayed and sparkled in the street, producing an intoxicating effect on the mob.

The procession was coming from the church in a continuous stream, breaking up into groups at the square. Before the altar, from which Pantaleone has been so recently dethroned, stood eight men, chosen to the rare privilege of raising the statue of St. Gonselvo. They were: Giovanni Curo, l'Ummalido, Mattao, Vincenzio Guanno, Rocco di Ceuzo, Benedette Gallante, Biagio di Clisci, Giovanni Senzapaura. Speechless they stood, conscious of their important duty, and somewhat agitated. They presented a powerful group, as they stood there, ears pierced by dangling gold earrings, and eyes bright with the gleam of religious fanaticism. Now and then they would feel their biceps and pulse as if to try their strength; and sometimes a faint smile would flit over their faces.

The statue of the patron Saint was of great size and enormous weight; the body was cast from dark bronze, the hands and head from silver.

"Forward!" came Mattao's order.

The people crowded from every side to see the procession. The windows clattered with every gust of wind. The interior of the temple was drowned in clouds of incense, and sounds of musical instruments rose intermittently to a clear pitch and disappeared into the mysterious distance. The eight men, now lost in the general scuffle, and dazed with a sort of religious fervor, stretched their arms, ready to start.

"One! . . . Two! . . . Three! . . ." cried Mattao.

With a concentrated effort they all tried to lift the statue from the altar. But the weight was too great, and the statue bent over a little to the left. The men had scarcely time to gain a firm hold on the pedestal. They leaned forward to retain their balance, but the less dextrous, among them Biagio di Clisci and Giovanni Curo, let the statue slip from their hands. It fell with all its weight to one side. Ummalido uttered a piercing cry.

"Look out! Look out!" shouted the people on every side when they noticed the danger that was threatening their patron Saint. A deafening uproar came from the square and drowned the voices.

Ummalido fell on his knees; his right hand was nailed flat by the statue. Standing thus on his knees, his glance was fastened to his hand, which he had no power to withdraw. His eyes expressed horror and torment, his mouth was distorted with pain, but he uttered no sound. Blood was dripping on the altar.

With a united effort his comrades tried to lift the statue, but that proved no easy task. Ummalido's mouth writhed with excruciating pain. The women standing near, shuddered in horror.

Finally the statue was lifted and Ummalido's hand removed from under it. The hand, crushed and bleeding, presented but a formless mass.

"Go home at once. Go home!" came the advice from some among the crowd, as they urged him gently toward the exits of the church.

One woman removed her apron and offered to bandage his arm. Ummalido refused. He stared silently at a group of men engaged in a quarrel around the statue.

"It's my turn."

"No, mine! Mine!"

"No, mine!"

Cicco Pono, Mattia Scarfarola, and Tommaso Clisci were each contending for Ummalido's place.

Ummalido approached the arguing men. His shapeless hand was dangling by his side, and with his second hand he was making his way through the crowd.

"The place belongs to me," he said simply, and offered his shoulder to support the statue. He set his teeth in fierce determination to suppress the infernal pain.

"What are you going to do?" asked Mattao.

"Whatever be the will of St. Gonselvo," he answered, and started on the procession together with the rest.

The crowd was stupefied.

During the procession his bleeding wound was gradually becoming black. Now and then someone would ask:

"Well, Umma, how do you feel?"

Ummalido did not answer, but marched in step with the music. He walked with heavy head under the broad canopy floating in the wind. The crowd was constantly growing in volume.

At the corner of a certain street Ummalido suddenly sank to the ground. The statue tipped slightly. Dismayed for a moment, the crowd slowed up. Soon, however, the procession was resumed. The place of Ummalido was taken by Mattia Scarfarola. Two relatives lifted the fainting man and carried him to the nearest house.

Anna di Ceuzo, an old woman, skilled in the art of healing, looked at the deformed and bleeding hand and shook her head.

"What can you do?"

In this case her art was powerless.

Ummalido recovered from the swoon and stubbornly retained his silence. He sat up and calmly examined his wound. The hand with its bones all crushed was evidently lost.

Two or three old peasants came up to look at it; by word or gesture each of them expressed the same thought.

"Who carried the Saint?" asked Ummalido.

"Mattia Scarfarola," they answered.

"And what is taking place there now?" he asked again.

"Vespers and music," was the answer.

The peasants bade him farewell, and left for the vespers. The sound of ringing bells was coming from the church.

One of the relatives placed a bucket of cold water near the wounded man and said:

"Dip your hand into it; we are going. The vesper-bells are calling."

Ummalido remained alone. The ringing changed its rhythm and grew louder. The day was nearing its end. It grew dark. Shaken by the wind, the branches of an olive tree struck against the pane.

Slowly Ummalido began to wash his hand. And as he removed the clots of blood it became apparent how really terrible the wound was.

"Useless," thought Ummalido; "the hand is lost. St. Gonselvo, I sacrifice it to Thee."

He took a knife and went out. All the streets were abandoned. The pious populace crowded the church. Above the houses, scarlet clouds, illumined by a September sunset, glided past like flocks in flight.

The people gathered at the church joined the voices of the choir to the accompaniment of music. The heat of human bodies and the smoke of burning candles made the atmosphere well-nigh stifling. The silver head of St. Gonselvo shone like a beacon above the crowd.

Ummalido entered. In the midst of general disorder he approached the altar.

"St. Gonselvo, I offer it to Thee," said he in a firm voice, holding the knife in his hand.

With these words he began to cut deep into the wrist of his right hand. The astounded crowd was struck dumb. The shapeless hand began to part from the arm. For a moment it dangled on the last tendons, then it fell at the feet of the Patron Saint into the bowl where money-offerings were deposited.

Then Ummalido lifted up the bloody stump and in a firm voice repeated:

"St. Gonselvo, I offer it to Thee."

GRAZIA DELEDDA

(1871–1936)

BORN in Sardinia in 1871, Grazia Deledda achieved conspicuous success in her novels and stories, which are for the most part concerned with the folk of her native Island. She wrote unaffectedly of the peasants, revealing a sense of actuality and a deep understanding of character.

The present version is translated by Walter Brooks, and is reprinted from his volume, *Retold in English*. Copyright, 1905, by Brentano's, by whose permission it is here included.

TWO MIRACLES

WITH eyes fastened upon the rosary of mother-of-pearl in her hand, "Zia" Batòra climbed the steep path which led from the village of Bitti up to the Church of Our Lady of Miracles, an unassuming edifice, famous throughout the entire island of Sardinia and so named because of the many miracles performed within its walls.

The fact that these manifestations before its modest altar had probably found their origin in the religious enthusiasm of the people, or at least been greatly exaggerated by popular superstition, did not prevent large crowds in need of either physical or mental succor from flocking to Bitti during the month of September to take part in the celebration in honor of Our Lady of Miracles.

The festival was one of the few upon which time had not laid its hand, and it still retained its awe-inspiring character and ancient glory. Mountains were crossed and valleys traversed on foot in order to reach the shrine of the wonder-working Madonna, who never failed to give in each successive year some new proof of her power.

"Zia" Batòra was a devoted follower of Our Lady of Miracles. On the first Monday of every month she took the path toward the church, telling her beads all the way, and during the three days of the feast she knelt there morning and evening and prayed fervently. In addition, she gave money for masses, processions, and novenas. She prayed to the Madonna for a miracle; she prayed for peace, for peace in her heart so restless and disturbed—for peace at once and without further watching and waiting—but always in vain. Days and months glided by, mass followed mass; novenas and processions succeeded one another, while bitterness and desolation became stagnant in the soul of "Zia" Batòra.

She could not forget—her heart was bruised and bleeding—and although supplied with every material want, she felt herself poorer than the most miserable beggar, and saw her happiness sink down beyond the desolate horizon of the future.

Batòra's house, with its carved wooden balconies, commanding a view of the church, stood out against the clear horizon in the ruddy September sunset, like the painted landscape in the background of the picture of the Resurrection over the altar. But the house was desolate and spiritually empty, as was the soul of her who occupied it—and yet it was so filled with all the material gifts of God.

. Sadurra, the only child of "Zia" Batòra, had fallen in love with a young man, poor and of humble birth. Because of her social position the mother rebelled against this affection as almost unnatural, since, besides being wealthy, she belonged to that aristocratic portion of the Sardinian people called "Principali," a class prominent and influential, and still imbued with the haughtiness of the Spaniards who were at one time the richest and most powerful of all the island's population.

But the beautiful Sadurra in her twenty-first year fled from the paternal roof to unite herself with the man of her heart, and the elopement gave rise to unlimited scandal in Bitti and the nearby villages.

The blow was a crushing one, and "Zia" Batòra was totally overcome. Never had mother loved a daughter as she loved hers. For twenty years since the murder of her husband she had concentrated all her affection, all her hope, on Sadurra, picturing for her a brilliant future, which naturally included a husband rich, esteemed, and belonging to the "Principali"; such a man as could avenge the death of the father.

Now, every wish, every hope, every affection had vanished, and "Zia" Batòra, kneeling on the hearthstone, cursed her daughter. She cursed the mother's milk which had given the child sustenance. She cursed her own gray hairs, and by the golden crucifix on her rosary she swore to never again think of her daughter except as a mortal enemy. And so she lived alone in a house void of comfort or hope. She saw herself dishonored, and felt keenly the triumph of those of her own position whom jealousy had made enemies.

No evidence, however, of grief or bitterness could be detected upon her pale and rigid features, none in her hard, cold, and sunken eyes nor on her thin, white lips.

"Batòra is strong," people said: "misfortune does not humble her."

But her heart was shattered so that she could not weep. She only hated and—prayed. Many a time after listening to the counsel of enemies, or even friends, she was prompted to pay an assassin to kill Peppe Nieglia, the husband of Sadurra; but religious fear had always stood in the way of such a crime.

She had made her will in favor of the Church of the Miracles, and day and night besought the merciful Madonna to give her peace, but, as always, in vain.

Eighteen months after the lamentable event she nursed the same hatred, and neither the knowledge that Sadurra was leading a life of misery and drudgery, nor the satisfaction of having more than once brutally repelled her entreaties for pardon, could console Batòra.

With eyes fastened upon the rosary of mother-of-pearl in her hand. "Zia" Batòra slowly climbed the steep path which led to the church.

In spite of the fact that at Bitti—contrary to the custom of the other Sardinian villages—the widows after a certain period resumed their bright-colored attire, she had always continued to dress in mourning, with the exception of two strips of silver lace in the form of a cross on the crown of her bonnet. These were half-concealed by a heavy veil, and were possibly some mysterious symbol of which Batòra alone knew the meaning. Her laced bodice, open in front, displayed a richly embroidered chemisette, the only luxury permitted in the costume of Bitti, and underneath the short skirt of alpaca was a longer white skirt of muslin.

A gaily dressed crowd filled the narrow streets and the open square in front of the church. Beggars at every turn held out their hands and in a whining and monotonous voice asked alms of passers-by. The neighboring villages had contributed to swell the multitude, and the market town of Bitti in the scintillating September sunlight presented a gorgeous picture, with its frame of fresh green fields in the distance.

"Zia" Batòra continued her ascent unmindful of the crowds, and, having arrived in front of the church, she stopped and made the sign of the cross before one of the innumerable processions which were passing.

It was a feature of the Festival of the Miracles that any devotee might pay for one of these processions. A contribution to the church of from one to fifty "scudi" caused the procession to start. First came a priest carrying a lighted taper, and then followed a line of worshipers from different villages with the banners of their religious societies. Each procession would make a single turn around the church, re-enter, and appear again on behalf of another contributor; so that in one short morning dozens of such processions might take place.

In contrast with all this solemnity, the frivolous minded were indulging in one of their native dances, the "duru-duru," on the opposite side of the square. The merriment was at its height in spite of dust and sun, and refreshment vendors were circulating among the crowd, offering consolation to the hungry and thirsty.

"Zia" Batòra entered the church. It was filled to overflowing with people from different localities, and different also in costume and speech, many of whom had come from miles away, with feet bare and heads uncovered. From the motley assemblage arose a confused murmur, amounting almost to an uproar, and all the women seemed to be talking at once, unconscious of the babel they were creating.

"Zia" Batòra found difficulty in making her way through the mass, and aroused energetic protests by her pushing and elbowing; but by dint of perseverance she finally succeeded in reaching the spot near the center of the church where she was accustomed to kneel.

"What is happening?" she asked of an acquaintance.

"It is a young girl possessed of an evil spirit," replied the person addressed in an excited tone. "After mass it will be exorcised, and the Lord grant that our Madonna may perform a miracle. The news has spread through the entire crowd, and every one is trembling with fear and horror. The lost soul is believed to have belonged to an apostate priest," she whispered mysteriously.

"Where does the girl come from?"

"From Alá. They say the spirit was driven out by a brother priest, and being refused admittance in heaven and purgatory, and even in hell, was forced to wander about the earth until it finally entered the body of this innocent child."

"How dreadful!"

"Yes; the poor thing is in continual torment, and acts as if she were mad. She foams at the mouth, shrieks and blasphemes, and her strength is marvelous for one of her age. She breaks everything within reach."

Batòra shuddered as she endeavored to get a glimpse of the pitiful spectacle.

"She is not yet in the church. They will bring her in, bound, after mass."

"But if the spirit is driven out of the child, will it not seek to enter the body of some other person?" asked Batòra.

"That I do not know. But if our Madonna performs the miracle she will make it complete by banishing the evil spirit from the earth forever. Perhaps in her mercy she will allow it to dwell in purgatory."

The mass began. Every one arose. The heat was intense, and the anticipation of the approaching ceremony held all spellbound.

Batòra alone was not absorbed by it. Her face was white and her eyes feverish, and though the latter were directed toward the altar they saw something entirely different.

Near Batòra were three women standing upon a bench, and one of them was holding in her arms a chubby infant with cheeks like roses. The laughter and playfulness of the babe were diverting the women and relieving the tension of delay. The young mother was pale and thin, but in spite of that her features showed traces of great beauty. It was Sadurra, in ill health and shabbily dressed. She saw her mother's cold and indifferent manner, and made an effort to restrain her tears.

"Not even one look at the 'bambino,' who is so pretty, and who in addition bears the name of its dead grandfather!" No! her mother was doubtless beside herself with rage, and was calling down curses on the curly head of the innocent. At the idea Sadurra could no longer refrain from weeping, and was tempted to leave the church.

But Batòra did not curse the "bambino," and the sight of it even softened the anger which the presence of Sadurra had aroused. She had never seen the child, and had not realized how deeply she could be affected. It was the first time, also, that she had seen her daughter since her marriage.

How changed she was! She seemed like a beggar. She seemed—"Zia" Batòra had not yet explored the depths of her heart. Under the layers of resentment and anger, perhaps some little pity for her daughter might be concealed.

Signora Santissima! How pretty the child is, and the eyes, how like its grandfather's. No! no! they are more like that vile race of the Nieglia.

The mass proceeded. The bell rang for the elevation of the Host, and for a moment all was hushed. "Zia" Batòra prayed, but only with her lips. She was conscious of nothing save the tumult of voices within her. Anger, humiliation, and regret; bitterness and tenderness; hate, pity, and love were mingled together in her heart, and engaged in a maddening struggle. The multitude of people sank upon their knees.

"Gezù, Gezù!" cried "Zia" Batòra, covering her face with her hands. "Nostra Signora mia! Have pity on me! Have pity on me!"

She felt the eyes of her daughter fixed upon her and experienced an inexpressible sensation of grief. She yearned to kiss the cheeks of her grandchild, and at the same time longed to dash its head against the wall. Sadurra had simply brought the infant for the purpose of stirring up the past, and her enemies were watching her humiliation with smiles of satisfaction!

"Dio Santissimo." It was torture! Would the mass never be finished?

The rapt attention grew more intense; morbid curiosity and fear had driven the crowd almost to a frenzy. Women fainted from heat and fatigue, and were trampled under foot. Even the merry-makers and vendors had pushed their way into the church. Behind the choir a group of gendarmerie added color to the picture.

"Zia" Batòra was nearly suffocated in her heavy bonnet and long black veil, and found herself pushed to the very foot of the bench on which Sadurra was standing. Her agitation was increased by fear of the supernatural, and she felt sure her trembling was noticeable to all about her.

At last a low murmur ran through the crowd. The child with the evil spirit was being brought in, and "Zia" Batòra caught a glimpse of her. The wasted little body was clad entirely in black, and the eyes were of a strange metallic color and shone with an unearthly light. The child was bound, but made no effort at resistance, nor did she utter a sound.

When, however, the ceremony of exorcising was finished and the crucifix presented to her to kiss, a piercing shriek which seemed to come from the evil spirit within rang out through the church. Men and women turned pale and held their breath. The child struck at the crucifix and spat upon it, and continued to utter inarticulate and terrifying cries.

On her knees at the altar rail, a woman was praying. She was the mother of the child, and her loud sobs and spasmodic weeping could be plainly heard. Batòra all at once felt her heart soften and was conscious of an unusual feeling of pity for the woman so grievously afflicted.

The crowd, having recovered from its fear, was no longer silent, and confused murmurs echoed and re-echoed from the opposite walls of the church. As the noise increased Batòra suddenly thought she heard her own name called by a mysterious voice. The woman of Alà seemed to be saying, "Why do you come here to bewail? What have you to desire, what have you to ask? I alone am unhappy. What mother can be so unfortunate? Batòra, Batòra, conquer your pride!" and her own name was repeated a thousand times by the echoes of the church. A wave of remorse and repentance surged through her heart, and a feeling of overwhelming tenderness prompted her to turn and kiss the cheek of the infant whose breath almost touched her face, but she could not; no, as yet she could not!

The heartrending spectacle at the altar, combined with such a display of maternal grief and love, had aroused in Batòra a series of bewildering sensations, and the sobs of the mother heard above the shrieks of the child had the effect upon her of acute physical pain. She knew not where nor how, but she felt herself suffocated, strangled.

The demented girl in her writhing had broken the cords which bound her, and it was necessary to summon the gendarmes in order to hold her down. The priests persisted in their efforts to make her kiss the crucifix, but the attempts only increased her blasphemy.

All of a sudden Batòra saw the mother of the child arise as if by inspiration and dry her tears. She took the crucifix from the hands of the priest and in an attitude of deepest reverence held it before the face of the child.

The little one was quiet in an instant. It was like enchantment. Her eyes melted into a fatigued and dreamy languor, and sinking into an attitude of prayer she repeated the "Ave Maria" in a voice subdued and full of piety.

"Figlia mia—daughter mine!" cried the mother, overcome with joy.

The crowd dropped to their knees, and with trembling voice responded to the "Ave Maria" of the child.

The miracle had been performed. The entire congregation gave vent to that sobbing and wailing which is the expression of fear of the supernatural—of the surprise and dread felt by the soul at the mysterious exhibition of its own simplicity.

"Zia" Batòra was one of these.

She returned to the village with the babe of Sadurra in her arms and its mother by her side, while the good people of Bitti said to one another, "This year our Madonna has performed not one, but two miracles."

Spain

INTRODUCTION

THE early epics and ballads of the Fourteenth and Fifteenth Centuries offer the first examples of the Spanish short story. The most interesting of the early indigenous Spanish stories are found in the epical Cid legends, one of which, *The Chronicle of the Cid*, contains a vast store of anecdotes and incidents. While the majority of these cannot properly be separated from the rest of the text, a few are independent stories. They are written with rare vigour and with that curiously effective emphasis which the epic writers managed to achieve through what would in modern writing be termed redundancy.

Among the very earliest writers of the more modern type of story was Prince Don Juan Manuel, grandson of San Fernando, whose collection of stories under the title *The Count Lucanor* were written to illustrate points in moral conduct. Though these were told ostensibly in order to exemplify the virtues of prudence and wisdom and kindness, they have none the less an independent interest. Don Juan exerted considerable influence over his followers.

There is more originality in the short romance of roguery, later developed in France by Le Sage, and still later in England by Fielding and Smollett. Mendoza's *Lazarillo de Tormes*, which belongs to the Golden Age of Spanish literature, is the earliest and one of the most famous of these picaresque romances. Alemán's *Guzmán de Alfarache*, no less celebrated, came a little later. Most of these novels are episodic (like *Gil Blas*, which was based upon them and their kind), so that the extraction of a chapter gives us in many instances a complete short story.

Interesting as these are, it was not until the great Cervantes produced his *Exemplary Novels*, that the Spanish story could be said to have reached a high point of development. Most of these are fairly long, and are indeed miniature novels. Among the contemporaries and immediate followers of Cervantes we find so many writers that it is extremely difficult to choose among them. Montalván, though better known as a dramatist, was the author of a much-read collection of tales.

Montalván was followed by writers who either wrote in his manner, or tried to imitate that of Cervantes and the earlier poets and romancers. Literature in the Seventeenth and Eighteenth Centuries suffered an eclipse coincident with the Spanish imperial decline, and it was not until the Nineteenth Century that the short story again came into its own.

Of the brilliant group that wrote during the early and middle years of the last century, Alarcon, Bécquer, and Alas have here been selected. Valera, Pardo-Bazán, Caballero and a score of others also contributed tales of high merit. Many recent writers, and in particular the "Group of '08," have discussed in short-story form the changing social order, but the leaders of young Spain, Benavente and Blásco-Ibañez, Baroja and "Azorín," have as a rule preferred the novel.

The Spaniards have not contributed very much to the development of the short story, though they have, over a period of nearly a thousand years, produced a multitude of readable and picturesque tales.

THE MIRACLE OF THE JEW

(Anonymous: 13th Century)

THE *Chronicle of the Cid* is a voluminous collection of adventures based upon the exploits of the celebrated Rodrigo Díaz de Bivar, who lived in the Tenth Century. Many ballads and several longer poems had made their appearance before the *Chronicle* was finally put together at the instigation of King Alfonso of Castile in the Thirteenth Century.

The episode of *The Miracle of the Jew* occurs toward the end of the book. It is a tale of wonder recounted for the glory of the warrior whose praises are celebrated throughout the entire work.

The present version is from the *Chronicle of the Cid*, translated by Robert Southey. There is no title in the original.

THE MIRACLE OF THE JEW

(From the *Chronicle of the Cid*, Book II)

NOW Don Garcia Tellez the Abbot, and the trusty Gil Diaz, were wont every year to make a great festival on the day of the Cid's departure, and on that anniversary they gave food and clothing to the poor, who came from all parts round about. And it came to pass when they made the seventh anniversary, that a great multitude assembled as they were wont to do, and many Moors and Jews came to see the strange manner of the Cid's body. And it was the custom of the Abbot Don Garcia Tellez, when they made that anniversary, to make a right noble sermon to the people: and because the multitude which had assembled was so great that the church could not hold them, they went out into the open place before the Monastery, and he preached unto them there. And while he was preaching there remained a Jew in the church, who stopped before the body of the Cid, looking at him to see how nobly he was there seated, having his countenance so fair and comely, and his long beard in such goodly order, and his sword Tizona in its scabbard in his left hand, and the strings of his mantle in his right, even in such manner as King Don Alfonso had left him, save only that the garments had been changed, it being now seven years since the body had remained there in that ivory chair. Now there was not a man in the church save this Jew, for all the others were hearing the preachment which the Abbot made. And when this Jew perceived that he was alone, he began to think within himself and say, "This is the body of the Ruydiez Cid, whom they say no man in the world ever took by the beard while he lived. I will take him by the beard now, and see what he can do to me." And with that he put forth his hand to pull the beard of the Cid; but before his hand could reach it, God, who would not suffer this thing to be done, sent his spirit into the body, and the Cid let the strings of his mantle go from his right hand, and laid hand on his sword Tizona, and drew it a full palm's length out of the scabbard. And when the Jew saw this, he fell upon his back for great fear, and began to cry out so loudly that all they who were without the Church heard him, and the Abbot broke off his preachment and went into the church to see what it might be. And when they came they found this Jew lying upon his back before the ivory chair, like one dead, for he had ceased to cry out, and had swooned away. And then the Abbot Don Garcia Tellez looked at the body of the Cid, and saw that his right hand was upon the hilt of the sword, and that he had drawn it out a full palm's length; and he was greatly amazed. And he called for holy water, and threw it in the face of the Jew, and with that the Jew came to himself. Then the Abbot asked him what all this had been, and he told him the whole truth; and he knelt down upon his knees before the Abbot, and besought him of his mercy that he would make a Christian of him, because of this great miracle which he had seen, and baptize him in the name of Jesus Christ, for he would live and die in his faith, holding all other to be but erroneous. And the Abbot baptized him in the name of the Holy Trinity, and gave him to name Diego Gil. And all who were there present were greatly amazed, and they made a great outcry and great rejoicings to God for this miracle, and for the power which He had shown through the body of the Cid in this manner; for it was plain that what the Jew said was verily and indeed true, because the posture of the Cid was changed. And from that day forward Diego Gil remained in the Monastery as long as he lived, doing service to the body of the Cid.

JUAN MANUEL

(*Ca.* 1280–1347)

PRINCE DON JUAN, son of the Infant Don Manuel, was one of the earliest writers in the Spanish vernacular. He was actively engaged in politics and warfare for the greater part of his life, and at one time plotted against the throne of Castile. After many years' intriguing he conquered Granada, then in the hands of the Moors, winning a victory which was universally celebrated in song and ballad. There followed more conspiracies against the Castilian sovereign, but ultimately a truce was called, and during the last years of his life, he devoted himself entirely to the service of his state.

This enterprising and heroic prince distinguished himself in the field of letters as well as on the field of battle. *Count Lucanor*, the volume from which the present story is taken, consists of forty-nine examples or cases, each illustrated by a story exemplifying some moral or ethical principle. It was not published until 1575.

The present version is reprinted from Thomas Roscoe's *Spanish Novelists*, London, no date. It is translated by Thomas Roscoe. The title of the story in the original is *Concerning What Happened to a Man That Had a Son, Who Said He Had a Great Many Friends*.

THE SON AND HIS FRIENDS

(From *Count Lucanor*, XXXVII)

ANOTHER time the Conde Lucanor was talking with his counselor Patronio, and said in this manner. "Patronio, according to my reckoning, I have a great many friends, who give me to understand, that, at the cost of their lives and substance, they would not fail to do everything to oblige me, and would not desert me for any chance that could befall. And now, according to your good judgment, I entreat that you will tell me in what manner I shall best be able to learn whether these friends would do for me as much as they say they would?" "My Lord Conde Lucanor," replied Patronio, "good friends are the best thing in the world; and you may well believe, that when a man most wants them, he will find fewer than he counted upon: and that, on the contrary, when the urgency is not great, it is difficult to prove who would show himself a true friend, were the time of need to arrive. However, that you may know what a true friend is, it will give me pleasure to acquaint you with what happened to a certain good man in regards to one of his sons, who said that he had many friends." And the Conde inquired how that had taken place.

THE HISTORY

"My Lord Conde Lucanor," said Patronio, "a certain good man had a son; and among other matters which he advised, he enjoined him always to endeavor to obtain a great number of friends; and the son did as he was told. He began to keep much company, and to share his substance among different individuals whom he esteemed as his friends, and ready to do anything in their power to pleasure him;—nay, insomuch as to venture their lives and substance, if need be, in his behalf. And one day this young man, conversing with his father, was asked whether he had done as he had been commanded, and had yet obtained many friends? And the son replied that he had; and in particular, that among others, there were ten of whom he was most assured, that never in any difficulty or necessity whatever would they be led to desert him. When the father heard this, he said he was greatly surprised that his son had been able in so short a time to obtain so many friends; and such as he, who was an old man, had never been fortunate enough to possess during his whole life, at all events never counting more than one friend and a half. And the son began to argue with him, maintaining that what he had said of his friends was only the truth.

"When the father saw that his son was so eager on their behalf, he said that he ought to proceed to prove it in the following manner. First, that he should kill a pig, and having put it into a sack, should go with it to the house of one of his friends, and when admitted there, tell him secretly—not it was a pig, but a man whom he had unhappily killed. Further, that if this fact should be made known, it would be quite impossible for him to escape with his life; and that all those who knew of it would be likely to share with him in the same fate. That his son should enjoin them, since they were his friends, not to reveal the fact; and that if need be, they should unite with him and defend him. And the youth did this: going to the house of his friends, he informed them of the fatal accident that had befallen him. They all, one after another, declared, that in all other matters they would serve him to the utmost, but that on such an occasion, which would endanger both their lives and property, they dare not assist him; beseeching him, at the same time, for the love of God, not to breathe a single being that he had been at their houses. Some of them, indeed, said that they would go to solicit on his behalf; and others observed that they would do as much, and, moreover, would not desert him even till after his execution, and that they would then give him honorable interment.

"And after the youth had thus tried the sincerity of all his friends, without finding any to receive him, he returned to his father, and related what had happened. And when the father saw that it so fell out, he said to his son, that he might now very well see how those who had lived long, and seen and experienced much in such a matter, knew more than their sons. He then added, that he himself had only one friend and a half, and that he might go and try them.

"The young man went accordingly to prove what his father had meant by half a friend, and he took the dead pig along with him. He called at the door of his father's half friend, and recounted to him first the unlucky adventure which had befallen him; that he had spoken with all his friends in vain, and beseeched him, by the regard he bore his father, to assist him now in this his utter need.

"And when his father's half friend saw this, he said that he had a regard for the father, but had no sort of love for or acquaintance with the son; but that for his father's sake, he was willing to assist him, and to conceal the affair. He then took the sack with the pig, and carried it into his orchard, where he deposited it in a deep furrow, and covered the spot with weeds and vegetables to conceal it from every eye.

"The youth then returned and acquainted his father with what had occurred in regard to this his half friend. He next ordered his son, on a certain day, when they should all be engaged in council, to start some question, and discuss it with this same friend very warmly, till at length he should deal him a hard blow in the face, which, when the opportunity served, was accordingly done. But the good man, on being smitten, only said, 'By my faith, young man, thou hast done ill; yet thou may'st be assured, that neither for this or other injury thou canst do, will I reveal what happened in the garden.' The son afterwards reported this to his father, who then told him to go to the house of his other friend, and he did so. And again he recounted all that had happened; and the good friend of his father directly said, that he would do all to save his life and his reputation. And it by chance happened that a man had been killed in that town, and none knew by whom; but several people having noticed the youth going along at night with the sack upon his shoulders, they concluded that he was no other than the murderer. In short, they informed of him, and the youth was taken and pronounced guilty of the offense; but his father's friend all the while exerted himself to compass his escape. And when he saw that there was no way left to save him from death, he said to the Alcalde, that he did not wish to have the sin of killing that young man upon his conscience, for, in fact, it was not he who had killed the man, but a son of his own, and the only one he had; and in this way did he succeed in saving the life of his friend's son, by the hard sacrifice of his own.

"And now, my Lord Count Lucanor, I have told you how friends are to be tried, and I told that this example is good, in order for a man to learn who are his friends in this world, and those whom he ought to put to the test before he trusts to them in any great exigency, so as to ascertain how far they would go along with him in a dangerous way. You may be certain, that if some few be good friends, yet the most part are fortune's friends, and according to its shifts and turns will they stick close or abandon you. And if you consider of this in a spiritual sense, everybody declares that he has friends, but when calamity or death approach, they too often find themselves driven to have recourse to the ministers of religion to intercede with God for them, who alone can help them, to whom they turn like the son of the good man. And such is the great goodness of the Saints, in particular of the Holy Mary, that they cease not to importune the Lord in a poor sinner's favor; and however much the importunity and the trouble they bear on his account, they refuse to inflict justice on him, just as the half friend of the young man's father would not inform of him though smitten by him in the face. And when the sinner finds no means of escape but turning to God, as the young man returned to his father, then does God, like the father and true friend, pitying man, who is his creature, act by him as did the good friend, for he even sent his own son Jesus Christ, who died for us without any fault, and whose freedom from all sin delivered man also from his state of sin, showing thereby that he was the true son of God, obedient and faithful, and full of love and mercy in all his acts.

"And now, Señor Count Lucanor, consider well what kind of friends be the most faithful and the best, and for whom ought a man most to exert himself in order to obtain their friendship." These reasons gave much satisfaction to the Count, and Don Juan being of opinion that this example was very excellent, caused it to be inserted in this book, and he also made these verses, to the following purport, which, being translated, were

> Man ne'er shall find so true a friend as he
> Who gave his life, man's race from death to free.

————————

DIEGO HURTADO DE MENDOZA

(1503–1574)

BORN of a noble family at Granada, Mendoza was primarily a man of action. We are told that he joined the army of Charles V in Italy where, "like Scipio, he devoted himself at once to literature and to war." He was ambassador in several Italian cities and was present at the Council of Trent. Some years later, having incurred the King's displeasure, he withdrew into retirement and wrote a history of the *War Against the Moors*. He was extraordinarily active as editor of ancient works, patron of the arts, and student; but it is chiefly to his picaresque romance, *Lazarillo de Tormes*, that he owes his fame in the modern world. This is probably the first of the so-called Romances of Roguery. Like most of the works of this kind, it is composed of a series of more or less connected incidents, from which one chapter has been selected for inclusion in this collection. It is characterized by great vivacity and good humour.

The present version is reprinted from Thomas Roscoe's *Spanish Novelists*, London, no date. The translation is by Thomas Roscoe. The title of the chapter is *How Lazaro Served a Bulero, and What Took Place*.

HOW LAZARO SERVED A BULERO

(From *Lazarillo de Tormes*)

THE fifth master that fortune threw in my way was a Bulero, or a dealer in papal indulgences—one of the most impudent and barefaced, yet cleverest rogues, that I have ever seen, or ever shall see. He practised all manner of deceit, and resorted to the most subtle inventions to gain his end. On his arrival at any place to present his credentials and open his traffic, the first thing he did was to send small presents of no great value to the clergy, by which means he would gain a civil reception—and perhaps assistance in his negotiations. He made himself acquainted with the character of these persons; when to some he would say, that he never spoke in Latin, but always preferred a chaste and elegant diction in his native tongue. To others again, he would talk Latin for two hours; at least so it would seem to those who heard him, although perhaps it was not half that time. When he found that no great success attended his usual endeavors, he would have recourse to artifice; but as a regular account of them would fill a volume, I will only recount one little maneuver, which will give you some idea of his genius and invention.

He had preached two or three days, at a place near Toledo, and had not neglected his usual offerings; but he found his indulgences go off but slowly, with very little appearance of improvement, for which he very heartily wished the good people at the devil. Being at his wit's end what to do, he invited all the people to the church the next morning to take his farewell. After supper that evening, he and the Alguazil sat down to enjoy themselves, and in the course of their entertainment some dispute arose, which increased to very high words. He called the Alguazil thief, to which the other retorted by calling him impostor. On this, the Bulero caught up a weapon lying near, and the Alguazil drew his sword to defend himself. The noise was so great, that neighbors ran in to inquire into the cause, and with some difficulty separated the enraged combatants. They continued, however, to revile each other with words, although, by reason of the house being filled with people, they could not vent their rage with blows; the Alguazil continually calling out that my master was an impostor, and that his indulgences were forged. The neighbors seeing that peace could not be restored, took away the Alguazil to another inn, to prevent mischief; and after some time, the uproar subsiding, we went to bed.

In the morning my master went to the church to preach his farewell sermon. The people were all there, murmuring about the authenticity of the bull, saying that the Alguazil had discovered it to them; and if they were indisposed towards the indulgences before, they were now little likely to purchase them. The reverend commissary ascended the pulpit, and commenced his sermon. He expatiated on the merits of the Pope's holy commission, and of the infallible virtues of the indulgences which the bull guaranteed. The sermon was proceeding in this manner when the Alguazil entered the church, and taking advantage of an opportunity, rose, and with a loud voice but discreet manner he addressed the congregation: "My good people; hear me but one word, and listen to whomsoever you please afterwards. I came here with yonder cheat who is now preaching to you, and, seduced by him, I promised to favor his deception and divide the gains. But as my conscience is uneasy at thus assisting to rob you of your money, I take this opportunity of declaring before you all that the bull is forged, and that the indulgences are false. And after this confession I beg you to bear witness, if at any future time this rogue meet with punishment as an impostor, that I am not implicated therein, but have done all in my power to expose him and warn you."

Many respectable people, to prevent the scandal of the thing proceeding further, wished to turn the Alguazil out of the church, but the reverend preacher would by no means permit such violence; and thus the Alguazil had the liberty of saying all he wished. When he was silent, my master rose and asked him if he wished to say more? on which he replied, "I could say plenty more concerning your rogueries, but for the present what I have said is sufficient."

The devout commissary of his holiness then threw himself on his knees in the pulpit, and casting his arms and eyes towards heaven, he exclaimed: "O Lord, to whom nothing is hidden, thou knowest the truth, and how cruelly I am calumniated. I forgive all that personally concerns me, but to that which relates to my holy calling I cannot be indifferent; inasmuch as many here may be induced to give credit to what has been falsely spoken, to the injury of their own souls and of my holy mission. I therefore pray thee, O Lord, to vouchsafe by a miracle to show the whole truth as to this matter. If I deal in falsehood and iniquity, may the pulpit on which I now kneel sink with me seven fathoms below the earth, so that I may never be heard of again,—and if what is said be false, and prompted by the devil to deprive these good people here of the comforts of which I am the bearer, let the author of the calumny be punished, so that all present may be convinced of his malice."

Hardly had my pious master finished his prayer, when the Alguazil fell from the place where he was standing, and with such a noise that the whole church resounded with the fall. His countenance became distorted, and he began to foam at the mouth, uttering frightful curses, and rolling about in the utmost apparent agony. At this wonderful interposition of Providence, the clamor became so great that no one could hear himself speak. Some were frightened, and cried, "Lord, Lord, have mercy on the sinner"; while others said, "It served him right for his false testimony—let him kick and go to the devil!"

Finally, however, some individuals went to his assistance, though not without evident fear, and tried to hold his arms and legs; but he gave them such fierce salutes, dealing his favors so vigorously and dexterously, that many were much hurt, and it required at least seventeen men to hold him down.

While this was proceeding, my sainted master was on his knees in the pulpit, his hands and eyes turned towards heaven, apparently filled with the divine essence, and utterly unconscious of the noises and disturbance around him, so completely was he wrapped in his heavenly meditations. Some approached him, and begged him, "for the love of God, to succor the poor wretch who was dying: and that, doubtless, at his intercession, the Lord would not prolong his sufferings."

The devout commissary, as though disturbed from a sweet vision, looked around him, first at the suppliants and then at the delinquent. "My good friends," said he slowly, "you ought not to ask a favor for him whom God has so signally chastised. But as he has commanded

that we should return good for evil, we may with more confidence
implore his pardon for the poor wretch who has dared to place an
obstacle in the way of his holy commission." Then, descending from
the pulpit, he desired them all to pray for the sinner, and that the devil
with which he was possessed might be cast out. The congregation
with one accord threw themselves on their knees, and commenced in
a low voice to repeat the litany; while my master, before he approached
the possessed sinner with the cross and holy water, turning his eyes
to heaven till the whites could only be seen, delivered a pious oration,
which drew tears from the eyes of the hearers. This being finished, he
commanded the holy bull to be brought and placed on the head of
the possessed, and immediately the sinner of an Alguazil began by
degrees to recover himself. Directly he was restored to consciousness,
he threw himself at the feet of the holy commissary, and implored his
pardon. He confessed that what he did was by the commandment of
the Devil, who was excessively annoyed at the appearance of the holy
man, and was fearful that he should lose his dominion over the people
if they were to purchase his indulgences. My master, in the most
benevolent manner, pardoned him, and interchanged kindnesses with
him, giving him advice very much to his comfort and advantage.
Great now was the demand for indulgences amongst the bystanders,
and not an individual would go from church without one, neither man,
woman nor child.

The news soon spread, and people came flocking from all parts, so
that no sermons were necessary in the church to convince them of the
benefits likely to result to the purchasers. The inn where we resided
was crowded with applicants, and wherever we went in that district,
thousands of indulgences were sold without a single sermon being
preached. I must confess that I, amongst many others, was deceived
at the time, and thought my master a miracle of sanctity; but hearing
the merriment which it afforded to the holy commissary and the Alguazil, I began to suspect that it originated in the peculiarly fertile invention of my master, and although young, from that moment I ceased
to be a child of grace; for I argued within myself, "If I, being an eye-
witness to such an imposition, could almost believe it, how many more,
amongst this poor innocent people, must be imposed on by these
robbers."

I quitted my fifth master at the end of four months, during which
I experienced some very fatiguing and unpleasant adventures.

———————————

MATEO ALEMÁN

(1547–*ca.* 1614)

LITTLE is known of Alemán, though it is stated that he was a native of Seville and was employed in the government service. He lived for a time in Mexico where he wrote certain works of no great importance. But he is remembered by his famous picaresque novel, *Guzmán de Alfarache*, which was published in 1599, and soon translated into all the languages of Europe. This romance depicts in vivid fashion the life of the underworld.

The present version is reprinted from Thomas Roscoe's *Spanish Novelists*, London, no date. The translation is by Thomas Roscoe. The full title of the chapter in the original is *How Guzmán Excited the Compassion of My Lord Cardinal, and What Ensued.*

GUZMAN AND MY LORD CARDINAL

(From *Guzmán de Alfarache*)

HAVING roused myself early one fine morning, according to custom, I went and seated myself at the door of a cardinal, concerning whom I had heard an excellent character, being one of the most charitably disposed in Rome. I had taken the trouble of getting one of my legs swelled, on which, notwithstanding what had passed, was to be seen a new ulcer, one that might set at defiance the most penetrating eye or probe of a surgeon. I had not this time omitted to have my face as pale as death; and thus, filling the air with horrible lamentations while I was asking alms, I moved the souls of the different domestics who came in and out to take pity upon me; they gave me something; but I was yet only beating up for game—it was their master I wanted. He at length made his appearance—I redoubled my cries and groans— I writhed in anguish;—and I then accosted him in these terms: "Oh! most noble Christian; thou friend of Christ and his afflicted ones! have pity upon me, a poor wretched sinner. Behold me cut down in the flower of my days;—may your excellency be touched with my extreme misery, for the sake of the sufferings of our dear Redeemer." The cardinal, who was really a pious man, stopped; and, after looking at me earnestly, turned to his attendants. "In the name of Christ, take this unhappy being, and bear him into my own apartments! let the rags that cover him be exchanged for fine linen; put him into a good bed—nay, into my own—and I will go into another room. I will tend on him; for in him do I verily see what must have been the sufferings of our Saviour.'" He was obeyed; and, oh, charity! how didst thou shame those lordly prelates who think Heaven in debt to them, if they do but look down on some poor wretch: while my good cardinal, not content with what he had done, ordered two surgeons to attend, recommending them to do all in their power to ease my agony, and to examine and cure my leg; after which they should be well recompensed. He then, bidding me be of good cheer, left me, to pursue his affairs; and the surgeons, to make the best of my case. They declared at once that it was useless, and that gangrene had already commenced. So seriously did they pronounce this, that, though I knew the effect was solely produced by staining my leg with a certain herb, I almost felt alarmed for the consequence. They then took out their case of instruments, called for a cauldron of hot water, for some fine linen, and a poultice. While these were in preparation, they questioned me as to the origin of my disease, how long I had had it, etc., etc.?—moreover, whether I drank wine, and what was my usual diet? To these, and to a hundred such interrogatories, I replied not a word; so great was my alarm at the terrific processes that appeared to be going on, in order to restore me to my pristine health and soundness. I was infinitely perplexed, not knowing to what saint to have recourse, for I was apprehensive there might not be a single one in heaven inclined to interfere in behalf of so thorough-paced a rascal. I recalled to mind the lesson I had so lately been taught at Gaeta, and had my misgivings that I might not escape even on such good terms as I had done there. The surgeons ranked high in their profession; and, after having curiously turned round my leg about twenty times, retired into another room to discuss the result of their observations. I remained in a state of horror not to be described; for it had got into my head that they would decide upon amputation; to learn which I crept softly towards the door to listen, fully resolved to reveal the imposture in so dreadful an alternative. "Sir," said one, "we may consult here forever, to little purport; he has got St. Anthony's fire." "No such thing," replied the other, "he has no more fire in his leg than I have in my hand: we might easily remove it in a couple of days." "You cannot be serious," said the first speaker. "By St. Comus, I know something of ulcers; and here, I maintain it, we have a gangrene." "No, no, friend," replied the second, "we have no ulcer—we have a rogue to deal with—nothing is the matter with him. I know the whole history of his ulcer, and how it was made. It is by no means very rare; for I know the herbs with which the impostor has prepared it, and the ingenious method in which they have been applied." The other seemed quite confounded at this assertion; but, ashamed of owning himself a dupe, he persisted in his former opinion: on which a pretty warm colloquy would have ensued, had not the more ingenious of the two had the sense to recommend first to examine the leg, and to end the dispute afterwards. "Look a little deeper into the matter," said he, "and you will see the fellow's knavery." "With all my heart. I will confess you are right, when I see there is no ulcer, or rather gangrene." "That is not enough," replied his colleague. "In acknowledging your error, you must also admit I am entitled to at least a third more fees than yourself." "By no means," retorted the other. "I have eyes to detect imposture as well as you; and I am of opinion we ought to divide the good cardinal's fees fairly between us." The dispute now waxed warm, and rather than give up his point, each declared that he would make the cardinal acquainted with the whole business.

In this dilemma I did not hesitate a moment—there was no time to lose—escape was impossible. I rushed into the presence of the faculty, and threw myself at their feet. With well-dissembled grief I thus addressed them: "Alas! my dear sirs, take pity upon an unfortunate fellow creature. Think, gentlemen, 'homo sum; nihil humani,' etc.: I am mortal like yourselves—you know the hard-heartedness of the great, and how the poor and forlorn are compelled to assume the most horrible shapes in order to soften their hardness; and in doing this what risks and sufferings do we not encounter, and all for so small a remuneration. Besides, what advantage will you get by exposing such a poor miserable sinner? You will certainly lose your fees, which you need not do if you will let us understand each other. You may rely on my discretion; the fear of consequences will keep me silent, and we may each benefit in our respective professions."

Upon this the men of physic again consulted, and at length came to the resolution of pocketing their fees, "secundum artem." Being all of one mind, we now begged to be ushered into the presence of the cardinal, and the surgeons then ordered me to be placed upon a couch, at the side of which they made an immense display of chirurgical instruments, dressings, etc.—again consulted, and after wrapping my leg in a great number of bandages, they desired that I might be put into a warm bed. His excellency, meanwhile, was full of anxiety to learn the state of my health, and whether there were any hopes of recovery? "My lord," replied one of the surgeons, "the patient is in a deplorable situation, gangrene has already begun; still, with time and care, there is a chance that he might recover, please God, but it will be a long affair." "And he is fortunate," said his coadjutor, "in having fallen into our hands; another day, and he was lost forever; but no doubt Providence must have directed him to the door of your excellency."

This account seemed to please the cardinal; it gave him occasion to display the truest Christian charity, and he desired that neither time nor skill might be spared in the endeavor to restore me to health. He also directed that I should be supplied with everything; and the surgeons on their part pledged themselves to do all that art could effect, and each of them to pay me a visit at least twice in the day; it being necessary to detect the slightest change that might occur in my present condition. They then withdrew, not a little to my consolation; for I could not but regard them while present, in the light of two executioners, who might fall upon me at any moment, or publish my imposition to the world. So far from this, however, they made me keep my apartment for three months, which to me seemed like so many ages, so difficult is it to give up the habit of gambling—or begging, with the tone of freedom they seem to include. In vain was I daintily lodged and fed, like his excellency himself; the *ennui* I felt was intolerable. I was incessantly beseeching the doctors to take pity on me, and bring the farce to a close, until they were at length compelled to yield to my importunity.

They left off dressing my leg, and, on its being reduced to its natural size, they acquainted the good cardinal with the fact, who was in raptures at the performance, under his auspices, of so great a cure. He rewarded them handsomely, and came to congratulate me on the miraculous event; and having acquitted myself well in his frequent visits to me, in regard both to my opinions and my principles, he imbibed a real kindness for me; and to give me a further proof of it, he gave me the situation of one of his confidential attendants—a species of honor I was too deeply sensible of to be able to refuse.

MIGUEL CERVANTES

(1547–1616)

CERVANTES' is the most brilliant name in all Spanish literature. He lived a life of romance and adventure and misery. Author of one of the greatest of all romances, *Don Quixote,* he also wrote satires and plays and a particular sort of long-short story, which he called the Exemplary Novel. In his preface to the collection of the twelve tales that compose it, he says: "I have bestowed on them the name of *Exemplary,* and if thou dost look well to it, there is not one of them from which thou couldst not derive a profitable example." But this was surely the same sort of excuse made by latter-day writers of pornography who declare that they depict vice in order to render it odious. It is more likely that Cervantes felt it incumbent upon him to excuse the short story form by endowing it with a moral purpose. The time was not yet ripe for an artist to set his story down for the simple reason that it was amusing, or beautiful, or true.

Rinconete and Cortadillo is one of the finest of the collection "in virtue of which Cervantes is acknowledged as the prince of story-tellers in the Spanish language." (Prof. J. D. M. Ford.)

The present version is reprinted from Thomas Roscoe's *Spanish Novelists*, London, no date. The translation is by Thomas Roscoe.

RINCONETE AND CORTADILLO

(From the *Exemplary Novels*)

ON the confines of Alcudia, between the provinces of Castile and Andalusia, might be seen a notable house of entertainment for travelers, called the *Little Windmill*. On one of the hottest days of summer, two boys were seen loitering about this place; one was about fourteen years of age, and the other might perhaps have attained his seventeenth year. They were both good looking, though in a sadly destitute condition; coats they had none; their trousers were of coarse linen, and, for want of better stockings, they were obliged to be contented with their bare skin.

It is true that their feet were covered, those of one being carefully bound in straw or rushes, while the shoes of the other were of so peculiar a formation, that it would seem the utmost ingenuity of the wearer had been displayed, in rendering them more than usually accessible to the elements of air and water. The head of one was partly covered by a scanty cap; the other wore a hat, though without seeming to trouble himself about its deficiency of crown and brim. The scanty remains of a shirt of the color of chamois leather partly adorned the neck and shoulders of the younger; while his companion had remedied the inconvenience of such a deficiency by the waistband of an old pair of trousers, covered with grease and completely in tatters, which hung suspended from his neck on his breast, and appeared to conceal a small bundle. In this repository of valuables was concealed a pack of cards of a different shape to those generally used; for by reason of their long service, the corners were so much worn, that they began to assume a circular shape, which had been rendered still more distinct by the application of the scissors, it being found that the circular form was the most durable. Both the youths were much sunburnt; their nails were begrimed with dirt, and their skin could hardly be called clean. One was armed with a broken sword, and the other with a yellow-handled knife, which completed their costume.

They sallied from the inn and seated themselves opposite each other, under a sort of covering which serves for a veranda in houses of that description; and the elder, bowing very politely to the other addressed him with all the air of a man of *ton*. "If I might take the liberty of addressing a gentleman of your distinguished appearance without the ceremony of introduction, I should inquire what part of the country has the honor of claiming you as a resident, and whither you intend to travel?"

"Señor Caballero," returned the other, with equal ceremony and politeness, "with respect to your first question, I am sorry that I am unable to satisfy your curiosity, being utterly ignorant of it myself; and, as to the second, I lament that I can afford you as little information, for I really don't know."

"Why, truly, sir," said he without the shirt, "if I might give an opinion, you certainly don't look as though you had dropped from heaven; and if you had, I should not think you would choose this place for your descent—consequently you must be going somewhere."

"That is very just," replied the one with the hat; "and yet I have told you the truth, for my country is no longer mine, my father having turned me out: and as to the future, I must trust to chance, which I dare say will put something in my way by which I may get an honest livelihood."

"And pray, may I ask whether you belong to any profession?" said the original querist.

"No other," replied the other, or younger, "than running like a hare, leaping like a deer, or using a pair of scissors very delicately, will fit me for."

"That is all very good and useful," said his companion, "for on next Holy Thursday you will find good employment in cutting paper ornaments for the church." "Ah, but my abilities in cutting do not lie that way," said the younger gentleman. "My father, by the blessing of Providence, is a tailor and shoemaker, and he taught me to cut out *antiparas*, which, as I dare say you know, are buskins, used by men in harvest—I obtained such a proficiency in the art, that I might have passed examination as a master, had not my bad fortune deprived me of my employment."

"That will happen to the best of us," remarked the elder cavalier, "and I have always heard that the best abilities have always the worst fortune. But I don't doubt a gentleman of your acquirements has some way of bettering his fortune; and, if my judgment don't deceive me, you possess some other accomplishments, which perhaps your modesty will not allow you to make public." "Why, that is very true," said he, of the shirt, laughing, "but, as you say, sir, they are not exactly for the public."

"Well, then,'" said the other, at the instant, "although I consider myself as discreet as most youth, yet, to give you some confidence in me, I will be open with you, and shall expect the same in return, for it is not without reason that fortune has thrown us together, and I am sure it will be to our loss if we do not become friends. You must know that my name is Pedro de Rincon, and I am a native of Fuenfrida, a place of some note, where my father is a minister of the church, that is to say, he sells the pope's indulgences, being, as the vulgar call him, the Bulero. As I assisted him in his traffic, I acquired such dexterity in making bargains, that few could obtain any advantage over me; but observing one day that I was fonder of the money I received, than of my business, he put a purse of dollars into my hand, and packed me off to Madrid to seek my fortune.

"Amongst the temptations of the city, the contents of my purse soon vanished, and I found myself at last possessed of more wit than fortune. I applied for assistance to those who had assisted *me* to spend my money, but it was perfectly astounding to see the want of recollection evinced by these wretches directly I made known my distress: some positively denied my acquaintance, while others dismissed me with their advice to be more cautious in future. I shrugged my shoulders, but suffered my lot patiently; and turned out to seek my fortune with such readiness, that I did not think of providing myself with any luxuries. I took what I thought most necessary, from the things which remained to me, and amongst others, these cards (at the same time drawing them from their concealment) from which I have managed to derive an honorable subsistence amongst the inns frequented by travelers. I always play at *Vingt-un*, which is a very excellent game for my purpose; and although you see the cards are somewhat the worse for wear, yet, I can assure you, they possess a marvelous virtue for those who understand them; indeed, they are become so familiar to me from long acquaintance, that I know them as well by the back as the front.

"Independently of these advantages, I learned of a certain ambassador a method of handling the cards, by which I am as much at home with their capabilities, as you are in the cutting of *antiparas*. So you see, my honorable sir, that I am in no danger of starving, for let me be in what place I may, there are always persons to be found who are willing to divert themselves with an innocent game; and he who has the least experience, is generally the loser. Now, for example, let us look out for a pigeon amongst these carriers within; we will sit down and play as though in earnest, and if any one wishes to make a third, you will see that he will be the first to lay down his cash."

"With all my heart," returned the younger adventurer, "and I feel much indebted for your frankness, in return for which I can do no otherwise than relate, in a few words, what concerns myself. I am a native of that goodly country situated between Salamanca and Medina del Campo. My father is a tailor, and taught me such a good use of the scissors, that, instead of cutting clothes, I learned to cut purses. My ambition, however, was not to be limited to the narrow precincts of a country village; and I was already disgusted with the treatment of a mother-in-law; leaving my home, therefore, I repaired to Toledo, where, giving a free scope to my abilities, I did wonders. There was no rosary, let it be hung ever so carefully, and no pocket however ingeniously contrived, that my fingers did not visit, or my scissors divide—even though they were guarded by the eyes of Argus. I can assure you, that, during the four months I resided in that city, I managed to escape all inconveniences. I was never caught between double doors; never taken off my guard; fell not into the hands of the constables, nor became the dupe of an informer.

"It is now, however, about eight days since, that a spy of the police gave notice of me to the corregidor, who, being a great admirer of people of talent, expressed an anxious desire to be acquainted with me; my extreme modesty, for which I am remarkable, prevented me that honor; for thinking myself neither by birth nor education qualified to move in such distinguished society, I was obliged to disappoint his worship, by withdrawing myself from Toledo. I effected my removal with such haste, that I actually did not allow myself time to procure a coach, to provide myself with linen, or indeed any of those conveniences with which gentlemen usually travel; and here I am as you see me."

"Really that was very amusing," said Rincon, grinning; "but now as we know each other, I think it is time to drop our gentility, and confess that we have not anything in the world but what we stand in."

"There is no use in mincing the matter," quoth Diego Cortado, for by such name he called himself, "it is even as you say; and since our friendship ought to be lasting, Señor Rincon, I think we should commence it by a proper manifestation of our feelings": and then rising, both the gentlemen embraced each other with great apparent cordiality and good will. This little ceremony completing their good understanding, they sat down to play with the above-mentioned cards, having cleaned them from dust and straw, though not from grease and certain deceitful signs; and in a few hands Cortado became as clever at the game as his master Rincon.

At this time one of the carriers came out, when seeing the two boys at play, he asked them whether they had any objection to a third, to which they good-naturedly consented. Fortune favored the boys so well that in less than half an hour the carrier lost twelve reals, and twenty-two maravedis, which in paying cost him just as many twinges of regret. The loser, however, seeing his adversaries were only boys, thought he could take his money from them again with impunity; but the one drew his piece of a sword, and the other handled his knife so formidably, that had not the carrier's companions come to his succor, it was likely to have gone ill with him.

At this time a troop of people passed on horseback, who, seeing the disturbance between the boys and the carrier, parted them, and told the former they were going to pass the night about a league further, whither, if they pleased, they might accompany them. "We will go with pleasure," said Rincon, "and anything we can do in return, we shall be most happy"; and, without further invitation, they jumped up on two of the mules and set forward with the party, leaving the carrier in no very enviable state of temper. The landlord could not help laughing at the dexterity of the young rogues; for he confessed he had overheard their conversation, and thus learned that the cards were false. At this discovery, the carrier could hardly contain himself for rage. He swore the most formidable oaths, and declared his intention of following the young sharpers and reclaiming his lost pieces—not that he valued the money, as he said; but from pure shame to think that so great a man as he should be cheated by two such very little rogues. His companion, however, endeavored to pacify him, saying, "It was much better to abide by the loss, than to get laughed at for his simplicity."

The two companions now congratulated themselves on their good fortune, and made themselves so useful to their fellow-travelers, that they were allowed to mount behind them the best part of the way; and although many opportunities occurred of exercising their professional abilities with advantage, yet they desisted, from the consideration that they might endanger their journey to Seville, whither they were going. However, on entering the city by the Aduana gate, Cortado was not able to resist the temptation of cutting open the portmanteau of a Frenchman, behind whom he was mounted. His knife was handy on all occasions, and he inflicted so grievous a wound on the valise, that he presently discovered its contents, and selected from them two shirts, a small sun-dial, and a memorandum book. These things, it is true, were of little value; but they served to replenish their purse, which was now exhausted, with twenty reals.

Having secured this, they went to view the city, of which they had heard so much; the cathedral excited their admiration, and they were astonished at the great concourse of people on the river. The galleys, likewise, did not escape their observation, and an involuntary sigh escaped from each, as his thoughts naturally anticipated the time when he might have a closer view of them.

They were surprised to see such a number of boys with baskets, plying for hire; and they took the opportunity of asking one the nature of his office—whether it was laborious—and what was the gain? It was an Asturian boy of whom they made the inquiry, and he replied, "That the business was easy enough—that they paid no duty—and that on some days they gained five reals, and on others six, as it might happen—with which they lived the life of a king—free to seek any master that paid them well—and then they enjoyed themselves after their own fashion."

This account of the Asturian pleased the two friends mightily; for the anticipation of carrying the goods of others seemed highly favorable to their peculiar abilities, and they forthwith determined to purchase the necessary equipment for their new profession. The Asturian told them it would be necessary to buy some small bags, and three baskets, for fish, flesh, and fruit—the bags to be used solely for bread; and that when provided with these necessaries, they were to attend in the mornings at the flesh-market, in the square of San Salvador—on fast-days at the fish-market—and in the evening they were to look for employment at the river side. This instruction the two friends committed to memory; and having purchased what was necessary with the spoils of the Frenchaman, they planted themselves the next morning in the square of San Salvador. They had not been there long, before their new baskets attracted the attention of the other boys, who soon flocked round them, anxious to know whence they came, and everything concerning them; to all which the friends gave those answers which might have been expected from young persons of their talent and discretion.

At this time a soldier and a student came up, who liking the cleanliness of the baskets, the former called Rincon, and the student beckoned Cortado. Rincon, by way of commencing his office, bowed very humbly to his employer, and said, "I hope your honor will not forget that I am a beginner."

"Never fear," said the soldier, "your reward shall not be amiss, for I can afford to be liberal—I am going to give a feast to-day to some friends of my mistress."

"Then pray load me as much as you please," returned the youth, "for I have both the will and the strength to carry the whole market; aye, and sugar to season it withal, if such be your honor's pleasure."

The soldier was so well pleased with the quickness of the youth, that he told him, if he desired to quit his present employment, he would take him into his service. Rincon replied with many thanks, saying, "That as he was so newly entered on the office, he wished to see whether it would turn out well or ill; but, in case of failure, he should not have the honor of serving so respectable a gentleman, because he had given his word to a priest." The soldier laughed, and gave him a good load, directing him to the house of his mistress, and desiring him to remember it well, as he would have occasion to go there often; he then gave him three quartos, and dismissed him. Rincon returned with the utmost speed to the square, lest he should lose an opportunity; for the Asturian had cautioned him to be diligent and trustworthy; although in carrying small fish, or such like commodity, there was no harm, he said, in taking a little from a quantity which could not be missed; but on no account to take it if there should be the least chance of detection, as credit was the soul of their trade.

Cortado returned just about the same time as Rincon, who, showing his companion the three quartos, asked him what luck he had met with? Cortado, putting his hand into his breast, drew out a purse which seemed to have been made in times past, but was nevertheless well stocked with money, and said, "His reverence has done me the favor to pay me with this purse, and with these two quartos; but take the purse, Rincon, lest his worship may change his mind." Rincon had hardly secreted the purse, when back came the student, perspiring at every pore, and in the utmost agitation and perplexity; coming to Cortado, "My good boy," said he, "have you by chance seen a purse of such and such marks, containing fifteen crowns of gold, three reals, and so many maravedis in quartos, only wanting the few pieces with which I paid for the meat which you carried?"

Cortado replied, without moving a muscle of his countenance, "All I can say to your reverence is, that your purse would not have been lost had you taken better care of it."

"That is but too true, sinner that I am," returned the student, "for had I taken better care of it, some rascal could never have robbed me."

"That is exactly what I think," said Cortado; "but as your reverence knows there is a remedy for all things but death, now I should advise your reverence to avail yourself of the first and principal, which is patience, for it is recommended by God. One day follows another; and he that gives takes away; so in like manner the time may arrive, that he who has stolen your purse may repent and restore it, even in better condition than he found it."

"That I will excuse," interrupted the student.

"For my part," continued Cortado, "I would not be the stealer of the purse for a trifle, for as your reverence is in sacred orders, it is neither more nor less than sacrilege."

"You say right," said the afflicted student, "for though I am no priest, but only the sacristan of a convent, the money I have lost is the third of a chaplain's salary, which is left in my charge, and therefore it is blessed and holy coin."

"As you have made your bread so must you eat it," said Cortado, in a condoling manner; "but the day of judgment will arrive, and then we shall see the rogue who was hardened enough to steal the chaplain's salary. And pray what might the situation of your friend be worth per annum, with regard to salary, Señor Sacristan?" asked Cortado, innocently.

"Salary of the devil," returned the sacristan, incensed beyond measure at what appeared to be trifling with him. "Is this a time to talk about salary? Tell me, my friend, do you know anything of the purse? if so, say; if not, God be with you; for I must go and have it cried."

"That is the best thing you can do," said Cortado, "and remember," he added, calling after him, "that you are very particular about the description of the purse, and the exact sum contained therein, for if you make the mistake of a single farthing, you will never see your purse again in this world; I only say this, sir, by way of advice."

"There is no fear of that, my friend," returned the sacristan. "I have it so truly in my memory that I shall not mistake a single thread." Saying this, he drew from his pocket a handkerchief to wipe the perspiration from his countenance; a movement not lost on Cortado, who immediately seemed to take a more vivid interest in the poor man's loss, and suggested several expedients for its recovery. The advice of Cortado was given in so vague a manner, that the sacristan was tempted to ask a repetition; during which, Cortado, taking advantage of the sacristan's anxiety, contrived to beguile him of his handkerchief, when, with many expressions of condolence, he took his leave, recommending him to use all diligence in the recovery of his property; and then returned to Rincon.

"What have you been so busy about with the student?" inquired his companion.

"Why, I have been listening to the poor gentleman's distress, which I protest has so affected me, that I was under the necessity of borrowing his handkerchief," replied the young wag, at the same time producing it, and applying it to his eyes.

The two young rogues then indulged in some merriment at the expense of the poor sacristan; but Cortado had not effected the latter transfer so secretly as to escape the observation of a lad who had been watching him. "Pray, gentlemen," said he, advancing towards them, "may I ask of what profession you call yourselves?" "We don't understand you, sir," replied Rincon. "I ask you, gentlemen, whether you are from Murcia," repeated the youth. "Neither from Murcia nor from Thebes," responded Cortado, "and if you have nothing further to say, I wish you a good morning."

"You don't choose to understand me, eh! my masters?" said the querist, "but I think I could soon make you understand—aye, and teach you to eat pap out of a spoon. What I wish to ask of you, gentlemen, is merely whether your honors are thieves, or no? although it is a useless question, because I already see that you are; but I must inquire with more reason, whether you have paid your footing to the Señor Monipodio?"

"Do thieves pay taxes in this country, my fair sir?" asked Rincon. "If they do not actually pay, at least they are registered by the Señor Monipodio, who is their father and their master; therefore I should counsel you to come with me for that purpose, or perhaps you will have cause to repent it."

"I always thought," said Cortado, "that thieving was a free trade, without any duty or impost; and if the professors paid at all, it was only at the stocks, or over the back and shoulders. But as every country has its own peculiar regulations, so we shall be happy to conform to yours, if we might make bold to ask a gentleman of your respectable appearance, to guide us to the abode of the worthy cavalier of whom you speak, where we will prove our proficiency in the science."

"That is well", said the other, "and you will see how well qualified our master is for his situation. Why! during the four years he has had charge of us, not more than four have suffered the capital punishment. But come along, and on the road I will explain to you a little of our vocabulary, which it will be necessary for you to know." During this walk, which was not very short, their new acquaintance instructed them in the language of the craft, very much to the edification of the novice. "And pray, sir," asked Rincon, "may I venture to inquire whether you are a thief yourself?" "Yes, sir; that is to say, by the blessing of God and the prayers of good people, I hope I shall be, although I am not yet out of my novitiate."

"Well," said Cortado, "you will excuse me for the remark; but although I have seen and heard a good deal, I never yet heard of thieving by the grace of God and the prayers of good people."

"Sir," replied the guide, "I am no theologian, and therefore cannot argue on the subject; but this I know, that everybody ought to praise God in the vocation to which Providence has been pleased to call him; and the more so as our master Monipodio has expressly ordered it."

"Doubtless that gentleman must be of a very religious turn," said Rincon, "since he makes his thieves praise God."

"He is the most exemplary man of our profession," returned the youth; "he orders that a part of everything which is stolen shall be set apart to buy oil for the lamp of an image in the city, which is possessed of marvelous virtue. Indeed, we have all seen the good effects of it; for it was but the other day, when a friend of ours was condemned to punishment for stealing two asses, and he bore it without a single cry, as though it was nothing, which can only be attributed to our regular devotion. And you must know that some of our club are so particular that they will not steal on a Friday, nor hold conversation with any woman on a Sabbath whose name is Mary."

"Indeed! this is most exemplary conduct," said Cortado; "but pray do not the priests sometimes order these religious persons to make restitution or penance?"

"No," returned the other, "because they never go to confession; and if letters of excommunication are taken out against them, they are not likely to know it, because they never go to church during the time they are read; excepting, indeed, at the great holiday, when the crowd of people gathered there makes it a matter of business."

"Pious rogues!" ejaculated Rincon. "And what is the harm of it?" cried the other. "Is it not much worse to be a heretic? or to murder your father and mother?" "Why, that certainly is very bad," said Rincon; "but as fortune is so kind as to allow us to be of this respectable fraternity, I must beg you, sir, to quicken your pace, for I am dying to see our respectable friend Monipodio, of whose virtues you have said so much." "Your praiseworthy impatience shall soon be gratified, for we are already arrived; but you must wait awhile at the portal, while I go within to see whether he is at leisure; for this is the hour he usually gives audience." The companions had just time to survey the house, which was not of the most promising appearance, when their guide reappeared, and called them in. They entered a small courtyard, paved with fanciful brickwork, of a bright red color: on one side was a bench with three legs; and on the other a broken jar, placed on a stand not in a much better condition. In another place was a rush mat, and in the middle was a space for flowers.

The boys observed everything attentively; and as the Señor Monipodio did not make his appearance, they took the liberty of entering the lower room, which adjoined the courtyard. There they beheld two fencing swords, with two shields of cork, suspended on pegs; a large bow without any case, and three more rush mats on the floor. On the front wall was placed an image of the Virgin, of no great merit in its workmanship; under which was seen a small basket, and a white basin; serving, as Rincon shrewdly conjectured, the former to receive alms, and the latter for holy water.

While they were waiting, there arrived two young men about twenty years of age, dressed as students; shortly afterwards came two of their brothers of the basket, and a blind man, who all walked about the open space without speaking a word to each other. Shortly after them came two elderly persons in spectacles; they looked grave and respectable, and carried in their hands good-sized rosaries. An old woman next arrived, who immediately on her entrance went to the image of the Virgin, and having taken the holy water with great devotion, prostrated herself before the image. Having indulged in this pious occupation some time, she arose, put a small offering into the basket, kissed the floor three times, lifted her hands and eyes to heaven, and then rejoined the others in the courtyard. Lastly appeared, to give additional grace to the company, two bravos, of most sinister aspect; with large whiskers, slouched hats, and ruffled collars. They were armed with enormous swords, several pistols, and targets hanging from their belts. The moment these worthies cast their eyes on the two friends, they came to them and inquired whether they belonged to the fraternity? Rincon answered in the affirmative, making great demonstration of respect, which the formidable appearance of the querists seemed to demand. At this moment arrived the long expected Señor Monipodio, to the great joy of the respectable company assembled.

He seemed about forty-five years of age, tall of stature, his countenance of a sullen hue, with sunken eyes, eyebrows joined in the center, and a black bushy beard. He was dressed in a shirt, and covered with a huge cloak reaching to his feet, on which were a pair of old shoes down at the heels. He wore loose trousers of linen, and a hat used by the lowest vagabonds, bell-shaped at the crown, and large in the brim. Across his shoulders was a belt, to which was suspended a short and stout sword. His hands were short, with fat fingers and long nails; and his feet were a pair, but not matched.

In short, the appearance of this gentleman, whose reputation had been so strenuously supported, was anything but favorable, he being, unfortunately, one of the most-ill-looking, misshapen barbarians in the world. The youth who had acted as guide to Rincon and his friend, now led them forward, and presented them to the dignitary, saying, "These are the two gentlemen of whom I spoke to your worhip. If you please, you can examine them, and see whether they are worthy to enter our brotherhood."

"That I will do with much pleasure," replied Monipodio, to whom, be it observed, the whole company bowed respectfully on his entrance, except the two bravos, who, considering themselves artists of a higher order, merely saluted him by touching their hats.

Monipodio, having made the tour of the courtyard to see his visitors, then asked the newcomers their profession, name, and country. Rincon answered that their profession did not need much explanation; and as to the rest, it was but of little importance, as such information was never expected from those who were to receive orders of distinction. "You are right, young man," returned the worthy, "it is always proper to conceal such truths;—for example, if business did not go well, it would not be very agreeable for your parents to see in the public book, that *so and so,* son of *so and so,* of such a place, stood in the pillory, or was flogged, on such a day, for such a theft; no, no, you are right; and to prevent such inconveniences, everybody ought to have a designation of his own choosing, therefore we only require your names."

This was complied with by the two candidates, when Monipodio said, "It is my pleasure, gentlemen, that henceforward you adopt the names of Rinconete and Cortadillo, for those which you at present bear, and which, I think, will be quite adapted to your pursuits. It is likewise necessary to make a private communication of the names of your parents, as it is a custom with us once a year to say masses for the souls of those that are no more, which expense is defrayed from a common fund, appropriated for the benefit of the community, such as paying the lawyer who defends us, the priest who advises us, and to reward those our worthy friends who, when a hue and cry is raised after any of our members, appease the losers, by telling them that God will punish the wicked." "These are excellent regulations," said Rinconete, who had already accommodated himself to his new appellation; "I cannot sufficiently admire the sagacity of their compiler; but, Señor, our parents have no need of the pious assistance of the brotherhood, being still in the land of the living. If a change should happily occur, we will not fail to inform you."

"That is well," said Monipodio; who then beckoned the boy who had introduced them. "Ganchoso," said the great man, "are the sentinels placed?" "Yes, sir, there are three placed to prevent any surprise." "Very good," returned the professor, "and now let us proceed to business! Rinconete, let me hear what are your attainments."

"Sir," replied he, "I possess a little spice of art; I can handle cards well, know how to turn an ace to a king, and little maneuvers of that sort. I know the table of chances better than the ten commandments, and have learnt that a stolen guinea is better than a borrowed crown." "That is very good as a beginning," said Monipodio, "but, as you must be aware, these are merely the groundwork of the art. However, with the assistance of a dozen lessons, by the blessing of God, I hope to make you a respectable artist." Rinconete bowed, and returned thanks to the master, who called on Cortadillo to state his qualifications.

"Sir," said Cortadillo, "I have learnt the rule of arithmetic, which says, 'put in two and take out five'; and I know how to dive into a pocket with ease and safety."

"Is that all?" said Monipodio. "That is all, to my misfortune," said Cortadillo.

"Never mind," said the professor, "you are in a good school, where, doubtless, you will soon improve, if you will follow my instructions."

"We have all the desire to improve in everything that touches our art and occupation," replied Rinconete.

"Very good," said Monipodio, "but I should like to know how you could endure, upon occasion, a dozen lashes without opening your lips, even as much as to say, 'This mouth is mine.'"

"We are not so misinstructed," said Cortadillo, "as not to know,

that what the tongue borrows sometimes the throat pays; and heaven
have mercy on the poor devil who does not know it is as easy to say
no, as *yes*."

"That is enough," said Monipodio, "I see you are a youth of talent;
I am quite satisfied with you, and shall enter you forthwith on our
company as a full member, without serving any novitiate, or paying
any duty." The company declared their full approbation of the award
of their superior, and complimented the newly elected brother; when
one of the sentinels came running in, saying, that the alguazil of vagabonds was coming towards the house at full speed.

"You need not disturb yourselves," said Monipodio to his friends,
some of whom began to evidence signs of embarrassment, "this alguazil
is a particular friend of mine, and never comes with any hostile intention; I will presently see what he wants." Every one was quieted with
this intimation, and Monipodio went to the door to speak to his friend,
with whom he was some little time in conversation. On his return, he
asked who had occupied the square of San Salvador that morning.

"I was there," replied the guide. "Then how is it that you have not
given notice of a purse, which you took there, containing fifteen gold
crowns, two reals, and some quartos," asked Monipodio. "Why, sir,"
replied the boy, "the fact is, that I have never seen the purse; I have
not taken it—worse luck for me—and I cannot imagine who has."

"No nonsense with me, sir," said Monipodio; "the purse must and
shall be forthcoming; the alguazil is an intimate friend, and has done
us great service." The boy protested, in the strongest terms, that he
had no knowledge of it; when Monipodio began to show symptoms
of ire. "No one shall dare to play tricks with me," said he, his eyes
sparkling with anger: "produce the purse, or take the consequences."
The boy again asserted his innocence, which only increased the master's
rage, and excited the feelings of the whole community against the
delinquent who had offended against the laws; when Rinconete,
finding it would be a serious disturbance, consulted a moment with
Cortadillo, who thought with him it would be better to appease the
anger of Monipodio: therefore, drawing forth the sacristan's purse,
he said, "Calm yourselves, my worthy masters, for here is the purse
which the alguazil requires, and likewise a handkerchief which my
companion borrowed from the same worthy gentleman this morning."
The countenance of the professor immediately brightened at this confession, and he exclaimed, "Cortadillo the Good, for by such distinction shall you henceforward be known—keep the handkerchief, and
content yourself this time with having rendered us a signal service;
for the sacristan, whose acquaintance you made this morning, is a relative of the alguazil, who is one of our best friends; therefore, we
must comply with the proverb, which says, 'To him who gives you a

fowl it is not much to send a leg'; and the alguazil winks at more in a single day, than we could compass in a hundred." Much approbation was manifested by the company at this generous act; and they fully agreed in the justice of the encomium bestowed on Cortadillo, who remained as proud of his title as other worthy and distinguished men, who have acquired the like honor from their virtues or other qualities.

Before the return of Monipodio, two girls entered the apartment, who from their address and manner, Rinconete easily guessed to belong to the community. They were welcomed very warmly by the two bravos, Chiquiznaque and Maniferro, the latter so called from having lost a hand by the course of law, and its place being supplied by one of iron. "Well, what news, my charmer?" said one. "What do you bring for the good of the club?" "You will see directly," replied one of the girls, called Gananciosa; "Silvatillo is coming."

She had hardly spoken these words, when a boy entered, bearing a large basket covered with a sheet. The good people seemed all very much delighted with the appearance of Silvatillo; and Monipodio, taking one of the rush mats, placed it in the middle, and invited his friends to place themselves round it; then, uncovering the basket, which contained abundance of eatables, he desired every one to carve for himself. There was no want of good-will in obeying this injunction, and the knives of the guests were put in requisition; Cortadillo making use of his scanty sword in lieu of a better and more appropriate weapon. The contents of the basket were soon dispatched; and some elderly gentlemen who were of the party, obtained permission to leave, having, as they said, some important business to attend. These reverend members of the community, it appeared, were of the utmost utility; obtaining access by the respectability of their age to houses of consideration, and then ascertaining their value, and facilities for plunder, with which they did not fail to acquaint their worthy employer.

The meal was scarcely finished before a disturbance was heard within, and one of the scouts came running in to inform them that the justice, followed by a whole *posse comitatus*, was advancing to the house. In an instant all was confusion; the remains of the feast were scattered on all sides. Bravos and priests, old and young, lame and blind, instantly betook themselves to their different hiding-places for refuge; and in an instant, the scene of hilarity became as tranquil as though there had been no revelers there. Cortadillo and his friend remained, because they knew not whither to fly; and Monipodio, secure in conscious innocence, as master of the house awaited the coming storm.

It proved after all a groundless alarm. The justice passed on his way to some other quarter, and the runaways were about to be recalled, when a cavalier was introduced, who seemed to be known to Monipodio, who ordered the bravos to be called down, but no others.

"How is it," said the cavalier, "that you have not executed my commands?"

"I do not know what has been done in the business," replied Monipodio, "but hear the artist who had the affair in hand, and I will answer for it he can give you good reason." He then called Chiquiznaque to give an account of his commission.

"Is it of the merchant in the crossway?" asked the man of office.

"The same," said the cavalier.

"Ah! I watched for him last night at the very door of his house," rejoined the bravo, "and when he came I looked him full in the face, which I found to be so very small, that there was positively not space enough for the fourteen slashes that you ordered me to give him; therefore I could not complete your destruction."

"My destruction!" echoed the cavalier, crossing himself. "God forbid! My instructions, I suppose the gentleman means to say."

"Yes," said the unperturbed Chiquiznaque, "that is what I mean. But lest you should say I am not a man of honor, and have neglected my duty, I gave the required number of slashes on the face of his lackey, who, I warrant, can show the marks."

"What use is that to me," said the cavalier; "I had rather that the master had seven than the lackey fourteen; however, you will have no more than the money I left, and I will bid you a good morning." Saying this, he took off his hat, and, bowing to the gentlemen, was about to leave, when Señor Monipodio caught him by the skirt. "Stay, sir, if you please," said he, "and as we have acted honorably in this affair, we shall expect you will do so likewise; there are twenty ducats wanting, which we must have before you leave."

"What do you call acting honorably?" said the cavalier. "Is it giving the punishment to the man that was intended for the master?"

"His honor forgets the proverb that says, 'Love me, love my dog,'" said Chiquiznaque. "And what the devil has that to do with the case?" asked the cavalier. "A great deal," replied the other, "for the same rule reversed must be equally true; therefore, 'Hate me, hate my dog,' is applicable here, and our conditions are thus honorably fulfilled."

"Come, your honor must not split straws with your servants," observed the professor, "but take my advice, and pay what has been honestly earned; and if you are contented to give an order that can be executed on the master; it shall be punctually performed."

"If you will do that," said the cavalier, "I'll pay it willingly." "It shall be done as I am a Christian," said the master. "I'll engage that Chiquiznaque shall make both master and man so like each other, that they shall not be known apart."

"Well, with this promise," said the cavalier, "take this chain for the twenty ducats owing, and forty on account of the business you have in hand. It is worth a thousand reals; but I shall require no change, as I think I shall have occasion shortly to send you to another friend of mine on the same errand." He then took a handsome gold chain from his neck, which was received with the utmost politeness by Monipodio, and Chiquiznaque promised on that very night to wait on the merchant. The cavalier went away very well contented; and the professor then called the members who were absent, and placing himself in the center, drew out his book of memorandums, and gave it to Rinconete to read aloud. The first part of the book was an account of the heavy business which had been paid for by their different employers, such as assassinations, slashing in the face with a poniard, maiming, etc. It began thus:

"Memorandum of the serious business for the week.

"First, The merchant of the crossway to receive fourteen cuts across the face—value fifty crowns—thirty received on account; to be executed by Chiquiznaque." "That is all for this week in that line," said Monipodio; "go on a few a leaves further, and see what is to be done under the article of cudgeling." Rinconete soon found the place, and found written: "Memorandum for cudgeling."

"First, The master of the Clover-flower eating-house a dozen stripes of the very best quality, at the rate of one crown each—time allowed, six days; to be executed by Maniferro." "You may soon rub that out," said Maniferro, "for this is the last night." "Is there any more, my boy?" asked Monipodio. "Yes, sir," said Rinconete, "there is one more. The hunchbacked tailor, commonly called the Goldfinch, six stripes of the best quality, by order of the lady who left the necklace—to be executed by Desmochado (the cropper)."

"I can't think how it is that Desmochado has not completed that order," said Monipodio. "The time has been up these two days." "I met him yesterday," said Maniferro, "and he told me the hunch-back had been ill and was confined to his house." "Ah! I thought so," returned the master; "for I always esteemed Desmochado a good artist and punctual in his obligations. There is no more, boy; pass on to common assaults." Rinconete found in another page as follows: "Memorandum of common business," such as "blacking the face with a bottle of ink"—"nailing a horn over the doors of cuckolds"—"pretenses at assassination"—"false alarms." "That is enough," said Monipodio; "I undertake all that business, because I make it a rule to keep secret little affairs of delicacy; and would rather nail up twenty horns, than give intelligence of one." The business of the day being then concluded, the names of the new members were entered in the book, during which one of the old respectable-looking gentlemen re-turned, to inform the professor that he had seen the gentleman from Malaga, who informed him that he was so much improved in his art, that now he should not be afraid to play with the very devil, and would wager that he could cheat him with clean cards. He had been prevented from waiting on the master since his tour by illness; but should not fail to be at the general rendezvous on Sunday morning. "I always said that Lovillo would arrive at eminence in his profession," said Monipodio; "he has the best hands I ever saw; and to be a good artist we must have good tools." "I have likewise seen the Jew who acts the clergyman," said the venerable reporter: "he has taken lodgings in the same house with some people whom he hopes to tempt at play; but he will not fail to attend on Sunday." "Ah! the Jew is a great scoundrel," said Monipodio: "I have long had great doubts of his honesty, by his never coming near me. Unless he conducts himself more orderly, I shall strip him of his gown. Have you anything more to say?" "Nothing more at present," returned the old gentleman.

"There, my children; take these fifty reals amongst you for the present," said the master, "and God bless and prosper you in your honest endeavors; and, on Sunday next, I shall expect everybody present without fail, as I have a lecture to give you on the improvement of our art." He then embraced Rinconete and Cortadillo, giving them in charge of their former guide, to conduct them to the boundaries of the walks allotted to them, where they were to be accountable for everything stolen from that district. The company then separated, and the two friends retired with their guide, highly edified and delighted with their visit.

PEDRO ANTONIO DE ALARCON

(1833–1891)

BORN in the province of Granada, Alarcón studied first for the law and then delved into theology. He made several unsuccessful efforts to sell his early writings. His first success was as editor of a small provincial paper. He was for a great part of his life engaged in political activities, was exiled, and was finally recalled to fill a position of honour. His best works are his novels and short stories.

The most famous of these is doubtless *The Tall Woman*, one of the classic ghost stories. It is remarkably well told, and exemplifies the writer's outstanding qualities of vivacity, invention, and ingenuity.

The present version is reprinted from *Modern Ghosts*, translated by Rollo Ogden. Copyright, 1890, by Harper & Bros., by whose permission it is here used.

THE TALL WOMAN

"HOW little we really know, my friends; how little we really know."

The speaker was Gabriel, a distinguished civil engineer of the mountain corps. He was seated under a pine tree, near a spring, on the crest of the Guadarrama. It was only about a league and a half distant from the palace of the Escurial, on the boundary line of the provinces of Madrid and Segovia. I know the place, spring, pine tree and all, but I have forgotten its name.

"Let us sit down," went on Gabriel, "as that is the correct thing to do, and as our programme calls for a rest here—here in this pleasant and classic spot, famous for the digestive properties of that spring, and for the many lambs here devoured by our noted teachers, Don Miguel Bosch, Don Máximo Laguna, Don Augustin Pascual, and other illustrious naturalists. Sit down, and I will tell you a strange and wonderful story in proof of my thesis, which is, though you call me an obscurantist for it, that supernatural events still occur on this terraqueous globe. I mean events which you cannot get into terms of reason, or science, or philosophy—as those 'words, words, words,' in Hamlet's phrase are understood (or are not understood) to-day."

Gabriel was addressing his animated remarks to five persons of different ages. None of them was young, though only one was well along in years. Three of them were, like Gabriel, engineers, the fourth was a painter, and the fifth was a *littérateur* in a small way. In company with the speaker, who was the youngest, we had all ridden up on hired mules from the Real Sitio de San Lorenzo to spend the day botanizing among the beautiful pine groves of Pequerinos, chasing butterflies with gauze nets, catching rare beetles under the bark of the decayed pines, and eating a cold lunch out of a hamper which we had paid for on shares.

This took place in 1875. It was the height of the summer. I do not remember whether it was Saint James's day or Saint Louis's; I am inclined to think it was Saint Louis's. Whichever it was, we enjoyed a delicious coolness at that height, and the heart and brain, as well as the stomach, were there in much better working order than usual.

When the six friends were seated, Gabriel continued as follows:

"I do not think you will accuse me of being a visionary. Luckily or unluckily, I am, if you will allow me to say so, a man of the modern world. I have no superstition about me, and am as much of a Positivist as the best of them, although I include among the positive data of nature all the mysterious faculties and feelings of the soul. Well, then, apropos of supernatural, or extra-natural, phenomena, listen to what I have

seen and heard, although I was not the real hero of the very strange
story I am going to relate, and then tell me what explanation of an
earthly, physical, or natural sort, however you may name it, can be
given of so wonderful an occurrence.

"The case was as follows. But wait! Pour me out a drop, for the
skin-bottle must have got cooled off by this time in that bubbling, crys-
talline-spring, located by Providence on this piny crest for the express
purpose of cooling a botanist's wine.

"Well, gentlemen, I do not know whether you ever heard of an
engineer of the roads corps named Telesforo X——; he died in 1860."

"No; I haven't."

"But I have."

"So have I. He was a young fellow from Andalusia, with a black
mustache; he was to have married the Marquis of Moreda's daughter,
but he died of jaundice."

"The very one," said Gabriel. "Well, then, my friend Telesforo, six
months before his death, was still a most promising young man, as
they say nowadays. He was good-looking, well-built, energetic, and
had the glory of being the first one in his class to be promoted. He had
already gained distinction in the practice of his profession through
some fine pieces of work. Several different companies were competing
for his services, and many marriageable women were also competing
for him. But Telesforo, as you said, was faithful to poor Joaquina
Moreda.

"As you know, it turned out that she died suddenly at the baths of
Santa Agueda, at the end of the summer of 1859. I was in Pau when
I received the sad news of her death, which affected me very much on
account of my close friendship with Telesforo. With her I had spoken
only once, in the house of her aunt, the wife of General Lopez, and I
certainly thought her bluish pallor a symptom of bad health. But, however that may be, she had a distinguished manner and a great deal of
grace, and was, besides, the only daughter of a title, and a title that
carried some comfortable thousands with it; so I felt sure my good
mathematician would be inconsolable. Consequently, as soon as I was
back in Madrid, fifteen or twenty days after his loss, I went to see him
very early one morning. He lived in elegant bachelor quarters in Lobo
Street—I do not remember the number, but it was near the Carrera de
San Jerónimo.

"The young engineer was very melancholy, although calm and apparently master of his grief. He was already at work, even at that hour,
laboring with his assistants over some railroad plans or other. He was
dressed in deep mourning.

"He greeted me with a long and close embrace, without so much as
sighing. Then he gave some directions to his assistants about the work

in hand, and afterwards led me to his private office at the farther end of the house. As we were on our way there he said, in a sorrowful tone and without glancing at me:

"'I am very glad you have come. Several times I have found myself wishing you were here. A very strange thing has happened to me. Only a friend such as you are can hear of it without thinking me either a fool or crazy. I want to get an opinion about it as calm and cool as science itself.

"'Sit down,' he went on when we had reached his office, 'and do not imagine that I am going to afflict you with a description of the sorrow I am suffering—a sorrow which will last as long as I live. Why should I? You can easily picture it to yourself, little as you know of trouble. And as for being comforted, I do not wish to be, either now, or later, or ever! What I am going to speak to you about, with the requisite deliberation, going back to the very beginning of the thing, is a horrible and mysterious occurrence, which was an infernal omen of my calamity and which has distressed me in a frightful manner.'

"'Go on,' I replied, sitting down. The fact was, I almost repented having entered the house as I saw the expression of abject fear on my friend's face.

"'Listen, then', said he, wiping the perspiration from his forehead.

"'I do not know whether it is due to some inborn fatality of imagination, or to having heard some story or other of the kind with which children are so rashly allowed to be frightened, but the fact is, that since my earliest years nothing has caused me so much horror and alarm as a woman alone, in the street, at a late hour of the night. The effect is the same whether I actually encounter her, or simply have an image of her in my mind.

"'You can testify that I was never a coward. I fought a duel once, when I had to, like any other man. Just after I had left the School of Engineers, my workmen in Despeñaperros revolted, and I fought them with stick and pistol until I made them submit. All my life long, in Jaen, in Madrid, and elsewhere, I have walked the streets at all hours, alone and unarmed, and if I have chanced to run upon suspicious-looking persons, thieves, or mere sneaking beggars, they have had to get out of my way or take to their heels. But if the person turned out to be a solitary woman, standing still or walking, and I was also alone, with no one in sight in any direction—then (laugh if you want to, but believe me) I would be all covered over with goose-flesh; vague fears would assail me; I would think about beings of the other world, about imaginary existences, and about all the superstitious stories which would make me laugh under other circumstances. I would quicken my pace, or else turn back, and would not get over my fright in the least until safe in my own house.

"'Once there I would fall a-laughing, and would be ashamed of my crazy fears. The only comfort I had was that nobody knew anything about it. Then I would dispassionately remind myself that I did not believe in goblins, witches, or ghosts, and that I had no reason whatever to be afraid of that wretched woman driven from her home at such an hour by poverty, or some crime, or accident, to whom I might better have offered help, if she needed it, or given alms. Nevertheless, the pitiable scene would be gone over again as often as a similar thing occurred—and remember that I was twenty-four years old, that I had experienced a great many adventures by night, and yet that I had never had the slightest difficulty of any sort with such solitary women in the streets after midnight! But nothing of what I have so far told you ever came to have any importance, since that irrational fear always left me as soon as I reached home, or saw any one else in the street, and I would scarcely recall it a few minutes afterwards, any more than one would recall a stupid mistake which had no result of any consequence.

"'Things were going on so, when, nearly three years ago (unhappily, I have good reason for knowing the date, it was the night of November 15-16, 1857), I was coming home at three in the morning. As you remember, I was living then in that little house in Jardines Street, near Montera Street. I had just come, at that late hour, a bitter, cold wind blowing at the time, out of a sort of a gambling-house—I tell you this, although I know it will surprise you. You know that I am not a gambler. I went into the place, deceived by an alleged friend. But the fact was, that as people began to drop in about midnight, coming from receptions or the theater, the play began to be very heavy, and one saw the gleam of gold in plenty. Then came bank-bills and notes of hand. Little by little I was carried away by the feverish and seductive passion, and lost all the money I had. I even went away owing a round sum, for which I had left my note behind me. In short, I ruined myself completely; and but for the legacy that came to me afterwards, together with the good jobs I have had, my situation would have been extremely critical and painful.

"'So I was going home, I say, at so late an hour that night, numb with the cold, hungry, ashamed, and disgusted as you can imagine, thinking about my sick old father more than about myself. I should have to write to him for money, and this would astonish as much as it would grieve him, since he thought me in very easy circumstances. Just before reaching my street, where it crosses Peligros Street, as I was walking in front of a newly built house, I perceived something in its doorway. It was a tall, large woman, standing stiff and motionless, as if made of wood. She seemed to be about sixty years old. Her bold and malignant eyes, unshadded by eyelashes, were fixed on mine like two daggers. Her toothless mouth made a horrible grimace at me, meant to be a smile.

"'The very terror or delirium of fear which instantly overcame me gave me somehow a most acute perception, so that I could distinguish at a glance, in the two seconds it took me to pass by that repugnant vision, the slightest details of her face and dress. Let me see if I can put together my impressions in the way and form in which I received them, as they were engraved ineffaceably on my brain in the light of the street-lamp which shone luridly over that ghastly scene. But I am exciting myself too much, though there is reason enough for it, as you will see further on. Don't be concerned, however, for the state of my mind. I am not yet crazy!

"'The first thing which struck me in that *woman*, as I will call her, was her extreme height and the breadth of her bony shoulders. Then, the roundness and fixity of her dry owl-eyes, the enormous size of her protruding nose, and the great dark cavern of her mouth. Finally, her dress, like that of a young woman of Avapiés—the new little cotton handkerchief which she wore on her head, tied under her chin, and a diminutive fan which she carried open in her hand, and with which, in affected modesty, she was covering the middle of her waist.

"'Nothing could be at the same time more ridiculous and more awful, more laughable and more taunting, than that little fan in those huge hands. It seemed like a make-believe scepter in the hands of such an old, hideous, and bony giantess! A like effect was produced by the showy percale handkerchief adorning her face by the side of that cut-water nose, hooked and masculine; for a moment I was led to believe (or I was very glad to) that it was a man in disguise.

"'But her cynical glance and harsh smile were those of hag, of a witch, an enchantress, a Fate, a—I know not what! There was something about her to justify fully the aversion and fright which I had been caused all my life long by women walking alone in the streets at night. One would have said that I had had a presentiment of that encounter from my cradle. One would have said that I was frightened by it instinctively, as every living being fears and divines, and scents, and recognizes, its natural enemy before ever being injured by it, before ever having seen it, and solely on hearing its tread.

"'I did not dash away in a run when I saw my life's sphinx. I restrained my impulse to do so, less out of shame and manly pride than out of fear lest my very fright should reveal to her who I was, or should give her wings to follow me, to overtake me—I do not know what. Panic like that dreams of dangers which have neither form nor name.

"'My house was at the opposite end of the long and narrow street, in which I was alone, entirely alone with that mysterious phantom whom I thought able to annihilate me with a word. How should I ever get home? Oh, how anxiously I looked towards that distant Montera Street, broad and well lighted, where there are policemen to be found at all hours! I decided finally to get the better of my weakness; to dissemble and hide that wretched fear; not to hasten my pace, but to keep on advancing slowly, even at the cost of years of health or life, and in this way, little by little, to go on getting nearer to my house, exerting myself to the utmost not to fall fainting on the ground before I reached it.

"'I was walking along in this way—I must have taken about twenty steps after leaving behind me the doorway where the woman with the fan was hidden, when suddenly a horrible idea came to me—horrible, yet very natural nevertheless—the idea that I would look back to see if my enemy was following me. One thing or the other I thought, with the rapidity of a flash of lightning: either my alarm has some foundation or it is madness; if it has any foundation, this woman will have started after me, will be overtaking me, and there is no hope for me on earth. But if it is madness, a mere supposition, a panic fright like any other, I will convince myself of it in the present instance, and for every case that may occur hereafter, by seeing that that poor old woman has stayed in that doorway to protect herself from the cold, or to wait till the door is opened; and thereupon I can go on to my house in perfect tranquillity, and I shall have cured myself of a fancy that causes me great mortification.

"'This reasoning gone through with, I made an extraordinary effort and turned my head. Ah, Gabriel!—Gabriel! how fearful it was! The tall woman had followed me with silent tread, was right over me, almost touching me with her fan, almost leaning her head on my shoulder.

"'Why was she doing it?—why, my Gabriel? Was she a thief? Was she really a man in disguise? Was she some malicious old hag who had seen that I was afraid of her? Was she a specter conjured up by my very cowardice? Was she a mocking phantasm of human self-deception?

"'I could never tell you all I thought in a single moment. If the truth must be told, I gave a scream and flew away like a child of four years who thinks he sees the Black Man. I did not stop running until I got out into Montera Street. Once there, my fear left me like magic. This in spite of the fact that that street also was deserted. Then I turned my head to look back to Jardines Street. I could see down its whole length. It was lighted well enough for me to see the tall woman, if she had drawn back in any direction, and, by Heaven! I could not see her, standing still, walking, or in any way! However, I was very careful not to go back into that street again. The wretch, I said to myself, has slunk into some other doorway. But she can't move without my seeing her.

"'Just then I saw a policeman coming up Caballero de Gracia

Street, and I shouted to him without stirring from my place. I told him that there was a man dressed as a woman in Jardines Street. I directed him to go round by the way of Peligros and Aduana Streets, while I would remain where I was, and in that way the fellow, who was probably a thief or murderer, could not escape us. The policeman did as I said. He went through Aduana Street, and as soon as I saw his lantern coming along Jardines Street I also went up it resolutely.

"'We soon met at about the middle of the block, without either of us having encountered a soul, although we had examined door after door.

"'"He has got into some house," said the policeman.

"'"That must be so," I replied, opening my door with the fixed purpose of moving to some other street the next day.

"'A few moments later I was in my room; I always carried my latchkey, so as not to have to disturb my good José. Nevertheless, he was waiting for me that night. My misfortunes of the 15th and 16th of November were not yet ended.

"'"What has happened?" I asked him, in surprise.

"'"Major Falcón was here," he replied, with evident agitation, "waiting for you from eleven till half-past two, and he told me that, if you came home to sleep, you had better not undress, as he would be back at daybreak."

"'Those words left me trembling with grief and alarm, as if they had predicted my own death to me. I knew that my beloved father, at his home in Jaen, had been suffering frequent and dangerous attacks of his chronic disease. I had written to my brothers that, if there should be a sudden and fatal termination of the sickness, they were to telegraph Major Falcón, who would inform me in some suitable way. I had not the slightest doubt, therefore, that my father had died.

"'I sat down in an arm-chair to wait for the morning and my friend, and, with them, the news of my great misfortune. God only knows what I suffered in those two cruel hours of waiting. All the while, three distinct ideas were inseparably joined in my mind; though they seemed unlike, they took pains, as it were, to keep in a dreadful group. They were: my losses at play, my meeting with the tall woman, and the death of my revered father.

"'Precisely at six Major Falcón came into my room, and looked at me in silence. I threw myself into his arms, weeping bitterly, and he exclaimed, caressing me:

"'"Yes, my dear fellow, weep, weep."'"

"My friend Telesforo," Gabriel went on, after having drained another glass of wine, "also rested a moment when he reached this point, and then he proceeded as follows:

"'If my story ended here, perhaps you would not find anything extraordinary or supernatural in it. You would say to me the same thing that men of good judgment said to me at that time: that every one who has a lively imagination is subject to some impulse of fear or other; that mine came from belated, solitary women, and that the old creature of Jardines Street was only some homeless waif who was going to beg of me when I screamed and ran.

"'For my part, I tried to believe that it was so. I even came to believe it at the end of several months. Still, I would have given years of my life to be sure that I was not again to encounter the tall woman. But, to-day, I would give every drop of my blood to be able to meet her again.'

"'What for?'

"'To kill her on the spot.'

"'I do not understand you.'

"'You will understand me when I tell you that I did meet her again, three weeks ago, a few hours before I had the fatal news of my poor Joaquina's death.'

"'Tell me about it, tell me about it!'

"'There is little more to tell. It was five o'clock in the morning. It was not yet fully light, though the dawn was visible from the streets looking towards the east. The street-lamps had just been put out, and the policemen had withdrawn. As I was going through Prado Street, so as to get to the other end of Lobo Street, the dreadful woman crossed in front of me. She did not look at me, and I thought she had not seen me.

"'She wore the same dress and carried the same fan as three years before. My trepidation and alarm were greater than ever. I ran rapidly across Prado Street as soon as she had passed, although I did not take my eyes off her, so as to make sure that she did not look back, and, when I had reached the other end of Lobo Street, I panted as if I had just swum an impetuous stream. Then I pressed on with fresh speed towards home, filled now with gladness rather than fear, for I thought that the hateful witch had been conquered and shorn of her power, from the very fact that I had been so near her and yet that she had not seen me.

"'But soon, and when I had almost reached this house, a rush of fear swept over me, in the thought that the crafty old hag had seen and recognized me, that she had made a pretense of not knowing me so as to let me get into Lobo Street, where it was still rather dark, and where she might set upon me in safety, that she would follow me, that she was already over me.

"'Upon this, I looked around—and there she was! There at my shoulder, almost touching me with her clothes, gazing at me with her horrible little eyes, displaying the gloomy cavern of her mouth, fanning herself in a mocking manner, as if to make fun of my childish alarm.

"'I passed from dread to the most furious anger, to savage and desperate rage. I dashed at the heavy old creature. I flung her against the wall. I put my hand to her throat. I felt of her face, her breast, the straggling locks of her gray hair until I was thoroughly convinced that she was a human being—a woman.

"'Meanwhile she had uttered a howl which was hoarse and piercing at the same time. It seemed false and feigned to me, like the hypocritical expression of a fear which she did not really feel. Immediately afterwards she exclaimed, making believe to cry, though she was not crying, but looking at me with her hyena eyes:

"'"Why have you picked a quarrel with me?"

"'This remark increased my fright and weakened my wrath.

"'"Then you remember," I cried, "that you have seen me somewhere else."

"'"I should say so, my dear," she replied, mockingly. "Saint Eugene's night, in Jardines Street, three years ago."

"'My very marrow was chilled.

"'"But who are you?" I asked, without letting go of her. "Why do you follow me? What business have you with me?"

"'"I am a poor weak woman," she answered, with a devilish leer. "You hate me, and you are afraid of me without any reason. If not, tell me, good sir, why you were so frightened the first time you saw me."

"'"Because I have loathed you ever since I was born. Because you are the evil spirit of my life."

"'"It seems, then, that you have known me for a long time. Well, look, my son, so have I known you."

"'"You have known me? How long?"

"'"Since before you were born! And when I saw you pass by me, three years ago, I said to myself, *that's the one.*"

"'"But what am I to you? What are you to me?"

"'"The devil!" replied the hag, spitting full in my face, freeing herself from my grasp, and running away with amazing swiftness. She held her skirts higher than her knees, and her feet did not make the slightest noise as they touched the ground.

"'It was madness to try to catch her. Besides, people were already passing through the Carrera de San Jerónimo, and in Prado Street, too. It was broad daylight. The tall woman kept on running or flying, as far as Huertas Street, which was now lighted up by the sun. There she stopped to look back at me. She waved her closed fan at me once or twice, threateningly, and then disappeared around a corner.

"'Wait a little longer, Gabriel. Do not yet pronounce judgment in this case, where my life and soul are concerned. Listen to me two minutes longer.

"'When I entered my house I met Colonel Falcón, who had just come to tell me that my Joaquina, my betrothed, all my hope and happiness and joy on earth, had died the day before in Santa Agueda. The unfortunate father had telegraphed Falcón to tell me—me, who should have divined it an hour before, when I met the evil spirit of my life! Don't you understand, now, that I must kill that born enemy of my happiness, that vile old hag, who is the living mockery of my destiny?

"'But why do I say kill? Is she a woman? Is she a human being? Why have I had a presentiment of her ever since I was born? Why did she recognize me when she first saw me? Why do I never see her except when some great calamity has befallen me? Is she Satan? Is she Death? Is she Life? Is she Antichrist? Who is she? What is she?'"

"I will spare you, my dear friends," continued Gabriel, "the arguments and remarks which I used to see if I could not calm Telesforo, for they are the same, precisely the same, which you are preparing now to advance to prove that there is nothing supernatural or superhuman in my story. You will even go further; you will say that my friend was half crazy; that he always was so; that, at least, he suffered from that moral disease which some call 'panic terror,' and others 'emotional insanity'; that, even granting the truth of what I have related about the tall woman, it must all be referred to chance coincidences of dates and events; and, finally, that the poor old creature could also have been crazy, or a thief, or a beggar, or a procuress— as the hero of my story said to himself in a lucid interval."

"A very proper supposition," exclaimed Gabriel's comrades; "that is just what we were going to say."

"Well, listen a few minutes longer, and you will see that I was mistaken at the time, as you are mistaken now. The one who unfortunately made no mistake was Telesforo. It is much easier to speak the word 'insanity' than to find an explanation for some things that happen on the earth."

"Speak, speak!"

"I am going to; and this time, as it is the last, I will pick up the thread of my story without first drinking a glass of wine."

"A few days after that conversation with Telesforo I was sent to the province of Albacete in my capacity as engineer of the mountain corps. Not many weeks had passed before I learned, from a contractor for public works, that my unhappy friend had been attacked by a dreadful form of jaundice; it had turned him entirely green, and he reclined in an arm-chair without working or wishing to see anybody, weeping night and day in the most inconsolable and bitter grief. The doctors had given up hope of his getting well.

"This made me understand why he had not answered my letters. I had to resort to Colonel Falcón as a source of news of him, and all the while the reports kept getting more unfavorable and gloomy.

"After an absence of five months I returned to Madrid the same day that the telegraph brought the news of the battle of Tetuan. I remember it as if it were yesterday. That night I bought the indispensable *Correspondencia de España*, and the first thing I read in it was the notice of Telesforo's death. His friends were invited to the funeral the following morning.

"You will be sure that I was present. As we arrived at the San Luis cemetery, whither I rode in one of the carriages nearest the hearse, my attention was called to a peasant woman. She was old and very tall. She was laughing sacrilegiously as she saw them taking out the coffin. Then she placed herself in front of the pall-bearers in a triumphant attitude and pointed out to them with a very small fan the passage-way they were to take to reach the open and waiting grave.

"At the first glance I perceived, with amazement and alarm, that she was Telesforo's implacable enemy. She was just as he had described her to me—with her enormous nose, her devilish eyes, her awful mouth, her percale handkerchief, and that diminutive fan which seemed in her hands the scepter of indecency and mockery.

"She immediately observed that I was looking at her, and fixed her gaze upon me in a peculiar manner, as if recognizing me, as if letting me know that she recognized me, as if acquainted with the fact that the dead man had told me about the scenes in Jardines Street and Lobo Street, as if defying me, as if declaring me the inheritor of the hate which she had cherished for my unfortunate friend.

"I confess that at the time my fright was greater than my wonder at those new *coincidences* and *accidents*. It seemed evident to me that some supernatural relation, antecedent to earthly life, had existed between the mysterious old woman and Telesforo. But for the time being my sole concern was about my own life, my own soul, my own happiness—all of which would be exposed to the greatest peril if I should really inherit such a curse.

"The tall woman began to laugh. She pointed at me contemptuously with the fan, as if she had read my thoughts and were publicly exposing my cowardice. I had to lean on a friend's arm to keep myself from falling. Then she made a pitying or disdainful gesture, turned on her heels, and went into the cemetery. Her head was turned towards me. She fanned herself and nodded to me at the same time. She sidled along among the graves with an indescribable, infernal coquetry, until at last she disappeared forever in that labyrinth of tombs.

"I say forever, since fifteen years have passed and I have never seen her again. If she was a human being she must have died before this;

if she was not, I rest in the conviction that she despised me too much to meddle with me.

"Now, then, bring on your theories! Give me your opinion about these strange events. Do you still regard them as entirely natural?"

GUSTAVO ADOLFO BÉCQUER

(1836—1870)

A NATIVE of Seville, Bécquer ran away from home while still a boy, and went to Madrid, where for many years he led a life of poverty. His entire life indeed was spent in executing what hack work he was able to get. He is known for his poems and fantastic tales, the latter written to a certain extent under the influence of the German Hoffmann. *Maese Pérez* is a good specimen of his art both as a teller of tales and a poet of fantasy. It is one of the recognized masterpieces of modern Spanish fiction.

The present version is reprinted from *Modern Ghosts*, translated by Rollo Ogden. Copyright, 1890, by Harper & Bros., by whose permission it is here used.

MAESE PÉREZ, THE ORGANIST

DO you see that man with the scarlet cloak, and the white plume in his hat, and the gold-embroidered vest? I mean the one just getting out of his litter and going to greet that lady—the one coming along after those four pages who are carrying torches? Well, that is the Marquis of Mascoso, lover of the widow, the Countess of Villapineda. They say that before he began paying court to her he had sought the hand of a very wealthy man's daughter, but the girl's father, who they say is a trifle close-fisted—but hush! Speaking of the devil—do you see that man closely wrapped in his cloak coming on foot under the arch of San Felipe? Well, he is the father in question. Everybody in Seville knows him on account of his immense fortune.

"Look—look at that group of stately men! They are the twenty-four knights. Aha! there's that Heming, too. They say that the gentlemen of the green cross have not challenged him yet, thanks to his influence with the great ones at Madrid. All he comes to church for is to hear the music.

"Alas! neighbor, that looks bad. I fear there's going to be a scuffle. I shall take refuge in the church, for, according to my guess, there will be more blows than *Paternosters*. Look, look! the Duke of Alcalá's people are coming round the corner of Saint Peter's Square, and I think I see the Duke of Medinasidonia's men in Dueñas Alley. Didn't I tell you? There—there! The blows are beginning. Neighbor, neighbor, this way before they close the doors!

"But what's that? They've left off. What's that light? Torches! a litter! It's the bishop himself! God preserve him in his office as many centuries as I desire to live myself! If it were not for him, half Seville would have been burned up by this time with these quarrels of the dukes. Look at them, look at them, the hypocrites, how they both press forward to kiss the bishop's ring!

"But come, neighbor—come into the church before it is packed full. Some nights like this it is so crowded that you could not get in if you were no larger than a grain of wheat. The nuns have a prize in their organist. Other sisterhoods have made Maese Pérez magnificent offers; nothing strange about that, though, for the very archbishop has offered him mountains of gold if he would go to the cathedral. But he would not listen to them. He would sooner die than give up his beloved organ. You don't know Maese Pérez? Oh, I forgot you had just come to the neighborhood. Well, he is a holy man; poor, to be sure, but as charitable as any man that ever lived. With no relative but a daughter, and no friend but his organ, he spends all his time in caring for the one and repairing the other. The organ is an old affair, you must know; but that makes no difference to him. He handles it so that its tone is a wonder. How he does know it! and all by touch, too, for did I tell you that the poor man was born blind?

"Humble, too, as the very stones. He always says that he is only a poor convent organist, when the fact is he could give lessons in *sol fa* to the very chapel master of the primate. You see, he began before he had teeth. His father had the same position before him, and as the boy showed such talent, it was very natural that he should succeed his father when the latter died. And what a touch he has, God bless him! He always plays well, always; but on a night like this he is wonderful. He has the greatest devotion to this Christmas Eve mass, and when the host is elevated, precisely at twelve o'clock, which is the time that Our Lord came into the world, his organ sounds like the voices of angels.

"But why need I try to tell you about what you are going to hear to-night? It is enough for you to see that all the elegance of Seville, the very archbishop included, comes to a humble convent to listen to him. And it is not only the learned people who can understand his skill that come; the common people, too, swarm to the church, and are still as the dead when Maese Pérez puts his hand to the organ. And when the host is elevated—when the host is elevated, then you can't hear a fly. Great tears fall from every eye, and when the music is over a long-drawn sigh is heard, showing how the people have been holding their breath all through.

"But come, come, the bells have stopped ringing, and the mass is going to begin. Hurry in. This is Christmas Eve for everybody, but for no one is it a greater occasion than for us."

So saying, the good woman who had been acting as *cicerone* for her neighbor pressed through the portico of the Convent of Santa Inés, and elbowing this one and pushing the other, succeeded in getting inside the church, forcing her way through the multitude that was crowding about the door.

The church was profusely lighted. The flood of light which fell from the altars glanced from the rich jewels of the great ladies, who, kneeling upon velvet cushions placed before them by pages, and taking their prayer-books from the hands of female attendants, formed a brilliant circle around the chancel lattice. Standing next that lattice, wrapped in their richly colored and embroidered cloaks, letting their green and red orders be seen with studied carelessness, holding in one hand their hats, the plumes sweeping the floor, and letting the other rest upon the polished hilts of rapiers or the jeweled handles of daggers, the twenty-four knights, and a large part of the highest nobility of Seville, seemed to be forming a wall for the purpose of keeping their wives and daughters from contact with the populace. The latter, swaying back and forth at the rear of the nave, with a noise like that of a rising surf, broke out into joyous acclamations as the archbishop was seen to come in. That dignitary seated himself near the high altar under a scarlet canopy, surrounded by his attendants, and three times blessed the people.

It was time for the mass to begin.

Nevertheless, several minutes passed before the celebrant appeared. The multitude commenced to murmur impatiently; the knights exchanged words with each other in a low tone; and the archbishop sent one of his attendants to the sacristan to inquire why the ceremony did not begin.

"Maese Pérez has fallen sick, very sick, and it will be impossible for him to come to the midnight mass."

This was the word brought back by the attendant.

The news ran instantly through the crowd. The disturbance caused by it was so great that the chief judge rose to his feet, and the officers came into the church, to enforce silence.

Just then a man of unpleasant face, thin, bony, and cross-eyed too, pushed up to the place where the archbishop was sitting.

"Maese Pérez is sick," he said; "the ceremony cannot begin. If you see fit, I will play the organ in his absence. Maese Pérez is not the best organist in the world, nor need this instrument be left unused after his death for lack of any one able to play it."

The archbishop nodded his head in assent, although some of the faithful, who had already recognized in that strange person an envious rival of the organist of Santa Inés, were breaking out in cries of displeasure. Suddenly a surprising noise was heard in the portico.

"Maese Pérez is here! Maese Pérez is here!"

At this shout, coming from those jammed in by the door, every one looked around.

Maese Pérez, pale and feeble, was in fact entering the church, brought in a chair which all were quarreling for the honor of carrying upon their shoulders.

The commands of the physicians, the tears of his daughter—nothing had been able to keep him in bed.

"No," he had said; "this is the last one, I know it. I know it, and I do not want to die without visiting my organ again, this night above all, this Christmas Eve. Come, I desire it, I order it; come, to the church!"

His desire had been gratified. The people carried him in their arms to the organ-loft. The mass began.

Twelve struck on the cathedral clock.

The introit came, then the Gospel, then the offertory, and the moment arrived when the priest, after consecrating the sacred wafer, took it in his hands and began to elevate it. A cloud of incense filled the church in bluish undulations. The little bells rang out in vibrating peals, and Maese Pérez placed his aged fingers upon the organ keys.

The multitudinous voices of the metal tubes gave forth a prolonged and majestic chord, which died away little by little, as if a gentle breeze had borne away its last echoes.

To this opening burst, which seemed like a voice lifted up to heaven from earth, responded a sweet and distant note, which went on swelling and swelling in volume until it became a torrent of overpowering harmony. It was the voice of the angels, traversing space, and reaching the world.

Then distant hymns began to be heard, intoned by the hierarchies of seraphim; a thousand hymns at once, mingling to form a single one, though this one was only an accompaniment to a strange melody which seemed to float above that ocean of mysterious echoes, as a strip of fog above the waves of the sea.

One song after another died away. The movement grew simpler. Now only two voices were heard, whose echoes blended. Then but one remained, and alone sustained a note as brilliant as a thread of light. The priest bowed his face, and above his gray head appeared the host. At that moment the note which Maese Pérez was holding

began to swell and swell, and an explosion of unspeakable joy filled
the church.

From each of the notes forming that magnificent chord a theme was
developed; and some near, others far away, these brilliant, those muffled, one would have said that the waters and the birds, the breezes
and the forests, men and angels, earth and heaven, were singing, each
in its own language, a hymn in praise of the Saviour's birth.

The people listened, amazed and breathless. The officiating priest
felt his hands trembling; for it seemed as if he had seen the heavens
opened and the host transfigured.

The organ kept on, but its voice sank away gradually, like a tone
going from echo to echo, and dying as it goes. Suddenly a cry was
heard in the organ-loft—a piercing, shrill cry, the cry of a woman.

The organ gave a strange, discordant sound, like a sob, and then
was silent.

The multitude flocked to the stairs leading up to the organ-loft,
towards which the anxious gaze of the faithful was turned.

"What has happened? What is the matter?" one asked the other,
and no one knew what to reply. The confusion increased. The excitement threatened to disturb the good order and decorum fitting within
a church.

"What was that?" asked the great ladies of the chief judge. He had
been one of the first to ascend to the organ-loft. Now, pale and displaying signs of deep grief, he was going to the archbishop, who was
anxious, like everybody else, to know the cause of the disturbance.

"What's the matter?"

"Maese Pérez has just expired."

In fact, when the first of the faithful rushed up the stairway, and
reached the organ-loft, they saw the poor organist fallen face down
upon the keys of his old instrument, which was still vibrating, while his
daughter, kneeling at his feet, was vainly calling to him with tears
and sobs.

"Good-evening, my dear Doña Baltasara. Are you also going to-
night to the Christmas Eve mass? For my part, I was intending to go
to the parish church to hear it, but what has happened—where is
Vicente going, do you ask? Why, where the crowd goes. And I must
say, to tell the truth, that ever since Maese Pérez died, it seems as if
a marble slab was on my heart whenever I go to Santa Inés. Poor dear
man! He was a saint! I know one thing—I keep a piece of his cloak
as a relic, and he deserves it. I solemnly believe that if the archbishop
would stir in the matter, our grandchildren would see his image among
the saints on the altars. But, of course, he won't do that. The dead
and absent have no friends, as they say. It's all the latest thing, nowa-

days; you understand me. What? You do not know what has happened? Well, it's true you are not exactly in our situations. From our house to the church, and from the church to our house—a word here and another one there—on the wing—without any curiosity whatever—I easily find out all the news.

"Well, then, it's a settled thing that the organist of San Roman— that squint-eye, who is always slandering other organists—that great blunderer, who seems more like a butcher than a master of *sol fa*—is going to play this Christmas Eve in Maese Pérez's old place. Of course, you know, for everybody knows it, and it is a public matter in all Seville, that no one dared to try it. His daughter would not, though she is a professor of music herself. After her father's death she went into the convent as a novice. Her unwillingness to play was the most natural thing in the world; accustomed as she was to those marvelous performances, any other playing must have appeared bad to her, not to speak of her desire to avoid comparisons. But when the sisterhood had already decided that in honor of the dead organist, and as a token of respect to his memory, the organ should not be played to-night, here comes this fellow along, and says that he is ready to play it.

"Ignorance is the boldest of all things. It is true, the fault is not his, so much as theirs who have consented to this profanation, but that is the way of the world. But, I say, there's no small bit of people coming. Any one would say that nothing had changed since last year. The same distinguished persons, the same elegant costumes, the crowding at the door, the same excitement in the portico, the same throng in the church. Alas! if the dead man were to rise, he would feel like dying again to hear his organ played by inferior hands. The fact is, if what the people of the neighborhood tell me is true, they are getting a fine reception ready for the intruder. When the time comes for him to touch the keys, there is going to break out a racket made by timbrels, drums, and horse-fiddlers, so that you can't hear anything else. But hush! there's the hero of the occasion going into the church. Goodness! what gaudy clothes, what a neckcloth, what a high and mighty air! Come, hurry up, the archbishop came only a moment ago, and the mass is going to begin. Come on; I guess this night will give us something to talk about for many a day!"

Saying this, the worthy woman, whom the reader recognizes by her abrupt talkativeness, went into the Church of Santa Inés, opening for herself a path, in her usual way, by shoving and elbowing through the crowd.

The ceremony had already begun. The church was as brilliant as the year before.

The new organist, after passing between the rows of the faithful in the nave, and going to kiss the archbishop's ring, had gone up to the organ-loft, where he was trying one stop of the organ after another, with an affected and ridiculous gravity.

A low, confused noise was heard coming from the common people clustered at the rear of the church, a sure augury of the coming storm, which would not be long in breaking.

"He is a mere clown," said some, "who does not know how to do anything, not even look straight."

"He is an ignoramus," said others, "who, after having made a perfect rattle out of the organ in his own church, comes here to profane Maese Pérez's."

And while one was taking off his cloak so as to be ready to beat his drum to good advantage, and another was testing his timbrel, and all were more and more buzzing out in talk, only here and there could one be found to defend even feebly that curious person, whose proud and pedantic bearing so strongly contrasted with the modest appearance and kind affability of Maese Pérez.

At last the looked-for moment arrived, when the priest, after bowing low and murmuring the sacred words, took the host in his hands. The bells gave forth a peal, like a rain of crystal notes; the transparent waves of incense rose, and the organ sounded.

But its first chord was drowned by a horrible clamor which filled the whole church. Bagpipes, horns, timbrels, drums, every instrument known to the populace, lifted up their discordant voices all at once.

The confusion and clangor lasted but a few seconds. As the noises began, so they ended, all together.

The second chord, full, bold, magnificent, sustained itself, pouring from the organ's metal tubes like a cascade of inexhaustible and sonorous harmony.

Celestial songs like those that caress the ear in moments of ecstasy; songs which the soul perceives, but which the lip cannot repeat; single notes of a distant melody, which sound at intervals, borne on the breeze; the rustle of leaves kissing each other on the trees with a murmur like rain; trills of larks which rise with quivering songs from among the flowers like a flight of arrows to the sky; nameless sounds, overwhelming as the roar of a tempest; fluttering hymns, which seemed to be mounting to the throne of the Lord like a mixture of light and sound—all were expressed by the organ's hundred voices, with more vigor, more subtle poetry, more weird coloring, than had ever been known before.

When the organist came down from the loft the crowd which pressed up to the stairway was so great, and their eagerness to see and greet him so intense, that the chief judge, fearing, and not without reason, that he would be suffocated among them all, ordered some of the officers to open a path for the organist, with their staves of office, so that he could reach the high altar, where the prelate was waiting for him.

"You perceive," said the archbishop, "that I have come all the way from my palace to hear you. Now, are you going to be as cruel as Maese Pérez? He would never save me the journey, by going to play the Christmas Eve mass in the cathedral."

"Next year," replied the organist, "I promise to give you the pleasure; since, for all the gold in the world, I would never play this organ again."

"But why not?" interrupted the prelate.

"Because," returned the organist, endeavoring to repress the agitation which revealed itself in the pallor of his face—"because it is so old and poor; one cannot express one's self on it satisfactorily."

The archbishop withdrew, followed by his attendants. One after another the litters of the great fold disappeared in the windings of the neighboring streets. The group in the portico scattered. The sexton was locking up the doors, when two women were perceived, who had stopped to cross themselves and mutter a prayer, and who were now going on their way into Dueñas Alley.

"What would you have, my dear Doña Baltasara?" one was saying. "That's the way I am. Every crazy person with his whim. The barefooted Capuchins might assure me that it was so, and I would not believe it. That man never played what we have heard. Why, I have heard him a thousand times in San Bartolomé, his parish church; the priest had to send him away he was so poor a player. You felt like plugging your ears with cotton. Why, all you need is to look at his face, and that is the mirror of the soul, they say. I remember, as if I was seeing him now, poor man—I remember Maese Pérez's face, nights like this, when he came down from the organ-loft, after having entranced the audience with his splendors. What a gracious smile! What a happy glow on his face! Old as he was, he seemed like an angel. But this creature came plunging down as if a dog were barking at him on the landing, and all the color of a dead man, while his—come, dear Doña Baltasara, believe me, and believe what I say: there is some great mystery about this."

Thus conversing, the two women turned the corner of the alley, and disappeared. There is no need of saying who one of them was.

Another year had gone by. The abbess of the Convent of Santa Inés and Maese Pérez's daughter were talking in a low voice, half hidden in the shadows of the church choir. The penetrating voice of the bell was summoning the faithful. A very few people were passing through the portico, silent and deserted, this year, and after taking holy water at the door, were choosing seats in a corner of the nave, where a handful of residents of the neighborhood were quietly waiting for the Christmas Eve mass to begin.

"There, you see," the mother superior was saying, "your fear is entirely childish; there is no one in the church. All Seville is trooping to the cathedral to-night. Play the organ, and do it without any distrust whatever. We are only a sisterhood here. But why don't you speak? What has happened? What is the matter with you?"

"I am afraid," replied the girl, in a tone of the deepest agitation. "Afraid! Of what?"

"I do not know—something supernatural. Listen to what happened last night. I had heard you say that you were anxious for me to play the organ for the mass. I was proud of the honor, and I thought I would arrange the stops and get the organ in good tune so as to give you a surprise to-day. Alone I went into the choir and opened the door leading to the organ-loft. The cathedral clock was striking just then, I do not know what hour; but the strokes of the bell were very mournful, and they were very numerous—going on sounding for a century, as it seemed to me, while I stood as if nailed to the threshold.

"The church was empty and dark. Far away there gleamed a feeble light, like a faint star in the sky; it was the lamp burning on the high altar. By its flickering light, which only helped to make the deep horror of the shadows the more intense, I saw—I saw—mother, do not disbelieve it—a man. In perfect silence, and with his back turned towards me, he was running over the organ-keys with one hand while managing the stops with the other. And the organ sounded, but in an indescribable manner. It seemed as if each note were a sob smothered in the metal tube, which vibrated under the pressure of the air compressed within it, and gave forth a low, almost imperceptible tone, yet exact and true.

"The cathedral clock kept on striking, and that man kept on running over the keys. I could hear his very breathing.

"Fright had frozen the blood in my veins. My body was as cold as ice, except my head, and that was burning. I tried to cry out, but I could not. That man turned his face and looked at me—no, he did not look at me, for he was blind. It was my father!"

"Nonsense, sister! Banish these fancies with which the adversary endeavors to overturn weak imaginations. Address a *Paternoster* and an *Ave Marie* to the archangel, Saint Michael, the captain of the celestial hosts, that he may aid you in opposing evil spirits. Wear on your neck a scapulary which has been pressed to the relics of Saint Pacomio, the counselor against temptations, and go, go quickly, and sit at the organ. The mass is going to begin, and the faithful are growing impatient. Your father is in heaven, and thence, instead of giving you a fright, will descend to inspire his daughter in the solemn service."

The prioress went to occupy her seat in the choir in the midst of the sisterhood. Maese Pérez's daughter opened the door of the organ-loft with trembling hand, sat down at the organ, and the mass began.

The mass began, and went on without anything unusual happening until the time of consecration came. Then the organ sounded. At the same time came a scream from Maese Pérez's daughter.

The mother superior, the nuns, and some of the faithful rushed up to the organ-loft.

"Look at him!—look at him!" cried the girl, fixing her eyes, starting from their sockets, upon the seat, from which she had risen in terror. She was clinging with convulsed hands to the railing of the organ-loft.

Everybody looked intently at the spot to which she directed her gaze. No one was at the organ, yet it went on sounding—sounding like the songs of the archangels in their bursts of mystic ecstasy.

"Didn't I tell you a thousand times, if I did once, dear Doña Baltasara—didn't I tell you? There is some great mystery about this. What! didn't you go last night to the Christmas Eve mass? Well, you must know, anyhow, what happened. Nothing else is talked about in the whole city. The archbishop is furious, and no wonder. Not to have gone to Santa Inés, not to have been present at the miracle—and all to hear a wretched clatter! That's all the inspired organist of San Bartolomé made in the cathedral, so persons who heard him tell me. Yes, I said so all the time. The squint-eye never could have played that. It was all a lie. There is some great mystery here. What do I think it was? Why, it was the soul of Maese Pérez."

LEOPOLDO ALAS

(1852—1901)

ALAS, who often wrote under the pseudonym of "Clarin," was born at Zamora. Studying first for the law, he went to Madrid, where he worked as journalist and literary critic. He was for some time a professor of Political Economy, and later of Law. His chief contributions to Spanish literature are novels and tales. *Adios, Cordera!* unlike his longer works, is a quiet and sentimental story, consistently charming and thoroughly Spanish.

The present version is translated by Walter Brooks, in the volume *Retold in English*, copyright, 1905, by Brentano's, by whose permission it is here used.

ADIOS, CORDERA!

THEY were three—always the same three—Rosa, Pinin, and "La Cordera."

The meadow "Somonte" was a triangular patch of velvety green spread out like a carpet at the foot of the hill. Its lower angle extended as far as the railway track from Oviedo to Gijon, and a telegraph post standing like a flag-pole in the corner of the field represented to Rosa and Pinin the world without; a world unknown, mysterious, and forever to be dreaded and ignored.

Pinin, after seriously considering the subject as he watched from day to day this tranquil and inoffensive post, finally came to the conclusion that it was trying its best to be simply a dried tree, nothing more, and to give the impression that its glass cups were some strange fruit, so he gained sufficient confidence to climb up almost to the wires. He never went as far as the cups, for they reminded him too strongly of some of the sacred vessels in the church, and he was able to shake off a feeling of awe only when he had slid down again and planted his feet safely on the green sod.

Rosa, less audacious, but more enamored of the unknown, contented herself with sitting beneath the telegraph post for hours at a time and listening to the wind as it drew a weird metallic song from the wires and mingled it with sighs from the heart of the pine.

At times these vibrations seemed to be music, and then again to Rosa they were whispers traveling along the wires from an unknown to an unknown. She had no curiosity to learn what people on opposite sides of the world were saying to one another. It mattered naught to her; she only listened to the sound with its melody and mystery.

"La Cordera," having lived to a mature age, was more matter-of-fact than her companions. She held aloof from contact with the world and contemplated the telegraph pole from a distance as purely an inanimate object of no use except to rub against.

"La Cordera" was a cow who had seen much of life, and for hours together she lay in the meadow passing her time meditating rather than feeding, enjoying the tranquillity of life, the gray sky, the peaceful earth, and seeking to improve her mind.

She joined in the games of the children, whose duty it was to guard her, and had she been able she would have smiled at the idea that Rosa and Pinin were charged with her care—she, "La Cordera!"—with keeping her in the pasture and preventing her from jumping the fence and straying along the railway track. Just as if she would be inclined to jump! Why should she meddle with the railway track?

It was *her* pleasure to graze quietly, selecting with care the choicest morsels without raising her head to look about in idle curiosity, and after that to lie down and either to meditate or else to taste the delights of simply not suffering; just to exist—that was all she cared to do; other things were dangerous undertakings. Her peace of mind had only been disturbed at the inauguration of the railway, when she had become almost beside herself with terror at seeing the first train pass. She had jumped the stone wall into the neighboring field and joined the other cattle in their wild antics; and her fear had lasted for several days, recurring with more or less violence every time the engine appeared at the mouth of the tunnel.

Little by little she realized that the train was harmless, a peril which always passed by, a catastrophe which threatened but did not strike. She therefore reduced her precautions and ceased to put herself on the defensive by lowering her head. Later on she gazed at the train without even getting up, and ended by entirely losing her antipathy and distrust and not looking at it at all.

In Rosa and Pinin the novelty of the railway produced impressions much more agreeable. In the beginning it brought excitement mixed with superstitious dread; the children danced wildly about and gave vent to loud shrieks; then there came a kind of quiet diversion, repeated several times a day as they watched the huge iron snake glide rapidly by with its burden of strange people.

But the railway and telegraph furnished incidents of only short duration, and these were soon swallowed up in the sea of solitude which surrounded the meadow "Somonte"; then no living being was to be seen, nor sound from the outside world to be heard.

Morning after morning under the burning rays of the sun and amid the hum of swarming insects the children and the cow watched for the approach of noon to return to the house, and on the long, melancholy afternoons they again awaited the coming of night.

The shadows lengthened, the birds became quiet, and here and there a star appeared in the darkest part of the sky. The souls of the children reflected the serenity of solemn and serious nature, and seated near "La Cordera" they maintained a dreamy silence, broken only now and then by the soft tinkle of the cowbell.

The children, inseparable as the two halves of a green fruit, were united in an affection existing by reason of their scanty knowledge of what was distinct in them and what made them two. This affection was extended to "La Cordera," the motherly cow, and as far as she was able she returned in her undemonstrative way the love of the children who were charged with guarding her. She showed wonderful patience and toleration when, included in their imaginative games, she was subjected to no very gentle usage, and gave evidence at all times of quiet and thoughtful consideration.

Only recently had Anton de Chinta, the children's father, acquired possession of the meadow "Somonte" and "La Cordera" enjoyed the privilege of such succulent pasture. She had previously been compelled to wander along the public roads and obtain her food from the scant herbage which grew along their borders.

In those times of poverty, Pinin and Rosa sought out for her the most favorable spots, and in many ways guarded her against the indignities to which animals are exposed who have to look for fodder on public lands, and in the lean and hungry days of the stable when hay was scarce and turnips not to be had the cow owed to the children a thousand little attentions which served to make life more bearable. Then, too, during those heroic times between the birth and weaning of her calves, when the inevitable question arose as to how much milk the Chintas should have and what was necessary for her own offspring, it was at such times that Pinin and Rosa were always found taking sides with "La Cordera." They would secretly let loose the young calf, which, wild with delight and stumbling over everything in its path, would rush to seek food and shelter underneath the ample body of its mother, while the latter would turn her head toward the children with a look of tenderness and gratitude.

Such ties could never be broken and such memories never be effaced.

Anton de Chinta had come to the conclusion that he was born under an unlucky star, and that his golden dreams of gradually increasing his stable were not to be fulfilled; for, having procured the one cow by means of a thousand economies and privations, he not only failed to acquire a second, but finally found himself behind in his rent. He saw in "La Cordera" his only available asset, and realized that she must be sold in spite of the fact that she was considered one of the family, and that his wife with her last breath had referred to the cow as their future mainstay.

As the mother lay upon her deathbed, in a room separated from the stable only by a partition of interwoven cornstalks, she turned her weary eyes toward "La Cordera" as if to silently entreat her to be a second mother to the children, and to supply that affection which the father could not understand.

Anton de Chinta appreciated this in an indefinite way, and consequently said nothing to the children of the necessity for selling the cow.

One Saturday morning at daybreak, he took advantage of the fact that Rosa and Pinin were still asleep, and started with a heavy heart for Gijon, driving "La Cordera" before him.

When the children awoke they were at a loss to explain the cause of his sudden departure, but felt sure the cow must have accompanied him much against her will; and when at evening the father, tired and

covered with dust, brought the animal back, and would give no explanation of his absence, the children apprehended danger.

The cow had not been sold. With the sophistry of tenderness and
affection he had put the selling price so high that no one would pay
it, and had scowled at any prospective purchaser presumptuous enough
even to approach the amount upon which he obstinately insisted. He
quieted his conscience with the argument that surely he had been
willing to sell; the fault lay with the others who were not willing to
pay "La Cordera's" value. So he had taken the road home again,
accompanied by a number of neighboring farmers who were driving
their livestock before them and experiencing more or less difficulty
according to the length of acquaintance between master and beast.

From the day when Pinin and Rosa began to suspect that there was
trouble in store they had no peace of mind, and their worst fears were
soon afterward confirmed by the appearance of the landlord with
threats of eviction.

"La Cordera" must therefore be sold, and perhaps only for the price
of a breakfast.

The following Saturday Pinin accompanied his father to a neighboring market-town, where the child looked in horror at the butchers
armed with their weapons of slaughter. To one of these the animal was
sold, and after being branded was driven back to her stable, the bell
tinkling sadly all the way.

Anton was silent, the eyes of the boy were red and swollen, and Rosa,
upon hearing of the sale, put her arms around "La Cordera's" neck
and sobbed.

The next few days were sad ones in the meadow "Somonte." "La
Cordera," ignorant of her fate, was as calm and placid as she would
continue to be up to the moment when the brutal blow of the axe
was given; but Pinin and Rosa could do nothing but lie stretched out
on the grass in continued silence, disconsolate in regard to the future.

They cast looks of hatred at the telegraph wires and the passing trains
which were connected with that world so distant from all their comprehension—the world which was robbing them of their only friend and
companion.

A few days later the separation took place; the butcher came and
brought the money agreed upon. He was asked by Anton to take a
draught of wine, and forced to listen to the extraordinary virtues of the
cow. The father could not believe that "La Cordera" was not going to
another master where she would be well treated and happy, and excited
by the wine and the weight of the money in his pocket, he continued
to extol her domestic qualities, her milk-giving capacity, and strength
under the yoke. The other only smiled as he realized what destiny
awaited her.

Pinin and Rosa, clasping one another's hands, stood watching the enemy from a distance, and thinking sadly of the past, with its memories of "La Cordera," and before she was finally led away they flung themselves upon her neck and covered it with kisses. The children followed some distance down the narrow road and formed a melancholy group with the indifferent driver and the reluctant cow. Finally they stopped and stood watching the animal as it slowly disappeared in the shadows of the bordering hedges.

Their foster mother was lost to them forever.

"Adios, Cordera!" cried Rosa, bursting into tears. "Adios, Cordera de mio alma."

"Adios, Cordera," repeated Pinin, his voice choked with emotion. "Adios," answered sadly and for the last time the distant cowbell, and then its piteous lamentation was lost among other sounds of the night.

Early the following day, Pinin and Rosa went to the meadow "Somonte." Never had its solitude been so oppressive; never had it seemed a desert waste until now.

Suddenly smoke appeared at the mouth of the tunnel, and then came the train. In a box-like car, pierced with narrow windows, could be seen the forms of closely packed cattle.

The children shook their fists at the train, more convinced than ever of the rapacity of the world.

"They are taking her to the slaughter!"

"Adios, Cordera!"

"Adios, Cordera!"

And Pinin and Rosa gazed with hatred upon the railway and the telegraph, those symbols of the cruel world which was taking away their companion of so many years for the satisfaction merely of its gluttonous appetite.

"Adios, Cordera!"

"Adios, Cordera!"

China

INTRODUCTION

CHINESE literature is one of the oldest, most varied, and extensive in the world, but though it includes a vast number of works on philosophy, religion, medicine, poetry, and the drama, it is comparatively poor in the realm of pure fiction, the novel and the short story. It appears that the narrative, related for its own sake alone, was held in contempt.

There are, however, two outstanding exceptions, in the form of collections of brief tales. Of these the first is the *Kin-Kou-Ki-Kuan*, or *Marvelous Tales, Ancient and Modern*, some forty short stories by a number of anonymous writers, brought together some time during the Fifteenth Century A.D. The other is the *Liao-Chai-Chih-I*, or *Strange Stories from a Chinese Studio*, edited by P'u Sung-Ling, who, though he did not write the stories, has been accorded a rank among the "immortal" writers of his land, doubtless because of the distinctly moral taste which governed his choice. P'u Sung-Ling lived during the brilliant Seventeenth Century, and since his day there has been very little added to the art of story-telling by the Chinese.

THE STORY OF MING-Y

(Anonymous: 15th Century A.D., or before)

The Story of Ming-Y is one of the most celebrated of the *Marvellous Tales, Ancient and Modern;* it appeals strongly to the Occidental because of the element of romance in it, and because it is without that didacticism that for us mars many otherwise charming Chinese stories. Yet even here the writer evidently feels it incumbent upon him to draw a moral.

This story is translated by Lafcadio Hearn, and appears in the volume *Some Chinese Ghosts*, copyright 1906 by Little, Brown and Company, by whose permission it is here reprinted.

THE STORY OF MING-Y

(From Marvellous Tales, Ancient and Modern)

FIVE hundred years ago, in the reign of the Emperor Houng-Wou, whose dynasty was *Ming*, there lived in the city of Genii, the city of Kwang-tchau-fu, a man celebrated for his learning and for his piety, named Tien-Pelou. This Tien-Pelou had one son, a beautiful boy, who for scholarship and for bodily grace and for polite accomplishments had no superior among the youths of his age. And his name was Ming-Y.

Now when the lad was in his eighteenth summer, it came to pass that Pelou, his father, was appointed Inspector of Public Instruction at the city of Tching-tou; and Ming-Y accompanied his parents thither. Near the city of Tching-tou lived a rich man of rank, a high commissioner of the government, whose name was Tchang, and who wanted to find a worthy teacher for his children. On hearing of the arrival of the new Inspector of Public Instruction, the noble Tchang visited him to obtain advice in this matter; and happening to meet and converse with Pelou's accomplished son, immediately engaged Ming-Y as a private tutor for his family.

Now as the house of this Lord Tchang was situated several miles from town, it was deemed best that Ming-Y should abide in the house of his employer. Accordingly the youth made ready all things necessary for his new sojourn and his parents, bidding him farewell, counseled him wisely, and cited to him the words of Lao-tseu and of the ancient sages:

> "By a beautiful face the world is filled with love; but Heaven may never be deceived thereby. Shouldst thou behold a woman coming from the East, look thou to the West; shouldst thou perceive a maiden approaching from the West, turn thy eyes to the East."

If Ming-Y did not heed this counsel in after days, it was only because of his youth and the thoughtlessness of a naturally joyous heart.

And he departed to abide in the house of Lord Tchang, while the autumn passed, and the winter also.

When the time of the second moon of spring was drawing near, and that happy day which the Chinese call *Hoa-tchao*, or, "The Birthday of a Hundred Flowers," a longing came upon Ming-Y to see his parents; and he opened his heart to the good Tchang, who not only gave him the permission he desired, but also pressed into his hand a silver gift of two ounces, thinking that the lad might wish to bring some little memento to his father and mother. For it is the Chinese custom, on the feast of Hoa-tchao, to make presents to friends and relations.

That day all the air was drowsy with blossom perfume, and vibrant with the droning of bees. It seemed to Ming-Y that the path he followed had not been trodden by any other for many long years; the grass was tall upon it; vast trees on either side interlocked their mighty and mossgrown arms above him, beshadowing the way; but the leafy obscurities quivered with birdsong, and the deep vistas of the wood were glorified by vapors of gold, and odorous with flower-breathings as a temple with incense. The dreamy joy of the day entered into the heart of Ming-Y; and he sat him down among the young blossoms, under the branches swaying against the violet sky, to drink in the perfume and the light, and to enjoy the great sweet silence. Even while thus reposing, a sound caused him to turn his eyes toward a shady place where wild peach-trees were in bloom; and he beheld a young woman, beautiful as the pinkening blossoms themselves, trying to hide among them. Though he looked for a moment only, Ming-Y could not avoid discerning the loveliness of her face, the golden purity of her complexion, and the brightness of her long eyes that sparkled under a pair of brows as daintily curved as the wings of the silk-worm butterfly outspread. Ming-Y at once turned his gaze away, and, rising quickly, proceeded on his journey. But so much embarrassed did he feel at the idea of those charming eyes peeping at him through the leaves, that he suffered the money he had been carrying in his sleeve to fall, without being aware of it. A few moments later he heard the patter of light feet running behind him, and a woman's voice calling him by name. Turning his face in great surprise, he saw a comely servant-maid, who said to him, "Sir, my mistress bade me pick up and return to you this silver which you dropped upon the road." Ming-Y thanked the girl gracefully, and requested her to convey his compliments to her mistress. Then he proceeded on his way through the perfumed silence, athwart the shadows that dreamed along the forgotten path, dreaming himself also, and feeling his heart beating with strange quickness at the thought of the beautiful being that he had seen.

It was just such another day when Ming-Y, returning by the same path, paused once more at the spot where the gracious figure had momentarily appeared before him. But this time he was surprised to perceive, through a long vista of immense trees, a dwelling that had previously escaped his notice—a country residence, not large, yet elegant to an unusual degree. The bright blue tiles of its curved and serrated double roof, rising above the foliage, seemed to blend their color with the luminous azure of the day; the green-and-gold designs of its carven porticos were exquisite artistic mockeries of leaves and flowers bathed in sunshine. And at the summit of terrace-steps before it, guarded by great porcelain tortoises, Ming-Y saw standing the mistress of the mansion— the idol of his passionate fancy—accompanied by the same waiting-maid who had borne to her his message of gratitude. While Ming-Y looked, he perceived that their eyes were upon him; they smiled and conversed together as if speaking about him; and, shy though he was, the youth found courage to salute the fair one from a distance. To his astonishment, the young servant beckoned him to approach; and opening a rustic gate half veiled by trailing plants bearing crimson flowers, Ming-Y advanced along the verdant alley leading to the terrace, with mingled feelings of surprise and timid joy. As he drew near, the beautiful lady withdrew from sight; but the maid waited at the broad steps to receive him, and said as he ascended:

"Sir, my mistress understands you wish to thank her for the trifling service she recently bade me do you, and requests that you will enter the house, as she knows you already by repute, and desires to have the pleasure of bidding you good-day."

Ming-Y entered bashfully, his feet making no sound upon a matting elastically soft as forest moss, and found himself in a reception-chamber vast, cool, and fragrant with scent of blossoms freshly gathered. A delicious quiet pervaded the mansion; shadows of flying birds passed over the bands of light that fell through the half-blinds of bamboo; great butterflies, with pinions of fiery color, found their way in, to hover a moment about the painted vases, and pass out again into the mysterious woods. And noiselessly as they, the young mistress of the mansion entered by another door, and kindly greeted the boy, who lifted his hands to his breast and bowed low in salutation. She was taller than he had deemed her, and supplely-slender as a beauteous lily; her black hair was interwoven with the creamy blossoms of the *chu-sha-kih;* her robes of pale silk took shifting tints when she moved, as vapors change hue with the changing of the light.

"If I be not mistaken," she said, when both had seated themselves after having exchanged the customary formalities of politeness, "my honored visitor is none other than Tien-chou, surnamed Ming-Y, educator of the children of my respected relative, the High Commissioner Tchang. As the family of Lord Tchang is my family also, I cannot but consider the teacher of his children as one of my own kin."

"Lady," replied Ming-Y, not a little astonished, "may I dare to inquire the name of your honored family, and to ask the relation which you hold to my noble patron?"

"The name of my poor family," responded the comely lady, "is

Ping—an ancient family of the city of Tching-tou. I am the daughter of a certain Sië of Moun-hao; Sië is my name, likewise; and I was married to a young man of the Ping family, whose name was Khang. By this marriage I became related to your excellent patron; but my husband died soon after our wedding, and I have chosen this solitary place to reside in during the period of my widowhood."

There was a drowsy music in her voice, as of the melody of brooks, the murmurings of spring; and such a strange grace in the manner of her speech as Ming-Y had never heard before. Yet, on learning that she was a widow, the youth would not have presumed to remain long in her presence without a formal invitation; and after having sipped the cup of rich tea presented to him, he arose to depart. Sië would not suffer him to go so quickly.

"Nay, friend," she said, "stay yet a little while in my house, I pray you; for, should your honored patron ever learn that you had been here, and that I had not treated you as a respected guest, and regaled you even as I would him, I know that he would be greatly angered. Remain at least to supper."

So Ming-Y remained, rejoicing secretly in his heart, for Sië seemed to him the fairest and sweetest being he had ever known, and he felt that he loved her more than his father and his mother. And while they talked the long shadows of the evening slowly blended into one violet darkness; the great citron-light of the sunset faded out; and those starry beings that are called the Three Councillors, who preside over life and death and the destinies of men, opened their cold bright eyes in the northern sky. Within the mansion of Sië the painted lanterns were lighted; the table was laid for the evening repast; and Ming-Y took his place at it, feeling little inclination to eat, and thinking only of the charming face before him. Observing that he scarcely tasted the dainties laid upon his plate, Sië pressed her young guest to partake of wine; and they drank several cups together. It was a purple wine, so cool that the cup into which it was poured became covered with vapory dew; yet it seemed to warm the veins with strange fire. To Ming-Y, as he drank, all things became more luminous as by enchantment; the walls of the chamber seemed to recede, and the roof to heighten; the lamps glowed like stars in their chains, and the voice of Sië floated to the boy's ears like some far melody heard through the spaces of a drowsy night. His heart swelled; his tongue loosened; and words flitted from his lips that he had fancied he could never dare to utter. Yet Sië sought not to restrain him, her lips gave no smile; but her long bright eyes seemed to laugh with pleasure at his words of praise, and to return his gaze of passionate admiration with affectionate interest.

"I have heard," she said, "of your rare talent, and of your many elegant accomplishments. I know how to sing a little, although I cannot claim to possess any musical learning; and now that I have the honor of finding myself in the society of a musical professor, I will venture to lay modesty aside, and beg you to sing a few songs with me. I should deem it no small gratification if you would condescend to examine my musical compositions."

"The honor and gratification, dear lady," replied Ming-Y, "will be mine; and I feel helpless to express the gratitude which the offer of so rare a favor deserves."

The serving-maid, obedient to the summons of a little silver gong, brought in the music and retired. Ming-Y took the manuscripts, and began to examine them with eager delight. The paper on which they were written had a pale yellow tint, and was light as a fabric of gossamer; but the characters were antiquely beautiful, as though they had been traced by the brush of Heï-song Ché-Tchoo himself—that divine Genius of Ink, who is no bigger than a fly; and the signatures attached to the compositions were the signatures of Youen-tchin, Kao-pien, and Thou-mou—might poets and musicians of the dynasty of Thang! Ming-Y could not repress a scream of delight at the sight of treasures so inestimable and so unique; scarcely could he summon resolution enough to permit them to leave his hands even for a moment.

"O Lady!" he cried, "these are veritably priceless things, surpassing in worth the treasures of all kings. This indeed is the handwriting of those great masters who sang five hundred years before our birth. How marvelously it has been preserved! Is not this the wondrous ink of which it was written: 'After centuries I remain firm as stone, and the letters that I make like lacquer'? And how divine the charm of this composition!—the song of Kao-pien, prince of poets, and Governor of Sze-tchouen five hundred years ago!"

"Kao-pien! darling Kao-pien!" murmured Sië, with a singular light in her yes. "Kao-pien is also my favorite. Dear Ming-Y, let us chant his verses together, to the melody of old—the music of those grand years when men were nobler and wiser than to-day."

And their voices rose through the perfumed night like the voices of the wonder-birds—of the Fung-hoang—blending together in liquid sweetness. Yet a moment, and Ming-Y, overcome by the witchery of his companion's voice, could only listen in speechless ecstasy, while the lights of the chamber swam dim before his sight, and tears of pleasure tickled down his cheeks.

So the ninth hour passed; and they continued to converse, and to drink the cool purple wine, and to sing the songs of the years of Thang, until far into the night. More than once Ming-Y thought of departing; but each time Sië would begin, in that silver-sweet voice of hers, so wondrous a story of the great poets of the past, and of the women whom they loved, that he became as one entranced; or she would sing for him a song so strange that all his senses seemed to die except that of hearing. And at last, as she paused to pledge him in a cup of wine, Ming-Y could not restrain himself from putting his arm about her round neck and drawing her dainty head close to him, and kissing the lips that were so much ruddier than the wine. Then their lips separated no more;—the night grew old, and they knew it not.

The birds awakened, the flowers opened their eyes to the rising sun, and Ming-Y found himself at last compelled to bid his lovely enchant-ress farewell. Sië, accompanying him to the terrace, kissed him fondly and said, "Dear boy, come hither as often as you are able—as often as your heart whispers you to come. I know you are not of those without faith and truth, who betray secrets; yet, being so young, you might also be sometimes thoughtless; and I pray you never to forget that only the stars have been the witness of our love. Speak of it to no living person, dearest; and take with you this little souvenir of our happy night."

And she presented him with an exquisite and curious little thing—a paper-weight in likeness of a côuchant lion, wrought from a jade-stone yellow as that created by a rainbow in honor of Kong-fu-tze. Tenderly the boy kissed the gift and the beautiful hand that gave it. "May the Spirits punish me," he vowed, "if ever I knowingly give you cause to reproach me, sweetheart!" And they separated with mutual vows.

That morning, on returning to the house of Lord Tchang, Ming-Y told the first falsehood which had ever passed his lips. He averred that his mother had requested him thenceforward to pass his nights at home, now that the weather had become so pleasant; for, though the way was somewhat long, he was strong and active, and needed both air and healthy exercise. Tchang believed all Ming-Y said, and offered no objection. Accordingly the lad found himself enabled to pass all his evenings at the house of the beautiful Sië. Each night they devoted to the same pleasures which had made their first acquaintance so charm-ing: they sang and conversed by turns; they played at chess—the learned game invented by Wu-Wang, which is an imitation of war; they composed pieces of weighty rhymes upon the flowers, the trees, the clouds, the streams, the birds, the bees. But in all accomplishments Sië far excelled her young sweetheart. Whenever they played at chess, it was always Ming-Y's general, Ming-Y's *tsiang*, who was surrounded and vanquished; when they composed verses, Sië's poems were ever superior to his in harmony of word-coloring, in elegance of form, in classic loftiness of thought. And the themes they selected were always the most difficult—those of the poets of the Thang dynasty; the songs they sang were also the songs of five hundred years before—the songs of Youen-tchin, of Thou-mou, of Kao-pien above all, high poet and ruler of the province of Sze-tchouen.

So the summer waxed and waned upon their love, and the luminous autumn came, with its vapors of phantom gold, its shadows of magical purple.

Then it unexpectedly happened that the father of Ming-Y, meeting his son's employer at Tching-tou, was asked by him: "Why must your boy continue to travel every evening to the city, now that the winter is approaching? The way is long, and when he returns in the morning he looks foredone with weariness. Why not permit him to slumber in my house during the season of snow?" And the father of Ming-Y, greatly astonished, responded: "Sir, my son has not visited the city, nor has he been to our house all this summer. I fear that he must have acquired wicked habits, and that he passes his nights in evil company—perhaps in gaming, or in drinking with the women of the flower-boats." But the High Commissioner returned:

"Nay! that is not to be thought of. I have never found any evil in the boy, and there are no taverns nor flower-boats nor any places of dissipation in our neighborhood. No doubt Ming-Y has found some amiable youth of his own age with whom to spend his evenings, and only told me an untruth for fear that I would not otherwise permit him to leave my residence. I beg that you will say nothing to him until I shall have sought to discover this mystery; and this very evening I shall send my servant to follow after him, and to watch whither he goes."

Pelou readily assented to this proposal, and promising to visit Tchang the following morning, returned to his home. In the evening, when Ming-Y left the house of Tchang, a servant followed him unobserved at a distance. But on reaching the most obscure portion of the road, the boy disappeared from sight as suddenly as though the earth had swallowed him. After having long sought after him in vain, the domestic returned in great bewilderment to the house, and related what had taken place. Tchang immediately sent a messenger to Pelou.

In the meantime Ming-Y, entering the chamber of his beloved, was surprised and deeply pained to find her in tears. "Sweetheart," she sobbed, wreathing her arms around his neck, "we are about to be separated forever, because of reasons which I cannot tell you. From the very first I knew this must come to pass, and nevertheless it seemed to me for the moment so cruelly sudden a loss, so unexpected a misfortune, that I could not prevent myself from weeping! After this night we shall never see each other again, beloved, and I know that you will not be able to forget me while you live; but I know also that you will become a great scholar, and that honors and riches will be showered upon you, and that some beautiful and loving woman will console you for my loss. And now let us speak no more of grief; but let us pass this last evening joyously, so that your recollection of me may not be a painful one, and that you may remember my laughter rather than my tears."

She brushed the bright drops away, and brought wine and music and the melodious *kin* of seven silken strings, and would not suffer Ming-Y to speak for one moment of the coming separation. And she sang him an ancient song about the calmness of summer lakes reflecting the blue of heaven only, and the calmness of the heart also, before the clouds of care and of grief and of weariness darken its little world. Soon they forgot their sorrow in the joy of song and wine; and those last hours seemed to Ming-Y more celestial than even the hours of their first bliss.

But when the yellow beauty of morning came their sadness returned, and they wept. Once more Sië accompanied her lover to the terrace steps; and as she kissed him farewell, she pressed into his hand a parting gift—a little brush-case of agate, wonderfully chiseled, and worthy the table of a great poet. And they separated forever, shedding many tears.

Still Ming-Y could not believe it was an eternal parting. "No!" he thought, "I shall visit her to-morrow; for I cannot live without her, and I feel assured that she cannot refuse to receive me." Such were the thoughts that filled his mind as he reached the house of Tchang, to find his father and his patron standing on the porch awaiting him. Ere he could speak a word, Pelou demanded:

"Son, in what place have you been passing your nights?"

Seeing that his falsehood had been discovered, Ming-Y dared not make any reply, and remained abashed and silent, with bowed head, in the presence of his father. Then Pelou, striking the boy violently with his staff, commanded him to divulge the secret; and at last, partly through fear of his parent, and partly through fear of the law which ordains that "*the son refusing to obey his father shall be punished with one hundred blows of the bamboo,*" Ming-Y faltered out the history of his love.

Tchang changed color at the boy's tale. "Child," exclaimed the High Commissioner, "I have no relative of the name of Ping; I have never heard of the woman you describe; I have never heard even of the house which you speak of. But I know also that you cannot dare to lie to Pelou, your honored father; there is some strange delusion in all this affair."

Then Ming-Y produced the gifts that Sië had given him—the lion of yellow jade, the brush-case of carven agate, also some original compositions made by the beautiful lady herself. The astonishment of Tchang was now shared by Pelou. Both observed that the brush-case of agate and the lion of jade bore the appearance of objects that had lain buried in the earth for centuries, and were of a workmanship beyond the power of living man to imitate; while the compositions proved to be veritable masterpieces of poetry, written in the style of the poets of the Dynasty of Thang.

"Friend Pelou," cried the High Commissioner, "let us immediately accompany the boy to the place where he obtained these miraculous things and apply the testimony of our senses to this mystery; the boy is no doubt telling the truth; yet his story passes my understanding." And all three proceeded toward the place of the habitation of Sië.

But when they had arrived at the shadiest part of the road, where the perfumes were most sweet and the mosses were greenest, and the fruits of the wild peach flushed most pinkly, Ming-Y, gazing though the groves, uttered a cry of dismay. Where the azure-tiled roof had risen against the sky, there was now only the blue emptiness of air; where the green-and-gold façade had been, there was visible only the flickering of leaves under the aureate autumn light; and where the broad terrace had extended, could be discerned only a ruin—a tomb so ancient, so deeply gnawed by moss, that the name graven upon it was no longer decipherable. The home of Sië had disappeared.

All suddenly the High Commissioner smote his forehead with his hand, and turning to Pelou, recited the well-known verse of the ancient poet Tching-Kou:

"Surely the peach-flowers blossom over the tomb of Sië-Thao."

"Friend Pelou," continued Tchang, "the beauty who bewitched your son was no other than she whose tomb stands there in ruin before us! Did she not say she was wedded to Ping Khang? There is no family of that name but Ping-Khang is indeed the name of a broad alley in the city near. There was a dark riddle in all that she said. She called herself Sië of Moun-Hiao; there is no person of that name, there is no street of that name; but the Chinese characters *Moun* and *Hiao*, placed together, form the character, 'Kiao.' Listen! The alley Ping-Khang, situated in the street Kiao, was the place where dwelt the great courtesans of the dynasty of Thang! Did she not sing the songs of Kao-pien? And upon the brush-case and the paper-weight she gave your son, are there not characters which read, '*Pure object of art belonging to Kao of the city of Pho-hai*'? That city no longer exists; but the memory of Kao-pien remains, for he was governor of the province of Sze-tchouen, and a mighty poet. And when he dwelt in the land of Chou, was not his favorite the beautiful wanton Sië—Sië-Thao, unmatched for grace among all the women of her day. It was he who made her a gift of those manuscripts of song; it was he who gave her those objects of rare art. Sië-Thao died not as other women die. Her limbs may have crumbled to dust; yet something of her still lives in this deep wood, her Shadow still haunts this shadowy place."

Tchang ceased to speak. A vague fear fell upon the three. The thin mists of the morning made dim the distances of green, and deepened the ghostly beauty of the woods. A faint breeze passed by, leaving a trail of blossom-scent—a last odor of dying flowers—thin as that which clings to the silk of a forgotten robe; and, as it passed, the trees seemed to whisper across the silence, "*Sië-Thao.*"

Fearing greatly for his son, Pelou sent the lad away at once to the city of Kwang-tchau-fu. And there in after years, Ming-Y obtained high dignities and honors by reason of his talents and his learning; and he married the daughter of an illustrious house, by whom he became the father of sons and daughters famous for their virtues and their accomplishments. Never could he forget Sië-Thao; and yet it is said that he never spoke of her—not even to his children when they begged him to tell them the story of two beautiful objects that always lay upon his writing table; a lion of yellow jade, and a brush-case of carven agate.

A FICKLE WIDOW

(Anonymous: 15th Century A.D., or before)

A FICKLE WIDOW, which also appeared originally in the *Marvellous Tales*, presents a striking contrast to *The Story of Ming-Y*. If the author was interested in pointing a moral, he was yet more interested in satirizing the frailties of human nature. It is impossible to tell whether there was a common source for this story and *The Matron of Ephesus* (the tale is retold by Anatole France), but in view of the lack of evidence it is reasonable to conclude that the Roman writer, like the Chinese, was inspired by a certain scepticism regarding the fidelity of the other sex.

This story is translated by R. K. Douglas, and appears in the volume *Chinese Stories*, published in 1893 by William Blackwood & Sons, publishers, by whose permission and that of Mr. R. K. Douglas it is here reprinted.

A FICKLE WIDOW

(From *Marvellous Tales, Ancient and Modern*)

AT a distance from the capital, and in the peaceful retirement of the country there dwelt many centuries ago a philosopher named Chwang, who led a pleasurable existence in the society of his third wife, and in the study of the doctrines of his great master, Lao-tsze.

Like many philosophers, Chwang had not been fortunate in his early married life. His first wife died young; his second he found it necessary to divorce, on account of misconduct; but in the companionship of the Lady T'ien he enjoyed a degree of happiness which had previously been denied him. Being a philosopher, however, he found it essential to his peace that he should occasionally exchange his domestic surroundings for the hillsides and mountain solitudes. On one such expedition he came unexpectedly on a newly made grave at the side of which was seated a young woman dressed in mourning, who was gently fanning the new mound. So strange a circumstance was evidently one into which a philosopher should inquire. He therefore approached the lady, and in gentle accents said, "May I ask what you are doing?"

"Well," replied the lady, "the fact is that this grave contains my husband. And, stupid man, just before he died he made me promise that I would not marry again until the soil above his grave should be dry. I watched it for some days, but it got dry so very slowly that I am fanning it to hasten the process." So saying she looked up into Chwang's face with so frank and engaging a glance that the philosopher at once decided to enlist himself in her service.

"Your wrists are not strong enough for such work," he said. "Let me relieve you at it."

"By all means," replied the lady briskly. "Here is the fan, and I shall owe you an everlasting debt of gratitude if you will fan it dry as quickly as possible."

Without more ado, Chwang set to work, and by the exercise of his magical powers he extracted every drop of moisture from the grave with a few waves of the fan. The lady was delighted with his success, and with the sunniest smile said, "How can I thank you sufficiently for your kindness! As a small mark of my gratitude, let me present you with this embroidered fan which I had in reserve; and as a token of my esteem, I really must ask you to accept one of my silver hairpins." With these words she presented the philosopher with the fan, and drawing out one of her ornamented hairpins, she offered it for his acceptance. The philosopher took the fan, but, possibly having the fear of Lady T'ien before his eyes, he declined the pin. The incident made him thoughtful, and as he seated himself again in his thatched hall, he sighed deeply.

"Why are you sighing?"' inquired the Lady T'ien, who happened to enter at that moment, "and where does the fan come from which you hold in your hand?"

Thus invited, Chwang related all that had passed at the tomb. As he proceeded with the tale, Lady T'ien's countenance fell, and when he had concluded she broke forth indignantly, inveighing against the young widow, who she vowed was a disgrace to her sex. So soon as she had exhausted her vituperations, Chwang quietly repeated the proverb, "Knowing men's faces is not like knowing their hearts." ·

Interpreting this use of the saying as implying some doubts as to the value of her protestations, Lady T'ien exclaimed:

"How dare you condemn all women as though they were all formed in the same mold with this shameless widow? I wonder you are not afraid of calling down a judgment on yourself for such an injustice to me, and others like me."

"What need is there of all this violence?" rejoined her husband. "Now, tell me, if I were to die, would you, possessed as you are of youth and beauty, be content to remain a widow for five, or even three years?"'

"A faithful minister does not serve two princes, and a virtuous woman never thinks of a second husband," sententiously replied the lady. "If fate were to decree that you should die, it would not be a question of three years or of five years, for never, so long as life lasted, would I dream of a second marriage."

"It is hard to say, it is hard to say," replied Chwang.

"Do you think," rejoined his wife, "that women are like men, destitute of virtue and devoid of justice? When one wife is dead you look out for another, you divorce this one and take that one; but we women are for one saddle to one horse. Why do you say these things to annoy me?"

With these words she seized the fan and tore it to shreds.

"Calm yourself," said her husband; "I only hope, if occasion offers, you will act up to your protestations."

Not many days after this Chwang fell dangerously ill, and as the symptoms increased in severity, he thus addressed his wife:

"I feel that my end is approaching, and that it is time I should bid you farewell. How unfortunate that you destroyed that fan the other day! You would have found it useful for drying my tomb."

"Pray, my husband, do not at such a moment suggest suspicions of me. Have I not studied the 'Book of Rites,' and have I not learned from it to follow one husband, and one only? If you doubt my sincerity, I will die in your presence to prove to you that what I say, I say in all faithfulness."

"I desire no more," replied Chwang; and then, as weakness overcame him, he added faintly, "I die. My eyes grow dim."

With these words he sank back motionless and breathless.

Having assured herself that her husband was dead, the Lady T'ien broke out into loud lamentations, and embraced the corpse again and again. For days and nights she wept and fasted, and constantly dwelt in her thoughts on the virtues and wisdom of the deceased. As was customary, on the death of so learned a man as Chwang, the neighbors all came to offer their condolences and to volunteer their assistance. Just as the last of these had retired, there arrived at the door a young and elegant scholar whose face was like a picture, and whose lips looked as though they had been smeared with vermilion. He was dressed in a violet silk robe, and wore a black cap, an embroidered girdle, and scarlet shoes. His servant announced that he was a Prince of the Kingdom of Tsoo, and he himself added by way of explanation:

"Some years ago I communicated to Chwang my desire to become his disciple. In furtherance of this purpose I came hither, and now, to my inexpressible regret, I find on my arrival that my master is dead."

To evince his respectful sorrow, the Prince at once exchanged his colored clothing for mourning garments, and prostrating himself before the coffin, struck his forehead four times on the ground, and sobbed forth, "Oh, learned Chwang, I am indeed unfortunate in not having been permitted to receive your instructions face to face. But to show my regard and affection for your memory, I will here remain and mourn for you a hundred days."

With these words he prostrated himself again four times, while he watered the earth with his tears. When more composed, he begged to be allowed to pay his respects to Lady T'ien, who, however, thrice declined to see him, and only at last consented when it was pointed out to her that, according to the most recondite authorities, the wives of deceased instructors should not refuse to see their husband's disciples.

After then receiving the Prince's compliments with downcast eyes, the Lady T'ien ventured just to cast one glance at her guest, and was so struck by his beauty and the grace of his figure, that a sentiment of more than interest suffused her heart. She begged him to take up his abode in her house, and when dinner was prepared, she blended her sighs with his. As a token of her esteem, so soon as the repast was ended, she brought him the copies of "The Classic of Nan-hwa," and the "Sûtra of Reason and of Virtue," which her husband had been in the habit of using, and presented them to the Prince. He, on his part, in fulfilment of his desire of mourning for his master, daily knelt and lamented by the side of the coffin, and thither also the Lady T'ien repaired to breathe her sighs. These constant meetings provoked short conversations, and the glances, which on these occasions were exchanged between them, gradually betook less of condolence and more of affection, as time went on. It was plain that already the Prince was half enamored, while the lady was deeply in love. Being desirous of learning some particulars about her engaging guest, she one evening summoned his servant to her apartment, and having plied him with wine, inquired from him whether his master was married.

"My master," replied the servant, "has never yet been married."

"What qualities does he look for in the fortunate woman he will choose for his wife?" inquired the lady.

"My master says," replied the servant, who had taken quite as much wine as was good for him, "that if he could obtain a renowned beauty like yourself, madam, his heart's desire would be fulfilled."

"Did he really say so? Are you sure you are telling me the truth?" eagerly asked the lady.

"Is it likely that an old man like me would tell you a lie?" replied the servant.

"If it be so, will you then act as a go-between and arrange a match between us?"

"My master has already spoken to me of the matter, and would desire the alliance above all things, if it were not for the respect due from a disciple to a deceased master, and for the animadversions to which such a marriage would give rise."

"But as a matter of fact," said the Lady T'ien, "the Prince was never my husband's disciple; and as to our neighbors about here, they are too few and insignificant to make their animadversions worth a thought."

The objections having thus been overcome, the servant undertook to negotiate with his master, and promised to bring word of the result at any hour of the day or night at which he might have anything to communicate.

So soon as the man was gone, the Lady T'ien gave way to excited impatience. She went backwards and forwards to the chamber of death, that she might pass the door of the Prince's room, and even listened at his window, hoping to hear him discussing with his servant the proposed alliance. All, however, was still until she approached the coffin, when she heard an unmistakable sound of hard breathing. Shocked and terrified, she exclaimed, "Can it be possible that the dead has come to life again!"

A light, however, relieved her apprehensions by discovering the form of the Prince's servant lying in a drunken sleep on a couch by the corpse. At any other time such disrespect to the deceased would have drawn from her a torrent of angry rebukes, but on this occasion she thought it best to say nothing, and on the next morning she accosted the defaulter without any reference to his escapade of the night before. To her eager inquiries the servant answered that his master was satisfied on the points she had combated on the preceding evening, but that there were still three unpropitious circumstances which made him hesitate.

"What are they?" asked the lady.

"First," answered the man, "my master says that the presence of the coffin in the saloon makes it difficult to conduct marriage festivities in ccordance with usage; secondly, that the illustrious Chwang having so deeply loved his wife, and that affection having been so tenderly returned by her in recognition of his great qualities, he fears that a second husband would probably not be held entitled to a like share of affection; and thirdly, that not having brought his luggage, he has neither the money nor the clothes necessary to play the part of a bridegroom."

"These circumstances need form no obstacle to our marriage," replied the lady. "As to the first objection, I can easily have the coffin removed into a shed at the back of the house; then as to the second, though my husband was a great Taoist authority, he was not by any means a very moral man. After his first wife's death he married a second, whom he divorced, and just before his own decease, he flirted outrageously with a widow whom he found fanning her husband's grave on the hill yonder. Why, then, should your master, young, handsome, and a prince, doubt the quality of my affection? Then as to the third objection, your master need not trouble himself about the expenses connected with our marriage; I will provide them. At this moment I have twenty taels of silver in my room, and these I will readily give him to provide himself clothes withal. Go back, then, and tell the Prince what I say, and remind that there is no time like the present, and that there could be no more felicitous evening for our marriage than that of to-day."

Carrying the twenty taels of silver in his hand, the servant returned to his master, and presently brought back word to the lady that the Prince was convinced by her arguments, and ready for the ceremony.

On receipt of this joyful news, Lady T'ien exchanged her mourning for wedding garments, painted her cheeks, reddened her lips, and ordered some villagers to carry Chwang's coffin into a hut at the back of the house, and to prepare for the wedding. She herself arranged the lights and candles in the hall, and when the time arrived stood ready to receive the Prince, who presently entered, wearing the insignia of his official rank, and dressed in a gayly embroidered tunic. Bright as a polished gem and a gold setting, the two stood beneath the nuptial torch, radiant with beauty and love. At the conclusion of the ceremony, with every demonstration of affection, the Prince led his bride by the hand into the nuptial chamber. Suddenly, as they were about to retire to rest, the Prince was seized with violent convulsions. His face became distorted, his eyebrows stood on end, and he fell to the ground, beating his breast with his hands.

The Lady T'ien, frantic with grief, embraced him, rubbed his chest, and when these remedies failed to revive him, called in his old servant.

"Has your master ever had any fits like this before?" she hurriedly inquired.

"Often," replied the man, "and no medicine ever alleviates his sufferings; in fact, there is only one thing that does.'"

"Oh, what is that?" asked the lady.

"The brains of a man, boiled in wine," answered the servant. "In Tsoo, when he has these attacks, the king, his father, beheads a male-factor and takes his brain to form the decoction; but how is it possible here to obtain such a remedy?"

"Will the brains of a man who has died a natural death do?" asked the lady.

"Yes, if forty-nine days have not elapsed since the death."

"My former husband's would do then. He has only been dead twenty days. Nothing will be easier than to open the coffin and take them out."

"But would you be willing to do it?"

"I and the Prince are now husband and wife. A wife with her body serves her husband, and should I refuse to do this for him out of regard for a corpse, which is fast becoming dust?"

So saying, she told the servant to look after his master, and seizing a hatchet, went straight to the hut to which the corpse had been removed. Having arranged the light conveniently, she tucked up her sleeves, clenched her teeth, and with both hands brought down the hatchet on the coffin-lid. Blow after blow fell upon the wood, and at the thirty-first stroke the plank yielded, and the head of the coffin was forced open. Panting with her exertions, she cast a glance on the corpse preparatory to her further grim office, when, to her inexpressible horror, Chwang sighed twice, opened his eyes, and sat up. With a piercing shriek she shrank backwards, and dropped the hatchet from her palsied hands.

"My dear wife," said the philosopher, "help me to rise."

Afraid to do anything else but obey, she assisted him out of the coffin and offered him support, while he led the way, lamp in hand, to her chamber. Remembering the sight that would there meet his eyes, the wretched woman trembled as they approached the door. What was her relief, however, to find that the Prince and his servant had disappeared. Taking advantage of this circumstance, she assumed every woman's wile, and in softest accents, said, "Ever since your death you have been in my thoughts day and night. Just now, hearing a noise in your coffin, and remembering how, in the tales of old, souls are said to return to their bodies, the hope occurred to me that it might be so in your case, and I took a hatchet to open your coffin. Thank Heaven and Earth my felicity is complete; you are once more by my side."

"Many thanks, madam," said Chwang, "for your deep consideration. But may I ask why you are dressed in such gay clothing."

"When I went to open your coffin, I had, as I say, a secret presentiment of my good fortune, and I dared not receive you back to life in mourning attire."

"Oh," replied her husband, "but there is one other circumstance which I should like to have explained. Why was not my coffin placed in the saloon, but tossed into a ruined barn?"

To this question Lady T'ien's woman's wit failed to supply an answer. Chwang looked at the cups and wine which formed the relics of the marriage feast, but made no other remark thereon, except to tell his wife to warm him some wine. This she did, employing all her most engaging wiles to win a smile from her husband; but he steadily rejected her advances, and presently, pointing with his finger over her shoulder, he said, "Look at those two men behind you."

She turned with an instinctive knowledge that she would see the Prince and his servant in the courtyard, and so she did. Horrified at the sight, she turned her eyes toward her husband, but he was not there. Again looking towards the courtyard she found that the prince and his servant had now disappeared, and that Chwang was once more at her side. Perceiving then the true state of the case, that the Prince and his servant were but Chwang's other self, which he by his magical power was able to project into separate existences, she saw that all attempts at concealment were vain; and taking her girdle from her waist, she tied it to a beam and hung herself on the spot.

So soon as life was extinct Chwang put his frail wife into the coffin from which he had lately emerged, and setting fire to his house, burnt it with its contents to ashes. The only things saved from the flames were the "Sûtra of Reason and of Virtue," and "The Classic of Nan-hwa," which were found by some neighbors, and carefully treasured.

As to Chwang, it is said that he set out on a journey towards the West. What his ultimate destination was is not known, but one thing is certain, and that is, that he remained a widower for the rest of his life.

P'U SUNG-LING

(1622—1679?)

THE *Strange Stories* of P'u Sung-Ling have delighted all classes in China for over two centuries, but about their editor we have little information. He was born in 1622 in the Province of Shantung. Though he studied in order to become a high government official, he was not especially interested in his academic work, and failed to secure his degree. To this failure the idea of his celebrated collection is supposed to be due. He is regarded by the Chinese as a master-critic of style and composition; even in translation it is possible to enjoy some of the niceties of expression in these stories, and their construction is always a delight. Here again, as in the earlier Chinese stories, we perceive the inherent passion of the Chinese for moralizing, though it will be admitted that they are highly skilled in the art of making their morality palatable.

This story is translated by Herbert A. Giles, and appears in the volume *Strange Stories from a Chinese Studio*, published by Kelly and Walsh, Shanghai, by whose permission and that of the translator, it is here reprinted. (The English publisher is T. Werner Laurie.)

THE VIRTUOUS DAUGHTER-IN-LAW

(From *Strange Stories from a Chinese Studio*)

AN TA-CH'ENG was a Chung-ch'ing man. His father, who had gained the master's degree, died early; and his brother Erh-ch'êng was a mere boy. He himself had married a wife from the Ch'ên family, whose name was Shan-hu; and this young lady had much to put up with from the violent and malicious disposition of her husband's mother. However, she never complained; and every morning dressed herself up smart, and went in to pay her respects to the old lady. Once when Ta-ch'êng was ill, his mother abused Shan-hu for dressing so nicely; whereupon Shan-hu went back and changed her clothes; but even then Mrs. An was not satisfied, and began to tear her own hair with rage. Ta-ch'êng, who was a very filial son, at once gave his wife a beating, and this put an end to the scene. From that moment his mother hated her more than ever, and although she was everything that a daughter-in-law could be, would never exchange a word with her. Ta-ch'êng then treated her in much the same way, that his mother might see he would have nothing to do with her; still the old lady wasn't pleased, and was always blaming Shan-hu for every trifle that occurred. "A wife," cried Ta-ch'êng, "is taken to wait upon her mother-in-law. This state of thing hardly looks like the wife doing her duty." So he bade Shan-hu begone, and sent an old maidservant to see her home: but when Shan-hu got outside the village-gate, she burst into tears, and said, "How can a girl who has failed in her duties as a wife ever dare to look her parents in the face? I had better die." Thereupon she drew a pair of scissors and stabbed herself in the throat, covering herself immediately with blood. The servant prevented any further mischief, and supported her to the house of her husband's aunt, who was a widow living by herself, and who made Shan-hu stay with her. The servant went back and told Ta-ch'êng, and he bade her say nothing to any one, for fear his mother should hear of it. In a few days Shan-hu's wound was healed, and Ta-ch'êng went off to ask his aunt to send her away. His aunt invited him in, but he declined, demanding loudly that Shan-hu should be turned out; and in a few moments Shan-hu herself came forth, and inquired what she had done. Ta-ch'êng said she had failed in her duty towards his mother; whereupon Shan-hu hung her head and made no answer, while tears of blood* trickled from her eyes and stained her dress all over. Ta-ch'êng was much touched by this spectacle, and went away without saying any more; but before long his mother heard all about it, and, hurrying off to the aunt's, began abusing her roundly. This the aunt would not stand, and said it was all the fault of her own bad temper, adding: "The girl has already left you, and do you still claim to decide with whom she is to live? Miss Ch'ên is staying with me, not your daughter-in-law; so you had better mind your own business." This made Mrs. An furious; but she was at a loss for an answer, and, seeing that the aunt was firm, she went off home abashed and in tears.

Shan-hu herself was very much upset, and determined to seek shelter elsewhere, finally taking up her abode with Mrs. An's elder sister, a lady of sixty odd years of age, whose son had died, leaving his wife and child to his mother's care. This Mrs. Yü was extremely fond of Shan-hu; and when she heard the facts of the case, said it was all her sister's horrid disposition, and proposed to send Shan-hu back. The latter, however, would not hear of this, and they continued to live together like mother and daughter; neither would Shan-hu accept the invitation of her two brothers to return home and marry some one else, but remained there with Mrs. Yü, earning enough to live upon by spinning and such work.

Ever since Shan-hu had been sent away, Ta-ch'êng's mother had been endeavoring to get him another wife; but the fame of her temper had spread far and wide, and no one would entertain her proposals. In three or four years Erh-ch'êng had grown up, and he had to be married first. His wife was a young lady named Tsang-ku, whose temper turned out to be something fearful, and far more ungovernable even than her mother-in-law's. When the latter only looked angry, Tsang-ku was already at the shrieking stage; and Erh-ch'êng, being of a very meek disposition, dared not side with either. Thus it came about that Mrs. An began to be in mortal fear of Tsang-ku; and whenever her daughter-in-law was in a rage she would try and

---

* Such is the Chinese idiom for what we should call "bitter" tears. This phrase is constantly employed in the notices of the death of a parent sent round to friends and relatives—Translator's note.

turn off her anger with a smile. She seemed never to be able to please
Tsang-ku, who in her turn worked her mother-in-law like a slave,
Ta-ch'êng himself not venturing to interfere, but only assisting his
mother in washing the dishes and sweeping the floor. Mother and son
would often go to some secluded spot, and there in secret tell their
griefs to one another; but before long Mrs. An was stretched upon a
sick-bed with nobody to attend to her except Ta-ch'êng. He watched
her day and night without sleeping, until both eyes were red and inflamed; and then when he went to summon the younger son to take
his place, Tsang-ku told him to leave the house. Ta-ch'êng now went
off to inform Mrs. Yü, hoping that she would come and assist; and
he had hardly finished his tale of woe before Shan-hu walked in. In
great confusion at seeing her, he would have left immediately had not
Shan held out her arms across the door; whereupon he bolted underneath them and escaped. He did not dare to tell his mother, and shortly
afterwards Mrs. Yü arrived, to the great joy of Ta-ch'êng's mother,
who made her stay in the house. Every day something nice was sent
for Mrs. Yü, and even when she told the servants that there was no
occasion for it, she having all she wanted at her sister's, the things still
came as usual. However, she kept none of them for herself, but gave
what came to the invalid, who gradually began to improve. Mrs. Yü's
grandson also used to come by his mother's orders, and inquire after
the sick lady's health, besides bringing a packet of cakes and so on
for her. "Ah, me!" cried Mrs. An, "what a good daughter-in-law
you have got, to be sure. What have you done to her?" "What sort
of a person was the one you sent away?" asked her sister in reply.
"She wasn't as bad as some one I know of," said Mrs. An, "though
not so good as yours." "When she was here you had but little to do,"
replied Mrs. Yü; "and when you were angry she took no notice of it.
How was she not as good?" Mrs. An then burst into tears, and saying
how sorry she was, asked if Shan-hu had married again; to which
Mrs. Yü replied that she did not know, but would make inquiries.
In a few more days the patient was quite well, and Mrs. Yü proposed
to return; her sister, however, begged her to stay, and declared she
should die if she didn't. Mrs. Yü then advised that Erh-ch'êng and his
wife should live in a separate house, and Erh-ch'êng spoke about it to
his wife; but she would not agree, and abused both Ta-ch'êng and
Mrs. Yü alike. It ended by Ta-ch'êng giving up a large share of the
property, and ultimately Tsang-ku consented, and a deed of separation
was drawn up. Mrs. Yü then went away, returning next day with a
sedan-chair to carry her sister back; and no sooner had the latter put
her foot inside Mrs. Yü's door, than she asked to see the daughter-in-
law, whom she immediately began to praise very highly. "Ah," said
Mrs. Yü, "she's a good girl, with her little faults like the rest of us;

but even if your daughter-in-law were as good as mine, you would not be able to appreciate her." "Alas!" replied her sister, "I must have been as senseless as a statue not to have seen what she was." "I wonder what Shan-hu, whom you turned out of doors, says of you?" rejoined Mrs. Yü. "Why, she swears at me, of course," answered Mrs. An. "If you examine yourself honestly and find nothing which should make people swear at you, is it at all likely you would be sworn at?" asked Mrs. Yü. "Well, all people are fallible," replied the other, "and as I know she is not perfect, I conclude she would naturally swear at me." "If a person has just cause for resentment, and yet does not indulge that resentment, it is obvious how he will repay kindness; or if any one has just cause for leaving another and yet does not do so, it is obvious how he will act under good treatment. Now, all the things that were sent when you were ill, and all the various little attentions, did not come from my daughter-in-law, but from yours." Mrs. An was amazed at hearing this, and asked for some explanation; whereupon Mrs. Yü continued, "Shan-hu has been living here for a long time. Everything she sent to you was bought with money earned by her spinning, and that, too, continued late into the night." Mrs. An here burst into tears, and begged to be allowed to see Shan-hu, who came in at Mrs. Yü's summons, and threw herself on the ground at her mother-in-law's feet. Mrs. An was much abashed, and beat her head with shame; but Mrs. Yü made it all up between them, and they became mother and daughter as at first. In about ten days they went home, and, as their property was not enough to support them, Ta-ch'êng had to work with his pen while his wife did the same with her needle. Erh-ch'êng was quite well off, but his brother would not apply to him, neither did he himself offer to help them. Tsang-ku, too, would have nothing to do with her sister-in-law, because she had been divorced; and Shan-hu in her turn, knowing what Tsang-ku's temper was, made no great efforts to be friendly. So the two brothers lived apart; * and when Tsang-ku was in one of her outrageous moods, all the others would stop their ears, till at length there was only her husband and the servants upon whom to vent her spleen. One day a maidservant of hers committed suicide, and the father of the girl brought an action against Tsang-ku for having caused her death. Erh-ch'êng went off to the mandarin's to take her place as defendant, but only got a good beating for his pains, as the magistrate insisted that Tsang-ku herself should appear and answer to the charge, in spite of all her friends could do. The consequence was she had her fingers squeezed † until the flesh was entirely taken off; and the magistrate

* A disgraceful state of things, in the eyes of the Chinese.—Translator's note.

† An illegal form of punishment, under the present dynasty, which authorizes only *bambooing* of two kinds.—Translator's note.

being a grasping man, a very severe fine was inflicted as well. Erh-ch'êng had now to mortgage his property before he could raise enough money to get Tsang-ku released; but before long the mortgage threatened to foreclose, and he was obliged to enter into negotiations for the sale of it to an old gentleman of the village named Jen. Now Mr. Jen knowing that half the property had belonged to Ta-ch'êng, said the deed of sale must be signed by the elder brother as well; however, when Ta-ch'êng reached his house, the old man cried out, "I am Mr. An, M.A.; who is this Jen that he should buy my property?" Then, looking at Ta-ch'êng, he added, "The filial piety of you and your wife has obtained for me in the realms below this interview"; upon which Ta-ch'êng said, "O father, since you have this power, help my younger brother." "The unfilial son and the vixenish daughter-in-law," said the old man, "deserve no pity. Go home and quickly buy back our ancestral property." "We have barely enough to live upon," replied Ta-ch'êng; "where, then, shall we find the necessary money?" "Beneath the crape myrtle-tree," answered his father, "you will find a store of silver, which you may take and use for this purpose." Ta-ch'êng would have questioned him further, but the old gentleman said no more, recovering consciousness shortly afterwards without knowing a word of what had happened. Ta-ch'êng went back and told his brother, who did not altogether believe the story; Tsang-ku, however, hurried off with a number of men, and had soon dug a hole four or five feet deep, at the bottom of which they found a quantity of bricks and stones, but no gold. She then gave up the idea and returned home, Ta-ch'êng having meanwhile warned his mother and wife not to go near the place while she was digging. When Tsang-ku left, Mrs. An went herself to have a look, and seeing only bricks and earth mingled together, she too, retraced her steps. Shan-hu was the next to go, and she found the hole full of silver bullion; and then Ta-ch'êng repaired to the spot and saw that there was no mistake about it. Not thinking it right to apply this heirloom to his own private use, he now summoned Erh-ch'êng to share it; and having obtained twice as much as was necessary to redeem the estate, the brothers returned to their homes. Erh-ch'êng and Tsang-ku opened their half together, when lo! the bag was full of tiles and rubbish. They at once suspected Ta-ch'êng of deceiving them, and Erh-ch'êng ran off to see how things were going at his brother's. He arrived just as Ta-ch'êng was spreading the silver on the table, and with his mother and wife rejoicing over their acquisition; and when he had told them what had occurred, Ta-ch'êng expressed much sympathy for him, and at once presented him with his own half of the treasure. Erh-ch'êng was delighted, and paid off the mortgage on the land, feeling very grateful to his brother for such kindness. Tsang-ku, however, declared it was a proof that Ta-ch'êng had been cheating him; "for how otherwise," argued she, "can you understand a man sharing anything with another, and then resigning his own half?"

Erh-ch'êng himself did not know what to think of it; but next day the mortgagee sent to say that the money paid in was all imitation silver, and that he was about to lay the case before the authorities. Husband and wife were greatly alarmed at this, and Tsang-ku exclaimed, "Well, I never thought your brother was as bad as this. He's simply trying to take your life." Erh-ch'êng himself was in a terrible fright, and hurried off to the mortgagee to entreat for mercy; but as the latter was extremely angry and would hear of no compromise, Erh-ch'êng was obliged to make over the property to him to dispose of himself. The money was then returned, and when he got home he found that two lumps had been cut through, showing merely an outside layer of silver, about as thick as an onion-leaf, covering nothing but copper within. Tsang-ku and Erh-ch'êng then agreed to keep the broken pieces themselves, but sent the rest back to Ta-ch'êng, with a message, saying that they were deeply indebted to him for all his kindness, and that they had ventured to retain two of the lumps of silver out of compliment to the giver; also that the property which remained to them was still equal to Ta-ch'êng's, that they had no use for much land, and accordingly had abandoned it, and that Ta-ch'êng could redeem it or not as he pleased. Ta-ch'êng, who did not perceive the intention in all this, refused to accept the land; however, Erh-ch'êng entreated him to do so, and at last he consented. When he came to weigh the money, he found it was five ounces short, and therefore bade Shan-hu pawn something from her jewel-box to make up the amount, with which he proceeded to pay off the mortgage. The mortgagee, suspecting it was the same money that had been offered him by Erh-ch'êng, cut the pieces in halves, and saw that it was all silver of the purest quality. Accordingly he accepted it in liquidation of his claim, and handed the mortgage back to Ta-ch'êng. Meanwhile, Erh-ch'êng had been expecting some catastrophe; but when he found that the mortgaged land had been redeemed, he did not know what to make of it. Tsang-ku thought that at the time of the digging Ta-ch'êng had concealed the genuine silver, and immediately rushed off to his house, and began to revile them all round. Ta-ch'êng now understood why they had sent him back the money; and Shan-hu laughed and said, "The property is safe; why, then, this anger?" Thereupon she made Ta-ch'êng hand over the deeds to Tsang-ku.

One night after this Erh-ch'êng's father appeared to him in a dream, and reproached him, saying, "Unfilial son, unfraternal brother, your hour is at hand. Wherefore usurp rights that do not belong to you?" In the morning Erh-ch'êng told Tsang-ku of his dream, and proposed to return the property to his brother; but she only laughed at him for a fool. Just then the eldest of his two sons, a boy of seven, died of small-pox, and this frightened Tsang-ku so that she agreed to restore the deeds. Ta-ch'êng would not accept them; and now the second child, a boy of three, died also; whereupon Tsang-ku seized the deeds, and threw them into her brother-in-law's house. Spring was over, but the land was in a terribly neglected state; so Ta-ch'êng set to work and put in in order again. From this moment Tsang-ku was a changed woman towards her mother- and sister-in-law; and when, six months later, Mrs. An died, she was so grieved that she refused to take any nourishment. "Alas!" cried she, "that my mother-in-law has died thus early, and prevented me from waiting upon her. Heaven will not allow me to retrieve my past errors." Tsang-ku had thirteen children,* but as none of them lived, they were obliged to adopt one of Ta-ch'êng's,** who, with his wife, lived to a good old age, and had three sons, two of whom took their doctor's degree. People said this was a reward for filial piety and brotherly love.

* Five is considered a large number for an ordinary Chinese woman.—Translator's note.
** In order to leave some one behind to look after their graves and perform the duties of ancestral worship. No one can well refuse to give a son to be adopted by a childless brother.—Translator's note.

Japan

INTRODUCTION

IN the Eighth Century A.D. (712) the annals of the chief families of Japan were collected in a work known as the *Kojiki*, or *Record of Ancient Matters*. This constituted the first writing of note in Japanese, but it was not until the appearance eight years later of the volume called *Nihongi*, or *Chronicles of Japan*, that Japanese literature can be said to have begun. The *Kojiki* was in the language of old Japan, while the *Nihongi* was in the classical Chinese, which superseded the Japanese and was in use until the Seventeenth Century. In the Eighteenth Century Motoori composed a work of forty-four volumes devoted to the elucidation of the *Kojiki* called *Exposition of the Record of Ancient Matters*. This has been declared by Chamberlain to be "perhaps the most admirable work of which Japanese erudition can boast."

In the first part of the Eleventh Century Murasaki-no-Shikibu, a lady of the great Fujiwara family, composed the *Genji Monogatari*, the first Japanese novel, a prose epic of contemporary life. Except for some volumes of poetry, among which may be named *Hundred Odes by a Hundred Poets* in the Thirteenth Century, and *Anthologies of the One-and-Twenty Reigns* gathered between the Eleventh and the Fifteenth Centuries, which constitute the classics of Japanese poetry, the period was not very productive.

Kiokutei Bakin (1767–1848) and Shikitei Samba (1775–1822) are authors whose fame has reached Europe. Both have written delightful stories of modern Japanese life. These, however, are for the most part too long for consideration here.

Japanese literature is rich in folk-tales, some of which have been translated by Lafcadio Hearn—but on the whole these belong rather to the category of folk lore than to that of narrative fiction.

During the golden era which began in the Seventeenth and extended into the Eighteenth Century, the drama and the novel flourished, but the short story was evidently neglected by serious artists. *The Forty-Seven Rônins*, the most famous story of the period, was never intended as a story at all, but an episode from history.

It is only in recent years, after the close of the Russo-Japanese war, when Occidental customs and ideas began to influence the Empire, that Japan has contributed genuine short stories. Since then a whole literature has developed, an integral branch of the literature of the entire modern world.

THE FORTY-SEVEN RONINS

(Anonymous: Early 18th Century)

THIS famous story is a relation of the most celebrated episode in the annals of modern Japan. It occurred in the year 1703, and within a few months had been used as the basis of a popular play. Before the middle of the century over fifty plays and operas and any number of tales and poems had been written round the vendetta. Practically nothing is known of the authorship of the stories, which form a considerable literature in themselves.

The present version, translated by A. B. Mitford, is reprinted from *The Fortnightly Review*, London, 1870, by permission of Macmillan and Co., owners of the copyright, who include it in Mitford's *Tales of Old Japan*.

THE FORTY-SEVEN RONINS

AT the beginning of the Eighteenth Century there lived a daimio, called Asano Takumi no Kami, the Lord of the Castle of Ako, in the province of Harima. Now it happened that an Imperial ambassador from the Court of the Mikado, having been sent to the Shogun at Yedo, Takumi no Kami and another noble called Kamei Sama, were appointed to receive and feast the envoy; and a high official, named Kira Kôtsuké no Suké, was named to teach them the proper ceremonies to be observed upon the occasion. The two nobles were accordingly forced to go daily to the castle to listen to the instructions of Kôtsuké no Suké. But this Kôtsuké no Suké was a man greedy of money, and as he deemed that the presents which the two daimios, according to time-honored custom, had brought him in return for his instruction, were mean and unworthy, he conceived a great hatred against them, and took no pains in teaching them, but on the contrary rather sought to make laughing-stocks of them. Takumi no Kami, restrained by a stern sense of duty, bore his insults with patience, but Kamei Sama, who had less control over his temper, was violently incensed and determined to kill Kôtsuké no Suké.

One night when his duties at the castle were ended, Kamei Sama returned to his own palace, and having summoned his councilors to a secret conference, said to them: "Kôtsuké no Suké has insulted Takumi no Kami and myself during our service in attendance on the Imperial envoy. This is against all decency, and I was minded to kill him on the spot; but I bethought me that if I did such a deed within the precincts of the castle, not only would my own life be forfeit, but my family and vassals would be ruined: so I stayed my hand. Still the life of such a wretch is a sorrow to the people, and to-morrow when I go to Court I will slay him: my mind is made up, and I will listen to no remonstrance." And as he spoke his face became livid with rage.

Now one of Kamei Sama's councilors was a man of great judgment, and when he saw from his lord's manner that remonstrance would be useless, he said: "Your lordship's words are law; your servant will make all preparations accordingly; and to-morrow, when your lordship goes to Court, if this Kôtsuké no Suké should again be insolent, let him die the death." And his lord was pleased at this speech, and waited with impatience for the day to break, that he might return to Court and kill his enemy.

But the councilor went home, and was much troubled, and thought anxiously about what his prince had said. And as he reflected, it occurred to him that since Kôtsuké no Suké had the reputation of being a miser he would certainly be open to a bribe, and that it was better to pay any sum, no matter how great, than that his lord and his house should be ruined. So he collected all the money he could, and, giving it to his servant to carry, rode off in the night to Kôtsuké no Suké's palace, and said to his retainers: "My master, who is now in attendance upon the Imperial envoy, owes much thanks to my Lord Kôtsuké no Suké, who has been at so great pains to teach him the proper ceremonies to be observed during the reception of the Imperial envoy. This is but a shabby present which he has sent by me, but he hopes that his lordship will condescend to accept it, and commends himself to his lordship's favor." And, with these words, he produced a thousand ounces of silver for Kôtsuké no Suké, and a hundred ounces to be distributed among his retainers.

When the latter saw the money their eyes sparkled with pleasure, and they were profuse in their thanks; and, begging the councilor to wait a little, they went and told their master of the lordly present which had arrived with a polite message from Kamei Sama. Kôtsuké no Suké in eager delight sent for the councilor into an inner chamber, and after thanking him, promised on the morrow to instruct his master carefully in all the different points of etiquette. So the councilor seeing the miser's glee rejoiced at the success of his plan; and having taken his leave returned home in high spirits. But Kamei Sama, little thinking how his vassal had propitiated his enemy, lay brooding over his vengeance, and on the following morning at daybreak went to Court in solemn procession.

When Kôtsuké no Suké met him his manner had completely changed, and nothing could exceed his courtesy. "You have come early to Court this morning, my Lord Kamei," said he. "I cannot sufficiently admire your zeal. I shall have the honor to call your attention to several points of etiquette to-day. I must beg your lordship to excuse my previous conduct, which must have seemed very rude; but I am naturally of a cross-grained disposition, so I pray you to forgive me." And as he kept on humbling himself and making fair speeches, the heart of Kamei Sama was gradually softened, and he renounced his intention of killing him. Thus, by the cleverness of his councilor, was Kamei Sama, with all his house, saved from ruin.

Shortly after this Takumi no Kami, who had sent no present, arrived at the castle, and Kôtsuké no Suké turned him into ridicule even more than before, provoking him with sneers and covered insults; but Takumi no Kami affected to ignore all this, and submitted himself patiently to Kôtsuké no Suké's orders.

This conduct, so far from producing a good effect, only made Kôtsuké no Suké despise him the more, until at last he said haughtily: "Here, my Lord of Takumi, the ribbon of my sock has come untied; be so good as to tie it up for me."

Takumi no Kami, although burning with rage at the affront, still thought that as he was on duty he was bound to obey, and tied up the ribbon of the sock. Then Kôtsuké no Suké, turning from him, petulantly exclaimed: "Why, how clumsy you are! You cannot so much as tie up the ribbon of a sock properly! Anyone can see that you are a boor from the country, and know nothing of the manners of Yedo." And with a scornful laugh he moved towards an inner room.

But the patience of Takumi no Kami was exhausted; this last insult was more than he could bear.

"Stop a moment, my lord," cried he.

"Well, what is it?" replied the other. And, as he turned round, Takumi no Kami drew his dirk, and aimed a blow at his head; but Kôtsuké no Suké, being protected by the Court cap which he wore, the wound was but a scratch, so he ran away; and Takumi no Kami, pursuing him, tried a second time to cut him down, but missing his aim, struck his dirk into a pillar. At this moment an officer, named Kajikawa Yosobei, seeing the affray, rushed up, and holding back the infuriated noble, gave Kôtsuké no Suké time to make good his escape.

Then there arose a great uproar and confusion, and Takumi no Kami was arrested and disarmed, and confined in one of the apartments of the palace under the care of the censors. A council was held, and the prisoner was given over to the safeguard of a daimio, called Tamura Ukiyô no Daibu, who kept him in close custody in his own house, to the great grief of his wife and of his retainers; and when the deliberations of the council were completed, it was decided that, as he had commited an outrage and attacked another man within the precincts of the palace, he must perform *hara kiri*, that is, commit suicide by disemboweling; his goods must be confiscated, and his family ruined. Such was the law. So Takumi no Kami performed *hara kiri*, his castle of Akô was confiscated, and his retainers, having become Rônins, some of them took service with other daimios, and others became merchants.

Now amongst these retainers was his principal councilor, a man called Oishi Kuranosuké, who with forty-six other faithful dependents formed a league to avenge their master's death by killing Kôtsuké no Suké. This Oishi Kuranosuké was absent at the castle of Akô at the time of the affray, which, had he been with his prince, would never have occurred; for, being a wise man, he would not have failed to propitiate Kôtsuké no Suké by sending him suitable presents; while the councilor who was in attendance on the prince at Yedo was a dullard, who neglected this precaution, and so caused the death of his master and the ruin of his house.

So Oishi Kuranosuké and his forty-six companions began to lay their plans of vengeance against Kôtsuké no Suké; but the latter was so well guarded by a body of men lent to him by a daimio called Uyésugi Sama, whose daughter he had married, that they saw that the only way of attaining their end would be to throw their enemy off his guard. With this object they separated, and disguised themselves, some as carpenters or craftsmen, others as merchants; and their chief, Kuranosuké, went to Kiôto, and built a house in the quarter called Yamashina, where he took to frequenting houses of the worst repute, and gave himself up to drunkenness and debauchery, as if nothing were further from his mind than revenge. Kôtsuké no Suké, in the meanwhile, suspecting that Takumi no Kami's former retainers would be scheming against his life, secretly sent spies to Kiôto, and caused a faithful account to be kept of all that Kuranosuké did. The latter, however, determined thoroughly to delude the enemy into a false security, went on leading a dissolute life with harlots and winebibbers. One day, as he was returning home drunk from some low haunt, he fell down in the street and went to sleep, and all the passers-by laughed him to scorn. It happened that a Satsuma man saw this, and said: "Is not this Oishi Kuranosuké, who was a councilor of Asano Takumi no Kami, and who, not having the heart to avenge his lord, gives himself up to women and wine? See how he lies drunk in the public street! Faithless beast! Fool and craven! Unworthy the name of a Samurai!"

And he trod on Kuranosuké's face as he slept, and spat upon him; but when Kôtsuké no Suké's spies reported all this at Yedo he was greatly relieved at the news, and felt secure from danger.

One day Kuranosuké's wife, who was bitterly grieved to see her husband lead this abandoned life, went to him and said: "My lord, you told me at first that your debauchery was but a trick to make your enemy relax in watchfulness. But indeed, indeed, this has gone too far. I pray and beseech you to put some restraint upon yourself."

"Trouble me not," replied Kuranosuké, "for I will not listen to your whining. Since my way of life is displeasing to you, I will divorce you, and you may go about your business; and I will buy some pretty young girl from one of the public-houses, and marry her for my pleasure. I am sick of the sight of an old woman like you about the house, so get you gone—the sooner the better."

So saying, he flew into a violent rage, and his wife, terror-stricken, pleaded piteously for mercy.

"Oh, my lord! unsay those terrible words! I have been your faithful wife for twenty years, and have borne you three children; in sickness and in sorrow I have been with you; you cannot be so cruel as to turn me out of doors now. Have pity! have pity!"

"Cease this useless wailing. My mind is made up, and you must go; and as the children are in my way also, you are welcome to take them with you."

When she heard her husband speak thus, in her grief she sought her eldest son, Oishi Chikara, and begged him to plead for her, and pray that she might be pardoned. But nothing would turn Kuranosuké from his purpose; so his wife was sent away, with the two younger children, and went back to her native place. But Oishi Chikara remained with his father.

The spies communicated all this without fail to Kôtsuké no Suké, and he, when he heard how Kuranosuké, having turned his wife and children out of doors and bought a concubine, was groveling in a life of drunkenness and lust, began to think that he had no longer anything to fear from the retainers of Takumi no Kami, who must be cowards, without the courage to avenge their lord. So by degrees he began to keep a less strict watch, and sent back half of the guard which had been lent to him by his father-in-law, Uyésugi Sama. Little did he think how he was falling into the trap laid for him by Kuranosuké, who, in his zeal to slay his lord's enemy, thought nothing of divorcing his wife and sending away his children! Admirable and faithful man!

In this way Kuranosuké continued to throw dust in the eyes of his foe, by persisting in his apparently shameless conduct; but his associates all went to Yedo, and, having in their several capacities as workmen and peddlers contrived to gain access to Kôtsuké no Suké's house, made themselves familiar with the plan of the building and the arrangement of the different rooms, and ascertained the character of the inmates, who were brave and loyal men, and who were cowards;

upon all of which matters they sent regular reports to Kuranosuké. And when at last it became evident from the letters which arrived from Yedo that Kôtsuké no Suké was thoroughly off his guard, Kuranosuké rejoiced that the day of vengeance was at hand; and, having appointed a trysting-place at Yedo, he fled secretly from Kiôto, eluding the vigilance of his enemy's spies. Then the forty-seven men, having laid all their plans, bided their time patiently.

It was now midwinter, the twelfth month of the year, and the cold was bitter. One night, during a heavy fall of snow, when the whole world was hushed, and peaceful men were stretched in sleep upon the mats, the Rônins determined that no more favorable opportunity could occur for carrying out their purpose. So they took counsel together, and having divided their band into two parties, assigned to each man his post. One band, led by Oishi Kuranosuké, was to attack the front gate, and the other, under his son Oishi Chikara, was to attack the rear of Kôtsuké no Suké's house; but as Chikara was only sixteen years of age, Yoshida Chiuzayémon was appointed to act as his guardian. Further it was arranged that a drum, beaten at the order of Kuranosuké, should be the signal for the simultaneous attack; and that if any one slew Kôtsuké no Suké and cut off his head he should blow a shrill whistle, as a signal to his comrades, who would hurry to the spot, and, having identified the head, carry it off to the temple called Sengakuji, and lay it as an offering before the tomb of their dead lord. Then they must report their deed to the Government, and await their sentence. To this the Rônins one and all pledged themselves. Midnight was fixed upon as the hour, and the forty-seven comrades, having made all ready for the attack, partook of a last farewell feast together, for on the morrow they must die. Then Oishi Kuranosuké addressed the band, and said:

"To-night we shall attack our enemy in his palace; his retainers will certainly resist us, and we shall be obliged to kill them. But to slay old men and women and children is a pitiful thing; therefore, I pray you each one to take great heed lest you kill a single helpless person." His comrades all applauded this speech, and so they remained, waiting for the hour of midnight to arrive.

When the appointed hour came, the Rônins set forth. The wind howled furiously, and the driving snow beat in their faces; but little cared they for wind or snow as they hurried on their road. At last they reached Kôtsuké no Suké's house, and divided themselves into two bands; and Chikara, with twenty-three men, went round to the back gate. Then four men, by means of a ladder of ropes which they hung on to the roof of the porch, effected an entry into the courtyard; and, as they saw signs that all the inmates of the house were asleep, they went into the porter's lodge where the guard slept, and, before the latter had time to recover from their astonishment, bound them. The terrified guard prayed hard for mercy, that their lives might he spared; and to this the Rônins agreed on condition that the keys of the gate should be given up; but the others tremblingly said that the keys were kept in the house of one of their officers, and that they had no means of obtaining them. Then the Rônins lost patience, and with a hammer smashed to shivers the big wooden bolt which secured the gate, and the doors flew open to the right and to the left. At the same time Chikara and his party broke in by the back gate.

Then Oishi Kuranosuké sent a messenger to the neighboring houses, bearing the following message: "We, the Rônins who were formerly in the service of Asano Takumi no Kami, are this night about to break into the palace of Kôtsuké no Suké, to avenge our lord. As we are neither night robbers nor ruffians, no hurt will be done to the neighboring houses. We pray you to set your minds at rest." And as Kôtsuké no Suké was hated by his neighbors for his covetousness, they did not unite their forces to assist him. Another precaution was yet taken. Lest any of the people inside should run out to call the relations of the family to the rescue, and these coming in force should interfere with the plans of the Rônins, Kuranosuké stationed ten of his men armed with bows on the roof of the four sides of the courtyard, with orders to shoot any retainers who might attempt to leave the place. Having thus laid all his plans and posted his men, Kuranosuké with his own hand beat the drum and gave the signal for attack.

Ten of Kôtsuké no Suké's retainers, hearing the noise, woke up; and, drawing their swords, rushed into the front room to defend their master. At this moment the Rônins, who had burst open the door of the front hall, entered the same room. Then arose a furious fight between the two parties, in the midst of which Chikara, leading his men through the garden, broke into the back of the house; and Kôtsuké no Suké, in terror of his life, took refuge, with his wife and female servants, in a closet in the veranda; while the rest of his retainers, who slept in the barrack outside the house, made ready to go to the rescue. But the Rônins who had come in by the front door, and were fighting with the ten retainers, ended by overpowering and slaying the latter without losing one of their own number; after which, forcing their way bravely towards the back rooms, they were joined by Chikara and his men, and the two bands were united in one.

By this time the remainder of Kôtsuké no Suké's men had come in, and the fight became general; and Kuranosuké, sitting on a campstool, gave his orders and directed the Rônins. Soon the inmates of the house perceived that they were no match for their enemy, so they tried to send out intelligence of their plight to Uyésugi Sama, their lord's father-in-law, begging him to come to the rescue with all the force at his command. But the messengers were shot down by the archers whom Kuranosuké had posted on the roof. So no help coming, they fought on in despair. Then Kuranosuké cried out with a loud voice: "Kôtuské no Suké alone is our enemy; let someone go inside and bring him forth dead or alive!"

Now in front of Kôtsuké no Suké's private room stood three brave retainers with drawn swords. The first was Kobayashi Héhachi, the second was Waku Handaiyu, and the third was Shimidzu Ikkaku, all good men and true, and expert swordsmen. So stoutly did these men lay about them that for awhile they kept the whole of the Rônins at bay, and at one moment even forced them back. When Oishi Kuranosuké saw this, he ground his teeth with rage, and shouted to his men: "What! did not every man of you swear to lay down his life in avenging his lord, and now are you beaten back by three men? Cowards, not fit to be spoken to! To die fighting in a master's cause should be the noblest ambition of a retainer!" Then turning to his own son Chikara, he said, "Here, boy! engage those men, and if they are too strong for you, die!"

Spurred by these words, Chikara seized a spear and gave battle to Waku Handaiyu, but could not hold his ground, and backing by degrees, was driven out into the garden, where he missed his footing and slipped into a pond; but as Handaiyu, thinking to kill him, looked down into the pond, Chikara cut his enemy in the leg and caused him to fall, and then crawling out of the water despatched him. In the meanwhile, Kobayashi Héhachi and Shimidzu Ikkaku had been killed by the other Rônins, and of all Kôtsuké no Suké's retainers not one fighting man remained. Chikara, seeing this, went with his bloody sword in his hand into a back room to search for Kôtsuké no Suké, but he only found the son of the latter, a young lord named Kira Sahioyé, who, carrying a halberd, attacked him, but was soon wounded and fled. Thus the whole of Kôtsuké no Suké's men having been killed, there was an end of the fighting; but as yet there was no trace of Kôtsuké no Suké to be found.

Then Kuranosuké divided his men into several parties and searched the whole house, but all in vain; women and children weeping were alone to be seen. At this the forty-seven men began to lose heart in regret, that after all their toil they had allowed their enemy to escape them, and there was a moment when in their despair they agreed to commit suicide together upon the spot; but they determined to make one more effort. So Kuranosuké went into Kôtsuké no Suké's sleeping-room, and touching the quilt with his hands, exlaimed, "I have just felt the bed-clothes and they are yet warm, and so methinks that our enemy is not far off. He must certainly be hidden somewhere in the house." Greatly excited by this, the Rônins renewed their search.

Now in the raised part of the room, near the place of honor, there was a picture hanging; taking down this picture, they saw that there was a large hole in the plastered wall, and on thrusting a spear in they could feel nothing beyond it. So one of the Rônins, called Yazama Jiutarô, got into the hole, and found that on the other side there was a little courtyard, in which there stood an outhouse for holding charcoal and firewood. Looking into the outhouse, he spied something white at the further end, at which he struck with his spear, when two armed men sprang out upon him and tried to cut him down, but he kept them back until one of his comrades came up and killed one of the two men and engaged the other, while Jiutarô entered the outhouse and felt about with his spear. Again seeing something white, he struck it with his lance, when a cry of pain betrayed that it was a man; so he rushed up, and the man in white clothes, who had been wounded in the thigh, drew a dirk and aimed a blow at him. But Jiutarô wrested the dirk from him, and clutching him by the collar, dragged him out of the outhouse. Then the other Rônin came up, and they examined the prisoner attentively, and saw that he was a noble-looking man, some sixty years of age, dressed in a white satin sleeping-robe, which was stained by the blood from the thigh-wound which Jiutarô had inflicted. The two men felt convinced that this was no other than Kôtsuké no Suké, and they asked him his name, but he gave no answer, so they gave the signal whistle, and all their comrades collected together at the call; then Oishi Kuranosuké, bringing a lantern, scanned the old man's features; and it was indeed Kôtsuké no Suké; and if further proof were wanting, he still bore a scar on his forehead where their master, Asano Takumi no Kami, had wounded him during the affray in the castle. There being no possibility of mistake, therefore Oishi Kuranosuké went down on his knees, and addressing the old man very respectfully, said:

"My lord, we are the retainers of Asano Takumi no Kami. Last year your lordship and our master quarreled in the palace, and our master was sentenced to *hara kiri*, and his family was ruined. We have come tonight to avenge him, as is the duty of faithful and loyal men. I pray your lordship to acknowledge the justice of our purpose. And now, my lord, we beseech you to perform *hara kiri*. I myself shall have the honor to act as your second, and when, with all humility, I shall have received your lordship's head, it is my intention to lay it as an offering upon the grave of Asano Takumi no Kami."

Thus, in consideration of the high rank of Kôtsuké no Suké, the Rônins treated him with the greatest courtesy, and over and over again entreated him to perform *hara kiri*. But he crouched speechless and trembling. At last Kuranosuké, seeing that it was vain to urge him to die the death of a nobleman, forced him down, and cut off his head with the same dirk with which Asano Takumi no Kami had killed himself. Then the forty-seven comrades, elated at having accomplished their design, placed the head in a bucket, and prepared to depart; but before leaving the house they carefully extinguished all the lights and fires in the place, lest by any accident a fire should break out and the neighbors suffer.

As they were on their way to Takanawa, the suburb in which the temple called Sengakuji stands, the day broke; and the people flocked out to see the forty-seven men, who, with their clothes and arms all blood-stained, presented a terrible appearance; and everyone praised them, wondering at their valor and faithfulness. But they expected every moment that Kôtsuké no Suké's father-in-law would attack them and carry off the head, so they determined to die nobly sword in hand. However, they reached Takanawa in safety, for Matsudaira Aki no Kami, one of the eighteen chief daimios of Japan, of whose house Asano Takumi no Kami had been a cadet, had been highly pleased when he heard of the last night's work, and he had made ready to assist the Rônins in case they were attacked. So Kôtsuké no Suké's father-in-law dared not pursue them.

At about seven in the morning they came opposite to the palace of Matsudaira Mutsu no Kami, the Prince of Sendai, and the prince hearing of it, sent for one of his councilors and said: "The retainers of Takumi no Kami have slain their lord's enemy, and are passing this way: I am filled with admiration at their devotion, so, as they must be tired and hungry after their night's work, do you go and invite them to come in here, and set some gruel and a cup of wine before them."

So the councilor went out and said to Oishi Kuranosuké, "Sir, I am a councilor of the Prince of Sendai, and my master bids me beg you, as you must be worn out after all you have undergone, to come in and partake of such poor refreshment as we can offer you. This is my message to you from my lord."

"I thank you, sir," replied Kuranosuké. "It is very good of his lordship to trouble himself to think of us. We shall accept his kindness gratefully."

So the forty-seven Rônins went into the palace, and were feasted with gruel and wine, and all the retainers of the Prince of Sendai came and praised them.

Then Kuranosuké turned to the councilor and said, "Sir, we are truly indebted to you for this kind hospitality; but as we have still to hurry to Sengakuji, we must needs humbly take our leave." And, after returning many thanks to their hosts, they left the palace of the Prince of Sendai and hastened to Sengakuji, where they were met by the abbot of the monastery, who went to the front gate to receive them, and led them to the tomb of Takumi no Kami.

And when they came to their lord's grave they took the head of Kôt-suké no Suké, and, having washed it clean in a well hard by, laid it as an offering before the tomb. When they had done this, they engaged the priests of the temple to come and read prayers while they burnt incense; first Oishi Kuranosuké burnt incense, and then his son Oishi Chikara, and after them the other forty-five men performed the same ceremony. Then Kuranosuké, having given all the money that he had by him to the abbot, said:

"When we forty-seven men shall have performed *hara kiri*, I beg you to bury us decently. I rely upon your kindness. This is but a trifle that I have to offer; such as it is, let it be spent in masses for our souls."

And the abbot, marveling at the faithful courage of the men, with tears in his eyes pledged himself to fulfil their wishes. So the forty-seven Rônins, with their minds at rest, waited patiently until they should receive the orders of the Government.

At last they were summoned to the Supreme Court, where the governors of Yedo and the public censors had assembled; and the sentence passed upon them was as follows: "Whereas, neither respecting the dignity of the city nor fearing the Government, having leagued yourselves together to slay your enemy, you violently broke into the house of Kira Kôtsuké no Suké by night and murdered him, the sentence of the Court is, that, for this audacious conduct, you perform *hara kiri*." When the sentence had been read, the forty-seven Rônins were divided into four parties, and handed over to the safe keeping of four different daimios; and sheriffs were sent to the palaces of those daimios in whose presence the Rônins were made to perform *hara kiri*. But, as from the very beginning they had all made up their minds that to this end they must come, they met their death nobly; and their corpses were carried to Sengakuji, and buried in front of the tomb of their master, Asano Takumi no Kami. And when the fame of this became noised abroad, the people flocked to pray at the graves of these faithful men.

Among those who came to pray was a Satsuma man, who, prostrating himself before the grave of Oishi Kuranosuké, said: "When I saw you lying drunk by the roadside at Yamashina, in Kiôto, I knew not that you were plotting to avenge your lord; and, thinking you to be a faithless man, I trampled on you and spat in your face as I passed. And now I have come to ask pardon and offer atonement for the insult of last year." With these words he prostrated himself again before the grave, and, drawing a dirk from his girdle, performed *hara kiri* and died. And the chief priest of the temple, taking pity upon him, buried him by the side of the Rônins; and his tomb still remains to be seen with those of the forty-seven comrades.

This is the end of the story of the Forty-seven Rônins.

MORI OGWAI

(1860—1922)

MORI OGWAI, who was at one time army surgeon general, was one of the most distinguished Japanese literary men. He has been indefatigable in his labors of translation and interpretation. His versions of the great works of European writers are considered among the finest in all modern Japanese literature. He also wrote important biographies, novels, and many excellent short stories.

This story, translated by Torao Taketomo, is reprinted from the volume *Paulownia*, copyright, 1918, by Duffield & Co., New York, by permission of the publisher.

THE PIER

THE pier is long—long——
The rails of four railroads cut straight and obliquely the beams of the iron bridge on which the long and short cross-beams are like the bars of a xylophone on which children play. Through the cracks of the cross-beams, that almost catch the heels of shoes and wooden clogs, here and there the black waves are shown, reflected on the white flashes of sunshine.

The sky has cleared into a deep blue. On the inside of the train where she was sitting with her husband starting to-day, she did not think the wind was blowing.

When leaving the jinrikisha, in which she rode from the station of Yokohama, and standing on this pier, she found that the wind of the fifth of March was still blowing as if to bite the skin, fluttering the skirts of the Azuma coat.

It is the Azuma coat in silver gray, which she loosely wears on her body, that carries the child of her husband, who is starting to-day, this day which is not far from the month of confinement.

She came with her hair in Sokuhatsu. Her boa is of white ostrich. Holding the light green umbrella with tassels, she walks along, surrounded by four or five maidservants.

The pier is long—long——
The big ships are anchoring on the right and the left of the pier. Some are painted in black, some in white.

The anchored ships are making a fence for the wind. Every time she leaves the place where there are ships, a gust of wind blows and flutters the skirts of her Azuma coat.

Two years ago, immediately after he was graduated from the university of literature, the count, her husband, had married her. It was during the previous year that she gave birth to her first child, a princess like a jewel. At the end of the year the husband became a Master of Ceremonies at the Court. And, now, he is starting to London, charged with his official duty.

In his newly made gray overcoat, flinging the cane with crooked handle, her husband is walking rapidly along the pier. The viscount, who is going with him, and whose height is taller by a head than his, also walks rapidly beside him, clad in a suit of similar color.

The French ship, on which her husband is about to go abroad, is anchoring at the extreme end of the right side of the pier.

A stool, like that which is used to repair the wires of a trolley, is stationed on the pier, and from it a gangplank is laid across to the bulwark.

While walking slowly, she sees her husband and the viscount, his companion, crossing the gangplank and entering the ship.

The group of people looking after them are standing, here and there, on the pier. Almost all of them are those who came to bid adieu to her husband and the viscount. Perhaps there are no other passengers on this ship about to sail who are so important and are looked at by so many people.

Some of them are going to the foot of the stool on which the gangplank is laid, and stop there to wait for their companions. Some of them are standing at the place, a bit before the stool, where the blocks and ropes are laid down.

Among these people there must be some who are intimately known to her husband, and some who know him but slightly. But, standing under this clear sky, they all seem dejected; or is it only her fancy?

The pier is long—long——

Following slowly after them, unconsciously she looks off to her right where there were many round windows on the side of the ship. The faces and chests of women are seen from one of those round windows. Three of them are from thirty to forty years of age; all with white aprons on their chests. They must be the waitresses of the ship. Supposing them to be the waitresses who wait on the passengers of the ship, on which her husband is on board, she feels envious of even those humble women.

There is also a woman at the bulwark, looking down on the pier, who wears a big bonnet with white cloth and carries a small leather bag in her hand. Two big eyes, as if painted with shadows, are shining on her wrinkled face above the large nose, like a hook. She looks like a Jewess. She also must be a traveler who is going on this ship. She is also envious of her.

The pier is long—long——

At last she arrives at the foot of the gangplank. Cautiously she carries her body, which has the second infant of her husband under the Azuma coat, and descends on the deck of the big, black-painted ship. She hands the umbrella to a maidservant.

Led by the people who have come to say farewell and were already on board, she goes back along the bulwark toward the prow. There are rooms for passengers at the end of the way, the numbers of which increase from twenty-seven to twenty-nine.

The viscount is standing at the entrance and addresses her.

"This is the room, madam."

Peeping into the room she finds two beds, under which the familiar packages and trunks are deposited. Her husband is standing before one of the beds.

"Look it through, madam. It is like this."

This is the room; she must look through it carefully. During the long, long voyage of her husband, this is the room where her dreams must come and go.

A man, who looks like the captain, comes, and, addressing her husband in French, guides him to the saloon of the ship. She follows her husband and the viscount and enters the room.

This is a spacious and beautiful saloon. Several tables are arranged, each bearing a flower basket. ... Gradually the people who came to say farewell gather into the room.

By the order of this man, who looks like the captain, a waiter brings forth many cups in the shape of morning-glories, and, pouring champagne into them, he distributes them among the people. Another waiter brings cakes, like those which are brought with ice cream, piled on a plate in the form of the well crib, and distributes them among the people.

The people who received the cups go one after another, and stand before her husband and the viscount, wishing them a happy voyage, and drink from the cups.

Sitting on a small chair beside the table, she is waiting for the time when the congratulations are at an end. During his busy moments, now and then, her husband lifts his eyes to her.

However, there is no more to be said to her before many people. Also, there is no more to be said to him, before many people.

The bell rings. Having bidden farewell to her husband and to the viscount the people are going out, one after another. She also follows them, saluting her husband and the viscount.

Again crossing the dangerous gangplank, she descends to the pier. She receives the light green umbrella from the hand of her maidservant, and raises it.

Her husband and the viscount are standing on the bulwark looking in her direction. She is looking up at them from under her umbrella. She feels that her eyes, as she looks up, are growing gradually larger and larger.

Again the bell rings. A few French sailors begin to untie the rope from the gangplank. A Japanese laborer in Hanten is standing on the stool like that which is used in repairing the trolley, preparing to draw down the gangplank. Hanging on the rope of the wheel, pulled by the man in Hanten, the gangplank at last leaves the bulwark.

The noon-gun of the city of Yokohama resounds. With this as a signal, the ship, from the hold of which for some time a noise has been issuing, silently begins to move.

The elderly Europeans, who seem to be a married couple, are standing at the bulwark. They are talking about something of a jolly nature with a white-haired old man who is standing on the pier, with one of his feet placed on an apparatus to roll the ropes, which looks like a big bobbin. They do not seem to regret the parting.

It looks as if the ship is moving. It looks as if the pier is moving. There seems to be the distance of a Pallaraxe between the place where her husband and the viscount are standing and the place where she is standing. She feels her eyes growing larger and larger.

Some of the people who are looking after them are running to the end of the pier. She cannot do such an immodest thing. Suddenly something white waves at the bulwark. It was a handkerchief waved by the hand of a woman who wears a big bonnet decorated with a white cloth. A tall man stands as the end of the pier, in red waistcoat and tan shoes. A white handkerchief waves also from the hand of this man. This also must be a parting in human life.

These two persons set the fashion, and the handkerchiefs are waved here and there. White things are waving also from the people who are looking after the group surrounding the count. She also grasps the batiste handkerchief which she has brought in her sleeve, but she cannot do such an immodest thing.

When the ship seemed to have left the pier, it turned its prow a bit to the right. The place where her husband and the viscount were standing has disappeared at last.

Still she can see a boy about fifteen or sixteen, standing at the stern, in a blue, cold-looking garment like a blouse. What mother is waiting for him in France? Or has he no parents? What is he looking at, standing by the rail at the stern?

Slowly she turned her feet and walked among the maidservants surrounding her.

The pier is long—long——

At the place where the black-painted ship was anchored, until a
short time ago, the water is glittering like the scales of fish, as the small
ripples are reflecting the pale sunshine.

SHIMAZAKI TOSON

(1871—1943)

SHIMAZAKI TOSON began writing as a poet of the new era, but after
the Russo-Japanese war, he turned to naturalistic fiction. He wrote
novels derived more or less directly from Europe, but in his short
stories he remained more genuinely Japanese. "Intimacy with nature," says the translator, "and intimacy with life," are felt throughout his little stories.

   This story, translated by Torao Taketomo, is reprinted from the
volume, *Paulownia*, copyright, 1918, by Duffield & Co., New York, by
permission of the publisher.

A DOMESTIC ANIMAL

HER first misfortune was at her birth; she came into the world
with short gray hair, overhanging ears, and fox-like eyes. Every
animal which is called by favor domestic has a certain quality which
attracts to itself the friendly feeling of man. But she did not have it.
Nothing in her countenance seemed to be favored by man. She was
entirely lacking in the usual qualifications of a domestic animal. Naturally she was deserted.
   However, she was also a dog, an animal which cannot live by itself.
She could not leave the hereditary habitat to be fed by people and then
go back to the wild native place of her remote ancestors. She began to
search after a suitable human house.
   This troublesome being strayed to the estate of Kin san, a planter,
when the building of the new wood-roofed rent house was just finished.
The house was built along the village road of Okubo, located in such
a manner as to enable one to go to the main street through the back
yard. The floor was high and the ground was dry. Moreover, there was
a narrow, dark, unoccupied space at the foot of the fence between this
house and the next, so that she could promptly hide herself in emergency. She lost no time in occupying this underground refuge.
   The urgent necessity was to get the food. There were two more rent
houses on this estate, which made four with the farm-like main house

where Kin san's family lived. These houses stood each against the other and trees with graceful branches were between them. Her sharp nose taught her first the direction toward the kitchen. As she was hungry, there was no time for choice. Peeled skins of fruits, cold, evil-smelling soup, corrupt remnants of dishes—she ate everything she could get. If these were not enough to satisfy her, she smelt around even the dust heap, and hunted as far as she could hunt. Some dirty socks were soaked in the wash-tub beside the well. Gladly, she drank the water from the tub.

There was an old Mokusei in the garden. She decided to make of their shade her resting place; stretching out her four legs on the ground, which was warmed by the sunshine through the leaves, she sighed or scratched the itchy spots. When it was evening she entered her underground retreat and lay down on the charcoal bags which were under the floor above. A large wash-tub she also tried. Sometimes she crept as far as the passage under the kitchen floor, and slept on the charcoals in the warm charcoal box. Thus she began her life.

Kin san's family, at this time, kept a piebald dog of brown and white, whose name was Pochi. This lively Pochi was the only being who welcomed her. Pochi seemed to have a sociable nature; he approached her politely scratching the ground. She made her return greeting by shaking her dirty tail.

But Kin san and the others who lived on his estate did not receive her as Pochi did. "Isn't it a great loss to be ugly, even among the animals," remarked one. "I might keep her, if she were a bit better," said another. All this was meaningless to her, and she was called Pup by these people who did not know. Each of the four houses had an "aunt," which was the name given to the hostess of the family. Not only these aunts, but also their children, laughed at and hated her and burst out railingly, calling her "Pup, pup." As for the "uncles," they were more dreadful. The least relaxing of her vigilance caused them to chase her. Many things were thrown at her—stones, clumps of clay, the iron fire-stick. Once a big club of the door guard was flung after her, and made a wound on her hind leg.

Gradually, she understood the human mind. The significant twist of the mouth, a gesture as if to pick up something, the shrugging of shoulders and the bitten lips—all sentiments expressed against her—showed to her the deep enmity of the hunter. One day she was almost driven to bay in Kin san's kitchen. Nobody knows how she was able to find the means of escape! People were crying: "Bring the rope—the rope, the rope!" She was desperate, and, running through the garden, where were the dwarf trees, she went toward the hot-house; turning around the barn, she escaped to the fields, where were the flowers to be sold on fête days.

"Gone, at last!" said one of the uncles. "Isn't she a troublesome thing?" replied Kin san, who laughed like a good-natured man.

It was not only once or twice that she met such hard experiences. But she was not a dog to be crushed down by this kind of hardship. She would hunt around for food with calm composure, with the appearance of saying: "This is my own territory." Boldly she stepped into the new kitchen of the rent house, or went up to the veranda with her dirty feet. She bit off the laces from the garden slippers, and played with the washed things of the aunts, smearing them with mud and dust. She had no regard for the human children. This family had a girl named Ko chan, who liked to come out to play in the yard, in big wooden clogs trailing on the ground. She chased this girl for fun. Sometimes, Ko chan would bring out a piece of tasty-looking cake and show it to her.

"Look here! Look here, Pup!"

Instantly she jumped at Ko chan.

"Oh, Pup is wicked, mamma!"

This was always Ko chan's cry for help. Then the aunt came hastily and called Ko chan.

"Run away, Ko chan!—quick! Why do you wear such big clogs?" By this time poor Ko chan had nothing left. She had taken the cake from the crying Ko chan, thus securing the sweets which are eaten by man. At such time, she usually licked the top of her nose with her red tongue.

Nevertheless, there was no intention of good or evil in her actions. These words she heard from the uncles and aunts of the estate, but nothing about them was known to her. She had no understanding of the etiquette and civility created by man. She was only a dog. Whether her action was impolite or not, that was not a question. She was only a poor animal, acting according to its nature.

The cold, scanty, miserable winter passed while she suffered this "better go away" treatment. It was a wonder that she did not die from hunger. The begging priest who used to come to Okubo every morning said that even he did not get much. As to the humble woman who took a child with her, she was refused mostly by "no business" or "nothing doing." Even human beings were in a sad state. How, then, could they spare to this ignorant and useless animal, this embarrassing dog, a bowlful of their cold rice? She roamed on the snow in the far-off places, and ate everything, even the skins of the orange.

Meanwhile, the spring has come. And at the time when the frost began to melt she seemed to be quite grown up. All the dogs, from Kin san's Pochi to Kuro of the bathing house, Aka of the timber-dealer's, and the fearful big dog which was kept at the neighboring planter's, gathered around her. Wherever she goes, she is followed by two or three dogs. So a comfortable place like that shade of Mokusei was overflowing with deep groans of dogs that sounded as if they wished to whisper or to flatter.

An aunt who came to the well-side with a hand-pail in her hand, saw this sight.

"My! "she said. "Pup was a female dog! I never noticed that!"

And the aunt of the new rent house, who happened to be there, also said:

"Neither did I!"

And the two aunts laughed, greatly amused.

She ought to be banished. Such was the argument which was raised in the estate of Kin san. Among the members of the four families, however, the arguments raged between two parties, the uncles and the aunts. According to the point of view which was insisted upon by the aunts, it was now different. She was not in the condition she was formerly, and it would be too pitiful if she were to have a baby. As is expected of those with experience, the aunts were sympathetic, comparing her with themselves. That may be so, but how awful it would be if she gave birth to children! This was the opinion held by the uncles. Indeed, there was nobody who was not anxious about her future.

She did not know anything about this.

Another day, a carriage stopped at the door of Kin san. There was something like a lidless box on this carriage, which was covered with a dirty straw mat. Her quick nose smelt out what was in the carriage.

Following after a policeman in uniform came a dubious looking man, who entered the house. But she was not roaming in such a dangerous place. Pochi, Kuro and the other dogs began to cry all at once. Now, uncles, aunts, and all people of the village came out.

"Dog hunter, mamma!"

Ko chan hid herself behind her mother.

People ran around the garden. Kin san's daughter, whose daily duty it was to water the flowers, ran out to the street with a dipper in her hand. A middle-school boy, who was painting a water-color picture, followed them, flinging away his tripod.

"Thither she escaped, hither she ran!"

The confusion itself was very extraordinary.

"Surely, Pup is killed," Ko chan said, trembling.

At last, she has escaped. A man with a big oak club in his hand, shook his head to his companion. "No use, no use," the policeman said and laughed when he went out the gate. With disappointed looks the two men drew away the empty carriage.

Anyway she had escaped with her life. And, by and by, her bosom became larger. Her eyes began to be shaded with the restless color. Now she must guard not only herself, but also her children within her womb. Thus the pleasant shade of Mokusei was no more the place for security. Even when she was comfortably lying on the moist earth, breathing out her agony for a while, she stood up as soon as she saw the shadow of a man. She could not be negligent even for a moment. To her eyes, there was nothing as merciless and cruel as the human being.

But, in spite of her fear, she could not leave the human house. How at ease she would be if, like other animals, she could go to a distant forest and give birth amid the green trees and grasses! Thus it might seem to the looker-on, but it was not so with her, she was unable to change her inherited nature.

It was just at the beginning of June that she finished her duty of motherhood. Four puppies appeared in the hot-house of Kin san. Two of them were beautiful piebald puppies of brown and while like that of Pochi, one was entirely black, and the other was of ambiguous gray, very much like herself!

Ah, it was in the morning of her motherhood that she first saw the smiles of human beings. It was also in that morning of her motherhood that she first had nourishing food since her birth.

"Pup—come, come."

Opening the paper screen of the kitchen, the aunt at Kin san's began to call her, as she has called her since that day.

Holland

INTRODUCTION

UNTIL comparatively recent times Holland has not produced very much in the way of short stories. Before the beginning of the modern period, and particularly the advent of Herman Heijermans, Dutch writers were more interested in philosophy, theology, poetry, the drama, and history.

But of the early writers Jacob Cats, affectionately known as Father Cats, after more than three centuries still retains his popularity. His fables, or *Emblems*, have from the Sixteenth Century until modern times been widely known among the Dutch people.

In recent years there have been very interesting revivals both of the drama and the novel. During the Nineteenth Century, however, one figure stands out among the novelists, E. D. Dekker, known under his pseudonym of Multatuli. His celebrated novel, *Max Havelaar*, which contains *The Story of Saïdjah*, was not only a dramatic revelation of conditions in Java, but a work of high independent artistic merit. But *Saïdjah* is an exception.

The modern writers, of whom Van Eeden and Couperus are now known throughout the world, have concentrated their attention chiefly upon the novel. One novelist, however, is better known as a dramatist and writer of short stories: Herman Heijermans is the dominating figure of modern Dutch literature.

As with the Belgians, the Dutch writers seem to have sought inspiration in their painting. The "Falkland" stories of Hiejermans are perfect literary counterparts of the pictures of Steen, Vermeer, and De Hoogh.

JACOB CATS

(1577–1660)

LAWYER, statesman, ambassador, and poet, Jacob Cats was born in Zeeland in 1577. After travelling and studying abroad he returned to Holland and practised law. During his long and active life he found time to write lyric poems, apologues and *Emblems,* which last were immensely popular.

Father Cats' fables are simple little tales recounted for the sake of their moral lessons. The fable here printed is characteristically trite in its philosophy, but it is easy to understand how the practical merchants who read Cats found in such things a comforting day-to-day rule of life.

The present version is made by the editors from two old English verse translations.

THE HIGHER THE FLIGHT, THE LOWER THE FALL

(From *Emblems*)

A TORTOISE—like certain men—once fell a prey to ambition. Puffed up with an overweening sense of his own importance, he desired to change his earthly lot for a more exalted one. His friends failed to recognize in him any extraordinary powers, doubtless because of their limited tortoise-like point of view. He was none the less resolved to convince the earthly creatures of his ability to shine in a sphere where *they* could never hope to rival him.

One day, seeing an eagle, the bird of Jupiter, alight after his journey through the clouds, he politely asked him to take him aloft, in order that he might prove to all tortoise-kind that he was eminently qualified to grace a position more exalted than that which he now held on earth; to be able to look down upon the glories of land and sea, to watch the glories of the rising sun high above the flat earth, where groveling tortoises are wont to regard things.

The eagle, who perceived at once the silly tortoise's vanity, answered that he was only too happy to comply with the tortoise's request. Seizing him quickly, he flew up into the air, so high that the tortoise could scarcely see the ground, and secretly wished he was down there at that moment. Higher and higher flew the bird, with the intention, as he declared, of showing the other as lofty and extensive a view as would best satisfy his ambitions.

A thousand feet below, the winding rivers looked like threads of silver; earth, sea and sky were bathed in one effulgent light—far too bright for the poor tortoise's eyes. Presently the eagle asked him how he was enjoying the change from his earthly home? Would he perhaps like to go higher still? Did he feel quite at home? How did he like being so high up in the sky?

The tortoise, in dismay, could not answer a syllable, and the eagle, with a shriek of scorn, released his grasp and let the tortoise go. The poor animal was dashed to pieces on the rocks below, learning too late, alas, of the evils that beset ambition.

So it is at courts when men of low degree and servile mind are suddenly elevated to high rank. How often are they raised up only to be cast down so much more quickly, and into what deep disgrace!

EDUARD DOUWES DEKKER

(Multatuli)

(1820—1887)

DEKKER was for many years an Assistant Resident official of the Dutch government in Java. Out of his bitter experiences he wrote his famous novel *Max Havelaar*, which exposes the cruelty and corruption of the Dutch in regard to the native population of Java. Dekker was also a dramatist, though his fame rests chiefly on his novel.

The Story of Saïdjah is a complete entity, introduced into *Max Havelaar* as an example of the sufferings undergone by the native Javanese under Dutch rule.

The present version is based upon the translation of *Max Havelaar* by Alphonse Nahuys, Edinburgh, 1868. It was made by the editors, who have omitted a number of long verse passages and here and there condensed a long and verbose passage.

THE STORY OF SAÏDJAH

(From *Max Havelaar*)

SAÏDJAH'S father had a buffalo, which he used for plowing his field. When this buffalo was taken away from him by the district chief at Parang-Koodjang he was very dejected, and spoke no word for many a day. For plowing time was come, and he feared that if the rice-field was not worked in time, the opportunity to sow would be lost, and lastly, that there would be no paddy to cut, and none to keep in the store-room of the house. I have here to tell readers who know Java, but not Bantam, that in that Residency there is personal landed property, which is not the case elsewhere. Saïdjah's father, then, was very uneasy. He feared that his wife would have no rice, nor Saïdjah himself, who was still a child, nor his little brothers and sisters. And the district chief, too, would denounce him to the Assistant Resident if he was behindhand in the payment of his taxes, for this is punished by the law. Saïdjah's father then took a poniard, which he had inherited from his father. It was not very handsome, but there were silver bands round the sheath, and at the end a silver plate. He sold it to a Chinaman in the capital, and came home with twenty-four guilders, with which he bought another buffalo.

Saïdjah, who was then about seven, soon made friends with the new buffalo. I purposely say "made friends," for it was indeed touching to see how the buffalo was attached to the little boy who watched over and fed him. Of this attachment I shall soon give an example. The large strong animal bends its heavy head to the right, to the left, or downwards, just as the pressure of the child's finger directs. Such a friendship the little Saïdjah had soon been able to make with the newcomer; and it seemed as if the encouraging voice of the child gave more strength to the heavy shoulders of the animal, when it tore open the stiff clay and traced its way in deep sharp furrows. The buffalo turned willingly, on reaching the end of the field, not losing an inch of ground when plowing backwards the new furrow, which was ever near the old, as if the *sawah* was a garden ground raked by a giant. Quite near were the *sawahs* of the father of Adinda (the child who was to marry Saïdjah), and when the little brothers of Adinda came to the limit of their fields, as the father of Saïdjah was there with his plow, the children called out merrily to each other, and each praised the strength and docility of his buffalo. But I believe that Saïdjah's buffalo was the best of all, perhaps because its master knew better how to speak to the animal, for buffaloes are very responsive to kind words.

Saïdjah was nine and Adinda six, when this buffalo was taken from Saïdjah's father by the chief. Saïdjah's father, who was very poor, thereupon sold to the Chinaman two silver curtain-hooks—inheritances from his wife's parents—for eighteen guilders, and with that money he bought a new buffalo. Saïdjah was very dejected, for he knew from Adinda's little brothers that the other buffalo had been driven to the capital, and he had asked his father if he had not seen the animal when he was there to sell the curtain-hooks. To this question his father refused to give an answer, and therefore the lad feared that his buffalo had been slaughtered, like the others which the chief had taken from the people. And Saïdjah wept much when he thought of the poor buffalo, which he had known for so long, and could eat nothing for days. It must be remembered that he was only a child.

The new buffalo soon got acquainted with the boy and obtained in the heart of Saïdjah the same place as his predecessor—alas, too soon, for the wax impressions of the heart are soon smoothed to make room for other writing. However this may be, the new buffalo was not so strong as the former: true, the old yoke was too large for his neck, but the poor animal was willing, like the other, and though Saïdjah could boast no more of the strength of his buffalo when he met Adinda's brothers at the boundaries, yet maintained that none surpassed his in willingness, and if the furrow was not so straight as before, or if lumps of earth had been turned but not cut, he willingly made this right as well as he could by means of his spade. Moreover, no buffalo had any such star on his forehead as this one had. The village priest himself said that there was good luck in the course of the hair-whorls on its shoulders.

Once when they were in the field, Saïdjah called in vain to his buffalo to make haste. The animal did not move. Saïdjah grew angry at this unusual refractoriness, and could not refrain from scolding. He called him a s——. Anyone who has been in India will understand me, and he who has not is the gainer if I spare him the explanation.

Saïdjah did not mean anything bad. He only used the word because he had often heard it used by others when they were dissatisfied with their buffaloes. But it was useless: his buffalo did not move. He shook his head as if to throw off the yoke, he blew and trembled, there was anguish in his blue eye, and the upper lip was curled, baring the gums.

"Fly, fly!" Adinda's brothers cried, "Fly, Saïdjah, there's a tiger!" And they all unyoked their buffaloes, and throwing themselves on their broad backs, galloped away through *sawahs*, irrigation, trenches, mud, brushwood, forest and jungle, along fields and roads, but when they tore panting and dripping with perspiration into the village of Badoer, Saïdjah was not with them. For when he had freed his buffalo from the yoke and mounted him as the others had done in order to escape, an unexpected jump made him lose his seat and fall to the ground. The tiger was very close. ... The buffalo, driven on by his own speed alone, and not of his own will, had gone further than Saïdjah, and scarcely had it conquered the momentum when it returned and, placing its big body, supported by its feet like a roof over the child, turned its horned head toward the tiger, which bounded forward—but for the last time. The buffalo caught him on his horns, and only lost some flesh, which the tiger took out of his neck. The tiger lay there with his belly torn open. Saïdjah was saved. Certainly there had been luck in the star on the buffalo's head.

When this buffalo had been taken away from Saïdjah's father and slaughtered, Saïdjah was just twelve, and Adinda was wearing *sarongs* and making figures on them. She had already learned to express thoughts in melancholy drawings on her tissue, for she had seen Saïdjah's sadness. And Saïdjah's father was also sad, but his mother still more so. For she had cured the wound in the neck of the faithful animal which had brought her child home unhurt. As often as she saw this wound, she thought how far the gashes of the tiger might have gone into the tender body of her child; and every time she put fresh dressing on the wound, she caressed the buffalo and spoke kindly to him, that the faithful animal might know how grateful a mother can be. Afterwards she hoped that the buffalo understood her, for he must have known why she wept when he was taken away, and that it was not Saïdjah's mother who caused him to be slaughtered. Some days afterward, Saïdjah's father fled out of the country, for he was afraid of being punished for not paying his taxes, and he had no other heirlooms to sell with which to buy another buffalo. His parents had left him but few things. However, he went on for some years after the loss of his last buffalo by working with hired animals: but that is a very unremunerative labor, and moreover sad for one who has had buffaloes of his own.

Saïdjah's mother died of grief, and his father, in a moment of dejection, left Bantam to find work in the Buitenzorg district. But he was punished with stripes because he had left Lebak without a passport, and brought back by the police to Badoer. There he was put in prison, because he was supposed to be mad, which I can well believe, and it was feared he would run amok in a moment of frenzy. But he was not long in prison, for he died soon after. What became of Saïdjah's brothers and sisters I do not know. The house they lived in at Badoer was empty for some time, and then fell down, for it was only built of bamboo covered with cane. A little dust and dirt covered the spot where there had been so much suffering. There are many such places in Lebak.

Saïdjah was already fifteen when his father set out for Buitenzorg, and he did not accompany him thither, because he had other plans in mind. He had been told that there were gentlemen in Batavia who drove in carriages, and that it would be easy to get work as a carriage boy, for which young lads are used, so as not to disturb the equilibrium of the two-wheeled carriage by too much motion. He would, they said, earn much that way if he behaved himself—perhaps in three years he would be able to save enough to buy two buffaloes. This was a pleasant prospect. With the proud gait of one who had conceived a grand idea, he entered Adinda's house one day after his father had gone away, and communicated his plans to her.

"Think of it," said he. "When I come back we shall be old enough to marry, and have enough to buy two buffaloes!"

"I will gladly marry you, Saïdjah, when you come back. I will spin and weave *sarongs* and *slendangs*, and be very diligent all the while."

"Oh, I believe you, Adinda, but—if I find you already married?"

"Saïdjah, you know very well I will marry nobody but you. My father promised me to your father."

"And you yourself—?"

"I shall marry you, you may be sure of that."

"When I come back, I will call from afar off."

"Who will hear it, if we are stamping rice in the village?"

"That is true, but Adinda—oh, yes, this is better: wait for me in the wood, under the Ketapan, where you gave me the Melatti flowers."

"But, Saïdjah, how am I to know when I am to go to the Ketapan?"

Saïdjah considered a moment and said: "Count the moons. I shall stay away three times twelve moons, not counting this moon. See, Adinda, at every new moon cut a notch in your rice block on the floor. When you have cut three times twelve lines, I will be under the Ketapan the next day. Do you promise to be there?"

"Yes, Saïdjah. I will be there, under the Ketapan, near the djatis, when you come back."

Thereupon Saïdjah tore a piece off his much-worn blue turban and gave it to Adinda to keep as a pledge, and then left her and Badoer. He walked many days, passing through Rankas-Belong, not yet capital of Lebak, through Warong-Goonoong, the home of the Assistant Resident, and the next day he came to Pamarangand, which lies in a garden. The day after, he came to Serang, and was astonished at the magnificence and size of the place, and the number of tiled stone houses. He had never before seen the like. He remained there a day, because he was tired, but in the coolness of the night he went his way, and the following day arrived at Tangerang. There he bathed in the river and rested at the home of an acquaintance of his father's who showed him how to make straw hats like those from Manila. He remained a day in order to learn the art, because he thought he might be able to turn it to use later on, if by chance he should fail to find other work in Batavia. The following day toward evening he thanked his host and departed. As soon as it was dark, and no one could see him, he took out the Melatti leaves Adinda had given him, for he was sad, thinking that he would not see her for so long. Neither on the first nor the second day had he realized how lonely he was, because he was captivated by the grand idea of earning money enough to buy two buffaloes, whereas his father had never had more than one, and was too excited over the prospect of seeing Adinda again to grieve over his departure. He had left her in anxious hope. The prospect of seeing her again so occupied his heart that on leaving Badoer and passing the tree, he felt something akin to joy, as if the thirty-six moons were already past. It had seemed that he had only to turn round to see Adinda waiting for him. But the further he went, the more did he realize the length of the period before him. There was something in his soul, that made him walk more slowly—he felt an affliction in his knees, and though it was not dejection that overcame him it was a mournful sadness. He thought of returning, but what would Adinda think of his want of courage?

Therefore he walked on, though not so fast as on the first day. He had the Melatti in his hand and often pressed them to his breast. He had aged much during the past few days, and could not understand how he had been able to live so calmly before, when Adinda was so near that he could see her as often as he liked. Now he could not recapture that calmness. Nor did he understand why, after having taken his leave, he had not gone back once again to see her. He recalled how recently he had quarreled with her about a cord she had made for her brother's kite, which had broken because there was some defect in her work. This made him lose a bet he had with the Tjipoeroet children. "How was it possible," he thought, "to have been angry over that with Adinda?" If there was a defect in the cord, and if the bet *was* lost, ought he to have been so rude and called her names? What, he wondered, if he died at Batavia without having asked her forgiveness? Would it not make him seem a wicked man? When it learned that he had died in a distant place, would not everyone at Badoer say, "It is well Saïdjah has died—he spoke insolently to Adinda!"

Thus his thoughts ran, uttered at first involuntarily and softly, soon in a quiet monologue, and finally in a melancholy song.

He arrived at Batavia, and asked a certain gentleman to take him into his service, which the gentleman did, because Saïdjah spoke no Malay—an advantage there, for servants who do not understand that language are not so corrupt as the others, who have been longer in touch with the Europeans. But Saïdjah soon learned Malay, though he behaved well, for he always remembered the two buffaloes he was going to buy. He grew tall and strong, because he ate every day—not always the case at Badoer. In the stable he was liked, and would certainly not have been rejected if he had asked the hand of the coachman's daughter. His master liked him so much that he soon promoted him to be a house servant, increased his wages, and continually made him presents, to show how pleased he was. Saïdjah's mistress had read Sue's novel, so popular for a short while, and always thought of Prince Djalma when she saw Saïdjah, and the young girls, too, understood better than before why the Javanese painter, Radeen Saleh, had been so successful at Paris. But they thought Saïdjah ungrateful when after almost three years he asked for his dismissal and a certificate of good behaviour. This could not be refused, and Saïdjah went on his journey with a joyful heart.

He counted the treasures he was carrying home. In a roll of bamboo he had his passport and certificate. In a case fastened to a leather girdle something heavy swung against his shoulder, but he enjoyed the feel of that, and no wonder! What would Adinda say? It contained thirty piastres—enough to buy three buffaloes! Nor was that all: on his back was a silver-covered sheath with his poniard. The hilt was indeed a fine one, for he had wound it round with a silk wrapper. And he had still more treasures! In the folds of his loin-cloth he kept a belt of silver links with gold clasps. True, the belt was short, but then Adinda was slender! Suspended by a cord round his neck, and under his clothes, he wore a silken bag in which were the withered Melatti leaves.

Is it to be wondered at that he stopped no longer at Sangerang than to visit the acquaintances who made such fine straw hats? That he said so little to the girls on his way who asked him whence he came and where he was going—the usual salutations; that he no longer thought Serang so beautiful (he who had learned to know Batavia); that he no longer hid himself behind the enclosure as he did three years before when he saw the Resident go riding out (he who had seen the much grander Lord at Buitenzorg, grandfather of the Emperor of Solo); that he paid little attention to the tales of those who went part of the way with him and gave news of Bantam-Kidool—is no wonder. No, he had sublime visions in his mind's eye. He looked for the Ketapan tree in the clouds when he was still far from Badoer. He caught at the air as if to embrace the form that was to meet him under the tree. He pictured to himself the face of Adinda, her head, her shoulders, saw the heavy chignon, black and glossy, confined in a net, hanging down her back; her large eyes glistening in dark reflection, the nostrils raised so proudly as a child (was it possible?), when he had vexed her; and the corner of her lips, when she smiled; and finally, her breasts, now doubtless swelling under her shawl. He could imagine her saying to him, "Welcome, Saïdjah! I have thought of you as I was spinning and weaving and stamping the rice on the floor which shows three times twelve lines cut by my hand. And I am under the Ketapan the first day of the new moon. Welcome, Saïdjah! I will be your wife."

That was the music that resounded in his ears and prevented him from listening to all the news that was told him on the road.

At last he saw the Ketapan, or rather a large, dark spot with many stars above it. That must be the Djati wood, near the tree where he should again see Adinda next morning, after sunrise. He sought in the dark and felt many trunks, finding at last a rough spot on the south side of a tree, and thrust his finger into a hole which Si-Panteh had cut with his knife to exorcise the Evil Spirit that had caused his mother's toothache, a short time before the birth of Panteh's little brother. That was the Ketapan he sought.

Yes, this was indeed the spot where he had looked upon Adinda for the first time with a different eye. She had become different from his other comrades. There she had given him the leaves. He sat down at the foot of the tree and looked at the stars, and when he saw a shooting-star he took it as a welcome of his return to Badoer, and wondered whether Adinda were now asleep, whether she had correctly cut the number of moons on the wood? How terrible if she had missed a moon, as if thirty-six were not quite enough! Had she, he wondered, made him some nice *sarongs* and *slendangs*? Who would now be living in her father's house? Then he thought of his childhood, and his mother, and how the buffalo had saved him from the tiger, of what would have become of Adinda if the buffalo had not been so faithful. He watched the sinking of the stars, and as each disappeared, he calculated how much nearer he was to Adinda. For she would certainly come at the first beam—at daybreak she would be there. Why had she not come the day before?

He was hurt that she had not anticipated the supreme moment that had lighted his soul for three years with indescribable brightness; unjust as he was in his selfishness, it seemed to him that Adinda ought to have been waiting for him. He complained unjustly, for the sun had not yet risen. But the stars were growing pale, and strange colors floated over the mountain tops, which appeared darker as they contrasted sharply with places elsewhere illuminated. Here and there something glowed in the east—arrows of gold and fire darted along the horizon, but disappeared again and seemed to fall down behind the impenetrable curtain which hid the day. It grew lighter and lighter around him: he now saw the landscape and could already distinguish a part of the wood behind which Badoer lay. There Adinda slept.

No, surely, she did not sleep! How could she? Did she not know that Saïdjah would be waiting for her? She had not slept the whole night certainly; the village night police had knocked at her door to ask why her lamp burned so long, and with a sweet laugh she had replied that she had vowed to weave a *slendang* which must be ready before the first day of the new moon. Or perhaps she had passed the night in darkness, sitting on the rice floor, counting with eager fingers the thirty-six lines. Or possibly amused herself by pretending that she miscalculated, and had counted the lines all over again each time, enjoying the delicious assurance that the thirty-six moons had come and gone since her Saïdjah had left her.

Now that it was becoming light, she would be busying herself with useless little things, glancing from time to time over the wide horizon, looking for the sun, the lazy sluggard!

There was a line of bluish red, touching the clouds and making their edges light. The arrows of fire shot higher and higher, and ran over the dark ground, illuminating wide spaces of the earth, meeting, crossing, unrolling, running, and at last uniting in vast patches of fire, painting the azure earth in pigments of shining gold. There was red, blue, and purple, yellow gold. God in Heaven—it was at last daybreak!— Adinda!

Saïdjah had never learned to pray, and it would have been a pity to teach him: a more devout prayer and a more fervent expression of gratitude than his would have been impossible. He would not to go Badoer: actually to see her again was not so wonderful as to await her coming. He sat down at the foot of the Ketapan, and his eyes wandered over the landscape. Nature smiled at him, and seemed to welcome him like a mother. Saïdjah was overjoyed at seeing again so many spots that reminded him of his earlier life. Though his eyes and thoughts wandered, his longing always reverted to the path which leads from Badoer to the Ketapan tree. His senses were wholly alive to Adinda. He saw the abyss to the left, where the earth was yellow, the spot where once a young buffalo had sunk down to the depths: they had all descended there with strong rattan cords, and Adinda's father had been the bravest of the rescue party. How Adinda had clapped her hands! Farther along, over there on the other side by the clump of cocoa-trees, whose leaves waved over the village, Si-Penah had fallen from a tree and been killed. How his mother had wailed—because, she said, Si-Penah was still such a little one—as if her grief had been less if he were larger! True, he *was* small, smaller and more fragile than Adinda.

There was no one on the little road leading from Badoer to the tree. —By and by she would come. It was still very early.

Saïdjah saw a squirrel spring playfully up the trunk of a cocoanut tree and run untiringly to and fro. He forced himself to stand and regard the animal, for this calmed his thoughts, which had been working hard since early morning. His thoughts then ran into song.

There was still no one on the little road.

He caught sight of a butterfly disporting joyously in the increasing warmth. ...

Still, there was no one on the little road. The sun climbed higher into the heavens, and it grew warm. ...

Still, no one appeared on the little road. ... No one.

She must have fallen asleep toward morning, weary with watching during the night, during many nights. She had not slept for weeks. That was it! Ought he to get up and go to Badoer? That would look as though he doubted her coming. ... That man over there was too far away, and Saïdjah did not wish to speak to anyone about Adinda. He would see her alone. Surely, surely, she would come soon!

He would wait. ...

But what if she were ill—dead?

Like a wounded stag he flew along the pathway toward the village. He saw nothing and heard nothing. Normally he would have heard, for there were men standing in the road at the entrance to the village, who cried out, "Saïdjah, Saïdjah!"

Was it his eagerness, or what, that prevented his finding Adinda's house? He had already run to the end of the village, and as if mad, he turned back, beating his head in despair to think that he had passed her house. But he soon found himself back at the entrance of the village, and—was it a dream! Again he had missed the house. Once more he flew back and suddenly stood still, and took his head in both hands to press out the madness that stunned him.

"Drunk, drunk!" he exclaimed. "I am drunk!"

The women of Badoer came out of their houses and saw with sorrow poor Saïdjah standing there, for they knew that he had been looking for Adinda's house, and that the house was no longer there. ...

When the chief of Parang-Koodjang had taken away the buffaloes belonging to Adinda's father, Adinda's mother had died of grief, and her baby sister soon after, for there was no one to suckle her. Adinda's father, fearing punishment for failing to pay his land taxes, had fled the district, taking with him Adinda and her brothers. He had heard how Saïdjah's father had been punished at Buitenzorg with stripes, because he had left Badoer without a passport. He had therefore not gone to Buitenzorg, nor to the Preangan, nor to Bantam, but to Tjilangkahan, bordering upon the sea. There he had hidden in the woods, awaiting the arrival of Pa-Ento, Pa-Lontah, Si-Penah, Pa-Ansive, Abdoel-Isma, and others who had been robbed of their buffaloes by the chief of Parang-Koodjang, all of whom feared punishment for failure to pay their taxes. There, during the night, they had taken possession of a fishing-boat, and gone to sea. They steered toward the west, as far as Java Head. There they turned northward, until they came in sight of Prince's Island, and sailed round the east coast, going thence to the Lampoons. That at least was what people whispered to one another in Lebak whenever there was any question about buffaloes or land-taxes.

But Saïdjah could scarcely understand what they told him. There was a buzzing in his ears, as if a gong were sounding in his head. He felt the blood throbbing convulsively in his temples; it seemed as though his head would burst under the pressure. He said nothing, and looked about stupefied, not seeing anything. At last he laughed horribly.

An old woman led him to her cottage. She would take care of the piteous fool. His laugh gradually became less horrible, but he still spoke no word. During the night the inmates of the hut were frightened by the sound of his voice. He sang out monotonously: "I don't know where I shall die!"

Some of the natives collected a little money in order to offer a sacrifice to the crocodile of the Tji-Udjiung, in order to cure Saïdjah, whom they thought insane. But he was not insane, for on a certain night when the moon was extraordinarily clear, he rose from his couch and quietly left the hut, and sought out the place where Adinda's house had stood. It was not easy to find it, for many houses had fallen down. But he recognized the spot by looking at the rays of moonlight that filtered down through the trees, as sailors measure their positions by lighthouses and mountain-tops.

That was the spot. There had Adinda lived!

Stumbling over half-decayed bamboos and pieces of fallen roof, he made his way to the sanctuary which he sought. He found some few remains of the enclosure still standing erect. There had been Adinda's room, and there was the bamboo pin on which she had hung her dress when she was retiring at night. The walls of the room were turned to dust. He took up a handful of it, pressed it to his lips, and breathed hard. ...

The next day he asked the old woman who had taken him in, where the rice-floor was, that stood in Adinda's house. The woman was glad at last to hear him speak, and ran through the village to look for the remains of the floor. She pointed out to Saïdjah the new proprietor, and Saïdjah followed in silence. He came to the rice-floor. On it he counted thirty-two lines. . . .

He gave the old woman piastres enough to buy a buffalo, and left Badoer. At Tjilangkahan he bought a fishing-boat, and after sailing for two days, reached the Lampoon Islands, where the insurgents had arisen against the Dutch rule. He joined a troop of Badoer men, not so much with the idea of fighting as of finding Adinda, for he was naturally tender-hearted, and more disposed to sorrow than to bitterness.

One day after the insurgents had suffered a defeat, he wandered through a village that had just been taken by the Dutch army, and was therefore in flames. Saïdjah knew that the defeated troop was composed largely of Badoer men. He wandered like a ghost among the houses that had not yet been burned. In one of them he found the dead body of Adinda's father with a bayonet wound in the breast. Near him lay the bodies of Adinda's three brothers, still boys—children, in fact.

Not far off lay the body of Adinda, naked and horribly mutilated.

A small piece of blue linen had penetrated into the gaping wound in the breast, which seemed to have made an end to a long struggle.

Saïdjah went off to meet some Dutch soldiers who were driving the surviving insurgents at the point of the bayonet into the fire of the burning houses. He went out to meet the broad bayonets, and pressed forward with all his might, until the steel was buried up to the hilt in his breast.

Not long after there was much rejoicing at Batavia for the new victory, which so added to the laurels of the Dutch-Indian army. And the Government wrote that tranquillity had been restored in the Lampoons. The King of Holland, enlightened by his statesmen, again rewarded so much heroism with many orders of knighthood.

HERMAN HEIJERMANS

(1864–1924)

HERMAN HEIJERMANS, JR. made his literary debut in 1892 with a
peasant novel, and though he continued to write fiction for many
years, he was chiefly engaged in writing plays and, in later life, in
managing his own theatre in Amsterdam. His now famous *Sketches*,
first issued under the pseudonym of Samuel Falkland, are known
simply as "Falklands." These are quaint and homely tales of the life
of the lower middle classes.

    Grandfather's Birthday Present is one of the most delightful of these
"Falklands." The present version was translated by Dr. A. van
C. P. Huizinga, especially for this collection. It is included by per-
mission of the author's heirs.

GRANDFATHER'S BIRTHDAY PRESENT

(From *Sketches*, by "Samuel Falkland")

POOR as they all were, not one of the family had ever been able
to rise even to a moderate state of prosperity. It was an invariable
rule among them to be constantly on the lookout for some miraculous
turn in the tide of fortune by which the chronically empty coffers
might be suddenly replenished.

Jet, the eldest daughter, had for a while been most successful, until
her husband was sent to the hospital. It was her idea to give grandfather a new Bible with a gold-plated clasp, while each of the grandchildren should give him some inconsiderable trifle. This plan entailed
no excessive outlay, which might be regretted later on.

Dirk was the next. He was six years younger than his sister. Three
other brothers and sisters had moved away while their mother was yet
alive. Dirk thought little of sister Jet's proposal; he was of the opinion
that if grandfather were to have a Bible with a gold clasp, he would
none the less continue to use the old Bible he had always read out of
with his wife. Besides, Dirk had ideas of his own; everyone had a right
to his convictions; *he* had not been inside a church for years, and he
would certainly vote against the Bible. No, if they were all to join in
making one gift, it was necessary to have everyone's assent. Now, he had
seen a perfectly stunning armchair in the window of a furniture store,
where all the prices had been reduced twenty per cent. In giving the

old man this, a few well-chosen words could be offered on the peculiar fitness of passing the last years of his life in rest. Besides, the chair in which he read his newspaper over by the window was a wreck; the springs were actually sticking out.

Mary was the second daughter. She had been separated from her husband (at the expense of the state!), and was now expecting her fourth child, before the decree was finally pronounced. She did not like the idea of the armchair. It was like Dirk to propose a thing of that sort! No one forced grandfather to sit on the springs of the old chair, and besides, was it not grandmother who had worn away its seat by constant use! Grandfather had said so a dozen times. If the whole family were going to give him a present, it should be something useful, and not stupid. Now, a winter coat, a warm muffler, a pair of gloves or some good stout slippers—these would be practical, and not nearly so expensive.

Piet and Frans, neither of whom had contributed anything to the family exchequer during the past year and had paid many visits to the pawnshop, had had to be helped out by grandfather. They made the greatest fuss of all, and were irrevocably set against the Bible, the armchair, *and* the winter coat. They had grandiose notions (without the wherewithal to realize them), and spoke of decorating the living-room with bunting and spruce, while grandfather was asleep and figured up the costs of a generous supply of raisins and brandy and gin.

Henk was the youngest son. He had recently signed up for service in the East Indies, and though he had long since spent the last of his premium money, it was his idea that the problem of deciding on a present (there were only four days left) should be solved by giving the old man a photograph of the entire family, children and grandchildren all together in one group. That would be a fine thing for everybody—especially for Henk himself, when he was far away in the Indies.

After some discussion, this proposal was accepted, and the next day, which was a Sunday, they all went to the photographer's and posed. Not one member of the family was absent, and even Toon, Jet's husband, who had left the hospital the night before with a thick growth of beard, managed to be present. The women—Mary, Truns and Jet—sat on chairs in the center of the group; the men—Dirk, Piet, Henk and Toon—stood behind them, Piet on the extreme left with his year-and-a-half old son, and Henk, in his new uniform, on the extreme right, with Santje, the youngest of Jet's squalling infants. The other five grandchildren knelt on the floor against their mother's knees.

They were fourteen in all—one more than the unlucky number. The photographer said that he had seldom had the pleasure of seeing a finer group in his studio. It was not easy, however, for the photographer to pose them: Piet's Willy kept up a continual howl, he was so afraid of the long-haired fellow who kept poking his head under that black cloth, and when the photographer shook his doll above the camera to attract the attention of the other youngsters, Willy set up such a scream that Truns had to get up from her chair to calm him. This continued fully a quarter of an hour, and when at last they could all get up, everyone was so on edge that they burst out laughing when anyone sighed or spoke. The first two exposures were unsuccessful: the first time Santje sneezed—on purpose, it seemed; and just as the photographer had counted three, Henk bawled out. The second time Mary's Charley stood up too soon, because he thought it was all over, Jet's Jan having pinched him. Each child received a box on the ears. After the wailing had subsided and everyone had sat stiff in his Sunday best, the third time all went well.

Nobody had expected that the photographer would ask for a cash payment, but as he knew Dirk well (Dirk worked in the drugstore opposite), he insisted; Dirk paid him two guilders on account, and the photographer promised that the picture would be ready Wednesday morning at ten o'clock.

"But what," asked Dirk prudently as they turned to go, "what if it shouldn't turn out right?" "In that event," replied the photographer, "you need not pay." "Very well, then," said Dirk with evident relief.

The whole affair was of course kept secret from grandfather. That is, he had been told about it before evening by not more than four of the family. Jet's Jan had called that afternoon with his sister, to ask for candy and two cents. "Grandfather," he said, "I know what you're going to get for your birthday: you'll never guess what it is."

The old man laughed, and taking his pipe from between his toothless jaws inquired, "It's pretty, is it, Jan?"

"We mustn't tell, grandpa."

"Is it something good to eat?"

"No. It would spoil your stomach!" he said, laughing.

"Is it something to read, eh?"

"You *can*."

"Something to sit on?"

"You *can*. Ha, ha!"

"Something to wear?"

"No, you can't wear it."

"Well, I don't think I can guess," smiled the old man contentedly.

Hoping that the two cents which he invariably received from the old man on Sundays might be increased to three, the youngster let slip a hint. "All of us—father, mother, Mary, Aunt Truns, Uncle Dirk, Uncle Piet, Uncle Henk all dressed up in his uniform, 'n all of us, had to sit still for it over half an hour."

"So," nodded grandfather, "and will it go in a frame?"

"I'm not allowed to tell that."

An hour later Henk came in for a glass of something to drink.

"Well, father," he said, "you'll be surprised next Wednesday. There'll be something you've never had the like of before. Jet wanted to give you a new Bible, Dirk preferred an armchair, and Mary a winter overcoat. But I put my foot down; I knew you wouldn't care for things like that. So I said—but you'll see. It's no fun if you know beforehand."

"I'll bet," said the old man, "I can guess what it is. I can smell it in the air."

"And I'll bet you," said the other, "even if you keep guessing all day and all night—" For a moment the old man sat pensively behind a cloud of blue tobacco smoke, then came out plump:

"It's something square. It has twenty-eight eyes, twenty-eight hands, twenty-eight ears, and fourteen mouths. I'm kind of warm, hey?"

"By Jiminy!" exclaimed Henk, "have they given it away already? Well, are you pleased?"

"I was just about to tell you," pursued grandfather, "that you ought to have a picture taken before you went to the Indies. We won't see each other soon again."

Later during the same day Dirk and Aunt Jet threw out further hints about the great surprise, and seemed so disappointed when they realized that others had revealed the secret. Now that it was no longer a secret everyone agreed that the photograph was, after all, the best present, so much better than a Bible would have been, or a chair or a coat. A family photograph was, after all, a present for everyone, and for all time. Grandfather was to have a large-sized copy in a frame, while the others would have ordinary unframed copies. Everyone looked forward with the keenest curiosity to seeing the picture, youngsters and grown-ups alike.

Tuesday evening after grandfather had retired (an old gentleman of seventy cannot stay up late), Dirk, Piet and Henk decorated the living-room in grand style. Bunting and spruce adorned the upper walls and made the place look as though it were for a wedding. Over the mirror they hung a pasteboard shield on which silver letters, cut by Truns, spelled out the following: *God Give You Many More Years Among Your Children and Grandchildren.* Round the arms and back of the chair in which Grandmother had died was a wreath of paper roses.

In order that the old man should not suspect what they were doing, they walked about in their stocking feet; and in order not to wake him they pinned the decorations with hairpins rather than hammer and nails. Jet and Mary had to go home with their hair down, for they had used up all their hairpins.

On the morning of the great festivity, the sun shone bright on the tulle curtains, and so gilded the flowers in the windows that it was impossible not to enter into a holiday mood. On this lovely morning the whole room, gay with bunting and spruce, was indeed overwhelmingly grand. At nine grandfather was given a large cup of tea in bed, with two slices of bread and butter. They had to keep him upstairs until the photograph should arrive at ten. The photographer had promised to deliver it to Dirk's by that time, and of course he would keep his word.

They were all dressed in their finest. Jet's Jan was rehearsing to himself the poem he was to address to grandfather when the old man should join them. His footsteps were now heard upstairs, pacing back and forth. He had already twice called down to inquire how long he was to be kept waiting.

On the stroke of ten, Dirk stepped into the little garden from the street. But his hands were empty and his countenance was woeful.

"Where's the picture?" gasped Jet, trembling with excitement. "Didn't he send it to you?"

"Haven't you got it with you?" asked Mary. "For goodness' sake, say something! What are you standing there like that for?"

"The old curmudgeon!" growled Dirk, clenching his fist. "He sent it all right, but with the bill to be collected on delivery."

"Collected on delivery!"

"Yes, and he promised to—I'd like to smash his teeth in for him! As if I wasn't going to pay him!"

"Then why didn't you give him the money?" inquired Truns in perfect innocence, though she had already determined not to pay her share until the picture had been delivered. "We're all good for our shares."

"What the devil!" snarled Dirk. "Do *you* run around with that much loose cash in your pocket? Did you expect me to pay it out of the drugstore cash-box?"

"Come, come," said Frans, trying to smooth matters, "nobody could expect you to do that. After all, didn't the photographer tell us all we didn't have to pay if the picture wasn't right? Cash on delivery, the idea! You can't ask people to buy a pig in a poke like that!"

"Well, it'll be a surprise for us all," said Piet, who was quite unconcerned over the matter of payment.

Just then Henk came in. "Well, where is it?" he asked, with the self-importance of one who had thought of the idea in the first place, and had already paid his share.

"We'll have to whistle for it," answered Jet. "That nasty photographer won't deliver it without his pay."

"Well—?"

"Well, nothing!" snapped Dirk. "I didn't have the twenty-seven fifty, so the messenger took it back."

"Good Lord," said Henk, "I thought you knew the fellow. You made the arrangements."

"Can I make the fellow deliver it?" said Dirk. "I went to see him, but he wasn't in; won't be back till the afternoon. If you'd paid your share, I wouldn't have looked such a fool."

"You can't tell me," said Henk, "that if you'd tried—"

"Are *you* so flush yourself?" replied Dirk heatedly. "Now, if we'd only bought the chair, we wouldn't have had to take something we hadn't seen."

In the midst of this quarreling the door squeaked, and grandfather appeared. He had already called three or four times from the top of the stairs. He wanted to know when he might come down, and was curious to learn the reason of the squabbling.

"Since you seem to have forgotten me," he beamed, "I thought I'd better take a look myself, eh, what?" He was nicely shaved and wore a clean white tie. He was smoking the new pipe Jan had brought him as his first present when he had sent up breakfast. He regarded the decorations with dimmed eyes.

"Congratulations, father!" cried Jet, kissing the old man's parchment-like cheeks, "and many happy returns!"

Then came all the others in turn, offering the old man birthday greetings, while he sat in the decorated armchair and read the inscription on the shield over the mirror. He thanked them in a trembling voice for their thoughtfulness while he nodded his head. After he had finished, he looked about expectantly for the big present. From six mouths he heard simultaneously the history of the tragic outcome, and the unspeakable turpitude of the photographer.

But toward evening happiness was restored: in order not to disappoint his numerous sons and daughters and grandchildren and dim the glory of their intended gift, grandfather himself made up the balance of the sum that was owing.

Hungary

INTRODUCTION

IT would be possible to begin the history of the short story in Hungary with the transplanted legends of St. Francis in the Ehrenfeld manuscript, one of the first books in Hungarian literature, dating from the Middle Ages. In the ballads and romances and epics of the Sixteenth and Seventeenth Centuries we have discovered episodes that might have been fitted into a framework showing the historical development in the art of narrative among the Hungarians. But as a matter of fact, the earlier centuries are barren of important short stories.

It was only in the Eighteenth Century that modern Hungarian literature really began. The Kisfaludi brothers, who came toward the end of the century, were among its pioneers. Karoly Kisfaludi, though better known as a dramatist, may be taken as a typical figure, and the story chosen to represent his achievement is in itself a capital example of the art.

The Nineteenth Century, crowded as it was with war, revolution, and political unrest, was the most fruitful period in Hungarian literature. Though the drama and the lyric poem were brought to a high point of development, the novel and the tale were no less assiduously developed. The two dominating figures of the time, so far as fiction is concerned, were Jokai and Mikszath. Both lived long lives and wrote a great deal; both were essentially national, and were loved by their people.

Of the more recent writers, Ferenc Molnar is the most distinguished. Unlike Jokai and Mikszath, Herczeg, Gyulay, and the rest, he is a cosmopolitan.

KAROLY KISFALUDI

(1788–1830)

KAROLY KISFALUDI and his brother Alexander are among the great pioneers in modern Hungarian literature. Though Karoly is chiefly celebrated as a dramatist, he managed, during his brief and adventurous life, to write some extraordinary short tales. He was, in the words of a Hungarian critic, "a thorough Bohemian, of a dreamy yet light-hearted disposition." A classic writer, he yet was able to impart to his stories an air of actuality which makes them seem as if they were written for the present generation. *The Invisible Wound* comprises most of the elements required by the strictest critics for the composition of a short story, and yet it conveys that indescribable quality of vitality that seems to persist in all art, regardless of rules and theories.

The translation of the story was made by Mr. Joseph Szebenyei for this volume, and appears here for the first time in English. Acknowledgment is hereby made to the translator for permission to use the MS.

THE INVISIBLE WOUND

EARLY one morning before the famous surgeon was even out of his bed he received an urgent caller who insisted that his case could not be postponed even for a minute; he demanded instant attention. The surgeon dressed hurriedly and rang for his valet.

"Let the patient come in," he said.

The man who entered appeared to belong to the best class of society. His pale face and nervous demeanor betrayed physical suffering. His right hand was tied up in a sling and, although he could control his features, a painful groan escaped from his lips now and again.

"Please be seated. What can I do for you?"

"I haven't been able to sleep for a week. There is some trouble with my right hand. I cannot make out what it is. It may be cancer or some other terrible disease. At first it did not bother me much, but lately it began to burn. I have not had a moment's relief. It pains me terribly. The pain increases hourly, becoming more and more agonizing and unbearable. I have come to town to consult you. If I have to bear it another hour, I shall go mad. I want you to burn it out or cut it out, or do something with it."

The surgeon reassured the patient by declaring that it was not perhaps necessary to operate.

"No, no," the man insisted. "It will have to be operated on. I came purposely to have the diseased part cut out. Nothing else can help."

He lifted his hand from the sling with considerable effort, and continued:

"I must ask you not to be surprised if you do not see any visible wound on my hand. The case is quite unusual."

The doctor assured the patient that he was not in the habit of being surprised at unusual things. Still, after looking at it, he dropped the hand in sheer astonishment, for there seemed to be absolutely nothing the matter with it. It looked like any other hand; it was not even discolored. Yet it was evident that the man suffered terrific pains, for the way he caught his right hand with his left when the doctor let it fall, demonstrated that fact quite conclusively.

"Where does it hurt you?"

He pointed to a round spot between the two large veins, but snatched the hand back when the physician cautiously touched the spot with the tip of his finger.

"Is that where it hurts?"

"Yes. Terribly."

"Do you feel the pressure when I place my finger on it?"

The man could not answer, but the tears that came into his eyes told the story.

"It's extraordinary. I can see nothing."

"Neither do I, but the pain is still there and I would rather die than go on this way."

The surgeon examined it all over again, with a microscope, took the man's temperature, and finally shook his head.

"The skin is perfectly healthy. The arteries are normal; not the slightest inflammation or swelling. It is as normal as any hand can be."

"I think it is a bit redder on the spot."

"Where?"

The stranger made a circle on the back of his hand about the size of a farthing: "Here."

The doctor looked at the man. He began to think that he had to deal with a lunatic.

"You will have to stay in town and I shall try to help you within the next few days," he said.

"I cannot wait a minute. Do not think, doctor, that I am insane, or under any delusion. This invisible wound hurts me terribly and I want you to cut out just that round part as far as the bone."

"I am not going to do it, sir."

"Why not?"

"Because there is nothing the matter with your hand. It is as healthy as my own."

"You seem to think I am a madman, or that I am deceiving you," said the patient as he drew out of his wallet a thousand-florin banknote and placed it on the table. "You see I am in earnest. The matter is important enough for me to pay a thousand for it. Please perform the operation."

"If you offered me all the money in the world I would not touch a healthy limb with the operating knife."

"Why not?"

"Because it would not be according to professional ethics. All the world would call you an idiot and would accuse me of taking advantage of your weakness, or declare that I could not diagnose a wound that did not exist."

"Very well, sir. Then I shall ask you another favor. I shall undertake the operation myself, though my left hand is rather clumsy at such things. All I will ask of you, is to take care of the wound after I operate on it."

The surgeon saw with astonishment that the man was quite serious, and watched him take off his coat and turn up his shirt sleeve. The man even took out his pocket knife, for want of any other instrument. Before the doctor could intervene, the stranger had made a deep incision in his hand.

"Stop," he shouted, afraid lest the sufferer should sever a vein. "Since you believe it must be done, very well, I'll do it."

He then prepared for the operation. When it came to the actual cutting the doctor advised his patient to turn his head away, for people are generally upset at the sight of their own blood.

"Quite unnecessary," said the other. "I must direct your hand so that you may know how far to cut."

The stranger took the operation stoically and was helpful with his directions. His hand never even trembled, and when the round spot had been carved out he sighed a sigh of happy relief, as if a load had been taken off his shoulders.

"You don't feel any pain now?" asked the surgeon.

"Not the least," he said with a smile. "It is as if the pain had been cut off and the slight irritation caused by the cutting seems like a cool breeze after a hot spell. Just let the blood run. It soothes me."

After the wound was bandaged, the stranger looked happy and contented. He was a changed man. He gratefully pressed the doctor's hand with his own left hand.

"I am very grateful to you, indeed."

The surgeon visited the patient at his hotel for several days after the operation and learned to respect the man, who occupied a high position in the county. He was learned and cultured, and was a member of one of the best families in the land.

After the wound was completely healed the stranger returned to his country home.

Three weeks later the patient again appeared at the surgeon's office. His hand was again in a sling and he complained of the same tormenting pain in the very spot where it hurt him before the operation.

His face looked like wax, and cold perspiration glistened on his brow. He sank into an armchair, and without saying a word held out his right hand for the doctor to look at.

"Good Lord, what has happened?"

"You didn't cut it deep enough," he groaned. "The pain returned; it is even worse than before. I am almost done for. I did not want to trouble you again, so I just bore it, but I can't bear it any longer. You must operate again."

The surgeon examined the spot. The place where he had operated was quite healed, and covered with fresh skin. Not one of the veins seemed disturbed, the pulse was normal. There was no fever, yet the man was trembling in every limb.

"I never experienced or heard anything like this before."

There was nothing to be done but to repeat the operation. Everything passed off as it had the first time. The pain stopped, and though the patient experienced a great relief, this time he failed to smile, and when he thanked the doctor it was with a sad and depressed expression.

"You needn't be surprised if I am back again in a month," he said as he took leave.

"You mustn't think of it."

"It is as sure as there's a God in heaven," he said, with an air of finality. "Au revoir."

· The surgeon discussed the case with several of his colleagues, each of whom expressed a different opinion. Not one, however, could offer a satisfactory explanation.

A month passed and the patient did not appear. Another few weeks, and then, instead of the patient, came a letter from his place of residence. The surgeon opened it with pleasure, thinking that the pain had not returned. The letter ran as follows:

"Dear Doctor: I do not want to leave you in any doubt as to the origin of my trouble, and do not care to carry the secret of it into my grave, or perhaps elsewhere. I wish to acquaint you with the history of my terrible illness. It has returned three times now and I do not intend to go on struggling against it any longer. I am only able to write this letter by placing a burning coal on the spot as an antidote against the hellish flames that burn it within.

"Six months ago I was a very happy man. I was rich and contented; I found pleasure in everything that appeals to a man of thirty-five. I married a year ago. It was a love match. A very beautiful, kindly and cultured young lady was my wife. She had been companion to a Countess not far from my estate. She loved me and her heart was full of gratitude. For six months the time passed happily, each day bringing greater happiness than the last. She would walk miles along the highway to meet me when I had to go to the town and would not stay away even at the home of her former mistress, where she often visited, for more than a few hours. Her longing for me made the others of her party uncomfortable. She would never dance with another man, and would confess it as a great crime if she happened to dream of some one else in her sleep. She was a lovely and innocent child.

"I can't say what it was that brought me to the belief that this was but pretense. Man is foolish enough to seek misery in the midst of his greatest happiness.

"She had a small sewing-table, the drawer of which she always kept locked. This began to torture me. I often noticed that she never left the key in the drawer and she never left it unlocked. What could she have to conceal so carefully? I became mad with jealousy. I did not believe her innocent eyes, her kisses and loving embraces. Perhaps all this was but cunning deceit?

"One day the Countess came to fetch her and managed to persuade her to spend the day at the Castle. I promised that I should follow later in the afternoon.

"The carriage had scarcely pulled out of the yard when I began trying to open the drawer of the sewing-table. One of the many keys I tried at last opened it. Rummaging among the many feminine effects under a folder of silk, I discovered a bundle of letters. One could recognize them at the first glance. They were, of course, love letters, tied together with a pink ribbon.

'I did not stop to consider that it was not honorable to commit such an indiscretion: looking for secrets of my wife's girlhood days! Something urged me to go on; perhaps they belonged to a later period— since she had borne my name? I untied the ribbon and read the letters one after the other.

"It was the most terrible hour of my life.

"They revealed the most unpardonable treachery ever committed against a man. They were written by one of my most intimate friends. And their tone. ... They revealed the tenderest intimacy and deepest passion. How he urged her to secrecy! What he said about stupid husbands! How he advised her what to do to keep her husband in ignorance! Every one of them had been written after our marriage. And I thought I was happy! I don't want to describe my feelings. I drank my poison to the least drop. Then I folded the letters and returned them to their hiding-place, locking the drawer again.

"I knew that if I did not go to the Castle she would return in the evening. That was precisely what happened. She sprang gayly out of the carriage and rushed to meet me on the porch, kissing and embracing me with the utmost tenderness. I pretended that nothing was amiss.

"We chatted, had supper together and went to bed as usual, each in our own room. I had by that time decided upon a course of action which I would carry out with the stubbornness of a maniac. What a miserable deception on the part of nature to endow sin with such an open face, I said to myself as I entered her room at midnight and looked at her beautiful innocent face as she slept. The poison had taken effect in my soul and had eaten itself through every vein of my body. I placed my right hand silently on her neck and pressed it with all my might. For a moment she opened her eyes and looked at me astounded, then closed them again and died. She did not make a move in self-defense, but died as quietly as though she were in a dream. She bore no grudge against me even for killing her. One drop of blood oozed through her lips and dropped on my hand—you know the spot. I only noticed it in the morning after it was already dried. We buried her without much ado. I lived out in the country on a private estate and there was no controlling authority to investigate. Besides, no one would have thought anything about the matter, for the woman was my wife. She had no relations and no friends, and there were no questions to answer. I purposely sent out notifications of her death after the funeral, in order to escape the importunities of other people.

"I felt no pangs of conscience. I had been cruel, but she had deserved it. I did not hate her. I could easily forget her. No murderer committed his deed with more indifference than I did.

"When I arrived at the house, the Countess had just driven up. She was too late for the funeral, as I intended she should be. She was under a tremendous strain. The terror and the unexpectedness of the news almost dazed her. She spoke in a queer manner and I could not make out her meaning as she tried to console me. I didn't listen to her with any interest, it is true, for I was in no need of consolation. Then she took hold of my hand in an intimate manner and said she would like to entrust a secret to me, adding that she hoped I would not take advantage of it.

"Then she said that she had entrusted a bundle of letters to my late wife; she could not possibly keep them at her own house owing to their peculiar character, and asked whether I would be good enough to return them to her. I felt a chill down my spine as I listened to her. With assumed calm I asked her what those contained? She trembled at the question and said:

"'Your wife was the most faithful and loyal woman I ever met. She did not ask what they contained; she even gave me her word never to look into them.'

"'Where did she keep your letters?'

"'She said she kept them under lock and key in the drawer of her sewing-table. They are tied with a pink ribbon. You will easily recognize them. Thirty letters in all.'

"I took her to the room where the sewing-table stood and opened the drawer. I took out the bundle and handed it to her.

"'Are these the letters?'

"She reached out for them eagerly. I dared not raise my eyes for fear she might read something in them. She left soon afterward.

"Exactly one week after the burial a stinging pain visited the spot on my hand where the drop of blood fell on that terrible night. The rest you know. I know it is nothing but auto-suggestion, but I cannot rid myself of it. It is my punishment for the hastiness and cruelty with which I murdered my innocent and lovely girl. I no longer try to struggle against it. I am going to join her and will try to obtain her pardon. She will surely forgive me. She will love me just as she loved me when she lived. I thank you, Doctor, for all you have done for me."

MAURUS JOKAI

(1825–1904)

JOKAI is the most famous of all Hungarian novelists. It has been said that "if all the persons whom he has called to life in his novels were to appear... the multitude would line the streets for more than a mile." So much for quantity; but Jokai was an artist as well. In his numerous short stories he was a keen if not a very subtle observer of the life about him. He led a very active life, as politician, journalist and editor. *A Ball* is characteristic of his skill as a narrator: the simplicity of the point of view shown in this story must not deceive the reader. Notice that the incidents are related in a letter from one prim young lady to another, neither of whom would for a moment be able to understand such shocking war stories as were to be told later by men like Stephen Crane and Ambrose Bierce.

The present translation, published anonymously, is reprinted from Jokai's *Hungarian Sketches in Peace and War*, Edinburgh, 1854.

A BALL

DEAREST ILMA: I am in despair! I am very ill, and in bed! Ah, I shall never dance a quadrille again. I will go into a convent, or marry, or make away with myself in some other way. Conceive what has happened to me! Oh, it is too dreadful! Too shocking! You never read such a thing in a romance.

You may have heard that the Hungarian troops marched through here last week after the battle of Branyisko; there was the greatest panic and confusion at the news of their approach. We expected that they would have set fire to the town, and pillaged and killed us—indeed, mamma said there was no knowing what horrors they might commit, and she desired me to scratch my face with my nails and disfigure myself in case they should wish to carry me off. Did you ever hear such an idea?

Well, ere long the National Guards marched in with their bands playing. Papa went to meet them with a deputation. Our servants all ran out to see the soldiers, and I could not find mamma anywhere; the day before, she had never ceased searching for a place to conceal herself in, never answering me when I called and looked for her; and if by chance I found her in a wardrobe, or in the clock, she scolded me severely for discovering her hiding-place.

As I was left quite alone, I thought the best thing I could do was to lay out the table with every sort of eatable and wine I could find, that at least these National Guards should not eat me, but find something else prepared for them; and I determined in my own mind to give them quietly everything they asked for, and let them see I did not fear them in the least. And then I waited with the utmost resignation to hear cries for help through the streets.

At last the sound of spurred footsteps and clinking swords echoed along the corridor, but no noise of swearing; *au contraire*, a very polite double knock at the door. In my terror or flurry, however, I had no power to say, Come in. But do not imagine they broke in the door with their muskets—not at all, they only repeated the knock and waited till I gave permission, in a trembling voice—expecting at least six dog-faced Tartars to enter, with square heads and skin caps—beards down to their girdles, and dressed in bear-hides with leather sacks over their shoulders to thrust their plunder into, and covered all over with pistols and knives, as I have heard mamma describe them. But conceive my surprise when, instead of all this, two young officers walked in, one fair and the other dark, but very well-dressed and just like other people.

They wore small fur cloaks across their shoulders, and under this a tight-fitting attila—no idea of skins or square heads; indeed, the dark one was quite a handsome youth. Their first action was to beg pardon for any inconvenience they might cause, to which I replied that I considered it no inconvenience whatever, and was ready to serve them in any way they wanted. The dark youth, glancing at the table, could scarcely refrain from a smile, which embarrassed me extremely, as I thought he must have supposed I had prepared all this on purpose for him. At last the other relieved my embarrassment by thanking me politely for my proffered services, and only begged I would show them an apartment where they could take some rest, as they were very tired, not having slept in a bed for six weeks, or lain down at all for two days. Poor creatures! I quite pitied them—not to have slept in a bed for six weeks!

"Indeed," I exclaimed, "it must have been very uncomfortable to have been obliged to sleep on a divan, or even in a camp-bed for six entire weeks!"

They both laughed. "On the bare ground—on the snow—under the open sky," they replied.

Oh, heavens! Even our servants would have died, had they been obliged to pass one winter's night out of doors. I begged them to follow me, and showed them our best room, in which there were two beds. As the servants were all out, I was going to make down the beds myself.

"Oh, we cannot allow that!" they both exclaimed. "We can do that ourselves," and, seeing they had need of rest, I bowed and hastened to leave them alone.

Scarcely had I reached my own room when I heard a terrible shriek which seemed to proceed from the apartment I had just left, and cries of "Help! Robbers! Murder!"

I knew the voice, but in my terror I could not remember whose it was, and still the cries continued: "Help! Murder!"

If you can imagine my situation, you may suppose that I never moved from the spot on which I stood till the voice, echoing through the rooms, at last approached my apartment. It was my dear mamma —but in what a plight. Her clothes all crumpled, her cap over her eyes, one of her shoes off, and her whole face as red as if she had come out of an oven. It was a long time before I could make out where she had been or what had happened to her. Well, only fancy: she had hidden in the very room where I had quartered my two guests, and where, do you think? In one of the beds, under all the feather quilts! Now you may imagine the rest, and the surprise of the National Guard officer when he threw himself down, half-dead with fatigue. Poor mamma had good reason to cry out, but what an idea, to hide there! After much trouble, I calmed her a little, and endeavored to persuade her that these National Guards had not come to rob or kill us; and finally I succeeded so far that she promised not to hide again, and I undertook to explain to the officers that mamma had the rheumatism and was obliged to get under all those feather beds by way of a vapor bath!

Meanwhile, our guests had scarcely time to fall asleep when an orderly arrived who desired to speak with them.

"You cannot see them at present," I replied. "They are both asleep; but you may wait, or come again."

"Where are they sleeping?" he asked.

I showed him the room, and without the slightest consideration as to whether it was proper to wake them, after being two whole days without rest, he walked coolly into the room. I expected they would have immediately cut the man in pieces for disturbing them, instead of which, in a few minutes, they both appeared, completely dressed, and followed the orderly without the slightest sign of displeasure. The Major had sent for them.

How strange this military life must be! How people can submit without the least resistance! I should be a very bad soldier indeed, for I always like to know beforehand why I am ordered to do a thing.

In about half an hour the officers returned—no ill-humor or sleepiness was visible; they did not even return to their rooms, but asked for mamma, and me and announced to us in very flattering terms that the officers' corps had improvised a ball for that night, to which we were invited, and then they immediately begged to engage me for a *Française*, a *Czardas*, and a *Polonaise* (there was to be no waltzing), and I naturally promised everything.

It was our first ball since the Carnival, and they seemed to enjoy the thoughts of it as much as I did, for they would not hear of sleeping any more.

Mamma, however, never ceased making every objection and difficulty she could think of.

"You have no ball-dress."

"My white dress, dear mamma. I only wore it once."

"It is old-fashioned."

"A little bow of National ribbon, and you will have the prettiest of new fashions," interrupted the dark officer.

"But my foot aches," persevered mamma.

"There is no absolute necessity for your dancing, dear mamma."

The officers did not laugh—out of politeness, and for the same reason mamma did not scold me until they had gone away.

"You foolish child," she said angrily, "to rush openly in the face of danger, and ruin yourself intentionally."

I thought mamma was afraid I should take cold, as she always was when I prepared for a ball, and to calm her fears I reminded her that there was to be no waltzing. This made her still more angry.

"You have no sense," she exclaimed. "Do you suppose they are giving this ball that they may dance? Not at all! It is all finesse—all a plot of the National Guards to get the young girls of the town together, when they will probably seize them and carry them off to Turkey."

"Ah, mamma, why, officers are not allowed to marry in time of war," I reminded her, laughing.

On this, she scolded me still more, called me a little goose, and told me I should find out to my cost; and with this threat she left me to prepare for the ball. I was busy enough until evening, getting everything ready. According to the officer's advice, I wore a broad, red-white-and-green ribbon as a sash, and my coiffure was a simple bouquet of white and red roses, to which the green leaves gave the National color. I never observed before how well these colors blend.

The two officers waited on us *en pleine parade*, and paid us so many compliments I could not imagine how they learned them all. I was obliged to laugh to put off my embarrassment.

"Well, you will see, tears will be the end of all this," said mamma, but nevertheless she continued arranging and altering something or other about my dress, so that if they did carry me off, they should at least find everything in order.

The officers accompanied us to the ball-room. I was already enjoying the idea of the effect which my National ribbon and our two beaux would produce, and, *entre nous*, I could not give up the hope that if all the others really had square heads, we should have the only two round ones in the room!

But great was my mistake and surprise. There was not one of my companions who had not at least twice as much National ribbon on her dress as I had, and as to the officers, our two cavaliers held but the third rank among them. None was more agreeable, more fascinating, handsomer, livelier than the other. How was it possible that men like these can shed so much blood!

There was one in particular who attracted my attention—not mine alone, but everybody's. He was a young captain—his strikingly handsome face and tall graceful figure became the braided attila so well, it seemed to have been molded on him. And then, his dancing! With what animation he went through the *Mazur* and *Czardas!* One could have rushed through the crowd to embrace him—I do not talk of myself. And, what was more than dancing, more than compliments, a *je ne sais quoi* in the large dark dreamy eyes. You cannot imagine *that!* It is not to be described—it bewildered, inspired, overpowered, and enchanted at the same moment. In less than an hour every girl in the room was in love with him. I do not except myself. If they are as irresistible in the field of battle, I do not know what could withstand them. Imagine my feelings when all at once he stepped up to me and requested the honor of the next quadrille!

Unfortunately, I was engaged. What would I not have given at that moment had a courier entered to call away my dancer!

"Perhaps the next one?" said the Captain, seating himself beside me.

I do not know what I said, or whether I replied at all; I only know I felt as I do when flying in a dream.

"But you will forget, perhaps, that you promised me?" he continued.

Had I not suddenly recollected myself, I should probably have told him that sooner could I forget my existence. However, I only replied in a very indifferent tone that I should not forget.

'But you do not know me!"

A country simpleton would have answered, in my place, "Among a hundred—among thousands! At the first glance!"

Not I! As if I were doing the simplest thing in the world, I took a single rosebud from my breast and gave it to him. "I shall know you by this," I said, without betraying the slightest agitation.

The Captain silently pressed the rose to his lips. I did not look, but I *knew* it. I would not have encountered his eyes, at that moment for all the world. He then left me and sat down under a mirror opposite. He did not dance, and seemed absorbed in his own reflections. Meanwhile, two *Czardas* and a *Polonaise* were danced, after which our quadrille would come. You may conceive how long the time appeared. These eternal *harom a tanczes* seemed absolutely to have no end. I never saw people dance so furiously, and although it was the third night since they had slept, nothing would tire them out. However, I amused myself pretty well by making the acquaintance of the Commander of the Battalion, Major Sch——, who is a most diverting person. His name is German, and though he speaks Hungarian shockingly, he will always speak it, even if he is addressed in German or French. Then he is most dreadfully deaf, and accustomed to such loud-toned conversation one would think the cannon were conversing together.

They say he is a very gallant soldier, but his appearance is not prepossessing—an uncouth, grotesque figure, with a long thin face, short-cut hair, and a grisly beard which is not all becoming. But the most amusing thing was that what I spoke he did not hear; and what he spoke I did not understand. He brought me over a box of bonbons—and I complained of the badness of confectionery in our town. He probably supposed from my grimace that somebody had offended me at the ball, and answered something from which—by the gesture which accompanied it—I could only infer that he intended cutting the offender in pieces; unless, indeed, what others would express under such circumstances may be the common gesticulation of men who live in war.

At last my quadrille came. The band played the symphony, and the dancers hastened to seek their partners. My heart almost burst from my dress when I saw my dancer approach and, bowing low, press the little flower to his heart. I fear my hand trembled as he took it in his, but I only smiled and made some observation about the music.

"Ah, you are carrying off my neighbor," cried the Major laughing, with one of his annihilating gesticulations.

As we joined the columns, somebody whispered behind us, "What a well-matched couple!"

Ah, Ilma, how happy I was! I felt, as we stood there hand in hand, as if his blood were flowing into mine, and mine into his!

We waited for the music, but before it could begin, the noise of horses' feet was heard galloping up the street and, at the same time, several cannon were fired at a distance, which made all the windows rattle. Suddenly an officer entered the ball-room with his *csako* on his head, and covered with mud, and announced that the enemy had attacked the outposts.

The Major had heard the cannon, and read from the courier's face what he could not understand from his words.

"Ah, that's right," he exclaimed clapping his hands, and again those fearful gestures by which people express killing. "We were only waiting for them, Messieurs; we must ask our ladies for a few moments' leave—just a few moments, Mesdames! We shall return immediately, and meantime you can rest."

And he hastened to put on his sword; all the other officers ran to get theirs, and I saw the gay, courtly, flattering expression suddenly change to angry, fierce, threatening countenances, but one and all seemed eager to start, as if they had expected it all along.

My dancer, too, forsook me to look for his sword and *csako*. His step was the firmest, his eye the keenest of all; if I had hitherto felt happiness—more than happiness—in looking at him, admiration, enthusiasm, now filled my breast. As he buckled on his sword a strange fever seemed to burn in all my veins; I could have wished to be in battle with him, to ride beside him, and dash with him into the midst of the enemy! He still had my rose in his hand and as he took up his *csako*, he placed it beside the cockade, and then he turned back as if he sought something through the crowd. Our eyes met—he hastened away, and the ball-room was empty.

Meanwhile, we remained alone as if nothing had happened. The Major had given orders that none should leave the room before his return. It was the longest hour I ever spent.

Many of us stood at the windows, listening to the cannon, and trying to guess the result, as they sounded nearer, now more distant. None judged it advisable to go home, as the combat might have ended in the streets, and they thought better to await the decision where we were.

Ere long the sounds began to recede further and further, till at last they ceased entirely. The civilians concluded by this that the National Guards had gained the victory. They were right. In less than a quarter of an hour we heard them return with great noise and clatter. And the officers entered the room gayly, as if nothing had happened. Many of them wiped something from their dress—perhaps mud or blood—and each hastened to find his partner.

"Where did we leave off?" cried one.

"At the quadrille," replied several at once, and began arranging the columns as if they had just come out of the supper room. My dancer and the Major were alone absent!

In vain my eyes were fixed on the door. Every instant some one entered, but not the one I sought. At last the Major appeared. He looked around and when he saw me, immediately approached, and, making a grotesque bow, without waiting for me to speak, "Fair lady," he said, "your dancer entreats your pardon for this breach of politeness, but he is unable with the best will to enjoy the happiness of dancing the *Française* with you, having been shot through the leg, which must be amputated above the knee."

Oh, Ilma! I shall never dance a quadrille again! I am very ill! I am overwhelmed by despair!

KALMAN MIKSZATH

(1849–1922)

Mikszath is one of the few Hungarian writers who is widely known outside his native land. An ardent patriot, he was all his life long a staunch defender of the principles of Hungarian independence. Into his literary work—which consists mostly of novels and tales—he poured all his love for the Hungarian people. His short stories, among the best ever written by a Hungarian, are vivid pictures of the life of his native country. *The Green Fly* is an especially amusing and well executed study in peasant psychology.

The translation of the story was made by Mr. Joseph Szebenyei for this volume, and appears here for the first time in English. Acknowledgment is hereby made to the translator for permission to use the MS.

THE GREEN FLY

THE old peasant, the richest man in the village, lay very ill at the point of death. God was holding judgment over him, pointing to him as an example for all mankind:

"Look at John Gal. What do you mortals imagine yourselves to be? You are nothing. Now, John Gal is really somebody. Even the county judge shakes his hand occasionally. The Countesses of the village come and visit him. He is the richest among you. Still, I could smite him. I did not have to send a hungry wolf to bite him, nor do I have to uproot a giant oak to fall upon and crush him. A tiny fly will do the work."

That is what actually happened. A fly bit his hand; it soon began to swell, becoming blacker and redder.

The priest and the lady of the Castle persuaded him to call a doctor.

He would have been willing to have the surgeon sent for, but they prevailed upon him to telegraph for a specialist to Budapest. Professor

Birli was chosen. One visit would cost three hundred florins, but that was money well spent.

"Nonsense," said the peasant, "that tiny fly couldn't have caused three hundred florins' worth of damage in me."

The Countess insisted and offered to pay the doctor's bill herself. This did the trick. John Gal was a proud peasant. The telegram was dispatched and a young man, slim and bespectacled—not at all imposing—arrived in the carriage that had been sent to meet him at the station.

Mrs. Gal, the young wife of the elderly peasant, received him at the gate.

"Are you the famous Doctor from Budapest?" she asked. "You had better come and look at my husband. He's making as much fuss over a fly-bitten hand as if he'd been bitten by an elephant."

This was absolutely untrue. John Gal had never said a word; never even mentioned the bite unless he was asked, and even then he was extremely curt. He lay on his bed indifferent and stoical. His head rested on a sheepskin, his pipe in his mouth.

"What's the trouble, old man?" asked the Doctor. "I understand a fly bit you."

"That's it," answered the peasant between his teeth.

"What sort of fly was it?"

"A green fly," he said curtly.

"You just question him, Doctor," interrupted the woman. "I shall have to look after my work. I have nine loaves in the oven."

"All right, *mother*," said the Doctor absent-mindedly.

She turned upon him immediately as if stung, her hands on her hips:

"Why, you're old enough to be my father!" she said, half offended and half flirting. "You don't seem to see well through those windows on your eyes."

She turned quickly about and the many starched skirts whirled like the wind as she walked out, erect with the sense of youth and strength.

The Doctor followed her with his eyes. She was devilish pretty, much younger than the doctor, and of course very much younger than her husband. He wanted to mutter some sort of apology, but she was gone before he could say a word.

"Well, let's see that hand. Does it hurt?"

"Quite a good deal," was the answer.

The Doctor examined the swollen hand, and his face assumed a grave look.

"Bad enough. It must have been a poisonous insect."

"Maybe," said John without the least emotion. "I could tell it wasn't an ordinary kind."

"It was a fly that had come from a dead body."

A mute curse was all John Gal vouchsafed for this information.

"It was lucky I arrived in time. We can still do something. To-morrow it would have been too late. You'd have been dead."

"That's strange," said the peasant, pressing the tobacco into his pipe with one thumb.

"Blood-poisoning works fast. We have no time to lose. You must harden your nerves, old man. Your arm will have to come off."

"My arm?" he asked with surprise and a touch of sarcasm, and a great deal of resignation.

"Yes. It has to be done."

John Gal did not say a word; he only shook his head and went on smoking.

"You see," the Doctor went on in his persuasive tone, "it will not hurt you. I shall put you to sleep and when you wake up you will be saved. Otherwise, to-morrow at this time you'll be as dead as a mouse. Not even God can save you."

"Oh, leave me alone," he said as though he were tired of so much talk; turned to the wall, and closed his eyes.

The Doctor was quite unprepared for such stubbornness. He left the room and went to have a word with the woman.

"How is my husband?" she asked with such indifference as she could muster, continuing her work at the same time in order to show her contempt for the Doctor.

"Bad enough. I just came to ask you to try and persuade him to let me amputate his arm."

"Good gracious!" she exclaimed, turning as white as the apron before her. "Must it be done?"

"He will die otherwise within twenty-four hours."

Her face turned red, as she took the Doctor by the arm. She dragged him into the sick-room and there, placing her hands on her hips, addressed him:

"Do I look like a woman who would be satisfied to be the wife of a cripple? I'd die of shame. There! Just look at him!" She turned to her husband and almost shouted: "Don't you let him cut your arm off, John. Don't you listen to him!"

The old peasant gave her a friendly look.

"Don't you worry, Kriska," he assured her. "There'll be no butchering here. I don't intend to die in pieces."

It was in vain that the Doctor spoke to the old man of the darkness of death and the beauties of life. It was to no purpose that he called the Countess from the Castle to plead his suit, and the priest and all the most eloquent and impressive talkers of the village. John Gal remained obdurate. He declined to be cut.

The resignation with which the peasant meets death, without bitterness, without reproach, and without vain tears, was expressed in the calm of his face and the tone of his voice. Death held no terrors for him. If his time was at hand, he was ready to go as his father and his grandfather had gone before him.

It was plain that nothing was to be gained through appeals to the old man to save himself. But at length the very real concern of the almost frantic doctor began to touch the old man's heart. He pitied the fellow's agitation. He was sorry that this man should be so grieved and, half-ridiculously, half-pathetically, John began to console the physician.

Suddenly the Doctor remembered that consideratic as of money will work wonders where a peasant is concerned. So he said:

"You'll have to pay the three hundred, you know, whether I amputate your arm or not. It would be wasting money not to have the operation. It only takes five minutes."

"Well, you can prescribe some ointment, just to be earning your fee," said the old man, as calmly as if he were bargaining over a pair of boots.

It was no use. Disgusted and disappointed, the Doctor left the man and went out for a walk to think matters over and discuss the problem with some of the village wiseacres. He found little good advice, however, and it was equally in vain to bring the notary and the Justice of the Peace to the patient's bedside. The young woman was always there to offset any wicked plan on the part of the Doctor, and she never missed an opportunity for putting in a word or two to strengthen the obduracy of her husband. The Doctor gave her a wicked glance now and again, and even shouted at her:

"You hold your tongue when men are in conference!" he said.

"The hen is somebody on the cock's dunghill," she retorted, swinging her body.

John Gal hastened to prevent a quarrel.

"Don't get too noisy, Kriska. You'd better get a bottle of wine for the visitors."

"From which barrel?" she asked.

"From the two-hecto barrel. But for my funeral-feast you'd better tap the three-hecto barrel: it's getting sour."

He was quite resigned to the idea of death. The visitors drank and left him to make his peace with God.

In the courtyard Doctor Birli met the hired man, a young, powerful-looking fellow, a man-of-all-work.

"Get the carriage ready, I shall be off in half-an-hour," he said to the man. "And tell Mrs. Gal I shall not stay for supper."

Outside the gate he stopped, undecided as to what to do next. Through the crack of the gate-door he saw the man go up to Mrs. Gal, and could not help seeing the coquettish look she gave him and the self-important bearing of the young fellow as he approached her. It was evident that they were playing with fire and that there was some understanding between them. All he had to do now was to get a little further information on the subject. There must be an old witch in the village who knows all about the love-affairs of the villagers, and who deals in love potions. The notary would surely know. He did.

"Old witch Rebek," he said. "She lives two doors away from the Gals."

The Doctor handed her two silver florins.

"I am in love with a woman, and I'd like something that would make her love *me*," he said.

"Oh, that can't be, my boy. You look like a scarecrow, and they don't usually fall in love with men like you."

"True, mother, but I could give her all the silks she wants and all the money she could spend. ..."

"And who be the woman?"

"Mrs. John Gal."

"You can pluck every rose, excepting those that are plucked."

That was just what the Doctor wanted to know.

"And who may the other man be?" he asked.

"Paul Nagy, the hired man. She must be in love with him, because she comes here often for potions. I gave her the last year's dust of three-year-old creepers to pour into his wine."

"And does John Gal suspect anything?"

"Smart as he may be, feminine wit beats him every time."

The Doctor returned to the Gal house and found the lovers still chatting, while the hired man wiped with a rag the backs of the horses that were now ready to take the Doctor to the station. She beckoned to him to approach. She dug her hand into her bosom as the city man approached, and drew out three hundred florins in bills.

"For your trouble, Doctor," she said, offering him the money.

"Right," said the Doctor, "but it will rest on your conscience, you pretty woman, that I did not deserve it more."

"My soul will bear it all right. Don't you worry."

"Very well. Just have my bag put into the carriage, while I say good-bye to your husband."

John Gal was lying exactly where he had been left. His pipe was unlit, and his eyes were closed as if he were taking a nap.

He looked up and cocked one eye as the door opened.

"I just came to say good-bye, Mr. Gal," said the Doctor.

"Are you going?" he asked with indifference.

"I have nothing to do here."

"Did the woman give you the money?"

"Yes. You've got a pretty wife, Mr. Gal. My, she's beautiful!"

The patient opened his other eye, and as he offered his good hand to the Doctor, he only said:

"Ain't she?"

"Her lovely lips are like cherries."

"So they are." There was almost a happy smile on his face.

"That loafer Paul will have a fine time with her, I daresay."

The old peasant began to tremble, and looked up.

"What was it you said, Doctor?"

The Doctor closed his lips suddenly as if he had said something he had not intended to say.

"Nonsense. It's none of my business. One has eyes and brains and one sees things, and comprehends things. I was suspicious the moment she refused to let me cut your arm off. Didn't *you* suspect anything? But now I understand. Of course, of course."

John Gal began to shake both his fists, forgetting for the moment that one of them was swollen. He groaned with pain.

"Oh, my arm, my arm! Don't say another word, Doctor."

"Not another word," said the other.

A deep groan broke forth from the sick man's chest as he clutched the Doctor's arm with his right.

"Which Paul, Doctor? Which Paul do you mean? Who is he?"

"You really mean to say you don't know? Paul Nagy, your hired man." The old peasant turned white. His lips were trembling and the blood rushed to his heart. His hand didn't hurt him a bit now. He suddenly slapped his forehead and looked up.

"What a stupid fool I was. I should have noticed long ago. ... That snake of a woman!"

"No use swearing at the woman, Mr. Gal. She has her youth; she's full of health and life. That's what. She may *yet* be quite innocent, but after all she'll have to get married after you're gone. ... And gone you'll be. ..."

The old peasant moved with an effort and turned to the Doctor, who continued speaking:

"You have nothing to lose if she marries a younger man after you are gone. You wouldn't know anything about it after you're under the earth. And, besides, you ought to be glad she'll have a handsome fellow for a husband. Good-looking chap, Paul!"

The old fellow was crunching his teeth. It sounded as if two tusks had been ground against each other.

"You mustn't be greedy, Mr. Gal. It would be a pity to let that wonderful body of hers waste away without embraces. Paul isn't a fool. He wouldn't let a woman like her pass him by without taking a bite. Besides, she'll have all your money, and the farm. The woman, too, would like to live. The only fool among you three is you, Mr. Gal."

The peasant groaned again and the perspiration covered his forehead. In his heart was bitterness almost ready to overflow.

"You see, Mr. Gal, it would be better to hug her with one arm than with none at all."

This was too much for the old man. He jumped up and extended his swollen arm toward the Doctor.

"Get your knife, Doctor, and cut away!"

FERENC MOLNAR

(1878—1952)

MOLNAR was born in 1878 in Budapest, the son, according to the translator of his plays, "of a wealthy Jewish merchant. He graduated from the Universities of Geneva and Budapest. His literary career was begun as a journalist at the age of eighteen." Though Molnar is best known as a dramatist, he was the author of a few novels and several short stories. His is a cynical and worldly-wise philosophy, yet tempered always by a certain sentiment, which is perceptible in the bitter little fable printed in these pages. *The Silver Hilt* is in effect a parable, related with grace, humour, and a certain curious sentiment.

The translation of the story was made by Mr. Joseph Szebenyei for this volume, and appears here for the first time in English. Acknowledgment is hereby made to the author and translator for permission to use the MS.

THE SILVER HILT

A NARROW ribbon of smoke wound its way lightly out of one of the many chimneys of the ancient feudal castle, and rose into the misty autumn dawn as the sun was just beginning to shine. Any well informed serf, noticing the smoke from the valley below, would have known that the cooks were not preparing breakfast for Count Scarlet, or as they called him in the Valley, the Red Scoundrel. In the castle of Count Scarlet the cooks were gentlemen, and never rose before seven in the morning. Any well-informed serf would know what the little ribbon of blue smoke meant. It was Maestro Conrad Superpollingerianus who rose so early. He was the Count's professional alchemist. He had come from Würzburg a year and a half before and had ever since been working at his alchemy without the least success.

Indeed, Maestro Conrad was already awake and up. He was standing by his fire in a long black coat. Over the fire boiled mysterious and strange-smelling concoctions. The man's long white beard reached to his knees, and whenever he wanted to stroke his beard (which was often) he had to bend down almost to the ground. Even then he could seldom reach the end of it.

He was surrounded by all sorts of mysterious instruments. On the walls hung mysterious charts showing the movements of the stars, and all the heavens were divided into those spheres by which one may read the whims of fate. Everywhere were ovens and smelting-furnaces built of brick, strong jars against which the fire of hell was futile, slabs of lead, shining quartz, enormous bellows which panted like the lungs of a fresh killed dragon, and in a corner on a richly carved stand, under a glass cover on a small velvet pillow, was one tiny bit of gold about half the size of a grain of rice.

The Maestro looked at this bit of gold and scratched his head. Count Scarlet had flown into a violent temper the night before. He was tired of having had him on his back for the past year and a half. The Maestro ate, drank and lived well, besides spending enormous sums for experiments, and he had not been able to make more than this tiny bit of gold. Once last year, the Count had determined to throw the Maestro out, when luckily the Maestro had succeeded in creating the gold. It is true that he had been able to do so only by inserting the gold—which he had bought—into the lead which he was supposed to have transformed. But Count Scarlet, cunning rascal though he was, had not discovered this. With the weirdest and most impressive ceremonies, exactly at the stroke of midnight, the Maestro put the stick of lead into the fire in the presence of the Count, and when they removed the jar from under the lead, the gold was discovered in the bottom of it.

And then the Maestro's trouble began. The Count demanded more gold.

"Until now," he said, "I believed that Superpollingerianus was the stupidest ox in the world. But now I am beginning to discover that he is not a fool, but an old scoundrel, who knows how to make gold but doesn't want to. If by to-morrow morning there is not a considerable lump of gold in the furnace, I will defy the coming generations, who will certainly brand me as a scoundrel for having done it, and will tear your whiskers out, Maestro, and have you dragged to the top of the highest tower of my castle and kicked off. *Quod dixi, dixi.*"

With that he turned on his heel, ate his supper, looked at his calendar to see in which of his villages there then was likely to be a little *jus primæ noctis,* and spreading some scented pomade on his scanty red mustache, he rode out of the castle.

I repeat, this happened at night. At dawn the next day, the Maestro was still scratching his head.

"Alas," sighed the Maestro, turning away from his strange-smelling concoction with disgust, "I cannot help myself. There can be no question about making gold, because I haven't even a worn copper. All the money I've been able to get out of Count Scarlet, I have sent to my illegitimate child. To think I have struggled through eighty-eight years of life by sheer deception, and now I cannot extricate myself from this predicament! That scoundrelly Scarlet will keep his promise. Only five years ago, for a similar offense, my honorable friend and colleague, Paphnucius Ratenowienis, was nailed to the gate of the castle by his ears, and made to look like a stray bat. Alas, how can I save myself?"

Thus wailed the Maestro, bending to the floor again and again to stroke his long whiskers.

Suddenly, in the midst of his distress, he heard footsteps in the corridor. In a moment the door opened, and in the middle of the diabolical kitchen stood Count Scarlet with threateningly puckered eyebrows. The Count was tall, lanky, freckled, with close-cropped red hair, and a wicked bony face. His hands were as large as beefsteaks. His knees stuck out from his tightly fitting trousers like two bunions. He lifted his aristocratic, hairy red hand, and his tiny pig eyes grinned searchingly:

"Well, Maestro!"

The Maestro suddenly grew limp and tried to sit down on the air. He gulped a big dry gulp, turned the color of onyx and faintingly whispered, "Well, what does that 'Well' mean?"

"It means what it means," said the Count coldly.

It was a terrible moment. The seriousness of the situation was accentuated by the fact that the Count had deviated from his usual custom, in rising at such an early hour. It was evident that he was in earnest about his threat. Deadly silence reigned in the room. Only the strange-smelling concoction of herbs boiled impertinently in the stillness of the room.

"Count," said the Maestro at last, "there is no gold."

"Then give me your whiskers," shouted the Count, and leaped toward the Maestro, who quickly threw his whiskers across his left shoulder so that they hung down over his back.

"Stop, sire!" he yelled in despair.

The Count was startled.

"What is it?"

"There is no gold," moaned the Maestro, "but there is something better."

"What?"

At this moment Maestro Superpollingerianus made an awful gulp, but this time it was no longer dry. His mouth watered at the thought of the fine lie that had just occurred to him. He felt that he was saved.

"What?" repeated the Count sternly.

"Something that is better than gold."

"The philosopher's stone?"

"No."

"What then?"

"The happiness of eternal love!" said the Maestro, and gulped again.

The Count stroked his nose. This was a sign of scepticism.

"Must I swallow this?" he asked. "Must I swallow this lie, too, as I have swallowed for a year and a half all the deceptions with which you have contrived to prolong your stay here, you shameless blot upon the heaven of science?"

To be undecided is half of believing, thought the Maestro and went on developing his lie with the greatest tranquillity.

"In the course of my experiments I have discovered the way to conquer the feminine heart."

The Count opened his eyes wide. He was known as an admirer of feminine charms, but had never had any success with ladies of rank. His face was gleaming with joy.

"I have ground silver into dust," continued the Maestro, "and boiled it in the juice of Asperula Odorato and then in the juice of the root of Azarum Europæum. These are the ingredients. But the chemical proportion that yields the magic is my own secret. *Ecce...*"

And he raised the lid of one of the pots. There were indeed bits of silver balls boiling in the juice of something that smelled horribly strange. He had cooked the whole mess the night before as a last chance.

"And—?"

"And of this silver dust I shall mold a thin sheet of silver plate; with that silver plate you will graciously cover the hilt of your sword and while you are courting the ladies keep your left hand on the hilt of the sword. There is no great lady, baroness, countess, duchess, or even queen, who will be able to resist the charm of this wizardry. With this sword you will have success with any lady in the world."

"Hm," said the Count, "may I have complete confidence?"

"Not the slightest chance of failure, sir."

The silver hilt was ready that same night.

"I am gaining time," said the Maestro to himself, and to save himself the trouble of bending down, he lifted his beard up over his arm and stroked it musingly.

The rumor soon spread throughout the district. In the neighborhood castles and fortresses, the great ladies dressed in gold-embroidered gowns, whispered and exchanged meaning glances, and everywhere conversation centered on the silver-hilted sword of Count Scarlet. Not three days had passed before Maestro Conrad Superpollingerianus had received eighteen offers from various other lords, promising him life-long positions, any amount of gold, together with board and lodging, if he would only communicate to them the secret of the chemical composition of the silver hilt. But the Scarlet Count bid more than any of them, and would not permit the Maestro to leave his castle.

On the fourth day he set out to conquer with his silver hilt. His first trip took him to the neighboring castle, whose lord was journeying in foreign lands. Only the beautiful Lady of the castle was at home, in company with her thirty-three ladies-in-waiting. For a long time, this had been the unsuccessful hunting-ground of the Scarlet Count, but now the women were waiting for him with a strange excitement and expectancy. All thirty-three of them wanted to receive the Count, and they all insisted that they were not afraid of the silver hilt. But the Lady of the Castle dismissed them and she, the model of faithfulness and womanly virtue, received the Count alone.

She lay resting on a large sofa when the Red Bone (that was what they called the Scarlet Count among themselves) entered the room. She rose and went to meet him, offering him a seat. The Lord sat down on a footstool and, as was customary with knights, held his sword between his knees. The Lady, who until now had not dared to cast even a glance at the sword, looked at it shyly. She was taken aback by the sight. The sword, studded with diamonds and precious stones, ended at the hilt in a simple silver sheet. It had an uncanny faded look about it and gleamed in the dimness of the room with a ghostly light.

They could not see the thirty-three women peeping in from behind the heavy drapery and curtains. But these women agreed that the Count looked irresistibly powerful, though they always before considered him ridiculous.

"It's fine weather," said the Red Bone.

"Yes, very fine," said the Lady, and was greatly relieved when she saw that the Count had not placed his hand on the hilt of the sword.

"Neither too warm nor too cold," said the Count.

"Very pleasant, indeed," said the Lady.

"At noon it's warm, but the nights are cool," the Count went on, "but to-night the sunset is the most wonderful of all, more wonderful indeed if one spends the time in the company of a beautiful woman."

And so saying, he placed his large red hand upon the silver hilt.

The Lady, who had been watching it with staring eyes, began to tremble a little. The heavy curtains began to move and a pleasant tremor passed through the veins of the women.

"He placed his hand on it," said those in front to those standing behind.

"He placed his hand on it... he did indeed!" the whisper passed around.

The Lady of the Castle could not take her eyes off the hand resting upon the hilt. The Red Count was talking away foolishly, but the Lady paid no attention to what he said.

"Eh," she said to herself, "the whole thing is a stupid superstition; why should I look at it at all?"

But as soon as she looked away, something constrained her to look back immediately. The Count drew his footstool nearer to her, grasping at the hilt with all his might. The lady grew frightened.

"Why are you afraid of me?" asked the Count with a smile. "I do not wish to hurt you. On the contrary..."

"Perhaps it would be better," whispered one of the women behind the curtain, "if we left them alone."

A soft, creeping noise could be heard, as the ladies, with their fingers on their lips, slipped away from behind the curtains.

"I have loved you for a long time," said the Red Scoundrel in a melting tone.

Something seemed to choke the woman, but she told herself it was only imagination.

"I adore you."

The woman could not take her eyes off his hand. And she pleaded: "If you love me, let go the hilt of your sword."

"Never," shouted Scarlet in the heat of his passion, and drew his chair closer.

The Lady was trembling like a leaf in an evening breeze.

"You are beautiful!" howled the Scarlet Bone. "You are as beautiful as the morning star, and I tell you frankly I am going to make you my own love."

His grip on the sword tightened.

"He will not let go of it," thought the terrified woman. "He will not let go of it. I am lost."

She made an attempt to stand up, but at that moment she felt the prickly hairs of a thin mustache on her lips. She wanted to scream, but the Count had already imprisoned her shoulders in his long, strong arms. Her beautiful head dropped like a flower, and she felt that the Scarlet Bone was holding her wilting head in the palm of his enormous hand. Kisses were beating heavily against her lips like hot rain.

"You are mine," said the Count between two kisses, still tightly grasping his sword with his left hand.

"I am yours," panted the Lady.

"What is the formula?" asked the Dark Blue Baron of the dying Maestro ten years later, for he had bought the scientist from the Scarlet Count for a hundred thousand gold pieces. He was a great lover of women and had seen that for the past ten years the Scarlet Count had virtually made a harvest of beautiful women by the magic of the Silver Hilt. "What is the formula?"

"By the Fires of Hell, there is no formula!" moaned the Maestro from his bed. "A silver hilt, a brass button, a tin spur, a golden horseshoe nail, it makes no difference. The man's bearing must announce that he is sure of himself—that is the formula. There is no escape from one who is sure of himself. But you must believe in the silver hilt, because if you do not, the women will not believe in it either. Now then: whether you believe in a silver hilt, a brass button, a tin spur, a golden horseshoe nail, your good manners, your beauty, your self-confidence or your discretion, it all amounts to the same thing. But now that I have told you this, O Dark Blue Baron, you will go to the women in vain with your silver hilt, because you will not believe in it any more. And the women will feel that you no longer believe in your own powers. And you will be defeated everywhere, O Dark Blue Ba..."

He could not finish the sentence, because the Dark Blue Baron struck him a blow on the head. He would have died anyway within the next ten minutes, but the Baron found it better to assist him in this manner.

So died Maestro Conrad Superpollingerianus, the gray-haired swindler, with the truth on his lips.

Russia

INTRODUCTION

R USSIA produced a literature of its own some centuries before the Nineteenth, but it was not a consistently characteristic product like that, for instance, of France or England. It is convenient, and not inaccurate, to name Gogol the father of modern Russian fiction, and since it is in fiction that the Russians are preeminent, Gogol may stand as a symbol of the beginnings. Pushkin, on the other hand, was a cosmopolitan of the Romantic school of Byron and Scott and Schiller. But one of his stories is included in this collection for its intrinsic merit, as well as to show the kind of tale that was widely popular throughout Europe at the time.

"We are all," said Dostoievsky, "descended from Gogol's *Cloak*." That story, too long for reprinting in a volume of this kind, was indeed a milestone. Gogol was essentially Russian, and in his best work he strikes for the first time "that truly Russian note of deep sympathy with the disinherited." (Thomas Seltzer.) And the note struck by Gogol is sounded again and again by later writers, from Dostoievsky to Gorky. The political conditions of Russia have from the very first been a determining factor in nearly every product of her literature. Even the greatest literary artists, like Turgenev and Chekhov, were unable or unwilling to write novels and stories simply as revelations of life or as a pastime for their readers: they sought, directly or indirectly, to better conditions as they saw them, to evoke pity for the downtrodden, to understand the ways of God and the meaning of life.

It is fortunate, and rather remarkable, that although the great story writers of the Nineteenth Century were constantly seeking to remedy the evils of their generation, they were at the same time artists who rarely sacrificed their art for ulterior motives. Tolstoy, the outstanding example of the preacher, was never able to forget that he was an artist.

Few countries can boast so many writers of the first order who deliberately adopted, developed, and respected the short story as did the Russians during the last century. Nearly all the great figures were either novelists or short story writers: nearly all the novelists wrote stories, and several later writers, like Chekhov and Kuprin and Gorky, are known chiefly through their shorter works.

It was Chekhov who finally brought the Russian short story to its present state of perfection, but despite the dozen odd volumes of tales, in which practically every variety of story is told, Chekhov's followers have managed to find new subjects and new methods of treatment.

Russia is here represented by ten stories. It was exceedingly difficult to select from among the many hundreds of available works precisely those which were the most readable and at the same time showed the development of the form.

ALEXANDER PUSHKIN

(1799–1837)

THOUGH Pushkin's fame is chiefly due to his genius as a poet, he is yet important as a writer of short stories. A Romanticist noticeably influenced by Byron, he was among the first Russians to write tales about his own people. Before his time the French influence predominated. He brought to the form a wealth of imagination and the touch of a poet.

The Snow Storm, contrasted with the other Russian stories in this collection, seems somewhat artificial; there is, none the less, something peculiarly indigenous in the background, and Russian in its treatment.

The present translation, by T. Keane, first appeared in *The Prose Tales of Alexander Pushkin*, published in 1894 by G. Bell & Sons, by whose permission it is here reprinted.

THE SNOW STORM

TOWARDS the end of the year 1811, a memorable period for us, the good Gavril Gavrilovitch R—— was living on his domain of Nenaradova. He was celebrated throughout the district for his hospitality and kind-heartedness. The neighbors were constantly visiting him: some to eat and drink; some to play at five kopek "Boston" with his wife, Praskovia Petrovna; and some to look at their daughter, Maria Gavrilovna, a pale, slender girl of seventeen. She was considered a wealthy match, and many desired her for themselves or for their sons.

Maria Gavrilovna had been brought up on French novels and consequently was in love. The object of her choice was a poor sub-lieutenant in the army, who was then on leave of absence in his village. It need scarcely be mentioned that the young man returned her passion with equal ardor, and that the parents of his beloved one, observing their mutual inclination, forbade their daughter to think of him, and received him worse than a discharged assessor.

Our lovers corresponded with one another and daily saw each other alone in the little pine wood or near the old chapel. There they exchanged vows of eternal love, lamented their cruel fate, and formed various plans. Corresponding and conversing in this way, they arrived quite naturally at the following conclusion:

If we cannot exist without each other, and the will of hard-hearted parents stands in the way of our happiness, why cannot we do without them?

Needless to mention that this happy idea originated in the mind of the young man, and that it was very congenial to the romantic imagination of Maria Gavrilovna.

The winter came and put a stop to their meetings, but their correspondence became all the more active. Vladimir Nikolaievitch in every letter implored her to give herself to him, to get married secretly, to hide for some time, and then to throw themselves at the feet of their parents, who would, without any doubt be touched at last by the heroic constancy and unhappiness of the lovers, and would infallibly say to them: "Children, come to our arms!"

Maria Gavrilovna hesitated for a long time, and several plans for a flight were rejected. At last she consented: on the appointed day she was not to take supper, but was to retire to her room under the pretext of a headache. Her maid was in the plot; they were both to go into the garden by the back stairs, and behind the garden they would find ready a sledge, into which they were to get, and then drive straight to the church of Jadrino, a village about five versts from Nenaradova, where Vladimir would be waiting for them.

On the eve of the decisive day, Maria Gavrilovna did not sleep the whole night; she packed and tied up her linen and other articles of apparel, wrote a long letter to a sentimental young lady, a friend of hers, and another to her parents. She took leave of them in the most touching terms, urged the invincible strength of passion as an excuse for the step she was taking, and wound up with the assurance that she should consider it the happiest moment of her life, when she should be allowed to throw herself at the feet of her dear parents.

After having sealed both letters with a Toula seal, upon which were engraved two flaming hearts with a suitable inscription, she threw herself upon her bed just before daybreak, and dozed off: but even then she was constantly being awakened by terrible dreams. First, it seemed to her that at the very moment when she seated herself in the sledge, in order to go and get married, her father stopped her, dragged her into a dark bottomless abyss, down which she fell headlong with an indescribable sinking of the heart. Then she saw Vladimir lying on the grass, pale and bloodstained. With his dying breath he implored her, in a piercing voice, to make haste and marry him.... Other fantastic and senseless visions floated before her, one after another. At last she arose, paler than usual, and with an unfeigned headache. Her father and mother observed her uneasiness; their tender solicitude and incessant inquiries: "What is the matter with you, Masha? Are you ill, Masha?" cut her to the heart. She tried to reassure them and to appear cheerful, but in vain.

The evening came. The thought that this was the last day she would pass in the bosom of her family weighed upon her heart. She was more dead than alive. In secret she took leave of everybody, of all the objects that surrounded her.

Supper was served; her heart began to beat violently. In a trembling voice she declared that she did not want any supper, and then took leave of her father and mother. They kissed her and blessed her as usual, and she could hardly restrain herself from weeping.

On reaching her own room, she threw herself into a chair and burst into tears. Her maid urged her to be calm and to take courage. Everything was ready. In half an hour Masha would leave forever her parents' house, her room, and her peaceful girlish life....

Out in the courtyard the snow was falling heavily; the wind howled, the shutters shook and rattled, and everything seemed to her to portend misfortune.

Soon all was quiet in the house: everyone was asleep. Masha wrapped herself in a shawl, put on a warm cloak, took her small box in her hand, and went down the back staircase. Her maid followed her with two bundles. They descended into the garden. The snowstorm had not subsided; the wind blew in their faces as if trying to stop the young criminal. With difficulty they reached the end of the garden. In the road a sledge awaited them. The horses, half-frozen with the cold, would not keep still; Vladimir's coachman was walking up and down in front of them, trying to restrain their impatience. He helped the young lady and her maid into the sledge, placed the box and the bundles in the vehicle, seized the reins, and the horses dashed off.

Having intrusted the young lady to the care of fate, and to the skill of Tereshka the coachman, we will return to our young lover.

Vladimir had spent the whole of the day in driving about. In the morning he paid a visit to the priest of Jadrino, and having come to an agreement with him after a great deal of difficulty, he then set out to seek for witnesses among the neighboring landowners. The first to whom he presented himself, a retired cornet of about forty years of age, and whose name was Dravin, consented with pleasure. The adventure, he declared, reminded him of his young days and his pranks in the

Hussars. He persuaded Vladimir to stay to dinner with him, and assured him that he would have no difficulty in finding the other two witnesses. And indeed, immediately after dinner, appeared the surveyor Schmidt, with mustache and spurs, and the son of the captain of police, a lad of sixteen years of age, who had recently entered the Uhlans. They not only accepted Vladimir's proposal, but even vowed that they were ready to sacrifice their lives for him. Vladimir embraced them with rapture, and returned home to get everything ready.

It had been dark for some time. He dispatched his faithful Tereshka to Nenaradova with his sledge and with detailed instructions, and ordered for himself the small sledge with one horse, and set out alone, without any coachman, for Jadrino, where Maria Gavrilovna ought to arrive in about a couple of hours. He knew the road well, and the journey would only occupy about twenty minutes altogether.

But scarcely had Vladimir issued from the paddock into the open field, when the wind rose and such a snowstorm came on that he could see nothing. In one minute the road was completely hidden; all surrounding objects disappeared in a thick yellow fog, through which fell the white flakes of snow; earth and sky became confounded. Vladimir found himself in the middle of the field, and tried in vain to find the road again. His horse went on at random, and at every moment kept either stepping into a snowdrift or stumbling into a hole, so that the sledge was constantly being overturned. Vladimir endeavored not to lose the right direction. But it seemed to him that more than half an hour had already passed, and he had not yet reached the Jadrino wood. Another ten minutes elapsed—still no wood was to be seen. Vladimir drove across a field intersected by deep ditches. The snowstorm did not abate, the sky did not become any clearer. The horse began to grow tired, and the perspiration rolled from him in great drops, in spite of the fact that he was constantly being half buried in the snow.

At last Vladimir perceived that he was going in the wrong direction. He stopped, began to think, to recollect, and compare, and he felt convinced that he ought to have turned to the right. He turned to the right now. His horse could scarcely move forward. He had now been on the road for more than an hour. Jadrino could not be far off. But on and on he went, and still no end to the field—nothing but snowdrifts and ditches. The sledge was constantly being overturned, and as constantly being set right again. The time was passing; Vladimir began to grow seriously uneasy.

At last something dark appeared in the distance. Vladimir directed his course towards it. On drawing near, he perceived that it was a wood.

"Thank Heaven," he thought, "I am not far off now." He drove along by the edge of the wood, hoping by and by to fall upon the well-known road or to pass round the wood; Jadrino was situated just behind it. He soon found the road, and plunged into the darkness of the wood, now denuded of leaves by the winter. The wind could not rage here; the road was smooth, the horse recovered courage, and Vladimir felt reassured.

But he drove on and on, and Jadrino was not to be seen; there was no end to the wood. Vladimir discovered with horror that he had entered an unknown forest. Despair took possession of him. He whipped the horse; the poor animal broke into a trot, but it soon slackened its pace, and in about a quarter of an hour it was scarcely able to drag one leg after the other, in spite of all the exertions of the unfortunate Vladimir.

Gradually the trees began to get sparser, and Vladimir emerged from the forest; but Jadrino was not to be seen. It must now have been midnight. Tears gushed from his eyes; he drove on at random. Meanwhile the storm had subsided, the clouds dispersed, and before him lay a level plain covered with a white, undulating carpet. The night was tolerably clear. He saw, not far off, a little village, consisting of four or five houses. Vladimir drove towards it. At the first cottage he jumped out of the sledge, ran to the window and began to knock. After a few minutes the wooden shutter was raised, and an old man thrust out his gray beard.

"What do you want?"

"Is Jadrino far from here?"

"Yes, yes! Is it far?"

"Not far; about ten versts."

At this reply, Vladimir grasped his hair and stood motionless, like a man condemned to death.

"Where do you come from?" continued the old man.

Vladimir had not the courage to answer the question.

"Listen, old man," said he, "can you procure me horses to take me to Jadrino?"

"How should we have such things as horses?" replied the peasant.

"Can I obtain a guide? I will pay him whatever he asks."

"Wait," said the old man, closing the shutter. "I will send my son out to you; he will guide you."

Vladimir waited. But a minute had scarcely elapsed when he began knocking again. The shutter was raised, and the beard again reappeared.

"What do you want?"

"What about your son?"

"He'll be out presently; he is putting on his boots. Are you cold? Come in and warm yourself."

"Thank you; send your son out quickly."

The door creaked; a lad came out with a cudgel and went on in front, at one time pointing out the road, at another searching for it among the drifted snow.

"What is the time?" Vladimir asked him.

"It will soon be daylight," replied the young peasant. Vladimir spoke not another word.

The cocks were crowing, and it was already light when they reached Jadrino. The church was closed. Vladimir paid the guide and drove into the priest's courtyard. His sledge was not there. What news awaited him!...

But let us return to the worthy proprietors of Nenaradova, and see what is happening there.

Nothing.

The old people awoke and went into the parlor, Gavril Gavrilovitch in a night-cap, and flannel doublet, Praskovia Petrovna in a wadded dressing-gown. The tea-urn (samovar) was brought in, and Gavril Gavrilovitch sent a servant to ask Maria Gavrilovna how she was and how she had passed the night. The servant returned saying that the young lady had not slept very well, but that she felt better now, and that she would come down presently into the parlor. And indeed, the door opened and Maria Gavrilovna entered the room and wished her father and mother good morning.

"How is your head, Masha?" asked Gavril Gavrilovitch.

"Better, papa," replied Masha.

"Very likely you inhaled the fumes from the charcoal yesterday," said Praskovia Petrovna.

"Very likely, mamma," replied Masha.

The day passed happily enough, but in the night Masha was taken ill. A doctor was sent for from the town. He arrived in the evening and found the sick girl delirious. A violent fever ensued, and for two weeks the poor patient hovered on the brink of the grave.

Nobody in the house knew anything about her flight. The letters, written by her the evening before, had been burnt; and her maid, dreading the wrath of her master, had not whispered a word about it to anybody. The priest, the retired cornet, the mustached surveyor, and the little Uhlan were discreet, and not without reason. Tereshka, the coachman, never uttered one word too much about it, even when he was drunk. Thus the secret was kept by more than half a dozen conspirators.

But Maria Gavrilovna herself divulged her secret during her delirious ravings. But her words were so disconnected, that her mother, who never left her bedside, could only understand from them that her daughter was deeply in love with Vladimir Nikolaievitch, and that probably love was the cause of her illness. She consulted her husband

and some of her neighbors, and at last it was unanimously decided that such was evidently Maria Gavrilovna's fate, that a woman cannot ride away from the man who is destined to be her husband, that poverty is not a crime, that one does not marry wealth, but a man, etc., etc. Moral proverbs are wonderfully useful in those cases where we can invent little in our own justification.

In the meantime the young lady began to recover. Vladimir had not been seen for a long time in the house of Gavril Gavrilovitch. He was afraid of the usual reception. It was resolved to send and announce to him an unexpected piece of good news: the consent of Maria's parents to his marriage with their daughter. But what was the astonishment of the proprietor of Nenaradova, when, in reply to their invitation, they received from him a half insane letter. He informed them that he would never set foot in their house again, and begged them to forget an unhappy creature whose only hope was death. A few days afterwards they heard that Vladimir had joined the army again. This was in the year 1812.

For a long time they did not dare to announce this to Masha, who was now convalescent. She never mentioned the name of Vladimir. Some months afterwards, finding his name in the list of those who had distinguished themselves and been severely wounded at Borodino, she fainted away, and it was feared that she would have another attack of fever. But, Heaven be thanked! the fainting fit had no serious consequences.

Another misfortune fell upon her: Gavril Gavrilovitch died, leaving her the heiress to all his property. But the inheritance did not console her; she shared sincerely the grief of poor Praskovia Petrovna, vowing that she would never leave her. They both quitted Nenaradova, the scene of so many sad recollections, and went to live on another estate.

Suitors crowded round the young and wealthy heiress, but she gave not the slightest hope to any of them. Her mother sometimes exhorted her to make a choice; but Maria Gavrilovna shook her head and became pensive. Vladimir no longer existed: he had died in Moscow on the eve of the entry of the French. His memory seemed to be held sacred by Masha; at least she treasured up everything that could remind her of him: books that he had once read, his drawings, his notes, and verses of poetry that he had copied out for her. The neighbors, hearing of all this, were astonished at her constancy, and awaited with curiosity the hero who should at last triumph over the melancholy fidelity of this virgin Artemisia.

Meanwhile the war had ended gloriously. Our regiments returned from abroad, and the people went out to meet them. The bands played the conquering songs: "Vive Henri-Quatre," Tyrolese waltzes and airs from "Joconde." Officers who had set out for the war almost mere lads returned grown men, with martial air, and their breasts decorated with crosses. The soldiers chatted gaily among themselves, constantly mingling French and German words in their speech. Time never to be forgotten! Time of glory and enthusiasm! How throbbed the Russian heart at the word "Fatherland!" How sweet were the tears of meeting! With what unanimity did we unite feelings of national pride with love for the Czar! And for him—what a moment!

The women, the Russian women, were then incomparable. Their enthusiasm was truly intoxicating, when, welcoming the conquerors, they cried "Hurrah!"

> "And threw their caps high in the air!"

What officer of that time does not confess that to the Russian women he was indebted for his best and most precious reward?

At this brilliant period Maria Gavrilovna was living with her mother in the province of ———, and did not see how both capitals celebrated the return of the troops. But in the districts and villages the general enthusiasm was, if possible, even still greater. The appearance of an officer in those places was for him a veritable triumph, and the lover in a plain coat felt very ill at ease in his vicinity.

We have already said that, in spite of her coldness, Maria Gavrilovna was, as before, surrounded by suitors. But all had to retire into the background when the wounded Colonel Bourmin of the Hussars, with the Order of St. George in his buttonhole and with an "interesting pallor," as the young ladies of the neighborhood observed, appeared at the castle. He was about twenty-six years of age. He had obtained leave of absence to visit his estate, which was contiguous to that of Maria Gavrilovna. Maria bestowed special attention upon him. In his presence her habitual pensiveness disappeared. It cannot be said that she coquetted with him, but a poet, observing her behaviour, would have said:

> "Se amor non e, che dunque?"

Bourmin was indeed a very charming young man. He possessed that spirit which is eminently pleasing to women: a spirit of decorum and observation, without any pretensions, and yet not without a slight tendency towards careless satire. His behavior towards Maria Gavrilovna was simple and frank, but whatever she said or did, his soul and eyes followed her. He seemed to be of a quiet and modest disposition, though report said that he had once been a terrible rake; but this did not injure him in the opinion of Maria Gavrilovna, who—like all young ladies in general—excused with pleasure follies that gave indication of boldness and ardor of temperament.

But more than everything else—more than his tenderness, more than his agreeable conversation, more than his interesting pallor, more than his arm in a sling—the silence of the young Hussar excited her curiosity and imagination. She could not but confess that he pleased her very much. Probably he, too, with his perception and experience, had already observed that she made a distinction between him and the others. How was it then that she had not yet seen him at her feet or heard his declaration? What restrained him? Was it timidity, inseparable from true love, or pride or the coquetry of a crafty wooer? It was an enigma to her. After long reflection, she came to the conclusion that timidity alone was the cause of it, and she resolved to encourage him by greater attention and, if circumstances should render it necessary, even by an exhibition of tenderness. She prepared a most unexpected dénouement, and waited with impatience for the moment of the romantic explanation. A secret, of whatever nature it may be, always presses heavily upon the human heart. Her stratagem had the desired success; at least Bourmin fell into such a reverie, and his black eyes rested with such fire upon her, that the decisive moment seemed close at hand. The neighbors spoke about the marriage as if it were a matter already decided upon, and good Praskovia Petrovna rejoiced that her daughter had at last found a lover worthy of her.

On one occasion the old lady was sitting alone in the parlor, amusing herself with a pack of cards, when Bourmin entered the room and immediately inquired for Maria Gavrilovna.

"She is in the garden," replied the old lady; "go out to her, and I will wait here for you."

Bourmin went, and the old lady made the sign of the cross and thought: "Perhaps the business will be settled to-day!"

Bourmin found Maria Gavrilovna near the pond, under a willow-tree, with a book in her hands, and in a white dress: a veritable heroine of romance. After the first few questions and observations, Maria Gavrilovna purposely allowed the conversation to drop, thereby increasing their mutual embarrassment, from which there was no possible way of escape except only by a sudden and decisive declaration.

And this is what happened: Bourmin, feeling the difficulty of his position, declared that he had long sought for an opportunity to open his heart to her, and requested a moment's attention. Maria Gavrilovna closed her book and cast down her eyes, as a sign of compliance with his request.

"I love you," said Bourmin. "I love you passionately...."

Maria Gavrilovna blushed and lowered her head still more. "I have acted imprudently in accustoming myself to the sweet pleasure of seeing and hearing you daily...." (Maria Gavrilovna recalled to mind the first letter of St. Preux) "But it is now too late to resist my fate; the remembrance of you, your dear incomparable image, will henceforth be the torment and the consolation of my life, but there still remains a grave duty for me to perform—to reveal to you a terrible secret which will place between us an insurmountable barrier.''

"That barrier has always existed," interrupted Maria Gavrilovna hastily. "I could never be your wife."

"I know," replied he calmly. "I know that you once loved, but death and three years of mourning.... Dear, kind Maria Gavrilovna, do not try to deprive me of my last consolation: the thought that you would have consented to make me happy, if..."

"Don't speak, for Heaven's sake, don't speak. You torture me."

"Yes, I know. I feel that you would have been mine, but I am the most miserable creature under the sun—I am already married!"

Maria Gavrilovna looked at him in astonishment.

"I am already married," continued Bourmin: "I have been married four years, and I do not know who is my wife, or where she is, or whether I shall ever see her again!"

"What do you say?" exclaimed Maria Gavrilovna. "How very strange! Continue: I will relate to you afterwards.... But continue, I beg of you."

"At the beginning of the year 1812," said Bourmin, "I was hastening to Vilna, where my regiment was stationed. Arriving late one evening at one of the post stations, I ordered the horses to be got ready as quickly as possible, when suddenly a terrible snow storm came on, and the post master and drivers advised me to wait till it had passed over. I followed their advice, but an unaccountable uneasiness took possession of me: it seemed as if someone were pushing me forward. Meanwhile the snowstorm did not subside. I could endure it no longer, and again ordering out the horses, I started off in the midst of the storm. The driver conceived the idea of following the course of the river, which would shorten our journey by three versts. The banks were covered with snow; the driver drove past the place where we should have come out upon the road, and so we found ourselves in an unknown part of the country. The storm did not cease; I saw a light in the distance, and I ordered the driver to proceed towards it. We reached a village; in the wooden church there was a light. The church was open. Outside the railings stood several sledges, and people were passing in and out through the porch.

" 'This way! this way!' cried several voices.

"I ordered the driver to proceed.

" 'In the name of Heaven, where have you been loitering?' said somebody to me. 'The bride has fainted away; the priest does not know what to do, and we were just getting ready to go back. Get out as quickly as you can.'

"I got out of the sledge without saying a word and went into the church, which was feebly lit up by two or three tapers. A young girl was sitting on a bench in a dark corner of the church; another girl was rubbing her temples.

" 'Thank God!' said the latter. 'You have come at last. You have almost killed the young lady.'

"The old priest advanced towards me, and said:

" 'Do you wish me to begin?'

" 'Begin, begin, father,' replied I absently.

"The young girl was raised up. She seemed to me not at all bad looking.... Impelled by an incomprehensible, unpardonable levity, I placed myself by her side in front of the pulpit; the priest hurried on; three men and a chambermaid supported the bride and only occupied themselves with her. We were married.

" 'Kiss each other!' said the witnesses to us.

"My wife turned her pale face towards me. I was about to kiss her, when she exclaimed: 'Oh! it is not he! It is not he!' and fell senseless.

"The witnesses gazed at me in alarm. I turned round and left the church without the least hindrance, flung myself into the kibitka and cried: 'Drive off!' "

"My God!" exclaimed Maria Gavrilovna. "And you do not know what became of your poor wife?"

"I do not know," replied Bourmin; "neither do I know the name of the village where I was married nor the post station where I set out from. At that time I attached so little importance to the wicked prank, that on leaving the church I fell asleep, and did not awake till the next morning after reaching the third station. The servant, who was then with me, died during the campaign, so that I have no hope of ever discovering the woman upon whom I played such a cruel joke, and who is now so cruelly avenged."

"My God! my God!" cried Maria Gavrilovna, seizing him by the hand. "Then it was you! And you do not recognize me?"

Bourmin turned pale—and threw himself at her feet.

NIKOLAI GOGOL

(1809–1852)

BORN in the Ukraine, Gogol was in many respects the founder of modern Russian literature. His stories of rural life collected under the title *Evenings on a Farm Near Dikanka* were enthusiastically received, and, because of their freshness and originality, exerted a profound and

lasting influence. To Gogol is chiefly due the credit for inaugurating
the modern Russian novel and short story.

The present version of *St. John's Eve* is reprinted from *Taras Bulba,
and Other Tales*, by permission of J. M. Dent and Sons, publishers.

ST. JOHN'S EVE

.(From *Evenings on a Farm Near Dikanka*)

THOMA GRIGOROVITCH had one very strange eccentricity:
to the day of his death he never liked to tell the same thing twice.
There were times when, if you asked him to relate a thing afresh, he
would interpolate new matter, or alter it so that it was impossible to
recognize it. Once upon a time, one of those gentlemen who like every
sort of frippery, and issue mean little volumes, no thicker than an
A B C book, every month, or even every week, wormed this same story
out of Thoma Grigorovitch, and the latter completely forgot about it.
But that same young gentleman, in the pea-green caftan, came from
Poltava, bringing with him a little book, and, opening it in the middle,
showed it to us. Thoma Grigorovitch was on the point of setting his
spectacles astride of his nose, but recollected that he had forgotten to
wind thread about them and stick them together with wax, so he passed
it over to me. As I understand something about reading and writing,
and do not wear spectacles, I undertook to read it. I had not turned two
leaves when all at once he caught me by the hand and stopped me.

"Stop! tell me first what you are reading."

I confess that I was a trifle stunned by such a question.

"What! what am I reading, Thoma Grigorovitch? Why, your own
words."

"Who told you that they were my words?"

"Why, what more would you have? Here it is printed: 'Related by
such and such a sacristan.'"

"Spit on the head of the man who printed that! he lies, the dog of
a Moscow peddler! Did I say that?' 'Twas just the same as though
one hadn't his wits about him!' Listen, I'll tell the tale to you on the
spot." We moved up to the table, and he began.

My grandfather (the kingdom of heaven be his! may he eat only
wheaten rolls and poppy-seed cakes with honey, in the other world!)
could tell a story wonderfully well. When he used to begin a tale you
could not stir from the spot all day, but kept on listening. He was not
like the story-teller of the present day, when he begins to lie, with a
tongue as though he had had nothing to eat for three days, so that you

snatch your cap and flee from the house. I remember my old mother was alive then, and in the long winter evenings when the frost was crackling out of doors, and had sealed up hermetically the narrow panes of our cottage, she used to sit at her wheel, drawing out a long thread in her hand, rocking the cradle with her foot, and humming a song, which I seem to hear even now.

The lamp, quivering and flaring up as though in fear of something, lighted up our cottage; the spindle hummed; and all of us children, collected in a cluster, listened to our grandfather, who had not crawled off the stove for more than five years, owing to his great age. But the wondrous tales of the incursions of the Zaporozhian Cossacks and the Poles, the bold deeds of Polkova, of Poltar-Kozhukh, and Sagaidatchnii, did not interest us so much as the stories about some deed of old, which always sent a shiver through our frames and made our hair rise upright on our heads. Sometimes such terror took possession of us in consequence of them, that, from that evening forward, Heaven knows how wonderful everything seemed to us. If one chanced to go out of the cottage after nightfall for anything, one fancied that a visitor from the other world had lain down to sleep in one's bed; and I have often taken my own smock, at a distance, as it lay at the head of the bed, for the Evil One rolled up in a ball! But the chief thing about grandfather's stories was, that he had never lied in all his life; and whatever he said was so was so.

I will now tell you one of his wonderful tales. I know that there are a great many wise people who copy in the courts, and can even read civil documents, but who, if you were to put into their hand a simple prayer-book, could not make out the first letter in it, and would show all their teeth in derision. These people laugh at everything you tell them. Along comes one of them—and doesn't believe in witches! Yes, glory to God that I have lived so long in the world! I have seen heretics to whom it would be easier to lie in confession than it would be to our brothers and equals to take snuff, and these folk would deny the existence of witches! But let them just dream about something and they won't even tell what it was! There, it is no use talking about them!

No one could have recognized the village of ours a little over a hundred years ago; it was a hamlet, the poorest kind of a hamlet. Half a score of miserable farmhouses, unplastered and badly thatched, were scattered here and there about the fields. There was not a yard or a decent shed to shelter animals or wagons. That was the way the wealthy lived: and if you had looked for our brothers, the poor—why, a hole in the ground—that was a cabin for you! Only by the smoke could you tell that a God-created man lived there. You ask why they lived so? It was not entirely through poverty: almost everyone led a raiding Cossack life, and gathered not a little plunder in foreign lands; it was rather because it was little use building up a good wooden house. Many folk were engaged in raids all over the country—Crimeans, Poles, Lithuanians! It was quite possible that their own countrymen might make a descent and plunder everything. Anything was possible.

In this hamlet a man, or rather a devil in human form, often made his appearance. Why he came, and whence, no one knew. He prowled about, got drunk, and suddenly disappeared as if into the air, leaving no trace of his existence. Then, behold, he seemed to have dropped from the sky again, and went flying about the street of the village, of which no trace now remains, and which was not more than a hundred paces from Dikanka. He would collect together all the Cossacks he met; then there were songs, laughter, and cash in plenty, and vodka flowed like water.... He would address the pretty girls, and give them ribbons, earrings, strings of beads—more than they knew what to do with. It is true that the pretty girls rather hesitated about accepting his presents: God knows, perhaps, what unclean hands they had passed through. My grandfather's aunt, who kept at that time a tavern, in which Basavriuk (as they called this devil-man) often caroused, said that no consideration on the earth would have induced her to accept a gift from him. But then, again, how avoid accepting? Fear seized on every one when he knit his shaggy brows, and gave a sidelong glance which might send your feet God knows whither: whilst if you did accept, then the next night some fiend from the swamp, with horns on his head, came and began to squeeze your neck, if there was a string of beads upon it, or bite your finger, if there was a ring upon it; or drag you by the hair, if ribbons were braided in it. God have mercy, then, on those who held such gifts! But there was the difficulty: it was impossible to get rid of them; if you threw them into the water, the diabolical ring or necklace would skim along the surface and into your hand.

There was a church in the village—St. Pantelei, if I remember rightly. There lived there a priest, Father Athanasii, of blessed memory. Observing that Basavriuk did not come to church even at Easter, he determined to reprove him and impose penance upon him. Well, he hardly escaped with his life. "Hark ye, sir!" he thundered in reply, "learn to mind your own business instead of meddling in other people's if you don't want that throat of yours stuck together with boiling kutya."*

What was to be done with this unrepentant man? Father Athanasii contented himself with announcing that any one who should make the acquaintance of Basavriuk would be counted a Catholic, an enemy of Christ's orthodox church, not a member of the human race.

---

* A dish of rice or wheat flour, with honey and raisins, which is brought to the church on the celebration of memorial masses.

In this village there was a Cossack named Korzh, who had a laborer whom people called Peter the Orphan—perhaps because no one remembered either his father or mother. The church elder, it is true, said that they had died of the pest in his second year; but my grandfather's aunt would not hear of that, and tried with all her might to furnish him with parents, although poor Peter needed them about as much as we need last year's snow. She said that his father had been in Zaporozhe, and had been taken prisoner by the Turks, amongst whom he underwent God only knows what tortures, until, having by some miracle disguised himself as a eunuch, he made his escape. Little cared the black-browed youths and maidens about Peter's parents. They merely remarked that if he only had a new coat, a red sash, a black lambskin cap with a smart blue crown on his head, a Turkish saber by his side, a whip in one hand and a pipe with handsome mountings in the other, he would surpass all the young men. But the pity was, that the only thing poor Peter had was a gray gaberdine with more holes in it than there are gold pieces in a Jew's pocket. But that was not the worst of it. Korzh had a daughter, such a beauty as I think you can hardly have chanced to see. My grandfather's aunt used to say—and you know that it is easier for a woman to kiss the Evil One than to call anyone else a beauty—that this Cossack maiden's cheeks were as plump and fresh as the pinkest poppy when, bathed in God's dew, it unfolds its petals, and coquets with the rising sun; that her brows were evenly arched over her bright eyes like black cords, such as our maidens buy nowadays, for their crosses and ducats, off the Moscow peddlers who visit the villages with their baskets; that her little mouth, at sight of which the youths smacked their lips, seemed made to warble the songs of nightingales; that her hair, black as the raven's wing, and soft as young flax, fell in curls over her shoulders, for our maidens did not then plait their hair in pigtails interwoven with pretty, bright-hued ribbons. Eh! may I never intone another alleluia in the choir, if I would not have kissed her, in spite of the gray which is making its way through the old wool which covers my pate, and of the old woman beside me, like a thorn in my side! Well, you know what happens when young men and maidens live side by side. In the twilight the heels of red boots were always visible in the place where Pidorka chatted with her Peter. But Korzh would never have suspected anything out of the way, only one day—it is evident that none but the Evil One could have inspired him—Peter took into his head to kiss the maiden's rosy lips with all his heart, without first looking well about him; and that same Evil One—may the son of a dog dream of the holy cross!—caused the old graybeard, like a fool, to open the cottage door at that moment. Korzh was petrified, dropped his jaw, and clutched at the door for support. Those unlucky kisses completely stunned him.

Recovering himself, he took his grandfather's hunting whip from the wall, and was about to belabor Peter's back with it, when Pidorka's little six-year-old brother Ivas rushed up from somewhere or other, and grasping his father's legs with his little hands, screamed out, "Daddy, Daddy! don't beat Peter!" What was to be done? A father's heart is not made of stone. Hanging the whip again upon the wall, he led Peter quietly from the house. "If you ever show yourself in my cottage again, or even under the windows, look out, Peter, for, by heaven, your black mustache will disappear; and your black locks, though wound twice about your ears will take leave of your pate, or my name is not Terentiy Korzh." So saying, he gave him such a taste of his fist in the nape of his neck, that all grew dark before Peter, and he flew headlong out of the place.

So there was an end of their kissing. Sorrow fell upon our turtle doves; and a rumor grew rife in the village that a certain Pole, all embroidered with gold, with mustaches, saber, spurs, and pockets jingling like the bells of the bag with which our sacristan Taras goes through the church every day, had begun to frequent Korzh's house. Now, it is well known why a father has visitors when there is a black-browed daughter about. So, one day, Pidorka burst into tears, and caught the hand of her brother Ivas. "Ivas, my dear! Ivas, my love! fly to Peter, my child of gold, like an arrow from a bow. Tell him all: I would have loved his brown eyes, I would have kissed his fair face, but my fate decrees otherwise. More than one handkerchief have I wet with burning tears. I am sad and heavy at heart. And my own father is my enemy. I will not marry the Pole, whom I do not love. Tell him they are making ready for a wedding, but there will be no music at our wedding: priests will sing instead of pipes and viols. I shall not dance with my bridegroom; they will carry me out. Dark, dark will be my dwelling of maple wood; and instead of chimneys, a cross will stand upon the roof."

Peter stood petrified, without moving from the spot, when the innocent child lisped out Pidorka's words to him. "And I, wretched man, had thought to go to the Crimea and Turkey, to win gold and return to thee, my beauty! But it may not be. We have been overlooked by the evil eye. I too shall have a wedding, dear one; but no ecclesiastics will be present at that wedding. The black crow instead of the pope will caw over me; the bare plain will be my dwelling; the dark blue cloud my roof-tree. The eagle will claw out my brown eyes; the rain will wash my Cossack bones, and the whirlwinds will dry them. But what am I? Of what should I complain? 'Tis clear God willed it so. If I am to be lost, then so be it!" and he went straight to the tavern.

My late grandfather's aunt was somewhat surprised at seeing Peter at the tavern, at an hour when good men go to morning mass; and stared at him as though in a dream when he called for a jug of brandy, about half a pailful. But the poor fellow tried in vain to drown his woe. The vodka stung his tongue like nettles, and tasted more bitter than wormwood. He flung the jug from him upon the ground.

"You have sorrowed enough, Cossack," growled a bass voice behind him. He looked round—it was Basavriuk! Ugh, what a face! His hair was like a brush, his eyes like those of a bull. "I know what you lack: here it is." As he spoke he jingled a leather purse which hung from his girdle and smiled diabolically. Peter shuddered. "Ha, ha, ha! how it shines!" he roared, shaking out ducats into his hands: "Ha, ha, ha! how it jingles! And I only ask one thing for a whole pile of such shiners."

"It is the Evil One!" exclaimed Peter. "Give me them! I'm ready for anything!"

They struck hands upon it, and Basavriuk said, "You are just in time, Peter: to-morrow is St. John the Baptist's day. Only on this one night in the year does the fern blossom. I will await you at midnight in the Bear's ravine."

I do not believe that chickens await the hour when the housewife brings their corn with as much anxiety as Peter awaited the evening. He kept looking to see whether the shadows of the trees were not lengthening, whether the sun was not turning red towards setting; and, the longer he watched, the more impatient he grew. How long it was! Evidently God's day had lost its end somewhere. But now the sun has set. The sky is red only on one side, and it is already growing dark. It grows colder in the fields. It gets gloomier and gloomier, and at last quite dark. At last! With heart almost bursting from his bosom, he set out and cautiously made his way down through the thick woods into the deep hollow called the Bear's ravine. Basavriuk was already waiting there. It was so dark that you could not see a yard before you. Hand in hand they entered the ravine, pushing through the luxuriant thorn-bushes and stumbling at almost every step. At last they reached an open spot. Peter looked about him; he had never chanced to come there before. Here Basavriuk halted.

"Do you see before you three hillocks? There are a great many kinds of flowers upon them. May some power keep you from plucking even one of them. But as soon as the fern blossoms, seize it, and look not round, no matter what may seem to be going on behind thee."

Peter wanted to ask some questions, but, behold, Basavriuk was no longer there. He approached the three hillocks—where were the flowers? He saw none! The wild steppe-grass grew all around, and hid everything in its luxuriance. But the lightning flashed; and before him was a whole bed of flowers, all wonderful, all strange: whilst amongst them there were also the simple fronds of fern. Peter doubted his senses, and stood thoughtfully before them, arms akimbo.

"What manner of prodigy is this? why, one can see these weeds ten times a day. What is there marvelous about them? Devil's-face must be mocking me!"

But behold! the tiny flower-bud of the fern reddened and moved as though alive. It was a marvel, in truth. It grew larger and larger, and glowed like a burning coal. The tiny stars of light flashed up, something burst softly, and the flower opened before his eyes like a flame, lighting the others about it.

"Now is the time," thought Peter and extended his hand. He saw hundreds of hairy hands reach also for the flower from behind him, and there was a sound of scampering in his rear. He half closed his eyes, and plucked sharply at the stalk, and the flower remained in his hand.

All became still.

Upon a stump sat Basavriuk, quite blue like a corpse. He did not move so much as a finger. His eyes were immovably fixed on something visible to him alone: his mouth was half open and speechless. Nothing stirred around. Ugh! it was horrible!—But then a whistle was heard, which made Peter's heart grow cold within him; and it seemed to him that the grass whispered, and the flowers began to talk among themselves in delicate voices, like little silver bells, whilst the trees rustled in murmuring contention;—Basavriuk's face suddenly became full of life, and his eyes sparkled. "The witch has just returned," he muttered between his teeth. "Hearken, Peter: a charmer will stand before you in a moment; do whatever she commands; if not—you are lost forever."

Then he parted the thorn-bushes with a knotty stick, and before him stood a tiny farmhouse. Basavriuk smote it with his fist, and the wall trembled. A large black dog ran out to meet them, and with a whine transformed itself into a cat and flew straight at his eyes.

"Don't be angry, don't be angry, you old Satan!" said Basavriuk, employing such words as would have made a good man stop his ears. Behold, instead of a cat, an old woman all bent into a bow, with a face wrinkled like a baked apple, and a nose and chin like a pair of nut-crackers.

"A fine charmer!" thought Peter; and cold chills ran down his back. The witch tore the flower from his hand, stooped and muttered over it for a long time, sprinkling it with some kind of water. Sparks flew from her mouth, and foam appeared on her lips.

"Throw it away," she said, giving it back to Peter.

Peter threw it, but what wonder was this? The flower did not fall straight to the earth, but for a long while twinkled like a fiery ball through the darkness, and swam through the air like a boat. At last it began to sink lower and lower, and fell so far away that the little star, hardly larger than a poppy-seed, was barely visible. "There!" croaked the old woman, in a dull voice; and Bosavriuk, giving him a spade, said, "Dig here Peter: you will find more gold than you or Korzh ever dreamed of."

Peter spat on his hands, seized the spade, pressed his foot on it, and turned up the earth, a second, a third, a fourth time. The spade clinked against something hard, and would go no farther. Then his eyes began to distinguish a small, iron-bound coffer. He tried to seize it, but the chest began to sink into the earth, deeper, farther and deeper still: whilst behind him he heard a laugh like a serpent's hiss.

"No, you shall not have the gold until you shed human blood," said the witch, and she led up to him a child of six, covered with a white sheet, and indicated by a sign that he was to cut off his head.

Peter was stunned. A trifle, indeed, to cut off a man's or even an innocent child's, head for no reason whatever! In wrath he tore off the sheet enveloping the victim's head, and behold! before him stood Ivas. The poor child crossed his little hands, and hung his head. Peter flew at the witch with the knife like a madman, and was on the point of laying hands on her.

"What did you promise for the girl?" thundered Basavriuk; and like a shot he was on his back. The witch stamped her foot; a blue flame flashed from the earth and illumined all within it. The earth became transparent as if molded of crystal; and all that was within it became visible as if in the palm of the hand. Ducats, precious stones, in chests and pots, were piled in heaps beneath the very spot they stood on. Peter's eyes flashed, his mind grew troubled.... He grasped the knife like a madman, and the innocent blood spurted into his eyes. Diabolical laughter resounded on all sides. Misshapen monsters flew past him in flocks. The witch, fastening her hands in the headless trunk like a wolf, drank its blood. His head whirled. Collecting all his strength, he set out to run. Everything grew red before him. The trees seemed steeped in blood, and burned and groaned. The sky glowed and threatened. Burning points, like lightning, flickered before his eyes. Utterly exhausted, he rushed into his miserable hovel and fell to the ground like a log. A deathlike sleep overpowered him.

Two days and two nights did Peter sleep, without once awakening. When he came to himself, on the third day, he looked long at all the corners of his hut; but in vain did he endeavor to recollect what had taken place; his memory was like a miser's pocket from which you cannot entice a quarter of a kopek. Stretching himself, he heard something clash at his feet. He looked; there were two bags of gold. Then only, as if in a dream, he recollected that he had been seeking for treasure, and that something had frightened him in the woods. But at what price he had obtained it, and how, he could by no means tell.

Korzh saw the sacks—and was mollified. "A fine fellow Peter, quite unequaled! yes, and did I not love him? Was he not to me as my own son?" And the old man repeated this fiction until he wept over it himself. Pidorka began to tell Peter how some passing gipsies had stolen Ivas; but he could not even recall him—to such a degree had the Devil's influence darkened his mind. There was no reason for delay. The Pole was dismissed and the wedding-feast prepared; rolls were baked, towels and handkerchiefs embroidered; the young people were seated at table; the wedding-loaf was cut; guitars, cymbals, pipes, viols sounded, and pleasure was rife.

A wedding in the olden times was not like one of the present day. My grandfather's aunt used to tell how the maidens—in festive head-dresses, of yellow, blue and pink ribbons, above which they bound gold braid; in thin chemisettes embroidered on all the seams with red silk, and strewn with tiny silver flowers; in morocco shoes, with high iron heels—danced the gorlitza as swimmingly as peacocks, and as wildly as the whirlwind; how the youths—with their ship-shaped caps upon their heads, the crowns of gold brocade, and two horns projecting, one in front and another behind, of the very finest black lambskin; in tunics of the finest blue silk with red borders—stepped forward one by one, their arms akimbo in stately form, and executed the gopak; how the lads—in tall Cossack caps, and light cloth gaberdines, girt with silver embroidered belts, their short pipes in their teeth—skipped before them and talked nonsense. Even Korzh as he gazed at the young people could not help getting gay in his old age. Guitar in hand, alternately puffing at his pipe and singing, a brandy-glass upon his head, the gray beard began the national dance amid loud shouts from the merrymakers.

What will not people devise in merry mood? They even began to disguise their faces till they did not look like human beings. On such occasions one would dress himself as a Jew, another as the devil; they would begin by kissing each other, and end by seizing each other by the hair. God be with them! you laughed till you held your sides. They dressed themselves in Turkish and Tatar garments. All upon them glowed like a conflagration, and then they began to joke and play pranks....

An amusing thing happened to my grandfather's aunt, who was at this wedding. She was wearing an ample Tatar robe, and, wineglass in hand, was entertaining the company. The Evil One instigated one man to pour vodka over her from behind. Another, at the same moment, evidently not by accident, struck a light, and held it to her. The flame flashed up, and poor aunt, in terror, flung her dress off, before them all. Screams, laughter, jests arose as if at a fair. In a word, the old folks could not recall so merry a wedding.

Pidorka and Peter began to live like a gentleman and lady. There was plenty of everything and everything was fine.... But honest folk shook their heads when they marked their way of living. "From the devil no good can come," they unanimously agreed. "Whence, except from the tempter of orthodox people, came this wealth? Where else could he have got such a lot of gold? Why, on the very day that he got rich, did Basavriuk vanish as if into thin air?"

Say, if you can, that people only imagine things! A month had not passed, and no one would have recognized Peter. He sat in one spot, saying no word to anyone; but continually thinking and seemingly trying to recall something. When Pidorka succeeded in getting him to speak, he appeared to forget himself, and would carry on a conversation, and even grow cheerful; but if he inadvertently glanced at the sacks, "Stop, stop! I have forgotten," he would cry, and again plunge into reverie and strive to recall something. Sometimes when he sat still a long time in one place, it seemed to him as though it were coming, just coming back to mind, but again all would fade away. It seemed as if he was sitting in the tavern: they brought him vodka; vodka stung him; vodka was repulsive to him. Some one came along and struck him on the shoulder; but beyond that everything was veiled in darkness before him. The perspiration would stream down his face, and he would sit exhausted in the same place.

What did not Pidorka do? She consulted the sorceresses; and they poured out fear, and brewed stomach ache—but all to no avail. And so the summer passed. Many a Cossack had mowed and reaped; many a Cossack, more enterprising than the rest, had set off upon an expedition. Flocks of ducks were already crowding the marshes, but there was not even a hint of improvement.

It was red upon the steppes. Ricks of grain, like Cossack's caps, dotted the fields here and there. On the highway were to be encountered wagons loaded with brushwood and logs. The ground had become more solid, and in places was touched with frost. Already had the snow begun to fall and the branches of the trees were covered with rime like rabbitskin. Already on frosty days the robin redbreast hopped about on the snow-heaps like a foppish Polish nobleman, and picked out grains of corn; and children, with huge sticks, played hockey upon the ice; while their fathers lay quietly on the stove, issuing forth at intervals with lighted pipes in their lips, to growl, in regular fashion, at the orthodox frost or to take the air, and thresh the grain spread out in the barn. At last the snow began to melt, and the ice slipped away: but Peter remained the same; and, the more time went on, the more morose he grew. He sat in the cottage as though nailed to the spot, with the sacks of gold at his feet. He grew averse to look at Pidorka; and still he thought of but one thing, still he tried to recall something, and got angry and ill-tempered because he could not. Often, rising wildly from his seat, he gesticulated violently and fixed his eyes on

something as though desirous of catching it: his lips moved as though
desirous of uttering some long-forgotten word, but remained speechless.
Fury would take possession of him: he would gnaw and bite his hands
like a man half crazy, and in his vexation would tear out his hair by
the handful, until, calming down, he would relapse into forgetfulness,
as it were, and then would again strive to recall the past and be again
seized with fury and fresh tortures. What visitation of God was this?

Pidorka was neither dead nor alive. At first it was horrible to her to
remain alone with him in the cottage; but, in course of time, the poor
woman grew accustomed to her sorrow. But it was impossible to recognize the Pidorka of former days. No blushes, no smiles; she was thin
and worn with grief, and had wept her bright eyes away. Once someone who took pity on her advised her to go to the witch who dwelt in the
Bear's ravine, and enjoyed the reputation of being able to cure every
disease in the world. She determined to try this last remedy: and finally
persuaded the old woman to come to her. This was on St. John's Eve,
as it chanced. Peter lay insensible on the bench, and did not observe
the newcomer. Slowly he rose, and looked about him. Suddenly he
trembled in every limb, as though he were on the scaffold: his hair
rose upon his head, and he laughed a laugh that thrilled Pidorka's
heart with fear.

"I have remembered, remembered!" he cried, in terrible joy; and,
swinging a hatchet round his head, he struck at the old woman with
all his might. The hatchet penetrated the oaken door nearly four
inches. The old woman disappeared; and a child of seven, covered in
a white sheet, stood in the middle of the cottage.... The sheet flew off.
"Ivas!" cried Pidorka, and ran to him; but the apparition became
covered from head to foot with blood, and illumined the whole room
with red light.

She ran into the passage in her terror, but, on recovering herself a
little, wished to help Peter. In vain! The door had slammed to behind
her, so that she could not open it. People ran up, and began to knock:
they broke in the door, as though there were but one mind among
them. The whole cottage was full of smoke; and just in the middle,
where Peter had stood, was a heap of ashes from whence smoke was still
rising. They flung themselves upon the sacks: only broken potsherds
lay there instead of ducats. The Cossacks stood with staring eyes and
open mouths, as if rooted to the earth, not daring to move a hair, such
terror did this wonder inspire in them.

I do not remember what happened next. Pidorka made a vow to go
upon a pilgrimage, collected the property left her by her father, and in
a few days it was as if she had never been in the village. Whither she
had gone, no one could tell. Officious old women would have despatched her to the same place whither Peter had gone; but a Cossack

from Kief reported that he had seen, in a cloister, a nun withered to a mere skeleton who prayed unceasingly. Her fellow-villagers recognized her as Pidorka by the tokens—that no one heard her utter a word; and that she had come on foot, and had brought a frame for the picture of God's mother, set with such brilliant stones that all were dazzled at the sight.

But this was not the end, if you please. On the same day that the Evil One made away with Peter, Basavriuk appeared again; but all fled from him. They knew what sort of a being he was—none else than Satan, who had assumed human form in order to unearth treasures; and, since treasures do not yield to unclean hands, he seduced the young. That same year, all deserted their earthen huts and collected in a village; but even there there was no peace an account of that accursed Basavriuk.

My late grandfather's aunt said that he was particularly angry with her because she had abandoned her former tavern, and tried with all his might to revenge himself upon her. Once the village elders were assembled in the tavern, and, as the saying goes, were arranging the precedence at the table, in the middle of which was placed a small roasted lamb, shame to say. They chattered about this, that and the other—among the rest about various marvels and strange things. Well, they saw something; it would have been nothing if only one had seen it, but all saw it, and it was this: the sheep raised his head; his goggling eyes became alive and sparkled; and the black, bristling mustache, which appeared for one instant, made a significant gesture at those present. All at once recognized Basavriuk's countenance in the sheep's head; my grandfather's aunt thought it was on the point of asking her for vodka. The worthy elders seized their hats and hastened home.

Another time, the church elder himself, who was fond of an occasional private interview with my grandfather's brandy-glass, had not succeeded in getting to the bottom twice, when he beheld the glass bowing very low to him. "Satan, take you, let us make the sign of the cross over you!" And the same marvel happened to his better half. She. had just begun to mix the dough in a huge kneading-trough when suddenly the trough sprang up. "Stop, stop! where are you going?" Putting its arms akimbo, with dignity, it went skipping all about the cottage. You may laugh, but is was no laughing matter to our grandfathers. And in vain did Father Athanasii go through the village with holy water, and chase the devil through all the streets with his brush. My late grandfather's aunt long complained that, as soon as it was dark, some one came knocking at her door and scratching at the wall.

Well! all appears to be quiet now, in the place where our village stands; but it was not so very long ago—my father was still alive—that

I remember how a good man could not pass the ruined tavern which a dishonest race had long managed for their own interest. From the smoke-blackened chimneys smoke poured out in a pillar and, rising high in the air, rolled off like a cap, scattering burning coals over the steppe; and Satan (the son of a dog should not be mentioned) sobbed so pitifully in his lair that the startled ravens rose in flocks from the neighboring oak-wood and flew through the air with wild cries.

IVAN TURGENEV

(1818–1883)

Born at Orel in 1818, Turgenev was educated in his native country. Though the greater part of his life was spent in Paris, he wrote invariably about his own people. He is one of the finest figures in Russian literature, surpassing all other Russians in beauty of language and form.

A Sportsman's Sketches was one of his earliest works. It is a collection of stories, from which The District Doctor has been chosen. The present translation is by Constance Garnett, and is published by William Heinemann.

THE DISTRICT DOCTOR

(From A Sportsman's Sketches)

ONE day in autumn on my way back from a remote part of the country I caught cold and fell ill. Fortunately the fever attacked me in the district town at the inn; I sent for the doctor. In half-an-hour the district doctor appeared, a thin, dark-haired man of middle height. He prescribed me the usual sudorific, ordered a mustard-plaster to be put on, very deftly slid a five-ruble note up his sleeve, coughing drily and looking away as he did so, and then was getting up to go home, but somehow fell into talk and remained. I was exhausted with feverishness; I foresaw a sleepless night, and was glad of a little chat with a pleasant companion. Tea was served. My doctor began to converse freely. He was a sensible fellow, and expressed himself with vigor and some humor. Queer things happen in the world: you may live a long while with some people, and be on friendly terms with them, and never once speak openly with them from your soul: with others you have scarcely time to get acquainted, and all at once you are pouring out to him—or he to you—all your secrets, as though you were at confession. I don't know how I gained the confidence of my new friend—anyway, with nothing to lead up to it, he told me a rather curious incident; and here I will report his tale for the information of the indulgent reader. I will try to tell it in the doctor's own words.

"You don't happen to know," he began in a weak and quavering voice (the common result of the use of unmixed Berezov snuff); "you don't happen to know the judge here, Mylov, Pavel Lukich?.... You don't know him?...Well, it's all the same." (He cleared his throat and rubbed his eyes.) "Well, you see, the thing happened, to tell you exactly without mistake, in Lent, at the very time of the thaws. I was sitting at his house—our judge's, you know—playing preference. Our judge is a good fellow, and fond of playing preference. Suddenly" (the doctor made frequent use of this word, suddenly) "they tell me, 'There's a servant asking for you.' I say, 'What does he want?' They say, 'He has brought a note—it must be from a patient.' 'Give me the note,' I say. So it is from a patient—well and good—you understand—it's our bread and butter.... But this is how it was: a lady, a widow, writes to me; she says, 'My daughter is dying. Come, for God's sake!' she says, 'and the horses have been sent for you.'... Well, that's all right. But she was twenty miles from the town, and it was midnight out of doors, and the roads in such a state, my word! And as she was poor herself, one could not expect more than two silver rubles, and even that problematic; and perhaps it might only be a matter of a roll of linen and a sack of oatmeal in payment. However, duty, you know, before everything: a fellow-creature may be dying. I hand over my cards at once to Kalliopin, the member of the provincial commission, and return home. I look; a wretched little trap was standing at the steps, with peasant's horses, fat—too fat—and their coat as shaggy as felt; and the coachman sitting with his cap off out of respect. 'Well,' I think to myself, 'it's clear, my friend, these patients aren't rolling in riches.' ... You smile; but I tell you, a poor man like me has to take everything into consideration. ...If the coachman sits like a prince, and doesn't touch his cap, and even sneers at you behind his beard, and flicks his whip—then you may bet on six rubles. But this case, I saw, had a very different air. 'However,' I think, 'there's no help for it; duty before everything.' I snatch up the most necessary drugs, and set off. Will you believe it? I only just managed to get there at all. The road was infernal: streams, snow, watercourses, and the dyke had suddenly burst there—that was the worst of it! However, I arrived at last. It was a little thatched house. There was a light in the windows; that meant they expected me. I was met by an old lady, very venerable, in a cap. 'Save her!' she says; 'she is dying.' I say, 'Pray don't distress yourself—where is the invalid?' 'Come this way.' I see a clean little room, a lamp in the corner; on the bed a girl of twenty, unconscious. She was in a burning heat, and breathing heavily—it was fever. There were two other girls, her sisters, scared and in tears. 'Yesterday,' they tell me, 'she was perfectly well and had a good appetite; this morning she complained of her head, and this evening, suddenly, you see, like this.' I say again: 'Pray don't be uneasy.' It's a doctor's duty, you know—and I went up to her and bled her, told them to put on a mustard-plaster, and prescribed a mixture. Meantime I looked at her; I looked at her, you know—there, by God! I had never seen such a face!—she was a beauty, in a word! I felt quite shaken with pity. Such lovely features; such eyes!... But, thank God! she became easier; she fell into a perspiration, seemed to come to her senses, looked round, smiled, and passed her hand over her face.... Her sisters bent over her. They ask, 'How are you?' 'All right,' she says, and turns away. I looked at her; she had fallen asleep. 'Well,' I say, 'now the patient should be left alone.' So we all went out on tiptoe; only a maid remained in case she was wanted. In the parlor there was a samovar standing on the table, and a bottle of rum; in our profession one can't get on without it. They gave me tea; asked me to stop the night.... I consented: where could I go, indeed, at that time of night? The old lady kept groaning. 'What is it?' I say. 'She will live; don't worry yourself; you had better take a little rest yourself; it is about two o'clock.' 'But will you send to wake me if anything happens?' 'Yes, yes.' The old lady went away, and the girls too went to their own room; they made up a bed for me in the parlor. Well, I went to bed—but I could not get to sleep, for a wonder! for in reality I was very tired. I could not get my patient out of my head. At last I could not put up with it any longer; I got up suddenly; I think to myself, 'I will go and see how the patient is getting on.' Her bedroom was next to the parlor. Well, I got up, and gently opened the door—how my heart beat! I looked in: the servant was asleep, her mouth wide open, and even snoring, the wretch! but the patient lay with her face towards me, and her arms flung wide apart, poor girl! I went up to her... when suddenly she opened her eyes and stared at me! 'Who is it? who is it?' I was in confusion. 'Don't be alarmed, madam,' I say; 'I am the doctor; I have come to see how you feel.' 'You the doctor?' 'Yes, the doctor, your mother sent for me from the town; we have bled you, madam; now pray go to sleep, and in a day or two, please God! we will set you on your feet again.' 'Ah, yes, yes, doctor, don't let me die... please, please.' 'Why do you talk like that? God bless you!' She is in a fever again, I think to myself; I felt her pulse; yes, she was feverish. She looked at me, and then took me by the hand. 'I will tell you why I don't want to die; I will tell you.... Now we are alone; and only, please don't you... not to any one... Listen. ...' I bent down; she moved her lips quite to my ear; she touched my

cheek with her hair—I confess my head went round—and began to
whisper.... I could make out nothing of it.... Ah, she was delirious!
.... She whispered and whispered, but so quickly, and as if it were not
in Russian; at last she finished, and shivering dropped her head on the
pillow, and threatened me with her finger: 'Remember, doctor, to no
one.' I calmed her somehow, gave her something to drink, waked the
servant, and went away."

At this point the doctor again took snuff with exasperated energy,
and for a moment seemed stupefied by its effects.

"However," he continued, "the next day, contrary to my expectations, the patient was no better. I thought and thought, and suddenly
decided to remain there, even though my other patients were expecting me. .... And you know one can't afford to disregard that; one's
practice suffers if one does. But, in the first place, the patient was really
in danger; and secondly, to tell the truth, I felt strongly drawn to her.
Besides, I liked the whole family. Though they were really badly off,
they were singularly, I may say, cultivated people.... Their father had
been a learned man, an author; he died, of course, in poverty, but he
had managed before he died to give his children an excellent education; he left a lot of books too. Either because I looked after the invalid
very carefully, or for some other reason, anyway, I can venture to say
all the household loved me as if I were one of the family.... Meantime
the roads were in a worse state than ever; all communications, so to
say, were cut off completely; even medicine could with difficulty be
got from the town.... The sick girl was not getting better. ... Day
after day, and day after day... but ... here...." (The doctor made
a brief pause.) "I declare I don't know how to tell you...." (He
again took snuff, coughed, and swallowed a little tea.) "I will tell
you without beating about the bush. My patient... how should I say?
... Well, she had fallen in love with me... or, no, it was not that
she was in love... however... really, how should one say?" (The
doctor looked down and grew red.) "No," he went on quickly, "in
love, indeed! A man should not over-estimate himself. She was an
educated girl, clever and well-read, and I had even forgotten my Latin,
one may say, completely. As to appearance" (the doctor looked himself over with a smile), "I am nothing to boast of there either. But God
Almighty did not make me a fool; I don't take black for white; I know
a thing or two; I could see very clearly, for instance, that Aleksandra
Andreyevna —that was her name—did not feel love for me, but had
a friendly, so to say, inclination—a respect or something for me.
Though she herself perhaps mistook this sentiment, anyway this was
her attitude; you may form your own judgment of it. But," added the
doctor, who had brought out all these disconnected sentences without
taking breath, and with obvious embarrassment, "I seem to be wander-

ing rather—you won't understand anything like this.... There, with your leave, I will relate it all in order."

He drank off a glass of tea, and began in a calmer voice.

"Well, then. My patient kept getting worse and worse. You are not a doctor, my good sir; you cannot understand what passes in a poor fellow's heart, especially at first, when he begins to suspect that the disease is getting the upper hand of him. What becomes of his belief in himself? You suddenly grow so timid; it's indescribable. You fancy then that you have forgotten everything you knew, and that the patient has no faith in you, and that other people begin to notice how distracted you are, and tell you the symptoms with reluctance; that they are looking at you suspiciously, whispering.... Ah! it's horrid! There must be a remedy, you think, for this disease, if one could find it. Isn't this it? You try—no, that's not it! You don't allow the medicine the necessary time to do good. ... You clutch at one thing, then at another. Sometimes you take up a book of medical prescriptions—here it is, you think! Sometimes, by Jove, you pick one out by chance, thinking to leave it to fate.... But meantime a fellow-creature's dying, and another doctor would have saved him. 'We must have a consultation,' you say; 'I will not take the responsibility on myself.' And what a fool you look at such times! Well, in time you learn to bear it; it's nothing to you. A man has died—but it's not your fault; you treated him by the rules. But what's still more torture to you is to see blind faith in you, and to feel yourself that you are not able to be of use. Well, it was just this blind faith that the whole of Aleksandra Andreyevna's family had in me; they had forgotten to think that their daughter was in danger. I, too, on my side assure them that it's nothing, but meantime my heart sinks into my boots. To add to our troubles, the roads were in such a state that the coachman was gone, for whole days together to get medicine. And I never left the patient's room; I could not tear myself away; I tell her amusing stories, you know, and play cards with her. I watch by her side at night. The old mother thanks me with tears in her eyes; but I think to myself, 'I don't deserve your gratitude.' I frankly confess to you—there is no object in concealing it now—I was in love with my patient. And Aleksandra Andreyevna had grown fond of me; she would not sometimes let any one be in her room but me. She began to talk to me, to ask me questions; where I had studied, how I lived, who are my people, whom I go to see. I feel that she ought not to talk; but to forbid her to—to forbid her resolutely, you know—I could not. Sometimes I held my head in my hands, and asked myself, 'What are you doing, villain?' ... And she would take my hand and hold it, give me a long, long look, and turn away, sigh, and say, 'How good you are!' Her hands were so feverish, her eyes so large and languid. ... 'Yes,' she says, 'you are a good, kind man; you are not like our neighbors. ... No, you are not like that. ... Why did I not know you till now!' 'Aleksandra Andreyevna, calm yourself,' I say. ... 'I feel, believe me, I don't know how I have gained ... but there, calm yourself. ... All will be right; you will be well again.' And meanwhile I must tell you," continued the doctor, bending forward and raising his eyebrows, "that they associated very little with the neighbors, because the smaller people were not on their level, and pride hindered them from being friendly with the rich. I tell you, they were an exceptionally cultivated family; so you know it was gratifying for me. She would only take her medicine from my hands... she would lift herself up, poor girl, with my aid, take it, and gaze at me. ... My heart felt as if it were bursting. And meanwhile she was growing worse and worse, worse and worse, all the time; she will die, I think to myself; she must die. Believe me, I would sooner have gone to the grave myself; and here were her mother and sisters watching me, looking into my eyes... and their faith in me was wearing away. 'Well? how is she?' 'Oh, all right, all right!' All right, indeed! My mind was failing me. Well, I was sitting one night alone again by my patient. The maid was sitting there too, and snoring away in full swing; I can't find fault with the poor girl, though; she was worn out too. Aleksandra Andreyevna had felt very unwell all the evening; she was very feverish. Until midnight she kept tossing about; at last she seemed to fall asleep; at least, she lay still without stirring. The lamp was burning in the corner before the holy image. I sat there, you know, with my head bent; I even dozed a little. Suddenly it seemed as though some one touched me in the side; I turned round. ... Good God! Aleksandra Andreyevna was gazing with intent eyes at me ... her lips parted, her cheeks seemed burning. 'What is it?' 'Doctor, shall I die?' 'Merciful Heavens!' 'No, doctor, no; please don't tell me I shall live ... don't say so. ... If you knew. ... Listen! for God's sake don't conceal my real position,' and her breath came so fast. 'If I can know for certain that I must die ... then I will tell you all—all!' 'Aleksandra Andreyevna, I beg!' 'Listen; I have not been asleep at all ... I have been looking at you a long while. ... For God's sake! ... I believe in you; you are a good man, an honest man; I entreat you by all that is sacred in the world—tell me the truth! If you knew how important it is for me. ... Doctor, for God's sake tell me. ... Am I in danger?' 'What can I tell you, Aleksandra Andreyevna, pray?' 'For God's sake, I beseech you!' 'I can't disguise from you,' I say, 'Aleksandra Andreyevna; you are certainly in danger; but God is merciful.' 'I shall die, I shall die.' And it seemed as though she were pleased, her face grew so bright; I was alarmed. 'Don't be afraid, don't be afraid! I am not frightened of death at all.' She suddenly sat up and leaned on her elbow. 'Now ... yes, now I can tell you that I thank you with my whole heart ... that you are kind and good—that I love you!' I stare at her, like one possessed; it was terrible for me, you know. 'Do you hear, I love you!' 'Aleksandra Andreyevna, how have I deserved——' 'No, no, you don't—you don't understand me.' ... And suddenly she stretched out her arms, and taking my head in her hands, she kissed it. ... Believe me, I almost screamed aloud. ... I threw myself on my knees, and buried my head in the pillow. She did not speak; her fingers trembled in my hair; I listen; she is weeping. I began to soothe her, to assure her. ... I really don't know what I did say to her. 'You will wake up the girl,' I say to her; 'Aleksandra Andreyevna, I thank you ... believe me ... calm yourself.' 'Enough, enough!' she persisted; 'never mind all of them; let them wake, then; let them come in—it does not matter; I am dying, you see. ... And what do you fear? why are you afraid? Lift up your head. ... Or, perhaps, you don't love me; perhaps I am wrong. ... In that case, forgive me.' 'Aleksandra Andreyevna, what are you saying! ... I love you, Aleksandra Andreyevna.' She looked straight into my eyes, and opened her arms wide. 'Then take me in your arms.' I tell you frankly, I don't know how it was I did not go mad that night. I feel that my patient is killing herself; I see that she is not fully herself; I understand, too, that if she did not consider herself on the point of death, she would never have thought of me; and, indeed, say what you will, it's hard to die at twenty without having known love; this was what was torturing her; this was why, in despair, she caught at me—do you understand now? But she held me in her arms, and would not let me go. 'Have pity on me, Aleksandra Andreyevna, and have pity on yourself,' I say. 'Why,' she says; 'what is there to think of? You know I must die. ...' This she repeated incessantly. ... 'If I knew that I should return to life, and be a proper young lady again, I should be ashamed ... of course, ashamed ... but why now?' 'But who has said you will die?' 'Oh, no, leave off! you will not deceive me; you don't know how to lie—look at your face. ...' 'You shall live, Aleksandra Andreyevna; I will cure you; we will ask your mother's blessing ... we will be united—we will be happy.' 'No, no, I have your word; I must die ... you have promised me ... you have told me. ...' It was cruel for me—cruel for many reasons. And see what trifling things can do sometimes; it seems nothing at all, but it's painful. It occurred to her to ask me, what is my name; not my surname, but my first name. I must needs be so unlucky as to be called Trifon. Yes, indeed; Trifon Ivanich. Every one in the house called me doctor. However, there's no help for it. I say, 'Trifon, madam.' She frowned, shook her head, and muttered something in French—ah, something unpleasant, of course!—and then she laughed—disagreeably too. Well, I spent the whole night with her in this way. Before morning I went away, feeling as though I were mad. When I went again into her room it was daytime, after morning tea. Good God! I could scarcely recognize her; people are laid in their grave looking better than that. I swear to you, on my honor, I don't understand—I absolutely don't understand —now, how I lived through that experience. Three days and nights my patient still lingered on. And what nights! What things she said to me! And on the last night—only imagine to yourself—I was sitting near her, and kept praying to God for one thing only: 'Take her,' I said, 'quickly, and me with her.' Suddenly the old mother comes unexpectedly into the room. I had already the evening before told her—the mother—there was little hope, and it would be well to send for a priest. When the sick girl saw her mother she said: 'It's very well you have come; look at us, we love one another—we have given each other our word.' 'What does she say, doctor? what does she say?' I turned livid. 'She is wandering,' I say; 'the fever.' But she: 'Hush, hush; you told me something quite different just now, and have taken my ring. Why do you pretend? My mother is good—she will forgive—she will understand—and I am dying. ... I have no need to tell lies; give me your hand.' I jumped up and ran out of the room. The old lady, of course, guessed how it was.

"I will not, however, weary you any longer, and to me too, of course, it's painful to recall all this. My patient passed away the next day. God rest her soul!" the doctor added, speaking quickly and with a sigh. "Before her death she asked her family to go out and leave me alone with her."

"'Forgive me,' she said; 'I am perhaps to blame towards you ... my illness ... but believe me, I have loved no one more than you ... do not forget me ... keep my ring.' "

The doctor turned away; I took his hand.

"Ah!" he said, "let us talk of something else, or would you care to play preference for a small stake? It is not for people like me to give way to exalted emotions. There's only one thing for me to think of; how to keep the children from crying and the wife from scolding. Since then, you know, I have had time to enter into lawful wedlock, as they say. ... Oh ... I took a merchant's daughter—seven thousand for her dowry. Her name's Akulina; it goes well with Trifon. She is an ill-tempered woman, I must tell you, but luckily she's asleep all day. ...Well, shall it be preference?"

We sat down to preference for halfpenny points. Trifon Ivanich won two rubles and a half from me, and went home late, well pleased with his success.

FEODOR DOSTOIEVSKY

(1821—1881)

DOSTOIEVSKY was born in 1821. When still a young man he was arrested on a trivial charge and sent to Siberia. Out of his experiences there he wrote a characteristic volume on prison life, in which the spirit of the man, his mysticism and his philosophy, are clearly revealed. Throughout his long novels he strove to show the suffering of his people and preached a philosophy of Christianity which has coloured Russian literature since his day. Many of Dostoievsky's stories are very long, but *The Christmas Tree and the Wedding*, one of the finest, comes within the limits of this book.

THE CHRISTMAS TREE AND THE WEDDING

THE other day I saw a wedding. ... But no! I would rather tell you about a Christmas tree. The wedding was superb. I liked it immensely. But the other incident was still finer. I don't know why it is that the sight of the wedding reminded me of the Christmas tree. This is the way it happened:

Exactly five years ago, on New Year's Eve, I was invited to a children's ball by a man high up in the business world, who had his connections, his circle of acquaintances, and his intrigues. So it seemed as though the children's ball was merely a pretext for the parents to come together and discuss matters of interest to themselves, quite innocently and casually.

I was an outsider, and, as I had no special matters to air, I was able to spend the evening independently of the others. There was another gentleman present who like myself had just stumbled upon this affair of domestic bliss. He was the first to attract my attention. His appearance was not that of a man of birth or high family. He was tall, rather thin, very serious, and well dressed. Apparently he had no heart for the family festivities. The instant he went off into a corner by himself the smile disappeared from his face, and his thick dark brows knitted into a frown. He knew no one except the host and showed every sign of being bored to death, though bravely sustaining the role of thorough enjoyment to the end. Later I learned that he was a provincial, had come to the capital on some important, brain-racking business, had brought a letter of recommendation to our host, and our host had taken him under his protection, not at all *con amore*. It was merely out of politeness that he had invited him to the children's ball.

They did not play cards with him, they did not offer him cigars. No one entered into conversation with him. Possibly they recognized the bird by its feathers from a distance. Thus, my gentleman, not knowing what to do with his hands, was compelled to spend the evening stroking his whiskers. His whiskers were really fine, but he stroked them so assiduously that one got the feeling that the whiskers had come into the world first and afterwards the man in order to stroke them.

There was another guest who interested me. But he was of quite a different order. He was a personage. They called him Julian Mastakovich. At first glance one could tell he was an honored guest and stood in the same relation to the host as the host to the gentleman of the whiskers. The host and hostess said no end of amiable things to him, were most attentive, wining him, hovering over him, bringing guests up to be introduced, but never leading him to any one else. I noticed tears glisten in our host's eyes when Julian Mastakovich remarked that he had rarely spent such a pleasant evening. Somehow I began to feel uncomfortable in this personage's presence. So, after amusing myself with the children, five of whom, remarkably well-fed young persons, were our host's, I went into a little sitting-room, entirely unoccupied, and seated myself at the end that was a conservatory and took up half the room.

The children were charming. They absolutely refused to resemble their elders, notwithstanding the efforts of mothers and governesses. In a jiffy they had denuded the Christmas tree down to the very last sweet and had already succeeded in breaking half of their playthings before they even found out which belonged to whom.

One of them was a particularly handsome little lad, dark-eyed, curly-haired, who stubbornly persisted in aiming at me with his wooden gun. But the child that attracted the greatest attention was his sister, a girl of about eleven, lovely as a Cupid. She was quiet and thoughtful, with large, full, dreamy eyes. The children had somehow offended her and she left them and walked into the same room that I had withdrawn into. There she seated herself with her doll in a corner.

"Her father is an immensely wealthy business man," the guests informed each other in tones of awe. "Three hundred thousand rubles set aside for her dowry already."

As I turned to look at the group from which I heard this news item issuing, my glance met Julian Mastakovich's. He stood listening to the insipid chatter in an attitude of concentrated attention, with his hands behind his back and his head inclined to one side.

All the while I was quite lost in admiration of the shrewdness our host displayed in the dispensing of the gifts. The little maid of the many-rubled dowry received the handsomest doll, and the rest of the gifts were graded in value according to the diminishing scale of the parents' stations in life. The last child, a tiny chap of ten, thin, red-haired, freckled, came into possession of a small book of nature stories without illustrations or even head and tail pieces. He was the governess's child. She was a poor widow, and her little boy, clad in a sorry-looking little nankeen jacket, looked thoroughly crushed and intimidated. He took the book of nature stories and circled slowly about the children's toys. He would have given anything to play with them. But he did not dare to. You could tell he already knew his place.

I like to observe children. It is fascinating to watch the individuality in them struggling for self-assertion. I could see that the other children's things had tremendous charm for the red-haired boy, especially a toy theater, in which he was so anxious to take a part that he resolved to fawn upon the other children. He smiled and began to play with them. His one and only apple he handed over to a puffy urchin whose pockets were already crammed with sweets, and he even carried another youngster pickaback—all simply that he might be allowed to stay with the theater.

. But in a few moments an impudent young person fell on him and gave him a pummeling. He did not dare even to cry. The governess came and told him to leave off interfering with the other children's games, and he crept away to the same room the little girl and I were in. She let him sit down beside her, and the two set themselves busily to dressing the expensive doll.

Almost half an hour passed, and I was nearly dozing off, as I sat there in the conservatory half listening to the chatter of the red-haired boy and the dowered beauty, when Julian Mastakovich entered suddenly. He had slipped out of the drawing-room under cover of a noisy scene among the children. From my secluded corner it had not escaped my notice that a few moments before he had been eagerly conversing with the rich girl's father, to whom he had only just been introduced. He stood still for a while reflecting and mumbling to himself, as if counting something on his fingers.

"Three hundred—three hundred—eleven—twelve—thirteen—sixteen—in five years! Let's say four per cent—five times twelve—sixty, and on these sixty——. Let us assume that in five years it will amount to—well, four hundred. Hm—hm! But the shrewd old fox isn't likely to be satisfied with four per cent. He gets eight or even ten, perhaps. Let's suppose five hundred, five hundred thousand, at least, that's sure. Anything above that for pocket money—hm—"

He blew his nose and was about to leave the room when he spied the girl and stood still. I, behind the plants, escaped his notice. He seemed to me to be quivering with excitement. It must have been his calculations that upset him so. He rubbed his hands and danced from place to place, and kept getting more and more excited. Finally, however, he conquered his emotions and came to a standstill. He cast a determined look at the future bride and wanted to move toward her, but glanced about first. Then, as if with a guilty conscience, he stepped over to the child on tip-toe, smiling, and bent down and kissed her head.

His coming was so unexpected that she uttered a shriek of alarm.

"What are you doing here, dear child?" he whispered, looking around and pinching her cheek.

"We're playing."

"What, with him?" said Julian Mastakovich with a look askance at the governess's child. "You should go into the drawing-room, my lad," he said to him.

The boy remained silent and looked up at the man with wide-open eyes. Julian Mastakovitch glanced round again cautiously and bent down over the girl.

"What have you got, a doll, my dear?"

"Yes, sir." The child quailed a little, and her brow wrinkled.

"A doll. And do you know, my dear, what dolls are made of?"

"No, sir," she said weakly, and lowered her head.

"Out of rags, my dear. You, boy, you go back to the drawing-room, to the children," said Julian Mastakovich, looking at the boy sternly.

The two children frowned. They caught hold of each other and would not part.

"And do you know why they gave you the doll?" asked Julian Mastakovich, dropping his voice lower and lower.

"No."

"Because you were a good, very good little girl the whole week."

Saying which, Julian Mastakovich was seized with a paroxysm of agitation. He looked round and said in a tone faint, almost inaudible with excitement and impatience:

"If I come to visit your parents will you love me, my dear?"

He tried to kiss the sweet little creature, but the red-haired boy saw that she was on the verge of tears, and he caught her hand and sobbed out loud in sympathy. That enraged the man.

"Go away! Go away! Go back to the other room, to your play-mates."

"I don't want him to. I don't want him to! You go away!" cried the girl. "Let him alone! Let him alone!" She was almost weeping.

There was a sound of footsteps in the doorway. Julian Mastakovich started and straightened up his respectable body. The red-haired boy was even more alarmed. He let go the girl's hand, sidled along the wall, and escaped through the drawing-room into the dining-room.

Not to attract attention, Julian Mastakovich also made for the dining-room. He was red as a lobster. The sight of himself in a mirror seemed to embarrass him. Presumably he was annoyed at his own ardor and impatience. Without due respect to his importance and dignity, his calculations had lured and pricked him to the greedy eagerness of a boy, who makes straight for his object—though this was not as yet an object; it only would be so in five years' time. I followed the worthy man into the dining-room, where I witnessed a remarkable play.

Julian Mastakovich, all flushed with vexation, venom in his look, began to threaten the red-haired boy. The red-haired boy retreated farther and farther until there was no place left for him to retreat to, and he did not know where to turn in his fright.

"Get out of here! What are you doing here? Get out, I say, you good-for-nothing! Stealing fruit, are you? Oh, so, stealing fruit! Get out, you freckle face, go to your likes!"

The frightened child, as a last desperate resort, crawled quickly under the table. His persecutor, completely infuriated, pulled out his large linen handkerchief and used it as a lash to drive the boy out of his position.

Here I must remark that Julian Mastakovich was a somewhat corpulent man, heavy, well-fed, puffy-cheeked, with a paunch and ankles as round as nuts. He perspired and puffed and panted. So strong was his dislike (or was it jealousy?) of the child that he actually began to carry on like a madman.

I laughed heartily. Julian Mastakovich turned. He was utterly confused and for a moment, apparently, quite oblivious of his immense importance. At that moment our host appeared in the doorway opposite. The boy crawled out from under the table and wiped his knees and elbows. Julian Mastakovich hastened to carry his handkerchief, which he had been dangling by the corner, to his nose. Our host looked at the three of us rather suspiciously. But, like a man who knows the world and can readily adjust himself, he seized upon the opportunity to lay hold of his very valuable guest and get what he wanted out of him.

"Here's the boy I was talking to you about," he said, indicating the red-haired child. "I took the liberty of presuming on your goodness in his behalf."

"Oh," replied Julian Mastakovich, still not quite master of himself.

"He's my governess's son," our host continued in a beseeching tone. "She's a poor creature, the widow of an honest official. That's why, if it were possible for you—"

"Impossible, impossible!" Julian Mastakovich cried hastily. "You must excuse me, Philip Alexeyevich, I really cannot. I've made inquiries. There are no vacancies, and there is a waiting list of ten who have a greater right—I'm sorry."

"Too bad," said our host. "He's a quiet, unobtrusive child."

"A very naughty little rascal, I should say," said Julian Mastakovich, wryly. "Go away, boy. Why are you here still? Be off with you to the other children."

Unable to control himself, he gave me a sidelong glance. Nor could I control myself. I laughed straight in his face. He turned away and asked our host, in tones quite audible to me, who that odd young fellow was. They whispered to each other and left the room, disregarding me.

I shook with laughter. Then I, too, went to the drawing-room. There the great man, already surrounded by the fathers and mothers and the host and the hostess, had begun to talk eagerly with a lady to whom he had just been introduced. The lady held the rich little girl's hand. Julian Mastakovich went into fulsome praise of her. He waxed ecstatic over the dear child's beauty, her talents, her grace, her excellent breeding, plainly laying himself out to flatter the mother, who listened scarcely able to restrain tears of joy, while the father showed his delight by a gratified smile.

The joy was contagious. Everybody shared in it. Even the children were obliged to stop playing so as not to disturb the conversation. The atmosphere was surcharged with awe. I heard the mother of the important little girl, touched to her profoundest depths, ask Julian Mastakovich in the choicest language of courtesy, whether he would honor them by coming to see them. I heard Julian Mastakovich accept the invitation with unfeigned enthusiasm. Then the guests scattered decorously to different parts of the room, and I heard them, with veneration in their tones, extol the business man, the business man's wife, the business man's daughter, and, especially, Julian Mastakovich.

"Is he married?" I asked out loud of an acquaintance of mine standing beside Julian Mastakovich.

Julian Mastakovich gave me a venomous look.

"No," answered my acquaintance, profoundly shocked by my—intentional—indiscretion.

Not long ago I passed the Church of ——. I was struck by the concourse of people gathered there to witness a wedding. It was a dreary day. A drizzling rain was beginning to come down. I made my way through the throng into the church. The bridegroom was a round, well fed, pot-bellied little man, very much dressed up. He ran and fussed about and gave orders and arranged things. Finally word was passed that the bride was coming. I pushed through the crowd, and I beheld a marvelous beauty whose first spring was scarcely commencing. But the beauty was pale and sad. She looked distracted. It seemed to me even that her eyes were red from recent weeping. The classic severity of every line of her face imparted a peculiar significance and solemnity to her beauty. But through that severity and solemnity, through the sadness, shone the innocence of a child. There was something inexpressibly naïve, unsettled and young in her features, which, without words, seemed to plead for mercy.

They said she was just sixteen years old. I looked at the bridegroom carefully. Suddenly I recognized Julian Mastakovich, whom I had not seen again in all those five years. Then I looked at the bride again —. Good God! I made my way, as quickly as I could, out of the church. I heard gossiping in the crowd about the bride's wealth—about her dowry of five hundred thousand rubles—so and so much for pocket money.

"Then his calculations were correct," I thought, as I pressed out into the street.

LEO TOLSTOY

(1828—1910)

TOLSTOY is the most celebrated of all Russian writers. This extraordinary man, after serving in the army and leading a wild and reckless life, was for half a century the great interpreter of the life of his country, and during the last thirty years a religious and social prophet. He was preëminent as a novelist, though his complete works include a large number of fairy tales and short stories.

The present version, by Louise and Aylmer Maude, is reprinted by permission of the translators and publisher, from *Twenty-Three Tales* by Leo Tolstoy, published by Humphrey Milford, Oxford University Press in the World's Classics Series. The title in the original runs *God Sees the Truth, but Waits*.

THE LONG EXILE

IN the town of Vladimir lived a young merchant named Ivan Dmitrich Aksionov. He had two shops and a house of his own.

Aksionov was a handsome, fair-haired, curly-headed fellow, full of fun, and very fond of singing. When quite a young man he had been given to drink, and was riotous when he had had too much; but after he married he gave up drinking, except now and then.

One summer Aksionov was going to the Nizhny Fair, and as he bade good-bye to his family, his wife said to him, "Ivan Dmitrich, do not start to-day; I have had a bad dream about you."

Aksionov laughed, and said, "You are afraid that when I get to the fair I shall go on a spree."

His wife replied: "I do not know what I am afraid of; all I know is that I had a bad dream. I dreamt you returned from the town, and when you took off your cap I saw that your hair was quite gray."

Aksionov laughed. "That's a lucky sign," said he. "See if I don't sell out all my goods, and bring you some presents from the fair."

So he said good-bye to his family, and drove away.

When he had traveled half-way, he met a merchant whom he knew, and they put up at the same inn for the night. They had some tea together, and then went to bed in adjoining rooms.

It was not Aksionov's habit to sleep late, and wishing to travel while it was still cool, he aroused his driver before dawn, and told him to put in the horses.

Then he made his way across to the landlord of the inn (who lived in a cottage at the back), paid his bill, and continued his journey.

When he had gone about twenty-five miles, he stopped for the horses to be fed. Aksionov rested awhile in the passage of the inn, then he stepped out into the porch, and, ordering a samovar to be heated, got out his guitar and began to play.

Suddenly a troika drove up with tinkling bells and an official alighted, followed by two soldiers. He came to Aksionov and began to question him asking him who he was and whence he came. Aksionov answered him, fully, and said, "Won't you have some tea with me?" But the official went on cross-questioning him and asking him, "Where did you spend last night? Were you alone, or with a fellow-merchant? Did you see the other merchant this morning? Why did you leave the inn before dawn?"

Aksionov wondered why he was asked all these questions, but he described all that had happened, and then added, "Why do you cross-question me as if I were a thief or a robber? I am traveling on business of my own, and there is no need to question me."

Then the official, calling the soldiers, said, "I am the police-officer of this district, and I question you because the merchant with whom you spent last night has been found with his throat cut. We must search your things."

They entered the house. The soldiers and the police-officer unstrapped Aksionov's luggage and searched it. Suddenly the officer drew a knife out of a bag, crying, "Whose knife is this?"

Aksionov looked, and seeing a blood-stained knife taken from his bag, he was frightened.

"How is it there is blood on this knife?"

Aksionov tried to answer, but could hardly utter a word, and only stammered: "I —don't know—not mine."

Then the police-officer said: "This morning the merchant was found in bed with his throat cut. You are the only person who could have done it. The house was locked from inside, and no one else was there. Here is this blood-stained knife in your bag, and your face and manner betray you! Tell me how you killed him, and how much money you stole?"

Aksionov swore he had not done it; that he had not seen the merchant after they had had tea together; that he had no money except eight thousand rubles of his own, and that the knife was not his. But his voice was broken, his face pale, and he trembled with fear as though he were guilty.

The police-officer ordered the soldiers to bind Aksionov and to put him in the cart. As they tied his feet together and flung him into the cart, Aksionov crossed himself and wept. His money and goods were taken from him, and he was sent to the nearest town and imprisoned there. Inquiries as to his character were made in Vladimir. The merchants and other inhabitants of that town said that in former days he used to drink and waste his time, but that he was a good man. Then the trial came on: he was charged with murdering a merchant from Ryazan, and robbing him of twenty thousand rubles.

His wife was in despair, and did not know what to believe. Her children were all quite small; one was a baby at her breast. Taking them all with her, she went to the town where her husband was in jail. At first she was not allowed to see him; but after much begging, she obtained permission from the officials, and was taken to him. When she saw her husband in prison-dress and in chains, shut up with thieves and criminals, she fell down, and did not come to her senses for a long time. Then she drew her children to her, and sat down near him. She told him of things at home, and asked about what had happened to him. He told her all, and she asked, "What can we do now?"

"We must petition the Czar not to let an innocent man perish."

His wife told him that she had sent a petition to the Czar, but it had not been accepted.

Aksionov did not reply, but only looked downcast.

Then his wife said, "It was not for nothing I dreamt your hair had turned gray. You remember? You should not have started that day." And passing her fingers through his hair, she said: "Vanya dearest, tell your wife the truth; was it not you who did it?"

"So you, too, suspect me!" said Aksionov, and, hiding his face in his hands, he began to weep. Then a soldier came to say that the wife and children must go away; and Aksionov said good-bye to his family for the last time.

When they were gone, Aksionov recalled what had been said, and when he remembered that his wife also had suspected him, he said to himself, "It seems that only God can know the truth; it is to Him alone we must appeal, and from Him alone expect mercy."

And Aksionov wrote no more petitions; gave up all hope, and only prayed to God.

Aksionov was condemned to be flogged and sent to the mines. So he was flogged with a knout, and when the wounds made by the knout were healed, he was driven to Siberia with other convicts.

For twenty-six years Aksionov lived as a convict in Siberia. His hair turned white as snow, and his beard grew long, thin, and gray. All his mirth went; he stooped; he walked slowly, spoke little, and never laughed, but he often prayed.

In prison Aksionov learned to make boots, and earned a little money, with which he bought *The Lives of the Saints*. He read this book when there was light enough in the prison; and on Sundays in the prison-church he read the lessons and sang in the choir; for his voice was still good.

The prison authorities liked Aksionov for his meekness, and his fellow-prisoners respected him: they called him "Grandfather," and "The Saint." When they wanted to petition the prison authorities about anything, they always made Aksionov their spokesman, and when there were quarrels among the prisoners they came to him to put things right, and to judge the matter.

No news reached Aksionov from his home, and he did not even know if his wife and children were still alive.

One day a fresh gang of convicts came to the prison. In the evening the old prisoners collected round the new ones and asked them what towns or villages they came from, and what they were sentenced for. Among the rest Aksionov sat down near the newcomers, and listened with downcast air to what was said.

One of the new convicts, a tall, strong man of sixty, with a closely-cropped gray beard, was telling the others what he had been arrested for.

"Well, friends," he said, "I only took a horse that was tied to a sledge, and I was arrested and accused of stealing. I said I had only taken it to get home quicker, and had then let it go; besides, the driver was a personal friend of mine. So I said, 'It's all right.' 'No,' said they, 'you stole it.' But how or where I stole it they could not say. I once really did something wrong, and ought by rights to have come here long ago, but that time I was not found out. Now I have been sent here for nothing at all. ... Eh, but it's lies I'm telling you; I've been to Siberia before, but I did not stay long."

"Where are you from?" asked some one.

"From Vladimir. My family are of that town. My name is Makar, and they also call me Semyonich."

Aksionov raised his head and said: "Tell me, Semyonich, do you know anything of the merchants Aksionov of Vladimir? Are they still alive?"

"Know them? Of course I do. The Aksionovs are rich, though their father is in Siberia: a sinner like ourselves, it seems! As for you, Gran'-dad, how did you come here?"

Aksionov did not like to speak of his misfortune. He only sighed, and said, "For my sins I have been in prison these twenty-six years."

"What sins?" asked Makar Semyonich.

But Aksionov only said, "Well, well—I must have deserved it!" He would have said no more, but his companions told the newcomers how Aksionov came to be in Siberia; how some one had killed a merchant, and had put the knife among Aksionov's things, and Aksionov had been unjustly condemned.

When Makar Semyonich heard this, he looked at Aksionov, slapped his own knee, and exclaimed, "Well, this is wonderful! Really wonderful! But how old you've grown, Gran'dad!"

The others asked him why he was so surprised, and where he had seen Aksionov before; but Makar Semyonich did not reply. He only said: "It's wonderful that we should meet here, lads!"

These words made Aksionov wonder whether this man knew who had killed the merchant; so he said, "Perhaps, Semyonich, you have heard of that affair, or maybe you've seen me before?"

"How could I help hearing? The world's full of rumors. But it's a long time ago, and I've forgotten what I heard."

"Perhaps you heard who killed the merchant?" asked Aksionov.

Makar Semyonich laughed, and replied: "It must have been him in whose bag the knife was found! If some one else hid the knife there, 'He's not a thief till he's caught,' as the saying is. How could any one put a knife into your bag while it was under your head? It would surely have woke you up."

When Aksionov heard these words, he felt sure this was the man who had killed the merchant. He rose and went away. All that night Aksionov lay awake. He felt terribly unhappy, and all sorts of images rose in his mind. There was the image of his wife as she was when he parted from her to go to the fair. He saw her as if she were present; her face and her eyes rose before him; he heard her speak and laugh. Then he saw his children, quite little, as they were at that time: one with a little cloak on, another at his mother's breast. And then he remembered himself as he used to be—young and merry. He remembered how he sat playing the guitar in the porch of the inn where he was arrested, and how free from care he had been. He saw, in his mind, the place where he was flogged, the executioner, and the people standing around; the chains, the convicts, all the twenty-six years of his prison life, and his premature old age. The thought of it all made him so wretched that he was ready to kill himself.

"And it's all that villain's doing!" thought Aksionov. And his anger was so great against Makar Semyonich that he longed for vengeance, even if he himself should perish for it. He kept repeating prayers all night, but could get no peace. During the day he did not go near Makar Semyonich, nor even look at him.

A fortnight passed in this way. Aksionov could not sleep at night, and was so miserable that he did not know what to do.

One night as he was walking about the prison he noticed some earth that came rolling out from under one of the shelves on which the prisoners slept. He stopped to see what it was. Suddenky Malar Semyonich crept out from under the shelf, and looked up at Aksionov with frightened face. Aksionov tried to pass without looking at him, but Makar seized his hand and told him that he had dug a hole under the wall, getting rid of the earth by putting it into his high-boots, and emptying it out every day on the road when the prisoners were driven to their work.

"Just you keep quiet, old man, and you shall get out too. If you blab, they'll flog the life out of me, but I will kill you first."

Aksionov trembled with anger as he looked at his enemy. He drew his hand away, saying, "I have no wish to escape, and you have no need to kill me; you killed me long ago! As to telling of you—I may do so or not, as God shall direct."

Next day, when the convicts were led out to work, the convoy soldiers noticed that one or other of the prisoners emptied some earth out of his boots. The prison was searched and the tunnel found. The Governor came and questioned all the prisoners to find out who had dug the hole. They all denied any knowledge of it. Those who knew would not betray Makar Semyonich, knowing he would be flogged almost to death. At last the Governor turned to Aksionov whom he knew to be a just man, and said:

"You are a truthful old man; tell me, before God, who dug the hole?"

Makar Semyonich stood as if he were quite unconcerned, looking at the Governor and not so much as glancing at Aksionov. Aksionov's lips and hands trembled, and for a long time he could not utter a word. He thought, "Why should I screen him who ruined my life? Let him pay for what I have suffered. But if I tell, they will probably flog the life out of him, and maybe I suspect him wrongly. And, after all, what good would it be to me?"

"Well, old man," repeated the Governor, "tell me the truth: who has been digging under the wall?"

Aksionov glanced at Makar Semyonich, and said, "I cannot say, your honor. It is not God's will that I should tell! Do what you like with me; I am in your hands."

However much the Governor tried, Aksionov would say no more, and so the matter had to be left.

That night, when Aksionov was lying on his bed and just beginning to doze, some one came quietly and sat down on his bed. He peered through the darkness and recognized Makar.

"What more do you want of me?" asked Aksionov, "Why have you come here?"

Makar Semyonich was silent. So Aksionov sat up and said, "What do you want? Go away, or I will call the guard!"

Makar Semyonich bent close over Aksionov, and whispered, "Ivan Dmitrich, forgive me!"

"What for?" asked Aksionov.

"It was I who killed the merchant and hid the knife among your things. I meant to kill you too, but I heard a noise outside, so I hid the knife in your bag and escaped out of the window."

Aksionov was silent, and did not know what to say. Makar Semyonich slid off the bed-shelf and knelt upon the ground. "Ivan Dmitrich," said he, "forgive me! For the love of God, forgive me! I will confess that it was I who killed the merchant, and you will be released and can go to your home."

"It is easy for you to talk," said Aksionov, "but I have suffered for you these twenty-six years. Where could I go to now?... My wife is dead, and my children have forgotten me. I have nowhere to go..."

Makar Semyonich did not rise, but beat his head on the floor. "Ivan Dmitrich, forgive me!" he cried. "When they flogged me with the knout it was not so hard to bear as it is to see you now... yet you had pity on me, and did not tell. For Christ's sake, forgive me, wretch that I am!" And he began to sob.

When Aksionov heard him sobbing he, too, began to weep.

"God will forgive you!" said he. "Maybe I am a hundred times worse than you." And at these words his heart grew light, and the longing for home left him. He no longer had any desire to leave the prison, but only hoped for his last hour to come.

In spite of what Aksionov had said, Makar Semyonich confessed his guilt. But when the order for his release came, Aksionov was already dead.

VLADIMIR KOROLENKO

(1853–1921)

KOROLENKO spent a great part of his life in exile. Much of his writing is based on incidents gathered in Siberia. It is surprising that his exile did not embitter him. His stories, which are half romances, are sympathetically and simply told.

　　The Old Bell-Ringer is one of his most beautiful tales.

　　The present version is by Maxim Lieber.

THE OLD BELL-RINGER

IT was growing dark.

　　The tiny village, nestling by the distant stream, in a pine forest, was merged in that twilight peculiar to starry spring nights, when the fog, rising from the earth, deepens the shadows of the woods and fills the open spaces with a silvery blue mist. ... Everything was still, pensive and sad. The village quietly slumbered.

　　The dark outlines of the wretched cabins were barely visible; here and there lights glimmered; now and then you could hear a gate creak; or a dog would suddenly bark and then stop. Occasionally, out of the dark, murmuring forest emerged the figure of a pedestrian, or that of a horseman; or a cart would jolt by. These were the inhabitants of lone forest hamlets going to their church for the great spring holiday.

　　The church stood on a gentle hill in the center of the village. The ancient belfry, tall and murky, was lost in the blue sky.

　　The creaking of the staircase could be heard as the old bell-ringer Mikheyich mounted to the belfry, and his little lantern, suspended in mid-air, looked like a star in space.

　　It was difficult for the old man to climb the staircase. His leg served him badly, and his eyes saw but dimly. ... An old man like him should have been at rest by now, but God spared him from death. He had buried his sons and his grandsons; he had accompanied old men and young men to their resting place, but he still lived on. 'Twas hard. Many the times he had greeted the spring holiday, and he could not remember how often he had waited in that very belfry the appointed hour. And now God had again willed that...

　　The old man went to the opening in the tower and leaned on the banister. In the darkness below, around the church, he made out the village cemetery in which the old crosses with their outstretched arms seemed to protect the ill-kept graves. Over these bowed here and there a few leafless birch trees. The aromatic odor of young buds, wafted to Mikheyich from below, brought with it a feeling of the melancholy of eternal sleep.

　　Where would he be a year hence? Would he again climb to this height, beneath the brass bell to awaken the slumbering night with its metallic peal, or would he be lying in a dark corner of the graveyard, under a cross? God knows!... He was prepared; in the meantime God granted him the happiness of greeting the holiday once more.

"Glory be to God!" His lips whispered the customary formula as his eyes looked up to the heaven bright with a million twinkling stars and made the sign of the cross.

"Mikheyich, ay, Mikheyich!" called out to him the tremulous voice of an old man. The aged sexton gazed up at the belfry, shading his unsteady, tear-dimmed eyes with his hand, trying to see Mikheyich.

"What do you want? Here I am," replied the bell-ringer, looking down from the belfry. "Can't you see me?"

"No, I can't. It must be time to ring. What do you say?"

Both looked at the stars. Myriads of God's lights twinkled on high. The fiery Wagoner was above them. Mikheyich meditated.

"No, not yet a while. ... I know when. ..."

Indeed he knew. He did not need a watch. God's stars would tell him when. ... Heaven and earth, the white cloud gently floating in the sky, the dark forest with its indistinct murmur and the rippling of the stream enveloped by the darkness—all that was familiar to him, part of him. Not in vain had he spent his life here.

The distant past arose before him. He recalled how for the first time he had mounted to this belfry with his father. Lord! how long ago that was, and yet how recent it seemed!... He saw himself a blond lad; his eyes sparkled; the wind—not the wind that raises the dust in the streets, but a strange one, that flaps its noiseless wings, tousled his hair. ... Way down below, tiny beings walked about, and the village huts looked small; the forest had receded, and the oval clearing on which the village stood seemed enormous, so endless...

"And there it is, all of it!" smiled the gray-haired old man, gazing at the little clearing. ... That was the way of life. As a young man one can not see the end of it. And now, there it was, as if in the palm of one's hand, from the beginning to the grave over there which he had fancied for himself in the corner of the cemetery. ... Well, glory be to God! it was time to rest. The burden of life he had borne honorably, and the damp earth seemed like his mother. ... Soon, very soon!...

But the hour had come. Mikheyich looked once more at the stars, took off his cap, made the sign of the cross, and grasped the bell-ropes. In a moment, the night air echoed with the resounding stroke. Another, a third, a fourth... one after the other, filling the quiescent, holy eve, there poured forth powerful, drawn-out, singing sounds.

The bell stopped. The church service had begun. Mikheyich had formerly been in the habit of going down to stand in the corner by the door in order to pray and hear the singing. This time he remained in the belfry. It was too much to walk the stairs, and, moreover, he felt rather tired. He sat down on the bench and, as he listened to the melting sounds of brass, fell to musing. About what? He would have been unable to say. ... The tower was dimly lit by the feeble light of his lantern. The still vibrating bells were invisible in the darkness; from time to time a faint murmur of singing in the church below reached him, and the night wind stirred the ropes attached to the iron tongues of the bells.

The old man let his head droop upon his breast, while his mind was confused with fancies. "Now they are singing a hymn," he thought, and imagined himself in church, where he heard the children's voices in the choir, and saw Father Naum, long since dead, leading the congregation in prayer; hundreds of peasants' heads rose and fell, like ripened stalks of grain before the wind. ... The peasants made the sign of the cross. ... All of these are familiar, although they are all dead. ... There he beheld his father's severe face; there was his brother fervently praying. And he also stood there, abloom with health and strength, filled with unconscious hope of happiness. ... And where was that happiness? ... For a moment, the old man's thoughts flared up, illuminating various episodes in his past life. ...

He saw hard work, sorrow, care... where was this happiness? A hard lot will trace furrows even in a young face, will bend a powerful back and teach him to sigh as it had taught his older brother.

There on the left, among the village women, with her head humbly bowed, stood his sweetheart. A good woman, may she inherit the kingdom of Heaven! How much she had suffered, poor woman. ... Constant poverty and work, and the inevitable sorrows of a woman's life will wither her beauty; her eyes will lose their luster, and instead of the customary serenity, dull fear of unexpected calamities will settle perpetually on her face. ... Well, then, where was her happiness? ...One son was left to them, their one hope and joy; but he was too weak to withstand temptation.

And there was his rich enemy, kneeling and praying to be forgiven for the many tears he had caused orphans to shed. He crossed himself ardently and struck his forehead against the ground. ... Mikheyich's heart boiled within him, and the dusky faces of the ikons frowned down upon human sorrow and human wickedness.

All that was past, behind him. For him the whole world was now bounded by this bell-tower, where the wind moaned in the darkness and stirred the ropes. ... "God be your judge!" muttered the old man, drooping his gray head, while tears rolled gently down his cheeks.

"Mikheyich, ay, Mikheyich! Have you fallen asleep up there?" shouted someone from below.

"What?" the old man answered, rising to his feet. "God! Have I really been sleeping? Such a thing never happened before!"

With quick, experienced hands he grasped the ropes. Below him, the peasant mob moved about like an ant-hill; banners, sparkling with gilt brocade, fluttered in the air. ... The procession made the circuit of the church, and soon the joyous call reached Mikheyich, "Christ is risen from the dead!"

The old man's heart responded fervently to this call. ... It seemed to him that the tapers were burning more brightly, and the crowd was more agitated; the banners seemed to be animated, and the wakened wind gathered the billows of sound on its wings, floated them up and blended then with the loud festal pealing of the bells.

Never before had old Mikheyich rung like this!

It seemed as if the old man's heart had passed into the lifeless brass, and the tones of the bells sang and laughed and wept, and, welding in a sublime stream of harmony, rose high and higher into a heaven resplendent with myriad stars, and, trembling, flowed down to earth.

A powerful bass bell proclaimed, "Christ is risen!" And two tenors, trembling with the alternate beats of their iron tongues, repeated joyfully, "Christ is risen!"

And two small sopranos, seemingly hastening so as not to be left behind, crowded in among the more powerful voices and, like little children, sang hurriedly, cheerfully, "Christ is risen!"

The old belfry seemed to tremble and shake, and the wind, flapping its wings in the old bell-ringer's face, repeated, "Christ is risen!"

The old heart forgot its life, full of cares and grief. The old bellringer forgot that his life was confined to the narrow limits of the dreary belfry, that he was alone in the world, like an old storm-broken stump. ...He heard those singing and weeping sounds that rose to heaven and fell again to the sorrowing earth, and it seemed to him that he was surrounded by his sons and grandsons, that he heard their joyful voices; the voices of young and old blend into a chorus and sing to him of happiness and joy which he had never tasted in his life. ... He pulled the ropes, while tears rolled down his cheeks, and his heart beat violently with the illusion of happiness. ...

Below, people listened and said to each other that never before had old Mikheyich rung so well.

Suddenly the large bell uttered an uncertain sound, and grew dumb. The smaller ones rang out an unfinished tone, and then stopped, as if abashed, to listen to the lugubrious echo of the prolonged and palpitating note gradually dying away upon the air. ... The old bell-ringer, utterly exhausted, fell back on the bench, and the last two tears trickled slowly down his pallid cheeks. ...

"Ho, there! Send up a substitute; the old bell-ringer has rung his final stroke."

VSEVOLOD GARSHIN

(1855–1888)

GARSHIN was all his life subject to melancholia. His work, consisting of only a score of stories, was influenced by his condition, and by his experiences in the Servian and Turkish wars. In 1888, sick with physical and mental torture, he killed himself. Garshin's stark realism has that pitifully beautiful quality which makes his stories endure. They are pessimistic but never morbid.

THE SIGNAL

SEMYON IVANOV was a track-walker. His hut was ten versts away from a railroad station in one direction and twelve versts away in the other. About four versts away there was a cotton mill that had opened the year before, and its tall chimney rose up darkly from behind the forest. The only dwellings around were the distant huts of the other track-walkers.

Semyon Ivanov's health had been completely shattered. Nine years before he had served right through the war as servant to an officer. The sun had roasted him, the cold frozen him, and hunger famished him on the forced marches of forty and fifty versts a day in the heat and the cold and the rain and the shine. The bullets had whizzed about him, but, thank God! none had struck him!

Semyon's regiment had once been on the firing line. For a whole week there had been skirmishing with the Turks, only a deep ravine separating the two hostile armies; and from morn till eve there had been a steady cross-fire. Thrice daily Semyon carried a steaming samovar and his officer's meals from the camp kitchen to the ravine. The bullets hummed about him and rattled viciously against the rocks. Semyon was terrified and cried sometimes, but still he kept right on. The officers were pleased with him, because he always had hot tea ready for them.

He returned from the campaign with limbs unbroken but crippled with rheumatism. He had experienced no little sorrow since then. He arrived home to find his father, an old man, and his little four-year-old son had died. Semyon remained alone with his wife. They could not do much. It was difficult to plow with rheumatic arms and legs. They could no longer stay in their village, so they started off to seek their fortune in new places. They stayed for a short time on the line, in Kherson and Donshchina, but nowhere found luck. Then the wife went out to service, and Semyon continued to travel about. Once he happened to ride on an engine, and at one of the stations the face of the station-master seemed familiar to him. Semyon looked at the station-master and the station-master looked at Semyon, and they recognized each other. He had been an officer in Semyon's regiment.

"You are Ivanov?" he said.

"Yes, your Excellency."

"How do you come to be here?"

Semyon told him all.

"Where are you off to?"

"I cannot tell you, sir."

"Idiot! What do you mean by 'cannot tell you'?"

"I mean what I say, your Excellency. There is nowhere for me to go to. I must hunt for work, sir."

The station-master looked at him, thought a bit, and said: "See here, friend, stay here a while at the station. You are married, I think. Where is your wife?"

"Yes, your Excellency, I am married. My wife is at Kursk, in service with a merchant."

"Well, write to your wife to come here. I will give you a free pass for her. There is a position as track-walker open. I will speak to the Chief on your behalf."

"I shall be very grateful to you, your Excellency," replied Semyon.

He stayed at the station, helped in the kitchen, cut firewood, kept the yard clean, and swept the platform. In a fortnight's time his wife arrived, and Semyon went on a hand-trolley to his hut. The hut was a new one and warm, with as much wood as he wanted. There was a little vegetable garden, the legacy of a former track-walker, and there was about half a dessiatin of plowed land on either side of the railway embankment. Semyon was rejoiced. He began to think of doing some farming, of purchasing a cow and a horse.

He was given all necessary stores—a green flag, a red flag, lanterns, a horn, hammer, screw-wrench for the nuts, a crow-bar, spade, broom, bolts, and nails: they gave him two books of regulations and a time-table of the trains. At first Semyon could not sleep at night, and learned the whole time-table by heart. Two hours before a train was due he would go over his section, sit on the bench at his hut, and look and listen whether the rails were trembling or the rumble of the train could be heard. He even learned the regulations by heart, although he could only read by spelling out each word.

It was summer; the work was not heavy; there was no snow to clear away, and the trains on that line were infrequent. Semyon used to go over his verst twice a day, examine and screw up nuts here and there, keep the bed level, look at the water-pipes, and then go home to his own affairs. There was only one drawback—he always had to get the inspector's permission for the least little thing he wanted to do. Semyon and his wife were even beginning to be bored.

Two months passed, and Semyon commenced to make the acquaintance of his neighbors, the track-walkers on either side of him. One was a very old man, whom the authorities were always meaning to relieve. He scarcely moved out of his hut. His wife used to do all his work. The other track-walker, nearer the station, was a young man, thin, but muscular. He and Semyon met for the first time on the line midway between the huts. Semyon took off his hat and bowed. "Good health to you, neighbor," he said.

The neighbor glanced askance at him. "How do you do?" he replied; then turned around and made off.

Later the wives met. Semyon's wife passed the time of day with her neighbor, but neither did she say much.

On one occasion Semyon said to her: "Young woman, your husband is not very talkative."

The woman said nothing at first, then replied: "But what is there for him to talk about? Every one has his own business. Go your way, and God be with you."

However, after another month or so they became acquainted. Semyon would go with Vasily along the line, sit on the edge of a pipe, smoke, and talk of life. Vasily, for the most part, kept silent, but Semyon talked of his village and of the campaign through which he had passed.

"I have had no little sorrow in my day," he would say; "and goodness knows I have not lived long. God has not given me happiness, but what He may give, so will it be. That's so, friend Vasily Stepanych."

Vasily Stepanych knocked the ashes out of his pipe against a rail, stood up, and said: "It is not luck which follows us in life, but human beings. There is no crueller beast on this earth than man. Wolf does not eat wolf, but man will readily devour man."

"Come, friend, don't say that; a wolf eats wolf."

"The words came into my mind and I said it. All the same, there is nothing crueller than man. If it were not for his wickedness and greed, it would be possible to live. Everybody tries to sting you to the quick, to bite and eat you up."

Semyon pondered a bit. "I don't know, brother," he said; "perhaps it is as you say, and perhaps it is God's will."

"And perhaps," said Vasily, "it is waste of time for me to talk to you. To put everything unpleasant on God, and sit and suffer, means, brother, being not a man but an animal. That's what I have to say." And he turned and went off without saying good-bye.

Semyon also got up. "Neighbor," he called, "why do you lose your temper?" But his neighbor did not look round, and kept on his way.

Semyon gazed after him until he was lost to sight in the cutting at the turn. He went home and said to his wife: "Arina, our neighbor is a wicked person, not a man."

However, they did not quarrel. They met again and discussed the same topics.

"Ah, friend, if it were not for men we should not be poking in these huts," said Vasily, on one occasion.

"And what if we are poking in these huts? It's not so bad. You can live in them."

"Live in them, indeed! Bah, you!... You have lived long and learned little, looked at much and seen little. What sort of life is there for a poor man in a hut here or there? The cannibals are devouring you. They are sucking up all your life-blood, and when you become old, they will throw you out just as they do husks to feed the pigs on. What pay do you get?"

"Not much, Vasily Stepanych—twelve rubles."

"And I, thirteen and a half rubles. Why? By the regulations the company should give us fifteen rubles a month with firing and lighting. Who decides that you should have twelve rubles, or I thirteen and a half? Ask yourself! And you say a man can live on that? You understand it is not a question of one and a half rubles or three rubles—even if they paid us each the whole fifteen rubles. I was at the station last month. The director passed through. I saw him. I had that honor. He had a separate coach. He came out and stood on the platform.... I shall not stay here long; I shall go somewhere, anywhere, follow my nose."

"But where will you go, Stepanych? Leave well enough alone. Here you have a house, warmth, a little piece of land. Your wife is a worker."

"Land! You should look at my piece of land. Not a twig on it—nothing. I planted some cabbages in the spring, just when the inspector came along. He said: 'What is this? Why have you not reported this? Why have you done this without permission? Dig them up, roots and all.' He was drunk. Another time he would not have said a word, but this time it struck him. Three rubles fine!..."

Vasily kept silent for a while, pulling at his pipe, then added quietly: "A little more and I should have done for him."

"You are hot-tempered."

"No, I am not hot-tempered, but I tell the truth and think. Yes, he will still get a bloody nose from me. I will complain to the Chief. We will see then!" And Vasily did complain to the Chief.

Once the Chief came to inspect the line. Three days later important personages were coming from St. Petersburg and would pass over the line. They were conducting an inquiry, so that previous to their journey it was necessary to put everything in order. Ballast was laid down, the bed was leveled, the sleepers carefully examined, spikes driven in a bit, nuts screwed up, posts painted, and orders given for yellow sand to be sprinkled at the level crossings. The woman at the neighboring hut turned her old man out to weed. Semyon worked for a whole week. He put everything in order, mended his kaftan, cleaned and polished his brass plate until it fairly shone. Vasily also worked hard. The Chief arrived on a trolley, four men working the handles and the levers, making the six wheels hum. The trolley traveled at twenty versts an hour, but the wheels squeaked. It reached Semyon's hut, and he ran out and reported in soldierly fashion. All appeared to be in repair.

"Have you been here long?" inquired the Chief.

"Since the second of May, your Excellency."

"All right. Thank you. And who is at hut No. 164?"

The traffic inspector (he was traveling with the Chief on the trolley) replied: "Vasily Spiridov."

"Spiridov, Spiridov.... Ah! is he the man against whom you made a note last year?"

"He is."

"Well, we will see Vasily Spirodov. Go on!" The workmen laid to the handles, and the trolley got under way. Semyon watched it, and thought, "There will be trouble between them and my neighbor."

About two hours later he started on his round. He saw some one coming along the line from the cutting. Something white showed on his head. Semyon began to look more attentively. It was Vasily. He had a stick in his hand, a small bundle on his shoulder, and his cheek was bound up in a handkerchief.

"Where are you off to?" cried Semyon.

Vasily came quite close. He was very pale, white as chalk, and his eyes had a wild look. Almost choking, he muttered: "To town—to Moscow—to the head office."

"Head office? Ah, you are going to complain, I suppose. Give it up! Vasily Stepanych, forget it."

"No, mate, I will not forget. It is too late. See! He struck me in the face, drew blood. So long as I live I will not forget. I will not leave it like this!"

Semyon took his hand. "Give it up, Stepanych. I am giving you good advice. You will not better things...."

"Better things! I know myself I shan't better things. You were right about Fate. It would be better for me not to do it, but one must stand up for the right."

"But tell me, how did it happen?"

"How? He examined everything, got down from the trolley, looked into the hut. I knew beforehand that he would be strict, and so I had put everything into proper order. He was just going when I made my complaint. He immediately cried out: 'Here is a Government inquiry coming, and you make a complaint about a vegetable garden. Here are privy councilors coming, and you annoy me with cabbages!' I lost patience and said something—not very much, but it offended him, and he struck me in the face. I stood still; I did nothing, just as if what he did was perfectly all right. They went off; I came to myself, washed my face, and left."

"And what about the hut?"

"My wife is staying there. She will look after things. Never mind about their roads."

Vasily got up and collected himself. "Good-bye, Ivanov. I do not know whether I shall get any one at the office to listen to me."

"Surely you are not going to walk?"

"At the station I will try to get on a freight train, and to-morrow I shall be in Moscow."

The neighbors bade each other farewell. Vasily was absent for some time. His wife worked for him night and day. She never slept, and wore herself out waiting for her husband. On the third day the commission arrived. An engine, luggage-van, and two first-class saloons; but Vasily was still away. Semyon saw his wife on the fourth day. Her face was swollen from crying and her eyes were red.

"Has your husband returned?" he asked. But the woman only made a gesture with her hands, and without saying a word went her way.

Semyon had learned when still a lad to make flutes out of a kind of reed. He used to burn out the heart of the stalk, make holes where necessary, drill them, fix a mouth-piece at one end, and tune them so well that it was possible to play almost any air on them. He made a number of them in his spare time, and sent them by his friends amongst the freight brakemen to the bazaar in the town. He got two kopeks apiece for them. On the day following the visit of the commission he left his wife at home to meet the six o'clock train, and started off to the forest to cut some sticks. He went to the end of his section—at this point the line made a sharp turn—descended the embankment, and struck into the wood at the foot of the mountain. About half a verst away there was a big marsh, around which splendid reeds for his flute grew. He cut a whole bundle of stalks and started back home. The sun was already dropping low, and in the dead stillness only the twittering of the birds was audible, and the crackle of the dead wood under his feet. As he walked along rapidly, he fancied he heard the clang of iron striking iron, and he redoubled his pace. There was no repair going on in his section. What did it mean? He emerged from the woods, the railway embankment stood high before him; on the top a man was squatting on the bed of the line busily engaged in something. Semyon commenced quietly to crawl up towards him. He thought it was some one after the nuts which secure the rails. He watched, and the man got up, holding a crow-bar in his hand. He had loosened a rail, so that it would move to one side. A mist swam before Semyon's eyes; he wanted to cry out, but could not. It was Vasily! Semyon scrambled up the bank, as Vasily with crow-bar and wrench slid headlong down the other side.

"Vasily Stepanych! My dear friend, come back! Give me the crow-bar. We will put the rail back; no one will know. Come back! Save your soul from sin!"

Vasily did not look back, but disappeared into the woods.

Semyon stood before the rail which had been torn up. He threw down his bundle of sticks. A train was due; not a freight, but a passenger-train. And he had nothing with which to stop it, no flag. He could not replace the rail and could not drive in the spikes with his bare hands. It was necessary to run, absolutely necessary to run to the hut for some tools. "God help me!" he murmured.

Semyon started running towards his hut. He was out of breath, but still ran, falling every now and then. He had cleared the forest; he was only a few hundred feet from his hut, not more, when he heard the distant hooter of the factory sound—six o'clock! In two minutes' time No. 7 train was due. "Oh, Lord! Have pity on innocent souls!" In his mind Semyon saw the engine strike against the loosened rail with its left wheel, shiver, careen, tear up and splinter the sleepers—and just there, there was a curve and the embankment seventy feet high, down which the engine would topple—and the third-class carriages would be packed ... little children.... All sitting in the train now, never dreaming of danger. "Oh, Lord! Tell me what to do! ... No, it is impossible to run to the hut and get back in time."

Semyon did not run on to the hut, but turned back and ran faster than before. He was running almost mechanically, blindly; he did not know himself what was to happen. He ran as far as the rail which had been pulled up; his sticks were lying in a heap. He bent down, seized one without knowing why, and ran on farther. It seemed to him the train was already coming. He heard the distant whistle; he heard the quiet, even tremor of the rails; but his strength was exhausted, he could run no farther, and came to a halt about six hundred feet from the awful spot. Then an idea came into his head, literally like a ray of light. Pulling off his cap, he took out of it a cotton scarf, drew his knife out of the upper part of his boot, and crossed himself, muttering, "God bless me!"

He buried the knife in his left arm above the elbow; the blood spurted out, flowing in a hot stream. In this he soaked his scarf, smoothed it out, tied it to the stick and hung out his red flag.

He stood waving his flag. The train was already in sight. The driver would not see him—would come close up, and a heavy train cannot be pulled up in six hundred feet.

And the blood kept on flowing. Semyon pressed the sides of the wound together so as to close it, but the blood did not diminish. Evidently he had cut his arm very deep. His head commenced to swim, black spots began to dance before his eyes, and then it became dark. There was a ringing in his ears. He could not see the train or hear the noise. Only one thought possessed him. "I shall not be able to keep standing up. I shall fall and drop the flag; the train will pass over me. Help me, O Lord!"

All turned black before him, his mind became a blank, and he dropped the flag; but the blood-stained banner did not fall to the ground. A hand seized it and held it high to meet the approaching train. The engineer saw it, shut the regulator, and reversed steam. The train came to a standstill.

People jumped out of the carriages and collected in a crowd. They saw a man lying senseless on the footway, drenched in blood, and another man standing beside him with a blood-stained rag on a stick.

Vasily looked around at all. Then, lowering his head, he said: "Bind me. I tore up a rail!"

ANTON CHEKHOV

(1860—1904)

CHEKHOV stands out as one of the greatest short story writers of the world. Although he received an M.D. degree, he never practiced medicine, but devoted himself to writing. His scientific studies were, however, of service to him. There seems to be no limit to the range of his knowledge of the human family. His situations are handled adroitly and with a strict economy of words.

In *The Bet* he shews all the cynicism, fatalism, bitterness, pettiness and viciousness that can result from a simple jest.

The present translation, by J. Middleton Murry and S. S. Koteliansky, is reprinted from *The Bet and Other Stories*, by permission of the publishers, George Allen & Unwin.

THE BET

IT was a dark autumn night. The old banker was pacing from corner to corner of his study, recalling to his mind the party he gave in the autumn fifteen years before. There were many clever people at the party and much interesting conversation. They talked among other things of capital punishment. The guests, among them not a few scholars and journalists, for the most part disapproved of capital punishment. They found it obsolete as a means of punishment, unfitted to a Christian State, and immoral. Some of them thought that capital punishment should be replaced universally by life-imprisonment.

"I don't agree with you," said the host. "I myself have experienced neither capital punishment nor life-imprisonment, but if one may judge *a priori*, then in my opinion capital punishment is more moral and more humane than imprisonment. Execution kills instantly, life-imprisonment kills by degrees. Who is the more humane executioner, one who kills you in a few seconds or one who draws the life out of you incessantly, for years?"

"They're both equally immoral," remarked one of the guests, "because their purpose is the same, to take away life. The State is not God. It has no right to take away that which it cannot give back, if it should so desire."

Among the company was a lawyer, a young man of about twenty-five. On being asked his opinion, he said:

"Capital punishment and life-imprisonment are equally immoral; but if I were offered the choice between them, I would certainly choose the second. It's better to live somehow than not to live at all."

There ensued a lively discussion. The banker who was then younger and more nervous suddenly lost his temper, banged his fist on the table, and turning to the young lawyer, cried out:

"It's a lie. I bet you two millions you wouldn't stick in a cell even for five years."

"If you mean it seriously," replied the lawyer, "then I bet I'll stay not five but fifteen."

"Fifteen! Done!" cried the banker. "Gentlemen, I stake two millions."

"Agreed. You stake two millions, I my freedom," said the lawyer.

So this wild, ridiculous bet came to pass. The banker, who at that time had too many millions to count, spoiled and capricious, was beside himself with rapture. During supper he said to the lawyer jokingly:

"Come to your senses, young man, before it's too late. Two millions are nothing to me, but you stand to lose three or four of the best years of your life. I say three or four, because you'll never stick it out any longer. Don't forget either, you unhappy man, that voluntary is much heavier than enforced imprisonment. The idea that you have the right to free yourself at any moment will poison the whole of your life in the cell. I pity you."

And now the banker, pacing from corner to corner, recalled all this and asked himself:

"Why did I make this bet? What's the good? The lawyer loses fifteen years of his life and I throw away two millions. Will it convince people that capital punishment is worse or better than imprisonment for life? No, no! all stuff and rubbish. On my part, it was the caprice of a well-fed man; on the lawyer's, pure greed of gold."

He recollected further what happened after the evening party. It was decided that the lawyer must undergo his imprisonment under the strictest observation, in a garden wing of the banker's house. It was agreed that during the period he would be deprived of the right to cross the threshold, to see living people, to hear human voices, and to receive letters and newspapers. He was permitted to have a musical instrument, to read books, to write letters, to drink wine and smoke tobacco. By the agreement he could communicate, but only in silence, with the outside world through a little window specially constructed for this purpose. Everything necessary, books, music, wine, he could receive in any quantity by sending a note through the window. The agreement provided for all the minutest details, which made the confinement strictly solitary, and it obliged the lawyer to remain exactly fifteen years from twelve o'clock of November 14th, 1870, to twelve o'clock of November 14th, 1885. The least attempt on his part to violate the conditions, to escape if only for two minutes before the time, freed the banker from the obligation to pay him the two millions.

During the first year of imprisonment, the lawyer, as far as it was possible to judge from his short notes, suffered terribly from loneliness and boredom. From his wing day and night came the sound of the piano. He rejected wine and tobacco. "Wine," he wrote, "excites desires, and desires are the chief foes of a prisoner; besides, nothing is more boring than to drink good wine alone," and tobacco spoiled the air in his room. During the first year the lawyer was sent books of a light character; novels with a complicated love interest, stories of crime and fantasy, comedies, and so on.

In the second year the piano was heard no longer and the lawyer asked only for classics. In the fifth year, music was heard again, and the prisoner asked for wine. Those who watched him said that during the whole of that year he was only eating, drinking, and lying on his bed. He yawned often and talked angrily to himself. Books he did not read. Sometimes at nights he would sit down to write. He would write for a long time and tear it all up in the morning. More than once he was heard to weep.

In the second half of the sixth year, the prisoner began zealously to study languages, philosophy, and history. He fell on these subjects so hungrily that the banker hardly had time to get books enough for him. In the space of four years about six hundred volumes were bought at his request. It was while that passion lasted that the banker received the following letter from the prisoner: "My dear jailer, I am writing these lines in six languages. Show them to experts. Let them read them. If they do not find one single mistake, I beg you to give orders to have a gun fired off in the garden. By the noise I shall know that my efforts have not been in vain. The geniuses of all ages and countries speak in different languages; but in them all burns the same flame. Oh, if you knew my heavenly happiness now that I can understand them!" The prisoner's desire was fulfilled. Two shots were fired in the garden by the banker's order.

Later on, after the tenth year, the lawyer sat immovable before his table and read only the New Testament. The banker found it strange that a man who in four years had mastered six hundred erudite volumes, should have spent nearly a year in reading one book, easy to understand and by no means thick. The New Testament was then replaced by the history of religions and theology.

During the last two years of his confinement the prisoner read an extraordinary amount, quite haphazard. Now he would apply himself to the natural sciences, then he would read Byron or Shakespeare. Notes used to come from him in which he asked to be sent at the same time a book on chemistry, a text-book of medicine, a novel, and some treatise on philosophy or theology. He read as though he were swimming in the sea among broken pieces of wreckage, and in his desire to save his life was eagerly grasping one piece after another.

The banker recalled all this, and thought:

"To-morrow at twelve o'clock he receives his freedom. Under the agreement, I shall have to pay him two millions. If I pay, it's all over with me. I am ruined forever..."

Fifteen years before he had too many millions to count, but now he was afraid to ask himself which he had more of, money or debts. Gambling on the Stock-Exchange, risky speculation, and the recklessness of which he could not rid himself even in old age, had gradually brought his business to decay; and the fearless, self-confident, proud man of business had become an ordinary banker, trembling at every rise and fall in the market.

"That cursed bet," murmured the old man clutching his head in despair.... "Why didn't the man die? He's only forty years old. He will take away my last farthing, marry, enjoy life, gamble on the Exchange, and I will look on like an envious beggar and hear the same words from him every day: 'I'm obliged to you for the happiness of my life. Let me help you.' No, it's too much! The only escape from bankruptcy and disgrace—is that the man should die."

The clock had just struck three. The banker was listening. In the house every one was asleep, and one could hear only the frozen trees whining outside the windows. Trying to make no sound, he took out of his safe the key of the door which had not been opened for fifteen years, put on his overcoat, and went out of the house. The garden was dark and cold. It was raining. A damp, penetrating wind howled in the garden and gave the trees no rest. Though he strained his eyes, the banker could see neither the ground, nor the white statues, nor the garden wing, nor the trees. Approaching the garden wing, he called the watchman twice. There was no answer. Evidently the watchman had taken shelter from the bad weather and was now asleep somewhere in the kitchen or the greenhouse.

"If I have the courage to fulfil my intention," thought the old man, "the suspicion will fall on the watchman first of all."

In the darkness he groped for the steps and the door and entered the hall of the garden-wing, then poked his way into a narrow passage and struck a match. Not a soul was there. Some one's bed, with no bed-clothes on it, stood there, and an iron stove loomed dark in the corner. The seals on the door that led into the prisoner's room were unbroken.

When the match went out, the old man, trembling from agitation, peeped into the little window.

In the prisoner's room a candle was burning dimly. The prisoner himself sat by the table. Only his back, the hair on his head and his hands were visible. Open books were strewn about on the table, the two chairs, and on the carpet near the table.

Five minutes passed and the prisoner never once stirred. Fifteen years' confinement had taught him to sit motionless. The banker tapped on the window with his finger, but the prisoner made no movement in reply. Then the banker cautiously tore the seals from the door and put the key into the lock. The rusty lock gave a hoarse groan and the door creaked. The banker expected instantly to hear a cry of surprise and the sound of steps. Three minutes passed and it was as quiet inside as it had been before. He made up his mind to enter.

Before the table sat a man, unlike an ordinary human being. It was a skeleton, with tight-drawn skin, with long curly hair like a woman's, and a shaggy beard. The color of his face was yellow, of an earthy shade; the cheeks were sunken, the back long and narrow, and the hand upon which he leaned his hairy head was so lean and skinny that it was painful to look upon. His hair was already silvering with gray, and no one who glanced at the senile emaciation of the face would have believed that he was only forty years old. On the table, before his bended head, lay a sheet of paper on which something was written in a tiny hand.

"Poor devil," thought the banker, "he's asleep and probably seeing millions in his dreams. I have only to take and throw this half-dead thing on the bed, smother him a moment with the pillow, and the most careful examination will find no trace of unnatural death. But, first, let us read what he has written here."

The banker took the sheet from the table and read:

"To-morrow at twelve o'clock midnight, I shall obtain my freedom and the right to mix with people. But before I leave this room and see the sun I think it necessary to say a few words to you. On my own clear conscience and before God who sees me I declare to you that I despise freedom, life, health, and all that your books call the blessings of the world.

"For fifteen years I have diligently studied earthly life. True, I saw neither the earth nor the people, but in your books I drank fragrant wine, sang songs, hunted deer and wild boar in the forests, loved women. . . . And beautiful women, like clouds ethereal, created by the magic of your poet's genius, visited me by night and whispered to me wonderful tales, which made my head drunken. In your books I climbed the summits of Elbruz and Mont Blanc and saw from there how the sun rose in the morning, and in the evening suffused the sky, the ocean and the mountain ridges with a purple gold. I saw from there how above me lightnings glimmered, cleaving the clouds; I saw green forests, fields, rivers, lakes, cities; I heard sirens singing, and the playing of the pipes of Pan; I touched the wings of beautiful devils who came flying to me to speak of God.... In your books I cast myself into bottomless abysses, worked miracles, burned cities to the ground, preached new religions, conquered whole countries....

"Your books gave me wisdom. All that unwearying human thought created in the centuries is compressed to a little lump in my skull. I know that I am cleverer than you all.

"And I despise your books, despise all wordly blessings and wisdom. Everything is void, frail, visionary and delusive as a mirage. Though you be proud and wise and beautiful, yet will death wipe you from the face of the earth like the mice underground; and your posterity, your history, and the immortality of your men of genius will be as frozen slag, burnt down together with the terrestrial globe.

"You are mad, and gone the wrong way. You take falsehood for truth and ugliness for beauty. You would marvel if suddenly apple and orange trees should bear frogs and lizards instead of fruit, and if roses should begin to breathe the odor of a sweating horse. So do I marvel at you, who have bartered heaven for earth. I do not want to understand you.

"That I may show you in deed my contempt for that by which you live, I waive the two millions of which I once dreamed as of paradise, and which I now despise. That I may deprive myself of my right to them, I shall come out from here five minutes before the stipulated term, and thus shall violate the agreement."

When he had read, the banker put the sheet on the table, kissed the head of the strange man, and began to weep. He went out of the wing. Never at any other time, not even after his terrible losses on the Exchange, had he felt such contempt for himself as now. Coming home, he lay down on his bed, but agitation and tears kept him a long time from sleeping....

The next morning the poor watchman came running to him and told him that they had seen the man who lived in the wing climb through the window into the garden. He had gone to the gate and disappeared. The banker instantly went with his servants to the wing and established the escape of his prisoner. To avoid unnecessary rumors he took the paper with the renunciation from the table and, on his return, locked it in his safe.

MAXIM GORKY

(1868—1936)

ALEXEI MAXIMOVITCH PYESHKOV, known as Gorky, which signifies "bitter," was born at Nijni Novgorod in 1868. He was orphaned at nine, and was then apprenticed to a bootmaker. He ran away and wandered all over Russia, plying various trades, and reading greedily all the books he could obtain. His experiences gave him a fund of material for his remarkable stories; stories which are filled with the vigour and pathos, the gentleness and bitterness of Russian life. At the height of his career he was exiled, and did not return to his native country until after the war.

Gorky specialized in the description of the class of outcasts which he knew best. Most of his short stories deal with these people.

The present version has been reprinted from Thomas Seltzer's

Best Russian Short Stories, Boni & Liveright, New York, by permission of Jarrolds, publishers, in whose volume, *Stories from Gorki*, it first appeared. The translator is R. N. Bain.

ONE AUTUMN NIGHT

ONCE in the autumn I happened to be in a very unpleasant and inconvenient position. In the town where I had just arrived and where I knew not a soul, I found myself without a farthing in my pocket and without a night's lodging.

Having sold during the first few days every part of my costume without which it was still possible to go about, I passed from the town into the quarter called "Yste," where were the steamship wharves— a quarter which during the navigation season fermented with boisterous, laborious life, but now was silent and deserted, for we were in the last days of October.

Dragging my feet along the moist sand, and obstinately scrutinizing it with the desire to discover in it any sort of fragment of food, I wandered alone among the deserted buildings and warehouses, and thought how good it would be to get a full meal.

In our present state of culture hunger of the mind is more quickly satisfied than hunger of the body. You wander about the streets, you are surrounded by buildings not bad-looking from the outside and— you may safely say it—not so badly furnished inside, and the sight of them may excite within you stimulating ideas about architecture, hygiene, and many other wise and high-flying subjects. You may meet warmly and neatly dressed folks—all very polite, and turning away from you tactfully, not wishing offensively to notice the lamentable fact of your existence. Well well, the mind of a hungry man is always better nourished and healthier than the mind of the well-fed man; and there you have a situation from which you may draw a very ingenious conclusion in favor of the ill fed.

The evening was approaching, the rain was falling, and the wind blew violently from the north. It whistled in the empty booths and shops, blew into the plastered window-panes of the taverns, and whipped into foam the wavelets of the river which splashed noisily on the sandy shore, casting high their white crests, racing one after another into the dim distance, and leaping impetuously over one another's shoulders. It seemed as if the river felt the proximity of winter, and was running at random away from the fetters of ice which the north wind might well have flung upon her that very night. The sky was heavy and dark; down from it swept incessantly scarcely visible drops of rain, and the melancholy elegy in nature all around me was emphasized by a couple of battered and misshapen willow-trees and a boat, bottom upwards, that was fastened to their roots.

The overturned canoe with its battered keel and the miserable old trees rifled by the cold wind—everything around me was bankrupt, barren, and dead, and the sky flowed with undryable tears.... Everything around was waste and gloomy... it seemed as if everything were dead, leaving me alone among the living, and for me also a cold death waited.

I was then eighteen years old—a good time!

I walked and walked along the cold wet sand, making my chattering teeth warble in honor of cold and hunger, when suddenly, as I was carefully searching for something to eat behind one of the empty crates, I perceived behind it, crouching on the ground, a figure in woman's clothes dank with the rain and clinging fast to her stooping shoulders. Standing over her, I watched to see what she was doing. It appeared that she was digging a trench in the sand with her hands—digging away under one of the crates.

"Why are you doing that?" I asked, crouching down on my heels quite close to her.

She gave a little scream and was quickly on her legs again. Now that she stood there staring at me, with her wide-open gray eyes full of terror, I perceived that it was a girl of my own age, with a very pleasant face embellished unfortunately by three large blue marks. This spoilt her, although these blue marks had been distributed with a remarkable sense of proportion, one at a time, and all were of equal size—two under the eyes, and one a little bigger on the forehead just over the bridge of the nose. This symmetry was evidently the work of an artist well inured to the business of spoiling the human physiognomy.

The girl looked at me, and the terror in her eyes gradually died out. ... She shook the sand from her hands, adjusted her cotton head-gear, cowered down, and said:

"I suppose you, too, want something to eat? Dig away then! My hands are tired. Over there"—she nodded her head in the direction of a booth—"there is bread for certain... and sausages too.... That booth is still carrying on business."

I began to dig. She, after waiting a little and looking at me, sat down beside me and began to help me.

We worked in silence. I cannot say now whether I thought at that moment of the criminal code, of morality, of proprietorship, and all the other things about which, in the opinion of many experienced persons, one ought to think every moment of one's life. Wishing to keep as close to the truth as possible, I must confess that apparently I was so deeply engaged in digging under the crate that I completely forgot about everything else except this one thing: What could be inside that crate?

The evening drew on. The gray, mouldy, cold fog grew thicker and thicker around us. The waves roared with a hollower sound than before, and the rain pattered down on the boards of that crate more loudly and more frequently. Somewhere or other the night-watchman began springing his rattle.

"Has it got a bottom or not?" softly inquired my assistant. I did not understand what she was talking about, and I kept silence.

"I say, has the crate got a bottom? If it has we shall try in vain to break into it. Here we are digging a trench, and we may, after all, come upon nothing but solid boards. How shall we take them off? Better smash the lock; it is a wretched lock."

Good ideas rarely visit the heads of women, but, as you see, they do visit them sometimes. I have always valued good ideas, and have always tried to utilize them as far as possible.

Having found the lock, I tugged at it and wrenched off the whole thing. My accomplice immediately stooped down and wriggled like a serpent into the gaping-open, four-cornered cover of the crate whence she called to me approvingly, in a low tone:

"You're a brick!"

Nowadays a little crumb of praise from a woman is dearer to me than a whole dithyramb from a man, even though he be more eloquent than all the ancient and modern orators put together. Then, however, I was less amiably disposed than I am now, and, paying no attention to the compliment of my comrade, I asked her curtly and anxiously:

"Is there anything?"

In a monotonous tone she set about calculating our discoveries.

"A basketful of bottles—thick furs—a sunshade—an iron pail."

All this was uneatable. I felt that my hopes had vanished.... But suddenly she exclaimed vivaciously:

"Aha! here it is!"

"What?"

"Bread... a loaf... it's only wet... take it!"

A loaf flew to my feet and after it herself, my valiant comrade. I had already bitten off a morsel, stuffed it in my mouth, and was chewing it....

"Come, give me some too!... And we mustn't stay here.... Where shall we go?" She looked inquiringly about on all sides.... It was dark, wet, and boisterous.

"Look! there's an upset canoe yonder... let us go there."

"Let us go then!" And off we set, demolishing our booty as we went, and filling our mouths with large portions of it.... The rain grew more violent, the river roared; from somewhere or other resounded a prolonged mocking whistle—just as if Someone great who feared nobody was whistling down all earthly institutions and along with them this horrid autumnal wind and us, its heroes. This whistling made my heart throb painfully, in spite of which I greedily went on eating, and in this respect the girl, walking on my left, kept even pace with me.

"What do they call you?" I asked her—why I know not.

"Natasha," she answered shortly, munching loudly.

I stared at her. My heart ached within me; and then I stared into the mist before me, and it seemed to me as if the inimical countenance of my Destiny was smiling at me enigmatically and coldly.

The rain scourged the timbers of the skiff incessantly, and its soft patter induced melancholy thoughts, and the wind whistled as it flew down into the boat's battered bottom through a rift, where some loose splinters of wood were rattling together—a disquieting and depressing sound. The waves of the river were splashing on the shore, and sounded so monotonous and hopeless, just as if they were telling something unbearably dull and heavy, which was boring them into utter disgust, something from which they wanted to run away and yet were obliged to talk about all the same. The sound of the rain blended with their splashing, and a long-drawn sigh seemed to be floating above the overturned skiff—the endless, laboring sigh of the earth, injured and exhausted by the eternal changes from the bright and warm summer to the cold, misty and damp autumn. The wind blew continually over the desolate shore and the foaming river—blew and sang its melancholy songs....

Our position beneath the shelter of the skiff was utterly devoid of comfort; it was narrow and damp, tiny cold drops of rain dribbled through the damaged bottom; gusts of wind penetrated it. We sat in silence and shivered with cold. I remembered that I wanted to go to sleep. Natasha leaned her back against the hull of the boat and curled herself up into a tiny ball. Embracing her knees with her hands, and resting her chin upon them, she stared doggedly at the river with wide-open eyes; on the pale patch of her face they seemed immense, because of the blue marks below them. She never moved, and this immobility and silence—I felt it—gradually produced within me a terror of my neighbor. I wanted to talk to her, but I knew not how to begin.

It was she herself who spoke.

"What a cursed thing life is!" she exclaimed plainly, abstractedly, and in a tone of deep conviction.

But this was no complaint. In these words there was too much of indifference for a complaint. This simple soul thought according to her understanding—thought and proceeded to form a certain conclusion which she expressed aloud, and which I could not confute for fear of contradicting myself. Therefore I was silent, and she, as if she had not noticed me, continued to sit there immovable.

"Even if we croaked... what then...?" Natasha began again, this time quietly and reflectively, and still there was not one note of complaint in her words. It was plain that this person, in the course of her reflections on life, was regarding her own case, and had arrived at the conviction that in order to preserve herself from the mockeries of life, she was not in a position to do anything else but simply "croak"—to use her own expression.

The clearness of this line of thought was inexpressibly sad and painful to me, and I felt that if I kept silence any longer I was really bound to weep.... And it would have been shameful to have done this before a woman, especially as she was not weeping herself. I resolved to speak to her.

"Who was it that knocked you about?" I asked. For the moment I could not think of anything more sensible or more delicate.

"Pashka did it all," she answered in a dull and level tone.

"And who is he?"

"My lover.... He was a baker."

"Did he beat you often?"

"Whenever he was drunk he beat me.... Often!"

And suddenly, turning towards me, she began to talk about herself, Pashka, and their mutual relations. He was a baker with red mustaches and played very well on the banjo. He came to see her and greatly pleased her, for he was a merry chap and wore nice clean clothes. He had a vest which cost fifteen rubles and boots with dress tops. For these reasons she had fallen in love with him, and he became her "creditor." And when he became her creditor, he made it his business to take away from her the money which her other friends gave to her for bonbons, and, getting drunk on this money, he would fall to beating her; but that would have been nothing if he hadn't also begun to "run after" other girls before her very eyes.

"Now, wasn't that an insult? I am not worse than the others. Of course that meant that he was laughing at me, the blackguard. The day before yesterday I asked leave of my mistress to go out for a bit, went to him, and there I found Dimka sitting beside him, drunk. And he, too, was half seas over. I said, 'You scoundrel, you!' And he gave me a thorough hiding. He kicked me and dragged me by the hair. But that was nothing to what came after. He spoiled everything I had on—left me just as I am now! How could I appear before my mistress? He spoiled everything... my dress and my jacket too—it was quite a new one; I gave a fiver for it... and tore my kerchief from my head.

.. Oh, Lord! What will become of me now?" she suddenly whined in a lamentable, overstrained voice.

The wind howled, and became ever colder and more boisterous.... Again my teeth began to dance up and down, and she, huddled up to avoid the cold, pressed as closely to me as she could, so that I could see the gleam of her eyes through the darkness.

"What wretches all you men are! I'd burn you all in an oven; I'd cut you in pieces. If any one of you was dying I'd spit in his mouth, and not pity him a bit. Mean skunks! You wheedle and wheedle, you wag your tails like cringing dogs, and we fools give ourselves up to you, and it's all up with us! Immediately you trample us underfoot.... Miserable loafers!"

She cursed us up and down, but there was no vigor, no malice, no hatred of these "miserable loafers" in her cursing that I could hear. The tone of her language by no means corresponded with its subject-matter, for it was calm enough, and the gamut of her voice was terribly poor.

Yet all this made a stronger impression on me than the most eloquent and convincing pessimistic books and speeches, of which I had read a good many and which I still read to this day. And this, you see, was because the agony of a dying person is much more natural and violent than the most minute and picturesque descriptions of death.

I felt really wretched—more from cold than from the words of my neighbor. I groaned softly and ground my teeth.

Almost at the same moment I felt two little arms about me—one of them touched my neck and the other lay upon my face—and at the same time an anxious, gentle, friendly voice uttered the question:

"What ails you?"

I was ready to believe that someone else was asking me this and not Natasha, who had just declared that all men were scoundrels, and expressed a wish for their destruction. But she it was, and now she began speaking quickly, hurriedly.

"What ails you, eh? Are you cold? Are you frozen? Ah, what a one you are, sitting there so silent like a little owl! Why, you should have told me long ago that you were cold. Come... lie on the ground ... stretch yourself out and I will lie... there! How's that? Now put your arms round me?... tighter! How's that? You shall be warm very soon now... And then we'll lie back to back.... The night will pass so quickly, see if it won't. I say... have you too been drinking...? Turned out of your place, eh?... It doesn't matter."

And she comforted me.... She encouraged me.

May I be thrice accursed! What a world of irony was in this single fact for me! Just imagine! Here was I, seriously occupied at this very time with the destiny of humanity, thinking of the reorganization of the social system, of political revolutions, reading all sorts of devilishly wise books whose abysmal profundity was certainly unfathomable by their very authors—at this very time, I say, I was trying with all my might to make of myself "a potent, active social force." It even seemed to me that I had partially accomplished my object; anyhow, at this time, in my ideas about myself, I had got so far as to recognize that I had an exclusive right to exist, that I had the necessary greatness to deserve to live my life, and that I was fully competent to play a great historical part therein. And a woman was now warming me with her body, a wretched, battered, hunted creature, who had no place and no value in life, and whom I had never thought of helping till she helped me herself, and whom I really would not have known how to help in any way even if the thought of it had occurred to me.

Ah! I was ready to think that all this was happening to me in a dream—in a disagreeable, an oppressive dream.

But, ugh! it was impossible for me to think that, for cold drops of rain were dripping down upon me, the woman was pressing close to me, her warm breath was fanning my face, and—despite a slight odor of vodka—it did me good. The wind howled and raged, the rain smote upon the skiff, the waves splashed, and both of us, embracing each other convulsively, nevertheless shivered with cold. All this was only too real, and I am certain that nobody ever dreamed such an oppressive and horrid dream as that reality.

But Natasha was talking all the time of something or other, talking kindly and sympathetically, as only women can talk. Beneath the influence of her voice and kindly words, a little fire began to burn up within me, and something inside my heart thawed in consequence.

Then tears poured from my eyes like a hailstorm, washing away from my heart much that was evil, much that was stupid, much sorrow and dirt which had fastened upon it before that night. Natasha comforted me.

"Come, come, that will do, little one! Don't take on! That'll do! God will give you another chance... you will right yourself and stand in your proper place again... and it will be all right...."

And she kept kissing me... many kisses did she give me... burning kisses... and all for nothing....

Those were the first kisses from a woman that had ever been bestowed upon me, and they were the best kisses too, for all the subsequent kisses cost me frightfully dear, and really gave me nothing at all in exchange.

"Come, don't take on so, funny one! I'll manage for you to-morrow if you cannot find a place." Her quiet, persuasive whispering sounded in my ears as if it came through a dream....

There we lay till dawn....

And when the dawn came, we crept from behind the skiff and went into the town.... Then we took friendly leave of each other and never met again, although for half a year I searched in every hole and corner for that kind Natasha, with whom I spent the autumn night just described.

If she be already dead—and well for her if it were so—may she rest in peace! And if she be alive... still I say "Peace to her soul!" And may the consciousness of her fall never enter her soul... for that would be a superfluous and fruitless suffering if life is to be lived....

LEONID ANDREYEV

(1871—1919)

Born in 1871 at Orel, Andreyev struggled for many years to earn a livelihood as a lawyer. He began writing in 1900, and was helped and encouraged by Gorky. The note of tragedy and fatalism that character-izes his plays and novels is present also in his numerous short stories, of which *Silence* is typical.

The present version, translated by John Cournos, was published by Brown Brothers, copyright, 1910. It is reprinted by permission of the present owners, Frank-Maurice, Inc.

SILENCE

ONE moonlit night in May, while the nightingales sang, Father Ignatius' wife entered his chamber. Her countenance expressed suffering, and the little lamp she held in her hand trembled. Approach-ing her husband, she touched his shoulder, and managed to say be-tween her sobs:

"Father, let us go to Verochka."

Without turning his head, Father Ignatius glanced severely at his wife over the rims of his spectacles, and looked long and intently, till she waved her unoccupied hand and dropped on a low divan.

"That one toward the other be so pitiless!" she pronounced slowly, with emphasis on the final syllables, and her good plump face was dis-torted with a grimace of pain and exasperation, as if in this manner she wished to express what stern people they were—her husband and daughter.

Father Ignatius smiled and arose. Closing his book, he removed his spectacles, placed them in the case and meditated. His long, black beard, inwoven with silver threads, lay dignified on his breast, and it slowly heaved at every deep breath.

"Well, let us go!" said he.

Olga Stepanovna quickly arose and entreated in an appealing, timid voice:

"Only don't revile her, father! You know the sort she is."

Vera's chamber was in the attic, and the narrow, wooden stair bent and creaked under the heavy tread of Father Ignatius. Tall and ponderous, he lowered his head to avoid striking the floor of the upper story, and frowned disdainfully when the white jacket of his wife brushed his face. Well he knew that nothing would come of their talk with Vera.

"Why do you come?" asked Vera, raising a bared arm to her eyes. The other arm lay on top of a white summer blanket hardly distinguishable from the fabric, so white, translucent and cold was its aspect.

"Verochka!" began her mother, but sobbing, she grew silent.

"Vera!" said her father, making an effort to soften his dry and hard voice. "Vera, tell us, what troubles you?"

Vera was silent.

"Vera, do not, we, your mother and I, deserve your confidence? Do we not love you? And is there someone nearer to you than we? Tell us about your sorrow, and believe me you'll feel better for it. And we too. Look at your aged mother, how much she suffers!"

"Verochka!"

"And I..." The dry voice trembled, truly something had broken in it. "And I... do you think I find it easy? As if I did not see that some sorrow is gnawing at you—and what is it? And I, your father, do not know what it is. Is it right that it should be so?"

Vera was silent. Father Ignatius very cautiously stroked his beard, as if afraid that his fingers would enmesh themselves involuntarily in it, and continued:

"Against my wish you went to St. Petersburg—did I pronounce a curse upon you, you who disobeyed me? Or did I not give you money? Or, you'll say, I have not been kind? Well, why then are you silent? There, you've had your St. Petersburg!"

Father Ignatius became silent, and an image arose before him of something huge, of granite, and terrible, full of invisible dangers and strange and indifferent people. And there, alone and weak, was his Vera and there they had lost her. An awful hatred against that terrible and mysterious city grew in the soul of Father Ignatius, and an anger against his daughter who was silent, obstinately silent.

"St. Petersburg has nothing to do with it," said Vera, morosely, and closed her eyes. "And nothing is the matter with me. Better go to bed, it is late."

"Verochka," whimpered her mother. "Little daughter, do confess to me."

"Akh, mamma!" impatiently Vera interrupted her.

Father Ignatius sat down on a chair and laughed.

"Well, then it's nothing?" he inquired, ironically.

"Father," sharply put in Vera, raising herself from the pillow, "you know that I love you and mother. Well, I do feel a little weary. But that will pass. Do go to sleep, and I also wish to sleep. And to-morrow, or some other time, we'll have a chat."

Father Ignatius impetuously arose so that the chair hit the wall, and took his wife's hand.

"Let us go."

"Verochka!"

"Let us go, I tell you!" shouted Father Ignatius. "If she has forgotten God, shall we..."

Almost forcibly he had led Olga Stepanovna out of the room, and when they descended the stairs, his wife, decreasing her gait, said in a harsh whisper:

"It was you, priest, who have made her such. From you she learned her ways. And you'll answer for it. Akh, unhappy creature that I am!"

And she wept, and, as her eyes filled with tears, her foot, missing a step, would descend with a sudden, jolt, as if she were eager to fall into some existent abyss below.

From that day Father Ignatius ceased to speak with his daughter, but she seemed not to notice it. As before she lay in her room, or walked about, continually wiping her eyes with the palms of her hands as if they contained some irritating foreign substance. And crushed between these two silent people, the jolly, fun-loving wife of the priest quailed and seemed lost, not knowing what to say or do.

Occasionally Vera took a stroll. A week following the interview she went out in the evening, as was her habit. She was not seen alive again, as on this evening she threw herself under the train, which cut her in two.

Father Ignatius himself directed the funeral. His wife was not present in church, as at the news of Vera's death she was prostrated by a stroke. She lost control of her feet, hands and tongue, and she lay motionless in the semi-darkened room when the church bells rang out. She heard the people, as they issued out of church and passed the house, intone the chants, and she made an effort to raise her hand, and to make a sign of the cross, but her hand refused to obey; she wished to say: "Farewell, Vera!" but the tongue lay in her mouth huge and heavy. And her attitude was so calm, that it gave one an impression of restfulness or sleep. Only her eyes remained open.

At the funeral, in church, were many people who knew Father Ignatius, and many strangers, and all bewailed Vera's terrible death, and tried to find in the movements and voice of Father Ignatius tokens of a deep sorrow. They did not love Father Ignatius because of his severity and proud manners, his scorn of sinners, for his unforgiving spirit, his envy and covetousness, his habit of utilizing every opportunity to extort money from his parishioners. They all wished to see him suffer, to see his spirit broken, to see him conscious in his two-fold guilt for the death of his daughter—as a cruel father and a bad priest—incapable of preserving his own flesh from sin. They cast searching glances at him, and he, feeling these glances directed toward his back, made efforts to hold erect its broad and strong expanse, and his thoughts were not concerning his dead daughter, but concerning his own dignity.

"A hardened priest!" said, with a shake of his head, Karzenoff, a carpenter, to whom Father Ignatius owed five rubles for frames.

And thus, hard and erect, Father Ignatius reached the burial ground, and in the same manner he returned. Only at the door of his wife's chamber did his spine relax a little, but this may have been due to the fact that the height of the door was inadequate to admit his tall figure. The change from broad daylight made it difficult for him to distinguish the face of his wife, but, after scrutiny, he was astonished at its calmness and because the eyes showed no tears. And there was neither anger, nor sorrow in the eyes—they were dumb, and they kept silent with difficulty, reluctantly, as did the entire plump and helpless body, pressing against the feather bedding.

"Well, how do you feel?" inquired Father Ignatius.

The lips, however, were dumb; the eyes also were silent. Father Ignatius laid his hand on her forehead; it was cold and moist, and Olga Stepanovna did not show in any way that she had felt the hand's contact. When Father Ignatius removed his hand there gazed at him, immobile two deep gray eyes, seeming almost entirely dark from the dilated pupils, and there was neither sadness in them, nor anger.

"I am going into my own room," said Father Ignatius, who began to feel cold and terror.

He passed through the drawing-room, where everything appeared neat and in order, as usual, and where, attired in white covers, stood tall chairs, like corpses in their shrouds. Over one window hung an empty wire cage, with the door open.

"Nastasya!" shouted Father Ignatius, and his voice seemed to him coarse, and he felt ill at ease because he raised his voice so high in these silent rooms, so soon after his daughter's funeral. "Nastasya!" he called out in a lower tone of voice, "where is the canary?"

"She flew away, to be sure."

"Why did you let it out?"

Nastasya began to weep, and wiping her face with the edges of her calico handkerchief, said through her tears:

"It was my young mistress's soul. Was it right to hold it?"

And it seemed to Father Ignatius that the yellow, happy little canary, always singing with inclined head, was really the soul of Vera, and if it had not flown away it wouldn't have been possible to say that Vera had died. He became even more incensed at the maidservant, and shouted:

"Off with you!"

And when Nastasya did not find the door at once he added:

"Fool!"

From the day of the funeral silence reigned in the little house. It was not stillness, for stillness is merely the absence of sounds; it was silence, because it seemed that they who were silent could say something but would not. So thought Father Ignatius each time he entered his wife's chamber and met that obstinate gaze, so heavy in its aspect that it seemed to transform the very air into lead, which bore down one's head and spine. So thought he, examining his daughter's music sheets, which bore imprints of her voice, as well as her books and her portrait, which she brought with her from St. Petersburg. Father Ignatius was accustomed to scrutinize the portrait in established order: First, he would gaze on the cheek upon which a strong light was thrown by the painter; in his fancy he would see upon it a slight wound, which he had noticed on Vera's cheek in death, and the source of which he could not understand. Each time he would meditate upon causes; he reasoned that if it was made by the train the entire head would have been crushed, whereas the head of Vera remained wholly untouched. It was possible that someone did it with his foot when the corpse was removed, or accidentally with a finger nail.

To contemplate at length upon the details of Vera's death taxed the strength of Father Ignatius, so that he would pass on to the eyes. These were dark, handsome, with long lashes, which cast deep shadows beneath, causing the whites to seem particularly luminous, both eyes appearing to be inclosed in black, mourning frames. A strange expression was given them by the unknown but talented artist; it seemed as if the space between the eyes and the object upon which they gazed there lay a thin, transparent film. It resembled somewhat the effect obtained by an imperceptible layer of dust on the black top of a piano, softening the shine of polished wood. And no matter how Father Ignatius placed the portrait, the eyes insistently followed him, but there was no speech in them, only silence; and this silence was so clear that it seemed it could be heard. And gradually Father Ignatius began to think that he heard silence.

Every morning after breakfast Father Ignatius would enter the drawing-room, throw a rapid glance at the empty cage and the other familiar objects, and seating himself in the armchair would close his eyes and listen to the silence of the house. There was something grotesque about this. The cage kept silence, stilly and tenderly, and in this silence were felt sorrow, and tears, and distant dead laughter. The silence of his wife, softened by the walls, continued insistent, heavy as lead, and terrible, so terrible that on the hottest day Father Ignatius would be seized by cold shivers. Continuous and cold as the grave, and mysterious as death, was the silence of his daughter. The silence itself seemed to share this suffering and struggled, as it were, with the terrible desire to pass into speech; however, something strong and cumbersome, as a machine, held it motionless and stretched it out as a wire. And somewhere at the distant end, the wire would begin to agitate and resound subduedly, feebly and plaintively. With joy, yet with terror, Father Ignatius would seize upon this engendered sound, and resting with his arms upon the arms of the chair, would lean his head forward, awaiting the sound to reach him. But the sound would break and pass into silence.

"How stupid!" muttered Father Ignatius, angrily, arising from the chair, still erect and tall. Through the window he saw, suffused with sunlight, the street, which was paved with round, even-sized stones, and directly across, the stone wall of a long, windowless shed. On the corner stood a cab-driver, resembling a clay statue, and it was difficult to understand why he stood there, when for hours there was not a single passer-by.

Father Ignatius had occasion for considerable speech outside his house. There was talking to be done with the clergy, with the members of his flock, while officiating at ceremonies, sometimes with acquaintances at social evenings; yet, upon his return he would feel invariably that the entire day he had been silent. This was due to the fact that with none of those people could he talk upon that matter which concerned him most, and upon which he would contemplate each night: Why did Vera die?

Father Ignatius did not seem to understand that now this could not be known, and still thought it was possible to know. Each night—all his nights had become sleepless—he would picture that minute when he and his wife, in dead midnight, stood near Vera's bed, and he entreated her: "Tell us!" And when in his recollection, he would reach these words, the rest appeared to him not as it was in reality. His closed eyes, preserving in their darkness a live and undimmed picture of that night, saw how Vera raised herself in her bed, smiled and tried to say something. And what was that she tried to say? That unuttered word of Vera's which should have solved all, seemed so near, that if one only had bent his ear and suppressed the beats of his heart, one could have heard it, and at the same time it was so infinitely, so hopelessly distant. Father Ignatius would arise from his bed, stretch forth his joined hands and, wringing them, would exclaim:

"Vera!"

And he would be answered by silence.

One evening Father Ignatius entered the chamber of Olga Stepanovna, whom he had not come to see for a week, seated himself at her head, and turning away from that insistent, heavy gaze, said:

"Mother! I wish to talk to you about Vera. Do you hear?"

Her eyes were silent, and Father Ignatius raising his voice, spoke sternly and powerfully, as he was accustomed to speak with penitents:

"I am aware that you are under the impression that I have been the cause of Vera's death. Reflect, however, did I love her less than you loved her? You reason absurdly. I have been stern; did that prevent her from doing as she wished? I have forfeited the dignity of a father, I humbly bent my neck, when she defied my malediction and departed —hence. And you—did you not entreat her to remain, until I commanded you to be silent? Did I beget cruelty in her? Did I not teach her about God, about humility, about love?"

Father Ignatius quickly glanced into the eyes of his wife, and turned away.

"What was there for me to do when she did not wish to reveal her sorrow? Did I not command her? Did I not entreat her? I suppose, in your opinion, I should have dropped on my knees before the maid, and cried like an old woman! How should I know what was going on in her head! Cruel, heartless daughter!"

Father Ignatius hit his knees with his fist.

"There was no love in her—that's what! As far as I'm concerned, that's settled, of course—I'm a tyrant! Perhaps she loved you—you, who wept and humbled yourself?"

Father Ignatius gave a hollow laugh.

"There's love for you! And as a solace for you, what a death she chose! A cruel, ignominious death. She died in the dust, in the dirt— as a d-dog who is kicked in the jaw." .

The voice of Father Ignatius sounded low and hoarse:

"I feel ashamed! Ashamed to go out in the street! Ashamed before the altar! Ashamed before God! Cruel, undeserving daughter! Accurst in thy grave!"

When Father Ignatius glanced at his wife she was unconscious, and revived only after several hours. When she regained consciousness her eyes were silent, and it was impossible to tell whether or not she remembered what Father Ignatius had said.

That very night—it was a moonlit, calm, warm and deathly still night in May—Father Ignatius, proceeding on his tiptoes, so as not to be overheard by his wife and the sick-nurse, climbed up the stairs and entered Vera's room. The window in the attic had remained closed since the death of Vera, and the atmosphere was dry and warm, with a light odor of burning that comes from heat generated during the day in the iron roof. The air of lifelessness and abandonment permeated the apartment, which for a long time had remained unvisited, and where the timber of the walls, the furniture and other objects gave forth a slight odor of continued putrescence. A bright streak of moonlight fell on the windowsill, and on the floor, and, reflected by the white, carefully washed boards, cast a dim light into the room's corners, while the white, clean bed, with two pillows, one large and one small, seemed phantom-like and aerial. Father Ignatius opened the window, causing to pour into the room a considerable current of fresh air, smelling of dust, of the nearby river and the blooming linden. An indistinct sound as of voices in chorus also entered occasionally; evidently young people rowed and sang.

Quietly treading with naked feet, resembling a white phantom, Father Ignatius made his way to the vacant bed, bent his knees and fell face down on the pillows, embracing them—on that spot where should have been Vera's face. Long he lay thus; the song grew louder, then died out; but he still lay there, while his long, black hair spread over his shoulders and the bed.

The moon had changed its position, and the room grew darker, when Father Ignatius raised his head and murmured, putting into his voice the entire strength of his long-suppressed and unconscious love and hearkening to his own words, as if it were not he who was listening, but Vera.

"Vera, daughter mine! Do you understand what you are to me, daughter? Little daughter! My heart, my blood and my life. Your father—your old father—is already gray, and also feeble."

The shoulders of Father Ignatius shook and the entire burdened figure became agitated. Suppressing his agitation, Father Ignatius murmured tenderly, as to an infant:

"Your old father entreats you. No, little Vera, he supplicates. He weeps. He never has wept before. Your sorrow, little child, your sufferings—they are also mine. Greater than mine."

Father Ignatius shook his head.

"Greater, Verochka. What is death to an old man like me? But you— if you only knew how delicate and weak and timid you are! Do you recall how you bruised your finger once and the blood trickled and you cried a little? My child! I know that you love me, love me intensely. Every morning you kiss my hand. Tell me, do tell me, what grief troubles your little head, and I—with these hands—shall smother your grief. They are still strong, Vera, these hands."

The hair of Father Ignatius shook.

"Tell me!"

Father Ignatius fixed his eyes on the wall, and wrung his hands.

"Tell me!"

Stillness prevailed in the room, and from afar was heard the prolonged and broken whistle of a locomotive.

Father Ignatius, gazing out of his dilated eyes, as if there had arisen suddenly before him the frightful phantom of the mutilated corpse, slowly raised himself from his knees, and with a credulous motion reached for his head with his hand, with spread and tensely stiffened fingers. Making a step toward the door, Father Ignatius whispered brokenly:

"Tell me!"

And he was answered by silence.

The next day, after an early and lonely dinner, Father Ignatius went to the graveyard, the first time since his daughter's death. It was warm, deserted and still; it seemed more like an illumined night. Following habit, Father Ignatius, with effort, straightened his spine, looked severely about him and thought that he was the same as formerly; he was conscious neither of the new, terrible weakness in his legs, nor that his long beard had become entirely white as if a hard frost had hit it. The road to the graveyard led through a long, direct street, slightly on an upward incline, and at its termination loomed the arch of the graveyard gate, resembling a dark, perpetually open mouth, edged with glistening teeth.

Vera's grave was situated in the depth of the grounds, where the sandy little pathways terminated, and Father Ignatius, for a considerable time, was obliged to blunder along the narrow footpaths, which led in a broken line between green mounds, by all forgotten and abandoned. Here and there appeared, green with age, sloping tombstones, broken railings and large, heavy stones planted in the ground, and seemingly crushing it with some cruel, ancient spite. Near one such stone was the grave of Vera. It was covered with fresh turf, turned yellow; around, however, all was in bloom. Ash embraced maple tree; and the widely spread hazel bush stretched out over the grave its bending branches with their downy, shaggy foliage. Sitting down on a neighboring grave and catching his breath, Father Ignatius looked around him, throwing a glance upon the cloudless, desert sky, where in complete immovability, hung the glowing sun disk—and here he only felt that deep, incomparable stillness which reigns in graveyards, when the wind is absent and the slumbering foliage has ceased its rustling. And anew the thought came to Father Ignatius that this was not a stillness but a silence. It extended to the very brick walls of the graveyard, crept over them and occupied the city. And it terminated only—in those gray, obstinate and reluctantly silent eyes.

Father Ignatius' shoulders shivered, and he lowered his eyes upon the grave of Vera. He gazed long upon the little tufts of grass uprooted together with the earth from some open, wind-swept field and not successful in adapting themselves to a strange soil; he could not imagine that there, under this grass, only a few feet from him, lay Vera. And this nearness seemed incomprehensible and brought confusion into the soul and a strange agitation. She, of whom Father Ignatius was accustomed to think as of one passed away forever into the dark depths of eternity, was here, close by—and it was hard to understand that she, nevertheless, was no more and never again would be. And in the mind's fancy of Father Ignatius it seemed that if he could only utter some word, which was almost upon his lips, or if he could make some sort of movement, Vera would issue forth from her grave and arise to the same height and beauty that was once hers. And not alone would she arise, but all corpses, intensely sensitive in their solemnly cold silence.

Father Ignatius removed his wide-brimmed black hat, smoothed down his disarranged hair and whispered:

"Vera!"

Father Ignatius felt ill at ease, fearing to be overheard by a stranger, and stepping on the grave he gazed around him. No one was present, and this time he repeated loudly:

"Vera!"

It was the voice of an aged man, sharp and demanding, and it was strange that a so-powerfully expressed desire should remain without answer.

"Vera!"

Loudly and insistently the voice called, and when it relapsed into silence, it seemed for a moment that somewhere from underneath came an incoherent answer. And Father Ignatius, clearing his ear of his long hair, pressed it to the rough, prickly turf.

"Vera, tell me!"

With terror, Father Ignatius felt pouring into his ear something cold as of the grave, which froze his marrow; Vera seemed to be speaking—speaking, however, with the same unbroken silence. This feeling became more racking and terrible, and when Father Ignatius forced himself finally to tear away his head, his face was pale as that of a corpse, and he fancied that the entire atmosphere trembled and palpitated from a resounding silence, and that this terrible sea was being swept by a wild hurricane. The silence strangled him; with icy waves it rolled through his head and agitated the hair; it smote against his breast, which groaned under the blows. Trembling from head to foot, casting around him sharp and sudden glances, Father

Ignatius slowly raised himself and with a prolonged and tortuous effort attempted to straighten his spine and to give proud dignity to his trembling body. He succeeded in this. With measured protractiveness, Father Ignatius shook the dirt from his knees, put on his hat, made the sign of the cross three times over the grave, and walked away with an even and firm gait, not recognizing, however, the familiar burial ground and losing his way.

"Well, here I've gone astray!" smiled Father Ignatius, halting at the branching of the footpaths.

He stood there for a moment, and, unreflecting, turned to the left, because it was impossible to stand and to wait. The silence drove him on. It arose from the green graves; it was the breath issuing from the gray, melancholy crosses; in thin, stifling currents it came from all pores of the earth, satiated with the dead. Father Ignatius increased his stride. Dizzy, he circled the same paths, jumped over graves, stumbled across railings, clutching with his hands the prickly, metallic garlands, and turning the soft material of his dress into tatters. His sole thought was to escape. He fled from one place to another, and finally broke into a dead run, seeming very tall and unusual in the flowing cassock, and his hair streaming in the wind. A corpse arisen from the grave could not have frightened a passer-by more than this wild figure of a man, running and leaping, and waving his arms, his face distorted and insane, and the open mouth breathing with a dull, hoarse sound. With one long leap, Father Ignatius landed on a little street, at one end of which appeared the small church, attached to the graveyard. At the entrance, on a low bench, dozed an old man, seemingly a distant pilgrim, and near him, assailing each other, were two quarreling old beggar women, filling the air with their oaths.

When Father Ignatius reached his home, it was already dusk, and there was light in Olga Stepanovna's chamber. Not undressing and without removing his hat, dusty and tattered, Father Ignatius approached his wife and fell on his knees.

"Mother... Olga... have pity on me!" he wept. "I shall go mad."

He dashed his head against the edge of the table and he wept with anguish, as one who was weeping for the first time. Then he raised his head, confident that a miracle would come to pass, that his wife would speak and would pity him.

"My love!"

With his entire big body he drew himself toward his wife—and met the gaze of those gray eyes. There was neither compassion in them, nor anger. It was possible his wife had forgiven him, but in her eyes there was neither pity, nor anger. They were dumb and silent.

And silent was the entire dark, deserted house.

Poland

INTRODUCTION

POLISH literature begins a thousand years ago, but until towards the middle of the last century there is very little prose fiction, and probably no single short story of outstanding merit. The history of Poland is so strikingly dramatic and her political vicissitudes so many and so varied that it is scarcely to be wondered at that the Poles failed to develop narrative fiction. One of the greatest Polish writers was Adam Mickiewicz (1798-1843), and though he wrote very little fiction he was largely instrumental in establishing a literary tradition.

With the novels of Mme. Orgaszo and Sienkiewicz Polish literature entered a new and very productive age. During the past two generations the short story has been assiduously developed by a dozen writers of exceptional talent. Prus and Szymański, Orzeszkowa, Sienkiewicz and Żeromski have utilized the form for the expression of their deepest convictions. Among the later writers who have written short stories are Reymont, Kaden-Bandrowski, and Mme. Rygier-Nalkowska.

HENRYK SIENKIEWICZ

(1846—1916)

SIENKIEWICZ was born at Wola Okrzejska in Lithuania. He studied at the University of Warsaw, and began writing at a comparatively early age. When he was thirty he went to the United States. In 1884 he published his first successful novel, *With Fire and Sword*. *Quo Vadis* came some years later. He was one of the most gifted of the Polish writers of stories, and *The Lighthouse Keeper of Aspinwall* is the best of his short tales.

The present version is reprinted from the volume *Yanko the Musician*, etc., translated by Jeremiah Curtin. Copyright, 1893, by Little, Brown & Co., of Boston, by whose permission it is used here.

THE LIGHTHOUSE KEEPER OF ASPINWALL

ON a time it happened that the lighthouse keeper in Aspinwall, not far from Panama, disappeared without a trace. Since he disappeared during a storm, it was supposed that the ill-fated man went to the very edge of the small, rocky island on which the lighthouse stood, and was swept out by a wave. This supposition seemed the more likely, as his boat was not found next day in its rocky niche. The place of lighthouse keeper had become vacant. It was necessary to fill this place at the earliest moment possible, since the lighthouse had no small significance for the local movement as well as for vessels going from New York to Panama. Mosquito Bay abounds in sandbars and banks. Among these, navigation, even in the daytime, is difficult; but at night, especially with the fogs which are so frequent on those waters warmed by the sun of the tropics, it is nearly impossible. The only guide at that time for the numerous vessels is the lighthouse.

The task of finding a new keeper fell to the United States consul living in Panama, and this task was no small one: first, because it was absolutely necessary to find a man within twelve hours; second, the man must be unusually conscientious—it was not possible, of course, to take the first comer at random; finally, there was an utter lack of candidates. Life on a tower is uncommonly difficult, and by no means enticing to people of the South, who love idleness and the freedom of vagrant life. That lighthouse keeper is almost a prisoner. He cannot leave his rocky island except on Sundays. A boat from Aspinwall brings him provisions and water once a day, and returns immediately; on the whole island, one acre in area, there is no inhabitant. The keeper lives in the lighthouse; he keeps it in order. During the day he gives signals by displaying flags of various colors to indicate changes of the barometer; in the evening he lights the lantern. This would be no great labor were it not that to reach the lantern at the summit of the tower he must pass over more than four hundred steep and very high steps; sometimes he must make this journey repeatedly during the day. In general, it is the life of a monk, and indeed more than that—the life of a hermit. It was not wonderful, therefore, that Mr. Isaac Falconbridge was in no small anxiety as to where he should find a permanent successor to the recent keeper; and it is easy to understand his joy when a successor announced himself most unexpectedly on that very day. He was a man already old, seventy years or more, but fresh, erect, with the movements and bearing of a soldier. His hair was perfectly white, his face as dark as that of a Creole; but, judging from his blue eyes, he did not belong to a people of the South. His face was somewhat downcast and sad, but honest. At the first glance he pleased Falconbridge. It remained only to examine him. Therefore the following conversation began:

"Where are you from?"

"I am a Pole."

"Where have you worked up to this time?"

"In one place and another."

"A lighthouse keeper should like to stay in one place."

"I need rest."

"Have you served? Have you testimonials of honorable government service?"

The old man drew from his bosom a piece of faded silk, resembling a strip of an old flag, unwound it, and said:

"Here are the testimonials. I received this cross in 1830. This second one is Spanish from the Carlist War; the third is the French legion; the fourth I received in Hungary. Afterward I fought in the States against the South; there they do not give crosses."

Falconbridge took the paper and began to read.

"H'm! Skavinski? Is that your name? H'm! Two flags captured in a bayonet attack. You were a gallant soldier."

"I am able to be a conscientious lighthouse keeper."

"It is necessary to ascend the tower a number of times daily. Have you sound legs?"

"I crossed the plains on foot." (The immense steppes between the East and California are called "the plains.")

"Do you know sea service?"

"I served three years on a whaler."

"You have tried various occupations."

"The only one I have not known is quiet."

"Why is that?"

The old man shrugged his shoulders. "Such is my fate."

"Still you seem to me too old for a lighthouse keeper."

"Sir," exclaimed the candidate suddenly in a voice of emotion, "I am greatly wearied, knocked about. I have passed through much, as you see. This place is one of those which I have wished for most ardently. I am old, I need rest. I need to say to myself, 'Here you will remain; this is your port.' Ah, sir, this depends now on you alone. Another time perhaps such a place will not offer itself. What luck that I was in Panama! I entreat you—as God is dear to me, I am like a ship which if it misses the harbor will be lost. If you wish to make an old man happy—I swear to you that I am honest, but—I have enough of wandering."

The blue eyes of the old man expressed such earnest entreaty that Falconbridge, who had a good, simple heart, was touched.

"Well," said he, "I take you. You are lighthouse keeper."

The old man's face gleamed with inexpressible joy.

"I thank you."

"Can you go to the tower to-day?"

"I can."

"Then good-bye. Another word—for any failure in service you will be dismissed."

"All right."

That same evening, when the sun had descended on the other side of the isthmus, and a day of sunshine was followed by a night without twilight, the new keeper was in his place evidently, for the lighthouse was casting its bright rays on the water as usual. The night was perfectly calm, silent, genuinely tropical, filled with a transparent haze, forming around the moon a great colored rainbow with soft, unbroken edges; the sea was moving only because the tide raised it. Skavinski on the balcony seemed from below like a small black point. He tried to collect his thoughts and take in his new position; but his mind was too much under pressure to move with regularity. He felt somewhat as a hunted beast feels when at last it has found refuge from pursuit on some inaccessible rock or in a cave. There had come to him, finally, an hour of quiet; the feeling of safety filled his soul with a certain unspeakable bliss. Now on that rock he can simply laugh at his previous wanderings, his misfortunes and failures. He was in truth like a ship whose masts, ropes, and sails had been broken and rent by a tempest, and cast from the clouds to the bottom of the sea—a ship on which the tempest had hurled waves and spat foam, but which still wound its way to the harbor. The pictures of that storm passed quickly through his mind as he compared it with the calm future now beginning. A part of his wonderful adventures he had related to Falconbridge; he had not mentioned, however, thousands of other incidents. It had been his misfortune that as often as he pitched his tent and fixed his fireplace to settle down permanently, some wind tore out the stakes of his tent, whirled away the fire, and bore him on toward destruction. Looking now from the balcony of the tower at the illuminated waves, he remembered everything through which he had passed. He had campaigned in the four parts of the world, and in wandering had tried almost every occupation. Labor-loving and honest, more than once had he earned money, and had always lost it in spite of every provision and the utmost caution. He had been a gold-miner in Australia, a diamond-digger in Africa, a rifleman in public service in the East Indies. He established a ranch in California—the drought ruined him; he tried trading with wild tribes in the interior of Brazil—his raft was wrecked on the Amazon; he himself alone, weaponless, and nearly naked, wandered in the forest for many weeks living on wild fruits, exposed every

moment to death from the jaws of wild beasts. He established a forg
in Helena, Arkansas, and that was burned in a great fire which con
sumed the whole town. Next he fell into the hands of Indians in th
Rocky Mountains, and only through a miracle was he saved by Ca
nadian trappers. Then he served as a sailor on a vessel running be
tween Bahia and Bordeaux, and as harpooner on a whaling-ship; bot
vessels were wrecked. He had a cigar factory in Havana, and was rob
bed by his partner while he himself was lying sick with the vomito. A
last he came to Aspinwall, and there was to be the end of his failures—
for what could reach him on that rocky island? Neither water nor fir
nor men. But from men Skavinski had not suffered much; he had me
good men oftener than bad ones.

But it seemed to him that all the four elements were persecuting him
Those who knew him said that he had no luck, and with that they ex
plained everything. He himself became somewhat of a monomaniac
He believed that some mighty and vengeful hand was pursuing hin
everywhere, on all lands and waters. He did not like, however, to speal
of this; only at times, when someone asked him whose hand that coul
be, he pointed mysteriously to the Polar Star, and said, "It comes fron
that place." In reality his failures were so continuous that they wer
wonderful, and might easily drive a nail into the head, especially of th
man who had experienced them. But Skavinski had the patience of an
Indian, and that great calm power of resistance which comes fron
truth of heart. In his time he had received in Hungary a number o
bayonet-thrusts because he would not grasp at a stirrup which wa
shown as means of salvation to him, and cry for quarter. In like man
ner he did not bend to misfortune. He crept up against the mountain a
industriously as an ant. Pushed down a hundred times, he began hi
journey calmly for the hundred and first time. He was in his way
most peculiar original. This old soldier, tempered, God knows in how
many fires, hardened in suffering, hammered and forged, had th
heart of a child. In the time of the epidemic in Cuba, the vomito at
tacked him because he had given to the sick all his quinine, of which
he had a considerable supply, and left not a grain to himself.

There had been in him also this wonderful quality—that after s
many disappointments he was ever full of confidence, and did not los
hope that all would be well yet. In winter he grew lively, and predicte
great events. He waited for these events with impatience, and live
with the thought of them whole summers. But the winters passed one afte
another, and Skavinski lived only to this—that they whitened his head
At last he grew old, began to lose energy; his endurance was becomin
more and more like resignation, his former calmness was tending to
ward supersensitiveness, and that tempered soldier was degeneratin
into a man ready to shed tears for any cause. Besides this, from time t

ime he was weighed down by a terrible homesickness which was roused
by any circumstance—the sight of swallows, gray birds like sparrows,
now on the mountains, or melancholy music like that heard on a time.
Finally, there was one idea which mastered him—the idea of rest. It
mastered the old man thoroughly, and swallowed all other desires and
hopes. This ceaseless wanderer could not imagine anything more to be
longed for, anything more precious, than a quiet corner in which to
rest, and wait in silence for the end. Perhaps specially because some
whim of fate had so hurried him over all seas and lands that he could
hardly catch his breath, did he imagine that the highest human happiness was simply not to wander. It is true that such modest happiness was
his due; but he was so accustomed to disappointments that he thought
of rest as people in general think of something which is beyond reach.
He did not dare to hope for it. Meanwhile, unexpectedly, in the course
of twelve hours he had gained a position which was as if chosen for him
out of all the world. We are not to wonder, then, that when he lighted
his lantern in the evening he became as it were dazed—that he asked
himself if that was reality, and he did not dare to answer that it was.
But at the same time reality convinced him with incontrovertible
proofs; hence hours one after another passed while he was on the balcony. He gazed, and convinced himself. It might seem that he was
looking at the sea for the first time in his life. The lens of the lantern
cast into the darkness an enormous triangle of light, beyond which the
eye of the old man was lost in the black distance completely, in the
distance mysterious and awful. But that distance seemed to run toward the light. The long waves following one another rolled out from
the darkness, and went bellowing toward the base of the island; and
then their foaming backs were visible, shining rose-colored in the light
of the lantern. The incoming tide swelled more and more, and covered
the sandy bars. The mysterious speech of the ocean came with a full-
ness more powerful and louder, at one time like the thunder of cannon,
at another like the roar of great forests, at another like the distant dull
sound of the voices of people. At moments it was quiet; then to the ears
of the old man came some great sigh, then a kind of sobbing, and again
threatening outbursts. At last the wind bore away the haze, but
brought black, broken clouds, which hid the moon. From the west it
began to blow more and more; the waves sprang with rage against the
rock of the lighthouse, licking with foam the foundation walls. In the
distance a storm was beginning to bellow. On the dark, disturbed expanse certain green lanterns gleamed from the masts of ships. These
green points rose high and then sank; now they swayed to the right, and
now to the left. Skavinski descended to his room. The storm began to
howl. Outside, people on those ships were struggling with night, with
darkness, with waves; but inside the tower it was calm and still. Even the

sounds of the storm hardly came through the thick walls, and only the measured tick-tack of the clock lulled the wearied old man to his slumber.

Hours, days, and weeks began to pass. Sailors assert that sometimes when the sea is greatly roused, something from out the midst of night and darkness calls them by name. If the infinity of the sea may call out thus, perhaps when a man is growing old, calls come to him, too, from another infinity still darker and more deeply mysterious; and the more he is wearied by life the dearer are those calls to him. But to hear them quiet is needed. Besides old age loves to put itself aside, as if with a foreboding of the grave. The lighthouse had become for Skavinski such a half grave. Nothing is more monotonous than life on a beacon-tower. If young people consent to take up this service they leave it after a time. Lighthouse keepers are generally men not young, gloomy, and confined to themselves. If by chance one of them leaves his lighthouse and goes among men, he walks in the midst of them like a person roused from deep slumber. On the tower there is a lack of minute impressions which in ordinary life teach men to adapt themselves to everything. All that a lighthouse keeper comes in contact with is gigantic and devoid of definitely outlined forms. The sky is one whole, the water another; and between those two infinities the soul of man is in loneliness. That is a life in which thought is continual meditation, and out of that meditation nothing rouses the keeper, not even his work. Day is like day as two beads in a rosary, unless changes of weather form the only variety. But Skavinski felt more happiness than ever in life before. He rose with the dawn, took his breakfast, polished the lens, and then sitting on the balcony gazed into the distance of the water; and his eyes were never sated with the pictures which he saw before him. On the enormous turquoise ground of the ocean were to be seen generally flocks of swollen sails gleaming in the rays of the sun so brightly that the eyes were blinking before the excess of light. Sometimes the ships, favored by the so-called trade winds, went in an extended line one after another, like a chain of sea-mews or albatrosses. The red casks indicating the channel swayed on the light wave with gentle movement. Among the sails appeared every afternoon gigantic grayish feather-like plumes of smoke. That was a steamer from New York which brought passengers and goods to Aspinwall, drawing behind it a frothy path of foam. On the other side of the balcony Skavinski saw, as if on his palm, Aspinwall and its busy harbor, and in it a forest of masts, boats, and craft; a little farther, white houses and the towers of the town. From the height of his tower the small houses were like the nest of sea-mews, the boats were like beetles, and the people moved around like small points on the white stone boulevard. From early morning a light eastern breeze brought a confused hum of human life, above which predominated the whistle of steamers. In the afternoon six o'clock came; the movements in the harbor began to cease; the mews hid themselves in the rents of the cliffs; the waves grew feeble and became in some sort lazy; and then on the land, on the sea, and on the tower came a time of stillness unbroken by anything. The yellow sands from which the waves had fallen back glittered like golden stripes on the width of the waters; the body of the tower was outlined definitely in blue. Floods of sunbeams were poured from the sky on the water and the sands and the cliff. At that time a certain lassitude full of sweetness seized the old man. He felt that the rest which he was enjoying was excellent; and when he thought that it would be continuous nothing was lacking to him.

Skavinski was intoxicated with his own happiness; and since a man adapts himself easily to improved conditions, he gained faith and confidence by degrees; for he thought that if men built houses for invalids, why should not God gather up at last His own invalids? Time passed, and confirmed him in this conviction. The old man grew accustomed to his tower, to the lantern, to the rock, to the sand-bars, to solitude. He grew accustomed also to the sea-mews which hatched in the crevices of the rock, and in the evening held meetings on the roof of the lighthouse. Skavinski threw to them generally the remnants of his food; and soon they grew tame, and afterward, when he fed them, a real storm of white wings encircled him, and the old man went among the birds like a shepherd among sheep. When the tide ebbed he went to the low sandbanks, on which he collected savory periwinkles and beautiful pearl shells of the nautilus, which receding waves had left on the sand. In the night by the moonlight and the tower he went to catch fish, which frequented the windings of the cliff in myriads. At last he was in love with his rocks and his treeless little island, grown over only with small thick plants exuding sticky resin. The distant views repaid him for the poverty of the island, however. During afternoon hours, when the air became very clear he could see the whole isthmus covered with the richest vegetation. It seemed to Skavinski at such times that he saw one gigantic garden—bunches of cocoa, and enormous musa, combined as it were in luxurious tufted bouquets, right there behind the houses of Aspinwall. Farther on, between Aspinwall and Panama, was a great forest over which every morning and evening hung a reddish haze of exhalations—a real tropical forest with its feet in stagnant water, interlaced with lianas and filled with the sound of one sea of gigantic orchids, palms, milk-trees, iron-trees, gum-trees.

Through his field-glass the old man could see not only trees and the broad leaves of bananas, but even legions of monkeys and great marabous and flocks of parrots, rising at times like a rainbow cloud over the forest. Skavinski knew such forests well, for after being wrecked on the Amazon he had wandered whole weeks among similar arches and thickets. He had seen how many dangers and deaths lie concealed under those wonderful and smiling exteriors. During the nights which he had spent in them he heard close at hand the sepulchral voices of howling monkeys, and the roaring of the jaguars; he saw gigantic serpents coiled like lianas on trees; he knew those slumbering forest lakes full of torpedo-fish and swarming with crocodiles; he knew under what a yoke man lives in those unexplored wildernesses in which are single leaves that exceed a man's size ten times—wildernesses swarming with blood-drinking mosquitoes, tree-leeches, and gigantic poisonous spiders. He had experienced that forest life himself, had witnessed it, had passed through it; therefore it gave him the greater enjoyment to look from his height and gaze on those *matos*, admire their beauty, and be guarded from their treacherousness. His tower preserved him from every evil. He left it only for a few hours on Sunday. He put on then his blue keeper's coat with silver buttons, and hung his crosses on his breast. His milk-white head was raised with a certain pride when he heard at the door, while entering the church, the Creoles say among themselves, "We have an honorable lighthouse keeper and not a heretic, though he is a Yankee." But he returned straightway after Mass to his island, and returned happy, for he had still no faith in the mainland. On Sunday also he read the Spanish newspaper which he bought in the town, or the *New York Herald*, which he borrowed from Falconbridge; and he sought in it European news eagerly. The poor old heart on that lighthouse tower, and in another hemisphere, was beating yet for its birthplace. At times too, when the boat brought his daily supplies and water to the island, he went down from the tower to talk with Johnson, the guard. But after a while he seemed to grow shy. He ceased to go to the town, to read the papers and to go down to talk politics with Johnson. Whole weeks passed in this way, so that no one saw him and he saw no one. The only signs that the old man was living were the disappearance of the provisions left on shore, and the light of the lantern kindled every evening with the same regularity with which the sun rose in the morning from the waters of those regions. Evidently, the old man had become indifferent to the world. Homesickness was not the cause, but just this—that even homesickness had passed into resignation. The whole world began now and ended for Skavinski on his island. He had grown accustomed to the thought that he would not leave the tower till his death, and he simply forgot that there was anything else besides it. Moreover, he had become a mystic; his mild blue eyes began to stare like the eyes of a child, and were as if fixed on something at a distance. In presence of a surrounding uncommonly simple and great, the old man was losing the feeling of personality; he was ceasing to exist as an individual, was becoming merged more and more in that which inclosed him. He did not understand anything beyond his environment; he felt only unconsciously. At last it seems to him that the heavens, the water, his rock, the tower, the golden sand-banks, and the swollen sails, the sea-mews, the ebb and flow of the tide—all form a mighty unity, one enormous mysterious' soul; that he is sinking in that mystery, and feels that soul which lives and lulls itself. He sinks and is rocked, forgets himself; and in that narrowing of his own individual existence, in that half-waking, half-sleeping, he has discovered a rest so great that it nearly resembles half-death.

But the awakening came.

On a certain day, when the boat brought water and a supply of provisions, Skavinski came down an hour later from the tower, and saw that besides the usual cargo there was an additional package. On the outside of this package were postage stamps of the United States, and the address: "Skavinski, Esq." written on coarse canvas.

The old man, with aroused curiosity, cut the canvas, and saw books; he took one in his hand, looked at it, and put it back; thereupon his hands began to tremble greatly. He covered his eyes as if he did not believe them; it seemed to him as if he were dreaming. The book was Polish—what did that mean? Who could have sent the book? Clearly, it did not occur to him at the first moment that in the beginning of his lighthouse career he had read in the *Herald*, borrowed from the consul, of the formation of a Polish society in New York, and had sent at once to that society half his month's salary, for which he had, moreover, no use on the tower. The society had sent him the books with thanks. The books came in the natural way; but at the first moment the old man could not seize those thoughts. Polish books in Aspinwall, on his tower, amid his solitude—that was for him something uncommon, a certain breath from past times, a kind of miracle. Now it seemed to him, as to those sailors in the night, that something was calling him by name with a voice greatly beloved and nearly forgotten. He sat for a while with closed eyes, and was almost certain that, when he opened them, the dream would be gone.

The package, cut open, lay before him, shone upon clearly by the afternoon sun, and on it was an open book. When the old man stretched his hand toward it again, he heard in the stillness the beating of his own heart. He looked; it was poetry. On the outside stood printed in great letters the title, underneath the name of the author. The name was not strange to Skavinski; he saw that it belonged to the great poet,* whose productions he had read in 1830 in Paris. Afterward, when campaigning in Algiers and Spain, he had heard from his countrymen of the growing fame of the great seer; but he was so ac-

* Mickiewicz (pronounced Mitskyevich), the greatest poet of Poland.

customed to the musket at that time that he took no book in 'hand. In 1849 he went to America, and in the adventurous life which he led he hardly ever met a Pole, and never a Polish book. With the greater eagerness, therefore, and with a livelier beating of the heart, did he turn to the title-page. It seemed to him then that on his lonely rock some solemnity is about to take place. Indeed it was a moment of great calm and silence. The clocks of Aspinwall were striking five in the afternoon. Not a cloud darkened the clear sky; only a few sea-mews were sailing through the air. The ocean was as if cradled to sleep. The waves on the shore stammered quietly, spreading softly on the sand. In the distance the white houses of Aspinwall, and the wonderful groups of palm, were smiling. In truth, there was something there solemn, calm, and full of dignity. Suddenly, in the midst of that calm of Nature, was heard the trembling voice of the old man, who read aloud as if to understand himself better:

"Thou art like health, O my birth-land Litva!*
How much we should prize thee he only can know who has lost thee.
Thy beauty in perfect adornment this day
I see and describe, because I am yearning for thee."

His voice failed Skavinski. The letters began to dance before his eyes: something broke in his breast, and went like a wave from his heart higher and higher, choking his voice and pressing his throat. A moment more he controlled himself, and read further:

"O Holy Lady, who guardest bright Chenstohova,
Who shinest in Ostrobrama and preservest
The castle town Novgrodek with its trusty people,
As Thou didst give me back to health in childhood,
When by my weeping mother placed beneath Thy care
I raised my lifeless eyelids upward,
And straightway walked unto Thy holy threshold,
To thank God for the life restored me,—
So by a wonder now restore us to the bosom of our birthplace."

The swollen wave broke through the restraint of his will. The old man sobbed, and threw himself on the ground; his milk-white hair was mingled with the sand of the sea. Forty years had passed since he had seen his country, and God knows how many since he heard his native speech; and now that speech had come to him itself—it had sailed to him over the ocean, and found him in solitude on another hemisphere —it so loved, so dear, so beautiful! In the sobbing which shook him there was no pain—only a suddenly aroused immense love, in the pres-

* Lithuania.

ence of which other things are as nothing. With that great weeping he had simply implored forgiveness of that beloved one, set aside because he had grown so old, had become so accustomed to his solitary rock, and had so forgotten it that in him even longing had begun to disappear. But now it returned as if by a miracle; therefore the heart leaped in him.

Moments vanished one after another; he lay there continually. The mews flew over the lighthouse, crying as if alarmed for their old friend. The hour in which he fed them with the remnants of his food had come; therefore, some of them flew down from the lighthouse to him; then more and more came, and began to pick and shake their wings over his head. The sound of the wings roused him. He had wept his fill, and had now a certain calm and brightness; but his eyes were as if inspired. He gave unwittingly all his provisions to the birds, which rushed at him with an uproar, and he himself took the book again. The sun had gone already behind the gardens and the forest of Panama, and was going slowly beyond the isthmus to the other ocean; but the Atlantic was full of light yet; in the open air there was still perfect vision; therefore, he read further:

"Now bear my longing soul to those forest slopes, to those green meadows."

At last the dusk obliterates the letters on the white paper—the dusk short as a twinkle. The old man rested his head on the rock, and closed his eyes. Then "She who defends bright Chenstohova" took his soul and transported it to "those fields colored by various grain." On the sky were burning yet those long stripes, red and golden, and on those brightnesses he was flying to beloved regions. The pine-woods were sounding in his ears; the streams of his native place were murmuring. He saw everything as it was; everything asked him, "Dost remember?" He remembers! he sees broad fields; between the fields, woods and villages. It is night now. At this hour his lantern usually illuminates the darkness of the sea; but now he is in his native village. His old head has dropped on his breast, and he is dreaming. Pictures are passing before his eyes quickly, and a little disorderly. He does not see the house in which he was born, for war had destroyed it; he does not see his father and mother, for they died when he was a child; but still the village is as if he had left it yesterday—the line of cottages with lights in the windows, the mound, the mill, the two ponds opposite each other, and thundering all night with a chorus of frogs. Once he had been on guard in that village all night; now that past stood before him at once in a series of views. He is an Uhlan again, and he stands there on guard; at a distance is the public-house; he looks with swimming eyes. There is thundering and singing and shouting amid the silence of the night, with voices of fiddles and bass-viols "U-ha! U-ha!" Then the Uhlans knock out fire with their horseshoes, and it is wearisome for him there on his horse. The hours drag on slowly; at last the lights are quenched; now as far as the eye reaches there is mist, and mist impenetrable; now the fog rises, evidently from the fields, and embraces the whole world with a whitish cloud. You would say, a complete ocean. But that is fields; soon the land-rail will be heard in the darkness, and the bitterns will call from the reeds. The night is calm and cool—in truth, a Polish night! In the distance the pine-wood is sounding without wind, like the roll of the sea. Soon dawn will whiten the east. In fact, the cocks are beginning to crow behind the hedges. One answers to another from cottage to cottage; the storks are screaming somewhere on high. The Uhlan feels well and bright. Someone had spoken of a battle to-morrow. Hei! that will go on, like all the others, with shouting, with fluttering of flaglets. The young blood is playing like a trumpet, though the night cools it. But it is dawning. Already night is growing pale; out of the shadows come forests, the thicket, a row of cottages, the mill, the poplars. The well is squeaking like a metal banner on a tower. What a beloved land, beautiful in the rosy gleams of the morning! Oh, the one land, the one land!

Quiet! the watchful picket hears that someone is approaching. Of course, they are coming to relieve the guard.

Suddenly some voice is heard above Skavinski:

"Here, old man! Get up! What's the matter?"

The old man opens his eyes, and looks with wonder at the person standing before him. The remnants of the dream-visions struggle in his head with reality. At last the visions pale and vanish. Before him stands Johnson, the harbor guide.

"What's this?" asked Johnson; "are you sick?"

"No."

"You didn't light the lantern. You must leave your place. A vessel from St. Geromo was wrecked on the bar. It is lucky that no one was drowned, or you would go to trial. Get into the boat with me; you'll hear the rest at the Consulate."

The old man grew pale; in fact he had not lighted the lantern that night.

A few days later, Skavinski was seen on the deck of a steamer, which was going from Aspinwall to New York. The poor man had lost his place. There opened before him new roads of wandering; the wind had torn that leaf away again to whirl it over lands and seas, to sport with it till satisfied. The old man had failed greatly during those few days, and was bent over; only his eyes were gleaming. On his new road of life he held at his breast his book, which from time to time he pressed with his hand as if in fear that too might go from him.

BOLESLAV PRUS

(Alexander Glowacki)

(1847–1912)

ALEXANDER GLOWACKI, known and loved among his people under the pen-name Prus, was born near Lublin in Poland, in 1847. His first novel was published in 1872, and from that time until his death in 1912, his literary activities were uninterrupted. He was a very prolific writer. "He believed in humanity, in civilization, in the creative power of good and light. He demanded national self-education... he yearned for the training of the will of the people, to whom he proclaimed that each man must find in himself the source of strength and energy." Prus's short stories are especially characteristic of the man's nature and art.

This story is translated—for the first time into English—by Sarka B. Hrbkova, by whose permission it is here printed.

THE HUMAN TELEGRAPH

ON her visit to the Orphanage recently the Countess X——witnessed an extraordinary scene. She beheld four boys wrangling over a torn book and pounding each other promiscuously with right sturdy and effective fists.

"Why, children, children—what does this mean—you are fighting!" cried the lady, greatly shocked. "For that—not one of you will get a taste of gingerbread and, besides, you'll have to go and kneel in the corner."

"He took Robinson Crusoe away from me," one boy ventured in extenuation of his offense.

"That's a lie! He took it himself!" burst out another.

"See how you lie!" shrieked a third boy at him. "Why you yourself took Robinson away from me!"

The Sister in charge explained to the Countess that in spite of the most watchful supervision similar scenes occurred often, because the children loved to read and the Orphanage lacked books.

A spark of some strange sensation lighted up the heart of the Countess. But as thinking wearied her, she strove to forget it. Not until some days later, when she was a guest at the home of the Chief Counselor where one had to discuss religious and philanthropic subjects, did it occur to her to mention it. Then she related at length the incident at the Orphanage and the explanation given by the Sister in charge.

The counselor, listening attentively, also experienced an odd sensation, and being more adept in thinking, he suggested that it would be a good idea to send some books to the orphans. In fact, he recalled that in his bookcases or in his trunk he had a whole collection of volumes going to waste which in bygone years he had purchased for his own children. But then—it was too laborious a task for him to go rummaging around to gather up the books.

That evening the counselor was a caller at the home of Mr. Z——, whose entire life was passed in performing trifling services to such representatives of humanity as comprise Classes VII to III of the official hierarchy. In his desire to please, the counselor related to Mr. Z—— what the Countess had witnessed at the Orphanage and what she had heard from the representative of the religious sisterhood. He added his own contribution that—ah—yes—that—really, books *ought* to be provided for the orphans.

"Nothing is simpler!" cried Mr. Z——. "To-morrow I am going to the office of the *Courier* and I'll see to it that an announcement of the book needs of the Orphanage is published."

The next day Mr. Z——very excitedly rushed into the editorial rooms of the *Courier*, imploring in the name of all the saints that it print an appeal to the public to donate books to the orphans.

He arrived at an opportune moment, for the paper needed matter for a few sensation-stirring lines. The reporter sat down at once and prepared an article headed: "A handful of children—under public care—suffering for lack of books.—The little tots are full of yearning.—Remember their famished souls!"

Then, whistling in satisfaction, he left for dinner.

A few days later on a Sunday, arriving with my friend, the physics professor, I encountered before the locked door of the editorial office a shabbily dressed man with hands as soiled as a chimney-sweep's and beside him a pale, thin little girl, illy clad, carrying a bundle of old books.

"What do you wish, sir?"

The sooty man raised his cap and answered timidly: "We have brought a few books, sir, for those 'famished' children that you wrote about."

The emaciated little girl curtsied and flushed as much as incipient anæmia permitted her to.

I took the books from her arms and put them in charge of the office-boy.

"What is your name, sir?" I asked.

"But, sir, what do you wish it for?" he responded, in embarrassment.

"Why, we must, of course, print the name of the donor of the books."

"Oh, that isn't necessary, please, sir. I am only a poor man working in the hat-factory. It isn't necessary."

And he went away with his thin little daughter.

Maybe it was because the professor of physics stood beside me that the thought of telegraphing by a new system occurred to me. The main station was the Orphanage, the receiving station the workman in the hat-factory. When the first gave the signal, "Attention," the second responded immediately. When one demanded, the other supplied. The rest of us were the telegraph poles.

STEFAN ŻEROMSKI

(1864–1925)

Żeromski is an intensely dynamic writer. Not so popular as his older contemporary Prus, he excels in the psychological analysis of his characters. In the story that follows, we feel the influence of the late Nineteenth Century Russian novelists. Żeromski began by writing stories of modern life, then produced a series of historical novels, and finally returned to his first manner. His short stories are sombre studies of character.

The present version, translated by Else C. M. Benecke, is reprinted from *Polish Tales*, Oxford University Press, by permission of the publisher.

FOREBODINGS

TWO SKETCHES

I HAD spent an hour at the railway station, waiting for the train to come in. I had stared indifferently at several ladies in turn who were yawning in the corners of the waiting-room. Then I had tried the effect of making eyes at a fair young girl with a small white nose, rosy cheeks, and eyes like forget-me-nots; she had stuck out her tongue (red as a field-poppy) at me, and I was now at a loss to know what to do next to kill time.

Fortunately for me two young students entered the waiting-room. They looked dirty from head to foot, mud-bespattered, untidy, and exhausted with traveling. One of them, a fair boy with a charming profile, seemed absent-minded or depressed. He sat down in a corner, took off his cap, and hid his face in his hands. His companion bought his ticket for him, sat down beside him, and grasped his hand from time to time.

"Why should you despair? All may yet be well. Listen, Anton."

"No, it's no good, he is dying, I know it . . . I know . . . perhaps he is dead already."

"Don't believe it! Has your father ever had this kind of attack before?"

"He has; he has suffered from his heart for three years. He used to drink at times. Think of it, there are eight of us, some are young children, and my mother is delicate. In another six months his pension would have been due. Terribly hard luck!"

"You are meeting trouble half-way, Anton."

The bell sounded, and the waiting-room became a scene of confusion. People seized their luggage and trampled on each other's toes; the porter who stood at the entrance-door was stormed with questions. There was bustle and noise everywhere. I entered the third-class carriage in which the fair-haired student was sitting. His friend had put him into it, settling him in the corner-seat beside the window, as if he were an invalid, and urging him to take comfort. It did not come easy to him, the words seemed to stick in his throat. The fair-haired boy's face twitched convulsively, and his eyelids closed over his moist eyes.

"Anton, my dear fellow," the other said, "well, you understand what I mean; God knows. You may be sure . . . confound it all!"

The second bell sounded, and then the third. The sympathizing friend stepped out of the carriage, and, as the train started, he waved an odd kind of farewell greeting, as if he were threatening him with his fists.

In the carriage were a number of poor people, Jews, women with enormously wide cloaks, who had elbowed their way to their seats, and sat chattering or smoking.

The student stood up and looked out of the window without seeing. Lines of sparks like living fire passed by the grimy window-pane, and balls of vapor and smoke, resembling large tufts of wool, were dashed to pieces and hurried to the ground by the wind. The smoke curled round the small shrubs growing close to the ground, moistened by the rain in the valley. The dusk of the autumn day spread a dim light over the landscape, and produced an effect of indescribable melancholy. Poor boy! Poor boy!

The loneliness of boundless sorrow was expressed in his weary look as he gazed out of the window. I knew that the pivot on which all his emotions turned was the anxiety of uncertainty, and that beyond the bounds of conscious thought an unknown loom was weaving for him a shadowy thread of hope. He saw, he heard nothing, while his vacant eyes followed the balls of smoke. As the train traveled along, I knew that he was miserable, tired out, that he would have liked to cry quietly. The thread of hope wound itself round his heart: Who could tell? perhaps his father was recovering, perhaps all would be well.

Suddenly (I knew it would come), the blood rushed from his face, his lips went pale and tightened; he was gazing into the far distance with wide-open eyes. It was as if a threatening hand, piercing the grief, loneliness and dread that weighed on him, was pointing at him, as if the wind were rousing him with the cry: "Beware!" His thread of hope was strained to breaking-point, and the naked truth, which he had not quite faced till that minute, struck him through the heart like a sword.

Had I approached him at that instant, and told him I was an omniscient spirit and knew his village well, and that his father was not lying dead, he would have fallen at my feet and believed, and I should have done him an infinite kindness.

But I did not speak to him, and I did not take his hand. All I wished to do was merely to watch him with the interest and insatiable curiosity which the human heart ever arouses in me.

"Let my fate go whither it listeth."
(Œdipus Tyrannus)

In the darkest corner of a ward, in the bed marked number twenty-four, a farm laborer of about thirty years of age had been lying for several months. A black wooden tablet, bearing the words "Caries tuberculosa," hung at the head of the bed, and shook at each movement of the patient. The poor fellow's leg had had to be amputated above the knee, the result of a tubercular decay of the bone. He was a peasant, a potato-grower, and his forefathers had grown potatoes before him. He was now on his own, after having been in two situations; had been married for three years and had a baby son with a tuft of flaxen hair. Then suddenly, from no cause that he could tell, his knee had pained him, and small ulcers had formed. He had afforded himself a carriage to the town, and there he had been handed over to the hospital at the expense of the parish.

He remembered distinctly how on that autumn afternoon he had driven in the splendid, cushioned carriage with his young wife, how they had both wept with fright and grief, and when they had finished crying had eaten hard-boiled eggs: but what had happened after that had all become blurred—indescribably misty. Yet only partially so.

Of the days in the hospital with their routine and monotony, creating an incomprehensible break in his life, his memory retained nothing; but the unchanging grief, weighing like a slab of stone on a grave, was ever present in his soul with inexorable and brutal force during these many months. He only half recalled the strange wonders that had been worked on him: bathing, feeding, probing into the wound, and later on the operation. He had been carried into a room full of gentlemen wearing aprons spotted with blood; he was conscious also of the mysterious, intrepid courage which, like a merciful hand, had supported him from that hour.

After having gazed at the awe-inspiring phenomena which surrounded him in the semicircle of the hospital theater, he had slept during the operation. His simple heart had not worked out the lesson which sleep, the greatest mistress on earth, teaches. After the operation everything had been veiled by mortal lassitude. This had continued, but in the afternoon and at night they had mixed something heavy, like a stone ball, into his drinking-cup, and waves of warmth had flowed to the toes of his healthy foot from the cup. Thoughts chased one another swiftly, like tiny quicksilver balls through some corner of his brain, and while he lay bathed in perspiration, and his eyelids closed of their own accord, not in sleep but in unconsciousness, he had been pursued by strange, half-waking visions.

Everything real seemed to disappear; only dimly lighted, vacant space remained, pervaded by the smell of chloroform. He seemed to be in the interior of a huge cone, stretching along the ground like a tunnel. Far away in the distance, where it narrowed towards the opening, there was a sparkling white spot; if he could get there, he might escape. He seemed to be traveling day and night towards that chink along unending spiral lines running within the surface of the tunnel; he traveled under compulsion and with great effort, slowly, like a snail, although within him something leaped up like a rabbit caught in a snare, or as if wings were fluttering in his soul. He knew what was beyond that chink. Only a few steps would lead him to the ridge under the wood . . . to his own four strips of potato-field! And whenever he roused himself mechanically from his apathy he had a vision of the potato-harvest. The transparent autumn haze in the fields was bringing objects that were far off into relief, and making them appear perfectly distinct. He saw himself together with his young wife, digging beautiful potatoes, large as their fists.

On the hillock, amid the stubble, the herdsmen were assembled in groups, their wallets slung round them; they were crouching on their heels, had collected dry juniper and lighted a fire; with bits of sticks they were scraping out the baked potatoes from the ashes. The rising smoke scented the air fragrantly with juniper.

At times, when he was better and more himself, when the fever tormented him less, he sank into the state of timidity and apprehension known only to those harassed almost beyond human endurance and to the dying. Fear oppressed him till his whole being shrank into something less than the smallest grain; he was hurled by fearful sounds and overawing obsessions into a bottomless abyss.

At last the wound on his foot began to heal, and the fever to abate. His mind returned from that other world to the familiar one, and to reflecting on what was taking place before his eyes. But the nature of these reflections had changed. Formerly he had felt self-pity arising from terror; now it was the wild hatred of the wounded man, his over-powering desire for revenge; his rage turned as fiercely even upon the unfortunate ones lying beside him as upon those who had maimed him. But another idea had taken even more powerfully possession of his mind; his thoughts darted forward like a pack of hounds on the trail, in frantic pursuit of the power which had thus passed sentence on him.

This condition of lonely self-torment lasted a long while, and increased his exasperation.

And then, one day, he noticed that his healthy foot was growing stiff and the ankle swelling. When the head-surgeon came on his daily rounds, the patient confided his fear to him. The doctor examined the emaciated limb, unobserved lanced the abscess, perceived that the probe reached to the bone, rubbed his hands together and looked into the peasant's face with a sad, doubtful look.

"This is a bad job, my good fellow. It may mean the other foot; was that what you were thinking of? And you are a bad subject. But we will do it for you here; you will be better off than in your cottage, we will give you plenty to eat." And he passed on, accompanied by his assistant. At the door he turned back, bent over the sick man, and furtively, so that no one should see, passed his hand kindly over his head.

The peasant's mind became a blank; it was as if some one had unawares dealt him a blow in the dark with a club. He closed his eyes and lay still for a long time . . . until an unknown feeling of calm came over him.

There is an enchanted, hidden spot in the human soul, fastened with seven locks, which no one and nothing but that picklock, bitter adversity, can open.

Through the lips of the self-blinded Œdipus, Sophocles makes mention of this secret place. Within it are hidden marvelous joy, sweet necessity, the highest wisdom.

As the poor fellow lay silently on his bed, the special conception that arose in his mind was that of Christ walking on the waves of the raging sea, quelling the storm.

Henceforward through long nights and wretched days he was looking at everything from an immeasurable distance, from a safe place, where all was calm and wholly well, whence everything seemed small, slightly ludicrous and foolish, and yet lovable.

"And may the Lord Jesus . . . may He give His peace to all people," he whispered to himself. "Never mind, this will do as well for me!"

————————————

Yiddish

INTRODUCTION

THE Yiddish, or Judæo-German, dialect was employed for general purposes some centuries before the beginning of what is known as Yiddish Literature. It is not until towards the end of the last century that a genuine Yiddish literature can be said to have existed. It came into being in Russia and Poland, and though, in Isaac Goldberg's words, "it has wandered from nation to nation seeking a home," most of the important living writers are now resident in the United States.

The Yiddish writers have developed a striking type of story, based to a certain extent upon modern Russian models, but at the same time rooted in the traditions of Jewish life. During the past few years Yiddish writers have produced many short stories of high merit.

The impulse that produced the modern Yiddish short story was due largely to Solomon Jacob Abromovitch and Isaac Loeb Peretz. A large number of writers followed in their footsteps, and it is from among them that the later tales here included have been selected.

Whatever may be the future of Yiddish as a literary language, it is certain that the movement of the past fifty years has produced many masterpieces.

The best of the Yiddish writers are interested largely in the ideas and aspirations of their own people, whether in Europe or America. They have set consciously to work to interpret Jewish life to the Jews themselves.

ISAAC LOEB PERETZ

(1851–1915)

BORN in Poland in 1851, Peretz is, according to Isaac Goldberg, "the greatest name in Yiddish literature." While his first work was written in Hebrew, he ultimately adopted Yiddish, the language of the masses which he wished to reach. He was one of the most highly gifted short story writers, and has exercised an incalculable influence over the Yiddish writers who followed him.

A Woman's Wrath, though it is technically Russian, is essentially Jewish in character.

This story is reprinted from the volume, *Yiddish Tales*, translated by Helena Frank, copyright, 1912, by The Jewish Publication Society of America, by whose permission it is here used.

A WOMAN'S WRATH

THE small room is dingy as the poverty that clings to its walls. There is a hook fastened to the crumbling ceiling, relic of a departed hanging lamp. The old, peeling stove is girded about with a coarse sack, and leans sideways toward its gloomy neighbor, the black, empty fireplace, in which stands an inverted cooking pot with a chipped rim. Beside it lies a broken spoon, which met its fate in unequal contest with the scrapings of cold, stale porridge.

The room is choked with furniture; there is a four-post bed with torn curtains. The pillows visible through their holes have no covers.

There is a cradle, with the large, yellow head of a sleeping child; a chest with metal fittings and an open padlock—nothing very precious left in there, evidently; further, a table and three chairs (originally painted red), a cupboard, now somewhat damaged. Add to these a pail of clean water and one of dirty water, an oven rake with a shovel, and you will understand that a pin could hardly drop onto the floor.

And yet the room contains *him* and *her* beside.

She, a middle-aged Jewess, sits on the chest that fills the space between the bed and the cradle.

To her right is the one grimy little window, to her left, the table. She is knitting a sock, rocking the cradle with her foot, and listening to *him* reading the Talmud at the table, with a tearful, Wallachian, singing intonation, and swaying to and fro with a series of nervous jerks. Some of the words he swallows, others he draws out; now he snaps at a word, and now he skips it; some he accentuates and dwells on lovingly, others he rattles out with indifference, like dried peas out of a bag. And never quiet for a moment. First he draws from his pocket a once red and whole handkerchief, and wipes his nose and brow, then he lets it fall into his lap, and begins twisting his earlocks or pulling at his thin, pointed, faintly grizzled beard. Again, he lays a pulled-out hair from the same between the leaves of his book, and slaps his knees. His fingers coming into contact with the handkerchief, they seize it, and throw a corner in between his teeth; he bites it, lays one foot across the other, and continually shuffles with both feet.

All the while his pale forehead wrinkles, now in a perpendicular, now in a horizontal, direction, when the long eyebrows are nearly lost below the folds of skin. At times, apparently, he has a sting in the chest, for he beats his left side as though he were saying the Al-Chets. Suddenly he leans his head to the left, presses a finger against his left nostril, and emits an artificial sneeze, leans his head to the right, and the proceeding is repeated. In between he takes a pinch of snuff, pulls himself together, his voice rings louder, the chair creaks, the table wobbles.

The child does not wake; the sounds are too familiar to disturb it.

And she, the wife, shriveled and shrunk before her time, sits and drinks in delight. She never takes her eye off her husband, her ear lets no inflection of his voice escape. Now and then, it is true, she sighs. Were he as fit for *this* world as he is for the *other* world, she would have a good time of it here, too—here, too—

"Ma!" she consoles herself, "who talks of honor? Not every one is worthy of both tables!"

She listens. Her shriveled face alters from minute to minute; she is nervous, too. A moment ago it was eloquent with delight. Now she remembers it is Thursday; there isn't a dreier to spend in preparation for Sabbath. The light in her face goes out by degrees, the smile fades, then she takes a look through the grimy window, glances at the sun. It must be getting late, and there isn't a spoonful of hot water in the house. The needles pause in her hand, a shadow has overspread her face. She looks at the child; it is sleeping less quietly, and will soon wake. The child is poorly, and there is not a drop of milk for it. The shadow on her face deepens into gloom, the needles tremble and move convulsively.

And when she remembers that it is near Passover, that her ear-rings and the festal candlesticks are at the pawnshop, the chest empty, the lamp sold, then the needles perform murderous antics in her fingers. The gloom on her brow is that of a gathering thunder-storm, lightnings play in her small, gray, sunken eyes.

He sits and "learns," unconscious of the charged atmosphere; does not see her let the sock fall and begin wringing her finger-joints; does not see that her forehead is puckered with misery, one eye closed, and the other fixed on him, her learned husband, with a look fit to send a chill through his every limb; does not see her dry lips tremble and her jaw quiver. She controls herself with all her might, but the storm is gathering fury within her. The least thing, and it will explode.

That least thing has happened.

He was just translating a Talmudic phrase with quiet delight, "And thence we derive that—" He was going on with "three,—" but the word "derive" was enough, it was the lighted spark, and her heart was the gunpowder. It was ablaze in an instant. Her determination gave way, the unlucky word opened the flood-gates, and the waters poured through, carrying all before them.

"Derived, you say, derived? Oh, derived may you be, Lord of the World," she exclaimed, hoarse with anger, "derived may you be! Yes! You!" she hissed like a snake. "Passover coming—Thursday—and the child ill—and not a drop of milk is there. Ha?"

Her breath gives out, her sunken breast heaves, her eyes flash.

He sits like one turned to stone. Then, pale and breathless, too, from fright, he gets up and edges toward the door.

At the door he turns and faces her, and sees that hand and tongue are equally helpless from passion; his eyes grow smaller; he catches a bit of handkerchief between his teeth, retreats a little further, takes a deeper breath, and mutters:

"Listen, woman, do you know what Bittul-Torah means? And not letting a husband study in peace, to be always worrying about livelihood, ha? And who feeds the little birds, tell me? Always this want of faith in God, this giving way to temptation, and taking thought for *this* world . . . foolish, ill-natured woman! Not to let a husband study! If you don't take care, you will go to Gehenna."

Receiving no answer, he grows bolder. Her face gets paler and paler, she trembles more and more violently, and the paler she becomes, and the more she trembles, the steadier his voice, as he goes on:

"Gehenna! Fire! Hanging by the tongue! Four death penalties inflicted by the court!"

She is silent, her face is white as chalk.

He feels that he is doing wrong, that he has no call to be cruel, that he is taking a mean advantage, but he has risen, as it were, to the top, and is boiling over. He cannot help himself.

"Do you know," he threatens her, "what Skiloh means? It means stoning, to throw into a ditch and cover up with stones! Srefoh—burning, that is, pouring a spoonful of boiling lead into the inside! Hereg—beheading, that means they cut off your head with a sword! Like this" (and he passes a hand across his neck). "Then Cheneck—strangling! Do you hear? To strangle! Do you understand? And all four for making light of the Torah! For Bittul-Torah!"

His heart is already sore for his victim, but he is feeling his power over her for the first time, and it has gone to his head. Silly woman! He had never known how easy it was to frighten her.

"That comes of making light of the Torah!" he shouts, and breaks off. After all, she might come to her senses at any moment, and take up the broom! He springs back to the table, closes the Gemoreh, and hurries out of the room.

"I am going to the house-of-study," he calls out over his shoulder in a milder tone, and shuts the door after him.

The loud voice and the noise of the closing door have waked the sick child. The heavy-lidded eyes open, the waxen face puckers, and there is a peevish wail. But she, beside herself, stands rooted to the spot, and does not hear.

"Ha!" comes hoarsely at last out of her narrow chest. "So that's it, is it? Neither this world nor the other. Hanging, he says, stoning, burning, beheading, strangling, hanging by the tongue, boiling lead poured into the inside, he says—for making light of the Torah—Hanging, ha, ha, ha!" (in desperation). "Yes, I'll hang, but *here, here!* And soon! What is there to wait for?"

The child begins to cry louder; still she does not hear.

"A rope! a rope!" she screams, and stares wildly into every corner. "Where is there a rope? I wish he mayn't find a bone of me left! Let me be rid of *one* Gehenna at any rate! Let him try it, let him be a mother for once, see how he likes it! I've had enough of it! Let it be an atonement! An end, an end! A rope, a rope!"

Her last exclamation is like a cry for help from out of a conflagration.

She remembers that they *have* a rope somewhere. Yes, under the stove—the stove was to have been tied round against the winter. The rope must be there still.

She runs and finds the rope, the treasure, looks up at the ceiling—the hook that held the lamp—she need only climb onto the table.

She climbs—

But she sees from the table that the startled child, weak as it is, has sat up in the cradle, and is reaching over the side—it is trying to get out—

"Mame, M-mame," it sobs feebly.

A fresh paroxysm of anger seizes her.

She flings away the rope, jumps off the table, runs to the child, and forces its head back into the pillow, exclaiming:

"Bother the child! It won't even let me hang myself! I can't even hang myself in peace! It wants to suck. What is the good? You will suck nothing but poison, poison, out of me, I tell you!"

"There, then, greedy!" she cries in the same breath, and stuffs her dried-up breast into his mouth.

"There, then, suck away—bite!"

SHOLOM ALEICHEM

(Sholom Rabinovitch)

(1859—1916)

RABINOVITCH, known everywhere by his pseudonym, Sholom Aleichem, was born in Russia. He is one of the most beloved figures in all Yiddish literature. In common with nearly all his contemporaries, he excels in the description of the pathos and tragedy of his people, though he was frequently able, as in *The Passover Guest*, to turn a tragic theme into a richly comic one.

The Passover Guest is quaintly humorous, though at the same time a bitter commentary on life. It is the artist's way of describing the lot of the Jew in the modern world.

This story is reprinted from the volume, *Yiddish Tales*, translated by Helena Frank, copyright, 1912, by the Jewish Publication Society of America, by whose permission and that of the Sholom Aleichem Foundation it is here reprinted.

THE PASSOVER GUEST

"I HAVE a Passover guest for you, Reb Yoneh, such a guest as you never had since you became a householder."

"What sort is he?"

"A real Oriental citron!"

"What does that mean?"

"It means a 'silken Jew,' a personage of distinction. The only thing against him is—he doesn't speak our language."

"What does he speak, then?"

"Hebrew."

"Is he from Jerusalem?"

"I don't know where he comes from, but his words are full of a's."

Such was the conversation that took place between my father and the beadle, a day before Passover, and I was wild with curiosity to see the "guest" who didn't understand Yiddish, and who talked with a's. I had already noticed, in synagogue, a strange-looking individual, in a fur cap, and a Turkish robe striped blue, red, and yellow. We boys crowded round him on all sides, and stared, and then caught it hot from the beadle, who said children had no business "to creep into a stranger's face" like that. Prayers over, every one greeted the stranger, and wished him a happy Passover, and he, with a sweet smile on his red cheeks set in a round gray beard, replied to each one, "Shalom! Shalom!" instead of our Sholom. This "Shalom! Shalom!" of his sent us boys into fits of laughter. The beadle grew very angry, and pursued us with slaps. We eluded him, and stole deviously back to the stranger, listened to his "Shalom! Shalom!" exploded with laughter, and escaped anew from the hands of the beadle.

I am puffed up with pride as I follow my father and his guest to our house, and feel how all my comrades envy me. They stand looking after us, and every now and then I turn my head, and put out my tongue at them. The walk home is silent. When we arrive, my father greets my mother with "a happy Passover!" and the guest nods his head so that his fur cap shakes. "Shalom! Shalom!" he says. I think of my comrades, and hide my head under the table, not to burst out laughing. But I shoot continual glances at the guest, and his appearance pleases me; I like his Turkish robe, striped yellow, red, and blue, his fresh red cheeks set in a curly gray beard, his beautiful black eyes that look out so pleasantly from beneath his bushy eyebrows. And I see that my father is pleased with him, too, that he is delighted with him. My mother looks at him as though he were something more than a man, and no one speaks to him but my father, who offers him the cushioned reclining-seat at table.

Mother is taken up with the preparations for the Passover meal, and Rikel the maid is helping her. It is only when the time comes for saying Kiddush that my father and the guest hold a Hebrew conversation. I am proud to find that I understand nearly every word of it. Here it is in full.

My father: "Nu?" (That means, "Won't you please say Kiddush?")
The guest: "Nu-nu!" (meaning, "Say it rather yourself!")
My father: "Nu-O?" ("Why not you?")
The guest: "O-nu?" ("Why should I?")
My father: "I-O!" ("You first!")
The guest: "O-ai!" ("*You* first!")
My father: "È-o-i!" ("I beg of you to say it!")
The guest: "Ai-o-ê!" ("I beg of you!")
My father: "Ai-e-o-nu?" ("Why should you refuse?")
The guest: "Oi-o-e-nu-nu!" ("If you insist, then I must.")

And the guest took the cup of wine from my father's hand, and recited a Kiddush. But what a Kiddush! A Kiddush such as we had never heard before, and shall never hear again. First, the Hebrew—all a's. Secondly, the voice, which seemed to come, not out of his beard, but out of the striped Turkish robe. I thought of my comrades, how they would have laughed, what slaps would have rained down, had they been present at that Kiddush.

Being alone, I was able to contain myself. I asked my father the Four Questions, and we all recited the Haggadah together. And I was elated to think that such a guest was ours, and no one else's.

Our sage who wrote that one should not talk at meals (may he forgive me for saying so!) did not know Jewish life. When shall a Jew find time to talk, if not during a meal? Especially at Passover, when there is so much to say before the meal and after it. Rikel the maid handed the water, we washed our hands, repeated the Benediction, mother helped us to fish, and my father turned up his sleeves, and started a long Hebrew talk with the guest. He began with the first question one Jew asks another:

"What is your name?"

To which the guest replied all in a's and all in one breath:

"Ayak Bakar Gashal Damas Hanoch Vassam Za'an Chafaf Tatzatz."

My father remained with his fork in the air, staring in amazement at the possessor of so long a name. I coughed and looked under the table, and my mother said, "Favele, you should be careful eating fish, or you might be choked with a bone," while she gazed at our guest with awe. She appeared overcome by his name, although unable to understand it. My father, who understood, thought it necessary to explain it to her.

"You see, Ayak Bakar, that is our Alef-Bes inverted. It is apparently their custom to name people after the alphabet."

"Alef-Bes! Alef-Bes!" repeated the guest with the sweet smile on his red cheeks, and his beautiful black eyes rested on us all, including Rikel the maid, in the most friendly fashion.

Having learned his name, my father was anxious to know whence, from what land he came. I understood this from the names of countries and towns which I caught, and from what my father translated for my mother, giving her a Yiddish version of nearly every phrase. And my mother was quite overcome by every single thing she heard, and Rikel the maid was overcome likewise. And no wonder! It is not every day that a person comes from perhaps two thousand miles away, from a land only to be reached across seven seas and a desert, the desert journey alone requiring forty days and nights. And when you get near to the land, you have to climb a mountain of which the top reaches into the clouds, and this is covered with ice, and dreadful winds blow there, so that there is peril of death! But once the mountain is safely climbed, and the land is reached, one beholds a terrestrial Eden. Spices, cloves, herbs, and every kind of fruit—apples, pears, and oranges, grapes, dates, and olives, nuts and quantities of figs. And the houses there are all built of deal, and roofed with silver, the furniture is gold (here the guest cast a look at our silver, spoons, forks, and knives), and brilliants, pearls, and diamonds bestrew the roads, and no one cares to take the trouble of picking them up, they are of no value there. (He was looking at my mother's diamond ear-rings, and at the pearls round her white neck.)

"You hear that?" my father asked her, with a happy face.

"I hear," she answered, and added: "Why don't they bring some over here? They could make money by it. Ask him that, Yoneh!"

My father did so, and translated the answer for my mother's benefit:

"You see, when you arrive there, you may take what you like, but when you leave the country, you must leave everything in it behind, too, and if they shake out of you no matter what, you are done for."

"What do you mean?" questioned my mother, terrified.

"I mean, they either hang you on a tree, or they stone you with stones."

The more tales our guest told us, the more thrilling they became, and just as we were finishing the dumplings and taking another sip or two of wine, my father inquired to whom the country belonged. Was there a king there? And he was soon translating, with great delight, the following reply:

"The country belongs to the Jews who live there, and who are called Sefardîm. And they have a king, also a Jew, and a very pious one, who wears a fur cap, and who is called Joseph ben Joseph. He is the high priest of the Sefardîm, and drives out in a gilded carriage, drawn by six fiery horses. And when he enters the synagogue, the Levites meet him with songs."

"There are Levites who sing in your synagogue?" asked my father, wondering, and the answer caused his face to shine with joy.

"What do you think?" he said to my mother. "Our guest tells me that in his country there is a temple, with priests and Levites and an organ."

"Well, and an altar?" questioned my mother, and my father told her:

"He says they have an altar, and sacrifices, he says, and golden vessels—everything just as we used to have it in Jerusalem."

And with these words my father sighs deeply, and my mother, as she looks at him, sighs also, and I cannot understand the reason. Surely we should be proud and glad to think we have such a land, ruled over by a Jewish king and high priest, a land with Levites and an organ, with an altar and sacrifices—and bright, sweet thoughts enfold me, and carry me away as on wings to that happy Jewish land where the houses are of pine-wood and roofed with silver, where the furniture is gold, and diamonds and pearls lie scattered in the street. And I feel sure, were I really there, I should know what to do—I should know how to hide things—they would shake nothing out of *me*. I should certainly bring home a lovely present for my mother, diamond ear-rings and several pearl necklaces. I look at the one mother is wearing, at her ear-rings, and I feel a great desire to be in that country. And it occurs to me, that after Passover I will travel there with our guest, secretly, no one shall know. I will only speak of it to our guest, open my heart to him, tell him the whole truth, and beg him to take me there, if only for a little while. He will certainly do so, he is a very kind and approachable person, he looks at every one, even at Rikel the maid, in such a friendly, such a very friendly way!

So I think, and it seems to me, as I watch our guest, that he has read my thoughts, and that his beautiful black eyes say to me: "Keep it dark, little friend, wait till after Passover, then we shall manage it!"

I dreamt all night long. I dreamt of a desert, a temple, a high priest, and a tall mountain. I climb the mountain. Diamonds and pearls grow on the trees, and my comrades sit on the boughs, and shake the jewels down onto the ground, whole showers of them, and I stand and gather them, and stuff them into my pockets, and, strange to say, however many I stuff in, there is still room! I stuff and stuff, and still there is room! I put my hand into my pocket, and draw out—not pearls and brilliants, but fruits of all kinds—apples, pears, oranges, olives, dates, nuts, and figs. This makes me very unhappy, and I toss from side to side. Then I dream of the temple, I hear the priests chant, and the Levites sing, and the organ play. I want to go inside and I cannot—Rikel the maid has hold of me, and will not let me go. I beg of her and scream and cry, and again I am very unhappy, and toss from side to side. I wake—and see my father and mother standing there, half dressed, both pale, my father hanging his head, and my mother wringing her hands, and with her soft eyes full of tears. I feel at once that something has gone very wrong, very wrong indeed, but my childish head is incapable of imagining the greatness of the disaster.

The fact is this: our guest from beyond the desert and the seven seas has disappeared, and a lot of things have disappeared with him: all the silver wine-cups, all the silver spoons, knives, and forks; all my mother's ornaments, all the money that happened to be in the house, and also Rikel the maid!

A pang goes through my heart. Not on account of the silver cups, the silver spoons, knives, and forks that have vanished; not on account of mother's ornaments or of the money, still less on account of Rikel the maid, a good riddance! But because of the happy, happy land whose roads were strewn with brilliants, pearls, and diamonds; because of the temple with the priests, the Levites, and the organ; because of the altar

and the sacrifices; because of all the other beautiful things that have
been taken from me, taken, taken, taken!

I turn my face to the wall, and cry quietly to myself.

S. LIBIN

(Israel Hurwitz)

(1872—1955)

ISRAEL HURWITZ, better known by his pseudonym, S. (or Z.) Libin,
was born in Russia in 1872. He wrote a number of short stories,
having specialized to a great extent in that form. Libin's best work
is found in his brief and homely sketches of Jewish domestic life among
the labouring classes of the large cities. He was for many years a
resident in the United States.

A Picnic reveals one of the amusing aspects of Jewish life. It is
related with lightness of touch and great good-humour.

This story is reprinted from the volume, Yiddish Tales, translated
by Helena Frank, copyright, 1912, by the Jewish Publication Society
of America, by whose permission, it is here used.

A PICNIC

ASK Shmuel, the capmaker, just for a joke, if he would like to come
for a picnic! He'll fly out at you as if you had invited him to a
swing on the gallows. The fact is, he and his Sarah once *went* for a
picnic, and the poor man will remember it all his days.

It was on a Sabbath towards the end of August. Shmuel came home
from work, and said to his wife:

"Sarah, dear!"

"Well, husband?" was her reply.

"I want to have a treat," said Shmuel, as though alarmed at the
boldness of the idea.

"What sort of a treat? Shall you go to the swimming-bath to-
morrow?"

"Ett! What's the fun of that?"

"Then, what have you thought of by way of an exception? A glass
of ice water for supper?"

"Not that, either."

"A whole siphon?"

Shmuel denied with a shake of the head.

"Whatever can it be!" wondered Sarah. "Are you going to fetch a pint of beer?"

"What should I want with beer?"

"Are you going to sleep on the roof?"

"Wrong again!"

"To buy some more carbolic acid, and drive out the bugs?"

"Not a bad idea," observed Shmuel, "but that is not it, either."

"Well, then, whatever is it, for goodness' sake! The moon?" asked Sarah, beginning to lose patience. "What have you been and thought of? Tell me once for all, and have done with it!"

And Shmuel said:

"Sarah, you know, we belong to a lodge."

"Of course I do!" and Sarah gave him a look of mingled astonishment and alarm. "It's not more than a week since you took a whole dollar there, and I'm not likely to have forgotten what it cost you to make it up. What is the matter now? Do they want another?"

"Try again!"

"Out with it!"

"I—want us, Sarah," stammered Shmuel,—"to go for a picnic."

"A picnic!" screamed Sarah. "Is that the only thing you have left to wish for?"

"Look here, Sarah, we toil and moil the whole year through. It's nothing but trouble and worry, trouble and worry. Call that living! When do we ever have a bit of pleasure?"

"Well, what's to be done?" said his wife, in a subdued tone.

"The summer will soon be over, and we haven't set eyes on a green blade of grass. We sit day and night sweating in the dark."

"True enough," sighed his wife, and Shmuel spoke louder:

"Let us have an outing, Sarah. Let us enjoy ourselves for once, and give the children a breath of fresh air, let us have a change, if it's only for five minutes!"

"What will it cost?" asks Sarah, suddenly, and Shmuel has soon made the necessary calculation.

"A family ticket is only thirty cents, for Yossele, Rivele, Hannahle, and Berele; for Resele and Doletzke I haven't to pay any carfare at all. For you and me, it will be ten cents there and ten back—that makes fifty cents. Then I reckon thirty cents for refreshments to take with us: a pineapple (a damaged one isn't more than five cents), a few bananas, a piece of watermelon, a bottle of milk for the children, and a few-rolls—the whole thing shouldn't cost us more than eighty cents at the outside."

"Eighty cents!" and Sarah clapped her hands together in dismay.

"Why, you can live on that two days, and it takes nearly a whole days' earning. You can buy an old ice-box for eighty cents, you can buy a pair of trousers—eighty cents!"

"Leave off talking nonsense!" said Shmuel, disconcerted. "Eighty cents won't make us rich. We shall get on just the same whether we have them or not. We must live like human beings one day in the year! Come, Sarah, let us go! We shall see lots of other people, and we'll watch them, and see how *they* enjoy themselves. It will do you good to see the world, to go where there's a bit of life! Listen, Sarah, what have you been to worth seeing since we came to America? Have you seen Brooklyn Bridge, or Central Park, or the Baron Hirsch baths?"

"You know I haven't!" Sarah broke in. "I've no time to go about sight-seeing. I only know the way from here to the market."

"And what do you suppose?" cried Shmuel. "I should be as great a greenhorn as you, if I hadn't been obliged to look everywhere for work. Now I know that America is a great big place. Thanks to the slack times, I know where there's an Eighth Street, and a One Hundred and Thirtieth Street with tin works, and an Eighty-fourth Street with a match factory. I know every single lane round the World Building. I know where the cable car line stops. But you, Sarah, know nothing at all, no more than if you had just landed. Let us go, Sarah, I am sure you won't regret it!"

"Well, you know best!" said his wife, and this time she smiled. "Let us go!"

And thus it was that Shmuel and his wife decided to join the lodge picnic on the following day.

Next morning they all rose much earlier than usual on a Sunday, and there was a great noise, for they took the children and scrubbed them without mercy. Sarah prepared a bath for Doletzke, and Doletzke screamed the house down. Shmuel started washing Yossele's feet, but as Yossele habitually went barefoot, he failed to bring about any visible improvement, and had to leave the little pair of feet to soak in a basin of warm water, and Yossele cried, too. It was twelve o'clock before the children were dressed and ready to start, and then Sarah turned her attention to her husband, arranged his trousers, took the spots out of his coat with kerosene, sewed a button onto his vest. After that she dressed herself, in her old-fashioned satin wedding dress. At two o'clock they set forth, and took their places in the car.

"Haven't we forgotten anything?" asked Sarah of her husband.

Shmuel counted his children and the traps. "No, nothing, Sarah!" he said.

Doletzke went to sleep, the other children sat quietly in their places. Sarah, too, fell into a doze, for she was tired out with the preparations for the excursion.

All went smoothly till they got some way up town, when Sarah gave a start.

"I don't feel very well—my head is so dizzy," she said to Shmuel.

"I don't feel very well, either," answered Shmuel. "I suppose the fresh air has upset us."

"I suppose it has," said his wife. "I'm afraid for the children."

Scarcely had she spoken when Doletzke woke up, whimpering, and was sick. Yossele, who was looking at her, began to cry likewise. The mother scolded him, and this set the other children crying. The conductor cast a wrathful glance at poor Shmuel, who was so frightened that he dropped the hand-bag with the provisions, and then, conscious of the havoc he had certainly brought about inside the bag by so doing, he lost his head altogether, and sat there in a daze. Sarah was hushing the children, but the look in her eyes told Shmuel plainly enough what to expect once they had left the car. And no sooner had they all reached the ground in safety than Sarah shot out:

"So, nothing would content him but a picnic? Much good may it do him! You're a workman, and workmen have no call to go gadding about!"

Shmuel was already weary of the whole thing, and said nothing, but he felt a tightening of the heart.

He took up Yossele on one arm and Resele on the other, and carried the bag with the presumably smashed-up contents besides.

"Hush, my dears! Hush, my babies!" he said. "Wait a little and mother will give you some bread and sugar. Hush, be quiet!" He went on, but still the children cried.

Sarah carried Doletzke, and rocked her as she walked, while Berele and Hannahle trotted alongside.

"He has shortened my days," said Sarah, "may his be shortened likewise."

Soon afterwards they turned into the park.

"Let us find a tree and sit down in the shade," said Shmuel. "Come, Sarah!"

'I haven't the strength to drag myself a step further," declared Sarah, and she sank down like a stone just inside the gate. Shmuel was about to speak, but a glance at Sarah's face told him she was worn out, and he sat down beside his wife without a word. Sarah gave Doletzke the breast. The other children began to roll about in the grass, laughed and played, and Shmuel breathed easier.

Girls in holiday attire walked about the park, and there were groups under the trees. Here was a handsome girl surrounded by admiring boys, and there a handsome young man encircled by a bevy of girls.

Out of the leafy distance of the park came the melancholy song of a workman; near by stood a man playing on a fiddle. Sarah looked about her and listened, and by degrees her vexation vanished. It is true that her heart was still sore, but it was not with the soreness of anger. She was taking her life to pieces and thinking it over, and it seemed a very hard and bitter one, and when she looked at her husband and thought of his life, she was near crying, and she laid her hands upon his knee. Shmuel also sat lost in thought. He was thinking about the trees and the roses and the grass, and listening to the fiddle. And he also was sad at heart.

"O Sarah!" he sighed, and he would have said more, but just at that moment it began to spot with rain, and before they had time to move there came a downpour. People started to scurry in all directions, but Shmuel stood like a statue.

"Shlimm-mazel, look after the children!" commanded Sarah. Shmuel caught up two of them, Sarah another two or three, and they ran to a shelter. Doletzke began to cry afresh.

"Mame, hungry!" began Berele.

"Hungry, hungry!" wailed Yossele. "I want to eat!"

Shmuel hastily opened the hand-bag, and then for the first time he saw what had really happened: the bottle had broken, and the milk was flooding the bag; the rolls and bananas were soaked, and the pine-apple (a damaged one to begin with) looked too nasty for words. Sarah caught sight of the bag, and was so angry, she was at a loss how to wreak vengeance on her husband. She was ashamed to scream and scold in the presence of other people, but she went up to him, and whispered fervently into his ear, "The same to you, my good man!"

The children continued to clamor for food.

"I'll go to the refreshment counter and buy a glass of milk and a few rolls," said Shmuel to his wife.

"Have you actually some money left?" asked Sarah. "I thought it had all been spent on the picnic."

"There are just five cents over."

"Well, then go and be quick about it. The poor things are starving."

Shmuel went to the refreshment stall, and asked the price of a glass of milk and a few rolls.

"Twenty cents, mister," answered the waiter.

Shmuel started as if he had burnt his finger, and returned to his wife more crestfallen than ever.

"Well, Shlimm-mazel, where's the milk?" inquired Sarah.

"He asked twenty cents."

"Twenty cents for a glass of milk and a roll? Are you Montefiore?" Sarah could no longer contain herself. "They'll be the ruin of us! If you want to go for another picnic, we shall have to sell the bedding."

The children never stopped begging for something to eat.

"But what are we to do?" asked the bewildered Shmuel.

"Do?" screamed Sarah. "Go home, this very minute!"

Shmuel promptly caught up a few children, and they left the park. Sarah was quite quiet on the way home, merely remarking to her husband that she would settle her account with him later.

"I'll pay you out," she said, "for my satin dress, for the hand-bag, for the pineapple, for the bananas, for the milk, for the whole blessed picnic, for the whole of my miserable existence."

"Scold away!" answered Shmuel. "It is you who were right. I don't know what possessed me. A picnic, indeed! You may well ask what next? A poor wretched workman like me has no business to think of anything beyond the shop."

Sarah, when they reached home, was as good as her word. Shmuel would have liked some supper, as he always liked it, even in slack times, but there was no supper given him. He went to bed a hungry man, and all through the night he repeated in his sleep:

"A picnic, oi, a picnic!"

ABRAHAM RAISIN

(1876—1953)

RAISIN is another of the Yiddish group who came from Russia, though he lived for some time in the United States. He is equally well-known among Yiddish readers as a poet and as a writer of stories.

The technical virtues of this popular and influential artist are particularly well exemplified in *The Kaddish*.

This story is reprinted from the volume, *Yiddish Tales*, translated by Helena Frank, copyright, 1912, by the Jewish Publication Society of America, by whose permission it is here used.

THE KADDISH

FROM behind the curtain came low moans, and low words of encouragement from the old and experienced *Bobbe*. In the room it was dismal to suffocation. The seven children, all girls, between twenty three and four years old, sat quietly each by herself, with drooping head, and waited for something dreadful.

At a little table near a great cupboard with books sat the "patriarch" Reb Selig Chanes, a tall, thin Jew, with a yellow, consumptive face. He was chanting in low, broken tones out of a big Gemoreh, and continually raising his head, giving a nervous glance at the curtain, and then, without inquiring what might be going on beyond the low moaning, taking up once again his sad, tremulous chant. He seemed to be suffering more than the woman in childbirth herself.

"Lord of the World!"—it was the eldest daughter who broke the stillness—"Let it be a boy for once! Help, Lord of the World, have pity!"

"Oi, thus might it be, Lord of the World!" chimed in the second.

And all the girls, little and big, with broken heart and prostrate spirit, prayed that there might be born a boy.

Reb Selig raised his eyes from the Gemoreh, glanced at the curtain, then at the seven girls, gave vent to a deep-drawn Oi, made a gesture with his hand, and said with settled despair, "She will give you another sister!"

The seven girls looked at one another in desperation; their father's conclusion quite crushed them, and they had no longer even the courage to pray.

Only the littlest, the four-year-old, in the torn frock, prayed softly: "Oi, please God, there will be a little brother."

"I shall die without a Kaddish!" groaned Reb Selig.

The time drags on, the moans behind the curtain grow louder, and Reb Selig and the elder girls feel that soon, very soon, the "grandmother" will call out in despair, "A little girl!" And Reb Selig feels that the words will strike home to his heart like a blow, and he resolves to run away.

He goes out into the yard, and looks up at the sky. It is midnight. The moon swims along so quietly and indifferently, the stars seem to frolic and rock themselves like little children, and still Reb Selig hears, in the "grandmother's" husky voice, "A girl!"

"Well, there will be no Kaddish! Verfallen!" he says, crossing the yard again. "There's no getting it by force!"

But his trying to calm himself is useless; the fear that it should be a girl only grows upon him. He loses patience, and goes back into the house.

But the house is in a turmoil.

"What is it, eh?"

"A little boy! Tate, a boy! Tatinke, as surely may I be well!" With this news the seven girls fall upon him with radiant faces.

"Eh, a little boy?" asked Reb Selig, as though bewildered, "eh? what?"

"A boy, Reb Selig, a Kaddish!" announced the "grandmother." "As soon as I have bathed him, I will show him you!"

"A boy... a boy..." stammered Reb Selig in the same bewilderment, and he leaned against the wall, and burst into tears like a woman.

The seven girls took alarm.

"That is for joy," explained the "grandmother." "I have known that happen before."

"A boy... a boy!" sobbed Reb Selig, overcome with happiness, "a boy... a boy... a Kaddish!"

The little boy received the name of Jacob, but he was called, by way of a talisman, Alter.

Reb Selig was a learned man, and inclined to think lightly of such protective measures; he even laughed at his Cheike for believing in such foolishness; but, at heart, he was content to have it so. Who could tell what might not be in it, after all? Women sometimes know better than men.

By the time Alterke was three years old, Reb Selig's cough had become worse, the sense of oppression on his chest more frequent. But he held himself morally erect, and looked death calmly in the face, as though he would say, "Now I can afford to laugh at you—I leave a Kaddish!"

"What do you think, Cheike," he would say to his wife, after a fit of coughing, "would Alterke be able to say Kaddish if I were to die to-day or to-morrow?"

"Go along with you, crazy pate!" Cheike would exclaim in secret alarm. "You are going to live a long while! Is your cough anything new?"

Selig smiled, "Foolish woman, she supposes I am afraid to die. When one leaves a Kaddish, death is a trifle."

Alterke was sitting playing with a prayer-book and imitating his father at prayer, "A num-num—a num-num."

"Listen to him praying!" and Cheike turned delightedly to her husband. "His soul is piously inclined!"

Selig made no reply, he only gazed at his Kaddish with a beaming face. Then an idea came into his head: Alterke will be a Tzaddik, will help him out of all his difficulties in the other world.

"Mame, I want to eat!" wailed Alterke, suddenly.

He was given a piece of the white bread which was laid aside, for him only, every Sabbath.

Alterke began to eat.

"Who bringest forth! Who bringest forth!" called out Reb Selig.

"Tan't!" answered the child.

"It is time you taught him to say grace," observed Cheike.

And Reb Selig drew Alterke to him and began to repeat with him. "Say: Boruch."

"Bo'uch," repeated the child after his fashion.

"Attoh."

"Attoh."

When Alterke had finished "Who bringest forth," Cheike answered piously Amen and Reb Selig saw Alterke, in imagination, standing in the synagogue and repeating Kaddish, and heard the congregation answer Amen, and he felt as though he were already seated in the Garden of Eden.

Another year went by, and Reb Selig was feeling very poorly. Spring had come, the snow had melted, and he found the wet weather more trying than ever before. He could just drag himself early to the synagogue, but going to the afternoon service had become a difficulty, and he used to recite the afternoon and later service at home, and spend the whole evening with Alterke.

It was late at night. All the houses were shut. Reb Selig sat at his little table, and was looking into the corner where Cheike's bed stood, and where Alterke slept beside her. Selig had a feeling that he would die that night. He felt very tired and weak, and with an imploring look he crept up to Alterke's crib, and began to wake him.

The child woke with a start.

"Alterke"—Reb Selig was stroking the little head—"come to me for a little!"

The child, who had had his first sleep out, sprang up, and went to his father.

Reb Selig sat down in the chair which stood by the little table with the open Gemoreh, lifted Alterke onto the table, and looked into his eyes.

"Alterke!"

"What, Tate?"

"Would you like me to die?"

"Like," answered the child, not knowing what "to die" meant, and thinking it must be something nice.

"Will you say Kaddish after me?" asked Reb Selig, in a strangled voice, and he was seized with a fit of coughing.

"Will say!" promised the child.

"Shall you know how?"

"Shall!"

"Well, now, say: Yisgaddal."

"Yisdaddal," repeated the child in his own way.

"Veyiskaddash."

"Veyistaddash."

And Reb Selig repeated the Kaddish with him several times.

The small lamp burnt low, and scarcely illuminated Reb Selig's yellow, corpse-like face, or the little one of Alterke, who repeated wearily the difficult. and to him unintelligible, words of the Kaddish. And

Alterke, all the while, gazed intently into the corner, where Tate's shadow and his own had a most fantastic and frightening appearance.

SHOLOM ASCH

(1880—1957)

SHOLOM ASCH (or Ash) was born in Poland, and is to-day regarded as one of the most gifted of recent Yiddish writers. He was the writer of plays (*The God of Vengeance* was produced in English and censored in New York), novels, and short stories. Like Peretz and certain others, he began writing in Hebrew, but, finding that there was only a small public he could reach by that medium, he soon turned to the Yiddish.

Abandoned is a story characteristic of the nervous style of this writer, brief, highly dramatic, and of compelling interest.

This story is reprinted from the *Pagan* magazine, the editor of which has authorized its inclusion in the present collection.

ABANDONED

WHEN Burih awoke he heard the baby crying, so with eyes still closed he called to his wife: "Golda! the brat is bawling."

Golda did not answer. He looked around and noticed that she wasn't in the house. He was rather surprised, but he thought: She must have gone to wash herself. He took a piece of linen and stuck it into the infant's mouth to stop its wailing. Then he started to dress.

While thus occupied, he began to figure how much he'd be able to "land" for the silver candlesticks he had "lifted" from the Zhobliner house. On the impulse of the moment he climbed up into the attic to examine "the goods." They were gone! He rummaged about everywhere... Gone!

Quickly clambering down again he hastened over to where his wife's things hung, and tore away the sheet covering them. They too were gone!... Only then did it begin to dawn on him that she had run away.

With whom?...

With Shloima Shlosser?... or Hayim'll Goob?...

"Well... let her run,—and be damned to her!... Who th' hell

cares?" he said to himself with forced unconcern, spitting on the walls. "That's a nice how-d-ye-do!... Ha-ha-ha-ha..."

He glanced at the baby.

"But what's to be done with the damned brat?" he murmured to himself reflectively. "If I only knew where she is I'd leave it right in front of her door... Take it!... it's yours!"

An evil thought suddenly flashed through his mind, causing him to grow pale, and bite his upper lip, while his hands trembled. He approached the infant, which lay uncovered, its dirty rag of a blanket kicked aside, its hands stuffed into its mouth, smiling vaguely into empty space... The shape of its mouth reminded him of some one... was it an old acquaintance?... He couldn't rightly remember...

He turned away from the child, put on his hat hurriedly, and went out, locking the door behind him. He walked on aimlessly, but with no peace of mind... The baby's cries kept ringing in his ears, as if it were calling to him... In fancy he could see it before him, kicking its little legs about, wailing frantically... No! he must turn back. ..."Oh, if I could get a-hold of her now!" he thought to himself, "I'd nab her by the throat and choke her!... choke her till her tongue stuck out, damn her!"

He entered a bakery, bought a roll, and went back to the house. The baby lay as before, uncovered, but smiling.

"Devil take the brat! he looks comfortable enough, the little cuss." ...And he left the house again. But he couldn't make himself walk on. All the time he fancied he heard the little one wailing... and it made him feel such a gnawing anguish at heart. ...

He clenched his fists and returned to the house. Now the baby was crying with a prolonged wail, "Mam-m-m-ma!... mam-m-m-ma!..."

"Your mamma, eh? The brat! ... Go and look for your precious mamma—plague take her!"

He took the child in his arms. It nestled up to him, seeking something eagerly with its little lips.

"Blast her ugly soul," he kept on cursing, while he patted the infant's cheek and body. "Don't cry, Shloimale... be quiet now... be quiet, I beg you."

The baby continued to seek with its little mouth, waved its hands about, and nodded its head, as if on the point of speaking. He drew it closer to him, at the same time looking about for some milk. He found a little on the stove, and soaked some of the roll in it. Then he began to feed the baby with a spoon, talking to it meanwhile, in a gentle voice. ... "Eat, sonny, eat. ... Your mother—devil take her—has deserted you. ... Even a dog doesn't abandon its young. ... She's worse than a dog. ... Don't cry. ... No, I won't abandon you ... on my word of honor, I won't."

When the baby had quieted down, he wrapped it in a cloth, and took it into the street.

His presence in the market-place created quite a stir. Burih Kulock* with a baby! ... From his "stand," Kradnick called out: "Hey, Kulock! where did you get the kid?"

Kradnick's wife got up excitedly, and hurried up to the baby with open arms. She wiped her face with her apron several times out of sheer gladness... laughed, and slapped the tiny urchin on the buttocks.

"Is he yours, Kulock? Well, I never!... Look at his little eyes ... if he don't look just like Marina! ... her nose—exactly! as I live! What a jewel of a lad!... Give him to me!..." She took the baby from him, and bounced it up and down. "There!... there! you little rascal."

Old man Kradnick, the "master" of the thieving gentry, got up slowly, approached the baby, examined it, and slapped Kulock on the back.

"Fine husky little chap!... He'll climb through a transom nimbly enough, all right. ... Who's the mother?"

"May she burn like a fire! ... She ran away, taking the candlesticks with her."

"And left you the kid?"

"Yes."

"That's bad... that's bad."

The old man scratched his head. The younger Kradnick approached and said to Kulock: "That's right. ... I guess you'll have to give up the profession now, and become a nurse. ... A fine trick she played you, eh?"

"Don't you be breaking your head about me. ... The Lord is a provider, and Kulock is Kulock!"

He took up the infant in his arms and started across the town. It seemed to him that people were pointing their fingers, and laughing, at him.

When he reached the wood on the outskirts of the town, he seated himself on a stone.

Round about not a soul was to be seen. The branches of the trees murmured sadly, as they shed their yellowed leaves... the sound of a distant stream was faintly audible, as it gurgled and splashed among the stones.

Burih put down the child near him, and regarded it with a feeling of bitterness. The baby stared at him silently, sucking its hand and looking as if absorbed in meditation. Kulock hadn't the least idea what to do with the child. For a fleeting moment he thought of abandoning it, but immediately a feeling of pity for the helpless mite, for his own

* Fist.

flesh and blood, drove the thought from his mind. He took the child in his arms again, and pressed its little body close to him, examining, meanwhile, all its features. He thought he recognized his own, in them, and felt a glad warmth in all his limbs at the idea.

"Little Kulock!" he cried to the baby; "yes, you're a little Kulock, all right; and you'll be a fine chap too, I'll bet. You'll climb through transoms, and ventilators, and garret-windows... break off locks, and steal calf-skin leather. ... And then you'll have children... and their mother will desert them. ... But—will you wander with your children from house to house begging for bread?... Who are you?... A Kulock, like me... you... I."

He laid the child down near the river-bank, and stood behind a tree to see what it would do. ... It pushed about with its legs, sucked its hands, and whimpered, as if in play. "Mam-m-a... mam-m-a."

He stole behind another tree, farther away, but he could still hear its cries. He glided thus from tree to farther and farther away, till he heard and saw nothing more. ... Then he took to his heels. But even as he ran, the infant's cries kept ringing in his ears. "It might be rolling down into the river," he thought suddenly. ... His head ached, and he felt a gnawing at his heart. ... But he kept on running. ...

Presently he stopped, looked around, and quickly retraced his steps.

He found the child crying aloud. He took it up in his arms, and approached the huts on the outskirts of the wood. ... Passing from door to door, he begged in a broken voice: "Give an orphan a little milk... give an orphan a little milk. ..."

DAVID PINSKI

(1872—1959)

DAVID PINSKI was born in Russia, but lived chiefly abroad, first in Germany, later in the United States and in Israel. He was preëminent as a dramatist and writer of stories. An artist of great culture and a finished stylist, he found in the proletariat the subject-matter of many of his plays and stories. His volume of tales *Temptations*, was once "censored" by the New York Society for the Suppression of Vice, on what grounds it still remains to be discovered.

In the Storm, which appears in *Temptations*, is one of the most effective and highly finished examples of the Yiddish short story.

Reprinted, in the translation by Isaac Goldberg, from *Temptations*, published by Brentano's, 1920, by whose permission it is here used.

IN THE STORM

A PIOUS woman told it to me as a warning to sinners, to the young, to the moderns.

Black clouds began to fleck the clear sky. Dense, heavy storm-clouds. At first far off, beyond the forest, but very soon they darkened the whole sky over the village. A violent wind lashed and drove them on, and they sped under its whip, angry and sullen, menacing. The wind—a tornado—raged in all the consciousness of its formidable power, raising pillars of dust as high as the driven clouds, tearing off roofs and uprooting trees.

Terror had descended upon the village. Bright day had of a sudden turned to night, such as well befitted the Sabbath of Repentance, the Sabbath before the Day of Atonement. ... As frightfully dark, as oppressively heavy as a pious Jew's heart.

Folks shut themselves up in their houses, fastening windows and locking doors. The earnest faces of the penitent Jews became still more earnest. The depressing moods of the Sabbath of Repentance waxed still more depressing. God was scolding. The sad voices of the psalm-singers became deeper and more tearful.

The darkness grew blacker and blacker. Then old Cheyne raised her eyes from the psalms, looked through her spectacles into the street, uttered "Au-hu!" with trembling heart and heaved a sigh.

For a while she sat gazing outside. She shook her head. Her whole soul was full of God's omnipotence.

It refused to grow lighter. The clouds passed by in endless procession, and the wind howled, whirling thick pillars of dust in its path.

She could recite psalms no longer. She removed her spectacles and placed them between the pages of her thick woman's prayer-book, rose from her seat and went into her daughter's room.

"What do you say to..."

She did not conclude her question. Her daughter was not there.

The old woman surveyed the room, looked into the kitchen, then returned to the room. Her daughter's bonnet was not in its place. With quivering hands she opened the closet. The jacket was missing!

She had gone! And she had warned her daughter, it seemed, not to go out to-day—that on the Sabbath of Repentance, at least, she might remain at home and not run off to that "Apostate," the former student.

Her aged countenance became as dark as the sky without. And her heart grew as furious as the storm. She gazed about the room as if seeking to vent her rage—strike somebody, break something.

"Oh, may she no longer be a daughter of mine!" escaped in angry outburst from her storming bosom, and she raised her hand to heaven.

She was not affrighted by the curse that her lips had uttered on this solemn Sabbath. At this moment she could curse and shriek the bitterest words. She could have seized her now by the hair, and slapped her face ruthlessly.

Suddenly she threw a shawl over her head and dashed out of the house.

She would hunt them both out and would visit an evil end upon both of them.

A flash of lightning rent the clouds, and was followed by reverberating thunder. Then flash upon flash of lightning and crash upon crash of thunder. One more blinding than the other, one louder than the other!

The horror of the population grew greater. That it should thunder on the Sabbath of Repentance, and in such demoniac fashion! All hearts were touched, all souls went out in prayer.

Old Cheyne, however, scarcely noticed this.

The wind blinded her eyes with dust, tore her scarf from her, blew her skirts about, twisted the wig on her old head.

She rushed along oblivious to all.

She neither heard nor saw anything before her. Within her it thundered and raged, it stormed and something drove her on. And before her all was dark, for her eyes were shot with blood.

Her small form grew even smaller. She strode along fairly doubled up, hastening breathlessly. She seemed to go faster than the wind. The wind lagged behind her. And whenever it caught up with her, it only spurred her on, and she quickened her step.

She did not look around, did not remark the inquisitive eyes that peered at her from behind the fastened windows by which she ran. She neither saw nor heard anything. Her entire being was merged with the fury of nature. Her thought was a curse, a horrible curse, a deadly curse. Not in words. But in her whole soul. Within her it cried, it thundered —drowning out the thunder of the black, angry clouds.

She stormed into the "apostate's" house. She opened the door with a loud bang and closed it with one even louder. Those in the room shuddered at the sudden intrusion and jumped to their feet. She cast a wild, hostile glance at them and dashed through the rooms, from one to the other, from the other to a third. She tore the doors open and slammed them behind her, accompanied by the thunder, as if in a wager as to which of them would make the panes and the windows rattle more violently. A little child took fright and began to cry. She ran from room to room, but neither he nor her daughter was there.

Then she flew back. On the threshold, however, she paused for a moment. She rolled her eyes heavenward and raised her arms to God.

"May flames devour this house!" came from her in a hoarse voice.

Then she departed, pulling the street door violently and leaving it open. The household stood agape, as if the storm itself had torn into the home. Out of sheer stupefaction the persons forgot to close their mouths.

Out of the clouds poured a drenching rain mixed with hail. The tempest seethed like a cauldron.

This boiling tempest, however, raged in Cheyne's bosom. Something stormed furiously within her. She no longer felt the ground beneath her. The flood soaked her through and through, but this could not restrain her. It served only to augment her savage mood.

She ran from house to house, wherever she might have expected to come upon her daughter and the "apostate." She stopped nowhere, uttered never a word, but dashed in and then sped out like a flash of lightning, leaving the household open-mouthed with astonishment.

She would find them! Even under the ground. And she did not stop her cursing and her maledictions.

As she rushed from the last house she paused for a moment. Whither now?

She turned homeward. Her heart told her that her daughter was now at home. Her lips muttered the most terrible imprecations, and the inner fury was at its height; the very air, it seemed to her, was laden with her cries, with her curses and oaths.

With a strong gust of wind, a flash of lightning and a crash of thunder, she tore into her home.

Her daughter was not there.

She sank upon a chair and burst into wailing.

There was a terrifying crash of thunder. One of those thunderclaps that work the most widespread havoc. Nature seemed to be shaking off the entire residue of energy that had been left to her by the hot summer.

The inhabitants of the village were rooted to the spot in terror. They looked about, then ventured a glance outside. Hadn't some misfortune occurred? The penitents buried their faces deeper than ever in their prayer-books, and more than ever their voices quivered.

Cheyne, however, had apparently not heard the thunder. She continued to wail, to wail bitterly. Then a wild cry issued from her throat, as wild as the thunder:

"May she not live to come home! May they bring her to me dead! O Lord of the universe!"

The clouds replied with a clap of thunder and the wind sped apace, shrieking.

Suddenly she arose and dashed out as before. The wind accompanied her. Now it thrust her forward from behind, now it ran ahead like a faithful dog, smiting all in its path, raising the dirt from the road and mixing it with the thick drops that fell from the clouds, which were still black, and with the seething drops that coursed from her burning eyes.

She was running to the road just beyond the village.

They had surely gone for a walk on the road, where they had been seen several times. She would meet them on the way, or in Jonah's inn near the big forest.

On the Gentile's lane, the last one of the village, the dogs in the yards heard her hastening steps upon the drenched earth. Some of them began to bark behind the gates, not caring to venture out into the rain; others were not so lazy and crawled out from under the gates with an angry yelping. She neither saw nor heard them, however. She only gazed far out over the road, which began at the lane, and ran along.

One dog seized her skirt, which had become heavy with water. She did not heed this, and dragged the animal along for part of the way, until it tired of keeping pace with her in the pelting downpour. So it released her skirt. For a moment it thought of seizing her in some other spot, but at once, with a sullen growl, it set out for its yard.

On the road the wind became still stronger. And the thunder re-echoed here with thousands of reverberations from the neighboring forest. Cheyne looked only straight before her, into the distance, through the dense, water-laden atmosphere.

The way was strewn with heaps of twigs and branches that had been severed by the lightning, and even, a few trees lay before her, torn up from their very roots, and charred.

"Would to God that the thunder would strike *them* even so!" she muttered.

She was consumed by an inner cry. Now she had found a definite form for all her curses. The thunder up yonder had torn it from her.

And she ran on, on. ...

But what is this here?

A few paces before her lie two persons. A man and a woman. With contorted visages. In writhing positions. Their faces black as earth, their eyes rolled back. Two corpses, struck by lightning.

There was a brilliant flash, followed by a deafening thunderclap.

She recognized her daughter.

More by her clothes than by her charred countenance; more by her entire figure than by the horribly staring whites of her eyes.

The girl's arm lay beneath that of the young man. The top of the open umbrella in the youth's hand had been burned off.

The old woman was on the point of shrieking a curse, of adding her thunder to the fury of the storm's thunder; her eyes flashed together with the lightning; in her heart there arose a devastating tempest.

She wished to cry out the most evil of words—that the dead maiden had earned her end. She desired to send after her the most wretched and degrading of names.

Suddenly, however, all grew black before her. A flood of molten lead seemed to pour into her head. Weariness and trembling fell upon her. Her garments, saturated with the rain, seemed to drag her to the earth. Her eyes were extinguished.

The thunder and lightning and shrieking of the wind broke out anew.

But within the old woman all was quiet, dark, dead. She sank to her knees before the corpse of her daughter, stretched over the body her trembling arms, and a dull flame flickered up in her eyes.

Her entire being quivered. Her teeth knocked together. And with a hoarse, toneless voice she gasped:

"My darling daughter! Hennye, my darling!"

The Scandinavian Countries

Iceland   Denmark
Norway   Sweden

INTRODUCTION

THERE are four groups included under the heading Scandinavian Countries: the Icelandic, the Danish, the Norwegian, and the Swedish. Though there is an interesting modern Icelandic literature from which short stories could be selected for inclusion in this collection, the contribution of Iceland has been chosen from the Old Norse literature, which flourished nearly a thousand years ago, and which has since that time affected all the Scandinavian countries, England, France, and Germany. On the other hand, the early beginnings of Danish, Swedish, and Norwegian literature are either too closely imitative of the Icelandic, or are not of themselves sufficiently interesting, and the most significant stories of those countries were written in the Nineteenth and Twentieth Centuries.

The Icelandic story is found imbedded in the *Eddas* and sagas, the great collections of mythology, religion, and history that were brought together between the Ninth and the Fourteenth Centuries. The first is the *Elder Edda*, written in verse, and collected by Samund the Wise before or about the year 1300. The *Prose*, or *Younger*, *Edda*, based largely upon the *Elder Edda*, was the work of Snorri Sturluson, who lived in the Thirteenth Century. The same writer composed the famous collection known as the *Heimskringla*.

The saga literature of Iceland is very extensive. Over two hundred volumes of these narratives are still in existence. Sagas were written and rewritten until the most finished products, like the *Volsunga Saga*, stand revealed as the work of genuine artists.

Iceland and Denmark have been in close relationship since the earliest days. The literature of Denmark dates back nearly a thousand years, but that country, like many others, does not emerge as a distinct

750

entity of interest to the world at large until the Nineteenth Century, although occasional figures like those of Ludwig Holberg and Oehlenschlager stand out as exceptions. The first of the modern writers is Hans Christian Andersen, a writer of genius whose fairy tales are the delight of the entire world. Meyer Goldschmidt, though he was of a more realistic turn of mind, developed a certain type of short story with rare skill and Drachmann, too, has done some excellent work in this form, though he was also a painter, poet, novelist, politician, and man of affairs.

With Jacobsen we come to the first outstanding Danish novelist. He is said to have initiated realistic and psychological fiction in Denmark, though his debt to Andersen is freely acknowledged.

Norway was separated in 1814 from Denmark, and not long after it set about forming a literature of its own. To Wergeland and Welhaven is due the credit of having initiated the movement that produced Ibsen and Björnson. But before these two came Asbjörnson and Moe, whose collections of stories served to show later writers the wealth of material that was ready to hand. It is well known that Ibsen made use of the Asbjörnson collections in writing his *Peer Gynt*.

Björnson, a dramatist, poet, novelist, writer of stories, and political leader, was a great national figure, dominating the intellectual life of his country for half a century. His short stories are exquisitely written idylls, whose influence was felt throughout all the Scandinavian countries. Of his younger contemporaries Alexander Kielland is probably the most important. Like Björnson he felt the influence of Europe, and used his knowledge of foreign literature the better to depict the people of his native land.

Among contemporary Norwegian writers Knut Hamsun and Johan Bojer stand supreme. Both are best known by their novels of modern life, though both wrote some plays and short stories. Hamsun wrote only a few of the latter: Bojer devoted more time to the form and produced a few literary masterpieces.

Sweden, like Denmark, has a literature that dates back to the Middle Ages, and even in the Eighteenth Century could boast of several writers, but the late Nineteenth was one of the richest periods in her literary annals. The first of the stories chosen for inclusion is one of August Strindberg's. During the closing years of the last century Strindberg was Sweden's most distinguished man of letters: dramatist, novelist and scientist, he wrote a few volumes of sketches and short stories, of which *Love and Bread* shows the best-known aspect of his sceptical philosophy. Selma Lagerlöf is chiefly known for her novels and stories of the country people among whom she lived.

The modern Swedish writers have brought the short story to a high point of technical perfection, but in so doing they have remained essentially products of their own land, if only by reason of their insistence upon local themes and the description of backgrounds that are familiar to them.

Iceland

SNORRI STURLUSON

(1178—1241)

SNORRI STURLUSON was born in Iceland of an old Icelandic family. He received a good education, acquired wealth through marriage, and became a powerful landowner. He made several visits to Norway, where he was well received at court. Later in life he was implicated in political quarrels and wars, and was finally murdered by his son-in-law. He wrote many sagas, the *Heimskringla*, and the *Prose*, or *Younger*, *Edda*. His work was founded upon oral tradition and the writings of the earlier poets and historians.

Sturluson's long works are full of episodes and incidents, many of which, like *Baldr's Bale*, are unified short stories.

This version is from the translation of *The Prose Edda*, by Arthur Gilchrist Brodeur, published by the American-Scandinavian Foundation, New York, 1916, by whose permission it is here included.

BALDR'S BALE

(From the *Prose Edda*)

NOW shall be told of those tidings which seemed of more consequence to the Æsir. The beginning of the story is this, that Baldr the Good dreamed great and perilous dreams touching his life. When he told these dreams to the Æsir, then they took counsel together; and this was their decision: to ask safety for Baldr from all kinds of dangers. And Frigg took oaths to this purport, that fire and water should spare Baldr, likewise iron and metal of all kinds, stones, earth, trees, sicknesses, beasts, birds, venom, serpents. And when that was done and made known, then it was a diversion of Baldr's and the Æsir, that he should stand up in the Thing, and all the others should some shoot at him, some hew at him, some beat him with stones; but whatsoever was done hurt him not at all, and that seemed to them all a very worshipful thing.

But when Loki Laufeyarson saw this, it pleased him ill that Baldr took no hurt. He went to Fensalir to Frigg, and made himself into the likeness of a woman. Then Frigg asked if that woman knew what the Æsir did at the Thing. She said that all were shooting at Baldr, and moreover, that he took no hurt. Then said Frigg: "Neither weapons nor trees may hurt Baldr: I have taken oaths of them all." Then the woman asked: "Have all things taken oaths to spare Baldr?" and Frigg answered: "There grows a tree-sprout alone westward of Valhall; it is called Mistletoe; I thought it too young to ask the oath of." Then straightway the woman turned away; but Loki took Mistletoe and pulled it up and went to the Thing.

Hödr stood outside the ring of men, because he was blind. Then spake Loki to him: "Why dost thou not shoot at Baldr?" He answered: "Because I see not where Baldr is; and for this also, that I am weapon-less." Then said Loki: "Do thou also after the manner of other men, and show Baldr honor as the other men do. I will direct thee where he stands; shoot at him with this wand." Hödr took Mistletoe and shot at Baldr, being guided by Loki: the shaft flew through Baldr, and he fell dead to the earth; and that was the greatest mischance that has ever befallen among gods and men.

Then, when Baldr was fallen, words failed all the Æsir, and their hands likewise to lay hold of him; each looked at the other, and all were of one mind as to him who had wrought the work, but none might take vengeance, so great a sanctuary was in that place. But when the Æsir tried to speak, then it befell first that weeping broke out, so that none might speak to the others with words concerning his grief. But Odin bore that misfortune by so much the worst, as he had most perception of how great harm and loss for the Æsir were in the death of Baldr.

Now when the gods had come to themselves, Frigg spake, and asked who there might be among the Æsir, who would fain have for his own all her love and favor: let him ride the road to Hel, and seek if he may find Baldr, and offer Hel a ransom if she will let Baldr come home to Ásgard. And he is named Hermódr the Bold, Odin's son, who undertook that embassy. Then Sleipnir was taken, Odin's steed, and led forward; and Hermódr mounted on that horse and galloped off.

The Æsir took the body of Baldr and brought it to the sea. Hringhorni is the name of Baldr's ship: it was greatest of all ships; the gods would have launched it and made Baldr's pyre thereon, but the ship stirred not forward. Then word was sent to Jötunheim after that giantess who is called Hyrrokkinn. When she had come, riding a wolf and having a viper for bridle, then she leaped off the steed; and Odin called to four berserks to tend the steed; but they were not able to hold it until they had felled it. Then Hyrrokkinn went to the prow of the boat and thrust it out at the first push, so that fire burst from the rollers, and all lands trembled. Thor became angry and clutched his hammer, and would straightway have broken her head, had not the gods prayed for peace for her.

Then was the body of Baldr borne out on shipboard; and when his wife, Nanna the daughter of Nep, saw that, straightway her heart burst with grief, and she died; she was borne to the pyre, and fire was kindled. Then Thor stood by and hallowed the pyre with Mjöllnir; and before his feet ran a certain dwarf which was named Litr; Thor kicked at him with his foot and thrust him into the fire, and he burned. People of many races visited this burning: First is to be told of Odin, how Frigg and the Valkyrs went with him, and his ravens; but Freyr drove in his chariot with the boar called Gold-mane, or Fearful-Tusk, and Heimdallr rode the horse called Gold-Top, and Freyja drove her cats. Thither came also much people of the Rime-Giants and the Hill-Giants. Odin laid on the pyre that gold ring which is called Draupnir; this quality attended it, that every ninth night there dropped from it eight gold rings of equal weight. Baldr's horse was led to the bale-fire with all his trappings.

Now this is to be told concerning Hermódr, that he rode nine nights through dark dales and deep, so that he saw not before he was come to the river Gjöll and rode onto the Gjöll-Bridge; which bridge is thatched with glittering gold. Módgudr is the maiden called who guards the bridge; she asked him his name and race, saying that the day before there had ridden over the bridge five companies of dead men; "but the bridge thunders no less under thee alone, and thou hast not the color of dead men. Why ridest thou hither on Hel-way?" He answered: "I am appointed to ride to Hel to seek out Baldr. Hast thou perchance seen Baldr on Hel-way?" She said that Baldr had ridden there over Gjöll's Bridge,—"but down and north lieth Hel-way."

Then Hermódr rode on till he came to Hel-gate; he dismounted from his steed and made his girths fast, mounted and pricked him with his spurs; and the steed leaped so hard over the gate that he came no-wise near to it. Then Hermódr rode home to the hall and dismounted from his steed, went into the hall, and saw sitting there in the high-seat Baldr, his brother; and Hermódr tarried there overnight. At morn Hermódr prayed Hel that Baldr might ride home with him, and told how great weeping was among the Æsir. But Hel said that in this wise it should be put to the test, whether Baldr were so all-beloved as had been said: "If all things in the world, quick and dead, weep for him, then he shall go back to the Æsir; but he shall remain with Hel if any gainsay it or will not weep." Then Hermódr arose; but Baldr led him out of the hall, and took the ring Draupnir and sent it to Odin for a remembrance. And Nanna sent Frigg a linen smock, and yet more gifts, and to Fulla a golden finger-ring.

Then Hermódr rode his way back, and came into Ásgard, and told all those tidings which he had seen and heard. Thereupon the Æsir sent óver all the world messengers to pray that Baldr be wept out of Hel; and all men did this, and quick things, and the earth, and stones, and trees, and all metals,—even as thou must have seen that these things weep when they come out of frost and into the heat. Then, when the messengers went home, having well wrought their errand, they found, in a certain cave, where a giantess sat: she called herself Thökk. They prayed her to weep Baldr out of Hel; she answered:

> *"Thökk will weep   waterless tears*
> *For Baldr's bale-fare;*
> *Living or dead,   I loved not the churl's son;*
> *Let Hel hold to that she hath!"*

And men deem that she who was there was Loki Laufeyarson, who hath wrought most ill among the Æsir.

REGIN'S TALE

(Anonymous: 12th Century)

THE *Volsunga Saga*, one of the most beautiful and highly finished of all the many Icelandic sagas, is a composite work based upon the *Elder Edda*, oral tradition, songs, and chronicles. Like most of the sagas, it consists of many incidents woven together.

The present version, translated by William Morris and Magnusson, is from *The Story of the Volsungs*, Camelot Series, London, no date. It is the fourteenth chapter, and the full title is *Regin's Tale of His Brothers, and of the Gold Called Andvari's Hoard*. It is reprinted by permission of the Morris trustees.

REGIN'S TALE

(From the *Volsunga Saga*)

"THUS the tale begins," said Regin. "Hreidmar was my father's name, a mighty man and a wealthy: and his first son was named Fafnir, his second Otter, and I was the third, and the least of them all both for prowess and good conditions, but I was cunning to work in iron, and silver, and gold, whereof I could make matters that availed somewhat. Other skill my brother Otter followed, and had another nature withal, for he was a great fisher, and above other men herein; in that he had the likeness of an otter by day, and dwelt ever in the river, and bare fish to bank in his mouth, and his prey would he ever bring to our father, and that availed him much: for the most part he kept him in his otter-gear, and then he would come home, and eat alone, and slumbering, for on the dry land he might see naught. But Fafnir was by far the greatest and grimmest, and would have all things about called his.

"Now," says Regin, "there was a dwarf called Andvari, who ever abode in that force,* which was called Andvari's force, in the likeness of a pike, and got meat for himself, for many fish there were in the force; now Otter, my brother, was ever wont to enter into the force, and bring fish aland, and lay them one by one on the bank. And so it befell that Odin, Loki, and Hœnir, as they went their ways, came to Andvari's force, and Otter had taken a salmon, and ate it slumbering upon the river bank; then Loki took a stone and cast it at Otter, so that he gat his death thereby; the gods were well content with their prey, and fell to flaying off the otter's skin; and in the evening they came to Hreidmar's house, and showed him what they had taken: thereon he laid hands on them, and doomed them to such ransom, as that they should fill the otter skin with gold, and cover it over without with red gold; to they sent Loki to gather gold together for them: he came to Ran, and got her net, and went therewith to Andvari's force, and cast the net before the pike, and the pike ran into the net and was taken. Then said Loki—

> "'What fish of all fishes,
>   Swims strong in the flood,
> But hath learnt little wit to beware?
>   Thine head must thou buy,
>   From abiding in hell,
> And find me the wan waters flame.'

He answered—

> "'Andvari folk call me,
>   Call Oinn my father,
> Over many a force have I fared;
>   For a Norn of ill-luck,
>   This life on me lay
> Through wet ways ever to wade.'

* Waterfall (Ice. *foss*, *fors*).

"So Loki beheld the gold of Andvari, and when he had given up the gold, he had but one ring left, and that also Loki took from him; then the dwarf went into a hollow of the rocks, and cried out that that gold-ring, yea and all the gold withal, should be the bane of every man who should own it thereafter.

"Now the gods rode with the treasure to Hreidmar, and fulfilled the otter-skin, and set it on its feet, and they must cover it over utterly with gold: but when this was done then Hreidmar came forth, and beheld yet one of the muzzle hairs, and bade them cover that withal; then Odin drew the ring, Andvari's loom, from his hand, and covered up the hair therewith; then sang Loki—

> "'Gold enow, gold enow,
>   A great weregild, thou hast,
> That my head in good hap I may hold;
>   But thou and thy son
>   Are naught fated to thrive,
> The bane shall it be of you both.'

"Thereafter," says Regin, "Fafnir slew his father and murdered him, nor got I aught of the treasure, and so evil he grew, that he fell to lying abroad, and begrudged any share in the wealth to any man, and so became the worst of all worms, and ever now lies brooding upon that treasure: but for me, I went to the king and became his master-smith; and thus is the tale told of how I lost the heritage of my father, and the weregild for my brother."

Denmark

HANS CHRISTIAN ANDERSEN

(1805–1875)

ANDERSEN was born at Odense. His parents were so poor that he had no chance at first of securing the education he wanted. At an early age he went to Copenhagen, tried to act, and failed. With the help of friends he was able eventually to attend the University. His earliest writings were verses and fantastic tales in the manner of Hoffmann, plays, and a few novels. In 1835 he published his first volume of fairy tales, which became at once immensely popular, bringing him fame and money. Throughout his long life he continued to write tales, novels, books of travel and plays, but it is chiefly his fairy tales that are remembered.

The Andersen fairy tale is different from all others of its kind. It is at its best a subtle prose poem, satiric, graceful, and harmonious. *The Shepherdess and the Sweep* is one of the loveliest of his works.

The present version, anonymously translated, is reprinted from an undated edition, published in London.

THE SHEPHERDESS AND THE SWEEP

HAVE you ever seen a very old wooden cabinet, quite black with age and carved all over with leaves and filigree-work? Such an one stood in a sitting-room, and had been in the family from the great-grandmother's time. It was covered from top to bottom with carved roses and tulips, amongst which there were the most extraordinary flourishes, and from these sprang the antlered heads of stags, whilst on the top, in the middle, stood a whole figure. He was ridiculous enough to look at, with goat's legs, short horns on his head, and a long beard, besides which he was constantly grinning, for it could not be called a laugh. The children christened him the GoatslegHighadjutantgeneral-militarycommandant, for that was a difficult name to pronounce, and a title not conferred upon many. To carve him cannot have been easy work, but there he stood, constantly looking at the table under the looking-glass, for there was the loveliest little china Shepherdess. Her shoes were gilt, and her dress neatly fastened up with a red rose, and then she had a gilt hat and a shepherdess's crook. She was, indeed, lovely. Close to her stood a little Sweep, as black as any coal, but he, too, was entirely made of china; he was quite as neat and clean as anyone else, for that he was a Sweep was, of course, only to represent something, and the potter could just as well have made a prince of him.

There he stood, with his face red and white, just like a girl, and that was a mistake, for it might have been blackened a little. He was close to the Shepherdess, and they had both been placed where they stood, which, being the case, they were naturally engaged to each other, and well suited they were, for they were made of the same china, and were both little.

Not far from them there was another figure, but three times as big, a Chinese, who could nod his head. He was also made of china, and pretended to be the Shepherdess's grandfather, though he could not prove it, so claimed authority over her, and had promised her to the Goatsleg-Highadjutantgeneralmilitarycommandant.

"You will have a husband," the old Chinese said, "who I almost believe is made of mahogany, and he has the whole cabinet full of plate, besides the valuables that are in the hidden drawers."

"I will not go into the dark cabinet," the little Shepherdess said, "for I have heard that he has eleven china wives in there."

"Then you will make the twelfth," the old Chinese said, "for this very night your marriage shall take place." He then nodded his head and fell asleep.

The little Shepherdess cried and looked at her dearly beloved china Sweep.

"I must ask you," she said, "to go with me out into the wide world, for here we cannot stay."

"Your will is my will," the little Sweep said. "Let us go at once, and I have no doubt by my calling I shall gain sufficient to keep you."

"Were we but safely down from the table," she said, "for I shall never be happy till we are out in the wide world."

He consoled her, and showed her where to put her little feet, on the projections and ornaments, within their reach, and they got safely to the floor, but when they looked towards the old cabinet all was confusion there. The stags stretched their heads further out, raising their antlers, and turned their necks from side to side. The GoatslegHighadjutantgeneralmilitarycommandant jumped high up into the air, and cried as loud as he could to the old Chinese, "They are now running away! they are now running away!"

At this they were frightened, and they jumped into the cupboard under the window-seat.

Here lay three or four packs of cards, which were not complete, and a little doll's theater, in which a play was being acted, and the Queens of hearts, diamonds, clubs and spades sat in the front row fanning themselves with their tulips, whilst behind them stood the Knaves, who seemed to be their pages. The plot of the play was the difficulties thrown in the way of two persons who wished to be married, and the little Shepherdess cried, for it was her own story.

"I cannot bear this," she said, "I must get out of the cupboard." But when they were out and looked up at the table, they saw the old Chinese was awake and his whole body shaking.

"Now the old Chinese is coming," the little Shepherdess cried, and fell down upon her china knees, she was in such a fright.

"I have an idea," the Sweep said. "Let us get into the potpourri-jar which stands there in the corner, where we can lie on rose-leaves and lavender, and throw salt in his eyes if he comes."

"That cannot help us," she said; "besides, I know that the old Chinese and the potpourri-jar were once engaged to each other, and there always remains some sort of tie between people with whom such a connection has existed. No, there is nothing left for us but to go out in the wide world."

"Have you really courage to go out with me into the wide world?" the Sweep asked. "Have you considered how large it is, and that we can never come back here?"

"Yes, I have," she answered.

The Sweep looked at her intently, and then said, "My way lies up the chimney, and that way I know well enough, and if you really have courage to go with me, we shall soon mount up so high that they will never be able to reach us."

And he led her to the grate.

"How black it looks up there!" she said, but still she went with him, and they had not gone far when he exclaimed, "Look, what a beautiful star is shining there above!"

It was a real star in the heavens shining down upon them, as if to show them the way. They crept on and climbed, and a dreadful way it was—so high, so high, but he held and lifted her, and showed her where to place her little china feet, till at last they reached the edge of the chimney, where they seated themselves, for they were very tired, as well they might be.

The sky, with all its stars, was above them, and below them lay all the roofs of the city, and they could see far around, so far out into the world. The poor Shepherdess had never imagined anything like it, and laying her little head on her Sweep's breast, she cried so that the gold was washed off her girdle.

"That is too much," she sobbed. "That I can never bear. The world is too large; oh, were I but back again on the table under the looking-glass! I shall never know happiness till I am back there. I have followed you into the world, and if you care for me you must now go back with me."

The Sweep spoke most reasonably and sensibly to her, spoke of the old Chinese, and of the GoatslegHighadjutantgeneralmilitarycommandant, but she sobbed so violently that he was obliged to do as she wished, though it was foolish.

They therefore climbed down again with much trouble and difficulty, and when they got near the bottom they stopped to listen, but all being quiet they stepped into the room. There lay the old Chinese on the floor; he had fallen off the table when he attempted to follow them, and there he lay broken into three pieces. His whole back had come off in one piece, and his head had rolled far off into a corner of the room.

"That is horrible!" the little Shepherdess said. "My old grandfather is broken to pieces, and it is our fault. Oh, I shall never survive it!" And she wrung her little hands.

"He can be riveted," the Sweep said. "He can very well be riveted.

Do not you give way so, for if they put a good strong rivet in his back and neck he will be as good as new again, and will be able to say many unpleasant things to us yet."

"Do you think so?" she said, and they then got on to the table again where they had always stood.

"It was not of much use going all the way we did," the Sweep said; "we might just as well have saved ourselves that trouble."

"Oh, if my poor old grandfather were but riveted," the Shepherdess said. "Will it cost very much?"

The family had him riveted, and he was in every way as good as new again, excepting that, owing to the rivet in his neck, he could no longer nod his head.

"You have grown proud since you were broken to pieces," the Goats-legHighadjutantgeneralmilitarycommandant said, "but I do not see any good reason for it. Now, am I to have her, or am I not?"

The Sweep and the little Shepherdess looked so beseechingly at the old Chinese, fearing that he would nod, but he could not. He did not choose to tell a stranger that he had a rivet in the back of his neck, so he was quiet, and the Shepherdess and Sweep remained together, loving each other till they got broken.

MEYER ARON GOLDSCHMIDT

(1819–1887)

GOLDSCHMIDT was for the greater part of his life actively engaged in editorial work. As editor of a satirical and political paper he threw himself whole-heartedly into the struggle for the establishment of liberal ideas. As a writer he excelled in his novels and tales of Jewish life. He is regarded as a great stylist, and in his typical novels and short stories he shows a firm grasp of character.

Henrik and Rosalie is considered one of his finest stories. It was originally published in his *Love Stories of Many Lands*, in 1867. The present version is translated by Minna Wreschner. It appeared in the *American Scandinavian Review*, July, 1922, and is here reprinted by permission of the editor.

HENRIK AND ROSALIE

THE fate that rules in matters of love is often singular, and its ways are inscrutable, not only in vital things but also in those of less importance, as this story will show.

Henrik Falk, student of divinity, had taken his fiancée, Rosalie Hvidbjerg, to the theater one evening to see Heiberg's *The Inseparables*. The following morning, as he was seated in his cozy student quarters at Regensen, smoking his pipe, he received the following note: "I consider it best that our engagement be broken.—Rosalie."

Henrik Falk's surprise upon reading this message can easily be understood; he put down his pipe, dressed quickly, and hastened to his fiancée's home. There he was told that Rosalie had gone away, but if he wished he could see her aunt. The aunt arrived but could give him no explanation, as she herself was in the dark about the whole affair. When Rosalie had returned from the theater the previous night, she had been very quiet; but soon after she had shown signs of great inward agitation and had said that to her the unpoetic relations which existed between Malle and Klister (main characters in the play), seemed unbearable, even wrong, and that probably all or at least the greater part of engaged couples were like that, or else sooner or later would assume that indifferent attitude toward each other, in which case she preferred to remain single. Whereupon she had written scores of letters, no doubt all to him, Henrik Falk, had again torn them up, one after the other, but had finally sent one letter to the post office. She did not go to bed, but packed her belongings and left by the morning train.

"You know," continued Rosalie's aunt. "I had really no control over her plans. She was here only on a visit and if she wanted to go to the— to other relatives of hers, I had no means of preventing her."

Which relatives, which uncle and aunt—for Rosalie's parents were dead—the lady would not tell; she said she had given her word of honor not to disclose the secret. They discussed the matter for some time, and in the course of the conversation Rosalie's aunt asked Henrik if he was certain that he had not in any way offended the young girl, of which he assured her most emphatically.

"Oh, well," said the aunt, "it is a difficult problem to handle such a young girl, only seventeen years of age, besides being of independent means. You know, Mr. Falk, she was really too young to become engaged. Next time you must be more cautious."

On his way home, and for several hours after, Henrik reviewed carefully his past life. He had to admit that there had been moments when he had—not exactly regretted, but almost regretted his engagement. Not because he had found any fault whatsoever with Rosalie; in the light in which he now viewed the situation, he asked himself what it was that at times had made him less appreciative of his good fortune, in fact so ungrateful that it was now difficult for him to realize his former feeling. When he examined his own heart, he remembered that even the previous day it had almost seemed to him as if Rosalie had been won too easily. They met at a dance shortly after he had finished college; later there was a casual meeting, a walk, a happy mood—and the word was said. He had been accepted, and fortune had bestowed upon him a happiness far greater than he had heretofore realized. Yes, that was the trouble, he had not appreciated his good luck; in his heart there had been an apathy, a lack of force and will, a want of enthusiasm which she undoubtedly had noticed, and now she had punished him cruelly but justly. In his present mood she appeared to him in all her loveliness which for some time he had almost overlooked. He saw her before his mind's eye more clearly than he had ever beheld her with his physical eye. And now it was all over! For among the qualities which heretofore he had hardly noticed or appreciated in her, one trait now seemed to stand out: she was determined and high-minded. It was due to her ideality and womanly loftiness, and to her lack of coquetry that she had immediately accepted him, and this romance he had dragged into mere prose and thereby become extremely unhappy himself.

For some time he grieved very much and, although his sorrow became less intense as time passed, it remained in his heart and made a great change in him.

To begin with, he gave up the study of theology. This desire had been as sudden as his engagement. He had discussed with Rosalie country life, parsonages, happiness, and before he knew it this had led him to speak the decisive word; later he had had a feeling that the way in which he had spoken contained a promise that he would lead her into his parsonage. This was the reason why he chose the study of theology. But now there was no reason why he should follow this profession. He had lost all desire either for parsonages or parsons' wives, or, in fact, for wives of any kind, and he decided to take up the study which he had originally preferred, and which in his present mood seemed to offer the greatest emancipation from his former plans, namely, medicine.

After five and a half years of hard study, Henrik Falk had finished and was ready to start out as a young physician. He decided to settle down in some provincial town, and this was especially due to the fact that in the course of time he had developed a certain romantic sentiment. In Copenhagen everything seemed to him so prosaic, while life in a small town, with visits to the neighboring villages, still offered an opportunity of finding innocence, spontaneity, romance and poetry.

He heard that there were prospects of acquiring a clientele in a small town in Jutland, and he immediately left for that place. But although the good-looking young doctor with the wistful smile made a pleasant impression, he immediately met with difficulties; there were not many apartments to be had, and the few that suited him the landlords did not like to rent to him for fear of offending his colleagues who were already established there. Just at that time a veterinary died and, having some available funds, Falk bought the veterinary's house from his widow and soon moved into these new quarters.

One day, not long afterwards, a man from the neighboring country drove up in front of the house and asked the doctor to follow him to his master's farm. Falk was pleased that the news of his establishment had already reached the farmers in the district; his new, hitherto unused doctor's stool was soon placed in the wagon, and the two drove off in silence.

After they got out of the town Falk asked the sullen driver, "What is the matter with your patient? What do you think has gone wrong?"

"He got a bone in his throat," replied the man.

"I see! Did you not try to slap him on the back?"

The man turned slowly toward the doctor, looked puzzled at him and said, "Very likely."

There the conversation ended, and after a while they arrived at the farm, which was situated at the edge, or almost at the edge of the heath. The farmer received the doctor, showed him the way to the parlor and sent for sandwiches and brandy, but Falk had no appetite; as a matter of fact he did not feel quite well. Finally the time came to look at the patient, and Falk was somewhat surprised when the farmer led him into the yard, through the stables, and stopped at a small isolated house situated in a morass which sent out a most unpleasant odor. The farmer opened the low door and took the doctor over to a pig.

"There he is," he said.

Henry Falk had entirely forgotten that he had moved into the house of a veterinary. The blood rushed to his cheeks and he cried, "What, do you expect me to cure your pig?"

The farmer answered, "Well, before you came we sent for Jespersen to cure the horse, but next time, if it so pleases our Lord, you shall treat the horse also. To-day you will have to be satisfied with the pig."

"Go to——with your pig and your horse."

"You should not use such ugly language," said the farmer, and colored slightly.

"That is just what I shall!" shouted the doctor. "And next time you have a sick beast, send for a veterinary and not for a practising physician. I have heard it said that to you farmers, nothing is too good for your beasts, but that you scarcely send for a veterinary when a human being is ill."

"Is that so!" said the farmer.

"Yes, that is so. And now let me get back to town immediately."

"Go ahead," replied the farmer. "Nobody is holding you back, neither you nor your foul words. You had better take them along with you."

"It just occurs to me," said the doctor, in a milder tone, "that there may be a misunderstanding somewhere. I moved into the house of Hansen, the veterinary, so that may explain the case."

"May be," answered the farmer.

"Will you please send the wagon for me?"

"No, our horses shall not drive you or your ugly words from this place—not unless you cure the pig first."

"Don't talk to me about your confounded pig."

Without another word the farmer took hold of the doctor so it hurt, pressing the latter's arms tightly up against his sides just above the hips, and by lifting him a little from the ground brought him into an almost horizontal position. In this fashion the farmer carried him outside, and not until they had reached some distance from the farm did he put him down, exclaiming. "Shame on you and your horrid language!"

Groaning with pain and anger the doctor cried, "You shall drive me home. You have my doctor's stool; if you keep it you are a thief."

The farmer returned to the house, fetched the stool and, laying two kroner upon it, said, "There you are, and once more shame on you!"

The doctor realized that he had lost out. He decided to start on his way home on foot, and in the meantime try to hire somebody to fetch his stool. Unfamiliar as he was with the neighborhood, he only remembered that when entering the farm he had turned to the left, so that in leaving he now turned to the right. But he entirely overlooked the fact that he had been put out on the opposite side, and the result was that he took the wrong direction. At first, owing to his agitated condition, he did not notice the surroundings, but when after a while he began to wonder that he had not yet reached the main road, he could no longer find even the path; nothing but wheel tracks could be seen in the heath. Besides, it was not only beginning to grow dark, but a cold rain had started, and a sharp wind was blowing.

He deliberated for a moment, trying to find his bearings, and as he considered carefully everything that had happened, he remembered suddenly that the farmer had not put him out by the front gate; he realized therefore that he had taken the wrong course and would have to go back almost as far as he had come. He did not want to pass the farm once more; and besides, he figured out that as the farm must be on his right hand and the town south of the farmstead, he would have to keep in a straight line toward the southeast. But the heath cannot be traversed by means of guesswork, and after a short time he absolutely lost his way among the heather, wet to the skin and surrounded by utter darkness.

The situation began indeed to seem perilous, and not without reason. The indisposition he had felt earlier in the day had increased. The blood hammered in his temples, and his head was hot and pained him considerably. His clothes were soaking wet, and he shivered with cold. He forced himself to go forward, walking in a straight line, and continued this course not so much because he had hopes of finding his way, but in order to get warm and not to collapse. Suddenly the heath seemed to change into meadowland. He discovered in the distance a house with lights in the windows, but a body of water separated him from it. He continued his way almost unconscious.

At this moment two women—one an elderly lady and the other a young girl of twenty-two or -three years of age—were sitting in the spacious, old-fashioned parlor on the estate Lundtofte. The old lady looked wise and placid; the young girl had a soulful face which might have been considered fitting for the heroine of a romance on an isolated estate. She had a dreamy expression, and her whole appearance denoted a charming simplicity, but at the same time there was something indescribable about her person, about her eyes, her complexion, her hair or perhaps the manner in which it was piled on her head, which did not belong in these surroundings, which seemed to conceal a memory and to rebel against the thought that the doors were closed, that no guest was expected, unknown though his name might be. To him who understood the language, this young figure expressed, not in plain letters but in music without words, that she had approached many a guest with a searching glance, but had again withdrawn after consulting something within herself which always in the last moment seemed to admonish her to wait. The poetic nimbus that surrounded her was expectancy—expectation of some romance, a beginning, pensive doubt as to whether it would ever happen, and at the same time a firm determination to give romance a trial for another year, even if her cheeks should grow a little paler in the waiting.

The head of the household was absent on a hunting party. He may not have been a very interesting man, but even a less entertaining person to whom one is accustomed, may by his absence leave a hole, an emptiness, which it is difficult to fill, especially in the country where the postman is not expected for another day or two, or where the farmhand has returned from his last trip to town with the wrong books from the circulating library or perhaps with no books at all. Fortunately Lundtofte had its own library. After impatiently putting aside her embroidery, the young girl fetched a copy of Oehlenschläger's poems, and at the request of the older lady began reading aloud. It was the romance about Aage and Else. Before she had reached the end, she suddenly stopped, exclaiming, "I wonder how these legends arise, about lovers who step forth from their graves? I am sure they are not taken from real life."

The old lady's reply led the conversation to the subject of ghosts; then with a jump it turned again to love, and once more drifted on to ghosts, until the young girl said: "It would be worth while meeting some one in this life who had the power and the will to appear to us after death."

The old lady replied: "Those who would do that for us, we probably do not see in the right light until they are in their graves."

Then silence followed in which each was occupied with her own thoughts.

Suddenly the maid appeared and said, "Someone is outside asking for shelter."

"What sort of person?" demanded the old lady.

"I don't know. He looks awful, as if he was steeped in his own clothes."

"Is he a journeyman?"

"No, he wears a white shirt—even though it is no longer white."

"I wonder who it can be? Ask him his name."

The maid left, but returned immediately, saying, "He is lying outside."

"What do you mean?"

"Yes, he is lying outside. I am afraid he is dead."

They all hurried into the hall. The young girl uttered a cry at the sight of Henry Falk, for he it was—our wandering doctor—as my reader no doubt has guessed. The old lady gave instructions to get a room ready, to put warm sheets on the bed, and so forth.

It took several days before the doctor regained consciousness, and when it happened, he experienced something which everyone in his own way may expect to encounter once in his life, namely, a miracle —something so wonderful and exquisite that it does not seem to come to us from natural sources according to rules and merits or even by accident, but must have befallen us by the grace of God.

Rosalie was sitting at his bedside, lovelier than ever, beautified through her very sacrifice, fairylike and glorified by the suddenness, the strangeness, and the enchantment of the whole occurrence.

How these two again joined the bond that had been torn asunder more than five years ago, my reader must picture for himself. Such reconciliations are made in words which have a strange and mysterious power over those by whom they are expressed and those for whom they are intended, but to everyone else they lose their wondrous sound.

It may be said, however, that the reconcilement was so much easier as Rosalie had never really thought that the connection had been broken entirely and, strange as it may sound, when she wrote her little note to Henrik she had a feeling, not as if the tie were cut forever, but rather as if it were being prolonged for an indefinite time. Let him who can explain it, though it is of no vital importance any more than the fact that it soon occurred to Henrik that he, too, had had the same feeling.

However this may be, there was one thing which still lingered in Rosalie's memory after the first rapture—in which the whole estate participated—had subsided, and which never ceased to have an exhilarating and refreshing influence on her married life: it was the delight she took in picturing to herself Henrik traversing the heath guided by her love, although ignorant thereof and even unwilling in his suffering condition. It seemed to her that she had seen with her own eyes life's poetry brought into reality, by his side, with her hand on his shoulder, leading him through the wet heather, forcing him forward step by step, toward the happiness which had once been lost. These memories were forever a source of great happiness to her, and every time the subject was discussed it brought to the doctor's face a tender and grateful smile, yet at the same time gave him an uncomfortable feeling which he carefully concealed, for he had not the heart to tell his wife in plain words that this wonderful, blessed, romantic turn in their lives was due to an unromantic pig who had got a bone in his throat.

JENS PETER JACOBSEN

(1847—1885)

JACOBSEN, who began writing under the influence of Hans Christian Andersen, soon developed into a novelist and short story writer of great originality. Though he was as deeply interested in natural science as in literature, during the course of his short life he was influential chiefly as a writer.

Two Worlds is typical of his poetic turn of mind, and reveals his technical skill as a story-teller. It is translated by H. Knudsen, first appeared in the *Pagan* magazine, and is here reprinted by permission of the editor.

TWO WORLDS

THE Salzach is not a merry river. On its eastern bank lies a little village, very gloomy, very poor, and strangely quiet.

Like a miserable flock of misshapen beggars who have been stopped by the river, without fare for the ferryman, stand the houses down there on the uttermost edge of the bank, their decayed shoulders leaning against each other, and grope hopelessly with their weather-beaten, crutch-like supports in the grayish river, while their dull windows stare from the background of their porches under the over-hanging thatch-roof brows—stare with a scowling expression of hateful chagrin at the happier houses on the opposite bank which are built singly, or two by two, in cozy company, and are scattered, here and there, over the green plains, far toward the golden misty distance. But about the poor houses there is no light; only depressing darkness and stillness, weighed down by the sound of the river which slowly, cease-lessly, rolls past, mumbling to itself on its way, so tired of life, so strangely absent minded.

The sun was setting, the locusts began to fill the air with their crystal-clear humming, which was carried over from the opposite shore by sud-den weak gusts of wind that kept rising and dying away in the thin reeds on the shore.

A little way up the river a boat was approaching.

A weak, emaciated woman was standing in one of the houses close by the shore, bent over the railing of the porch, and looking toward the boat. She was shading her eyes with her almost transparent hand, for, up there where the boat was, the rays of the sun lay golden and sharply glittering on the water, as if it were sailing on a mirror of gold.

Through the clear dusk shone the woman's wax-pale face, as if it had light in itself. Distinct and sharp, it could be seen, just as one sees the white foam which even in the darkest nights whitens the waves of the ocean. Full of fear, her hopeless eyes were searching; a strangely weak-minded smile lay about her tired mouth, but the vertical wrinkles in her protruding forehead nevertheless spread a shadow of the decision of despair over her entire face.

The bell began to toll in the small village church.

She turned from the sunset, and rocked her head to and fro, as if she sought to escape the sound of the bells, while she mumbled almost as an answer to the continuous ringing:

"I cannot wait. I cannot wait."

But the sound continued.

As if in pain, she walked back and forth on the veranda. The shadows of despair had grown deeper, and she drew her breath heavily, like one who is forced to tears and cannot cry.

In long, long years she had suffered from a painful malady which never let her rest, whether lying down or walking. She had consulted one "wise" woman after another. She had dragged herself from one "holy" spring to another, but without avail. Finally she had gone on the September pilgrimage to St. Bartholomew; and here an old one-eyed man had advised her to tie together a bouquet of edelweiss and a splinter of glass, a huck of corn, and some ferns from a graveyard, a lock of her hair and a splinter from a coffin, and this she was to throw toward a young woman who was healthy and fresh and who came toward her across flowing water. Then the malady would leave her and pass to the other.

And now she had this bouquet hidden under her shawl, and up there on the river came a boat, the first since she had tied the magic posy. She had again stepped to the railing of the porch. The boat was so near, she could see that there were six passengers on board. Strangers they looked to be. At the prow stood the puntsman with his pole. At the rudder sat a lady, and close by her a young man who watched while she steered according to the directions of the puntsman. The others sat in the middle of the boat.

The sick woman bent far over the railing. Every line in her face was taut, and her hand was under her shawl. The blood beat at her temples. Her breathing almost stopped; with quivering nostrils, flaming cheeks, and wide-open staring eyes, she awaited the arrival of the boat.

Already the voices of the travelers could be heard—now clearly and now as a muffled murmur.

"Happiness," one of them was saying, "is an absolutely pagan idea. You cannot find the word in a single place in the New Testament."

"Salvation?" questioned another.

"No. Now listen," someone said; "it is true that the ideal conversation gets as far away as possible from what one is talking about; but that, it seems to me, we could best do by turning back to what we started with."

"Very well, then. The Greeks..."

"First the Phœnicians!"

"What do you know about the Phœnicians?"

"Nothing! But why should the Phœnicians always be skipped?"

The boat was now opposite the house, and just as it passed someone on board lighted his cigarette. The light fell in a few short flashes on the lady at the helm, and in the reddish glare one beheld a fresh, girlish face with a happy smile about the parted lips and a dreamy expression in the clear eyes that looked up to the dark sky. The light went out. A slight splash was heard, as of something thrown into the water, and the boat drifted past.

About a year later. The sun was setting amidst banks of heavy, deeply glowing clouds which cast a blood-red reflection over the dark waters of the river. A fresh wind blew over the plains. There were no locusts—only the murmur of the river, and the whispering of the reeds. In the distance a boat was coming down the stream.

The old woman was down by the edge of the river. ... After she had thrown her magic bouquet towards the young girl she had fainted, and the strong emotion—perhaps also the new doctor who had recently arrived in the vicinity—had worked a change in her malady. For months her condition improved, and finally she regained her health entirely. In the beginning she was as if intoxicated by this feeling of health; but it did not last long. She grew downhearted and sorrowful, restless and full of despair, for she was constantly pursued by the picture of the young girl in the boat. It seemed to her the girl was kneeling at her feet and looked at her with pleading eyes. Later the vision vanished, but she knew that it was still there. The girl kept moaning all the time. Then she grew silent, but visible again. Presently the vision was always before her, pale and emaciated, staring at her with unnaturally large wondering eyes. ...

This evening she was down at the river's edge; she had a stick in her hand, and she drew cross after cross in the soft mud; now and again she arose and listened; then she bent down and drew crosses again.

Presently the bell began to toll.

She carefully finished the last cross, put the stick away, kneeled down and prayed. Then she walked into the river till it reached her armpits. She folded her hands and let herself down into the black water. The water took her, pulled her down into its depths, and rolled on, as ever, heavy and sad, past the village, past the fields—away.

The boat was very near now. The same young people were on board who had helped each other steer the year before, and they were on their wedding-trip. He sat at the helm; she stood in the middle of the boat, draped in a large gray shawl, with a little red hood over her head... stood leaning against the short sailless mast, and hummed.

They drifted past the house. She nodded happily to the helmsman, looked up to the sky, and began to sing; sang hummingly as she leaned against the mast with her eyes lifted toward the drifting clouds... a song filled with happiness triumphant.

Norway

PETER CHRISTEN ASBJÖRNSEN

(1812–1878)

JÖRGEN MOE

(1813–1880)

BOTH Asbjörnsen and Moe came from the country, and belonged to families in modest circumstances. They made friends while preparing for a university career. Influenced by the Grimms, they set out to study the folklore of their country, and in their first collection of tales, which appeared in 1841, they produced a work of striking interest and genuine originality. "This volume," says John Gade, "was perhaps the greatest single event in the whole movement of that generation toward a more truly national culture."

The Smith Who Could Not Get into Hell is a highly artistic treatment of a bit of ancient folklore. It is reprinted, in the translation by Helen and John Gade, from *Norwegian Fairy Tales*, American-Scandinavian Foundation, New York, 1924, by permission of the Foundation.

THE SMITH WHO COULD NOT GET INTO HELL

IN the days when Our Lord and St. Peter walked on earth, they came once upon a time, to a smith who had made a bargain with the devil to belong to him after seven years if during that time he could be the master of all other smiths; and both the smith and the devil had signed their names to this contract. That was why the smith had set up over his smithy door a big sign which read: "Here lives the master of all masters!"

When Our Lord came along and saw this, He went in.

"Who are you?" he said to the smith.

"Read what's over the door," said the smith, "and if you can't read, you'll have to wait till some one comes along to help you."

Before Our Lord could answer, a man came along leading a horse which he wanted the smith to shoe.

"Won't you let me shoe him?" said Our Lord.

"You can try," said the smith; "you can't do it so badly but that I can fix it again."

So Our Lord went out and cut off one of the horse's forelegs, put it in the forge, made the shoe glowing hot, sharpened the calks and nails and drove them home and then put the leg, whole and perfect, back on the horse. When that was done, he took the other front leg and did the same, and after putting that leg back, took the two hind legs, first the right and then the left, put them in the forge till the shoes were white with heat, sharpened calks and nails and drove them in and finally put these legs, too, back on the horse.

The smith stood by all the time watching Him.

"You're not such a bad smith, after all," he said.

"Do you think so?" said Our Lord.

Soon after the smith's mother came to tell him dinner was ready. She was old and wrinkled, bent double, and barely able to walk.

"Now you mark carefully what you see," said Our Lord, and He took the old woman, put her into the forge, and changed her into a beautiful young girl.

"I repeat what I've said," said the smith, "you're quite a smith. Over my door stands: 'Here lives the master of all masters,' but even if I have to say it myself, 'We live and learn,'" and, so saying, he went home to eat his dinner. When he came back to the smithy, a man rode up and wanted his horse shod. Our Lord and St. Peter were still there.

"I'll do it in a jiffy," said the smith; "I've just learned a new way of shoeing which isn't so bad when the days are short." So he began to cut and break till he had taken off the horse's four legs. "For," said he, "I don't see why one should bother to take them one by one."

He put the legs into the forge just as he had seen Our Lord do, heaped on a lot of coal, and told the apprentices to work the bellows hard. But it turned out just as one might have expected; the legs burnt up, and the smith had to pay for the horse. That did not please him at all.

Just then a poor old hag came hobbling along, and the smith thought that, though he had not succeeded in one thing, he was sure to with the other, so he grabbed the old woman and put her into the forge, paying no attention to her cries and prayers.

"Old as you are, you don't know what's good for you," said the smith; "you'll be a young girl again in a minute, and I won't charge you a cent for the forging." But it went no better with the old woman than with the horse's legs.

"That was a shame," said Our Lord.

"Oh, she won't be missed," answered the smith; "but the devil ought to be ashamed: he is hardly keeping to what stands over my door."

"Suppose I were to give you three wishes, what would they be?" said Our Lord.

"Just try," said the smith, "and you'll find out."

Our Lord asked him what they were.

"Well, then, I wish, first, that whenever I tell someone to climb up into the pear tree outside the smithy wall, he will have to stay there till I tell him he may come down again," said the smith. "Next, I wish that when I beg anyone to sit down in the armchair in the workroom, he will have to stay there till I myself beg him to get up again, and, lastly, whenever I ask someone to creep into the steel mesh purse I have in my pocket, he will have to stay there till I give him leave to creep out again."

"You've wished very foolishly," said St. Peter; "first of all, you should have asked for God's grace and friendship."

"I didn't dare ask for anything so great," said the smith, whereupon Our Lord and St. Peter bade him good-bye and left.

Well, time wore on, and when the seven years were up, the devil came, according to the terms of the contract, to fetch the smith.

"Are you ready?" he asked, poking his nose in at the smithy door.

"Well, first I should really like to make a head to this nail," answered the smith. "Meanwhile you just climb up into the pear tree and pick a pear to munch on. You must be both hungry and thirsty after your trip."

The devil thanked him for the kind offer, and climbed up into the pear tree.

"Well, now, as I consider this job," said the smith, "I'm afraid it will take me at least four years to make a head to this nail, for the iron is as hard as the deuce; all that time you can't come down, but you'll get a good rest sitting up there."

The devil begged and implored for all he was worth to be allowed to come down, but it did no good. At last he had to promise to do as the smith said and not to come back for four years.

"Now you may come down again," said the smith.

When the time was up, there was the devil again to fetch the smith.

"Now you must be ready," said the devil. "You must have made a head on that nail by this time."

"Yes, I've got the head on," said the smith, "but you've come a little too soon all the same, for I haven't sharpened the point yet. While I'm sharpening the nail, you may sit down in my armchair and rest, for I am sure you must be tired."

"Thanks," said the devil, sitting down in the armchair. But no sooner was he seated than the smith told him that, as he looked his work over, he was afraid it would take him at least four years to sharpen the nail and that the devil would have to sit there while he worked.

At first the devil begged him politely to let him out of the chair, but then he got angry and began to threaten him. The smith kept making all kinds of excuses, saying it was the fault of the iron which was hard as the deuce, and he tried to console the devil by telling him how comfortable he was in the armchair and that he would certainly let him out in four years on the stroke of the clock.

At last the devil saw there was nothing for it but to promise that he would not come for the smith till the four years were over.

"Well, then, you can get up," said the smith, and the devil hustled off as fast as ever he could.

In four years he came back to fetch the smith.

"Well, now you *must* be ready," said the devil, poking his nose in at the smithy door.

"Yes, I'm Johnny-on-the-spot," said the smith, "ready to go whenever you say so. But just listen, there's one thing I've thought over and wanted to ask you about for ever so long. Is it true, as they say, that the devil can make himself as small as he wants to?"

"Of course it's true," answered the devil.

"Then I really think you might do me the favor of creeping into my steel-mesh purse to see if there are any holes in it," said the smith. "I'm so afraid I might lose my traveling money."

"Why, certainly," said the devil, making himself so tiny he could crawl into the purse, and in a trice the smith snapped it shut.

"Yes; it is whole and perfect everywhere," said the devil, inside the purse.

"You are probably right," said the smith, "but a stitch in time saves nine, so I think I'll solder the joints a little, just to make sure." Whereupon, he put the purse into the forge and made it glowing hot.

"Oh, me!—are you mad?" shrieked the devil. "Don't you know I'm inside the purse?"

"I'm sorry I can't help you," said the smith; "there's an old saying that you must strike while the iron is hot." At this, he took his great sledge-hammer, laid the purse on the anvil, and basted it for all he was worth.

"Oh, ouch, oh!" shrieked the devil. "Oh, please let me out, and I'll promise faithfully never to come back again."

"Well, now, I guess the joints are pretty well soldered," said the smith, "so I'll let you out."

So the smith opened the purse, and the devil jumped out and rushed off in such a hurry, he did not even dare to look back.

As the smith thought over the whole matter, he thought he had made a mistake in falling out with the devil. "For if I don't get into heaven," he said to himself, "I might be without lodgings, since I'm on bad terms with the fellow who rules in hell."

He decided he might as well try now as later to see whether he could get into either heaven or hell; then he would know what was in store for him. So he shouldered his hammer and started off.

When he had gone quite a bit, he came to the crossroads where they branched off to heaven and hell, and there he met a tailor's apprentice, shuffling along with his pressing iron in his hand.

"How do you do?" said the smith. "Where are you going?"

"To heaven, if I can only get in," answered the tailor.

"Well, I'm afraid, we can't keep company very long," answered the smith. "I thought I'd first try hell, for I know the devil slightly from old days. "

So they said good-bye, and each went his way. The smith, who was a big, husky fellow, walked more quickly than the tailor, and it took him only a short time to reach the gates of hell. He told the watchman to say there was someone waiting outside who wanted to speak to the devil.

"Go out and ask who it is," said the devil to the watchman, who hurried off to do his bidding.

"Tell him it's the smith who owned the purse," said the smith. "He'll know, and beg him kindly to let me in at once, for I'm pretty tired, having worked till noon, and been walking ever since."

When the devil heard who it was, he ordered the watchman to lock all the nine locks of hell. "And put an extra bolt on, too," he said, "for if that fellow gets in, he'll raise an awful row in hell."

"There's no use hanging around here," said the smith to himself, when he heard how fast everything was being locked. "I'll have to try heaven." So he turned around and went back till he reached the crossroads, where he took the road the tailor had taken.

As he was angry at having gone so far in vain, he hurried along, and reached the gates of heaven just as St. Peter opened them wide enough to let the thin tailor squeeze through. The smith was some six or seven feet off. "There's no time to lose," he thought, and he hurled his hammer at the crack of the gate, just as the tailor was slipping through.

If the smith did not get through the crack, then I don't know what has become of him.

BJÖRNSTJERNE BJÖRNSON

(1832–1910)

BJORNSON was one of the founders of modern Norwegian literature and as dramatist, poet, novelist, moralist and politician he was a leader of his people. His novel, *Synnöve Solbakken*, one of his earliest works, appeared in 1857. Among his numerous and varied later writings his short tales are not the least interesting. *The Father* is a masterpiece in brief.

The present version was translated by R. B. Anderson and published in the volume *The Bridal March*, Boston, 1881.

THE FATHER

THE man whose story is here to be told was the wealthiest and most influential person in his parish; his name was Thord Overaas. He appeared in the priest's study one day, tall and earnest.

"I have gotten a son," said he, "and I wish to present him for baptism."

"What shall his name be?"

"Finn—after my father."

"And the sponsors?"

They were mentioned, and proved to be the best men and women of Thord's relations in the parish.

"Is there anything else?" inquired the priest, and looked up.

The peasant hesitated a little.

"I should like very much to have him baptized by himself," said he, finally.

"That is to say on a week-day?"

"Next Saturday, at twelve o'clock noon."

"Is there anything else?" inquired the priest.

"There is nothing else;" and the peasant twirled his cap, as though he were about to go.

Then the priest rose. "There is yet this, however," said he, and walking toward Thord, he took him by the hand and looked gravely into his eyes: "God grant that the child may become a blessing to you!"

One day sixteen years later, Thord stood once more in the priest's study.

"Really, you carry your age astonishingly well, Thord," said the priest; for he saw no change whatever in the man.

"That is because I have no troubles," replied Thord.

To this the priest said nothing, but after a while he asked: "What is your pleasure this evening?"

"I have come this evening about that son of mine who is to be confirmed to-morrow."

"He is a bright boy."

"I did not wish to pay the priest until I heard what number the boy would have when he takes his place in church to-morrow."

"He will stand number one."

"So I have heard; and here are ten dollars for the priest."

"Is there anything else I can do for you?" inquired the priest, fixing his eyes on Thord.

"There is nothing else."

Thord went out.

Eight years more rolled by, and then one day a noise was heard outside of the priest's study, for many men were approaching, and at their head was Thord, who entered first.

The priest looked up and recognized him.

"You come well attended this evening, Thord," said he.

"I am here to request that the banns may be published for my son; he is about to marry Karen Storliden, daughter of Gudmund, who stands here beside me."

"Why, that is the richest girl in the parish."

"So they say," replied the peasant, stroking back his hair with one hand.

The priest sat a while as if in deep thought, then entered the names in his book, without making any comments, and the men wrote their signatures underneath. Thord laid three dollars on the table.

"One is all I am to have," said the priest.

"I know that very well; but he is my only child, I want to do it handsomely."

The priest took the money.

"This is now the third time, Thord, that you have come here on your son's account."

"But now I am through with him," said Thord, and folding up his pocket-book he said farewell and walked away.

The men slowly followed him.

A fortnight later, the father and son were rowing across the lake, one calm, still day, to Storliden to make arrangements for the wedding.

"This thwart is not secure," said the son, and stood up to straighten the seat on which he was sitting.

At the same moment the board he was standing on slipped from under him; he threw out his arms, uttered a shriek, and fell overboard.

"Take hold of the oar!" shouted the father, springing to his feet and holding out the oar.

But when the son had made a couple of efforts he grew stiff.

"Wait a moment!" cried the father, and began to row toward his son. Then the son rolled over on his back, gave his father one long look, and sank.

Thord could scarcely believe it; he held the boat still, and stared at the spot where his son had gone down, as though he must surely come to the surface again. There rose some bubbles, then some more, and finally one large one that burst; and the lake lay there as smooth and bright as a mirror again.

For three days and three nights people saw the father rowing round and round the spot, without taking either food or sleep; he was dragging the lake for the body of his son. And toward morning of the third day he found it, and carried it in his arms up over the hills to his gard.

It might have been about a year from that day, when the priest, late one autumn evening, heard someone in the passage outside of the door, carefully trying to find the latch. The priest opened the door, and in walked a tall, thin man, with bowed form and white hair. The priest looked long at him before he recognized him. It was Thord.

"Are you out walking so late?" said the priest, and stood still in front of him.

"Ah, yes! it is late," said Thord, and took a seat.

The priest sat down also, as though waiting. A long, long silence followed. At last Thord said:

"I have something with me that I should like to give to the poor; I want it to be invested as a legacy in my son's name."

He rose, laid some money on the table, and sat down again. The priest counted it.

"It is a great deal of money," said he.

"It is half the price of my gard. I sold it to-day."

The priest sat long in silence. At last he asked, but gently:

"What do you propose to do now, Thord?"

"Something better."

They sat there for a while, Thord with downcast eyes, the priest with his eyes fixed on Thord. Presently the priest said, slowly and softly:

"I think your son has at last brought you a true blessing."

"Yes, I think so myself," said Thord, looking up, while two big tears coursed slowly down his cheeks.

JOHAN BOJER

(1872—1959)

BORN at Orkedalsovan, Bojer spent much of his early life in the rural districts of his country. He became interested in politics as a young man, and his first book was a satirical work with a political background. His most significant works (though he also wrote a few plays) are his novels and tales. Among the former the best known are *The Great Hunger* and *The Power of a Lie*. He travelled widely.

His short story, *Skobelef*, translated by Sigurd B. Hustvedt, appeared originally in the *American-Scandinavian Review*, July, 1922, and is here reprinted by permission of the editor.

SKOBELEF

S KOBELEF was a horse.
  This was in the days when the church bells of a Sunday morning sent out their summons, not over moribund highways and slumberous farmsteads, but over a parish waiting to be wakened into life by the sustained, solemn calling of those brazen tongues. The bells rang, rang, till the welkin rang again:

> *Come, come,*
> *Old and young,*
> *Old and young,*
> *Rich man, poor man,*
> *Dalesman, fisherman, man from the hills,*
> *The forest, the fields,*
> *The strand, the fells,*
>
> *Mads from Fallin, and Anders from Berg,*
> *And Ola from Rein,*
> *And Mette from Naust,*
> *And Mari and Kari from Densta-lea,*
> *Lea, lea,*
> *Come, come,*
> *Come, come,*
> *Come.*

And so the roads grew black with people on their way to church, some walking and some riding. Old codgers wheezed past, stick in one hand, hat in the other, their coats under their arms, and their gray homespun trousers tucked into boots shiny with grease. The women trundled along carrying shawls and hymn-books, and scenting the breeze with their perfumed handkerchiefs. Out on the lake, bordered with hills and farms, appeared row-boats driven over the water by sturdy oarsmen; from across the fjord swept the sail-boats; far up in the mountains it seemed as if the cattle even stopped grazing; and the boy who was watching them put the goat-horn to his lips and blew a stout blast down toward the folks at home. In those times Sunday was both holy day and holiday.

Looking back after these many years, I have a vivid impression that all the world was sunshine and green forests on a day like that. The old church, brown with tar, standing amidst the crowns of mighty trees, seemed then to be more than just a building; there was something supernatural about it, as if it knew all there was to be known. Many hundreds of years had passed over it. It had seen the dead when they were still alive, when they went to church like ourselves. The surrounding graveyard was a little village of wooden crosses and stone slabs; and the grass grew wild between the leaning monuments. We knew well enough that the sexton mowed it and fed it to his cows; so that when we got a drink of milk at his house we felt as if we were quaffing the very souls of the departed, a kind of angelic milk from which we drew transcendental virtues with every draft.

We boys used to stand outside the church and do as our elders did—size up the people that arrived after us. We judged by appearances, and they all knew it. The cripple made himself look smaller than ever so as to hide in the crowd; the dandies ran the gauntlet of both friendly and unfriendly eyes, and pretty women looked down and smiled. We youngsters searched the gathering throng for someone to admire, some heroic figure we should like to resemble when we ourselves one day should be grown up. There was the new teacher, for instance, stalking along in his homespun with his coat buttoned tight, with a white necktie, top hat, and umbrella. He was at least one stage above the farmer. Not a doubt about it, we too were going to attend the normal school. So we thought, at any rate, until a butcher came up from the city, wearing a suit of blue duffle, a white waistcoat with a gold watch-chain, cuffs, a dazzling white collar, and a straw hat. He was a perfect revelation. With such an exemplar before us it was easy to decide that we were to become butcher's apprentices as soon as we were old enough.

Many were the magnates that paraded through our day dreams. Still it was with no ordinary emotion that we laid eyes for the first time on a city lawyer. His was a truly royal presence. Even his nose had its appropriate ornament, a pair of gold eye-glasses. Our ambitions soared beyond all bounds. Whatever our hopes of higher education might be, most of us were bent on carrying our studies far enough to impair our vision and so to justify the use of gold-rimmed glasses.

Then came Skobelef. And Skobelef was a horse.

For weeks busy little feet had been bringing the tidings to all corners of the parish. Peter Lo had bought a registered stallion that was not simply a horse but a whole Arabian Nights' entertainment. It took six men to lead him ashore from the steamer. Only one man could have turned the trick alone, and that was Peter Lo himself. For the most part the horse walked on his hind legs. He kept whinnying even in his sleep. He was so fierce that he had already killed a number of men. His name was Skobelef. And what do you suppose they fed him? It was neither hay nor oats nor bran; not much! Skobelef's fodder was nothing less than eggnog, made with whiskey, at that. It was common talk that Peter Lo and the stallion munched this provender together out of the same crib. They required stimulants, the two of them.

To return to that particular Sunday—we were standing at the church keeping an impatient lookout across the parish. Peter Lo was bound for the house of worship, driving none other than Skobelef himself.

The long line of vehicles came rolling in from the valleys. It picked up reinforcements at every crossroad until it was like a regular bridal procession. That day we kept our eyes on the horses and estimated the people in the gigs according to their dumb, driven cattle. A whole fated universe passed in review, animals fat and lean, jaded and fiery, old big-bellied nags with long necks and prominent backbones and heads sagging with each step toward the ground under the burden of unceasing tribulation; prosperous-looking brutes that gave manifest proof of good crops and bank deposits. Look at that brood-mare; she has weaned many a colt and therefore carries her head high and surveys the world with maternal eyes. Here and there you can pick out fjord ponies with ragged haunches, stamping against the grade and sweating with the weight of the heavy gig, some of them so small that they make you think of mice. There comes a big old bay with huge watery eyes and quivering knees, looking about as if to ask why there is no Sabbath for the likes of him. Don't miss the physiognomies of those virtuous, censorious fillies proclaiming the vanity of vanities, and just behind them wild young gallants neighing at the world in general. Have a look at that bay gelding. Why is his belly all spattered with mud? That's easy. He is from a mountain farm; early this morning he had to wade through heath and marsh, across brooks and rivers on the way to the parish below, where his master could borrow a cart. He has another tough time coming before he gets back home. Talk about long processions! But what has become of Peter Lo? Where is Skobelef?

At last, there someone comes driving behind all the others. He is still far away beyond the farmhouses. Never mind, he is gaining ground at a pretty smart pace. Hundreds of eyes are fixed in rapt attention.

The church bells rang out. Most of the horses had been unhitched and were tied to the big ash trees; there they stood with their heads buried in bags of hay, grinding at their dinners and gazing absently about. All of a sudden they jerked their heads up, and even the most raw-boned skates made shift to arch their necks as they stared down the road.

Enter Peter Lo. Enter Skobelef.

He came trotting along before the gig, a broad black hulk, his fetlocks dancing, his mane sweeping in billows down his neck, his eyes shooting fire two red prize ribbons waving at his ears. He raised his head and snuffed the breeze, monarch of all he surveyed; then he lifted up his voice and split the welkin—believe me, that was a trumpet call that fetched the echoes out of the mountains. In the gig sat Peter Lo, holding the reins relaxed, a very debonair man not over thirty-five, broad of shoulder, vigorous, smiling out of a corner of his mouth above his chin-whiskers. It was certainly too bad that his wife, sitting beside him, was so much older than he; her every feature drooped, her red cheeks drooped, her eyes drooped, the corners of her mouth drooped; she always spoke in whimpering tones. As for Peter Lo himself, he had a weakness for all things pretty, even for such as were not his own. As Skobelef neighed to his affinities, Peter Lo glanced at good friends of his own among the crowd and smiled. Skobelef came to a stop, but got a cut of the whip; he reared and got another stroke; then he bounded up the road toward the parsonage, the crowd in his wake, we boys flying ahead like birds on the wing.

It was a circus to watch Peter Lo maneuver Skobelef out from the shafts of the gig and over toward the stable door. Peter Lo for sure looked swell that day; the horse must have lent him a new dignity, his gray suit was so well brushed and he wore a stiff hat just like the teacher's. But every now and then his polished boots flew up in the air. The crowd stared for all they were worth. Too soon the magic horse disappeared behind the stable door; presently Peter Lo came out again brushing the horse hairs from his hands. He picked his way carefully so as not to soil those shiny boots as he walked down to the church. The crowd trekked after him. Peter Lo mounted the steps to the hall and walked in. The congregation followed at his heels. Peter Lo sat down in one of the pews, opened a hymn book, and began to sing. The congregation did likewise, and the singing rose in volume.

But on this particular day we youngsters kept watch and ward outside the stable door. It was a mighty good thing it was locked; there was no telling what Skobelef would do if he got loose on his own account. The cold chills ran down our spines as we heard him rattling his halter and stamping on the floor. Now and again the walls shook with his neighing. Talk about thrills! We stood still, put our heads together, and spoke in whispers.

It was a great day for the horses, too. The mares under the ash trees lost their appetites and stood all the while arching their necks and trying to look like two-year-olds. Stallions and geldings had that day caught sight of a rival whose eyes flashed with arrogance. Do you suppose they would put up with that sort of thing! They pawed the ground furiously and shook the air with protests from all sides.

At last the bells rang again. The congregation came out, but the greater number had no thought of hitching up their own horses. The yard was jammed with people wanting to see Peter Lo lead Skobelef out of the stable.

The man himself approached. The eyes of all waiting upon him, he strolled along talking to the sexton as if he were an ordinary mortal.

Yet he had already acquired certain of the gestures that the parson was accustomed to make use of in the pulpit.

The people gradually drew back from the road. One circumspect man dragged his gig away from the middle of the yard. The women took refuge on the landings of the barns. It was just as well to be on the safe side, but everybody wanted to see what was going on.

Peter Lo unlocked the stable door and disappeared from view. A seven-fold thunder of neighing sounded from within, the halter rattled, heavy hoofs drummed against the floor, and the next minute a black barrel of a body appeared on the threshold. Skobelef flung his battlecry to the four winds; Peter Lo was hurled aloft, but landed on his feet some distance out in the yard. Women shrieked. Old men jumped out of the way, hats flying right and left. Peter Lo and Skobelef started to dance around the yard. Skobelef snorted and foamed so that his dark body was dappled with froth; he had no mind to be led toward the gig; he reared, pummeled the air with his hoofs, and plunged from side to side, while a pair of shining boots kept cutting strange capers through space. It was an apocalyptic vision, something to dream about. The yard was swept clean of vehicles and people in a trice. It had been changed into a ball-room for Peter Lo and Skobelef. Peter Lo yelled at the stallion, and the stallion screamed at the universe and at Peter Lo. On went the dance. Finally Skobelef seemed bound to enter the parsonage and have a chat with the preacher's wife; but Peter Lo got ahead of him and planted his splendid boots with a resounding thump against the steps, so that Skobelef succeeded only in tearing down the railing. Peter Lo grew red in the face. Skobelef's whole body had become a mass of foam. The women gasped out shivering sighs, "Oh, oh!"

At last the wild beast was forced between the shafts. As the reins were loosened he rose on his hind legs, and the lash fell on his neck; he pranced about on all fours with arched neck and flaring nostrils. Then Peter Lo's wife came up, gathering her shawl around her shoulders, and—believe it or not—stepped calmly into the gig while the earthquake was still going on. Now Peter Lo knew that the victory was his; he put his hand on the dashboard and leaped up besides his wife; the horse reared, his eyes shot fire, the foam flew, the whip cracked, and the next second the whole show dissolved in a cloud of dust rushing along beyond the farmhouses.

We stood rooted to the spot. The other men began bashfully to hitch up their own horses. There was really nothing at all left to look at.

From that day Skobelef was an influential personality throughout the parish. To tell the truth, Peter Lo and Skobelef took on together a sort of higher individuality that drew the popular gaze as they flashed by. It seemed as if they were whipping the whole neighborhood up to a more rapid tempo. The farmers came to be men of honor so far as their horses were concerned, fed them well, and groomed them with the utmost care. They drove at a brisker pace along the roads, their speech acquired an added dash of humor, they laughed in the face of heaven and earth, their thoughts assumed a new boldness. On Sundays, as the congregation stood outside the church admiring Skobelef and Peter Lo, a fresh source of vitality seemed to be manifesting itself; men saw with their own eyes the very embodiment of animal spirits, they sensed something venerable in brute strength, they caught the chanted praise of rippling muscles. It began to dawn on them that life is not a mere medley of sins and sorrows, that life on earth has a glory of its own.

As time passed, Peter Lo gave increasing attention to his clothes. He took to reading books, to wearing a white collar, to using a handkerchief when he blew his nose about the precincts of the church. He imitated the sheriff's mannerisms of speech. He knew quite well that he and Skobelef had become the local cynosures; and this persuasion lent him a feeling of responsibility and a desire to serve as a pattern for the herd. If the truth must be told, it was not only we boys who prayed, "Good Lord, help us to be like Peter Lo when we get big!" By no means! The grownups, too, tried to ape his manner. "You are brushing your shoes just the way Peter Lo does," one man would say to another. "And you are wearing a white collar, just like Peter Lo's," they would say. Skobelef, imported to ennoble the rural breed of horse flesh, had become a spiritual force, an educational institution for the entire countryside.

Peter Lo was not quite so fortunate. He could not be happy except in the society of the stallion. He lost interest in work. He was in his element only when racing down the county roads behind his crony, or when he and Skobelef together conducted revival services beneath the very walls of the church. The rumor spread that he had taken to sleeping in the stable. Gossip would have it that horse and man were coming to resemble each other. Skobelef smiled out of the corner of his mouth when he met with his affinities, and Peter Lo greeted good friends at church with something like a whinny in his voice.

Peter Lo's lot was not altogether enviable. He had a fondness for all things pretty, not excepting those that belonged to his neighbors. And when he got into an unusually bad scrape, he made a most pathetic figure. Then he would go to church and take holy communion. Many a time we saw him come driving, not the wild stallion but an old mare. His sour-visaged wife, wrapped in her shawl, would be sitting in the cart, at one side of which walked the sexton, and at the other side Peter Lo, with bowed head. On such a day he would have his mind made up to listen to the sermon with folded hands and not once to glance in the direction of the women's pews—afterward he would step forward to the altar and partake of the sacrament. These penitential pilgrimages occasioned more than one good laugh. "Peter has had a sorry adventure again," people would say.

A day or two later you would see him tearing down the highway with Skobelef. So he kept on laying up stores of gayety and æsthetic appreciation of the beautiful, until his conduct became more reprehensible than ever. His wife insisted upon Skobelef's deportation from the farm; it was impossible to convert Peter to virtuous ways so long as he maintained a companionship of that sort.

Meanwhile, round about in the parish there grew up a numerous race of black, prancing horses, and the wheels rumbled faster on all the roads. A whinnying joy of life took sovereign possession of the community. Men lifted up their heads and cast jovial eyes on their surroundings, women plucked up courage actually to laugh out loud, and young folks discovered anew the pleasures of the dance.

But Skobelef was not to reach old age. He broke out of the stable one night and ran off in the mountains to find his affinities, who were accustomed to graze there during the summer.

When Peter Lo came along and saw the empty stable, he started shouting clamorous complaints; he evidently suspected at once that misfortune had stamped her mark upon his brow. He had a pretty shrewd idea where his comrade had fled; and witnesses reported that the whole day long they heard Peter Lo tramping over the hills neighing just like Skobelef, calling and coaxing his old chum.

At last he found him. Skobelef was standing up to his neck in a marsh far off in the foothills. He had fought so hard to extricate himself that he had broken one of his forelegs, out of which protruded splinters of bone. The flies had stung his eyes till they bled.

Peter wiped his pal's eyes with a tuft of grass and gave him a raw egg and a shot of whiskey. For a little while he let his own tears roll, but finally there was nothing to do but to draw his knife.

After that day Peter Lo drove more slowly along the roads. His head bent lower and his whiskers turned gray.

Now he is an old man; but he still dresses better than most of his neighbors and affects a city brogue as before. When someone reminds him of Skobelef, his eyes grow dim. "Yes, yes," he replies; "Skobelef was not like other horses. He was a regular high school; he taught us all a thing or two."

Sweden

AUGUST STRINDBERG

(1849–1912)

AUGUST STRINDBERG, born of a poor and humble family, is one of the most celebrated figures in modern European literature. He engaged in many professions during his youth, and was a writer of plays, novels, scientific and philological works, and stories. He was one of the chief innovators in the modern Naturalistic movement. His powerful studies of contemporary life are personal and psychological interpretations of society according to his own peculiar philosophy.

Love and Bread is typically Strindbergian in its cynicism. The present anonymous translation was published in *Short Story Classics*. Copyright, 1907, by P. F. Collier & Son, by whose permission it is here reprinted.

LOVE AND BREAD

WHEN young Gustaf Falk, the assistant councilor, made his ceremonial proposal for Louise's hand to her father, the old gentleman's first question was: "How much are you earning?"

"Not more than a hundred kroner a month. But Louise—"

"Never mind the rest," interrupted Falk's prospective father-in-law; "you don't earn enough."

"Oh, but, Louise and I love each other so dearly! We are so sure of one another."

"Very likely. However, let me ask you: is twelve hundred a year the sum total of your resources?"

"We first became acquainted at Lidingö."

"Do you make anything besides your government salary?" persisted Louise's parent.

"Well, yes, I think we shall have sufficient. And then, you see, our mutual affection—"

"Yes, exactly; but let's have a few figures."

"Oh," said the enthusiastic suitor, "I can get enough by doing extra work!"

"What sort of work? And how much?"

"I can give lessons in French, and also translate. And then I can get some proofreading."

"How much translation?" queried the elder, pencil in hand.

"I can't say exactly, but at present I am translating a French book at the rate of ten kroner per folio."

"How many folios are there altogether?"

"About a couple of dozen, I should say."

"Very well. Put this at two hundred and fifty kroner. Now, how much else?"

"Oh, I don't know. It's a little uncertain."

"What, you are not certain, and you intend to marry? You seem to have queer notions of marriage, young man! Do you realize that there will be children, and that you will have to feed and clothe them, and bring them up?"

"But," objected Falk, "the children may not come so very soon. And we love each other so dearly, that—"

"That the arrival of children may be prophesied quite safely." Then, relenting, Louise's father went on:

"I suppose you are both set on marrying, and I don't doubt but what you are really fond of each other. So it seems as though I should have to give my consent after all. Only make good of the time that you are engaged to Louise by trying to increase your income."

Young Falk flushed with joy at this sanction, and demonstratively kissed the old man's hand. Heavens, how happy he was—and his Louise, too! How proud they felt the first time they went out walking together arm in arm, and how everybody noticed the radiant happiness of the engaged couple!

In the evenings he came to see her, bringing with him the proof-sheets he had undertaken to correct. This made a good impression on papa, and earned the industrious young man a kiss from his betrothed. But one evening they went to the theater for a change, and drove home in a cab, the cost of that evening's entertainment amounting to ten kroner. Then, on a few other evenings, instead of giving the lessons, he called at the young lady's house to take her for a little walk.

As the day set for the wedding drew near, they had to think about making the necessary purchases to furnish their flat. They bought two handsome beds of real walnut, with substantial spring mattresses and soft eiderdown quilts. Louise must have a blue quilt, as her hair was blond. They, of course, also paid a visit to the house-furnisher's, where they selected a lamp with a red shade, a pretty porcelain statuette of Venus, a complete table service with knives, forks, and fine glassware. In picking out the kitchen utensils they were benefited by mamma's advice and aid. It was a busy time for the assistant councilor—rushing about to find a house, looking after the workmen, seeing that all the furniture was got together, writing out checks, and what not.

Meanwhile it was perfectly natural that Gustaf could earn nothing extra. But when they were once married he would easily make it up. They intended to be most economical—only a couple of rooms to start with. Anyhow, you could furnish a small apartment better than a large one. So they took a first-floor apartment at six hundred kroner, consisting of two rooms, kitchen, and larder. At first Louise said she would prefer three rooms on the top landing. But what did it matter, after all, so long as they sincerely loved each other?

At last the rooms were furnished. The sleeping chamber was like a small sanctuary, the beds standing side by side like chariots taking their course along life's journey. The blue quilts, the snowy sheets, and the pillow-spreads embroidered with the young people's initials amorously intertwined, all had a bright and cheerful appearance. There was a tall, elegant screen for the use of Louise, whose piano—costing twelve hundred kroner—stood in the other chamber, which served as sitting-room, dining-room, and study, in one. Here, too, stood a large walnut writing-desk and dining-table, with chairs to match; a large gilt-framed mirror, a sofa, and a bookcase added to the general air of comfort and coziness.

The marriage ceremony took place on a Saturday night, and late on Sunday morning the happy young couple were still asleep. Gustaf rose first. Although the bright light of day was peering in through the shutters, he did not open them, but lit the red-shaded lamp, which threw a mysterious rosy glow over the porcelain Venus. The pretty young wife lay there languid and content; she had slept well, and had not been awakened—as it was Sunday—by the rumbling of early market wagons. Now the church bells were ringing joyfully, as if to celebrate the creation of man and woman.

Louise turned over, while Gustaf retired behind the screen to put on a few things. He went out into the kitchen to order lunch. How dazzlingly the new copper and tin utensils gleamed and glistened! And all was his own—his and hers. He told the cook to go to the neighboring restaurant, and request that the lunch be sent in. The proprietor knew about it; he had received full instructions the day before. All he needed now was a reminder that the moment had come.

The bridegroom thereupon returns to the bedchamber and taps softly: "May I come in?"

A little scream is heard. Then: "No, dearest; just wait a minute!"

Gustaf lays the table himself. By the time the lunch arrives from the restaurant, the new plates and cutlery and glasses are set out on the fresh, white linen cloth. The bridal bouquet lies beside Louise's place. As she enters the room in her embroidered morning wrapper, she is greeted by the sunbeams. She still feels a little tired, so he makes her take an armchair, and wheels it to the table. A drop or two of liqueur enlivens her; a mouthful of caviar stimulates her appetite. Fancy what mamma would say if she saw her daughter drinking spirits! But that's the advantage of being married you know; then you can do whatever you please.

The young husband waits most attentively upon his fair bride. What a pleasure, too! Of course he has had good luncheons before, in his bachelor days; but what comfort or satisfaction had he ever derived from them? None. Thus he reflects while consuming a plate of oysters and a glass of beer. What numbskulls they are, those bachelors, not to marry! And how selfish! Why, there ought to be a tax on them, as on dogs. Louise is not quite so severe, urging gently and sweetly that perhaps the poor fellows who elect the single state are subjects of pity. No doubt if they could afford to marry, they would—she thinks. Gustaf feels a slight pang at his heart. Surely happiness is not to be measured by money. No, no; but, but—Well, never mind, there will soon be lots of work, and then everything will run smoothly. For the present there is this delicious roast partridge with cranberry sauce to be considered, and the Burgundy. These luxuries, together with some fine artichokes, cause the young wife a moment's alarm, and she timidly asks Gustaf if they can afford living on such a scale. But Gustaf pours more wine into the glass of his little Louise, reassuring her and softening those groundless fears. "One day is not every day," he says; "and people ought to enjoy life when they can. Ah, how beautiful life is!"

At six o'clock an elegant carriage, with two horses, pulls up before the door, and the bridal pair take a drive. Louise is charmed as they roll along through the park, reclining there so comfortably, while they meet acquaintances on foot, who bow to them in obvious astonishment and envy. The assistant councilor has made a good match, they must think; he has chosen a girl with money. And they, poor souls, have to walk. How much pleasanter to ride, without effort, leaning against these soft cushions! It is symbolical of agreeable married life.

The first month was one of unceasing enjoyment—balls, parties, dinners, suppers, theaters. Still, the time they spent at home was really the best of all! It was a delightful sensation to carry Louise off home, from her parents, at night, when they would do as they pleased under their own roof. Arriving at the flat, they would make a little supper, and then they would sit comfortably, chatting until a late hour. Gustaf was all for economy—the theory of it, that is to say. One day the young bride and housekeeper tried smoked salmon with boiled potatoes. How she relished it, too! But Gustaf demurred, and when smoked salmon day came round again he invested in a brace of partridges. These he bought at the market for a krone, exulting over the splendid bargain, of which

Louise did not approve. She had once bought a pair for less money. Besides, to eat game was extravagant. However, it would not do to disagree with her husband about such a trifling matter.

After a couple of months more Louise Falk became strangely indisposed. Had she caught cold? Or had she perchance been poisoned by the metal kitchen utensils ? The doctor who was called in merely laughed, and said it was all right—a queer diagnosis, to be sure, when the young lady was seriously ailing. Perhaps there was arsenic in the wall-paper. Falk took some to a chemist, bidding him make a careful analysis. The chemist's report stated the wall-paper to be quite free from any harmful substance.

His wife's sickness not abating, Gustaf began to investigate on his own account, his studies in a medical book resulting in a certainty as to her ailment. She took warm foot-baths, and in a month's time her state was declared entirely promising. This was sudden—sooner than they had expected; yet how lovely to be papa and mamma! Of course the child would be a boy—no doubt of that; and one must think of a name to give him. Meanwhile, though, Louise took her husband aside, and reminded him that since their marriage he had earned nothing to supplement his salary, which had proved far from sufficient. Well, it was true they had lived rather high, but now a change should be made, and everything would be satisfactory!

Next day the assistant councilor went to see his good friend the barrister, with a request that he indorse a promissory note. This would allow him to borrow the money that would be needed to meet certain unavoidable forthcoming expenses—as Falk made clear to his friend. "Yes," agreed the man of law, "marrying and raising a family is an expensive business. I have never been able to afford it."

Falk felt too much ashamed to press his request, and when he returned home, empty-handed, was greeted with the news that two strangers had been to the house, and had asked for him. They must be lieutenants in the army, thought Gustaf, friends belonging to the garrison of Fort Vaxholm. No, he was told, they could not have been lieutenants; they were much older-looking men. Ah, then they were two fellows he used to know in Upsala; they had probably heard of his marriage, and had come to look him up. Only the servant said they were not from Upsala, but were Stockholmers, and carried sticks. Mysterious —very; but no doubt they would come back.

Then the young husband went marketing again. He bought strawberries—at a bargain, of course.

"Just fancy," he triumphantly exclaimed to his housewife, "a pint of these large strawberries for a krone and a half, at this time of year!"

"Oh, but Gustaf dear, we can't afford that sort of thing!"

"Never mind, darling; I have arranged for some extra work."

"But what about our debts?"

"Debts? Why, I'm going to make a big loan, and pay them all off at once that way."

"Ah," objected Louise, "but won't this simply mean a new debt?"

"No matter if it does. It will be a respite, you know. But why discuss such unpleasant things? What capital strawberries, eh, dear? And don't you think a glass of sherry would go well now after the strawberries?"

Upon which the servant was sent out for a bottle of sherry—the best, naturally.

When Falk's wife awoke from her afternoon nap on the sofa that day, she apologetically reverted to the subject of debt. She hoped he would not be angry at what she had to say. Angry? No, of course not. What was it? Did she want some money for the house? Louise explained:

"The grocer has not been paid, the butcher has threatened us, and the livery-stable man also insists on having his bill settled."

"Is that all?" replied the assistant councilor. "They shall be paid at once—to-morrow—every farthing. But let's think of something else. How would you like to go out for a little drive to the park? You'd rather not take a carriage? All right, then, there's the tramway; that will take us to the park."

So they went to the park, and they had dinner in a private room at the Alhambra Restaurant. It was great fun, too, because the people in the general dining-room thought they were a frisky young pair of lovers. This idea amused Gustaf, though Louise seemed a trifle depressed, especially when she saw the bill. They could have had a good deal at home for that amount.

The months go by, and now arises the need for actual preparation— a cradle, infant's clothing, and so forth.

Falk has no easy time raising the money. The livery-stable man and the grocer refuse further credit, for they, too, have families to feed. What shocking materialism!

At length the eventful day arrives. Gustaf must secure a nurse, and even while holding his new-born daughter in his arms is called out to pacify his creditors. The fresh responsibilities weigh heavily upon him; he almost breaks down under the strain. He succeeds, it is true, in getting some translation to do, but how can he perform the work when at every touch and turn he is obliged to run errands? In this frame of mind he appeals to his father-in-law for help. The old gentleman receives him coldly:

"I will help you this once, but not again. I have little enough myself, and you are not my only child."

Delicacies must be provided for the mother, chicken and expensive wine. And the nurse has to be paid.

Fortunately, Falk's wife is soon on her feet again. She is like a girl once more, with a slender figure. Her pallor is quite becoming. Louise's father talks seriously to his son-in-law, however:

"Now, no more children, if you please, unless you want to be ruined."

For a brief space the junior Falk family continued to live on love and increasing debts. But one day bankruptcy knocked at the door. The seizure of the household effects was threatened. Then the old man came and took away Louise and her child, and as they rode off in a cab he made the bitter reflection that he had lent his girl to a young man, who had given her back after a year, dishonored. Louise would willingly have stayed with Gustaf, but there was nothing more to subsist upon. He remained behind, looking on while the bailiffs—those men with the sticks—denuded the flat of everything, furniture, bedding, crockery, cutlery, kitchen utensils, until it was stripped bare.

Now began real life for Gustaf. He managed to get a position as proofreader on a newspaper which was published in the morning, so that he had to work at his desk for several hours each night. As he had not actually been declared a bankrupt, he was allowed to keep his place in the government service, although he could hope for no more promotion. His father-in-law made the concession of letting him see his wife and child on Sundays, but he was never permitted to be alone with them. When he left, in the evening, to go to the newspaper office, they would accompany him to the gate, and he would depart in utter humiliation of soul. It might take him perhaps twenty years to pay off all his obligations. And then—yes, what then? Could he then support his wife and child? No, probably not. If, in the meantime, his father-in-law should die, they would be left without a home. So he must be thankful even to the hard-hearted old man who had so cruelly separated them.

Ah, yes, human life itself is indeed hard and cruel! The beasts of the field find maintenance easily enough, while of all created beings man alone must toil and spin. It is a shame, yes, it is a crying shame, that in this life everybody is not provided with gratuitous partridges and strawberries.

SELMA LAGERLÖF

(1858–1940)

SELMA LAGERLÖF came of a family of landowners, from that part of rural Sweden which she described in many of her most delightful books, particularly in *Gösta Berling's Saga*. In her youth she taught for a little, making time to write occasionally, until public recogni-

tion and material success enabled her to devote all her energy to
literary work. Her books, which include novels, travel sketches,
plays, and stories, reveal a personality deeply conscious of its environment. In 1909 Selma Lagerlöf received the Nobel Prize for literature.

The Eclipse is translated by Velma Swanston Howard. It originally
appeared in the *American-Scandinavian Review*, December, 1922. For
permission to reprint, thanks are due to the editor and the translator.

THE ECLIPSE

THERE were Stina of Ridgecôte and Lina of Birdsong and Kajsa
of Littlemarsh and Maja of Skypeak and Beda of Finn-darkness
and Elin, the new wife on the old soldier's place, and two or three other
peasant women besides—all of them lived at the far end of the parish,
below Storhöjden, in a region so wild and rocky none of the big farm
owners had bothered to lay hands on it.

One had her cabin set up on a shelf of rock, another had hers put up
at the edge of a bog, while a third had one that stood at the crest of a
hill so steep it was a toilsome climb getting to it. If by chance any of
the others had a cottage built on more favorable ground, you may be
sure it lay so close to the mountain as to shut out the sun from autumn
fair time clear up to Annunciation Day.

They each cultivated a little potato patch close by the cabin, though
under serious difficulties. To be sure, there were many kinds of soil
there at the foot of the mountain, but it was hard work to make the
patches of land yield anything. In some places they had to clear away
so much stone from their fields, it would have built a cow-house on a
manorial estate; in some they had dug ditches as deep as graves, and
in others they had brought their earth in sacks and spread it on the bare
rocks. Where the soil was not so poor, they were forever fighting the
tough thistle and pigweed which sprang up in such profusion you would
have thought the whole potato land had been prepared for their benefit.

All the livelong day the women were alone in their cabins; for even
where one had a husband and children, the man went off to his work
every morning and the children went to school. A few among the older
women had grown sons and daughters, but they had gone to America.
And some there were with little children, who were always around, of
course; but these could hardly be regarded as company.

Being so much alone, it was really necessary that they should meet
sometimes over the coffee cups. Not that they got on so very well together, nor had any great love for each other; but some liked to keep

posted on what the others were doing, and some grew despondent living like that, in the shadow of the mountain, unless they met people now and then. And there were those, who needed to unburden their hearts, and talk about the last letter from America, and those who were naturally talkative and jocular, and who longed for opportunity to make use of these happy God-given talents.

Nor was it any trouble at all to prepare for a little party. Coffee-pot and coffee cups they all had of course, and cream could be got at the manor, if one had no cow of one's own to milk; fancy biscuits and small cakes one could, at a pinch, get the dairyman's driver to fetch from the municipal bakery, and country merchants who sold coffee and sugar were to be found everywhere. So, to get up a coffee party was the easiest thing imaginable. The difficulty lay in finding an occasion.

For Stina of Ridgecôte, Lina of Birdsong, Kajsa of Littlemarsh, Maja of Skypeak, Béda of Finn-darkness, and Elin, the new wife at the old soldier's, were all agreed that it would never do for them to celebrate in the midst of the common everyday life. Were they to be that wasteful of the precious hours which never return, they might get a bad name. And to hold coffee parties on Sundays or great Holy Days was out of the question; for then the married women had husband and children at home, which was quite company enough. As for the rest—some liked to attend church, some wished to visit relatives, while a few preferred to spend the day at home, in perfect peace and stillness, that they might really feel it was a Holy Day.

Therefore they were all the more eager to take advantage of every possible opportunity. Most of them gave parties on their name-days, though some celebrated the great event when the wee little one cut its first tooth, or when it took its first steps. For those who received money-letters from America that was always a convenient excuse, and it was also in order to invite all the women of the neighborhood to come and help tack a quilt or stretch a web just off the loom.

All the same, there were not nearly as many occasions to meet as were needed. One year one of the women was at her wit's end. It was her turn to give a party, and she had no objection to carrying out what was expected of her; but she could not seem to hit upon anything to celebrate. Her own name-day she could not celebrate, being named Beda, as Beda has been stricken out of the almanac. Nor could she celebrate that of any member of her family, for all her dear ones were resting in the churchyard. She was very old, and the quilt she slept under would probably outlast her. She had a cat of which she was very fond. Truth to tell, it drank coffee just as well as she did; but she could hardly bring herself to hold a party for a cat!

Pondering, she searched her almanac again and again, for there she felt she must surely find the solution of her problem.

She began at the beginning, with "The Royal House" and "Signs and Forecasts," and read on, right through to "Markets and Postal Transmittances for 1912," without finding anything.

As she was reading the book for the seventh time, her glance rested on "Eclipses." She noted that that year, which was the year of our Lord nineteen-hundred twelve, on April seventeenth there would be a solar eclipse. It would begin at twenty minutes past high noon and end at 2.40 o'clock, and would cover nine-tenths of the sun's disk.

This she had read before, many times, without attaching any significance to it; but now, all at once, it became dazzlingly clear to her.

"Now I have it!" she exclaimed.

But it was only for a second or two that she felt confident; and then she put the thought away, fearing that the other women would just laugh at her.

The next few days, however, the idea that had come to her when reading her almanac kept recurring to her mind, until at last she began to wonder whether she hadn't better venture. For when she thought about it, what friend had she in all the world she loved better than the Sun? Where her hut lay not a ray of sunlight penetrated her room the whole winter long. She counted the days until the Sun would come back to her in the spring. The Sun was the only one she longed for, the only one who was always friendly and gracious to her and of whom she could never see enough.

She looked her years, and felt them, too. Her hands shook as if she were in a perpetual chill and when she saw herself in the looking-glass, she appeared so pale and washed out, as if she had been lying out to bleach. It was only when she stood in a strong, warm, down-pouring sunshine that she felt like a live human being and not a walking corpse.

The more she thought about it, the more she felt there was no day in the whole year she would rather celebrate than the one when her friend the Sun battled against darkness, and after a glorious conquest, came forth with new splendor and majesty.

The seventeenth of April was not far away, but there was ample time to make ready for a party. So, on the day of the eclipse Stina, Lina Kajsa, Maja, and the other women all sat drinking coffee with Beda at Finn-darkness. They drank their second and their third cups, and chatted about everything imaginable. For one thing, they said they couldn't for the life of them understand why Beda should be giving a party.

Meanwhile, the eclipse was under way. But they took little notice of it. Only for a moment, when the sky turned blackish gray, when all nature seemed under a leaden pall, and there came driving a howling wind with sounds as of the Trumpet of Doom and the lamentations of Judgment Day—only then did they pause and feel a bit awed.

But here they each had a fresh cup of coffee, and the feeling soon passed.

When all was over, and the Sun stood out in the heavens so beamingly happy—it seemed to them it had not shone with such brilliancy and power the whole year—they saw old Beda go over to the window, and stand with folded hands. Looking out toward the sunlit slope, she sang in her quavering voice:

> "Thy shining sun goes up again,
> I thank Thee, O my Lord!
> With new-found courage, strength and hope,
> I raise a song of joy."

Thin and transparent, old Beda stood there in the light of the window, and as she sang the sunbeams danced about her, as if wanting to give her, also, of their life and strength and color.

When she had finished the old hymn-verse she turned and looked at her guests, as if in apology.

"You see," she said, "I haven't any better friend than the Sun, and I wanted to give her a party on the day of her eclipse. I felt that we should come together to greet her, when she came out of her darkness."

Now they understood what old Beda meant, and their hearts were touched. They began to speak well of the Sun. "She was kind to rich and poor alike, and when she came peeping into the hut on a winter's day, she was as comforting as a glowing fire on the hearth. Just the sight of her smiling face made life worth living, whatever the troubles one had to bear."

The women went back to their homes after the party, happy and content. They somehow felt richer and more secure in the thought that they had a good, faithful friend in the Sun.

PER HALLSTRÖM

(1866—1960)

PER HALLSTRÖM travelled widely. He was for some time an analytical chemist in Chicago, and his work shows traces of foreign influence. He brought the art of writing stories to a high point of perfection and is one of the few Scandinavian masters of that form.

The Falcon is translated by Herbert G. Wright. It first appeared in the American-Scandinavian Review, October, 1920, and is reprinted by permission of the editor.

THE FALCON

S IR ENGUERRAND rode out hunting every day, and generally with his red, gold-embroidered glove on, for only the flight of the Iceland falcon with his tinkling bells could awaken music within him and make him breathe the keen, light morning air with joy, as he were drinking an animating wine. One day the falcon had driven a heron bleeding into a marsh behind a copse, where the huntsman found it and broke its neck, but the falcon himself was gone. Whether he had been attracted by a fresh prey, or had shunned the brown water, or by some caprice had let himself be thrown aloft and carried away by the wind—in vain they searched; in vain they called caressing names; in vain they let the sound of the horn beat against every height. Sir Enguerrand struck the trembling mouth of the head falconer with his glove until the blood flowed, and rode home at a gallop over the tufts of grass, his lips closed still more firmly and his eyelids lowered still more gloomily over the listless pupils—and the falcon was not found.

But Renaud found him, caught by the thong round his foot in a briarbush, motionless, awaiting death from starvation with a firm grip of the branch, one wing hanging, the other raised defiantly, the narrow head stretched forward threateningly with eyes fixed and beak keen— beautiful he was amidst the blood-red berries. Renaud's hand trembled with eagerness as he disentangled the thong from the thorns, as the bells jingled about his fingers on the ring with the mark of Sir Enguerrand. He called aloud with joy, when the sharp claws cut into his sinewy arm, and he was his, the falcon with the broadest breast and the longest wings and the proudest eyes of burning gold.

He was all the more his, since he would never be able to show him to anyone, for he knew that rigorous laws protected the sport of the knights. In the forest he would build a cage for him; early in the morning he would steal thither, before the bird had shaken off the cold; over the fields they would go together, sweeping with their gaze the white upper regions; they would become fond of each other, as they let the sunshine rise and fall over their heads and the wind carry off their silent thoughts, and the falcon would never miss his red glove nor the restraint of his pearl-bedecked hood. He fastened him again and ran toward the pool. Soon he came back with a duck which he had killed with a stone, and the falcon took it, and Renaud's heart was benumbed with intoxication, for it was a sign that the falcon did not despise him and would be his.

And the falcon became his. He bent his head forward to listen, his eyes calm and watchful, when the frosty twigs cracked under Renaud's step in the silence of the morning. He sprang lightly down from his cage and stretched himself toward his hand and flapped his wings as if to fly—this was merely a reminder—and so they hastened out to the expanses of the moors, which were gradually becoming light.

Their eyes gazed sharply at the dark red sky. Black lay the hills and the sparse thickets, and the trees slept on, their boughs heavy with silent birds. But the sky became brighter, flaming with gold and red, and the lines of the fields became blue, and the owl flew low over the ground seeking her hiding-place, and the day-birds stretched their wings and chirped gently on account of the cold, and their flight stood black against the glimmering air. But Renaud and his falcon hastened past, for these were sparrows and thrushes—no prey for them. Down toward the marshes the herons were already shrieking and flying with long strokes of the wing in wide circles; there was their prey. There the falcon was cast aloft, his breast already distended and his wings ready to beat, and Renaud saw him turn to gold in the sunshine, stood with blind eyes and whirling brain, whilst the bird grew smaller against the deep azure, and he heard how the sound of his bells mocked the cries of the herons.

They circled like wheels in their fear. Now they thought to dart down to the shore and hide their long necks and stupid, terrified heads with the backward-leaning crests under the dark trees; now they tried in hesitating uncertainty to rise up in a spiral, relying on their broad wings to carry them higher than the enemy could pursue, and they wavered like reeds with the pale terror of their hearts.

But the falcon from the beginning picked out one of the strongest, one of those which at once flew aloft, for he loved to try his strength and feel keen, light air beneath his wings, and he raised himself as quickly and unswervingly as if he had circled about a sunbeam. Soon he was highest. Less than a sparrow he seemed, but something in the position of his wings, in the concentrated strength of his body, gave one an idea of the flashing wildness of his eyes and of his extended claws— and suddenly he fell, heavy as steel, on the neck of his defenseless, upward-turning prey, and the two sank like a stone, hardly whirling even a wing's breadth. Then Renaud ran and swam and waded to get there quickly, before the heron, stupefied by the blow, could pull itself together and in the wildness of despair use its keen beak; but the falcon dealt the death-blow sharply and quickly, and turned his large eyes, already calmed, toward his master, for he did not love to stain his feathers with blood, and waited to have the warm heart given him.

Afterwards he did not fly again that day; when Renaud threw him aloft and ran with an enticing call, he beat his wings a few times and settled on his shoulder again in proud coldness against the laughing face of the boy. He seemed to despise all trifling, and Renaud soon ceased, while his look acquired the far-gazing seriousness of the falcon's. He became more devoted to him than to anything he had possessed. It seemed to him that the falcon was his own soul, his longing with broad wings and victorious glance. But there was pain in his love, gloomy foreboding of misfortune, and at times he feared lest the bird should fly from him in indifference, disappear with a mocking sound of bells, and it would be like death, so void. Or it seemed to him that the falcon was honor, resplendent with sunshine in the azure air, which now rested on his shoulder for fresh journeys. In the midst of his joy he was oppressed by his insignificance; he scarcely dared to look at the bird, and his heart ached that he would never share his joy, that his gaze would never soften at the sight of his master, and he fled to the land of dreams.

He laid himself down in the middle of the moor with red heather under his head; while the clouds glided past like the fates of men, light and heavy, concentrated within firm lines or scattered in flight, always with the invisible hand of the wind on his shoulder, and the bushes bent down their rustling golden twigs, and Renaud told stories to his falcon.

King Arthur had come again from the sea of Brittany. His sword Excalibur, blue like the night sky in cold weather, was handed him again; his twelve knights raised their heavy heads from the table of stone and shook off their sleep; the ground rang under their steps. Gareth was present, the Prince's son, who dressed as a scullion and turned Lynnette's echoing mockery into love. Renaud was also there, a noble born, and his horse pranced under him, and the falcon, who now slept with lowered head, sat erect on his hand and sought his glance with eyes resplendent with joy and the golden sun of the heroic sagas.

But the clouds glided past like the fates of men, were driven all dark one above the other, and formed an arch of gigantic blocks, where the rays of the sun fell through the openings, pale and sharp as spears, and the falcon dreamed gloomy dreams of impotent wrath and awoke with a shriek.

Wandering boys soon caught sight of Sir Enguerrand's bird in Renaud's hand; the knight's menials seized him and led him to the castle, and he shivered when the falcon was taken from him, motionless and proud as always, without turning his bent neck, without a glance from his cold, calm eyes. The bird was taken to his master, but he had not even a caress for the favorite he had missed, for he had allowed himself to be touched by ignoble hands. Sir Enguerrand gazed down in silence at Renaud, and in his mind there settled more and more distinctly the memory of an old game-law of the days when the noble's foot lay steel-shod on the neck of the people, and pleasures fluttered inviolable about his shoulders—and his eyebrows closed about the certainty that the old law had never been repealed. The law provided that he who stole a falcon with the mark of a knight on its foot should pay twelve sols of silver or six ounces of flesh from his ribs under the beak of a famished bird of prey.

Sir Enguerrand knew of Renaud's poverty and looked at his brown, naked breast. He stretched out his hand, and touched it with a testing, unfeeling gesture. Then he sent a message to the neighboring castle, which raised its pointed roofs above the forest, and invited the seneschal and his two daughters to be his guests three days later and see some falcons fly, after they had heightened the solemnity of a thief's punishment by their presence—and they were to come before dawn.

Renaud's eyes had been dilated by the darkness of his prison, they were black and immobile and the pupils merely contracted as they slowly grew brighter and reflected the torn clouds and rising sun in the east. Behind Sir Enguerrand was borne the Iceland falcon, his claws sharply fastened in the glove and a hood over his keen, hungry eyes which had not seen food for three days.

But farther behind swayed a line of color which burned and flamed. Six light-colored horses, almost blue in the dawn, were led by pages at a gallop, and red velvet cloths were lifted from their curved necks. The carriage that they drew was red, and in it gold shone heavily over the delicate breasts and slender arms of the seneschal's daughters. Six mounted damsels followed with hair as blonde as corn and their pointed feet playing under the folds of their skirts. Six huntsmen blew notes, which seemed to dance and turn round like wheels out of the mouths of the crooked horns, and the lines of the plain also danced and dashed past one another in a wine-colored mist, while the clouds above had shining borders like butterflies' wings.

They formed a semi-circle, plume by plume, shoulder by shoulder, round a bush where the prisoner was tied. As the horse-cloths fluttered in the wind, red penetrated deep into the shadow, gloomy like hopeless longing, and red burned in the sunshine, light as victorious jubilation. The noble ladies' supple necks leaned forward out of the carriage, and their conical hoods formed one line with the sloping contours of their shoulders. They were like herons, Renaud thought, and he almost expected them to utter shrill cries when the notes of the horns fell far away like projected stones, and all grew silent. But when he saw them more clearly, with their thin, straight lips and strangely dreamy eyes, which were always directed in cold ecstasy toward something infinitely distant, and the indolent white hands in their laps and the long folds of their robes, then they seemed to him wondrously beautiful like the richest images of saints with dimly burning candle flames at their feet, and it pained him that they should see him bound. He let his eyes run on, past the damsels—pretty, shy birds, whom he would have liked to frighten with a whistle—past the retainer's red faces and mouths gaping with curiosity, past the brown plain, where he had run until he was tired and dreamed until he was weary.

He knew the fate that awaited him, but when the Iceland falcon was brought forward, and he understood that this was the bird which was to execute the punishment, he laughed with joy. His heart throbbed with pride, as when they were his—the bird and the long sunny day and the fields with listening winds and swaying trees with the yellow leaves of autumn. When the falcon had again beheld the light and accustomed himself to seeing, he gathered his strength for flight and waited to be cast aloft from the bearer, whilst his eyes sought for prey in the air—they were keen and fierce with hunger and flamed as with sparks, and they had no memories in their depths, they recognized none. But Renaud's eyes looked anxiously inquiring into the bird's and were moistened with sorrow not to meet their gaze. They should have reflected his days of daring and longing, his contempt and his dreams on the red heather, but they merely waited greedily for prey, cold and cruel, like the curiosity of the people or the jest on Sir Enguerrand's thin lips. He felt the pang of grief more bitterly than before, and turned his head aside to recollect himself, with his eyelids closed about fluttering thoughts.

He lay thus, while the herald read aloud the law, "twelve sols in silver—six ounces of flesh from near the heart—thus Sir Enguerrand protects the pleasures of the nobles." He did not look up, when his skin was cut open, so that the smell of blood should attract the falcon, and when it plunged its beak in his breast, he did not utter a cry, merely quivered, so that the bird's eyes flashed angrily, and it stretched out its wings as if about to flap them.

The seneschal's daughters leaned their heads forward with a gleam of interest in their strangely dreamy eyes, but they did not raise their hands from their laps, and their robes lay as before in unruffled folds. The horses snorted at the smell of blood and stamped on the frosty ground, so that the red cloths fluttered in the blue pallor of the morning air; but Renaud lay silent, and the huntsmen stood in vain with distended cheeks and their horns at their lips, ready to drown his cry of pain.

The first pang had torn at his most delicate fibers; it was as if his heart would go with it, but afterwards he had almost grown insensible with satisfaction, with dizzy torpor, and as the blood flowed warm from the wound, and the keen beak tore at his breast, Renaud dreamed himself in the lofty azure atmosphere of his dreams, and he understood all, death and honor, and he felt how it burned and dazzled—the golden sun of the heroic sagas.

When Sir Enguerrand thought that the six ounces of the law were fulfilled, he gave the signal to his men to blow, and the falcon was lifted off, satiated with blood, his eyes again filled with calm pride. The procession was again set in motion, with greater mirth than before, toward the reeds which shone yellow in the distance; but Renaud could not be wakened. He had dreamed himself to death. They merely unbound him and let him lie with red heather beneath his head.

But the Iceland falcon was never allowed to sit on his master's hand, for Sir Enguerrand did not love to drink from a goblet on which the lips of another had imprinted a kiss.

———————

Belgium

INTRODUCTION

IT was not until 1880 that the Belgians could claim to have established an indisputably original literature of their own. Before that time a few national writers, like Henri Conscience, made a sporadic appearance, but either they joined the ranks of French writers in Paris or they remained more or less isolated phenomena in their own country.

Midway between the earlier period and the foundation of Max Waller's epoch-making magazine, *La Jeune Belgique*, in 1880, stood Charles de Coster, whose *Legend of Tyl Ulenspiegel* is now regarded as one of the chief sources of inspiration to the generations that followed. But De Coster died before the opening of the period that marks the birth of a genuine Belgian literature.

Modern Belgium is rich in prose fiction. Though Maeterlinck specialized in the drama and the essay, and Verhaeren was essentially a poet, the most significant products of the Belgians were their novels and stories. Lemonnier's first important novel appeared in 1881. Demolder, Delattre, Virrès, Eekhoud, Rodenbach, and a score of others have all struck roots into the soil of their native land; and nearly all of them have written short stories. As anyone may see at a glance, the story as practised by the Belgians is quite as much a painting as a narrative. The Maeterlinck, Lemonnier and Verhaeren stories in the present collection are little more than paintings in the manner of the earlier Flemish artists transferred to the medium of literature.

There runs through modern Belgian literature a melancholy note that is attributable doubtless to the tragic history of that small country, a mysterious and mystic insistence upon the darker aspects of life; above all, a sense of the picturesque decay of a nation once immensely prosperous and powerful.

There are a few comic writers, chief among them Léopold Courouble, but these are exceptional: it is in the peasant studies of Lemonnier and Eekhoud and Demolder, and the mood pictures of Maeterlinck and Verhaeren and Rodenbach, that the Belgians have found their most satisfactory medium of expression.

CHARLES DE COSTER

(1827—1879)

CHARLES-THÉODORE-HENRY DE COSTER, "the father of Belgian literature," was born at Munich in 1827. He studied in Belgium, and at a
comparatively early age entered a bank, where he spent the greater
part of his life. His writing was done sporadically. Apart from *Tyl
Ulenspiegel*, his most important work is the *Flemish Legends*. It was not
until after his death that he was recognized as a master of prose
fiction. *Tyl Ulenspiegel*, the composition of which took the author some
ten years, is already regarded as one of the classics of Belgian literature.

The *Mysterious Picture* is found in Section 33 of the First Book.
Translated by Geoffrey Whitworth in the volume, *The Legend of Tyl
Ulenspiegel*, published by Chatto and Windus, by whose permission it is
here used. There is no title in the original.

THE MYSTERIOUS PICTURE

(From *The Legend of the Glorious Adventures of Tyl Ulenspiegel*)

ULENSPIEGEL came at last to the palace of the Landgrave.
There two captains of artillery were playing dice upon the steps
of the palace, and one of them, a red-haired man of gigantic stature,
soon noticed Ulenspiegel as he approached modestly upon his ass,
gazing down upon them and their game.

"What do you want?" said the captain, "you fellow, with your
starved pilgrim's face?"

"I am extremely hungry," answered Ulenspiegel, "and if I am a
pilgrim, it is against my will."

"An you are hungry," replied the captain, "go, eat the next gallows-
cord you come to, for such cords are prepared for vagabonds like you."

"Sir Captain," answered Ulenspiegel, "only give me the fine golden
cord you wear on your hat, and I will go straightway and hang myself
by the teeth from that fat ham which I see hanging over there at the
cook-shop."

The captain asked him where he came from. Ulenspiegel told him,
"From Flanders."

"What do you want?"

"To show His Highness the Landgrave one of my pictures. For I am
a painter."

"If it is a painter that you are," said the captain, "and from Flanders, come in and I will lead you to my master."

When he had been brought before the Landgrave, Ulenspiegel saluted thrice and again.

"May Your Highness deign," said he, "to excuse my presumption in daring to come and lay before these noble feet a picture I have made for Your Highness, wherein I have had the honor to portray Our Lady the Virgin in her royal attire."

And then after a moment's pause:

"It may be that my picture may please Your Highness," he continued, "and in that case I am sufficiently presumptuous to hope that I might aspire even unto this fine chair of velvet where sat in his lifetime the painter that is lately deceased and ever to be regretted by Your Magnanimity."

Now, the picture which Ulenspiegel showed him was very beautiful, and when the Landgrave had inspected it he told Ulenspiegel to sit down on the chair, for that he would certainly make him his court painter. And the Landgrave kissed him on both cheeks most joyously, and Ulenspiegel sat down on the chair.

"Of a truth, you are a very talkative fellow," said the Landgrave, looking him up and down.

"May it please Your Lordship," answered Ulenspiegel, "Jeff—my donkey—has dined most excellently well on thistles, but as for me, I have seen nothing but misery these three days past, and have had nothing to nourish me but the mists of expectation."

"You shall soon have some better fare than that," answered the Landgrave, "but where is this donkey of yours?"

"I left him on the Grande Place," Ulenspiegel said, "opposite the palace; and I should be most obliged if he could be given lodging for the night, some straw, and a little fodder."

The Landgrave gave immediately instructions to one of his pages that Ulenspiegel's donkey should be treated even as his own.

The hour for supper soon arrived, and the meal was like a wedding festival. Hot meats smoked in the dishes, wine flowed like water, while Ulenspiegel and the Landgrave grew both as red as burning coals. Ulenspiegel also became very merry, but His Highness was somewhat pensive even in his cups.

"Our painter," said he suddenly, "will have to paint our portrait, for it is a great satisfaction to a mortal prince to bequeath to his descendants the memory of his countenance."

"Sir Landgrave," answered Ulenspiegel, "your will is my pleasure. Nevertheless, I cannot help feeling sorry at the thought that if Your Lordship is painted by himself he will feel lonely perhaps, all there in solitary state through the ages to come. Surely he should be accompanied by his noble wife, Madame the Landgravine, by her lords and ladies, and by his captains and most warlike officers of state. In the midst of these My Lord and his Lady will shine like twin suns surrounded by lanterns."

"Well, painter mine, and how shall I have to pay you for this mighty work?"

"One hundred florins, either now or later, just as you will."

"Here they are, in advance," said the Landgrave.

"Most compassionate master," said Ulenspiegel as he took the money, "you have filled my lamp with oil, and now it shall burn bright in your honor."

On the next day Ulenspiegel asked the Landgrave to let him see those persons who were to have the honor of being painted. And first there came before him the Duke of Lüneburg, Commander of the infantry of the Landgrave. He was a stout man who carried with difficulty his great paunch swollen with food. He went up to Ulenspiegel and whispered in his ear, "When you paint my portrait, see that you take off half my fat at least, else will I order my soldiers to have you hung."

The Duke passed on. And next day there came a noble lady with a hump on her back and a bosom as flat as a sword-blade.

"Sir painter," said she, "unless you remove the hump on my back and give me a couple of others in the place where they should be, verily, I will have you drawn and quartered as if you were a prisoner."

The lady went away, and now there appeared a young maid-of-honor, fair, fresh and comely, only that she lacked three teeth under her upper lip.

"Sir painter," said she, "if you do not paint me smiling and showing through my parted lips a perfect set of teeth, I'll have you chopped up into small pieces at the hands of my gallant. There he is, look at him."

And she pointed to that captain of artillery who a while ago had been playing dice on the palace steps. And she went her way.

The procession continued until at last Ulenspiegel was left alone with the Landgrave. The Landgrave said to him, "My friend, let me warn you that if your painting has the misfortune to be inaccurate or false to all these various physiognomies by so much as a single feature, I will have your throat cut as if you were a chicken."

"If I am to have my head cut off," thought Ulenspiegel, "if I am to be drawn and quartered, chopped up into small pieces and finally hung, I should do better to paint no portrait at all. I must consider what is best to be done."

"And where is the hall," he asked the Landgrave, "which I am to adorn with all these likenesses?"

"Follow me," said the Landgrave. And he brought him to a large room with great bare walls. "This is the hall," he said.

"I should be very grateful," said Ulenspiegel, "if some curtains could be hung right along the walls, so that my paintings may be protected from the flies and the dust."

"Certainly," said the Landgrave.

When the curtains had been hung as directed, Ulenspiegel asked if he might have three apprentices to help him with the mixing of his colors. This was done, and for thirty days Ulenspiegel and the apprentices spent the whole of their time feasting and carousing together, with every extravagance of meat and drink. And the Landgrave looked on at it all. But at last, on the thirty-first day, he came and thrust his nose in at the door of the chamber where Ulenspiegel had begged him not to enter.

"Well, Tyl," he said, "and where are the portraits?"

"They are not finished," answered Ulenspiegel.

"When shall I be able to see them?"

"Not just yet," said Ulenspiegel.

On the six-and-thirtieth day the Landgrave again thrust his nose inside the door.

"Well, Tyl," he inquired, "how, now?"

"Ah, Sir Landgrave," said Ulenspiegel, "the portraits are getting on."

On the sixtieth day the Landgrave grew very angry and, coming right into the room, "Show me the pictures at once," he cried.

"I will do so," answered Ulenspiegel, "but pray have the kindness not to draw the curtains until you have summoned hither the lords and captains and ladies of your court."

"Very well," said the Landgrave, and at his command the aforesaid notabilities appeared. Ulenspiegel took his stand in front of the curtain, which was still carefully drawn.

"My Lord Landgrave," he said "and you, Madame the Landgravine, and you, my Lord of Lüneburg, and you others, fine ladies and valiant captains, know that behind this curtain have I portrayed to the best of my abilities, your faces, every one warlike or gentle, as the case may be. It will be quite easy for each one of you to recognize himself. And that you are anxious to see yourselves is only natural. But I pray you, have patience and suffer me to speak a word or two before the curtain is drawn. Know this, fair ladies and valiant captains: all you that are of noble blood shall behold my paintings and rejoice. But if there be any among you that is of low or humble birth, such an one will see nothing but a blank wall. So there! And now, have the goodness to open wide your noble eyes."

And so saying, Ulenspiegel drew the curtain.

"Remember," said he again, "only they of noble birth can see my pictures, whether they be lords or ladies." And again, presently: "He of low birth is blind to my pictures, but he who clearly sees, that man is a nobleman without a doubt."

At that, everyone present opened wide his eyes, pretending—you may be sure—to see, and failing to recognize the various faces, and pointing themselves out to one another, though in reality they beheld nothing at all but a bare wall. And for this they were each and all secretly ashamed. Suddenly the court jester, who was standing by, jumped three feet in the air and jangled his bells.

"Take me for a villain," he cried, "a most villainous villain, I verily will affirm and assert and say with trumpets and fanfares that there I see a wall, a blank white wall and nothing but a wall, so help me God and his saints!"

Ulenspiegel said, "When fools 'gin talking, time for wise men to be walking."

And he was about to leave the palace when the Landgrave stopped him.

"Fool in your folly," said he, "you make boast that you go through the world praising what is good and fair and making mock of foolery, and you have dared to make open game of so many and so high-born ladies, and of their yet more noble lords, bringing ridicule on the pride of their nobility! Of a truth, I tell you that the day will come when you will hang for your free speech."

"If the cord is of gold," said Ulenspiegel, "it will break with dread of my approach."

"Stay," said the Landgrave. "Here is the first bit of your rope." And he gave him fifteen florins.

"All thanks to you," said Ulenspiegel, "and I promise you that every tavern on the road shall have a thread of it, a thread of that gold which makes Crœsuses of all those rascally tavern-keepers."

And off he went on his donkey, holding his head up high in the air, with the plume in his cap wagging joyously in the breeze.

MAURICE MAETERLINCK

(1862—1949)

MAURICE MAETERLINCK was born at Ghent in 1862. He studied for the law, but left for Paris after a short career as a lawyer. In Paris he became acquainted with several writers who exercised considerable influence over him. Maeterlinck's chief contributions to contemporary literature are his plays and his essays.

The Massacre of the Innocents was the earliest published work of this writer. It appeared in 1886 in a small magazine. It is a skilfully constructed tale, in which the background and details are strikingly similar to the early paintings of the Flemish school.

The translation, by Barrett H. Clark, was made especially for this collection. Originally reprinted by permission of the author.

THE MASSACRE OF THE INNOCENTS

ON Friday the 26th of December about supper time, a little shepherd came into Nazareth crying terribly.

Some peasants who were drinking ale at the Blue Lion threw open the shutters to look into the village orchard, and saw the lad running across the snow. They recognized him as Korneliz' son, and shouted at him from the window: "What's the matter? Go to bed, you!"

But the boy answered in a voice of terror, telling them that the Spaniards had come, having already set fire to the farm, hanged his mother from a chestnut bough, and bound his nine little sisters to the trunk of a large tree. The peasants quickly came forth from the inn, surrounded the boy and plied him with questions. He went on to tell them that the soldiers were clad in steel armor and mounted on horseback, that they had seized the cattle of his uncle, Petrus Krayer, and would soon enter the wood with the sheep and cattle.

They all ran to the Golden Sun, where Korneliz and his brother-in-law were drinking ale, while the innkeeper hastened out into the village to spread the news of the approach of the Spaniards.

There was great excitement in Nazareth. Women threw open windows and peasants ran forth from their houses carrying lights which they extinguished as soon as they came to the orchard, where it was bright as midday, because of the snow and the full moon. They gathered round Korneliz and Krayer in the public square before the inn. Many had brought pitchforks and rakes. They took counsel, speaking in tones of terror, out under the trees.

As they were uncertain what to do, one of them ran to fetch the curé, who owned the farm that was worked by Korneliz. He came forth from his house with the keys of the church, in company with the sacristan, while all the others followed him to the churchyard, where he proclaimed from the top of the tower that he could see nothing, either across the fields or in the wood, but that there were red clouds in the direction of his farm. Over all the rest of the horizon the sky was blue and filled with stars.

After deliberating a long while in the churchyard, they decided to hide in the wood which the Spaniards were to come through, attack them if they were not too numerous, and recover Petrus Krayer's cattle and any booty they might have taken at the farm.

The men armed themselves with forks and spades while the women remained with the curé by the church. Looking for a favorable place for an ambuscade, the men reached a hilly spot near a mill at the edge of the wood, where they could see the fire glowing against the stars of night. They took up their position under some enormous oaks by the side of an ice-covered pond.

A shepherd, who was called the Red Dwarf, mounted to the top of the hill in order to warn the miller, who had already stopped his mill when he saw flames on the horizon. But he allowed the peasant to enter, and the two went to a window to look out over the countryside.

The moon shone down brightly upon the conflagration, and the men could see a long procession of people wending their way across the snow. After they had done watching, the Dwarf went down again to the others waiting in the wood. They could soon distinguish in the distance four riders behind a herd of cattle browsing over the fields. As they stood, clad in their blue breeches and red mantles, looking about by the pond's edge under trees made luminous by the heavy snowfall, the sacristan showed them a box-hedge, and behind this they crouched.

The Spaniards, driving before them flocks and cattle, made their way over the ice, and when the sheep came to the hedge and began nibbling at the greenery, Korneliz broke through, the others following him into the moonlight, armed with their forks. There was then a great massacre in the presence of the huddled sheep and cows, that looked on frightened at the terrible slaughter under the light of the moon.

When they had killed the men and their horses, Korneliz went out into the fields toward the blazing farm, while the others stripped the dead. Then they all returned to the village with the flocks and cattle. The women, who were looking out toward the dense wood from behind the churchyard walls, saw them coming out from among the trees and in company with the curé ran to meet them. They all returned dancing amid laughing children and barking dogs. As they made merry under the pear-trees, where the Dwarf had hung lanterns as for a kermesse, they asked the curé what ought to be done next. They decided to send a cart for the body of the woman who had been hanged and her nine little girls, and bring them all back to the village. The sisters of the dead woman and various other relatives got into the cart, and the curé as well, for he was old and very fat and could walk only with the greatest difficulty. They drove off into the wood, and in silence reached the wide open fields, where they saw the dead soldiers, stripped naked, and the horses lying on their backs on the shining ice among the trees.

They went on toward the farm, which was still burning in the midst of the open fields.

When they reached the orchard of the burning house, they stopped short before the garden gate and looked upon the terrible tragedy. Korneliz' wife hung, naked, from the branches of a huge chestnut. He himself climbed up a ladder into the branches of the tree, below which his nine little girls awaited their mother on the lawn. Korneliz made his way through the arching boughs overhead when all at once, outlined against the bright snow, he caught sight of the crowd beneath, looking up at him. Weeping, he signed to them to come to his help, and they came into the garden, and the sacristan, the Red Dwarf, the innkeepers of the Blue Lion and the Golden Sun, the curé carrying a lantern, and several other peasants, climbed into the snow-covered chestnut to cut down the body of the hanged woman. The women took the body into their arms at the foot of the tree, as those other women once received Our Lord Jesus Christ.

She was buried on the following day, and for the next week nothing unusual occurred in Nazareth, but the next Sunday famished wolves ran through the village after High Mass, and the snow fell until noon. Then the sun came out and shone bright in the sky, and the peasants went home to dinner as usual, and dressed for Benediction.

At this time there was no one out on the square, for it was bitter cold. Only dogs and chickens wandered here and there among the trees, and sheep nibbled at the triangular spot of grass, and the curé's maid swept the snow in the garden.

Then a troop of armed men crossed the stone bridge at the far end of the village, and pulled up at the orchard. A few peasants came out of their houses, but hurried back terror-stricken when they saw that the horsemen were Spaniards, and went to their windows to watch what was going to happen. There were thirty horsemen, in armor. They gathered round an old man with a white beard. Each horseman carried with him a foot-soldier dressed in yellow or red. These dismounted and ran about over the snow to warm themselves, while a number of armored soldiers also dismounted.

They made their way toward the Golden Sun and knocked at the door. It was opened with some hesitancy, and the Spaniards entered, warmed themselves before the fire, and demanded ale. They then left the inn, taking with them pots, pitchers, and bread for their companions, and the old man with the white beard who stood waiting among his soldiers. As the street was still deserted, the commanding officer sent off some horsemen behind the houses to guard the village on the side facing the open country, and ordered the footmen to bring to him all children two years old or under, as he intended to massacre them, in accordance with what is written in the Gospel of St. Matthew.

The men went first to the small inn of the Green Cabbage and the barber's hut, which stood close to each other in the central part of the street. One of them opened the pigsty and a whole litter of pigs escaped and roamed about through the village. The innkeeper and the barber came out of their houses and humbly inquired of the soldiers what was wanted, but the Spaniards understood no Flemish, and entered the houses in search of the children. The innkeeper had one who, dressed in its little shirt, was sitting on the dinner table, crying. One of the soldiers took it in his arms and carried it off out under the apple trees, while its parents followed weeping. The foot-soldiers next threw open the stables of the barrel-maker, the blacksmith, and the cobbler, and cows, calves, asses, pigs, goats and sheep wandered here and there over the square. When they broke the windows of the carpenter's house, a number of the wealthiest and oldest peasants of the parish gathered in the street and advanced toward the Spaniards. They respectfully took off their caps and hats to the velvet-clad chief, asking him what he intended to do, but he too did not understand their language, and one of them ran off to get the curé. He was about to go to Benediction, and was putting on his golden chasuble in the sacristy. The peasants cried, "The Spaniards are in the orchard!" Terror-stricken, he ran to the church door, followed by the choir-boys carrying their censers and candles. From the door he could see the cattle and other animals set loose from their stables wandering over the grass and snow, the Spanish horsemen, the foot-soldiers before the doors of the houses, horses tied to trees all along the street, and men and women supplicating the soldier who carried the child still clad in its shirt. He hastened into the churchyard, the peasants turning anxiously toward him, their priest, who arrived like a god covered with gold, out there among the pear-trees. They pressed close about him as he stood facing the white-bearded man. He spoke both in Flemish and Latin, but the officer slowly shrugged his shoulders to show that he failed to understand.

The parishioners inquired of him in undertones, "What does he say? What is he going to do?" Others, seeing the curé in the orchard, emerged cautiously from their huts, and women hastily came near and whispered in small groups among themselves, while the soldiers who had been besieging the inn, came out again when they saw the crowd assembling in the square.

Then he who held the innkeeper's child by one leg, cut off its head with a stroke of the sword. The peasants saw the head fall, and the body bleeding on the ground. The mother gathered it to her arms, forgetting the head, and ran toward her house. On the way she stumbled against a tree, fell flat on the snow and lay in a faint, while the father struggled with two soldiers.

Some of the younger peasants threw stones and wood at the Spaniards, but the horsemen rallied and lowered their lances, the women scattered in all directions, while the curé with his other parishioners, shrieked with horror to the accompaniment of the noises made by the sheep, geese, and dogs.

As the soldiers went off once more down the street, they were quiet again, waiting to see what would happen. A group went into the shop of the sacristan's sisters, but came out again without touching the seven women, who were on their knees praying within. Then they entered the inn of the Hunchback of St. Nicholas. There too the door was instantly opened in the hope of placating them, but when they appeared again in the midst of a great tumult, they carried three children in their arms, and were surrounded by the Hunchback, his wife and daughters, who were begging for mercy with clasped hands. When the soldiers came to their leader they laid the children down at the foot of an elm, all dressed in their Sunday clothes. One of them, who wore a yellow dress, got up and ran with unsteady feet toward the sheep. A soldier ran after it with his naked sword. The child died with its face on the earth. The others were killed near the tree. The peasants and the innkeeper's daughters took flight, screaming, and went back to their houses. Alone in the orchard, the curé fell to his knees and begged the Spaniards, in a piteous voice, with arms crossed over his breast, going from one to the other on his knees, while the father and mother of the murdered children, seated on the snow, wept bitterly as they bent over the lacerated bodies.

As the foot-soldiers went along the street they noticed a large blue farmhouse. They tried to break in the door, but this was of oak and studded with huge nails. They therefore took tubs which were frozen in a pond near the entrance, and used them to enter the house from the second story windows.

There had been a kermesse in this house: relatives had come to feast on waffles, hams, and custards. At the sound of the smashing of windows they crouched together behind the table, still laden with jugs and dishes. The soldiers went to the kitchen and after a savage fight in which many were wounded, they seized all the small boys and girls, and a little servant who had bitten the thumb of one soldier, left the house and closed the door behind them to prevent their being followed.

Those who had no children cautiously came forth from their houses and followed the soldiers at a distance. They could see them throw down their victims on the ground before the old man, and cold-bloodedly massacre them with lances or swords. Meanwhile men and women crowded the windows of the blue farmhouse and the barn, cursing and raising their arms to heaven as they contemplated the pink, red, and white clothes of their motionless children on the ground among the trees. Then the soldiers hanged the servant from the Half Moon Inn on the other side of the street. There was a long silence in the village.

It had now become a general massacre. Mothers escaped from their houses, trying to flee through vegetable and flower gardens out into the open country, but mounted soldiers pursued them and drove them back into the street. Peasants, with caps held tight between their hands, fell to their knees before the soldiers who dragged off their little ones, and dogs barked joyously amid the disorder. The curé, his hands raised heavenward, rushed back and forth from house to house and out among the trees, praying in desperation like a martyr. The soldiers, trembling from the cold, whistled in their fingers as they moved about, or stood idly with their hands in their pockets, their swords under their arms, in front of houses that were being entered. Small groups in all directions, seeing the fear of the peasants, were entering the farmhouses, and in every street similar scenes were enacted. The market-gardener's wife, who lived in an old hut with pink tiles near the church, pursued with a chair two soldiers who were carrying off her children in a wheelbarrow. She was terribly sick when she saw her children die, and made to sit on a chair against a tree.

Other soldiers climbed into the lime trees in front of a farmhouse painted the color of lilacs, and made their way in by taking off the tiles. When they reappeared on the roof, the parents with extended arms followed them until the soldiers forced them back, finding it necessary finally to strike them over the head with their swords before they could shake themselves free and return again to the street below.

One family, who had concealed themselves in the cellar of a large house, stood at the gratings and wildly lamented, while the father desperately brandished his pitchfork through the grating. Outside, an old bald-headed fellow sat on a manure-heap, sobbing to himself. In the square a woman dressed in yellow had fainted away, her weeping husband holding her up by the arms against a pear-tree. Another woman, in red, clutched her little girl, whose hands had been cut off, and lifted the child's arms to see whether she could move. Still another woman was escaping toward the open country, the soldiers running after her among the haystacks, which stood out in sharp relief against the snow-covered fields.

Before the Four Sons of Aymon confusion reigned. The peasants had made a barricade while the soldiers encircled the inn, unable to effect an entrance. They were trying to climb up to the sign-board by means of the vines, when they caught sight of a ladder behind the garden gate. Setting this against the wall, they scaled it, one after another. But the landlord and his family threw down at them tables and chairs, crockery and cradles from the window, upsetting ladder and soldiers together.

In a wooden cottage at the outskirts of the village another group of soldiers came upon an old woman washing her children in a tub before the open fire. She was old and deaf, and did not hear them when they entered. Two soldiers carried off the tub with the children in it, while the bewildered old woman set off in pursuit, carrying the clothes which she had been about to put on the infants. Out in the village she saw traces of blood, swords in the orchard, smashed cradles in the open streets, women praying and wringing their hands over their dead children, and began to scream and strike the soldiers who had to set down the tub in order to defend themselves. The curé hurried over to her, his hands still folded over his chasuble, and entreated the Spaniards for mercy, in the presence of the naked children screaming in the tub. Other soldiers came up, bound the distracted mother to a tree, and went off with the children.

The butcher, having hidden his baby girl, leaned against the front of his shop with apparent unconcern. A foot-soldier and one of the armed horsemen entered his home and found the child in a copper pot. The butcher desperately seized a knife and rushed off in pursuit, but the soldiers disarmed him and suspended him by the hands from some hooks in the wall, where he kicked and wriggled among his dead animals until evening.

Round the churchyard a multitude gathered in front of a long low green farmhouse. The proprietor wept bitterly as he stood in his doorway. He was a fat, jolly-looking man, and happened to arouse the compassion of a few soldiers who sat near the wall in the sunlight, patting a dog. The soldier who was taking off his child made gestures as if to convey the meaning, "What can I do? I'm not to blame!"

One peasant who was being pursued leaped into a boat near the stone bridge, and, with his wife and children, rowed quickly across that part of the pond that was not frozen. The Spaniards, who dared not follow, walked angrily among the reeds by the shore. They climbed into the willows along the bankside, trying to reach the boat with their lances. Unable to do so, they continued to threaten the fugitives, who drifted out over the dark water.

The orchard was still thronged with people: it was there, in the presence of the white-bearded commanding officer, that most of the children were being murdered. The children who were over two and could just walk, stood together eating bread and jam, staring in wide-eyed wonder at the massacre of their helpless playmates, or gathered round the village fool, who was playing his flute.

All at once there was a concerted movement in the village, and the peasants made off in the direction of the castle that stood on rising ground at the far end of the street. They had caught sight of their lord on the battlements, watching the massacre. Men and women, young and old, extended their hands toward him in supplication as he stood there in his velvet cloak and golden cap like a king in Heaven. But he only raised his hands and shrugged his shoulders to show that he was powerless, while the people supplicated him in growing despair, kneeling with heads bared in the snow, and crying piteously. He turned slowly back into his tower. Their last hope had vanished.

When all the children had been killed, the weary soldiers wiped their swords on the grass and ate their supper among the pear-trees, then mounting in pairs, they rode out of Nazareth across the bridge over which they had come.

The setting sun turned the wood into a flaming mass, dyeing the village a blood red. Utterly exhausted, the curé threw himself down in the snow before the church, his servant standing at his side. They both looked out into the street and the orchard, which were filled with peasants dressed in their Sunday clothes. Before the entrances of many houses were parents holding the bodies of children on their knees, still full of blank amazement, lamenting over their grievous tragedy. Others wept over their little ones where they had perished, by the side of a cask, under a wheelbarrow, or by the pond. Others again carried off their dead in silence. Some set to washing benches, chairs, tables, bloody underclothes, or picking up the cradles that had been hurled into the street. Many mothers sat bewailing their children under the trees, having recognized them by their woolen dresses. Those who had had no children wandered through the square, stopping by grief-stricken mothers, who sobbed and moaned. The men, who had stopped crying, doggedly pursued their strayed beasts to the accompaniment of the barking of dogs; others silently set to work mending their broken windows and damaged roofs.

As the moon quietly rose through the tranquil sky, a sleepy silence fell upon the village, where at last the shadow of no living thing stirred.

CAMILLE LEMONNIER

(1844–1913)

LEMONNIER has, from the very beginning of his career in 1863, remained an interpreter of Belgian life, and particularly of the life of the peasants. His novels are powerful exhibitions of the brutality of humankind, yet penetrated with a moving beauty of form and style. Lemonnier wrote several volumes of short stories, of which many reveal the melancholy aspect of old Flemish towns.

The Soul of Veere is highly characteristic of this latter type of story.

It originally appeared in a volume entitled *It Was in Summer*, first published in 1900. The translation by Barrett H. Clark, here printed for the first time, is included by permission of Albin Michel, publisher, Paris.

THE SOUL OF VEERE

LITTLE Pietje, who belonged to the inn on the public square, asked me whether I had ever seen the boy who was always "playing his little tunes?" Now, what did she mean by that? I had been in Veere three days and had seen no one answering to her description. Good heavens, I thought to myself, can there be anyone in Veere foolish enough to do that? It would be quite useless to play music there, as the houses are invariably closed, while only on the rarest occasions do you see at a window the face of an old man, an old woman, or a pretty girl in one of those flat caps with metal plaques over the temples. Why, there would be no one to listen to him! In the strange little village of Veere, they all look like mummies on exhibition behind their little squares of green or blue glass.

That is my impression of the place. If by chance I had happened to hear that boy playing his little tunes through the streets, I would have put my finger to my lips as a warning not to disturb the silence that reigned in the depths of those houses. The sun itself, in scattered flecks of gold, sleeps in the middle of the street. It is long since it fell sick trying to reawaken the town that was once alive and is now fallen into a deep slumber. Its light dies on the threshold of houses, like the footstep of a beggar who returns morning after morning to a door which no one ever opens. The shades within have bolted their doors.

If I live to be a hundred I shall never forget that street in Veere, nor the little houses jutting out over sidewalks that look as though they were clasping hands in prayer. It is all so far away from life that one has doubts of one's own existence: only a faint shadow precedes you, and you are not quite sure at first whither it leads. But it leads in the direction of the churchyard, where all else has gone. Over there behind the ramparts lies the open sea with its ships, while overhead the arching sky, heavy with clouds, bears down upon the expanse of the sea. In that town I felt I was dying myself, that my feeble heart beat so faintly, while my fingers made some slight sign of life toward the sun.

"That little Pietje was trying to take advantage of my credulity," I said to myself. "Or else she's talking about something that happened long ago, before everyone had died here."

At that moment the carillon sang out its sweet little song. It reminded one of a Sunday afternoon in summer at grandfather's, as the ld man sat watching the dust filter in from the street under the door, is hands crossed over the head of his cane. The air it played sounded ke that of some old broken music-box. The sounds trickled lazily own from the belfry and saddened me; it was as if I had suddenly eard the song that sang the last agonies of old Veere.

The town hall in the public square was a pretty building, as delica- ely decorated as a reliquary; it had tall statues in the niches, of kings nd saints. I suppose—but who now knows the history of Veere?— made up my mind that it was doubtless the carillon to which the trange-eyed child had referred. And I thought almost contemptuously f those old statues, so outmoded on their daises, looking out always oward the open sea. They had stood there for centuries, with heads igidly fixed, waiting for something that never happened. Possibly hose shadowy eyes, carved out of stone, were watching for the return f fleets that one day long since set sail out of the harbor. Near the quare stood an old church steeple, the key of which has for ages eposed at the bottom of the sea.

The irony of it all, I mused with a smile. Everyone had left the town, nd was now along the ramparts that extended all the way out to the unes. Only a few old people were left—aged folk with dirty, smudgy ttle shadows under their noses like the greenish mold that comes after eath. And yet the stone images, with their swords and scepters, seem s though they were actually in command over the living.

I went to the tower and kicked three resounding blows at the gate. did it mainly as a sort of mockery, knowing well that no one in the olitude of that ancient House of God would respond. I also wanted to ear what a noise could be made among the shadows of death. I was mazed at the sudden opening of the door and the appearance of handsome young man with strange eyes. He wore a short jacket of elvet with the silver clasps ordinarily worn by the men of Zeeland. Ie carried an accordion such as is sold in the harbor shops and played y sailors at sea, when of an evening they draw silver tones from it, now ippling quickly and now long drawn out. The young man looked as hough he had been rudely awakened out of a dream. Was this, I vondered, the boy who, as Pietje, said, was always "playing his little unes"?

He walked by me without so much as turning his head, passing along ink-tinted walls, long straight windows of aged glass, and little ardens planted with cabbage and onions. He slowly crossed the public quare, while once again the little carillon rang out in crystal tones, inging its sad song of the ultimate agony of Veere. The wind softly cattered the notes and sent them flying over the roofs of houses in the irection of the sea. The singular young man placed the accordion gainst his shoulder, and with his fingers on the stops, expanded and

contracted the bellows of the instrument. The air he played seemed t
have a meaning for himself alone. Bending his head down close to h
accordion, he smiled the smile of a man who no longer belongs to th
life. I thought I understood deep down in my soul that some secre
cause had affected the boy's reason, attuning it at the same time to th
mystery of the village of Veere. But I could not have explained it.

Then something occurred that troubled me. The young man looke
up at the tower, saw the great lords standing in their niches, and the
out over the distant sea, his eyes glistening with a light as of another da
The accordion played on faster and more furiously with a kind of mac
ness, and it seemed as though the ancient soul of the town were suc
denly set to vibrating under the deft fingers of the player. He made h
way on and on through the streets, dancing a quaint step like a sailor
hornpipe. He shook the ground under foot with his heels, whirled abou
holding the accordion high above his head, and quickly brought
down until it almost touched the paved walk; then balanced himse
in one spot with an affected grace, eyes closed and face set in an ecstat
and ceremonious smile—always to the accompaniment of that rhythm
ical and feverish dance music, palpitating with all the abandoned arde
of a murderer or a lover.

Then in those miniature houses there was a gradual animation, an
the reappearance of life that seemed to have slept for ages behi
closed doors, awaiting only the coming of the pale young man wi
the accordion. Behind the windows there was laughter on the fac
of young girls with their white headdresses decorated with quai
spirals sticking out like antennæ. All the pretty girls of Veere we
there behind their lace curtains, with mouths agape like roses
a cloud of bees. Seeing them thus emerge out of the deep shadows ar
come, with fresh complexions, to their windows, I imagined the
homes to be real dolls' houses brought to life by enchantment—t
houses of all the dolls of Veere, with their lovely bare arms tanned l
the salt air, their great bulged skirts, their little colored heads ar
eyes tinted like the sea.

So the musician went here and there through the streets, his wild ai
changing to sad and plaintive strains that brought tears to the eye
These were like the melancholy tunes played at sea during the nigl
by some little cabin boy. It was the soul of Veere, silently weeping ov
her lost love, sighing regretfully over all the lovely girls who now l
asleep with crosses over them, for the handsome young men who we
to sea and never returned. Finally the sounds of the accordion di
away far off among the dunes.

When I returned to the inn I said to Pietje:

"You were right. There is a boy in this town who plays his lit
tunes. Doubtless he is a soul in torment. Do they know what evil bef

him?" The little cat-eyed creature laughed and pointed to a man seated over by the window:

"Ask him," she said. "He can tell you better than I could."

Well, the story was quite commonplace, after all. It seems that one day the lad had fallen in love with one of those doll-like creatures who come to the windows. One evening he had come to her house to dance and play the accordion. Other boys were also in the habit of coming to the same house, and they too paid their court to the girl. When the lad wept, she would say to him, "What do you expect? I love you, but I love him, too—the boy over by the door, and I love the boy who's coming here after you leave.... I love them all!" Once from behind the hedge he had caught sight of her in the arms of the youth who had come before him. He quickly drew his knife, and killed both the girl and the boy.

"And from that day to this," continued the man who was telling the story, "he wanders through the streets, playing his little tunes. He's quite inoffensive: children throw stones at him and the girls laugh. He doesn't understand."

But I could not quite believe that this was the true version. Things are true only in appearance: behind even the most obvious facts there lurks a secret meaning: this must be sought for, for it is the more beautiful of the two. I therefore said to myself that this boy was the soul of Veere. I now understand why he came out of the church door. You, little town of Veere, and that poor half-witted musician are both tainted with the same quiet madness. It is as if the winds of the sea had turned your heads. Something has gone never to return, something that is lamented by your carillon, that sobs in the notes of that accordian.

At Veere there is always a strange young man who walks off in the direction of the dunes and looks out over the broad expanse of the sea.

EMILE VERHAEREN

(1855–1920)

EMILE VERHAEREN was one of the most widely read poets of modern Belgium. Influenced at first by the French Parnassiens and Naturalists, he ultimately developed a style and a philosophy of his own. He began work in the eighties. A large part of his writings are poems, but in his plays and short stories, clearly the work of a poet, he achieves effects of striking power.

One Night is translated by Keene Wallis, and appears in the volume, *Five Tales by Emile Verhaeren*, Albert and Charles Boni, New York, 1924, by whose permission it is here used.

ONE NIGHT

"I'LL be back directly," the best friend I have in the world called to me as he raced down the stairs of the great inn where we had just put up in the outskirts of a decayed city of old Spain.

I saw him disappear, then I heard his last "Be right back," mingled with the sound of his retreating footsteps. Left alone, I went to the balcony and leaned over. Folk, haughty in their dirt and rags, strutted through the arcades. Indescribable beggars blocked the doorways. Dogs howled at the windows of convents or at the many crucifixes which gave the quarter the appearance of an abandoned graveyard. Dusk increased the mystery of the streets. In the bloody sunset the houses seemed the habitations of ghosts. I could see into a window. I felt that a disquietude ran from chamber to chamber of that house, then the room, into which I was looking was filled with people of somber aspect who suddenly prostrated themselves before a great Christ hanging on the wall between flickering candles and votive wreaths, and seeming to run living blood.

Suddenly, at the end of a lane the first lamp twinkled into emerald light. I looked at my watch. An hour had passed since my friend's departure. An overmastering anxiety rose within me. From the moment when I had first begun to look out over this ancient city, fear had been gradually inflaming my fancies. I imagined my friend meeting with a mishap, being robbed, murdered. I did not know in which direction he had gone, nor with what intent. I began to conjure up horrors, ascribing his disappearance to the workings of an alien and hostile influence.

I scrutinized the passers-by, only to find them equivocal. There were old women, cavernous from illness and senility, children almost naked, whimpering until their mothers pressed them to their dry breasts; then came men, burly brutes with long staffs at the end of which was something shiny. A fiery team plunged past with a wild clash of iron-shod hoofs.

The darkness grew thicker and thicker. Unbroken chains of lights glowed along the thoroughfares. One belfry after another awoke and great bells began to peal.

Not far from me a church with yawning doors was engulfing the multitude. The disappearance of the antlike creatures into this gigantic mouth assumed in my eyes a disquieting significance. Had not my poor companion been carried along by the crowd and thrust willy-nilly into this depth of the unknown, out of which arose a ponderous gnashing and crunching of bronze upon bell-metal?

I must have uttered a cry, because an old man who some time since had stopped on the other side of the street to look at me, and who seemed to be seeking an excuse to address me, said something unintelligible and then went away, looking back reproachfully, enigmatically.

I was fairly twitching with anxiety. Our old-fashioned suite was many-cornered, crammed with little nooks in which the darkness piled up, compressed into dread intensity. I dressed hurriedly and began to ransack the city in all directions, rationally at first, then quite feverishly.

I thought I saw my friend now among the loiterers who leaned over the parapets of a stone bridge, now in the recesses of a cellar where frightful sots lurched about a bar, now under a gigantic candelabrum, whose fitfully flickering light illumined a bas-relief of a battle between serpents and eagles.

Every time I banished one of these ideas my head whirled the more. My eyes smarted and my heart was as if in a vise. I resolved to return. But hardly had I taken a step before the object of my anxiety changed. I ceased to worry about my friend and feared only for myself. Whether he was lost or killed, I must return at once! Oh, that nocturnal flight! Through black streets whose house-fronts leered so horribly! Towers loomed up out of sable squares as if built upon the Unknown to reach the stars. Wine-cellars resounded with oaths and brawlings and the sound of my footsteps, reechoed from the angles and doorways of colossal houses, was like a cannonade. More mysterious than before and more implacably hostile the passers-by appeared. Could I ask them to direct me? They were garroters, assassins ready to stick a knife into my back. I walked in the middle of the street, casting stealthy glances over my shoulder, knowing that I was ghostly pale, and fearing above all that my fear would be noticed. A little hunchback peddling matches approached me. I sprang back to avoid him. A cocotte whispered silly words in my ear. I quickened my pace, not daring to thrust her from me bodily. In a glazed arcade, one of those hideous cloaked beggars, such as had disquieted me ever since I started out, stood blocking the passage with his sweeping gestures. I wheeled about. And the hour was striking overhead in the cathedral with a sound of swords clashing in combat.

Suddenly I saw, right before my eyes, the inn where we were staying. Trembling, I put the key in the lock. What awaited me behind the door? My friend had so completely vanished from my thoughts that I did not even ask myself whether he might have returned yet. I searched all the crannies of our suite, one after the other; looked under the armchairs, sofas, and beds with a lighted candle, opened and quickly closed the cubbies, locked the door and carefully rearranged the furniture, and was frightened by my very eagerness to allay my fear. I loaded my revolver. In my bedroom I took the most elaborate precautions. To what end? I certainly did not mean to try to go to sleep. I began to read, my eyes glued to the pages, but my attention really occupied with what might be lurking behind the door, outside the window. I could hear the steps of a fellow-lodger coming up the stair, moving to the rhythm of my anxiety. Somebody stopped on my floor. I jumped up out of bed, thinking of burglars. A dazzling idea came to me: to notify the police. I half dressed myself, but the moment I got to the street all my fever laid hold of me again. Should I jostle those beggars who stood like figures on a monument, and lose myself once more in the labyrinth of night from which I had emerged by miracle? Should I renew my former unrest? And work myself up to madness? I reascended the stairs, and when I stood in front of my lodging, I trembled to think what might have happened in my absence.

I remember I sank down on the threshold with my arms hanging limp and weary, while at the same time I seemed to be raised and thrust away by a thousand unfeeling hands. I heard the noisy speech of other lodgers who were coming up the stairs. Nearer they came. Leaning over the landing I thought to make them a sign, to appeal to them, to say something at least, and then involuntarily I huddled back against the wall, mute, with bated breath, and as I hid myself I thought that all my blood had gone out of me, that I was collapsing. They filed past without seeing me, then vanished into their several lodgings.

I was enraged at myself for not having addressed them. I even climbed one flight to knock at the end of a passage when the last comer had disappeared. When I got there I fled hastily down again.

All at once I sprang downstairs four steps at a time and came out into the street, not knowing what I was doing.

A night-watchman loomed up in front of me. "I come," I said, "to get you to see about a theft which has just been committed on my premises."

The man followed me, and the few words which he spoke dispelled my nightmare. At that moment I was not aware what a comedy I was playing.

When we reached the threshold of my lodging I would have dared to go into my room and hunt in every nook and corner, and go to sleep at last in complete tranquillity. The watchman searched the sitting-room, the bath-room, lighting his flashlight, and made the rounds of the whole suite. In order to give weight to my words—which lay very lightly upon me—I pretended that a jewel-case had been lying on this taboret between the candlestick and the traveling bag, and that the case had disappeared. With increasing zeal I vented my indignation on the sharpers who lounge around hotels and prey on travelers, and inveighed against the authorities, who never seem to be able to bring the guilty to justice. I must have overdone it, because the watchman smiled, and I saw the faintest trace of incredulity in his eyes. I grew angry.

"I am certain," I explained, "that an hour ago a—a valuable medallion, set in pearls and inlaid with arabesques, was in that case."

And as the man interrupted me to assure me that the reputation of the house had never been questioned, and that the vicinity was the quietest in the city, I answered that while I was in bed I had suddenly been awakened by a scratching sound like that of a diamond on glass, or of an object being drawn across a marble-topped table, that as I jumped up a man went out, slamming the door behind him. As to the case, it had four copper nails on the under side, and the sound of one of these scraping on something was what had wakened me.

The watchman looked me straight in the eyes.

"Follow me," he said, "and make your complaint to the Captain."

But to this I would not consent. I excused myself, saying that my friend would not be back for quite a while. My friend now meant nothing to me but a subterfuge—and I dared not for a single second leave our papers and other valuables unguarded in this suspicious place.

Again that smile in the watchman's eye. I wanted to knock him down. Suddenly the door opened and he who had been the prime cause of my dread, whom I had vainly, yes, madly, sought all through the city, stepped in. I threw myself on his neck and asked him where in the world he had been and what had kept him so long. I quickly drew him aside and gave him a detailed account of the adventure. The watchman pretended not to notice. He understood. Quite seriously, for in my aroused state the least mockery would have ruined everything, he and my friend agreed that a complaint should be lodged next day and that, to give me justice and punish the guilty, the questionable neighborhoods in the vicinity of the barracks and the docks should be systematically searched.

But in the light of day the city seemed to me so peaceful, so cloister-like, so restful, that I could think only of enjoying to the full the charms of its antique works of art and the melancholy splendor of its decaying relics.

Jugoslavia

INTRODUCTION

THE Jugoslavs form a national unit and are ethnologically part of the Slavonic race. Jugoslav literature begins with translations of the Bible by Cyril and Methodius, the "Slavonic Apostles," about the middle of the Ninth Century. During the first period of the nation's literary history, from the Twelfth to the Fifteenth Century, several biographies and chronicles were produced.

Toward the end of the Fourteenth Century and until the beginning of the Nineteenth Century the Jugoslavs fell under the domination of the Turks, who practically arrested national life. There were, however, those who, despite this catastrophe, tried to carry on the traditions of their literature.

The deliverance from Turkish rule brought with it a gradual revival. At first, however, little was written in the Jugoslav languages (Serbian, Croatian, and Slovenian), because the printing presses throughout the country had been destroyed by the Turks. The books imported from Russia were printed in Russian, and were not familiar to the mass of readers. Dositey Obradovich (1739—1811), writing in the vernacular, became immensely popular, so much so that he was appointed Minister of Public Education, in which capacity he established the first Serbian college at Belgrade.

Vuk Karajich (1787—1864) is considered by many as the father of modern Serbian literature. He collected some ten volumes of national poetry and songs which served as an inspirational source for other writers.

The Jugoslavs have as yet no great novelist, but they have some successful short story writers, among whom Dr. Lazarevich (1851—1890) takes high rank. Another popular author is Stefan Sremacs, whom literary critics have dubbed the "Serbian Dickens." Sima Matavulj, another much read author, paints vivid pictures of the Dalmatian and Montenegrin Serbians in his delightful stories.

The division designated as "Jugoslav" includes the political groups speaking the Serbian, Croatian, and Slovenian tongues. Certain territories which were before 1914 under Austrian rule are now joined with Serbia, forming Jugoslavia.

The short story is a comparatively recent development. In the three examples included in the present volume no one can fail to observe the folk element, which characterizes the work of the best Jugoslav writers.

Croatian

ANTUN GUSTAV MATOŠ

(1873–1914)

ANTUN GUSTAV MATOŠ was the son of a village schoolmaster. Shortly after his birth he was taken to Zagreb, where he received his early education. Later he went to Vienna and studied veterinary medicine, but as that failed to interest him he went to Prague. Being without a degree, he was drafted into the army as a private. He was sent to prison for violating some military rule, but escaped to Belgrade, where he played in the orchestra of the Royal Theatre. After many wanderings through Europe, he was pardoned and returned to Zagreb, where he worked as a journalist and teacher. There he did a great deal of miscellaneous writing. He died of cancer in 1914. Matoš was a literary radical and a "Realist." As critic, teacher, and novelist, he did more than any other prose writer to develop a native Croatian literature.

The Neighbor is one of his most vivid short stories. It is here published for the first time in English. The translation is by Ivan Mladineo, to whom thanks are due for permission to use it.

THE NEIGHBOR

HE was very tired. While cooling himself at a window of his apartment on the second floor, his thoughts wandered afar. He had had to leave his country on account of debts. His family had turned him away, not without giving him the necessary expenses for his journey to America. He stopped off at Geneva and began gambling, winning at poker from the Slavic, especially the Bulgarian, students. When one of the students committed suicide, because of his losses, by drowning himself in the lake, Tkalac stopped gambling and conceived a happy thought: he would rent a larger apartment, buy a few mats and start giving lessons in fencing and later on in boxing (having learned this latter sport from a Parisian expert).

By means of the sword he made his way into the highest social circles, securing excellent recommendations, especially for Russia. After the wonderful match which placed him among the world champions, he made preparations to move to Paris. For the first time in his life he had managed to save money. The young, eccentric, cosmopolitan ladies, in particular, were paying him in a princely fashion. He started paying off his debts in his native country. Everyone was won over by his behavior, which was undeniably good, being a heritage from a long line of heroic borderland officers, noblemen of Laudon's time. Like most of our frivolous men, he remained good at heart—a childish, almost girlish, soul shining from his yellowish, eagle-like eyes; and a black, manly beard accentuated his rapacious profile, as it does in all our mountaineer descendants of *hajduks* and *uskoks*. Though he loved much, not a single woman did he really like, because at bottom he remained somewhat of a Don Quixote, dreaming of the ideal woman like all men who are brought up on the ideals of chivalry.

From the huge yard, transformed into a garden, was wafted an agreeable breeze. A canary was heard singing from a nearby window, and elsewhere a sweetly grieving strain from a Chopin ballad was audible. Tkalac followed the curling smoke of his cigarette, dreaming, with eyes open, like a savage. Suddenly he winced. On his bare, perspiring neck, he felt some drops. He wiped them off with his handkerchief, but, alas, rain again, and from a clear June sky. The young man turned his head, and above, from the upper window among the flower-pots and blossoms, there blushed a beautiful woman who lacked words to excuse herself and was powerless to turn her eyes from his confused countenance.

"Along with your beautiful flowers, you are also watering nettle, madame," he finally said in his foreign French which, reminding them so much of a child's prattle, caused him to be well liked by the ladies.

"I am too far away to be hurt," she retorted, continuing to observe him with childish surprise.

"But there is also nettle without thorns."

"I am quite poor in botany, but I am willing to accept what you say."

"Please do not go, madame; it is wonderful to look up to heaven and you in that blue sky surrounded by those beautiful flowers."

"You are a foreigner, I gather, from your accent and manner of speech."

"I am, to my sorrow. I am an army officer who has failed and, as you doubtless know, I teach fencing and boxing."

"Yes, I have read about you in the newspapers. You are on the path of glory."

"Miserable glory! But even that is better than stealing. What can one do? A man must work. Should my plans succeed, I shall go to Paris and, besides, teach horseback-riding. I am a passionate equestrian, and you cannot understand how I feel here without my horse. At the sight of a fine horse I become as sad as a Bedouin. We horsemen alone know that a horse and a horseman may become one; not a horse's soul in a human body—naturally!''

"You are a survival of extinct centaurs! And have you found an Amazon?"

Tkalac noticed how suddenly she paled and then blushed, and his eyes, darkening, filled with a surprising moisture, which confused her. He wanted to reply with warmth and great affection, but among the flowers there remained only a short greeting and a suppressed and siren-like giggle.

Thus they became acquainted.

In the evening, Tkalac did not wish to go to the city for dinner. He felt ashamed about something. The presence of a stranger embarrassed him. In the evening, in the dark room, lying on a leather sofa which served also as a bed, he felt utterly unhappy and alone. He thought of his dead mother who had spoiled him—her only child; even as a cadet he had had to go to her bed every morning before she arose. His memories turned to his father, a colonel, the real "bruder Jovo," red of face with a white mustache, hard as a provost's stick, wearing his civilian clothes as though they were on a hanger, and those red, dilapidated morning slippers. Even as an officer he dared not light a cigarette in the presence of his father without first asking for permission. He remembered, when taking his departure, the sudden burst of tears which flowed like molten iron, the burning of which he still felt on his cheeks.

"Be righteous, Pero, not being successful as a soldier. Even be a laborer, but remain honest as all your ancestors. Here is a revolver which may be of use to you, even for yourself, in case of any shame you may commit, to yourself or to me. It is better to die honorably than to live in disgrace."

And Tkalac found, in the disorder of his luggage, which was like that of a gipsy's, a photograph, and although it was quite dark, a lady, somewhat gray-haired, stepped out of the picture—she was still of a girlish build, pale, attractive, dark-eyed, with a permanent, sad smile—and this foreigner, after two years of dissipation, pressed this dear, lifeless relic to his lips, weeping like a child before going to sleep, great big tears; and consoled by the shadow of his dead mother, he fell asleep without so much as removing his clothes.

He was abruptly awakened by a tapping on the window. Knowing every emotion except fear, he was greatly surprised and thought he was suffering from hallucination. The tapping on the window was repeated, once, twice, three times. He rose, approached, and noticed a key dangling from a string which had been lowered from the floor above. Fastened to the key was a gingerbread heart bought at a fair. It was then near midnight. Silence reigned everywhere with the exception of the sound of a passing automobile on the street and the singing, accompanied by a mandolin, of some Italian laborers in the distance.

"We were to a fair on the outskirts of France, and remembering that you were alone, I brought you this present. This is not my home. I am a Frenchwoman who considers loneliness a misfortune and really believe that you are very unhappy alone there in the darkness of your gloomy, empty rooms."

"Thank you, thank you," he said, untying the gift, and still under the sway of the memories that had lulled him to sleep. His voice trembled with restrained sobs. Leaning back over the window sill and untying the string, he looked up to her, transformed in the soft and tepid light of the gentle full moon.

"Oh, how beautiful you are, my charming neighbor! If you could only realize what a gift you have made and what happiness you have brought to me by this cake, you would, perhaps, have reconsidered your act, because, in holding this dry heart, I feel as though I had a part of your heart and your soul."

"Ah, speak quietly, lest the neighbors should hear."

"Do not fear! Below live people who are always travelling."

Tkalac then leaped up and with the hand of a gymnast, took hold of the ledge of the outer window, hanging with his back and his whole body over the deep, dark, and black yard as over an abyss.

"Ah, for God's sake! What are you doing, you maniac? Should this old rotted wood give, you would break your neck. I beg you, as a brother, a son, a god, I implore you, enter your room! Have mercy!"

Suddenly she began weeping and his grasp loosening, he almost fell from the window. He felt a warm moisture upon his forehead, like a tear.

"Oh, my dear, charming, kind neighbor, were I not afraid of grieving you, I would this instant dive into the abyss as into a pool of water, because something fell on my forehead like a dewdrop, from that beautiful, refreshing heaven of yours."

"Mercy, mercy! Have mercy on me and yourself, you madman," she proceeded to beg, hardly able, out of great fear and sympathy, to utter a sound. "I will allow you everything, everything, you understand, if you will enter your room and be sensible."

As the wood of the window creaked and broke, she uttered a suppressed screech, while he, with one great swing, fell into his room with a loud and cheerful laugh.

"Until now I hung between you and darkness, between life and death, and now life and happiness look upon me from your moonlit window, my dear beautiful neighbor!"

As before, he lay on the window-sill, looking at her, her shadow, interwoven in the moonlight, surrounded by warm and luminous stars, and she silently observed this new, unusual man. They conversed in silence, with their eyes, for a long time, until finally she said:

"I like you because you have not insisted upon my word and do not ask anything of me. Good night; it is necessary to save those minutes. Good night and thank you, my neighbor!"

"Ah, stay a little longer! Tell me, at least, how I should call you?"

"My Christian name is Valentina."

"Beautiful name! Once upon a time, if I remember correctly, a beautiful princess was thus called."

"Yes, Valentina of Milan. And what is your name?"

"Peter, vulgar Peter."

"Good night, dear Mr. Peter, and 'au revoir.' Soon my husband will come."

"Who?"

"My husband!"

"Eh! Good night!"

Husband! He had never thought of that. Suddenly a cold sweat appeared on his brow. He went out and roamed until dawn around the quiet, moonlit lake, filled with the reflection of bright stars which resembled greenish sparkling fireflies.

He was just about to lie down, when a tap, tap, tap sounded on the window pane. His charming neighbor appeared, just like the dawn, golden and blushing, rose-like and white, in a lace morning gown, her lovely blue eyes still heavy with sleep. She held a little finger to her red, sinful lips, luscious and sanguine, as a sign of silence.

"I found no peace throughout the night," he whispered, pale and weary.

"Do not fear. I understand you. Do not fear, Peter; I am true to you alone!"

And only the trembling of a flower from her breath remained, as Tkalac extended his hungry arms towards the quiet, blooming window, lit by the first rays of the sun, while from above was heard the unpleasant voice of a man, severely rolling his r's.

This was repeated daily for two weeks.

Valentina was very much surprised when Tkalac disappeared without leaving a trace. She became ill from worry and torment. One rainy evening her husband told her in a puzzling way that he was awaiting a very important guest and that they would remain alone. She thought it would be some tiresome business matter, some tedious signing of papers; and while at supper, she almost fainted on hearing Peter's steps on the upper floor. Notwithstanding all her questioning, her husband refused to explain this unexpected visit.

Like a thunderbolt from a clear sky, the servant announced that "Monsieur Kalak" sends his card and wishes to enter.

She did not recognize him at first; so emaciated had he become in the few days. Her husband arose, changed the expression on his bloated, otherwise quite pleasing face adorned with spectacles and a blond mustache, wiped his bald head and wheezed harshly, like one suffering from asthma. The visitor bowed courteously and in military fashion, kissed with visible embarrassment the hand of his hostess, sat down, and, after a brief, unpleasant silence, addressed his host.

"I am very glad Monsieur Colignon, that you received me so gallantly, and, as I see, you have not advised madame regarding my coming. If there still exists some knighthood these days, it consists in that honorable and sensible people eliminate every unpleasantness with as little trouble as possible."

"Very well, very well," broke in the host, breathing heavily. "I have thoroughly inquired and learned all about you to-day, and I know that your affairs are in good condition and that you have a glorious future before you, though, relatively, very difficult. As a man of affairs and business, I guess your intention and the cause for your presence. You have no acquaintance here nor any countrymen of yours; in your native country you have no reason, presumably, to look for help. Therefore, as your neighbor, you wish to turn to me, offering no more security than your energy and your indubitable honesty. You have begged me for the presence of my wife to show me that in such a delicate matter you fear not even such a—pardon!—embarrassing witness. I have, sir, no children from heaven, and although a man of means, I sympathize with everything young and fit for life."

"But pardon me."

"Allow me, allow me, my dear 'Kalak.' I am really not as wealthy as they say, but I will always have enough to help you in your eventual establishment. It is known to me that your institution prospers excellently, and I feel proud that you should, notwithstanding your great acquaintance with foreign, especially, Slavic, aristocracy, turn to me, an ordinary citizen and business man."

"You are absolutely wrong, my dear neighbor," the young man gasped with difficulty, and paled as though he were going to fall from his chair.

Deep, asthmatic breathing. The ticking of a clock mingled with the wild, loud throbbing of hearts. Valentina's eyes became glassy.

"From your words, dear neighbor, I see that you are better than I ever dreamed, and my mission, therefore, is so much more painful and distressing. If I had known this, I never would have determined to undertake this step," came from Tkalac as from a tomb, and Colignon began to look around fearfully, thinking that he must deal with a dangerous, gorilla-like lunatic.

"Well, what is it? What is it?" he breathed with great effort, meantime kicking his petrified wife under cover of the table to convey his alarm. She did not feel his nudges, so paralyzed was her moral and physical strength.

"No, sir, I have not come for money, but I came for her, for your wife, for Valentina, for my dear——"

"Are you sane?" sighed the host, rushing towards the window as if wanting to cry "Fire." Tkalac almost brought him back to his chair with his burning, feverish gaze.

"Yes, sir, you have spoken correctly. I am an honest man, so honest that I am unable to lie, and I would kill and I would die before stealing another man's wife, robbing the love that belongs to another, especially of such a sympathetic man as you. I love your wife, your wife loves me, and I came to-night to tell you this honestly and openly, and to take her with me," continued Tkalac, placing a revolver on the table. "Here, sir, do not fear! I am not a lunatic, I am not a criminal, and you may, if you find no other exit, take this gun and shoot me here like an ordinary vagabond and burglar."

And again there was a painful, grievous, fatal silence; difficult, asthmatic breathing, then the ticking of watches as of hearts, and the beating of hearts as of watches.

"Why, what do I hear? Is all this possible; tell me, tell me, Valentina? Why, it is not, it is not, it cannot be true; say it isn't, Valentina, my dear little Valentina," sobbed the husband.

"Peter Tkalac, peer of Zvečaj castle, is poor, has no more a uniform, but he remains an officer and never tells lies!" The young man, with his chest expanded, spoke energetically, as if commanding his troops. Valentina's glassy eyes revived; slowly, as if awakening, she arose and stepped toward Peter and said, looking at him from head to foot:

"Whether you are an Austrian, Hungarian, Slovak, or what not, you should know that I am a Frenchwoman, and that in France it is not customary for lovers to denounce their sweethearts to their husbands. Monsieur Colignon, I have in fact liked his type, although I have not given myself to him; but from now on I hate him deeply and let that foreigner consider himself slapped. Good-bye, gentlemen!"— and she swept from the room.

"Noble sir, Monsieur 'Kalak,' do you need any help? I am at your service," said Colignon to the young man, who staggered out of the room as though he were drunk and feeling like a whipped cur.

The servant ran after him into the hallway.

"Pardon, sir, you have forgotten your revolver!"

Slovenian

IVAN CANKAR

(18–?–1919)

CANKAR was one of the most promising of the younger group of Slovenian writers. He had established a solid reputation as novelist, dramatist, and writer of short stories. His most significant work was produced late in his life. The volume, *Dream Visions*, from which *Children and Old Folk* is selected, appeared in 1917.

This story is here published for the first time in English. The translation is by Helen P. Hlacha, to whom thanks are due for permission to use it.

CHILDREN AND OLD FOLK

EACH night, before they went to bed, the children used to chat together. Seating themselves on the ledge of the broad oven, they uttered whatever came into their minds. Through the dim window the evening twilight peered into the room with dream-laden eyes. Out of every corner the silent shadows drifted upwards, carrying strange stories with them.

They spoke of whatever came to their minds, but to their minds came only pleasant stories of sunlight and warmth interwoven with love and hope. The whole future was one long bright holiday; no Lent, between Christmas and Eastertide. Over there, somewhere behind the flowered curtain, all life, blinking and throbbing, silently poured from the light into light. Words were whispered and only half understood. No story had any beginning, nor definite form. No story had an end. At times all four children spoke at once, yet none confused the other. All gazed enthralled into a beauteous heavenly light where each word was clear and true, where each story had a clear and living face, and each tale its glorious finish.

The children bore so marked a resemblance to one another that in the dim twilight the face of the youngest, four-year-old Tonchek, could not be distinguished from that of the ten-year-old Loizka, the eldest. All had thin, narrow faces and large, wide-open eyes—introspective eyes.

That evening, something unknown from an unknown place reached with violent hand into that heavenly light and struck pitilessly among the holidays, the stories, and legends. The post had brought tidings that the father "had fallen" on Italian soil. Something unknown, new, strange, entirely incomprehensible rose before them. It stood there, tall and broad, but had neither face, nor eyes, nor mouth. Nowhere did it belong, not to that clamorous life before the church and on the street, nor to that warm twilight around the oven, nor to the stories.

It was nothing joyful, but neither was it particularly sorrowful, for it was dead; because it had no eyes that it might by their look reveal wherefore and whence, and no mouth that it might explain by words. Thought stood humbly and timidly before that enormous apparition as before a great black wall, motionless. It approached the wall, and stared dumb and ponderous.

"But when will he come back?" asked Tonchek, wonderingly.

Loizka nudged him with an angry look. "How can he come back if he has fallen?"

All lapsed into silence. They stood before that great black wall, and beyond it they could not see.

"I'm going to war, too!" unexpectedly announced seven-year-old Matiche, as if he had swiftly hit up the right thought. That was evidently all that it was necessary to say.

"You're too small," admonished four-year-old Tonchek in a deep voice. Tonchek still wore dresses!

Milka, the thinnest and sickliest of them, who was wrapped in her mother's large shawl and resembled a wayfarer's pack, asked in her soft little voice from somewhere out of the shadows, "What is war like? Tell us, Matiche, tell us that story!"

Matiche explained, "Well, war is like this. People stab each other with knives, cut each other down with swords, and shoot each other with guns. The more you stab and cut down, the better it is. Nobody says anything to you, 'cause that's how it has to be. That's war."

"But why do they stab and cut each other down?" Milka insisted.

"For the Emperor!" said Matiche, and all were silent.

In the dim distance before their clouded eyes appeared something mighty, glistening with the radiance of glory. They sat motionless, their breaths barely daring to escape their mouths, as in church at the benediction.

Then Matiche again swiftly gathered his thoughts; possibly just to dispel the silence which lay so heavy over them. "I'm going to war, too. Against the enemy."

"What is the enemy like? Has he horns?" suddenly inquired the thin voice of Milka.

"'Course he has, else how could he be the enemy?" seriously, almost angrily replied Tonchek in emphatic tones. And now not even Matiche himself knew the correct answer.

"I don't think he—has them!" he said slowly, haltingly.

"How can he have horns? He's a person like us," voiced Loizka unwillingly. Then, reconsidering, she added, "Only he has no soul."

After a lengthy pause Tonchek inquired, "But how does a person fall in the war? Like this, backward?" And he illustrated the point.

"They kill him to death!" calmly explained Matiche.

"Father promised to bring me a gun."

"How can he bring you a gun if he has fallen?" Loizka roughly retorted.

"And they killed him—to death?"

"To death."

Through the youthful and wide-open eyes silence and sorrow stared into darkness, into something unknown, to heart and mind inconceivable.

At the same time on a bench before the cottage sat the grandfather and grandmother. The last red rays of the sun glowed through the dark foliage in the garden. The evening was silent except for a smothered, prolonged sob, already grown hoarse, which came from the stable. In all probability it was the wail of the young mother who had gone there to tend the livestock.

The two old people sat deeply bowed, close to one another, and held each other's hands as they had not done for a long time. They gazed into the heavenly afterglow with eyes devoid of tears, and did not speak.

Serbian

LAZA K. LAZAREVICH

(1851–1890)

AFTER completing his law studies at Belgrade, Lazarevich received a government fellowship in medicine, and in 1872 began studying in Berlin. Seven years later, having received his degree, he returned to Belgrade, where he filled important official positions in his capacity as physician. He died in Belgrade in 1890, probably of tuberculosis. Lazarevich is one of the most gifted and popular of Serbian writers. His literary works were many and varied.

Of his many stories of the life of his native land, *At the Well* (first published in 1881) is considered one of the finest. It is here published for the first time in English. The translation is by I. Altaraz, Ph.D., to whom thanks are due for permission to use it.

AT THE WELL

DENSE clouds of flakes, like white ghosts, are driven by the howling wind and swept in all directions until they hang like tiny white crystals on man's whiskers and horse's mane.—That's what I always say: If there aren't any flies to bother you, there is frost. Feet are frozen, eyes water. Not even brandy has the power to warm one's heart, and you look about for a hospitable home to offer you welcome.

Well, by God, I know where I'm going! I'll go to Mathias Jenadich, over yonder, where a jug of brandy hangs at all times on the plum tree in front of his house. Whoso passes by may drink.—So Mathias likes it. Should you happen to cross his threshold, his entire family will treat you like a lord. There is no use talking about it; one has to see it with one's own eyes. What a home! What a communal family—a whole army of people! Come some evening when they expect you, and one of the daughters-in-law will be sure to meet you on the road with a torch in her hand. The second will wait in the orchard, a third in front of the stable, a fourth will chase the dogs, a fifth will welcome you into the kitchen, and a sixth will lead you into the sitting room—just like a wedding, indeed! Everybody is jolly, modest, satisfied. Heaven help you should you start a fight with anyone in that home. There are six sons always ready like soldiers. One of them is a real soldier, serving the flag in Belgrade.

There is no need for harvesters or any other help; they themselves can furnish plenty of hands. The plows are in constant use; and when pork dealers come to examine the hogs, Mathias may well be proud of his.

I knew Arsen when he was only a young fellow. He would sit in front of Burmas' house and play on his shepherd's flute. For Burmas had a daughter. And what a wench! People say if she looked at one with her fiery eyes one was apt to be burned. But Arsen became accustomed to her eyes. With his left arm on the gate, he said to her: "I am ashamed to speak to father, and afraid to approach grandfather. I couldn't do it even if I knew you never would be mine."

Anoka was not bashful. She looked cunningly at him, leaned a little over the gate and concealing her anger, said: "Well, then, don't do it. I shall marry Philip Marichich."

"Do you think I would let you marry anyone but me? Anyone daring to touch you would not be sure of his life."

Anoka, like a spoiled child, stamped her foot, flashed her eyes at him and retorted: "Would you rather see me knitting my life away like a spinster? You don't say!"

Arsen heard no more. Coming nearer, he snatched her wrist and drew her to him. Her determined protests grew weaker. She thrilled at the touch of a man's arm encircling her waist. She would have been a less wilful girl if old Burmas had not spoiled her. What could her father have done? Some years ago the plague had taken his other children, so that now he guarded Anoka as one would some precious drops of water.

That evening Arsen came home in a melancholy mood. Contrary to his habit, he first went into the wine cellar and took a stiff drink, the first time he had ever done so. He returned to the yard, sat down on a block of wood where he remained long after dark, absorbed by nocturnal sounds. In the kitchen on the hearth, flaming tongues shot out and licked the iron cauldron suspended by chains from the ceiling. A newly discovered fire was burning in Arsen's heart. In the surrounding darkness he discerned human forms, dogs crossing the yard, oxen returning from pasture; he heard the trampling of horses in their stalls; he recognized his brother Nenad returning from the city. A hen jumped from the mulberry tree, looked round sleepily, and flew to another branch. Already a mouse dared to nibble at the block on which Arsen was sitting.

He felt dizzy, and became frightened at his heart beats. Suddenly he began to laugh, stupidly, for no reason at all. As he laughed and cried intermittently, he had a hazy vision of Anoka. He leaned against a barrel, and felt as though he were dying. But it was strangely agreeable, because he pictured himself in Anoka's embrace and riding on Ostoyich's wild horse. A feeling that comes of being drunk for the first time.

He had slept but a short time when Velinka, looking for something with a torch, found him. She trembled on seeing him with a jug in his hand. Drawing closer, she touched his shoulder, saying, "Darling." Arsen opened his bloodshot eyes.

"You are drunk, my jolly fellow."

Arsen, aware of his condition, replied jovially, "Drunk!"

"Why so, my happy fellow?"

"Why, because I want to kill Philip Marichich." He lifted the jug, threw it on the ground, where it broke, and laughed. Velinka also began to laugh. "What did Philip do to you, my darling?"

"He wants to have Anoka."

"Well, let him have her."

"But I won't have it!" He wanted to rise and leave the place, but fell back. Velinka laughed heartily and asked, "What, darling; then you want her?"

"Of course I do." Upon that he grew confused, turned to the barrel and moaned brokenly: "Why did brother marry? I want to also—naturally!" He slapped his knee for emphasis. Velinka laughed again and exclaimed: "Woe is me, my child, you shall have her, my darling, don't fear. I shall speak to father, he will tell grandmother, and she will manage the affair to your satisfaction with grandfather. Come, now, let me help you in. Grandfather must not see you in your present condition. Go to sleep now. Don't fear—we will get you a girl—even if it be Anoka!"

"By God, I care only for her!"

Velinka led her drunken brother-in law into the room, covered him with a blanket, and returned to the kitchen to announce the news to the other womenfolk. No one was overjoyed at the news.

"She is no good for our home!"

"She is a coquette!"

"Not alone that, but spoiled. God be with us!"

"She is an intriguer!"

Mathias Jenadich is a very old man. His forehead is disfigured by the scar of an old wound inflicted while he fought in Hajduk Veljko's fort. The whole village calls him "grandpa." His wife has been long dead. His older brother left a widow who now acts with him as the head of the house, sharing with him the duties of the Elders' Council of the community. Her name is Radoyka, and her place at the table is at grandfather's right. Radoyka must give her consent to a thing before grandfather approves. He would, for instance, ask, "What think you, dear sister-in-law, about buying Marichich's meadow?" "Just as you please, my brother, you have a man's brain."

Grandfather's oldest son, Blagoye, Arsen's father, is the third member of the home council. The rest of the family listens and obeys. The three elders sometimes leave the house intentionally, to give the children a chance to play to their heart's desire, the women to talk as much as they might please and the men to smoke freely. The moment, however, one of the "big three" steps into the house, every one becomes quiet and busy.

Grandpa, being an old man, would frequently behave like a child. At times he would lose his temper for the least trifle, then he would rage, scold, and, in his excitement, strike at the nearest one. Again, he would be gentle, generous, play with the youngsters, give them coppers. Then again, for no reason in the world, he would begin to cry: "I am left alone in this world like a withered tree on a mountain."

Youth has its frivolity, old age its senility.

The day following Arsen's adventure, Blagoye came to Radoyka with a serious mien, saying, "Auntie! Arsen, God forgive us, is crazy about Burmas' devil of a girl."

"Arsen? Is that the boy who was a major last summer?"

"That's the one."

"Did you say Burmas' dare-devil?"

"Yes."

"Anoka?"

"The same."

"She is no good for our house."

"No, no! I think so too. But Arsen, the Lord forgive us our sins, is deeply in love with her. Velinka tells me he behaved badly last night."

"How! What did he do?"

"Please don't say anything to grandpa."

"Never."

"Velinka told me he was drunk, and that he threatened to kill Philip Marichich, because, you know—this fellow is after Anoka."

"What do you say?" Grandma meditated a while, then said, "I'll take the matter to grandpa and see what he says."

"Please don't mention a thing about last night, you know."

"God forbid!"

Radoyka went to grandpa and told him the story; he was obviously worried. After a silence he looked at the old woman and said: "You know, my dear sister-in-law, it is just as you say. But I have heard our old people say that it does no good to break young people's hearts and disregard their desires. I believe our community has some eighty souls."

"By far more."

"Thank God! Why, then, shouldn't Anoka be able to adjust herself and become one of us?"

"God bless your words."

Several days later Anoka said to one of her friends, "I knew everything would turn out favorably! I am the prettiest girl in the nine villages hereabout!" She took a mirror from a little box under her blouse and began to primp her curly hair.

After becoming one of the members of the *zadruga* Jedanich, she remained the same spoiled girl as of old. She was always vain and obstinate; she would never do what was required of her, being always ready with a retort:

"I didn't do this in my father's house!"

"Why should I knead dough for a whole army? One loaf of bread is sufficient for me and my Arsen!"

The women did not dare to say anything. Once in a while they mentioned something to their husbands, but who would dare tell anything to Radoyka or grandpa?

For some time they suffered and kept her mischief secret. All of them worked for her and obeyed her will. There was something commanding and tyrannical in her behavior which made one a slave to her every wish. Though her sisters-in-law gossiped and criticized her among themselves, they would always defend and protect her before the older members and strangers. God alone knows how long things would have gone on like this, if Anoka, after having been nearly six months in the family, had not made life a hell for all. She would not help them by planting cabbage, neither would she want to stay home to take care of a child. She went so far as to request better dresses than the rest of the women wore. Poor Arsen tried to explain to her that Radoyka and grandpa buy the same dress material for all members of the family, and that he could not think of asking for an extra silk jacket for her. The answer was, that she did not marry grandpa and that she would instantly return to her father's home. If her husband was such a coward, her father surely would buy her everything she wanted. Arsen felt he was between the devil and the deep sea. If she would only cease looking at him with her big, fiery eyes, he would then surely know how to manage her....

Anoka's fury grew day by day and she invented all kinds of tricks with which to tease the people in the house. She would chase the dogs into the kitchen, and would allow them to eat up the meat in the pot. She would open the faucets of the kegs in the cellar, so the wine would flow out. The bread in the oven always burned if she was to watch it. On working days, for instance, she would put on holiday attire. It became worse and worse. The women couldn't stand it any longer. Once, when it was Anoka's turn to be the *redara* (housekeeper) she left home and went to the fair. Then the sisters-in-law gathered secretly.

"I don't know, dear sisters, what great wrong we have committed that we should have to suffer so much."

"Neither do I know."

"That's a great punishment and a great misfortune."

"God alone can help us."

"No, it cannot go on like this any more."

"Let us talk to grandma, and she will take it up with grandpa."

"You talk to her, Selena."

"Why I?"

"Didn't she accuse you of having stolen her bracelet?"

"Didn't she call your husband a barbarous priest?"

"Well, she accused Miryana of being the daughter of paupers."

"She called Velinka's child a bastard."

The women would hardly have said anything had not Radoyka been a silent witness to these painful incidents. Then too, Arsen, after seeing Anoka tear her new jacket while running through the bushes, went to complain to grandpa.

Arsen was a quiet man. From his childhood he had always obeyed. He couldn't even go to the market with a load of wood without having received direct instructions as to how much to ask, and for how much he might sell it.

Grandpa was sittting alone in the room when Arsen entered. Being so old, and not being able to work outside, his people gave him the task of shelling beans.

Arsen removed his cap and reached for grandpa's hand. Grandpa looked angry. He did not move, withdrew his hand and said dryly:

"All right!"

"Grandpa, please I beg—your pardon... there is no use hiding it from you any longer.... I am to be blamed for everything. I have brought shame into our house."

The old man observed him severely.

"No use, grandpa, don't be angry."

Grandpa lifted his head, pushed the dish with the beans, and remained angry.

"I know everything. What kind of a man are you, eh? Do you think that you are going to destroy my freedom and the happiness of my house?"

Arsen, simple soul that he was, stood speechless on discovering that grandpa was informed about everything.

"Dear grandpa, I do not know what to do. Forgive me."

Arsen reached again for grandpa's hand, but the latter refused it.

"Get out of here, don't profane and disgrace this place. Are you a man?"

Arsen, hiding his face in his waistcoat, said, almost crying:

"Do with me and with her whatever you please. Kill me and drive her away. God be with you. But don't push me like a dog—have mercy."

Grandpa's beard trembled.

He used all effort to hide his excitement. He looked up, stretched his legs, and said with amazing self-reliance:

"My son, you have chosen her. Did I tell you to do it?"

"Far be it from me to say that. I alone am the guilty one."

Grandpa pulled his beard; he looked severe and asked seriously:

"And shall I right the wrong?"

"God first and then you."

"Yes! but I don't know how."

Radoyka would have noticed the childish, cunning expression around grandpa's eyes.

"God will help you do it," said Arsen.

"And you... why... you don't love her?"

Arsen felt embarrassed. He would rather have died of shame. Grandpa looked directly into his eyes.

"She is ungrateful."

"I know, I know! But I am asking you, if you care for her?"

Arsen said nothing. He would have liked to escape but grandpa watched him closely.

"It must be," said Arsen, "that Burmas has spoiled her awfully. You know she was his only child."

Grandpa remarked impatiently:

"Hear ye, boy, what I am asking of you? I want to know if you love Anoka? Tell me!"

Arsen lowered his head, hid his face, moved his shoulders clumsily and said in a bashful way:

"I don't know."

"Well, you ought to know. I shall judge by your answer, and don't come later on to complain."

"No, I won't."

From the expression on grandpa's face, one could easily see that he had made up his mind, and that he was satisfied with his plans.

The same evening all the men were sitting around the table, for it was supper time. Radoyka was the only woman among them. The other women had their supper in the kitchen. Two or three women were serving at the table.

It was Anoka's turn to serve.

Two other women walked in and out with dishes and food. Anoka leaned against the door and made faces.

Grandpa gave her a terrific look. All were speechless. Radoyka felt all the blood rushing to her head. Anoka did not even notice it!

After supper everybody made a sign of the cross, waiting for grandpa's sign for leaving the room.

But the old man pushed aside a crust of bread, the spoon, the knife, and the wooden dish. He rested his head on his palm, looked around and fixed his eyes on Anoka.

She was on pins and needles, dropped her arms, stretched her strong and beautiful body, and moved to leave the room.

"Wait, my daughter," said the old man, with an unusually clear voice.

The whole community was startled.

Grandpa continued in the same voice:

"Daughter, I hear... you feel a stranger in my house and with my folks."

Grandpa again quietly said:

"I will not tolerate it as long as I live. My home shall never be a prison for any of my children. I understand that those women over there"—and he pointed in the direction of the kitchen—"are treating you badly. They forget that I am still the boss here."

Anoka read malicious thoughts on grandpa's lips. Hatred and fear possessed her heart.

"They are teasing you. They want you to work and to slave for them. You are not from a common family. Oh, no!"

He made every effort to look kind, sweet, and tender. Anoka felt uncomfortable.

"I won't permit anything of this kind any longer. I am an old and weak man, and cannot stand any quarrels. I now..."

His face looked severe, his lips trembled. He yelled out to the whole community:

"Hear ye all, you, Radoyka, too, and you, Blagoye, and the rest of you: I now command all of you and your wives to obey this woman here"—pointing to Anoka—"I don't want her to do anything more in the house, so that her aristocratic hands won't get dirty. God shall forsake any one who shall not obey her, or would insult her in any way."

He arose, poor old man, with an attempt at dignity, which appeared pathetic and sad.

Now all crossed themselves, got up, silently passed Anoka, careful not to touch her.

A fury possessed Anoka. She ran into the kitchen and triumphantly shouted out:

"Did you hear it all?"

As if women could fail to hear!

"Make a bed for me under the linden tree. I wish grandpa's cushion, Radoyka's little pillow, Blagoye's woolen blanket; and I want you, Petriya, whose brother is in jail, to take a stick, to chase the chickens from the trees, and to keep watch all through the night. God shall punish any one that does not obey my orders. Didn't you hear grandpa say so?"

God be with us! How funny human beings sometimes are!

Nobody objected. A strange fear went into all of them. Grandpa's words, "God shall forsake!" still rang in everybody's ears.

Arsen hid himself in the thrashing floor, lowered his head and tried to sleep, but in vain. Sleep is not like a blanket that you can put over your head whenever you like.

Anoka had her will.

But she couldn't sleep as easily as she thought she might. She never before had this feeling of isolation and solitude. With no roof over her head she felt like a wild rider without reins, or like a sailboat on the open sea. She felt her heart burning, and no one to console her. But she remained stubborn.

"I command you not to slumber over there. Do you want to be punished by God?" she said to Petriya.

The moon was overhead. Everything was so quiet. Anoka's heart was breaking and something was slowly dying within her.

She couldn't go on like this any longer, but what was to be done? Should she return to her father—what could she tell him?—"Grandpa has ordered everybody to obey my will." No, she couldn't say anything like this. And then, this terrible night will also have its end, and soon the dawn will break and the sun will shine on all God's creatures. But she, disgraceful person, what shall she do? Could she be more furious than she is? To be quiet—but how? To surrender? No!

The thoughts played a wild dance in her head, crossing, mingling and intermingling.

She felt very tired. Passions, love, hatred, hunger and thirst all disappeared. Her eyelids were heavy like lead, and still they would not close. She felt so miserable and lonesome that she would have gladly disappeared into nothingness. But sleep could not be commanded by grandpa, neither did it fear him.

Anoka got up. She looked at the dark figure of Petriya sitting near her.

She felt as if something in her heart were breaking. Suddenly, and with great force, a Christlike feeling of compassion swept over her, and she burst out:

"Petriya, go to sleep!"

Petriya said nothing, dropped the stick, and was about to leave.

"Petriya!"

Petriya trembled, stopped as if petrified. My God, what a new mood! What is going to happen now?

"Petriya, dear sister, forgive me!"

Her woman's heart softened; she understood and melted.

"Anoka, my dear soul, may God forgive you!"

"Petriya, my sister ..."

She took Petriya by the hand, brought her closer, and embraced her; both were crying.

How sweetly they cried—like children.

Everything is so quiet—not a sound under the sky; two women embrace, cry, and pet each other. Anoka kisses her over and over; Petriya kisses her on the neck and on the forehead. The moon raised its eyebrows in wonder.

"Petriya, my darling, I shall die! You shall bathe me, sister, when I am gone. Cover me with basil. Bite into an apple and place it then into my coffin. You are the only one that loves me."

"Don't say that, my dear little fool. Everybody loves you."

"No, no, I know. Nobody does."

"How can you know this, my dear, when you never even spoke to us? I would rather die now myself than let anyone say something against you."

"And grandpa?"

"Our grandpa is an old and kind man. Approach him penitently and you will find out for yourself."

"Good, I'll go to him.... Good-bye, my dear, and forever, if I should die."

Petriya covered her mouth with her hand. Anoka took Petriya's hand and put it around her neck:

"If I die don't speak evil of me, Petriya! And now go, please."

"I won't leave you, as long as I live."

"I pray you as I pray God."

"And where will you go?"

"Leave me. I feel wonderful now. Leave me, may God help you. For the love of your child, leave me."

Petriya hid behind the house, to see where Anoka would go. But the night still ruled, so Petriya could not see that Anoka went to grandpa's door and sat down on the threshold.

Grandpa, too, had not closed his eyes all night.

The first cocks crow, the earliest messengers of a new day and a new life. Never until now did Anoka find this song to be so beautiful.

Grandpa sat up, threw off his blanket, crossed himself and continued squatting on his bed in the darkness, with conflicting thoughts passing through his mind.

Again the cocks crow.

Grandpa arose to go as usually to the well.

On the threshold, through the faint light of the early dawn, he noticed a human figure.

"Who are you, there?"

"It is me, grandpa, Anoka! I want to die. Forgive me, if you can."

Grandpa stopped, swayed, and almost fell.

"My child, it is sinful to talk like that. Look at my hair, not even the sheep's wool is whiter."

Anoka grasped the hem of his cloak which hung down from his shoulders, and kissed it.

"I have sinned awfully. I destroyed the harmony of your home. Forgive me, for God's sake!"

Nothing easier than to make an old man cry. Tears rolled down his cheeks. He took her head in both his hands and kissed her.

"Come in."

She followed him into the room.

"Sit down there."

She sat on a stool, and grandpa on the edge of the bed.

"Shell some of these beans."

She did so. Grandpa looked at her with joy. Both remained silent, without uttering a sound, yet their hearts spoke. Day began to reign.

"Follow me."

She went with him into the stable, and fed the horses, at grandpa's command. She was not afraid of them, not even of Blagoye's fiery mare, that usually kicked and bit.

"Now, come here."

He took her to the sty. She cut nine pumpkins and threw them to the pigs.

The people in the house woke up, came out and timidly followed them with their eyes, taking care not to be seen. Arsen was so afraid and confused that he climbed a walnut tree, hid in the branches, and wondered at the unusual scene.

Grandpa looked rejuvenated. He skipped rather than walked.

"Come to the well!"

They reached it.

"Draw some water."

Anoka did so.

"Pour some."

Anoka poured, and grandpa splashed his face and head.

"Dry me."

Anoka began to dry his head carefully. It was easy to wipe away the water, but an old man's eyes are weak and tears continued to roll down his cheeks.

Grandpa noticed some folks standing in the yard.

"Come nearer, all of you. Why don't you wash yourselves? Don't you see Anoka is waiting to pour for all of you? Yes, all of you. Poor girl, she will do it. But if she were to ask somebody to do the same for her, there would be three hundred growlings."

Rather timidly, the men and women came closer to the well. And like well-bred, citified people, they each said to Anoka: "Thank you!"

Arsen's face shone with happiness. He too reached the well, spread his feet, bent forward, and held out his hands.

"Pour!"

She did so.

Arsen was in the seventh heaven.

"And how fine you pour! Take it easy, I am getting wet. Stop, not so, not so."

She rolled up his sleeves, and with her right hand poured.

"That's right, God bless you."

Petriya ran around, tears rolling down her cheeks, telling something to one woman, questioning another.

Grandpa, overwhelmed with joy, went into his room, opened an old wooden box, took out a string of pearls, put it carefully in a spotted handkerchief, hid it under his waist, and returned to the well.

They were through with washing. They all felt as if they were standing on holy ground and listening to a sacred choral chant: "The Lord blessed the waters of the earth...." If by chance someone in the group would have given a sign, all would have fallen on their knees and prayed. Grandpa looked around with shining dignity and pride. Dear old fellow!

"You are fine people. No one here to pour water for Anoka."

All of them jumped and reached the coop.

"Too late now. I like to do it myself. Come, my child, wash yourself!"

It is hard to say whether grandpa's hands were shivering, or Anoka's heart trembling. He dried her with his own towel, and hung the string of pearls around her neck.

"She did everything by herself, poor child. But I will repeat what I said last night, and every one of you shall remember it: 'May God forsake anyone who insults her.' "

Heaven looks down on earth and smiles with joy looking at human affairs in amazement. What a funny two-legged creature is man! He gazes into the sky, opens his arms in despair, exclaims in mysterious sounds, prays and waits and wonders. Something unknown to man burns in his bosom; his soul expands and rises like holy incense longing for communion with the universe.... By God, it was always so!

Czechoslovakia

INTRODUCTION

CZECH literature is usually considered as beginning with the writings of the great reformer, John Huss, who was born in the 1360's. He was a man of wide interests. For a time he was rector of the University of Prague, and in 1415 was burned at the stake in Constance for his heretical preachings. There are few other great names in early Czech literature, for men like Comenius are pre-eminent not so much for literary writings as for ideas. In the 16th century Bohemia fell under Austrian influence, and the use of the Czech language was either forbidden or discouraged; but with the beginning of the Nineteenth Century there came a period of great literary activity. It was during the second half of the century that writers of fiction came to the fore. Čech, Neruda, Vrchlický, Jirásek and a dozen others were serious literary artists.

The Czech short story has been considerably influenced by the literature of the Russians, although there is perceptible in the best work of the Czechs a genuine folk element and a deep patriotic feeling.

JAN NERUDA

(1834–1891)

NERUDA was one of the most prominent Czech authors of the Nineteenth Century. As poet, dramatist, editor, critic, novelist, and story writer, he contributed much that was original and beautiful to the growing literature of his country. Born in Prague in 1834, he spent the greater part of his life engaged in editorial and literary work. *The Vampire* is a highly finished technical achievement.

The present version, translated by Šarka B. Hrbková, is reprinted by permission of the translator and publisher, from Hrbkova's *Czechoslovak Stories*. Copyright, 1920, by Duffield & Co., New York.

THE VAMPIRE

THE excursion steamer brought us from Constantinople to the shore of the island of Prinkipo and we disembarked. The number of passengers was not large. There was one Polish family, a father, a mother, a daughter and her bridegroom, and then we two. Oh, yes, I must not forget that when we were already on the wooden bridge which crosses the Golden Horn to Constantinople, a Greek, a rather youthful man, joined us. He was probably an artist, judging by the portfolio he carried under his arm. Long black locks floated to his shoulders, his face was pale, and his black eyes were deeply set in their sockets. In the first moment he interested me, especially for his obligingness and for his knowledge of local conditions. But he talked too much, and I then turned away from him.

All the more agreeable was the Polish family. The father and mother were good-natured, fine people, the lover a handsome young fellow, of direct and refined manners. They had come to Prinkipo to spend the summer months for the sake of the daughter, who was slightly ailing. The beautiful pale girl was either just recovering from a severe illness or else a serious disease was just fastening its hold upon her. She leaned upon her lover when she walked and very often sat down to rest, while a frequent dry little cough interrupted her whispers. Whenever she coughed, her escort would considerately pause in their walk. He always cast upon her a glance of sympathetic suffering and she would look back at him as if she would say: "It is nothing. I am happy!" They believed in health and happiness.

On the recommendation of the Greek, who departed from us immediately at the pier, the family secured quarters in the hotel on the hill. The hotel-keeper was a Frenchman and his entire building was equipped comfortably and artistically, according to the French style.

We breakfasted together and when the noon heat had abated somewhat we all betook ourselves to the heights, where in the grove of Siberian stone-pines we could refresh ourselves with the view. Hardly had we found a suitable spot and settled ourselves when the Greek appeared again. He greeted us lightly, looked about and seated himself only a few steps from us. He opened his portfolio and began to sketch.

"I think he purposely sits with his back to the rocks so that we can't look at his sketch," I said.

"We don't have to," said the young Pole. "We have enough before us to look at." After a while he added, "It seems to me he's sketching us in as a sort of background. Well—let him!"

We truly did have enough to gaze at. There is not a more beautiful or more happy corner in the world than that very Prinkipo! The political martyr, Irene, contemporary of Charles the Great, lived there for a month as an exile. If I could live a month of my life there I would be happy for the memory of it for the rest of my days! I shall never forget even that one day spent at Prinkipo.

The air was as clear as a diamond, so soft, so caressing, that one's whole soul swung out upon it into the distance. At the right beyond the sea projected the brown Asiatic summits; to the left in the distance purpled the steep coasts of Europe. The neighboring Chalki, one of the nine islands of the "Prince's Archipelago," rose with its cypress forests into the peaceful heights like a sorrowful dream, crowned by a great structure—an asylum for those whose minds are sick.

The Sea of Marmora was but slightly ruffled and played in all colors like a sparkling opal. In the distance the sea was as white as milk, then rosy, between the two islands a glowing orange and below us it was beautifully greenish blue, like a transparent sapphire. It was resplendent in its own beauty. Nowhere were there any large ships—only two small craft flying the English flag sped along the shore. One was a steamboat as big as a watchman's booth, the second had about twelve oarsmen, and when their oars rose simultaneously molten silver dripped from them. Trustful dolphins darted in and out among them and drove with long, arching flights above the surface of the water. Through the blue heavens now and then calm eagles winged their way, measuring the space between two continents.

The entire slope below us was covered with blossoming roses whose fragrance filled the air. From the coffee-house near the sea music was carried up to us through the clear air, hushed somewhat by the distance.

The effect was enchanting. We all sat silent and steeped our souls completely in the picture of paradise. The young Polish girl lay on the grass with her head supported on the bosom of her lover. The pale oval of her delicate face was slightly tinged with soft color, and from her blue eyes tears suddenly gushed forth. The lover understood, bent down and kissed tear after tear. Her mother also was moved to tears, and I—even I—felt a strange twinge.

"Here mind and body both must get well," whispered the girl. "How happy a land this is!"

"God knows I haven't any enemies, but if I had I would forgive them here!" said the father in a trembling voice.

And again we became silent. We were all in such a wonderful mood —so unspeakably sweet it all was! Each felt for himself a whole world of happiness and each one would have shared his happiness with the whole world. All felt the same—and so no one disturbed another. We had scarcely even noticed that the Greek, after an hour or so, had arisen, folded his portfolio and with a slight nod had taken his departure. We remained.

Finally after several hours, when the distance was becoming over-spread with a darker violet, so magically beautiful in the south, the mother reminded us it was time to depart. We arose and walked down towards the hotel with the easy, elastic steps that characterize carefree children. We sat down in the hotel under the handsome veranda.

Hardly had we been seated when we heard below the sounds of quarreling and oaths. Our Greek was wrangling with the hotel-keeper, and for the entertainment of it we listened.

The amusement did not last long. "If I didn't have other guests," growled the hotel-keeper and ascended the steps towards us.

"I beg you to tell me, sir," asked the young Pole of the approaching hotel-keeper, "who is that gentleman? What's his name?"

"Eh—who knows what the fellow's name is?" grumbled the hotel-keeper, and he gazed venomously downwards. "We call him the Vampire."

"An artist?"

"Fine trade! He sketches only corpses. Just as soon as someone in Constantinople or here in the neighborhood dies, that very day he has a picture of the dead one completed. That fellow paints them before-hand—and he never makes a mistake—just like a vulture!"

The old Polish woman shrieked affrightedly. In her arms lay her daughter pale as chalk. She had fainted.

In one bound the lover had leaped down the steps. With one hand he seized the Greek and with the other reached for the portfolio.

We ran down after him. Both men were rolling in the sand. The contents of the portfolio were scattered all about. On one sheet, sketched with a crayon, was the head of the young Polish girl, her eyes closed and a wreath of myrtle on her brow.

SVATOPLUK ČECH

(1846—1908)

ČECH was educated at various schools in different parts of his native country. After graduating from a gymnasium in Prague he studied law for a little, but eventually turned to journalism, and was editor successively of several of the leading Czech literary journals. He was immensely prolific. Several epic poems, many volumes of verse, novels, essays, and a dozen books of short stories are among his literary achievements.

Foltýn's Drum, translated by Sarka B. Hrbkova, is reprinted by permission of the translator and publisher, from Hrbkova's Czecho-slovak Stories. Copyright, 1920, by Duffield & Co., New York.

FOLTÝN'S DRUM

OLD Foltýn hung on his shoulder his huge drum, venerable relic of glorious patriarchal ages, and went out in front of the castle. It seemed as if indulgent time had spared the drummer for the sake of the drum. The tall, bony figure of Foltýn—standing in erect perpendicularity in soldier fashion, wrapped in a sort of uhlan cape, with a face folded in numberless furrows, in which, however, traces of fresh color and bright blue eyes preserved a youthful appearance, with a bristly gray beard and gray stubble on his double chin, a broad scar on his forehead, and a dignified uniformity in every motion—was the living remnant of the former splendor of the nobility.

Old Foltýn was the gate-keeper at the castle, an honor which was an inheritance in the Foltýn family. As in the Middle Ages, vassal families devoted themselves exclusively to the service of their ruler, so the Foltýn family for many generations had limited its ambitions to the rank of gate-keepers, stewards, granary-masters, herdsmen and game-wardens in the service of the noble proprietors of the castle. Indeed one member of the family had become a footman for one of the former masters and thereby the boast and proud memory of his numerous kinsmen.

Well, then, old Foltýn stepped forth with his drum before the castle, to all appearances as if he wished to drum forth the mayor and the councilmen to some exceedingly important official duty, but in truth, alas, to noisefully assemble an army of old women to their work on the noble domain.

He slightly inclined his head and swung the sticks over the ancient drum. But what was that? After several promising beginnings he suddenly concluded his performance by a faint tap. I am convinced that many an old woman, hearing that single indistinct sound, dropped her spoon in amazement and pricked up her ears. When that mysterious sound was followed by no other she doubtless threw a shawl over her gray braids and running to the cottage across the way, met its occupant and read on her lips the same question her own were forming: "What happened to old Foltýn that he finished his afternoon artistic performance with such an unheard of turn?"

It happened thus: If you had stood in Foltýn's place at the stated moment and if you had had his falcon eyes you would have descried beyond the wood at the turn of the wagon-road some sort of dark object which with magic swiftness approached the village. Later you would have distinguished a pair of horses and a carriage of a type never before seen in those regions.

When the gate-keeper had arrived at this result of his observation, he recovered suddenly from the absolute petrifaction into which he had been bewitched by the appearance of the object and raced as fast as his legs would allow back to the castle.

Beruška, the steward's assistant, was just bidding a painful farewell to a beautiful cut of the roast over which the fork of his chief was ominously hovering when Foltýn with his drum burst into the room without even rapping. He presented a remarkable appearance. He was as white as chalk, his eyes were staring blankly, on his forehead were beads of sweat, while he moved his lips dumbly and waved his drumstick in the air. With astonishment all turned from the table toward him and were terrified in advance at the news whose dreadful import was clearly manifested in the features of the old man.

"The nob—nobility!" he stuttered after a while.

"Wh—what?" burst forth the steward, dropping his fork on the plate.

"The nobility—beyond the wood—" answered Foltýn with terrible earnestness.

The steward leaped from his place at the table, seized his Sunday coat and began, in his confusion, to draw it on over his striped dressing-gown. His wife, for some unaccountable reason, began to collect the silver from the table. Miss Melanie swished as she fled across the room. Beruška, alone stood unmoved, looking with quiet satisfaction at his chief, whom Nemesis had suddenly overtaken at his customary culling of the choicest pieces of the roast.

In order to interpret these events I must explain that our castle, possibly for its distance and lack of conveniences, was very little in favor with its proprietors. From the period of the now deceased old master, who sojourned here a short time before his death, it had not beheld a single member of the noble family within its weatherbeaten walls. The rooms on the first floor, reserved for the nobility, were filled with superfluous luxury. The spiders, their only occupants, let themselves down on fine threads from the glitteringly colored ceilings to the soft carpets and wove their delicate webs around the ornamentally carved arms of chairs, upholstered in velvet. The officials and servants in the castle knew their masters only by hearsay. They painted them as they could, with ideal colors, to be sure. From letters, from various rumors carried from one manor to the next, from imagination, they put together pictures of all these personages who, from a distance, like gods, with invisible hands reached out and controlled their destinies. In clear outlines there appeared the images of barons, baronesses, the young baronets and sisters, the maids, nurses, the wrinkled, bewigged proctor, the English governess with a sharp nose, the fat footman, the peculiarities of each were known to them to the minutest detail. But to behold these constant objects of their dreams and discussions, these ideals of theirs, face to face, was for them a prospect at once blinding and terrifying.

In the castle, feverish excitement reigned. From the upper rooms echoed the creaking of folding-doors, the noise of furniture being pushed hither and thither, the whisking of brooms and brushes. The steward's wife ran about the courtyard from the chicken house to the stables without a definite purpose. The steward hunted up various keys and day-books and charged the blame for all the disorder on the head of Beruška, who, suspecting nothing, was just then in the office, rubbing perfumed oil on his blond hair. Old Foltýn stood erect in the driveway with his drum swung from his shoulder, every muscle in his face twitching violently as he extended his hand with the drumstick in the direction of the approaching carriage as if, like Joshua of old, he execrated it, commanding it to tarry in the village until all was in readiness. Through his old brain there flashed visions of splendidly ornamented portals, maids of honor, schoolboys, an address of welcome, flowers on the pathway.... But the carriage did not pause. With the speed of the wind it approached the castle. One could already see on the road from the village the handsome bays with flowing, bright manes and the liveried coachman glittering on the box. A blue-gray cloud of dust arose above the carriage and enveloped a group of gaping children along the wayside. Hardly had Foltýn stepped aside a little and doffed his shaggy cap, hardly had the soft white silhouette of Melanie disappeared in the ground-floor window, when the eminent visitors rattled into the driveway.

In the carriage sat a gentleman and a lady. He was of middle age, wore elegant black clothes and had a smooth, oval, white face with deep shadows around the eyes. He appeared fatigued and sleepy, and yawned at times. The lady was young, a fresh-looking brunette with a fiery, active glance. She was dressed in light colors and with a sort of humorous, coquettish smile she gazed all around.

When they entered the driveway, where practically all the occupants of the castle welcomed them with respectful curtsies, the dark gentleman fixed his weary, drowsy eyes on old Foltýn who stood in the foreground with loosely hanging mustaches, with endless devotion in his honest blue eyes, and with an expression of contrite grief in his wrinkled face, his patriarchal drum at his hip.

The baron looked intently for a while at this interesting relic of the inheritance from his ancestors, then the muscles of the languid face twitched and his lordship relieved his mood by loud, candid laughter. The bystanders looked for a moment with surprise from the baron to the gate-keeper and back again. Then they regarded it as wise to express their loyalty by blind imitation of his unmistakable example and they all laughed the best they knew how. The steward and his wife laughed somewhat constrainedly, the light-minded Beruška and the coachman with the lackey, most heartily. Even the baroness smiled slightly in the most bewitching manner.

Old Foltýn at that moment presented a picture which it is not easy to describe. He looked around several times, paled and reddened by turns, patted down his cape and gray beard in embarrassment and his gaze finally slid to the fatal drum. It seemed to him that he comprehended it all. He was crushed.

After a few condescending words to the others the nobility betook themselves to their quarters, leaving for the time being on the occupants of the lower floors the impression that they were the most handsome and the happiest couple in all the world.

After a while we behold both in the general reception-room. The master rocks carelessly in the easy-chair and sketches a likeness of old Foltýn on the covers of some book. The baroness, holding in her hand a naked antique statuette, looks about the room searchingly.

"Advise me, Henry. Where shall I place it?"

"You should have left it where it was."

"Not at all! We are inseparable. I would have been lonesome for these tender, oval, marble features."

"But if you haul her around this way over the world she won't last whole very long."

"Never fear! I'll guard her like the apple of my eye. You saw that I held the box containing her on my lap throughout the journey."

"You might better get a pug-dog, my dear!"

The baroness flashed an angry glance at her husband. Her lips opened to make response to his offensive levity, but she thought better of it. She held the statuette carefully and swished disdainfully past the baron in the direction of a rounded niche in the wall. She was just about to deposit her charming burden when suddenly, as if stung by a serpent, she recoiled and extended a finger towards her husband. The dust of many years accumulated in the niche had left its gray trace.

"Look" she cried.

"Look!" he repeated, pointing towards the ceiling. From the bouquet of fantastic flowers there hung a long, floating cobweb on which an ugly spider was distinctly swinging.

"You wouldn't listen to my warnings. Well, here you have an introduction to that heavenly rural idyll of which you raved."

The baroness drew down her lips in disgust at the spider and in displeasure at her husband's remark. Violently she rang the bell on the table. The fat footman in his purple livery appeared.

"Tell them down below to send some girl here to wipe down the dust and cobwebs," the lovely mistress said to him with frowning brow.

She sat down opposite her husband, who was smiling rather maliciously and gazed with vexation at her beloved statuette.

A considerable time passed, but no maid appeared. The baroness showed even greater displeasure in her countenance, while the baron smiled more maliciously than ever.

The footman's message caused great terror below on account of the dust and the cobwebs and no less embarrassment on account of the request for a maid. After long deliberation and discussion they seized upon Foltýn's Marianka as a drowning man grasps at a straw. After many admonitions from old Foltýn who hoped through his daughter to make up for the unfortunate drum, they drew out the resisting girl from the gate-keeper's lodge. The steward's wife with her own hands forced on Marianka her own yellow silk kerchief with a long fringe which she folded across her bosom, placed an immense sweeping-brush in her hands, and thus arrayed the footman led his trembling victim into the master's apartments.

The baroness had just stamped her foot angrily and approached the door when it softly opened and Marianka, pale as the wall, with down-cast eye, appeared in it. The unkind greeting was checked on the baroness' lips. The charm of the simple maid surprised her. Slender she was and supple as a reed, her features gentle and childishly rounded, the rich brown hair contrasting wonderfully with her fresh white skin, and her whole appearance breathing the enchantment of earliest springtime.

"Here, dear child!" she said to her, agreeably, pointing to the floating cobweb.

The girl bowed awkwardly, and for an instant under her light lashes there was a flash of dark blue as she stepped timidly forward. The brush did not reach the cobweb. She had to step up on her tiptoes. Her entire face flushed with a beautiful red glow, her dark-blue eye lifted itself towards the ceiling, her delicate white throat was in full outline, and below it there appeared among the fringes of the yellow shawl a string of imitation corals on the snowwhite folds of her blouse. Add to this the dainty foot of a princess and acknowledge—it was an alluring picture.

When all that was objectionable had been removed, the baroness tapped Marianka graciously on the shoulder and asked, "What is your name?"

"Marie Foltýnova," whispered the girl.

"Foltýn? Foltýn? What is your father?"

"The gate-keeper, your Grace!"

"Doubtless the man with the drum," suggested the baron, and a light smile passed over his face.

"Go into the next room and wait for me," said the baroness to the girl. When she had departed, the baroness turned to her husband with these words: "A charming maiden. What do you think of her?"

"Well, it's a matter of taste."

"I say—charming! Unusually beautiful figure, a most winsome face and withal—such modesty!"

"The statuette is threatened with a rival."

"Jokes aside, what do you say to my training her to be a lady's maid? To taking her into service? What do you say to it?"

"That your whims are, in truth, quite varied," he answered, yawning.

The baroness indulged her whim with great energy. She immediately asked the girl if she would like to go to the city with her and, not even waiting for her answer, engaged her at once in her service, rechristened her Marietta, described in brilliant colors the position of a lady's maid, and, at the end, made her a present of a pair of slightly worn slippers and a coquettish house cap.

Old Foltýn was fairly numbed with joyous surprise when Marianka, with the great news, returned to him. Even in his dreams he would not have thought that his daughter would be chosen by fate to become the glittering pendant to that footman of whose relationship the entire Foltýn family boasted. Instantly he forgot the incident of the drum, his gait became sturdier and his eyes glowed like a youth's.

Several days passed. The baroness continued enthusiastic about the delights of country life and devoted herself with great eagerness to the education of Marietta as a lady's maid. Marietta often stood in front of the mirror wearing the coquettish cap and holding in her soft hand the large tuft of many-colored feathers which the mistress had purchased for her for brushing off the dust. Often, too, she sat on the low stool, her eyes gazing dreamily somewhere into the distance, where, in imagination, she saw tall buildings, beautifully dressed people, and splendid equipages. Frequently she would bury her head in her hands, and lose herself in deep thought. The baron would sit idly in the easy-chair, smoking and yawning. The steward and his wife rid themselves of all fears of their eminent guests. Beruška made friends with the purple footman, playing "Twenty-six" with him in the office behind closed doors when they lighted their pipes.

Once towards evening the baroness, with her beautifully bound "Burns," stepped out into the flower-covered arbor in the park from which place there was a distant and varied view and where she hoped to await the nightingale concert which for several evenings had echoed in the neighborhood of the castle. The baron rebuked the footman for his fatness and ordered him to begin reducing by taking a walk out into the fields. The steward and his wife were putting up fruit behind closed doors. Melanie had a toothache.

In this idyllic, peaceful moment it occurred to old Foltýn that

Marianka was lingering an unusually long time in the apartments of the nobility. He disposed of the thought, but it returned soon again. The thought became every moment more and more obtrusive.

"What is she doing there so long?" he growled into his mustaches. "The mistress is not in the house."

Involuntarily he went into the gallery and walked about a while, listening intently to sounds from above. Then he ventured on the steps, urged by an irresistible force. On tiptoes he reached the corridor of the first floor. He stole to the footman's door and pressed the knob. It was closed. He crept to the door of the reception-room. Suddenly he paused. Within could be heard a voice—the voice of the baron. Distinctly he heard these words: "Don't be childish! Foolish whims! The world is different from what the priests and your simple-minded parents have painted it for you. I will make you happy. Whatever you wish, you will get—beautiful clothes, jewels, money—all. I will make your father a butler, steward, maybe even something higher. You will be in the city yourself. Now, my little dove, don't be ashamed, lift up your lovely eyes. God knows I never saw more beautiful ones!"

Foltýn stood as if thunderstruck. All the blood receded from his face. Horror and fright were depicted in it. He stooped down to the keyhole. Within he beheld the baron wholly changed. In his pale, handsome countenance there was not a single trace of sleepiness, and his dark eyes flashed with passion underneath the thin, proud brows. Uplifting by the chin Marianka's beautiful face, flushed deep scarlet with shame, he gazed lustfully upon her heaving bosom. Her eyes were cast down, in one hand she held the statuette, in the other the tousled tuft of variegated feathers.

Foltýn put his hands up to his gray head. Anguish contracted his throat. Through his head rushed a whirl of terrible thoughts. Already he had reached for the door-knob, then quickly jerked his hand away. No! To have the baron learn that Marianka's father had listened to his words, to stand, shamed, and apprehended in an abominable deed before his own servant—no, that must not be! All of Foltýn's inborn loyalty rose in opposition. But what was he to do?

In the office was the footman. He would send him upstairs on some pretext. No sooner thought of than he hastened down. But the office was closed and perfect silence reigned within. Beruška and the footman who had but recently been playing cards inside were not at home. One was in the courtyard, the other out for a health promenade.

In desperation Foltýn ran down the corridor. Suddenly he paused in front of the jail-room. He stood but a moment and then burst open the door, seized the immense drum hanging there, hung it over his shoulder and ran out into the driveway. Wildly he swung the drumsticks, bowed his head, and then a deafening rattle resounded. He beat the drum until beads of sweat stood out on his brow.

The steward, hearing the clatter, turned as pale as death. "In God's name, Foltýn has gone mad," he burst out. He flew to the driveway. There he beheld Beruška, holding a card hand of spades in one hand and the collar of the unsummoned drummer in the other.

"Are you drunk?" shouted the clerk.

Foltýn continued obstinately to beat the drum. From all sides figures came running in the dusk.

The steward came to Beruška's assistance. "Stop, you maniac!" he thundered at Foltýn. "Don't you know the baron is already sleeping? I'll drive you out of service immediately."

"Oh, just let him stay in service," sounded the voice of the baron behind them. "He is a capital drummer." Then he passed through the bowing crowd, whistling and switching his riding-boots with his whip. He was going for a walk.

When the baroness, attracted hither by the mysterious sound of the drum, had returned from the nightingales' concert and entered the reception-room, she beheld in the middle of it her beautiful, beloved statuette broken into many bits. From the weeping eyes of Marietta whom she summoned before her she at once learned the perpetrator. In great wrath she dismissed her from service on the spot. Short was the dream of tall buildings, beautiful people and splendid equipages!

At noon of the next day Foltýn stood in front of the castle and drummed the peasants to their labors. At the same time he gazed towards the forest road down which the noble carriage with marvelous speed was receding into the distance. When the carriage disappeared in the forest Foltýn breathed a sigh of relief, dropped the drumsticks and shook his head. And then the thought came into his head that, like the drum, he no longer belonged to the present era of the world. As to the cause of the disturbance of the day before he preserved an obstinate silence unto the day of his death.

———————

Modern Greece

INTRODUCTION

FOR at least two centuries there has been a continuous and at times brilliant literary activity in the land of Sophocles, and the work of the Nineteenth Century, both in quantity and quality, compares favorably with that of the other Balkan states. But even the Greeks themselves admit that it is scarcely possible to regard the modern writers without thinking of the ancient past, and that this past is in many respects a serious handicap to the development of a wholly new and original tradition.

The Nineteenth Century Greeks have taken the short story and made it the chief vehicle of their life and thought. This may be accounted for by the fact that the form is primarily a modern product, little used by the ancients, and consequently offered a free field to the writer who sought to express himself with more or less originality.

Most of the Greek story writers are chiefly concerned with the life of their own day and their own land.

Foremost of all the modern Greeks is Bikelas, who is known by all readers of the language and beloved as the author of numerous tales and stories of Greek life. Papadiamantis, Moraitidis, Vlahos, Bikelas, Rados, Anninos and Xenopoulos are among the best writers of the past half-century.

DEMETRIOS BIKELAS

(1835–1908)

BIKELAS was born at Hermopolis on the Island of Syra in 1835. He began writing as a young man, and in spite of a long residence abroad as a business man, he continued his literary work. He wrote verse and prose, and made several translations of classic works. In 1879 he published his first story, *Loukis Laros*, which was widely popular, both among the Greeks and abroad. Bikelas' stories are characteristically Greek, though the writer's wide acquaintance with other literatures is evident.

THE PRIEST'S TALE

WE were talking about dogs.
        Dinner was just over, and the ladies had gone out on the
balcony to watch the clouds reddening under the rays of the setting
sun, while we still lingered over our coffee and cigars. My nephew
Andrew —who does not smoke yet, or secretly if at all—was playing in
a corner with his dog. Although his noisy frolic did not amuse the
older people gathered around the table, or aid their peaceable diges-
tion, nobody cared to complain, for Andrew was our host's only son
and the dog was Andrew's favorite companion. Still, it was easy to see
that we should all have been glad to be rid of the animal's company.

Perceiving this, my brother-in-law sent him out of the room, in spite
of his master's ill-concealed discontent.

Quiet was once more restored, and conversation began again with
renewed activity. Naturally we spoke of the exile and his various
qualities—of his breed in particular and of dogs generally. One thing
led to another, and the subject of hydrophobia finally came up.
Andrew showed a lively interest in the matter, and asked the village
priest, who was one of the guests, if he had known of many mad dogs
in the country.

"No, not many, but they are by no means unknown," replied Father
Seraphim; and among others he told us of a fine dog he had been
obliged to kill because he believed it to be mad.

Andrew kept interrupting the priest with questions; how did Father
Seraphim know that the dog was mad? how had it become mad? what
had it done? how did he kill it?

The boy's inquiries and the father's courteous replies gave me no
little information on the subject.

"Speaking of mad dogs," said my brother-in-law, disregarding his
son's last question, "what would you say, Andrew, if Father Seraphim
were to tell you that he had seen a mad man?"

"A mad man!" cried Andrew, and we all began to overwhelm the
priest with questions. "How? Where? When? Tell us about it! How
did it end?"

Father Seraphim's thick brows contracted at our host's words, and
he made no answer. His silence and melancholy look showed that the
recollection was too painful to be revived willingly. But seeing us all

curious and impatient to hear the story, he overcame his reluctance, straightened himself up in his chair, took off his cap, put it on the table, and passing his hand over his forehead two or three times, he looked quietly at each of us, one after the other, and then began in these words:

"You all know the place called 'The Old Eyrie,' just up there at the end of the village. As you remember, our graveyard is a little farther on to the west; there are vineyards on the right, while the mountain lies to the left, and between them the road that leads from 'The Eyrie' to the graveyard. Half way along this road and on the side toward the mountain, you must have noticed a large pine-tree standing alone. Its ancient branches make a kind of shady oasis in the parched and arid land. Every time I pass there, my heart stands still at the sight of this pine, and in the sighing of the wind through its branches I always hear the name of the unhappy Christos.

"Thirteen years have passed since then—it was about the middle of August. For several days it had been rumored that a wolf was prowling near the village. Old Mitros, who had built his little cottage that same year close by 'The Eyrie,' told how he had been awakened one night by the barking of his dog, and opening his window had seen an enormous wolf outside his garden wall. He had snatched his gun and fired, but failed to kill the beast, and saw it reeling away in the moonlight with its tail down. He was too frightened to reload and fire a second time. The shepherds told of a similar encounter, so that the village was full of rumors that we had a dangerous wolf in the neighborhood, and the peasants slept with one eye open, always thinking of their flocks.

"The danger was even greater than they knew, for it was not a mere hungry wolf that they had to deal with, but a she-wolf—and mad.

"One afternoon—it was a Monday—Christos was pasturing his father's sheep near the pine I spoke of. He was sitting in the shade scouring an old milk basin, when suddenly he saw his sheep running in terror and crowding close together. He looked toward the graveyard, and there, only twenty paces off, he saw the wolf, bristling for the attack and showing her terrible teeth.

"He instantly jumped to his feet, and seized a stone. As a rule, wolves are afraid of men and run away; but Heaven keep you from a mad wolf!"

Father Seraphim took up his cap mechanically and put it on his head. "Let me give you a piece of advice, my friends, although I hope you may never stand in need of it. You are hardly likely to meet a mad wolf, but if you are ever attacked by a mad dog, and have no weapon or club stout enough to break its head, take care of your hands above everything else. If you use your hands against the beast, it will bite you. You, who wear the European dress, have your hats; I have my priest's cap; the peasant has his fez: use anything—no matter what—to protect your hands.

"Christos had no chance to escape. Instead of running away when she saw him rise, the wolf rushed upon him, and before he had even time to throw his stone, her fore-paws pressed against his right side, and her teeth were fastened in his breast.

"The stone fell from his fingers, but his hands were free.

"Of all the young men of the village, Christos was the tallest; he was strong and fearless—a true *pallicare;* and, as we all know, danger often makes even the coward brave. Suddenly he dropped his right arm and tightly squeezed the wolf's neck under his armpit, while with his left he clutched her head and tried to strangle her.

"The struggle was frightful. The teeth and claws of the mad beast dug into the poor fellow's side; he could not use his knife, because to draw it from his girdle he would have had to let go the wolf's neck, which he still held with his left hand. He could not move his right arm without loosening his vise-like grasp upon her, and he dared not call for help, for he knew too well that he had no strength to waste in shouting.

"At last they fell to the ground, clasped in a horrible embrace. Christos was on the top, but the wolf had her head free against his breast, and she tore it savagely, in her efforts to release herself.

"Christos felt himself growing weak, and began to lose courage, when suddenly he heard the voice of old Mitros:

" 'Hold fast, Christos, I'm coming!'

"The sheep in their flight had come to the old man's cottage. Much surprised, he opened his door, and saw Christos in the distance wrestling with the wolf. He hastily snatched his gun from the wall, and started on a run as fast as his old legs would carry him.

"When he reached the pine-tree and saw the two upon the ground, he did not dare to shoot at the beast, for fear of wounding the man. But Christos took fresh heart at the thought of help, and, pushing the wolf's head as far as he could away from his breast, cried, 'Fire!' The old man lost no time in pressing the muzzle of his gun against the beast's ear, and fired. The wolf rolled over, dead."

Father Seraphim was silent for some minutes. None of us disturbed him, for we saw that he had more to tell us, and waited.

Meanwhile the sun had set, and it was growing dark in the corners of the room. The ladies were still out on the balcony, and we could hear snatches of their merry talk and laughter.

"My friends," continued the priest, "do you know what I was just thinking about? It is a thought that comes to me often; I was thinking of what our ignorance costs us. How many evils we could avoid, or at least lessen if we only knew a little more. But who is there to teach us? We are making progress, it is true, but we are still far behind.

Would you believe that in all the villages of this district there is not a single doctor, or even a pharmacy! I do not know if anything of the kind has been printed at Athens, but certainly we have never had here any book or pamphlet giving directions how to avoid or cure the commonest diseases—I do not mean hydrophobia, but the simple ailments of which our little children die. But never mind that now; those things will come in time.

"When Christos came home leaning on the old man's shoulder, wounded and bloody, with his clothes torn, the whole village was in commotion. I was told at once of what had happened, and went to see him. He lived with his father in that little house in the street by the church. On the ground-floor there is a storeroom and an oil-press, while above there are two small chambers, which are reached by a stairway built on the outside facing the road."

"Where the schoolmaster lives now?" asked Andrew.

"Yes, that's the place. When I arrived I found the greatest difficulty in getting near Christos. The neighbors' wives had filled the two rooms and were pressing round the young man, with the best intentions, no doubt, but only making confusion, and hindering instead of helping.

"The first thing to do was not to wash away the blood or mend the torn clothes, but to cauterize the poor boy's wounds. Nobody had thought of that, or of anything else but to get some of the herb that is supposed to cure madness. I did my best to persuade them to send Christos at once to the hospital in Athens; but they would not hear of it. They kept talking of the 'mad plant,' and nothing but the 'mad plant'! This was the only remedy; but unfortunately no one in the village had any of it!"

"What herb is it?" I asked the priest, interrupting him.

Everybody at the table turned to me, and I couldn't help blushing under all those eyes. I saw that my interruption did not find favor, and repented my untimely question; too late I perceived that it was not an opportune moment for botanical inquiries.

"I cannot describe it to you, because I have never seen it," replied Father Seraphim. "I think it grows at Salamis; it is the secret of the monks of Phaneromeni, and is quite a source of revenue to them."*

I was satisfied with this explanation, and bent my head in silence, while the priest covered my embarrassment by turning to the other guests, and continued:—

* The reader will perceive that the priest is speaking of a period prior to the discoveries of M. Pasteur.

The monks' ointment is made of the powdered insect *Mylabris* and the root of the *Cynachum erectum* (or *Marsdenia erecta*), a plant identified by Fraas as the Απόκυνον of the ancients, which bore also the names κυνόμοοον and Παρδαλιαγχες: in modern popular Greek it is called ψόφιος (dead beast) and Λυδδόκορτον (mad plant).

"With great difficulty I managed to persuade Christos and the men —or rather women—who surrounded him, and it was at last decided to take him to Athens. He wanted to put off going until the next day; but I insisted, and finally prevailed upon him to start at once, by offering to go with him. So we mounted our donkeys and set out. The neighbors' wives showered good wishes upon us, but it was easy to see that they thought medical skill a poor substitute for the virtues of the mad plant.

"We reached Athens very late; I left Christos at the hospital, and returned to my parsonage in the middle of the night.

"As I said before, all this happened on Monday. Thursday Christos came home, still suffering from the cauterization, but he seemed well otherwise, and in a few days the burns were quite healed.

"But the peasants had no confidence in hospital treatment. Their fears arose not from the delay in cauterizing the wounds, but from the failure to apply the mad plant, without which how could any one expect to avert the terrible disease? Everybody felt uneasy whenever Christos came in sight; anxious mothers called their children away so that he might not meet them; and men humored him—as though to avoid all chance of making him angry. In a word, the village was on its guard. Even Christos himself seemed to mistrust the success of his cure. His hesitancy in answering my greeting, his furtive look at the passers-by while I was talking with him—all these and many other things besides made me fear that the poor fellow was not without a secret dread, and I pitied him from the bottom of my heart. My friends, imagine the torment, the agony a man must suffer when he suspects that he carries within him the germ of such a malady, and is waiting day by day for it to break forth!"

"And the worst of it is," said my brother-in-law, "that this very fear helps to bring on the attack. Only a little while ago I was reading an article on this subject, in a scientific review. The dread that seizes so many people when they are bitten by a dog—a dread that they try to conceal, either from pride or a desire to save their friends anxiety—is in itself a disease. The morbid state aggravates the consequences of the bite and of the cauterization. These causes of themselves often produce tetanus, and hydrophobia and tetanus have many points of resemblance. This is what the doctors tell us. But what good does that do, if they cannot give us at the same time some means of controlling or getting rid of this secret fear? I am waiting to hear from our medical friends on this point. But I beg your pardon, father, for interrupting you."

"Without ever having read anything of the kind," replied the priest, "I have often thought of that.

"Meanwhile the weeks passed by, and the peasants were beginning to forget what had happened, or at least had stopped talking about it, when suddenly one morning toward the end of September the boy's father came to tell me that Christos was not well.

" 'What's the matter with him?'

" 'I don't know; he's feverish, and has no appetite.'

"I went to see him without delay, and found him lying on the floor with his cloak under him. He was quiet, but pale and troubled about himself. He told me that he couldn't breathe, and that he felt stifled every now and then for lack of air. I offered him a little milk, and urged him to drink it. He sat up and took the cup in his hands; but as soon as he brought it near his lips, he began to shiver with disgust. I had barely time to take the cup from him when he was seized with terrible spasms, and I thought he was dying; but gradually he came to himself.

" 'Ah!' he cried, 'it's my father's fault; if he had only got the mad plant for me, I shouldn't be dying now—mad!'

"I tried to persuade him that it was a mere derangement of the stomach, and said all I could to comfort him, but, alas! without believing what I said. Then I left him, promising to come back in the evening—for I had to perform the marriage service in the most distant village of my parish. Such is the life of a priest: sorrow and joy; marriage and death —ah, well—

"Before I reached home that evening I heard that Christos was delirious and violent. His father was waiting for me at the parsonage, and wanted me to help to move the poor boy to another house, where he could be on the ground-floor. The neighbors insisted on this; they were afraid he would get out on the street and bite every one he met. Where he was they could not prevent him from jumping out of the window, and they wished to have him on the ground-floor—where they could keep better watch. The peasants were afraid, and their fear made them savage. I saw that if Christos became dangerous they might shoot him without mercy.

"I lost no time in going up to his room, and fortunately found him in one of his intervals of quiet. He was sitting on the floor with his elbows on his knees and his head in his hands. The furniture was all in disorder, and broken dishes were lying about. I admit I was a little frightened. It was rash to go in alone, but I could not turn back even if I had wished; so I went up to him, and laying my hand on his head repeated a prayer.

"When I was done he made the sign of the cross, and kissed my hand.

" 'You are not very comfortable here, my dear Christos,' said I. 'Come, let us go to your uncle's; the house is empty, and you'll be better there. Won't you come?'

"He rose without a word, and then said quietly: 'I don't want anybody to see me; please ask them to stay away.'

"I opened the door, and although there was no one there, I cried out,—

" 'Go away, all of you; go home!—There, Christos, the street is empty; let us go.'

" 'I can't bear the light, father; it hurts me.'

"The sun was near its setting, and its rays streamed into the room through the open door. Christos put on his cloak, and pulling the hood over his eyes, gave me his hand. He followed me to his uncle's house. I stayed with him a long time, trying my best to comfort him, and it was night when I came away.

"As I opened the door to go out, I thought I saw men with guns standing there in the darkness.

"I shut the door and locked it, taking the key with me. The peasants gathered about me and plied me with questions about Christos. I told them he was going to die, and implored them in the name of the merciful Father to let him die in peace. The poor men were not heartless— in their way they sincerely pitied their friend and comrade; but the instinct of self-preservation is stronger than pity, and fear fills the heart of the ignorant with the passion of wild beasts."

Just then the ladies came in to join us, for the cool evening air had driven them in from the balcony.

"What, are you still in the dark!" said my sister. "Father Seraphim's story must have been very interesting. Won't you tell us about it? I'm sure we should be interested too." And she ordered the lights to be brought.

"What became of Christos?" asked Andrew, in a whisper.

The priest closed his eyes and stretched out his hand.

I do not care to dwell upon the meaning of this gesture. Was he allowed to die in quiet—or did they kill him?

The servant came in with the lighted candles, and we talked of other things.

Roumania

INTRODUCTION

ROUMANIAN literature was slow in developing, chiefly because of the political vicissitudes of the country, which was at various periods under Slavonic, Greek, and Turkish domination. Its first period (1550-1710) witnessed the translation of the Bible, the liturgy and homilies. Few names stand out, though Miron Costin, whose writings rank as classical, wrote a portion of the history of Moldavia.

The second period (1710-1830) sees Roumanian entrenched as the authorized language of the Church. Towards the end of the Eighteenth Century, Roumanian literature slowly began to develop, and here we find the early beginnings of poetry and belles lettres. The first novel to be translated was the *Æthiopica* of Heliodorus. Prose translations of the *Odyssey* and *Iliad* followed. The individuality of the poets was more marked, for they soon advanced from translation to original creation. An acquaintance with Western forms led to a development of poetical composition.

Éminescu (1849-1889) was the greatest Roumanian poet. By his masterly handling of rhythm and verse, his simple language, deep thought, and plastic expression, he created a school of poetry which has dominated the thought and expression of Roumanian writers up to the present time.

In prose, we do not find the same progress as in poetry, until comparatively recent times. Under the influence of Maiorescu (born 1839), a group of national writers gathered around the newly founded periodical, *Convorbiri Literare*. Among them were J. Creanga, who embodied in his tales the spirit of the Moldavian peasantry; and Caragiale (1852?-1912), who has written several volumes of excellently contrived short stories, besides a number of dramas. Popovici-Banatzeanu and Slavici are other gifted writers. Sadoveanu and Beza are likewise reckoned among the most distinguished writers of Roumanian tales.

Two foreigners, both queens, have closely identified themselves with Roumanian literature—"Carmen Xylva" and the late Queen Marie.

I. L. CARAGIALE

(1852?–1912)

CARAGIALE first came to the attention of his country's readers through the pages of *Convorbiri Literare*, a literary periodical to which he contributed several short stories. Maiorescu, Roumania's most distinguished critic, became at once interested in this new author, and under his influence, Caragiale quickly assumed a place of importance among the writers of his country. Prof. S. Mehedintzi, in a preface to *Roumanian Stories*, writes: "Caragiale, our most noted dramatic author, is ... a man of culture, literary and artistic in the highest sense of the word. *The Easter Torch* ranks him high among the great short-story writers."

This story, translated by Lucy Byng, appeared in *Roumanian Stories*, published in 1921 by John Lane, by whose permission, and that of the translator, it is here reprinted.

THE EASTER TORCH

LEIBA ZIBAL, mine host of Podeni, was sitting, lost in thought, by a table placed in the shadow in front of the inn; he was awaiting the arrival of the coach which should have come some time ago; it was already an hour behind time.

The story of Zibal's life is a long and cheerless one: when he is taken with one of his feverish attacks it is a diversion for him to analyze one by one the most important events in that life.

Huckster, seller of hardware, jobber, between whiles even rougher work perhaps, seller of old clothes, then tailor, and bootblack in a dingy alley in Jassy; all this had happened to him since the accident whereby he lost his situation as office boy in a big wine-shop. Two porters were carrying a barrel down to a cellar under the supervision of the lad Zibal. A difference arose between them as to the division of their earnings. One of them seized a piece of wood that lay at hand and struck his comrade on the forehead, who fell to the ground covered in blood. At the sight of the wild deed the boy gave a cry of alarm, but the wretch hurried through the yard, and in passing gave the lad a blow. Zibal fell to the ground fainting with fear. After several months in bed he returned to his master, only to find his place filled up. Then began a hard struggle for existence, which increased in difficulty after his marriage with Sura. Their hard lot was borne with patience. Sura's brother, the innkeeper of Podeni, died; the inn passed into Zibal's hands, and he carried on the business on his own account.

Here he had been for the last five years. He had saved a good bit of money and collected good wine—a commodity that will always be worth good money. Leiba had escaped from poverty, but they were all three sickly, himself, his wife, and his child, all victims of malaria, and men are rough and quarrelsome in Podeni—slanderous, scoffers, revilers, accused of vitriol throwing. And the threats! A threat is very terrible to a character that bends easily beneath every blow. The thought of a threat worked more upon Leiba's nerves than did his attacks of fever.

"Oh, wretched Gentile!" he thought, sighing.

This "wretched" referred to Gheorghe—wherever he might he!—a man between whom and himself a most unpleasant affair had arisen.

Gheorghe came to the inn one autumn morning, tired with his walk; he was just out of hospital—so he said—and was looking for work. The innkeeper took him into his service. But Gheorghe showed himself to be a brutal and a sullen man. He swore continually, and muttered to himself alone in the yard. He was a bad servant, lazy and insolent, and he stole. He threatened his mistress one day when she was pregnant, cursing her, and striking her on the stomach. Another time he set a dog on little Strul.

Leiba paid him his wages at once, and dismissed him. But Gheorghe would not go: he asserted with violence that he had been engaged for a year. Then the innkeeper sent to the town hall to get guards to remove him.

Gheorghe put his hand swiftly to his breast, crying: "Jew!" and began to rail at his master. Unfortunately a cart full of customers arrived at that moment. Gheorghe began to grin, saying: "What frightened you, Master Leiba? Look, I am going now." Then bending fiercely over the bar towards Leiba, who drew back as far as possible, he whispered: "Expect me on Easter Eve; we'll crack red eggs together, Jew! You will know then what I have done to you, and I will answer for it."

Just then, customers entered the inn.

"May we meet in good health at Easter, Master Leiba!" added Gheorghe as he left.

Leiba went to the town hall, then to the sub-prefecture to denounce the threatener, begging that he might be watched. The sub-prefect was a lively young man; he first accepted Leiba's humble offering, then he began to laugh at the timid Jew, and make fun of him. Leiba tried hard to make him realize the gravity of the situation and pointed out how isolated the house stood from the village, and even from the high road. But the sub-prefect, with a more serious air, advised him to be prudent; he must not mention such things, for, truly, it would arouse the desire to do them in a village where men were rough and poor, ready to break the law.

A few days later an official with two riders came to see him about Gheorghe; he was "wanted" for some crime.

If only Leiba had been able to put up with him until the arrival of these men! In the meanwhile, no one knew the whereabouts of Gheorghe. Although this had happened some time ago, Gheorghe's appearance, the movement as though he would have drawn something from his breast, and the threatening words had all remained deeply impressed upon the mind of the terror-stricken man. How was it that that memory remained so clear?

It was Easter Eve.

From the top of the hill, from the village lying among the lakes about two miles away, came the sound of church bells. One hears in a strange way when one is feverish, now so loud, now so far away. The coming night was the night before Easter, the night of the fulfilment of Gheorghe's promise.

"But perhaps they have caught him by now!"

Moreover, Zibal only means to stay at Podeni till next quarter-day. With his capital he could open a good business in Jassy. In a town, Leiba would regain his health, he would go near the police station—he could treat the police, the commissionaires, the sergeants. Who pays well gets well guarded.

In a large village, the night brings noise and light, not darkness and silence as in the isolated valley of Podeni. There is an inn in Jassy—there in the corner, just the place for a shop! An inn where girls sing all night long, a Café Chantant. What a gay and rousing life! There, at all hours of the day and night, officials and their girls, and other dirty Christians will need entertainment.

What is the use of bothering oneself here where business keeps falling off, especially since the coming of the railway which only skirts the marshes at some distance?

"Leiba," calls Sura from within, "the coach is coming, one can hear the bells."

The Podeni valley is a ravine enclosed on all sides by wooded hills. In a hollow towards the south lie several deep pools caused by the springs which rise in the hills; above them lie some stretches of ground covered with bushes and rushes. Leiba's hotel stands in the center of the valley, between the pools and the more elevated ground to the north; it is an old stone building, strong as a small fortress: although the ground is marshy, the walls and cellars are very dry.

At Sura's voice Leiba raises himself painfully from his chair, stretching his tired limbs; he takes a long look towards the east; not a sign of the diligence.

"It is not coming; you imagined it," he replied to his wife, and sat down again.

Very tired, the man crossed his arms on the table, and laid his head upon them, for it was burning. The warmth of the spring sun began to strike the surface of the marshes and a pleasant lassitude enveloped his nerves, and his thoughts began to run riot as a sick man's will, gradually taking on strange forms and colors.

Gheorghe—Easter Eve—burglars—Jassy—the inn in the center of the town—a gay restaurant doing well—restored health.

And he dozed.

Sura and the child went without a great deal up here.

Leiba went to the door of the inn and looked out on to the road.

On the main road there was a good deal of traffic, an unceasing noise of wheels accompanied by the rhythmic sound of horses' hoofs trotting upon the smooth asphalt.

But suddenly the traffic stopped, and from Copou a group of people could be seen approaching, gesticulating and shouting excitedly.

The crowd appeared to be escorting somebody: soldiers, a guard and various members of the public. Curious onlookers appeared at every door of the inn.

"Ah," thought Leiba, "they have laid hands on a thief."

The procession drew nearer. Sura detached herself from the others, and joined Leiba on the steps of the inn.

"What is it, Sura?" he asked.

"A madman escaped from Golia."

"Let us close the inn so that he cannot get at us."

"He is bound now, but a while ago he escaped. He fought with all the soldiers. A rough Gentile in the crowd pushed a Jew against the madman and he bit him on the cheek."

Leiba could see well from the steps; from the stair below Sura watched with the child in her arms.

It was, in fact, a violent lunatic held on either side by two men: his wrists were tightly bound over each other by a thick cord. He was a man of gigantic stature with a head like a bull, thick black hair, and hard, grizzled beard and whiskers. Through his shirt, which had been torn in the struggle, his broad chest was visible, covered, like his head, with a mass of hair. His feet were bare; his mouth was full of blood, and he continually spat out hair which he had bitten from the Jew's beard.

Every one stood still. Why? The guards unbound the lunatic's hands. The crowd drew to one side, leaving a large space around him. The madman looked about him, and his fierce glance rested upon

Zibal's doorway; he gnashed his teeth, made a dash for the three steps, and in a flash, seizing the child's head in his right hand and Sura's in his left, he knocked them together with such force that they cracked like so many fresh eggs. A sound was heard, a scrunching impossible to describe, as the two skulls cracked together.

Leiba, with bursting heart, like a man who falls from an immense height, tried to cry out: "The whole world abandons me to the tender mercies of a madman!" But his voice refused to obey him.

"Get up, Jew!" cried someone, beating loudly upon the table with a stick.

"It's a bad joke!" said Sura from the doorway of the inn, "thus to frighten the man out of his sleep, you stupid peasant!"

"What has scared you, Jew?" asked the wag, laughing. "You sleep in the afternoon, eh? Get up, customers are coming, the mail coach is arriving."

And, according to his silly habit which greatly irritated the Jew, he tried to take his arm and tickle him.

"Let me alone!" cried the innkeeper, drawing back and pushing him away with all his might. "Can you not see that I am ill? Leave me in peace."

The coach arrived at last, nearly three hours late. There were two passengers who seated themselves together with the driver, whom they had invited to share their table.

The conversation of the travellers threw a light upon recent events. At the highest posting station, a robbery with murder had been committed during the night in the inn of a Jew. The murdered innkeeper should have provided a change of horses. The thieves had taken them, and while other horses were being found in the village the curious travellers could examine the scene of the crime at their leisure. Five victims! But the details! From just seeing the ruined house one could believe it to have been some cruel vendetta or the work of some religious fanatic. In stories of sectarian fanaticism one heard occasionally of such extravagant crimes.

Leiba shook with a violent access of fever and listened aghast.

What followed must have undoubtedly filled the driver with respect. The young passengers were two students, one of philosophy, the other of medicine; they were returning to amuse themselves in their native town. They embarked upon a violent academic discussion upon crime and its causes, and, to give him his due, the medical student was better informed than the philosopher.

Atavism; alcoholism and its pathological consequences; defective birth; deformity; Paludism; then nervous disorders! Such and such conquest of modern science—but the case of reversion to type! Darwin, Häckel, Lombroso. At the case of reversion to type, the driver opened wide his eyes in which shone a profound admiration for the conquests of modern science.

"It is obvious," added the medical student. "The so-called criminal proper, taken as a type, has unusually long arms, and very short feet, a flat and narrow forehead, and a much developed occiput. To the experienced eye his face is characteristically coarse and bestial; he is rudimentary man: he is, as I say, a beast which has but lately got used to standing on its hind legs only, and to raising its head towards the sky, towards the light."

At the age of twenty, after so much excitement, and after a good repast with wine so well vinted and so well matured as Leiba's, a phrase with a lyrical touch came well even from a medical student.

Between his studies of Darwin and Lombroso, the enthusiastic youth had found time to imbibe a little Schopenhauer—"towards the sky, towards the light!"

Leiba was far from understanding these "illuminating" ideas. Perhaps for the first time did such grand words and fine subtleties of thought find expression in the damp atmosphere of Podeni. But that which he understood better than anything, much better even, than the speaker, was the striking illustration of the theory: the case of reversion to type he knew in flesh and blood, it was the portrait of Gheorghe. This portrait, which had just been drawn in broad outline only, he could fill in perfectly in his own mind, down to the most minute details.

The coach had gone. Leiba followed it with his eyes until, turning to the left, it was lost to sight round the hill. The sun was setting behind the ridge to the west, and the twilight began to weave soft shapes in the Podeni valley.

The gloomy innkeeper began to turn over in his mind all that he had heard. In the dead of night, lost in the darkness, a man, two women and two young children, torn without warning from the gentle arms of sleep by the hands of beasts with human faces, and sacrificed one after the other, the agonized cries of the children cut short by the dagger ripping open their bodies, the neck slashed with a hatchet, the dull rattle in the throat with each gush of blood through the wound; and the last victim, half-distraught, in a corner, witness of the scene, and awaiting his turn. A condition far worse than execution was that of the Jew without protection in the hands of the Gentile—skulls too fragile for such fierce hands as those of the madman just now.

Leiba's lips, parched with fever, trembled as they mechanically followed his thoughts. A violent shivering fit seized him; he entered the porch of the inn with tottering steps.

"There is no doubt," thought Sura, "Leiba is not at all well, he is really ill; Leiba has got 'ideas' into his head. Is not that easy to understand after all he has been doing these last days, and especially after what he has done to-day?"

He had had the inn closed before the lights were lit, to remain so until the Sabbath was ended. Three times had some customers knocked at the door, calling to him, in familiar voices, to undo it. He had trembled at each knock and had stood still, whispering softly and with terrified eyes:

"Do not move—I want no Gentiles here."

Then he had passed under the portico, and had listened at the top of the stone steps by the door which was secured with a bar of wood. He shook so that he could scarcely stand, but he would not rest. The most distressing thing of all was that he had answered Sura's persistent questions sharply, and had sent her to bed, ordering her to put out the light at once. She had protested meanwhile, but the man had repeated the order curtly enough, and she had had unwillingly to submit, resigning herself to postponing to a later date any explanation of his conduct.

Sura had put out the lamp, had gone to bed, and now slept by the side of Strul.

The woman was right. Leiba was really ill.

Night had fallen. For a long time Leiba had been sitting, listening by the doorway which gave on to the passage.

What is that?

Indistinct sounds came from the distance—horses trotting, the noise of heavy blows, mysterious and agitated conversations. The effort of listening intently in the solitude of the night sharpens the sense of hearing; when the eye is disarmed and powerless, the ear seems to struggle to assert its power.

But it was not imagination. From the road leading hither from the main road came the sound of approaching horses. Leiba rose, and tried to get nearer to the big door in the passage. The door was firmly shut by a heavy bar of wood across it, the ends of which ran into holes in the wall. At his first step the sand scrunching under his slippers made an indiscreet noise. He drew his feet from his slippers, and waited in the corner. Then, without a sound that could be heard by an unexpectant ear, he went to the door in the corridor, just as the riders passed in front of it at walking pace. They were speaking very low to each other, but not so low but that Leiba could quite well catch these words:

"He has gone to bed early."

"Supposing he has gone away?"

"His turn will come; but I should have liked—"

No more was intelligible; the men were already some distance away. To whom did these words refer? Who had gone to bed or gone away?

Whose turn would come another time? Who would have liked something? And what was it he wanted? What did they want on that by-road—a road only used by anyone wishing to find the inn?

An overwhelming sense of fatigue seemed to overcome Leiba.

Could it be Gheorghe?

Leiba felt as if his strength was giving way, and he sat down by the door. Eager thoughts chased each other through his head, he could not think clearly or come to any decision.

Terrified, he reëntered the inn, struck a match, and lighted a small petroleum lamp.

It was an apology for a light; the wick was turned so low as to conceal the flame in the brass receiver; only by means of the opening round the receiver could some of the vertical shafts of light penetrate into a gloom that was like the darkness of death—all the same it was sufficient to enable him to see well into the familiar corners of the inn. Ah! How much less is the difference between the sun and the tiniest spark of light than between the latter and the gloom of blindness.

The clock on the wall ticked audibly. The monotonous sound irritated Leiba. He put his hand over the swinging pendulum, and stayed its movement.

His throat was parched. He was thirsty. He washed a small glass in a three-legged tub by the side of the bar and tried to pour some good brandy out of a decanter; but the mouth of the decanter began to clink loudly on the edge of the glass. This noise was still more irritating. A second attempt, in spite of his effort to conquer his weakness, met with no greater success.

Then, giving up the idea of the glass, he let it fall gently into the water, and drank several times out of the decanter. After that he pushed the decanter back into its place; as it touched the shelf it made an alarming clatter. For a moment he waited, appalled by such a catastrophe. Then he took the lamp, and placed it in the niche of the window which lighted the passage: the door, the pavement, and the wall which ran at right angles to the passage, were illuminated by almost imperceptible streaks of light.

He seated himself near the doorway and listened intently.

From the hill came the sound of bells ringing in the Resurrection morning. It meant that midnight was past, day was approaching. Ah! If only the rest of this long night might pass as had the first half!

The sound of sand trodden underfoot! But he was sitting in the corner, and had not stirred; a second noise, followed by many such. There could be no doubt someone was outside, here, quite near. Leiba rose, pressing his hand to his heart, and trying to swallow a suspicious lump in his throat.

There were several people outside—and Gheorghe! Yes, he was there; yes, the bells on the hill had rung the Resurrection.

They spoke softly:

"I tell you he is asleep. I saw when the lights went out."

"Good, we will take the whole nest."

"I will undo the door, I understand how it works. We must cut an opening—the beam runs along here."

He seemed to feel the touch of the men outside as they measured the distance on the wood. A big gimlet could be heard boring its way through the dry bark of the old oak. Leiba felt the need of support; he steadied himself against the door with his left hand while he covered his eyes with the right.

Then, through some inexplicable play of the senses, he heard, from within, quite loud and clear:

"Leiba! Here comes the coach."

It was surely Sura's voice. A warm ray of hope! A moment of joy! It was just another dream! But Leiba drew his left hand quickly back; the point of the tool, piercing the wood at that spot, had pricked the palm of his hand.

Was there any chance of escape? Absurd! In his burning brain the image of the gimlet took inconceivable dimensions. The instrument, turning continually, grew indefinitely, and the opening became larger and larger, large enough at last to enable the monster to step through the round aperture without having to bend. All that surged through such a brain transcends the thoughts of man; life rose to such a pitch of exaltation that everything seen, heard, felt, appeared to be enormous, the sense of proportion became chaotic.

The work outside was continued with method and perseverance. Four times in succession Leiba had seen the sharp steel tooth pierce through to his side and draw back again.

"Now, give me the saw," said Gheorghe.

The narrow end of a saw appeared through the first hole, and started to work with quick, regular movements. The plan was easy to understand; four holes in four corners of one panel; the saw made cuts between them; the gimlet was driven well home in the center of the panel. when the piece became totally separated from the main body of the wood it was pulled out; through the opening thus made a strong hand inserted itself, seized the bar, pushed it to one side and—Gentiles are in Leiba's house.

In a few moments, this same gimlet would cause the destruction of Leiba and his domestic hearth. The two executioners would hold the victim prostrate on the ground, and Gheorghe, with heel upon his body, would slowly bore the gimlet into the bone of the living breast as he had done into the dead wood, deeper and deeper, till it reached the heart, silencing its wild beatings and pinning it to the spot.

Leiba broke into a cold sweat; the man was overcome by his own imagination, and sank softly to his knees as though life were ebbing from him under the weight of this last horror, overwhelmed by the thought that he must abandon now all hope of saving himself.

"Yes! Pinned to the spot," he said, despairingly. "Yes! Pinned to the spot."

He stayed a moment, staring at the light by the window. For some moments he stood aghast, as though in some other world, then he repeated with quivering eyelids:

"Yes! Pinned to the spot."

Suddenly a strange change took place in him, a complete revulsion of feeling; he ceased to tremble, his despair disappeared, and his face, so discomposed by the prolonged crisis, assumed an air of strange serenity. He straightened himself with the decision of a strong and healthy man who makes for an easy goal.

The line between the two upper punctures of the panel was finished. Leiba went up, curious to see the working of the tool. His confidence became more pronounced. He nodded his head as though to say: "I still have time."

The saw cut the last fiber near the hole towards which it was working, and began to saw between the lower holes.

"There are still three," thought Leiba, and with the caution of the most experienced burglar he softly entered the inn. He searched under the bar, picked up something, and went out again as he entered, hiding the object he had in his hand as though he feared somehow the walls might betray him, and went back on tiptoe to the door.

Something terrible had happened; the work outside had ceased— there was nothing to be heard.

"What is the matter? Has he gone? What has happened?" flashed through the mind of the man inside. He bit his lower lip at such a thought, full of bitter disappointment.

"Ha, ha!" It was an imaginary deception; the work began again, and he followed it with the keenest interest, his heart beating fast. His decision was taken, he was tormented by an incredible desire to see the thing finished.

"Quicker!" he thought, with impatience. "Quicker!"

Again the sound of bells ringing on the hill.

"Hurry up, old fellow, the daylight will catch us!" said a voice outside, as though impelled by the will of the man within.

The work was pushed on rapidly. Only a few more movements and all the punctures in the panel would be united.

At last!

Gently the drill carried out the four-sided piece of wood. A large and supple hand was thrust in; but before it reached the bars it sought two screams were heard, while, with great force, Leiba enclosed it with the free end of the noose, which was round a block fixed to the cellar door.

The trap was ingeniously contrived: a long rope fastened round a block of wood; lengthwise, at the place where the sawn panel had disappeared, was a spring-ring which Leiba held open with his left hand, while at the same time his right hand held the other end taut. At the psychological moment he sprang the ring, and rapidly seizing the free end of the rope with both hands he pulled the whole arm inside by a supreme effort.

In a second the operation was complete. It was accompanied by two cries, one of despair, the other of triumph: the hand is "pinned to the spot." Footsteps were heard retreating rapidly: Gheorghe's companions were abandoning to Leiba the prey so cleverly caught.

The Jew hurried into the inn, took the lamp and with a decided movement turned up the wick as high as it would go: the light concealed by the metal receiver rose gay and victorious, restoring definite outlines to the nebulous forms around.

Zibal went into the passage with the lamp. The burglar groaned terribly; it was obvious from the stiffening of his arm that he had given up the useless struggle. The hand was swollen, the fingers were curved as though they would seize something. The Jew placed the lamp near it—a shudder, the fever is returning. He moved the light quite close, until, trembling, he touched the burglar's hand with the burning chimney; a violent convulsion of the fingers was followed by a dull groan. Leiba was startled at the sight of this phenomenon.

Leiba trembled—his eyes betrayed a strange exaltation. He burst into a shout of laughter which shook the empty corridor and resounded in the inn.

Day was breaking.

Sura woke up suddenly—in her sleep she seemed to hear a terrible moaning. Leiba was not in the room. All that had happened previously returned to her mind. Something terrible had taken place. She jumped out of bed and lighted the candle. Leiba's bed had not been disturbed. He had not been to bed at all.

Where was he? The woman glanced out of the window; on the hill in front shone a little group of small bright lights, they flared and jumped, now they died away, now, once more, soared upwards. They told of the Resurrection. Sura undid the window; then she could hear groans from down by the door. Terrified, she hurried down the stairs. The corridor was lighted up. As she emerged through the doorway, the woman was astonished by a horrible sight.

Upon a wooden chair, his elbows on his knees, his beard in his hand sat Leiba. Like a scientist, who, by mixing various elements, hopes to surprise one of nature's subtle secrets which has long escaped and worried him, Leiba kept his eyes fixed upon some hanging object, black and shapeless, under which, upon another chair of convenient height, there burnt a big torch. He watched, without turning a hair, the process of decomposition of the hand which most certainly would not have spared him. He did not hear the groans of the unhappy being outside: he was more interested, at present, in watching than in listening.

He followed with eagerness each contortion, every strange convulsion of the fingers till one by one they became powerless. They were like the legs of a beetle which contract and stretch, waving in agitated movement, vigorously, then slower and slower until they lie paralyzed by the play of some cruel child.

It was over. The roasted hand swelled slowly and remained motionless. Sura gave a cry.

"Leiba!"

He made a sign to her not to disturb him. A greasy smell of burnt flesh pervaded the passage: a crackling and small explosions were heard.

"Leiba! What is it?" repeated the woman.

It was broad day. Sura stretched forward and withdrew the bar. The door opened outwards, dragging with it Gheorghe's body, suspended by the right arm. A crowd of villagers, all carrying lighted torches, invaded the premises.

"What is it? What is it?"

They soon understood what had happened. Leiba, who up to now had remained motionless, rose gravely to his feet. He made room for himself to pass, quietly pushing the crowd to one side.

"How did it happen, Jew?" asked someone.

"Leiba Zibal," said the innkeeper in a loud voice, and with a lofty gesture, "goes to Jassy to tell the Rabbi that Leiba Zibal is a Jew no longer. Leiba Zibal is a Christian—for Leiba Zibal has lighted a torch for Christ."

And the man moved slowly up the hill, towards the sunrise, like the prudent traveller who knows that the long journey is not achieved with hasty steps.

MARIE, QUEEN OF ROUMANIA

(1875–1935)

JUST as one never thinks of Conrad as anything but an English writer, so one considers Queen Marie as Roumanian. She became, at the age of fifteen, the wife of the future King Ferdinand. Her work shows that she soon learnt the secrets of her adopted country, and that she won the hearts of the Roumanian peasantry. Her stories constitute the autobiography of a rich mind developed by contact with a country still by no means exploited for literary purposes.

This story was written in English, and was originally reprinted by permission of the author.

WHAT VASILE SAW

IT was night.

A gusty wind swept over the plain; the cold was intense. Very far above, the stars shone quite small as though they had withdrawn as far as possible from the cold upon earth, but the thick snow that covered the fields so white that it radiated a faint light over the ground. From time to time the wind stirred the sleeping surface, chasing it along in small clouds which rose straight into the air as though seeking escape from their tormentor.

A gloomy night, a sad night—the sort of night when one can imagine spirits abroad. When the howling of the wind abated, a sinister sound would occasionally roll through the night—a far-off boom that held within it the voice of war.

Near the road which was faintly distinguishable even in the night as a dark line where many feet had sullied the snow's whiteness, sat a shivering group of soldiers, huddled over an almost extinguished fire.

The wind seemed to single them out as special object of its fury, dashing the snowdrifts against them as foaming waves against a rock. The soldiers had pulled their collars up over their ears and their caps well down over their foreheads, but neither fur nor cloth could protect them against the icy storm.

There were about a dozen soldiers in all, three or four bearded old fellows and one quite young man, guarding a handful of ragged prisoners who sat round the last embers of the fire in postures of mournful resignation. Their bowed heads were sunk upon their drawn-up knees, thus hiding their alien faces from the snow as well as from the looks of those who regarded them, half with pity, half with contempt; their gloveless hands were cracked and swollen by the frost, and a faint tremor shook their bodies with spasms of either cold, sorrow or fear—perhaps all three!

Their burly guardians paid little attention to them; in short sentences which the wind seemed to rend, they were talking to their only young companion who stood leaning on his gun as in summer shepherds lean upon their staffs.

Quite a boy he was, eighteen or nineteen perhaps. He was staring into the night with a dreamy expression in his large green eyes. The snowflakes whirled about him, settling in layers upon the fur of his cap, catching even on to his eyelashes that were long and extraordinarily strong; this made him pass his hand occasionally over his face.

"Vasile, the fire is going out!" growled one of the elder men. "Before this damned night is over, we shall all die of cold!"

"We ought not to have lost our way," grumbled one of the others.

"We did not do so on purpose," said the first again, a certain Andrei Scurtu, leader of the small detachment in charge of the prisoners. His temper was as short as his name and the others treated him with irritated docility.

"How can one drag even prisoners beyond a certain distance with frozen feet; we were to have reached the village before night—well, we have not—more's the pity. If we freeze here before morning, we shall probably only be a few of many, and the fault will neither be ours nor God's."

"Whose fault is it then?" asked someone.

"That is no business of yours or mine," snapped Scurtu.

"It is the fault of war," said another old fellow, one Petre Pasca, who had not yet spoken.

"War, war!" grumbled Scurtu, "war comes as a dry summer, or a flood when the seeds are young."

"But a war like this!" objected another.

"Those German fiends are the devil's own!" said another as he vainly tried to stir up the dying embers.

"May the devil take them, then," said Scurtu, and to emphasize his words he spat into the cinders.

Vasile turned his young frost-bitten face towards his elders.

"I am sorry for those prisoners," he said.

"Sorry!" Several voices were raised in protest. "Sorry for these foreign dogs!"

"They are young and far from their homes," explained Vasile.

"And we, where are we then?"

"We are still on our Roumanian soil!"

"It is not their fault if we are!"

A gust of wind whirled up a great wave of snow and each man turned so as to meet the onslaught with his back.

"A night for wolves," said one.

"A night for the devil," said another.

"A night for the dead," said a third.

"Vasile, we shall freeze if we find no wood," said Scurtu again.

"Where can one find wood in this desert?" answered Vasile still using his gun as a shepherd's staff.

"Thy legs are young," began Petre Pasca, "and, after all, the night is not so very dark. ..."

"Not so very dark because of the snow," said someone from the other side of the cinders.

"It is the devil's night," repeated one of the men with a groan.

"Vasile, thy legs are young..." persisted Petre Pasca, and old Scurtu who had been struggling to light a cigarette, looked up.

"Aye, aye, thy legs are young, why not search for some wood?"

"I am here to guard the prisoners," protested Vasile, clacking his feet one against the other, but otherwise not shifting his position.

"A dog could guard them!" exclaimed Scurtu. "Besides I am here in command."

Someone laughed hoarsely.

"Thy old one would be proud of thy honors!"

"Leave my old one alone," snapped Scurtu; "she was young in her day and has borne me many children, mostly boys."

"Where are they?"

Scurtu shrugged his shoulders and made a deprecating gesture with his hands.

"God alone knows with this war... and then the Boches..." he added vaguely after a pause.

"They know how to fight," said someone.

"They are the devil's own," repeated a voice out of the dark.

"That does not help us much," said another.

"No, but their cannons would!" sneered Scurtu who after many efforts with his flint had managed to light a damp cigarette.

"Even now do you not hear them?" asked Vasile.

"Curse them!" said several voices together and then there was silence a while, the wind alone filling the night with its howl.

"Vasile," began Petre again, who was a persistent fellow, "thy legs are young and there must be wood somewhere, and the night is not so very dark. ..."

"If we do not find something to burn we shall all be dead before morning," Scurtu agreed with slow nods of his head. "Shoulder thy gun, Vasile, and go and search—anything will do."

Vasile shrugged his shoulders. "As you will," he said, slinging his gun upon his back and without further protest set out, wading with stiff movements through the deep uneven snow, little caring which way he went, for verily where could he find fuel?... it was night... the plain was bare... there were no huts anywhere, no trees, no enclosures, nothing... not even an old wooden well... what could he find?... Stumbling and resigned, Vasile tramped into the night's immensity.

As he trudged along in the dark Vasile had many thoughts, confused thoughts, but thoughts nevertheless, and even visions, happy visions that had nothing to do with either winter or war.

He saw a fruitful valley through which ran a long, long dusty road leading to a village half hidden amongst fruit-trees. It was the hour of sunset and a herd of oxen was returning along the road guarded by a youth who sauntered behind them, a green switch in his hand. The youth was whistling a melancholy peace-filled "doïna," whistling it over and over again—always the same doïna. ...

Unconsciously Vasile's lips tried to whistle the tune, but they were cracked by the frost and only a few weird notes rang out into the night.

But the youth was still sauntering along the road at sunset; the dust raised by the oxen powdered his hands and his face. ...

The road was long, but there was no hurry; neither the youth nor the creatures cared much about time.

On reaching the village the solemn gray oxen turned each one to his stable... the herd diminishing as the youth went along.

He flourished his switch in the air as he advanced still whistling his song.

Some little children with a family of earth-colored pigs that had been grubbing in the road scurried away on all sides as they passed. The pigs had curly little tails and ridiculous stiff, skipping movements, the children were noisy and half naked, scarcely covered by their ragged shirts.

In front of nearly each house large pyramids of pumpkins had been heaped up and long strings of scarlet "ardei" hung from the porches like giant necklaces of barbaric beads. A haze of dust and lazy content lay over the entire village; it was all full of peace... peace... peace... and the youth was striding back to his love. ...

Vasile stumbled over something in the dark and came heavily down on his knees. The fall was soft, as the snow was deep, but the warm visions vanished. He was once more alone and shivering in the night, whilst out of the far distance the cannon's voice forced reality back upon him.

"Wood—wood! I was to find wood," he grumbled. "Where in this damned desert is there any wood I wonder! My God, what a night!

The wind cuts like a whip and the snow it drives into my face pricks like pine-needles,—but where in the devil am I to find wood!"

Vasile stood still slapping his sides with his numbed hands. In his aimless wanderings he had not stuck to the road; he had just blindly tramped into the night. He could not see much, but here and there were darker patches in the snow where its covering was thin; shapeless mounds that might be anything, a heap of stones, a dead horse, a rotting pile of straw—in the uncanny solitude of the night they might also have a more sinister meaning—anything was possible in time of war. ...

Vasile shuddered, and again the vision of the peaceful village rose before him: once more he saw the pyramids of orange pumpkins and from behind some hedge a girl's clear voice took up the refrain of the "doïna" the youth had been whistling. ...

"But I must find wood!" exclaimed Vasile, driving away those pictures of peace. "The others are freezing and I cannot go on wandering all the night."

Again he looked about him and it seemed to him that he perceived the darker line of the high road not very far off—it would be easier walking on the high road.

Slowly and painfully he began picking his way towards that trodden path; the ground was uneven, he was weary, his feet terribly cold.

All of a sudden he stood still with a start—what was that over there? Three gaunt specters standing side by side—three weird solitary skeletons rising dimly out of the night!

His heart began to beat, a sudden moisture wetted the middle of his palms—what was it! How devilish lonely was the night! But after all why should he be afraid? Ghosts were ghosts—pretty harmless—to meet a live Bosch were surely worse! But at that moment in his heart of hearts Vasile was not certain that he would not have preferred a Bosch!

Overcoming his reluctance with an effort, Vasile strode towards the three specters which stood quite still allowing him to approach—three crosses! three solitary weather-beaten crosses of wood! three forsaken graves!

Vasile crossed himself instinctively, murmuring under his breath a prayer for the dead. He stood gazing in a dazed way at those three melancholy effigies, vaguely wondering the end of whose road they marked. Were they soldiers' graves? or the graves of women? or perhaps of little children... of little children who had died of hunger and frost? Since the war so many children had died of hunger and frost. ...

Then with a start Vasile realized that the crosses were made of wood ...of heavy wood! Had he not been sent out into the night to find wood?...

As one who stares at an unexpectedly discovered treasure upon which he dare not lay hand, Vasile remained standing before the three crosses, fascinated by the wood, yet not daring to touch them and at the same time unwilling to move on.

A terrible temptation rose within him: why not tear up one of those crosses and carry it off to feed the dying fire he had left! After all the dead are dead! Their sleep is so profound that they cannot hear what is being done above their heads! Thank God that they sleep so profoundly, for who otherwise could even contemplate such a thought!

Going a few steps nearer, he laid his hand upon the first cross. As he did so, a great revulsion of feeling came over him—No! such an act was sacrilege—the dead must be honored, even above the living. Such an act would surely be condemned by both God and Man. The dead cannot defend themselves; each one is at the mercy of him who passes by—therefore must a grave be respected as one respects the altar steps of a church... it were verily impossible to lay hands upon its cross, the last tribute paid to one who upon earth someone had surely loved!

Then again the voice of temptation rose in Vasile's soul. The dead are dead, their sufferings are passed, whilst over there men were freezing for want of wood, brave men who were doing their duty; surely, surely it were better to despoil the dead than let the living die—brave soldiers defending their country! If the dead had voices, they would cry to him to take their crosses—all their crosses! to warm the country's defenders—to warm brave soldiers who were dying of cold. ...

With a rapid movement Vasile seized the first cross and tried to pull it from the frozen ground. ... The cross resisted—resisted like a tree with roots deep down in the ground, resisted like a living creature defending a sacred spot. But Vasile's blood was up—the resistance he met with awoke the instinct of strife that lies dormant in each man. The stubborn cross became an opponent he had to overcome.

The strangest of struggles then ensued upon that forsaken plain—the wind howling like furies let loose whilst the young man wrestled with the wooden cross! The inert symbol offered a resistance that was almost human, and the youth fought desperately as though he had an enemy to overthrow.

Both arms clasped round the cross, as though it had been a living creature, Vasile pulled and shoved and shook the stubborn monument that would not yield to his strength. The perspiration ran like rain down his cheeks. He had thrown his cap from him and taken the gun from his back; with a persistence that had in it something of hatred, Vasile fought, fought with all his might!

Suddenly the cross gave way... gave way so suddenly that Vasile fell with it to the ground where he remained stretched above his fallen opponent—his opponent that was naught but a wooden cross!

The light of battle still in his eyes, Vasile lay awhile gasping; each time he drew in his breath, it was like a sob he could not hold back. The wind howled around him, whipping up crystals of frozen snow into his face. ....

But he had won! The cross had been uprooted; he had found wood for the fire of the living... so all was well. ...

The fire had gone out—even the embers had died down and with them all talk. Like thrown-away bundles of old clothes the captives and captors sat in mute resignation round the dead cinders; there was little difference between them in this night of suffering.

A faint sound of someone approaching came to them out of the dark. For the moment nothing could be seen, and then suddenly Vasile stood before them dragging behind him something heavy and black like a shadow.

Wood!

A shout of joy rose from the circle seated around the ashes, a sound of unutterable relief rang in the cracked voices greeting Vasile's return; and several men rose instinctively, searching for their flints with stiff fingers so numbed that they would scarcely obey.

Vasile said nothing. He was breathing heavily. This walk back through the night had been like a battle— a battle against wind and snow and cold—and especially a battle against his conscience. Therefore said he nothing; but with a movement of finality let the heavy cross fall at the feet of those who had been waiting. ...

Scurtu was the first to realize of what nature was the fuel Vasile had brought and something like a curse fell from his lips: "It is a cross," he muttered, "a cross... a cross!"

Others rose to examine the longed-for wood Vasile had brought and exclamations of all kinds arose.

The prisoners raised their heads and stared with sullen eyes at those who were talking. But Vasile was dumb. Overcome by fatigue, he sank down into the snow.

"A cross!" cried Scurtu. "How dare he bring a cross!"

"But it is wood and we are cold," hazarded someone.

"That may be as it may be, but we cannot burn a cross!"

"It were sacrilege!"

"God would curse us!"

"And the dead also!"

"Yet we are cold and the dead are dead. ..."

"What good to the dead if we freeze?"

"We have our country to defend!"

"There are so many dead without crosses!"

"For shame! Who dares burn a cross!"

Thus did exclamations fly from all tongues at once. Only Vasile and the prisoners were silent. Shame, weariness and a dull feeling of resent-ment filled Vasile's soul—what could he do! He had found nothing else. ...

The men's voices rose and fell in a wrangle that had within it notes of strife. The wind added to the discussion stormy gusts of fury that outcried those small voices of humans in dispute. ...

"I will not allow it!" It was Scurtu's voice raised to an angry pitch. "Rather would I see you all freeze to death and I with you, than allow Christ's cross to be burnt!"

The old fellow stood his ground. There was something of the look of a rugged bear about him as he faced his companions. The snow lay thick upon him, his ugly old countenance was blue with cold, he stamped his frozen feet, clapped his hands together, beat them against his sides in futile efforts for keeping off the frost, but being the head of his party, no persuasions nor threats could make him change his mind: "Rather die, rather freeze than commit the mortal sin of burning the holy Sign of Christ. ..!"

Silence had fallen upon the suffering group of half-frozen men. Hud-dled together like lost sheep with heads buried in their arms, they lay around the cold ashes, enemy beside enemy, suffering having leveled every distance—after all they were all men before God and the cruel-ties of the winter's night!

A little apart lay Vasile, his head resting upon the cross he had drag-ged with such trouble from so far. Sleep did not come to him. Although the cold numbed his never very acute faculties, Vasile was pondering over the problems of life.

Why war? why suffering and cold and sacrifices when life might be easy—why? why? Why a God in the Heavens... too far off? Why symbols and superstitions and prejudices that had no clear meaning, no real use? Why hatred between nations? Why death and abominations of all sorts? Why? Why?...

The wind raged around him. Vasile occasionally raised a hand, stif-fened by cold, to wipe the driven snow from his eyes.

Why winter after summer? Why distance and longing, and things that never can be again? Why? Why?

Vasile did not understand.

He raised himself to a sitting posture; why was the night so dark? What did it all mean?

Ah! but over there, there was a faint light? Was dawn coming? Was the deadly vigil soon coming to an end?

Vasile watched intently the light he seemed to see right over there in the distance—was it dawn? Could it be dawn at last? But it did not spread, yet it seemed moving—it *was* moving! It was coming nearer. ...It was coming *his* way!

When afterwards... in full daylight Vasile tried to relate what
he had seen—the others—those who had been sleeping, would never
quite believe his tale—yet they had been sleeping, those others, and
Vasile, he had been awake!—but even thus is man—like Thomas of old:
he wants to touch so as to be able to believe. ...

What Vasile saw was a white figure coming steadily towards him
over the snow, a white figure all wrapped in light—and the figure itself
was the light, and so luminous was that figure that Vasile never understood why it did not awake the others from their sleep.

A long trail of brightness remained in the wake of the moving figure
—a path of glory marked by Holy Feet. ... For it was the Son of Man
who was coming over the snow towards Vasile—it was the Son of
God!

Out of the night He came—a figure so glorious that Vasile sank to
his knees, tearing his cap from his head, folding his numbed hands.

Forgotten all suffering, all conflict! forgotten the many doubts, the
many questions that had made heavy his soul.

Now he was but a watcher in the dark, a lost child to whom God had
come! An ineffable ecstasy filled his being—for the Man of Light was
coming towards him, Vasile—Vasile, the soldier who had stolen a cross
from the dead!

But what was it that the Son of God was bearing on his shoulders—
something dark and heavy and enormously large. ...

His Cross! Christ too was carrying His Cross, why? oh! why?...

So lightly did He come over the snow, the Cross seemed no weight
for His shoulders, yet Vasile's shoulders still remembered the weight
they had borne.

The luminous Figure did not pause before the young soldier, but
Vasile had a fleeting glimpse of the angelic compassion in his eyes. ...
Slowly the Holy One passed the spot where Vasile knelt, and going
straight up to the circle of sleeping soldiers, he stepped amongst them
and Vasile saw—saw with his own eyes how the Son of God cast his
Cross upon the cinders and how a glorious flame shot up from them,
licking the sides of the Cross till the Cross itself was as a great torch of
light!

Christ had brought his own Cross, had brought it to make a fire, so
that the country's brave defenders should not die of cold!

After that Vasile remembered but dimly what had happened; on his
knees he had dragged himself towards the holy flame, upon his knees
... and then in a swoon he had fallen beside the saving flame. ...

Day had come.

One after another the sleepers awoke, and, oh! marvel! the cinders
that had been cold and dead so early in the night were now red-hot

and a blessed glow irradiated from them, a glow so intense and life-giving that winter-cold seemed but the specter of a terror that had passed.

Each man came gradually back from the realm of dreams with the sensation that something marvelous had happened, his body warmed and his soul overflowing with a gladness he could not explain. Even the pale prisoners had in their eyes a strange reflection of something resembling joy. ...

With a loud voice he tried to make menacing, Scurtu called upon Vasile—had he disobeyed orders? had he burnt the cross whilst his chief had been asleep?

But, no! Over there lay the cross, like a dead man with arms out-stretched, and beside the heavy wood on the snow knelt Vasile, with hands clasped, staring into the rising sun. ...

Scurtu crossed himself.

"Vasile!" he called. "Vasile! What seest thou in the face of the rising sun?"

Vasile turned towards him—there was a wondrous light in his eyes, but he did not answer—and Scurtu never knew what vision Vasile was following as he stared into the face of the rising sun.

Bulgaria

INTRODUCTION

BULGARIAN literature is still in its infancy. The first Bulgarian grammar was published in 1835. This was the work of the monk Neophyt Rilski (1793—1881) who was responsible for the opening of some of the first schools in Bulgaria. Among the writers of this earlier period were George Rakowski (1818—1867), whose patriotic works stimulated the national zeal, Christo Boteff (1847—1876) and Petko Slaveïkoff (died 1895), whose poems molded the modern poetical language and exercised a great influence over the people. One of the most distinguished men of letters is Ivan Vazoff (born 1850), whose poetry and prose are distinguished for their literary finish. Dimitr Ivanov (born 1878) is one of the younger writers who has displayed rare qualities in several volumes of short stories. Under the pen-name of Elin-Pelin he is well known to all readers of the Bulgarian language. It is to Ivanov that especial credit is due for describing the little-known peasant class of his country.

DIMITR IVANOV

(Elin-Pelin)

(1878—1949)

ELIN-PELIN, whose real name was Dimitr Ivanov (born in 1878 near Sofia), was one of the common people. As a village teacher he spread enlightenment among his fellow-countrymen. Wishing to win their confidence, he "lived among the peasants and in the repression of self he found the power to create." In his stories the spiritual life of the Bulgarian countryman is depicted as in a mirror.

The motives of his first collection of stories are as simple as folk-songs and, like them, were born of the emotions of life. The first collection of his tales was published in 1904.

In the author's second collection of stories not only Bulgarian peasants and villagers but many Mohammedan types appear in refreshing variety. *The Commissioner's Christmas* presents a characteristic sketch of the peasants of Bulgaria's hinterland.

This story, here translated for the first time into English, by Sarka B. Hrbkova, is reprinted by permission of the translator.

THE COMMISSIONER'S CHRISTMAS

"WE'LL get there in plenty of time, sir. Yes, we'll get there yet before daylight's gone. See—there's the village over yonder at the foot of the hill! Do you see it? As soon as we cross that low ridge we can say we're there." And the young driver, swinging his whip above the backs of his lean horses, shouted lustily to spur them on: "Vyee hey! Vyee! Sirs!"

The four wheels of the light coach splattered worse than ever through the soft mud of the country road. The rickety skeleton of the coach rattled dismally through the cheerless, dreary plain soaked by the late December rains.

The country lad shouted once more to his horses, settled himself more comfortably on the box, slapped his wet cap on his thick cape and, in a carefree voice, started up a gay tune.

"What's your name, boy?" inquired a fat man bundled up in a wolf-skin coat, who sat inside the coach.

The lad continued his song.

"Ho, boy!" cried the man in a loud, harsh voice.

"What?" The boy turned around.

"Name! Your name? What's your name?"

"Ondra."

"Ah, ah, Ondra. Clever lad, you are! All of you have become clever. Sly, you country bumpkins. You only know how to lie and deceive. And how you do put on! I watch 'em at court. Sheep—little lambkins—of innocence—but really regular wolves! They play with the judges!"

"We're just simple folk, sir, and they only slander us. You just think so, but we're really not bad like that. Our peasant people deceive only out of ignorance. Ignorance and poverty."

"Ah! So that's it! Because of poverty! Cursed clods! They complain of ignorance and poverty, and guzzle like fish!"

"You think it's prosperity they're suffering from, sir? From being overprosperous? No! Not from prosperity. Drink—guzzle? Yes, they all drink. To feel a bit happier, not because they're well off. That's something a man like you can set down in his note-book."

"Ah! It looks to me as if you, too, had had a drink, friend! You're still too young for that ; your whiskers haven't sprouted yet. Those peasants of yours—just write it down—are a lost lot—lost, that's what!"

"You write it down, sir! We don't know how to write," said the boy and turning to his skinny horses, he called "Vyee, vyee, sirs!" and lapsed into deep thought.

The horses hesitated for a moment, as if they, too, were thinking.

The man put up the big collar of his wolf cloak, disappeared inside it and he, too, lost himself in meditation.

A crow with ruffled wings settled on a solitary tree beside the road and swinging on a dry twig croaked mournfully, while it, too, ruminated. Even the somber wintry weather seemed in a gray reflective mood, portending a gloomy Christmas on the morrow. Across the heavens thick scraggly storm-clouds crept and broke heavily beneath a cold blue sky. The earth was submerged in mud and moisture. The vistas of villages, streams, distant forests and mountains darkened, lifeless and distorted, before them. On the plains here and there glistened great pools, all cloudy, cold and glassy like the eyes of a corpse.

The small coach slowly wallowed through the deep soft mud, wading in, wading out, twisting and turning. A loose board on the side of it constantly, monotonously, dismally and senselessly rattled and banged mercilessly on the nerves of the corpulent gentleman in the fur coat. Finally, losing all patience, he opened his collar, thrust out his fat face, and shouted: "What is that horrible rattle? Devil take it!"

"It's only a loose clapboard, sir. It bangs away like a learned man : no sense to its rattle at all!"

"You're clever, Ondra, very clever! You know how to fool the young girls, I'll bet. You fellows marry young and have pretty wives."

The gentleman thrust back the tall collar of his fur coat in his attempt at jocularity.

"Say what you will, the married women are better! I know it! And you, sir, have an errand in our village, I take it?"

"I'm the court commissioner."

Ondra turned round and inspected his fare with a penetrating look.

"On official service, I suppose?"

"Service, of course. One of your fine fellows played a trick on me, but this time I'll fix him properly. I've got one official paper in my hands that'll catch him right. I got wind of the fact that this fellow was deceiving us—and I'll search him out in the evening. Believe me, he'll have cause to remember me and this Christmas! I'll confiscate all his rye—every grain of it! Not only to teach him what's what, but to set an example to all the rest of you not to try to fool the authorities. You cheat the merchants, you cheat the townspeople; you sell them spoiled eggs and rancid butter. But just wait, you peasant brood, you can't cheat the courts! We know how to punish you! What you need is the lash—a stout Russian knout—that's the only way to teach you! You've all become drunkards, low-down trash. You're failing to meet your taxes—you're destroyers of the State! Our patriotic interests are suffering! I wish I could be Czar for at least two days, and I'd fix you all *my* way! I'd make angels of all of you; yes, sir, angels! Pity I'm not the Czar!"

The court commissioner unbuttoned his fur coat, inside of which he squirmed like a chick breaking out of its shell.

"Oh, but Mr. Commissioner, God created the world and calculated that women don't need beards, so he didn't give them beards. He figured that an ass needs long ears, so he gave a pair to every donkey," answered Ondra with feigned simplicity.

"Stop your silly chatter and get along. It's getting dark, and I've got to get back to celebrate Christmas with my family. You charge too much, you imp! Three leu for twenty kilometers! You surely know how to skin us. Hurry up, will you: drive faster or those jades of yours will go to sleep!"

"Vyee, there! Vyee, sirs!" shouted Ondra, swinging his whip in the air.

"Sirs, you call them? Sirs! Better call them 'brothers,'" commented the commissioner in a rage.

"They'd resent that, Mr. Commissioner! I'd insult 'em if I didn't call 'em sirs. Why, they're regular gentlemen! *Their* service is official: they run on a regular schedule. In the morning they get up; at a certain hour we water them and give them their feed. Then we harness them up, they go, you might say, to their offices: they pull till evening. Have supper at a regular hour, drink water, 'read the news,' so to speak, and —sleep. Regular official life!"

"Where did you get your drinks, friend? Stop your jabbering and get on, or I'll be late. You've got a sly look, fellow, sly!"

"There're no wolves about, Mr. Commissioner, don't fear," the driver said in such a tone that the honorable court official looked round with apprehensive eyes.

"I'm not afraid of wolves, friend, but of the cold weather. I haven't time to nurse a cold."

They jogged on silently for a while.

"So you're on an official mission? Who's going to get scorched this time?" Ondra turned a serious face toward his passenger.

The commissioner waited for a while before answering. "Why shouldn't you know? Stanoycho they call him, little man with a thick neck."

"I know him. So you're going to take his rye, are you? He's a poor fellow, Mr. Commissioner; let him off this time. It's Christmas, you know, and all that!"

"Poor fellow, yes, but a regular devil!" The commissioner lapsed into silence. Darkness was falling. The horses could barely crawl to the top of the hill beyond which lay the village. Ondra no longer urged them on, nor swung his long whip above them. He stopped his talk, he no longer sang, and was lost in meditation.

When they reached the summit and started down on the other side, night had come, but there was still no sign of the village. A cold penetrating wind blew over the land buried under the mire. Scattered clouds moved up toward the mountains. The blue vault of the frosty sky cleared up, widened and lifted to greater heights. Soon stars, cold and glistening, appeared on its surface. The air was perceptibly chillier. The horses plodded on slowly, sluggishly.

"Whip 'em up! Hurry up! You lazybones! We'll freeze to death!" shrieked the furious commissioner.

Ondra indifferently shouted to the horses and drowsily swung his whip over their heads, but as before they wearily, inertly dragged on the coach as if they had heard nothing at all.

Ondra was thinking of the miserable Stanoycho whose rye the commissioner was going to confiscate early next morning.

"It was you brought me this misfortune, Ondra," Stanoycho would say to him, and when he'd be through blaming him, he'd ask Ondra to join his family in their meal, and then he'd weep. Yes, he would surely weep. Stanoycho's heart was soft. Ondra knew that.

He must help the poor fellow, contrive to tell him to hide his rye overnight and sweep the granary clean, or else all the coming year he'd be stretching his lean ears in hunger. Yes, he must do something!

Nothing was distinguishable but mud—deep, thick mud. The road lost itself in the mire, and led nowhere except into more mud.

Ondra pulled up the lines and stopped the horses.

"I'm afraid we're in danger of losing our way, Mr. Commissioner!" And the lad peered intently into the darkness.

The commissioner looked gravely at the driver's face on which not a trace of his former mischief was visible.

"Boy, open your eyes, or I'll not answer for the consequences. You'll get a thrashing."

Ondra jerked the reins, swished his whip and cried, "Hold on tight, Mr. Commissioner!" Far off in the distance before them the lights of the village glimmered. The distant echoes of dogs' barking was carried to them. A few feet to the right of them glistened the pearly surface of a great pool of motionless water. The coach turned its course in that direction.

"What's that?" asked the commissioner.

"A swamp, Mr. Commissioner. The road leads right through it. It's shallow, don't be afraid. Only a few holes here and there. I usually miss 'em whether I go by wagon or on foot. Vyee, there, sirs! Hold tight, Mr. Commissioner!"

The horses plunged into the cold water, which mirrored the starry sky. They proceeded more and more cautiously as they began to sink deeper and deeper into the mire. The dead surface of the pearl-green water broke into lively motion.

"Stop, you cattle!" cried the commissioner in terror, drawing his coat tightly round him. "You'll drown me, you fool! Can't you see the coach is filling with water! Stop! Stop!"

Ondra stopped. The coach sank in to the bottom, standing in the middle of a swamp whose margin was lost in the impenetrable blackness.

"Ho! Go ahead!" bawled Ondra to his horses. His powerful young voice reëchoed through the night. Near by some wild ducks fluttered excitedly and vanished in the dark.

"Guess we, too, have to turn into moor-hens and wade out," said Ondra thoughtfully, "or else—"

"Oh, you idiot! Just wait till we get out of this! I'll break every bone in your body! We'll drown here like rats! You ass!"

"No, we won't drown, Mr. Commissioner, we won't drown, don't be afraid. In this darkness anyone would miss the way. Just be calm," said Ondra, and began to examine the harness. Then he proceeded to buckle and unbuckle various straps, swearing loudly, tying, untying, cursing incessantly. Finally he resumed his place on the driver's seat, swung his whip and shouted, "Vyee, there! Go on!"

The horses pulled and went forward. Suddenly one of them slipped loose from the shaft and staggered ahead in the mire, free of the harness. The other horse stood still with the coach.

"Ho, you! What's happened now?" shrieked the commissioner.

"Stop, you! Dorcha, Dorcha!" called Ondra to the liberated horse, and began to coax it to come back.

But the animal, frightened by the water, turned round and warily made its way back in the direction of the shore, where it gradually lost itself to view, wholly oblivious of the pleadings of his master.

The commissioner stood up excitedly in the coach, terror written on every feature.

At that instant Ondra quickly leaped onto the other horse and, following in Dorcha's path, continued to call loudly, "Dorcha, Dorcha, wait! Come back—Dorcha, Dorcha!"

"Where are you going? Stop! What are you doing, you cattle? You crazy fool! Oh, you lousy peasant! I'll fix you!"

In the darkness only merry laughter was his response.

"Oh, you cattle, so you're leaving me here! To perish! For the beasts to devour me! Boy, don't do it, please, I beg you!" implored the commissioner in a trembling voice.

"Don't be afraid, don't be afraid, Mr. Commissioner," sounded Ondra's voice. "No wild beasts here in the swamp. Just wrap up, so you don't take cold. To-morrow morning—early, bright and early—I'll come. There's hay in the coach, make yourself a bed. I'll not charge you for the night's lodging!"

"Boy, don't joke," pleaded the commissioner. "Don't leave me! Come back! Pull me out of here!"

"It's dark, sir, very dark. I can't see a thing! And my horse has run away! How can I help you? I can't do it!"

The commissioner heard the mocking voice wafted back out of the darkness. Terrified at the prospect, alone there in the middle of the dismal swamp, he burst into tearful entreaty.

"Ondra, come back! Please—please! I'll pay you well—pay you anything! Help me out of this! I'll die here! I have children! They're waiting for me! It's Christmas! Have you no heart?" His voice broke in desperation. He listened, but no answer came. Then, as if bereft of his senses, he howled out into the unanswering darkness: "Ho, fellow! Cattle! You ox! You beast! Come back! Take me out of this! Have pity! My children! Christmas! You peasant cur! You dog!"

And sinking back into the coach, he drew his fur coat about him and burst out crying like a child.

But the black night gave no answer.

———————————

South America

INTRODUCTION

FROM the very earliest years following the conquest of Spanish America in the Sixteenth Century there have been Spanish-American writers, and though some of the most famous of them, like Alarcón and Garcilaso de la Vega, belong rather to Spanish literature proper, there remains a sufficiently large body of writings to warrant the use of the term Spanish-American literature. Yet before the Nineteenth Century, the situation was not very different from that in North America, where writers produced a body of literature more or less directly related to that of the mother country.

But for the purposes of this collection, the early Colonial period, indeed the entire period up to the beginning of the last century, may be disregarded so far as the short story is concerned. To trace the history of fiction in Spanish America, it would be necessary to treat practically every country from Mexico to Argentina and Chile. All the Spanish-American countries have their writers, and all have produced short stories. The five tales here included as representative have been taken from Costa Rica, Brazil, Venezuela, Nicaragua and Peru, though it would have been easy to find others as excellent in Colombia, Mexico, Cuba or the Argentine.

Though the writers of Spanish America have been directly or indirectly influenced by Europe, especially by Spain and France (and, in the case of Brazil, by Portugal), the past fifty years have seen the development of work as truly native and free of direct imitation as that of the best North American writers. The theories of art and the "schools" and movements of the rest of the world have inevitably left their mark on the Spanish Americans, but they have striven to depict the scenes that are familiar to them, and to describe the people they know best.

It can hardly be said that Spanish America has produced a Maupassant, but on the other hand, neither has North America. Blanco-Fombona, Darío, Machado de Assis, Fernández-García, and García-Calderón have alone written stories that are quite as good as any that have been produced in the United States during the past generation.

Costa Rica

RICARDO FERNÁNDEZ-GARCÍA

(1867—1951)

FERNÁNDEZ-GARCÍA was born in the province of Alejuela, Costa Rica, in 1867. He received his early education in Paris, but returned to his native land in 1878, to discover that he had to learn his own language over again. His earliest literary efforts were in French, though they were inspired by his readings from Fenimore Cooper. It was early in the nineties that his work attracted the attention of Rubén Darío. The best-known of all his writings is the volume *Costa Rican Tales*. These are vivid simple narratives, "transcriptions of the national life."

The present version, translated by Gray Casement, from the volume, *Costa Rican Tales*, copyright, 1905, by Burrows Co., Cleveland, is here reprinted by permission of the translator.

CHIVALRY

ONE night in the month of July, four horsemen, well mounted, emerged from an hacienda in Uruca and rode hurriedly along the highway to the joining of the road to San Antonio de Belén, where they stopped.

"Here we must separate," said one of them. "May you have good luck, Ramón," he added, searching in the darkness for his friend's hand.

"Adiós, Salvador, adiós," replied the one spoken to, in a voice trembling with emotion. The two men, without letting go of each other's hands, drew together until their stirrups touched, and embraced warmly.

"Adiós, adiós"—"Good luck."

After a last embrace, long and affectionate, both started off in different directions, each escorted by one of the two horsemen who had just witnessed the sad scene of farewell. Those who followed the highroad did not get very far. At the Ciruelas river they fell into the hands of a picket of soldiers who carried them prisoners to the Alejuela Barracks. The other two fugitives, for fugitives they were, kept on, with better fortune, along the San Antonio road. The darkness did not permit them to see where they were going, so that the travellers had to trust to the instinct of their horses to avoid the bad places or to get out of them. Luckily it did not rain, which would have been one more hindrance to the rapid march that the critical situation in which Salvador Moreno found himself necessitated, for he was being eagerly searched for on account of his share in the attack made the night before on the Cuartel Principal in San José. The revolutionary uprising had failed through the fault of those who were to have brought men from the neighboring towns, with the intention of arming them when the Cuartel had surrendered, and of laying siege to the other ones.

Not one of them appeared at the critical moment, and the few valiant ones who had surprised the garrison asleep at two o'clock in the morning, had to abandon at daybreak the conquest which had cost them so much blood.

Salvador did not answer the questions which from time to time his companion asked him. Absorbed in his thoughts he lived over again the happenings of last night's bloody drama; the meeting in the house of one of the conspirators, the irritating wait for those who did not come, the fear of a betrayal, the doubts and hesitations of the last hour, finally the moment of marching, the gate of the Cuartel opened by the hand of a traitor, the hand-to-hand fight with the guard, the gallantry of the officers meeting death at their posts. But more than all there harassed him the vision of a young lieutenant running up hurriedly, saber in hand, to aid his comrades, whom he had laid low by a shot at barely arm's length. In vain he tried to make himself believe that it was a legitimate act of warfare. An internal voice cried out in the tribunal of his conscience against the blood that had been shed. Salvador Moreno was a high-strung, refined man to whom the brutality of force was repugnant. At the same time his indomitable and lofty spirit could not bend itself to the political despotism which is killing us like a shameful chronic sore. In the conspiracy he had seen the shaking off of the heavy yoke, the dignity of his country avenged, and the triumph of liberty. To gain all that, the sacrifice of his life had not seemed too much. Now his sorrow was very great, his patriotic illusions had disappeared like the visions of a beautiful dream when one awakens, and his heart was throbbing with wrath against those who through their cowardice had caused the daring attempt to fail. With keen regret he thought of his comrades uselessly sacrificed, of the agony of a brave young fellow whom he had carried out of the Cuartel in his arms, mortally wounded. Clear and exact the events of the combat went marching through his mind, some of which were atrocious, worthy of savages, others irresistibly comical, like that of the boastful fellow who withdrew from the gate of the Cuartel to go in search of his revolver which he pretended to have forgotten; and always persistent and sad, the vision of the lieutenant falling without a cry, his hand at his breast. Afterwards the despair at the failure, that retreat at daybreak through the deserted streets of the capital, the interminable hours of anguish, hidden with Ramón Solares under some sacks in the country house of a friend, listening to the voices of those who were searching for them. Finally the sheltering night, the hurried flight, the gloomy future, forbidding as the wrath of the enraged dictator. In order to aid their escape the fugitives had agreed to follow different roads; Salvador Moreno chose the one to Puntarenas, passing through San Antonio de Belén, and the plains of Carmen. Ramón Solares preferred the San Carlos route, with the idea of seeking refuge in Nicaragua by land, where the two friends were to meet if Salvador should succeed in escaping the vigilance of the authorities of the port.

Both were accompanied by trusty retainers who knew the country and were of proved courage. It was Fate that decided in this case, and we have already seen that she declared in favor of Salvador Moreno, who without meeting a soul, arrived at the highroad to Puntarenas at one o'clock in the morning, while his friend, chained in his prison, offered prayers that he might succeed in escaping from those who pursued him. At three o'clock he passed through Atenas and at six in the morning he and his companion arrived at the gates of San Mateo. But now the horses could endure no more. It was part of the fugitive's plan to pass the day hidden in a friendly and secure house on the plains of Surubres, although now this was not possible, on account of the fatigue of the horses and the danger of the young conspirator's being recognized in passing through the village, in spite of the fact that he was wearing the costume of a countryman. It was necessary then to decide on something.

"Don Salvador," said the guide, "three hundred yards from here there lives an acquaintance of mine, who is a man you can trust. If you like we can dismount here, so that we shan't have to pass through San Mateo in the daytime."

"Very well, let us go there."

The two men spurred their horses and a few minutes afterwards arrived at a house situated a short distance from the road. Through the unbarred gate they entered, saluted by the barking of three thin, mangy dogs. At this disturbance an old and corpulent countryman came out on the veranda.

"Buenos días, 'Nor José," said the guide.

"Buenos días, Pedro," replied the old man. "How goes it?"

"Well; and how are you? How are the girls getting on?"

"Very well, thank you. Why don't you get off a while and rest?" added the old fellow.

The horseman dismounted and Salvador dropped, half dead with fatigue, on the settle that stood on the veranda. While he was stretching his aching legs, 'Nor José and Pedro unsaddled the horses and the latter confided to the old man that his companion was fleeing the country. Hurriedly he told him a story which he made up as he went on; something about a quarrel in which machetes had been flourished in the air. The old man did not insist on the details, promising to keep quiet about the unlooked for guests in his house.

Pedro went to take the horses to the pasture and Salvador accepted with pleasure the coffee which the youngest daughter of 'Nor José served him. The old man was proud of having a son-in-law the *jefe politico* of San Mateo, who had married his oldest daughter, a handsome girl, so people said. Noticing that his guest was getting sleepy he conducted him to a cot bed that he might rest.

Five minutes afterwards the fugitive was sleeping like a log. The night came on without Salvador's awakening from the deep slumber into which he had fallen, his bones aching and his nerves being unstrung by the fatigue and emotions he had endured.

Pedro had improved the time by bathing the horses in the neighboring river and giving them a good feed of corn. This task ended, he took a nap for a couple of hours, which was sufficient to restore to his muscles the necessary energy; and as it was not two o'clock in the afternoon, he shared the frugal dinner of his host.

On hearing the church bells of San Mateo tolling "Las animas" he resolved to awaken Salvador, which was not an easy thing to do. For all that he shook him, it was impossible to overcome the stupor which held him fast. Finally he opened his eyes, looking about in a dazed way without comprehending, until Pedro's voice insisting on the urgency of taking the road made him remember the reality of the situation. Salvador got up with difficulty; each movement that he made aroused a dormant pain in his body, which was agitated by a painful, feverish sensation. A little glass of cognac produced the necessary reaction, and the odor of supper already served began to remind him that he had been fasting for many hours.

While Salvador was devouring a chicken, which at Pedro's request the daughter of 'Nor José had cooked, the latter, seated on a bench, observed him closely. Naturally keen, he had scented the fact that beneath the short jacket was hidden a person who was not accustomed to wear it. The attentiveness of Pedro to Salvador, the respect with which he talked to him, were indications that this man belonged to a higher class of society than his garb would imply. This was evident; but looking well into the matter, what difference did it make to him that the stranger was who he was?

A five-dollar bill which Salvador put in his hand completely confirmed that old man's suspicions. In a little while Pedro entered to give notice that the horses were ready and Salvador, in bidding farewell, warmly squeezed the hand of his chance host, who almost fell over himself in his salutations and wishes for a safe journey. They were already going out to the veranda, when a boy came running up with the news that 'Nor José's oldest daughter was very ill. About to give birth to a child she had suffered a fall with bad consequences.

The old man was very much alarmed and Salvador tried to calm him, advising him to call a doctor.

"We have no doctor here," replied 'Nor José, much distressed, "and while one is coming from Alejuela the girl may die."

Salvador, who was a warm-hearted fellow, did not hesitate a moment.

"Let us go and see her," he said. "I am a doctor."

The old man, surprised and pleased, did not know what to say.

"May God pay you, señor, may God pay you!" he finally murmured with tears in his eyes. Pedro, plainly anxious, improved the moment when the countryman went to get his hat and call his daughter, to whisper in Salvador's ear that the sick woman was no less than the wife of the *jefe politico*, who must already have had orders to capture him.

"No matter, Pedro. It is my duty not to allow this poor woman to die. Let us go at once."

The old man, who returned hurriedly, heard these last words. "May God pay you, señor," he said again in a low voice. Pedro took the old man behind him on the crupper and Salvador the girl. After fifteen minutes of fast riding, the four stopped in front of the *jefe politico's* office.

The house was full of gossipers of the neighborhood, who had come in armed with infallible remedies which they were anxious to apply to the sufferer. The friends of the *jefe politico*, gathered together in the dining-room about a bottle of white rum, told discreetly, for the comfort of the official, of similar cases which finally had ended happily.

The arrival of her father and sister called forth a groan from the sick one, who in her rôle of a first-time mother considered herself as good as dead.

"Enter, enter, doctor!" exclaimed the old man, politely addressing the fugitive, whom nobody in the midst of the general confusion had as yet noticed. Judging by his costume, those present took him for one of those country quacks who live on the ignorance and avarice of the country people. Salvador examined the sick woman carefully and was convinced that, although the case was a serious one, it would not be difficult to save her. Without loss of time he took such measures as the circumstances demanded, and from that moment he thought only of the life of the little human creature which depended on his care. In vain Pedro reminded him many times of the great peril he was incurring in that house; nothing could make him withdraw.

'Nor José and the *jefe politico*, feeling more at ease after hearing the doctor's opinion, went to join the circle of friends, who had already given a good account of the first bottle of rum. When the second was opened, tongues began to get loosened, and the conversation acquired an animation which it lacked at the beginning.

Incidentally they talked of the revolution which had just taken place, and 'Nor José, who, on account of the isolation in which he lived, was ignorant of it all, made them tell him of what had happened, listening to the story with anxiety. On learning that it was the Cuartel Principal which had been attacked, he asked his son-in-law whether he had news of Rafael, his son, who was one of the garrison.

"I don't know anything about him," replied the *jefe politico*. "I suppose that there is no news, since they have not sent me any word. Nevertheless in order to feel easy I am going to telegraph to San José."

When the despatch was written it was sent to the telegraph office.

Salvador did not leave his patient, encouraging her with cheering words to bear her pains with fortitude. Pedro, ill at ease, was watching the street, near the horses which were dozing with their heads low down.

At ten o'clock at night a long telegram came for the *jefe politico*. As he was reading it his hands trembled slightly. Suddenly a violent exclamation broke from his lips.

On hearing it, the people present got up as though to ask the cause, but the *jefe politico* without speaking a word conducted his father-in-law to a neighboring room. There, without any preamble, he told him that his son had been killed in the attack of the night before, and that Doctor Salvador Moreno was supposed to have been his slayer, and that he was then trying to escape from the country.

The poor old man, falling limp into a chair, wept bitterly over the death of his son. After a while he aroused himself with an expression of unspeakable wrath and the tears dried up in his eyes, which now shone like red-hot coals. "Salvador Moreno," he murmured in a hoarse voice. "I won't forget that name."

"I have heard it," said the *jefe politico*. "I believe it is that of a young doctor recently come back from Europe."

One of the women neighbors interrupted the conversation with the glad news of the birth of a strong and healthy man-child. Both were going in to see it, but it was not yet time for them to enter.

Pedro, always uneasy, had hardly heard the news when he went in search of 'Nor José to ask him to remind his companion of the urgency of starting.

"Tell Don Salvador that it is already very late and that I am waiting for him," he said forgetting to use the assumed name. On hearing this name the old man became petrified. Then he exclaimed with fury:

"Don Salvador! Don Salvador Moreno! That's the doctor's name, isn't it so?"

"Yes. Did he tell you?"

Without replying, 'Nor José went to a corner of the room where a machete was leaning against the wall. He drew it from its scabbard and with an expression of unheard-of ferocity went toward the apartment of his daughter.

At that moment, the door opened. Upon the bed lay the mother, very pale, but her eyes and lips were smiling. With his sleeves rolled up and absorbed in his task, Salvador was bathing the new born child in a wash basin. On seeing this the angry father felt a surge of generous feeling invade his heart. That man was the slayer of his Rafael; that was the terrible truth; but that same man who had shed the blood of his son had just saved another bit of his soul at the risk of his liberty and perhaps of his very life. He stood looking at the peaceful scene; the happy mother, the anxious and busy neighbors, and the doctor, very earnest, coddling the child, whose cries seemed to ask pardon for the savior of its mother.

The old man drew back slowly, letting go of the machete. After a moment of hesitation, he passed his rough hand across his face and drawing near to the fugitive said in a hoarse and trembling voice:

"Don Salvador, I beg you to go soon, because you are in great danger in this house."

Brazil

J. M. MACHADO DE ASSIS

(1839—1908)

BORN at Rio de Janeiro of poor parents, Joaquim Maria Machado de Assis began his literary career at an early age, although it was not for some years that he succeeded in establishing a reputation. Long before his death he was regarded as the chief exponent of modern Brazilian literature. About 1880 he first became generally known, and until the end of his life he wrote industriously. He is best known for his rather pessimistic but finely conceived and well-written psychological novels and short stories.

The Attendant's Confession is one of his characteristic tales. The pre-

THE ATTENDANT'S CONFESSION

SO you really think that what happened to me in 1860 is worth while writing down? Very well. I'll tell you the story, but on the condition that you don't divulge it before my death. You'll not have long to wait—a week at most; I am a marked man.

I could have told you the story of my whole life, which holds many other interesting details: but that would require time, courage and paper. There is plenty of paper, to be sure, but my courage is at low ebb, and as for the time that is yet left me, it may be compared to the life of a candle-flame. Soon to-morrow's sun will rise—a demon sun as impenetrable as life itself. So good-bye, my dear sir; read this and bear me no ill will; pardon me those things that will appear evil to you and do not too much complain if there rises a disagreeable odor which is not exactly that of the rose. You asked me for a human document. Here it is. Ask me for neither the empire of the Great Mogul nor a photograph of the Maccabees; but request, if you will, my dead man's shoes, and I'll will them to you and none other.

You already know that this took place in 1860. The year before, about the month of August, at the age of forty-two, I had become a theologian—that is, I copied the theological studies of a priest at Nictheroy, an old college-chum, who thus tactfully gave me my board and lodging. In that same month of August, 1859, he received a letter from the vicar of a small town in the interior, asking if he knew of an intelligent, discreet, and patient person who would be willing, in return for generous wages, to serve as attendant to the invalid Colonel Felisbert. The priest proposed that I take the place, and I accepted it eagerly, for I was tired of copying Latin quotations and ecclesiastic formulas. First I went to Rio de Janeiro to take leave of a brother who lived at the capital, and from there I left for the little village of the interior.

Arriving there, I heard bad reports concerning the colonel. He was pictured to me as a disagreeable, harsh, exacting fellow; nobody could endure him, not even his own friends. He had used more attendants than medicines. In fact he had broken the faces of two of them. But to all this I replied that I had no fear of persons in good health, still less of invalids. So, after first visiting the vicar, who confirmed all that I had heard and recommended to me charity and forbearance, I turned toward the colonel's residence.

I found him on the veranda of his house, stretched out on a chair and suffering greatly. He received me fairly well. At first he examined me silently, piercing me with his feline eyes: then a kind of malicious smile spread over his features, which were rather hard. Finally he declared that all the attendants he had ever engaged hadn't been worth a button, that they slept too much, were impudent and spent their time flirting with the servants; two of them were even thieves.

"And you, are you a thief?"

"No, sir."

Then he asked me my name. Scarcely had I uttered it when he made a gesture of astonishment.

"Your name is Colombo?"

"No, sir. My name is Procopio José Gomes Vallongo."

Vallongo?—He came to the conclusion that this was no Christian name and proposed thenceforth to call me simply Procopio. I replied that it should be just as he pleased.

If I recall this incident, it is not only because it seems to me to give a good picture of the colonel, but also to show you that my reply made a very good impression upon him. The next day he told the vicar so, adding that he had never had a more sympathetic attendant. The fact is, we lived a regular honeymoon that lasted one week.

From the dawn of the eighth day I knew the life of my predecessors —a dog's life. I no longer slept. I no longer thought of anything, I was showered with insults and laughed at them from time to time with an air of resignation and submission, for I had discovered that this was a way of pleasing him. His impertinences proceeded as much from his malady as from his temperament. His illness was of the most complicated: he suffered from aneurism, rheumatism and three or four minor affections. He was nearly sixty, and had been accustomed since his fifth year to having everybody at his beck and call. That he was surly, one could well forgive; but he was also very malicious. He took pleasure in the grief and the humiliation of others. At the end of three months I was tired of putting up with him and had made up my mind to leave; only the opportunity was lacking.

But that came soon enough. One day, when I was a trifle late in giving him a massage, he took his cane and struck me with it two or three times. That was the last straw. I told him on the spot that I was through with him and I went to pack my trunk. He came later to my room; he begged me to remain, assured me that there wasn't anything to be angry at, that I must excuse the ill-humoredness of old age. ... He insisted so much that I agreed to stay.

"I am nearing the end, Procopio," he said to me that evening. "I can't live much longer, I am upon the verge of the grave. You shall go to my burial, Procopio. Under no circumstances will I excuse you. You shall go, you shall pray over my tomb. And if you don't," he added, laughing, "my ghost will come at night and pull you by the legs. Do you believe in souls of the other world, Procopio?"

"Nonsense!"

"And why don't you, you blockhead?" he replied passionately, with distended eyes.

That is how he was in his peaceful intervals; what he was like during his raging attacks, you may well imagine!

He struck me no more with his cane, but his insults were the same, if not worse. With time I became hardened, I no longer heeded anything; I was an ignoramus, a camel, a bumpkin, an idiot, a loggerhead —I was everything! It must further be understood that I alone was favored with these pretty names. He had no relatives; there had been a nephew, but he had died of consumption. As to friends, those who came now and then to flatter him and indulge his whims made him but a short visit, five or ten minutes at the most. I alone was always present to receive his dictionary of insults. More than once I resolved to leave him; but as the vicar would implore me not to abandon the colonel I always yielded in the end.

Not only were our relations becoming very much strained, but I was in a hurry to get back to Rio de Janeiro. At forty-two years of age one does not easily accustom oneself to perpetual seclusion with a brutal, snarling old invalid, in the depths of a remote village. Just to give you an idea of my isolation, let it suffice to inform you that I didn't even read the newspapers; outside of some more or less important piece of news that was brought to the colonel, I knew nothing of what was doing in the world. I therefore yearned to get back to Rio at the first opportunity, even at the cost of breaking with the vicar. And I may as well add—since I am here making a general confession—that having spent nothing of my wages, I was itching to squander them at the capital.

Very probably my chance was approaching. The colonel was rapidly getting worse. He made his will, the notary receiving almost as many insults as did I. The invalid's treatment became more strict; short intervals of peace and rest became rarer then ever for me. Already I had lost the meager measure of pity that made me forget the old sufferer's excesses; inside of me seethed a cauldron of aversion and hatred. At the beginning of the month of August I decided definitely to leave. The vicar and the doctor, finally accepting my explanations, asked me but a few days' more service. I gave them a month. At the end of that time I would depart, whatever might be the condition of the invalid. The vicar promised to find me a substitute.

Now for what happened. On the evening of the 24th of August

the colonel had a violent attack of anger; he struck me, he called me the vilest names, he threatened to shoot me; finally he threw a plate of porridge that was too cold for him square in my face. The plate struck the wall and was shattered into a thousand fragments.

"You'll pay me for it, you thief!" he bellowed.

For a long time he grumbled. Towards eleven o'clock he gradually fell asleep. While he slept I took a book out of my pocket, a translation of an old d'Arlincourt romance which I had found lying about, and began to read it in his room, at a small distance from his bed. I was to wake him at midnight to give him his medicine; but, whether it was due to fatigue or to the influence of the book, I too, before reaching the second page, fell asleep. The cries of the colonel awoke me with a start; in an instant I was up. Apparently in a delirium, he kept shrieking the same cries; finally he seized his water-bottle and threw it at my face. I could not get out of the way in time; the bottle hit me in the left cheek, and the pain was so acute that I almost lost consciousness. With a leap I rushed upon the invalid; I tightened my hands around his neck; he struggled several moments; I strangled him.

When I beheld that he no longer breathed, I stepped back in terror. I cried out; but nobody heard me. Then, approaching the bed once more, I shook him, to bring him back to life. It was too late; the aneurism had burst, and the colonel was dead. I went into the adjoining room, and for two hours I did not dare to return. It is impossible for me to express all that I felt during that time. It was intense stupefaction, a kind of vague and vacant delirium. It seemed to me that I saw faces grinning on the walls; I heard muffled voices. The cries of the victim, the shrieks before the struggle and during its wild moments, continued to reverberate within me, and the air, in whatever direction I turned, seemed to shake with convulsions. Do not imagine that I am inventing pictures or aiming at verbal style. I swear to you that I heard distinctly voices that were crying at me: "Murderer! Murderer!"

All was quiet in the house. The tick-tick of the clock, very even, slow, dryly metrical, increased the silence and solitude. I put my ear to the door of the room, in hope of hearing a groan, a word, an insult, anything that would be a sign of life, that might bring back peace to my conscience; I was ready to let myself be struck ten, twenty, a hundred times, by the colonel's hand. But, nothing—all was silent. I began to pace the room aimlessly; I sat down, I brought my hands despairingly to my head; I repented ever having come to the place.

"Cursed be the hour in which I ever accepted such a position," I cried. And I flamed with resentment against the priest of Nictheroy, against the doctor, the vicar—against all those who had produced the place for me and forced me to remain there so long. They, too, I convinced myself, were accomplices in my crime.

As the silence finally terrified me, I opened a window, in the hope of hearing at least the murmuring of the wind. But no wind was blowing. The night was peaceful. The stars were sparkling with the indifference of those who remove their hats before a passing funeral procession and continue to speak of other things. I remained at the window for some time, my elbows on the sill, my gaze seeking to penetrate the night, forcing myself to make a mental summary of my life so that I might escape the present agony. I believe it was only then that I thought clearly about the penalty of my crime. I saw myself already accused and threatened with dire punishment. From this moment fear complicated my feeling of remorse. I felt my hair stand on end. A few minutes later I saw three or four human shapes spying at me from the terrace, where they seemed to be waiting in ambush; I withdrew; the shapes vanished into the air; it had been an hallucination.

Before daybreak I bandaged the wounds that I had received in the face. Then only did I pluck up enough courage to return to the other room. Twice I started, only to turn back; but it must be done, so I entered. Even then, I did not at first go to the bed. My legs shook, my heart pounded. I thought of flight; but that would have been a confession of the crime. ... It was on the contrary very important for me to hide all traces of it. I approached the bed. I looked at the corpse, with its widely distended eyes and its mouth gaping, as if uttering the eternal reproach of the centuries: "Cain, what hast thou done with thy brother?" I discovered on the neck the marks of my nails; I buttoned the shirt to the top, and drew the bed-cover up to the dead man's chin. Then I called a servant and told him that the colonel had died towards morning; I sent him to notify the vicar and the doctor.

The first idea that came to me was to leave as soon as possible under the pretext that my brother was ill; and in reality I had received, several days before, from Rio, a letter telling me that he was not at all well. But I considered that my immediate departure might arouse suspicion, and I decided to wait. I laid out the corpse myself, with the assistance of an old, near-sighted negro. I remained continually in the room of the dead. I trembled lest something out of the way should be discovered. I wanted to assure myself that no mistrust be read upon the faces of the others; but I did not dare to look any person in the eye. Everything made me impatient; the going and coming of those who, on tiptoe, crossed the room; their whisperings; the ceremonies and the prayers of the vicar. ... The hour having come, I closed the coffin, but with trembling hands, so trembling that somebody noticed it and commented upon it aloud, compassionately.

"Poor Procopio! Despite what he has suffered from his master, he is strongly moved."

It sounded like irony to me. I was anxious to have it all over with.

We went out. Once in the street the passing from semi-obscurity to day-light dazed me and I staggered. I began to fear that it would no longer be possible for me to conceal the crime. I kept my eyes steadily fixed upon the ground and took my place in the procession. When all was over, I breathed once more. I was at peace with man. But I was not at peace with my conscience, and the first nights, naturally, I spent in restlessness and affliction. Need I tell you that I hastened to return to Rio de Janeiro, and that I dwelt there in terror and suspense, although far removed from the scene of the crime? I never smiled; I scarcely spoke; I ate very little; I suffered hallucinations and nightmares. ...

"Let the dead rest in peace," they would say to me. "Such gloom is beyond all reason."

And I was happy to find how people interpreted my symptoms; I praised the dead man highly, calling him a good soul, surly, in truth, but with a heart of gold. And as I spoke in such wise, I convinced myself, at least for a few moments at a time. Another interesting phenomenon was taking place within me—I tell it to you because you will perhaps make some useful deduction from it—and that was, although I had very little religion in me, I had a mass sung for the eternal rest of the colonel at the Church of the Blessed Sacrament. I sent out no invitations to it, I did not whisper a word of it to anybody; I went there alone. I knelt during the whole service and made many signs of the cross. I paid the priest double and distributed alms at the door, all in the name of the deceased.

I wished to deceive nobody. The proof of this lies in the fact that I did all this without letting anybody know. To complete this incident, I may add that I never mentioned the colonel without repeating, "May his soul rest in peace!" And I told several funny anecdotes about him, some amusing caprices of his. ...

About a week after my arrival at Rio I received a letter from the vicar. He announced that the will of the colonel had been opened and that I was there designated as his sole heir. Imagine my stupefaction! I was sure that I had read wrongly; I showed it to my brother, to friends; they all read the same thing. It was there in black and white: I was really the sole heir of the colonel. Then suddenly it occurred to me that this was a trap to catch me; but then I considered that there were other ways of arresting me, if the crime had been discovered. Moreover, I knew the vicar's honesty, and I was sure that he would not be a party to such a plan. I reread the letter five times, ten times, a hundred times; it was true. I was the colonel's sole heir!

"How much was he worth?" my brother asked me.

"I don't know, but I know that he was very wealthy."

"Really, he's proved that he was a very true friend to you."

"He certainly was—he was. ..."

Thus, by a strange irony of fate, all the colonel's wealth came into my hands. At first I thought of refusing the legacy. It seemed odious to take a sou of that inheritance; it seemed worse than the reward of a hired assassin. For three days this thought obsessed me; but more and more I was thrust against this consideration: that my refusal would not fail to awake suspicion. Finally I settled upon a compromise; I would accept the inheritance and would distribute it in small sums, secretly.

This was not merely scruple on my part, it was also the desire to redeem my crime by virtuous deeds; and it seemed the only way to recover my peace of mind and feel that accounts were straight.

I made hurried preparations and left. As I neared the little village the sad event returned obstinately to my memory. Everything about the place, as I looked at it once again, suggested tragic deeds. At every turn in the road I seemed to see the ghost of the colonel loom. And despite myself, I evoked in my imagination his cries, his struggles, his looks on that horrible night of the crime. ...

Crime or struggle? Really, it was rather a struggle; I had been attacked, I had defended myself; and in self-defense. ... It had been an unfortunate struggle, a genuine tragedy. This idea gripped me. And I reviewed all the abuse he had heaped upon me; I counted the blows, the names. ... It was not the colonel's fault, that I knew well; it was his affliction that made him so peevish and even wicked. But I pardoned all, everything! ... The worst of it was the end of that fatal night. ... I also considered that in any case the colonel had not long to live. His days were numbered; did not he himself feel that? Didn't he say every now and then, "How much longer have I to live? Two weeks, or one, perhaps less?"

This was not life; it was slow agony, if one may so name the eternal martyrdom of that poor man. ... And who knows, who can say that the struggle and his death were not simply a coincidence? That was after all quite possible, it was even most probable; careful weighing of the matter showed that it couldn't have been otherwise. At length this idea, too, engraved itself upon my mind. ...

Something tugged at my heart as I entered the village; I wanted to run back; but I dominated my emotions and I pressed forward. I was received with a shower of congratulations. The vicar communicated to me the particulars of the will, enumerated the pious gifts, and, as he spoke, praised the Christian forbearance and the faithfulness which I had shown in my care of the deceased, who, despite his temper and brutality, had so well demonstrated his gratitude.

"Certainly," I said, looking nervously around.

I was astounded. Everybody praised my conduct. Such patience, such devotion. The first formalities of the inventory detained me for a while; I chose a solicitor; things followed their course in regular fashion.

During this time there was much talk of the colonel. People came and told me tales about him, but without observing the priest's moderation. I defended the memory of the colonel. I recalled his good qualities, his virtues; had he not been austere?...

"Austere!" they would interrupt. "Nonsense! He is dead, and it's all over now. But he was a regular demon!"

And they would cite incidents and relate the colonel's perversities, some of which were nothing less than extraordinary.

Need I confess it? At first I listened to all this talk with great curiosity; then, a queer pleasure penetrated my heart, a pleasure from which, sincerely, I tried to escape. And I continued to defend the colonel; I explained him, I attributed much of the fault-finding to local animosity; I admitted, yes, I admitted that he had been a trifle exacting, somewhat violent. ...

"Somewhat! Why he was as furious as a snake!" exclaimed the barber.

And all—the collector, the apothecary, the clerk—all were of the same opinion. And they would start to relate other anecdotes. They reviewed the entire life of the deceased. The old folks took particular delight in recalling the cruelties of his youth. And that queer pleasure, intimate, mute, insidious, grew within me—a sort of moral tapeworm whose coils I tore out in vain, for they would immediately form again and take firmer hold than ever.

The formalities of the inventory afforded me a little relief; moreover, public opinion was so unanimously unfavorable to the colonel that little by little the place lost the lugubrious aspect that had at first struck me. At last I entered into possession of the legacy, which I converted into land-titles and cash.

Several months had elapsed, and the idea of distributing the inheritance in charity and pious donations was by no means so strong as at first it had been; it even seemed to me that this would be sheer affectation. I revised my initial plan; I gave away several insignificant sums to the poor; I presented the village church with a few new ornaments; I gave several thousand francs to the Sacred House of Mercy, etc. I did not forget to erect a monument upon the colonel's grave—a very simple monument, all marble, the work of a Neapolitan sculptor who remained at Rio until 1866, and who has since died, I believe, in Paraguay.

Years have gone by. My memory has become vague and unreliable. Sometimes I think of the colonel, but without feeling again the terrors of those early days. All the doctors to whom I have described his afflictions have been unanimous as regards the inevitable end in store for the invalid, and were indeed surprised that he should so long have resisted. It is just possible that I may have involuntarily exaggerated the description of his various symptoms; but the truth is that he was sure of sudden death, even had this fatality not occurred. ...

Good-bye, my dear sir. If you deem these notes not totally devoid of value reward me for them with a marble tomb, and place there for my epitaph this variant which I have made of the divine Sermon on the Mount:

"Blessed are they who possess, for they shall be consoled."

Peru

VENTURA GARCÍA-CALDERÓN

(1890—1956)

GARCÍA-CALDERON, born at Lima of an old Peruvian family, was one of the most distinguished critics and literary historians of South America. He was also a fastidious writer of verse. His short stories are clearly the work of a poet, and are characterized by an extreme delicacy of style and treatment.

The Legend of Pygmalion is translated by Isaac Goldberg especially for this collection and included by his permission. It has never before appeared in English.

THE LEGEND OF PYGMALION

I. THE ARTIST

WHEN Pygmalion had finished that statue, he smiled. The enchanted smile of children discovering the world! Truly it was perfect, unsurpassable. Just as the ancient sculptors of idols venerated the deity created by themselves, so would he gladly have fallen to his knees in adoration. About him, on rough pedestals or on the ground, close by, farther off, on shelves or on the window seats, a marble populace rigid in attitudes of grace and abandon. All the dreams of a now declining youth lay there as in a living quarry. This was why, out of a maternal modesty, he forbade access to his atelier. What could others be seeking in this abode? Only curiosity or the desire to carp could bring them. And here he had bared his soul.

There were blocks as vague as chrysalides of thought; in others, only the hinted outlines of a hip. There the chisel had traced coarse furrows as if Pygmalion, in the grip of the creative demon, had cracked the marble with heavy blows, in his eagerness to impart to this inert matter the living gesture. And successive sketches of a work, from the confused embryo to the perfect image, revealed sadly the painful task of conception.

But amid all these sister images, amid this white populace united by the kinship of a selfsame fever and a selfsame pain, none could equal in victorious rapture the virgin Galatea, bending her light head over the mirror of her hand, the better to admire its graceful negligence. Pygmalion had informed her with the evanescent and legendary delicacy of Psyche.

The imagination added short wings to the lightness of the feet; the softness of the stomach recalled the vases of the school of Athens; the arms formed such a glorious chain that, joining to embrace a favorite, they could hold him fast till death.

Pygmalion gazed at his palms, still white with dust, doubting that he had completed this marvel with hands that were destined to die. It was possible, then, for the human artificer to wrest from the gods the secret of beauty. Without self-deception, with that clairvoyance of the hours of loftiest judgment, he knew that this time, by a miracle, he had fashioned the eternal masterpiece. Ah, how he remembered his failures before the uncompleted marbles, when his idea lingered and, face to face with the truncated form, he felt his hands so clumsy and his mind so dull! This was an agony that no death relieved. Bitter tears, towering rages, almost an iconoclastic fury, at the disproportion between his petty accomplishment and the cherished ideal.

II. THE MIRACLE

Evening descended upon these virginal forms. But the white mass resisted the shadows, and when the walls were draped in mourning, these bodies still shed light. The very gloom lent them grace and the illusion of nakedness. At this hour Pygmalion could feel them throb with a life that was different from the changeless existence of marble. Twilight tinged their limbs with its ruddy flame and on their breasts the setting sun traced a lingering hand.

That evening the zephyrs pulsed with voluptuousness. From the near-by sea where Venus ruled in her naked chastity, came an enervating languor. First Pygmalion kissed her naked feet, nestling his feverish head against her nubile thighs. Then, with a brusque movement, he arose on the pedestal and sealed her speechless lips with the human compact of a kiss. It was the first kiss of love. He lowered his eyes in shame. Suddenly, however, they grew wide with amazement and thrilling terror before the miracle: the statue had come to life and was stirring. A blush of blood rose to its cheeks. A tremor of life rippled down from its neck to its rosy feet. Slowly, slowly, with rhythmic pauses, the breasts began to rise. And the terrified lashes fluttered before the light.

Now he no longer doubted. His hands became as tender as a gardener's. At their touch, the marble lost all weight and hardness. The tresses became as black as if the night had been kneaded into them, but the eyes acquired the luminosity of the sea.

She did not speak; she smiled with an expression of astonishment upon her radiant face. Like a child in a cradle she stretched out a hand to touch Pygmalion's hair. As she parted the dark locks, she laughed. It was a clear laughter. He spoke a few words, and for the first time her smooth forehead wrinkled in an effort to understand.

She was lulled in a tender stupor, for doubtless life is more fatiguing than motionless eternity. Delirious, as if after infinite labors he were about to lose his greatest work, Pygmalion watched for signs of life. In her repose, Galatea, with her arms crossed over her bosom, her lips supine and on her face such a sleeping abandon, evoked not the proud image of a marble goddess but that of sad flesh seeking the shelter of love. By divine consent she had been fashioned, not of common clay, but of pure marble. And, as in the hours of creation, so he too felt divine.

All that night he kept vigil over this tender life. At the first glimmer of daybreak his amazement was repeated. All trace of marmorean life had disappeared in Galatea. Perhaps in her flesh there remained the polished softness where caresses glide. But in her lips and in her arms, in the hair that cascaded over her shoulders, there were an earthly grace and frailty. Only in her eyes without pupils there floated the vagueness of an Olympian remembrance.

She did not speak because she had been eternal. Doubtless, with the light there entered into her mind a confused perception of earthly things. Her soul was like those Hindu blocks of ivory whereon one may sculpture alike the goatish visage of the satyr and the face of Pallas Athena.

III. THE INITIATION

Pygmalion became her master and her guide. This manner of teaching filled him with a confused intoxication, like to that of one who models the cherished image in wax. And, as the features of human beauty are adumbrated in the hazy sketch, so in this ingenuous child appeared—with a more than terrestrial charm—the first restlessness of womanhood. No longer did she wander among the slabs of the atelier; nor did she lie upon the marble blocks, so crude and full of possibilities, into which her body seemed ready to merge and thus suddenly return to its primal element. Perhaps some dim memory induced in her a preference for the nearness of this pure material. Standing, she assumed always the attitude of a goddess. And when she reclined in meditation, she became the supple form that advances in the procession of the Panathenæa.

Aureoled thus in pure, resplendent white, at every hour before the astonished artist she repeated the miracle of a dream come true. From the depths of his soul there rose to Pygmalion's lips thanks with no definite goal, fervor for that blind Fate which had been so kindly. Art, his sculpture, did not appear to him, as in past hours of ennui, the sterile labors of a solitary fanatic, but the glorious replacement of the unknown God, for he, like God, could create in living flesh. What mattered mortal sleeplessness while waiting for the inspiration that never came, the untranscribable madness of night and the cold disillusionment of the morrow, which daily dies, the grievous solitude of him who dreams because every aspiring ecstasy is a punishment! To create, to feel one's hands strong as claws for molding all the clay in the world, to be for a moment God after having so many times been wretched and powerless!

The urgency of tears wrinkled his features. In his veins began the prostration of one about to pray. On his knees now, he twined his arms around her strong legs, which were almost virile like those of the hermaphrodite. Intoxicating as the perfumes of the nocturnal woods, as those wines that madden thirst, there breathed from her youth a feline aroma. It was the odor that sent the centaurs galloping with their voracious nostrils opened wide.

Thought Pygmalion: "Why is a kiss not enough? Why, from our double nature of horse and man rises the harshness of possession? Lust, thou art blended even with the highest purity!"

And on one voluptuous evening, Galatea, with her clear pupils dilated, learned the wonder and the terror of being a woman. For that avid lover, woman, or all womankind incarnate in a single insuperable body, there were madnesses of possession, cries, sighs, languorous tendernesses until dawn, fatigue resembling death, divine deaths from which one does not wish to rise. Before the changing spectacle of that sea were repeated the childish stammerings, the interrupted vows that lovers in all times have invented to lull and deceive the brevity of love.

The waves, with their unceasing restlessness, gave them an image of life's inconstancy. But they did not understand its lesson.

IV. WEARINESS

Thought Pygmalion, not daring to say it in words: "O godly form, despite your divine origin, you shall die. Worm and rot, instead of the eternity that I have dreamed. To reveal to myself my godly powers, I subjected you to the law of death. But I'll not be able to bear that you should die. Let me die instead, and let my flesh rot; but you must remain unchangeable, immune to time. Ah, why did I teach you love!"

With a nameless anguish he espied in his perfect companion each hollow and wrinkle. Then began sad days of terrible memory when love, having reached the summit, descends the hill with wings folded across her soft shoulders. But no, as in earthly passion, blindness prolonged his affection, save that in Pygmalion's eyes, unfortunately, was the clairvoyance of the artist accustomed to notice in the skin of the marble as in the flesh, the coarse grain and the future crack. In the hue of dawn his artist's nerves at times tingled to exasperation. He would surprise in the face of the sleeping woman that fatigue which changes all beauty. The delicate charm of her abandon still provoked kisses, even as does a sleeping child; but the breasts were losing their supple firmness, no longer pointing as before their desires to the skies.

In the corners of his studio Pygmalion meditated, weeping: "You have given me everything, and yet... You have revealed to me felicities the mere memory of which makes me swoon. But happiness, like grief, can weary us. Because I did not know that dreams, translated to earth, are corrupted, I wished to endow you with an inferior reality, that of life. Ah, beautiful creations should remain eternal! And behold me now, sad and loving, vacillating between an unholy crime, that I may not witness the misery of a perfection destined to-morrow to be sullied, and the most human, the deepest desire to let you live, though my dream be shattered, that I may not lose—O cowardice!—this daily commerce of happiness."

Pygmalion joined his hands and wept. From the sea came those raucous accents that to great hearts are as cooings. His impatient hands trembled anew with the fever for new forms.

But for a few days the aridity of an unbounded fatigue followed upon this plenitude. Art seemed to him a new lie invented to satisfy the need of adoration. It was as servility and a superstition worthy of slaves.

If Galatea cried, his pity returned convulsively. And though she did not understand his words, he said to her in that low voice in which dreams are told or children are spoken to: "O my Galatea, do not weep. My reason for living is these creatures of marble. You, at least, have felt the possibility of eternal being. But I, an earthly creature with divine promptings, do not resign myself to death. Though my cherished dreams float off on the wind, my finest enthusiasms shall have been for a fleeting moment part of eternity. At least let not the evidences of my madness die. A little of our wretched nature remains living in our eternal labors. My friend, my wife, tell me that you understand my grief."

But the sweetly unknowing one could only weep. In a brief space her eyes had lost their clearness of rare and luminous stones; her breasts were no longer clusters tipped with the pink grape; wasted was the line of the hips.

She was journeying to her ruin, pale and austere as the statue of Fate. Through need of sharpening her agony, she recalled the olden shining hours of vows and kisses, as if a wasted face could rouse in her beloved the selfsame worship that her inviolate beauty had won. Daily, between one who aspired to self-perfection and his conquered, abandoned companion, the separation increased.

Pygmalion would not deceive her with creatures of flesh, but with new dreams.

Galatea compared herself with those pure sisters of the atelier, envying the immutable virtue of the stone that knows neither grief nor age. After these human lusts she began to feel the selfsame yearning of the gods: self-annihilation.

But, wretched creature that she was, she could not die at her wish.

v. FEVER

And because on one dazzling morning the light revealed her deformation, Pygmalion foresaw her inevitable fate. Without wakening her, when night came he took his chisel and struck her bosom a blow. There came the roar of the sea, unfailing and intermittent, like Fate herself. And in the gloom that is so favorable to the dreams of the poets, Pygmalion said: "Why art thou so cruel, O Beauty? It were better that I should be blind. Why does human ugliness so much offend me, and why dream if every dead dream becomes a corpse?"

His hands felt the cold body. He trembled as he divined the new miracle: Galatea was returning to the original marble. Her body was acquiring the firmness and the inert smoothness of the pure divine matter. Her tresses grew fixed in salient lines like hard veins. And even a tear on her cheek had turned to stone.

Oh, wonder of the creative soul, emotion of death or of miracle! To remedy the imperfections of this ruined flesh his ancient frenzy returned. He groped in the dark for his chisel and hammer. All that night he chiseled. In the wondrous silence the blows of his hammer seemed like the throbs of a vast bosom. To this human matter conquered by grief—this shroud with which we come into the world—succeeded a flesh resistant to the centuries, indomitably firm, incorruptible and pure. In this gloom and silence so favorable to perennial creation, Pygmalion felt his hands agitated by a quivering of wings. At moments they rose caressingly to form a shield upon each breast; he was yet too close to the image of the ardent woman for the statue not to appear still docile to the slavery of life and love. But after this loving interlude there resounded anew, as vehement as cries of victory, as wild as shouts of jubilation, thunderous and rhythmical, the blows of the hammer that were to resuscitate this marble life.

VI. THE MELODY OF GRIEF

A pale dawn hovered. With the first gleams the sea awoke, stretching its golden scales. Across the heavens as purple as martyred flesh flew black arrows of birds. And a beam came to encircle like a collar the neck of Galatea.

Pygmalion, wearied after that night, lay sleeping. Awakening, he rubbed his eyes that were freighted with visions, for this had doubtless been a nightmare. The statue was not his, his Galatea Victrix. The lips had lost their curve of a taut bow. With the human precision of pupils these eyes told the grief of living. A maternal milk films and conquers these breasts; the hips have lost their softness; the fragile frame is bent toward Mother Earth. Instead of the statue of potent Beauty, all night long he has been sculpturing the very face of grief. His hands, formerly as exact as pupils, have deceived him, and now his eyes, too, must be deceiving him. No pain is comparable to that of the creator before whose piercing sight is unfolded the sterile perspective of an uninspired future.

Death is preferable, when consoling vanity does not come to suggest victorious to-morrows. He who has known the anguish of the perishable is no longer capable of eternal masterpieces. He was punished in his divinity for having adored the imperfect creatures of this world.

And he was like a man weeping over a ruin.

Venezuela

RUFINO BLANCO-FOMBONA

(1874–1944)

BLANCO-FOMBONA was born at Caracas, in Venezuela, in 1874. He came of an old and aristocratic family of Spanish descent. His extraordinary activities, not only as a writer, but as politician, revolutionary soldier, and government employee, together with his picturesque personal exploits, all contributed to make him one of the most interesting figures in Spanish-America. He travelled in many parts of the world. His writings include criticism, poetry, political essays, novels, and short stories, the first collection of which appeared in 1900. Of *Creole Democracy*, perhaps his finest short story, Dr. Goldberg has said that "not many tales that have come out of South America can match it."

The present version, revised from an earlier version, is here printed by permission of the translator, Isaac Goldberg.

CREOLE DEMOCRACY

THE hamlet of Camoruco stands at one of the gateways to the Plains. The wagon-road cuts the little settlement squarely and neatly in two, like the parting of a dandy's hair. Stretched out upon the savanna, the village consists of two rows of houses which stand in a file along the edge of the road, and seem to peer furtively upon the passer-by. They look like a double row of sparrows upon two parallel telegraph wires. Close by flows the Guárico, an abundant stream that irrigates the pampas; in its sands slumbers the skate-fish and on its banks, with half-open jaws, the lazy alligators take their noonday rest.

It was election time; a governor of the Department was to be chosen. For certain political reasons the interest of an appreciable part of the Republic was centered upon the contest. *El Faro (The Lighthouse)*, a backwoods sheet which had been established for the occasion, declared its opening number: "Perhaps for the first time in Camoruco, the elections will cease to be the work of a group of petty politicians, mere vote-manufacturers; perhaps for the first time in Camoruco the elective fabric will be woven by the unsullied hands of the people."

The number of candidates had dwindled to two. On the eve of the election the local bosses, wealthy cattle-breeders of the district, brought into the neighboring town, which served as a business center for the shacks of the outlying settlements, herds of peons, submissive farm hands, good, simple plainsmen, ignorant of everything, even of what they were to do in the next day's election; for these peons, rounded up like cattle, were the citizens, that is to say, the voters. The apparel of most of them consisted of drill trousers and striped shirts; on their feet, hempen sandals; on their heads, the high-crowned, wide-brimmed sombrero, or the saffron-colored *pelo de guama;* around their waists, slung diagonally like a baldric, the red and blue sash; in their right hands, like a cane, they carried the peasant weapon, the ever-present *machete.* A goodly number of these simple citizens were of medium height, muscular, bronzed by the sun and by their mixed blood, and recalled the classic plainsmen of Apure and Arauca,—those terrible centaurs of General Páez, in the armies of Bolívar, those mighty warriors who captured the Spanish war vessels on horseback, at the point of the lance, and of whom a hundred and fifty attacked six thousand of Morillo's soldiers, as in the *Queseras del Medio*,—those heroes of the pampas who live in history, on canvas, in ballads, in epic, and above all, in the popular imagination.

The parties concerned in the election, like the candidates, were two. The efforts of the party-leaders were directed towards herding the largest possible number of men. Each faction in Camoruco was quartered in its own district; one to the north, the other to the south of the village. As new groups of peons continued to arrive, the bosses of each side would spy upon each other to see how many voters were being added to their rival's forces. "See here," they would say to some trusted farm hand, "go and take a look at those dunderheads." Meanwhile party-hacks were going from group to group, explaining the procedure of the morrow's election. But despite all explanations, the simple rustics displayed a certain suspiciousness. Many believed that plans for an armed uprising were afoot. In one of the groups, particularly, a feeling of mistrust grew apace. Wild talk arose. "Elections!" scoffed one *vaquero*, as chubby and brown as a sausage. "Before long we'll be hearing Pum Pum!—and then, ho, for stabbing hides!"

To this bit of grim humor in the face of possible tragedy another *vaquero* added: "Yes. Soon we'll be hearing 'Two shots, boys, then out with your *machetes*.'"

This was a slogan familiar to everybody, and many smiled bitterly at the memories it awoke. "Two shots, boys, then out with your *machetes*." This was the cry of the revolutionary officers in time of battle, for, lacking ammunition as they generally did, the method of the rebels was to fire one or two rounds and then charge upon the enemy battalions with their naked blades. The government mausers, however, would always wreak swift vengeance and in a few minutes the battlefield would be heaped with the corpses of the insurgents. But the few who succeeded in reaching the soldiers alive would avenge their fallen comrades, for in a hand-to-hand struggle a heavy gun is a hindrance rather than a help and against the furious *machete* neither the bayonet nor anything else can avail. One must then choose between death or flight.

"What I don't like about all this business," declared one of the peons, "is that they don't tell a fellow the truth. If we're going to war, let's go; but let 'em not hide it from us."

All agreed that the complaint was justified. If they knew the truth they could at least bid farewell to their wives, their children, their mothers.

"They take us for hens."

"No, not for hens, but for chattering magpies."

"That's right. They're not afraid that we'll run off into hiding like so many hens or women, but that we'll squeal on them, that we'll betray the uprising and inform the commissary or the magistrate."

Then an old, experienced mulatto, with a grayish head and a forehead furrowed by a deep scar, began to quell the dissension. "That's the way those things are done, boys. In '92, when we started a revolt in El Totum under General Crespo..." And he plunged into his memories of army life. They all listened to him with pleasure, for the old plainsman, in his way and for his kind, was a true *causeur*. In the midst of the reminiscences one of the party-leaders called from a distance to the talkative old fellow. "Hey, Ramón, old boy!"

Old Ramón, before answering, tried to finish his tale by cutting it short. But the boss called again: "Ramón, old boy, come here!" For he wanted old Ramón to give "the boys" to understand, and to understand himself, that the events of the next day had nothing to do with warfare, but only with electing a president of the Department.

Evening began to fall. Darkness drew its curtains of funeral velvet across the verdant plain, across the road, here yellow and there spotted with red patches; across the radiant azure of the heavens. The sounds of night began to be heard: the rustling of the breeze, the lowing of cattle, the shrilling of grasshoppers, the croaking of frogs. The wakening stars pierced the first shadows and descended to bathe their luminous eyes in the Guárico, and as it mirrored their gold the river flowed gently onward in the night, like a golden Pactolus. Eight o'clock strikes. Camoruco is going to sleep, for the little hamlet arises with the dawn; and it closes its eyes when the stars begin to open theirs. Only from the headquarters of the two political factions there continues to be heard now the strumming of a guitar, now the plaint of a creole song. Bottles have been circulating freely during the afternoon, and that restlessness, that wailing of the guitar and the làmentation of that song are only the result of the brandy of the plains which, when it does not make for ferocity, makes for melancholy, and when it does not shed blood, sheds tears. The strains of a folk-song rise in the air:

> "Two kisses my poor soul treasures,
> That never forgot shall be:
> The last that I gave my mother,
> And the first that I gave to thee.

> On the door that leads to the prison
> Is written in chalk this verse:
> 'Tis here that the good man turns bad man,
> And the bad man changes to worse."

Presently one of the party-leaders appears before the circle from which the song is rising. "How about someone to go and take a look at what's doing yonder?" he suggests. "Yonder" meant the other faction. A thousand voices seemed to reply: "I." "I." "I."

The man chosen for the errand was a *vaquero* of some twenty years, dark, robust, beardless, with tiny eyes as black as two *paraperas*. As he rose to go on his errand, the unsuccessful volunteers began to taunt him:

"How can they send that cow?"

"Be sure to cry out loud, now, when you want us to come to your help."

"Here's a woman to go along and keep you company."

The boss intervened. "Peace, gentlemen, peace; and everybody to bed. To-morrow we conquer the enemy." But despite the presence of his leader the chosen man retorted with three or four coarse gibes and left. As he stalked along the road he thought: "What do those scoundrels imagine? That we'll conquer the enemy to-morrow? I wish the row broke out to-night! They think I'm afraid. I oughtn't to have listened to them. The beasts!"

The road was deserted. Everything was veiled in shadow. A fine drizzle began to fall. As the youth walked meditatively along there came to his ears from the distance, on the rainy wings of the breeze, snatches of music. Those of the other party were having a good time, too. The young plainsman thought again of his companions' jests, and growled: "The beasts!"

Suddenly it seemed to him that he could dimly make out a form in the darkness and he placed himself on guard. The form was approaching from the opposite direction. As it came near, the youth recognized an old man belonging to the hostile faction. "Where are you going, old man?"

"Taking the fresh air hereabouts."

"Taking the fresh air! You're a spy! And you're out to spy on us!"

"Spy? So is your mother, you scoundrel!"

There were no more words. Two *machetes* cleaved the darkness and the old man, his head split in two, was stretched in the mire, under the rain, dying like a dog.

The youth ran off at once to his leader and not without a certain boastfulness told, in the presence of all, just what had occurred.

"Kill an old man!" jeered one of the group. "Why not an old woman?"

The leader sternly rebuked the young plainsman. "You have committed a crime, a needless crime. They'll soon be after you. I can't do a thing. Quick! Off to the mountains!"

The boy was perplexed. What? Flee to the mountains, run away like

a wild animal? Then it was true that this was a crime? But—the devil!
Wasn't that old man one of the enemy?

"Be off, friend. I'll bring the news to your ranch."

The youth vanished amid the thin drizzle into the gloom...

His flight betrayed him. ... At last, wearied of his wandering,
hazardous existence, he delivered himself up "to justice."... The
morning when they sentenced him, finding himself condemned without hope of reprieve to the penal settlement, the poor fellow burst
into tears before the court, sobbing: "But weren't we supposed to
conquer them? Weren't they our enemies?"

Nicaragua

RUBÉN DARÍO

(1867—1916)

RUBÉN DARÍO is one of the few Spanish-American writers who have
won international celebrity. He first became known as a boy poet,
but soon after his sensational appearance in the field of literature, he
became a journalist. His travels began at an early age. He was in the
diplomatic service and represented his country in several cities abroad.
Of a rather melancholy and neurotic temperament, he had none the
less an extremely varied and active career, and in spite of his diplomatic
and other duties he continued to write. Though he is best known
as a poet, he is the author of several short stories and books of travel.
His volume of prose tales and poems called *Azul* (1888) attracted notice
in Europe. It is from this collection that *The Deaf Satyr* is selected.
This charming idyll exemplifies Darío's outstanding qualities of style
and literary form.

The present version is translated by Isaac Goldberg especially for this
collection and included by his permission.

THE DEAF SATYR

THERE dwelt near Mount Olympus a satyr, and he was the ancient
king of his forest. The gods had said to him: "Rejoice, the woods
are yours; be a merry rascal, hunt the nymphs and let your flute be
heard." And the satyr took his pleasure.

On a day that father Apollo was playing his divine lyre, the satyr left his dominions, daring to ascend the sacred mount and surprise the long-haired god. Whereupon the god punished him by turning him as deaf as a rock. In vain from the denseness of the forest filled with birds poured trills and sounded gentle cooing. The satyr heard nothing. Philomel, over his tangled hair that was crowned with vine shoots, sang songs that halted the streams in their course and turned the pale roses a blushing red. He remained impassive or howled with savage laughter, leaping in joyous wantonness when, through the openings of the branches, he espied a white round hip that the sun was caressing with its golden light. The animals fawned upon him as a master to be obeyed.

Before his eyes, to divert him danced choruses of bacchantes aflame with their mad fever; close by him, providing the musical accompaniment, were the adolescent fauns, beautiful youths, who caressed him reverently with their smiles; and though he heard no voice, nor the sound of the castanets, he found pleasure after his own fashion. Thus did this bearded king with the goatish feet pass his days.

He was a capricious satyr.

He had two court counselors: a lark and an ass. The first had lost her prestige when the satyr went deaf. Formerly, when, weary with lust, he softly played his flute, the lark accompanied him.

Afterward, in his great forest, where he could not hear even the voice of Olympian thunder, the patient animal of the long ears served him as mount, while the lark, at break of dawn, flew out of his hands, singing on her flight to the skies.

The forest was vast. To the lark belonged the tree-tops; to the ass, the pasture. The lark was greeted by the first gleams of dawn; she drank dew in the shoots; she awoke the oak, singing to it, "Old oak, awake." She rejoiced in a kiss from the sun; she was beloved by the morning star. And the blue firmament so vast knew that she, so tiny, dwelt beneath its immensity. The ass (though he had not yet conversed with Kant) was an expert in philosophy, according to common report. The satyr, who saw him browsing in the pasture, swaying his ears with a solemn air, held such a thinker in high esteem. In those days the ass was not so famous as to-day. As he moved his jaws, one could hardly have imagined that men yet would write in his praise: Daniel Heinsius, in Latin; Passerat, Buffon and the great Hugo, in French; Posada and Valderrama, in Spanish.

Phlegmatically, if the flies bit him, he would frighten them off with his tail, kick from time to time and send forth, under the vault of the woods, the strange noise of his throat. He was the petted favorite there. As he took his midday nap on the dark and grateful earth, the plants and flowers gave out their sweetest scents. And the great trees inclined their foliage to lend him shade.

It was in those days that Orpheus, affrighted at the misery of mankind, bethought himself to flee to the woods, where the trunks and the stones would understand him and listen in ecstasy, and where he could tremble with harmony and the fire of love and life to the sounds of his instrument.

When Orpheus plucked his lyre there was a smile on the countenance of Apollo. Demeter thrilled with pleasure. The palm-trees shed their pollen, the seeds burst, the lions gently moved their manes. Once a carnation flew from its stem transformed into a red butterfly, and a star came down from the heavens in thrall and became a fleur de lis.

What forest better than the forest of the satyr, whom he would enchant, where he would be held as a demigod; a forest all joy, and dancing, and beauty, and voluptuousness; where nymphs and bacchantes were ever fondled and ever virginal; where there were grapes and roses and the noise of the sistrum, and where the goat-footed king danced drunk before his fauns, making gestures like Silenus?

He went with his wreath of laurel, his lyre, his proud poet's mien, erect and radiant.

He came to where the wild and hairy satyr ruled, and at his request for hospitality, he sang. He sang of great Jove, of Eros and Aphrodite, of the graceful centaurs and of the ardent bacchantes; he sang the cup of Dionysus, and the thyrsus that strikes the joyous air, and of Pan, emperor of the mountains, sovereign of the woods, god-satyr who, too, could sing. He sang the intimacies of the air and earth, the great mother. Thus he expounded the melody of an Æolian harp, the murmuring of a grove, the hoarse whisper of a shell, and the harmonious notes that issue from the syrinx. He sang of verse which flies down from the sky and pleases the gods, of verse which accompanies the barbiton in the ode and beats time in the pæan. He sang the breasts of tepid snow and the cups of wrought gold, and the throat of the bird and the glory of the sun.

And from the very beginning of his canticle the light of day shone with brighter gleams. The huge trunks were moved and there were roses that shed their petals and lilies that bent over languorously as in a tender swoon. For Orpheus, with the music of his rhythmic lyre, made the lions to moan and the very stones to weep. The most furious of the bacchantes had grown silent and listened to him as in a trance. A virgin naiad who never had been profaned by so much as a single glance of the satyr, drew timorously near to the singer and said to him, "I love you..." Philomel had flown down and alighted upon the lyre, like the Anacreontic bird. Now only the voice of Orpheus resounded. Nature thrilled to the hymn. Venus, who was in the near-by skies, asked from afar in her heavenly voice, "Can Apollo, perchance, be here?"

And in all that vastness of wondrous harmony, the only one who did not hear was the deaf satyr.

When the poet had ended, he said to the satyr, "Did you like my song? If you did, I shall remain with you in the forest."

The satyr looked at his two counselors. They must settle what he could not understand. That glance asked an opinion.

"Master," spoke the lark, forcing her throat to make its loudest sounds, "let him remain who thus has sung for us. Behold, his lyre is beautiful and powerful. He has offered you the grandeur and the radiance that you have beheld to-day in your forest. He has given you his harmony. Master, I understand these things. When the naked dawn has come and the world awakes, I rise to the highest skies and shed from yonder heights the invisible pearls of my trills, and my melody fills the air amid the morning brightness, and is the gladness of all space. I, then, tell you that Orpheus has sung well, and is of the elect of the gods. His music intoxicated the whole forest. The eagles drew near and flew above our heads, the flowering bushes gently swayed their mysterious censers, the bees left their cells to come and listen. As for me, O Master were I in your place I should yield to him my garland of vine-shoots and my thyrsus. There exist two powers: the real and the ideal. What Hercules would do with his wrists, Orpheus does with his inspiration. With a single blow the robust god could shatter Mount Athos itself. Orpheus, with the potency of his triumphant voice, could subdue Nemea's lion and the wild boar of Erimanthus. Of men, some have been born to forge metals, others to wrest from the soil the ears of wheat, others to fight in bloody wars, and others still to teach, to glorify, and to sing. If I am your cupbearer and I give you wine, it is the joy of your palate; if I offer you a hymn, it is the joy of your soul."

As the lark sang her song, Orpheus accompanied her on his instrument, and a vast, overpowering lyric gust escaped from the green and fragrant wood. The deaf satyr was getting restless. Who was this strange visitor? Why had the mad, voluptuous dance abruptly ceased before him? What said his two counselors?

Ah, the lark has sung, but the satyr could not hear! At last he turned his gaze toward the ass.

Was his opinion desired? Very well, then; before the vast, sonorous forest, underneath the sacred blue, the ass moved his head from one side to the other, austerely, obstinately, silently, like a philosopher in thought.

Then, with his cloven hoof, the satyr struck the ground, wrinkled his brow with displeasure, and unheedingly exclaimed, pointing out to Orpheus the road from the forest:

"No!"

The echo reached to neighboring Olympus, and from the mountain, where the gods were at play, resounded a chorus of formidable guffaws that were afterward called Homeric.

Orpheus strode sadly from the forest of the deaf satyr, almost ready to hang himself upon the first laurel tree that he encountered on the road.

He did not hang himself, however; he married Eurydice.

The United States

INTRODUCTION

IT need hardly be said that the literature of the United States is a direct offshoot of that of England. The writings of the early Colonial period differ from the contemporaneous writings of the mother country, when they differ at all, only in subject-matter. It was only natural that the Puritan influence should predominate in New England for a long time after the arrival of the *Mayflower* in 1620; as a matter of fact, it is still a potent force in American life and art.

American fiction is therefore a late growth. Charles Brockden Brown (1771-1810) is usually regarded as the first novelist, but it was James Fenimore Cooper (1789-1851) and Washington Irving (1783-1859) who, by their genuinely American stories and undoubted talents as writers, first won places for themselves among the readers of the new land.

The earlier years of the Nineteenth Century witnessed the sporadic appearance of such writers as Irving, men who turned their hand to the short-story form and utilized it for the interpretation of what was later termed the American Scene; but not until the advent of Poe can it be properly asserted that the short story came into its own. Poe's stories are probably the most famous as they were certainly the most influential of any written within the past four centuries. But he had at least one contemporary who was as great an artist as he: Hawthorne, though primarily a novelist, began writing excellent short stories as early as the thirties. Poe's followers—those both directly influenced by him as well as those who were not—were numerous. Among the more important may be mentioned Rose Terry Cooke (1827-1892) and Fitz-James O'Brien (1828-1862). Somewhat later several writers of distinction played important rôles in the development of the short story: Sarah Orne Jewett, Bret Harte, Henry James, Frank Stockton, H. C. Bunner, William Dean Howells, are only a few of a far larger group that contributed a mass of short-story literature to American letters. Steadily, from the seventies to the present day, American writers have studied the form, consciously treating it as an artistic medium of expression, with the result that during the past twenty-five to thirty years the American story has been brought to a point of technical perfection which is unsurpassed. The most celebrated of all modern American story-writers was Sydney W. Porter, known as O. Henry, who did more to popularize his craft than any other of his generation.

The whole aspect and the spirit of American literature has changed since the death of O. Henry in 1910. The occasionally inspired "unknowns" of the eighties and nineties, like Bierce and Crane, were discovered and put into vogue during the last few years. But even before that Dreiser had blazed the trail, and when the War came, there was a new "school" ready to turn the short story to their own ends. With the advent of Anderson and Dreiser (who turned to the short story long after he had begun his career as a novelist), of Willa Cather and a hundred others, the writers of the late Nineteenth Century seemed outmoded. The new writers had, among other things, shown a remarkable talent for exposing the absurdity and complacency of the nationalistic idealism of the Brahmin writers; they were naturalistic on the whole, and they represented a national tendency of thought. This naturalistic impulse necessarily aroused antagonism among the satirists and the idealists, observable in the stories of James Branch Cabell; but in spite of them the trend of the time is toward the depiction and interpretation of all aspects of contemporary life and thought.

WASHINGTON IRVING

(1783–1859)

WASHINGTON IRVING was born in New York City in 1783, during the British occupation. He was in the diplomatic service for the greater part of his productive years, and wrote several of his books abroad. In many ways Irving is a product of the Eighteenth Century. Of his numerous historical works, biographies and travel sketches, several are still read with pleasure. His most famous collection of stories is *The Sketch Book* (1819), which contains *Rip Van Winkle* and the story that follows in these pages. *The Specter Bridegroom* is one of the earliest examples of the American short story.

THE SPECTER BRIDEGROOM

(From *The Sketch Book*)

> "He that supper for is dight,
> He lyes full cold, I trow, this night!
> Yestreen to chamber I him led,
> This night Gray-steel has made his bed!"
> —*Sir Eger, Sir Grahame* and *Sir Gray-steel.*

ON the summit of one of the heights of the Odenwald, a wild and romantic tract of Upper Germany that lies not far from the confluence of the Main and the Rhine, there stood, many many years since, the Castle of the Baron Von Landshort. It is now quite fallen to decay, and almost buried among beech trees and dark firs; above which, however, its old watch-tower may still be seen struggling, like the former possessor I have mentioned, to carry a high head, and look down upon a neighboring country.

The Baron was a dry branch of the great family of Katzenellenbogen, and inherited the relics of the property and all the pride of his ancestors. Though the warlike disposition of his predecessors had much impaired the family possessions, yet the Baron still endeavored to keep up some show of former state. The times were peaceable, and the German nobles, in general, had abandoned their inconvenient old castles, perched like eagles' nests among the mountains, and had built more convenient residences in the valleys; still the Baron remained proudly drawn up in his little fortress, cherishing with hereditary inveteracy all the old family feuds; so that he was on ill terms with some of his nearest neighbors, on account of disputes that had happened between their great-great-grandfathers.

The Baron had but one child, a daughter; but Nature, when she grants but one child, always compensates by making it a prodigy; and so it was with the daughter of the Baron. All the nurses, gossips, and country cousins, assured her father that she had not her equal for beauty in all Germany; and who should know better than they? She had, moreover, been brought up with great care, under the superintendence of two maiden aunts, who had spent some years of their early life at one of the little German courts, and were skilled in all the branches of knowledge necessary to the education of a fine lady. Under their instructions, she became a miracle of accomplishments. By the time she was eighteen she could embroider to admiration, and had worked whole histories of the saints in tapestry with such strength of expression in their countenances that they looked like so many souls in purgatory.

She could read without great difficulty, and had spelled her way through several church legends, and almost all the chivalric wonders of the Heldenbuch. She had even made considerable proficiency in writing, could sign her own name without missing a letter, and so legibly that her aunts could read it without spectacles. She excelled in making little good-for-nothing ladylike knick-knacks of all kinds; was versed in the most abstruse dancing of the day; played a number of airs on the harp and guitar; and knew all the tender ballads of the Minne-lieders by heart.

Her aunts, too, having been great flirts and coquettes in their younger days, were admirably calculated to be vigilant guardians and strict censors of the conduct of their niece; for there is no duenna so rigidly prudent, and inexorably decorous, as a superannuated coquette. She was rarely suffered out of their sight; never went beyond the domains of the castle, unless well attended, or, rather, well watched; had continual lectures read to her about strict decorum and implicit obedience; and, as to the men—pah! she was taught to hold them at such distance and distrust that, unless properly authorized, she would not have cast a glance upon the handsomest cavalier in the world—no, not if he were even dying at her feet.

The good effects of this system were wonderfully apparent. The young lady was a pattern of docility and correctness. While others were wasting their sweetness in the glare of the world, and liable to be plucked and thrown aside by every hand, she was coyly blooming into fresh and lovely womanhood under the protection of those immaculate spinsters, like a rosebud blushing forth among guardian thorns. Her aunts looked upon her with pride and exultation, and vaunted that though all the other young ladies in the world might go astray, yet, thank Heaven, nothing of the kind could happen to the heiress of Katzenellenbogen.

But however scantily the Baron Von Landshort might be provided with children, his household was by no means a small one, for Providence had enriched him with abundance of poor relations. They, one and all, possessed the affectionate disposition common to humble relatives; were wonderfully attached to the Baron, and took every possible occasion to come in swarms and enliven the castle. All family festivals were commemorated by these good people at the Baron's expense; and when they were filled with good cheer, they would declare that there was nothing on earth so delightful as these family meetings, these jubilees of the heart.

The Baron, though a small man, had a large soul, and it swelled with satisfaction at the consciousness of being the greatest man in the little world about him. He loved to tell long stories about the stark old warriors whose portraits looked grimly down from the walls around, and he found no listeners equal to those who fed at his expense. He was much given to the marvelous, and a firm believer in all those supernatural tales with which every mountain and valley in Germany abounds. The faith of his guests even exceeded his own, they listened to every tale of wonder with open eyes and mouth, and never failed to be astonished, even though repeated for the hundredth time. Thus lived the Baron Von Landshort, the oracle of his table, the absolute monarch of his little territory, and happy, above all things, in the persuasion that he was the wisest man of the age.

At the time of which my story treats there was a great family gathering at the castle, on an affair of the utmost importance: it was to receive the destined bridegroom of the Baron's daughter. A negotiation had been carried on between the father and an old nobleman of Bavaria, to unite the dignity of their houses by the marriage of their children. The preliminaries had been conducted with proper punctilio. The young people were betrothed without seeing each other, and the time was appointed for the marriage ceremony. The young Count Von Altenburg had been recalled from the army for the purpose, and was actually on his way to the Baron's to receive his bride. Missives had even been received from him, from Wurtzburg, where he was accidentally detained, mentioning the day and hour when he might be expected to arrive.

The castle was in a tumult of preparation to give him a suitable welcome. The fair bride had been decked out with uncommon care. The two aunts had superintended her toilet, and quarreled the whole morning about every article of her dress. The young lady had taken advantage of their contest to follow the bent of her own taste; and fortunately it was a good one. She looked as lovely as youthful bridegroom could desire; and the flutter of expectation heightened the luster of her charms.

The suffusions that mantled her face and neck, the gentle heaving of the bosom, the eye now and then lost in reverie, all betrayed the soft tumult that was going on in her little heart. The aunts were continually hovering around her; for maiden aunts are apt to take great interest in affairs of this nature: they were giving her a world of staid counsel, how to deport herself, what to say, and in what manner to receive the expected lover.

The Baron was no less busied in preparations. He had, in truth, nothing exactly to do; but he was naturally a fuming, bustling little man, and could not remain passive when all the world was in a hurry. He worried from top to bottom of the castle, with an air of infinite anxiety; he continually called the servants from their work to exhort them to be diligent, and buzzed about every hall and chamber, as idle, restless, and importunate as a bluebottle fly on a warm summer's day.

In the meantime, the fatted calf had been killed; the forests had rung with the clamor of the huntsmen; the kitchen was crowded with good cheer; the cellars had yielded up whole oceans of *Rhein-wein* and *Ferne-wein*, and even the great Heidelberg Tun had been laid under contribution. Everything was ready to receive the distinguished guest with *Saus und Braus* in the true spirit of German hospitality—but the guest delayed to make his appearance. Hour rolled after hour. The sun that had poured his downward rays upon the rich forests of the Oden-wald, now just gleamed along the summits of the mountains. The Baron mounted the highest tower, and strained his eyes in hopes of catching a distant sight of the Count and his attendants. Once he thought he beheld them; the sound of horns came floating from the valley, pro-longed by the mountain echoes: a number of horsemen were seen far below, slowly advancing along the road; but when they had nearly reached the foot of the mountain they suddenly struck off in a different direction. The last ray of sunshine departed—the bats began to flit by in the twilight—the road grew dimmer and dimmer to the view; and nothing appeared stirring in it but now and then a peasant lagging homeward from his labor.

While the old castle of Landshort was in this state of perplexity, a very interesting scene was transacting in a different part of the Oden-wald.

The young Count Von Altenburg was tranquilly pursuing his route in that sober jog-trot way in which a man travels toward matrimony when his friends have taken all the trouble and uncertainty of court-ship off his hands, and a bride is waiting for him, as certainly as a dinner at the end of his journey. He had encountered at Wurtzburg a youth-ful companion in arms, with whom he had seen some service on the frontiers: Herman Von Starkenfaust, one of the stoutest hands and worthiest hearts of German chivalry, who was now returning from the army. His father's castle was not far distant from the old fortress of Landshort, although a hereditary feud rendered the families hostile and strangers to each other.

In the warm-hearted moment of recognition, the young friends re-lated all their past adventures and fortunes, and the Count gave the whole history of his intended nuptials with a young lady whom he had never seen, but of whose charms he had received the most enrapturing descriptions.

As the route of the friends lay in the same direction, they agreed to perform the rest of their journey together; and, that they might do it more leisurely, set off from Wurtzburg at an early hour, the Count having given directions for his retinue to follow and overtake him.

They beguiled their wayfaring with recollections of their military scenes and adventures; but the Count was apt to be a little tedious, now and then, about the reputed charms of his bride, and the felicity that awaited him.

In this way they had entered among the mountains of the Odenwald, and were traversing one of its most lonely and thickly wooded passes. It is well known that the forests of Germany have always been as much infested with robbers as its castles by specters; and, at this time, the former were particularly numerous, from the hordes of disbanded soldiers wandering about the country. It will not appear extraordinary, therefore, that the cavaliers were attacked by a gang of these stragglers in the midst of the forest. They defended themselves with bravery, but were nearly overpowered when the Count's retinue arrived to their assistance. At sight of them the robbers fled, but not until the Count had received a mortal wound. He was slowly and carefully conveyed back to the city of Wurtzburg, and a friar summoned from a neighboring convent, who was famous for his skill in administering to both soul and body. But half of his skill was superfluous; the moments of the unfortunate Count were numbered.

With his dying breath he entreated his friend to repair instantly to the castle of Landshort, and explain the fatal cause of his not keeping his appointment with his bride. Though not the most ardent of lovers, he was one of the most punctilious of men, and appeared earnestly solicitous that this mission should be speedily and courteously executed. "Unless this is done," said he, "I shall not sleep quietly in my grave!" He repeated these last words with peculiar solemnity. A request, at a moment so impressive, admitted no hesitation. Starkenfaust endeavored to soothe him to calmness; promised faithfully to execute his wish, and gave him his hand in solemn pledge. The dying man pressed it in acknowledgment, but soon lapsed into delirium—raved about his bride—his engagements—his plighted word; ordered his horse, that he might ride to the castle of Landshort, and expired in the fancied act of vaulting into the saddle.

Starkenfaust bestowed a sigh and a soldier's tear on the untimely fate of his comrade; and then pondered on the awkward mission he had undertaken. His heart was heavy, and his head perplexed; for he was to present himself an unbidden guest among hostile people, and to damp their festivity with tidings fatal to their hopes. Still there were certain whisperings of curiosity in his bosom to see this far-famed beauty of Katzenellenbogen so cautiously shut up from the world; for he was a passionate admirer of the sex, and there was a dash of eccentricity and enterprise in his character that made him fond of all singular adventure.

Previous to his departure, he made all due arrangements with the holy fraternity of the convent for the funeral solemnities of his friend, who was to be buried in the cathedral of Wurtzburg, near some of his illustrious relatives; and the mourning retinue of the Count took charge of his remains.

It is now high time that we should return to the ancient family of Katzenellenbogen, who were impatient for their guest, and still more for their dinner; and to the worthy little Baron, whom we left airing himself on the watch-tower.

Night closed in, but still no guest arrived. The Baron descended from the tower in despair. The banquet, which had been delayed from hour to hour, could no longer be postponed. The meats were already overdone, the cook in an agony, and the whole household had the look of a garrison that had been reduced by famine. The Baron was obliged reluctantly to give orders for the feast without the presence of the guest. All were seated at table, and just on the point of commencing, when the sound of a horn from without the gate gave notice of the approach of a stranger. Another long blast filled the old courts of the castle with its echoes, and was answered by the warder from the walls. The Baron hastened to receive his future son-in-law.

The drawbridge had been let down, and the stranger was before the gate. He was a tall gallant cavalier, mounted on a black steed. His countenance was pale, but he had a beaming, romantic eye, and an air of stately melancholy. The Baron was a little mortified that he should have come in this simple, solitary style. His dignity for a moment was ruffled, and he felt disposed to consider it a want of proper respect for the important occasion, and the important family with which he was to be connected. He pacified himself, however, with the conclusion that it must have been youthful impatience which had induced him thus to spur on sooner than his attendants.

"I am sorry," said the stranger, "to break in upon you thus un-seasonably—"

Here the Baron interrupted him with a world of compliments and greetings; for, to tell the truth, he prided himself upon his courtesy and his eloquence. The stranger attempted, once or twice, to stem the torrent of words, but in vain; so he bowed his head and suffered it to flow on. By the time the Baron had come to a pause they had reached the inner court of the castle; and the stranger was again about to speak, when he was once more interrupted by the appearance of the female part of the family, leading forth the shrinking and blushing bride. He gazed on her for a moment as one entranced; it seemed as if his whole soul beamed forth in the gaze, and rested upon that lovely form. One of the maiden aunts whispered something in her ear; she made an effort to speak; her moist blue eye was timidly raised, gave a shy glance of inquiry on the stranger, and was cast again to the ground. The words died away; but there was a sweet smile playing about her lips, and a soft dimpling of the cheek, that showed her glance had not been unsatisfactory. It was impossible for a girl of the fond age of eighteen, highly predisposed for love and matrimony, not to be pleased with so gallant a cavalier.

The late hour at which the guest had arrived left no time for parley. The Baron was peremptory, and deferred all particular conversation until the morning, and led the way to the untasted banquet.

It was served up in the great hall of the castle. Around the walls hung the hard-favored portraits of the heroes of the house of Katzen-ellenbogen, and the trophies which they had gained in the field and in the chase. Hacked corselets, splintered jousting spears, and tattered banners were mingled with the spoils of sylvan warfare: the jaws of the wolf and the tusks of the boar grinned horribly among crossbows and battle-axes, and a huge pair of antlers branched immediately over the head of the youthful bridegroom.

The cavalier took but little notice of the company or the entertainment. He scarcely tasted the banquet, but seemed absorbed in admiration of his bride. He conversed in a low tone, that could not be overheard—for the language of love is never loud; but where is the female ear so dull that it cannot catch the softest whisper of the lover? There was a mingled tenderness and gravity in his manner that appeared to have a powerful effect upon the young lady. Her color came and went, as she listened with deep attention. Now and then she made some blushing reply, and when his eye was turned away she would steal a sidelong glance at his romantic countenance, and heave a gentle sigh of tender happiness. It was evident that the young couple were completely enamored. The aunts, who were deeply versed in the mysteries of the heart, declared that they had fallen in love with each other at first sight.

The feast went on merrily, or at least noisily, for the guests were all blessed with those keen appetites that attend upon light purses and mountain air. The Baron told his best and longest stories, and never had he told them so well, or with such great effect. If there was anything marvelous, his auditors were lost in astonishment; and if anything facetious, they were sure to laugh exactly in the right place. The Baron, it is true, like most great men, was too dignified to utter any joke but a dull one: it was always enforced, however, by a bumper of excellent Hoch-heimer; and even a dull joke, at one's own table, served up with jolly old wine, is irresistible. Many good things were said by poorer and keener wits that would not bear repeating, except on similar occasions; many sly speeches whispered in ladies' ears that almost convulsed them with suppressed laughter; and a song or two roared out by a poor, but merry and broadfaced cousin of the Baron, that absolutely made the maiden aunts hold up their fans.

Amid all this revelry, the stranger-guest maintained a most singular and unseasonable gravity. His countenance assumed a deeper cast of dejection as the evening advanced, and, strange as it may appear, even the Baron's jokes seemed only to render him the more melancholy. At times he was lost in thought, and at times there was a perturbed and restless wandering of the eye that bespoke a mind but ill at ease. His conversation with the bride became more and more earnest and mysterious. Lowering clouds began to steal over the fair serenity of her brow, and tremors to run through her tender frame.

All this could not escape the notice of the company. Their gaiety was chilled by the unaccountable gloom of the bridegroom; their spirits were infected; whispers and glances were interchanged, accompanied by shrugs and dubious shakes of the head. The song and the laugh grew less and less frequent: there were dreary pauses in the conversation, which were at length succeeded by wild tales and supernatural legends. One dismal story produced another still more dismal, and the Baron nearly frightened some of the ladies into hysterics with the history of the goblin horseman that carried away the fair Leonora—a dreadful, but true story, which has since been put into excellent verse, and is read and believed by all the world.

The bridegroom listened to this tale with profound attention. He kept his eyes steadily fixed on the Baron, and, as the story drew to a close, began gradually to rise from his seat, growing taller and taller, until, in the Baron's entranced eye, he seemed almost to tower into a giant. The moment the tale was finished, he heaved a deep sigh, and took a solemn farewell of the company. They were all amazement. The Baron was perfectly thunderstruck.

"What! going to leave the castle at midnight? Why, everything was prepared for his reception; a chamber was ready for him if he wished to retire."

The stranger shook his head mournfully and mysteriously: "I must lay my head in a different chamber to-night!"

There was something in this reply, and the tone in which it was uttered, that made the Baron's heart misgive him; but he rallied his forces, and repeated his hospitable entreaties. The stranger shook his head silently, but positively, at every offer; and, waving his farewell to the company, stalked slowly out of the hall. The maiden aunts were absolutely petrified—the bride hung her head, and a tear stole to her eye.

The Baron followed the stranger to the great court of the castle, where the black charger stood pawing the earth and snorting with impatience. When they had reached the portal, whose deep archway was dimly lighted by a cresset, the stranger paused, and addressed the Baron in a hollow tone of voice, which the vaulted roof rendered still more sepulchral. "Now that we are alone," said he, "I will impart to you the reason of my going. I have a solemn, an indispensable engagement—"

"Why," said the Baron, "cannot you send some one in your place?"

"It admits of no substitute—I must attend it in person—I must away to Wurtzburg cathedral—"

"Ay," said the Baron, plucking up spirit, "but not until to-morrow—to-morrow you shall take your bride there."

"No! no!" replied the stranger, with tenfold solemnity, "my engagement is with no bride—the worms! the worms expect me! I am a dead man—I have been slain by robbers—my body lies at Wurtzburg—at midnight I am to be buried—the grave is waiting for me—I must keep my appointment!"

He sprang on his black charger, dashed over the drawbridge, and the clattering of his horse's hoofs was lost in the whistling of the nightblast.

The Baron returned to the hall in the utmost consternation, and related what had passed. Two ladies fainted outright; others sickened at the idea of having banqueted with a specter. It was the opinion of some that this might be the wild huntsman famous in German legend. Some talked of mountain sprites, of wood-demons, and of other supernatural beings, with which the good people of Germany have been so grievously harrassed since time immemorial. One of the poor relations ventured to suggest that it might be some sportive evasion of the young cavalier, and that the very gloominess of the caprice seemed to accord with so melancholy a personage. This, however, drew on him the indignation of the whole company, and especially of the Baron, who looked upon him as little better than an infidel; so that he was fain to abjure his heresy as speedily as possible, and come into the faith of the true believers.

But, whatever may have been the doubts entertained, they were completely put to an end by the arrival, next day, of regular missives confirming the intelligence of the young Count's murder, and his interment in Wurtzburg cathedral.

The dismay at the castle may well be imagined. The Baron shut himself up in his chamber. The guests who had come to rejoice with him could not think of abandoning him in his distress. They wandered about the courts, or collected in groups in the hall, shaking their heads and shrugging their shoulders at the troubles of so good a man; and sat longer than ever at table, and ate and drank more stoutly than ever, by way of keeping up their spirits. But the situation of the widowed bride was the most pitiable. To have lost a husband before she had even embraced him—and such a husband! If the very specter could be so gracious and noble, what must have been the living man? She filled the house with lamentations.

On the night of the second day of her widowhood, she had retired to her chamber, accompanied by one of her aunts, who insisted on sleeping with her. The aunt, who was one of the best tellers of ghost stories in all Germany, had just been recounting one of her longest, and had fallen asleep in the very midst of it. The chamber was remote, and overlooked a small garden. The niece lay pensively gazing at the beams of the rising moon, as they trembled on the leaves of an aspen tree before the lattice. The castle clock had just told midnight, when a soft strain of music stole up from the garden. She rose hastily from her bed and stepped lightly to the window. A tall figure stood among the shadows of the trees. As it raised its head, a beam of moonlight fell upon the countenance. Heaven and earth! She beheld the Specter Bridegroom! A loud shriek at that moment burst upon her ear, and her aunt, who had been awakened by the music, and had followed her silently to the window, fell into her arms. When she looked again, the specter had disappeared.

Of the two females, the aunt now required the most soothing, for she was perfectly beside herself with terror. As to the young lady, there was something, even in the specter of her lover, that seemed endearing. There was still the semblance of manly beauty; and though the shadow of a man is but little calculated to satisfy the affections of a lovesick girl, yet, where the substance is not to be had, even that is consoling. The aunt declared that she would never sleep in that chamber again; the niece, for once, was refractory, and declared as strongly that she would sleep in no other in the castle: the consequence was that she had to sleep in it alone; but she drew a promise from her aunt not to relate the story of the specter, lest she should be denied the only melancholy pleasure left her on earth—that of inhabiting the chamber over which the guardian shade of her lover kept its nightly vigils.

How long the good old lady would have observed this promise is uncertain, for she dearly loved to talk of the marvelous, and there is a triumph in being the first to tell a frightful story; it is, however, still quoted in the neighborhood, as a memorable instance of female secrecy, that she kept it to herself for a whole week; when she was suddenly absolved from all further restraint by intelligence brought to the breakfast-table one morning that the young lady was not to be found. Her room was empty—the bed had not been slept in—the window was open—and the bird had flown!

The astonishment and concern with which the intelligence was received can only be imagined by those who have witnessed the agitation which the mishaps of a great man cause among his friends. Even the poor relations paused for a moment from the indefatigable labors of the trencher; when the aunt, who had at first been struck speechless, wrung her hands and shrieked out, "The goblin! the goblin! She's carried away by the goblin!"

In a few words she related the fearful scene of the garden, and concluded that the specter must have carried off his bride. Two of the domestics corroborated the opinion, for they had heard the clattering of a horse's hoofs down the mountain about midnight, and had no doubt that it was the specter on his black charger, bearing her away to the tomb. All present were struck with the direful probability; for events of the kind are extremely common in Germany, as many well-authenticated histories bear witness.

What a lamentable situation was that of the poor Baron! What a heartrending dilemma for a fond father, and a member of the great family of Katzenellenbogen! His only daughter had either been rapt away to the grave, or he was to have some wood-demon for a son-in-law, and, perchance, a troop of goblin grandchildren. As usual, he was completely bewildered, and all the castle in an uproar. The men were ordered to take horse and scour every road and path and glen of the Odenwald. The Baron himself had just drawn on his jack-boots, girded on his sword, and was about to mount his steed to sally forth on the doubtful quest, when he was brought to a pause by a new apparition. A lady was seen approaching the castle, mounted on a palfrey attended by a cavalier on horseback. She galloped up to the gate, sprang from her horse, and falling at the Baron's feet, embraced his knees. It was his lost daughter, and her companion—the Specter Bridegroom! The Baron was astounded. He looked at his daughter, then at the specter, and almost doubted the evidence of his senses. The latter, too, was wonderfully improved in his appearance, since his visit to the world of spirits. His dress was splendid, and set off a noble figure of manly symmetry. He was no longer pale and melancholy. His fine countenance was flushed with the glow of youth, and joy rioted in his large dark eyes.

The mystery was soon cleared up. The cavalier (for, in truth, as you must have known all the while, he was no goblin) announced himself as Sir Herman Von Starkenfaust. He related his adventure with the young Count. He told how he had hastened to the castle to deliver the unwelcome tidings, but that the eloquence of the Baron had interrupted him in every attempt to tell his tale. How the sight of the bride had completely captivated him, and that to pass a few hours near her he had tacitly suffered the mistake to continue. How he had been sorely perplexed in what way to make a decent retreat, until the Baron's goblin stories had suggested his eccentric exit. How, fearing the feudal hostility of the family, he had repeated his visits by stealth—had haunted the garden beneath the young lady's window—had wooed— had won—had borne away in triumph—and, in a word, had wedded, the fair.

Under any other circumstances the Baron would have been inflexible, for he was tenacious of paternal authority and devoutly obstinate in all family feuds; but he loved his daughter; he had lamented her as lost; he rejoiced to find her still alive; and, though her husband was of a hostile house, yet, thank Heaven, he was not a goblin. There was something, it must be acknowledged, that did not exactly accord with his notions of strict veracity, in the joke the knight had passed upon him of his being a dead man; but several old friends present, who had served in the wars, assured him that every stratagem was excusable in love, and that the cavalier was entitled to especial privilege, having lately served as a trooper.

Matters therefore, were happily arranged. The Baron pardoned the young people on the spot. The revels at the castle were resumed. The poor relations overwhelmed this new member of the family with loving-kindness; he was so gallant, so generous—and so rich. The aunts, it is true, were somewhat scandalized that their system of strict seclusion and passive obedience should be so badly exemplified, but attributed all to their negligence in not having the windows grated. One of them was particularly mortified at having her marvelous story marred, and that the only specter she had ever seen should turn out a counterfeit; but the niece seemed perfectly happy at having found him substantial flesh and blood—and so the story ends.

NATHANIEL HAWTHORNE

(1804—1864)

HAWTHORNE was born at Salem, Mass., in 1804. He came of an old Puritan family, and to the end of his life was influenced by his early environment and his New England temperamental heritage. Before he went abroad as consul for the American government he had written a number of stories and sketches of New England life, and in 1850 had won many readers and considerable fame with his novel, *The Scarlet Letter*. Hawthorne's stories, which are essentially American in subject-matter, are among the masterpieces of our literature of fiction. Hawthorne understood, as few others have done, the limitations and the possibilities of the form.

Mrs. Bullfrog is one of his most delightful tales. It is reprinted from *Mosses from an Old Manse*, 1837, by permission of Houghton Mifflin & Company.

MRS. BULLFROG

(From *Mosses from an Old Manse*)

IT makes me melancholy to see how like fools some very sensible people act in the matter of choosing wives. They perplex their judgments by a most undue attention to little niceties of personal appearance, habits, disposition, and other trifles which concern nobody but the lady herself. An unhappy gentleman resolving to wed nothing short of perfection keeps his heart and hand till both get so old and withered that no tolerable woman will accept them. Now, this is the very height of absurdity. A kind Providence has so skilfully adapted sex to sex and the mass of individuals to each other that, with certain obvious exceptions, any male and female may be moderately happy in the married state. The true rule is to ascertain that the match is fundamentally a good one, and then to take it for granted that all minor objections, should there be such, will vanish if you let them alone. Only put yourself beyond hazard as to the real basis of matrimonial bliss, and it is scarcely to be imagined what miracles in the way of reconciling smaller incongruities connubial love will effect.

For my own part, I freely confess that in my bachelorship I was precisely such an over-curious simpleton as I now advise the reader not to be. My early habits had gifted me with a feminine sensibility and too exquisite refinement. I was the accomplished graduate of a dry-goods store where by dint of ministering to the whims of the fine ladies, and suiting silken hose to delicate limbs, and handling satins, ribbons, chintzes, calicoes, tapes, gauze and cambric needles, I grew up a very ladylike sort of a gentleman. It is not assuming too much to affirm that the ladies themselves were hardly so ladylike as Thomas Bullfrog. So painfully acute was my sense of female imperfection, and such varied excellence did I require in the woman whom I could love, that there was an awful risk of my getting no wife at all or of being driven to perpetrate matrimony with my own image in the looking-glass. Besides the fundamental principle already hinted at, I demanded the fresh bloom of youth, pearly teeth, glossy ringlets, and the whole list of lovely items, with the utmost delicacy of habits and sentiments, a silken texture of mind, and, above all, a virgin heart. In a word, if a young angel just from Paradise, yet dressed in earthly fashion, had come and offered me her hand, it is by no means certain that I should have taken it. There was every chance of my becoming a most miserable old bachelor, when by the best luck in the world I made a journey into another State, and was smitten by and smote again, and wooed, won and married the present Mrs. Bullfrog, all in the space of a fortnight.

Owing to these extempore measures, I not only gave my bride credit for certain perfections which have not as yet come to light, but also overlooked a few trifling defects, which, however, glimmered on my perception long before the close of the honeymoon. Yet, as there was no mistake about the fundamental principle aforesaid, I soon learned, as will be seen, to estimate Mrs. Bullfrog's deficiencies and superfluities at exactly their proper value.

The same morning that Mrs. Bullfrog and I came together as a unit we took two seats in the stage-coach and began our journey toward my place of business. There being no other passengers, we were as much alone and as free to give vent to our raptures as if I had hired a hack for the matrimonial jaunt. My bride looked charming in a green silk calash and riding-habit of pelisse cloth; and whenever her red lips parted with a smile, each tooth appeared like an inestimable pearl. Such was my passionate warmth that—we had rattled out of the village, gentle reader, and were lonely as Adam and Eve in Paradise— I plead guilty to no less freedom than a kiss. The gentle eye of Mrs. Bullfrog scarcely rebuked me for the profanation. Emboldened by her indulgence, I threw back the calash from her polished brow and suffered my fingers, white and delicate as her own, to stray among those dark and glossy curls which realized my daydreams of rich hair.

"My love," said Mrs. Bullfrog, tenderly, "you will disarrange my curls."

"Oh, no, my sweet Laura," replied I, still playing with the glossy ringlets. "Even your fair hand could not manage a curl more delicately than mine. I propose myself the pleasure of doing up your hair in papers every evening at the same time with my own."

"Mr. Bullfrog," repeated she, "you must not disarrange my curls."

This was spoken in a more decided tone than I had happened to hear until then from my gentlest of all gentle brides. At the same time she put up her hand and took mine prisoner, but merely drew it away from the forbidden ringlet, and then immediately released it. Now, I am a fidgety little man and always love to have something in my fingers; so that, being debarred from my wife's curls, I looked about me for any other plaything. On the front seat of the coach there was one of those small baskets in which travelling ladies who are too delicate to appear at a public table generally carry a supply of gingerbread, biscuits and cheese, cold ham, and other light refreshments, merely to sustain nature to the journey's end. Such airy diet will sometimes keep them in pretty good flesh for a week together. Laying hold of this same little basket, I thrust my hand under the newspaper with which it was carefully covered.

"What's this, my dear?" cried I, for the black neck of a bottle had popped out of the basket.

"A bottle of Kalydor, Mr. Bullfrog," said my wife, coolly taking the basket from my hands and replacing it on the front seat.

There was no possibility of doubting my wife's word, but I never knew genuine Kalydor such as I use for my own complexion to smell so much like cherry-brandy. I was about to express my fears that the lotion would injure her skin, when an accident occurred which threatened more than a skin-deep injury. Our Jehu had carelessly driven over a heap of gravel and fairly capsized the coach, with the wheels in the air and our heels where our heads should have been. What became of my wits I cannot imagine: they have always had a perverse trick of deserting me just when they were most needed; but so it chanced that in the confusion of our overthrow I quite forgot that there was a Mrs. Bullfrog in the world. Like many men's wives, the good lady served her husband as a stepping-stone. I had scrambled out of the coach and was instinctively settling my cravat, when somebody brushed roughly by me and I heard a smart thwack upon the coachman's ear.

"Take that, you villain!" cried a strange, hoarse voice. "You have ruined me, you blackguard! I shall never be the woman I have been."

And then came a second thwack, aimed at the driver's other ear, but which missed it and hit him on the nose, causing a terrible effusion of blood. Now, who or what fearful apparition was inflicting this punishment on the poor fellow remained an impenetrable mystery to me. The blows were given by a person of grisly aspect with a head almost bald and sunken cheeks, apparently of the feminine gender, though hardly to be classed in the gentler sex. There being no teeth to modulate the voice, it had a mumbled fierceness—not passionate, but stern —which absolutely made me quiver like calves'-foot jelly. Who could the phantom be? The most awful circumstance of the affair is yet to be told, for this ogre—or whatever it was—had a riding-habit like Mrs. Bullfrog's, and also a green silk calash dangling down her back by the strings. In my terror and turmoil of mind I could imagine nothing less than that the Old Nick at the moment of our overturn had annihilated my wife and jumped into her petticoats. This idea seemed the more probable since I could nowhere perceive Mrs. Bullfrog alive, nor, though I looked very sharp about the coach, could I detect any traces of that beloved woman's dead body. There wouldn't have been a comfort in giving her Christian burial.

"Come, sir! bestir yourself! Help this rascal to set up the coach," said the hobgoblin to me; then, with a terrific screech to three countrymen at a distance, "Here, you fellows! Ain't you ashamed to stand off when a poor woman is in distress?"

The countrymen, instead of fleeing for their lives, came running at full speed, and laid hold of the topsy-turvy coach. I also, though a small-sized man, went to work like a son of Anak. The coachman, too, with the blood still streaming from his nose, tugged and toiled most manfully, dreading, doubtless, that the next blow might break his head. And yet, bemauled as the poor fellow had been, he seemed to glance at me with an eye of pity, as if my case were more deplorable than his. But I cherished a hope that all would turn out a dream, and seized the opportunity, as we raised the coach, to jam two of my fingers under the wheel, trusting that the pain would awaken me.

"Why, here we are all to rights again!" exclaimed a sweet voice, behind.—"Thank you for your assistance, gentlemen.—My dear Mr. Bullfrog, how you perspire! Do let me wipe your face.—Don't take this little accident too much to heart, good driver. We ought to be thankful that none of our necks are broken!"

"We might have spared one neck out of the three," muttered the driver, rubbing his ear and pulling his nose, to ascertain whether he had been cuffed or not. "Why, the woman's a witch!"

I fear that the reader will not believe, yet it is positively a fact, that there stood Mrs. Bullfrog with her glossy ringlets, curling on her brow and two rows of Orient pearls gleaming between her parted lips, which wore a most angelic smile. She had regained her riding-habit and calash from the grisly phantom, and was in all respects the lovely woman who had been sitting by my side at the instant of our overturn. How she had happened to disappear, and who had supplied her place, and whence she did now return, were problems too knotty for me to solve. There stood my wife: that was the one thing certain among a heap of mysteries. Nothing remained but to help her into the coach and plod on through the journey of the day and the journey of life as comfortably as we could. As the driver closed the door upon us I heard him whisper to the three countrymen.

"How do you suppose a fellow feels shut up in the cage with a she-tiger?"

Of course this query could have no reference to my situation; yet, unreasonable as it may appear, I confess that my feelings were not altogether so ecstatic as when I first called Mrs. Bullfrog mine. True, she was a sweet woman and an angel of a wife; but what if a gorgon should return amid the transports of our connubial bliss and take the angel's place! I recollected the tale of a fairy who half the time was a beautiful woman and half the time a hideous monster. Had I taken that very fairy to be the wife of my bosom? While such whims and chimeras were flitting across my fancy I began to look askance at Mrs. Bullfrog, almost expecting that the transformation would be wrought before my eyes.

To divert my mind I took up the newspaper which had covered the little basket of refreshments, and which now lay at the bottom of the coach blushing with a deep-red stain and emitting a potent spirituous fume from the contents of the broken bottle of Kalydor. The paper was two or three years old, but contained an article of several columns in which I soon grew wonderfully interested. It was the report of a trial for breach of promise of marriage, giving the testimony in full, with fervid extracts from both the gentleman's and lady's amatory correspondence. The deserted damsel had personally appeared in court, and had borne energetic evidence to her lover's perfidy and the strength of her blighted affections. On the defendant's part, there had been an attempt, though insufficiently sustained, to blast the plaintiff's character, and a plea, in mitigation of damages, on account of her unamiable temper. A horrible idea was suggested by the lady's name.

"Madam," said I, holding the newspaper before Mrs. Bullfrog's eyes —and, though a small, delicate and thin-visaged man, I feel assured that I looked very terrific—"Madam," repeated I, through my shut teeth, "were you the plaintiff in this cause?"

"Oh, my dear Mr. Bullfrog!" replied my wife, sweetly; "I thought all the world knew that."

"Horror! horror!" exclaimed I, sinking back on the seat.

. Covering my face with both hands, I emitted a deep and deathlike groan, as if my tormented soul were rending me asunder. I, the most exquisitely fastidious of men, and whose wife was to have been the most delicate and refined of women, with all the fresh dewdrops glittering on her virgin rosebud of a heart! I thought of the glossy ringlets and pearly teeth, I thought of the Kalydor, I thought of the coachman's bruised ear and bloody nose, I thought of the tender love-secrets which she had whispered to the judge and jury, and a thousand tittering auditors, and gave another groan.

"Mr. Bullfrog!" said my wife.

As I made no reply, she gently took my hands within her own, removed them from my face and fixed her eyes steadfastly on mine.

"Mr. Bullfrog," said she, not unkindly, yet with all the decision of her strong character, "let me advise you to overcome this foolish weakness and prove yourself to the best of your ability as good a husband as I will be a wife. You have discovered, perhaps, some little imperfections in your bride. Well, what did you expect? Women are not angels; if they were, they would go to heaven for husbands—or, at least, be more difficult in their choice on earth."

"But why conceal those imperfections?" interposed I, tremulously.

"Now, my love, are not you a most unreasonable little man?" said Mrs. Bullfrog, patting me on the cheek. "Ought a woman to disclose her frailties earlier than the wedding-day? Few husbands, I assure you, make the discovery in such good season, and still fewer complain that these trifles are concealed too long. Well, what a strange man you are! Poh! you are joking."

"But the suit for breach of promise!" groaned I.

"Ah! and is that the rub?" exclaimed my wife. "Is it possible that you view that affair in an objectionable light? Mr. Bullfrog, I never could have dreamed it. Is it an objection that I have triumphantly defended myself against slander and vindicated my purity in a court of justice? Or do you complain because your wife has shown the proper spirit of a woman, and punished the villain who trifled with her affections?"

"But," persisted I, shrinking into a corner of the coach, however, for I did not know precisely how much contradiction the proper spirit of a woman would endure—"but, my love, would it not have been more dignified to treat the villain with the silent contempt he merited?"

"That is all very well, Mr. Bullfrog," said my wife, slyly, "but in that case where would have been the five thousand dollars which are to stock your drygoods store?"

"Mrs. Bullfrog, upon your honor," demanded I, as if my life hung upon her words, "is there no mistake about those five thousand dollars?"

"Upon my word and honor, there is none," replied she. "The jury gave me every cent the rascal had, and I have kept it all for my dear Bullfrog."

"Then, thou dear woman," cried I, with an overwhelming gush of tenderness, "let me fold thee to my heart! The basis of matrimonial bliss is secure, and all thy little defects and frailties are forgiven. Nay, since the result has been so fortunate, I rejoice at the wrongs which drove thee to this blessed lawsuit, happy Bullfrog that I am!"

EDGAR ALLAN POE

(1809–1849)

POE was born at Boston in 1809, and left an orphan while still in his infancy. He was adopted by a tobacco merchant and taken to Virginia. As a child he was sent to England for his early education, returning to Richmond in 1820. He attended the University of Virginia, but was forced to leave because of his weakness for drink and gambling. He engaged in editorial work for some time, wrote verses, criticism, and short stories. The stories of Poe are justly regarded as among the world's very finest examples of the form. He was influenced to a certain extent by the fantastic tales of the German, Hoffmann, and in turn he influenced nearly every writer, especially the Europeans, since his day. He brought the short story to a point of technical perfection which has never been surpassed.

The Tell-Tale Heart first appeared in a magazine in 1843, and is reprinted from the *Collected Works*.

THE TELL-TALE HEART

TRUE!—nervous—very, very dreadfully nervous I had been and am! but why *will* you say that I am mad? The disease had sharpened my senses—not destroyed—not dulled them. Above all was the sense of hearing acute. I heard all things in the heaven and in the earth. I heard many things in hell. How, then, am I mad? Hearken! and observe how healthily—how calmly I can tell you the whole story.

It is impossible to tell how first the idea entered my brain; but once conceived, it haunted me day and night. Object there was none. Passion there was none. I loved the old man. He had never wronged me. He had never given me insult. For his gold I had no desire. I think it was his eye! Yes, it was this! One of his eyes resembled that of a vulture —a pale blue eye, with a film over it. Whenever it fell upon me, my blood ran cold; and so by degrees—very gradually—I made up my mind to take the life of the old man, and thus rid myself of the eye forever.

Now this is the point. You fancy me mad. Madmen know nothing. But you should have seen *me*. You should have seen how wisely I proceeded—with what caution—with what foresight —with what dissimulation I went to work!

I was never kinder to the old man than during the whole week before I killed him. And every night, about midnight, I turned the latch of his door and opened it—oh, so gently! And then, when I had made an opening sufficient for my head, I put in a dark lantern, all closed, closed, so that no light shone out, and then I thrust in my head. Oh, you would have laughed to see how cunningly I thrust it in! I moved it slowly—very, very slowly, so that I might not disturb the old man's sleep. It took me an hour to place my whole head within the opening so far that I could see him as he lay upon his bed. Ha!—would a madman have been so wise as this? And then, when my head was well in the room, I undid the lantern cautiously—oh, so cautiously—cautiously (for the hinges creaked)—I undid it just so much that a single thin ray fell upon the vulture eye. And this I did for seven long nights—every night just at midnight—but I found the eye always closed; and so it was impossible to do the work; for it was not the old man who vexed me, but his Evil Eye. And every morning, when the day broke, I went boldly into the chamber, and spoke courageously to him, calling him by name in a hearty tone, and inquiring how he had passed the night. So you see he would have been a very profound old man, indeed, to suspect that every night, just at twelve, I looked in upon him while he slept.

Upon the eighth night I was more than usually cautious in opening the door. A watch's minute hand moves more quickly than did mine. Never before that night had I *felt* the extent of my own powers—of my sagacity. I could scarcely contain my feelings of triumph. To think that there I was, opening the door, little by little, and he not even to dream of my secret deeds or thoughts. I fairly chuckled at the idea; and perhaps he heard me; for he moved on the bed suddenly, as if startled. Now you may think that I drew back—but no. His room was as black as pitch with the thick darkness (for the shutters were close fastened, through fear of robbers), and so I knew that he could not see the opening of the door, and I kept pushing it on steadily, steadily.

I had my head in, and was about to open the lantern, when my thumb slipped upon the tin fastening, and the old man sprang up in bed, crying out: "Who's there?"

I kept quite still and said nothing. For a whole hour I did not move a muscle, and in the meantime I did not hear him lie down. He was still sitting up in the bed listening;—just as I have done, night after night, hearkening to the death watches in the wall.

Presently I heard a slight groan, and I knew it was the groan of mortal terror. It was not a groan of pain or grief—oh, no!—it was the low stifled sound that arises from the bottom of the soul when over-charged with awe. I knew the sound well. Many a night, just at mid-night, when all the world slept, it has welled up from my own bosom, deepening, with its dreadful echo, the terrors that distracted me. I say I knew it well. I knew what the old man felt, and pitied him, although I chuckled at heart. I knew that he had been lying awake ever since the first slight noise, when he had turned in the bed. His fears had been ever since growing upon him. He had been trying to fancy them cause-less, but could not. He had been saying to himself: "It is nothing but the wind in the chimney—it is only a mouse crossing the floor," or "it is merely a cricket which has made a single chirp." Yes, he has been trying to comfort himself with these suppositions; but he had found all in vain. *All in vain;* because Death, in approaching him, had stalked with his black shadow before him, and enveloped the victim. And it was the mournful influence of the unperceived shadow that caused him to feel—although he neither saw nor heard—to *feel* the presence of my head within the room.

When I had waited a long time, very patiently, without hearing him lie down, I resolved to open a little—a very, very little crevice in the lantern. So I opened it—you cannot imagine how stealthily, stealthily —until, at length, a single dim ray, like the thread of the spider, shot from out the crevice and full upon the vulture eye.

It was open—wide, wide open—and I grew furious as I gazed upon it. I saw it with perfect distinctness—all a dull blue, with a hideous veil over it that chilled the very marrow in my bones; but I could see nothing else of the old man's face or person: for I had directed the ray, as if by instinct, precisely upon the damned spot.

And now—have I not told you that what you mistake for madness is but over-acuteness of the senses?—now, I say, there came to my ears a low, dull, quick sound, such as a watch makes when enveloped in cotton. I knew *that* sound well too. It was the beating of the old man's heart. It increased my fury, as the beating of a drum stimulates the soldier into courage.

But even yet I refrained and kept still. I scarcely breathed. I held the lantern motionless. I tried how steadily I could maintain the ray upon the eye. Meantime the hellish tattoo of the heart increased. It grew quicker and quicker, and louder and louder every instant. The old man's terror *must* have been extreme! It grew louder, I say, louder every moment!—do you mark me well? I have told you that I am nervous: so I am. And now at the dead hour of night, amid the dreadful silence of that old house, so strange a noise as this excited me to uncontrollable terror. Yet, for some minutes longer I refrained and stood still. But the beating grew louder, louder! I thought the heart must burst. And now a new anxiety seized me—the sound would be heard by a neighbor! The old man's hour had come! With a loud yell, I threw open the lantern and leaped into the room. He shrieked once— once only. In an instant I dragged him to the floor, and pulled the heavy bed over him. I then smiled gaily, to find the deed so far done. But, for many minutes, the heart beat on with a muffled sound. This, however, did not vex me; it would not be heard through the wall. At length it ceased. The old man was dead. I removed the bed and examined the corpse. Yes, he was stone, stone dead. I placed my hand upon the heart and held it there many minutes. There was no pulsation. He was stone dead. His eye would trouble me no more.

If still you think me mad, you will think so no longer when I describe the wise precautions I took for the concealment of the body. The night waned, and I worked hastily, but in silence. First of all I dismembered the corpse. I cut off the head and the arms and the legs.

I then took up three planks from the flooring of the chamber, and deposited all between the scantlings. I then replaced the boards so cleverly, so cunningly, that no human eye—not even *his*—could have detected anything wrong. There was nothing to wash out—no stain of any kind—no blood-spot whatever. I had been too wary for that. A tub had caught all—ha! ha!

When I had made an end of these labors, it was four o'clock—still dark as midnight. As the bell sounded the hour, there came a knocking at the street door. I went down to open it with a light heart—for what had I *now* to fear? There entered three men, who introduced themselves, with perfect suavity, as officers of the police. A shriek had been heard by a neighbor during the night: suspicion of foul play had been aroused; information had been lodged at the police office, and they (the officers) had been deputed to search the premises.

I smiled—for *what* had I to fear? I bade the gentlemen welcome. The shriek, I said, was my own in a dream. The old man, I mentioned, was absent in the country. I took my visitors all over the house. I bade them search—search *well*. I led them, at length, to *his* chamber. I showed them his treasures, secure, undisturbed. In the enthusiasm of my confidence, I brought chairs into the room, and desired them *here* to rest from their fatigues, while I myself, in the wild audacity of my perfect triumph, placed my own seat upon the very spot beneath which reposed the corpse of the victim.

The officers were satisfied. My *manner* had convinced them. I was singularly at ease. They sat, and while I answered cheerily, they chatted familiar things. But, ere long, I felt myself getting pale and wished them gone. My head ached, and I fancied a ringing in my ears: but still they sat and still chatted. The ringing became more distinct:—it continued and became more distinct: I talked more freely to get rid of the feeling: but it continued and gained definitiveness—until, at length, I found that the noise was *not* within my ears.

No doubt I now grew *very* pale;—but I talked more fluently, and with a heightened voice. Yet the sound increased—and what could I do? It was *a low, dull, quick sound—much such a sound as a watch makes when enveloped in cotton.* I gasped for breath—and yet the officers heard it not. I talked more quickly—more vehemently; but the noise steadily increased. Why *would* they not be gone? I paced the floor to and fro with heavy strides, as if excited to fury by the observation of the men—but the noise steadily increased. Oh, God; what *could* I do? I foamed—I raved—I swore! I swung the chair upon which I had been sitting, and grated it upon the boards, but the noise arose over all and continually increased. It grew louder—louder—*louder!* And still the men chatted pleasantly, and smiled. Was it possible they heard not? Almighty God!—no, no! They heard!—they suspected!—they *knew!*—they were making a *mockery* of my horror!—this I thought, and this I think. But anything was better than this agony! Anything was more tolerable than this derision! I could bear those hypocritical smiles no longer! I felt that I must scream or die!—and now—again!—hark! louder! louder! louder! *louder!*—

"Villains!" I shrieked, "dissemble no more! I admit the deed!—tear up the planks!—here, here!—it is the beating of his hideous heart!"

MARK TWAIN

(Samuel L. Clemens)

(1835–1910)

SAMUEL LANGHORNE CLEMENS, universally known under his pen-name of Mark Twain, was born at Florida, Mo., in 1835. His early education was fragmentary. He spent some years of his youth as a journeyman printer, wandering from town to town. At the age of seventeen he worked on a Mississippi boat, and later went West with his brother. In Nevada he began to write for the newspapers. In 1869 he achieved his first great success with *Innocents Abroad,* based on his experiences in Europe. Then followed a long period of travelling, lecturing, business enterprise, and writing. He is one of the best-known American authors throughout the world. Though Mark Twain's brief sketches can for the most part hardly be considered short stories, there are a few, like that which follows, that may legitimately be included in the category. It is reprinted from *Sketches, New and Old,* 1875.

JOURNALISM IN TENNESSEE

(From Sketches, New and Old)

I WAS told by the physician that a Southern climate would improve my health, and so I went down to Tennessee, and got a berth on the *Morning Glory and Johnson County War-Whoop* as associate editor. When I went on duty I found the chief editor sitting tilted back in a three-legged chair with his feet on a pine table. There was another pine table in the room and another afflicted chair, and both were half buried under newspapers and scraps and sheets of manuscript. There was a wooden box of sand, sprinkled with cigar stubs and "old soldiers," and a stove with a door hanging by its upper hinge. The chief editor had a long-tailed black frock coat on, and white linen pants. His boots were small and neatly blacked. He wore a ruffled shirt, a large seal ring, a standing collar of obsolete pattern, and a checkered neckerchief with the ends hanging down. Date of costume about 1848. He was smoking a cigar, and trying to think of a word, and in pawing his hair he had rumpled his locks a good deal. He was scowling fearfully, and I judged that he was concocting a particularly knotty editorial. He told me to take the exchanges and skim

through them and write up the "Spirit of the Tennessee Press," condensing into the article all of their contents that seemed of interest.
I wrote as follows:—

SPIRIT OF THE TENNESSEE PRESS

The editors of the *Semi-Weekly Earthquake* evidently labor under a misapprehension with regard to the Ballyhack railroad. It is not the object of the company to leave Buzzardville off to one side. On the contrary, they consider it one of the most important points along the line, and consequently can have no desire to slight it. The gentlemen of the *Earthquake* will, of course, take pleasure in making the correction.

John W. Blossom, Esq., the able editor of the Higginsville *Thunderbolt and Battle Cry of Freedom*, arrived in the city yesterday. He is stopping at the Van Buren House.

We observe that our contemporary of the Mud Springs *Morning Howl*, has fallen into the error of supposing that the election of Van Werter is not an established fact, but he will have discovered his mistake before this reminder reaches him, no doubt. He was doubtless misled by incomplete election returns.

It is pleasant to note that the city of Blathersville is endeavoring to contract with some New York gentleman to pave its well-nigh impassable streets with the Nicholson pavement. The *Daily Hurrah* urges the measure with ability, and seems confident of ultimate success.

I passed my manuscript over to the chief editor for acceptance, alteration, or destruction. He glanced at it and his face clouded. He ran his eye down the pages, and his countenance grew portentous. It was easy to see that something was wrong. Presently he sprang up and said—

"Thunder and lightning! Do you suppose I am going to speak of those cattle that way? Do you suppose my subscribers are going to stand such gruel as that? Give me the pen!"

I never saw a pen scrape and scratch its way so viciously, or plow through another man's verbs and adjectives so relentlessly. While he was in the midst of his work, somebody shot at him through the open window, and marred the symmetry of my ear.

"Ah," said he, "that is that scoundrel Smith, of the *Moral Volcano*— he was due yesterday." And he snatched a navy revolver from his belt and fired. Smith dropped, shot in the thigh. The shot spoiled Smith's aim, who was just taking a second chance, and he crippled a stranger. It was me. Merely a finger shot off.

Then the chief editor went on with his erasures and interlineations. Just as he finished them a hand-grenade came down the stove-pipe, and the explosion shivered the stove into a thousand fragments. However, it did no further damage, except that a vagrant piece knocked a couple of my teeth out.

"That stove is utterly ruined," said the chief editor.

I said I believed it was.

"Well, no matter—don't want it this kind of weather. I know the man that did it. I'll get him. Now, *here* is the way this stuff ought to be written."

I took the manuscript. It was scarred with erasures and interlineations till its mother wouldn't have known it if it had had one. It now read as follows:—

SPIRIT OF THE TENNESSEE PRESS

The inveterate liars of the *Semi-Weekly Earthquake* are evidently endeavoring to palm off upon a noble and chivalrous people another of their vile and brutal falsehoods with regard to that most glorious conception of the Nineteenth Century, the Ballyhack railroad. The idea that Buzzardville was to be left off at one side originated in their own fulsome brains—or rather in the settlings which *they* regard as brains. They had better swallow this lie if they want to save their abandoned reptile carcasses the cowhiding they so richly deserve.

That ass, Blossom, of the Higginsville *Thunderbolt and Battle Cry of Freedom*, is down here again sponging at the Van Buren.

We observe that the besotted blackguard of the Mud Spring *Morning Howl* is giving out, with his usual propensity for lying, that Van Werter is not elected. The heaven-born mission of journalism is to disseminate truth; to eradicate error; to educate, refine and elevate the tone of public morals and manners, and make all men more gentle, more virtuous, more charitable, and in all ways better, and holier, and happier; and yet this black-hearted scoundrel degrades his great office persistently to the dissemination of falsehood, calumny, vituperation, and vulgarity.

Blathersville wants a Nicholson pavement—it wants a jail and a poorhouse more. The idea of a pavement in a one-horse town composed of two gin-mills, a blacksmith's shop, and that mustard-plaster of a newspaper, the *Daily Hurrah!* The crawling insect, Buckner, who edits the *Hurrah*, is braying about this business with his customary imbecility, and imagining that he is talking sense.

"Now *that* is the way to write—peppery and to the point. Mush-and-milk journalism gives me the fan-tods."

About this time a brick came through the window with a splintering crash, and gave me a considerable of a jolt in the back. I moved out of range—I began to feel in the way.

The chief said, "That was the Colonel, likely. I've been expecting him for two days. He will be up, now, right away."

He was correct. The Colonel appeared in the door a moment afterward with a dragoon revolver in his hand.

He said, "Sir, have I the honor of addressing the poltroon who edits this mangy sheet?"

"You have. Be seated, sir. Be careful of the chair, one of its legs is gone. I believe I have the honor of addressing the putrid liar, Col. Blatherskite Tecumseh?"

"Right, sir. I have a little account to settle with you. If you are at leisure we will begin."

"I have an article on the 'Encouraging Progress of Moral and Intellectual Development in America,' to finish, but there is no hurry. Begin."

Both pistols rang out their fierce clamor at the same instant. The chief lost a lock of his hair, and the Colonel's bullet ended its career in the fleshy part of my thigh.

The Colonel's left shoulder was clipped a little. They fired again. Both missed their men this time, but I got my share, a shot in the arm. At the third fire both gentlemen were wounded slightly, and I had a knuckle chipped. I then said I believed I would go out and take a walk, as this was a private matter, and I had a delicacy about participating in it further. But both gentlemen begged me to keep my seat, and assured me that I was not in the way.

They then talked about the elections and the crops while they reloaded, and I fell to tying up my wounds. But presently they opened fire again with animation, and every shot took effect—but it is proper to remark that five out of the six fell to my share. The sixth one mortally wounded the Colonel, who remarked, with fine humor, that he would have to say good morning now, as he had business up town. He then inquired the way to the undertaker's and left.

The chief turned to me and said, "I am expecting company to dinner, and shall have to get ready. It will be a favor to me if you will read proofs and attend to the customers."

I winced a little at the idea of attending to the customers, but I was too bewildered by the fusillade that was still ringing in my ears to think of anything to say.

He continued, "Jones will be here at three—cowhide him. Gillespie will call earlier, perhaps—throw him out of the window. Ferguson will be along about four—kill him. That is all for to-day, I believe. If you have any odd time, you may write a blistering article on the police—give the Chief Inspector rats. The cowhides are under the table; weapons in the drawer—ammunition there in the corner—lint and bandages up there in the pigeon-holes. In case of accident, go to Lancet, the surgeon, downstairs. He advertises—we take it out in trade."

He was gone. I shuddered. At the end of the next three hours I had been through perils so awful that all peace of mind and all cheerfulness were gone from me. Gillespie had called and thrown *me* out of the window. Jones arrived promptly, and when I got ready to do the cowhiding he took the job off my hands. In an encounter with a stranger, not in the bill of fare, I had lost my scalp. Another stranger, by the name of Thompson, left me a mere wreck and ruin of chaotic rags. And at last, at bay in the corner, and beset by an infuriated mob of editors, blacklegs, politicians, and desperadoes, who raved and swore and flourished their weapons about my head till the air shimmered with glancing flashes of steel, I was in the act of resigning my berth on the paper, when the chief arrived, and with him a rabble of charming and enthusiastic friends. Then ensued a scene of riot and carnage such as no human pen, or steel one either, could describe. People were shot, probed, dismembered, blown up, thrown out of the window. There was a brief tornado of murky blasphemy, with a confused and frantic war-dance glimmering through it, and then all was over. In five minutes there was silence, and the gory chief and I sat alone and surveyed the sanguinary ruin that strewed the floor around us.

He said, "You'll like this place when you get used to it."

I said, "I'll have to get you to excuse me; I think maybe I might write to suit you after a while; as soon as I had had some practice and learned the language I am confident I could. But, to speak the plain truth, that sort of energy of expression has its inconveniences, and a man is liable to interruption. You see that yourself. Vigorous writing is calculated to elevate the public, no doubt, but then I do not like to attract so much attention as it calls forth. I can't write with comfort when I am interrupted so much as I have been to-day. I like this berth well enough, but I don't like to be left here to wait on the customers. The experiences are novel, I grant you, and entertaining too, after a fashion, but they are not judiciously distributed. A gentleman shoots at you through the window and cripples *me;* a bomb-shell comes down the stove-pipe for your gratification and sends the stove-door down my throat; a friend drops in to swap compliments with you, and freckles *me* with bullet-holes till my skin won't hold my principles; you go to dinner, and Jones comes with his cowhide, Gillespie throws me out of the window, Thompson tears all my clothes off, and an entire stranger takes my scalp with the easy freedom of an old acquaintance; and in less than five minutes all the blackguards in the country arrive in their war-paint, and proceed to scare the rest of me to death with their tomahawks. Take it altogether, I never had such a spirited time in all my life as I have had to-day. No; I like you, and I like your calm unruffled way of explaining things to the customers, but you see I am not used to it. The Southern heart is too impulsive; Southern hospitality is too lavish with the stranger. The paragraphs which I have written to-day, and into whose cold sentences

your masterly hand has infused the fervent spirit of Tennesseean journalism, will wake up another nest of hornets. All that mob of editors
will come—and they will come hungry, too, and want somebody for
breakfast. I shall have to bid you adieu. I decline to be present at
these festivities. I came South for my health, I will go back on the
same errand, and suddenly. Tennesseean journalism is too stirring
for me."

After which we parted with mutual regret, and I took apartments at
the hospital.

AMBROSE BIERCE

(1839–1914?)

BIERCE was born in Ohio in 1839. He served as an officer in the Civil
War, and in 1866 went to California, six years later proceeding to
England. Before that time he had begun to write those brief sketches
and stories which have only in recent years become widely known.
Between 1877 and 1884, having returned to California, he edited a magazine. He was last heard of in Mexico in 1914, and is supposed to
have died there that year. Bierce's stories are remarkable achievements.
They are highly finished psychological studies cast in fiction form,
of a tragic or satirical turn.

The story of *The Man and the Snake* was published in the volume
Tales of Soldiers and Civilians. Copyright, 1891, by E. L. G. Steele.
Reprinted by permission of Chatto and Windus, who include it in a vol-
ume entitled *In the Midst of Life.*

THE MAN AND THE SNAKE

(From *Tales of Soldiers and Civilians*)

*It is of veritabyll report, and attested of so many that there be nowe of wyse
and learned none to gaynsaye it, that ye serpente hys eye hath a magnetick pro-
pertie that whosoe falleth into its svasion is drawn forwards in despyte of his
wille, and perisheth miserabyll by ye creature hys byte.*

STRETCHED at ease upon a sofa, in gown and slippers, Harker
Brayton smiled as he read the foregoing sentence in old Morryster's
"Marvells of Science." "The only marvel in the matter," he said to
himself, "is that the wise and learned in Morryster's day should have
believed such nonsense as is rejected by most of even the ignorant in
ours."

A train of reflection followed—for Brayton was a man of thought —and he unconsciously lowered his book without altering the direction of his eyes. As soon as the volume had gone below the line of sight, something in an obscure corner of the room recalled his attention to his surroundings. What he saw, in the shadow under his bed, were two small points of light, apparently about an inch apart. They might have been reflections of the gas jet above him, in metal nail heads; he gave them but little thought and resumed his reading. A moment later something—some impulse which it did not occur to him to analyze—impelled him to lower the book again and seek for what he saw before. The points of light were still there. They seemed to have become brighter than before, shining with a greenish luster which he had not at first observed. He thought, too, that they might have moved a trifle—were somewhat nearer. They were still too much in the shadow, however, to reveal their nature and origin to an indolent attention, and he resumed his reading. Suddenly something in the text suggested a thought which made him start and drop the book for the third time to the side of the sofa, whence, escaping from his hand, it fell sprawling to the floor, back upward. Brayton, half-risen, was staring intently into the obscurity beneath the bed, where the points of light shone with, it seemed to him, an added fire. His attention was now fully aroused, his gaze eager and imperative. It disclosed, almost directly beneath the foot rail of the bed, the coils of a large serpent—the points of light were its eyes! Its horrible head, thrust flatly forth from the innermost coil and resting upon the outermost, was directed straight toward him, the definition of the wide, brutal jaw and the idiotlike forehead serving to show the direction of its malevolent gaze. The eyes were no longer merely luminous points; they looked into his own with a meaning, a malign significance.

A snake in a bedroom of a modern city dwelling of the better sort is, happily, not so common a phenomenon as to make explanation altogether needless. Harker Brayton, a bachelor of thirty-five, a scholar, idler, and something of an athlete, rich, popular, and of sound health, had returned to San Francisco from all manner of remote and unfamiliar countries. His tastes, always a trifle luxurious, had taken on an added exuberance from long privation; and the resources of even the Castle Hotel being inadequate for their perfect gratification, he had gladly accepted the hospitality of his friend, Dr. Druring, the distinguished scientist. Dr. Druring's house, a large, old-fashioned one in what was now an obscure quarter of the city, had an outer and visible aspect of reserve. It plainly would not associate with the contiguous elements of its altered environment, and appeared to have developed some of the eccentricities which come of isolation. One of these was a "wing," conspicuously irrelevant in point of architecture, and no less rebellious in the matter of purpose; for it was a combination of laboratory, menagerie, and museum. It was here that the doctor indulged the scientific side of his nature in the study of such forms of animal life as engaged his interest and comforted his taste—which, it must be confessed, ran rather to the lower forms. For one of the higher types nimbly and sweetly to recommend itself unto his gentle senses, it had at least to retain certain rudimentary characteristics allying it to such "dragons of the prime" as toads and snakes. His scientific sympathies were distinctly reptilian; he loved nature's vulgarians and described himself as the Zola of zoölogy. His wife and daughters, not having the advantage to share his enlightened curiosity regarding the works and ways of our ill-starred fellow-creatures, were, with needless austerity, excluded from what he called the Snakery, and doomed to companionship with their own kind; though, to soften the rigors of their lot, he had permitted them, out of his great wealth, to outdo the reptiles in the gorgeousness of their surroundings and to shine with a superior splendor.

Architecturally, and in point of "furnishing," the Snakery had a severe simplicity befitting the humble circumstances of its occupants, many of whom, indeed, could not safely have been intrusted with the liberty which is necessary to the full enjoyment of luxury, for they had the troublesome peculiarity of being alive. In their own apartments, however, they were under as little personal restraint as was compatible with their protection from the baneful habit of swallowing one another; and, as Brayton had thoughtfully been apprised, it was more than a tradition that some of them had at divers times been found in parts of the premises where it would have embarrassed them to explain their presence. Despite the Snakery and its uncanny associations—to which, indeed, he gave little attention—Brayton found life at the Druring mansion very much to his mind.

Beyond a smart shock of surprise and a shudder of mere loathing, Mr. Brayton was not greatly affected. His first thought was to ring the call bell and bring a servant; but, although the bell cord dangled within easy reach, he made no movement toward it; it had occurred to his mind that the act might subject him to the suspicion of fear, which he certainly did not feel. He was more keenly conscious of the incongruous nature of the situation than affected by its perils; it was revolting, but absurd.

The reptile was of a species with which Brayton was unfamiliar. Its length he could only conjecture; the body at the largest visible part seemed about as thick as his forearm. In what way was it dangerous, if in any way? Was it venomous? Was it a constrictor? His knowledge of nature's danger signals did not enable him to say; he had never deciphered the code.

If not dangerous, the creature was at least offensive. It was *de trop*—"matter out of place"—an impertinence. The gem was unworthy of the setting. Even the barbarous taste of our time and country, which had loaded the walls of the room with pictures, the floor with furniture, and the furniture with *bric-à-brac,* had not quite fitted the place for this bit of the savage life of the jungle. Besides—insupportable thought!—the exhalations of its breath mingled with the atmosphere which he himself was breathing!

These thoughts shaped themselves with greater or less definition in Brayton's mind, and begot action. The process is what we call consideration and decision. It is thus that we are wise and unwise. It is thus that the withered leaf in an autumn breeze shows greater or less intelligence than its fellows, falling upon the land or upon the lake. The secret of human action is an open one—something contracts our muscles. Does it matter if we give to the preparatory molecular changes the name of will?

Brayton rose to his feet and prepared to back softly away from the snake, without disturbing it, if possible, and through the door. People retire so from the presence of the great, for greatness is power, and power is a menace. He knew that he could walk backward without obstruction, and find the door without error. Should the monster follow, the taste which had plastered the walls with paintings had consistently supplied a rack [of murderous Oriental weapons from which he could snatch one so suit the occasion. In the meantime the snake's eyes burned with a more pitiless malevolence than ever.

Brayton lifted his right foot free of the floor to step backward. That moment he felt a strong aversion to doing so.

"I am accounted brave," he murmured; "is bravery, then, no more than pride? Because there are none to witness the shame shall I retreat?"

He was steadying himself with his right hand upon the back of a chair, his foot suspended.

"Nonsense!" he said aloud; "I am not so great a coward as to fear to seem to myself afraid."

He lifted the foot a little higher by slightly bending the knee, and thrust it sharply to the floor—an inch in front of the other! He could not think how that occurred. A trial with the left foot had the same result; it was again in advance of the right. The hand upon the chair back was grasping it; the arm was straight, reaching somewhat backward. One might have seen that he was reluctant to lose his hold. The snake's malignant head was still thrust forth from the inner coil as before, the neck level. It had not moved, but its eyes were now electric sparks, radiating an infinity of luminous needles.

The man had an ashy pallor. Again he took a step forward, and another, partly dragging the chair, which, when finally released, fell upon the floor with a crash. The man groaned; the snake made neither sound nor motion, but its eyes were two dazzling suns. The reptile itself was wholly concealed by them. They gave off enlarging rings of rich and vivid colors, which at their greatest expansion successively vanished like soap bubbles; they seemed to approach his very face, and anon were an immeasurable distance away. He heard, somewhere, the continual throbbing of a great drum, with desultory bursts of far music, inconceivably sweet, like the tones of an æolian harp. He knew it for the sunrise melody of Memnon's statue, and thought he stood in the Nileside reeds, hearing, with exalted sense, that immortal anthem through the silence of the centuries.

The music ceased; rather, it became by insensible degrees the distant roll of a retreating thunderstorm. A landscape, glittering with sun and rain, stretched before him, arched with a vivid rainbow, framing in its giant curve a hundred visible cities. In the middle distance a vast serpent, wearing a crown, reared its head out of its, voluminous convolutions and looked at him with his dead mother's eyes. Suddenly this enchanting landscape seemed to rise swiftly upward, like the drop scene at a theater, and vanished in a blank. Something struck him a hard blow upon the face and breast. He had fallen to the floor; the blood ran from his broken nose and his bruised lips. For a moment he was dazed and stunned, and lay with closed eyes, his face against the door. In a few moments he had recovered, and then realized that his fall, by withdrawing his eyes, had broken the spell which held him. He felt that now, by keeping his gaze averted, he would be able to retreat. But the thought of the serpent within a few feet of his head, yet unseen—perhaps in the very act of springing upon him and throwing its coils about his throat—was too horrible. He lifted his head, stared again into those baleful eyes, and was again in bondage.

The snake had not moved, and appeared somewhat to have lost its power upon the imagination; the gorgeous illusions of a few moments before were not repeated. Beneath that flat and brainless brow its black, beady eyes simply glittered, as at first, with an expression unspeakably malignant. It was as if the creature, knowing its triumph assured, had determined to practice no more alluring wiles.

Now ensued a fearful scene. The man, prone upon the floor, within a yard of his enemy, raised the upper part of his body upon his elbows, his head thrown back, his legs extended to their full length. His face was white between its gouts of blood; his eyes were strained open to their uttermost expansion. There was froth upon his lips; it dropped off in flakes. Strong convulsions ran through his body, making almost serpentine undulations. He bent himself at the waist, shifting his legs from side to side. And every movement left him a little nearer to the snake. He thrust his hands forward to brace himself back, yet constantly advanced upon his elbows.

Dr. Druring and his wife sat in the library. The scientist was in rare good humor.

"I have just obtained, by exchange with another collector," he said, "a splendid specimen of the *Ophiophagus.*"

"And what may that be?" the lady inquired with a somewhat languid interest.

"Why, bless my soul, what profound ignorance! My dear, a man who ascertains after marriage that his wife does not know Greek, is entitled to a divorce. The *Ophiophagus* is a snake which eats other snakes."

"I hope it will eat all yours," she said, absently shifting the lamp. "But how does it get the other snakes? By charming them, I suppose."

"That is just like you, dear," said the doctor, with an affection of petulance. "You know how irritating to me is any allusion to that vulgar superstition about the snake's power of fascination."

The conversation was interrupted by a mighty cry which rang through the silent house like the voice of a demon shouting in a tomb. Again and yet again it sounded, with terrible distinctness. They sprang to their feet, the man confused, the lady pale and speechless with fright. Almost before the echoes of the last cry had died away the doctor was out of the room, springing up the staircase two steps at a time. In the corridor, in front of Brayton's chamber, he met some servants who had come from the upper floor. Together, they rushed at the door without knocking. It was unfastened, and gave way. Brayton lay upon his stomach on the floor, dead. His head and arms were partly concealed under the foot rail of the bed. They pulled the body away, turning it upon the back. The face was daubed with blood and froth, the eyes were wide open, staring—a dreadful sight!

"Died in a fit," said the scientist, bending his knee and placing his hand upon the heart. While in that position he happened to glance under the bed. "Good God!" he added; "how did this thing get in here?"

He reached under the bed, pulled out the snake, and flung it, still coiled, to the center of the room, whence, with a harsh, shuffling sound, it slid across the polished floor till stopped by the wall where it lay without motion. It was a stuffed snake; its eyes were two shoe buttons.

BRET HARTE

(1839–1902)

FRANCIS BRET HARTE was born at Albany in 1839, and after receiving an ordinary school education, went to California, in 1854. He tried teaching and mining, but without success, and then worked as compositor on a San Francisco paper. During that time he published a few verses and sketches. On the appearance of *The Luck of Roaring Camp* in the *Overland Monthly*, he was hailed as a man of exceptional talent—as indeed he was. It was he who popularized the Western story. Such tales as *The Luck of Roaring Camp* and *The Outcasts of Poker Flat* are typical of Harte at his best. He was often over-sentimental and at times he wrote primarily in order to exhibit a trick-ending, in the manner of O. Henry, but the story included in this volume shows that he could interpret and describe human beings in a masterly fashion.

This story is reprinted from the volume *The Luck of Roaring Camp*, etc. Copyright, 1872, by Houghton Mifflin & Co., Boston, by whose permission it is here used.

THE OUTCASTS OF POKER FLAT

AS Mr. John Oakhurst, gambler, stepped into the main street of Poker Flat on the morning of the 23d of November, 1850, he was conscious of a change in its moral atmosphere since the preceding night. Two or three men, conversing earnestly together, ceased as he approached, and exchanged significant glances. There was a Sabbath lull in the air, which, in a settlement unused to Sabbath influences, looked ominous.

Mr. Oakhurst's calm, handsome face betrayed small concern in these indications. Whether he was conscious of any predisposing cause was another question. "I reckon they're after somebody," he reflected: "likely it's me." He returned to his pocket the handkerchief with which he had been wiping away the red dust of Poker Flat from his neat boots, and quietly discharged his mind of any further conjecture.

In point of fact, Poker Flat was "after somebody." It had lately suffered the loss of several thousand dollars, two valuable horses, and a prominent citizen. It was experiencing a spasm of virtuous reaction, quite as lawless and ungovernable as any of the acts that had provoked it. A secret committee had determined to rid the town of all improper persons. This was done permanently in regard to two men who were then hanging from the boughs of a sycamore in the gulch, and temporarily in the banishment of certain other objectionable characters. I regret to say that some of these were ladies. It is but due to the sex, however, to state that their impropriety was professional, and it was only in such easily established standards of evil that Poker Flat ventured to sit in judgment.

Mr. Oakhurst was right in supposing that he was included in this category. A few of the committee had urged hanging him as a possible example and a sure method of reimbursing themselves from his pockets of the sums he had won from them. "It's agin justice," said Jim Wheeler, "to let this yer young man from Roaring Camp—an entire stranger—carry away our money." But a crude sentiment of equity residing in the breasts of those who had been fortunate enough to win from Mr. Oakhurst overruled this narrower local prejudice.

Mr. Oakhurst received his sentence with philosophic calmness, none the less coolly that he was aware of the hesitation of his judges. He was too much of a gambler not to accept fate. With him life was at best an uncertain game, and he recognized the usual percentage in favor of the dealer.

A body of armed men accompanied the deported wickedness of Poker Flat to the outskirts of the settlement. Besides Mr. Oakhurst, who was known to be a coolly desperate man, and for whose intimidation the armed escort was intended, the expatriated party consisted of a young woman familiarly known as "The Duchess"; another who had won the title of "Mother Shipton"; and "Uncle Billy," a suspected sluice-robber and confirmed drunkard. The cavalcade provoked no comments from the spectators, nor was any word uttered by the escort. Only when the gulch which marked the uttermost limit of Poker Flat was reached, the leader spoke briefly and to the point. The exiles were forbidden to return at the peril of their lives.

As the escort disappeared, their pent-up feelings found vent in a few hysterical tears from the Duchess, some bad language from Mother Shipton, and a Parthian volley of expletives from Uncle Billy. The philosophic Oakhurst alone remained silent. He listened calmly to Mother Shipton's desire to cut somebody's heart out, to the repeated statements of The Duchess that she would die in the road, and to the alarming oaths that seemed to be bumped out of Uncle Billy as he rode forward. With the easy good humor characteristic of his class, he insisted upon exchanging his own riding-horse, "Five-spot," for the sorry mule which the Duchess rode. But even this act did not draw the party into any closer sympathy. The young woman readjusted her somewhat draggled plumes with a feeble, faded coquetry; Mother Shipton eyed the possessor of "Five-spot" with malevolence, and Uncle Billy included the whole party in one sweeping anathema.

The road to Sandy Bar—a camp that, not having as yet experienced the regenerating influences of Poker Flat, consequently seemed to offer some invitation to the emigrants—lay over a steep mountain range. It was distant a day's severe travel. In that advanced season the party soon passed out of the moist, temperate regions of the foothills into the dry, cold, bracing air of the Sierras. The trail was narrow and difficult. At noon the Duchess, rolling out of her saddle upon the ground, declared her intention of going no farther, and the party halted.

The spot was singularly wild and impressive. A wooded amphitheater surrounded on three sides by precipitous cliffs of naked granite, sloped gently toward the crest of another precipice that overlooked the valley. It was, undoubtedly, the most suitable spot for a camp, had camping been advisable. But Mr. Oakhurst knew that scarcely half the journey to Sandy Bar was accomplished, and the party were not equipped or provisioned for delay. This fact he pointed out to his companions curtly, with a philosophic commentary on the folly of "throwing up their hand before the game was played out." But they were furnished with liquor, which in this emergency stood them in place of food, fuel, rest and prescience. In spite of his remonstrances, it was not long before they were more or less under its influence. Uncle Billy passed rapidly from a bellicose state into one of stupor, the Duchess became maudlin, and Mother Shipton snored. Mr. Oakhurst alone remained erect, leaning against a rock, calmly surveying them.

Mr. Oakhurst did not drink. It interfered with a profession which required coolness, impassiveness, and presence of mind, and, in his own language, he "couldn't afford it." As he gazed at his recumbent fellow exiles, the loneliness begotten of his pariah trade, his habits of life, his very vices, for the first time seriously oppressed him. He bestirred himself in dusting his black clothes, washing his hands and face, and other acts characteristic of his studiously neat habits, and for a moment forgot his annoyance. The thought of deserting his weaker and more pitiable companions never perhaps occurred to him. Yet he could not help feeling the want of that excitement which, singularly enough, was most conducive to that calm equanimity for which he was notorious. He looked at the gloomy walls that rose a thousand feet sheer above the circling pines around him, at the sky ominously clouded, at the valley below, already deepening into shadow; and, doing so, suddenly he heard his own name called.

A horseman slowly ascended the trail. In the fresh, open face of the newcomer Mr. Oakhurst recognized Tom Simson, otherwise known as "The Innocent," of Sandy Bar. He had met him some months before over a "little game," and had, with perfect equanimity, won the entire fortune—amounting to some forty dollars—of that guileless youth. After the game was finished, Mr. Oakhurst drew the youthful speculator behind the door and thus addressed him: "Tommy, you're a good little man, but you can't gamble worth a cent. Don't try it ever again." He then handed him his money back, pushed him gently from the room, and so made a devoted slave of Tom Simson.

There was a remembrance of this in his boyish and enthusiastic greeting of Mr. Oakhurst. He had started, he said, to go to Poker Flat to seek his fortune. "Alone?" No, not exactly alone; in fact (a giggle), he had run away with Piney Woods. Didn't Mr. Oakhurst remember Piney? She that used to wait on the table at the Temperance House? They had been engaged a long time, but old Jake Woods had objected, and so they had run away, and were going to Poker Flat to be married, and here they were. And they were tired out, and how lucky it was they had found a place to camp, and company. All this the Innocent delivered rapidly, while Piney, a stout, comely damsel of fifteen, emerged from behind the pine tree, where she had been blushing unseen, and rode to the side of her lover.

Mr. Oakhurst seldom troubled himself with sentiment, still less with propriety; but he had a vague idea that the situation was not fortunate. He retained, however, his presence of mind sufficiently to kick Uncle Billy, who was about to say something, and Uncle Billy was sober enough to recognize in Mr. Oakhurst's kick a superior power that would not bear trifling. He then endeavored to dissuade Tom Simson from delaying further, but in vain. He even pointed out the fact that there was no provision, nor means of making a camp. But, unluckily, the Innocent met this objection by assuring the party that he was provided with an extra mule loaded with provisions, and by the discovery of a rude attempt at a log house near the trail. "Piney can stay with Mrs. Oakhurst," said the Innocent, pointing to the Duchess, "and I can shift for myself."

Nothing but Mr. Oakhurst's admonishing foot saved Uncle Billy from bursting into a roar of laughter. As it was, he felt compelled to retire up the cañon until he could recover his gravity. There he confided the joke to the tall pine trees, with many slaps of his leg, contortions of his face, and the usual profanity. But when he returned to the party, he found them seated by a fire—for the air had grown strangely chill and the sky overcast—in apparently amicable conversation. Piney was actually talking in an impulsive girlish fashion to the Duchess, who was listening with an interest and animation she had not shown for many days. The Innocent was holding forth, apparently with equal effect, to Mr. Oakhurst and Mother Shipton, who was actually relaxing into amiability. "Is this yer a d—d picnic?" said Uncle Billy, with inward scorn, as he surveyed the sylvan group, the glancing firelight, and the tethered animals in the foreground. Suddenly an idea mingled with the alcoholic fumes that disturbed his brain. It was apparently of a jocular nature, for he felt impelled to slap his leg again and cram his fist into his mouth.

As the shadows crept slowly up the mountain, a slight breeze rocked the tops of the pine trees and moaned through their long and gloomy aisles. The ruined cabin, patched and covered with pine boughs, was set apart for the ladies. As the lovers parted, they unaffectedly exchanged a kiss, so honest and sincere that it might have been heard above the swaying pines. The frail Duchess and the malevolent Mother Shipton were probably too stunned to remark upon this last evidence of simplicity, and so turned without a word to the hut. The fire was replenished, the men lay down before the door, and in a few minutes were asleep.

Mr. Oakhurst was a light sleeper. Toward morning he awoke benumbed and cold. As he stirred the dying fire, the wind, which was now blowing strongly, brought to his cheek that which caused the blood to leave it—snow!

He started to his feet with the intention of awakening the sleepers, for there was no time to lose. But turning to where Uncle Billy had been lying, he found him gone. A suspicion leaped to his brain, and a curse to his lips. He ran to the spot where the mules had been tethered —they were no longer there. The tracks were already rapidly disappearing in the snow.

The momentary excitement brought Mr. Oakhurst back to the fire with his usual calm. He did not waken the sleepers. The Innocent slumbered peacefully, with a smile on his good-humored, freckled face; the virgin Piney slept beside her frailer sisters as sweetly as though attended by celestial guardians; and Mr. Oakhurst, drawing his blanket over his shoulders, stroked his mustaches and waited for the dawn. It came slowly in a whirling mist of snowflakes that dazzled and confused the eye. What could be seen of the landscape appeared magically changed. He looked over the valley, and summed up the present and future in two words, "Snowed in!"

A careful inventory of the provisions, which, fortunately for the party, had been stored within the hut, and so escaped the felonious fingers of Uncle Billy, disclosed the fact that with care and prudence they might last ten days longer. "That is," said Mr. Oakhurst *sotto voce* to the Innocent, "if you're willing to board us. If you ain't—and perhaps you'd better not—you can wait till Uncle Billy gets back with provisions." For some occult reason, Mr. Oakhurst could not bring himself to disclose Uncle Bill's rascality, and so offered the hypothesis that he had wandered from the camp and had accidentally stampeded the animals. He dropped a warning to the Duchess and Mother Shipton, who, of course, knew the facts of their associate's defection. "They'll find out the truth about us *all* when they find out anything," he added significantly, "and there's no good frightening them now."

Tom Simson not only put all his worldly store at the disposal of Mr. Oakhurst, but seemed to enjoy the prospect of their enforced seclusion. "We'll have a good camp for a week, and then the snow'll melt, and we'll all go back together." The cheerful gayety of the young man and Mr. Oakhurst's calm infected the others. The Innocent, with the aid of pine boughs, extemporized a thatch for the roofless cabin, and the Duchess directed Piney in the rearrangement of the interior with a taste and tact that opened the blue eyes of that provincial maiden to their fullest extent. "I reckon now you're used to fine things at Poker Flat," said Piney. The Duchess turned away sharply to conceal something that reddened her cheeks through their professional tint, and Mother Shipton requested Piney not to "chatter." But when Mr. Oakhurst returned from a weary search for the trail, he heard the sound of happy laughter echoed from the rocks. He stopped in some alarm, and his thoughts first naturally reverted to the whiskey, which he had prudently cached. "And yet it don't somehow sound like whiskey," said the gambler. It was not until he caught sight of the blazing fire through the still blinding storm, and the group around it, that he settled to the conviction that it was "square fun."

Whether Mr. Oakhurst had cached his cards with the whiskey as something debarred the free access of the community, I cannot say. It was certain that, in Mother Shipton's words, he "didn't say 'cards' once" during that evening. Haply the time was beguiled by an accordion, produced somewhat ostentatiously by Tom Simson from his pack. Notwithstanding some difficulties attending the manipulation of this instrument, Piney Woods managed to pluck several reluctant melodies from its keys, to an accompaniment by the Innocent on a pair of bone castanets. But the crowning festivity of the evening was reached in a rude camp-meeting hymn, which the lovers, joining hands, sang with great earnestness and vociferation. I fear that a certain defiant tone and Covenanter's swing to its chorus, rather than any devotional quality, caused it speedily to infect the others, who at last joined in the refrain:—

> "I'm proud to live in the service of the Lord,
> And I'm bound to die in his army."

The pines rocked, the storm eddied and whirled above the miserable group, and the flames of their altar leaped heavenward, as if in token of the vow.

At midnight the storm abated, the rolling clouds parted, and the stars glittered keenly above the sleeping camp. Mr. Oakhurst, whose professional habits had enabled him to live on the smallest possible amount of sleep, in dividing the watch with Tom Simson somehow managed to take upon himself the greater part of that duty. He excused himself to the Innocent by saying that he had "often been a week without sleep." "Doing what?" asked Tom. "Poker!" replied Oakhurst sententiously. "When a man gets a streak of luck—nigger-luck—he don't get tired. The luck gives in first. Luck," continued the gambler reflectively," is a mighty queer thing. All you know about it for certain is that it's bound to change. And it's finding out when it's going to change that makes you. We've had a streak of bad luck since we left Poker Flat—you come along, and, slap, you get into it, too. If you can hold your cards right along you're all right. For," added the gambler, with cheerful irrelevance—

> "'I'm proud to live in the service of the Lord,
> And I'm bound to die in his army.'"

The third day came, and the sun, looking through the white-curtained valley, saw the outcasts divide their slowly decreasing store of provisions for the morning meal. It was one of the peculiarities of that mountain climate that its rays diffused a kindly warmth over the wintry landscape, as if in regretful commiseration of the past. But it revealed drift on drift of snow piled high around the hut—a hopeless, uncharted, trackless sea of white lying below the rocky shores to which the castaways still clung. Through the marvelously clear air the smoke of the pastoral village of Poker Flat rose miles away. Mother Shipton saw it, and from a remote pinnacle of her rocky fastness hurled in that direction a final malediction. It was her last vituperative attempt, and perhaps for that reason was invested with a certain degree of sublimity. It did her good, she privately informed the Duchess. "Just you go out there and cuss, and see." She then set herself to the task of amusing "the child," as she and the Duchess were pleased to call Piney. Piney was no chicken, but it was a soothing and original theory of the pair thus to account for the fact that she didn't swear and wasn't improper.

When night crept up again through the gorges, the reedy notes of the accordion rose and fell in fitful spasms and long-drawn gasps by the flickering camp-fire. But music failed to fill entirely the aching void left by insufficient food, and a new diversion was proposed by Piney,—story-telling. Neither Mr. Oakhurst nor his female companions caring to relate their personal experiences, this plan would have failed too, but for the Innocent. Some months before he had chanced upon a stray copy of Mr. Pope's ingenious translation of the Iliad. He now proposed to narrate the principal incidents of that poem—having thoroughly mastered the argument and fairly forgotten the words—in the current vernacular of Sandy Bar. And so for the rest of that night the Homeric demigods again walked the earth. Trojan bully and wily Greek wrestled in the winds, and the great pines in the cañon seemed to bow to the wrath of the son of Peleus. Mr. Oakhurst listened with quiet satisfaction. Most especially was he interested in the fate of "Ash-heels," as the Innocent persisted in denominating the "swift-footed Achilles."

So, with small food and much of Homer and the accordion, a week passed over the heads of the outcasts. The sun again forsook them, and again from leaden skies the snowflakes were sifted over the land. Day by day closer around them drew the snowy circle, until at last they looked from their prison over drifted walls of dazzling white, that towered twenty feet above their heads. It became more and more difficult to replenish their fires, even from the fallen trees beside them, now half hidden in the drifts. And yet no one complained. The lovers turned from the dreary prospect and looked into each other's eyes, and were happy. Mr. Oakhurst settled himself coolly to the losing game before him. The Duchess, more cheerful than she had been, assumed the care of Piney. Only Mother Shipton—once the strongest of the party—seemed to sicken and fade. At midnight on the tenth day she called Oakhurst to her side. "I'm going," she said, in a voice of querulous weakness, "but don't say anything about it. Don't waken the kids. Take the bundle from under my head, and open it." Mr. Oakhurst did so. It contained Mother Shipton's rations for the last week, untouched. "Give 'em to the child," she said, pointing to the sleeping Piney. "You've starved yourself," said the gambler. "That's what they call it," said the woman querulously, as she lay down again, and, turning her face to the wall, passed quietly away.

The accordion and the bones were put aside that day, and Homer was forgotten. When the body of Mother Shipton had been committed to the snow, Mr. Oakhurst took the Innocent aside, and showed him a pair of snow-shoes, which he had fashioned from the old pack-saddle. "There's one chance in a hundred to save her yet," he said, pointing to Piney; "but it's there," he added, pointing toward Poker Flat. "If you can reach there in two days, she's safe." "And you?" asked Tom Simson. "I'll stay here," was the curt reply.

The lovers parted with a long embrace. "You are not going, too?" said the Duchess, as she saw Mr. Oakhurst apparently waiting to accompany him. "As far as the cañon," he replied. He turned suddenly and kissed the Duchess, leaving her pallid face aflame, and her trembling limbs rigid with amazement.

Night came, but not Mr. Oakhurst. It brought the storm again and the whirling snow. Then the Duchess, feeding the fire, found that some one had quietly piled beside the hut enough fuel to last a few days longer. The tears rose to her eyes, but she hid them from Piney.

The women slept but little. In the morning, looking into each other's faces, they read their fate. Neither spoke, but Piney, accepting the position of the stronger, drew near and placed her arm around the Duchess's waist. They kept this attitude for the rest of the day. That night the storm reached its greatest fury, and, rending asunder the protecting vines, invaded the very hut.

Toward morning they found themselves unable to feed the fire, which gradually died away. As the embers slowly blackened, the Duchess crept closer to Piney, and broke the silence of many hours: "Piney, can you pray?" "No, dear," said Piney simply. The Duchess, without knowing exactly why, felt relieved, and, putting her head upon Piney's shoulder, spoke no more. And so reclining, the younger and purer pillowing the head of her soiled sister upon her virgin breast, they fell asleep.

The wind lulled as if it feared to waken them. Feathery drifts of snow, shaken from the long pine boughs, flew like white winged birds, and settled about them as they slept. The moon through the rifted clouds looked down upon what had been the camp. But all human stain, all trace of earthly travail, was hidden beneath the spotless mantle mercifully flung from above.

They slept all that day and the next, nor did they waken when voices and footsteps broke the silence of the camp. And when pitying fingers brushed the snow from their wan faces, you could scarcely have told from the equal peace that dwelt upon them which was she that had sinned. Even the law of Poker Flat recognized this, and turned away, leaving them still locked in each other's arms.

But at the head of the gulch, on one of the largest pine trees, they found the deuce of clubs pinned to the bark with a bowie-knife. It bore the following, written in pencil in a firm hand:—

†

BENEATH THIS TREE
LIES THE BODY
OF

JOHN OAKHURST

WHO STRUCK A STREAK OF BAD LUCK
ON THE 23D OF NOVEMBER 1850,
AND
HANDED IN HIS CHECKS
ON THE 7TH DECEMBER 1850

↓

And pulseless and cold, with a derringer by his side and a bullet in his heart, though still calm as in life, beneath the snow lay he who was at once the strongest and yet the weakest of the outcasts of Poker Flat.

HENRY JAMES

(1843–1915)

HENRY JAMES, JR., was born in New York City in 1843. He was educated for the most part abroad. A good deal of his early writing was done in America, but early in the seventies he settled in England, and except for a few short trips to the States, he spent his life here. A short time before his death he became an English subject. James was one of the most remarkable literary artists this country has produced. His earlier short stories are related with an extraordinary power and a fine command of English. They are chiefly studies in character. His later stories, shorter and far more compact, are masterly technical achievements.

The Story in It appeared in the collection entitled *The Better Sort,* copyright, 1903, by Methuen and Co., by whose permission it is here reprinted.

THE STORY IN IT

I

THE weather had turned so much worse that the rest of the day was certainly lost. The wind had risen and the storm gathered force; they gave from time to time a thump at the firm windows and dashed even against those protected by the veranda their vicious splotches of rain. Beyond the lawn, beyond the cliff, the great wet brush of the sky dipped deep into the sea. But the lawn, already vivid with the touch of May, showed a violence of watered green; the budding shrubs and trees repeated the note as they tossed their thick masses, and the cold, troubled light, filling the pretty drawing-room, marked the spring afternoon as sufficiently young. The two ladies seated there in silence could pursue without difficulty—as well as, clearly, without interruption—their respective tasks; a confidence expressed, when the noise of the wind allowed it to be heard, by the sharp scratch of Mrs. Dyott's pen at the table where she was busy with letters.

Her visitor, settled on a small sofa that, with a palm-tree, a screen, a stool, a stand, a bowl of flowers and three photographs in silver frames, had been arranged near the light wood-fire as a choice "corner"—Maud Blessingbourne, her guest, turned audibly, though at intervals neither brief nor regular, the leaves of a book, covered in lemon-colored paper and not yet despoiled of a certain fresh crispness. This effect of the volume, for the eye, would have made it, as presumably the newest French novel—and evidently, from the attitude of the reader, "good"—consort happily with the special tone of the room, a consistent air of selection and suppression, one of the finer æsthetic evolutions. If Mrs. Dyott was fond of ancient French furniture, and distinctly difficult about it, her inmates could be fond—with whatever critical cocks of charming darkbraided heads over slender sloping shoulders—of modern French authors. Nothing had passed for half an hour—nothing, at least, to be exact, but that each of the companions occasionally and covertly intermitted her pursuit in such a manner as to ascertain the degree of absorption of the other without turning round. What their silence was charged with, therefore, was not only a sense of the weather, but a sense, so to speak, of its own nature. Maud Blessingbourne, when she lowered her book into her lap, closed her eyes with a conscious patience that seemed to say she waited; but it was nevertheless she who at last made the movement representing a snap of their tension. She got up and stood by the fire, into which she looked a minute; then came round and approached the window as if to see what was really going on. At this Mrs. Dyott wrote with refreshed intensity. Her little pile of letters had grown, and if a look of determination was compatible with her fair and slightly faded beauty, the habit of attending to her business could always keep pace with any excursion of her thought. Yet she was the first who spoke.

"I trust your book has been interesting."

"Well enough; a little mild."

A louder throb of the tempest had blurred the sound of the words. "A little wild?"

"Dear, no—timid and tame; unless I've quite lost my sense."

"Perhaps you have," Mrs. Dyott placidly suggested—"reading so many."

Her companion made a motion of feigned despair. "Ah, you take away my courage for going to my room, as I was just meaning to, for another."

"Another French one?"

"I'm afraid."

"Do you carry them by the dozen——"

"Into innocent British homes?" Maud tried to remember. "I believe I brought three—seeing them in a shop window as I passed through town. It never rains but it pours! But I've already read two."

"And are they the only ones you do read?"

"French ones?" Maud considered. "Oh, no. D'Annunzio."

"And what's that?" Mrs. Dyott asked as she affixed a stamp.

"Oh, you dear thing!" Her friend was amused, yet almost showed pity. "I know you don't read," Maud went on; "but why should you? *You* live!"

"Yes—wretchedly enough," Mrs. Dyott returned, getting her letters together. She left her place, holding them as a neat, achieved handful, and came over to the fire, while Mrs. Blessingbourne turned once more to the window, where she was met by another flurry.

Maud spoke then as if moved only by the elements. "Do you expect him through all this?"

Mrs. Dyott just waited, and it had the effect, indescribably, of making everything that had gone before seem to have led up to the question. This effect was even deepened by the way she then said, "Whom do you mean?"

"Why, I thought you mentioned at luncheon that Colonel Voyt was to walk over. Surely he can't."

"Do you care very much?" Mrs. Dyott asked.

Her friend now hesitated. "It depends on what you call 'much.' If you mean should I like to see him—then certainly."

"Well, my dear, I think he understands you're here."

"So that as he evidently isn't coming," Maud laughed, "it's particularly flattering! Or rather," she added, giving up the prospect again, "it would be, I think, quite extraordinarily flattering if he did. Except that, of course," she subjoined, "he might come partly for you."

" 'Partly' is charming. Thank you for 'partly.' If you *are* going upstairs, will you kindly," Mrs. Dyott pursued, "put these into the box as you pass?"

The younger woman, taking the little pile of letters, considered them with envy. "Nine! You *are* good. You're always a living reproach!"

Mrs. Dyott gave a sigh. "I don't do it on purpose. The only thing, this afternoon," she went on, reverting to the other question, "would be their not having come down."

"And as to that you don't know."

"No—I don't know." But she caught even as she spoke a ra-tat-tat of the knocker, which struck her as a sign. "Ah, there!"

"Then I go." And Maud whisked out.

Mrs. Dyott, left alone, moved with an air of selection to the window, and it was as so stationed, gazing out at the wild weather, that the visitor, whose delay to appear spoke of the wiping of boots and the disposal of drenched mackintosh and cap, finally found her. He was tall, lean, fine, with little in him, on the whole, to confirm the titular in the "Colonel Voyt" by which he was announced. But he had left the army, and his reputation for gallantry mainly depended now on his fighting Liberalism in the House of Commons. Even these facts, however, his aspect scantly matched; partly, no doubt, because he looked, as was usually said, un-English. His black hair, cropped close, was lightly powdered with silver, and his dense glossy beard, that of an emir or a caliph, and grown for civil reasons, repeated its handsome color and its somewhat foreign effect. His nose had a strong and shapely arch, and the dark gray of his eyes was tinted with blue. It had been said of him—in relation to these signs—that he would have struck you as a Jew had he not, in spite of his nose, struck you so much as an Irishman. Neither responsibility could in fact have been fixed upon him, and just now, at all events, he was only a pleasant, weather-washed, wind-battered Briton, who brought in from a struggle with the elements that he appeared quite to have enjoyed a certain amount of unremoved mud and an unusual quantity of easy expression. It was exactly the silence ensuing on the retreat of the servant and the closed door that marked between him and his hostess the degree of this ease. They met, as it were, twice: the first time while the servant was there and the second as soon as he was not. The difference was great between the two encounters, though we must add in justice to the second that its marks were at first mainly negative. This communion consisted only in their having drawn each other for a minute as close as possible—as possible, that is, with no help but the full clasp of hands. Thus they were mutually held, and the closeness was at any rate such that, for a little, though it took account of dangers, it did without words. When words presently came the pair were talking by the fire, and she had rung for tea. He had by this time asked if the note he had despatched to her after breakfast had been safely delivered.

"Yes, before luncheon. But I'm always in a state when—except for some extraordinary reason—you send such things by hand. I knew, without it, that you had come. It never fails. I'm sure when you're there—I'm sure when you're not."

He wiped, before the glass, his wet mustache. "I see. But this morning I had an impulse."

"It was beautiful. But they make me as uneasy, sometimes, your impulses, as if they were calculations; make me wonder what you have in reserve."

"Because when small children are too awfully good they die? Well, I *am* a small child compared to you—but I'm not dead yet. I cling to life."

He had covered her with his smile, but she continued grave. "I'm not half so much afraid when you're nasty."

"Thank you! What then did you do," he asked, "with my note?"

"You deserve that I should have spread it out on my dressing-table—or left it, better still, in Maud Blessingbourne's room."

He wondered while he laughed. "Oh, but what does *she* deserve?"

It was her gravity that continued to answer. "Yes—it would probably kill her."

"She believes so in you?"

"She believes so in *you*. So don't be *too* nice to her."

He was still looking, in the chimney-glass, at the state of his beard—brushing from it, with his handkerchief, the traces of wind and wet. "If she also then prefers me when I'm nasty, it seems to me I ought to satisfy her. Shall I now, at any rate, see her?"

"She's so like a pea on a pan over the possibility of it that she's pulling herself together in her room."

"Oh, then, we must try and keep her together. But why, graceful, tender, pretty too—quite, or almost—as she is, doesn't she remarry?"

Mrs. Dyott appeared—and as if the first time—to look for the reason. "Because she likes too many men."

It kept up his spirits. "And how many *may* a lady like——?"

"In order not to like any of them too much? Ah, that, you know, I never found out—and it's too late now. When," she presently pursued, "did you last see her?"

He really had to think. "Would it have been since last November or so?—somewhere or other where we spent three days."

"Oh, at Surredge? I know all about that. I thought you also met afterwards."

He had again to recall. "So we did! Wouldn't it have been somewhere at Christmas? But it wasn't by arrangement!" he laughed, giving with his forefinger a little pleasant nick to his hostess's chin. Then as if something in the way she received this attention put him back to his question of a moment before. "Have you kept my note?"

She held him with her pretty eyes. "Do you want it back?"

"Ah, don't speak as if I did take things——!"

She dropped her gaze to the fire. "No, you don't; not even the hard things a really generous nature often would." She quitted, however, as if to forget that, the chimney-place. "I put it *there!*"

"You've burnt it? Good!" It made him easier, but he noticed the next moment on a table the lemon-colored volume left there by Mrs. Blessingbourne, and, taking it up for a look, immediately put it down. "You might, while you were about it, have burnt that too."

"You've read it?"

"Dear, yes. And you?"

"No," said Mrs. Dyott; "it wasn't for me Maud brought it."

It pulled her visitor up. "Mrs. Blessingbourne brought it?"

"For such a day as this." But she wondered. "How you look! Is it so awful?"

"Oh, like his others." Something had occurred to him; his thought was already far. "Does she know?"

"Why, anything."

But the door opened too soon for Mrs. Dyott, who could only murmur quickly—

"Take care!"

II

It was in fact Mrs. Blessingbourne, who had under her arm the book she had gone up for—a pair of covers that this time showed a pretty, a candid blue. She was followed next minute by the servant, who brought in tea, the consumption of which, with the passage of greetings, inquiries and other light civilities between the two visitors, occupied a quarter of an hour. Mrs. Dyott meanwhile, as a contribution to so much amenity, mentioned to Maud that her fellow-guest wished to scold her for the books she read—a statement met by this friend with the remark that he must first be sure about them. But as soon as he had picked up the new volume he broke out into a frank "Dear, dear!"

"Have you read that too?" Mrs. Dyott inquired. "How much you'll have to talk over together! The other one," she explained to him, "Maud speaks of as terribly tame."

"Ah, I must have that out with her! You don't feel the extraordinary force of the fellow?" Voyt went on to Mrs. Blessingbourne.

And so, round the hearth, they talked—talked soon, while they warmed their toes, with zest enough to make it seem as happy a chance as any of the quieter opportunities their imprisonment might have involved. Mrs. Blessingbourne did feel, it then appeared, the force of the fellow, but she had her reserves and reactions, in which Voyt was much interested. Mrs. Dyott rather detached herself, mainly gazing, as she leaned back, at the fire; she intervened, however, enough to relieve Maud of the sense of being listened to. That sense, with Maud, was too apt to convey that one was listened to for a fool. "Yes, when I read a novel I mostly read a French one," she had said to Voyt in answer to a question about her usual practice; "for I seem with it to get hold more of the real thing—to get more life for my money. Only I'm not so infatuated with them but that sometimes for months and months on end I don't read any fiction at all."

The two books were now together beside them. "Then when you begin again you read a mass?"

"Dear, no. I only keep up with three or four authors."

He laughed at this over the cigarette he had been allowed to light.

"I like your 'keeping up,' and keeping up in particular with 'authors.'"

"One must keep up with somebody," Mrs. Dyott threw off.

"I dare say I'm ridiculous," Mrs. Blessingbourne conceded without heeding it; "but that's the way we express ourselves in my part of the country."

"I only alluded," said Voyt, "to the tremendous conscience of your sex. It's more than mine can keep up with. You take everything too hard. But if you can't read the novel of British and American manufacture, heaven knows I'm at one with you. It seems really to show our sense of life as the sense of puppies and kittens."

"Well," Maud more patiently returned, "I'm told all sorts of people are now doing wonderful things; but somehow I remain outside."

"Ah, it's *they*, it's our poor twangers and twaddlers who remain outside. They pick up a living in the street. And who indeed would want them in?"

Mrs. Blessingbourne seemed unable to say, and yet at the same time to have her idea. The subject, in truth, she evidently found, was not so easy to handle. "People lend me things, and I try; but at the end of fifty pages——"

"There you are! Yes—heaven help us!"

"But what I mean," she went on, "isn't that I don't get wofully weary of the eternal French thing. What's *their* sense of life?"

"Ah, *voilà!*" Mrs. Dyott softly sounded.

"Oh, but it *is* one; you can make it out," Voyt promptly declared. "They do what they feel, and they feel more things than we. They strike so many more notes, and with so different a hand. When it comes to any account of a relation, say, between a man and a woman —I mean an intimate or a curious or a suggestive one—where are we compared to them? They don't exhaust the subject, no doubt," he admitted; "but we don't touch it, don't even skim it. It's as if we denied its existence, its possibility. You'll doubtless tell me, however, he went on, "that as all such relations *are* for us, at the most, much simpler, we can only have all round less to say about them."

She met this imputation with the quickest amusement. "I beg your pardon. I don't think I shall tell you anything of the sort. I don't know that I even agree with your premise."

"About such relations?" He looked agreeably surprised. "You think we make them larger?—or subtler?"

Mrs. Blessingbourne leaned back, not looking, like Mrs. Dyott, at the fire, but at the ceiling. "I don't know what I think."

"It's not that she doesn't know," Mrs. Dyott remarked. "It's only that she doesn't say."

But Voyt had this time no eye for their hostess. For a moment he watched Maud. "It sticks out of you, you know, that you've yourself written something. Haven't you—and published? I've a notion I could read *you*."

"When I do publish," she said without moving, "you'll be the last one I shall tell. I *have*," she went on, "a lovely subject, but it would take an amount of treatment——!"

"Tell us then at least what it is."

At this she again met his eyes. "Oh, to tell it would be to express it, and that's just what I can't do. What I meant to say just now," she added, "was that the French, to my sense, give us only again and again, forever and ever, the same couple. There they are once more, as one has had them to satiety, in that yellow thing, and there I shall certainly again find them in the blue."

"Then why do you keep reading about them?" Mrs. Dyott demanded.

Maud hesitated. "I don't!" she sighed. "At all events, I shan't any more. I give it up."

"You've been looking for something, I judge," said Colonel Voyt, "that you're not likely to find. It doesn't exist."

"What is it?" Mrs. Dyott inquired.

"I never look," Maud remarked, "for anything but an interest."

"Naturally. But your interest," Voyt replied, "is in something different from life."

"Ah, not a bit! I *love* life—in art, though I hate it anywhere else. It's the poverty of the life those people show, and the awful bounders, of both sexes, that they represent."

"Oh, now we have you!" her interlocutor laughed. "To me, when all's said and done, they seem to be—as near as art can come—in the truth of the truth. It can only take what life gives it, though it certainly may be a pity that that isn't better. Your complaint of their monotony is a complaint of their conditions. When you say we get always the same couple what do you mean but that we get always the same passion? Of course we do!" Voyt declared. "If what you're looking for is another, that's what you won't anywhere find."

Maud for a while said nothing, and Mrs. Dyott seemed to wait. "Well, I suppose I'm looking, more than anything else, for a decent woman."

"Oh, then, you mustn't look for her in pictures of passion. That's not her element nor her whereabouts."

Mrs. Blessingbourne weighed the objection. "Doesn't it depend on what you mean by passion?"

"I think one can mean only one thing: the enemy to behavior."

"Oh, I can imagine passions that are, on the contrary, friends to it."

Her interlocutor thought. "Doesn't it depend perhaps on what you mean by behavior?"

"Dear, no. Behavior is just behavior—the most definite thing in the world."

"Then what do you mean by the 'interest' you just now spoke of? The picture of that definite thing?"

"Yes—call it that. Women aren't *always* vicious, even when they're——"

"When they're what?" Voyt asked.

"When they're unhappy. They can be unhappy and good."

"That one doesn't for a moment deny. But can they be 'good' and interesting?"

"That must be Maud's subject!" Mrs. Dyott explained. "To show a woman who *is*. I'm afraid, my dear," she continued, "you could only show yourself."

"You'd show then the most beautiful specimen conceivable"—and Voyt addresssed himself to Maud. "But doesn't it prove that life is, against your contention, more interesting than art? Life you embellish and elevate; but art would find itself able to do nothing with you, and, on such impossible terms, would ruin you."

The color in her faint consciousness gave beauty to her stare. " 'Ruin' me?"

"He means," Mrs. Dyott again indicated, "that you would ruin 'art.' ".

"Without, on the other hand"—Voyt seemed to assent—"its giving at all a coherent impression of you."

"She wants her romance cheap!" said Mrs. Dyott.

"Oh, no—I should be willing to pay for it. I don't see why the romance—since you give it that name—should be all, as the French inveterately make it, for the women who are bad."

"Oh, they pay for it!" said Mrs. Dyott.

"*Do* they?"

"So, at least"—Mrs. Dyott a little corrected herself—"one has gathered (for I don't read your books, you know!) that they're usually shown as doing."

Maud wondered, but looking at Voyt, "They're shown often, no doubt, as paying for their badness. But are they shown as paying for their romance?"

"My dear lady," said Voyt, "their romance *is* their badness. There isn't any other. It's a hard law, if you will, and a strange, but goodness has to go without that luxury. Isn't to *be* good just exactly, all round, to go without?" He put it before her kindly and clearly—regretfully too, as if he were sorry the truth should be so sad. He and she, his pleasant eyes seemed to say, would, had they had the making of it, have made it better. "One has heard it before—at least *I* have; one has heard your question put. But always, when put to a mind not merely muddled, for an inevitable answer. 'Why don't you, *cher monsieur*, give us the drama of virtue?' 'Because, *chère madame*, the high privilege of virtue is precisely to avoid drama.' The adventures of the honest lady? The honest lady hasn't—can't possibly have—adventures."

Mrs. Blessingbourne only met his eyes at first, smiling with a certain intensity. "Doesn't it depend a little on what you call adventures?"

"My poor Maud," said Mrs. Dyott, as if in compassion for sophistry so simple, "adventures are just adventures. That's all you can make of them!"

But her friend went on, for their companion, as if without hearing. "Doesn't it depend a good deal on what you call drama?" Maud spoke as one who had already thought it out. "Doesn't it depend on what you call romance?"

Her listener gave these arguments his very best attention. "Of course you may call things anything you like—speak of them as one thing and mean quite another. But why should it depend on anything? Behind these words we use—the adventure, the novel, the drama, the romance, the situation, in short, as we most comprehensively say—behind them all stands the same sharp fact that they all, in their different ways, represent."

"Precisely!" Mrs. Dyott was full of approval.

Maud, however, was full of vagueness. "What great fact?"

"The fact of a relation. The adventure's a relation; the relation's an adventure. The romance, the novel, the drama are the picture of one. The subject the novelist treats is the rise, the formation, the development, the climax, and for the most part the decline, of one. And what is the honest lady doing on that side of the town?"

Mrs. Dyott was more pointed. "She doesn't so much as *form* a relation."

But Maud bore up. "Doesn't it depend, again, on what you call a relation?"

"Oh," said Mrs. Dyott, "if a gentleman picks up her pocket-handkerchief——"

"Ah, even that's one," their friend laughed, "if she has thrown it to him. We can only deal with one that *is* one."

"Surely," Maud replied. "But if it's an innocent one——?"

"Doesn't it depend a good deal," Mrs. Dyott asked, "on what you call innocent?"

"You mean that the adventures of innocence have so often been the material of fiction? Yes," Voyt replied; "that's exactly what the bored reader complains of. He has asked for bread and been given a stone. What is it but, with absolute directness, a question of interest, or, as people say, of the story? What's a situation undeveloped but a subject lost? If a relation stops, where's the story? If it doesn't stop, where's the innocence? It seems to me you must choose. It would be very pretty if it were otherwise, but that's how we flounder. Art is our flounderings shown."

Mrs. Blessingbourne—and with an air of deference scarce supported perhaps by its sketchiness—kept her deep eyes on this definition. "But sometimes we flounder out."

It immediately touched in Colonel Voyt the spring of a genial derision. "That's just where I expected *you* would! One always sees it come."

"He has, you notice," Mrs. Dyott parenthesised to Maud, "seen it come so often; and he has always waited for it and met it."

"Met it, dear lady, simply enough! It's the old story, Mrs. Blessingbourne. The relation is innocent that the heroine gets out of. The book is innocent that's the story of her getting out. But what the devil—in the name of innocence—was she doing *in?*"

Mrs. Dyott promptly echoed the question. "You have to be in, you know, to *get* out. So there you are already with your relation. It's the end of your goodness."

"And the beginning," said Voyt, "of your play!"

"Aren't they all, for that matter, even the worst," Mrs. Dyott pursued, "supposed *some* time or other to get out? But if, meanwhile, they've been in, however briefly, long enough to adorn a tale——"

"They've been in long enough to point a moral. That is to point ours!" With which, and as if a sudden flush of warmer light had moved him, Colonel Voyt got up. The veil of the storm had parted over a great red sunset.

Mrs. Dyott also was on her feet, and they stood before his charming antagonist who, with eyes lowered and a somewhat fixed smile, had not moved. "We've spoiled her subject!" the elder lady sighed.

"Well," said Voyt, "it's better to spoil an artist's subject than to spoil his reputation. I mean," he explained to Maud with his indulgent manner, "his appearance of knowing what he has got hold of, for that, in the last resort, is his happiness."

She slowly rose at this, facing him with an aspect as handsomely mild as his own. "You can't spoil my happiness."

He held her hand an instant as he took leave. "I wish I could add to it!"

III

When he had quitted them and Mrs. Dyott had candidly asked if her friend had found him rude or crude, Maud replied—though not immediately—that she had feared showing only too much that she found him charming. But if Mrs. Dyott took this, it was to weigh the sense. "How could you show it too much?"

"Because I always feel that that's my only way of showing anything. It's absurd, if you like," Mrs. Blessingbourne pursued, "but I never know, in such intense discussions, what strange impression I may give."

Her companion looked amused. "Was it intense?"

"*I* was," Maud frankly confessed.

"Then it's a pity you were so wrong. Colonel Voyt, you know, is right." Mrs. Blessingbourne at this gave one of the slow, soft, silent headshakes to which she often resorted and which, mostly accompanied by the light of cheer, had somehow, in spite of the small obstinacy that smiled in them, a special grace. With this grace, for a moment, her friend, looking her up and down, appeared impressed, yet not too much so to take, the next minute, a decision. "Oh, my dear, I'm sorry to differ from anyone so lovely—for you're awfully beautiful to-night, and your frock's the very nicest I've ever seen you wear. But he's as right as he can be."

Maud repeated her motion. "Not so right, at all events, as he thinks he is. Or perhaps I can say," she went on, after an instant, "that I'm not so wrong. I do know a little what I'm talking about."

Mrs. Dyott continued to study her. "You *are* vexed. You naturally don't like it—such destruction."

"Destruction?"

"Of your illusion."

"I *have* no illusion. If I had, moreover, it wouldn't be destroyed. I have, on the whole, I think, my little decency."

Mrs. Dyott stared. "Let us grant it for argument. What, then?"

"Well, I've also my little drama."

"An attachment?"

"An attachment."

"That you shouldn't have?"

"That I shouldn't have."

"A passion?"

"A passion."

"Shared?"

"Ah, thank goodness, no!"

Mrs. Dyott continued to gaze. "The object's unaware——?"

"Utterly."

Mrs. Dyott turned it over. "Are you sure?"

"Sure."

"That's what you call your decency? But isn't it," Mrs. Dyott asked, "rather *his?*"

"Dear, no. It's only his good fortune."

Mrs. Dyott laughed. "But yours, darling—your good fortune: where does *that* come in?"

"Why, in my sense of the romance of it."

"The romance of what? Of his not knowing?"

"Of my not wanting him to. If I did"—Maud had touchingly worked it out—"where would be my honesty?"

The inquiry, for an instant, held her friend; yet only, it seemed, for a stupefaction that was almost amusement. "Can you want or not want as you like? Where in the world, if you don't want, is your romance?"

Mrs. Blessingbourne still wore her smile, and she now, with a light gesture that matched it, just touched the region of her heart. "There!"

Her companion admiringly marveled. "A lovely place for it, no doubt!—but not quite a place, that I can see, to make the sentiment a relation."

"Why not? What more is required for a relation for *me?*"

"Oh, all sorts of things, I should say! And many more, added to those, to make it one for the person you mention."

"Ah, that I don't pretend it either should be or *can* be. I only speak for myself."

It was said in a manner that made Mrs. Dyott, with a visible mixture of impressions, suddenly turn away. She indulged in a vague movement or two, as if to look for something; then again found herself near her friend, on whom with the same abruptness, in fact with a strange sharpness, she conferred a kiss that might have represented either her tribute to exalted consistency or her idea of a graceful close of the discussion. "You deserve that one should speak *for* you!"

Her companion looked cheerful and secure. "How *can* you, without knowing——?"

"Oh, by guessing! It's not——?"

But that was as far as Mrs. Dyott could get. "It's not," said Maud, "anyone you've ever seen."

"Ah, then, I give you up!"

And Mrs. Dyott conformed, for the rest of Maud's stay, to the spirit of this speech. It was made on a Saturday night, and Mrs. Blessingbourne remained till the Wednesday following, an interval during which, as the return of fine weather was confirmed by the Sunday, the two ladies found a wider range of action. There were drives to be taken, calls made, objects of interest seen, at a distance; with the effect of much easy talk and still more easy silence. There had been a question of Colonel Voyt's probable return on the Sunday, but the whole time passed without a sign from him, and it was merely mentioned by Mrs. Dyott, in explanation, that he must have been suddenly called, as he was so liable to be, to town. That this in fact was what had happened he made clear to her on Thursday afternoon, when, walking over again late, he found her alone. The consequence of his Sunday letters had been his taking, that day, the 4.15. Mrs. Voyt had gone back on Thursday, and he now, to settle on the spot the question of a piece of work begun at his place, had rushed down for a few hours in anticipation of the usual collective move for the week's end. He was to go up again by the later train, and had to count a little—a fact accepted by his hostess with the hard pliancy of practice—his present happy moments. Too few as these were, however, he found time to make of her an inquiry or two not directly bearing on their situation. The first was a recall of the question for which Mrs. Blessingbourne's entrance on the previous Saturday had arrested the answer. Did that lady know of anything between them?

"No. I'm sure. There's one thing she does know," Mrs. Dyott went on; "but it's quite different and not so very wonderful."

"What, then, is it?"

"Well, that she's herself in love."

Voyt showed his interest. "You mean she told you?"

"I got it out of her."

He showed his amusement. "Poor thing! And with whom?"

"With you."

His surprise, if the distinction might be made, was less than his wonder. "You got that out of her too?"

"No—it remains in. Which is much the best way for it. For you to know it would be to end it."

He looked rather cheerfully at sea. "Is that then why you tell me?"

"I mean for her to know you know it. Therefore it's in your interest not to let her."

"I see," Voyt after a moment returned. "Your real calculation is that my interest will be sacrificed to my vanity—so that, if your other idea is just, the flame will in fact, and thanks to her morbid conscience, expire by her taking fright at seeing me so pleased. But I promise you," he declared, "that she sha'n't see it. So there you are!" She kept her eyes on him and had evidently to admit, after a little, that there she was. Distinct as he had made the case, however, he was not yet quite satisfied. "Why are you so sure that I'm the man?"

"From the way she denies you."

"You put it to her?"

"Straight. If you hadn't been she would, of course, have confessed to you—to keep me in the dark about the real one."

Poor Voyt laughed out again. "Oh, you dear souls!"

"Besides," his companion pursued, "I was not in want of that evidence."

"Then what other had you?"

"Her state before you came—which was what made me ask you how much you had seen her. And her state after it," Mrs. Dyott added. "And her state," she wound up, "while you were here."

"But her state while I was here was charming."

"Charming. That's just what I say."

She said it in a tone that placed the matter in its right light—a light in which they appeared kindly, quite tenderly, to watch Maud wander away into space with her lovely head bent under a theory rather too big for it. Voyt's last word, however, was that there was just enough in it —in the theory—for them to allow that she had not shown herself, on the occasion of their talk, wholly bereft of sense. Her consciousness, if they let it alone—as they of course after this, mercifully must—*was*, in the last analysis, a kind of shy romance. Not a romance like their own, a thing to make the fortune of any author up to the mark—one who should have the invention or who *could* have the courage; but a small, scared, starved, subjective satisfaction that would do her no harm and nobody else any good. Who but a duffer—he stuck to his contention—would see the shadow of a "story" in it?

JAMES LANE ALLEN

(1849–1925)

JAMES LANE ALLEN was born near Lexington, Ky., in 1849. He was largely self-educated, and began writing at a comparatively early age. His novels and stories are the expression for the most part of Southern life and character.

King Solomon of Kentucky is a typical story, leisurely, vivid and without obvious artifice. The story is reprinted from the volume *Flute and Violin*, Century Co., 1891, by permission of the James Lane Allen Estate and the publishers.

KING SOLOMON OF KENTUCKY

IT had been a year of strange disturbances—a desolating drought, a hurly-burly of destructive tempests, killing frosts in the tender valleys, mortal fevers in the tender homes. Now came tidings that all day the wail of myriads of locusts was heard in the green woods of Virginia and Tennessee; now that Lake Erie was blocked with ice on the very verge of summer, so that in the Niagara new rocks and islands showed their startling faces. In the Blue-grass Region of Kentucky countless caterpillars were crawling over the ripening apple orchards and leaving the trees as stark as when tossed in the thin air of bitter February days.

Then, flying low and heavily through drought and tempest and frost and plague, like the royal presence of disaster, that had been but heralded by its mournful train, came nearer and nearer the dark angel of the pestilence.

M. Xaupi had given a great ball only the night before in the dancing-rooms over the confectionery of M. Giron—that M. Giron who made the tall pyramids of méringues and macaroons for wedding suppers, and spun around them a cloud of candied webbing as white and misty as the veil of the bride. It was the opening cotillon party of the summer. The men came in blue cloth coats with brass buttons, buff waistcoats, and laced and ruffled shirts; the ladies came in white satins with ethereal silk overdresses, embroidered in the figure of a gold beetle or an oak leaf of green. The walls of the ballroom were painted to represent landscapes of blooming orange-trees, set here and there in clustering tubs; and the chandeliers and sconces were lighted with innumerable wax-candles, yellow and green and rose.

Only the day before, also, Clatterbuck had opened for the summer a new villa-house, six miles out in the country, with a dancing-pavilion in a grove of maples and oaks, a pleasure-boat on a sheet of crystal water, and a cellar stocked with old sherry, Sauterne, and Château Margaux wines, with anisette, "Perfect Love," and Guigholet cordials.

Down on Water Street, near where now stands a railway station, Hugh Lonney, urging that the fear of cholera was not the only incentive to cleanliness, had just fitted up a sumptuous bathhouse, where cold and shower baths might be had at twelve and a half cents each, or hot ones at three for half a dollar.

Yes, the summer of 1833 was at hand, and there must be new pleasures, new luxuries; for Lexington was the Athens of the West and the Kentucky Birmingham.

Old Peter Leuba felt the truth of this, as he stepped smiling out of his little music-store on Main Street, and, rubbing his hands briskly together, surveyed once more his newly arranged windows, in which were displayed gold and silver epaulets, bottles of Jamaica rum, garden seeds from Philadelphia, drums and guitars and harps. Dowees & Grant felt it in their drug-store on Cheapside, as they sent off a large order for calomel and superior Maccoboy, rappee, and Lancaster snuff. Bluff little Daukins Tegway felt it, as he hurried on the morning of that day to the office of the *Observer and Reporter*, and advertised that he would willingly exchange his beautiful assortment of painted muslins and Dunstable bonnets for flax and feathers. On the threshold he met a florid farmer, who had just offered ten dollars' reward for a likely runaway boy with a long fresh scar across his face; and to-morrow the paper would contain one more of those tragical little cuts, representing an African slave scampering away at the top of his speed, with a stick swung across his shoulder and a bundle dangling down his back. In front of Postlethwaite's Tavern, where now stands the Phœnix Hotel, a company of idlers, leaning back in Windsor chairs and planting their feet against the opposite wall on a level with their heads, smoked and chewed and yawned, as they discussed the administration of Jackson and arranged for the coming of Daniel Webster in June, when they would give him a great barbecue, and roast in his honor a buffalo bull taken from the herd emparked near Ashland. They hailed a passing merchant, who, however, would hear nothing of the bull, but fell to praising his Rocky Mountain beaver and Goose Creek salt; and another, who turned a dead ear to Daniel Webster, and invited them to drop in and examine his choice essences of peppermint, bergamot, and lavender.

But of all the scenes that might have been observed in Lexington on that day, the most remarkable occurred in front of the old courthouse at the hour of high noon. On the mellow stroke of the clock in the steeple above the sheriff stepped briskly forth, closely followed by a man of powerful frame, whom he commanded to station himself on the pavement several feet off. A crowd of men and boys had already collected in anticipation, and others came quickly up as the clear voice of the sheriff was heard across the open public square and old market-place.

He stood on the topmost of the courthouse steps, and for a moment looked down on the crowd with the usual air of official severity.

"Gentlemen," he then cried out sharply, "by an ordah of the cou't I now offah this man at public sale to the highes' biddah. He is able-bodied but lazy, without visible property or means of suppoht, an' of dissolute habits. He is therefoh adjudged guilty of high misdemeanahs, an' is to be sole into labah foh a twelve-month. How much, then, am I offahed foh the vagrant? How much am I offahed foh ole King Sol'mon?"

Nothing was offered for old King Solomon. The spectators formed themselves into a ring around the big vagrant and settled down to enjoy the performance.

"Staht 'im, somebody."

Somebody started a laugh, which rippled around the circle.

The sheriff looked on with an expression of unrelaxed severity, but catching the eye of an acquaintance on the outskirts, he exchanged a lightning wink of secret appreciation. Then he lifted off his tight beaver hat, wiped out of his eyes a little shower of perspiration which rolled suddenly down from above, and warmed a degree to his theme.

"Come, gentlemen," he said, more suasively, "it's too hot to stan' heah all day. Make me an offah! You all know ole King Sol'mon; don't wait to be interduced. How much, then, to staht 'im? Say fifty dollahs!

Twenty-five! Fifteen! Ten! Why, gentlemen! Not *ten* dollahs? Re-membah this is the Blue-grass Region of Kentucky—the land of Boone an' Kenton, the home of Henry Clay!" he added, in an oratorical *crescendo*.

"He ain't wuth his victuals," said an oily little tavern-keeper folding his arms restfully over his own stomach and cocking up one piggish eye into his neighbor's face. "He ain't wuth his 'taters."

"Buy 'im foh 'is rags!" cried a young law-student, with a Blackstone under his arm, to the town rag-picker opposite, who was unconsciously ogling the vagrant's apparel.

"I *might* buy 'im foh 'is *scalp*," drawled a farmer, who had taken part in all kinds of scalp contests and was now known to be busily engaged in collecting crow scalps for a match soon to come off between two rival counties.

"I think I'll buy 'im foh a hat-sign," said a manufacturer of ten-dollar Castor and Rhorum hats. This sally drew merry attention to the vagrant's hat, and the merchant felt rewarded.

"You'd bettah say the town ought to buy 'im an' put 'im up on top of the cou't-house as a scarecrow foh the cholera," said someone else.

"What news of the cholera did the stage-coach bring this mohning?" quickly inquired his neighbor in his ear; and the two immediately fell into low, grave talk, forgot the auction, and turned away.

"Stop, gentlemen, stop!" cried the sheriff, who had watched the rising tide of good-humor, and now saw his chance to float in on it with spreading sails. "You're runnin' the price in the wrong direction —down, not up. The law requires that he be sole to the highes' biddah, not the lowes'. As loyal citizens, uphole the constitution of the com-monwealth of Kentucky an' make me an offah; the man is really a great bargain. In the first place, he would cos' his ownah little or nothin', because, as you see, he keeps himself in cigahs an' clo'es; then, his main article of diet is whisky—a supply of which he always has on han'. He don't even need a bed, foh you know he sleeps jus' as well on any dooh-step; noh a chair, foh he prefers to sit roun' on the curbstones. Re-membah, too, gentlemen, that ole King Sol'mon is a Virginian—from the same neighborhood as Mr. Clay. Remembah that he is well edu-cated, that he is an *awful* Whig, an' that he has smoked mo' of the stumps of Mr. Clay's cigahs than any other man in existence. If you don't b'lieve *me*, gentlemen, yondah goes Mr. Clay now; call *him* ovah an' ask 'im foh yo'se'ves."

He paused, and pointed with his right forefinger towards Main Street, along which the spectators, with a sudden craning of necks, beheld the familiar figure of the passing statesman.

"But you don't need *any*body to tell you these fac's, gentlemen," he continued. "You merely need to be reminded that ole King Sol'mon is no ohdinary man. Mo'ovah he has a kine heaht, he nevah spoke a rough wohd to anybody in this worl', an' he is as proud as Tecumseh of his good name an' charactah. An', gentlemen," he added, bridling with an air of mock gallantry and laying a hand on his heart, "if anythin' fu'thah is required in the way of a puffect encomium, we all know that there isn't anothah man among us who cuts as wide a swath among the ladies. The'foh, if you have any appreciation of virtue, any magnanimity of heaht; if you set a propah valuation upon the descendants of Virginia, that mothah of Presidents; if you believe in the pure laws of Kentucky as the pioneer bride of the Union; if you love America an' love the worl'—make me a gen'rous, high-toned offah foh ole King Sol'mon!"

He ended his peroration amid a shout of laughter and applause, and, feeling satisfied that it was a good time for returning to a more practical treatment of his subject, proceeded in a sincere tone:

"He can easily earn from one to two dollahs a day, an' from three to six hundred a yeah. There's not anothah white man in town capable of doin' as much work. There's not a niggah han' in the hemp factories with such muscles an' such a chest. *Look* at 'em! An', if you don't b'lieve me, step fo'wahd and *feel* 'em. How much, then, is bid foh' im?"

"One dollah!" said the owner of a hemp factory, who had walked forward and felt the vagrant's arm, laughing, but coloring up also as the eyes of all were quickly turned upon him. In those days it was not an unheard-of thing for the muscles of a human being to be thus examined when being sold into servitude to a new master.

"Thank you!" cried the sheriff, cheerily. "One precinc' heard from! One dollah! I am offahed one dollah foh ole King Sol'mon. One dollah foh the king! Make it a half. One dollah an' a half. Make it a half. One dol-dol-dol-dollah!"

Two medical students, returning from lectures at the old Medical Hall, now joined the group, and the sheriff explained:

"One dollah is bid foh the vagrant ole King Sol'mon, who is to be sole into labah foh a twelvemonth. Is there any othah bid? Are you all done? One dollah, once—"

"Dollah and a half," said one of the students, and remarked half jestingly under his breath to his companion. "I'll buy him on the chance of his dying. We'll dissect him."

"Would you own his body if he *should* die?"

"If he dies while bound to me, I'll arrange *that*."

"One dollah an' a half," resumed the sheriff; and falling into the tone of a facile auctioneer he rattled on:

"One dollah an' a half foh ole Sol'mon—sol, sol sol,—do, re, mi, fa, sol—do, re, mi, fa, sol! Why, gentlemen, you can set the king to music!"

All this time the vagrant had stood in the center of that close ring of jeering and humorous bystanders—a baffling text from which to have preached a sermon on the infirmities of our imperfect humanity. Some years before, perhaps as a master-stroke of derision, there had been given to him that title which could but heighten the contrast of his personality and estate with every suggestion of the ancient sacred magnificence; and never had the mockery seemed so fine as at this moment, when he was led forth into the streets to receive the lowest sentence of the law upon his poverty and dissolute idleness. He was apparently in the very prime of life—a striking figure, for nature at least had truly done some royal work on him. Over six feet in height, erect, with limbs well shaped and sinewy, with chest and neck full of the lines of great power, a large head thickly covered with long reddish hair, eyes blue, face beardless, complexion fair but discolored by low passions and excesses—such was old King Solomon. He wore a stiff, high, black Castor hat of the period, with the crown smashed in and the torn rim hanging down over one ear; a black cloth coat in the style, ragged and buttonless; a white cotton shirt, with the broad collar crumpled, wide open at the neck and down his sunburnt bosom; blue jeans pantaloons, patched at the seat and the knees; and ragged cotton socks that fell down over the tops of his dusty shoes, which were open at the heels.

In one corner of his sensual mouth rested the stump of a cigar. Once during the proceedings he had produced another, lighted it, and continued quietly smoking. If he took to himself any shame as the central figure of this ignoble performance, no one knew it. There was something almost royal in his unconcern. The humor, the badinage, the open contempt, of which he was the public target, fell thick and fast upon him, but as harmlessly as would balls of pitch upon a coat of mail. In truth, there was that in his great, lazy, gentle, good-humored bulk and bearing which made the gibes seem all but despicable. He shuffled from one foot to the other as though he found it a trial to stand up so long, but all the while looking the spectators full in the eyes without the least impatience. He suffered the man of the factory to walk round him and push and pinch his muscles as calmly as though he had been the show bull at a country fair. Once only, when the sheriff had pointed across the street at the figure of Mr. Clay, he had looked quickly in that direction with a kindling light in his eye and a passing flush on his face. For the rest, he seemed like a man who has drained his cup of human life and has nothing left him but to fill again and drink without the least surprise or eagerness.

The bidding between the man of the factory and the student had gone slowly on. The price had reached ten dollars. The heat was intense, the sheriff tired. Then something occurred to revivify the scene. Across the market-place and towards the steps of the courthouse there suddenly came trundling along in breathless haste a huge old negress, carrying on one arm a large shallow basket containing apple crab-lanterns and fresh gingerbread. With a series of half-articulate grunts and snorts she approached the edge of the crowd and tried to force her way through. She coaxed, she begged, she elbowed and pushed and scolded, now laughing, and now with a passion of tears in her thick, ex-cited voice. All at once, catching sight of the sheriff, she lifted one pon-derous brown arm, naked to the elbow, and waved her hand to him above the heads of those in front.

"Hole on, marster! Hole on!" she cried, in a tone of humorous en-treaty. "Don' knock 'im off till I come! Gim *me* bid at 'im!"

The sheriff paused and smiled. The crowd made way tumultuously, with broad laughter and comment.

Stan' aside theah an' let Aun' Charlotte in!"

"*Now* you'll see biddin'!"

"Get out of the way foh Aun' Charlotte!"

"Up, my free niggah! Hurrah foh Kentucky!"

A moment more and she stood inside the ring of spectators, her basket on the pavement at her feet, her hands plumped akimbo into her fath-omless sides, her head up, and the soft, motherly eyes turned eagerly upon the sheriff. Of the crowd she seemed unconscious, and on the vagrant before her she had not cast a single glance.

She was dressed with perfect neatness. A red and yellow Madras kerchief was bound about her head in a high coil, and another was crossed over the bosom of her stiffly starched and smoothly ironed blue cottonade dress. Rivulets of perspiration ran down over her nose, her temples, and around her ears, and disappeared mysteriously in the creases of her brown neck. A single drop accidentally hung glistening like a diamond on the circlet of one of her large brass earrings.

The sheriff looked at her a moment, smiling, but a little disconcerted The spectacle was unprecedented.

"What do you want heah, Aun' Charlotte?" he asked, kindly. "You can't sell yo' pies an' gingerbread heah."

"I don' *wan*' sell no pies en gingerbread," she replied, contemptu-ously. "I wan' bid on *him*," and she nodded sidewise at the vagrant.

"White folks allers sellin' niggahs to wuk fuh *dem*; I gwine buy a white man to wuk fuh *me*. En he gwine t' git a mighty hard mistiss, you heah *me*!"

The eyes of the sheriff twinkled with delight.

"Ten dollahs is offahed foh ole King Sol'mon. Is theah any othah bid? Are you all done?"

"'Leben," she said.

Two young ragamuffins crawled among the legs of the crowd up to her basket and filched pies and cake beneath her very nose.

"Twelve!" cried the student, laughing.

"Thirteen!" She laughed too, but her eyes flashed.

"*You are bidding against a niggah*," whispered the student's companion in his ear.

"So I am; let's be off," answered the other, with a hot flush on his proud face.

Thus the sale was ended, and the crowd variously dispersed. In a distant corner of the courtyard the ragged urchins were devouring their unexpected booty. The old negress drew a red handkerchief out of her bosom, untied a knot in a corner of it, and counted out the money to the sheriff. Only she and the vagrant were now left on the spot.

"You have bought me. What do you want me to do?" he asked quietly.

"Lohd, honey!" she answered, in a low tone of affectionate chiding. "I don' wan' you to do *nothin'*! I wuzn' gwine t' 'low dem white folks to buy you. Dey'd wuk you till you dropped dead. You go 'long en do ez you please."

She gave a cunning chuckle of triumph in thus setting at naught the ends of justice, and, in a voice rich and musical with affection, she said, as she gave him a little push:

"You bettah be gittin' out o' dis blazin' sun. G' on home! I be 'long by-en-by."

He turned and moved slowly away in the direction of Water Street, where she lived; and she, taking up her basket, shuffled across the market-place towards Cheapside, muttering to herself the while:

"I come mighty nigh gittin' dah too late, foolin' 'long wid dese pies. Sellin' *him* 'ca'se he don' wuk! Umph! If all de men in dis town dat don' wuk wuz to be tuk up en sole, d' wouldn' be 'nough money in de town to buy 'em. Don' I see 'em settin' roun' dese taverns f'om mohnin' till night?"

She snorted out her indignation and disgust, and sitting down on the sidewalk, under a Lombardy poplar, uncovered her wares and kept the flies away with a locust bough, not discovering in her alternating good and ill humor, that half of them had been filched by her old tormentors.

This was the memorable scene enacted in Lexington on that memorable day of the year 1833—a day that passed so briskly. For whoever met and spoke together asked the one question: Will the cholera come to Lexington? And the answer always gave a nervous haste to business —a keener thrill to pleasure. It was of the cholera that the negro woman heard two sweet passing ladies speak as she spread her wares on the sidewalk. They were on their way to a little picture-gallery just opened opposite M. Giron's ball-room, and in one breath she heard them discussing their toilets for the evening and in the next several portraits by Jouett.

So the day passed, the night came on, and M. Xaupi gave his brilliant ball. Poor old Xaupi—poor little Frenchman! whirled as a gamin of Paris through the mazes of the Revolution, and lately come all the way to Lexington to teach the people how to dance. Hop about blithely on thy dry legs, basking this night in the waxen radiance of manners and melodies and graces! Where will be thy tunes and airs to-morrow! Ay, smile and prompt away! On and on! Swing corners, ladies and gentlemen! Form the basket! Hands all round!

While the bows were still darting across the strings, out of the low, red east there shot a long, tremulous bow of light up towards the zenith. And then, could human sight have beheld the invisible, it might have seen hovering over the town, over the ballroom, over M. Xaupi, the awful presence of the plague.

But knowing nothing of this, the heated revelers went merrily home in the chill air of the red and saffron dawn. And knowing nothing of it also, a man awakened on the door-step of a house opposite the ballroom, where he had long since fallen asleep. His limbs were cramped and a shiver ran through his frame. Staggering to his feet, he made his way down to the house of Free Charlotte, mounted to his room by means of a stairway opening on the street, threw off his outer garments, kicked off his shoes, and taking a bottle from a closet pressed it several times to his lips with long outward breaths of satisfaction. Then, casting his great white bulk upon the bed, in a minute more he had sunk into a heavy sleep—the usual drunken sleep of old King Solomon.

He, too, had attended M. Xaupi's ball, in his own way and in his proper character, being drawn to the place for the pleasure of seeing the fine ladies arrive and float in, like large white moths of the summer night, of looking in through the open windows as the many-colored waxen lights and the snowy arms and shoulders, of having blown out to him the perfume and the music; not worthy to go in, being the lowest of the low, but attending from a door-step of the street opposite —with a certain rich passion in his nature for splendor and revelry and sensuous beauty.

About 10 o'clock the sunlight entered through the shutter and awoke him. He threw one arm up over his eyes to intercept the burning rays. As he lay outstretched and stripped of grotesque rags, it could be better seen in what a mold nature had cast his figure. His breast, bare and tanned, was barred by full, arching ribs and knotted by crossing muscles; and his shirt-sleeve, falling away to the shoulder from his bent arm, revealed its crowded muscles in the high relief of heroic bronze. For although he had been sold as a vagrant, old King Solomon had in earlier years followed the trade of a digger of cellars, and the strenuous use of mattock and spade had developed every sinew to the utmost. His whole person, now half naked and in repose, was full of the suggestions of unspent power. Only his face, swollen and red, only his eyes, bloodshot and dull, bore the impress of wasted vitality. There, all too plainly stamped, were the passions long since raging and still on fire.

The sunlight had stirred him to but a low degree of consciousness, and some minutes passed before he realized that a stifling, resinous fume impregnated the air. He sniffed it quickly; through the window seemed to come the smell of burning tar. He sat up on the edge of the bed and vainly tried to clear his thoughts.

The room was a clean but poor habitation—uncarpeted, white-washed, with a piece or two of the cheapest furniture, and a row of pegs on one wall, where usually hung those tattered coats and panta-loons, miscellaneously collected, that were his purple and fine linen. He turned his eyes in this direction now and noticed that his clothes were missing. The old shoes had disappeared from their corner; the cigar stumps, picked up here and there in the streets according to his wont, were gone from the mantelpiece. Near the door was a large bundle tied up in a sheet. In a state of bewilderment, he asked himself what it all meant. Then a sense of the silence in the street below pos-sessed him. At this hour he was used to hear noises enough—from Hugh Lonney's new bathhouse on one side, from Harry Sikes's barber shop on the other.

A mysterious feeling of terror crept over and helped to sober him. How long had he lain asleep? By degrees he seemed to remember that two or three times he had awakened far enough to drink from the bottle under his pillow, only to sink again into heavier stupefaction. By de-grees, too, he seemed to remember that other things had happened—a driving of vehicles this way and that, a hurrying of people along the street. He had thought it the breaking-up of M. Xaupi's ball. More than once had not some one shaken and tried to arouse him? Through the wall of Harry Sikes's barber shop had he not heard cries of pain—sobs of distress?

He staggered to the window, threw open the shutters, and, kneeling at the sill, looked out. The street was deserted. The houses opposite were closed. Cats were sleeping in the silent doorways. But as he looked up and down he caught sight of people hurrying along cross-streets. From a distant lumber yard came the muffled sound of rapid hammer-ings. On the air was the faint roll of vehicles—the hush and the vague noises of a general terrifying commotion.

In the middle of the street below him a keg was burning, and, as he looked, the hoops gave way, the tar spread out like a stream of black lava, and a cloud of inky smoke and deep-red furious flame burst up-ward through the sagging air. Just beneath the window a common cart had been backed close up to the door of the house. In it had been thrown a few small articles of furniture, and on the bottom bedclothes had been spread out as if for a pallet. While he looked old Charlotte hurried out with a pillow.

He called down to her in a strange, unsteady voice:

"What is the matter? What are you doing, Aunt Charlotte?"

She uttered a cry, dropped the pillow, and stared up at him. Her face looked dry and wrinkled.

"My God! De chol'ra's in town! I'm waitin' on you! Dress, en come down en fetch de bun'le by do dooh." And she hurried back into the house.

But he continued leaning on his folded arms, his brain stunned by the shock of the intelligence. Suddenly he leaned far out and looked down at the closed shutters of the barber shop. Old Charlotte reappeared.

"Where is Harry Sikes?" he asked.

"Dead en buried."

"When did he die?"

"Yestidd'y evenin'."

"What day is this?"

"Sadd'y."

M. Xaupi's ball had been on Thursday evening. That night the cholera had broken out. He had lain in his drunken stupor ever since. Their talk had lasted but a minute, but she looked up anxiously and urged him.

"D' ain' no time to was'e, honey! D' ain' no time to was'e. I done got dis cyart to tek you 'way in, en I be ready to start in a minute. Put yo' clo'es on en bring de bun'le wid all yo' yudder things in it."

With incredible activity she climbed into the cart and began to roll up the bedclothes. In reality she had made up her mind to put him into the cart, and the pallet had been made for him to lie and finish his drunken sleep on, while she drove him away to a place of safety.

Still he did not move from the window-sill. He was thinking of Harry Sikes, who had shaved him many a time for nothing. Then he suddenly called down to her:

"Have many died of the cholera? Are there many cases in town?"

She went on with her preparations and took no notice of him. He repeated the question. She got down quickly from the cart and began to mount the staircase. He went back to bed, pulled the sheet up over him, and propped himself up among the pillows. Her soft, heavy footsteps slurred on the stairway as though her strength were failing, and as soon as she entered the room she sank into a chair, overcome with terror. He looked at her with a sudden sense of pity.

"Don't be frightened," he said, kindly. "It might only make it the worse for you,"

"I can't he'p it, honey," she answered, wringing her hands and rocking herself to and fro; "de ole niggah can' he'p it. If de Lohd jes spah me to git out'n dis town wid you! Honey, ain' you able to put on yo' clo'es?"

"You've tied them all up in the sheet."

"De Lohd he'p crazy old niggah!"

She started up and tugged at the bundle, and laid out a suit of his clothes, if things so incongruous could be called a suit.

"Have many people died of the cholera?"

"Dey been dyin' like sheep 'ev since yestidd'y mohnin'—all day, en all las' night, en dis mohnin'! De man he done lock up de huss, en dey been buryin' 'em in cyarts. En de grave-diggah he done run away, en hit look like d' ain' nobody to dig de graves."

She bent over the bundle, tying again the four corners of the sheet. Through the window came the sound of the quick hammers driving nails. She threw up her arms into the air, and then seizing the bundle dragged it rapidly to the door.

"You heah dat? Dey nailin' up cawfins in de lumbah-yahd! Put on yo' clo'es, honey, en come on."

A resolution had suddenly taken shape in his mind.

"Go on away and save your life. Don't wait for me; I'm not going. And good-bye, Aunt Charlotte, in case I don't see you any more. You've been very kind to me—kinder than I deserved. Where have you put my mattock and spade?"

He said this very quietly, and sat up on the edge of the bed, his feet hanging down, and his hand stretched out towards her.

"Honey," she explained, coaxingly, from where she stood, "can't you sobah up a little en put on yo' clo'es? I gwine to tek you 'way to de country. You don' wan' no tools. You can' dig no cellahs now. De chol'ra's in town en de people's dyin' like sheep."

"I expect they will need me," he answered.

She perceived now that he was sober. For an instant her own fear was forgotten in an outburst of resentment and indignation.

"Dig graves fuh 'em, when dey put you up on de block en sell you same ez you wuz a niggah! Dig graves fuh 'em, when dey allers callin' you names on de street en makin' fun o' you!"

"They are not to blame. I have brought it on myself."

"But we can' stay heah en die o' de chol'ra!"

"You mustn't stay. You must go away at once."

"But if I go, who gwine tek cyah o' you?"

"Nobody."

She came quickly across the room to the bed, fell on her knees, clasped his feet to her breast, and looked up into his face with an expression of imploring tenderness. Then, with incoherent cries and with sobs and tears, she pleaded with him—pleaded for dear life; his and her own.

It was a strange scene. What historian of the heart will ever be able to do justice to those peculiar ties which bound the heart of the negro in years gone by to a race of not always worthy masters? This old Virginia nurse had known King Solomon when he was a boy playing with her young master, till that young master died on the way to Kentucky.

At the death of her mistress she had become free with a little property. By thrift and industry she had greatly enlarged this. Years passed and she became the only surviving member of the Virginian household, which had emigrated early in the century to the Blue-grass Region. The same wave of emigration had brought in old King Solomon from the same neighborhood. As she had risen in life, he had sunk. She sat on the sidewalks selling her fruits and cakes; he sat on the sidewalks more idle, more ragged and dissolute. On no other basis than these facts she began to assume a sort of maternal pitying care of him, patching his rags, letting him have money for his vices, and when, a year or two before, he had ceased working almost entirely, giving him a room in her house and taking in payment what he chose to pay.

He brushed his hand quickly across his eyes as she knelt before him now, clasping his feet to her bosom. From coaxing him as an intractable child, she had, in the old servile fashion, fallen to imploring him, with touching forgetfulness of their real relations:

"O my marseter! O my marseter Solomon! Go 'way en save yo' life, en tek yo' po' ole niggah wid you!"

But his resolution was formed, and he refused to go. A hurried footstep paused beneath the window and a loud voice called up. The old nurse got up and went to the window. A man was standing by the cart at her door.

"For God's sake, let me have this cart to take my wife and little children away to the country! There is not a vehicle to be had in town. I will pay you—" He stopped, seeing the distress on her face.

"Is he dead?" he asked, for he knew of her care of old King Solomon.

"He *will* die!" she sobbed. "Tilt de t'ings out on de pavement. I gwine t' stay wid 'im en tek cyah o' 'im."

A little later, dressed once more in grotesque rags and carrying on his shoulder a rusty mattock and a rusty spade, old King Solomon appeared in the street below and stood looking up and down it with an air of anxious indecision. Then shuffling along rapidly to the corner of Mill Street, he turned up towards Main.

Here a full sense of the terror came to him. A man, hurrying along with his head down, ran full against him and cursed him for the delay:

"Get out of my way, you old beast!" he cried, "If the cholera would carry you off it would be a blessing to the town."

Two or three little children, already orphaned and hungry, wandered past, crying and wringing their hands. A crowd of negro men with the muscles of athletes, some with naked arms, some naked to the waist, their eyes dilated, their mouths hanging open, sped along in tumultuous disorder. The plague had broken out in the hemp factory and scattered them beyond control.

He grew suddenly faint and sick. His senses swam, his heart seemed to cease beating, his tongue burned, his throat was dry, his spine like ice. For a moment the contagion of deadly fear overcame him, and, unable to stand, he reeled to the edge of the sidewalk and sat down.

Before him along the street passed the flying people—men on horseback with their wives behind and children in front, families in carts and wagons, merchants in two-wheeled gigs and sulkies. A huge red and yellow stagecoach rolled ponderously by, filled within, on top, in front, and behind with a company of riotous students of law and of medicine. A rapid chorus of voices shouted to him as they passed:

"Good-bye, Solomon!"

"The cholera'll have you befoah sunset!"

"Better be diggin' yoah grave, Solomon! That'll by yoah last cellah."

"Dig us a big wine cellah undah the Medical Hall while we are away."

"And leave yo' body there! We want yo' skeleton."

"Good-bye, old Solomon!"

A wretched carry-all passed with a household of more wretched women; their tawdry and gay attire, their haggard and painted and ghastly faces, looking horrible in the blaze of the pitiless sunlight. They, too, simpered and hailed him and spent upon him their hardened and degraded badinage. Then there rolled by a high-swung carriage, with the most luxurious of cushions, upholstered with morocco, with a coat-of-arms, a driver and a footman in livery, and drawn by sparkling, prancing horses. Lying back on the satin cushions a fine gentleman; at the window of the carriage two rosy children, who pointed their fingers at the vagrant and turned and looked into their father's face, so that he leaned forward, smiled, leaned back again, and was whirled away to a place of safety.

Thus they passed him, as he sat down on the sidewalk—even physicians from their patients, pastors from their stricken flocks. Why should not he flee? He had no ties, except the faithful affection of an old negress. Should he not at least save her life by going away, seeing that she would not leave him?

The orphaned children wandered past again, sobbing more wearily. He called them to him.

"Why do you not go home? Where is your mother?" he asked.

"She is dead in the house," they answered; "and no one has come to bury her."

Slowly down the street was coming a short funeral train. It passed—a rude cortege: a common cart, in the bottom of which rested a box of plain boards containing the body of the old French dancing-master; walking behind it, with a cambric handkerchief to his eyes, the old French confectioner; at his side, wearing the robes of his office and carrying an umbrella to ward off the burning sun, the beloved Bishop Smith; and behind them, two by two and with linked arms, perhaps a dozen men, most of whom had been at the ball.

No head was lifted or eye turned to notice the vagrant seated on the sidewalk. But when the train had passed he rose, laid his mattock and spade across his shoulder, and stepping out into the street, fell into line at the end of the procession.

They moved down Short Street to the old burying-ground, where the Baptist churchyard is to-day. As they entered it, two grave-diggers passed out and hurried away. Those before them had fled. They had been at work but a few hours. Overcome with horror at the sight of the dead arriving more and more rapidly, they, too, deserted that post of peril. No one was left. Here and there in the churchyard could be seen bodies awaiting interment. Old King Solomon stepped quietly forward and, getting down into one of the half-finished graves, began to dig.

The vagrant had happened upon an avocation.

All summer long, Clatterbuck's dancing-pavilion was as silent in its grove of oaks as a temple of the Druids, and his pleasure-boat nestled in its moorings, with no hand to feather an oar in the little lake. All summer long, no athletic young Kentuckians came to bathe their white bodies in Hugh Lonney's new bathhouse for twelve and a half cents, and no one read Daukins Tegway's advertisement that he was willing to exchange his Dunstable bonnets for flax and feathers. The likely runaway boy, with a long, fresh scar across his face, was never found, nor the buffalo bull roasted for Daniel Webster, and Peter Leuba's guitars were never thrummed on any moonlit verandas. Only Dewees and Grant were busy, dispensing, not snuff, but calomel.

Grass grew in the deserted streets. Gardens became little wildernesses of rank weeds and riotous creepers. Around shut window-lattices roses clambered and shed their perfume into the poisoned air, or dropped their faded petals to strew the echoless thresholds. In darkened rooms family portraits gazed on sad vacancy or looked helplessly down on rigid sheeted forms.

In the trees of poplar and locust along the streets the unmolested birds built and brooded. The oriole swung its hempen nest from a bough over the door of the spider-tenanted factory, and in front of the old Medical Hall the blue-jay shot up his angry crest and screamed harshly down at the passing bier. In a cage hung against the wall of a house in a retired street a mocking-bird sung, beat its breast against the bars, sung more passionately, grew silent and dropped dead from its perch, never knowing that its mistress had long since become a clod to its full-throated requiem.

Famine lurked in the wake of the pestilence. Markets were closed. A few shops were kept open to furnish necessary supplies. Now and then some old negro might have been seen, driving a meat-wagon in from the country, his nostrils stuffed with white cotton saturated with camphor. Oftener the only visible figure in the streets was that of a faithful priest going about among his perishing fold, or that of the bishop moving hither and thither on his ceaseless ministrations.

But over all the ravages of that terrible time there towered highest the solitary figure of that powerful grave-digger, who, nerved by the spectacle of the common misfortune, by one heroic effort rose for the time above the wrecks of his own nature. In the thick of the plague, in the very garden spot of the pestilence, he ruled like an unterrified king. Through days unnaturally chill with gray cloud and drizzling rain, or unnaturally hot with the fierce sun and suffocating damps that appeared to steam forth from subterranean cauldrons, he worked unfaltering, sometimes with a helper, sometimes with none. There were times when, exhausted, he would lie down in the half-dug graves and there sleep until able to go on; and many a midnight found him under the spectral moon, all but hidden by the rank nightshade as he bent over to mark out the lines of one of those narrow mortal cellars.

Nature soon smiles upon her own ravages and strews our graves with flowers, not as memories, but for other flowers when the spring returns.

It was one cool, brilliant morning late in that autumn. The air blew fresh and invigorating, as though on the earth there were no corruption, no death. Far southward had flown the plague. A spectator in the open court-square might have seen many signs of life returning to the town. Students hurried along, talking eagerly. Merchants met for the first time and spoke of the winter trade. An old negress, gayly and neatly dressed, came into the market-place, and sitting down on a sidewalk displayed her yellow and red apples and fragrant gingerbread. She hummed to herself an old cradle-song, and in her soft, motherly black eyes shone a mild, happy radiance. A group of young ragamuffins eyed her longingly from a distance. Court was to open for the first time since the spring. The hour was early, and one by one the lawyers passed slowly in. On the steps of the courthouse three men were standing: Thomas Brown, the sheriff, old Peter Leuba, who had just walked over from his music store on Main Street; and little M. Giron, the French confectioner. Each wore mourning on his hat, and their voices were low and grave.

"Gentlemen," the sheriff was saying, "it was on this very spot the day befoah the cholera broke out that I sole 'im as a vagrant. An' I did the meanes' thing a man can evah do. I hel' 'im up to public ridicule foh his weaknesses an' made spoht of 'is infirmities. I laughed at 'is povahty an' 'is ole clo'es. I delivahed on 'im as complete an oration of sarcastic detraction as I could prepare on the spot, out of my own meanness an' with the vulgah sympathies of the crowd. Gentlemen, if I only had that crowd heah now, an' ole King Sol'mon standin' in the midst of it, that I might ask 'im to accept a humble public apology, offahed from the heaht of one who feels himself unworthy to shake 'is han'! But, gentlemen, that crowd will nevah reassemble. Neahly ev'ry man of them is dead, an' ole King Sol'mon buried them."

"He buried my friend Adolphe Xaupi," said François Giron, touching his eyes with his handkerchief.

"There is a case of my best Jamaica rum for him whenever he comes for it," said old Leuba, clearing his throat.

"But, gentlemen, while we are speakin' of ole King Sol'mon we ought not to fohget who it is that has suppohted 'im. Yondah she sits on the sidewalk, sellin' 'er apples an' gingerbread."

The three men looked in the direction indicated.

"Heah comes ole King Sol'mon now," exclaimed the sheriff.

Across the open square the vagrant was seen walking slowly along with his habitual air of quiet, unobtrusive preoccupation. A minute more and he had come over and passed into the courthouse by a side door.

"Is Mr. Clay to be in court to-day?"

"He is expected, I think."

"Then let's go in; there will be a crowd."

"I don't know; so many are dead."

They turned and entered and found seats quietly as possible; for a strange and sorrowful hush brooded over the court-room. Until the bar assembled, it had not been realized how many were gone. The silence was that of a common overwhelming disaster. No one spoke with his neighbor, no one observed the vagrant as he entered and made his way to a seat on one of the meanest benches, a little apart from the others. He had not sat there since the day of his indictment for vagrancy. The judge took his seat and, making a great effort to control himself, passed his eyes slowly over the court-room. All at once he caught sight of old King Solomon sitting against the wall in an obscure corner; and before any one could know what he was doing, he hurried down and walked up to the vagrant and grasped his hand. He tried to speak, but could not. Old King Solomon had buried his wife and daughter—buried them one clouded midnight, with no one present but himself.

Then the oldest member of the bar started up and followed the example; and then the other members, rising by a common impulse, filed slowly back and one by one wrung that hard and powerful hand. After them came the other persons in the court-room. The vagrant, the grave-digger, had risen and stood against the wall, at first with a white face and a dazed expression, not knowing what it meant; afterwards, when he understood it, his head dropped suddenly forward and his tears fell thick and hot upon the hands that he could not see. And his were not the only tears. Not a man in the long file but paid his tribute of emotion as he stepped forward to honor that image of sadly eclipsed but still effulgent humanity. It was not grief, it was not gratitude, nor any sense of making reparation for the past. It was the softening influence of an act of heroism, which makes every man feel himself a brother hand in hand with every other—such power has a single act of moral greatness to reverse the relations of men, lifting up one, and bringing all others to do him homage.

It was the coronation scene in the life of old King Solomon of Kentucky.

SARAH ORNE JEWETT

(1849–1909)

SARAH ORNE JEWETT was born at South Berwick, Maine, in 1849. She was one of the leading exponents of New England life in fiction. She came of an old and cultured family. In 1887 she published her first book, *Deephaven*, a study of New England life in the form of an autobiography. This was followed by a number of other books, novels and short stories concerned with the life and character of New England folk.

Miss Tempy's Watchers is reprinted from *The King of Folly Island*, etc. Copyright, 1888, Houghton Mifflin & Co., by whose permission it is here used.

MISS TEMPY'S WATCHERS

THE time of year was April; the place was a small farming town in New Hampshire, remote from any railroad. One by one the lights had been blown out in the scattered houses near Miss Tempy Dent's; but as her neighbors took a last look out-of-doors, their eyes turned with instinctive curiosity toward the old house, where a lamp burned steadily. They gave a little sigh. "Poor Miss Tempy!" said more than one bereft acquaintance; for the good woman lay dead in her north chamber, and the light was a watcher's light. The funeral was set for the next day, at one o'clock.

The watchers were two of the oldest friends, Mrs. Crowe and Sarah Ann Binson. They were sitting in the kitchen, because it seemed less awesome than the unused best room, and they beguiled the long hours by steady conversation. One would think that neither topics nor opinions would hold out, at that rate, all through the long spring night; but there was a certain degree of excitement just then, and the two women had risen to an unusual level of expressiveness and confidence. Each had already told the other more than one fact that she had determined to keep secret; they were again and again tempted into statements that either would have found impossible by daylight. Mrs. Crowe was knitting a blue yarn stocking for her husband; the foot was already so long that it seemed as if she must have forgotten to narrow it at the proper time. Mrs. Crowe knew exactly what she was about, however; she was of a much cooler disposition that Sister Binson, who made futile attempts at some sewing, only to drop her work into her lap whenever the talk was most engaging.

Their faces were interesting—of the dry, shrewd, quick-witted New England type, with thin hair twisted neatly back out of the way. Mrs. Crowe could look vague and benignant, and Miss Binson was, to quote her neighbors, a little too sharp-set; but the world knew that she had need to be, with the load she must carry of supporting an inefficient widowed sister and six unpromising and unwilling nieces and nephews. The eldest boy was at last placed with a good man to learn the mason's trade. Sarah Ann Binson, for all her sharp, anxious aspect, never defended herself, when her sister whined and fretted. She was told every week of her life that the poor children never would have had to lift a finger if their father had lived, and yet she had kept her steadfast way with the little farm, and patiently taught the young people many useful things, for which, as everybody said, they would live to thank her. However pleasureless her life appeared to outward view, it was brimful of pleasure to herself.

Mrs. Crowe, on the contrary, was well to do, her husband being a rich farmer and an easy-going man. She was a stingy woman, but for all that she looked kindly; and when she gave away anything, or lifted a finger to help anybody, it was thought a great piece of beneficence, and a compliment, indeed, which the recipient accepted with twice as much gratitude as double the gift that came from a poorer and more generous acquaintance. Everybody liked to be on good terms with Mrs. Crowe. Socially she stood much higher than Sarah Ann Binson. They were both old schoolmates and friends of Temperance Dent, who had asked them, one day, not long before she died, if they would not come together and look after the house, and manage everything, when she was gone. She may have had some hope that they might become closer friends in this period of intimate partnership, and that the richer woman might better understand the burdens of the poorer. They had not kept the house the night before; they were too weary with the care of their old friend, whom they had not left until all was over.

There was a brook which ran down the hillside very near the house, and the sound of it was much louder than usual. When there was silence in the kitchen, the busy stream had a strange insistence in its wild voice, as if it tried to make the watchers understand something that related to the past.

"I declare, I can't begin to sorrow for Tempy yet. I am so glad to have her at rest," whispered Mrs. Crowe. "It is strange to set here without her, but I can't make it clear that she has gone. I feel as if she had got easy and dropped off to sleep, and I'm more scared about waking her up than knowing any other feeling."

"Yes," said Sarah Ann. "It's just like that, ain't it? But I tell you we are goin' to miss her worse than we expect. She's helped me through with many a trial, has Temperance. I ain't the only one who says the same, neither."

These words were spoken as if there were a third person listening; somebody besides Mrs. Crowe. The watchers could not rid their minds of the feeling that they were being watched themselves. The spring wind whistled in the window crack, now and then, and buffeted the little house in a gusty way that had a sort of companionable effect. Yet, on the whole, it was a very still night, and the watchers spoke in a half-whisper.

"She was the freest-handed woman that ever I knew," said Mrs. Crowe, decidedly. "According to her means, she gave away more than anybody. I used to tell her 't wa'n't right. I used really to be afraid that she went without too much, for we have a duty to ourselves."

Sister Binson looked up in a half-amused, unconscious way, and then recollected herself.

Mrs. Crowe met her look with a serious face. "It ain't so easy for me to give as it is for some," she said simply, but with an effort which was made possible only by the occasion. "I should like to say, while Tempy is laying here yet in her own house, that she has been a constant lesson to me. Folks are too kind, and shame me with thanks for what I do. I ain't such a generous woman as poor Tempy was, for all she had nothin' to do with, as one may say."

Sarah Binson was much moved at this confession, and was even pained and touched by the unexpected humility. "You have a good many calls on you"—she began, and then left her kind little compliment half finished.

"Yes, yes, but I've got means enough. My disposition's more of a cross to me as I grow older, and I made up my mind this morning that Tempy's example should be my pattern henceforth." She began to knit faster than ever.

"''Tain't no use to get morbid: that's what Tempy used to say herself," said Sarah Ann, after a minute's silence. "Ain't it strange to say 'used to say?'" and her own voice choked a little. "She never did like to hear folks git goin' about themselves."

"''Twas only because they're apt to do it so as other folks will say 'twasn't so, an' praise 'em up," humbly replied Mrs. Crowe, "and that ain't my object. There wa'n't a child but what Tempy set herself to work to see what she could do to please it. One time my brother's folks had been stopping here in the summer, from Massachusetts. The children was all little, and they broke up a sight of toys, and left 'em when they were going away. Tempy come right up after they rode by, to see if she couldn't help me set the house to rights, and she caught me just as I was going to fling some of the clutter into the stove. I was kind of tired out, starting 'em off in season. 'Oh, give me them!' says she, real pleading; and she wropped 'em up and took 'em home with her when she went, and she mended 'em up and stuck 'em together, and made some young one or other happy with every blessed one. You'd thought I'd done her the biggest favor. 'No thanks to me. I should ha' burnt 'em, Tempy,' says I."

"Some of 'em came to our house, I know," said Miss Binson. "She'd take a lot o' trouble to please a child, 'stead o' shoving of it out o' the way, like the rest of us when we're drove.

"I can tell you the biggest thing she ever done, and I don't know's there's anybody left but me to tell it. I don't want it forgot," Sarah Binson went on, looking up at the clock to see how the night was going. "It was that pretty-looking Trevor girl, who taught the Corners school, and married so well afterwards, out in New York State. You remember her, I dare say?"

"Certain," said Mrs. Crowe, with an air of interest.

"She was a splendid scholar, folks said, and give the school a great start; but she'd overdone herself getting her education, and working to pay for it, and she all broke down one spring, and Tempy made her come and stop with her a while—you remember that? Well, she had an uncle, her mother's brother, out in Chicago, who was well off and friendly, and used to write to Lizzie Trevor, and I dare say make her some presents; but he was a lively, driving man, and didn't take time to stop and think about his folks. He hadn't seen her since she was a little girl. Poor Lizzie was so pale and weakly that she just got through the term o' school. She looked as if she was just going straight off in a decline. Tempy, she cosseted her up a while, and then, next thing folks knew, she was tellin' round how Miss Trevor had gone to see her uncle, and meant to visit Niagary Falls on the way, and stop over night. Now I happened to know, in ways I won't dwell on to explain, that the poor girl was in debt for her schoolin' when she come here, and her last

quarter's pay had just squared it off at last, and left her without a
cent ahead, hardly; but it had fretted her thinking of it, so she paid
it all; those might have dunned her that she owed it to. An' I taxed
Tempy about the girl's goin' off on such a journey till she owned up,
rather'n have Lizzie blamed, that she'd given her sixty dollars, same's
if she was rolling in riches, and sent her off to have a good rest and
vacation."

"Sixty dollars!" exclaimed Mrs. Crowe. "Tempy only had ninety
dollars a year that came in to her; rest of her livin' she got by helpin'
about, with what she raised off this little piece o' ground, sand one
side an' clay the other. An' how often I've heard her tell, years ago,
that she'd rather see Niagary than any other sight in the world!"

The women looked at each other in silence; the magnitude of the
generous sacrifice was almost too great for their comprehension.

"She was just poor enough to do that!" declared Mrs. Crowe at last,
in an abandonment of feeling. "Say what you may, I feel humbled to
the dust," and her companion ventured to say nothing. She never had
given away sixty dollars at once, but it was simply because she never
had it to give. It came to her very lips to say in explanation, "Tempy
was so situated"; but she checked herself in time, for she would not
betray her own loyal guarding of a dependent household.

"Folks say a great deal of generosity, and this one's being public-
sperited, and that one free-handed about giving," said Mrs. Crowe,
who was a little nervous in the silence. "I suppose we can't tell the
sorrow it would be to some folks not to give, same's 'twould be to me
not to save. I seem kind of made for that, as if 'twas what I'd got to do.
I should feel sights better about it if I could make it evident what I was
savin' for. If I had a child, now, Sarah Ann," and her voice was a little
husky,—"if I had a child, I should think I was heapin' of it up because
he was the one trained by the Lord to scatter it again for good. But
here's Mr. Crowe and me, we can't do anything with money, and both
of us like to keep things same's they've always been. Now Priscilla
Dance was talking away like a mill-clapper, week before last. She'd
think I would go right off and get one o' them new-fashioned gilt-and-
white papers for the best room, and some new furniture, an' a marble-
top table. And I looked at her, all struck up. "Why,' says I, 'Priscilla,
that nice old velvet paper ain't hurt a mite. I shouldn't feel 'twas my
best room without it. Dan'el says 'tis the first thing he can remember
rubbin' his little baby fingers on to it, and how splendid he thought
them red roses was.' I maintain," continued Mrs. Crowe stoutly, "that
folks wastes sights o' good money doin' just such foolish things. Tearin'
out the insides o' meetin'-houses, and fixin' the pews different; 'twas
good enough as 'twas with mendin'; then times come, an' they want to
put it all back same's 'twas before."

This touched upon an exciting subject to active members of that parish. Miss Binson and Mrs. Crowe belonged to opposite parties and had at one time come as near hard feelings as they could, and yet escape them. Each hastened to speak of other things and to show her untouched friendliness.

"I do agree with you," said Sister Binson, "that few of us know what use to make of money, beyond everyday necessities. You've seen more o' the world than I have, and know what's expected. When it comes to taste and judgment about such things, I ought to defer to others"; and with this modest avowal the critical moment passed when there might have been an improper discussion.

In the silence that followed, the fact of their presence in a house of death grew more clear than before. There was something disturbing in the noise of a mouse gnawing at the dry boards of a closet wall near by. Both the watchers looked up anxiously at the clock; it was almost the middle of the night, and the whole world seemed to have left them alone with their solemn duty. Only the brook was awake.

"Perhaps we might give a look upstairs now," whispered Mrs. Crowe, as if she hoped to hear some reason against their going just then to the chamber of death; but Sister Binson rose, with a serious and yet satisfied countenance, and lifted the small lamp from the table. She was much more used to watching than Mrs. Crowe, and much less affected by it. They opened the door into a small entry with a steep stairway; they climbed the creaking stairs, and entered the cold upper room on tiptoe. Mrs. Crowe's heart began to beat very fast as the lamp was put on a high bureau, and made long, fixed shadows about the walls. She went hesitatingly toward the solemn shape under its white drapery, and felt a sense of remonstrance as Sarah Ann gently, but in a businesslike way, turned back the thin sheet.

"Seems to me she looks pleasanter and pleasanter," whispered Sarah Ann Binson impulsively, as they gazed at the white face with its wonderful smile. "To-morrow 'twill all have faded out. I do believe they kind of wake up a day or two after they die, and it's then they go." She replaced the light covering, and they both turned quickly away; there was a chill in this upper room.

"'Tis a great thing for anybody to have got through, ain't it?" said Mrs. Crowe softly, as she began to go down the stairs on tiptoe. The warm air from the kitchen beneath met them with a sense of welcome and shelter.

"I don't know why it is, but I feel as near again to Tempy down here as I do up there," replied Sister Binson. "I feel as if the air was full of her, kind of. I can sense things, now and then, that she seems to say. Now I never was one to take up with no nonsense of sperits and such, but I declare I felt as if she told me just now to put some more wood into the stove."

Mrs. Crowe preserved a gloomy silence. She had suspected before this that her companion was of a weaker and more credulous disposition than herself. "'Tis a great thing to have got through," she repeated, ignoring definitely all that had last been said. "I suppose you know as well as I that Tempy was one that always feared death. Well, it's all put behind her now; she knows what 'tis." Mrs. Crowe gave a little sigh, and Sister Binson's quick sympathies were stirred toward this other old friend, who also dreaded the great change.

"I'd never like to forgit almost those last words Tempy spoke plain to me," she said gently, like the comforter she truly was. "She looked up at me once or twice, that last afternoon after I come to set by her, and let Mis' Owen go home; and I says, 'Can I do anything to ease you, Tempy?' and the tears come into my eyes so I couldn't see what kind of a nod she give me. 'No, Sarah Ann, you can't, dear', says she; and then she got her breath again, and says she, looking at me real meanin', 'I'm only a-gettin' sleepier and sleepier; that's all there is,' says she, and smiled up at me kind of wishful, and shut her eyes. I knew well enough all she meant. She'd been lookin' out for a chance to tell me, and I don' know's she ever said much afterwards."

Mrs. Crowe was not knitting; she had been listening too eagerly. "Yes, 'twill be a comfort to think of that sometimes," she said, in acknowledgment.

"I know that old Dr. Prince said once, in evenin' meetin', that he'd watched by many a dyin' bed, as we well knew, and enough o' his sick folks had been scared o' dyin' their whole lives through; but when they come to the last, he'd never seen one but was willin', and most were glad, to go. ''Tis as natural as bein' born or livin' on,' he said. I don't know what had moved him to speak that night. You know he wa'n't in the habit of it, and 'twas the monthly concert of prayer for foreign missions anyways," said Sarah Ann; "but 'twas a great stay to the mind to listen to his words of experience."

"There never was a better man," responded Mrs. Crowe, in a really cheerful tone. She had recovered from her feeling of nervous dread, the kitchen was so comfortable with lamplight and firelight; and just then the old clock began to tell the hour of twelve with leisurely whirring strokes.

Sister Binson laid aside her work, and rose quickly and went to the cupboard. "We'd better take a little to eat," she explained. "The night will go fast after this. I want to know if you went and made some o' your nice cupcake, while you was home to-day?" she asked, in a pleased tone; and Mrs. Crowe acknowledged such a gratifying piece of thoughtfulness for this humble friend who denied herself all luxuries.

Sarah Ann brewed a generous cup of tea, and the watchers drew their chairs up to the table presently, and quelled their hunger with good country appetites. Sister Binson put a spoon into a small, old-fashioned glass of preserved quince, and passed it to her friend. She was most familiar with the house, and played the part of hostess. "Spread some o' this on your bread and butter," she said to Mrs. Crowe. "Tempy wanted me to use some three or four times, but I never felt to. I know she'd like to have us comfortable now, and would urge us to make a good supper, poor dear."

"What excellent preserves she did make!" mourned Mrs. Crowe. "None of us has got her light hand at doin' things tasty. She made the most o' everything, too. Now, she only had that one old quince-tree down in the far corner of the piece, but she'd go out in the spring and tend to it, and look at it so pleasant, and kind of expect the old thorny thing into bloomin'."

"She was just the same with folks," said Sarah Ann. "And she'd never git more'n a little apernful o' quinces, but she'd have every mite o' goodness out o' those, and set the glasses up onto her best-room closet shelf, *so* pleased. 'Twa'n't but a week ago to-morrow mornin' I fetched her a little taste o' jelly in a teaspoon; and she says 'Thank ye,' and took it, an' the minute she tasted it she looked up at me as worried as could be. 'Oh, I don't want to eat that,' says she. 'I always keep that in case o' sickness.' 'You're goin' to have the good o' one tumbler yourself,' says I. 'I'd just like to know who's sick now, if you ain't!' An' she couldn't help laughin', I spoke up so smart. Oh, dear me, how I shall miss talkin' over things with her! She always sensed things, and got just the p'int you meant."

"She didn't begin to age until two or three years ago, did she?" asked Mrs. Crowe. "I never saw anybody keep her looks as Tempy did. She looked young long after I begun to feel like an old woman. The doctor used to say 'twas her young heart, and I don't know but what he was right. How she did do for other folks! There was one spell she wasn't at home a day to a fortnight. She got most of her livin' so, and that made her own potatoes and things last her through. None o' the young folks could get married without her, and all the old ones was disappointed if she wa'n't round when they was down with sickness and had to go. An' cleanin', or tailorin' for boys, or rug-hookin',—there was nothin' but what she could do as handy as most. 'I do love to work,'— ain't you heard her say that twenty times a week?"

Sarah Ann Binson nodded, and began to clear away the empty plates. "We may want a taste o' somethin' more towards mornin'," she said. "There's plenty in the closet here; and in case some comes from a distance to the funeral, we'll have a little table spread after we get back to the house."

"Yes, I was busy all the mornin'. I've cooked up a sight o' things to bring over," said Mrs. Crowe. "I felt 'twas the last I could do for her."

They drew their chairs near the stove again, and took up their work. Sister Binson's rocking-chair creaked as she rocked; the brook sounded louder than ever. It was more lonely when nobody spoke, and presently Mrs. Crowe returned to her thoughts of growing old.

"Yes, Tempy aged all of a sudden. I remember I asked her if she felt as well as common, one day, and she laughed at me good. There, when Mr. Crowe begun to look old, I couldn't help feeling as if somethin' ailed him, and like as not 'twas somethin' he was goin' to git right over, and I dosed him for it stiddy, half of one summer."

"How many things we shall be wanting to ask Tempy!" exclaimed Sarah Ann Binson, after a long pause. "I can't make up my mind to doin' without her. I wish folks could come back just once, and tell us how 'tis where they've gone. Seems then we could do without 'em better."

The brook hurried on, the wind blew about the house now and then; the house itself was a silent place, and the supper, the warm fire, and an absence of any new topics for conversation made the watchers drowsy. Sister Binson closed her eyes first, to rest them for a minute; and Mrs. Crowe glanced at her compassionately, with a new sympathy for the hard-worked little woman. She made up her mind to let Sarah Ann have a good rest, while she kept watch alone; but in a few minutes her own knitting was dropped, and she, too, fell asleep. Overhead, the pale shape of Tempy Dent, the outworn body of that generous, loving-hearted, simple soul, slept on also in its white raiment. Perhaps Tempy herself stood near, and saw her own life and its surroundings with new understanding. Perhaps she herself was the only watcher.

Later, by some hours, Sarah Ann Binson woke with a start. There was a pale light of dawn outside the small windows. Inside the kitchen, the lamp burned dim. Mrs. Crowe awoke, too.

"I think Tempy'd be the first to say 'twas just as well we both had some rest," she said, not without a guilty feeling.

Her companion went to the outer door, and opened it wide. The fresh air was none too cold, and the brook's voice was not nearly so loud as it had been in the midnight darkness. She could see the shapes of the hills, and the great shadows that lay across the lower country. The east was fast growing bright.

"'Twill be a beautiful day for the funeral," she said, and turned again, with a sigh, to follow Mrs. Crowe up the stairs.

HENRY CUYLER BUNNER

(1855–1896)

BUNNER's fame rests on the work he published in the last fifteen years of his life. Born at Oswego, N. Y., he went when he was very young to New York for his education. It soon became apparent that literature was to be his career, and he joined the staff of the *Arcadian*. Later he became the editor of *Puck*. The first of Bunner's stories to meet with success was *The Midge* (1886), a tale of New York life. Then followed a number of others which were subsequently collected in several volumes, *Short Sixes* (1891) among them. His stories are distinguished by simplicity of motive, and are related with subtle humour and an underlying pathos, escaping any sentimentality.

A Letter and a Paragraph is reprinted from *Stories of H. C. Bunner*, copyright, 1891, 1896, by Charles Scribner's Sons, by permission of the publishers.

A LETTER AND A PARAGRAPH

I

THE LETTER

New York, Nov. 16, 1883.

MY DEAR WILL:—

You cannot be expected to remember it, but this is the fifth anniversary of my wedding-day, and to-morrow—it will be to-morrow before this letter is closed—is my birthday—my fortieth. My head is full of those thoughts which the habit of my life moves me to put on paper, where I can best express them; and yet which must be written for only the friendliest of eyes. It is not the least of my happiness in this life that I have one friend to whom I can unlock my heart as I can to you.

The wife has just been putting your namesake to sleep. Don't infer that, even on the occasion of this family feast, he has been allowed to sit up until half past eleven. He went to bed properly enough, with a tear or two, at eight; but when his mother stole into his room just now, after her custom, I heard his small voice raised in drowsy inquiry; and I followed her, and slipped the curtain of the doorway aside, and looked. But I did not go into the room.

The shaded lamp was making a yellow glory in one spot—the head of the little brass crib where my wife knelt by my boy. I saw the little face, so like hers, turned up to her. There was a smile on it that I knew was a reflection of hers. He was winking in a merry half-attempt to keep awake; but wakefulness was slipping away from him under the charm of that smile I could not see. His brown eyes closed, and opened for an instant, and closed again as the tender, happy hush of a child's sleep settled down upon him, and he was gone where we in our heavier slumbers shall hardly follow him. Then, before I could see my wife's face as she bent and kissed him, I let the curtain fall, and crept back here, to sit by the last of the fire, and see that sacred sight again with the spiritual eyes, and to dream wonderingly over the unspeakable happiness that has in some mysterious way come to me, undeserving.

I tell you, Will, that moment was to me like one of those moments of waking that we know in childhood, when we catch the going of a dream too subtly sweet to belong to this earth—a glad vision, gone before our eyes can open wide; not to be figured into any earthly idea, leaving in its passage a joy so high and fine that the poets tell us it is a memory of some heaven from which our young souls are yet fresh.

You can understand how it is that I find it hard to realize that there can be such things in my life; for you know what that life was up to a few years ago. I am like a man who has spent his first thirty years in a cave. It takes more than a decade above ground to make him quite believe in the sun and the blue of the sky.

I was sitting just now before the hearth, with my feet in the bearskin rug you sent us two Christmases ago. The light of the low wood fire was chasing the shadows around the room, over my books and my pictures, and all the fine and gracious luxuries with which I may now make my eyes and my heart glad, and pamper the tastes that grow with feeding. I was taking count, so to speak, of my prosperity—the material treasures, the better treasure that I find in such portion of fame as the world has allotted me, and the treasure of treasures across the threshold of the next room—in the next room? No—there, here, in every room, in every corner of the house, filling it with peace, is the gentle and holy spirit of love.

As I sat and thought, my mind went back to the day that you and I first met, twenty-two years ago—twenty-two in February next. In twenty-two years more I could not forget that hideous first day in the city room of the *Morning Record*. I can see the great gloomy room, with its meager gas-jets lighting up, here and there, a pale face at a desk, and bringing out in ghastly spots the ugliness of the ink-smeared walls. A winter rain was pouring down outside. I could feel its chill and damp in the room, though little of it was to be seen through the grimy window-panes. The composing room in the rear sent a smell of ink and benzine to permeate the moist atmosphere. The rumble and shiver of the great presses printing the weekly came up from below. I sat there in my wet clothes and waited for my first assignment. I was eighteen, poor as a church mouse, green, desperately hopeful after a boy's fashion, and with nothing in my head but the Latin and Greek of my one single year at college. My spirit had sunk down far out of sight. My heart beat nervously at every sound of that awful city editor's voice, as he called up his soldiers one by one and assigned them to duty. I could only silently pray that he would "give me an easy one," and that I should not disgrace myself in the doing of it. By Jove, Will, what an old martinet Baldwin was, for all his good heart! Do you remember that sharp, crackling voice of his, and the awful "Be brief! be brief!" that always drove all capacity for condensation out of a man's head, and set him to stammering out his story with wordy incoherence? Baldwin is on the *Record* still. I wonder what poor devil is trembling at this hour under that disconcerting adjuration.

A wretched day that was! The hours went slow as grief. Smeary little bare-armed fiends trotted in from the composing-room and out again, bearing fluttering galley-proofs. Bedraggled, hollow-eyed men came in from the streets and set their soaked umbrellas to steam against the heater, and passed into the lion's den to feed him with news, and were sent out again to take up their half cooked umbrellas and so forth to forage for more. Everyone, I thought, gave me one brief glance of contempt and curiosity, and put me out of his thoughts. Everyone had some business—everyone but me. The men who had been waiting with me were called up one by one and detailed to work. I was left alone.

Then a new horror came to torture my nervously active imagination. Had my superior officer forgotten his new recruit? Or could he find no task mean enough for my powers? This filled me at first with a sinking shame, and then with a hot rage and sense of wrong. Why should he thus slight me? Had I not a right to be tried, at least? Was there any duty he could find that I would not perform or die? I would go to him and tell him that I had come there to work; and would make him give me the work. No, I should simply be snubbed, and sent to my seat like a schoolboy, or perhaps discharged on the spot. I must bear my humiliation in silence.

I looked up and saw you entering, with your bright, ruddy boy's face shining with wet, beaming a greeting to all the room. In my soul I cursed you, at a venture, for your lightheartedness and your look of cheery self-confidence. What a vast stretch of struggle and success set you above me—you, the reporter, above me, the novice! And just then awful summons—"Barclay! Barclay!"—I shall hear that strident note at the judgment day. I went in and got my orders, and came out with them, all in a sort of daze that must have made Baldwin think me an idiot. And then you came up to me and scraped acquaintance in a desultory way, to hide your kind intent; and gave me a hint or two as to how to obtain a full account of the biennial meeting of the Post-Pliocene

Mineralogical Society, or whatever it was, without diving too deeply into the Post-Pliocene period. I would have fought for you to the death, at that moment.

'Twas a small matter, but the friendship begun in manly and helpful kindness has gone on for twenty-two years in mutual faith and loyalty; and the growth dignifies the seed.

A sturdy growth it was in its sapling days. It was in the late spring that we decided to take the room together in St. Mark's Place. A big room and a poor room, indeed, on the third story of that "battered caravanserai," and for twelve long years it held us and our hopes and our despairs and our troubles and our joys.

I don't think I have forgotten one detail of that room. There is the generous old fireplace, insultingly bricked up by modern poverty, all save the meager niche that holds our fire—when we can have a fire. There is the great second-hand table—our first purchase—where we sit and work for immortality in the scant intervals of working for life. Your drawer, with the manuscript of your *Concordance of Political Economy*, is to the right. Mine is to the left; it holds the unfinished play, and the poems that might better have been unfinished. There are the two narrow cots—yours to the left of the door as you enter; mine to the right.

How strange that I can see it all so clearly, now that all is different!

Yet I can remember myself coming home at one o'clock at night, dragging my tired feet up those dark, still, tortuous stairs, gripping the shaky baluster for aid. I open the door—I can feel the little old-fashioned brass knob in my palm even now—and I look to the left. Ah, you are already at home and in bed. I need not look toward the table. There is money—a little—in the common treasury; and, in accordance with our regular compact, I know there stand on that table twin bottles of beer, half a loaf of rye bread, and a double palm's-breadth of Swiss cheese. You are staying your hunger in sleep: for one may not eat until the other comes. I will wake you up, and we shall feast together and talk over the day that is dead and the day that is begun.

Strange, is it not, that I should have some trouble to realize that this is only a memory,—I, with my feet in the bearskin rug that it would have beggared the two of us, or a dozen like us, to purchase in those days. Strange that my mind should be wandering on the crude work of my boyhood and my early manhood. I who have won name and fame, as the world would say. I, to whom young men come for advice and encouragement, as to a tried veteran! Strange that I should be thinking of a time when even your true and tireless friendship could not quench a subtle hunger at my heart, a hunger for a more dear and intimate comradeship. I, with the tenderest of wives scarce out of my sight; even in her sleep she is no further from me than my own soul.

Strangest of all this, that the mad agony of grief, the passion of desolation that came upon me when our long partnership was dissolved for ever, should now be nothing but a memory, like other memories, to be summoned up out of the resting-places of the mind, toyed with, idly questioned, and dismissed with a sigh and a smile! What a real thing it was just ten years ago; what a very present pain! Believe me, Will,— yes, I want you to believe this—that in those first hours of loneliness I could have welcomed death; death would have fallen upon me as calmly as sleep has fallen upon my boy in the room beyond there.

You knew nothing of this then; I suppose you but half believe it now; for our parting was manly enough. I kept as stiff an upper lip as you did, for all there was less hair on it. Perhaps it seems extravagant to you. But there was a deal of difference between our cases. You had turned your pen to money-making, at the call of love; you were going to Stillwater to marry the judge's daughter, and to become a great land-owner and mayor of Stillwater and millionaire—or what is it now? And much of this you foresaw or hoped for, at least. Hope is something. But for me? I was left in the third-story of a poor lodging-house in St. Mark's Place, my best friend gone from me; with neither remembrance nor hope of Love to live on, and with my last story back from *all* the magazines.

We will not talk about it. Let me get back to my pleasant library with the books and the pictures and the glancing fire-light, and me with my feet in your bearskin rug, listening to my wife's step in the next room.

To your ear, for our communion has been so long and so close that to either one of us the faintest inflection of the other's voice speaks clearer than formulated words; to your ear there must be something akin to a tone of regret—regret for the old days—in what I have just said. And would it be strange if there were? A poor soldier of fortune who had been set to a man's work before he had done with his meager boyhood, who had passed from recruit to a place of a young veteran in that great, hard-fighting, unresting pioneer army of journalism; was he the man, all of a sudden, to stretch his toughened sinews out and let them relax in the glow of the home hearth? Would not his legs begin to twitch for the road; would he not be wild to feel again the rain in his weatherbeaten face? Would you think it strange if at night he should toss in his white, soft bed, longing to change it for a blanket on the turf, with the broad procession of sunlit worlds sweeping over his head, beyond the blue spaces of the night? And even if the dear face on the pillow next him were to wake and look at him with reproachful surprise; and even if warm arms drew him back to his new allegiance; would not his heart in dreams go throbbing to the rhythm of the drum or the music of songs sung by the camp-fire?

It was so at the beginning, in the incredible happiness of the first year, and even after the boy's birth. Do you know, it was months before I could accept that boy as a *fact?* If, at any moment, he had vanished from my sight, crib and all, I should not have been surprised. I was not sure of him until he began to show his mother's eyes.

Yes, even in those days some of the old leaven worked in me. I had moments of that old barbaric freedom which we used to rejoice in—that feeling of being answerable to nothing in the world save my own will—the sense of untrammeled, careless power.

Do you remember the night that we walked till sunrise? You remember how hot it was at midnight, when we left the office, and how the moonlight on the statue above the City Hall seemed to invite us fieldward, where no gaslight glared, no torches flickered. So we walked idly northward, through the black, silence-stricken down-town streets; through that feverish, unresting central region that lies between the vileness of Houston Street and the calm and spacious dignity of the brownstone ways, where the closed and darkened dwellings looked like huge tombs in the pallid light of the moon. We passed the suburban belt of shanties; we passed the garden-girt villas beyond them, and it was from the hill above Spuyten Duyvil that we saw the first color of the morning upon the face of the Palisades.

It would have taken very little in that moment to set us off to tramping the broad earth, for the pure joy of free wayfaring. What was there to hold us back? No tie of home or kin. All we had in the world to leave behind us was some futile scribbling on various sheets of paper. And of that sort of thing both our heads were full enough. I think it was but the veriest chance that, having begun that walk, we did not go on and get our fill of wandering, and ruin our lives.

Well, that same wild, adventurous spirit came upon me now and then. There were times when, for the moment, I forgot that I had a wife and a child. There were times when I remembered them as a burden. Why should I not say this? It is the history of every married man,—at least of every manly man,—though he be married to the best woman in the world. It means no lack of love. It is as unavoidable as the leap of the blood in you that answers a trumpet-call.

At first I was frightened, and fought against it as against something that might grow upon me. I reproached myself for disloyalty in thought. Ah! what need had *I* to fight? What need had I to choke down rebellious fancies, while my wife's love was working that miracle that makes two spirits one?

What is it, this union that comes to us as a surprise, and remains for all outside an incommunicable mystery? What is this that makes our unmarried love seem so slight and childish a thing? You and I, who know it, know that it is no mere fruit of intimacy and usage, although in its growth it keeps pace with these. We know that in some subtle way, it has been given to a man to see a woman's soul as he sees his own, and to a woman to look into a man's heart as if it were, indeed, hers. But the friend who sits at my table, seeing that my wife and I understand each other at a simple meeting of the eyes, makes no more of it than he does of the glance of intelligence which, with close friends, often takes the place of speech. He never dreams of the sweet delight with which we commune together in a language that he cannot understand—that he cannot hear—a language that has no formulated words, feeling answering feeling.

It is not wonderful that I should wish to give expression to the gratitude with which I have seen my life made to blossom thus; my thankfulness for the love which has made me not only a happier, but, I humbly believe, a wiser and a better-minded man. But I know too well the hopelessness of trying to find words to describe what, were I a poet, my best song might but faintly, faintly echo.

I thought I heard a rustle behind me just now. In a little while my wife will come softly into the room, and softly up to where I am sitting, stepping silently across your bearskin rug, and will lay one hand softly on my left shoulder, while the other slips down this arm with which I write, until it falls and closes lightly, yet with loving firmness, on my hand that holds the pen. And I shall say, "Only the last words to Will and his wife, dear." And she will release my hand, and will lift her own, I think, to caress the patch of gray hair on my temple; it is a way she has, as though it were some pitiful scar, and she will say, "Give them my love, and tell them they must not fail us this Christmas. I want them to see how our Willy has grown." And when she says "Our Willy," the hand on my shoulder will instinctively close a little, clingingly; and she will bend her head, and put her face close to mine, and I shall turn and look into her eyes.

Bear with me, my dear Will, until I have told you I have written this letter and what it means. I have concealed one thing from you for the last six months. I have disease of the heart, and the doctor has told me that I may die at any moment. Somehow, I think—I know the moment is close at hand; I shall soon go to that narrow cot on the right of the door, and I do not believe I shall wake up in the morning with the sun in my eyes, to look across the room and see that its companion is gone.

For I am in the old room, Will, as you know, and it is not ten years since you went away, but two days. The picture that has seemed real to me as I wrote these pages is fading, and the thin gas-jet flickers and sinks as it always did in these first morning hours. I can hear the roar of the last Harlem train swell and sink, and the sharp clink of car-bells breaks the silence that follows. The wind is gasping and struggling in the chimney, and blowing a white powdery ash down on the hearth. I have just burnt my poems and the play. Both the table drawers are empty now; and soon enough the two empty chairs will stare at each other across the bare table. What a wild dream have I dreamt in all this emptiness! Just now, I thought indeed that it was true. I thought I heard a woman's step behind me, and I turned—

Peace be with you, Will, in the fulness of your love. I am going to sleep. Perhaps I shall dream it all again, and shall hear that soft footfall when the turn of the night comes, and the pale light through the ragged blind, and the end of a long loneliness.

After I am dead, I wish you to think of me not as I was, but as I wanted to be. I have tried to show you that I have led by your side a happier and dearer life of hope and aspiration than the one you saw. I have tried to leave your memory a picture of me that you will not shrink from calling up when you have a quiet hour and time for thought of the friend whom you knew well; but whom you may, perhaps, know better now that he is dead.

REGINALD BARCLAY.

II

THE PARAGRAPH

(From the *New York Herald* of Nov. 18, 1883.)

Reginald Barclay, a journalist, was found dead in his bed at 15. St. Mark's Place, yesterday morning. No inquest was held, as Mr. Barclay had been known to be suffering from disease of the heart, and his death was not unexpected. The deceased came originally from Oneida County, and was regarded as a young journalist of considerable promise. He had been for some years on the city staff of the *Record*, and was the correspondent of several out-of-town papers. He had also contributed to the monthly magazines, occasional poems and short stories, which showed the possession, in some measure, of the imaginative faculty. Mr. Barclay was about thirty years of age, and unmarried.

O. HENRY

(William Sydney Porter)

(1862–1910)

WILLIAM SYDNEY PORTER—who wrote under the pen-name "O. Henry"—was born at Greensboro, N. C., in 1862. He received only the rudiments of an education. As a young man he went to Texas, working in the General Land Office and later in a bank. He was implicated in a business deal and served a short prison sentence. While in prison he began writing stories for the magazines. By the time of his death he was one of the most popular story writers in the country. Between the time of his death and 1920 his work became known throughout the entire English-speaking world. He is one of the ablest short-story writers who ever lived: fertile in invention, clever, amusing, and amazingly deft in the handling of the trick plot. Though he is limited in the subject-matter which he treats, and too fond of telling a story simply for the sake of the point, he must be accorded the credit of perfecting his own type of story.

Supply and Demand appears in the volume *Options*, copyright, 1909, by Harper & Bros., by whose permission it is here used.

SUPPLY AND DEMAND

FINCH keeps a hats-cleaned-by-electricity-while-you-wait establishment, nine feet by twelve, in Third Avenue. Once a customer, you are always his. I do not know his secret process, but every four days your hat needs to be cleaned again.

Finch is a leathern, sallow, slow-footed man, between twenty and forty. You would say he had been brought up a bushelman in Essex Street. When business is slack he likes to talk, so I had my hat cleaned even oftener than it deserved, hoping Finch might let me into some of the secrets of the sweatshops.

One afternoon I dropped in and found Finch alone. He began to anoint my headpiece de Panama with his mysterious fluid that attracted dust and dirt like a magnet.

"They say the Indians wear 'em under water," said I, for a leader.

"Don't you believe it," said Finch. "No Indian or white man could stay under water that long. Say, do you pay much attention to politics? I see in the paper something about a law they've passed called 'the law of supply and demand.'"

I explained to him as well as I could that the reference was to a politico-economical law, and not to a legal statute.

"I didn't know," said Finch. "I heard a good deal about it a year or so ago, but in a one-sided way."

"Yes," said I, "political orators use it a great deal. In fact, they never give it a rest. I suppose you heard some of those cart-tail fellows spouting on the subject over here on the east side."

"I heard it from a king," said Finch—"the white king of a tribe of Indians in South America."

I was interested but not surprised. The big city is like a mother's knee to many who have strayed far and found the roads rough beneath their uncertain feet. At dusk they come home and sit upon the door-step. I know a piano player in a cheap café who has shot lions in Africa, a bell-boy who fought in the British army against the Zulus, an express-driver whose left arm had been cracked like a lobster's claw for a stew-pot of Patagonian cannibals when the boat of his rescuers hove in sight. So a hat-cleaner who had been a friend of a king did not oppress me.

"A new band?" asked Finch, with his dry, barren smile.

"Yes," said I, "and half an inch wider." I had had a new band five days before.

"I meets a man one night," said Finch, beginning his story—"a man brown as snuff, with money in every pocket, eating schweinerknuckel in Schlagel's. That was two years ago, when I was a hose-cart driver for No. 98. His discourse runs to the subject of gold. He says that certain mountains in a country down South that he calls Gaudymala is full of it. He says the Indians wash it out of the streams in plural quantities.

"'Oh, Geronimo!' says I. 'Indians! There's no Indians in the South,' I tell him, 'except Elks, Maccabees, and the buyers for the fall dry-goods trade. The Indians are all on the reservations,' says I.

"'I'm telling you this with reservations,' says he. 'They ain't Buffalo Bill Indians; they're squattier and more pedigreed. They call 'em Inkers and Aspics, and they was old inhabitants when Mazuma was King of Mexico. They wash the gold out of the mountain streams,' says the brown man, 'and fill quills with it; and then they empty 'em into red jars till they are full; and then they pack it in buckskin sacks of one arroba each—an arroba is twenty-five pounds—and store it in a stone house, with an engraving of a idol with marceled hair, playing a flute, over the door.'

"'How do they work off this unearth increment?' I asks.

"'They don't,' says the man. 'It's a case of "Ill fares the land with the great deal of velocity where wealth accumulates and there ain't any reciprocity."'

"After this man and me got through our conversation, which left him dry of information, I shook hands with him and told him I was

THE UNITED STATES—O. HENRY 1025

sorry I couldn't believe him. And a month afterward I landed on the coast of this Gaudymala with $1,300 that I had been saving up for five years. I thought I knew what Indians liked, and I fixed myself accordingly. I loaded down four pack-mules with red woolen blankets, wrought-iron pails, jeweled side combs for the ladies, glass necklaces, and safety-razors. I hired a black mozo, who was supposed to be a mule-driver and an interpreter too. It turned out that he could interpret mules all right, but he drove the English language much too hard. His name sounded like a Yale key when you push it in wrong side up, but I called him McClintock, which was close to the noise.

"Well, this gold village was forty miles up in the mountains, and it took us nine days to find it. But one afternoon McClintock led the other mules and myself over a rawhide bridge stretched across a precipice five thousand feet deep, it seemed to me. The hoofs of the beasts drummed on it just like before George M. Cohan makes his first entrance on the stage.

"This village was built of mud and stone, and had no streets. Some few yellow-and-brown persons popped their heads out-of-doors, looking about like Welsh rabbits with Worcester sauce on 'em. Out of the biggest house, that had a kind of a porch around it, steps a big white man, red as a beet in color, dressed in fine tanned deerskin clothes, with a gold chain around his neck, smoking a cigar. I've seen United States Senators of his style of features and build, also head-waiters and cops.

"He walks up and takes a look at us, while McClintock disembarks and begins to interpret to the lead mule while he smokes a cigarette.

"'Hello, Buttinsky,' says the fine man to me. 'How did you get in the game? I didn't see you buy any chips. Who gave you the keys of the city?'

"'I'm a poor traveler', says I. 'Especially mule-back. You'll excuse me. Do you run a hack line or only a bluff?'

"'Segregate yourself from your pseudo-equine quadruped', says he, 'and come inside.'

"He raises a finger, and a villager runs up.

"'This man will take care of your outfit,' says he, 'and I'll take care of you.'

"He leads me into the biggest house, and sets the chairs and a kind of a drink the color of milk. It was the finest room I ever saw. The stone walls was hung all over with silk shawls, and there was red and yellow rugs on the floor, and jars of red pottery and Angora goat skins, and enough bamboo furniture to misfurnish half a dozen sea-side cottages.

"'In the first place,' says the man, 'you want to know who I am. I'm sole lessee and proprietor of this tribe of Indians. They call me the

Grand Yacuma, which is to say King or Main Finger of the bunch. I've got more power here than a chargé d'affaires, a charge of dynamite, and a charge account at Tiffany's combined. In fact, I'm the Big Stick, with as many extra knots on it as there is on the record run of the *Lusitania.* Oh, I read the papers now and then,' says he. 'Now, let's hear your entitlements,' he goes on, 'and the meeting will be open.'

"'Well,' says I, 'I am known as one W. D. Finch. Occupation, capitalist. Address, 541 East Thirty-second—'

"'New York,' chips in the Noble Grand. 'I know', says he, grinning. 'It ain't the first time you've seen it go down on the blotter.' I can tell by the way you hand it out. Well, explain, "capitalist."'

"I tells this boss plain what I come for and how I come to came.

"'Gold-dust?' says he, looking as puzzled as a baby that's got a feather stuck on its molasses finger. 'That's funny. This ain't a gold-mining country. And you invested all your capital on a stranger's story? Well, well! These Indians of mine—they are the last of the tribe of Peches—are simple as children. They know nothing of the purchasing power of gold. I'm afraid you've been imposed on,' says he.

"'Maybe so,' says I, 'but it sounded pretty straight to me.'

"'W. D.,' says the King, all of a sudden, 'I'll give you a square deal. It ain't often I get to talk to a white man, and I'll give you a show for your money. It may be these constituents of mine have a few grains of gold-dust hid away in their clothes. To-morrow you may get out these goods you've brought up and see if you can make any sales. Now, I'm going to introduce myself unofficially. My name is Shane—Patrick Shane. I own this tribe of Peche Indians by right of conquest—single handed and unafraid. I drifted up here four years ago, and won 'em by my size and complexion and nerve. I learned their language in six weeks—it's easy: you simply emit a string of consonants as long as your breath holds out and then point at what you're asking for.

"'I conquered 'em, spectacularly,' goes on King Shane, 'and then I went at 'em with economical politics, law, sleight-of-hand, and a kind of New England ethics and parsimony. Every Sunday, or as near as I can guess at it, I preach to 'em in the council-house (I'm the council) on the law of supply and demand. I praise supply and knock demand. I use the same text every time. You wouldn't think, W. D.,' says Shane, 'that I had poetry in me, would you?'

"'Well,' says I, 'I wouldn't know whether to call it poetry or not.'

"'Tennyson,' says Shane, 'furnishes the poetic gospel I preach. I always considered him the boss poet. Here's the way the text goes:

> "For, not to admire, if a man could learn it, were more
> Than to walk all day like a Sultan of old in a garden of spice."

"'You see, I teach 'em to cut out demand—that supply is the main thing. I teach 'em not to desire anything beyond their simplest needs. A little mutton, a little cocoa, and a little fruit brought up from the coast—that's all they want to make 'em happy. I've got 'em well trained. They make their own clothes and hats out of a vegetable fiber and straw, and they're a contented lot. It's a great thing,' winds up Shane, 'to have made a people happy by the inculvitation of such simple institutions.'

"Well, the next day, with the King's permission, I has the McClintock open up a couple of sacks of my goods in the little plaza of the village. The Indians swarmed around by the hundred and looked the bargain-counter over. I shook red blankets at 'em, flashed finger-rings and earbobs, tried pearl necklaces and side-combs on the women, and a line of red hosiery on the men. 'Twas no use. They looked on like hungry graven images, but I never made a sale. I asked McClintock what was the trouble. Mac yawned three or four times, rolled a cigarette, made one or two confidential side remarks to a mule, and then condescended to inform me that the poeple had no money.

"Just then up strolls King Patrick, big and red and royal as usual, with the gold chain over his chest and his cigar in front of him.

"'How's business, W. D.?' he asks.

"'Fine,' says I. 'It's a bargain-day rush. I've got one more line of goods to offer before I shut up shop. I'll try 'em with safety-razors. I've got two gross that I bought at a fire sale.'

"Shane laughs till some kind of mameluke or private secretary he carries with him has to hold him up.

"'O my sainted Aunt Jerusha!' says he, 'ain't you one of the Babes in the Woods, W. D.? Don't you know that no Indians ever shave? They pull out their whiskers instead.'

"'Well,' says I, 'that's just what these razors would do for 'em—they wouldn't have any kick coming if they used 'em once.'

"Shane went away, and I could hear him laughing a block, if there had been any block.

"'Tell 'em, says I to McClintock, 'it ain't money I want—tell 'em I'll take gold-dust. Tell 'em I'll allow 'em sixteen dollars an ounce for it in trade. That's what I'm out for—the dust.'

"Mac interprets, and you'd have thought a squadron of cops had charged the crowd to disperse it. Every uncle's nephew and aunt's niece of 'em faded away inside of two minutes.

"At the royal palace that night me and the King talked it over.

"'They've got the dust hid out somewhere,' says I, 'or they wouldn't have been so sensitive about it.'

"'They haven't,' says Shane. 'What's this gag you've got about gold? You been reading Edward Allen Poe? They ain't got any gold.'

"'They put it in quills,' says I, 'and then they empty it in jars, and then into sacks of twenty-five pounds each. I got it straight.'

"'W. D.,' says Shane, laughing and chewing his cigar, 'I don't often see a white man, and I feel like putting you on. I don't think you'll get away from here alive, anyhow, so I'm going to tell you. Come over here.'

"He draws aside a silk fiber curtain in a corner of the room and shows me a pile of buckskin sacks.

"'Forty of 'em,' says Shane. 'One arroba in each one. In round numbers, $220,000 worth of gold-dust you see there. It's all mine. It belongs to the Grand Yacuma. They bring it all to me. Two hundred and twenty thousand dollars—think of that, you glass-bead peddler,' says Shane—'and all mine.'

"'Little good it does you,' says I, contemptuously and hatefully. 'And so you are the government depository of this gang of moneyless moneymakers? Don't you pay enough interest on it to enable one of your depositors to buy an Augusta (Maine) Pullman carbon diamond worth $220 for $4.85?'

"'Listen,' says Patrick Shane, with the sweat coming out on his brow. 'I'm confident with you, as you have, somehow, enlisted my regards. Did you ever,' he says, 'feel the avoirdupois power of gold—not the troy weight of it, but the sixteen-ounces-to-the-pound force of it?'

"'Never,' says I. 'I never take in any bad money.'

"Shane drops down on the floor and throws his arms over the sacks of gold-dust.

"'I love it,' says he. 'I want to feel the touch of it day and night. It's my pleasure in life. I come in this room, and I'm a king and a rich man. I'll be a millionaire in another year. The pile's getting bigger every month. I've got the whole tribe washing out the sands in the creeks. I'm the happiest man in the world, W. D. I just want to be near this gold, and know it's mine and it's increasing every day. Now, you know,' says he, 'why my Indians wouldn't buy your goods. They can't. They bring all the dust to me. I'm their king. I've taught 'em not to desire or admire. You might as well shut up shop.'

"'I'll tell you what you are,' says I. 'You're a plain, contemptible miser. You preach supply and you forget demand. Now, supply,' I goes on, 'is never anything but supply. On the contrary,' says I, 'demand is a much broader sylogism and assertion. Demand includes the rights of our women and children, and charity and friendship, and even a little begging on the street corners. They've both got to harmonize equally. And I've got a few things up my commercial sleeve yet,' says I, 'that may jostle your preconceived ideas of politics and economy.'

"The next morning I had McClintock bring up another mule-load of goods to the plaza and open it up. The people gathered around the same as before.

"I got out the finest line of necklaces, bracelets, hair-combs, and earrings that I carried, and had the women put 'em on. And then I played trumps.

"Out of my last pack I opened up a half gross of hand-mirrors, with solid tinfoil backs, and passed 'em around among the ladies. That was the first introduction of looking-glasses among the Peche Indians.

"Shane walks by with his big laugh.

"'Business looking up any?' he asks.

"'It's looking at itself right now,' says I.

"By-and-by a kind of a murmur goes through the crowd. The women had looked into the magic crystal and seen that they were beautiful, and were confiding the secret to the men. The men seemed to be urging the lack of money and the hard times just before the election, but their excuses didn't go.

"Then was my time.

"I called McClintock away from an animated conversation with his mules and told him to do some interpreting.

"'Tell 'em, says I, 'that gold-dust will buy for them these befitting ornaments for kings and queens of the earth. Tell 'em the yellow sand they wash out of the waters for the High Sanctified Yacomay and Chop Suey of the tribe will buy the precious jewels and charms that will make them beautiful and preserve and pickle them from evil spirits. Tell 'em the Pittsburgh banks are paying four per cent. interest on deposits by mail, while this get-rich-frequently custodian of the public funds ain't even paying attention. Keep telling 'em, Mac,' says I, 'to let the gold-dust family do their work. Talk to 'em like a born anti-Bryanite,' says I. 'Remind 'em that Tom Watson's gone back to Georgia,' says I.

"McClintock waves his hand affectionately at one of his mules, and then hurls a few stickfuls of minion type at the mob of shoppers.

"A gutta-percha Indian man, with a lady hanging on his arm, with three strings of my fish-scale jewelry and imitation marble beads around her neck, stands up on a block of stone and makes a talk that sounds like a man shaking dice in a box to fill aces and sixes.

"'He says,' says McClintock, 'that the people not know that gold-dust will buy their things. The women very mad. The Grand Yacuma tell them it no good but for keep to make bad spirits keep away.'

"'You can't keep bad spirits away from money,' says I.

"'They say,'' goes on McClintock, 'the Yacuma fool them. They raise plenty row.'

"'Going! Going!' says I. 'Gold-dust or cash takes the entire stock.

The dust weighed before you, and taken at sixteen dollars the ounce —the highest price on the Gaudymala coast.'

"Then the crowd disperses all of a sudden, and I don't know what's up. Mac and me packs away the hand-mirrors and jewelry they had handed back to us, and we had the mules back to the corral they had set apart for our garage.

"While we was there we hear great noises of shouting, and down across the plaza runs Patrick Shane, hotfoot, with his clothes ripped half off, and scratches on his face like a cat had fought him hard for every one of its lives.

"'They're looting the treasury, W. D.,' he sings out. 'They're going to kill me and you, too. Unlimber a couple of mules at once. We'll have to make a get-away in a couple of minutes.'

"'They've found out,' says I, 'the truth about the law of supply and demand.'

"'It's the women, mostly,' says the King. 'And they used to admire me so!'

"'They hadn't seen looking-glasses then,' says I.

"'They've got knives and hatchets,' says Shane; 'hurry!'

"'Take that roan mule,' says I. 'You and your law of supply! I'll ride the dun, for he's two knots per hour the faster. The roan has a stiff knee, but he may make it,' says I. 'If you'd included reciprocity in your political platform I might have given you the dun,' says I.

"Shane and McClintock and me mounted our mules and rode across the rawhide bridge just as the Peches reached the other side and began firing stones and long knives at us. We cut the thongs that held up our end of the bridge and headed for the coast."

A tall, bulky policeman came into Finch's shop at that moment and leaned an elbow on the showcase. Finch nodded at him friendly.

"I heard down at Casey's", said the cop, in rumbling, husky tones, "that there was going to be a picnic of the Hat-Cleaners' Union over at Bergen Beach, Sunday. Is that right?"

"Sure," said Finch. "There'll be a dandy time."

"Gimme five tickets," said the cop, throwing a five-dollar bill on the showcase.

"Why," said Finch, "ain't you going it a little too—"

"Go to h—," said the cop. "You got 'em to sell, ain't you? Somebody's got to buy 'em. Wish I could go along."

I was glad to see Finch so well thought of in his neighborhood.

And then in came a wee girl of seven, with dirty face and pure blue eyes and smutched and insufficient dress.

"Mamma says," she recited shrilly, "that you must give me eighty cents for the grocer and nineteen for the milkman and five cents for me to buy hokey-pokey with—but she didn't say that," the elf concluded, with a hopeful but honest grin.

Finch shelled out the money, counting it twice, but I noticed that the total sum that the small girl received was one dollar and four cents.

"That's the right kind of a law," remarked Finch, as he carefully broke some of the stitches of my hatband so that it would assuredly come off within a few days—"the law of supply and demand. But they've both got to work together. I'll bet," he went on, with his dry smile, "she'll get jelly beans with that nickel—she likes 'em. What's supply if there's no demand for it?"

"What ever became of the King?" I asked, curiously.

"Oh, I might have told you," said Finch. "That was Shane came in and bought the tickets. He came back with me, and he's on the force now."

STEPHEN CRANE

1871—1900)

CRANE has only recently received due credit for his stories. True, his *Red Badge of Courage* made quite a stir in the nineties, but apart from that book, he was not well-known until some four or five years ago. He was a free-lance writer to the end of his short life. His best work is found in his few volumes of short tales, war stories and stories of contemporary life. He was a war-correspondent in the Balkans and Cuba, though he wrote his most striking war stories before he had ever witnessed a battle. He was not a trick-story writer; he was neither facile nor ingenious; his work at its best is the sound product of an honest artist.

This story is from *Men, Women, and Boats*, published in 1921 by Boni & Liveright, New York. It is here reprinted by permission of Alfred A. Knopf.

A DARK-BROWN DOG

A CHILD was standing on a street-corner. He leaned with one shoulder against a high board fence and swayed the other to and fro, the while kicking carelessly at the gravel.

Sunshine beat upon the cobbles, and a lazy summer wind raised yellow dust which trailed in clouds down the avenue. Clattering trucks moved with indistinctness through it. The child stood dreamily gazing.

After a time, a little dark-brown dog came trotting with an intent air down the sidewalk. A short rope was dragging from his neck. Occasionally he trod upon the end of it and stumbled.

He stopped opposite the child, and the two regarded each other. The dog hesitated for a moment, but presently he made some little advances with his tail. The child put out his hand and called him. In an apologetic manner the dog came close, and the two had an interchange of friendly pattings and waggles. The dog became more enthusiastic with each moment of the interview, until with his gleeful caperings he threatened to overturn the child. Whereupon the child lifted his hand and struck the dog a blow upon the head.

This thing seemed to overpower and astonish the little dark-brown dog, and wounded him to the heart. He sank down in despair at the child's feet. When the blow was repeated, together with an admonition in childish sentences, he turned over upon his back, and held his paws in a peculiar manner. At the same time with his ears and his eyes he offered a small prayer to the child.

He looked so comical on his back, and holding his paws peculiarly, that the child was greatly amused and gave him little taps repeatedly, to keep him so. But the little dark-brown dog took this chastisement in the most serious way, and no doubt considered that he had committed some grave crime, for he wriggled contritely and showed his repentance in every way that was in his power. He pleaded with the child and petitioned him, and offered more prayers.

At last the child grew weary of this amusement and turned toward home. The dog was praying at the time. He lay on his back and turned his eyes upon the retreating form.

Presently he struggled to his feet and started after the child. The latter wandered in a perfunctory way toward his home, stopping at times to investigate various matters. During one of these pauses he discovered the little dark-brown dog who was following him with the air of a footpad.

The child beat his pursuer with a small stick he had found. The dog lay down and prayed until the child had finished, and resumed his journey. Then he scrambled erect and took up the pursuit again.

On the way to his home the child turned many times and beat the dog, proclaiming with childish gestures that he held him in contempt as an unimportant dog, with no value save for a moment. For being this quality of animal the dog apologized and eloquently expressed regret, but he continued stealthily to follow the child. His manner grew so very guilty that he slunk like an assassin.

When the child reached his doorstep, the dog was industriously ambling a few yards in the rear. He became so agitated with shame when he again confronted the child that he forgot the dragging rope. He tripped upon it and fell forward.

The child sat down on the step and the two had another interview. During it the dog greatly exerted himself to please the child. He performed a few gambols with such abandon that the child suddenly saw him to be a valuable thing. He made a swift, avaricious charge and seized the rope.

He dragged his captive into a hall and up many long stairways in a dark tenement. The dog made willing efforts, but he could not hobble very skilfully up the stairs because he was very small and soft, and at last the pace of the engrossed child grew so energetic that the dog became panic-stricken. In his mind he was being dragged toward a grim unknown. His eyes grew wild with the terror of it. He began to wiggle his head frantically and to brace his legs.

The child redoubled his exertions. They had a battle on the stairs. The child was victorious because he was completely absorbed in his purpose, and because the dog was very small. He dragged his acquirement to the door of his home, and finally with triumph across the threshold.

No one was in. The child sat down on the floor and made overtures to the dog. These the dog instantly accepted. He beamed with affection upon his new friend. In a short time they were firm and abiding comrades.

When the child's family appeared, they made a great row. The dog was examined and commented upon and called names. Scorn was leveled at him from all eyes, so that he became much embarrassed and drooped like a scorched plant. But the child went sturdily to the center of the floor, and, at the top of his voice, championed the dog. It happened that he was roaring protestations, with his arms clasped about the dog's neck, when the father of the family came in from work.

The parent demanded to know what the blazes they were making the kid howl for. It was explained in many words that the infernal kid wanted to introduce a disreputable dog into the family.

A family council was held. On this depended the dog's fate, but he in no way heeded, being busily engaged in chewing the end of the child's dress.

The affair was quickly ended. The father of the family, it appears, was in a particularly savage temper that evening, and when he perceived that it would amaze and anger everybody if such a dog were allowed to remain, he decided that it should be so. The child, crying softly, took his friend off to a retired part of the room to hobnob with him, while the father quelled a fierce rebellion of his wife. So it came to pass that the dog was a member of the household.

He and the child were associated together at all times save when the child slept. The child became a guardian and a friend. If the large folk kicked the dog and threw things at him, the child made loud and violent objections. Once when the child had run, protesting loudly, with tears raining down his face and his arms outstretched, to protect his friend, he had been struck in the head with a very large saucepan from the hand of his father, enraged at some seeming lack of courtesy in the dog. Ever after, the family were careful how they threw things at the dog. Moreover, the latter grew very skilful in avoiding missiles and feet. In a small room containing a stove, a table, a bureau and some chairs, he would display strategic ability of a high order, dodging, feinting and scuttling about among the furniture. He could force three or four people armed with brooms, sticks and handfuls of coal, to use all their ingenuity to get in a blow. And even when they did, it was seldom that they could do him a serious injury or leave any imprint.

But when the child was present these scenes did not occur. It came to be recognized that if the dog was molested, the child would burst into sobs, and as the child, when started, was very riotous and practically unquenchable, the dog had therein a safeguard.

However, the child could not always be near. At night, when he was asleep, his dark-brown friend would raise from some black corner a wild, wailful cry, a song of infinite loneliness and despair, that would go shuddering and sobbing among the buildings of the block and cause people to swear. At these times the singer would often be chased all over the kitchen and hit with a great variety of articles.

Sometimes, too, the child himself used to beat the dog, although it is not known that he ever had what truly could be called a just cause. The dog always accepted these thrashings with an air of admitted guilt. He was too much of a dog to try to look to be a martyr or to plot revenge. He received the blows with deep humility, and furthermore he forgave his friend the moment the child had finished, and was ready to caress the child's hand with his little red tongue.

When misfortune came upon the child, and his troubles overwhelmed him, he would often crawl under the table and lay his small distressed head on the dog's back. The dog was ever sympathetic. It is not to be supposed that at such times he took occasion to refer to the unjust beatings his friend, when provoked, had administered to him.

He did not achieve any notable degree of intimacy with the other members of the family. He had no confidence in them, and the fear that he would express at their casual approach often exasperated them exceedingly. They used to gain a certain satisfaction in underfeeding him, but finally his friend the child grew to watch the matter with some care, and when he forgot it, the dog was often successful in secret for himself.

So the dog prospered. He developed a large bark, which came wondrously from such a small rug of a dog. He ceased to howl persistently at night. Sometimes, indeed, in his sleep, he would utter little yells, as from pain, but that occurred, no doubt, when in his dreams he encountered huge flaming dogs who threatened him direfully.

His devotion to the child grew until it was a sublime thing. He wagged at his approach; he sank down in despair at his departure. He could detect the sound of the child's step among all the noises of the neighborhood. It was like a calling voice to him.

The scene of their companionship was a kingdom governed by this terrible potentate, the child; but neither criticism nor rebellion ever lived for an instant in the heart of the one subject. Down in the mystic, hidden fields of his little dog-soul bloomed flowers of love and fidelity and perfect faith.

The child was in the habit of going on many expeditions to observe strange things in the vicinity. On these occasions his friend usually jogged aimfully along behind. Perhaps, though, he went ahead. This necessitated his turning around every quarter-minute to make sure the child was coming. He was filled with a large idea of the importance of these journeys. He would carry himself with such an air! He was proud to be the retainer of so great a monarch.

One day, however, the father of the family got quite exceptionally drunk. He came home and held carnival with the cooking utensils, the furniture and his wife. He was in the midst of this recreation when the child, followed by the dark-brown dog, entered the room. They were returning from their voyages.

The child's practised eye instantly noted his father's state. He dived under the table, where experience had taught him was a rather safe place. The dog, lacking skill in such matters, was, of course, unaware of the true condition of affairs. He looked with interested eyes at his friend's sudden dive. He interpreted it to mean: Joyous gambol. He started to patter across the floor to join him. He was the picture of a little dark-brown dog en route to a friend.

The head of the family saw him at this moment. He gave a huge howl of joy, and knocked the dog down with a heavy coffee-pot. The dog, yelling in supreme astonishment and fear, writhed to his feet and ran for cover. The man kicked out with a ponderous foot. It caused the dog to swerve as if caught in a tide. A second blow of the coffee-pot laid him upon the floor.

Here, the child, uttering loud cries, came valiantly forth like a knight. The father of the family paid no attention to these calls of the child, but advanced with glee upon the dog. Upon being knocked down twice in swift succession, the latter apparently gave up all hope of escape. He rolled over on his back and held his paws in a peculiar manner. At the same time with his eyes and his ears he offered up a small prayer.

But the father was in a mood for having fun, and it occurred to him that it would be a fine thing to throw the dog out of the window. So he reached down and, grabbing the animal by a leg, lifted him, squirming, up. He swung him two or three times hilariously about his head, and then flung him with great accuracy through the window.

The soaring dog created a surprise in the block. A woman watering plants in an opposite window gave an involuntary shout and dropped a flower-pot. A man in another window leaned perilously out to watch the flight of the dog. A woman who had been hanging out clothes in a yard began to caper wildly. Her mouth was filled with clothes-pins, but her arms gave vent to a sort of exclamation. In appearance she was like a gagged prisoner. Children ran whooping.

The dark-brown body crashed in a heap on the roof of a shed five stories below. From thence it rolled to the pavement of an alleyway.

The child in the room far above burst into a long, dirge-like cry, and toddled hastily out of the room. It took him a long time to reach the alley, because his size compelled him to go downstairs backward, one step at a time, and holding with both hands to the step above.

When they came for him later, they found him seated, by the body of his dark-brown friend.

THEODORE DREISER

(1871—1945)

THEODORE DREISER came from the Middle West. For some years a journalist, he wrote his first novel, *Sister Carrie*, out of his deep conviction of the bitterness and sorrow and stupidity of modern life. This was followed by other novels, but it is not until recently that Dreiser has found a large reading public. His short stories are part and parcel of the man's work. "What," asks Sherwood Anderson, "has Dreiser given us? A fine growing and glowing tradition, a new sense of the value of our own lives, a new interest in the life about us, in offices, streets and houses."

The Lost Phœbe is reprinted by permission of Constable & Co., publishers.

THE LOST PHŒBE

THEY lived together in a part of the country which was not so prosperous as it had once been, about three miles from one of those small towns that, instead of increasing in population, is steadily decreasing. The territory was not very thickly settled; perhaps a house every other mile or so, with large areas of corn- and wheat-land and fallow fields that at odd seasons had been sown to timothy and clover. Their particular house was part log and part frame, the log portion being the old original home of Henry's grandfather. The new portion, of now rain-beaten, time-worn slabs, through which the wind squeaked in the chinks at times, and which several overshadowing elms and a butternut-tree made picturesque and reminiscently pathetic, but a little damp, was erected by Henry when he was twenty-one and just married.

That was forty-eight years before. The furniture inside, like the house outside, was old and mildewy and reminiscent of an earlier day. You have seen the what-not of cherry wood, perhaps, with spiral legs and fluted top. It was there. The old-fashioned four poster bed, with its ball-like protuberances and deep curving incisions, was there also, a sadly alienated descendant of an early Jacobean ancestor. The bureau of cherry was also high and wide and solidly built, but faded-looking, and with a musty odor. The rag carpet that underlay all these sturdy examples of enduring furniture was a weak, faded, lead-and-pink-colored affair woven by Phœbe Ann's own hands, when she was fifteen years younger than she was when she died. The creaky wooden loom on which it had been done now stood like a dusty, bony skeleton, along with a broken rocking-chair, a worm-eaten clothes-press—Heaven knows how old— a lime-stained bench that had once been used to keep flowers on outside the door, and other decrepit factors of household utility, in an east room that was a lean-to against this so-called main portion. All sorts of other broken-down furniture were about this place; an antiquated clothes-horse, cracked in two of its ribs; a broken mirror in an old cherry frame, which had fallen from a nail and cracked itself three days before their youngest son, Jerry, died; an extension hat-rack, which once had had porcelain knobs on the ends of its pegs; and a sewing-machine, long since outdone in its clumsy mechanism by rivals of a newer generation.

The orchard to the east of the house was full of gnarled old apple-trees, worm-eaten as to trunks and branches, and fully ornamented with green and white lichens, so that it had a sad, greenish-white, silvery effect in moonlight. The low outhouses, which had once housed chickens, a horse or two, a cow, and several pigs, were covered with patches of moss as to their roof, and the sides had been free of paint for so long that they were blackish gray as to color, and a little spongy. The picket-fence in front, with its gate squeaky and askew, and the side fences of the stake-and-rider type were in an equally run-down condition. As a matter of fact, they had aged synchronously with the persons who lived here, old Henry Reifsneider and his wife Phœbe Ann.

They had lived here, these two, ever since their marriage, forty-eight years before, and Henry had lived here before that from his childhood up. His father and mother, well along in years when he was a boy, had invited him to bring his wife here when he had first fallen in love and decided to marry; and he had done so. His father and mother were the companions of himself and his wife for ten years after they were married, when both died; and then Henry and Phœbe were left with their five children growing lustily apace. But all sorts of things had happened since then. Of the seven children, all told, that had been born to them, three had died; one girl had gone to Kansas; one boy had gone to Sioux Falls, never even to be heard of after; another boy had gone to Washington; and the last girl lived five counties away in the same State, but was so burdened with cares of her own that she rarely gave them a thought. Time and a common-place home life that had never been attractive had weaned them thoroughly, so that, wherever they were, they gave little thought as to how it might be with their father and mother.

Old Henry Reifsneider and his wife Phœbe were a loving couple. You perhaps know how it is with simple natures that fasten themselves like lichens on the stones of circumstance and weather their days to a crumbling conclusion. The great world sounds widely, but it has no call for them. They have no soaring intellect. The orchard, the meadow, the cornfield, the pig-pen, and the chicken-lot measure the range of their human activities. When the wheat is headed it is reaped and threshed; when the corn is browned and frosted it is cut and shocked; when the timothy is in full head it is cut, and the haycock erected. After that comes winter, with the hauling of grain to market, the sawing and splitting of wood, the simple chores of fire-building, meal-getting, occasional repairing and visiting. Beyond these and the changes of weather—the snows, the rains, and the fair days—there are no immediate, significant things. All the rest of life is a far-off, clamorous phantasmagoria, flickering like Northern lights in the night, and sounding as faintly as cowbells tinkling in the distance.

Old Henry and his wife Phœbe were as fond of each other as it is possible for two old people to be who have nothing else in this life to be fond of. He was a thin old man, seventy when she died, a queer, crotchety person with coarse gray-black hair and beard, quite straggly and unkempt. He looked at you out of dull, fishy, watery eyes that had deep-brown crow's-feet at the sides. His clothes, like the clothes of many farmers, were aged and angular and baggy, standing out at the pockets, not fitting about the neck, protuberant and worn at elbow and knee. Phœbe Ann was thin and shapeless, a very umbrella of a woman, clad in shabby black, and with a black bonnet for her best wear. As time had passed, and they had only themselves to look after, their movements had become slower and slower, their activities fewer and fewer. The annual keep of pigs had been reduced from five to one grunting porker, and the single horse which Henry now retained was a sleepy animal, not over-nourished and not very clean. The chickens, of which formerly there was a large flock, had almost disappeared, owing to ferrets, foxes, and the lack of proper care, which produces disease. The former healthy garden was now a straggling memory of itself, and the vines and flower-beds that formerly ornamented the windows and dooryard had now become choking thickets. A will had been made which divided the small tax-eaten property equally among the remaining four, so that it was really of no interest to any of them. Yet these two lived together in peace and sympathy, only that now and then old Henry would become unduly cranky, complaining almost invariably that something had been neglected or mislaid which was of no importance at all.

"Phœbe, where's my corn-knife? You ain't never minded to let my things alone no more."

"Now you hush, Henry," his wife would caution him in a cracked and squeaky voice. "If you don't, I'll leave yuh. I'll git up and walk out of here some day, and then where would y' be? Y' ain't got anybody but me to look after yuh, so yuh just behave yourself. Your corn knife's on the mantel where it's allus been unless you've gone an' put it sum-mers else."

Old Henry, who knew his wife would never leave him in any cir-cumstances, used to speculate at times as to what he would do if she were to die. That was the one leaving that he really feared. As he climbed on the chair at night to wind the old, long-pendulumed, double-weighted clock, or went finally to the front and the back door to see that they were safely shut in, it was a comfort to know that Phœ-be was there, properly ensconced on her side of the bed, and that if he stirred restlessly in the night, she would be there to ask what he wanted.

"Now, Henry, do lie still! You're as restless as a chicken."

"Well, I can't sleep, Phœbe."

"Well, yuh needn't roll so, anyhow. Yuh kin let me sleep."

This usually reduced him to a state of somnolent ease. If she wanted a pail of water, it was a grumbling pleasure for him to get it; and if she did rise first to build the fires, he saw that the wood was cut and placed within easy reach. They divided this simple world nicely be-tween them.

As the years had gone on, however, fewer and fewer people had called. They were well-known for a distance of as much as ten square miles as old Mr. and Mrs. Reifsneider, honest, moderately Christian, but too old to be really interesting any longer. The writing of letters had become an almost impossible burden too difficult to continue or even negotiate via others, although an occasional letter still did arrive from the daughter in Pemberton County. Now and then some old friend stopped with a pie or cake or a roasted chicken or duck, or merely to see that they were well; but even these kindly minded visits were no longer frequent.

One day in the early spring of her sixty-fourth year Mrs. Reifsneider took sick, and from a low fever passed into some indefinable ailment which, because of her age, was no longer curable. Old Henry drove to Swinnerton, the neighboring town, and procured a doctor. Some friends called, and the immediate care of her was taken off his hands. Then one chill spring night she died, and old Henry, in a fog of sorrow and uncertainty, followed her body to the nearest graveyard, an unattractive space with a few pines growing in it. Although he might have gone to the daughter in Pemberton or sent for her, it was really too much trouble and he was too weary and fixed. It was suggested to him at once by one friend and another that he come to stay with them awhile, but he did not see fit. He was so old and so fixed in his notions and so accustomed to the exact surroundings he had known all his days, that he could not think of leaving. He wanted to remain near where they had put his Phœbe; and the fact that he would have to live alone did not trouble him in the least. The living children were notified and the care of him offered if he would leave, but he would not.

"I kin make a shift for myself," he continually announced to old Dr. Morrow, who had attended his wife in this case. "I kin cook a little, and besides, it don't take much more'n coffee an' bread in the mornin's to satisfy me. I'll get along now well enough. Yuh just let me be." And after many pleadings and proffers of advice, with supplies of coffee and bacon and baked bread duly offered and accepted, he was left to himself. For a while he sat idly outside his door brooding in the spring sun. He tried to revive his interest in farming, and to keep himself busy and free from thought by looking after the fields, which of late had been much neglected. It was a gloomy thing to come in of an evening, however, or in the afternoon and find no shadow of Phœbe where everything suggested her. By degrees he put a few of her things away. At night he sat beside his lamp and read in the papers that were left him occasionally or in a Bible that he had neglected for years, but he could get little solace from these things. Mostly he held his hand over his mouth and looked at the floor as he sat and thought of what had become of her, and how soon he himself would die. He made a great business of making his coffee in the morning and frying himself a little bacon at night; but his appetite was gone. The shell in which he had been housed so long seemed vacant, and its shadows were suggestive of immedicable griefs. So he lived quite dolefully for five long months, and then a change began.

It was one night, after he had looked after the front and the back door, wound the clock, blown out the light, and gone through all the selfsame motions that he had indulged in for years, that he went to bed not so much to sleep as to think. It was a moonlight night. The green-lichen-covered orchard just outside and to be seen from his bed where he now lay was a silvery affair sweetly spectral. The moon shone through the east windows, throwing the pattern of the panes on the wooden floor, and making the old furniture, to which he was accustomed, stand out dimly in the room. As usual he had been thinking of Phœbe and the years when they had been young together, and of the children who had gone, and the poor shift he was making of his present days. The house was coming to be in a very bad state indeed. The bed-clothes were in disorder, and not clean, for he made a wretched shift of washing. It was a terror to him. The roof leaked, causing things, some of them, to remain damp for weeks at a time, but he was getting into that brooding state where he would accept anything rather than exert himself. He preferred to pace slowly to and fro or to sit and think.

By twelve o'clock of this particular night he was asleep, however, and by two had waked again. The moon by this time had shifted to a position on the western side of the house, and it now shone in through the windows of the living-room and those of the kitchen beyond. A certain combination of furniture—a chair near a table, with his coat on it, the half-open kitchen door casting a shadow, and the position of a lamp near a paper—gave him an exact representation of Phœbe leaning over the table as he had often seen her do in life. It gave him a great start. Could it be she—or her ghost? He had scarcely ever believed in spirits; and still—— He looked at her fixedly in the feeble half-light, his old hair tingling oddly at the roots, and then sat up. The figure did not move. He put his thin legs out of the bed and sat looking at her, wondering if this could really be Phœbe. They had talked of ghosts often in their lifetime, of apparitions and omens; but they had never agreed that such things could be. It had never been a part of his wife's creed that she could have a spirit that could return to walk the earth. Her after-world was quite a different affair, a vague heaven, no less, from which the righteous did not trouble to return. Yet here she was now, bending over the table in her black skirt and gray shawl, her pale profile outlined against the moonlight.

"Phœbe," he called, thrilling from head to toe and putting out one bony hand, "have yuh come back?"

The figure did not stir, and he arose and walked uncertainly to the door, looking at it fixedly the while. As he drew near, however, the apparition resolved itself into its primal content—his old coat over the high-backed chair, the lamp by the paper, the half-open door.

"Well," he said to himself, his mouth open, "I thought shore I saw her." And he ran his hand strangely and vaguely through his hair, the while his nervous tension relaxed. Vanished as it had, it gave him the idea that she might return.

Another night, because of this first illusion, and because his mind was now constantly on her and he was old, he looked out of the window that was nearest his bed and commanded a hen-coop and pig-pen and a part of the wagon-shed, and there, a faint mist exuding from the damp of the ground, he thought he saw her again. It was one of those little wisps of mist, one of those faint exhalations of the earth that rise in a cool night after a warm day, and flicker like small white cypresses of fog before they disappear. In life it had been a custom of hers to cross this lot from her kitchen door to the pig-pen to throw in any scrap that was left from her cooking, and here she was again. He sat up and watched it strangely, doubtfully, because of his previous experience, but inclined, because of the nervous titillation that passed over his body, to believe that spirits really were, and that Phœbe, who would be concerned because of his lonely state, must be thinking about him, and hence returning. What other way would she have? How otherwise could she express herself? It would be within the province of her charity so to do, and like her loving interest in him. He quivered and watched it eagerly; but, a faint breath of air stirring, it wound away toward the fence and disappeared.

A third night, as he was actually dreaming, some ten days later, she came to his bedside and put her hand on his head.

"Poor Henry!" she said. "It's too bad."

He roused out of his sleep, actually to see her, he thought, moving from his bed-room into the one living-room, her figure a shadowy mass of black. The weak straining of his eyes caused little points of light to flicker about the outlines of her form. He arose, greatly astonished, walked the floor in the cool room, convinced that Phœbe was coming back to him. If he only thought sufficiently, if he made it perfectly clear by his feeling that he needed her greatly, she would come back, this kindly wife, and tell him what to do. She would perhaps be with him much of the time, in the night, anyhow; and that would make him less lonely, this state more endurable.

In age and with the feeble it is not such a far cry from the subtleties of illusion to actual hallucination, and in due time this transition was made for Henry. Night after night he waited, expecting her return. Once in his weird mood he thought he saw a pale light moving about the room, and another time he thought he saw her walking in the orchard after dark. It was one morning when the details of his lonely state were virtually unendurable that he woke with the thought that she was not dead. How he had arrived at this conclusion it is hard to say. His mind had gone. In its place was a fixed illusion. He and Phœbe had had a senseless quarrel. He had reproached her for not leaving his pipe where he was accustomed to find it, and she had left. It was an aberrated fulfillment of her old jesting threat that if he did not behave himself she would leave him.

"I guess I could find yuh ag'in," he had always said. But her cackling threat had always been:

"Yuh'll not find me if I ever leave yuh. I guess I kin git some place where yuh can't find me."

This morning when he arose he did not think to build the fire in the customary way or to grind his coffee and cut his bread, as was his wont, but solely to meditate as to where he should search for her and how he should induce her to come back. Recently the one horse had been dispensed with because he found it cumbersome and beyond his needs. He took down his soft crush hat after he had dressed himself, a new glint of interest and determination in his eye, and taking his black crook cane from behind the door, where he had always placed it, started out briskly to look for her among the nearest neighbors. His old shoes clumped soundly in the dust as he walked, and his gray-black locks, now grown rather long, straggled out in a dramatic fringe or halo from under his hat. His short coat stirred busily as he walked, and his hands and face were peaked and pale.

"Why, hello, Henry! Where's yuh goin' this mornin'?" inquired Farmer Dodge, who, hauling a load of wheat to market, encountered him on the public road. He had not seen the aged farmer in months, not since his wife's death, and he wondered now, seeing him looking so spry.

"Yuh ain't seen Phœbe, have yuh?" inquired the old man, looking up quizzically.

"Phœbe who?" inquired Farmer Dodge, not for the moment connecting the name with Henry's dead wife.

"Why, my wife Phœbe o' course. Who do yuh s'pose I mean?" He stared up with a pathetic sharpness of glance from under his shaggy, gray eyebrows.

"Wall, I'll swan, Henry, yuh ain't jokin', are yuh?" said the solid Dodge, a pursy man, with a smooth, hard red face. "It can't be your wife yuh're talkin' about. She's dead."

"Dead! Shucks!" retorted the demented Reifsneider. "She left me early this mornin', while I was sleepin'. She allus got up to build the fire, but she's gone now. We had a little spat last night, an' I guess that's the reason. But I guess I kin find her. She's gone over to Matilda Race's; that's where she's gone."

He started briskly up the road, leaving the amazed Dodge to stare in wonder after him.

"Well, I'll be switched!" he said aloud to himself. "He's clean out'n his head. That poor old feller's been livin' down there till he's gone outen his mind. I'll have to notify the authorities." And he flicked his whip with great enthusiasm. "Geddap!" he said, and was off.

Reifsneider met no one else in this poorly populated region until he reached the whitewashed fence of Matilda Race and her husband three miles away. He had passed several other houses en route, but these not being within the range of his illusion were not considered. His wife, who had known Matilda well, must be here. He opened the picket-gate which guarded the walk, and stamped briskly up to the door.

"Why, Mr. Reifsneider," exclaimed old Matilda herself, a stout woman, looking out of the door in answer to his knock, "what brings yuh here this mornin'?"

"Is Phœbe here?" he demanded eagerly.

"Phœbe who? What Phœbe?" replied Mrs. Race, curious as to this sudden development of energy on his part.

"Why, my Phœbe, o' course. My wife Phœbe. Who do yuh s'pose? Ain't she here now?"

"Lawsy me!" exclaimed Mrs. Race, opening her mouth. "Yuh pore man! So you're clean out'n your mind now. Yuh come right in and sit down. I'll git yuh a cup o' coffee. O' course your wife ain't here; but yuh come in an' sit down. I'll find her fer yuh after a while. I know where she is."

The old farmer's eyes softened, and he entered. He was so thin and pale a specimen, pantalooned and patriarchal, that he aroused Mrs. Race's extremest sympathy as he took off his hat and laid it on his knees quite softly and mildly.

"We had a quarrel last night, an' she left me," he volunteered.

"Laws! laws!" sighed Mrs. Race, there being no one present with whom to share her astonishment as she went to her kitchen. "The pore man! Now somebody's just got to look after him. He can't be allowed to run around the country this way lookin' for his dead wife. It's turrible."

She boiled him a pot of coffee and brought in some of her new-baked bread and fresh butter. She set out some of her best jam and put a couple of eggs to boil, lying whole-heartedly the while.

"Now yuh stay right there, Uncle Henry, till Jake comes in, an' I'll send him to look for Phœbe. I think it's more'n likely she's over to Swinnerton with some o' her friends. Anyhow, we'll find out. Now yuh just drink this coffee an' eat this bread. Yuh must be tired. Yuh've had a long walk this mornin'." Her idea was to take counsel with Jake, "her man," and perhaps have him notify the authorities.

She bustled about, meditating on the uncertainties of life, while old Reifsneider thrummed on the rim of his hat with his pale fingers and later ate abstractedly of what she offered. His mind was on his wife, however, and since she was not here, or did not appear, it wandered vaguely away to a family by the name of Murray, miles away in another direction. He decided after a time that he would not wait for Jake Race to hunt his wife but would seek her for himself. He must be on, and urge her to come back.

"Well, I'll be goin'," he said, getting up and looking strangely about him. "I guess she didn't come here after all. She went over to the Murrays', I guess. I'll not wait any longer, Mis' Race. There's a lot to do over to the house to-day." And out he marched in the face of her protests, taking to the dusty road again in the warm spring sun, his cane striking the earth as he went.

It was two hours later that this pale figure of a man appeared in the Murrays' doorway, dusty, perspiring, eager. He had tramped all of five miles, and it was noon. An amazed husband and wife of sixty heard his strange query, and realized also that he was mad. They begged him to stay to dinner, intending to notify the authorities later and see what could be done; but though he stayed to partake of a little something, he did not stay long, and was off again to another distant farmhouse, his idea of many things to do and his need of Phœbe impelling him. So it went for that day and the next and the next, the circle of his inquiry ever widening.

The process by which a character assumes the significance of being peculiar, his antics weird, yet harmless, in such a community is often involute and pathetic. This day, as has been said, saw Reifsneider at other doors, eagerly asking his unnatural question, and leaving a trail of amazement, sympathy, and pity in his wake. Although the authorities were informed—the county sheriff, no less—it was not deemed advisable to take him into custody; for when those who knew old Henry, and had for so long, reflected on the condition of the county insane asylum, a place which, because of the poverty of the district, was of staggering aberration and sickening environment, it was decided to let him remain at large; for, strange to relate, it was found on investigation that at night he returned peaceably enough to his lonesome domicile there to discover whether his wife had returned, and to brood in loneliness until the morning. Who would lock up a thin, eager, seeking old man with iron-gray hair and an attitude of kindly, innocent inquiry, particularly when he was well-known for a past of only kindly servitude and reliability? Those who had known him best rather agreed that he should be allowed to roam at large. He could do no harm. There were many who were willing to help him as to food, old clothes, the odds and ends of his daily life—at least at first. His figure after a time became not so much a commonplace as an accepted curiosity, and the replies, "Why, no, Henry; I ain't see her," or "No, Henry; she ain't been here to-day," more customary.

For several years thereafter then he was an odd figure in the sun and rain, on dusty roads and muddy ones, encountered occasionally in strange and unexpected places, pursuing his endless search. Undernourishment, after a time, although the neighbors and those who knew his history gladly contributed from their store, affected his body; for he walked much and ate little. The longer he roamed the public highway in this manner, the deeper became his strange hallucination; and finding it harder and harder to return from his more and more distant pilgrimages, he finally began taking a few utensils with him from his home, making a small package of them, in order that he might not be compelled to return. In an old tin coffee-pot of large size he placed a small tin cup, a knife, fork, and spoon, some salt and pepper, and to the outside of it, by a string forced through a pierced hole, he fastened a plate, which could be released, and which was his woodland table. It was no trouble for him to secure the little food that he needed, and with a strange, almost religious dignity, he had no hesitation in asking for that much. By degrees his hair became longer and longer, his once black hat became an earthen brown, and his clothes threadbare and dusty.

For all of three years he walked, and none knew how wide were his perambulations, nor how he survived the storms and cold. They could not see him, with homely rural understanding and forethought, sheltering himself in haycocks, or by the sides of cattle, whose warm bodies protected him from the cold, and whose dull understandings were not opposed to his harmless presence. Overhanging rocks and trees kept him at times from the rain, and a friendly hay-loft or corn-crib was not above his humble consideration.

The involute progression of hallucination is strange. From asking at doors and being constantly rebuffed or denied, he finally came to the conclusion that although his Phœbe might not be in any of the houses at the doors of which he inquired, she might nevertheless be within the sound of his voice. And so, from patient inquiry, he began to call sad, occasional cries, that ever and anon waked the quiet landscapes and ragged hill regions, and set to echoing his thin "O-o-o Phœbe! O-o-o Phœbe!" It had a pathetic, albeit insane, ring, and many a farmer of plowboy came to know it even from afar and say, "There goes old Reifsneider."

Another thing that puzzled him greatly after a time and after many hundreds of inquiries was, when he no longer had any particular dooryard in view and no special inquiry to make, which way to go. These crossroads, which occasionally led in four or even six directions, came after a time to puzzle him. But to solve this knotty problem, which became more and more of a puzzle, there came to his aid another hallucination. Phœbe's spirit or some power of the air or wind or nature would tell him. If he stood at the center of the parting of the ways, closed his eyes, turned thrice about, and called "O-o-o Phœbe!" twice, and then threw his cane straight before him, that would surely indicate which way to go for Phœbe, or one of these mystic powers would surely govern its direction and fall! In whichever direction it went, even though, as was not infrequently the case, it took him back along the path he had already come, or across fields, he was not so far gone in his mind but that he gave himself ample time to search before he called again. Also the hallucination seemed to persist that at some time he would surely find her. There were hours when his feet were sore, and his limbs weary, when he would stop in the heat to wipe his seamed brow, or in the cold to beat his arms. Sometimes, after throwing away his cane, and finding it indicating the direction from which he had just come, he would shake his head wearily and philosophically, as if contemplating the unbelievable or an untoward fate, and then start briskly off. His strange figure came finally to be known in the farthest reaches of three or four counties. Old Reifsneider was a pathetic character. His fame was wide.

Near a little town called Watersville, in Green County, perhaps four miles from that minor center of human activity, there was a place or precipice locally known as the Red Cliff, a sheer wall of red sandstone, perhaps a hundred feet high, which raised its sharp face for half a mile or more above the fruitful cornfields and orchards that lay beneath, and which was surmounted by a thick grove of trees. The slope that slowly led up to it from the opposite side was covered by a rank growth of beech, hickory, and ash, through which threaded a number of wagontracks crossing at various angles. In fair weather it had become old Reifsneider's habit, so inured was he by now to the open, to make his bed in some such patch of trees as this to fry his bacon or boil his eggs at the foot of some tree before laying himself down for the night. Occasionally, so light and inconsequential was his sleep, he would walk at night. More often, the moonlight or some sudden wind stirring in the trees or a reconnoitering animal arousing him, he would sit up and think, or pursue his quest in the moonlight or the dark, a strange, unnatural, half wild, half savage-looking but utterly harmless creature, calling at lonely road crossings, staring at dark and shuttered houses, and wondering where, where Phœbe could really be.

That particular lull that comes in the systole-diastole of this earthly ball at two o'clock in the morning invariably aroused him, and though he might not go any farther he would sit up and contemplate the darkness or the stars, wondering. Sometimes in the strange processes of his mind he would fancy that he saw moving among the trees the figure of his lost wife, and then he would get up to follow, taking his utensils, always on a string, and his cane. If she seemed to evade him too easily he would run, or plead, or, suddenly losing track of the fancied figure, stand awed or disappointed, grieving for the moment over the almost insurmountable difficulties of his search.

It was in the seventh year of these hopeless peregrinations, in the dawn of a similar springtime to that in which his wife had died, that he came at last one night to the vicinity of this selfsame patch that crowned the rise to the Red Cliff. His far-flung cane, used as a divining-rod at the last crossroads, had brought him hither. He had walked many, many miles. It was after ten o'clock at night, and he was very weary. Long wandering and little eating had left him but a shadow of his former self. It was a question now not so much of physical strength but of spiritual endurance which kept him up. He had scarcely eaten this day, and now, exhausted, he set himself down in the dark to rest and possibly to sleep.

Curiously on this occasion a strange suggestion of the presence of his wife surrounded him. It would not be long now, he counseled with himself, although the long months had brought him nothing, until he should see her, talk to her. He fell asleep after a time, his head on his knees. At midnight the moon began to rise, and at two in the morning, his wakeful hour, was a large silver disk shining through the trees to the east. He opened his eyes when the radiance became strong, making a silver pattern at his feet and lighting the woods with strange lusters and silvery, shadowy forms. As usual, his old notion that his wife must be near occurred to him on this occasion, and he looked about him with a speculative, anticipatory eye. What was it that moved in the distant shadows along the path by which he had entered—a pale, flickering will-o'-the-wisp that bobbed gracefully among the trees and riveted his expectant gaze? Moonlight and shadows combined to give it a strange form and a stranger reality, this fluttering of bog-fire or dancing of wandering fireflies. Was it truly his lost Phœbe? By a circuitous route it passed about him, and in his fevered state he fancied that he could see the very eyes of her, not as she was when he last saw her in the black dress and shawl but now a strangely younger Phœbe, gayer, sweeter, the one whom he had known years before as a girl. Old Reifsneider got up. He had been expecting and dreaming of this hour all these years, and now as he saw the feeble light dancing lightly before him he peered at it questioningly, one thin hand in his gray hair.

Of a sudden there came to him now for the first time in many years the full charm of her girlish figure as he had known it in boyhood, the pleasing, sympathetic smile, the brown hair, the blue sash she had once worn about her waist at a picnic, her gay, graceful movements. He walked around the base of the tree, straining with his eyes, forgetting for once his cane and utensils, and following eagerly after. On she moved before him, a will-o'-the-wisp of the spring, a little flame above her head, and it seemed as though among the small saplings of ash and beech and the thick trunks of hickory and elm that she signaled with a young, a lightsome hand.

"O Phœbe! Phœbe!" he called. "Have yuh really come? Have yuh really answered me?" And hurrying faster, he fell once, scrambling lamely to his feet, only to see the light in the distance dancing illusively on. In and on he hurried until he was fairly running, brushing his ragged arms against the trees, striking his hands and face against impending twigs. His hat was gone, his lungs were breathless, his reason quite astray, when coming to the edge of the cliff he saw her below among a silvery bed of apple-trees now blooming in the spring.

"O Phœbe!" he called. "O Phœbe! Oh, no, don't leave me!" And feeling the lure of a world where love was young and Phœbe as this vision presented her, a delightful epitome of their quondam youth, he gave a gay cry of "Oh, wait, Phœbe!" and leaped.

Some farmer-boys, reconnoitering this region of bounty and prospect some few days afterward, found first the tin utensils tied together under the tree where he had left them, and then later at the foot of the cliff, pale, broken, but elate, a molded smile of peace and delight upon his lips, his body. His old hat was discovered lying under some low-growing saplings the twigs of which had held it back. No one of all the simple population knew how eagerly and joyously he had found his lost mate.

SHERWOOD ANDERSON

(1876–1941)

SHERWOOD ANDERSON was born at Clyde, Ohio, in 1876. Though he had written stories before, it was not until 1916 that he published his first book, *Windy McPherson's Son*. Anderson's short stories—particularly those in the volume *Winesburg, Ohio*—are about as different from the suavely clever products of Harte and O. Henry as anything could be. They are concerned first and last with human beings: plot and technique—in short, the framework—are almost entirely disregarded in an effort to present what appears to the writer as the truth.

Sophistication is reprinted from *Winesburg, Ohio*. Copyright by Jonathan Cape, by whose permission it is here used.

SOPHISTICATION

IT was early evening of a day in the late fall, and the Winesburg County Fair had brought crowds of country people into town. The day had been clear and the night came on warm and pleasant. On the Trunion Pike, where the road after it left town stretched away between berry fields now covered with dry brown leaves, the dust from passing wagons arose in clouds. Children, curled into little balls, slept on the straw scattered on wagon beds. Their hair was full of dust and their fingers black and sticky. The dust rolled away over the fields and the departing sun set it ablaze with colors.

In the main street of Winesburg crowds filled the stores and the sidewalks. Night came on, horses whinnied, the clerks in the stores ran madly about, children became lost and cried lustily, an American town worked terribly at the task of amusing itself.

Pushing his way through the crowds in Main Street, young George Willard concealed himself in the stairway leading to Doctor Reefy's office and looked at the people. With feverish eyes he watched the faces drifting past under the store lights. Thoughts kept coming into his head and he did not want to think. He stamped impatiently on the wooden steps and looked sharply about. "Well, is she going to stay with him all day? Have I done all this waiting for nothing?" he muttered.

George Willard, the Ohio village boy, was fast growing into manhood and new thoughts had been coming into his mind. All that day, amid the jam of people at the Fair, he had gone about feeling lonely. He was about to leave Winesburg to go away to some city where he hoped to get work on a city newspaper and he felt grown up. The mood that had taken possession of him was a thing known to men and unknown to boys. He felt old and a little tired. Memories awoke in him. To his mind his new sense of maturity set him apart, made of him a half-tragic figure. He wanted someone to understand the feeling that had taken possession of him after his mother's death.

There is a time in the life of every boy when he for the first time takes the backward view of life. Perhaps that is the moment when he crosses the line into manhood. The boy is walking through the street of his town. He is thinking of the future and of the figure he will cut in the world. Ambitions and regrets awake within him. Suddenly something happens; he stops under a tree and waits as for a voice calling his name. Ghosts of old things creep into his consciousness; the voices outside of himself whisper a message concerning the limitations of life. From being quite sure of himself and his future he becomes not at all sure. If he be an imaginative boy a door is torn open and for the first time he looks out upon the world, seeing, as though they marched in procession before him, the countless figures of men who before his time have come out of nothingness into the world, lived their lives and again disappeared into nothingness. The sadness of sophistication has come to the boy. With a little gasp he sees himself as merely a leaf blown by the wind through the streets of his village. He knows that in spite of all the stout talk of his fellows he must live and die in uncertainty, a thing blown by the winds, a thing destined like corn to wilt in the sun. He shivers and looks eagerly about. The eighteen years he has lived seem but a moment, a breathing space in the long march of humanity. Already he hears death calling. With all his heart he wants to come close to some other human, touch someone with his hands, be touched by the hand of another. If he prefers that the other be a woman, that is because he believes that a woman will be gentle, that she will understand. He wants, most of all, understanding.

When the moment of sophistication came to George Willard his mind turned to Helen White, the Winesburg banker's daughter. Always he had been conscious of the girl growing into womanhood as he grew into manhood. Once on a summer night when he was eighteen, he had walked with her on a country road and in her presence had given way to an impulse to boast, to make himself appear big and significant in her eyes. Now he wanted to see her for another purpose. He wanted to tell her of the new impulses that had come to him. He had tried to make her think of him as a man when he knew nothing of manhood and now he wanted to be with her and to try to make her feel the change he believed had taken place in his nature.

As for Helen White, she also had come to a period of change. What George felt, she in her young woman's way felt also. She was no longer a girl and hungered to reach into the grace and beauty of womanhood. She had come home from Cleveland, where she was attending college, to spend a day at the Fair. She also had begun to have memories. During the day she sat in the grand-stand with a young man, one of the instructors from the college, who was a guest of her mother's. The young man was of a pedantic turn of mind and she felt at once he would not do for her purpose. At the Fair she was glad to be seen in his company as he was well dressed and a stranger. She knew that the fact of his presence would create an impression. During the day she was happy, but when night came on she began to grow restless. She wanted to drive the instructor away, to get out of his presence. While they sat together in the grand-stand and while the eyes of former schoolmates were upon them, she paid so much attention to her escort that he grew interested. "A scholar needs money. I should marry a woman with money," he mused.

Helen White was thinking of George Willard even as he wandered gloomily through the crowds thinking of her. She remembered the summer evening when they had walked together and wanted to walk with him again. She thought that the months she had spent in the city, the going to theaters and the seeing of great crowds wandering in lighted thoroughfares, had changed her profoundly. She wanted him to feel and be conscious of the change in her nature.

The summer evening together that had left its mark on the memory of both the young man and woman had, when looked at quite sensibly, been rather stupidly spent. They had walked out of town along a country road. Then they had stopped by a fence near a field of young corn and George had taken off his coat and let it hang on his arm. "Well, I've stayed here in Winesburg—yes—I've not yet gone away but I'm growing up," he had said. "I've been reading books and I've been thinking. I'm going to try to amount to something in life.

"Well," he explained, "that isn't the point. Perhaps I'd better quit talking."

The confused boy put his hand on the girl's arm. His voice trembled. The two started to walk back along the road toward town. In his desperation George boasted, "I'm going to be a big man, the biggest that ever lived here in Winesburg," he declared. "I want you to do something, I don't know what. Perhaps it is none of my business. I want you to try to be different from other women. You see the point. It's none of my business I tell you. I want you to be a beautiful woman. You see what I want."

The boy's voice failed and in silence the two came back into town and went along the street to Helen White's house. At the gate he tried to say something impressive. Speeches he had thought out came into his head, but they seemed utterly pointless. "I thought—I used to think— I had it in my mind you would marry Seth Richmond. Now I know you won't," was all he could find to say as she went through the gate and toward the door of her house.

On the warm fall evening as he stood in the stairway and looked at the crowd drifting through Main Street, George thought of the talk beside the field of young corn and was ashamed of the figure he had made of himself. In the street the people surged up and down like cattle confined in a pen. Buggies and wagons almost filled the narrow thoroughfare. A band played and small boys raced along the sidewalk, diving between the legs of men. Young men with shining red faces walked awkwardly about with girls on their arms. In a room above one of the stores, where a dance was to be held, the fiddlers tuned their instruments. The broken sounds floated down through an open window and out across the murmur of voices and the loud blare of the horns of the band. The medley of sounds got on young Willard's nerves. Everywhere, on all sides, the sense of crowding, moving life closed in about him. He wanted to run away by himself and think. "If she wants to stay with that fellow she may. Why should I care? What difference does it make to me?" he growled and went along Main Street and through Hern's grocery into a side street.

George felt so utterly lonely and dejected that he wanted to weep but pride made him walk rapidly along, swinging his arms. He came to Westley Moyer's livery barn and stopped in the shadows to listen to a group of men who talked of a race Westley's stallion, Tony Tip, had won at the Fair during the afternoon. A crowd had gathered in front of the barn and before the crowd walked Westley, prancing up and down and boasting. He held a whip in his hand and kept tapping the ground. Little puffs of dust arose in the lamplight. "Hell, quit your talking," Westley exclaimed. "I wasn't afraid, I knew I had 'em beat all the time. I wasn't afraid."

Ordinarily George Willard would have been intensely interested in the boasting of Moyer, the horseman. Now it made him angry. He turned and hurried away along the street. "Old wind-bag," he spluttered. "Why does he want to be bragging? Why don't he shut up?"

George went into a vacant lot and as he hurried along, fell over a pile of rubbish. A nail protruding from an empty barrel tore his trousers. He sat down on the ground and swore. With a pin he mended the torn place and then arose and went on. "I'll go to Helen White's house, that's what I'll do. I'll walk right in. I'll say that I want to see her. I'll walk right in and sit down, that's what I'll do," he declared, climbing over a fence and beginning to run.

On the veranda of Banker White's house Helen was restless and distraught. The instructor sat between the mother and daughter. His talk wearied the girl. Although he had also been raised in an Ohio town, the instructor began to put on the airs of the city. He wanted to appear cosmopolitan. "I like the chance you have given me to study the background out of which most of our girls come," he declared. "It was good of you, Mrs. White, to have me down for the day." He turned to Helen and laughed. "Your life is still bound up with the life of this town?" he asked. "There are people here in whom you are interested?" To the girl his voice sounded pompous and heavy.

Helen arose and went into the house. At the door leading to a garden at the back she stopped and stood listening. Her mother began to talk. "There is no one here fit to associate with a girl of Helen's breeding," she said.

Helen ran down a flight of stairs at the back of the house and into the garden. In the darkness she stopped and stood trembling. It seemed to her that the world was full of meaningless people saying words. Afire with eagerness she ran through a garden gate and turning a corner by the banker's barn, went into a little side street. "George!

Where are you, George?" she cried, filled with nervous excitement. She stopped running, and leaned against a tree to laugh hysterically. Along the dark little street came George Willard, still saying words. "I'm going to walk right into her house. I'll go right in and sit down," he declared as he came up to her. He stopped and stared stupidly. "Come on," he said and took hold of her hand. With hanging heads they walked away along the street under the trees. Dry leaves rustled under foot. Now that he had found her George wondered what he had better do and say.

At the upper end of the fair ground, in Winesburg, there is a half decayed old grand-stand. It has never been painted and the boards are all warped out of shape. The fair ground stands on top of a low hill rising out of the valley of Wine Creek and from the grand-stand one can see at night, over a cornfield, the lights of the town reflected against the sky.

George and Helen climbed the hill to the fair ground, coming by the path past Waterworks Pond. The feeling of loneliness and isolation that had come to the young man in the crowded streets of his town was both broken and intensified by the presence of Helen. What he felt was reflected in her.

In youth there are always two forces fighting in people. The warm unthinking little animal struggles against the thing that reflects and remembers, and the older, the more sophisticated thing had possession of George Willard. Sensing his mood, Helen walked beside him filled with respect. When they got to the grand-stand they climbed up under the roof and sat down on one of the long bench-like seats.

There is something memorable in the experience to be had by going into a fair ground that stands at the edge of a Middle Western town on a night after the annual fair has been held. The sensation is one never to be forgotten. On all sides are ghosts, not of the dead, but of living people. Here, during the day just passed, have come the people pouring in from the town and the country around. Farmers with their wives and children and all the people from the hundreds of little frame houses have gathered within these board walls. Young girls have laughed and men with beards have talked of the affairs of their lives. The place has been filled to overflowing with life. It has itched and squirmed with life and now it is night and the life has all gone away. The silence is almost terrifying. One conceals oneself standing silently beside the trunk of a tree and what there is of a reflective tendency in his nature is intensified. One shudders at the thought of the meaninglessness of life while at the same instant and if the people of the town are his people, one loves life so intensely that tears come into the eyes.

In the darkness under the roof of the grand-stand, George Willard sat beside Helen White and felt very keenly his own insignificance in the scheme of existence. Now that he had come out of town where the presence of the people stirring about, busy with a multitude of affairs, had been so irritating the irritation was all gone. The presence of Helen renewed and refreshed him. It was as though her woman's hand was assisting him to make some minute readjustment of the machinery of his life. He began to think of the people in the town where he had always lived with something like reverence. He had reverence for Helen. He wanted to love and to be loved by her, but he did not want at the moment to be confused by her womanhood. In the darkness he took hold of her hand and when she crept close put a hand on her shoulder. A wind began to blow and he shivered. With all his strength he tried to hold and to understand the mood that had come upon him. In that high place in the darkness the two oddly, sensitive human atoms held each other tightly and waited. In the mind of each was the same thought. "I have come to this lonely place and here is this other," was the substance of the thing felt.

In Winesburg the crowded day had run itself out into the long night of the late fall. Farm horses jogged away along lonely country roads pulling their portion of weary people. Clerks began to bring samples of goods in off the sidewalks and lock the doors of stores. In the Opera House a crowd had gathered to see a show and further down Main Street the fiddlers, their instruments tuned, sweated and worked to keep the feet of youth flying over a dance floor.

In the darkness in the grand-stand Helen White and George Willard remained silent. Now and then the spell that held them was broken and they turned and tried in the dim light to see into each other's eyes. They kissed but that impulse did not last. At the upper end of the fair ground a half dozen men worked over horses that had raced during the afternoon. The men had built a fire and were heating kettles of water. Only their legs could be seen as they passed back and forth in the light. When the wind blew the little flames of the fire danced crazily about.

George and Helen arose and walked away into the darkness. They went along a path past a field of corn that had not yet been cut. The wind whispered among the dry corn blades. For a moment during the walk back into town the spell that held them was broken. When they had come to the crest of Waterworks Hill they stopped by a tree and George again put his hands on the girl's shoulders. She embraced him eagerly and then again they drew quickly back from that impulse. They stopped kissing and stood a little apart. Mutual respect grew big in them. They were both embarrassed and to relieve their embarrassment dropped into the animalism of youth. They laughed and began to pull and haul at each other. In some way chastened and purified by the mood they had been in they became, not man and woman, not boy and girl, but excited little animals.

It was so they went down the hill. In the darkness they played like two splendid young things in a young world. Once, running swiftly forward, Helen tripped George and he fell. He squirmed and shouted. Shaking with laughter, he rolled down the hill. Helen ran after him. For just a moment she stopped in the darkness. There is no way of knowing what woman's thoughts went through her mind but, when the bottom of the hill was reached and she came up to the boy, she took his arm and walked beside him in dignified silence. For some reason they could not have explained they had both got from their silent evening together the thing needed. Man or boy, woman or girl, they had for a moment taken hold of the thing that makes the mature life of men and women in the modern world possible.

WILLA CATHER

(1876—1947)

WILLA SIBERT CATHER was born at Winchester, Va., in 1876. She was for some years engaged in newspaper work, and was until 1912 associate editor of *McClure's Magazine*. Her novels, *My Antonia* and *A Lost Lady*, are among the best modern American fiction. In her volume *Youth and the Bright Medusa* she offers a variety of well-written short stories. Miss Cather described with honesty and power the characters and scenes she knew and understood.

A Wagner Matinée is reprinted from *Youth and the Bright Medusa*. Copyright, 1920, by Alfred A. Knopf, New York, and William Heinemann, London, by whose permission it is here used.

A WAGNER MATINÉE

I RECEIVED one morning a letter, written in pale ink on glossy blue-lined note-paper, and bearing the postmark of a little Nebraska village. This communication, worn and rubbed, looking as if it had been carried for some days in a coat pocket that was none too clean, was from my Uncle Howard, and informed me that his wife had been left a small legacy by a bachelor relative, and that it would be necessary for her to go to Boston to attend the settling of the estate. He requested me to meet her at the station and render her whatever services might be necessary. On examining the date indicated as that of her arrival, I found it to be no later than to-morrow. He had characteristically delayed writing until, had I been away from home for a day, I must have missed my aunt altogether.

The name of my Aunt Georgiana opened before me a gulf of recollection so wide and deep that, as the letter dropped from my hand, I felt suddenly a stranger to all the present conditions of my existence, wholly ill at ease and out of place amid the familiar surroundings of my study. I became, in short, the gangling farm-boy my aunt had known, scourged with chilblains and bashfulness, my hands cracked and sore from the corn husking. I sat again before her parlor organ fumbling the scales with my stiff red fingers, while she, beside me, made canvas mittens for the huskers.

The next morning, after preparing my landlady for a visitor, I set out for the station. When the train arrived. I had some difficulty in finding my aunt. She was the last of the passengers to alight, and it was not until I got her into the carriage that she seeemed really to recognize me. She had come all the way in a day coach; her linen duster had become black with soot and her black bonnet gray with dust during the journey. When we arrived at my boarding house the landlady put her to bed at once and I did not see her again until the next morning.

Whatever shock Mrs. Springer experienced at my aunt's appearance, she considerately concealed. As for myself, I saw my aunt's battered figure with that feeling of awe and respect with which we behold explorers who have left their ears and fingers north of Franz-Joseph Land or their health somewhere along the Upper Congo. My Aunt Georgiana had been a music teacher at the Boston Conservatory, somewhere back in the later sixties. One summer, while visiting in the little village among the Green Mountains where her ancestors had dwelt for generations, she had kindled the callow fancy of my uncle, Howard Carpenter, then an idle, shiftless boy of twenty-one. When she returned to her duties in Boston, Howard followed her, and the upshot of this infatuation was that she eloped with him, eluding the reproaches of her family and the criticism of her friends by going with him to the Nebraska frontier. Carpenter, who, of course, had no money, took up a homestead in Red Willow County, fifty miles from the railroad. There they had measured off their land themselves, driving across the prairie in a wagon, to the wheel of which they had tied a red cotton handkerchief, and counting its revolutions. They built a dugout in the red hillside, one of those cave dwellings whose inmates so often reverted to primitive conditions. Their water they got from the lagoons where the buffalo drank, and their slender stock of provisions was always at the mercy of roving Indians. For thirty years my aunt had not been farther than fifty miles from the homestead.

I owed to this woman most of the good that ever came my way in my boyhood, and had a reverential affection for her. During the years when I was riding here for my uncle, my aunt, after cooking the three meals—the first of which was ready at six o'clock in the morning—and putting the six children to bed, would often stand until midnight at her ironing-board, with me at the kitchen table beside her, hearing me recite Latin declensions and conjugations, gently shaking me when my drowsy head sank down over a page of irregular verbs. It was to her, at her ironing or mending, that I read my first Shakespeare, and her old textbook on mythology was the first that ever came into my empty hands. She taught me my scales and exercises on the little parlor organ which her husband had bought her after fifteen years during which she had not so much as seen a musical instrument. She would sit beside me by the hour, darning and counting, while I struggled with the "Joyous Farmer." She seldom talked to me about music, and I understood why. Once when I had been doggedly beating out some easy passages from an old score of *Euryanthe* I had found among her music books, she came up to me and, putting her hands over my eyes, gently drew my head back upon her shoulder, saying tremulously, "Don't love it so well, Clark, or it may be taken from you."

When my aunt appeared on the morning after her arrival in Boston, she was still in a semi-somnambulant state. She seemed not to realize that she was in the city where she had spent her youth, the place longed for hungrily half a lifetime. She had been so wretchedly train-sick throughout the journey that she had no recollection of anything but her discomfort, and, to all intents and purposes, there were but a few hours of nightmare between the farm in Red Willow County and my study on Newbury Street. I had planned a little pleasure for her that afternoon, to repay her for some of the glorious moments she had given me when we used to milk together in the straw-thatched cowshed and she, because I was more than usually tired, or because her husband had spoken sharply to me, would tell me of the splendid performance of the *Huguenots* she had seen in Paris, in her youth.

At two o'clock the Symphony Orchestra was to give a Wagner program, and I intended to take my aunt; though, as I conversed with her, I grew doubtful about her enjoyment of it. I suggested our visiting the Conservatory and the Common before lunch, but she seemed altogether too timid to wish to venture out. She questioned me absently about various changes in the city, but she was chiefly concerned that she had forgotten to leave instructions about feeding half-skimmed milk to a certain weakling calf, "old Maggie's calf, you know, Clark," she explained, evidently having forgotten how long I had been away. She was further troubled because she had neglected to tell her daughter about the freshly opened kit of mackerel in the cellar, which would spoil if it were not used directly.

I asked her whether she had ever heard any of the Wagnerian operas, and found that she had not, though she was perfectly familiar with their respective situations, and had once possessed the piano score of *The Flying Dutchman*. I began to think it would be best to get her back to Red Willow County without waking her, and regretted having suggested the concert.

From the time we entered the concert hall, however, she was a trifle less passive and inert, and for the first time seemed to perceive her surroundings. I had felt some trepidation lest she might become aware of her queer country clothes, or might experience some painful embarrassment at stepping suddenly into the world to which she had been dead for a quarter of a century. But, again, I found how superficially I had judged her. She sat looking about her with eyes as impersonal, almost as stony, as those with which the granite Rameses in a museum watches the froth and fret that ebbs and flows about his pedestal. I have seen this same aloofness in old miners who drift into the Brown hotel at Denver, their pockets full of bullion, their linen soiled, their haggard faces unshaven; standing in the thronged corridors as solitary as though they were still in a frozen camp on the Yukon.

The matinée audience was made up chiefly of women. One lost the contour of faces and figures, indeed any effect of line whatever, and there was only the color of bodices past counting, the shimmer of fabrics soft and fine, silky and sheer; red, mauve, pink, blue, lilac, purple, écru, rose, yellow, cream, and white, all the colors that an impressionist finds in a sunlit landscape, with here and there the dead shadow of a frock coat. My Aunt Georgiana regarded them as though they had been so many daubs of tube-paint on a palette.

When the musicians came out and took their places, she gave a little stir of anticipation, and looked with quickening interest down over the rail at that invariable grouping, perhaps the first wholly familiar thing that had greeted her eye since she had left old Maggie and her weakling calf. I could feel how all those details sank into her soul, for I had not forgotten how they had sunk into mine when I came fresh from plowing forever and forever between green aisles of corn, where, as in a treadmill, one might walk from daybreak to dusk without perceiving a shadow of change. The clean profiles of the musicians, the gloss of their linen, the dull black of their coats, the beloved shapes of the instruments, the patches of yellow light on the smooth, varnished bellies of the 'cellos and the bass viols in the rear, the restless, wind-tossed forest of fiddle necks and bows—I recalled how, in the first orchestra I ever heard, those long bow-strokes seemed to draw the heart out of me, as a conjurer's stick reels out yards of paper ribbon from a hat.

The first number was the *Tannhäuser* overture. When the horns drew out the first strain of the "Pilgrims' Chorus," Aunt Georgiana clutched my coat sleeve. Then it was I first realized that for her this broke a silence of thirty years. With the battle between the two motives, with the frenzy of the Venusberg theme and its rippings of strings, there came to me an overwhelming sense of the waste and wear we are so powerless to combat; and I saw again the tall, naked house on the prairie, black and grim as a wooden fortress; the black pond where I had learned to swim, its margin pitted with sun-dried cattle tracks; the rain gullied clay banks about the naked house, the four dwarf ash seedlings where the dish-cloths were always hung to dry before the kitchen door. The world there was the flat world of the ancients; to the east, a cornfield that stretched to daybreak; to the west, a corral that reached to sunset; between, the conquests of peace, dearer-bought than those of war.

The overture closed, my aunt released my coat sleeve, but she said nothing. She sat staring dully at the orchestra. What, I wondered, did she get from it? She had been a good pianist in her day, I knew, and her musical education had been broader than that of most music teachers of a quarter of a century ago. She had often told me of Mozart's operas and Meyerbeer's, and I could remember hearing her sing, years ago, certain melodies of Verdi. When I had fallen ill, with a fever in her house she used to sit by my cot in the evening—when the cool night wind blew in through the faded mosquito netting tacked over the window and I lay watching a certain bright star that burned red above the cornfield—and sing "Home to our mountains, O let us return!" in a way fit to break the heart of a Vermont boy near dead of homesickness already.

I watched her closely through the prelude to *Tristan and Isolde*, trying vainly to conjecture what that seething turmoil of strings and winds might mean to her, but she sat mutely staring at the violin bows that drove obliquely downward, like the pelting streaks of rain in a summer shower. Had this music any message for her? Had she enough left to at all comprehend this power which had kindled the world since she had left it. I was in a fever of curiosity, but Aunt Georgiana sat silent upon her peak in Darien. She preserved this utter immobility throughout the number from *The Flying Dutchman*, though her fingers worked mechanically upon her black dress, as if, of themselves, they were recalling the piano score they had once played. Poor hands! They had been stretched and twisted into mere tentacles to hold and lift and knead with; on one of them a thin worn band that had once been a wedding ring. As I pressed and gently quieted one of these groping hands, I remembered with quivering eyelids their services for me in other days.

Soon after the tenor began the "Prize Song," I heard a quick drawn breath, and turned to my aunt. Her eyes were closed, but the tears were glistening on her cheeks, and I think, in a moment more, they were in my eyes as well. It never really dies, then—the soul which can suffer so excruciatingly and so interminably; it withers to the outward eye only; like that strange moss which can lie on a dusty shelf half a century, and yet, if placed in water, grow green again. She wept so throughout the development and elaboration of the melody.

During the intermission before the second half, I questioned my aunt and found that the "Prize Song" was not new to her. Some years before there had drifted to the farm in Red Willow County a young German, a tramp cow-puncher, who had sung in the chorus at Bayreuth when he was a boy, along with the other peasant boys and girls. On a Sunday morning he used to sit on his gingham-sheeted bed in the hands' bedroom which opened off the kitchen, cleaning the leather of his boots and saddle, singing the "Prize Song," while my aunt went about her work in the kitchen. She had hovered over him until she had prevailed upon him to join the country church, though his sole fitness for this step, in so far as I could gather, lay in his boyish face, and his possession of this divine melody. Shortly afterward, he had gone to town on the Fourth of July, been drunk for several days, lost his money at a faro table, ridden a saddled Texas steer on a bet, and disappeared with a fractured collar-bone. All this my aunt told me huskily, wanderingly, as though she were talking in the weak lapses of illness.

"Well, we have come to better things than the old *Trovatore* at any rate, Aunt Georgie?" I queried, with a well-meant effort at jocularity.

Her lip quivered and she hastily put her handkerchief up to her mouth. From behind it she murmured, "And you have been hearing this ever since you left me, Clark?" Her question was the gentlest and saddest of reproaches.

The second half of the program consisted of four numbers from the *Ring*, and closed with Siegfried's funeral march. My aunt wept quietly but almost continuously, as a shallow vessel overflows in a rain-storm. From time to time her dim eyes looked up at the lights, burning softly under their dull glass globes.

The deluge of sound poured on and on; I never knew what she found in the shining current of it; I never knew how far it bore her, or past what happy islands. From the trembling of her face, I could well believe that before the last number she had been carried out where the myriad graves are, into the gray, nameless burying grounds of the sea, or into some world of death vaster yet, where, from the beginning of the world, hope has lain down with hope and dream with dream and, renouncing, slept.

The concert was over; the people filed out of the hall chattering and laughing, glad to relax and find the living level again, but my kinswoman made no effort to rise. The harpist slipped the green felt cover over his instrument; the flute-players shook the water from their mouthpieces; the men of the orchestra went out one by one, leaving the stage to the chairs and music stands, empty as a winter cornfield.

I spoke to my aunt. She burst into tears and sobbed pleadingly. "I don't want to go, Clark, I don't want to go!"

I understood. For her, just outside the concert hall, lay the black pond with the cattle-tracked bluffs; the tall, unpainted house, with weather-curled boards, naked as a tower; the crook-backed ash seedlings where the dish-cloths hung to dry; the gaunt, moulting turkeys picking up refuse about the kitchen door.

JAMES BRANCH CABELL

(1879—1958)

CABELL was born in Virginia, and except for a few brief intervals he resided there continuously. Among his score of volumes, most of which are romantic and satirical novels, are a few charmingly related short tales. The collection called *The Certain Hour* is a delicately written cycle of stories around actual or imagined episodes in the lives of various authors. *A Brown Woman* is one of the best of these.

A Brown Woman is reprinted from *The Certain Hour*. Copyright, 1916, by Robert M. McBride & Co., New York, by permission of the publisher.

A BROWN WOMAN

"BUT I must be hurrying home now," the girl said, "for it is high time I were back in the hayfields."

"Fair shepherdess," he implored, "for heaven's sake, let us not cut short the *pastorelle* thus abruptly."

"And what manner of beast may that be, pray?"

"'Tis a conventional form of verse, my dear, which we at present strikingly illustrate. The plan of a *pastorelle* is simplicity's self: a gentleman, which I may fairly claim to be, in some fair rural scene—such as this—comes suddenly upon a rustic maiden of surpassing beauty. He naturally falls in love with her, and they say all manner of fine things to each other."

She considered him for a while before speaking. It thrilled him to see the odd tenderness that was in her face. "You always think of saying and writing fine things, do you not, sir?"

"My dear," he answered, gravely, "I believe that I was undoubtedly guilty of such folly until you came. I wish I could make you understand how your coming has changed everything."

"You can tell me some other time," the girl gaily declared, and was about to leave him.

His hand detained her, very gently. "Faith, but I fear not, for already my old hallucinations seem to me incredible. Why, yesterday I thought it the most desirable of human lots to be a great poet"—the gentleman laughed in self-mockery. "I positively did. I labored every day toward becoming one. I lived among books, esteemed that I was doing something of genuine importance as I gravely tinkered with alliteration and metaphor and antithesis and judicious paraphrases of the ancients. I put up with life solely because it afforded material for versification; and, in reality, believed the destruction of Troy was providentially ordained lest Homer lack subject matter for an epic. And as for loving, I thought people fell in love in order to exchange witty rhymes."

His hand detained her, very gently. ... Indeed, it seemed to him he could never tire of noting her excellencies. Perhaps it was that splendid light poise of her head he chiefly loved; he thought so at least, just now. Or was it the wonder of her walk, which made all other women he had ever known appear to mince and hobble, like rusty toys? Something there was assuredly about this slim brown girl which recalled an untamed and harmless woodland creature; and it was that, he knew, which most poignantly moved him, even though he could not name it. Perhaps it was her bright kind eyes, which seemed to mirror the tranquillity of forests. ...

"You gentry are always talking of love," she marveled.

"Oh," he said, with acerbity, "oh, I don't doubt that any number of beet-gorging squires and leering, long-legged Oxford dandies——" He broke off here, and laughed contemptuously, "Well, you are beautiful, and they have eyes as keen as mine. And I do not blame you, my dear, for believing my designs to be no more commendable than theirs—no, not at all."

But his mood was spoiled, and his tetchy vanity hurt, by the thought of stout well-set fellows having wooed this girl; and he permitted her to go without protest.

Yet he sat alone for a while upon the fallen tree-trunk, humming a contented little tune. Never in his life had he been happier. He did not venture to suppose that any creature so adorable could love such a sickly hunchback, such a gargoyle of a man, as he was; but that Sarah was fond of him, he knew. There would be no trouble in arranging with her father for their marriage, most certainly; and he meant to attend to that matter this very morning, and within ten minutes. So Mr. Alexander Pope was meanwhile arranging in his mind a suitable wording for his declaration of marital aspirations.

Thus John Gay found him presently and roused him from phrase-spinning. "And what shall we do this morning, Alexander?" Gay was always demanding, like a spoiled child, to be amused.

Pope told him what his own plans were, speaking quite simply, but with his countenance radiant. Gay took off his hat and wiped his forehead, for the day was warm. He did not say anything at all.

"Well——?" Mr. Pope asked, after a pause.

Mr. Gay was dubious. "I had never thought that you would marry," he said. "And—why, hang it, Alexander! to grow enamored of a milkmaid is well enough for the hero of a poem, but in a poet it hints at injudicious composition."

Mr. Pope gesticulated with thin hands and seemed upon the verge of eloquence. Then he spoke unanswerably. "But I love her," he said.

John Gay's reply was a subdued whistle. He, in common with the other guests of Lord Harcourt, at Nuneham Courtney, had wondered what would be the outcome of Mr. Alexander Pope's intimacy with Sarah Drew. A month earlier the poet had sprained his ankle upon Amshot Heath, and this young woman had found him lying there, entirely helpless, as she returned from her evening milking. Being hale of person, she had managed to get the little hunchback to her home unaided. And since then Pope had often been seen with her.

This much was common knowledge. That Mr. Pope proposed to marry the heroine of his misadventure afforded a fair mark for raillery, no doubt, but Gay, in common with the run of educated England in 1718, did not aspire to be facetious at Pope's expense. The luxury was too costly. Offend the dwarf in any fashion, and were you the proudest duke at Court or the most inconsiderable rhymester in Petticoat Lane, it made no difference; there was no crime too heinous for "the great Mr. Pope's" next verses to charge you with, and, worst of all, there was no misdoing so out of character that his adroit malignancy could not make it seem plausible.

Now, after another pause, Pope said, "I must be going now. Will you not wish me luck?"

"Why, Alexander—why, hang it!" was Mr. Gay's observation, "I believe that you are human after all, and not just a book in breeches."

He thereby voiced a commentary patently uncalled-for, as Mr. Pope afterward reflected. Mr. Pope was then treading toward the home of old Frederick Drew. It was a gray morning in late July.

"I love her," Pope had said. The fact was undeniable; yet an expression of it necessarily halts. Pope knew, as every man must do who dares conserve his energies to annotate the drama of life rather than play a part in it, the nature of that loneliness which this conservation breeds. Such persons may hope to win a posthumous esteem in the library, but it is at the bleak cost of making life a wistful transaction with foreigners. In such enforced aloofness Sarah Drew had come to him—strong, beautiful, young, good and vital, all that he was not—and had serenely befriended "the great Mr. Pope," whom she viewed as a queer decrepit little gentleman of whom within a week she was unfeignedly fond.

"I love her," Pope had said. Eh, yes, no doubt; and what, he fiercely demanded of himself, was he—a crippled scribbler, a bungling artisan of phrases—that he should dare to love this splendid and deep-bosomed goddess? Something of youth awoke, possessing him—something of that high ardor which, as he cloudily remembered now, had once controlled a boy who dreamed in Windsor Forest and with the lightest of hearts planned to achieve the impossible. For what is more difficult of attainment than to achieve the perfected phrase, so worded that to alter a syllable of its wording would be little short of sacrilege?

"What whimwhams!" decreed the great Mr. Pope, aloud. "Verse-making is at best only the affair of idle men who write in their closets and of idle men who read there. And as for him who polishes phrases, whatever be his fate in poetry, it is ten to one but he must give up all the reasonable aims of life for it."

No, he would have no more loneliness. Henceforward Alexander Pope would be human—like the others. To write perfectly was much; but it was not everything. Living was capable of furnishing even more than the raw material of a couplet. It might, for instance, yield content.

For instance, if you loved, and married, and begot, and died, with the seriousness of a person who believes he is performing an action of real importance, and conceded that the perfection of any art, whether it be that of verse-making or of rope-dancing, is at best a by-product of life's conduct; at worst, you probably would not be lonely. No; you would be at one with all other fat-witted people, and there was no greater blessing conceivable.

Pope muttered, and produced his notebook, and wrote tentatively. Wrote Mr. Pope:

> "The bliss of man (could pride that blessing find)
> Is not to act or think beyond mankind;
> No powers of body or of soul to share
> But what his nature and his state can bear."

"His state!" yes, undeniably, two sibilants collided here. "His wit?" —no, that would be flat-footed awkwardness in the management of your vowel-sounds; the lengthened "a" was almost requisite. ... Pope was fretting over the imbroglio when he absent-mindedly glanced up to perceive that his Sarah, not irrevocably offended, was being embraced by a certain John Hughes—who was a stalwart, florid, personable individual, no doubt, but, after all, only an unlettered farmer.

The dwarf gave a hard, wringing motion of his hands. The diamond —Lord Bolingbroke's gift—which ornamented Pope's left hand cut into the flesh of his little finger, so cruel was the gesture; and this little finger was bleeding as Pope tripped forward, smiling. A gentleman does not incommode the public by obtruding the ugliness of a personal wound.

"Do I intrude?" he queried. "Ah, well! I also have dwelt in Arcadia." It was bitter to comprehend that he had never done so.

The lovers were visibly annoyed; yet, if an interruption of their pleasant commerce was decreed to be, it could not possibly have sprung, as they soon found, from a more sympathetic source.

These were not subtle persons. Pope had the truth from them within ten minutes. They loved each other; but John Hughes was penniless, and old Frederick Drew was, in consequence, obdurate.

"And, besides, he thinks you mean to marry her!" said John Hughes.

"My dear man, he pardonably forgets that the utmost reach of my designs in common reason would be to have her as my kept mistress for a month or two," drawled Mr. Pope. "As concerns yourself, my good fellow, the case is somewhat different. Why, it is a veritable romance—an affair of Daphne and Corydon—although, to be unpardonably candid, the plot of your romance, my young Arcadians, is not the most original conceivable. I think that the dénouement need not baffle our imaginations."

The dwarf went toward Sarah Drew. The chary sunlight had found the gold in her hair, and its glint was brightly visible to him. "My dear—" he said. His thin long fingers touched her capable hand. It was a sort of caress—half-timid. "My dear, I owe my life to you. My body is at most a flimsy abortion such as a night's exposure would have made more tranquil than it is just now. Yes, it was you who found a caricature of the sort of man that Mr. Hughes here is, disabled, helpless, and—for reasons which doubtless seemed to you sufficient—contrived that this unsightly parody continue in existence. I am not lovable, my dear. I am only a hunchback, as you can see. My aspirations and my sickly imaginings merit only the derision of a candid clean-souled being such as you are." His finger-tips touched the back of her hand again. "I think there was never a maker of enduring verse who did not at one period or another long to exchange an assured immortality for a sturdier pair of shoulders. I think—I think that I am prone to speak at random," Pope said, with his half-drowsy smile. "Yet, none the less, an honest man, as our kinsmen in Adam average, is bound to pay his equitable debts."

She said, "I do not understand."

"I have perpetrated certain jingles," Pope returned. "I had not comprehended until to-day they are the only children I shall leave behind me. Eh, and what would you make of them, my dear, could ingenuity contrive a torture dire enough to force you into reading them!... Misguided people have paid me for contriving these jingles. So that I have money enough to buy you from your father just as I would purchase one of his heifers. Yes, at the very least I have money, and I have earned it. I will send your big-thewed adorer—I believe that Hughes is the name?—£500 of it this afternoon. That sum, I gather, will be sufficient to remove your father's objection to your marriage with Mr. Hughes."

Pope could not but admire himself tremendously. Moreover, in such matters no woman is blind. Tears came into Sarah's huge brown eyes. This tender-hearted girl was not thinking of John Hughes now. Pope noted the fact with the pettiest exultation. "Oh, you—you are good." Sarah Drew spoke as with difficulty.

"No adjective, my dear, was ever applied with less discrimination. It is merely that you have rendered no inconsiderable service to posterity, and merit a reward."

"Oh, and indeed, indeed, I was always fond of you——" The girl sobbed this.

She would have added more, no doubt, since compassion is garrulous, had not Pope's scratched hand dismissed a display of emotion as not entirely in consonance with the rules of the game.

"My dear, therein you have signally honored me. There remains only to offer you my appreciation of your benevolence toward a sickly monster, and to entreat for my late intrusion—however unintentional—that forgiveness which you would not deny, I think, to any other impertinent insect."

"Oh, but we have no words to thank you, sir——!" Thus Hughes began.

"Then don't attempt it, my good fellow. For phrase-spinning, as I can assure you, is the most profitless of all pursuits." Whereupon Pope bowed low, wheeled, walked away. Yes, he was wounded past sufferance; it seemed to him he must die of it. Life was a farce, and Destiny an overseer who hiccoughed mandates. Well, all that even Destiny could find to gloat over, he reflected, was the tranquil figure of a smallish gentleman switching at the grass-blades with his cane as he sauntered under darkening skies.

For a storm was coming on, and the first big drops of it were splattering the terrace when Mr. Pope entered Lord Harcourt's mansion.

Pope went straight to his own rooms. As he came in there was a vivid flash of lightning, followed instantaneously by a crashing, splitting noise, like that of universes ripped asunder. He did not honor the high uproar with attention. This dwarf was not afraid of anything except the commission of an error in taste.

Then, too, there were letters for him, laid ready on the writing-table. Nothing of much importance he found there.—Here, though, was a rather diverting letter from Eustace Budgell, that poor fool, abjectly thanking Mr. Pope for his advice concerning how best to answer the atrocious calumnies on Budgell then appearing in *The Grub-Street Journal*—and reposing, drolly enough, next the proof-sheets of an anonymous letter Pope had prepared for the forthcoming issue of that publication, wherein he sprightlily told how Budgell had poisoned Dr. Tindal, after forging his will. For even if Budgell had not in point of fact been guilty of these particular peccadilloes, he had quite certainly committed the crime of speaking lightly of Mr. Pope, as "a little envious animal," some seven years ago; and it was for this grave indiscretion that Pope was dexterously goading the man into insanity, and eventually drove him to suicide. ...

The storm made the room dark and reading difficult. Still, this was an even more amusing letter, from the all-powerful Duchess of Marlborough. In as civil terms as her sick rage could muster, the frightened woman offered Mr. Pope £1,000 to suppress his verbal portrait of her, in the character of Atossa, from his *Moral Essays;* and Pope straightway decided to accept the bribe, and afterward to print his verses unchanged. For the hag, as he reflected, very greatly needed to be taught that in this world there was at least one person who did not quail before her tantrums. There would be, moreover, even an elementary justice in thus robbing her who had robbed England at large. And, besides, her name was Sarah. ...

Pope lighted four candles and set them before the long French mirror. He stood appraising his many curious deformities while the storm raged. He stood sidelong, peering over his left shoulder, in order to see the outline of his crooked back. Nowhere in England, he reflected, was there a person more pitiable and more repellent outwardly.

"And, oh, it would be droll," Pope said, aloud, "if our exteriors were ever altogether parodies. But time keeps a diary in our faces, and writes a monstrously plain hand. Now, if you take the first letter of Mr. Alexander Pope's Christian name, and the first and last letters of his surname, you have A. P. E.," Pope quoted, genially. "I begin to think that Dennis was right. What conceivable woman would not prefer a well-set man of five-and-twenty to such a withered abortion? And what does it matter, after all, that a hunchback has dared to desire a shapely brown-haired woman?"

Pope came more near to the mirror. "Make answer, you who have dared to imagine that a goddess was ever drawn to descend into womanhood except by kisses, brawn and a clean heart."

Another peal of thunder bellowed. The storm was growing furious. "Yet I have had a marvelous dream. Now I awaken. I must go on in the old round. As long as my wits preserve their agility I must be able to amuse, to flatter and, at need, to intimidate the patrons of that ape in the mirror, so that they will not dare refuse me the market-value of my antics. And Sarah Drew has declined an alliance such as this in favor of a fresh-colored complexion and a pair of straight shoulders!"

Pope thought a while. "And a clean heart! She bargained royally, giving love for nothing less than love. The man is rustic, illiterate; he never heard of Aristotle, he would be at a loss to distinguish between a trochee and a Titian, and if you mentioned Boileau to him would probably imagine you were talking of cookery. But he loves her. He would forfeit eternity to save her a toothache. And, chief of all, she can make this robust baby happy, and she alone can make him happy. And so, she gives, gives royally—she gives, God bless her!"

Rain, sullen rain, was battering the window. "And you—you hunchback in the mirror, you maker of neat rhymes—pray, what had you to offer? A coach-and-six, of course, and pin-money and furbelows and in the end a mausoleum with unimpeachable Latin on it! And—*paté sur paté*—an unswerving devotion which she would share on almost equal terms with the Collected Works of Alexander Pope. And so she chose—chose brawn and a clean heart."

The dwarf turned, staggered, fell upon his bed. "God, make a man of me, make me a good brave man. I loved her—oh, such as I am, You know that I loved her! You know that I desire her happiness above all things. Ah, no, for You know that I do not at bottom. I want to hurt, to wound all living creatures, because they know how to be happy, and I do not know how. Ah, God, and why did You decree that I should never be an obtuse and comely animal such as this John Hughes is? I am so tired of being 'the great Mr. Pope,' and I want only the common joys of life."

The hunchback wept. It would be too curious to anatomize the writhings of his proud little spirit.

Now someone tapped upon the door. It was John Gay. He was bidden to enter, and, complying, found Mr. Pope yawning over the latest of Tonson's publications.

Gay's face was singularly portentous. "My friend," Gay blurted out, "I bring news which will horrify you. Believe me, I would never have mustered the pluck to bring it did I not love you. I cannot let you hear it first in public and unprepared, as, otherwise, you would have to do."

"Do I not know you have the kindest heart in all the world? Why, so outrageous are your amiable defects that they would be the public derision of your enemies if you had any," Pope returned.

The other poet evinced an awkward comminglement of consternation and pity. "It appears that when this storm arose—why, Mistress Drew was with a young man of the neighborhood—a John Hewet——" Gay was speaking with unaccustomed rapidity.

"Hughes, I think," Pope interrupted, equably.

"Perhaps—I am not sure. They sought shelter under a haycock. You will remember that first crash of thunder, as if the heavens were in demolishment? My friend, the reapers who had been laboring in the fields —who had been driven to such protection as the trees or hedges afforded——"

"Get on!" a shrill voice cried; "for God's love, man, get on!" Mr. Pope had risen. This pallid shaken wisp was not in appearance the great Mr. Pope whose ingenuity had enabled Homeric warriors to excel in the genteel.

"They first saw a little smoke. ... They found this Hughes with one arm about the neck of Mistress Drew, and the other held over her face, as if to screen her from the lightning. They were both"—and here Gay hesitated. "They were both dead," he amended.

Pope turned abruptly. Nakedness is of necessity uncouth, he held, whether it be the body or the soul that is unveiled. Mr. Pope went toward a window which he opened, and he stood thus looking out for a brief while.

"So she is dead," he said. "It is very strange. So many rare felicities of curve and color, so much of purity and kindliness and valor and mirth, extinguished as one snuffs a candle! Well, I am sorry she is dead, for the child had a talent for living and got such joy out of it. ... Hers was a lovely happy life, but it was sterile. Already nothing remains of her but dead flesh which must be huddled out of sight. I shall not perish thus entirely, I believe. Men will remember me. Truly a mighty foundation for pride! when the utmost I can hope for is but to be read in one island, and to be thrown aside at the end of one age. Indeed, I am not even sure of that much. I print, and print, and print. And when I collect my verses into books, I am altogether uncertain whether to look upon myself as a man building a monument, or burying the dead. It sometimes seems to me that each publication is but a solemn funeral of many wasted years. For I have given all to the verse-making. Granted that the sacrifice avails to rescue my name from oblivion, what will it profit me when I am dead and care no more for men's opinions than Sarah Drew cares now for what I say of her? But then she never cared. She loved John Hughes. And she was right."

He made an end of speaking, still peering out of the window with considerate narrowed eyes.

The storm was over. In the beech-tree opposite a wren was raising optimistic outcry. The sun had won his way through a black-bellied shred of cloud; upon the terrace below, a dripping Venus and Perseus were glistening as with white fire. Past these, drenched gardens, the natural wildness of which was judiciously restrained with walks, ponds, grottoes, statuary and other rural elegancies, displayed the intermingled brilliancies of diamonds and emeralds, and glittered as with pearls and rubies where tempest-battered roses were reviving in assertiveness.

"I think the storm is over," Mr. Pope remarked. "It is strange how violent are these convulsions of nature. ... But nature is a treacherous blowsy jade, who respects nobody. A gentleman can but shrug under her onslaughts, and henceforward civilly avoid them. It is a consolation to reflect that they pass quickly."

He turned as in defiance. "Yes, yes! It hurts. But I envy them. Yes, even I, that ugly spiteful hornet of a man! 'the great Mr. Pope,' who will be dining with the proudest people in England within the hour and gloating over their deference! For they presume to make a little free with God occasionally, John, but never with me. And *I* envy these dead young fools. ... You see, they loved each other, John. I left them, not an hour ago, the happiest of living creatures. I looked back once. I pretended to have dropped my handkerchief. I imagine they were talking of their wedding-clothes, for this broad-shouldered Hughes was matching poppies and field-flowers to her complexion. It was a scene out of Theocritus. I think Heaven was so well pleased by the tableau that Heaven hastily resumed possession of its enactors in order to prevent any after-happenings from belittling that perfect instant."

"Egad, and matrimony might easily have proved an anti-climax," Gay considered.

"Yes; oh, it is only Love that is blind, and not the lover necessarily. I know. I suppose I always knew at the bottom of my heart. This hamadryad was destined in the outcome to dwindle into a village housewife, she would have taken a lively interest in the number of eggs the hens were laying, she would even have assured her children, precisely in the way her father spoke of John Hughes, that young people ordinarily have foolish fancies which their rational elders agree to disregard. But as it is, no Eastern queen—not Semele herself—left earth more nobly—"

Pope broke off short. He produced his notebook, which he never went without, and wrote frowningly, with many erasures. "H'm, yes," he said; and he read aloud:

"When Eastern lovers feed the funeral fire,
On the same pile the faithful fair expire;
Here pitying heaven that virtue mutual found,
And blasted both that it might neither wound.
Hearts so sincere the Almighty saw well pleased,
Sent His own lightning and the victims seized."

Then Pope made a grimace. "No; the analogy is trim enough, but the lines lack fervor. It is deplorable how much easier it is to express any emotion other than that of which one is actually conscious." Pope had torn the paper half-through before he reflected that it would help to fill a printed page. He put it in his pocket. "But, come now, I am writing to Lady Mary this afternoon. You know how she loves oddities. Between us—with prose as the medium, of course, since verse should, after all, confine itself to the commemoration of heroes and royal persons—I believe we might make of this occurrence a neat and moving *pastorelle*—I should say, pastoral, of course, but my wits are woolgathering."

Mr. Gay had the kindest heart in the universe. Yet he, also, had dreamed of the perfected phrase, so worded that to alter a syllable of its wording would be little short of sacrilege. Eyes kindling, he took up a pen. "Yes, yes, I understand. Egad, it is an admirable subject. But, then, I don't believe I ever saw these lovers——?"

"John was a well-set man of about five-and-twenty," replied Mr. Pope; "and Sarah was a brown woman of eighteen years, three months and fourteen days."

Then these two dipped their pens and set about a moving composition, which has to-day its proper rating among Mr. Pope's Complete Works.

————————————

Reading List

A brief selective bibliography of the works in English consulted in the preparation of this volume.

G. Maspero, *Popular Stories of Ancient Egypt.*
James H. Breasted, *Ancient Times.*
Gilbert Murray, *Ancient Greek Literature.*
Marcus S. Dimsdale, *A History of Latin Literature.*
A. W. Ward and A. R. Waller, editors, *The Cambridge History of English Literature.*
Edmund Gosse, *Modern English Literature.*
William P. Trent, and others, editors, *The Cambridge History of American Literature.*
F. L. Pattee, *History of American Literature Since 1870.*
Reuben Levy, *Persian Literature.*
E. G. Brown, *A Literary History of Persia.*
Clément Huart, *A History of Arabic Literature.*
Herbert A. Giles, *A History of Chinese Literature.*
W. G. Aston, *A History of Japanese Literature.*
Leo Wiener, *Anthology of Russian Literature.*
K. Waliszewski, *A History of Russian Literature.*
R. Dyboski, *Periods of Polish Literary History.*
R. Dyboski, *Modern Polish Literature.*
Count Lützow, *A History of Bohemian Literature.*
Edward Dowden, *A History of French Literature.*
A. A. Macdonnell, *A History of Sanskrit Literature.*
Frederick Reidl, *A History of Hungarian Literature.*
Calvin Thomas, *A History of German Literature.*
Richard Garnett, *A History of Italian Literature.*
J. Fitzmaurice-Kelly, *A History of Spanish Literature.*
J. D. M. Ford, *Main Currents of Spanish Literature.*
Isaac Goldberg, *Studies in Spanish-American Literature.*
F. W. Horn, *History of the Literature of the Scandinavian North.*

Index